GOSH, IT MUST BE A LONG WAY TO DEATH VALLEY, MICKEY
NO!! JUST A JUMP FROM HERE MINNIE!!

WALT DISNEY'S

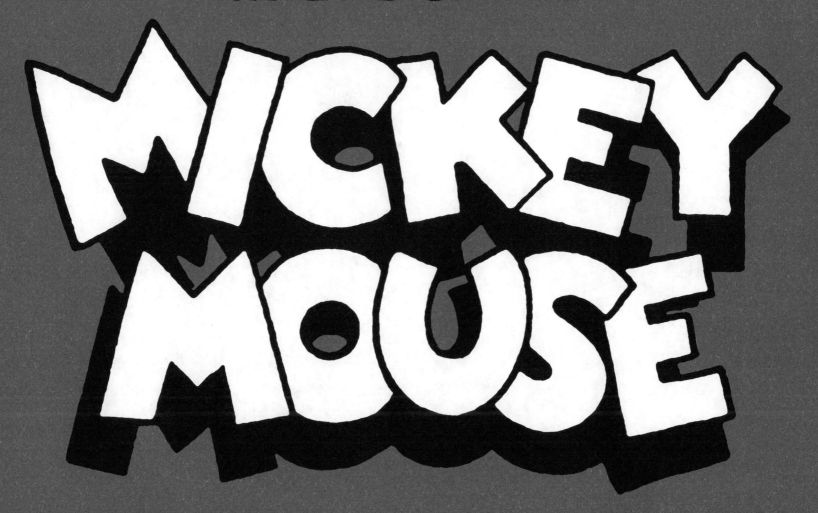

MICKEY MOUSE

BY FLOYD GOTTFREDSON

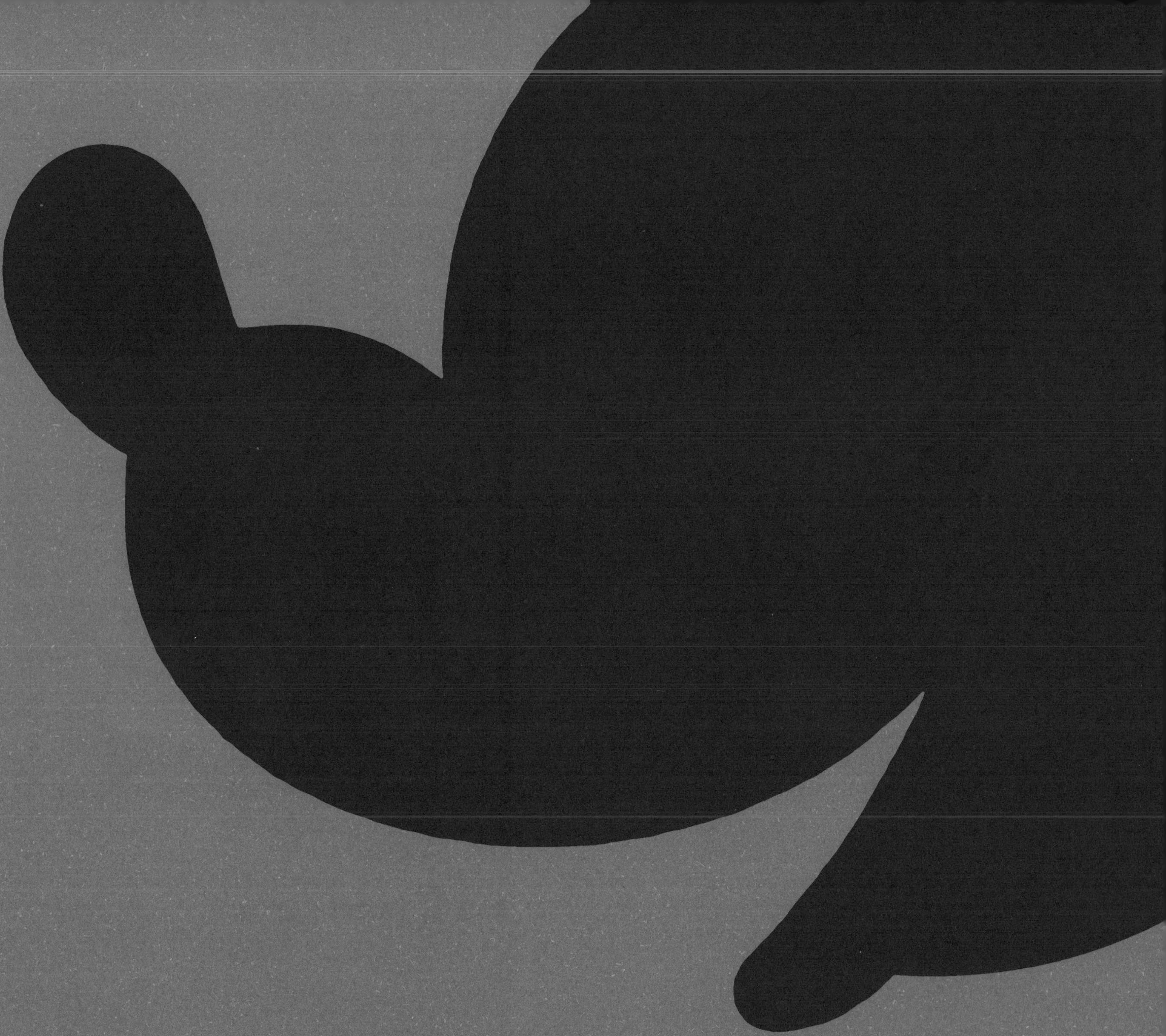

WALT DISNEY'S

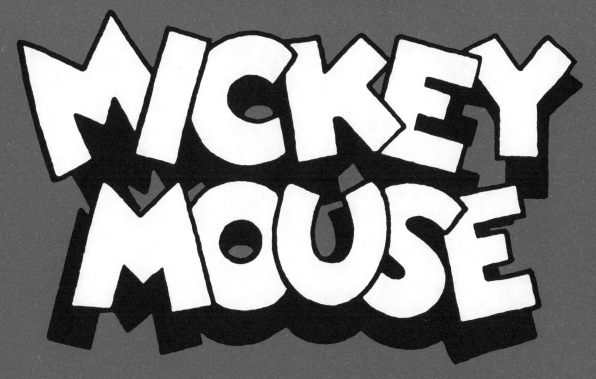

MICKEY MOUSE

BY FLOYD GOTTFREDSON

"RACE TO DEATH VALLEY"

Series Editors: David Gerstein and Gary Groth

FANTAGRAPHICS BOOKS

The Floyd Gottfredson Library

Series Editors: DAVID GERSTEIN and GARY GROTH
Series Designer: JACOB COVEY
Production: PAUL BARESH
Associate Publisher: ERIC REYNOLDS
Publishers: GARY GROTH AND KIM THOMPSON

To receive a free catalogue of graphic novels, newspaper strip reprints, prose novels, art books, cultural criticism and essays, and more, call 1-800-657-1100 or visit our website at Fantagraphics.com.

Distributed in the U.S. by W.W. Norton and Company, Inc. (800-233-4830)
Distributed in Canada by Canadian Manda Group (fax 888-563-8327)
Distributed in the U.K. by Turnaround Distribution (44 (0)20 8829-3002)
Distributed to comic stores by Diamond Comics Distributors (800-452-6642 x215)

ISBN 978-1-60699-441-2

Printed in Singapore

OPPOSITE: Publicity drawing, May 1930. Pencils and lettering attributed to Floyd Gottfredson, inker unknown. Image courtesy Gunnar Andreassen.

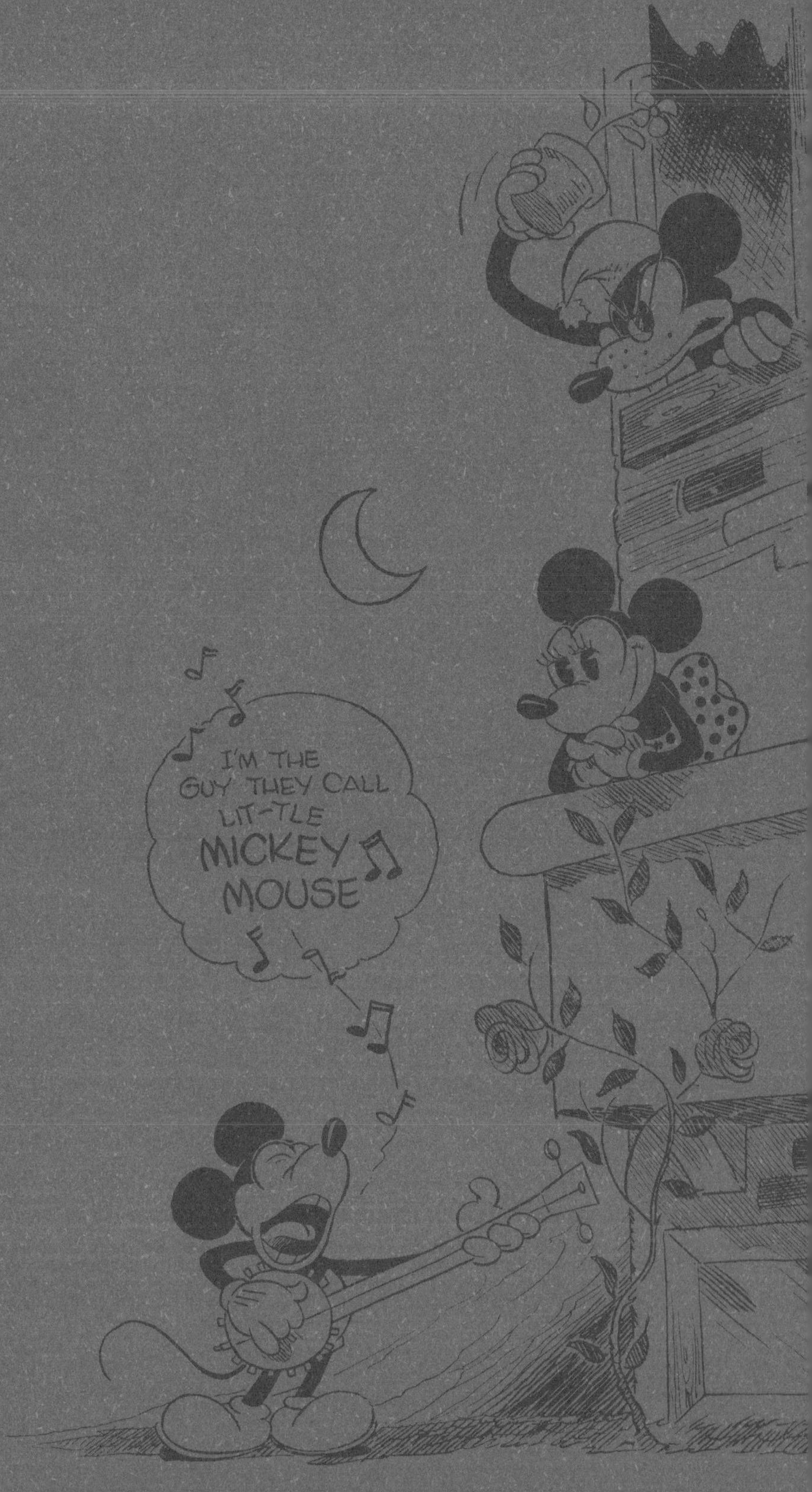
I'M THE GUY THEY CALL LIT-TLE MICKEY MOUSE

I WAS FIVE YEARS OLD in 1979, when Floyd Gottfredson's Mickey Mouse introduced me to comics. Mickey's youthful enthusiasm and determination inspired my own. I've wanted to possess a complete collection of Gottfredson's unforgettable work for three decades. It is an honor for me to help make the Floyd Gottfredson Library happen at last.

I have an entire world of Mickey and Gottfredson aficionados to thank for support and contributions. First and foremost are Ken Shue, Disney Publishing Worldwide's Vice President of Global Art and Design Development, and his Secretary Iliana Lopez, who first enabled us to access, sort, repair, and remaster Gottfredson's strips from the studio's surviving master materials. Next come collectors Bill Blackbeard, Leonardo Gori, Thomas Jensen, and Cole Johnson— who provided better quality strips at times when the masters were damaged or missing—and Disney Account Manager Jesse Post, who as Fantagraphics' liason was always there for me in a pinch.

Numerous other scholars contributed artwork, essays, knowledge, and archival items to this volume. I am indebted to Director Rebecca Cline and Director emeritus David R. Smith at the Walt Disney Archives. I'd also like to thank Thomas Andrae, Gunnar Andreassen, Michael Barrier, Alberto Becattini, Jerry Beck, Geoffrey Blum, Luca Boschi, Karsten Bracker, Didier Ghez, Shane Glines, Jonathan Gray, Linda Gramatky Smith, Joakim Gunnarsson, the Hake's Americana staff (including Alex Winter, Terence Kean, and Deak Stagemeyer), J. B. Kaufman, Mark Kausler, Floyd Norman, Devyn Samara, Charles Shopsin, Warren Spector, Francesco Stajano, Tom Stathes, Fredrik Strömberg, and Germund Von Wowern.

I'd also like thank others who have provided critical support and encouragement. First and foremost come my parents, Susan and Larry Gerstein, and my brother Ben. Then come friends including—but not limited to—Céline and Stefan Allirol-Molin, Christopher and Nicky Barat, Christopher Burns, Byron Erickson, Bob Foster, Andy Hershberger, Lars Jensen, Carl Keil, Thad Komorowski, Raquel Lopez Fernandez, Christopher Meyer, Martin Olsen, Tarkan Rosenberg, Kwongmei To, Joe and Esther Torcivia, and Wilbert Watts.

A special tip of the mouse ears goes to John Clark, Susan Kolberg, and Travis Seitler, my colleagues at Gemstone Publishing's late Disney comics department. You all mean so much.

And finally—thanks, Floyd—for everything.

—David Gerstein
January 2011

TABLE of CONTENTS

TABLE of CONTENTS

The Gottfredson Archives: Essays and Archival Features

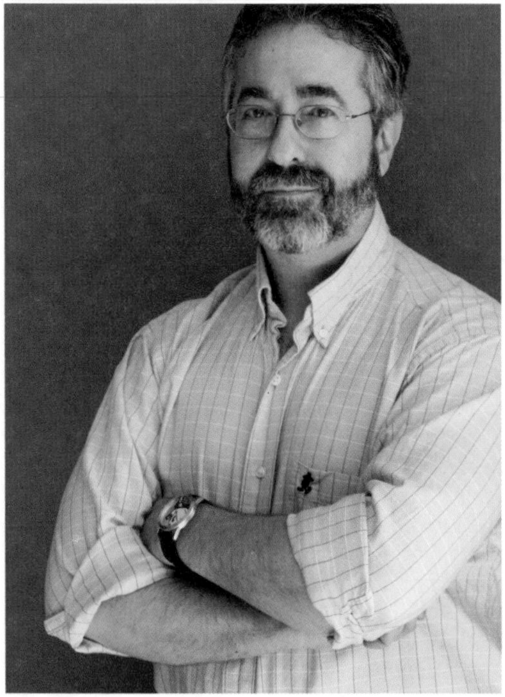

ABOVE: Warren Spector, Creative Director of *Disney Epic Mickey*.

THE MASTER OF Mickey Epics

» INTRODUCTION BY WARREN SPECTOR

THERE HAVE BEEN amazing Disney comic strip and comic book artists over the years. If you're reading this, you already know that. There are wonderful artists and writers at work today. But you already know that, too. However, when I think about Disney comics, two names come to mind before all others.

The first is Carl Barks; the second, Floyd Gottfredson.

Barks was the duck-meister, a master of framing, pacing and characterization whose work seemed special to me, as to many other comic fans, from the time I was a young child.

Gottfredson was a little different—still special, but special in his own way. For starters, when you think about Gottfredson you think of Mickey Mouse, not Donald. But beyond, Gottfredson seems a master of a different sort than "the good duck artist." When I thought—and think—of Floyd Gottfredson's work, what has always come to mind is his use of line and panel layout in the simulation of motion. I think of long-form storytelling, of high adventure and, at times, of low humor more than a little reminiscent of the early Mickey cartoons when Ub Iwerks and Walt Disney were working out what made the mouse tick—heck, though the world may not know it, Gottfredson probably contributed as much to Mickey's core personality as either of his better-known contemporaries.

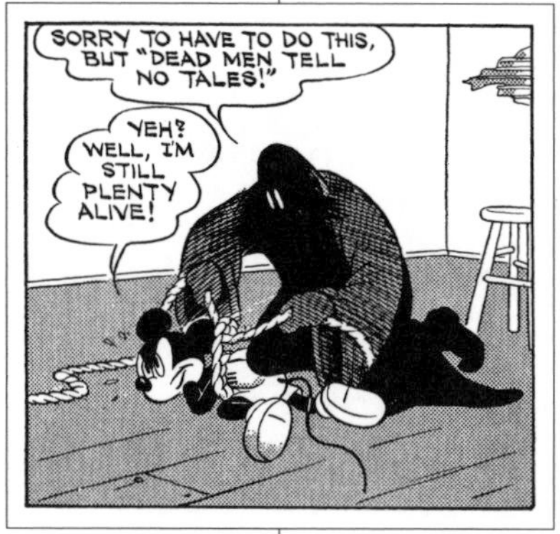
SORRY TO HAVE TO DO THIS, BUT "DEAD MEN TELL NO TALES!"
YEH? WELL, I'M STILL PLENTY ALIVE!

When I think of Barks, I think of amazing, colorful moments frozen in time. When I think of Gottfredson, I think of simple, black and white moments that seem endlessly inventive, artfully animated (if only in my imagination) and exhilaratingly alive.

In a sense, where Barks represents for me an independent-minded, painterly artist with a unique world-view and his own, inimitable story sense, Gottfredson represents a more cinematic approach and the near-perfect embodiment of Walt Disney's vision. I realize that could sound demeaning, as if Gottfredson was less creative or original than Barks, but that's not true at all. Carving out your own space in the context of creative constraints put in place by others is an art, one few are willing to tackle and fewer do extremely well.

I understand the challenges Gottfredson must have faced as well as anyone, having worked on a game project called *Disney Epic Mickey*, where my team and I had to offer players a Mickey Mouse suited to the medium of video games while remaining true to Walt's vision! Making art in the context of someone else's creation is an amazing feat and no one—no one—has ever done it better than Floyd Gottfredson.

The Mickey strips feel like what Walt and Ub would have done if they'd pioneered a medium of still images rather than one of images in motion, a medium where readers would return, reliably, for weeks, even months on end. That's no surprise, given that Gottfredson picked up the Mickey strip in May 1930, in the middle of a story begun by Walt himself. But as time went on, and Mickey became a more established star on screen, in books and, yes, in comic strips, Gottfredson took the character places Walt, Ub and the animators and directors who followed could only dream of.

This accomplishment was a product of Gottfredson's talent, of course, but the increasing scope and scale of the Mickey dailies was also a

YAAAAHH! COME ON UP! I DARE YA TO! I DARE YA TO!
WELL-- I WARNED YA!
3-10

result of some characteristics inherent in the comic strip medium. The depth of Mickey's character was expressed in ways it had never been—could never be—on screen, until and unless Mickey moved from shorts to features, and maybe not even then. The simple fact of the matter is that Gottfredson could count on his audience returning day after day, week after week, even month after month, allowing him to weave stories of greater depth and complexity than Walt or Ub or any of the Disney short subject animators could. Seven minutes isn't a lot of time to tell a story, not compared with seven weeks or even seven months, and Gottfredson took full advantage of that.

In addition to time—lots of time—Gottfredson had another tool at his disposal. Words. It may seem odd to single out a comic strip guy for giving Mickey his "voice," given that the mouse made his mark as the first talking cartoon star while comic strips are, clearly, a silent medium. But while screen star Mickey was squeaking and squawking, speaking in monosyllables and short spurts when he spoke at all, Mickey in the comics talked a blue streak. Mickey was "talkier" even in the earliest Walt-written comics strips than in movies, but words became an ever-more important part of Mickey's character under Gottfredson's "direction."

Thanks to long-form storytelling and dialogue, Gottfredson probably did more to establish the basic nature of the character than anyone this side of Walt himself. For Ub Iwerks, Mickey was an adventurous mime; for Walt, he was often an aw-shucks country boy; for Floyd Gottredson, he was an actor, and the variety of situations Mickey tackled in the comic strips was incredible, far broader than he ever encountered onscreen. And the basic combination of visual and verbal humor that came to characterize Mickey Mouse got its start on the printed page, first under Walt and, later, under Gottfredson and the writers and artists he worked with.

At the end of the day, though there's great beauty in Floyd Gottfredson's visuals, his artistry doesn't stem from breathtaking composition or exquisitely detailed, "Barksian" background illustrations. He didn't seem to care much about anatomy or believability (despite Walt's interest in bringing those artistic values to the screen). Floyd Gottfredson was, plain and simple, a story guy, an adventure guy and a Mickey guy. The artwork is always in the service of story—as it should be in anything with the name "Disney" attached.

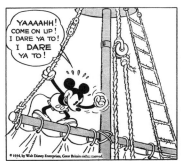

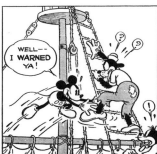

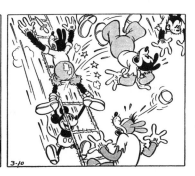

More than anything else, what shines through in Floyd Gottfredson's work is Mickey's *character*—the youthful enthusiasm, the determined optimism, the hopeful self-confidence, the MacGyver-like ingenuity. Gottfredson captured the heart of Mickey's character, defining and refining the core characteristics that have—almost miraculously—made him as relevant today as he was in 1928.

As a creator of character-driven, story-based video games, I routinely turn to Carl Barks for visual inspiration and general story tips, but I turn to Floyd Gottfredson for insight into the heart of Mickey's character and for Mickey-specific storytelling ideas. And that's a legacy to be proud of; one to be envied, as far as I'm concerned. I suspect that, once you've read *this* book, you'll agree. •

THE TRAP DOOR LEADING TO THE HYPNOTIC RAY ROOM IS FAR OUT OF MICKEY'S REACH. BUT....
!!!
I USED TO POLE-VAULT AROUND TH' FARM, I WONDER IF....

Warren Spector began his game industry career in 1983 with tabletop gaming company Steve Jackson Games and, later, TSR. His videogame career began in 1989 with Origin Systems, where he produced games in the Ultima, Underworld *and* System Shock *series, among others. In 1997, Warren founded Ion Storm-Austin where he directed the award-winning shooter/stealth/RPG game* Deus Ex. *He left Ion Storm in 2004, after the release of* Deus Ex: Invisible War *and* Thief: Deadly Shadows, *to found Junction Point Studios. Junction Point was acquired by The Walt Disney Company in July 2007 and in November 2010 released its first title,* Disney Epic Mickey, *a hybrid platform/adventure/RPG for the Nintendo Wii. Warren lives in Austin, TX with his wife, writer, Caroline Spector, and too many animals, games, guitars and books (comic and otherwise).*

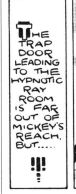

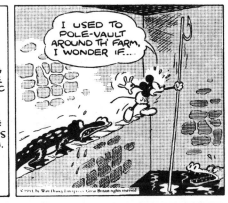

OPPOSITE: Self-confidence: from "Mickey Mouse Outwits the Phantom Blot" (August 11, 1939).

ABOVE: Enthusiasm: from "The Captive Castaways" (March 10, 1934).

RIGHT: Ingenuity: from "Blaggard Castle" (January 27, 1933).

OF MOUSE & MAN

FLOYD GOTTFREDSON AND THE MICKEY MOUSE CONTINUITIES
1930-1931: THE EARLY YEARS

» FOREWORD BY THOMAS ANDRAE

A small black mouse rides the rapids in a barrel. The river waters are fierce, yet he is forced to travel onward. Should he give up and swim to shore, he would face mob justice at the hands of a posse—who mistakenly believe him a desperate criminal. He must reach safety at the river's end; where he can safely build a case for his innocence, find the gold mine that his enemies would steal, and hatch a plan to rescue his true love from prison. But what's that? He hears a horrific rushing sound up ahead—a deadly waterfall! He struggles against the current to no effect. Certain doom rages closer and closer...

TO MANY, this scene from the 1930 comic strip adventure, "Mickey Mouse in Death Valley," may seem incongruous with the image we have inherited of Mickey Mouse. This is not the sweet, diffident mouse we are accustomed to. We forget that audiences growing up in the 1930s—and into the 1950s—knew two radically different Mickeys, the mouse of the animated cartoons and that of the newspaper comic strips. As comics historian Bill Blackbeard puts it, the comic strip Mickey was "a death-defying, tough, steel-gutted mouse... who kept the kids of 1933 rapt with his adventures on pirate dirigibles, cannibal islands, and bullet-tattered fighter planes."[1] Whereas the screen Mickey was famed for his romantic idylls and musical hijinks with Minnie, the comic strip mouse had little time for romance: he was involved in life-and-death struggles which could not be won through tricks of animation magic.

By the early 1930s, Mickey had become an international star whose popularity rivaled that of Charlie Chaplin (one of the celebrities Walt Disney used to model the mouse). Children and adults flocked to watch his latest screen exploits, and intellectuals pondered his immense popularity, declaring Disney one of the great graphic minds of the twentieth century.

Not surprisingly, the world's image of the mouse is that of the screen Mickey. Nonetheless, as this book series will demonstrate, Mickey had some of his finest moments in the newspapers, and his was virtually the only nationally syndicated strip which offered adult cliffhangers in the funny animal genre. Animated cartoons in 1930 were strings of gags, held together by fairly simple plots and brought to their climax by some concluding joke. Personalities rarely developed beyond the requirements of the gags. Comic strip adventures offered an alternative to this type of story. Serialized over three or four months, they were

allowed time to build complex plots and rounded characters. And the combination of graphics with written narration and dialog made them a striking mixture of media, something between a cartoon and a novel.

Though Walt Disney supervised all his cartoon shorts, they were still group efforts, passing through many sets of hands and becoming diluted in the process. The *Mickey* strips, though still produced by a team, were primarily the work of one man who at various times was responsible for plotting, drawing, inking, and editing. As a result, a single personal vision emerged. This one man was the main *Mickey Mouse* artist to draw the strip for over 45 years, until he retired in the mid-1970s. Though it never bore his name, it always bore his mark. In the late 1960s, diligent fans sought him out, and he began at last to receive the acclaim he deserved. The man's name was Floyd Gottfredson.

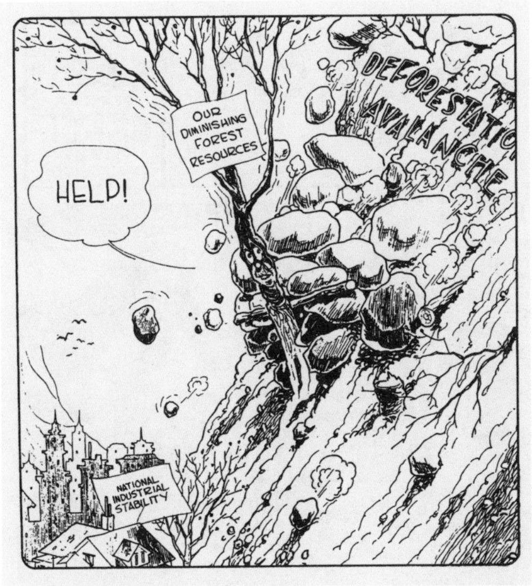
HELP!
OUR DIMINISHING FOREST RESOURCES
DEFORESTATION AVALANCHE
NATIONAL INDUSTRIAL STABILITY

Like the strip he drew, Gottfredson's biography reads like a piece of Americana: "I was born May 5, 1905," he recalled, "in, believe it or not, a railway station in Kaysville, Utah. I was raised in a small town, Siggud, 180 miles south of Salt Lake City."[2] The future mouse-artist's interest in drawing was sparked by an accident he suffered at the age of eleven. His mother had sent him to church on Sunday, but Floyd and a cousin decided to go hunting instead. Young Gottfredson had been taught never to point a gun, so he carried the rifle with the barrel turned inward. As he handed it to his cousin, the gun was thought to have caught on a twig, and Floyd shot himself badly in the arm.

This accident changed his whole life. No longer could he play outside with other children; he had to stay home, recuperating from nine operations to repair the damaged limb. To have some indoor activity, he developed an interest in art, which bloomed under his mother's encouragement. Gottfredson's sister, Mrs. Jessie Furby, fondly recalls that one of Floyd's first drawings was a portrait of his mother, made while sitting at her knee.[3] Since there were no art schools in the vicinity, he began taking drawing lessons by correspondence. To earn money for the lessons, he worked door to door, selling copies of a book recounting his grandfather's experiences fighting Blackhawk Indians in Utah.

Gottfredson's father opposed this budding art career, feeling that his son should get a job like other boys. After all, the family was poor and badly needed money. But the injury to Gottfredson's hand would not allow him to hold a regular job. Like other great artists who have turned tragedy to advantage, he persisted, and, drawing with his bad hand, he eventually developed a drawing style that compensated for his physical limitations. Because he had lost most of the flexibility in his hand, he had to draw by moving his entire arm—something that is taught in penmanship classes, but which artists are rarely trained to do. This gave his drawings a sweep and flair few others attain.

The accident also profoundly shaped Gottfredson's values, forming ideals with which he later imbued his comic strip. Like Mickey, he was something of an outsider, a country lad in the city who constantly had to prove himself. Not only did Gottfredson's father oppose his art career; many of the neighbors believed that a disabled kid who stayed home sketching would never amount to anything.

During his convalescence, Gottfredson read a small stack of Horatio Alger books. "I belonged to an organization called the Lone Scouts. They had a national magazine, and my uncle wrote to them and told them about my accident and asked other kids to write to me. Kids from all over the country sent me letters and things, including 42 Horatio Alger books. After that I gravitated to boys' adventure books and detective stories."[4] This diet of pulp and punch provided raw material for the character of Mickey in

OPPOSITE: Floyd Gottfredson outside the Disney Studio, January 1930. Image courtesy Michael Barrier.

LEFT: Gottfredson drew this political cartoon for an American Tree Association cartooning contest in 1928. It won second place. Image courtesy Alberto Becattini.

BELOW: Mickey flees from his adoring fans. Publicity drawing, May 1930. Pencils attributed to Floyd Gottfredson, inker unknown. Image courtesy Gunnar Andreassen.

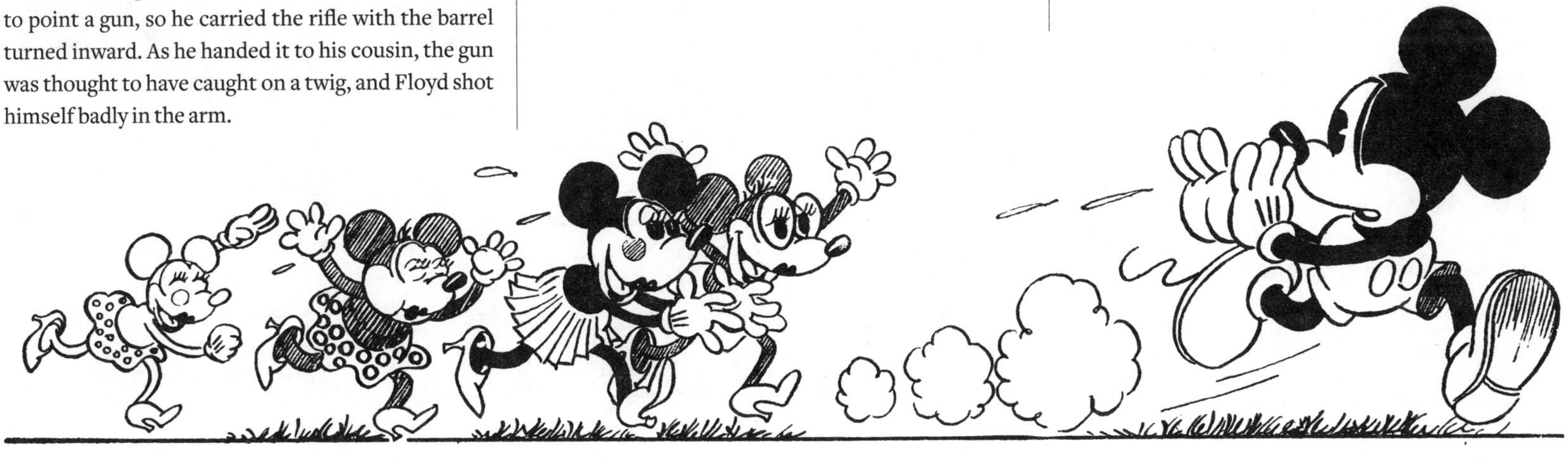

future adventures: the mouse would become another Horatio Alger hero, struggling to overcome his lack of size, strength, and advantage.

Gottfredson's first professional job was that of projectionist and advertising artist for a small movie theater chain. In 1926 he began taking another correspondence course, with the Federal Schools of Illustrating and Cartooning. About a third of the way through, the school started finding work for him. Soon he was drawing four cartoons a month for *Contact,* an automobile journal, and occasional cartoons for the *Salt Lake City Telegram* and a Farm Bureau magazine, the *Utah Farmer*. In 1928, at the suggestion of Federal Schools, he entered a national cartoon contest and placed second. On the strength of this showing, he quit his job as projectionist and moved his family to Los Angeles, hoping to find work as a newspaper cartoonist. But he could not find a position with any of the papers and was forced to resume his former occupation.

His decision to apply at the Disney Studio was the result of a chance encounter that had all the marks of destiny. "Late in 1929, the theater I was working in was torn down to extend the street through the site, and I was out of work. I was looking on what was then known as 'film row' [Vermont Avenue], where all the film exchanges were located, when I saw a one-sheet movie poster of Mickey Mouse in front of the exchange that distributed Walt Disney's films. As a projectionist in Utah I had run all of Walt's and Ub Iwerks' *Oswald the Lucky Rabbit* films, but I had never seen or heard of Mickey Mouse. Out of curiosity, I went in, and the fellow there told me about Walt creating Mickey after losing Oswald to his distributor. He said that Walt was going to New York the next week to hire artists. I rushed home to get my portfolio, went to the Studio, and got the job that afternoon."[5]

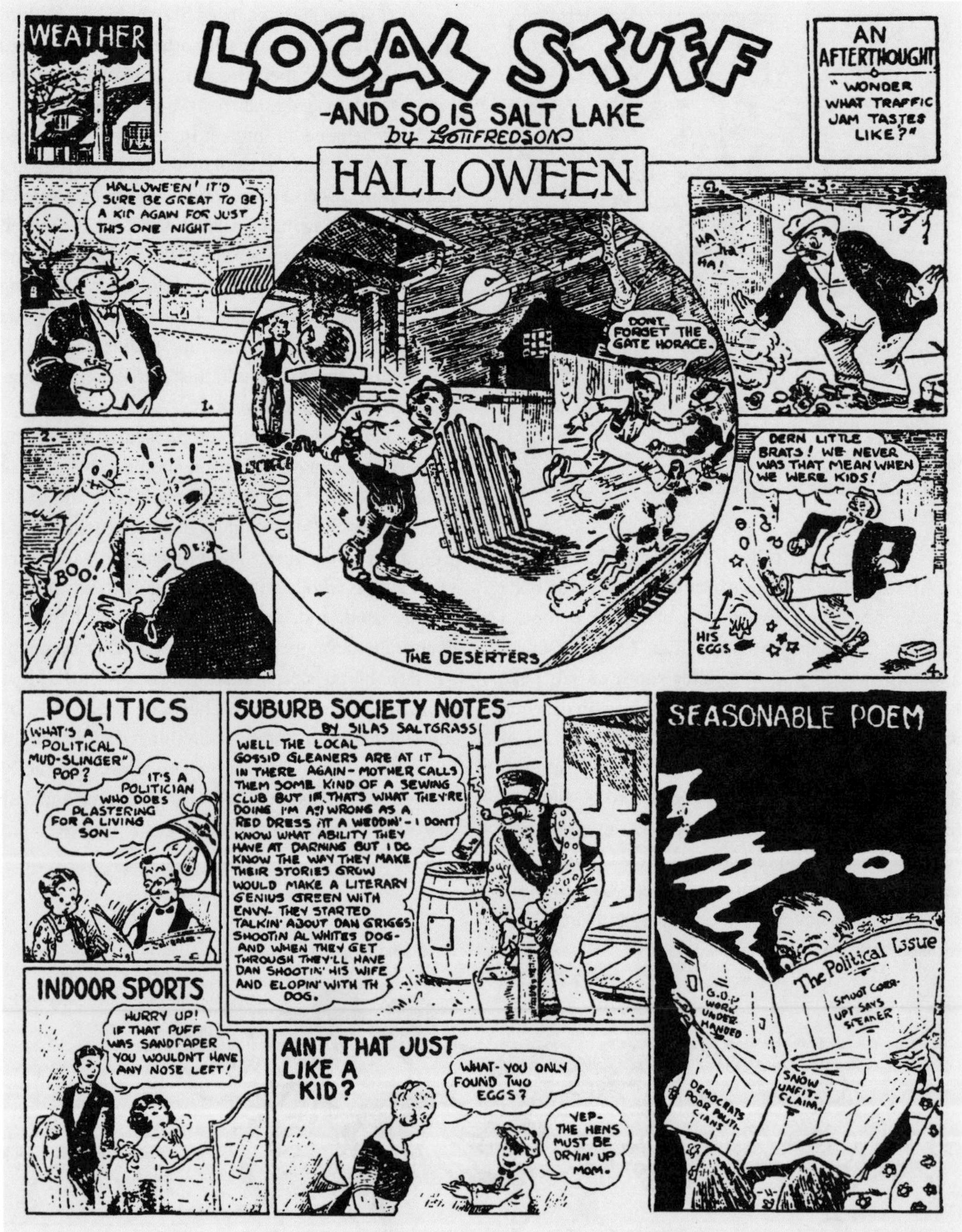
WEATHER
LOCAL STUFF
-AND SO IS SALT LAKE
by GOTTFREDSON
AN AFTERTHOUGHT
"WONDER WHAT TRAFFIC JAM TASTES LIKE?"
HALLOWEEN
HALLOWE'EN! IT'D SURE BE GREAT TO BE A KID AGAIN FOR JUST THIS ONE NIGHT—
DONT FORGET THE GATE HORACE.
THE DESERTERS
HA! HA! HA!
BOO!
DERN LITTLE BRATS! WE NEVER WAS THAT MEAN WHEN WE WERE KIDS!
HIS EGGS
POLITICS
WHAT'S A "POLITICAL MUD-SLINGER" POP?
IT'S A POLITICIAN WHO DOES PLASTERING FOR A LIVING SON—
SUBURB SOCIETY NOTES
BY SILAS SALTGRASS
WELL THE LOCAL GOSSIP GLEANERS ARE AT IT IN THERE AGAIN - MOTHER CALLS THEM SOME KIND OF A SEWING CLUB BUT IF THATS WHAT THEY'RE DOING I'M AS WRONG AS A RED DRESS AT A WEDDIN' - I DONT KNOW WHAT ABILITY THEY HAVE AT DARNING BUT I DO KNOW THE WAY THEY MAKE THEIR STORIES GROW WOULD MAKE A LITERARY GENIUS GREEN WITH ENVY- THEY STARTED TALKIN' ABOUT DAN GRIGGS SHOOTIN AL WHITES DOG- AND WHEN THEY GET THROUGH THEY'LL HAVE DAN SHOOTIN' HIS WIFE AND ELOPIN' WITH TH DOG.
SEASONABLE POEM
The Political Issue
INDOOR SPORTS
HURRY UP! IF THAT PUFF WAS SANDPAPER YOU WOULDN'T HAVE ANY NOSE LEFT!
AINT THAT JUST LIKE A KID?
WHAT- YOU ONLY FOUND TWO EGGS?
YEP- THE HENS MUST BE DRYIN' UP MOM.

RIGHT: One of young Floyd's gag cartoons for the *Salt Lake City Telegram*. Another "Seasonable Poem" vignette can be seen—if one looks closely—in the newspaper shown in the *Mickey Mouse* strip for March 20, 1931. Image courtesy Alberto Becattini.

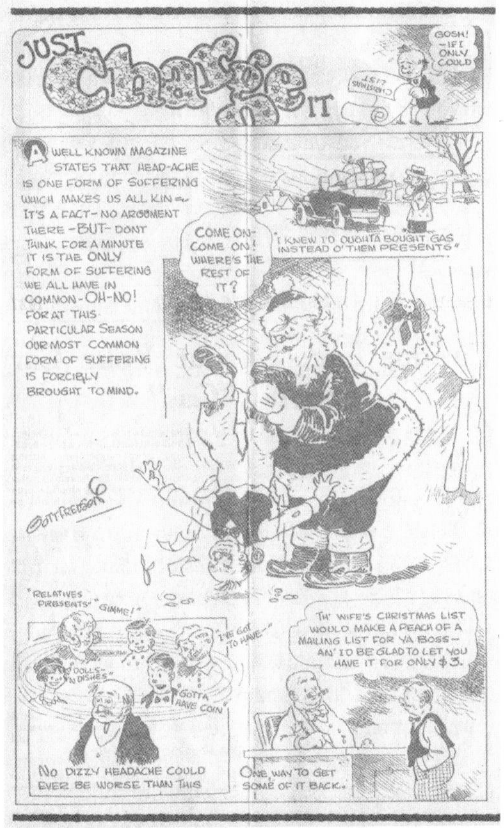
JUST Change IT
GOSH! — IF I ONLY COULD
CHRISTMAS LIST
A WELL KNOWN MAGAZINE STATES THAT HEAD-ACHE IS ONE FORM OF SUFFERING WHICH MAKES US ALL KIN — IT'S A FACT — NO ARGUMENT THERE — BUT — DONT THINK FOR A MINUTE IT IS THE ONLY FORM OF SUFFERING WE ALL HAVE IN COMMON — OH — NO! FOR AT THIS PARTICULAR SEASON OUR MOST COMMON FORM OF SUFFERING IS FORCIBLY BROUGHT TO MIND.
COME ON — COME ON! WHERE'S THE REST OF IT?
"I KNEW I'D OUGHTA BOUGHT GAS INSTEAD O' THEM PRESENTS"
GOTTFREDSON
"RELATIVES PRESENTS"
"GIMME!"
"I'VE GOT TO HAVE—"
"DOLLS — 'N DISHES"
"GOTTA HAVE COIN"
NO DIZZY HEADACHE COULD EVER BE WORSE THAN THIS
TH' WIFE'S CHRISTMAS LIST WOULD MAKE A PEACH OF A MAILING LIST FOR YA BOSS — AN' I'D BE GLAD TO LET YOU HAVE IT FOR ONLY $3.
ONE WAY TO GET SOME OF IT BACK.

When Gottfredson expressed interest in becoming a newspaper cartoonist, Disney talked him out of the idea. King Features Syndicate had asked for a *Mickey Mouse* comic strip, and Disney already had artists at work on it. So he hired Gottfredson as an *inbetweener*, the entry-level position for would-be animators. Perhaps as a concession, however, he did make Gottfredson backup man on the strip. This decision was to lead to Gottfredson becoming the *Mickey* strip artist after all.

Perhaps because Disney had always wanted to be a comic strip artist himself, he wrote *Mickey Mouse* in its early months. Ub Iwerks, who did the final design of Mickey's appearance and almost single-handedly animated the first *Mickey* cartoons, did the drawing. Another artist, Win Smith, inked Iwerks' pencils. When Iwerks quit Disney's to open his own cartoon studio, Smith took over the pencil work as well. "But four months after the strip started, Win had a blowup with Walt," Gottfredson recalled. "Walt was trying to get him to take over the writing because he didn't have time for it anymore. Because of Walt's prodding, Smith quit; and since Walt hired me as backup man on the strip, he asked me to take it over. By now I had become very interested in animation and told Walt I'd rather stay in it. So Walt asked me to take over the strip for two weeks until he found another artist to do it. Nothing further was ever said about it, and I continued to draw the *Mickey* daily for 45 years—until my retirement in October 1975."[6]

The first strips had loose continuity; they presented a gag-centered "story" adapted from early *Mickey* and *Oswald* cartoons. The initial week's sequence, based on the first produced Mickey short, *Plane Crazy*, reflected Disney's rural origins. As we shall see (page 231), it was set in a barnyard and shows the mouse on a haystack dreaming of becoming an aviator like his hero Lindbergh.[7] The humor was based on animation-styled gags with Mickey using a dachshund like a rubber band to power his plane and a turkey's feathers as a tailfin. The 1929 cartoon *Jungle Rhythm*, recently released at the time, provided a plot beginning during the second week: Mickey finds himself marooned on a jungle island. A gag unique to the strip was later reused in another jungle cartoon, *The Castaway* (1931): Mickey tricks a crocodile into swallowing a lion that is chasing him, then uses the lion's tail to tie the croc's jaws shut. In the comic strip, however, the gag is stilted, broken into three static panels and lacking the fast, zany pacing of the later animation. Clearly, the strip needed new focus—but in what direction?

The nudge came from King Features, who had observed the growing popularity of radio serials like *Amos 'n' Andy*. Serialized strips like Sidney Smith's *The Gumps* and Roy Crane's *Wash Tubbs* were fast replacing gag-a-day comics, and in March 1930, the syndicate asked Disney to turn *Mickey Mouse* into a more serious continuity. Disney complied, and the first true adventure story, "Mickey Mouse in Death Valley," began on April 1. Gottfredson assumed the art chores in April, with his first strip being published on May 5. Disney continued doing the writing for two more weeks. Then Gottfredson took over as both artist and writer until late 1932. After that, as manager of the comic strip department, he began to bring in other writers and inkers. Though the strip was no longer a solo effort, Gottfredson continued to plot each continuity and draw the pencil art, setting both the storyline and the visual style.[8]

The first segment of "Mickey Mouse in Death Valley" is based on a 1929 cartoon called *Haunted House*, in which Mickey has a confrontation with the Grim Reaper. Needing greater mystery to build suspense and provide a framework for the strip's plot, Disney had replaced the Reaper with a mysterious

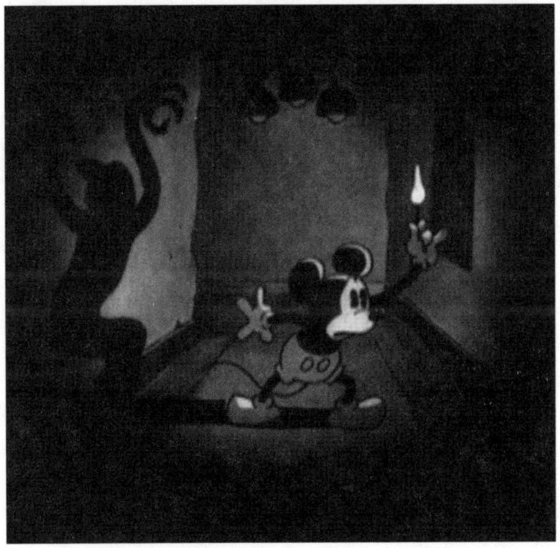

LEFT: Gottfredson feature from *Contact*, December 1927. Image courtesy Gunnar Andreassen.

ABOVE: Mickey's shadow becomes the Grim Reaper in *Haunted House* (1929). The comics' Fox made a relatively more believable scare.

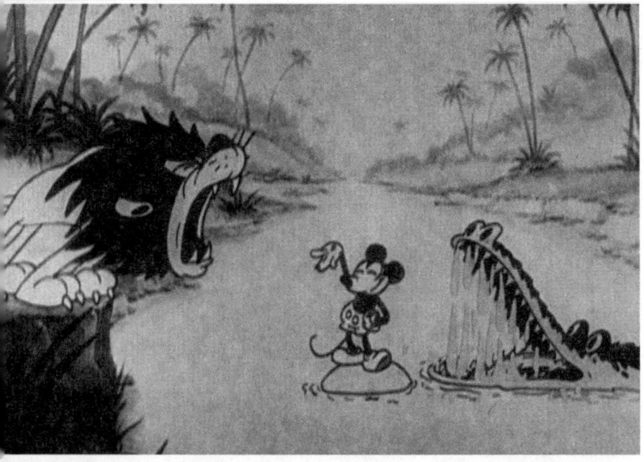

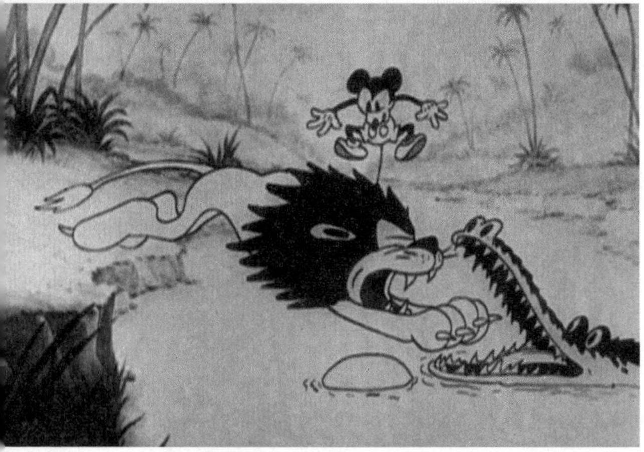

ABOVE: Some early gags simply worked better in cartoons than comics—as when *The Castaway* (1931) reused a sequence from the February 1, 1930 daily.

OPPOSITE: Floyd Gottfredson in the Comic Strip Department library, September 1975.

black-clad figure called the Fox. Such figures were standard fare in the movie serials of the twenties through the fifties and a mainstay of Saturday morning matinees. Given his threatening appearance and secretive manner, it comes as a surprise—explained at story's end—that the Fox occasionally acts as Mickey's helper. Despite the haunted house motif, the real threat in this story is economic, not gothic.

The villains are Pegleg Pete—an oversized alley cat with a wooden leg who serves as Mickey's chief nemesis in the cartoons—and Sylvester Shyster, a top-hatted rat that Disney created for the strip. Shyster, as his name implies, is a crooked lawyer with designs on Minnie's inheritance, which includes a secret gold mine. The plot derives, of course, from the melodramatic clichés of silent cinema which were so popular in the years prior to the *Mickey* strip. Mickey is the stalwart youth who rescues his kidnapped sweetheart, then sets out to save her fortune by recovering a stolen map.

The threat posed by Shyster and Pete seems particularly apt when we consider that the story appeared only months after the great stock market crash of 1929. Villains in the early melodramas had often represented oppressive economic forces, taking the form of heartless landlords and scheming swindlers. These stereotyped figures offered audiences a way of negotiating the tensions caused by America's transition from a self-sufficient agrarian culture to an industrial society governed by the pursuit of profit. The shyster figure, however, had an immediate appeal to audiences in the 1930s. At the nadir of the Depression (1930-1933), many films were made featuring corrupt lawyers, crooked politicians, and sleazy newspapermen.[9]

The shyster also appeared as a fast-talking city con man—an embodiment of the great moral weaknesses people feared in urban life. In American folklore, rural America (and later, the small town) was enshrined as an Arcadian Eden, free of the corruption of the urban metropolis. The shyster thus seemed to embody all that was wrong with the nation, offering a tangible, easily understood threat. But as Andrew Bergman points out, it was not the hand in the till but the emptiness of the till that was the problem. The films' blaming the shyster suggested that it was not failed institutions but individual con men that were the problem and getting rid of crooks was the answer, not overhauling the economy. Thus, ironically, blaming such scapegoats only reinforced the institutions which had brought the country to its crisis.

Gottfredson's next story, the first he wrote entirely by himself, also involves an economic threat. "Mr. Slicker and the Egg Robbers" makes explicit the urban nature of the menace that was implicit in Sylvester Shyster. Slicker is a con artist who turns Minnie's head with his city ways at the same time that her father is threatened with bankruptcy.

Again the melodramatic and the Depression's concerns dovetail and the shyster is blamed for the economic crisis. To ensure that Minnie will marry him, Slicker carries out a plan that throws the entire community into destitution. Mickey's defeat of Slicker both saves Minnie from the proverbial Fate Worse Than Death and restores economic security, offering a happy ending for Depression readers.

"Slicker" is a transitional story that moves from the barnyard and what Horst Schroeder calls the "rustic anarchy" of the strip's first weeks to the small-town no-man's land in which Mickey would reside for the rest of the decade.[10] The small-town setting provided a community in which more sophisticated adventures could take place. In "Slicker," Gottfredson introduced two themes that would characterize some of his best later stories: the sensational crime and the mysterious master criminal whose activities force Mickey to play amateur detective.

At the same time, the story shows Gottfredson experimenting. "Death Valley" had been a mixture of horror story and western; this time, the artist mixed two other genres, the romance and the crime drama. At the same time, he slowly perfected the difficult blend of humor and sustained suspense required by an adventure serial. We can watch as Gottfredson learns to deepen his villains, approaching the combination of mystery and sinister suspense that will characterize his most famous criminal masterminds.

1 Bill Blackbeard, "Mickey Mouse and the Phantom Artist," in *The Comic Book Book*, ed. Don Thompson and Dick Lupoff (New Rochelle: Arlington House, 1973), p. 38.

2 Series of interviews with Floyd Gottfredson, September 27 and December 12, 1979 and February 26, 1981.

3 Mrs. Furby recalls that "when Floyd's arm was shot, the doctors decided to amputate. My dear mother said, 'No,' and wouldn't permit it. That's when they tried nine operations and saved it as best as they could in those 'horse and buggy' days. [Do you] call it a Mother's Faith? Or Providence? I prefer to think yes to both!" From a letter to Bruce Hamilton, April 19, 1988.

4 Gottfredson interviews.

5 Ibid.

6 Ibid. Research shows that Walt—or someone—did briefly try another artist on the strip in June 1930. See "Sharing the Spotlight" in this volume, page 265.

7 Charles A. Lindbergh, an American aviator, became a national hero in 1927, piloting his *Spirit of St. Louis* in the world's first nonstop solo flight across the Atlantic.

8 See the contents pages for a rundown of other artists and writers who worked on this volume's *Mickey* strips.

9 Andrew Bergman, *We're In the Money: Depression America and Its Films* (New York: Harper and Row, 1971), p. 18.

10 Horst Schroeder, Introduction to *Walt Disney's Goofy: Best Comics* (New York: Abbeville Press, 1979), p. 13.

In effect, Gottfredson was serving his apprenticeship during his first two years. And while he was learning to draw and craft stories, he was adapting to the continuity art form. For him to do a "serious" funny animal adventure, it required two things that were also needed in real-life adventure strips. First, Gottfredson had to master the serial format. Each strip had to end on a puzzle or cliffhanger that would make readers turn to the next day's strip. The opening panel had to summarize the immediately preceding action, so that readers who missed a day or two could still follow the story; and the entire strip had to advance the general plot. Not easy.

Second—and in the funny animal realm, this can be credited as his invention—Gottfredson had to make Mickey's perils realistic and threatening enough to create suspense, yet keep them tongue-in-cheek. Humor could not rely too heavily on slapstick, nor on the physically outlandish events that propelled the cartoons, because this would disturb the suspension of disbelief necessary to carry an adventure story.

In short, the *Mickey* strips required a very delicate balance of conflicting elements. In this volume, we see Gottfredson beginning to achieve that balance and to pioneer a new genre of comics—the funny animal adventure story. •

Thomas Andrae (Ph.D. University of California, Berkeley) is an internationally recognized authority on social theory and Cultural Studies and an instructor at California State University East Bay. He is co-founder and senior editor of Discourse: Journal for Theoretical Studies in Media and Culture. *His work has been reprinted in academic collections including* American Media and Mass Culture (*University of California Press, 1987*) *and* A Comics Studies Reader (*University Press of Mississippi, 2008*). *He is the author of* Carl Barks and the Disney Comic Book: Unmasking the Myth of Modernity; Creators of the Superheroes; *and* TV Nation: Prime Time Television and the Politics of the Sixties (*forthcoming*); *and co-author of Bob Kane's autobiography,* Batman & Me *and (with Mel Gordon)* Siegel and Shuster's Funnyman: The First Jewish Superhero.

FLOYD GOTTFREDSON, THE MICKEY STRIP ...AND ME

A
WALT DISNEY
MICKEY MOUSE
IN TECHNICOLOR
DISTRIBUTED BY
R·K·O RADIO PICTURES
INC.
COPYRIGHT MCMXLI WALT DISNEY PRODUCTIONS
ALL RIGHTS RESERVED

» *Appreciation by Floyd Norman*

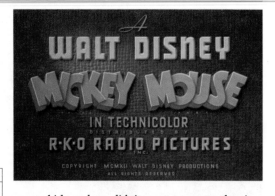

LIKE MOST KIDS, I first became aware of the famous Mouse while reading the monthly comic book *Walt Disney's Comics and Stories*. As a young person in the 1940s, I knew Floyd Gottfredson's work from its reprints in these comic books. But I didn't even know there was a Mickey Mouse comic *strip*, and I knew nothing about Floyd Gottfredson. All the published comics were credited to Walt. Of course, I saw the Mickey cartoons on the big screen in our local theater, and I remember how different the later screen Mickey was from the scrappy, adventurous little guy I read in the comics.

I still remember the love I had for Gottfredson's Mouse and how real he seemed to me. I had no idea how much a part of my life Mickey would become as I followed my career path. Initially, I dreamed of working in comics, but that was soon followed by an interest in animation. Clearly, the Walt Disney Studio was my destiny.

Years passed, and eventually I found myself inside Walt's magic factory serving an animation apprenticeship. While visiting the scene-planning department one day, I happened across a piece of original Disney art. It was the Mickey Mouse title card that preceded every Disney Mickey cartoon. An image I had seen countless times up on the big screen when I was a child. Yet, here it was in front of me, and I could actually touch what I considered a magical piece of Disney history.

As my colleagues and I continued our tour of the Disney Studio, we made our way up a flight of stairs in an older building. A group of gentlemen sat at their drawing tables working away. I'm embarrassed to say we had no idea who they were, but they quickly introduced themselves. The gentleman drawing Donald Duck was Al Taliaferro, and the artist drawing Mickey was Floyd Gottfredson. It appeared I had finally met the man who had given me so much delight as a kid and inspired me to become a Disney artist.

I still regret my meeting with Floyd Gottfredson was so brief that day. However, we were young kids and we didn't want to waste the time of these wonderful Disney artists. I saw Mr. Gottfredson a few times after that initial meeting, but sadly I never got to know him that well. The Disney veterans were a good deal older than myself and my colleagues, and we were reluctant to make a nuisance of ourselves. In time, I did get to know Floyd's son, an animation artist whose first name happens to be the same as my last. Norman Gottfredson soon became a friend, and I still find the "name thing" rather curious.

As an animation artist, I worked on many a Mickey animated segment for the *Disneyland* TV show, but I didn't join Disney's Comic Strip Department until the early 1980s, where I considered myself a cartoon utility man of sorts. I would, on occasion fill in for a writer who was ill or on vacation. Sometimes, that even meant writing the *Mickey Mouse* comic strip. Over time, I worked on it more and more.

MICKEY'S RECENT FEATS OF HEROISM HAVE CAUSED SOME TENSION IN THE UNDERWORLD!
GET 'IM, BOYS!
©1990 The Walt Disney Company
POW
BAM
SORRY, GUYS, I HAVE NO TIME FOR THIS... I'VE GOT A DATE WITH MINNIE...
SOCK
BOP!
...AND SHE'LL KILL ME IF I'M LATE!!
OOF!
Distributed by King Features Syndicate

ABOVE: An early 1940s title card—and a late 1950s rediscovery for young Floyd Norman.

RIGHT: The opening scene of Floyd Norman's first Mickey daily strip serial paid homage to Gottfredson's first strip (compare with May 5, 1930 daily, later in this volume). Art by Alex Howell; image courtesy Thomas Jensen.

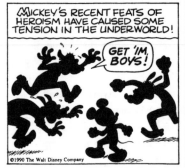

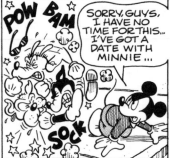

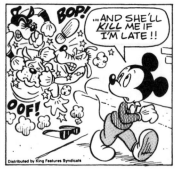

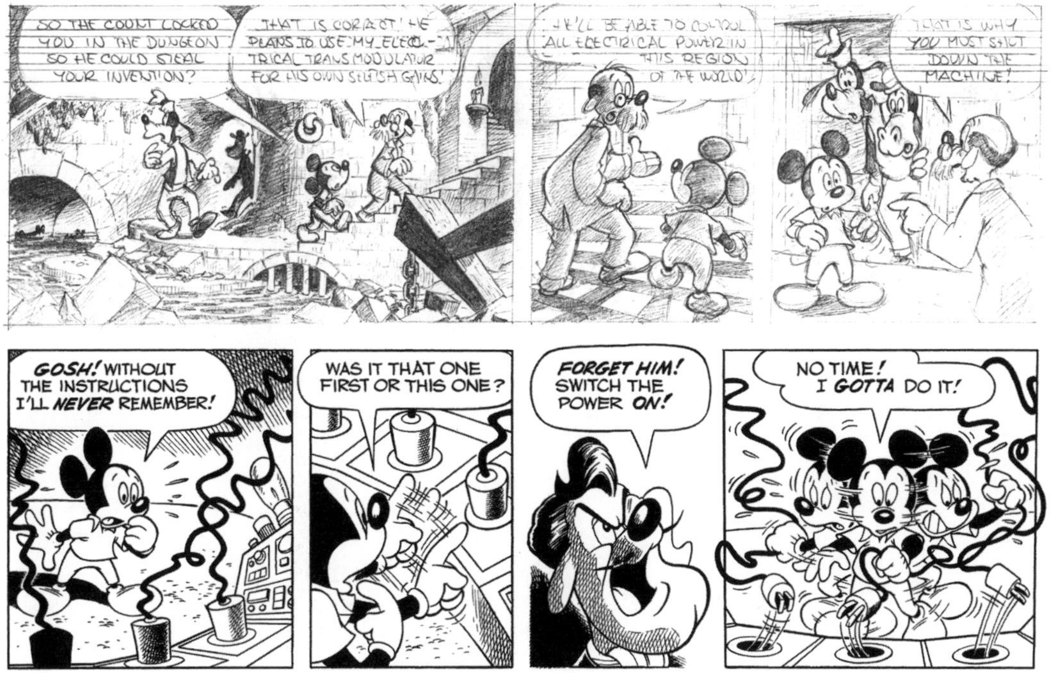
SO THE COUNT LOCKED YOU IN THE DUNGEON SO HE COULD STEAL YOUR INVENTION?
THAT IS CORRECT! HE PLANS TO USE MY ELECTRICAL TRANSMODULATOR FOR HIS OWN SELFISH GAINS!
HE'LL BE ABLE TO CONTROL ALL ELECTRICAL POWER IN THIS REGION OF THE WORLD!
THAT IS WHY YOU MUST SHUT DOWN THE MACHINE!
GOSH! WITHOUT THE INSTRUCTIONS I'LL NEVER REMEMBER!
WAS IT THAT ONE FIRST OR THIS ONE?
FORGET HIM! SWITCH THE POWER ON!
NO TIME! I GOTTA DO IT!

ABOVE: Mickey, Goofy, and Horace face wicked Count Dupree in Norman's last Mickey daily strip story—one that was shelved before inks had been completed. Art by Rick Hoover, c. 1995.

The strip had evolved over the years. The editorial styling and even the art styling had changed. As Floyd Gottfredson grew older, Mickey seemed to have aged with him. I don't suppose there was any way around such a change. Floyd had been drawing Mickey Mouse since the 1930s. Clearly, their lives were intertwined. What else could one expect? Mickey was no longer the scrappy, cheeky little guy from his early years. No longer the explorer heading off into the jungles of Africa or the frozen wastes of the North Pole, Mickey had settled into a cozy suburban lifestyle, and morphed into a cartoon version of Ozzie Nelson.

King Features Syndicate insisted that Disney continue their gag-a-day newspaper format even after Floyd retired. Once I found myself the ongoing writer of the *Mickey Mouse* comic strip, I pleaded with Disney and the syndicate to allow me to bring back the real Mickey we knew and loved. I was so eager to write Mickey adventures for the daily strip, even though all insisted that doing daily gags would be the only way to keep the strip alive. I persisted, and eventually King allowed me to write ongoing Mickey continuities. They limited me to three-week storylines, but I sometimes fudged and pushed it to four. I had achieved my greatest joy: writing Mickey adventures much like the stories I read as a kid! I was fortunate to have editors who never restricted what I could write, as long as my stories stayed within the bounds of Disney propriety.

It may sound odd, but I never had a moment of difficulty writing Mickey Mouse. Thanks to Floyd Gottfredson's wonderful portrayals, I knew the characters so well that my stories almost seemed to write themselves. I simply needed to put Mickey and Goofy in a situation and listen to what they would say. It would seem my childhood passion for Floyd's comics enabled me to absorb the process by osmosis. Clearly, it was in my blood now, and this old storyteller wasn't about to complain.

Yet, in spite of the fun I was having, the *Mickey Mouse* comic strip was eventually cancelled, or rather new stories stopped being produced for it. The strip went all-reprint, and I had to stop producing my final storyline right in the middle. Both Disney and the syndicate agreed it was time to retire the famous mouse.

I look back on my days with Mickey Mouse as a delightful time. In many ways, Mickey has touched me and become more real than ever. I've had the opportunity to work with most of Mickey's creators, from Walt Disney to Ub Iwerks. I've known Mickey's voices, Jimmy MacDonald and Wayne Allwine. I've worked with the Disney animators who gave life to Mickey on the big screen, and I was given the opportunity to write the comic strip I so loved as a kid. I grew up on the stories of Floyd Gottfredson, Bill Walsh and so many other talented individuals.

Back in 1930, Walt Disney had his hands full, so he needed one of his talented staffers to write and draw the Mickey Mouse comic strip. Floyd Gottfredson stepped up and took on the temporary job. A job that lasted over forty years and gave us incredible adventures, memorable characters and a hero that would make Indiana Jones proud. Thank you, Mr. Gottfredson, for a job well done. •

Floyd Norman started work with Disney as an animation artist on Sleeping Beauty *(1959), then moved to the story department with* The Jungle Book *(1967)—making him Disney's first African-American story man, and enabling him to work with Walt on the last film that the "Old Maestro" personally supervised. After a storied career elsewhere, including work as writer/producer of* Sesame Street *animated segments, Norman rejoined Disney in the 1980s, working first for the Comic Strip Department and then as an animator on Disney and Pixar feature films. Floyd received a Disney Legends Award in 2007 for his animation contributions.*

MICKEY MOUSE IN DEATH VALLEY

APRIL 1, 1930

–

SEPTEMBER 20, 1930

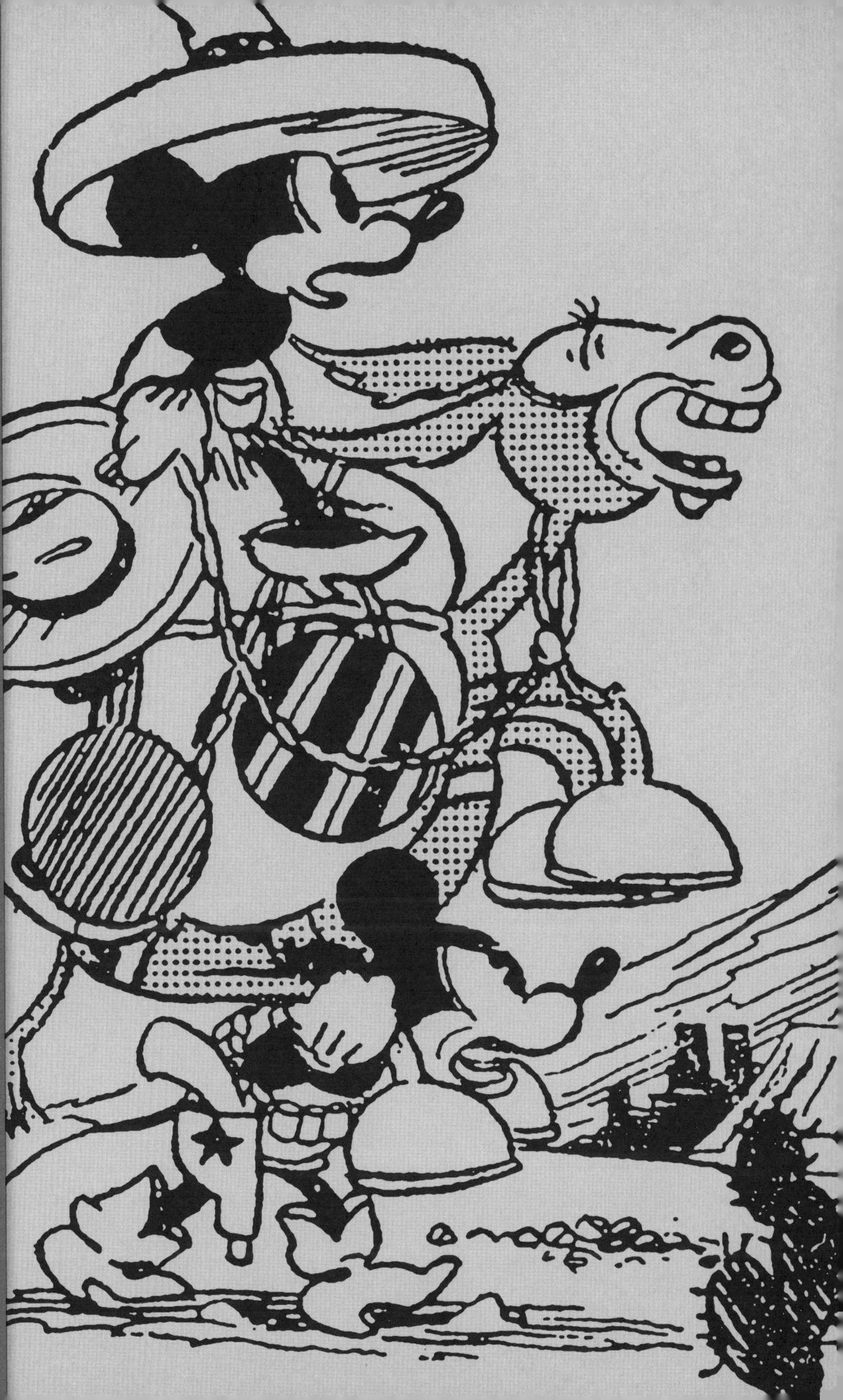

MICKEY MOUSE

REGISTERED U.S. PATENT OFFICE

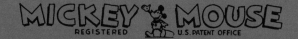

AN INDEBTED VALLEY

Neither Walt Disney nor Floyd Gottfredson hit the ground running when it came to comics. Caught flat-footed by a King Features request that the Mickey strip become more adventure-oriented, Disney set out in "Death Valley" to mimic *The Gumps*, then the most popular humor-adventure strip. But a look at "Death Valley" quickly reveals a hodge-podge of additional influences as well. In the effort to get away from the gaggier style of earlier Mickey strips, an anything-goes ethic prevailed in the fledgling comic strip department, and the result was a Mickey adventure like few others.

As created by Sidney Smith, *The Gumps* revolved around a family; an adventurous family, to be sure, but still a domestic unit of father (Andy), mother (Min), and son (Chester). By contrast, Mickey and Minnie were at the time high school age teens, whose unmarried status lent itself to a very different set of relationship crises. In particular, Minnie could face the threats of traditional melodrama-style villains, as she does here.

Then came the cliffhangers. In another nod to melodrama, "Death Valley" repeatedly threatens Mickey with drowning, hanging, and other Pauline-like perils—similar in concept to thrills he would face in the future, but made scarier here by a more gothic artistic style and by the overall lack of a humorous touch. More suited to older readers than to Mickey's younger fans, the scares would be deployed with more taste and skill later on.

In the same vein, "Death Valley" also contains a typical 1930s usage of cartoon weapons. Bad guys are quick to stick 'em up in the desert; good guys (including Mickey) are forced to carry their own guns for self-defense. At the time, Wild West-themed adventure stories generally invoked such "trueshot cowboy" imagery without a second thought. As in Disney's oft-seen "Pecos Bill" (in *Melody Time* [1948]) and *Pirates of the Caribbean* movies, the mayhem was intended as fantastic and over-the-top.

Finally, we'd like to draw your attention to other cultural references included in the story. As initial writer, Walt Disney set a standard for engaging nods to popular songs. "Tomorrow, tomorrow, how happy we will be" (April 1) opens the chorus to Roy Turk's "(I'll Be In My Dixie Home Again) To-Morrow," then an Eddie Cantor standard. When Mickey speaks of "climb[ing] the golden stairs" to Sylvester's law office (April 4), the remark is a nod to F. Heiser's 1884 jubilee favorite, "Climbing Up De Golden Stairs." Even "You'd Be Surprised" (June 27) and "Looking At the World Through Rose-Colored Glasses" (July 10) were then the titles of songs.

And when Mickey, entering Sylvester's office through the window, shouts "Lafayette!—We are here!" (April 11), he is actually quoting General John Pershing, who in 1917 used that phrase to salute the memory of Revolutionary War hero Marquis de Lafayette. [DG]

OPPOSITE, TOP: This oft-reprinted introductory strip, drawn by Win Smith in early 1930, was designed for newspapers that picked up *Mickey Mouse* mid-continuity. Its alternate name for Pegleg Pete seems never to have been used again.

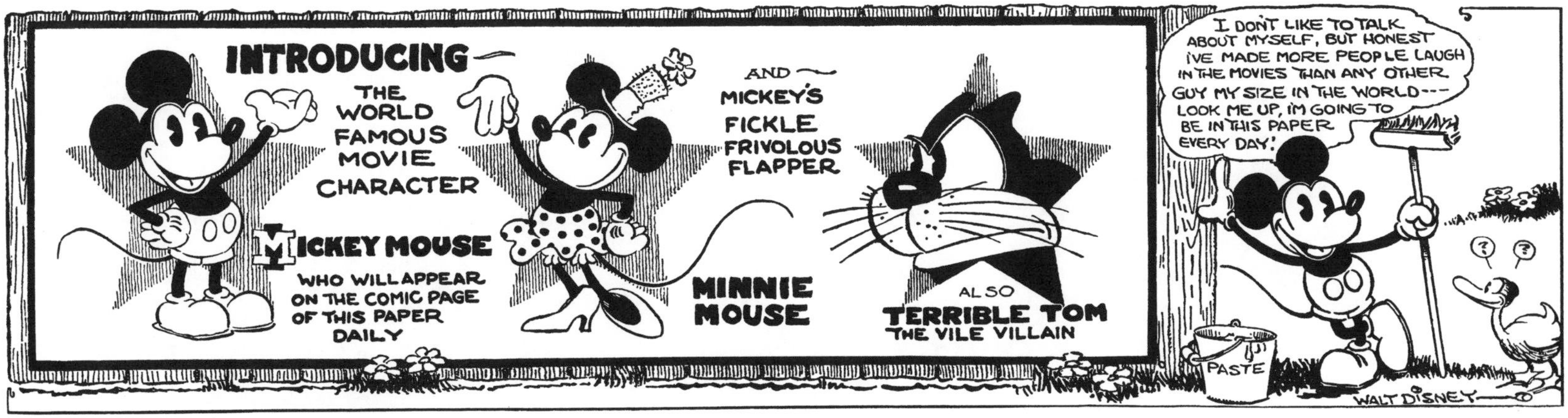
INTRODUCING—
THE WORLD FAMOUS MOVIE CHARACTER
MICKEY MOUSE
WHO WILL APPEAR ON THE COMIC PAGE OF THIS PAPER DAILY
MINNIE MOUSE
AND— MICKEY'S FICKLE FRIVOLOUS FLAPPER
ALSO
TERRIBLE TOM
THE VILE VILLAIN
I DON'T LIKE TO TALK ABOUT MYSELF, BUT HONEST I'VE MADE MORE PEOPLE LAUGH IN THE MOVIES THAN ANY OTHER GUY MY SIZE IN THE WORLD--- LOOK ME UP, I'M GOING TO BE IN THIS PAPER EVERY DAY!
? ?
PASTE
WALT DISNEY

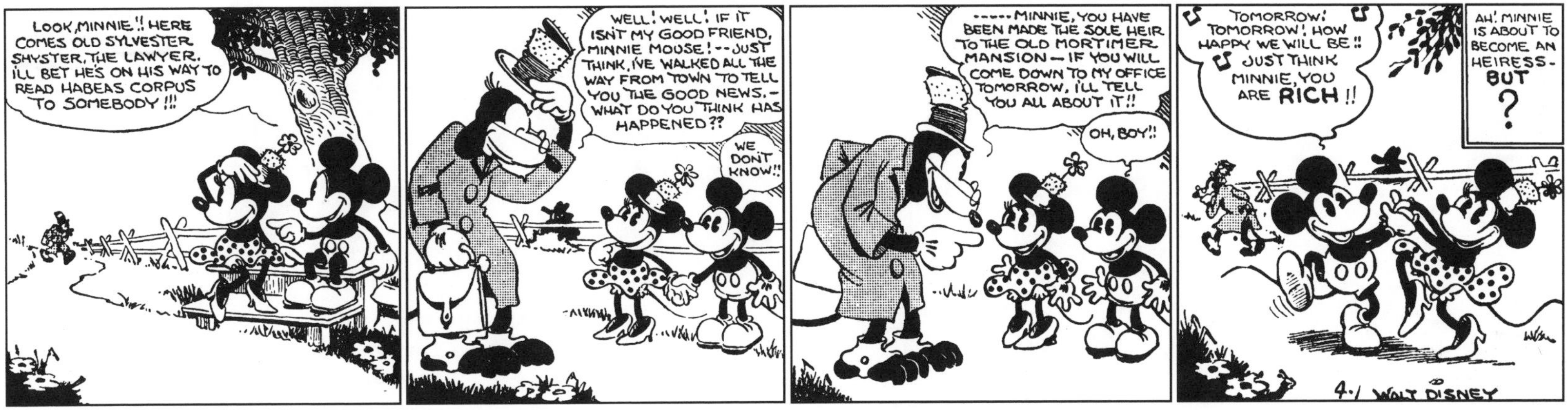
LOOK, MINNIE!! HERE COMES OLD SYLVESTER SHYSTER, THE LAWYER. I'LL BET HE'S ON HIS WAY TO READ HABEAS CORPUS TO SOMEBODY!!!
WELL! WELL! IF IT ISN'T MY GOOD FRIEND, MINNIE MOUSE! -- JUST THINK, I'VE WALKED ALL THE WAY FROM TOWN TO TELL YOU THE GOOD NEWS. - WHAT DO YOU THINK HAS HAPPENED??
WE DON'T KNOW!!
-----MINNIE, YOU HAVE BEEN MADE THE SOLE HEIR TO THE OLD MORTIMER MANSION - IF YOU WILL COME DOWN TO MY OFFICE TOMORROW, I'LL TELL YOU ALL ABOUT IT!!
OH, BOY!!
TOMORROW! TOMORROW! HOW HAPPY WE WILL BE!! JUST THINK MINNIE, YOU ARE RICH!!
AH! MINNIE IS ABOUT TO BECOME AN HEIRESS - BUT ?
4-1 WALT DISNEY

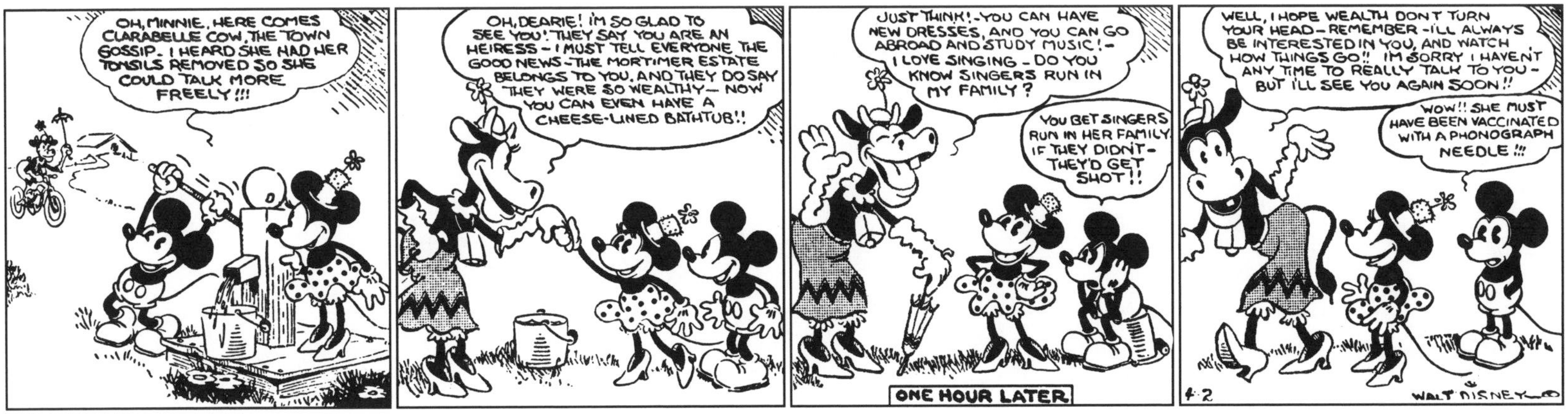
OH, MINNIE, HERE COMES CLARABELLE COW, THE TOWN GOSSIP. I HEARD SHE HAD HER TONSILS REMOVED SO SHE COULD TALK MORE FREELY!!!
OH, DEARIE! I'M SO GLAD TO SEE YOU! THEY SAY YOU ARE AN HEIRESS - I MUST TELL EVERYONE THE GOOD NEWS - THE MORTIMER ESTATE BELONGS TO YOU, AND THEY DO SAY THEY WERE SO WEALTHY - NOW YOU CAN EVEN HAVE A CHEESE-LINED BATHTUB!!
JUST THINK! - YOU CAN HAVE NEW DRESSES, AND YOU CAN GO ABROAD AND STUDY MUSIC! - I LOVE SINGING - DO YOU KNOW SINGERS RUN IN MY FAMILY?
YOU BET SINGERS RUN IN HER FAMILY. IF THEY DIDN'T - THEY'D GET SHOT!!
ONE HOUR LATER
WELL, I HOPE WEALTH DON'T TURN YOUR HEAD - REMEMBER - I'LL ALWAYS BE INTERESTED IN YOU, AND WATCH HOW THINGS GO!! I'M SORRY I HAVEN'T ANY TIME TO REALLY TALK TO YOU - BUT I'LL SEE YOU AGAIN SOON!!
WOW!! SHE MUST HAVE BEEN VACCINATED WITH A PHONOGRAPH NEEDLE!!!
4-2 WALT DISNEY

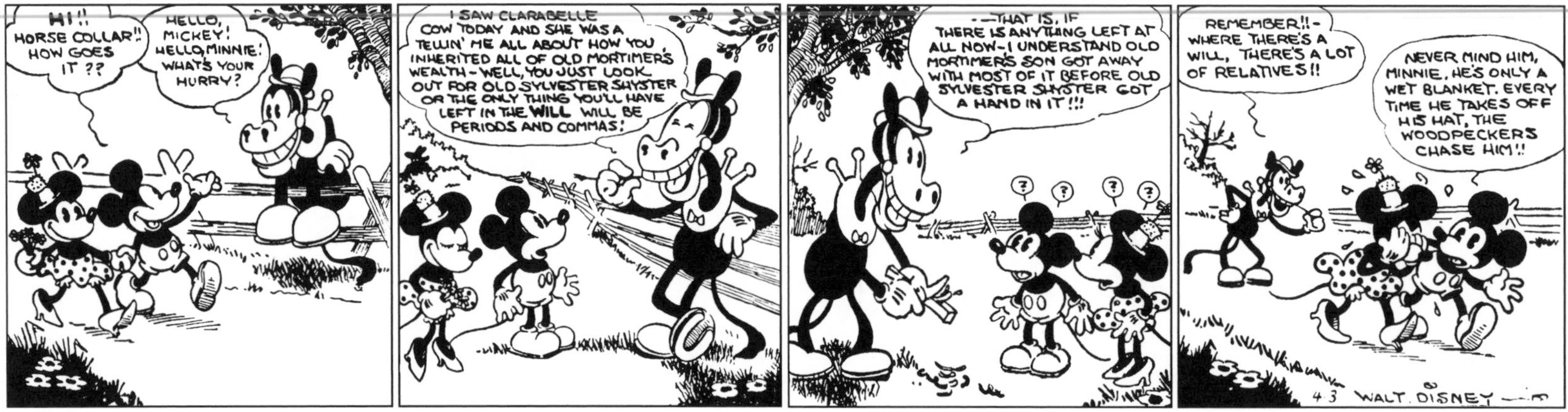
HI!! HORSE COLLAR!! HOW GOES IT ??
HELLO, MICKEY! HELLO, MINNIE! WHAT'S YOUR HURRY?
I SAW CLARABELLE COW TODAY AND SHE WAS A TELLIN' ME ALL ABOUT HOW YOU INHERITED ALL OF OLD MORTIMER'S WEALTH - WELL, YOU JUST LOOK OUT FOR OLD SYLVESTER SHYSTER OR THE ONLY THING YOU'LL HAVE LEFT IN THE **WILL** WILL BE PERIODS AND COMMAS!
--THAT IS, IF THERE IS ANYTHING LEFT AT ALL NOW - I UNDERSTAND OLD MORTIMER'S SON GOT AWAY WITH MOST OF IT BEFORE OLD SYLVESTER SHYSTER GOT A HAND IN IT!!!
REMEMBER!! - WHERE THERE'S A WILL, THERE'S A LOT OF RELATIVES!!
NEVER MIND HIM, MINNIE, HE'S ONLY A WET BLANKET. EVERY TIME HE TAKES OFF HIS HAT, THE WOODPECKERS CHASE HIM!!
43 WALT. DISNEY

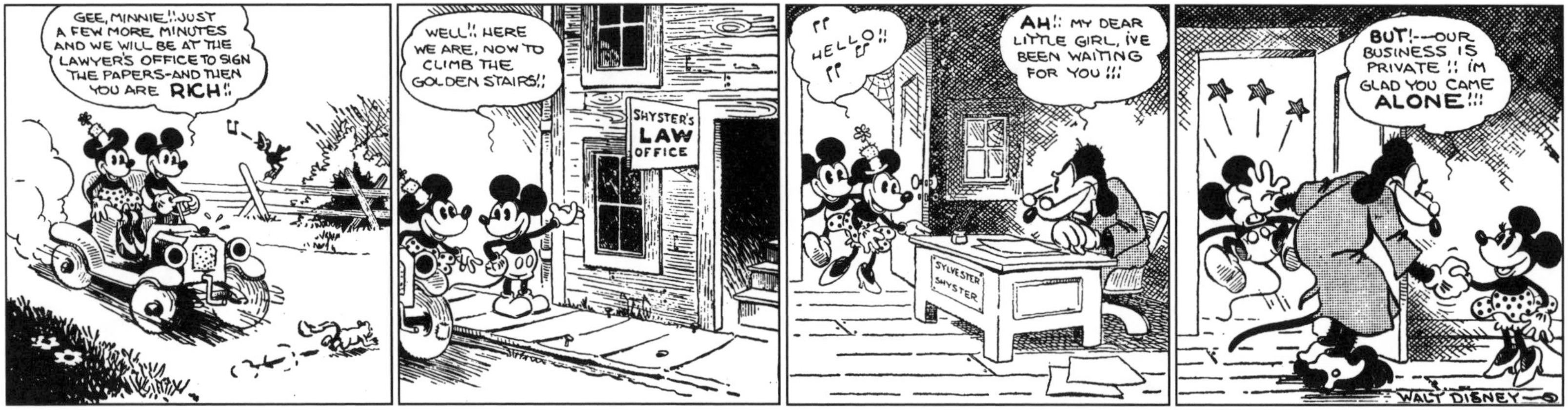
GEE, MINNIE!! JUST A FEW MORE MINUTES AND WE WILL BE AT THE LAWYER'S OFFICE TO SIGN THE PAPERS - AND THEN YOU ARE **RICH**!!
WELL!! HERE WE ARE, NOW TO CLIMB THE GOLDEN STAIRS!!
SHYSTER'S LAW OFFICE
HELLO!!
AH!! MY DEAR LITTLE GIRL, I'VE BEEN WAITING FOR YOU!!!
SYLVESTER SHYSTER
BUT!--OUR BUSINESS IS PRIVATE!! I'M GLAD YOU CAME **ALONE**!!!
WALT DISNEY

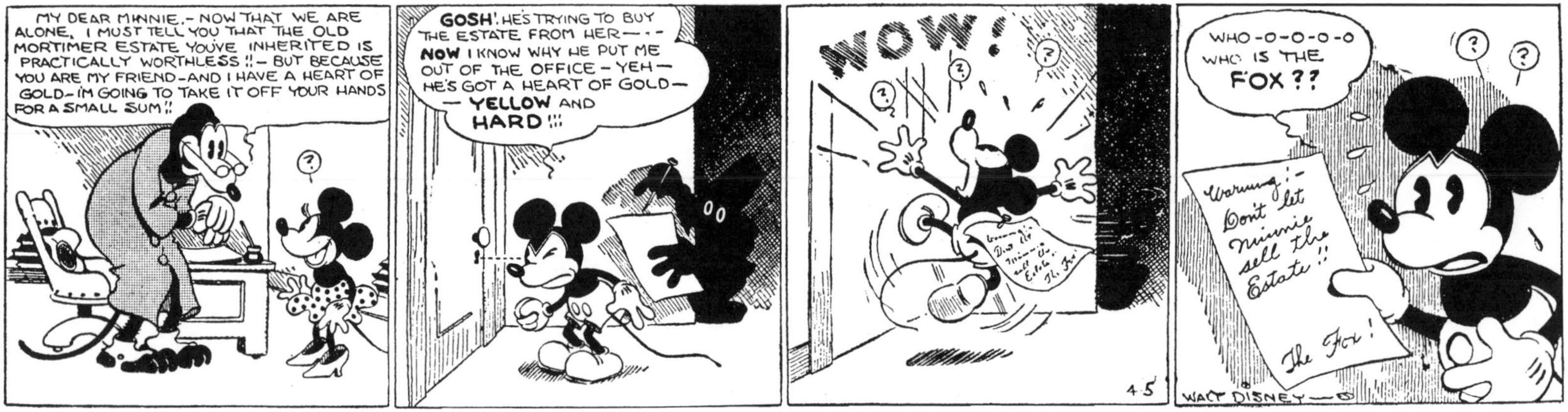
MY DEAR MINNIE, - NOW THAT WE ARE ALONE, I MUST TELL YOU THAT THE OLD MORTIMER ESTATE YOU'VE INHERITED IS PRACTICALLY WORTHLESS!! - BUT BECAUSE YOU ARE MY FRIEND - AND I HAVE A HEART OF GOLD - I'M GOING TO TAKE IT OFF YOUR HANDS FOR A SMALL SUM!!
GOSH! HE'S TRYING TO BUY THE ESTATE FROM HER--- **NOW** I KNOW WHY HE PUT ME OUT OF THE OFFICE - YEH - HE'S GOT A HEART OF GOLD - - **YELLOW** AND **HARD**!!!
WOW!
45
WHO-O-O-O-O WHO IS THE **FOX**??
Warning!! - Don't let Minnie sell the Estate!! The Fox!
WALT DISNEY

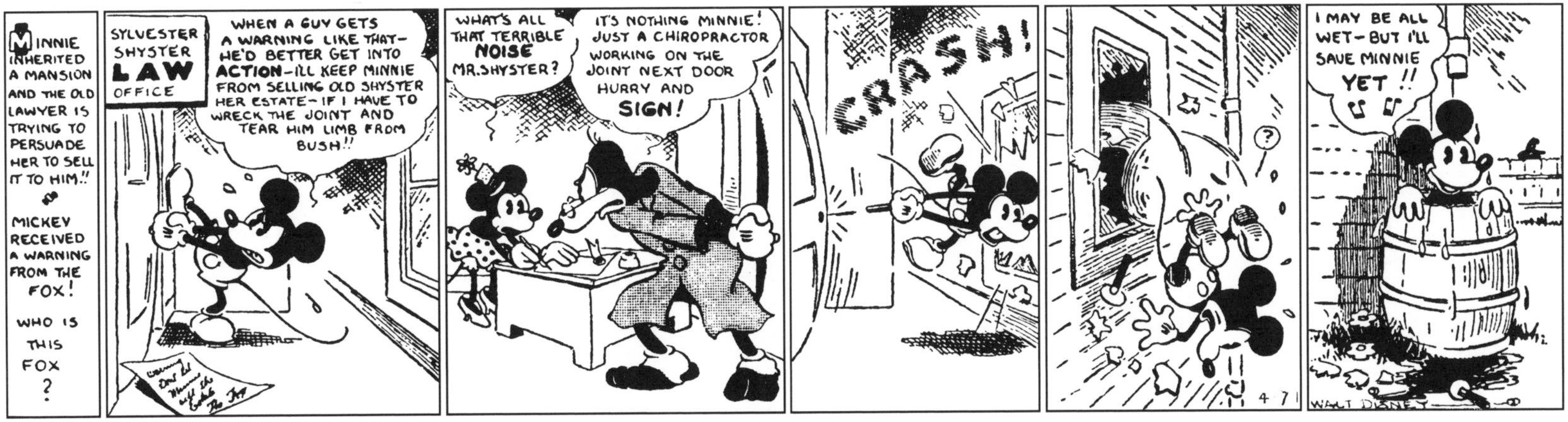
MINNIE INHERITED A MANSION AND THE OLD LAWYER IS TRYING TO PERSUADE HER TO SELL IT TO HIM!!
MICKEY RECEIVED A WARNING FROM THE FOX!
WHO IS THIS FOX ?
SYLVESTER SHYSTER LAW OFFICE
WHEN A GUY GETS A WARNING LIKE THAT—HE'D BETTER GET INTO ACTION—I'LL KEEP MINNIE FROM SELLING OLD SHYSTER HER ESTATE—IF I HAVE TO WRECK THE JOINT AND TEAR HIM LIMB FROM BUSH!!
WHAT'S ALL THAT TERRIBLE NOISE MR. SHYSTER?
IT'S NOTHING MINNIE! JUST A CHIROPRACTOR WORKING ON THE JOINT NEXT DOOR HURRY AND SIGN!
CRASH!
I MAY BE ALL WET—BUT I'LL SAVE MINNIE YET!!
4-7
WALT DISNEY

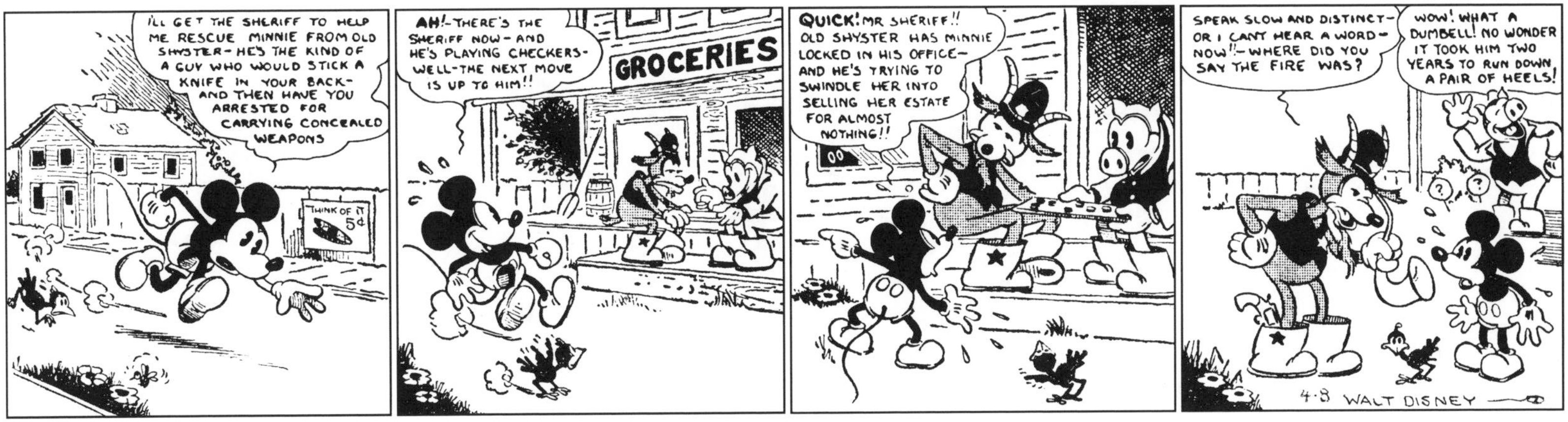
I'LL GET THE SHERIFF TO HELP ME RESCUE MINNIE FROM OLD SHYSTER—HE'S THE KIND OF A GUY WHO WOULD STICK A KNIFE IN YOUR BACK—AND THEN HAVE YOU ARRESTED FOR CARRYING CONCEALED WEAPONS
THINK OF IT 5¢
AH!—THERE'S THE SHERIFF NOW—AND HE'S PLAYING CHECKERS—WELL—THE NEXT MOVE IS UP TO HIM!!
GROCERIES
QUICK! MR SHERIFF!! OLD SHYSTER HAS MINNIE LOCKED IN HIS OFFICE—AND HE'S TRYING TO SWINDLE HER INTO SELLING HER ESTATE FOR ALMOST NOTHING!!
SPEAK SLOW AND DISTINCT—OR I CANT HEAR A WORD—NOW!—WHERE DID YOU SAY THE FIRE WAS?
WOW! WHAT A DUMBELL! NO WONDER IT TOOK HIM TWO YEARS TO RUN DOWN A PAIR OF HEELS!
4-8 WALT DISNEY

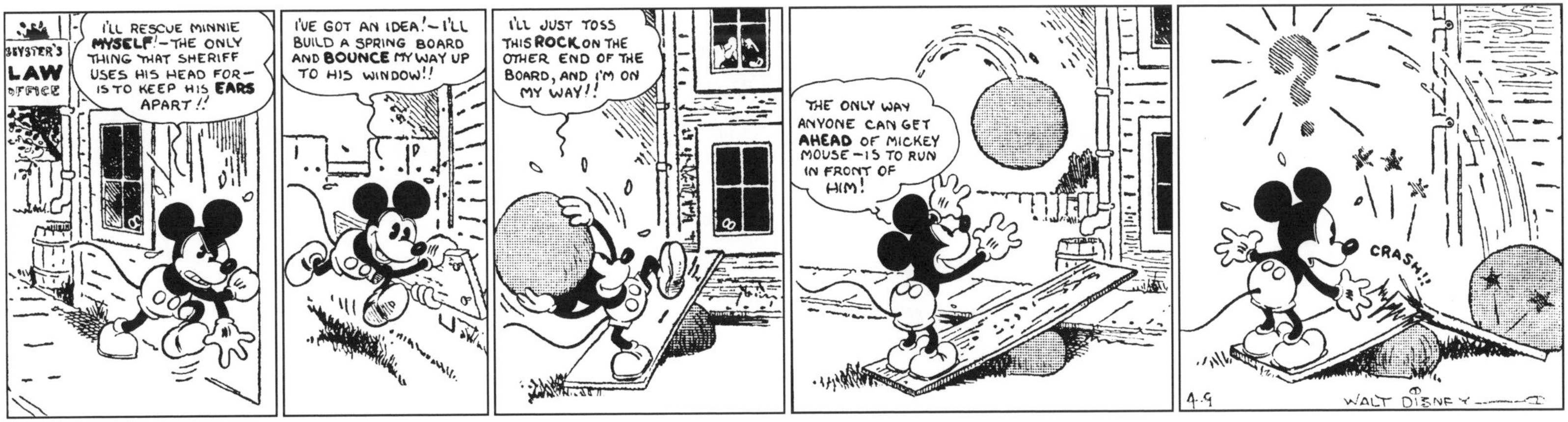
SHYSTER'S LAW OFFICE
I'LL RESCUE MINNIE MYSELF!—THE ONLY THING THAT SHERIFF USES HIS HEAD FOR—IS TO KEEP HIS EARS APART!!
I'VE GOT AN IDEA!—I'LL BUILD A SPRING BOARD AND BOUNCE MY WAY UP TO HIS WINDOW!!
I'LL JUST TOSS THIS ROCK ON THE OTHER END OF THE BOARD, AND I'M ON MY WAY!!
THE ONLY WAY ANYONE CAN GET AHEAD OF MICKEY MOUSE—IS TO RUN IN FRONT OF HIM!
CRASH!!
4-9
WALT DISNEY

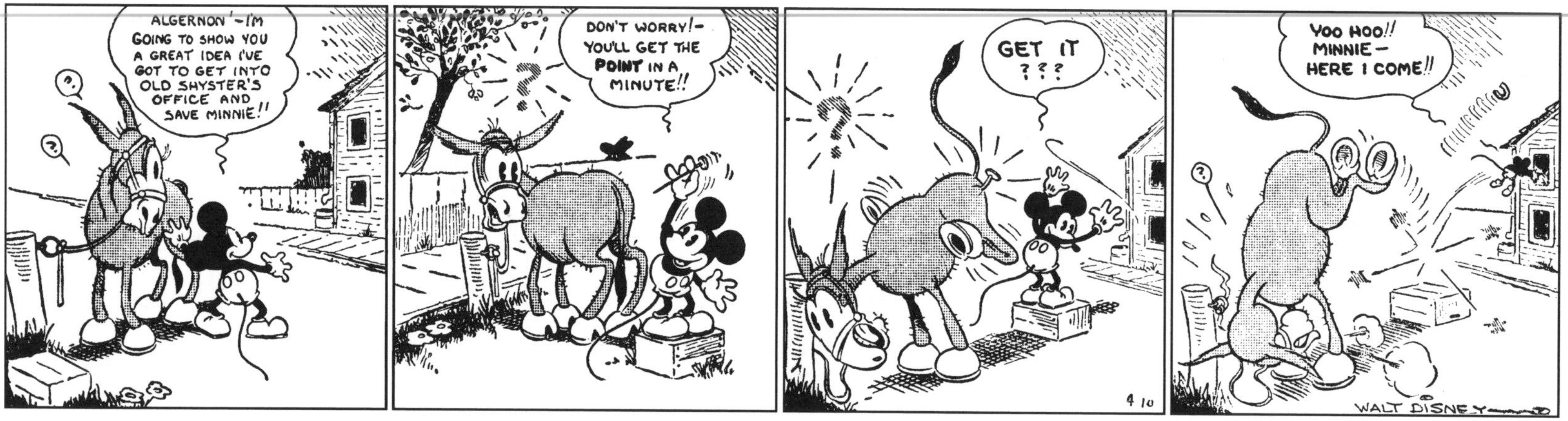
ALGERNON'—I'M GOING TO SHOW YOU A GREAT IDEA I'VE GOT TO GET INTO OLD SHYSTER'S OFFICE AND SAVE MINNIE!!
?
?
DON'T WORRY!—YOU'LL GET THE POINT IN A MINUTE!!
?
GET IT ???
?
YOO HOO!! MINNIE—HERE I COME!!
?
4 10
WALT DISNEY

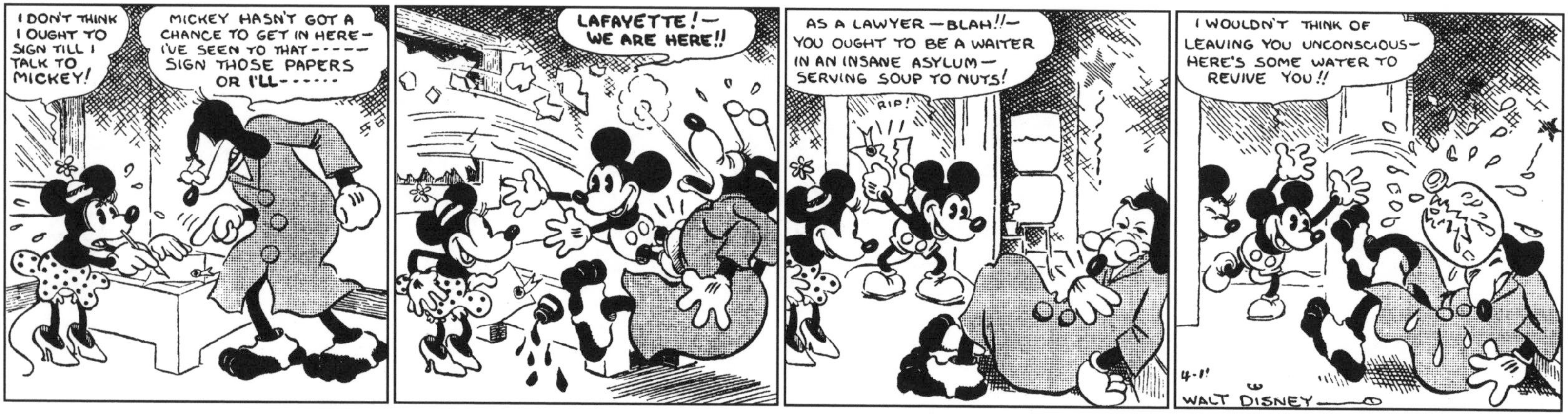
I DON'T THINK I OUGHT TO SIGN TILL I TALK TO MICKEY!
MICKEY HASN'T GOT A CHANCE TO GET IN HERE—I'VE SEEN TO THAT----- SIGN THOSE PAPERS OR I'LL-----
LAFAYETTE!—WE ARE HERE!!
AS A LAWYER—BLAH!!—YOU OUGHT TO BE A WAITER IN AN INSANE ASYLUM—SERVING SOUP TO NUTS!
RIP!
I WOULDN'T THINK OF LEAVING YOU UNCONSCIOUS—HERE'S SOME WATER TO REVIVE YOU!!
4-11
WALT DISNEY

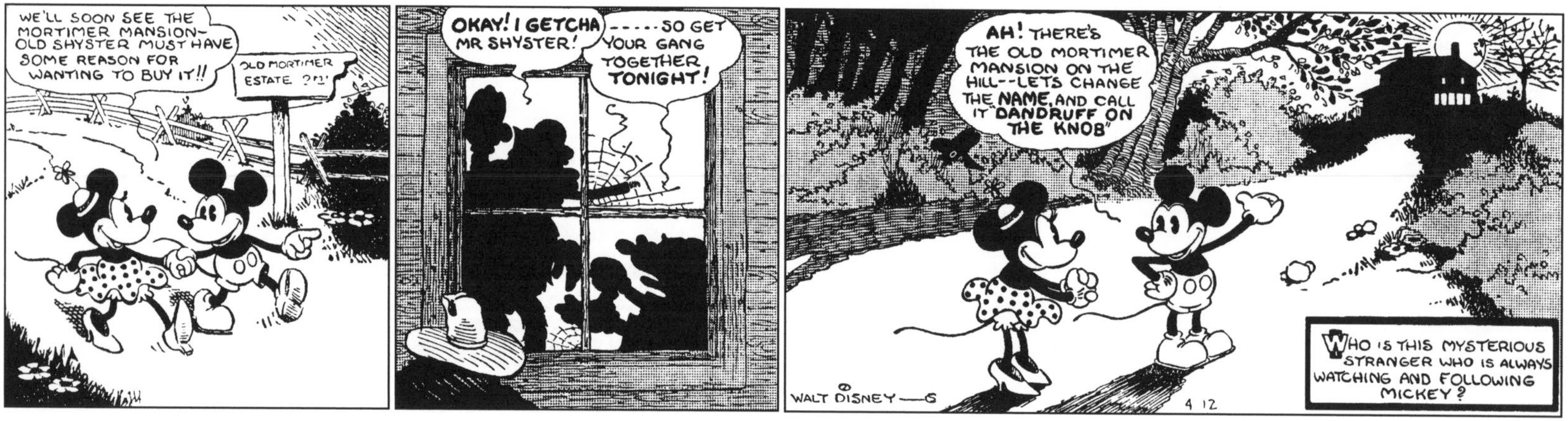
WE'LL SOON SEE THE MORTIMER MANSION—OLD SHYSTER MUST HAVE SOME REASON FOR WANTING TO BUY IT!!
OLD MORTIMER ESTATE ?!!
OKAY! I GETCHA MR SHYSTER!
-----SO GET YOUR GANG TOGETHER TONIGHT!
AH! THERE'S THE OLD MORTIMER MANSION ON THE HILL--LETS CHANGE THE NAME AND CALL IT "DANDRUFF ON THE KNOB"
WHO IS THIS MYSTERIOUS STRANGER WHO IS ALWAYS WATCHING AND FOLLOWING MICKEY?
WALT DISNEY
4 12

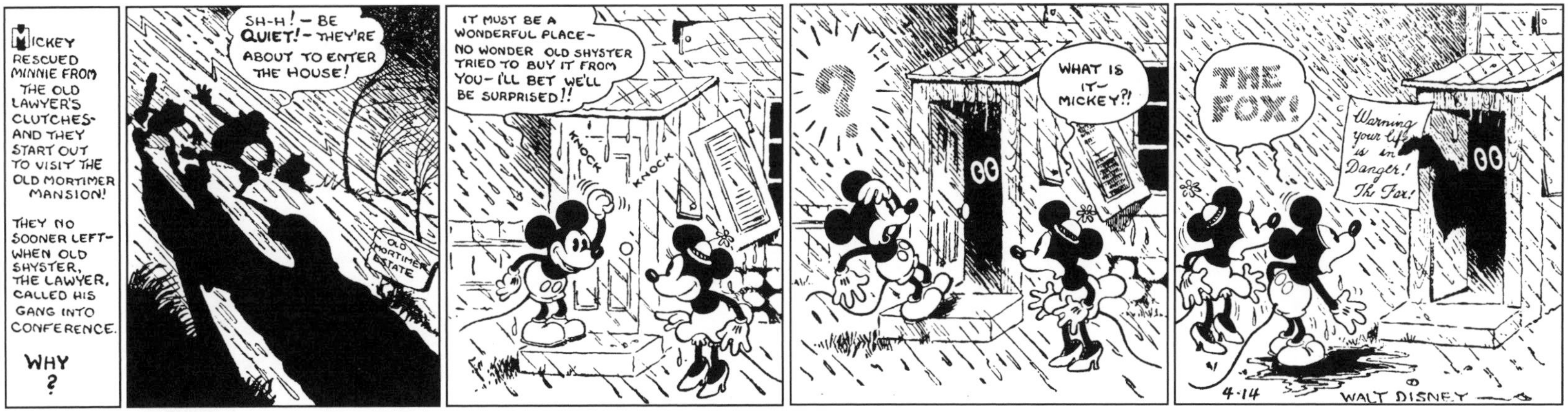
MICKEY RESCUED MINNIE FROM THE OLD LAWYER'S CLUTCHES- AND THEY START OUT TO VISIT THE OLD MORTIMER MANSION!
THEY NO SOONER LEFT- WHEN OLD SHYSTER, THE LAWYER, CALLED HIS GANG INTO CONFERENCE.
WHY ?
SH-H! - BE QUIET! - THEY'RE ABOUT TO ENTER THE HOUSE!
OLD MORTIMER ESTATE
IT MUST BE A WONDERFUL PLACE- NO WONDER OLD SHYSTER TRIED TO BUY IT FROM YOU- I'LL BET WE'LL BE SURPRISED!!
KNOCK
KNOCK
?
WHAT IS IT- MICKEY?!
THE FOX!
Warning your life is in Danger! The Fox!
4·14
WALT DISNEY

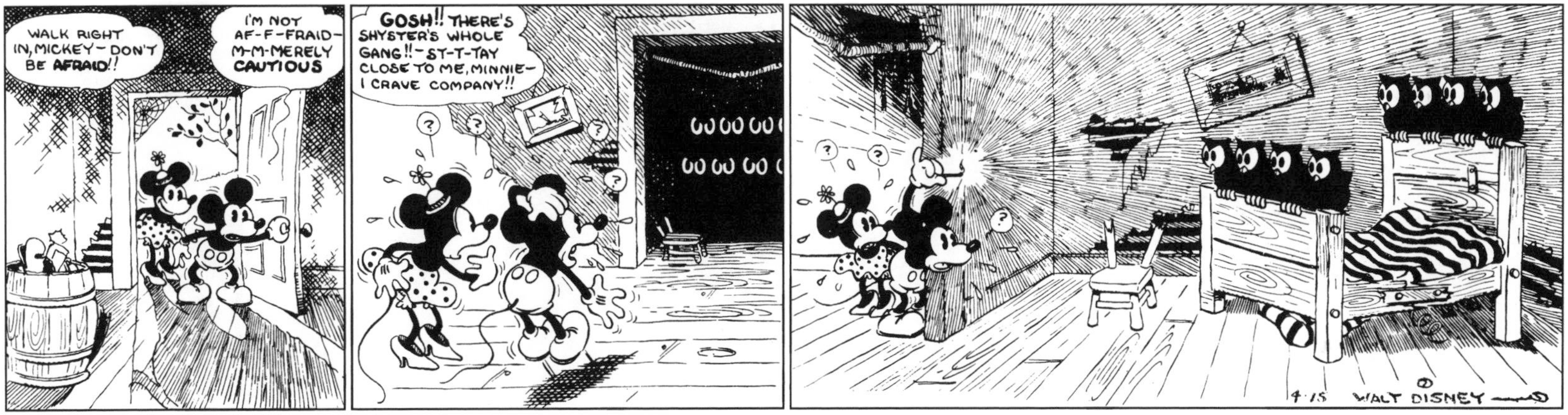
WALK RIGHT IN, MICKEY- DON'T BE AFRAID!!
I'M NOT AF-F-FRAID- M-M-MERELY CAUTIOUS
GOSH!! THERE'S SHYSTER'S WHOLE GANG!!- ST-T-TAY CLOSE TO ME, MINNIE- I CRAVE COMPANY!!
4·15
WALT DISNEY

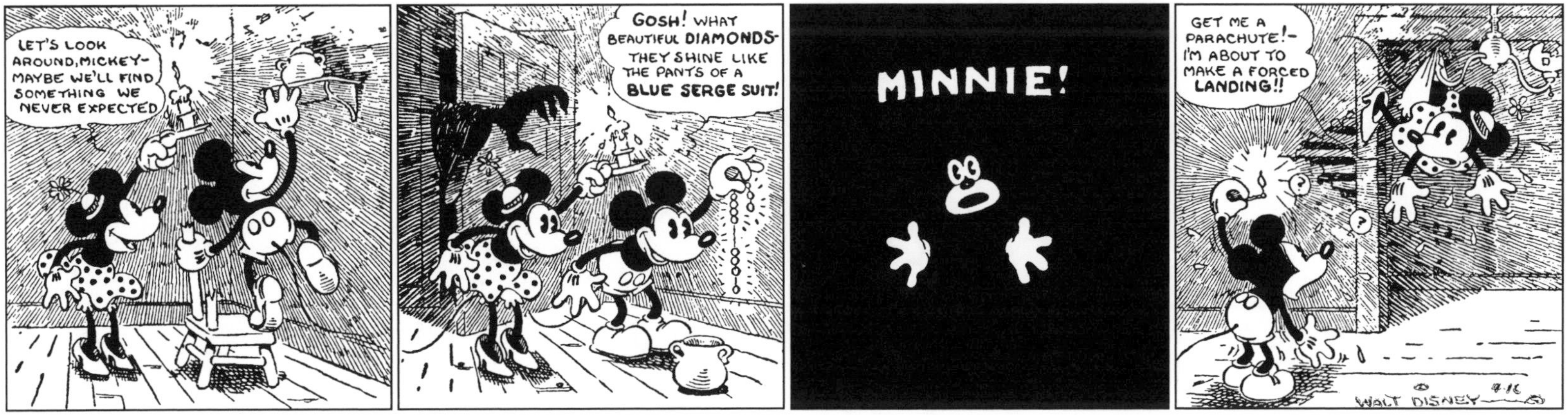
LET'S LOOK AROUND, MICKEY- MAYBE WE'LL FIND SOMETHING WE NEVER EXPECTED
GOSH! WHAT BEAUTIFUL DIAMONDS- THEY SHINE LIKE THE PANTS OF A BLUE SERGE SUIT!
MINNIE!
GET ME A PARACHUTE!- I'M ABOUT TO MAKE A FORCED LANDING!!
4·16
WALT DISNEY

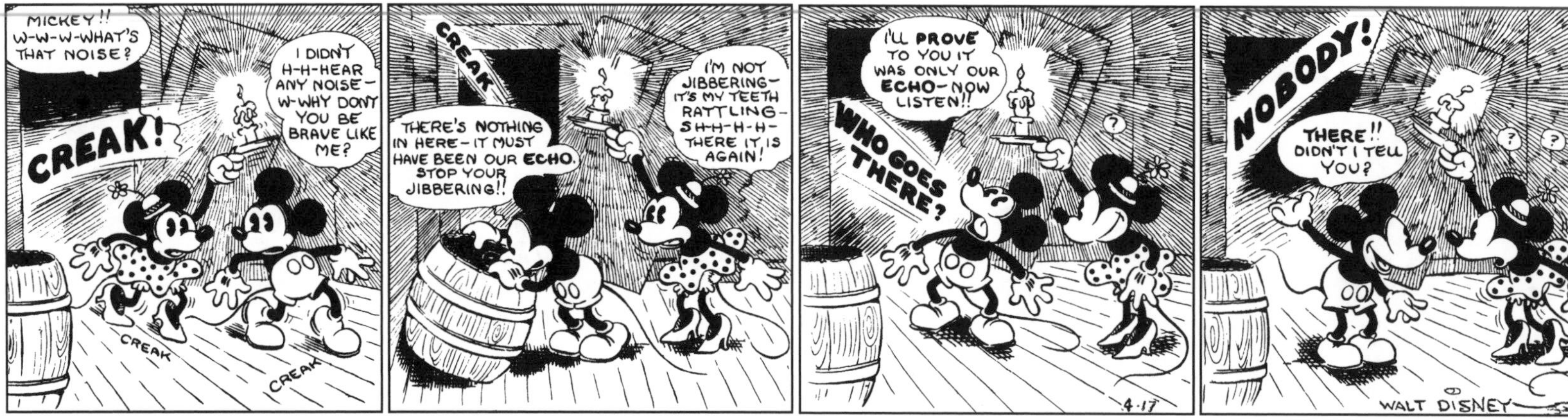
MICKEY!! W-W-W-WHAT'S THAT NOISE?
I DIDN'T H-H-HEAR ANY NOISE— W-WHY DON'T YOU BE BRAVE LIKE ME?
CREAK!
CREAK
CREAK
CREAK
THERE'S NOTHING IN HERE—IT MUST HAVE BEEN OUR ECHO. STOP YOUR JIBBERING!!
I'M NOT JIBBERING— IT'S MY TEETH RATTLING— S-H-H-H-H— THERE IT IS AGAIN!
I'LL PROVE TO YOU IT WAS ONLY OUR ECHO—NOW LISTEN!!
WHO GOES THERE?
NOBODY!
THERE!! DIDN'T I TELL YOU?
4-17
WALT DISNEY

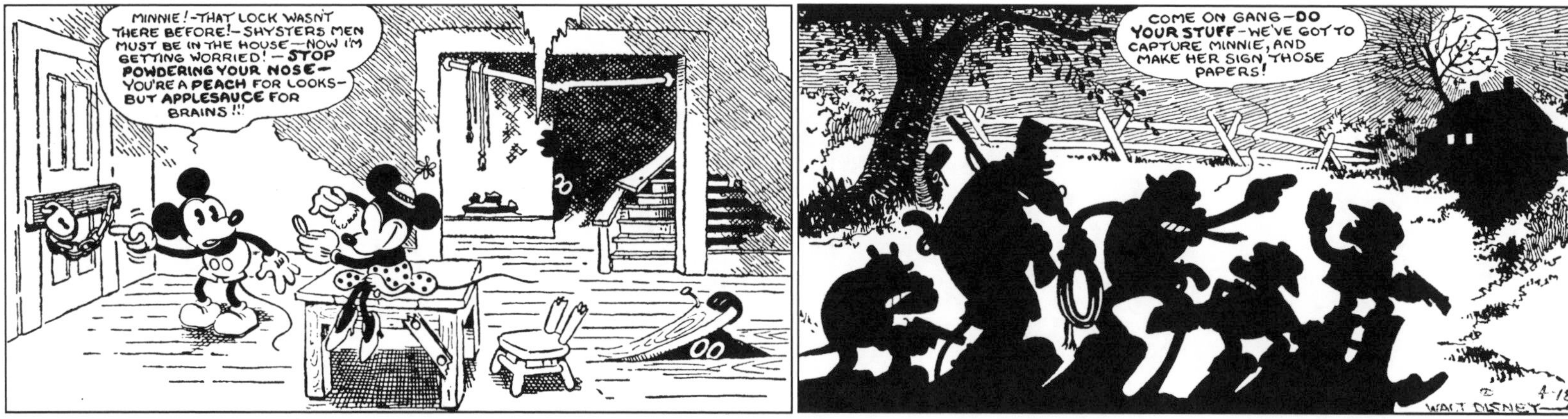
MINNIE!—THAT LOCK WASN'T THERE BEFORE!—SHYSTERS MEN MUST BE IN THE HOUSE—NOW I'M GETTING WORRIED!—STOP POWDERING YOUR NOSE— YOU'RE A PEACH FOR LOOKS— BUT APPLESAUCE FOR BRAINS!!!
COME ON GANG—DO YOUR STUFF—WE'VE GOT TO CAPTURE MINNIE, AND MAKE HER SIGN THOSE PAPERS!
4-18
WALT DISNEY

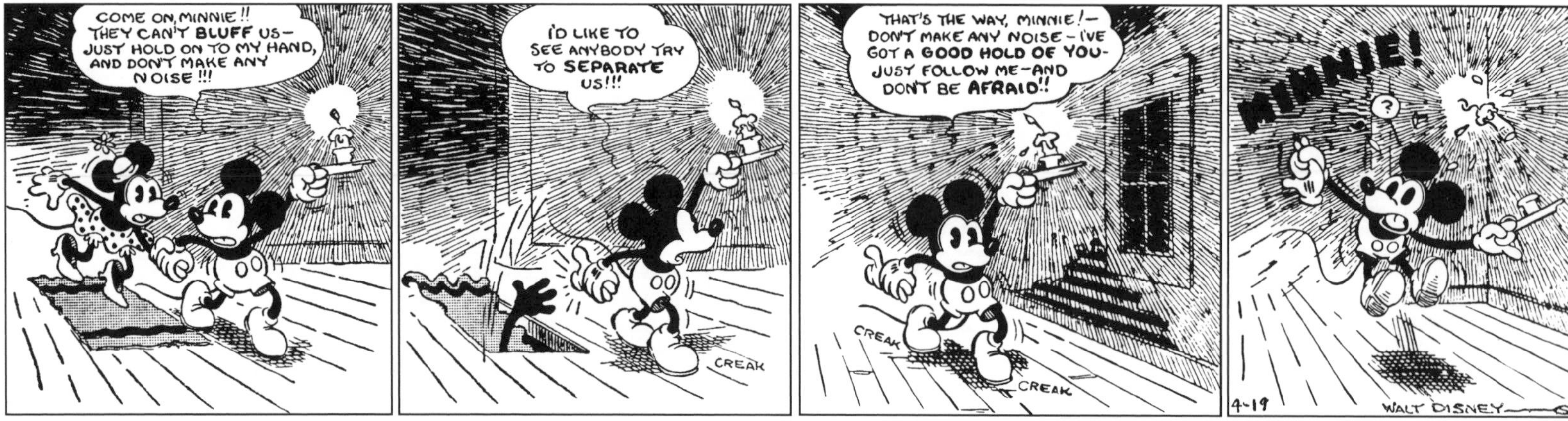
COME ON, MINNIE!! THEY CAN'T BLUFF US— JUST HOLD ON TO MY HAND, AND DON'T MAKE ANY NOISE!!!
I'D LIKE TO SEE ANYBODY TRY TO SEPARATE US!!!
CREAK
THAT'S THE WAY, MINNIE!— DON'T MAKE ANY NOISE—I'VE GOT A GOOD HOLD OF YOU— JUST FOLLOW ME—AND DON'T BE AFRAID!!
CREAK
CREAK
MINNIE!
4-19
WALT DISNEY

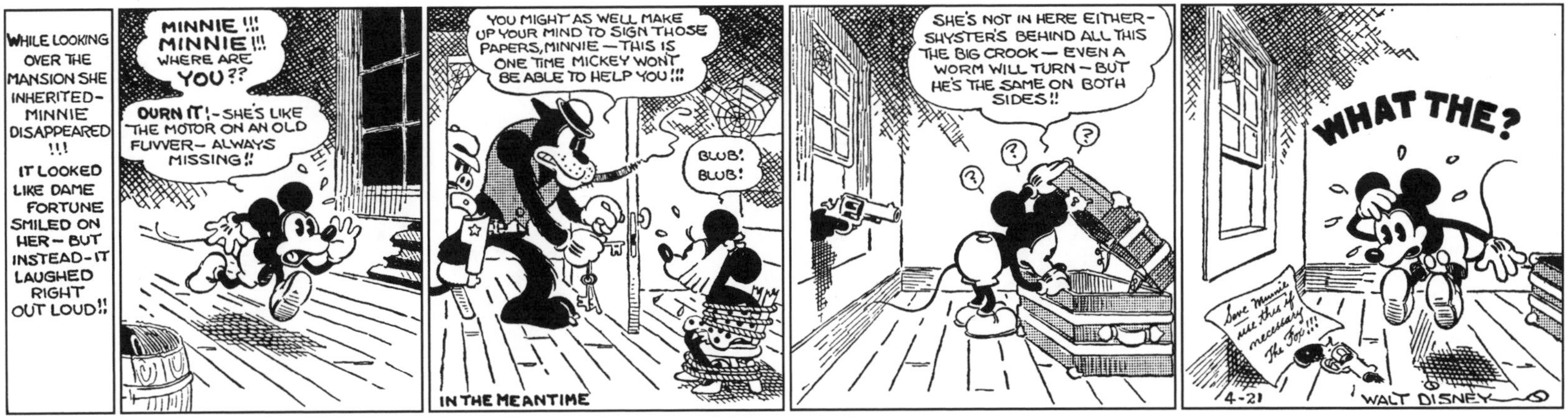
WHILE LOOKING OVER THE MANSION SHE INHERITED—MINNIE DISAPPEARED!!! IT LOOKED LIKE DAME FORTUNE SMILED ON HER—BUT INSTEAD—IT LAUGHED RIGHT OUT LOUD!!
MINNIE!!! MINNIE!!! WHERE ARE YOU??
DURN IT!—SHE'S LIKE THE MOTOR ON AN OLD FLIVVER—ALWAYS MISSING!!
YOU MIGHT AS WELL MAKE UP YOUR MIND TO SIGN THOSE PAPERS, MINNIE—THIS IS ONE TIME MICKEY WON'T BE ABLE TO HELP YOU!!!
BLUB! BLUB!
IN THE MEANTIME
SHE'S NOT IN HERE EITHER—SHYSTER'S BEHIND ALL THIS THE BIG CROOK—EVEN A WORM WILL TURN—BUT HE'S THE SAME ON BOTH SIDES!!
WHAT THE?
Save Minnie use this if necessary The Fox!!!
4-21
WALT DISNEY

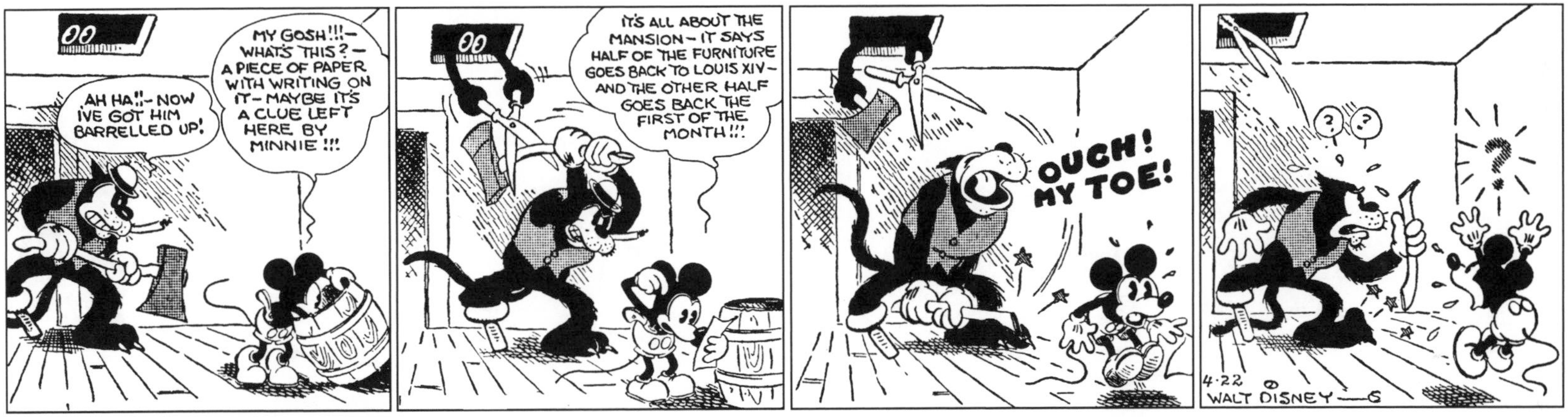
AH HA!!—NOW I'VE GOT HIM BARRELLED UP!
MY GOSH!!!—WHAT'S THIS?—A PIECE OF PAPER WITH WRITING ON IT—MAYBE IT'S A CLUE LEFT HERE BY MINNIE!!!
IT'S ALL ABOUT THE MANSION—IT SAYS HALF OF THE FURNITURE GOES BACK TO LOUIS XIV—AND THE OTHER HALF GOES BACK THE FIRST OF THE MONTH!!!
OUCH! MY TOE!
4-22
WALT DISNEY

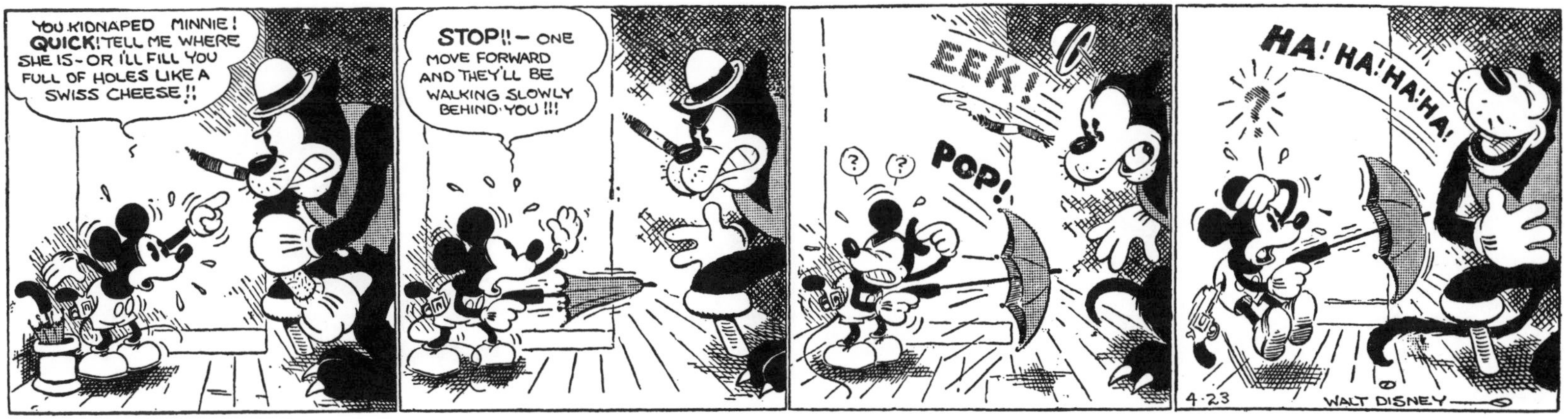
YOU KIDNAPED MINNIE! QUICK! TELL ME WHERE SHE IS—OR I'LL FILL YOU FULL OF HOLES LIKE A SWISS CHEESE!!
STOP!!—ONE MOVE FORWARD AND THEY'LL BE WALKING SLOWLY BEHIND YOU!!!
EEK!
POP!
HA! HA! HA! HA! HA!
4-23
WALT DISNEY

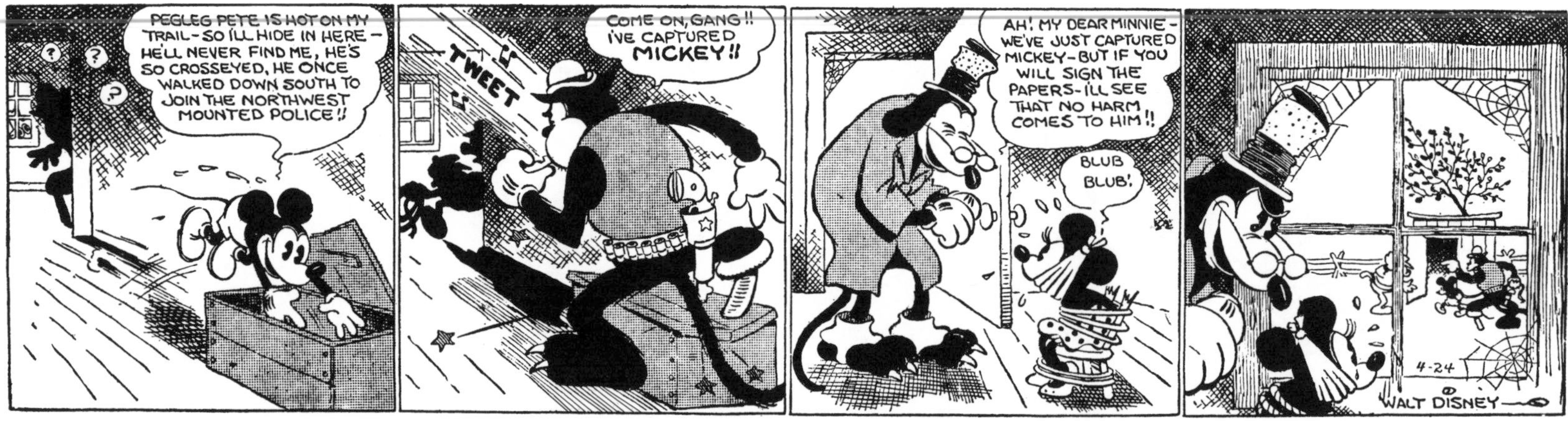
PEGLEG PETE IS HOT ON MY TRAIL-SO I'LL HIDE IN HERE-HE'LL NEVER FIND ME, HE'S SO CROSSEYED, HE ONCE WALKED DOWN SOUTH TO JOIN THE NORTHWEST MOUNTED POLICE!!
TWEET
COME ON, GANG!! I'VE CAPTURED MICKEY!!
AH! MY DEAR MINNIE-WE'VE JUST CAPTURED MICKEY-BUT IF YOU WILL SIGN THE PAPERS-I'LL SEE THAT NO HARM COMES TO HIM!!
BLUB BLUB!
4-24
WALT DISNEY

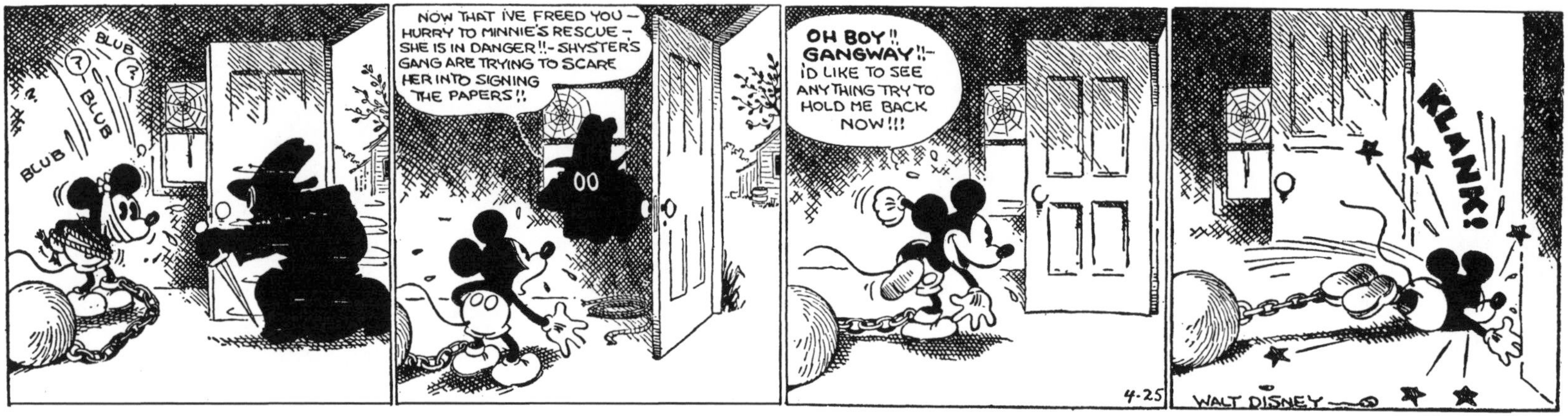
BLUB
BLUB
BLUB
NOW THAT I'VE FREED YOU-HURRY TO MINNIE'S RESCUE-SHE IS IN DANGER!!-SHYSTER'S GANG ARE TRYING TO SCARE HER INTO SIGNING THE PAPERS!!
OH BOY!! GANGWAY!!-I'D LIKE TO SEE ANYTHING TRY TO HOLD ME BACK NOW!!!
4-25
KLANK!
WALT DISNEY

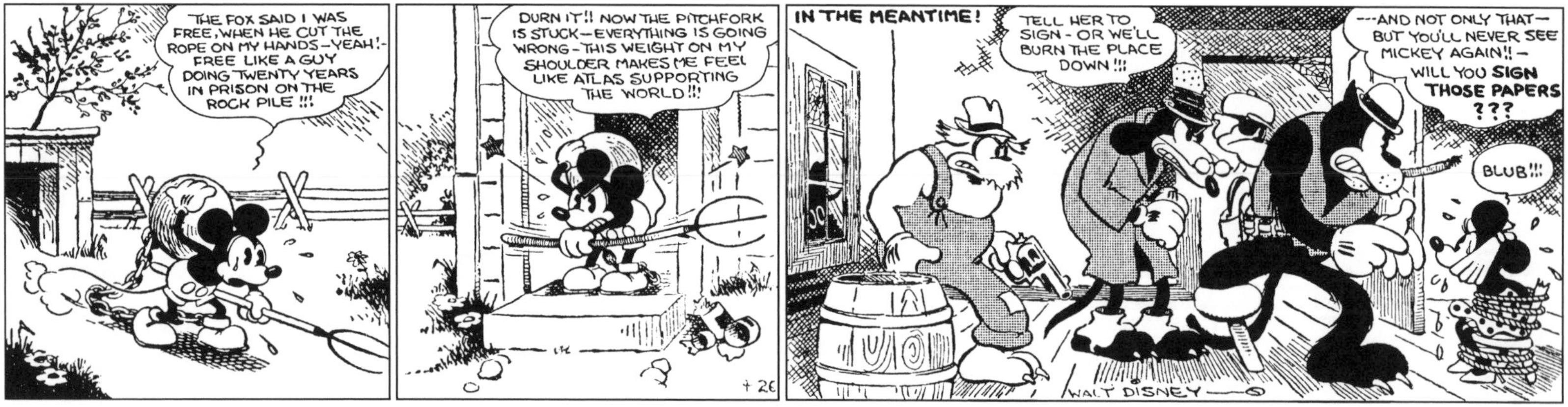
THE FOX SAID I WAS FREE, WHEN HE CUT THE ROPE ON MY HANDS-YEAH!-FREE LIKE A GUY DOING TWENTY YEARS IN PRISON ON THE ROCK PILE!!!
DURN IT!! NOW THE PITCHFORK IS STUCK-EVERYTHING IS GOING WRONG-THIS WEIGHT ON MY SHOULDER MAKES ME FEEL LIKE ATLAS SUPPORTING THE WORLD!!!
IN THE MEANTIME!
TELL HER TO SIGN-OR WE'LL BURN THE PLACE DOWN!!!
---AND NOT ONLY THAT-BUT YOU'LL NEVER SEE MICKEY AGAIN!!-WILL YOU SIGN THOSE PAPERS???
BLUB!!!
WALT DISNEY

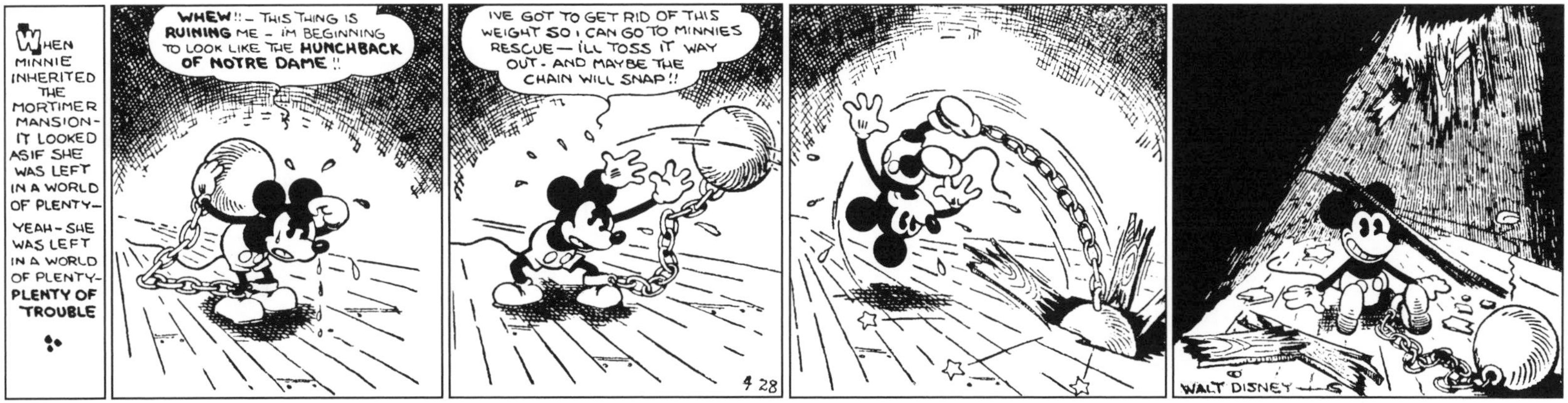
WHEN MINNIE INHERITED THE MORTIMER MANSION- IT LOOKED ASIF SHE WAS LEFT IN A WORLD OF PLENTY-
YEAH-SHE WAS LEFT IN A WORLD OF PLENTY- PLENTY OF TROUBLE
WHEW!! - THIS THING IS RUINING ME - IM BEGINNING TO LOOK LIKE THE HUNCHBACK OF NOTRE DAME !!
IVE GOT TO GET RID OF THIS WEIGHT SO I CAN GO TO MINNIES RESCUE - ILL TOSS IT WAY OUT - AND MAYBE THE CHAIN WILL SNAP!!
4 28
WALT DISNEY

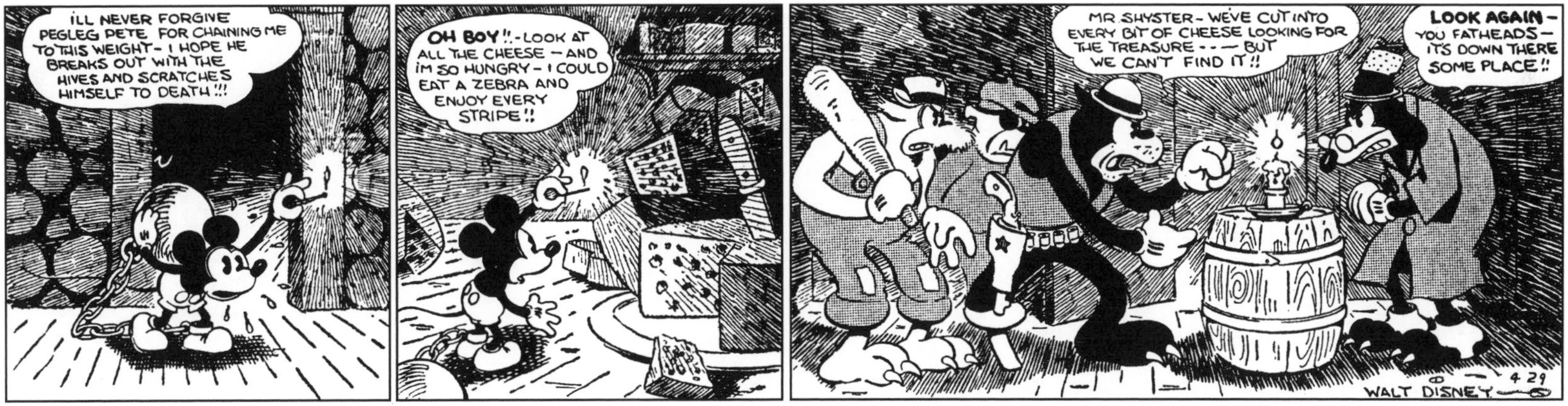
ILL NEVER FORGIVE PEGLEG PETE FOR CHAINING ME TO THIS WEIGHT - I HOPE HE BREAKS OUT WITH THE HIVES AND SCRATCHES HIMSELF TO DEATH!!!
OH BOY!! - LOOK AT ALL THE CHEESE - AND IM SO HUNGRY - I COULD EAT A ZEBRA AND ENJOY EVERY STRIPE!!
MR SHYSTER - WEVE CUT INTO EVERY BIT OF CHEESE LOOKING FOR THE TREASURE - - - BUT WE CAN'T FIND IT!!
LOOK AGAIN - YOU FATHEADS - ITS DOWN THERE SOME PLACE!!
4 29
WALT DISNEY

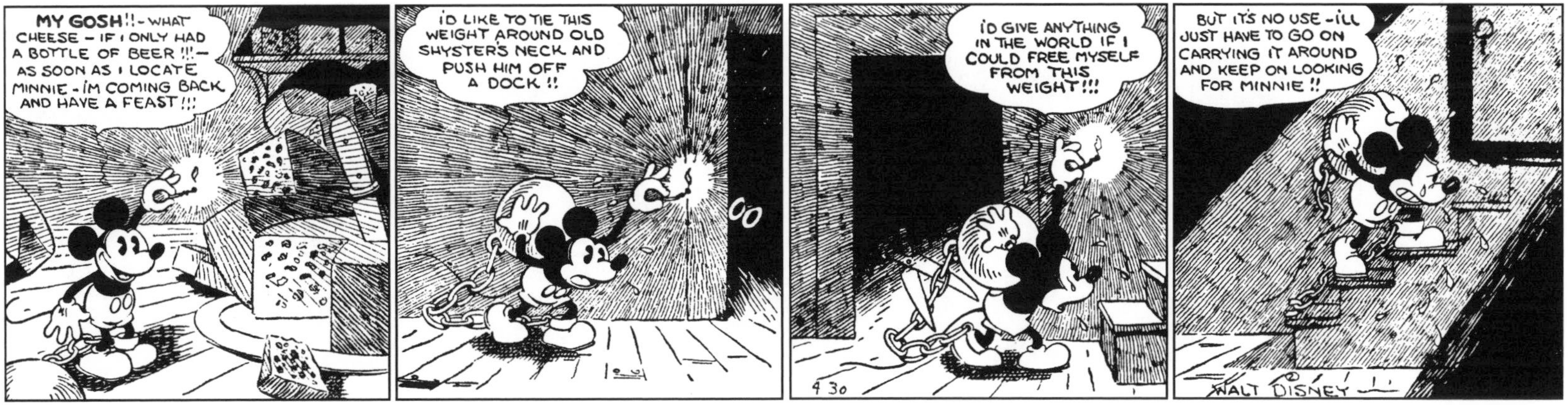
MY GOSH!! - WHAT CHEESE - IF I ONLY HAD A BOTTLE OF BEER!!! - AS SOON AS I LOCATE MINNIE - IM COMING BACK AND HAVE A FEAST!!!
ID LIKE TO TIE THIS WEIGHT AROUND OLD SHYSTER'S NECK AND PUSH HIM OFF A DOCK!!
ID GIVE ANYTHING IN THE WORLD IF I COULD FREE MYSELF FROM THIS WEIGHT!!!
BUT ITS NO USE - ILL JUST HAVE TO GO ON CARRYING IT AROUND AND KEEP ON LOOKING FOR MINNIE!!
4 30
WALT DISNEY

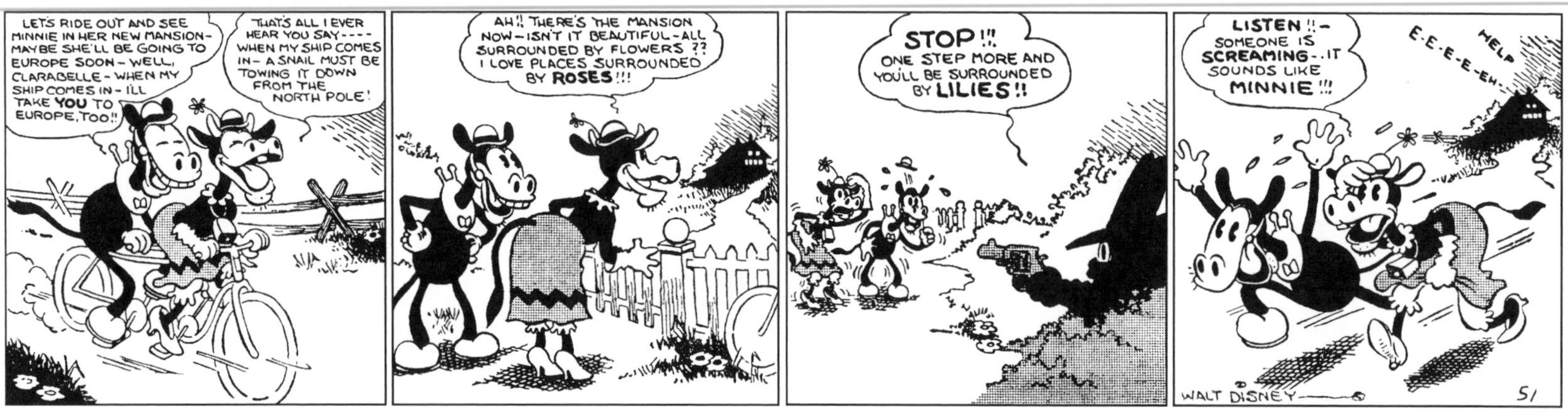
LET'S RIDE OUT AND SEE MINNIE IN HER NEW MANSION- MAYBE SHE'LL BE GOING TO EUROPE SOON - WELL, CLARABELLE - WHEN MY SHIP COMES IN - I'LL TAKE YOU TO EUROPE, TOO!!
THAT'S ALL I EVER HEAR YOU SAY---- WHEN MY SHIP COMES IN - A SNAIL MUST BE TOWING IT DOWN FROM THE NORTH POLE!
AH!! THERE'S THE MANSION NOW - ISN'T IT BEAUTIFUL - ALL SURROUNDED BY FLOWERS ?? I LOVE PLACES SURROUNDED BY ROSES!!!
STOP!!! ONE STEP MORE AND YOU'LL BE SURROUNDED BY LILIES!!
LISTEN!! - SOMEONE IS SCREAMING - IT SOUNDS LIKE MINNIE!!!
HELP
E-E-E-E-EH
WALT DISNEY
51

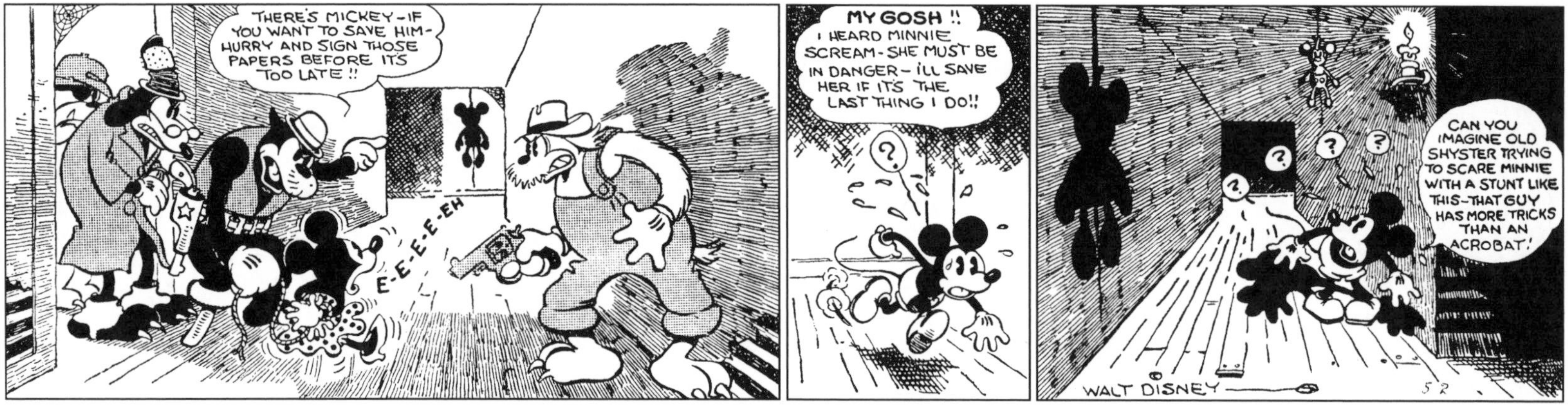
THERE'S MICKEY - IF YOU WANT TO SAVE HIM - HURRY AND SIGN THOSE PAPERS BEFORE IT'S TOO LATE!!
E-E-E-E-EH
MY GOSH!! I HEARD MINNIE SCREAM - SHE MUST BE IN DANGER - I'LL SAVE HER IF IT'S THE LAST THING I DO!!
CAN YOU IMAGINE OLD SHYSTER TRYING TO SCARE MINNIE WITH A STUNT LIKE THIS - THAT GUY HAS MORE TRICKS THAN AN ACROBAT!
WALT DISNEY
52

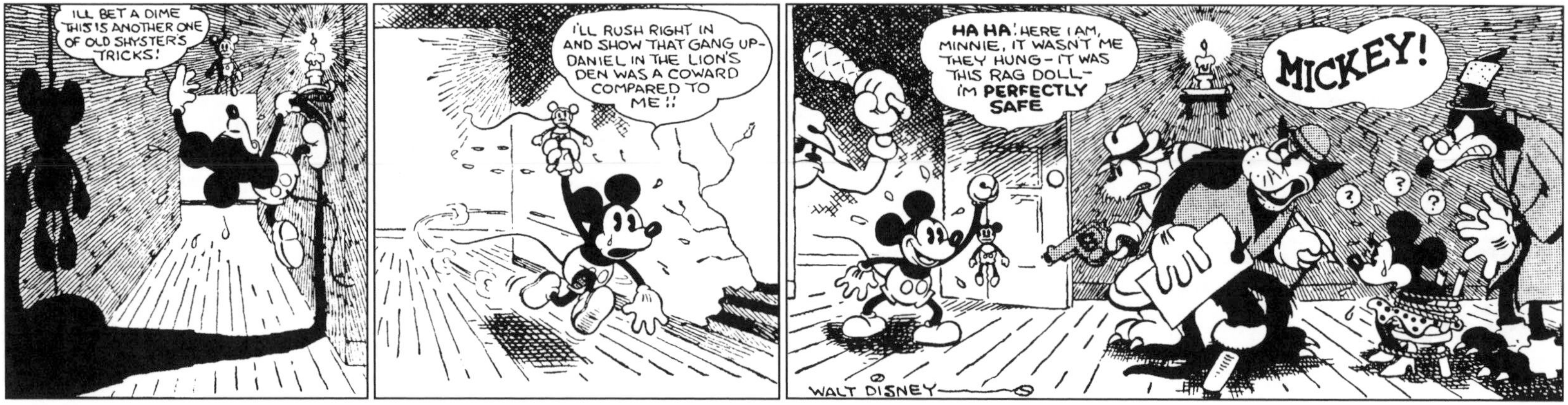
I'LL BET A DIME THIS IS ANOTHER ONE OF OLD SHYSTER'S TRICKS!
I'LL RUSH RIGHT IN AND SHOW THAT GANG UP - DANIEL IN THE LION'S DEN WAS A COWARD COMPARED TO ME!!
HA HA! HERE I AM, MINNIE, IT WASN'T ME THEY HUNG - IT WAS THIS RAG DOLL - I'M PERFECTLY SAFE
MICKEY!
WALT DISNEY

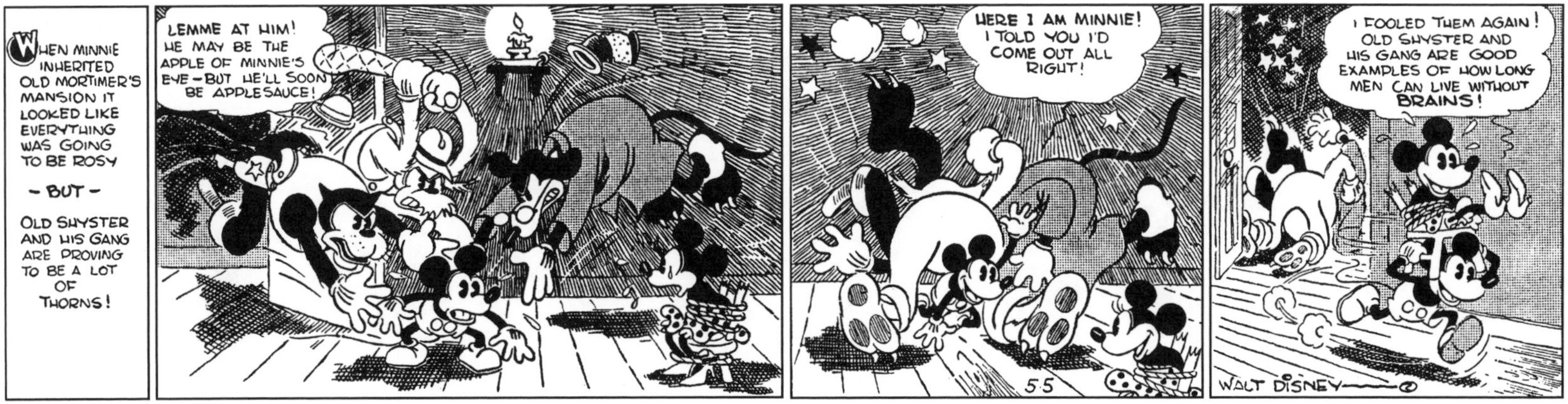
WHEN MINNIE INHERITED OLD MORTIMER'S MANSION IT LOOKED LIKE EVERYTHING WAS GOING TO BE ROSY
- BUT -
OLD SHYSTER AND HIS GANG ARE PROVING TO BE A LOT OF THORNS!
LEMME AT HIM! HE MAY BE THE APPLE OF MINNIE'S EYE—BUT HE'LL SOON BE APPLESAUCE!
HERE I AM MINNIE! I TOLD YOU I'D COME OUT ALL RIGHT!
5·5
I FOOLED THEM AGAIN! OLD SHYSTER AND HIS GANG ARE GOOD EXAMPLES OF HOW LONG MEN CAN LIVE WITHOUT BRAINS!
WALT DISNEY

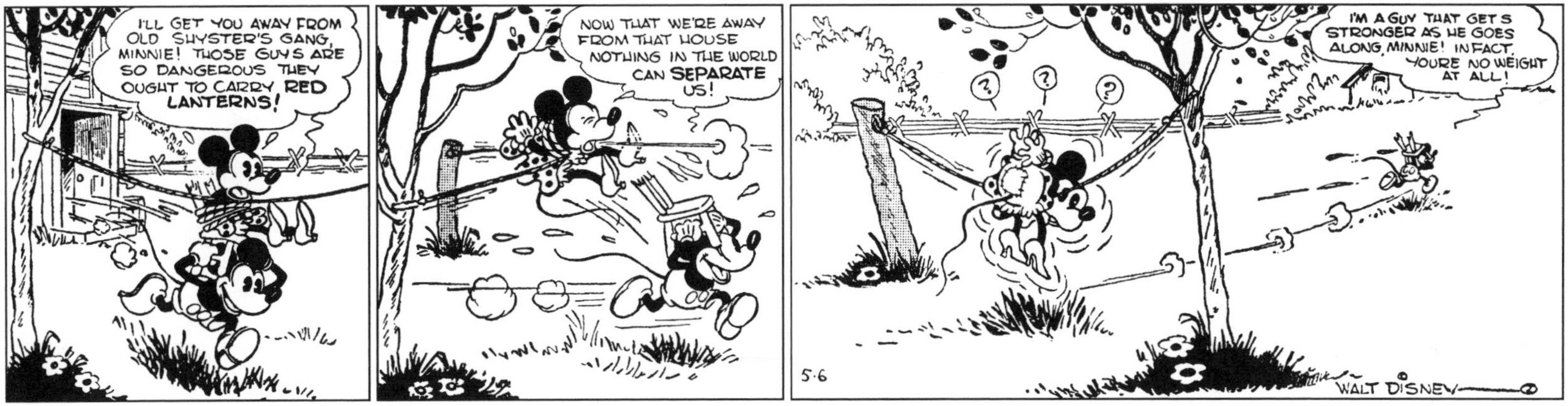
I'LL GET YOU AWAY FROM OLD SHYSTER'S GANG, MINNIE! THOSE GUYS ARE SO DANGEROUS THEY OUGHT TO CARRY RED LANTERNS!
NOW THAT WE'RE AWAY FROM THAT HOUSE NOTHING IN THE WORLD CAN SEPARATE US!
?
?
?
I'M A GUY THAT GETS STRONGER AS HE GOES ALONG, MINNIE! IN FACT, YOU'RE NO WEIGHT AT ALL!
5·6
WALT DISNEY

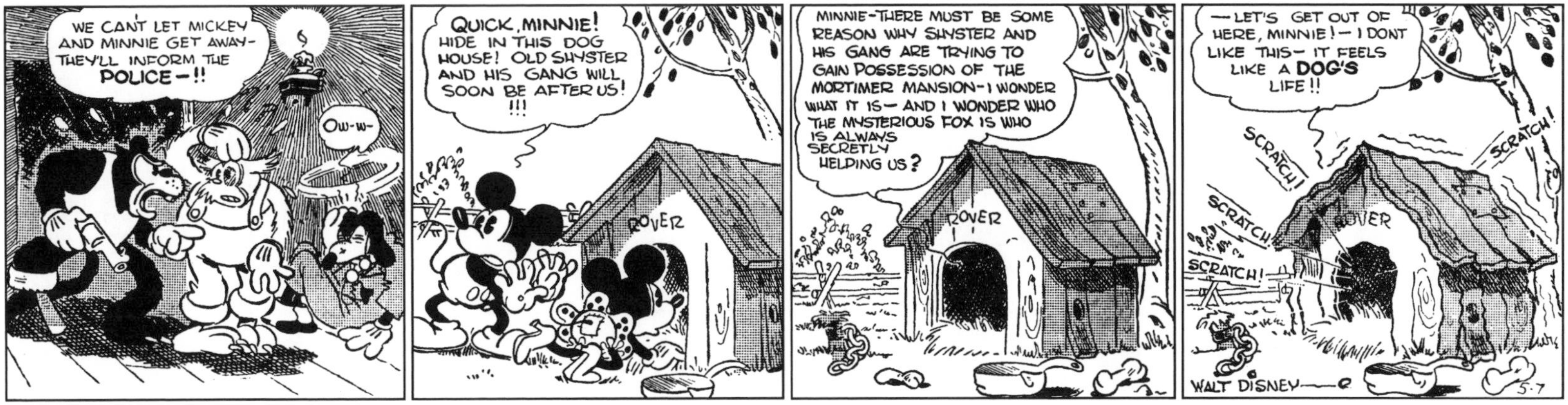
WE CAN'T LET MICKEY AND MINNIE GET AWAY—THEY'LL INFORM THE POLICE—!!
OW-W-
QUICK, MINNIE! HIDE IN THIS DOG HOUSE! OLD SHYSTER AND HIS GANG WILL SOON BE AFTER US! !!!
ROVER
MINNIE—THERE MUST BE SOME REASON WHY SHYSTER AND HIS GANG ARE TRYING TO GAIN POSSESSION OF THE MORTIMER MANSION—I WONDER WHAT IT IS—AND I WONDER WHO THE MYSTERIOUS FOX IS WHO IS ALWAYS SECRETLY HELPING US?
ROVER
—LET'S GET OUT OF HERE, MINNIE!—I DONT LIKE THIS—IT FEELS LIKE A DOG'S LIFE!!
SCRATCH!
SCRATCH!
SCRATCH!
SCRATCH!
ROVER
WALT DISNEY
5·7

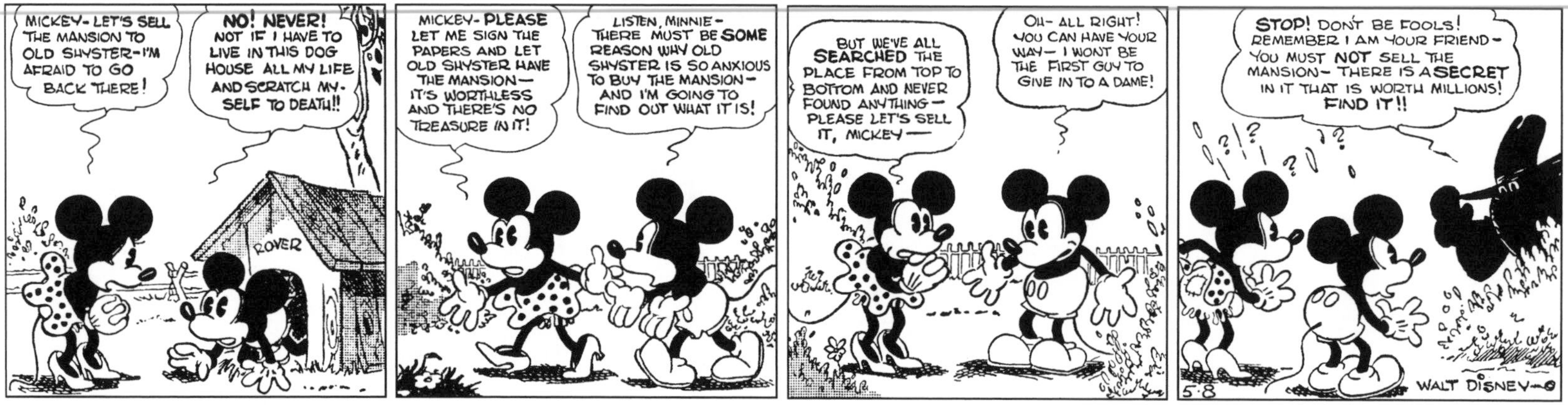
MICKEY- LET'S SELL THE MANSION TO OLD SHYSTER-I'M AFRAID TO GO BACK THERE!
NO! NEVER! NOT IF I HAVE TO LIVE IN THIS DOG HOUSE ALL MY LIFE AND SCRATCH MY-SELF TO DEATH!!
ROVER
MICKEY- PLEASE LET ME SIGN THE PAPERS AND LET OLD SHYSTER HAVE THE MANSION— IT'S WORTHLESS AND THERE'S NO TREASURE IN IT!
LISTEN, MINNIE- THERE MUST BE SOME REASON WHY OLD SHYSTER IS SO ANXIOUS TO BUY THE MANSION- AND I'M GOING TO FIND OUT WHAT IT IS!
BUT WE'VE ALL SEARCHED THE PLACE FROM TOP TO BOTTOM AND NEVER FOUND ANYTHING- PLEASE LET'S SELL IT, MICKEY—
OH- ALL RIGHT! YOU CAN HAVE YOUR WAY- I WONT BE THE FIRST GUY TO GIVE IN TO A DAME!
STOP! DON'T BE FOOLS! REMEMBER I AM YOUR FRIEND- YOU MUST NOT SELL THE MANSION- THERE IS A SECRET IN IT THAT IS WORTH MILLIONS! FIND IT!!
5·8
WALT DISNEY

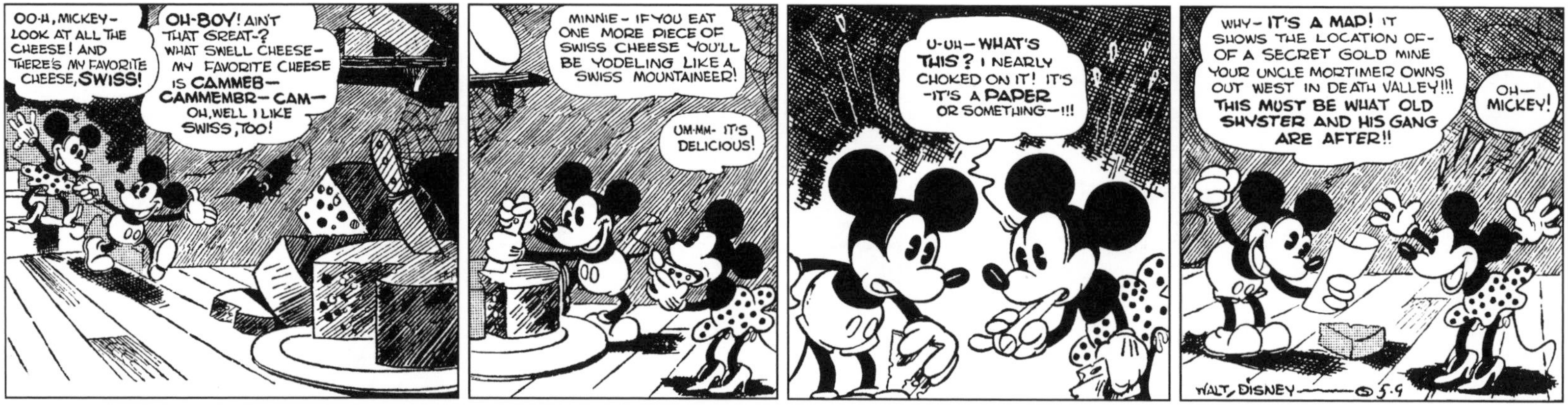
OO-H, MICKEY- LOOK AT ALL THE CHEESE! AND THERE'S MY FAVORITE CHEESE, SWISS!
OH-BOY! AIN'T THAT GREAT-? WHAT SWELL CHEESE- MY FAVORITE CHEESE IS CAMMEB- CAMMEMBR- CAM- OH, WELL I LIKE SWISS, TOO!
MINNIE- IF YOU EAT ONE MORE PIECE OF SWISS CHEESE YOU'LL BE YODELING LIKE A SWISS MOUNTAINEER!
UM-MM- IT'S DELICIOUS!
U-UH- WHAT'S THIS? I NEARLY CHOKED ON IT! IT'S -IT'S A PAPER OR SOMETHING—!!!
WHY- IT'S A MAP! IT SHOWS THE LOCATION OF- OF A SECRET GOLD MINE YOUR UNCLE MORTIMER OWNS OUT WEST IN DEATH VALLEY!!! THIS MUST BE WHAT OLD SHYSTER AND HIS GANG ARE AFTER!!
OH— MICKEY!
WALT DISNEY 5·9

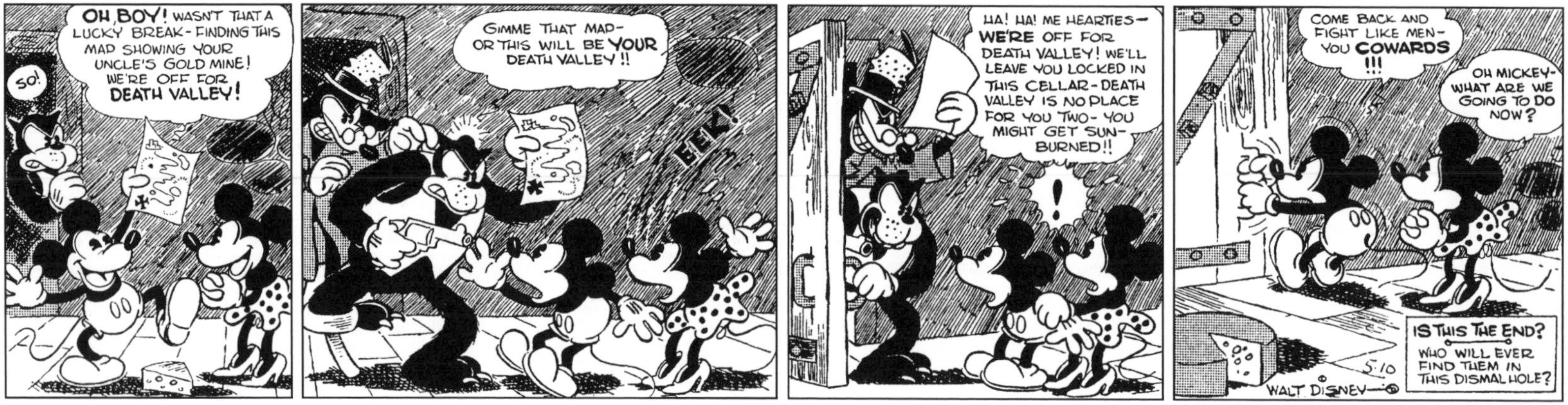
OH, BOY! WASN'T THAT A LUCKY BREAK- FINDING THIS MAP SHOWING YOUR UNCLE'S GOLD MINE! WE'RE OFF FOR DEATH VALLEY!
SO!
GIMME THAT MAP- OR THIS WILL BE YOUR DEATH VALLEY!!
EEK!
HA! HA! ME HEARTIES- WE'RE OFF FOR DEATH VALLEY! WE'LL LEAVE YOU LOCKED IN THIS CELLAR- DEATH VALLEY IS NO PLACE FOR YOU TWO- YOU MIGHT GET SUN-BURNED!!
!
COME BACK AND FIGHT LIKE MEN- YOU COWARDS!!!
OH MICKEY- WHAT ARE WE GOING TO DO NOW?
IS THIS THE END? WHO WILL EVER FIND THEM IN THIS DISMAL HOLE?
5·10
WALT DISNEY

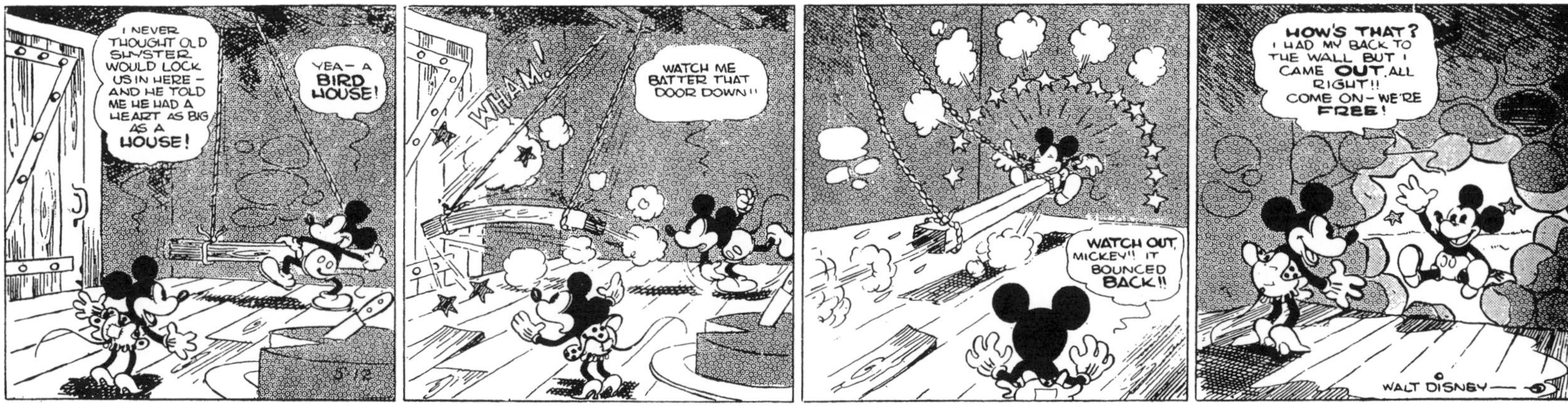
I NEVER THOUGHT OLD SHYSTER WOULD LOCK US IN HERE – AND HE TOLD ME HE HAD A HEART AS BIG AS A HOUSE!
YEA– A BIRD HOUSE!
5/12
WHAM!
WATCH ME BATTER THAT DOOR DOWN!!
WATCH OUT, MICKEY!! IT BOUNCED BACK!!
HOW'S THAT? I HAD MY BACK TO THE WALL BUT I CAME OUT ALL RIGHT!! COME ON– WE'RE FREE!
© WALT DISNEY

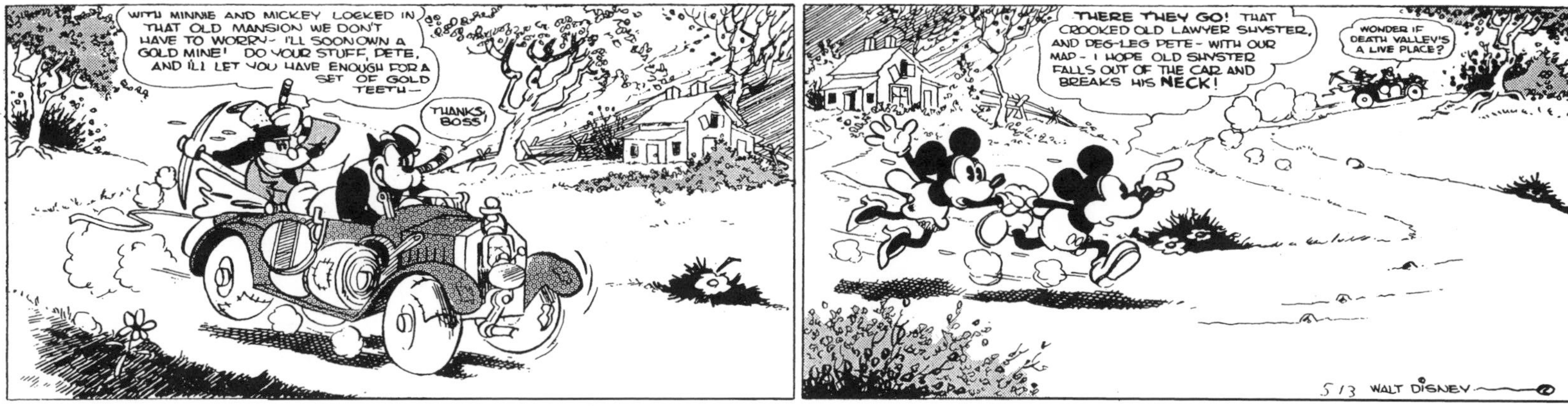
WITH MINNIE AND MICKEY LOCKED IN THAT OLD MANSION WE DON'T HAVE TO WORRY– I'LL SOON OWN A GOLD MINE! DO YOUR STUFF, PETE, AND I'LL LET YOU HAVE ENOUGH FOR A SET OF GOLD TEETH–
THANKS, BOSS!
THERE THEY GO! THAT CROOKED OLD LAWYER SHYSTER, AND PEG-LEG PETE– WITH OUR MAP– I HOPE OLD SHYSTER FALLS OUT OF THE CAR AND BREAKS HIS NECK!
WONDER IF DEATH VALLEY'S A LIVE PLACE?
5/13 WALT DISNEY

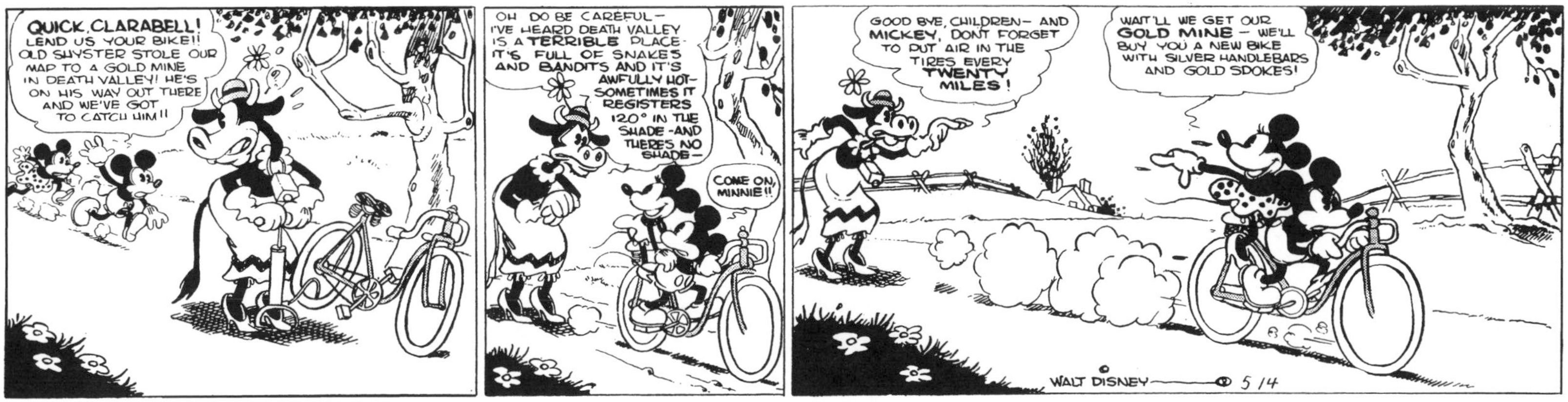
QUICK, CLARABELL! LEND US YOUR BIKE!! OLD SHYSTER STOLE OUR MAP TO A GOLD MINE IN DEATH VALLEY! HE'S ON HIS WAY OUT THERE AND WE'VE GOT TO CATCH HIM!!
OH DO BE CAREFUL– I'VE HEARD DEATH VALLEY IS A TERRIBLE PLACE– IT'S FULL OF SNAKES AND BANDITS AND IT'S AWFULLY HOT– SOMETIMES IT REGISTERS 120° IN THE SHADE–AND THERE'S NO SHADE–
COME ON, MINNIE!!
GOOD BYE, CHILDREN– AND MICKEY, DON'T FORGET TO PUT AIR IN THE TIRES EVERY TWENTY MILES!
WAIT'LL WE GET OUR GOLD MINE– WE'LL BUY YOU A NEW BIKE WITH SILVER HANDLEBARS AND GOLD SPOKES!
© WALT DISNEY 5/14

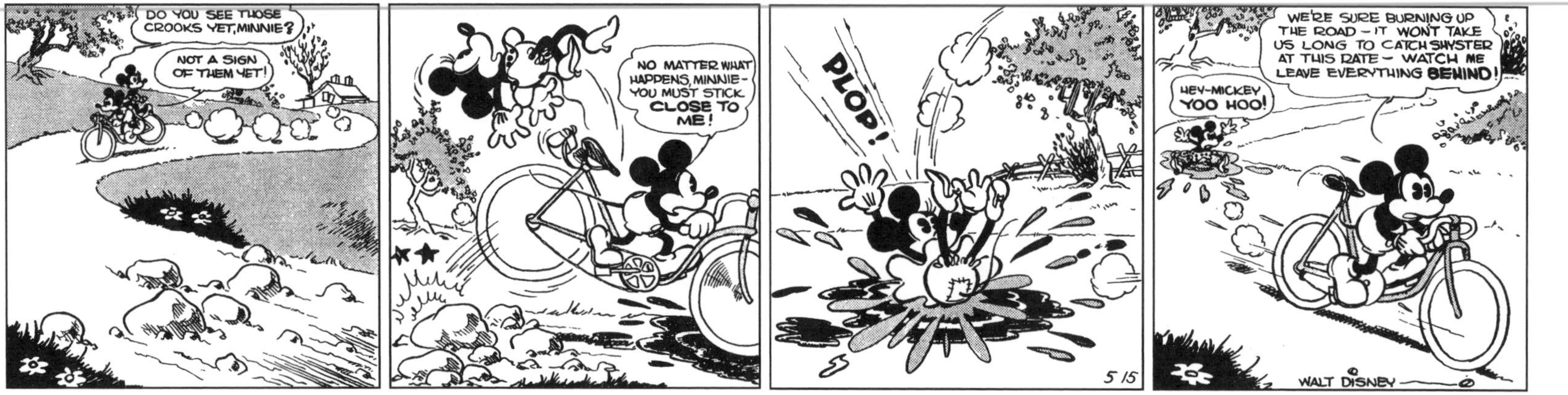
DO YOU SEE THOSE CROOKS YET, MINNIE?
NOT A SIGN OF THEM YET!
NO MATTER WHAT HAPPENS, MINNIE— YOU MUST STICK CLOSE TO ME!
PLOP!
5 15
WE'RE SURE BURNING UP THE ROAD — IT WON'T TAKE US LONG TO CATCH SHYSTER AT THIS RATE — WATCH ME LEAVE EVERYTHING BEHIND!
HEY-MICKEY YOO HOO!
WALT DISNEY

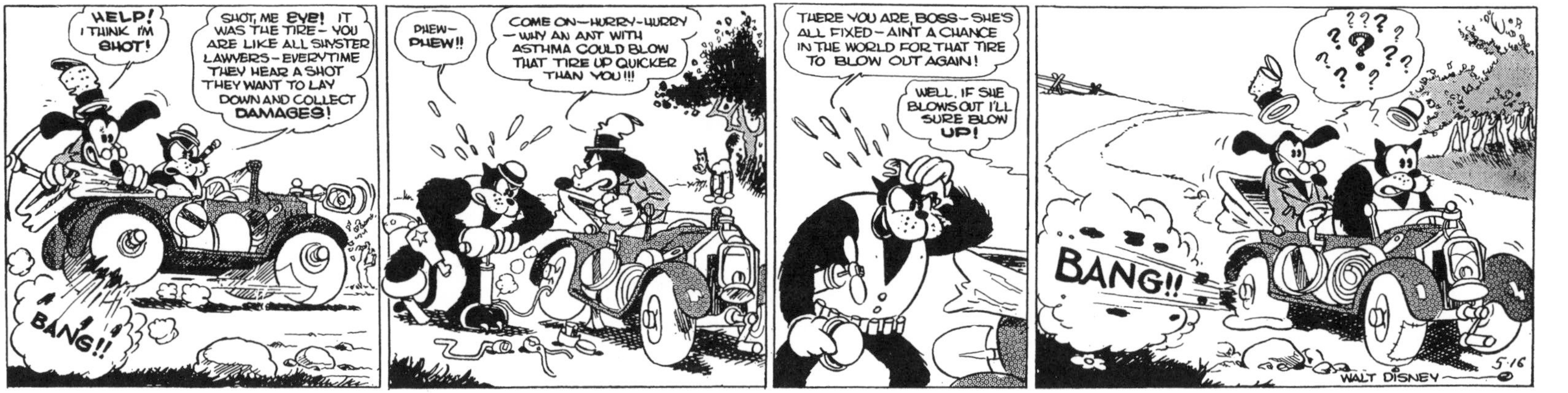
HELP! I THINK I'M SHOT!
SHOT, ME EYE! IT WAS THE TIRE — YOU ARE LIKE ALL SHYSTER LAWYERS — EVERYTIME THEY HEAR A SHOT THEY WANT TO LAY DOWN AND COLLECT DAMAGES!
BANG!!
PHEW— PHEW!!
COME ON—HURRY-HURRY —WHY AN ANT WITH ASTHMA COULD BLOW THAT TIRE UP QUICKER THAN YOU!!!
THERE YOU ARE, BOSS— SHE'S ALL FIXED— AINT A CHANCE IN THE WORLD FOR THAT TIRE TO BLOW OUT AGAIN!
WELL, IF SHE BLOWS OUT I'LL SURE BLOW UP!
BANG!!
5-16
WALT DISNEY

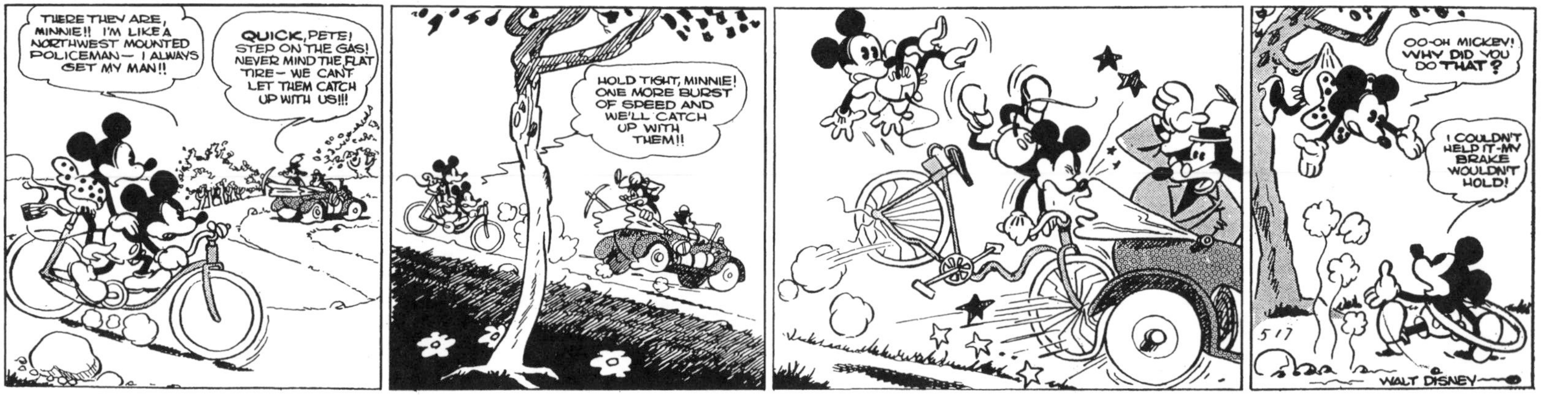
THERE THEY ARE, MINNIE!! I'M LIKE A NORTHWEST MOUNTED POLICEMAN— I ALWAYS GET MY MAN!!
QUICK, PETE! STEP ON THE GAS! NEVER MIND THE FLAT TIRE— WE CAN'T LET THEM CATCH UP WITH US!!!
HOLD TIGHT, MINNIE! ONE MORE BURST OF SPEED AND WE'LL CATCH UP WITH THEM!!
OO-OH MICKEY! WHY DID YOU DO THAT?
I COULDN'T HELP IT-MY BRAKE WOULDN'T HOLD!
5 17
WALT DISNEY

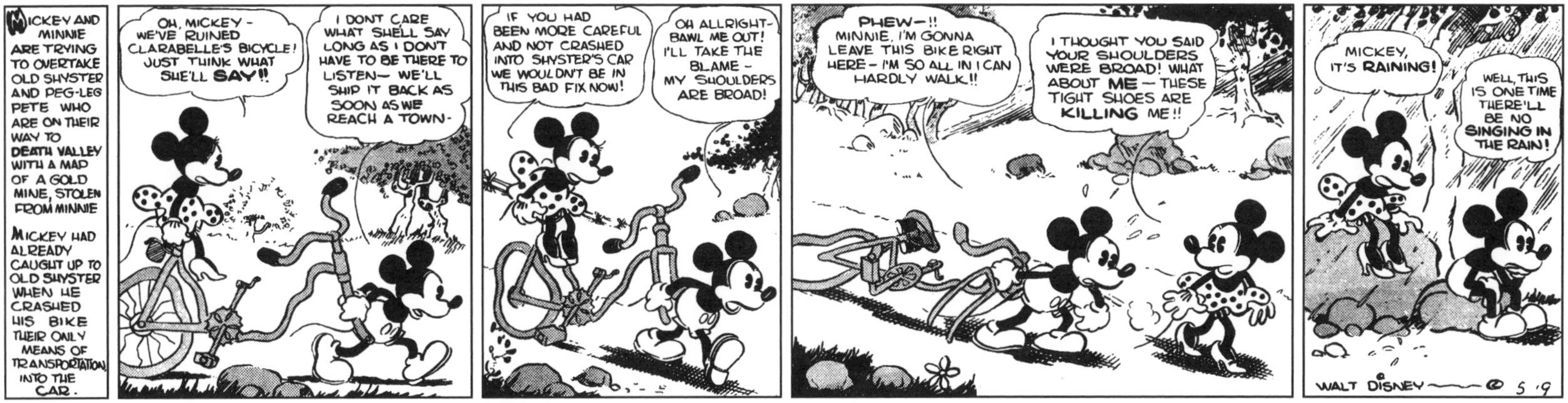
MICKEY AND MINNIE ARE TRYING TO OVERTAKE OLD SHYSTER AND PEG-LEG PETE WHO ARE ON THEIR WAY TO DEATH VALLEY WITH A MAP OF A GOLD MINE, STOLEN FROM MINNIE
MICKEY HAD ALREADY CAUGHT UP TO OLD SHYSTER WHEN HE CRASHED HIS BIKE THEIR ONLY MEANS OF TRANSPORTATION, INTO THE CAR.
OH, MICKEY - WE'VE RUINED CLARABELLE'S BICYCLE! JUST THINK WHAT SHE'LL SAY!!
I DONT CARE WHAT SHELL SAY LONG AS I DON'T HAVE TO BE THERE TO LISTEN— WE'LL SHIP IT BACK AS SOON AS WE REACH A TOWN-
IF YOU HAD BEEN MORE CAREFUL AND NOT CRASHED INTO SHYSTER'S CAR WE WOULDN'T BE IN THIS BAD FIX NOW!
OH ALLRIGHT- BAWL ME OUT! I'LL TAKE THE BLAME - MY SHOULDERS ARE BROAD!
PHEW-!! MINNIE, I'M GONNA LEAVE THIS BIKE RIGHT HERE- I'M SO ALL IN I CAN HARDLY WALK!!
I THOUGHT YOU SAID YOUR SHOULDERS WERE BROAD! WHAT ABOUT ME — THESE TIGHT SHOES ARE KILLING ME!!
MICKEY, IT'S RAINING!
WELL, THIS IS ONE TIME THERE'LL BE NO SINGING IN THE RAIN!
WALT DISNEY
5 19

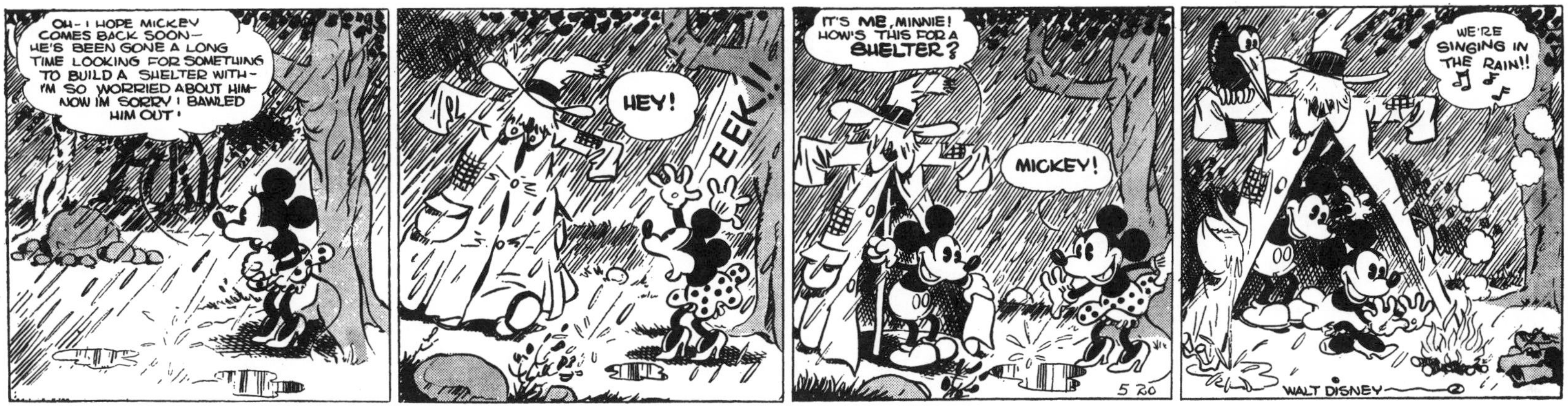
OH- I HOPE MICKEY COMES BACK SOON— HE'S BEEN GONE A LONG TIME LOOKING FOR SOMETHING TO BUILD A SHELTER WITH— I'M SO WORRIED ABOUT HIM- NOW I'M SORRY I BAWLED HIM OUT!
HEY!
EEK!!
IT'S ME, MINNIE! HOW'S THIS FOR A SHELTER?
MICKEY!
5 20
WE'RE SINGING IN THE RAIN!!
WALT DISNEY

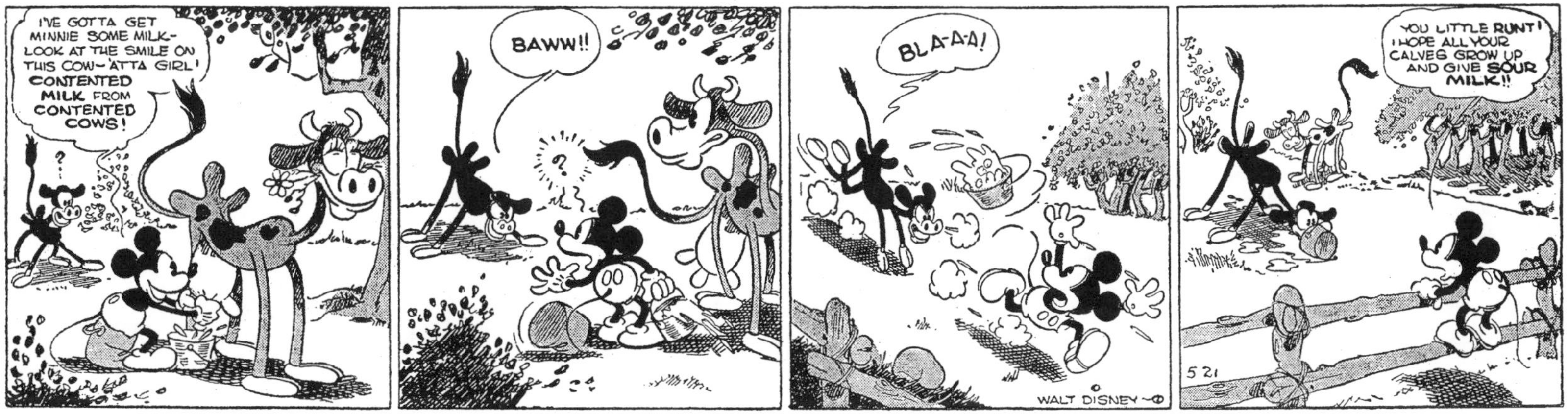
I'VE GOTTA GET MINNIE SOME MILK- LOOK AT THE SMILE ON THIS COW- 'ATTA GIRL! CONTENTED MILK FROM CONTENTED COWS!
?
BAWW!!
?
BLA-A-A!
WALT DISNEY
YOU LITTLE RUNT! I HOPE ALL YOUR CALVES GROW UP AND GIVE SOUR MILK!!
5 21

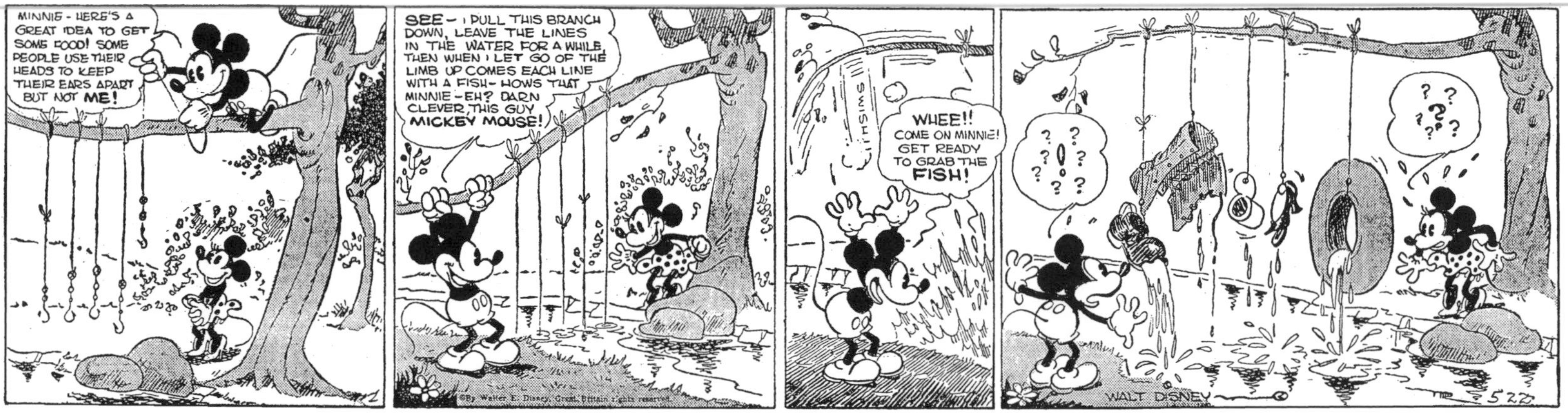
MINNIE - HERE'S A GREAT IDEA TO GET SOME FOOD! SOME PEOPLE USE THEIR HEADS TO KEEP THEIR EARS APART BUT NOT ME!
SEE - I PULL THIS BRANCH DOWN, LEAVE THE LINES IN THE WATER FOR A WHILE, THEN WHEN I LET GO OF THE LIMB UP COMES EACH LINE WITH A FISH - HOWS THAT MINNIE - EH? DARN CLEVER, THIS GUY MICKEY MOUSE!
SWISH
WHEE!! COME ON MINNIE! GET READY TO GRAB THE FISH!
WALT DISNEY
5.22

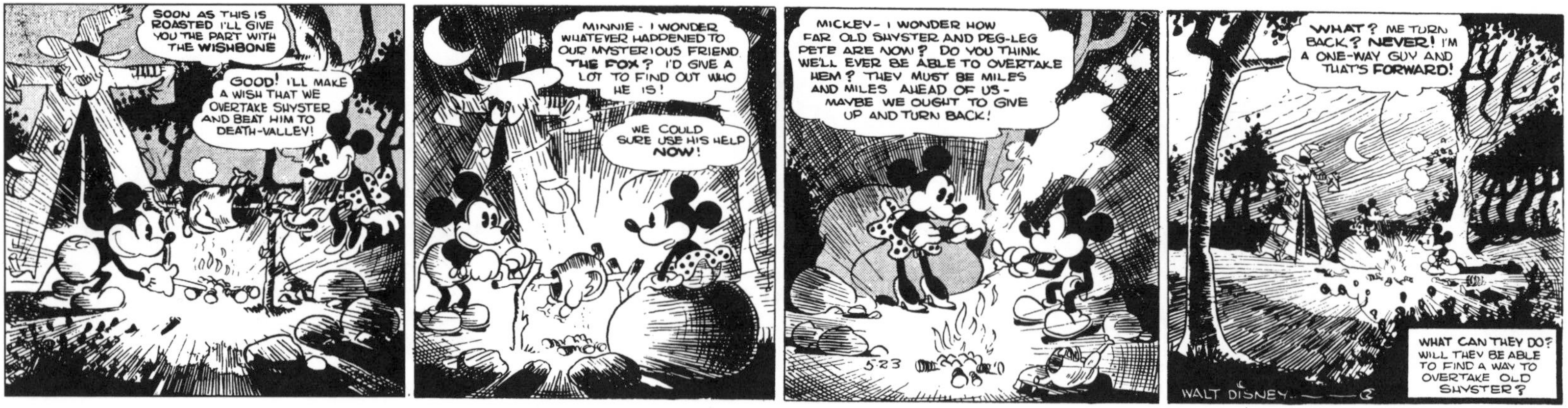
SOON AS THIS IS ROASTED I'LL GIVE YOU THE PART WITH THE WISHBONE
GOOD! I'LL MAKE A WISH THAT WE OVERTAKE SHYSTER AND BEAT HIM TO DEATH-VALLEY!
MINNIE - I WONDER WHATEVER HAPPENED TO OUR MYSTERIOUS FRIEND THE FOX? I'D GIVE A LOT TO FIND OUT WHO HE IS!
WE COULD SURE USE HIS HELP NOW!
MICKEY - I WONDER HOW FAR OLD SHYSTER AND PEG-LEG PETE ARE NOW? DO YOU THINK WE'LL EVER BE ABLE TO OVERTAKE HEM? THEY MUST BE MILES AND MILES AHEAD OF US - MAYBE WE OUGHT TO GIVE UP AND TURN BACK!
5.23
WHAT? ME TURN BACK? NEVER! I'M A ONE-WAY GUY AND THAT'S FORWARD!
WHAT CAN THEY DO? WILL THEY BE ABLE TO FIND A WAY TO OVERTAKE OLD SHYSTER?
WALT DISNEY

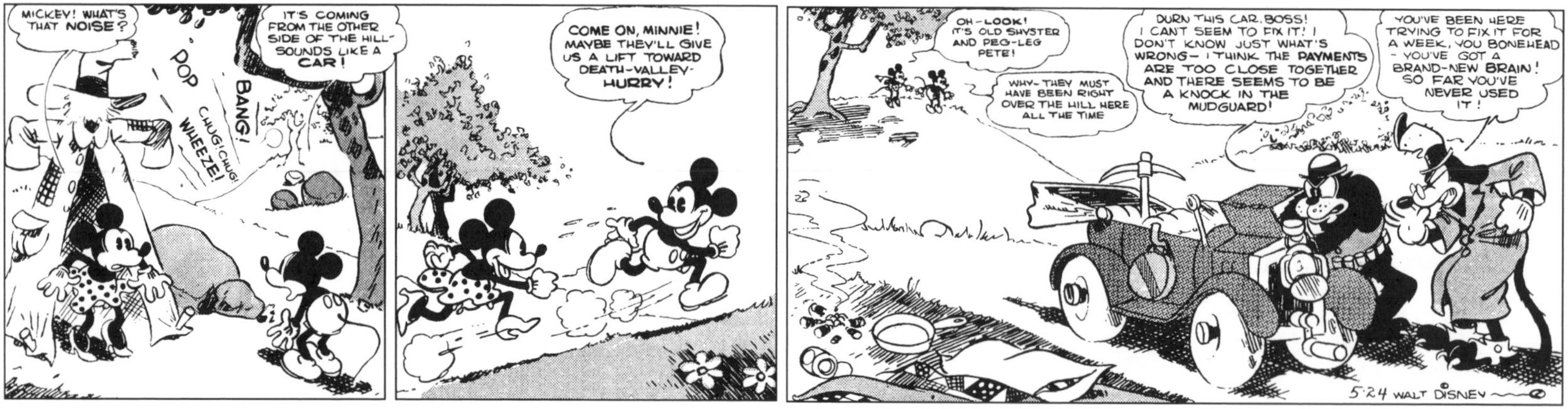
MICKEY! WHAT'S THAT NOISE?
POP
BANG!
CHUG! CHUG!
WHEEZE!
IT'S COMING FROM THE OTHER SIDE OF THE HILL - SOUNDS LIKE A CAR!
COME ON, MINNIE! MAYBE THEY'LL GIVE US A LIFT TOWARD DEATH-VALLEY - HURRY!
OH - LOOK! IT'S OLD SHYSTER AND PEG-LEG PETE!
WHY - THEY MUST HAVE BEEN RIGHT OVER THE HILL HERE ALL THE TIME
DURN THIS CAR, BOSS! I CAN'T SEEM TO FIX IT! I DON'T KNOW JUST WHAT'S WRONG - I THINK THE PAYMENTS ARE TOO CLOSE TOGETHER AND THERE SEEMS TO BE A KNOCK IN THE MUDGUARD!
YOU'VE BEEN HERE TRYING TO FIX IT FOR A WEEK, YOU BONEHEAD - YOU'VE GOT A BRAND-NEW BRAIN! SO FAR YOU'VE NEVER USED IT!
5.24 WALT DISNEY

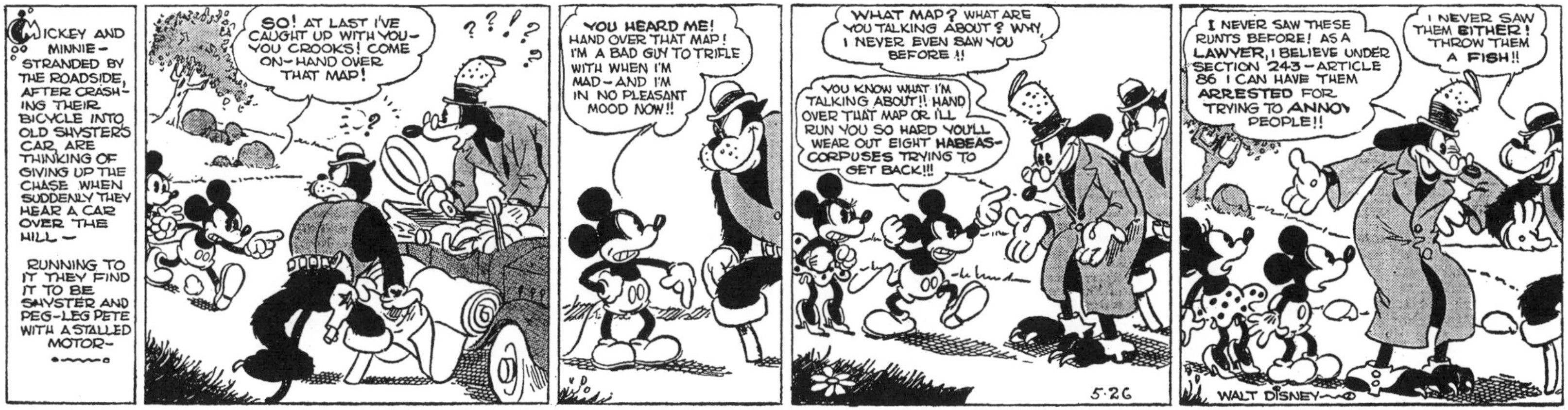
MICKEY AND MINNIE – STRANDED BY THE ROADSIDE, AFTER CRASHING THEIR BICYCLE INTO OLD SHYSTER'S CAR, ARE THINKING OF GIVING UP THE CHASE WHEN SUDDENLY THEY HEAR A CAR OVER THE HILL –
RUNNING TO IT THEY FIND IT TO BE SHYSTER AND PEG-LEG PETE WITH A STALLED MOTOR –
SO! AT LAST I'VE CAUGHT UP WITH YOU – YOU CROOKS! COME ON – HAND OVER THAT MAP!
? ? ! ?
YOU HEARD ME! HAND OVER THAT MAP! I'M A BAD GUY TO TRIFLE WITH WHEN I'M MAD – AND I'M IN NO PLEASANT MOOD NOW!!
WHAT MAP? WHAT ARE YOU TALKING ABOUT? WHY, I NEVER EVEN SAW YOU BEFORE!!
YOU KNOW WHAT I'M TALKING ABOUT!! HAND OVER THAT MAP OR I'LL RUN YOU SO HARD YOU'LL WEAR OUT EIGHT HABEAS-CORPUSES TRYING TO GET BACK!!!
5·26
I NEVER SAW THESE RUNTS BEFORE! AS A LAWYER, I BELIEVE UNDER SECTION 243 – ARTICLE 86 I CAN HAVE THEM ARRESTED FOR TRYING TO ANNOY PEOPLE!!
I NEVER SAW THEM BITHER! THROW THEM A FISH!!
WALT DISNEY

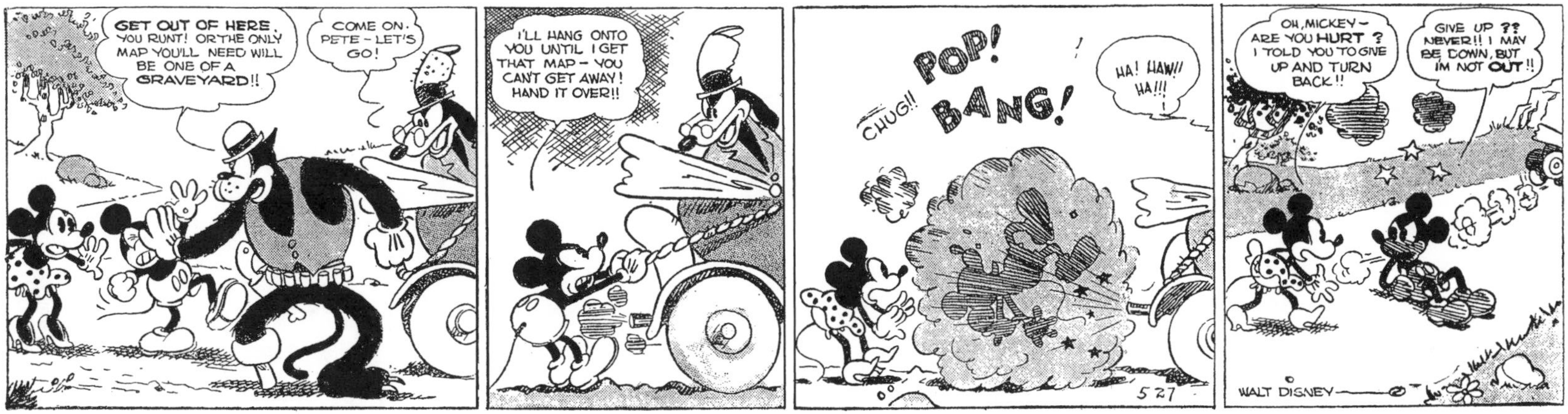
GET OUT OF HERE, YOU RUNT! OR THE ONLY MAP YOU'LL NEED WILL BE ONE OF A GRAVEYARD!!
COME ON, PETE – LET'S GO!
I'LL HANG ONTO YOU UNTIL I GET THAT MAP – YOU CAN'T GET AWAY! HAND IT OVER!!
CHUG!! POP! BANG!
HA! HAW!! HA!!!
5·27
OH, MICKEY – ARE YOU HURT? I TOLD YOU TO GIVE UP AND TURN BACK!!
GIVE UP ?? NEVER!! I MAY BE DOWN, BUT I'M NOT OUT!!
WALT DISNEY

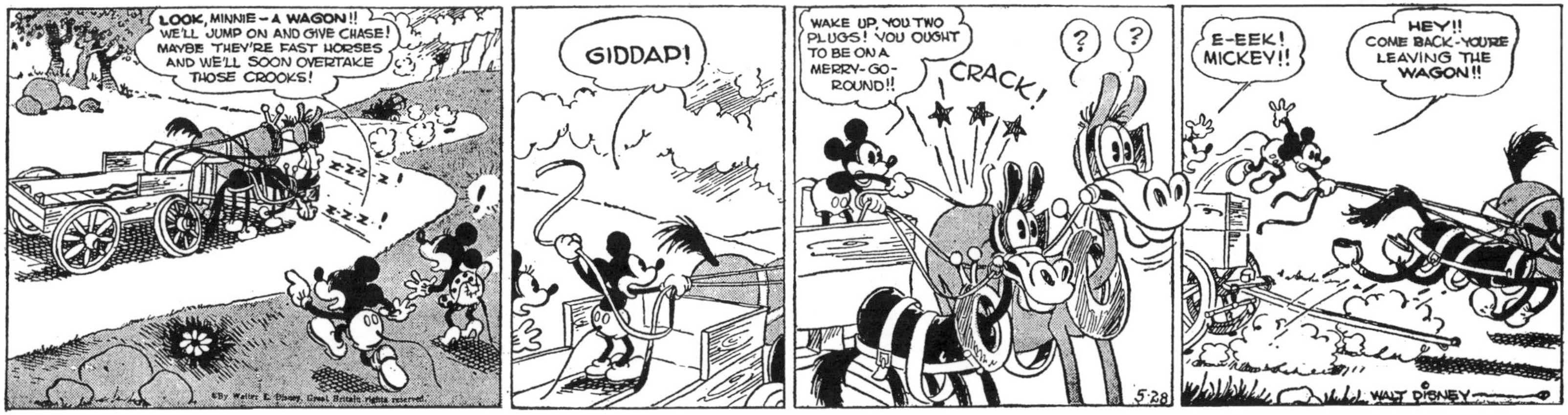
LOOK, MINNIE – A WAGON!! WE'LL JUMP ON AND GIVE CHASE! MAYBE THEY'RE FAST HORSES AND WE'LL SOON OVERTAKE THOSE CROOKS!
Z-Z-Z-Z!
Z-Z-Z!
©By Walter E. Disney, Great Britain rights reserved.
GIDDAP!
WAKE UP, YOU TWO PLUGS! YOU OUGHT TO BE ON A MERRY-GO-ROUND!!
CRACK!
? ?
5·28
E-EEK! MICKEY!!
HEY!! COME BACK – YOU'RE LEAVING THE WAGON!!
WALT DISNEY

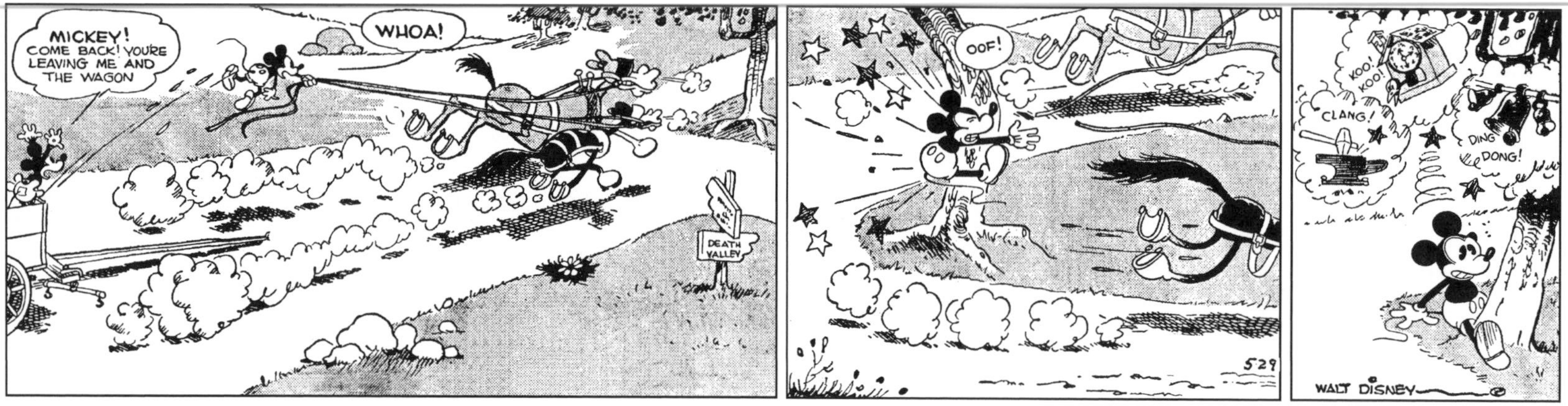
MICKEY! COME BACK! YOU'RE LEAVING ME AND THE WAGON
WHOA!
DEATH VALLEY
OOF!
529
KOO! KOO!
CLANG!
DING DONG!
WALT DISNEY

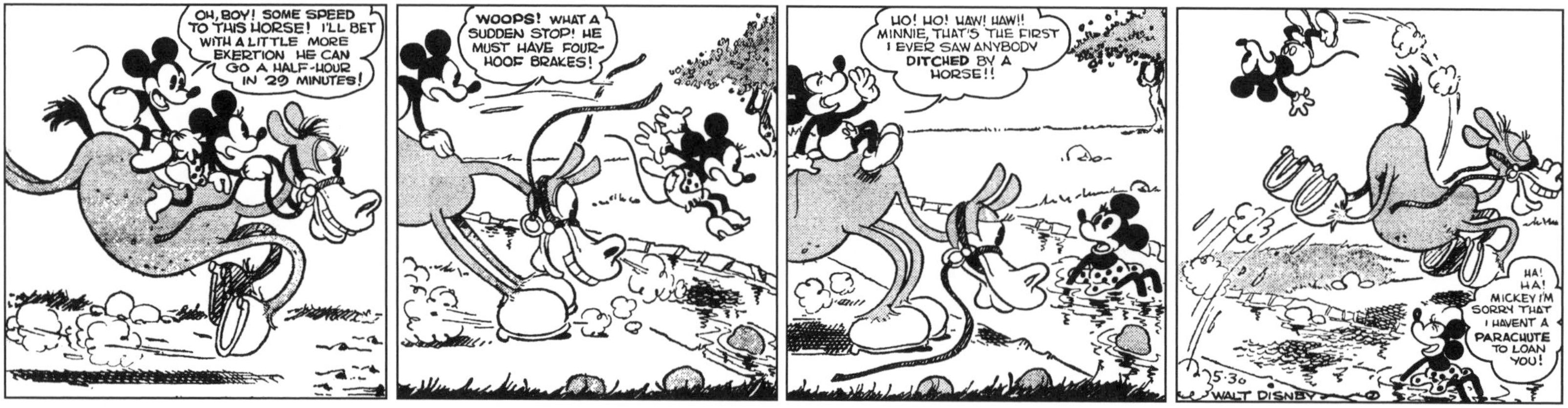
OH, BOY! SOME SPEED TO THIS HORSE! I'LL BET WITH A LITTLE MORE EXERTION HE CAN GO A HALF-HOUR IN 29 MINUTES!
WOOPS! WHAT A SUDDEN STOP! HE MUST HAVE FOUR-HOOF BRAKES!
HO! HO! HAW! HAW!! MINNIE, THAT'S THE FIRST I EVER SAW ANYBODY DITCHED BY A HORSE!!
HA! HA! MICKEY I'M SORRY THAT I HAVENT A PARACHUTE TO LOAN YOU!
5-30
WALT DISNEY

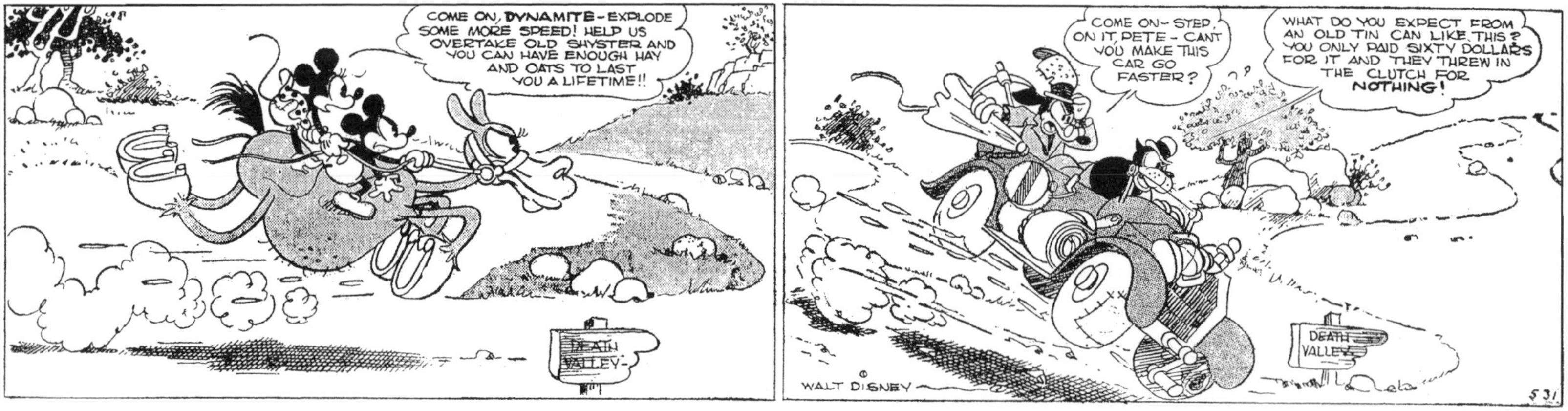
COME ON, DYNAMITE - EXPLODE SOME MORE SPEED! HELP US OVERTAKE OLD SHYSTER AND YOU CAN HAVE ENOUGH HAY AND OATS TO LAST YOU A LIFETIME!!
DEATH VALLEY
COME ON - STEP ON IT, PETE - CANT YOU MAKE THIS CAR GO FASTER?
WHAT DO YOU EXPECT FROM AN OLD TIN CAN LIKE THIS? YOU ONLY PAID SIXTY DOLLARS FOR IT AND THEY THREW IN THE CLUTCH FOR NOTHING!
DEATH VALLEY
WALT DISNEY
531

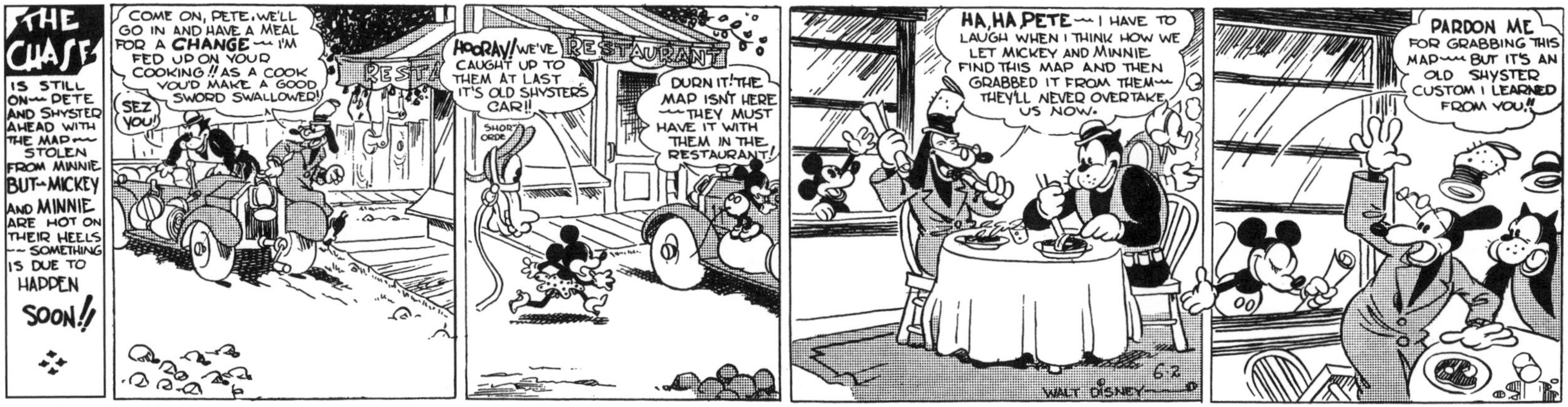
THE CHASE IS STILL ON— PETE AND SHYSTER AHEAD WITH THE MAP— STOLEN FROM MINNIE BUT—MICKEY AND MINNIE ARE HOT ON THEIR HEELS —SOMETHING IS DUE TO HAPPEN SOON!!
COME ON, PETE, WE'LL GO IN AND HAVE A MEAL FOR A CHANGE— I'M FED UP ON YOUR COOKING!! AS A COOK YOU'D MAKE A GOOD SWORD SWALLOWER!
SEZ YOU!
RESTA
HOORAY! WE'VE CAUGHT UP TO THEM AT LAST IT'S OLD SHYSTER'S CAR!!
RESTAURANT
DURN IT! THE MAP ISN'T HERE —THEY MUST HAVE IT WITH THEM IN THE RESTAURANT!
HA, HA PETE— I HAVE TO LAUGH WHEN I THINK HOW WE LET MICKEY AND MINNIE FIND THIS MAP AND THEN GRABBED IT FROM THEM— THEY'LL NEVER OVERTAKE US NOW.
6-2
WALT DISNEY
PARDON ME FOR GRABBING THIS MAP— BUT IT'S AN OLD SHYSTER CUSTOM I LEARNED FROM YOU!!

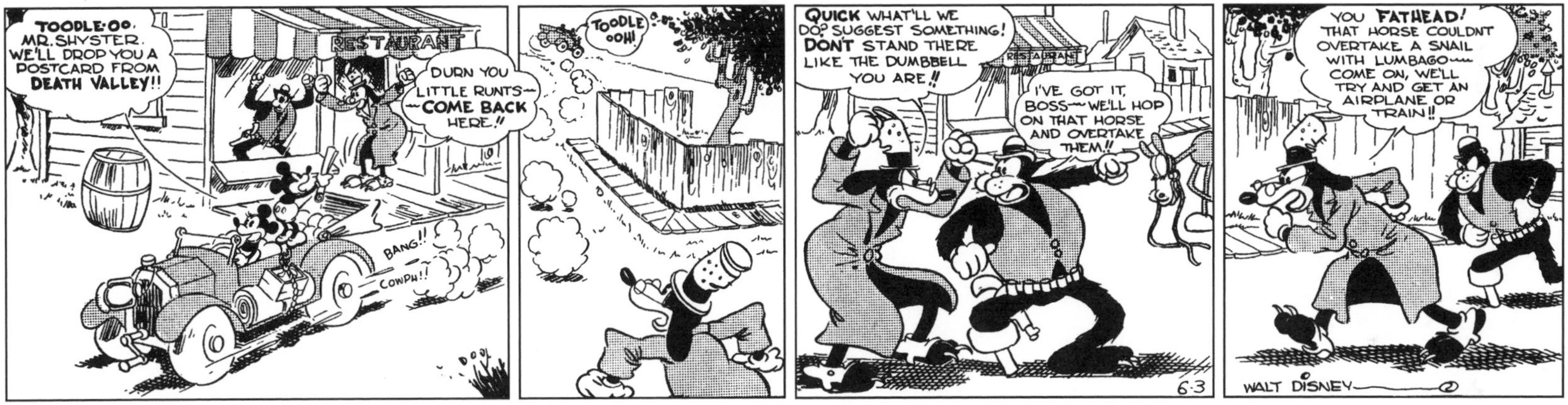
TOODLE-OO, MR. SHYSTER. WE'LL DROP YOU A POSTCARD FROM DEATH VALLEY!!
RESTAURANT
DURN YOU LITTLE RUNTS— —COME BACK HERE!!
BANG!!
COWPH!!
TOODLE OOH!
QUICK WHAT'LL WE DO? SUGGEST SOMETHING! DON'T STAND THERE LIKE THE DUMBELL YOU ARE!!
RESTAURANT
I'VE GOT IT, BOSS— WE'LL HOP ON THAT HORSE AND OVERTAKE THEM!!
6-3
YOU FATHEAD! THAT HORSE COULDN'T OVERTAKE A SNAIL WITH LUMBAGO— COME ON, WE'LL TRY AND GET AN AIRPLANE OR TRAIN!!
WALT DISNEY

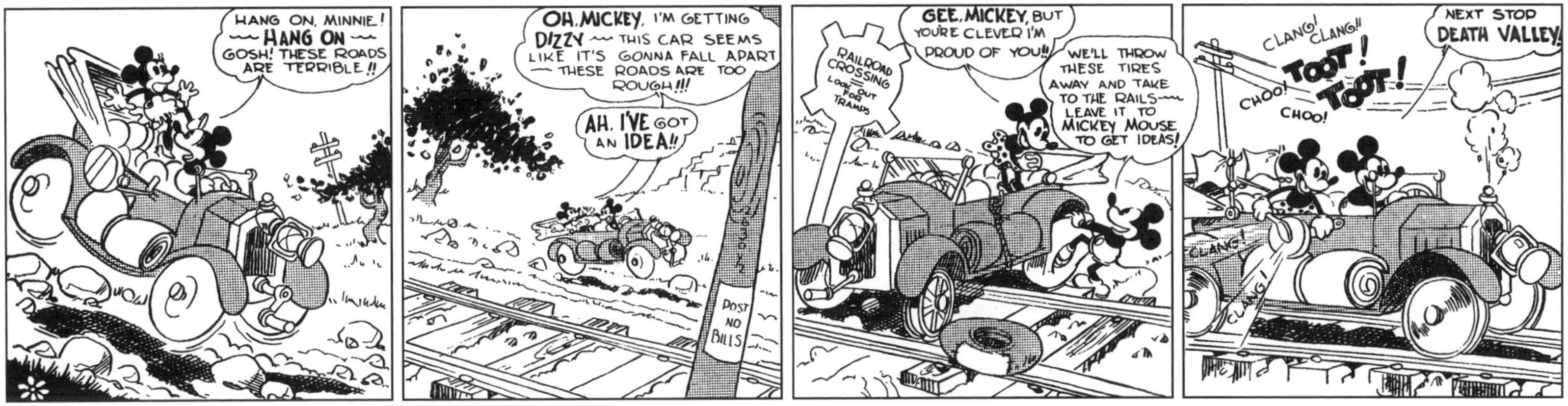
HANG ON, MINNIE! —HANG ON— GOSH! THESE ROADS ARE TERRIBLE!!
OH, MICKEY, I'M GETTING DIZZY— THIS CAR SEEMS LIKE IT'S GONNA FALL APART —THESE ROADS ARE TOO ROUGH!!!
AH, I'VE GOT AN IDEA!!
POST NO BILLS
RAILROAD CROSSING LOOK OUT FOR TRAMPS
GEE, MICKEY, BUT YOU'RE CLEVER I'M PROUD OF YOU!!
WE'LL THROW THESE TIRES AWAY AND TAKE TO THE RAILS— LEAVE IT TO MICKEY MOUSE TO GET IDEAS!
CLANG! CLANG!!
CHOO! TOOT! TOOT! CHOO!
NEXT STOP DEATH VALLEY!
CLANG! CLANG!

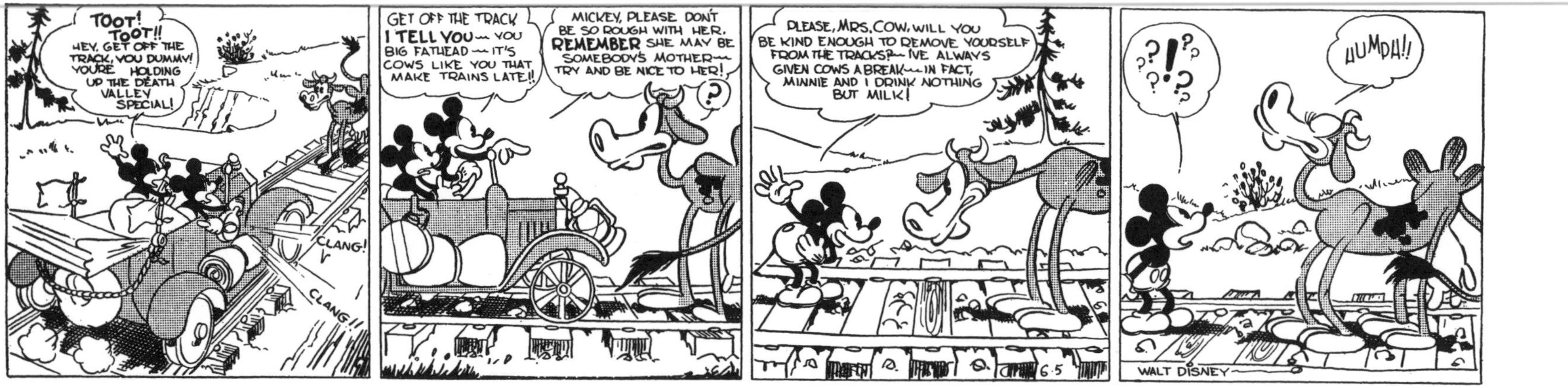
TOOT! TOOT!! HEY, GET OFF THE TRACK, YOU DUMMY! YOU'RE HOLDING UP THE DEATH VALLEY SPECIAL!
CLANG!
CLANG!!
GET OFF THE TRACK I TELL YOU— YOU BIG FATHEAD— IT'S COWS LIKE YOU THAT MAKE TRAINS LATE!!
MICKEY, PLEASE DON'T BE SO ROUGH WITH HER. REMEMBER SHE MAY BE SOMEBODY'S MOTHER— TRY AND BE NICE TO HER!
?
PLEASE, MRS. COW, WILL YOU BE KIND ENOUGH TO REMOVE YOURSELF FROM THE TRACKS?— I'VE ALWAYS GIVEN COWS A BREAK— IN FACT, MINNIE AND I DRINK NOTHING BUT MILK!
6-5
HUMPH!!
WALT DISNEY

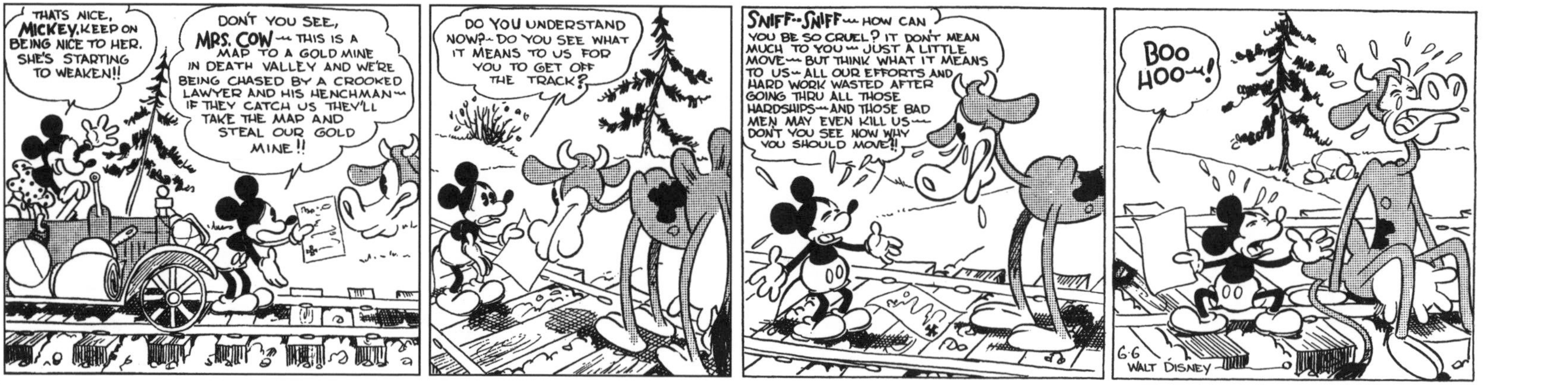
THAT'S NICE, MICKEY. KEEP ON BEING NICE TO HER. SHE'S STARTING TO WEAKEN!!
DON'T YOU SEE, MRS. COW— THIS IS A MAP TO A GOLD MINE IN DEATH VALLEY AND WE'RE BEING CHASED BY A CROOKED LAWYER AND HIS HENCHMAN— IF THEY CATCH US THEY'LL TAKE THE MAP AND STEAL OUR GOLD MINE!!
DO YOU UNDERSTAND NOW?— DO YOU SEE WHAT IT MEANS TO US FOR YOU TO GET OFF THE TRACK?
SNIFF-SNIFF— HOW CAN YOU BE SO CRUEL? IT DON'T MEAN MUCH TO YOU— JUST A LITTLE MOVE— BUT THINK WHAT IT MEANS TO US— ALL OUR EFFORTS AND HARD WORK WASTED AFTER GOING THRU ALL THOSE HARDSHIPS— AND THOSE BAD MEN MAY EVEN KILL US— DON'T YOU SEE NOW WHY YOU SHOULD MOVE?!!
BOO HOO—!
6-6
WALT DISNEY

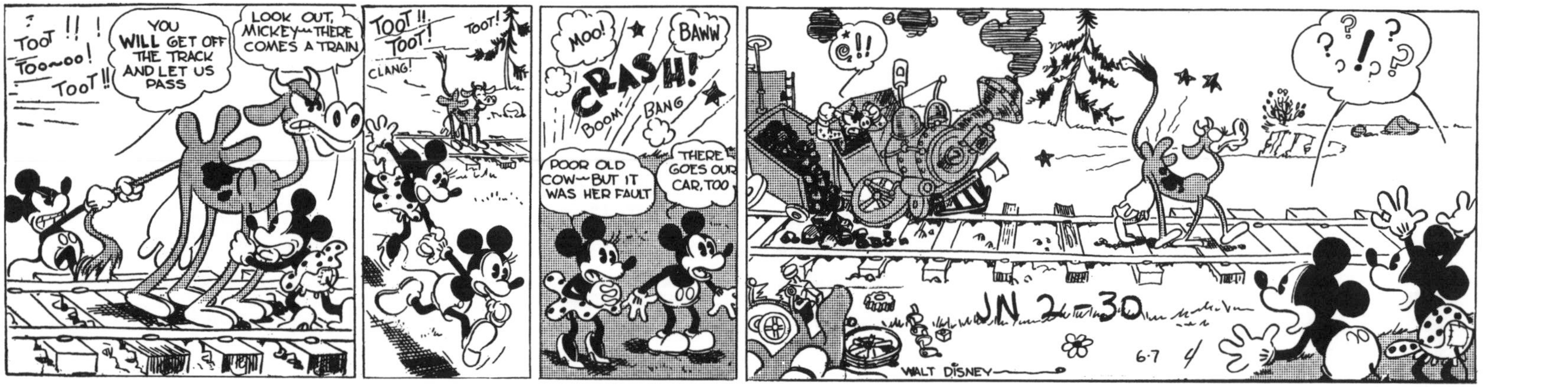
TOOT!!! TOO-OO! TOOT!!
YOU WILL GET OFF THE TRACK AND LET US PASS
LOOK OUT, MICKEY— THERE COMES A TRAIN
TOOT!! TOOT! TOOT!
CLANG!
MOO!
BAWW
CRASH!
BOOM
BANG
POOR OLD COW— BUT IT WAS HER FAULT
THERE GOES OUR CAR, TOO
JN 2-30
6-7
WALT DISNEY

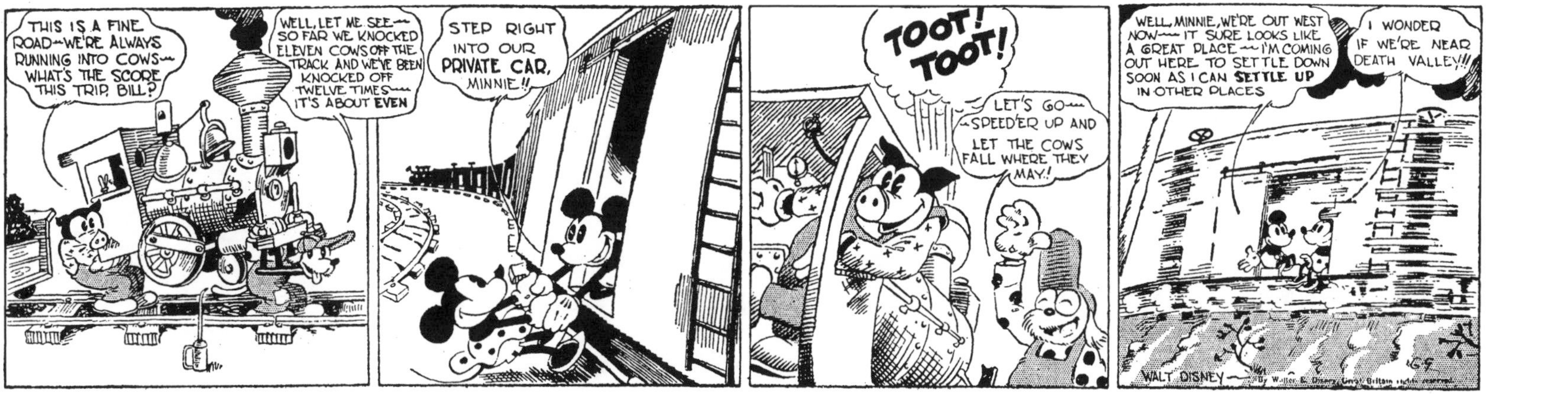
THIS IS A FINE ROAD — WE'RE ALWAYS RUNNING INTO COWS — WHAT'S THE SCORE THIS TRIP, BILL?
WELL, LET ME SEE — SO FAR WE KNOCKED ELEVEN COWS OFF THE TRACK AND WE'VE BEEN KNOCKED OFF TWELVE TIMES — IT'S ABOUT EVEN
STEP RIGHT INTO OUR PRIVATE CAR, MINNIE!!
TOOT! TOOT!
LET'S GO — SPEED'ER UP AND LET THE COWS FALL WHERE THEY MAY!
WELL, MINNIE, WE'RE OUT WEST NOW — IT SURE LOOKS LIKE A GREAT PLACE — I'M COMING OUT HERE TO SETTLE DOWN SOON AS I CAN SETTLE UP IN OTHER PLACES
I WONDER IF WE'RE NEAR DEATH VALLEY!!
WALT DISNEY
6-9

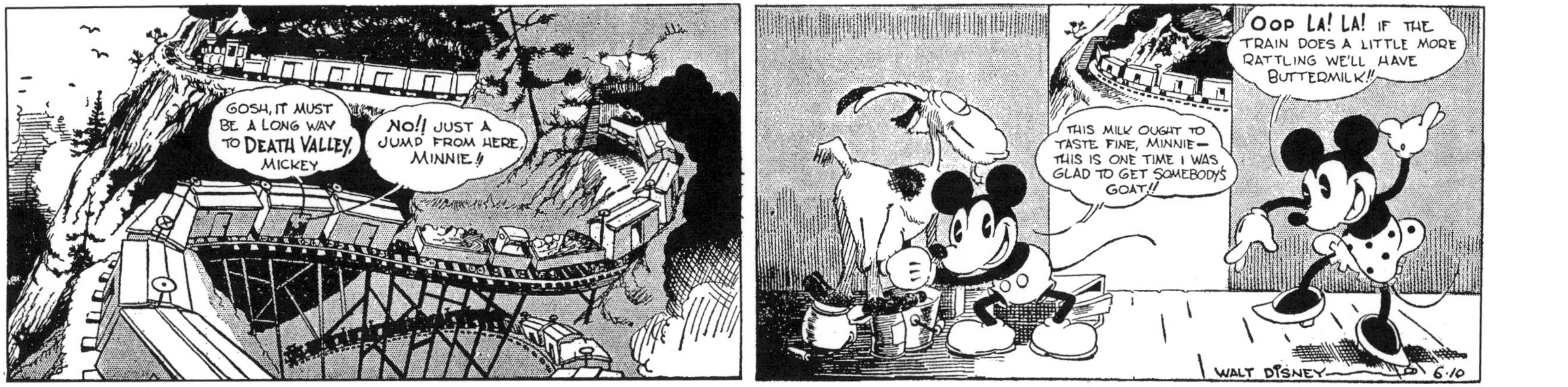
GOSH, IT MUST BE A LONG WAY TO DEATH VALLEY, MICKEY
NO!! JUST A JUMP FROM HERE, MINNIE!!
THIS MILK OUGHT TO TASTE FINE, MINNIE — THIS IS ONE TIME I WAS GLAD TO GET SOMEBODY'S GOAT!!
OOP LA! LA! IF THE TRAIN DOES A LITTLE MORE RATTLING WE'LL HAVE BUTTERMILK!!
WALT DISNEY
6-10

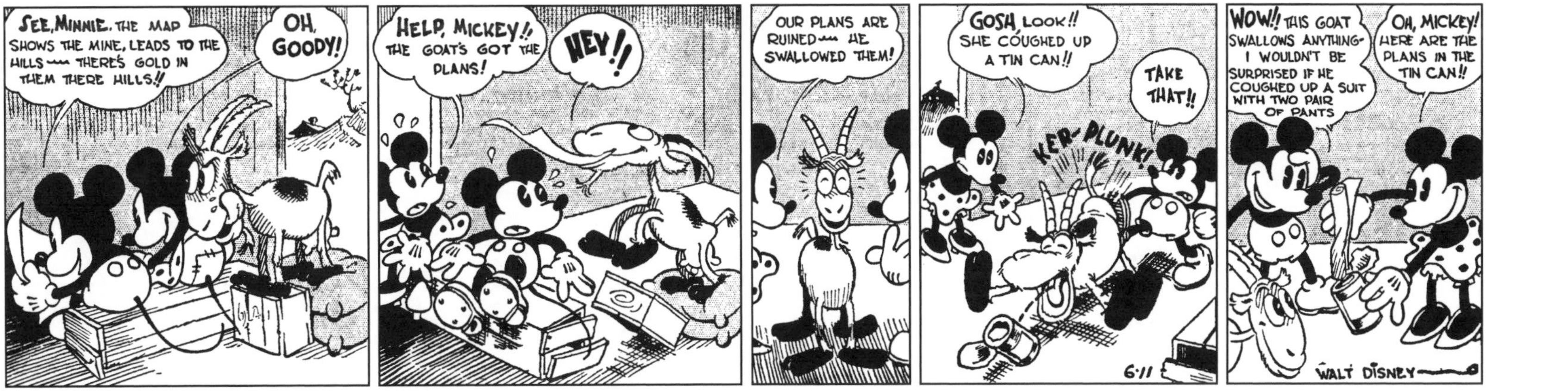
SEE, MINNIE, THE MAP SHOWS THE MINE, LEADS TO THE HILLS — THERE'S GOLD IN THEM THERE HILLS!!
OH, GOODY!
HELP, MICKEY!! THE GOAT'S GOT THE PLANS!
HEY!!
OUR PLANS ARE RUINED — HE SWALLOWED THEM!
GOSH, LOOK!! SHE COUGHED UP A TIN CAN!!
TAKE THAT!!
KER-PLUNK!
6-11
WOW!! THIS GOAT SWALLOWS ANYTHING — I WOULDN'T BE SURPRISED IF HE COUGHED UP A SUIT WITH TWO PAIR OF PANTS
OH, MICKEY! HERE ARE THE PLANS IN THE TIN CAN!!
WALT DISNEY

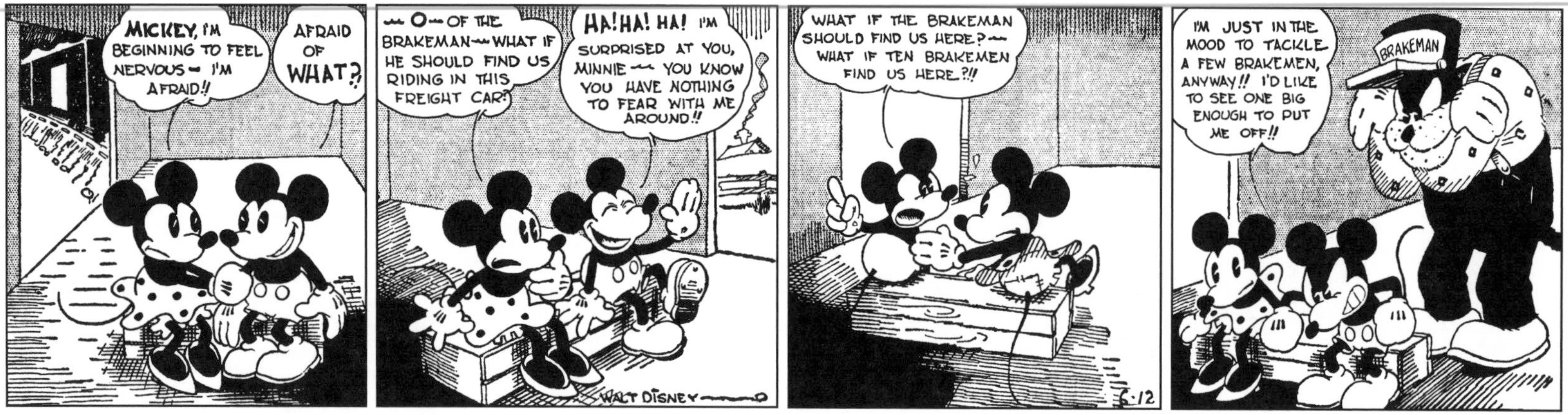
MICKEY, I'M BEGINNING TO FEEL NERVOUS — I'M AFRAID!!
AFRAID OF WHAT?
— O — OF THE BRAKEMAN — WHAT IF HE SHOULD FIND US RIDING IN THIS FREIGHT CAR?
HA! HA! HA! I'M SURPRISED AT YOU, MINNIE — YOU KNOW YOU HAVE NOTHING TO FEAR WITH ME AROUND!!
WALT DISNEY
WHAT IF THE BRAKEMAN SHOULD FIND US HERE? — WHAT IF TEN BRAKEMEN FIND US HERE?!!
6-12
I'M JUST IN THE MOOD TO TACKLE A FEW BRAKEMEN, ANYWAY!! I'D LIKE TO SEE ONE BIG ENOUGH TO PUT ME OFF!!
BRAKEMAN

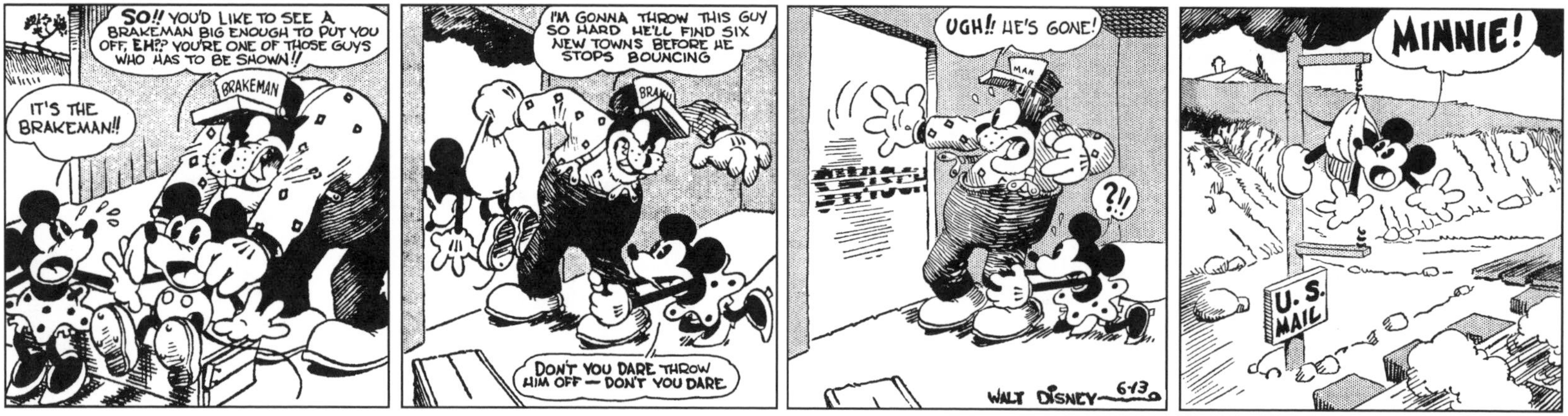
SO!! YOU'D LIKE TO SEE A BRAKEMAN BIG ENOUGH TO PUT YOU OFF, EH?? YOU'RE ONE OF THOSE GUYS WHO HAS TO BE SHOWN!!
IT'S THE BRAKEMAN!!
BRAKEMAN
I'M GONNA THROW THIS GUY SO HARD HE'LL FIND SIX NEW TOWNS BEFORE HE STOPS BOUNCING
DON'T YOU DARE THROW HIM OFF — DON'T YOU DARE
UGH!! HE'S GONE!
?!!
WALT DISNEY 6-13
MINNIE!
U.S. MAIL

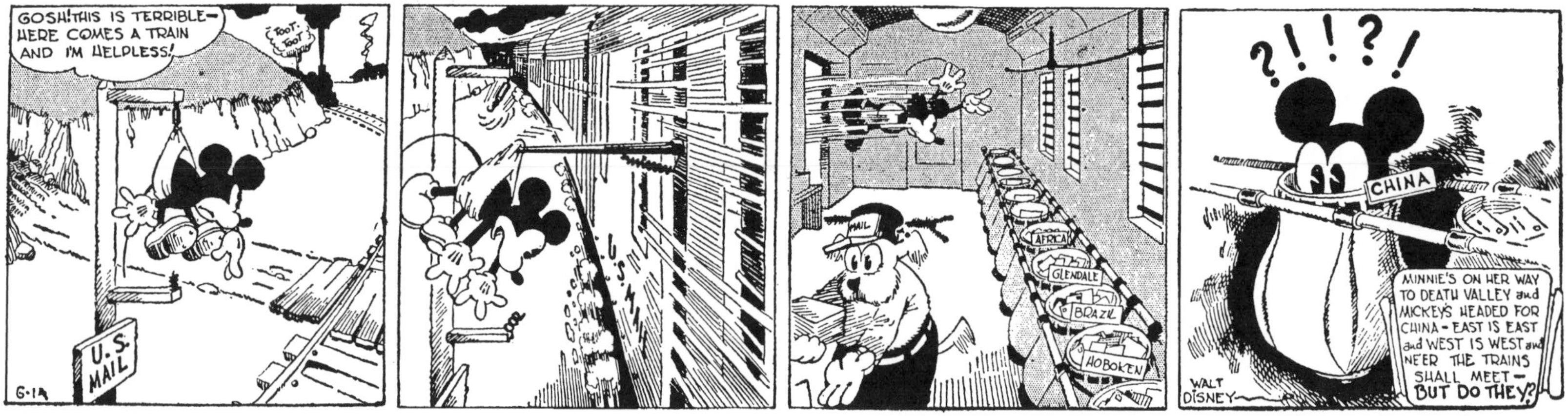
GOSH! THIS IS TERRIBLE — HERE COMES A TRAIN AND I'M HELPLESS!
TOOT-TOOT
U.S. MAIL
6-14
MAIL
AFRICA
GLENDALE
BRAZIL
HOBOKEN
?!!?!
CHINA
WALT DISNEY
MINNIE'S ON HER WAY TO DEATH VALLEY and MICKEY'S HEADED FOR CHINA — EAST IS EAST and WEST IS WEST and NE'ER THE TRAINS SHALL MEET — BUT DO THEY?

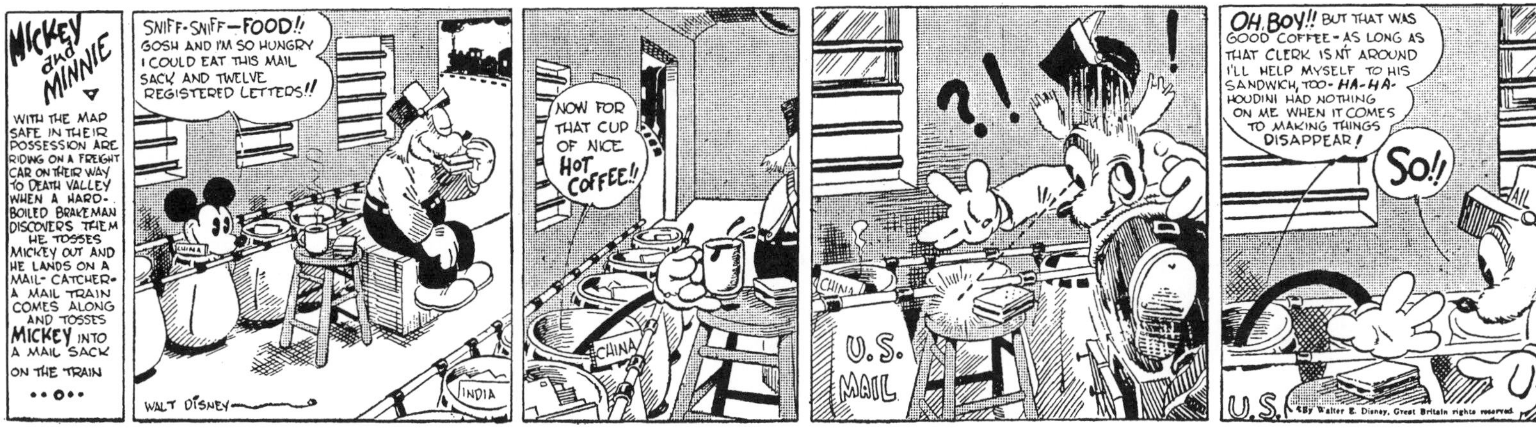
MICKEY and MINNIE
WITH THE MAP SAFE IN THEIR POSSESSION ARE RIDING ON A FREIGHT CAR ON THEIR WAY TO DEATH VALLEY WHEN A HARD-BOILED BRAKEMAN DISCOVERS THEM HE TOSSES MICKEY OUT AND HE LANDS ON A MAIL-CATCHER-A MAIL TRAIN COMES ALONG AND TOSSES MICKEY INTO A MAIL SACK ON THE TRAIN
• • O • •
SNIFF-SNIFF—FOOD!! GOSH AND I'M SO HUNGRY I COULD EAT THIS MAIL SACK AND TWELVE REGISTERED LETTERS!!
CHINA
INDIA
WALT DISNEY
NOW FOR THAT CUP OF NICE HOT COFFEE!!
CHINA
?! !
CHINA
U.S. MAIL
OH, BOY!! BUT THAT WAS GOOD COFFEE-AS LONG AS THAT CLERK IS N'T AROUND I'LL HELP MYSELF TO HIS SANDWICH, TOO-HA-HA-HOUDINI HAD NOTHING ON ME WHEN IT COMES TO MAKING THINGS DISAPPEAR!
SO!!
U.S.
©By Walter E. Disney, Great Britain rights reserved
6·16

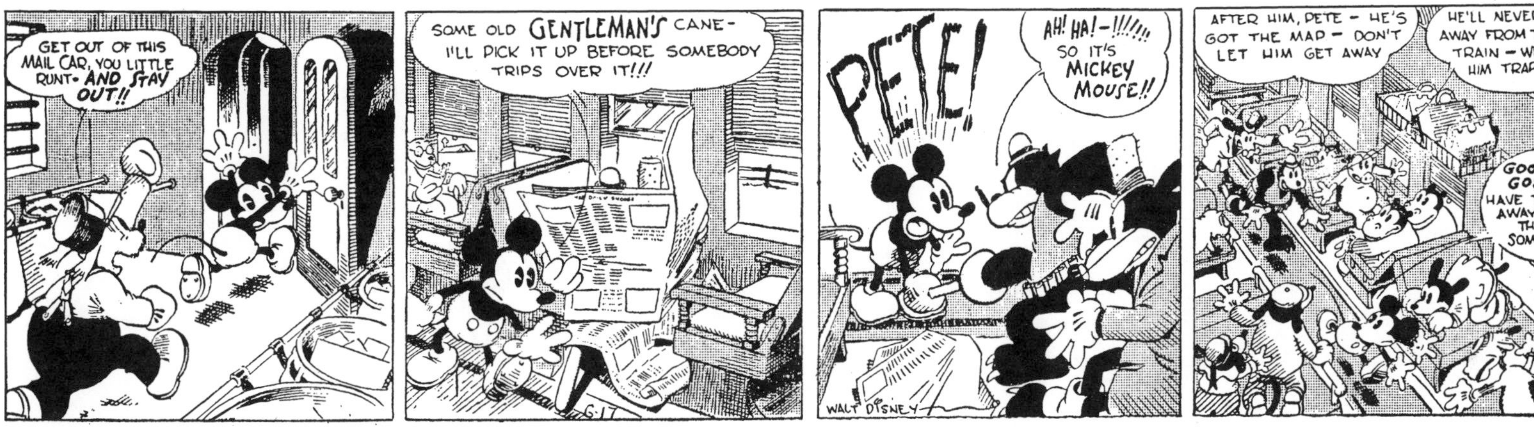
GET OUT OF THIS MAIL CAR, YOU LITTLE RUNT-AND STAY OUT!!
SOME OLD GENTLEMAN'S CANE-I'LL PICK IT UP BEFORE SOMEBODY TRIPS OVER IT!!!
6·17
PETE!
AH! HA!-!!!!!! SO IT'S MICKEY MOUSE!!
WALT DISNEY
AFTER HIM, PETE - HE'S GOT THE MAP - DON'T LET HIM GET AWAY
HE'LL NEVER GET AWAY FROM THIS TRAIN - WE'VE GOT HIM TRAPPED!!
GOOD GOSH! I HAVE TO GET AWAY FROM THEM SOMEHOW!

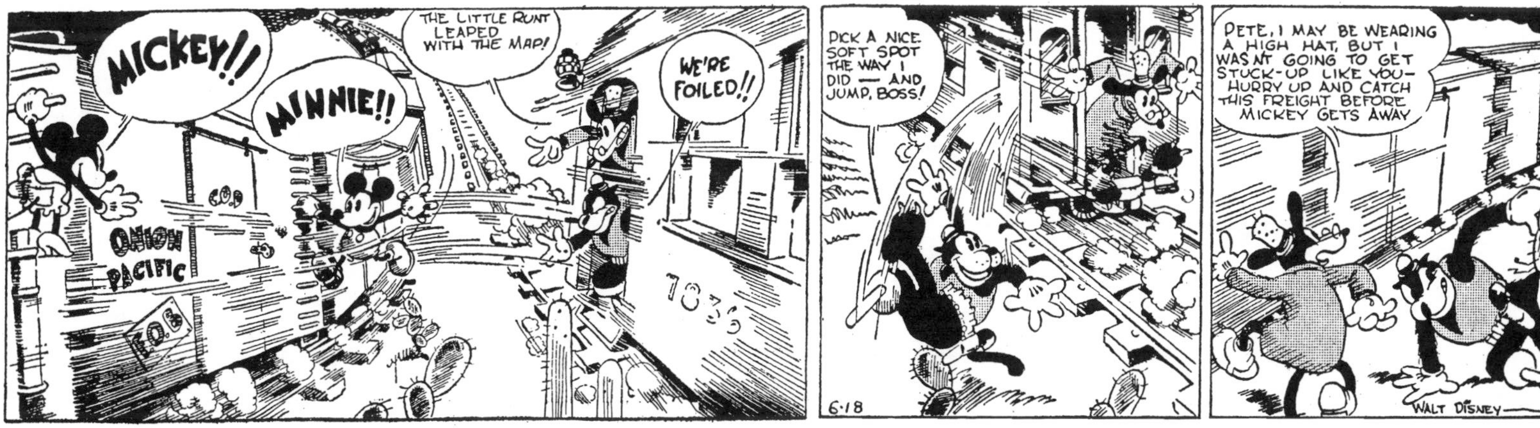
MICKEY!!!
MINNIE!!
THE LITTLE RUNT LEAPED WITH THE MAP!
WE'RE FOILED!!
ONION PACIFIC
F.O.B.
7036
PICK A NICE SOFT SPOT THE WAY I DID — AND JUMP, BOSS!
6·18
PETE, I MAY BE WEARING A HIGH HAT, BUT I WAS N'T GOING TO GET STUCK-UP LIKE YOU-HURRY UP AND CATCH THIS FREIGHT BEFORE MICKEY GETS AWAY
WALT DISNEY

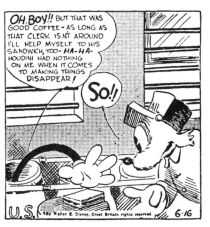

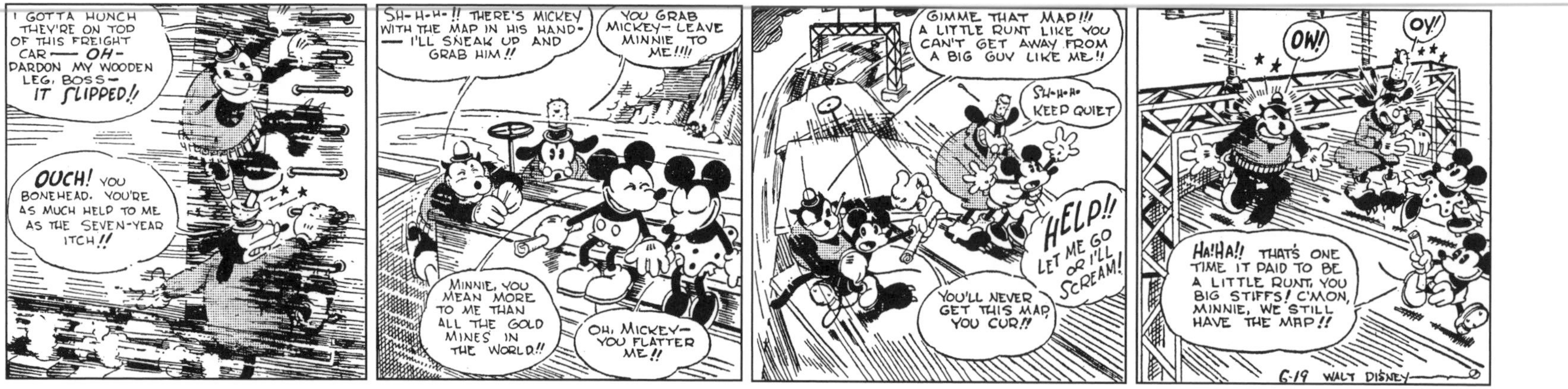
I GOTTA HUNCH THEY'RE ON TOP OF THIS FREIGHT CAR — OH — PARDON MY WOODEN LEG, BOSS — IT SLIPPED!!
OUCH! YOU BONEHEAD. YOU'RE AS MUCH HELP TO ME AS THE SEVEN-YEAR ITCH!!
SH-H-H-!! THERE'S MICKEY WITH THE MAP IN HIS HAND — I'LL SNEAK UP AND GRAB HIM!!
YOU GRAB MICKEY — LEAVE MINNIE TO ME!!!!
MINNIE, YOU MEAN MORE TO ME THAN ALL THE GOLD MINES IN THE WORLD!!
OH, MICKEY — YOU FLATTER ME!!
GIMME THAT MAP!!! A LITTLE RUNT LIKE YOU CAN'T GET AWAY FROM A BIG GUY LIKE ME!!
SH-H-H- KEEP QUIET
HELP!! LET ME GO OR I'LL SCREAM!
YOU'LL NEVER GET THIS MAP, YOU CUR!!
OW!
OY!
HA!HA!! THAT'S ONE TIME IT PAID TO BE A LITTLE RUNT, YOU BIG STIFFS! C'MON, MINNIE, WE STILL HAVE THE MAP!!
6-19 WALT DISNEY

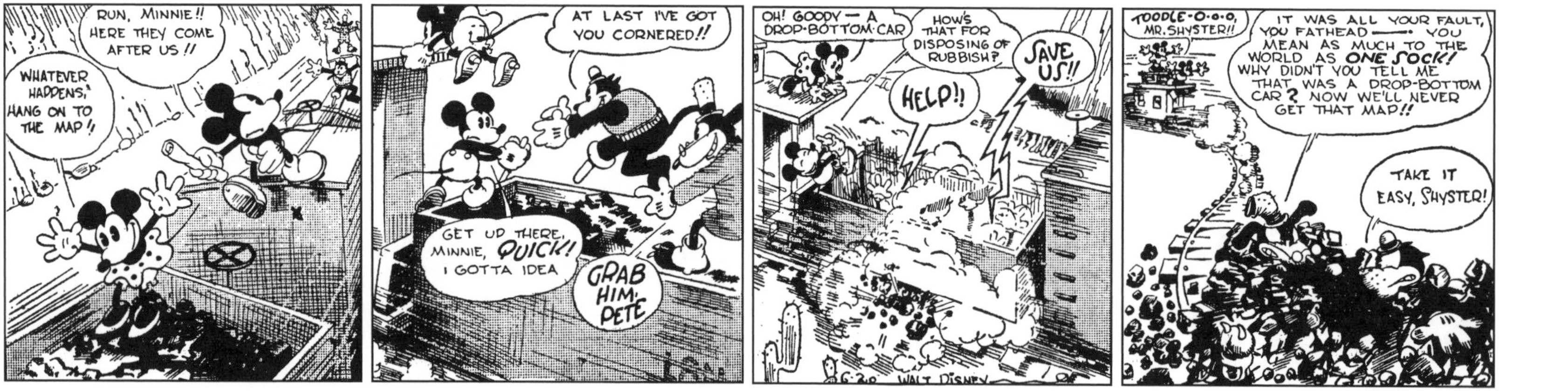
RUN, MINNIE!! HERE THEY COME AFTER US!!
WHATEVER HAPPENS, HANG ON TO THE MAP!!
AT LAST I'VE GOT YOU CORNERED!!
GET UP THERE, MINNIE, QUICK!! I GOTTA IDEA
GRAB HIM, PETE
OH! GOODY — A DROP-BOTTOM CAR
HOW'S THAT FOR DISPOSING OF RUBBISH?
HELP!!
SAVE US!!
6-20 WALT DISNEY
TOODLE-O-O-O, MR. SHYSTER!!
IT WAS ALL YOUR FAULT, YOU FATHEAD — YOU MEAN AS MUCH TO THE WORLD AS ONE SOCK!! WHY DIDN'T YOU TELL ME THAT WAS A DROP-BOTTOM CAR? NOW WE'LL NEVER GET THAT MAP!!
TAKE IT EASY, SHYSTER!

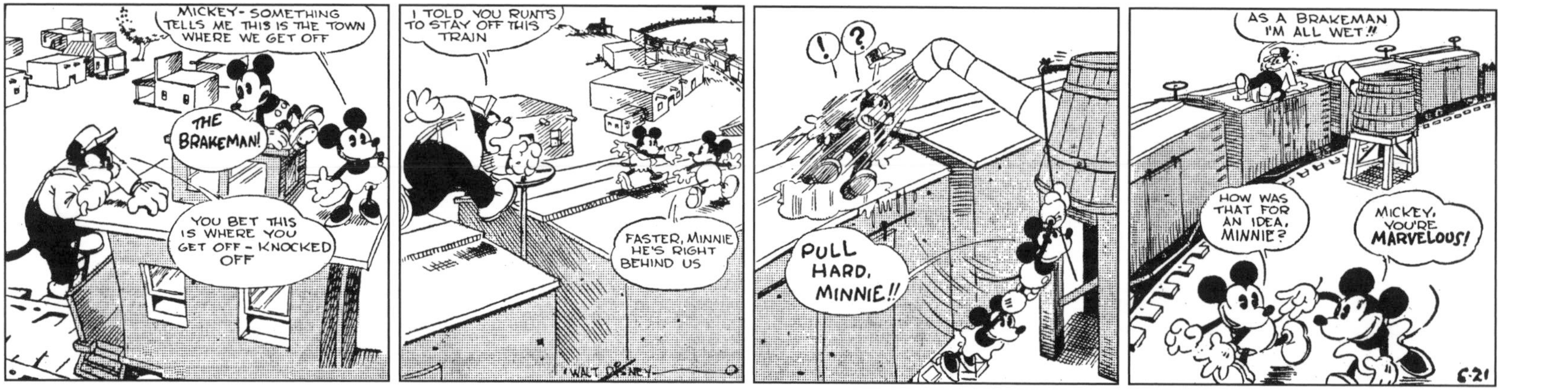
MICKEY — SOMETHING TELLS ME THIS IS THE TOWN WHERE WE GET OFF
THE BRAKEMAN!
YOU BET THIS IS WHERE YOU GET OFF — KNOCKED OFF
I TOLD YOU RUNTS TO STAY OFF THIS TRAIN
FASTER, MINNIE HE'S RIGHT BEHIND US
WALT DISNEY
! ?
PULL HARD, MINNIE!!
AS A BRAKEMAN I'M ALL WET!!
HOW WAS THAT FOR AN IDEA, MINNIE?
MICKEY, YOU'RE MARVELOUS!
6-21

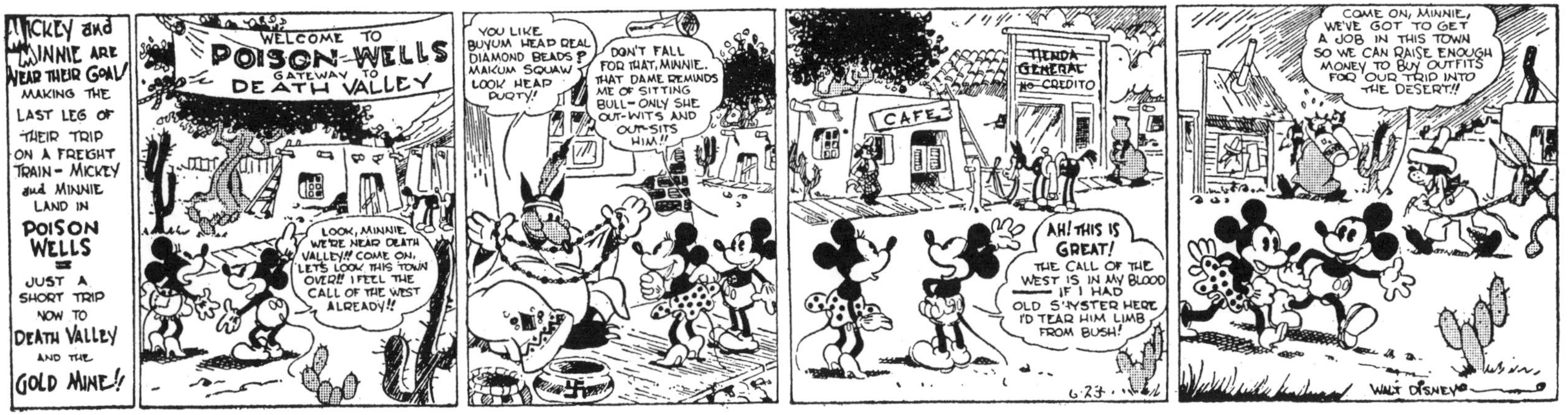
MICKEY and MINNIE ARE NEAR THEIR GOAL! MAKING THE LAST LEG OF THEIR TRIP ON A FREIGHT TRAIN - MICKEY and MINNIE LAND IN POISON WELLS = JUST A SHORT TRIP NOW TO DEATH VALLEY AND THE GOLD MINE!!
WELCOME TO POISON WELLS GATEWAY TO DEATH VALLEY
LOOK, MINNIE WE'RE NEAR DEATH VALLEY!! COME ON, LET'S LOOK THIS TOWN OVER!! I FEEL THE CALL OF THE WEST ALREADY!!
YOU LIKE BUYUM HEAP REAL DIAMOND BEADS? MAKUM SQUAW LOOK HEAP PURTY!
DON'T FALL FOR THAT, MINNIE. THAT DAME REMINDS ME OF SITTING BULL - ONLY SHE OUT-WITS AND OUT-SITS HIM!!
TIENDA GENERAL NO CREDITO
CAFE
AH! THIS IS GREAT! THE CALL OF THE WEST IS IN MY BLOOD - IF I HAD OLD S'HYSTER HERE I'D TEAR HIM LIMB FROM BUSH!
6-23
COME ON, MINNIE, WE'VE GOT TO GET A JOB IN THIS TOWN SO WE CAN RAISE ENOUGH MONEY TO BUY OUTFITS FOR OUR TRIP INTO THE DESERT!!
WALT DISNEY

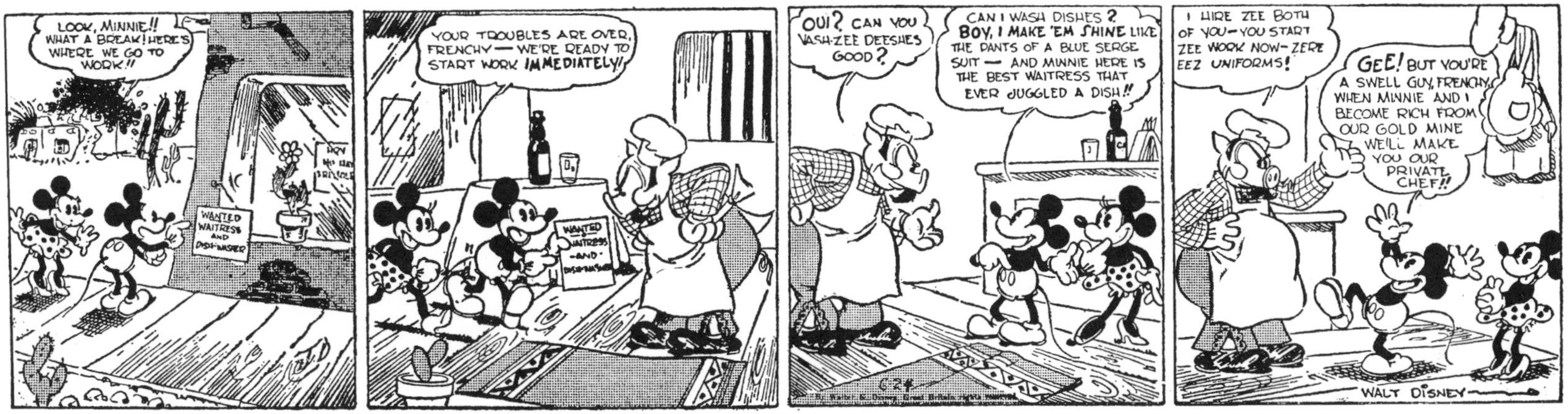
LOOK, MINNIE!! WHAT A BREAK! HERE'S WHERE WE GO TO WORK!!
WANTED WAITRESS AND DISH-WASHER
YOUR TROUBLES ARE OVER, FRENCHY - WE'RE READY TO START WORK IMMEDIATELY!
WANTED WAITRESS -AND- DISH-WASHER
OUI? CAN YOU VASH-ZEE DEESHES GOOD?
CAN I WASH DISHES? BOY, I MAKE 'EM SHINE LIKE THE PANTS OF A BLUE SERGE SUIT - AND MINNIE HERE IS THE BEST WAITRESS THAT EVER JUGGLED A DISH!!
6-24
I HIRE ZEE BOTH OF YOU - YOU START ZEE WORK NOW - ZERE EEZ UNIFORMS!
GEE! BUT YOU'RE A SWELL GUY, FRENCHY, WHEN MINNIE AND I BECOME RICH FROM OUR GOLD MINE WE'LL MAKE YOU OUR PRIVATE CHEF!!
WALT DISNEY

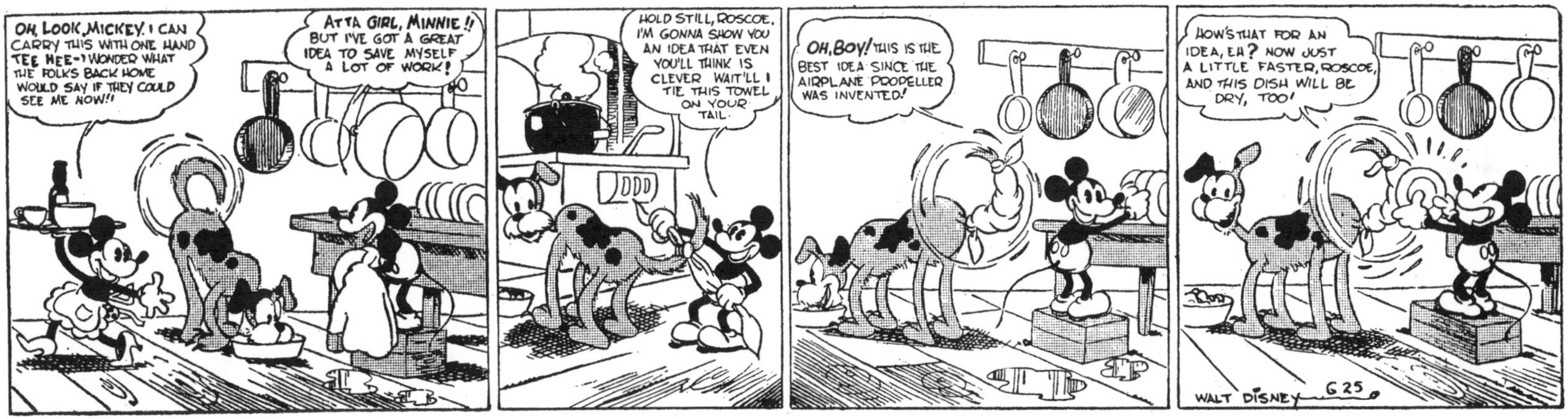
OH, LOOK, MICKEY. I CAN CARRY THIS WITH ONE HAND TEE HEE - I WONDER WHAT THE FOLKS BACK HOME WOULD SAY IF THEY COULD SEE ME NOW!!
ATTA GIRL, MINNIE!! BUT I'VE GOT A GREAT IDEA TO SAVE MYSELF A LOT OF WORK!
HOLD STILL, ROSCOE, I'M GONNA SHOW YOU AN IDEA THAT EVEN YOU'LL THINK IS CLEVER WAIT'LL I TIE THIS TOWEL ON YOUR TAIL.
OH, BOY! THIS IS THE BEST IDEA SINCE THE AIRPLANE PROPELLER WAS INVENTED!
HOW'S THAT FOR AN IDEA, EH? NOW JUST A LITTLE FASTER, ROSCOE, AND THIS DISH WILL BE DRY, TOO!
WALT DISNEY 6-25

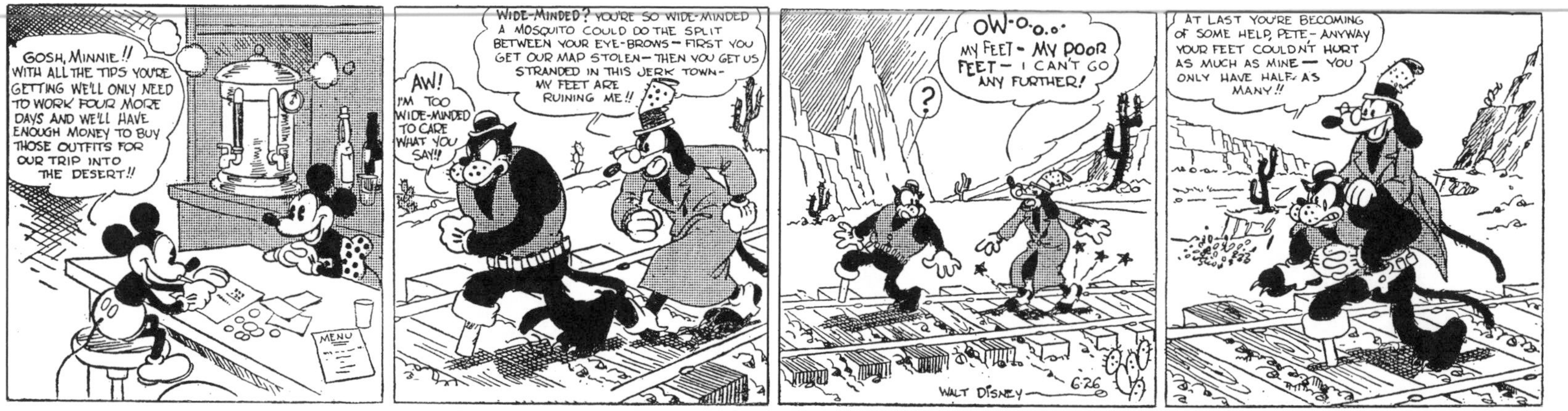
GOSH, MINNIE!! WITH ALL THE TIPS YOU'RE GETTING WE'LL ONLY NEED TO WORK FOUR MORE DAYS AND WE'LL HAVE ENOUGH MONEY TO BUY THOSE OUTFITS FOR OUR TRIP INTO THE DESERT!!
MENU
WIDE-MINDED? YOU'RE SO WIDE-MINDED A MOSQUITO COULD DO THE SPLIT BETWEEN YOUR EYE-BROWS — FIRST YOU GET OUR MAP STOLEN — THEN YOU GET US STRANDED IN THIS JERK TOWN — MY FEET ARE RUINING ME!!
AW! I'M TOO WIDE-MINDED TO CARE WHAT YOU SAY!!
OW-O-O-O-
MY FEET — MY POOR FEET — I CAN'T GO ANY FURTHER!
?
WALT DISNEY
6-26
AT LAST YOU'RE BECOMING OF SOME HELP, PETE — ANYWAY YOUR FEET COULDN'T HURT AS MUCH AS MINE — YOU ONLY HAVE HALF AS MANY!!

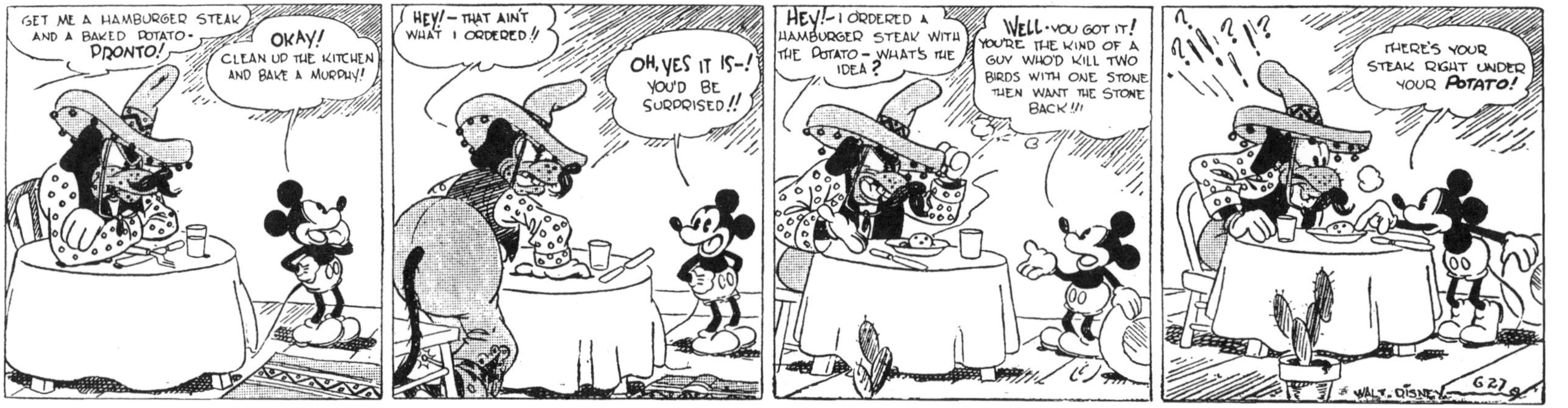
GET ME A HAMBURGER STEAK AND A BAKED POTATO — PRONTO!
OKAY! CLEAN UP THE KITCHEN AND BAKE A MURPHY!
HEY! — THAT AIN'T WHAT I ORDERED!!
OH, YES IT IS —! YOU'D BE SURPRISED!!
HEY! — I ORDERED A HAMBURGER STEAK WITH THE POTATO — WHAT'S THE IDEA?
WELL — YOU GOT IT! YOU'RE THE KIND OF A GUY WHO'D KILL TWO BIRDS WITH ONE STONE THEN WANT THE STONE BACK!!!
?!!?!?!?
THERE'S YOUR STEAK RIGHT UNDER YOUR POTATO!
WALT DISNEY
6-27

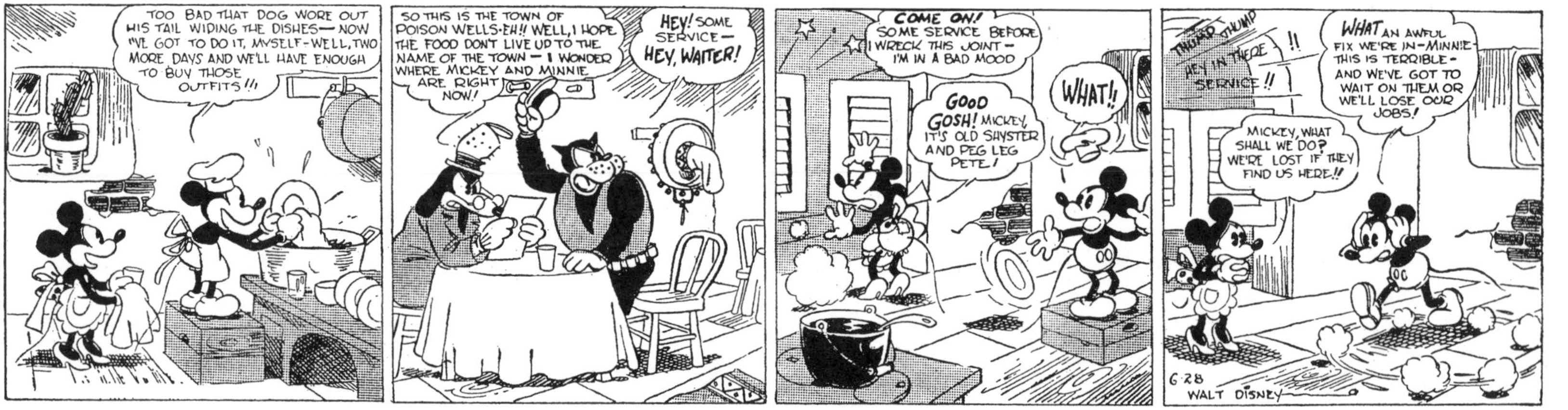
TOO BAD THAT DOG WORE OUT HIS TAIL WIPING THE DISHES — NOW WE'VE GOT TO DO IT, MYSELF — WELL, TWO MORE DAYS AND WE'LL HAVE ENOUGH TO BUY THOSE OUTFITS!!
SO THIS IS THE TOWN OF POISON WELLS — EH!! WELL, I HOPE THE FOOD DON'T LIVE UP TO THE NAME OF THE TOWN — I WONDER WHERE MICKEY AND MINNIE ARE RIGHT NOW!
HEY! SOME SERVICE — HEY, WAITER!
COME ON! SOME SERVICE BEFORE I WRECK THIS JOINT — I'M IN A BAD MOOD
GOOD GOSH! MICKEY, IT'S OLD SHYSTER AND PEG LEG PETE!
WHAT!!
THUMP THUMP
HEY IN THERE — SERVICE!!
WHAT AN AWFUL FIX WE'RE IN — MINNIE — THIS IS TERRIBLE — AND WE'VE GOT TO WAIT ON THEM OR WE'LL LOSE OUR JOBS!
MICKEY, WHAT SHALL WE DO? WE'RE LOST IF THEY FIND US HERE!!
6-28
WALT DISNEY

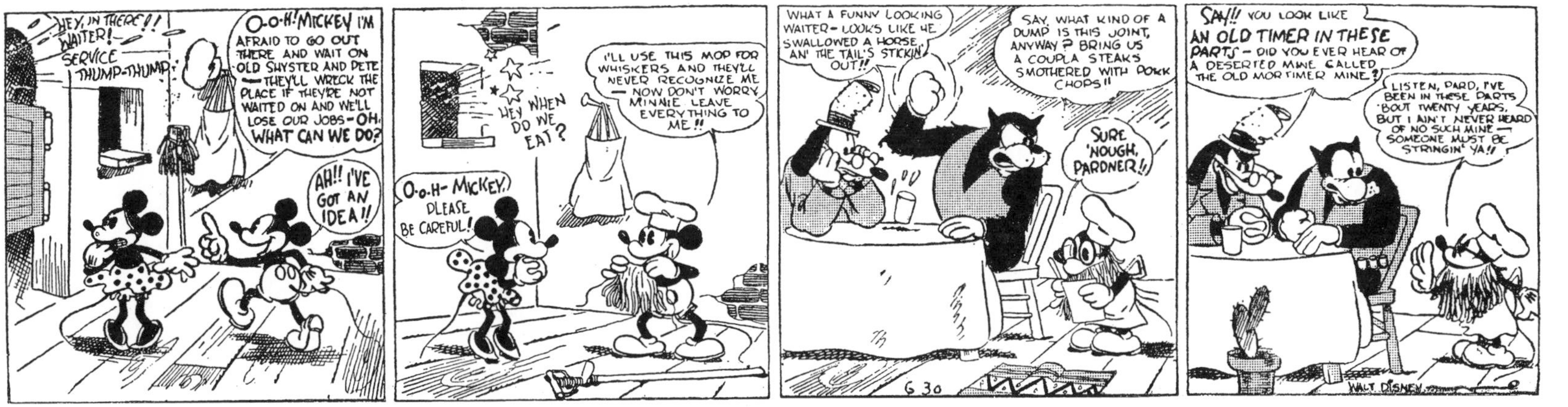
HEY, IN THERE!! WAITER! SERVICE
THUMP-THUMP
O-O-H! MICKEY I'M AFRAID TO GO OUT THERE AND WAIT ON OLD SHYSTER AND PETE —THEY'LL WRECK THE PLACE IF THEY'RE NOT WAITED ON AND WE'LL LOSE OUR JOBS—OH, WHAT CAN WE DO?
AH!! I'VE GOT AN IDEA!!
HEY WHEN DO WE EAT?
I'LL USE THIS MOP FOR WHISKERS AND THEY'LL NEVER RECOGNIZE ME —NOW DON'T WORRY, MINNIE LEAVE EVERYTHING TO ME!!
O-O-H-MICKEY, PLEASE BE CAREFUL!
WHAT A FUNNY LOOKING WAITER—LOOKS LIKE HE SWALLOWED A HORSE, AN' THE TAIL'S STICKIN' OUT!!
SAY, WHAT KIND OF A DUMP IS THIS JOINT, ANYWAY? BRING US A COUPLA STEAKS SMOTHERED WITH PORK CHOPS!!
SURE 'NOUGH, PARDNER!!
6 30
SAY!! YOU LOOK LIKE AN OLD TIMER IN THESE PARTS—DID YOU EVER HEAR OF A DESERTED MINE CALLED THE OLD MORTIMER MINE?
LISTEN, PARD, I'VE BEEN IN THESE PARTS 'BOUT TWENTY YEARS, BUT I AIN'T NEVER HEARD OF NO SUCH MINE— SOMEONE MUST BE STRINGIN' YA!!
WALT DISNEY

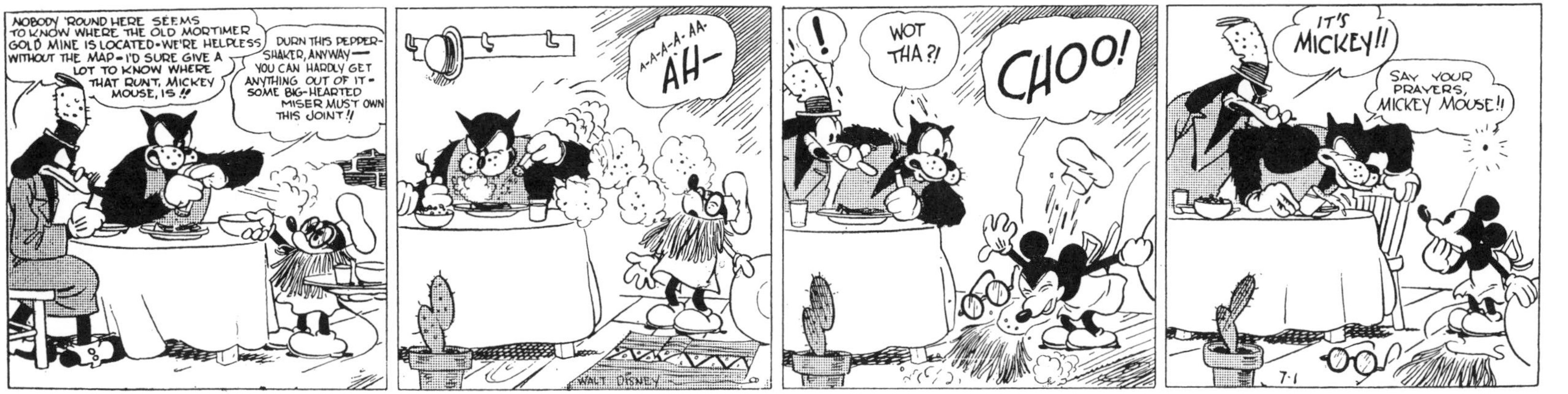
NOBODY 'ROUND HERE SEEMS TO KNOW WHERE THE OLD MORTIMER GOLD MINE IS LOCATED—WE'RE HELPLESS WITHOUT THE MAP—I'D SURE GIVE A LOT TO KNOW WHERE THAT RUNT, MICKEY MOUSE, IS!!
DURN THIS PEPPER-SHAKER, ANYWAY— YOU CAN HARDLY GET ANYTHING OUT OF IT— SOME BIG-HEARTED MISER MUST OWN THIS JOINT!!
A-A-A-A-AA- AH-
WALT DISNEY
!
WOT THA?!
CHOO!
IT'S MICKEY!!
SAY YOUR PRAYERS, MICKEY MOUSE!!
7·1

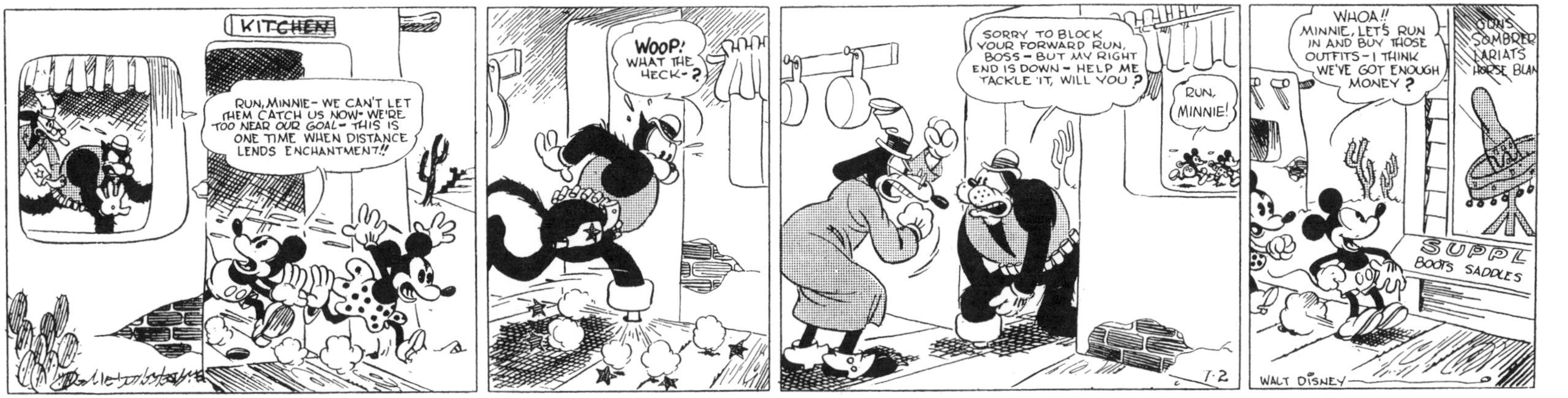
KITCHEN
RUN, MINNIE—WE CAN'T LET THEM CATCH US NOW—WE'RE TOO NEAR OUR GOAL—THIS IS ONE TIME WHEN DISTANCE LENDS ENCHANTMENT!!
WOOP! WHAT THE HECK-?
SORRY TO BLOCK YOUR FORWARD RUN, BOSS—BUT MY RIGHT END IS DOWN—HELP ME TACKLE IT, WILL YOU?
RUN, MINNIE!
7·2
WHOA!! MINNIE, LET'S RUN IN AND BUY THOSE OUTFITS—I THINK WE'VE GOT ENOUGH MONEY?
GUNS SOMBRER LARIATS HORSE BLAN
SUPPL
BOOTS SADDLES
WALT DISNEY

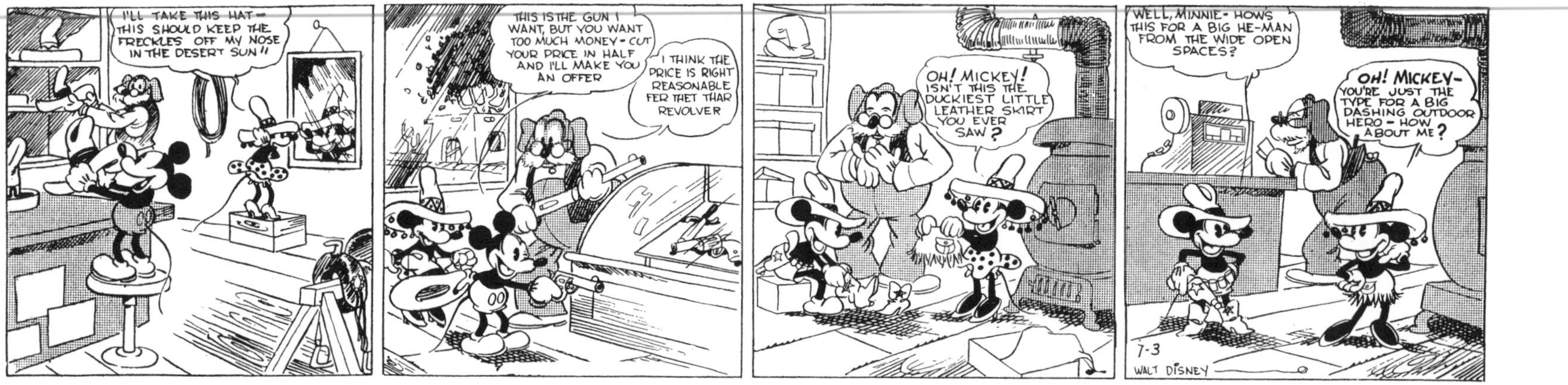
I'LL TAKE THIS HAT— THIS SHOULD KEEP THE FRECKLES OFF MY NOSE IN THE DESERT SUN!!
THIS IS THE GUN I WANT, BUT YOU WANT TOO MUCH MONEY—CUT YOUR PRICE IN HALF AND I'LL MAKE YOU AN OFFER
I THINK THE PRICE IS RIGHT REASONABLE FER THET THAR REVOLVER
OH! MICKEY! ISN'T THIS THE DUCKIEST LITTLE LEATHER SKIRT YOU EVER SAW?
WELL, MINNIE- HOWS THIS FOR A BIG HE-MAN FROM THE WIDE OPEN SPACES?
OH! MICKEY— YOU'RE JUST THE TYPE FOR A BIG DASHING OUTDOOR HERO—HOW ABOUT ME?
7-3
WALT DISNEY

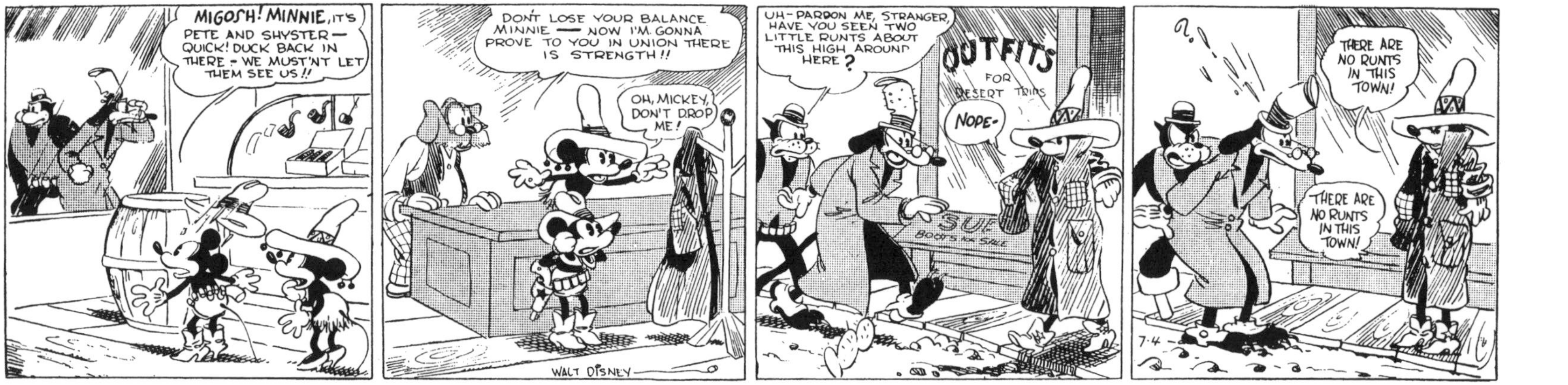
MIGOSH! MINNIE, IT'S PETE AND SHYSTER— QUICK! DUCK BACK IN THERE - WE MUST'NT LET THEM SEE US!!
DON'T LOSE YOUR BALANCE MINNIE — NOW I'M GONNA PROVE TO YOU IN UNION THERE IS STRENGTH!!
OH, MICKEY, DON'T DROP ME!
WALT DISNEY
UH-PARDON ME, STRANGER, HAVE YOU SEEN TWO LITTLE RUNTS ABOUT THIS HIGH AROUND HERE?
OUTFITS FOR DESERT TRIPS
NOPE-
THERE ARE NO RUNTS IN THIS TOWN!
THERE ARE NO RUNTS IN THIS TOWN!
7-4

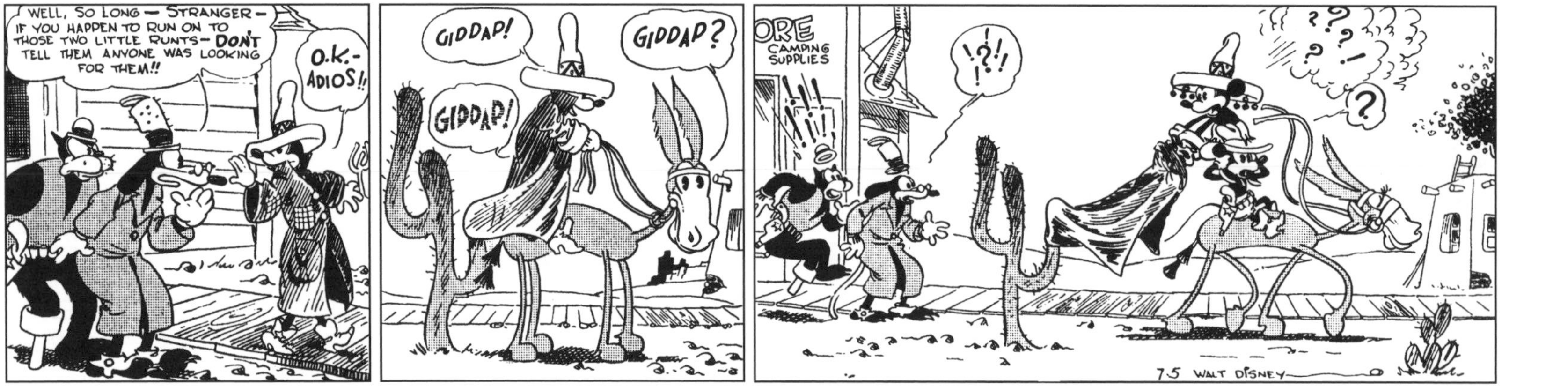
WELL, SO LONG — STRANGER— IF YOU HAPPEN TO RUN ON TO THOSE TWO LITTLE RUNTS— DON'T TELL THEM ANYONE WAS LOOKING FOR THEM!!
O.K.- ADIOS!!
GIDDAP!
GIDDAP?
GIDDAP!
CAMPING SUPPLIES
!?!!
7-5 WALT DISNEY

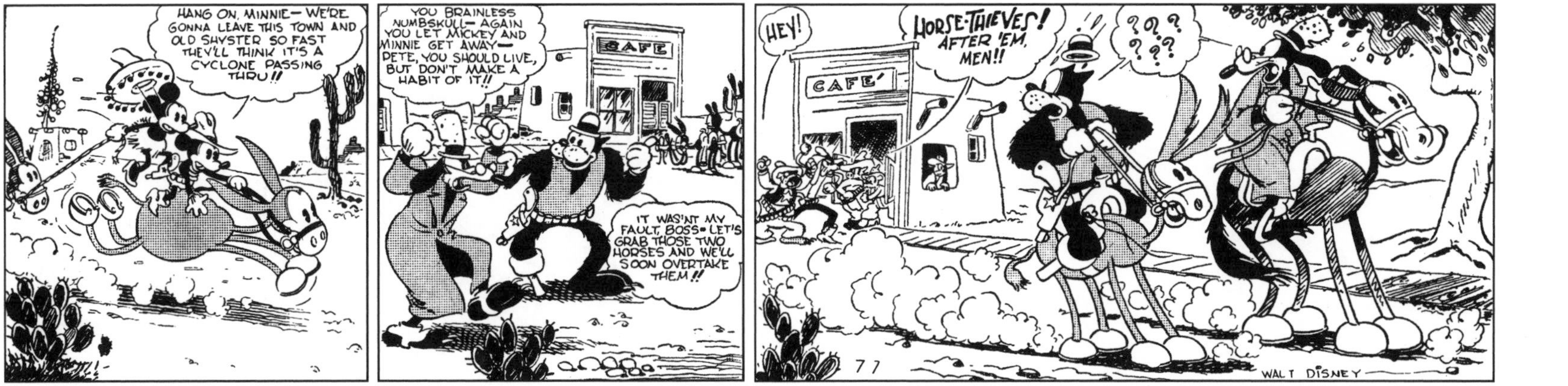
HANG ON, MINNIE— WE'RE GONNA LEAVE THIS TOWN AND OLD SHYSTER SO FAST THEY'LL THINK IT'S A CYCLONE PASSING THRU!!
CAFE
YOU BRAINLESS NUMBSKULL— AGAIN YOU LET MICKEY AND MINNIE GET AWAY— PETE, YOU SHOULD LIVE, BUT DON'T MAKE A HABIT OF IT!!
IT WAS'NT MY FAULT, BOSS• LET'S GRAB THOSE TWO HORSES AND WE'LL SOON OVERTAKE THEM!!
HEY!
CAFE'
HORSE-THIEVES! AFTER 'EM, MEN!!
? ? ? ? ? ?
7 7
WALT DISNEY

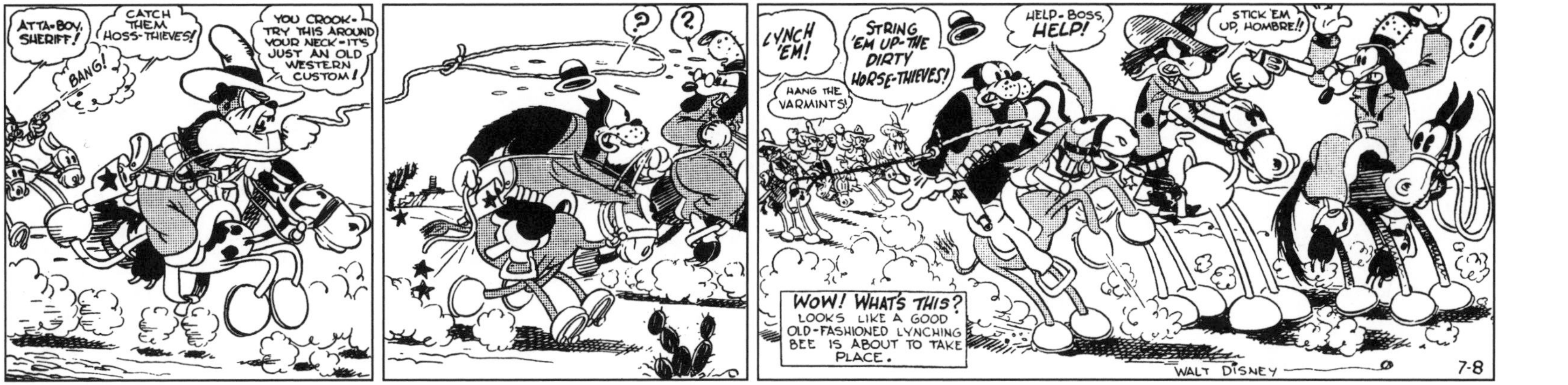
ATTA-BOY, SHERIFF!
CATCH THEM HOSS-THIEVES!
YOU CROOK— TRY THIS AROUND YOUR NECK-IT'S JUST AN OLD WESTERN CUSTOM!
BANG!
?
?
LYNCH 'EM!
STRING 'EM UP-THE DIRTY HORSE-THIEVES!
HANG THE VARMINTS!
HELP-BOSS, HELP!
STICK 'EM UP, HOMBRE!!
!
WOW! WHAT'S THIS? LOOKS LIKE A GOOD OLD-FASHIONED LYNCHING BEE IS ABOUT TO TAKE PLACE.
WALT DISNEY
7-8

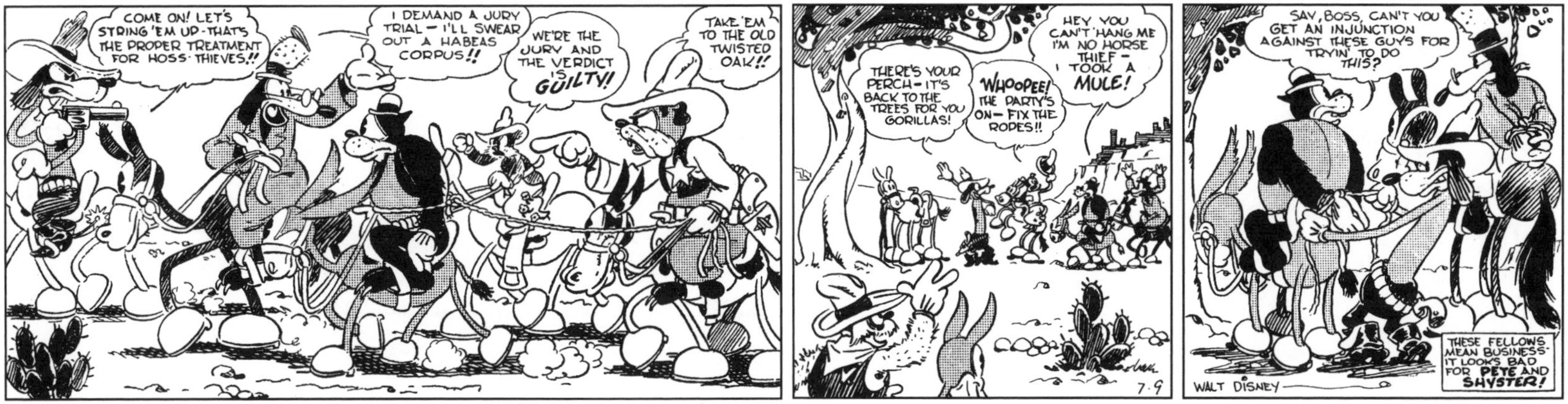
COME ON! LET'S STRING 'EM UP-THAT'S THE PROPER TREATMENT FOR HOSS-THIEVES!!
I DEMAND A JURY TRIAL— I'LL SWEAR OUT A HABEAS CORPUS!!
WE'RE THE JURY AND THE VERDICT IS GUILTY!
TAKE 'EM TO THE OLD TWISTED OAK!!
THERE'S YOUR PERCH— IT'S BACK TO THE TREES FOR YOU GORILLAS!
WHOOPEE! THE PARTY'S ON— FIX THE ROPES!!
HEY YOU CAN'T HANG ME I'M NO HORSE THIEF— I TOOK A MULE!
7-9
SAY, BOSS, CAN'T YOU GET AN INJUNCTION AGAINST THESE GUYS FOR TRYIN' TO DO THIS?
THESE FELLOWS MEAN BUSINESS- IT LOOKS BAD FOR PETE AND SHYSTER!
WALT DISNEY

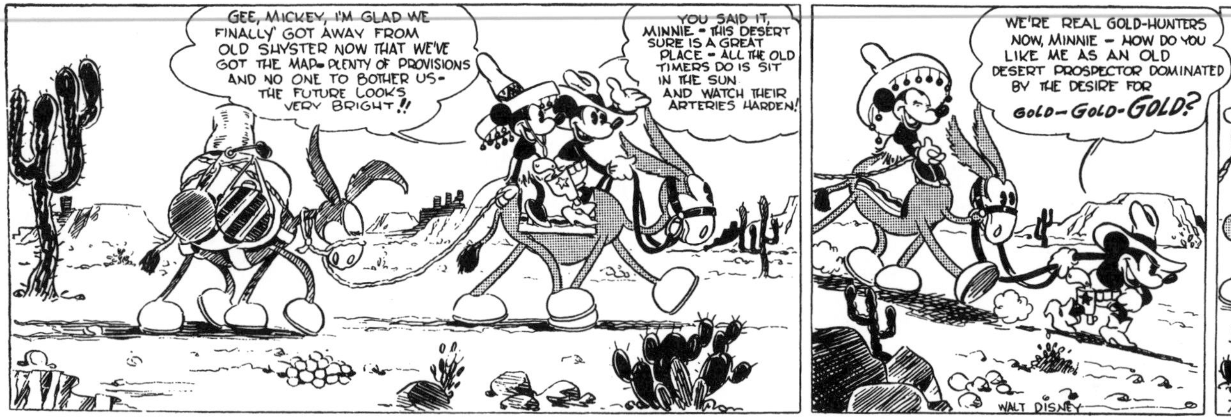
GEE, MICKEY, I'M GLAD WE FINALLY GOT AWAY FROM OLD SHYSTER NOW THAT WE'VE GOT THE MAP- PLENTY OF PROVISIONS AND NO ONE TO BOTHER US- THE FUTURE LOOKS VERY BRIGHT!!
YOU SAID IT, MINNIE - THIS DESERT SURE IS A GREAT PLACE - ALL THE OLD TIMERS DO IS SIT IN THE SUN AND WATCH THEIR ARTERIES HARDEN!
WE'RE REAL GOLD-HUNTERS NOW, MINNIE - HOW DO YOU LIKE ME AS AN OLD DESERT PROSPECTOR DOMINATED BY THE DESIRE FOR GOLD-GOLD-GOLD?
LOO-KIN'- AT THE WORLD THROUGH ROSE-COLORED GLASS-ES
WALT DISNEY
7-10

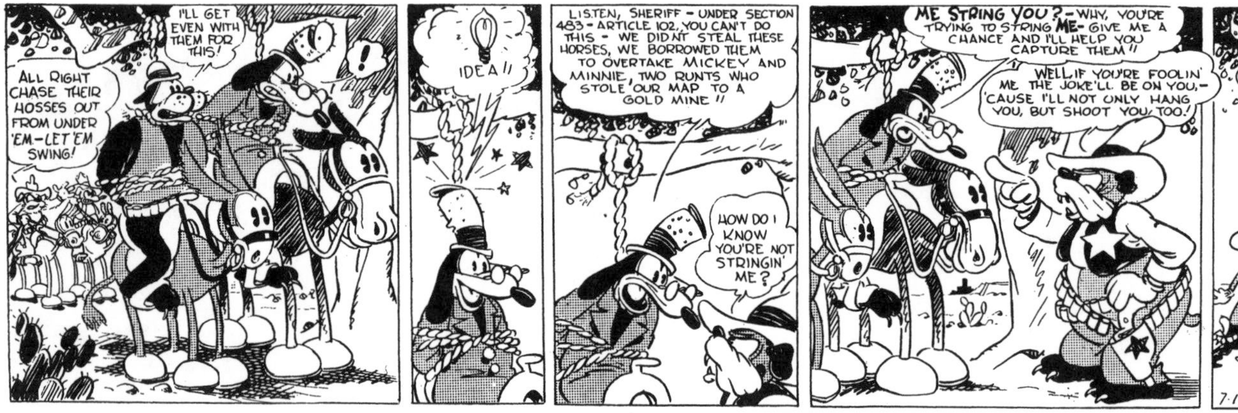
I'LL GET EVEN WITH THEM FOR THIS!
ALL RIGHT CHASE THEIR HOSSES OUT FROM UNDER 'EM-LET 'EM SWING!
IDEA!!
LISTEN, SHERIFF - UNDER SECTION 483 - ARTICLE 102, YOU CAN'T DO THIS - WE DIDN'T STEAL THESE HORSES, WE BORROWED THEM TO OVERTAKE MICKEY AND MINNIE, TWO RUNTS WHO STOLE OUR MAP TO A GOLD MINE!!
HOW DO I KNOW YOU'RE NOT STRINGIN' ME?
ME STRING YOU?-WHY, YOU'RE TRYING TO STRING ME- GIVE ME A CHANCE AND I'LL HELP YOU CAPTURE THEM!!
WELL, IF YOU'RE FOOLIN' ME THE JOKE'LL BE ON YOU,- 'CAUSE I'LL NOT ONLY HANG YOU, BUT SHOOT YOU, TOO!
COME ON- UNTIE THEM AND LET'S GET GOIN', BUT KEEP A CLOSE WATCH ON THESE TWO HOMBRES!!
7-11
WALT DISNEY

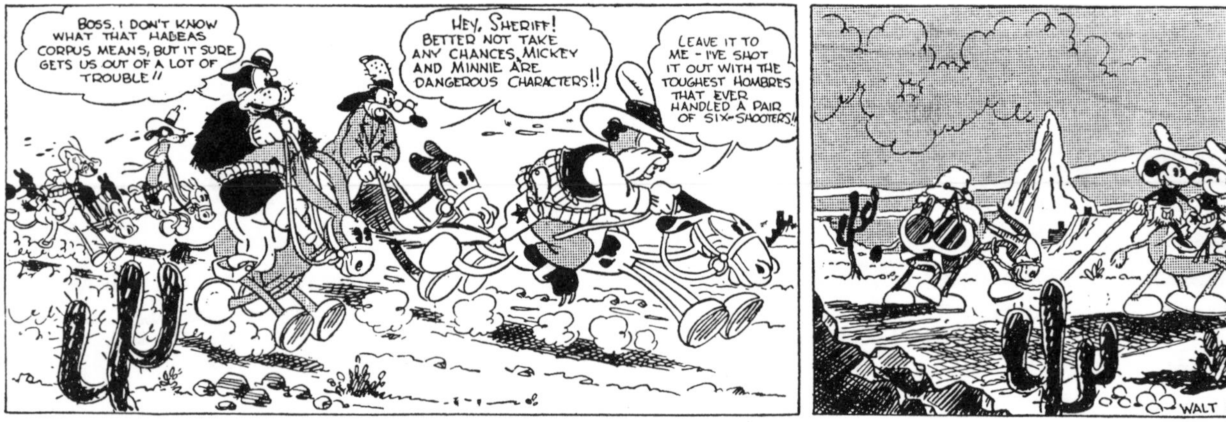
BOSS, I DON'T KNOW WHAT THAT HABEAS CORPUS MEANS, BUT IT SURE GETS US OUT OF A LOT OF TROUBLE!!
HEY, SHERIFF! BETTER NOT TAKE ANY CHANCES, MICKEY AND MINNIE ARE DANGEROUS CHARACTERS!!
LEAVE IT TO ME - I'VE SHOT IT OUT WITH THE TOUGHEST HOMBRES THAT EVER HANDLED A PAIR OF SIX-SHOOTERS!!
MICKEY AND MINNIE ARE AS HAPPY AS TWO LOVE BIRDS, NOT KNOWING WHAT THOSE TWO EGGS, PETE AND SHYSTER, ARE UP TO-
WALT DISNEY
7-12

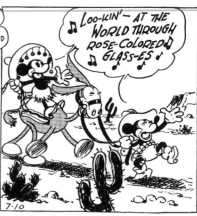

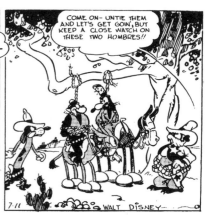

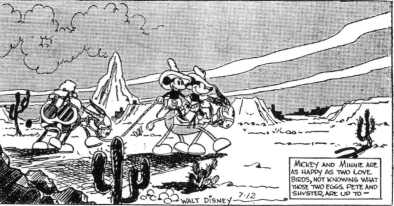

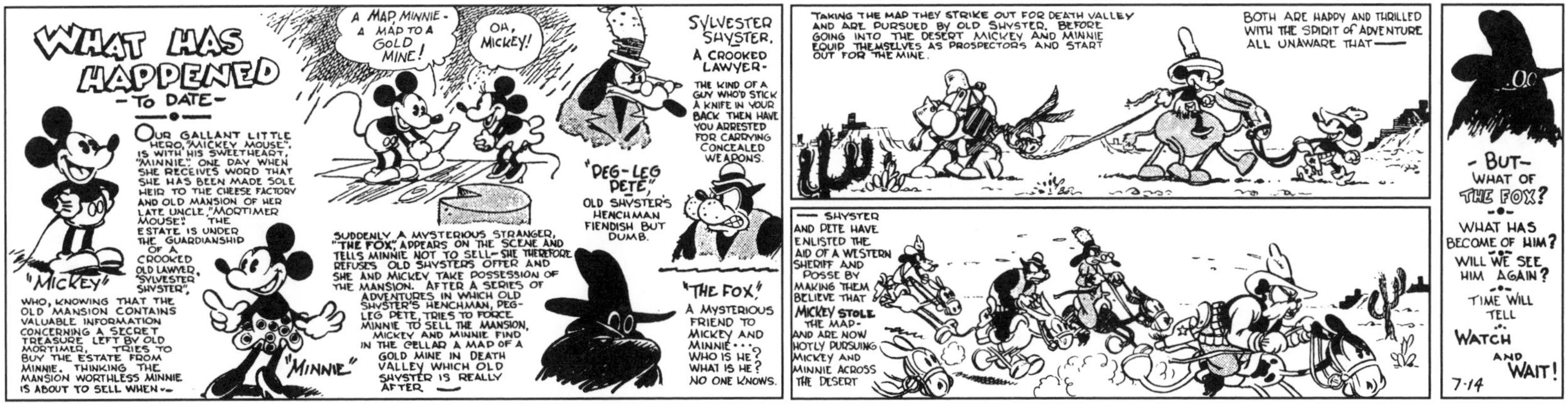
WHAT HAS HAPPENED -TO DATE-
OUR GALLANT LITTLE HERO, "MICKEY MOUSE", IS WITH HIS SWEETHEART, "MINNIE." ONE DAY WHEN SHE RECEIVES WORD THAT SHE HAS BEEN MADE SOLE HEIR TO THE CHEESE FACTORY AND OLD MANSION OF HER LATE UNCLE, "MORTIMER MOUSE." THE ESTATE IS UNDER THE GUARDIANSHID OF A CROOKED OLD LAWYER, "SYLVESTER SHYSTER",
"MICKEY"
WHO, KNOWING THAT THE OLD MANSION CONTAINS VALUABLE INFORMATION CONCERNING A SECRET TREASURE LEFT BY OLD MORTIMER, TRIES TO BUY THE ESTATE FROM MINNIE. THINKING THE MANSION WORTHLESS MINNIE IS ABOUT TO SELL WHEN--
"MINNIE"
A MAP, MINNIE - A MAP TO A GOLD MINE!
OH, MICKEY!
SUDDENLY A MYSTERIOUS STRANGER, "THE FOX," APPEARS ON THE SCENE AND TELLS MINNIE NOT TO SELL-SHE THEREFORE REFUSES OLD SHYSTERS OFFER AND SHE AND MICKEY TAKE POSSESSION OF THE MANSION. AFTER A SERIES OF ADVENTURES IN WHICH OLD SHYSTER'S HENCHMAN, PEG-LEG PETE, TRIES TO FORCE MINNIE TO SELL THE MANSION, MICKEY AND MINNIE FIND IN THE CELLAR A MAP OF A GOLD MINE IN DEATH VALLEY WHICH OLD SHYSTER IS REALLY AFTER —
SYLVESTER SHYSTER. A CROOKED LAWYER-
THE KIND OF A GUY WHO'D STICK A KNIFE IN YOUR BACK THEN HAVE YOU ARRESTED FOR CARRYING CONCEALED WEAPONS.
"DEG-LEG PETE," OLD SHYSTER'S HENCHMAN FIENDISH BUT DUMB.
"THE FOX," A MYSTERIOUS FRIEND TO MICKEY AND MINNIE... WHO IS HE? WHAT IS HE? NO ONE KNOWS.
TAKING THE MAP THEY STRIKE OUT FOR DEATH VALLEY AND ARE PURSUED BY OLD SHYSTER. BEFORE GOING INTO THE DESERT MICKEY AND MINNIE EQUIP THEMSELVES AS PROSPECTORS AND START OUT FOR THE MINE.
BOTH ARE HAPPY AND THRILLED WITH THE SPIRIT OF ADVENTURE ALL UNAWARE THAT——
—— SHYSTER AND PETE HAVE ENLISTED THE AID OF A WESTERN SHERIFF AND POSSE BY MAKING THEM BELIEVE THAT MICKEY STOLE THE MAP- AND ARE NOW HOTLY PURSUING MICKEY AND MINNIE ACROSS THE DESERT
- BUT- WHAT OF THE FOX?
WHAT HAS BECOME OF HIM?
WILL WE SEE HIM AGAIN?
TIME WILL TELL
WATCH AND WAIT!
7-14

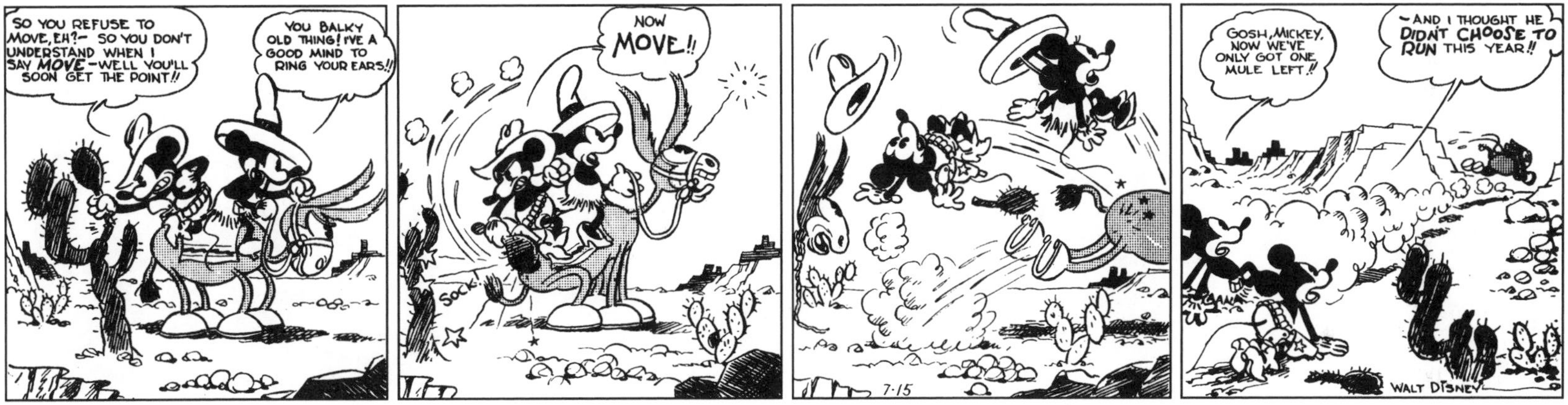
SO YOU REFUSE TO MOVE, EH?- SO YOU DON'T UNDERSTAND WHEN I SAY MOVE-WELL YOU'LL SOON GET THE POINT!!
YOU BALKY OLD THING! I'VE A GOOD MIND TO RING YOUR EARS!!
NOW MOVE!!
SOCK
7-15
GOSH, MICKEY, NOW WE'VE ONLY GOT ONE MULE LEFT!!
-AND I THOUGHT HE DIDN'T CHOOSE TO RUN THIS YEAR!!
WALT DISNEY

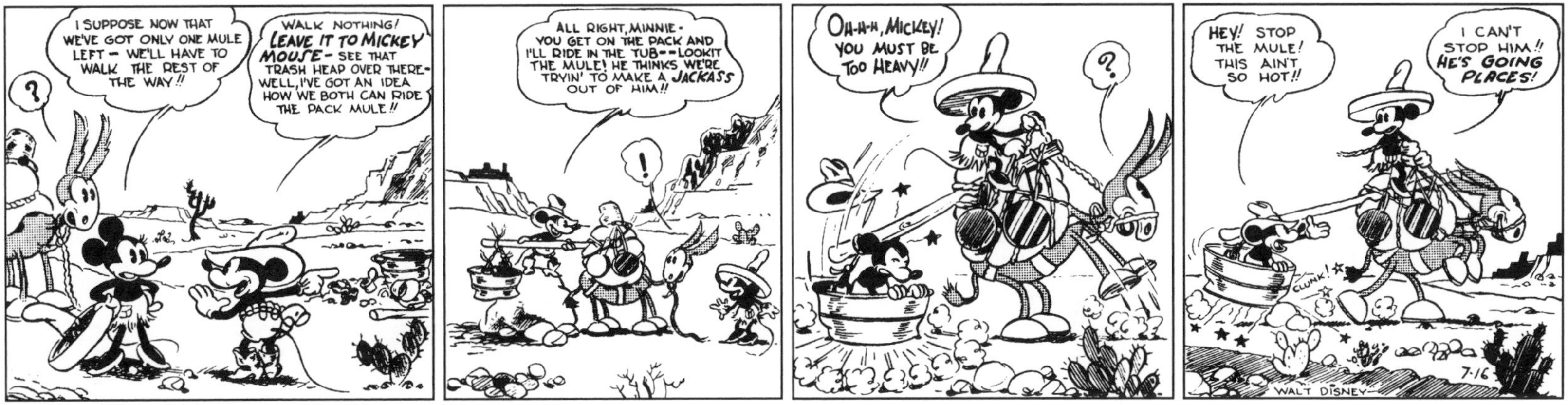
I SUPPOSE NOW THAT WE'VE GOT ONLY ONE MULE LEFT - WE'LL HAVE TO WALK THE REST OF THE WAY!!
?
WALK NOTHING! LEAVE IT TO MICKEY MOUSE - SEE THAT TRASH HEAP OVER THERE-WELL, I'VE GOT AN IDEA HOW WE BOTH CAN RIDE THE PACK MULE!!
ALL RIGHT, MINNIE - YOU GET ON THE PACK AND I'LL RIDE IN THE TUB--LOOKIT THE MULE! HE THINKS WE'RE TRYIN' TO MAKE A JACKASS OUT OF HIM!!
!
OH-H-H, MICKEY! YOU MUST BE TOO HEAVY!!
?
HEY! STOP THE MULE! THIS AIN'T SO HOT!!
I CAN'T STOP HIM!! HE'S GOING PLACES!
CLUNK!
7-16
WALT DISNEY

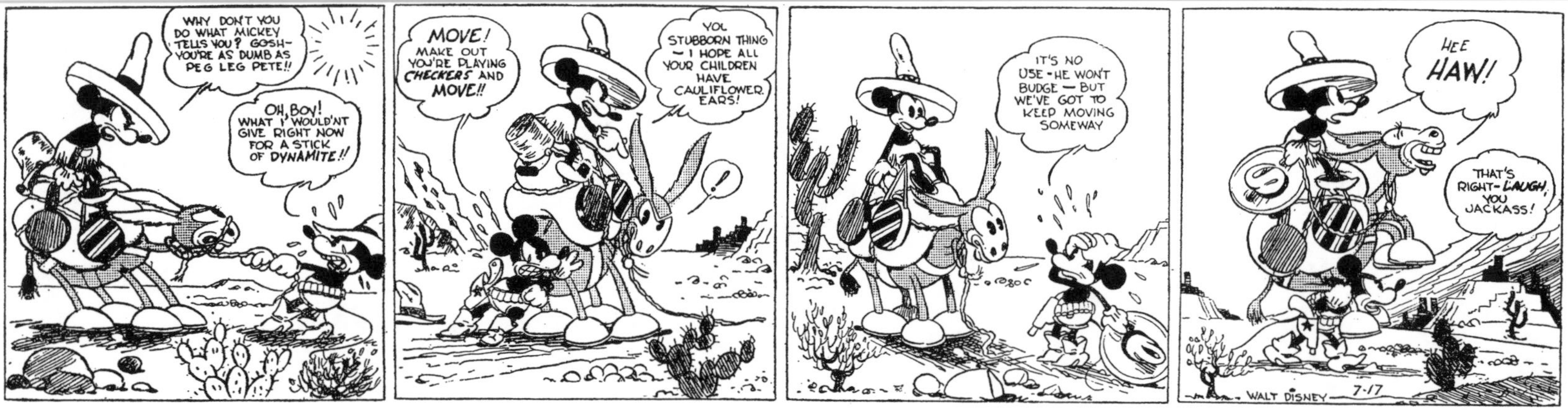
WHY DON'T YOU DO WHAT MICKEY TELLS YOU? GOSH-YOU'RE AS DUMB AS PEG LEG PETE!!
OH, BOY! WHAT I WOULD'NT GIVE RIGHT NOW FOR A STICK OF DYNAMITE!!
MOVE! MAKE OUT YOU'RE PLAYING CHECKERS AND MOVE!!
YOU STUBBORN THING — I HOPE ALL YOUR CHILDREN HAVE CAULIFLOWER EARS!
!
IT'S NO USE-HE WON'T BUDGE — BUT WE'VE GOT TO KEEP MOVING SOMEWAY
HEE HAW!
THAT'S RIGHT-LAUGH, YOU JACKASS!
WALT DISNEY 7-17

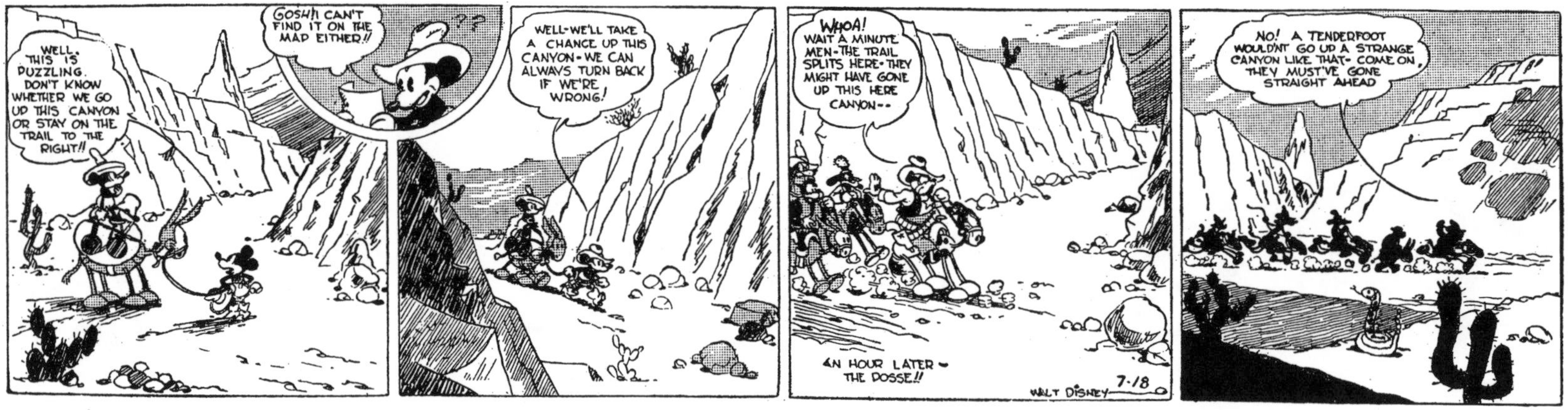
WELL, THIS IS PUZZLING. DON'T KNOW WHETHER WE GO UP THIS CANYON OR STAY ON THE TRAIL TO THE RIGHT!!
GOSH! I CAN'T FIND IT ON THE MAP EITHER!!
??
WELL-WE'LL TAKE A CHANCE UP THIS CANYON-WE CAN ALWAYS TURN BACK IF WE'RE WRONG!
WHOA! WAIT A MINUTE MEN-THE TRAIL SPLITS HERE-THEY MIGHT HAVE GONE UP THIS HERE CANYON--
AN HOUR LATER — THE POSSE!!
WALT DISNEY 7-18
NO! A TENDERFOOT WOULDN'T GO UP A STRANGE CANYON LIKE THAT- COME ON, THEY MUST'VE GONE STRAIGHT AHEAD

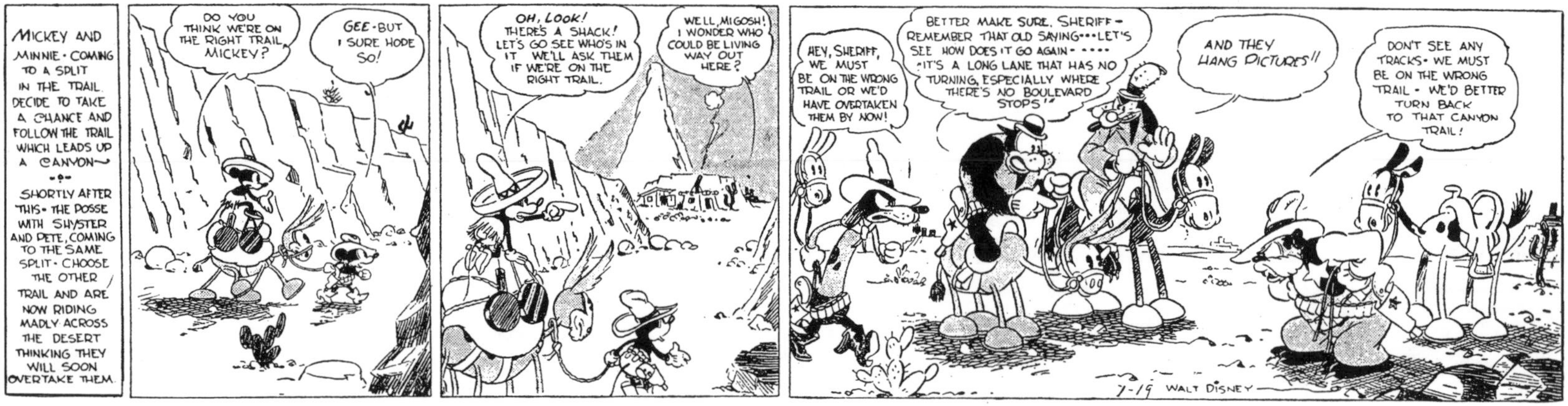
MICKEY AND MINNIE-COMING TO A SPLIT IN THE TRAIL. DECIDE TO TAKE A CHANCE AND FOLLOW THE TRAIL WHICH LEADS UP A CANYON~
SHORTLY AFTER THIS-THE POSSE WITH SHYSTER AND PETE, COMING TO THE SAME SPLIT-CHOOSE THE OTHER TRAIL AND ARE NOW RIDING MADLY ACROSS THE DESERT THINKING THEY WILL SOON OVERTAKE THEM.
DO YOU THINK WE'RE ON THE RIGHT TRAIL, MICKEY?
GEE-BUT I SURE HOPE SO!
OH, LOOK! THERE'S A SHACK! LET'S GO SEE WHO'S IN IT WE'LL ASK THEM IF WE'RE ON THE RIGHT TRAIL.
WELL, MIGOSH! I WONDER WHO COULD BE LIVING WAY OUT HERE?
HEY, SHERIFF, WE MUST BE ON THE WRONG TRAIL OR WE'D HAVE OVERTAKEN THEM BY NOW!
BETTER MAKE SURE, SHERIFF — REMEMBER THAT OLD SAYING--- LET'S SEE HOW DOES IT GO AGAIN----"IT'S A LONG LANE THAT HAS NO TURNING, ESPECIALLY WHERE THERE'S NO BOULEVARD STOPS"
AND THEY HANG PICTURES!!
DON'T SEE ANY TRACKS-WE MUST BE ON THE WRONG TRAIL - WE'D BETTER TURN BACK TO THAT CANYON TRAIL!
7-19 WALT DISNEY

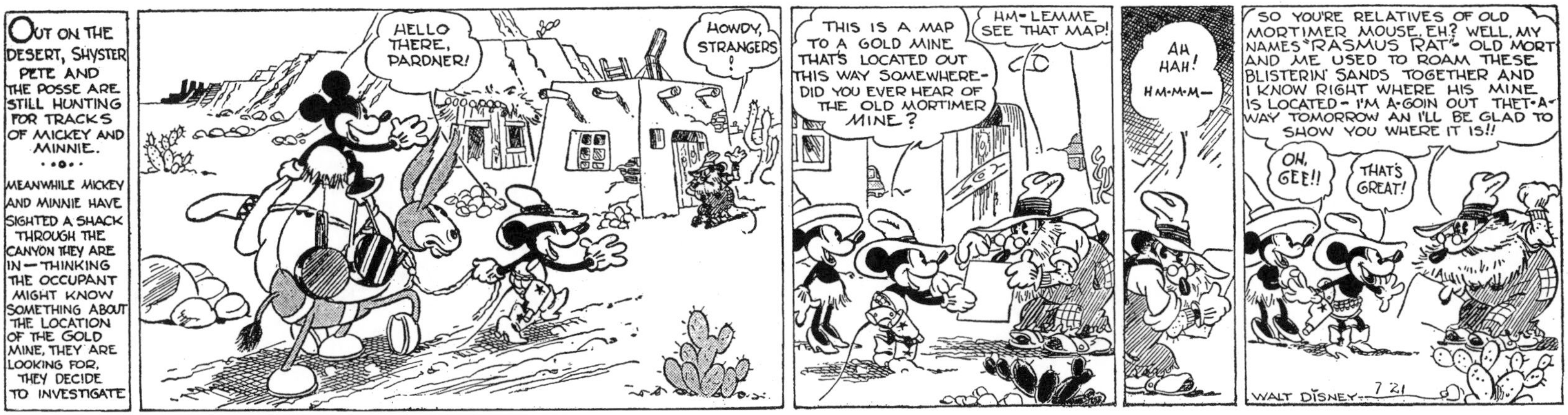
OUT ON THE DESERT, SHYSTER PETE AND THE POSSE ARE STILL HUNTING FOR TRACKS OF MICKEY AND MINNIE.
MEANWHILE MICKEY AND MINNIE HAVE SIGHTED A SHACK THROUGH THE CANYON THEY ARE IN—THINKING THE OCCUPANT MIGHT KNOW SOMETHING ABOUT THE LOCATION OF THE GOLD MINE, THEY ARE LOOKING FOR, THEY DECIDE TO INVESTIGATE
HELLO THERE, PARDNER!
HOWDY, STRANGERS!
THIS IS A MAP TO A GOLD MINE THAT'S LOCATED OUT THIS WAY SOMEWHERE-DID YOU EVER HEAR OF THE OLD MORTIMER MINE?
HM-LEMME SEE THAT MAP!
AH HAH! HM-M-M—
SO YOU'RE RELATIVES OF OLD MORTIMER MOUSE, EH? WELL, MY NAMES "RASMUS RAT"- OLD MORT AND ME USED TO ROAM THESE BLISTERIN' SANDS TOGETHER AND I KNOW RIGHT WHERE HIS MINE IS LOCATED- I'M A-GOIN OUT THET-A-WAY TOMORROW AN I'LL BE GLAD TO SHOW YOU WHERE IT IS!!
OH, GEE!!
THAT'S GREAT!
WALT DISNEY
7-21

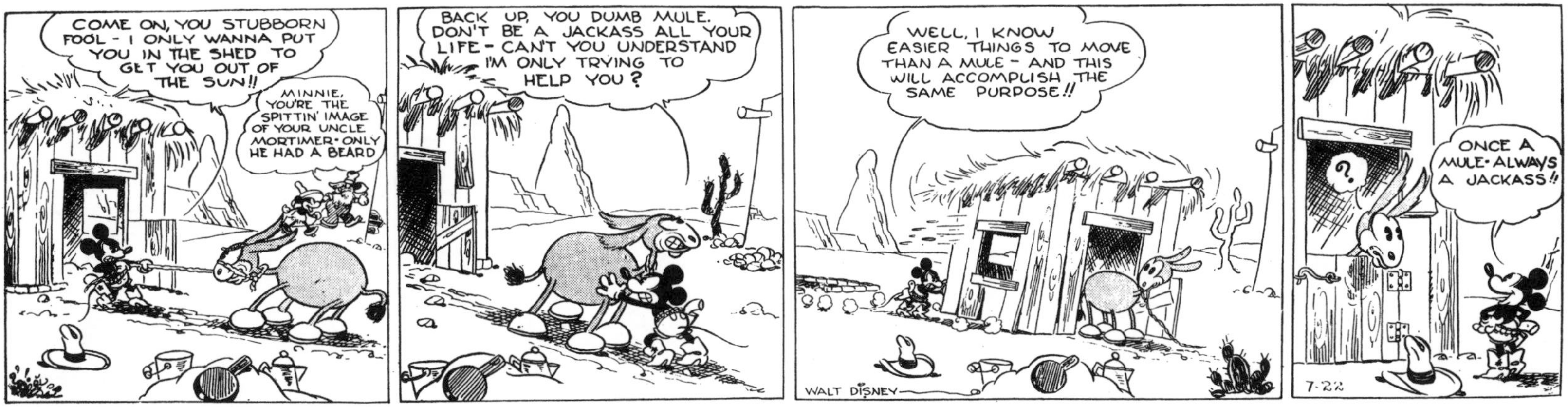
COME ON, YOU STUBBORN FOOL- I ONLY WANNA PUT YOU IN THE SHED TO GET YOU OUT OF THE SUN!!
MINNIE, YOU'RE THE SPITTIN' IMAGE OF YOUR UNCLE MORTIMER- ONLY HE HAD A BEARD
BACK UP, YOU DUMB MULE. DON'T BE A JACKASS ALL YOUR LIFE- CAN'T YOU UNDERSTAND I'M ONLY TRYING TO HELP YOU?
WELL, I KNOW EASIER THINGS TO MOVE THAN A MULE- AND THIS WILL ACCOMPLISH THE SAME PURPOSE!!
WALT DISNEY
?
ONCE A MULE-ALWAYS A JACKASS!!
7-22

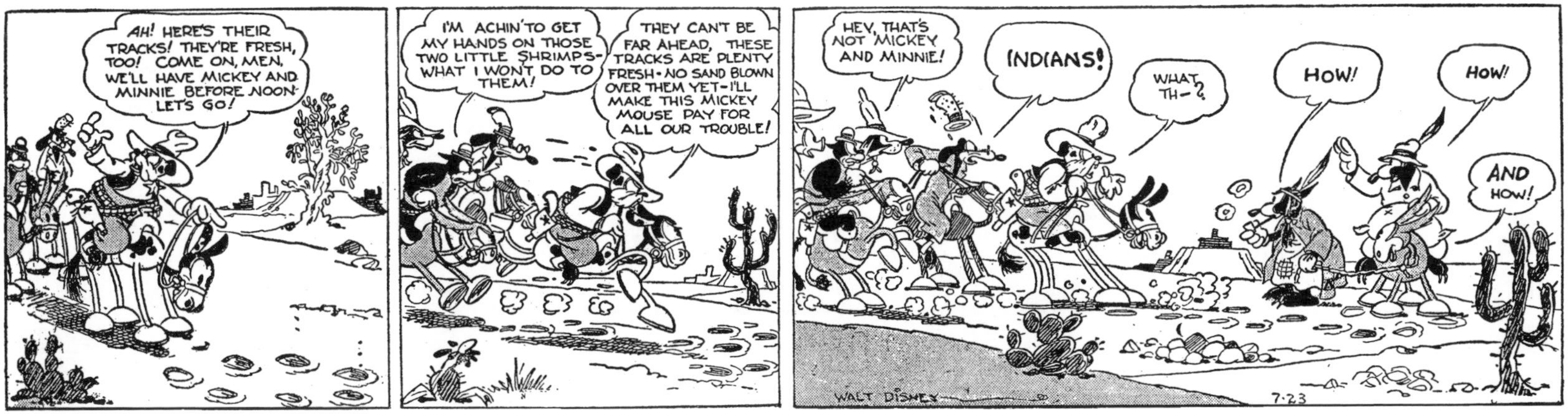
AH! HERE'S THEIR TRACKS! THEY'RE FRESH, TOO! COME ON, MEN, WE'LL HAVE MICKEY AND MINNIE BEFORE NOON-LET'S GO!
I'M ACHIN' TO GET MY HANDS ON THOSE TWO LITTLE SHRIMPS-WHAT I WONT DO TO THEM!
THEY CAN'T BE FAR AHEAD, THESE TRACKS ARE PLENTY FRESH- NO SAND BLOWN OVER THEM YET- I'LL MAKE THIS MICKEY MOUSE PAY FOR ALL OUR TROUBLE!
HEY, THAT'S NOT MICKEY AND MINNIE!
INDIANS!
WHAT TH-?
HOW!
HOW!
AND HOW!
WALT DISNEY
7-23

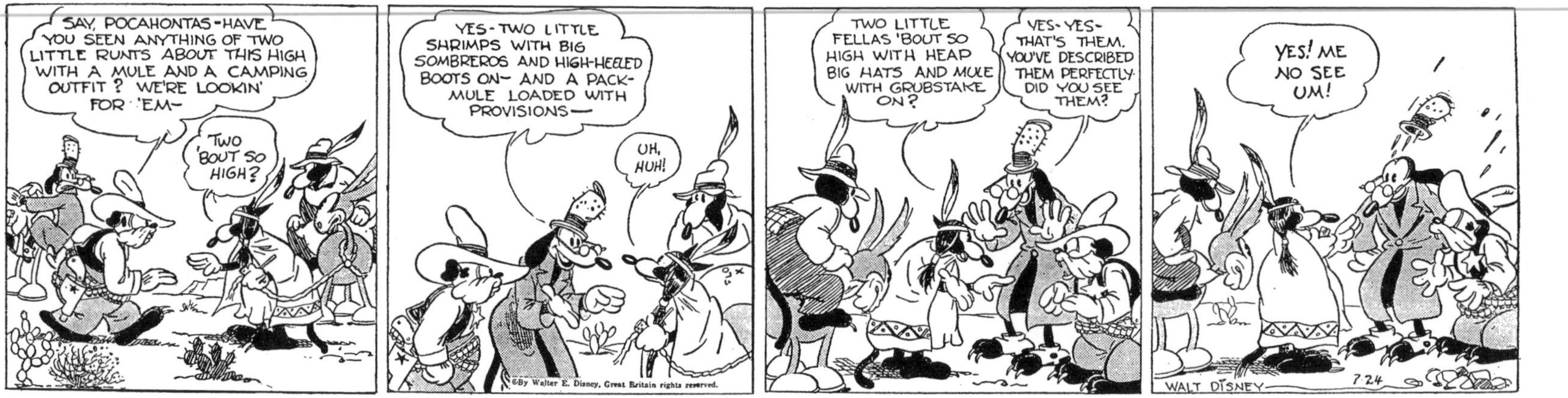
SAY, POCAHONTAS-HAVE YOU SEEN ANYTHING OF TWO LITTLE RUNTS ABOUT THIS HIGH WITH A MULE AND A CAMPING OUTFIT? WE'RE LOOKIN' FOR 'EM—
TWO 'BOUT SO HIGH?
YES- TWO LITTLE SHRIMPS WITH BIG SOMBREROS AND HIGH-HEELED BOOTS ON- AND A PACK-MULE LOADED WITH PROVISIONS—
UH, HUH!
©By Walter E. Disney, Great Britain rights reserved.
TWO LITTLE FELLAS 'BOUT SO HIGH WITH HEAP BIG HATS AND MULE WITH GRUBSTAKE ON?
YES- YES- THAT'S THEM. YOU'VE DESCRIBED THEM PERFECTLY- DID YOU SEE THEM?
YES! ME NO SEE UM!
WALT DISNEY
7-24

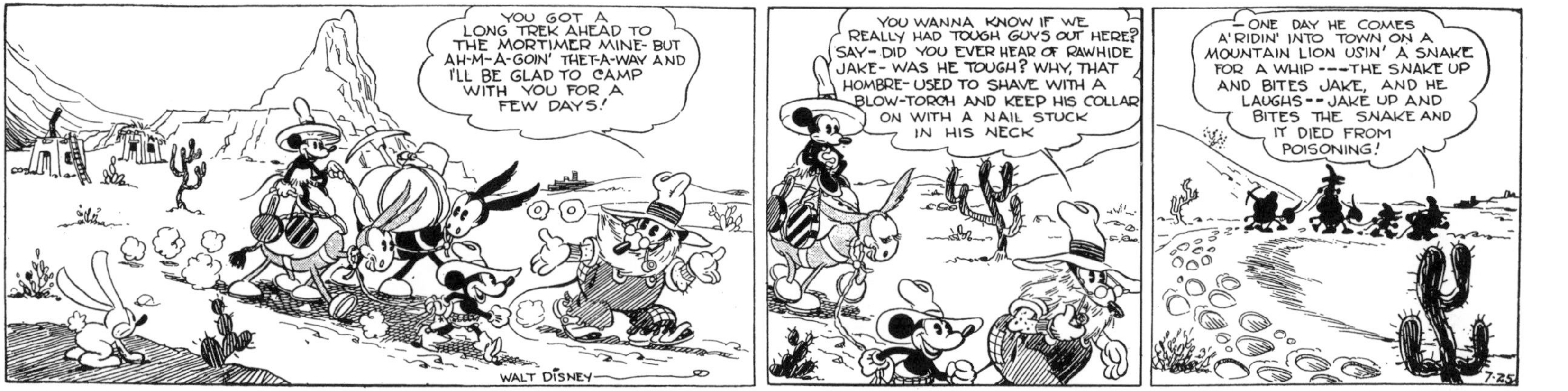
YOU GOT A LONG TREK AHEAD TO THE MORTIMER MINE- BUT AH-M-A-GOIN' THET-A-WAY AND I'LL BE GLAD TO CAMP WITH YOU FOR A FEW DAYS!
WALT DISNEY
YOU WANNA KNOW IF WE REALLY HAD TOUGH GUYS OUT HERE? SAY- DID YOU EVER HEAR OF RAWHIDE JAKE- WAS HE TOUGH? WHY, THAT HOMBRE- USED TO SHAVE WITH A BLOW-TORCH AND KEEP HIS COLLAR ON WITH A NAIL STUCK IN HIS NECK
—ONE DAY HE COMES A'RIDIN' INTO TOWN ON A MOUNTAIN LION USIN' A SNAKE FOR A WHIP ——THE SNAKE UP AND BITES JAKE, AND HE LAUGHS—JAKE UP AND BITES THE SNAKE AND IT DIED FROM POISONING!
7-25

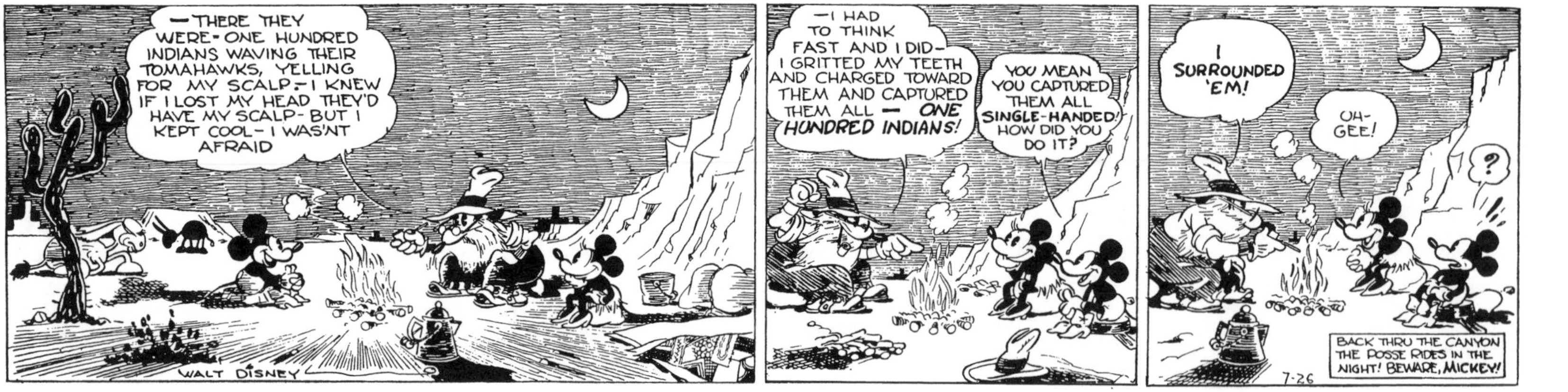
—THERE THEY WERE- ONE HUNDRED INDIANS WAVING THEIR TOMAHAWKS, YELLING FOR MY SCALP- I KNEW IF I LOST MY HEAD THEY'D HAVE MY SCALP- BUT I KEPT COOL- I WAS'NT AFRAID
WALT DISNEY
—I HAD TO THINK FAST AND I DID- I GRITTED MY TEETH AND CHARGED TOWARD THEM AND CAPTURED THEM ALL — ONE HUNDRED INDIANS!
YOU MEAN YOU CAPTURED THEM ALL SINGLE-HANDED! HOW DID YOU DO IT?
I SURROUNDED 'EM!
UH- GEE!
?
BACK THRU THE CANYON THE POSSE RIDES IN THE NIGHT! BEWARE, MICKEY!
7-26

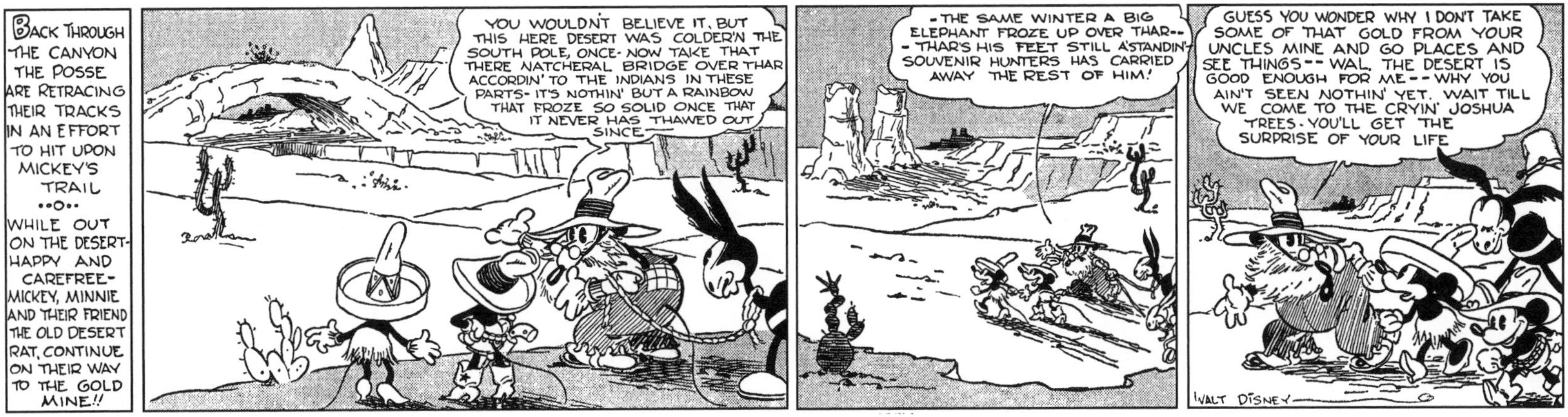
BACK THROUGH THE CANYON THE POSSE ARE RETRACING THEIR TRACKS IN AN EFFORT TO HIT UPON MICKEY'S TRAIL
••O••
WHILE OUT ON THE DESERT- HAPPY AND CAREFREE- MICKEY, MINNIE AND THEIR FRIEND THE OLD DESERT RAT, CONTINUE ON THEIR WAY TO THE GOLD MINE!!
YOU WOULDN'T BELIEVE IT, BUT THIS HERE DESERT WAS COLDER'N THE SOUTH POLE, ONCE- NOW TAKE THAT THERE NATCHERAL BRIDGE OVER THAR ACCORDIN' TO THE INDIANS IN THESE PARTS- IT'S NOTHIN' BUT A RAINBOW THAT FROZE SO SOLID ONCE THAT IT NEVER HAS THAWED OUT SINCE—
-THE SAME WINTER A BIG ELEPHANT FROZE UP OVER THAR-- -THAR'S HIS FEET STILL A'STANDIN'- SOUVENIR HUNTERS HAS CARRIED AWAY THE REST OF HIM!
GUESS YOU WONDER WHY I DON'T TAKE SOME OF THAT GOLD FROM YOUR UNCLE'S MINE AND GO PLACES AND SEE THINGS-- WAL, THE DESERT IS GOOD ENOUGH FOR ME--WHY YOU AIN'T SEEN NOTHIN' YET. WAIT TILL WE COME TO THE CRYIN' JOSHUA TREES- YOU'LL GET THE SURPRISE OF YOUR LIFE
WALT DISNEY

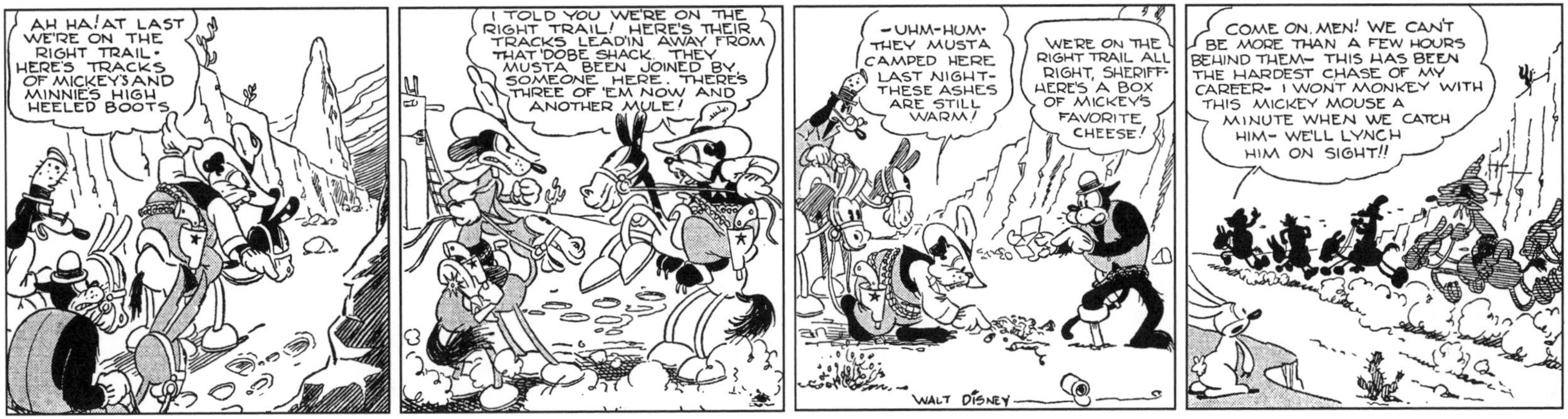
AH HA! AT LAST WE'RE ON THE RIGHT TRAIL- HERE'S TRACKS OF MICKEY'S AND MINNIE'S HIGH HEELED BOOTS
I TOLD YOU WE'RE ON THE RIGHT TRAIL! HERE'S THEIR TRACKS LEAD'IN AWAY FROM THAT 'DOBE SHACK. THEY MUSTA BEEN JOINED BY SOMEONE HERE. THERE'S THREE OF 'EM NOW AND ANOTHER MULE!
-UHM-HUM- THEY MUSTA CAMPED HERE LAST NIGHT- THESE ASHES ARE STILL WARM!
WE'RE ON THE RIGHT TRAIL ALL RIGHT, SHERIFF- HERE'S A BOX OF MICKEY'S FAVORITE CHEESE!
WALT DISNEY
COME ON, MEN! WE CAN'T BE MORE THAN A FEW HOURS BEHIND THEM- THIS HAS BEEN THE HARDEST CHASE OF MY CAREER- I WON'T MONKEY WITH THIS MICKEY MOUSE A MINUTE WHEN WE CATCH HIM- WE'LL LYNCH HIM ON SIGHT!!

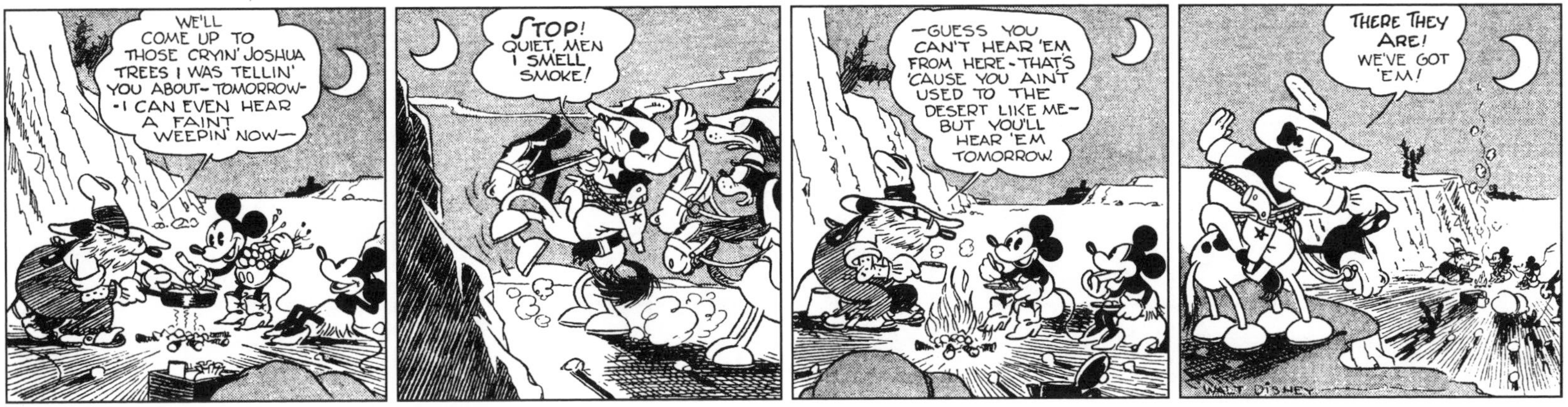
WE'LL COME UP TO THOSE CRYIN' JOSHUA TREES I WAS TELLIN' YOU ABOUT- TOMORROW- -I CAN EVEN HEAR A FAINT WEEPIN' NOW—
STOP! QUIET, MEN I SMELL SMOKE!
-GUESS YOU CAN'T HEAR 'EM FROM HERE- THAT'S 'CAUSE YOU AIN'T USED TO THE DESERT LIKE ME- BUT YOU'LL HEAR 'EM TOMORROW.
THERE THEY ARE! WE'VE GOT 'EM!
WALT DISNEY

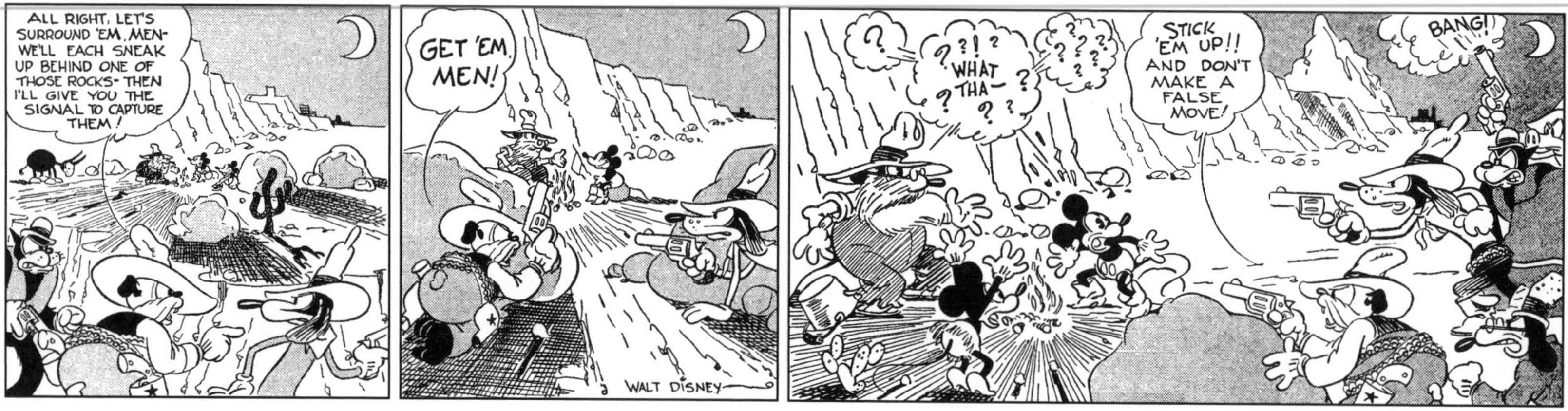
ALL RIGHT, LET'S SURROUND 'EM, MEN- WE'LL EACH SNEAK UP BEHIND ONE OF THOSE ROCKS- THEN I'LL GIVE YOU THE SIGNAL TO CAPTURE THEM!
GET 'EM, MEN!
WALT DISNEY
?
? ?! ? WHAT THA- ? ? ? ?
? ? ? ? ? ? ?
STICK 'EM UP!! AND DON'T MAKE A FALSE MOVE!
BANG!!

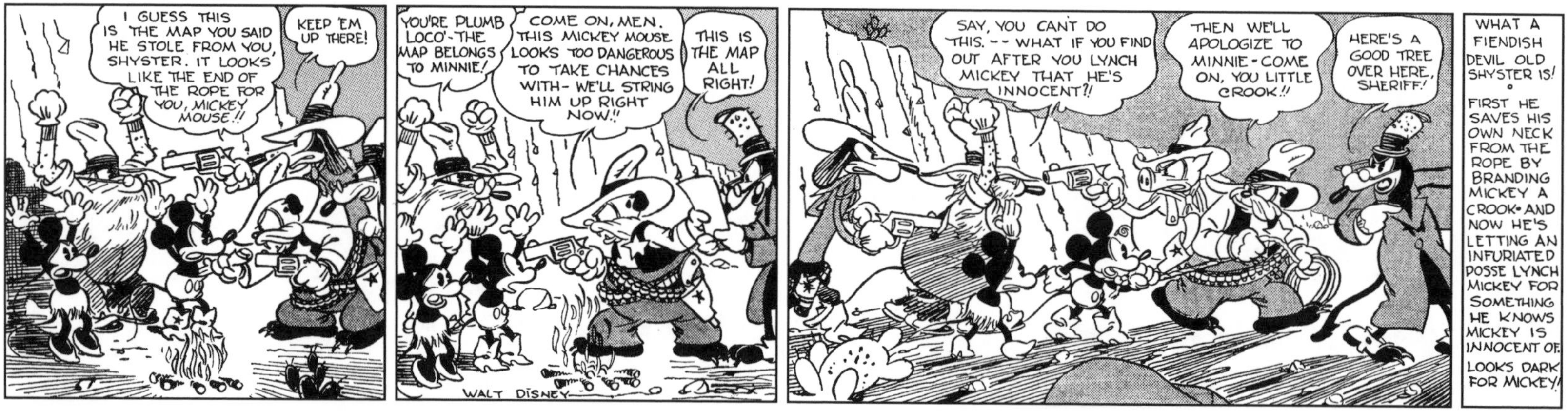
I GUESS THIS IS THE MAP YOU SAID HE STOLE FROM YOU, SHYSTER. IT LOOKS LIKE THE END OF THE ROPE FOR YOU, MICKEY MOUSE!!
KEEP 'EM UP THERE!
YOU'RE PLUMB LOCO'-THE MAP BELONGS TO MINNIE!
COME ON, MEN. THIS MICKEY MOUSE LOOKS TOO DANGEROUS TO TAKE CHANCES WITH- WE'LL STRING HIM UP RIGHT NOW!!
THIS IS THE MAP ALL RIGHT!
WALT DISNEY
SAY, YOU CAN'T DO THIS.-- WHAT IF YOU FIND OUT AFTER YOU LYNCH MICKEY THAT HE'S INNOCENT?!
THEN WE'LL APOLOGIZE TO MINNIE-COME ON, YOU LITTLE CROOK!!
HERE'S A GOOD TREE OVER HERE, SHERIFF!
WHAT A FIENDISH DEVIL OLD SHYSTER IS!
FIRST HE SAVES HIS OWN NECK FROM THE ROPE BY BRANDING MICKEY A CROOK- AND NOW HE'S LETTING AN INFURIATED POSSE LYNCH MICKEY FOR SOMETHING HE KNOWS MICKEY IS INNOCENT OF.
LOOKS DARK FOR MICKEY!

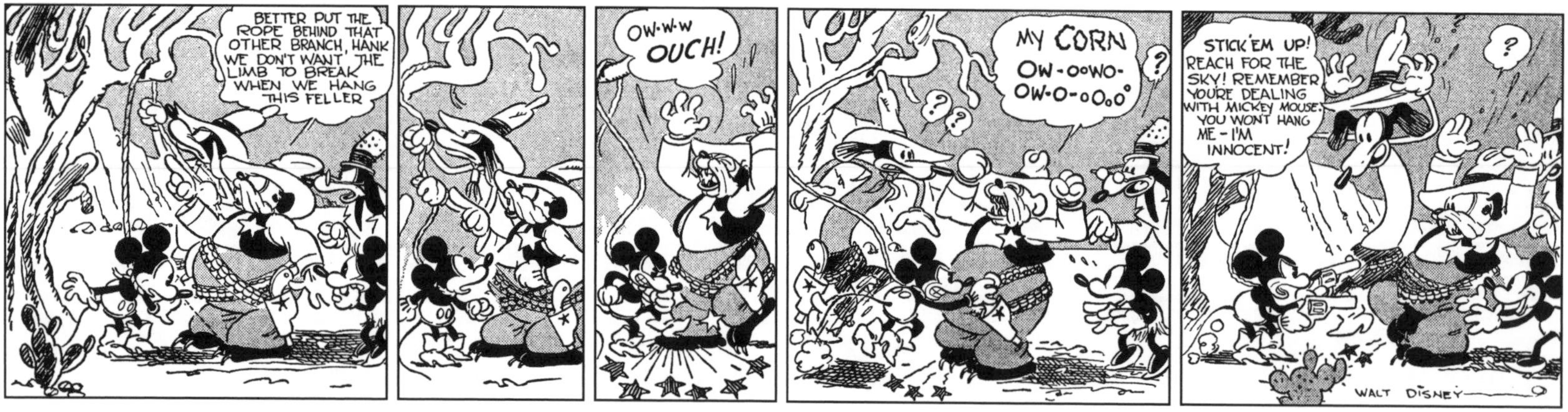
BETTER PUT THE ROPE BEHIND THAT OTHER BRANCH, HANK WE DON'T WANT THE LIMB TO BREAK WHEN WE HANG THIS FELLER
OW-W-W OUCH!
MY CORN OW-OOWO-OW-O-OOOO
? ? ?
?
STICK 'EM UP! REACH FOR THE SKY! REMEMBER YOU'RE DEALING WITH MICKEY MOUSE. YOU WONT HANG ME- I'M INNOCENT!
?
WALT DISNEY

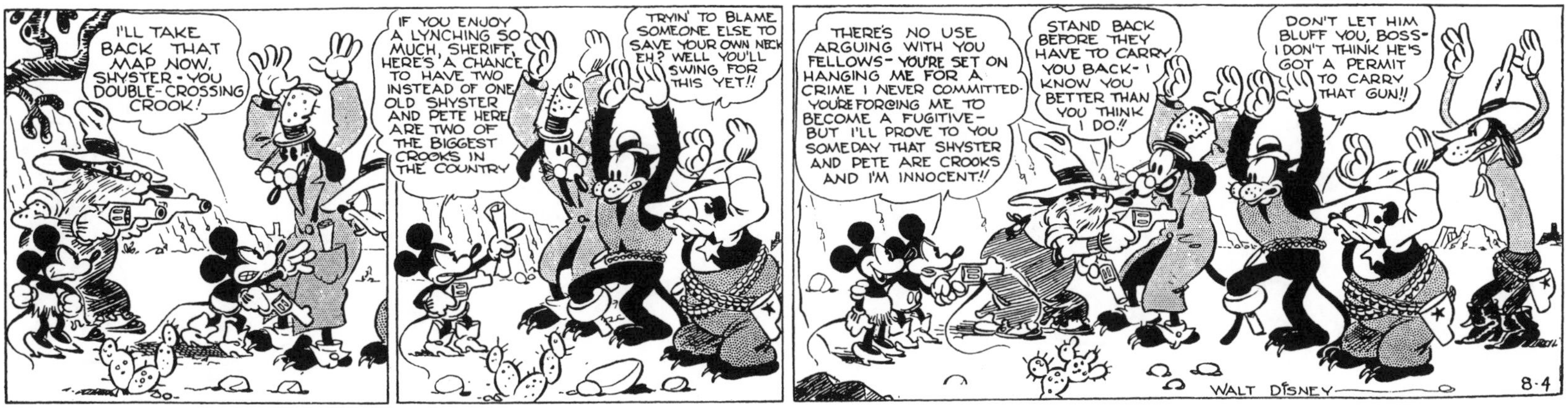
I'LL TAKE BACK THAT MAP NOW, SHYSTER - YOU DOUBLE-CROSSING CROOK!
IF YOU ENJOY A LYNCHING SO MUCH, SHERIFF, HERE'S A CHANCE TO HAVE TWO INSTEAD OF ONE. OLD SHYSTER AND PETE HERE ARE TWO OF THE BIGGEST CROOKS IN THE COUNTRY
TRYIN' TO BLAME SOMEONE ELSE TO SAVE YOUR OWN NECK EH? WELL YOU'LL SWING FOR THIS YET!!
THERE'S NO USE ARGUING WITH YOU FELLOWS - YOU'RE SET ON HANGING ME FOR A CRIME I NEVER COMMITTED - YOU'RE FORCING ME TO BECOME A FUGITIVE - BUT I'LL PROVE TO YOU SOMEDAY THAT SHYSTER AND PETE ARE CROOKS AND I'M INNOCENT!!
STAND BACK BEFORE THEY HAVE TO CARRY YOU BACK - I KNOW YOU BETTER THAN YOU THINK I DO!!
DON'T LET HIM BLUFF YOU, BOSS - I DON'T THINK HE'S GOT A PERMIT TO CARRY THAT GUN!!
WALT DISNEY
8·4

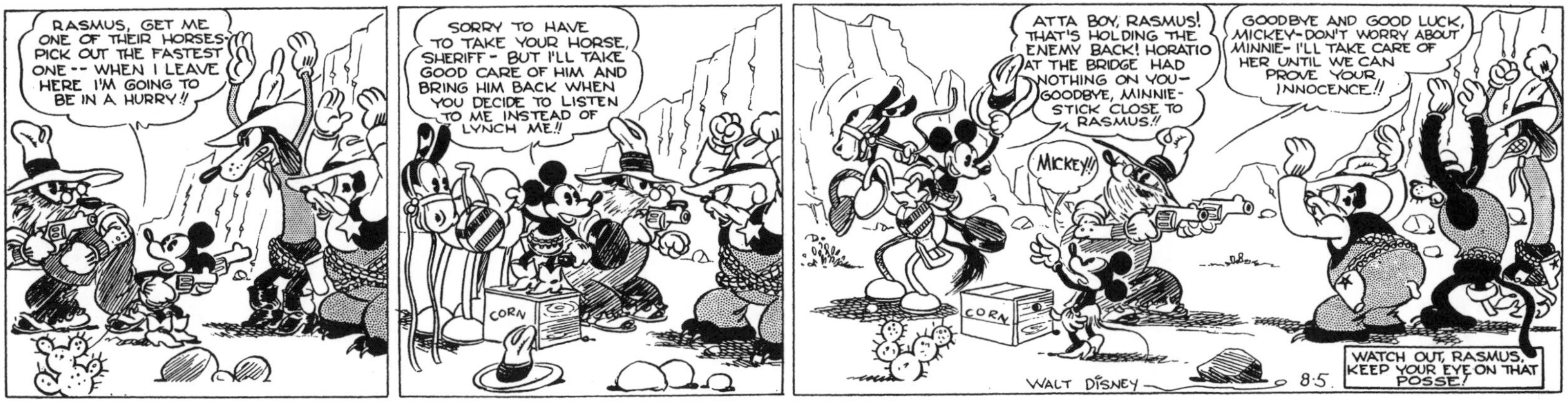
RASMUS, GET ME ONE OF THEIR HORSES - PICK OUT THE FASTEST ONE -- WHEN I LEAVE HERE I'M GOING TO BE IN A HURRY!!
SORRY TO HAVE TO TAKE YOUR HORSE, SHERIFF - BUT I'LL TAKE GOOD CARE OF HIM AND BRING HIM BACK WHEN YOU DECIDE TO LISTEN TO ME INSTEAD OF LYNCH ME!!
CORN
ATTA BOY, RASMUS! THAT'S HOLDING THE ENEMY BACK! HORATIO AT THE BRIDGE HAD NOTHING ON YOU - GOODBYE, MINNIE - STICK CLOSE TO RASMUS!!
MICKEY!!
GOODBYE AND GOOD LUCK, MICKEY - DON'T WORRY ABOUT MINNIE - I'LL TAKE CARE OF HER UNTIL WE CAN PROVE YOUR INNOCENCE!!
CORN
WALT DISNEY
8·5
WATCH OUT, RASMUS, KEEP YOUR EYE ON THAT POSSE!

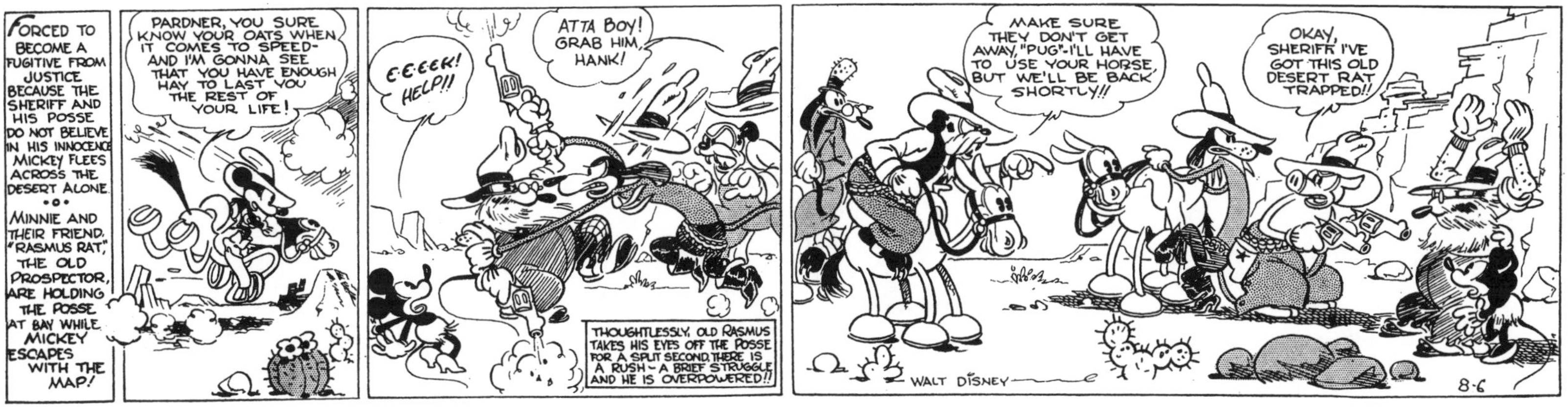
FORCED TO BECOME A FUGITIVE FROM JUSTICE BECAUSE THE SHERIFF AND HIS POSSE DO NOT BELIEVE IN HIS INNOCENCE MICKEY FLEES ACROSS THE DESERT ALONE
MINNIE AND THEIR FRIEND, "RASMUS RAT," THE OLD PROSPECTOR, ARE HOLDING THE POSSE AT BAY WHILE MICKEY ESCAPES WITH THE MAP!
PARDNER, YOU SURE KNOW YOUR OATS WHEN IT COMES TO SPEED - AND I'M GONNA SEE THAT YOU HAVE ENOUGH HAY TO LAST YOU THE REST OF YOUR LIFE!
E-E-EEK! HELP!!
ATTA BOY! GRAB HIM, HANK!
THOUGHTLESSLY, OLD RASMUS TAKES HIS EYES OFF THE POSSE FOR A SPLIT SECOND. THERE IS A RUSH - A BRIEF STRUGGLE AND HE IS OVERPOWERED!!
MAKE SURE THEY DON'T GET AWAY, "PUG" - I'LL HAVE TO USE YOUR HORSE, BUT WE'LL BE BACK SHORTLY!!
OKAY, SHERIFF! I'VE GOT THIS OLD DESERT RAT TRAPPED!!
WALT DISNEY
8·6

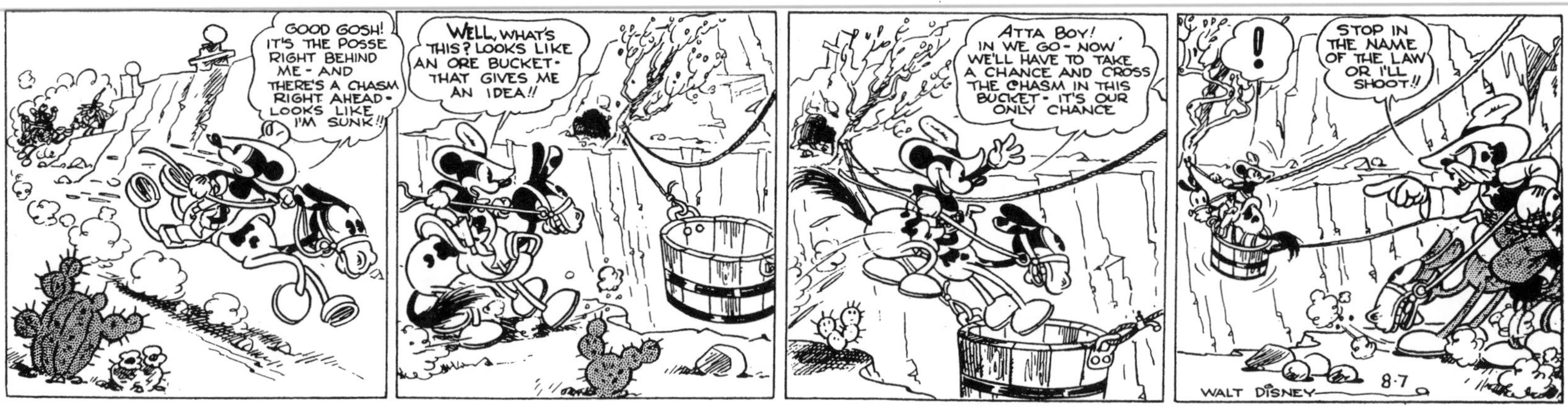
GOOD GOSH! IT'S THE POSSE RIGHT BEHIND ME - AND THERE'S A CHASM RIGHT AHEAD - LOOKS LIKE I'M SUNK!!
WELL, WHAT'S THIS? LOOKS LIKE AN ORE BUCKET - THAT GIVES ME AN IDEA!!
ATTA BOY! IN WE GO - NOW WE'LL HAVE TO TAKE A CHANCE AND CROSS THE CHASM IN THIS BUCKET - IT'S OUR ONLY CHANCE
!
STOP IN THE NAME OF THE LAW OR I'LL SHOOT!!
WALT DISNEY
8·7

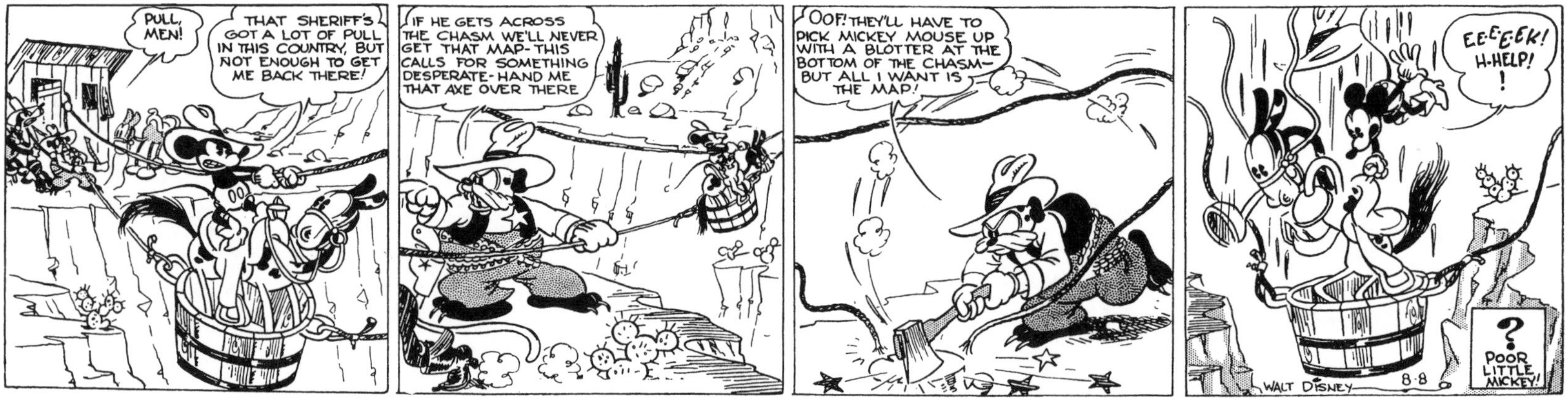
PULL, MEN!
THAT SHERIFF'S GOT A LOT OF PULL IN THIS COUNTRY, BUT NOT ENOUGH TO GET ME BACK THERE!
IF HE GETS ACROSS THE CHASM WE'LL NEVER GET THAT MAP - THIS CALLS FOR SOMETHING DESPERATE - HAND ME THAT AXE OVER THERE
OOF! THEY'LL HAVE TO PICK MICKEY MOUSE UP WITH A BLOTTER AT THE BOTTOM OF THE CHASM - BUT ALL I WANT IS THE MAP!
EE-E-E-EK! H-HELP! !
? POOR LITTLE MICKEY!
WALT DISNEY
8·8

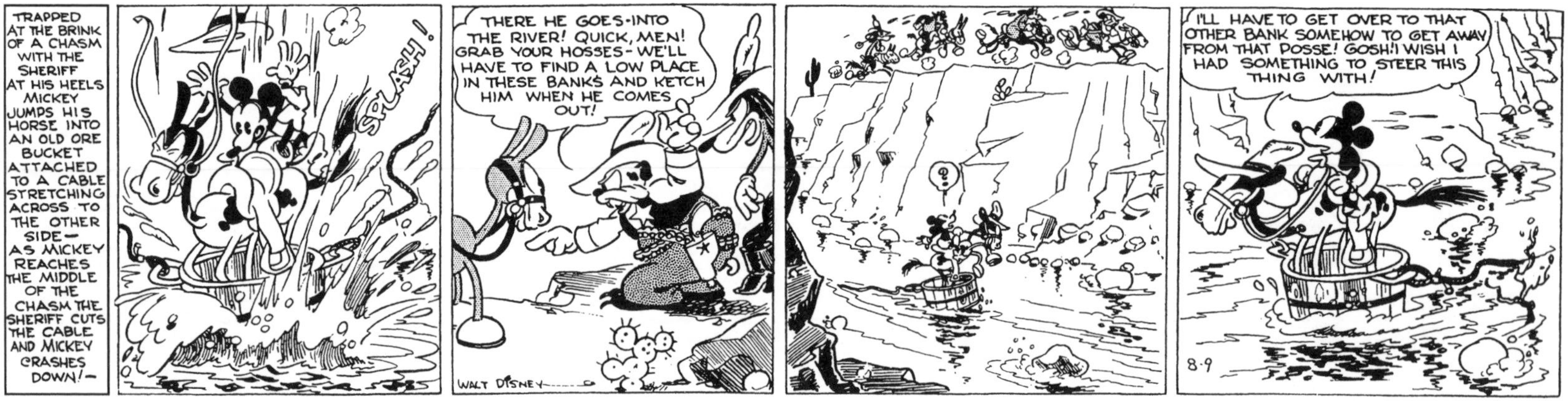
TRAPPED AT THE BRINK OF A CHASM WITH THE SHERIFF AT HIS HEELS MICKEY JUMPS HIS HORSE INTO AN OLD ORE BUCKET ATTACHED TO A CABLE STRETCHING ACROSS TO THE OTHER SIDE— AS MICKEY REACHES THE MIDDLE OF THE CHASM THE SHERIFF CUTS THE CABLE AND MICKEY CRASHES DOWN!—
SPLASH!
THERE HE GOES - INTO THE RIVER! QUICK, MEN! GRAB YOUR HOSSES - WE'LL HAVE TO FIND A LOW PLACE IN THESE BANKS AND KETCH HIM WHEN HE COMES OUT!
WALT DISNEY
?
I'LL HAVE TO GET OVER TO THAT OTHER BANK SOMEHOW TO GET AWAY FROM THAT POSSE! GOSH! I WISH I HAD SOMETHING TO STEER THIS THING WITH!
8·9

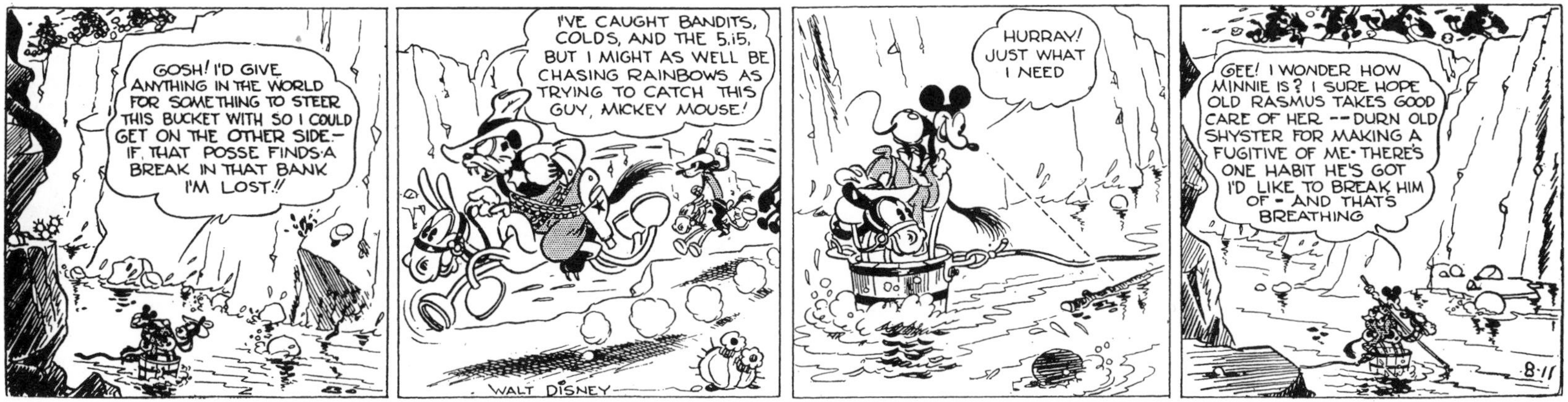
GOSH! I'D GIVE ANYTHING IN THE WORLD FOR SOMETHING TO STEER THIS BUCKET WITH SO I COULD GET ON THE OTHER SIDE— IF THAT POSSE FINDS A BREAK IN THAT BANK I'M LOST!!
I'VE CAUGHT BANDITS, COLDS, AND THE 5.15, BUT I MIGHT AS WELL BE CHASING RAINBOWS AS TRYING TO CATCH THIS GUY, MICKEY MOUSE!
WALT DISNEY
HURRAY! JUST WHAT I NEED
GEE! I WONDER HOW MINNIE IS? I SURE HOPE OLD RASMUS TAKES GOOD CARE OF HER -- DURN OLD SHYSTER FOR MAKING A FUGITIVE OF ME - THERE'S ONE HABIT HE'S GOT I'D LIKE TO BREAK HIM OF - AND THAT'S BREATHING
8-11

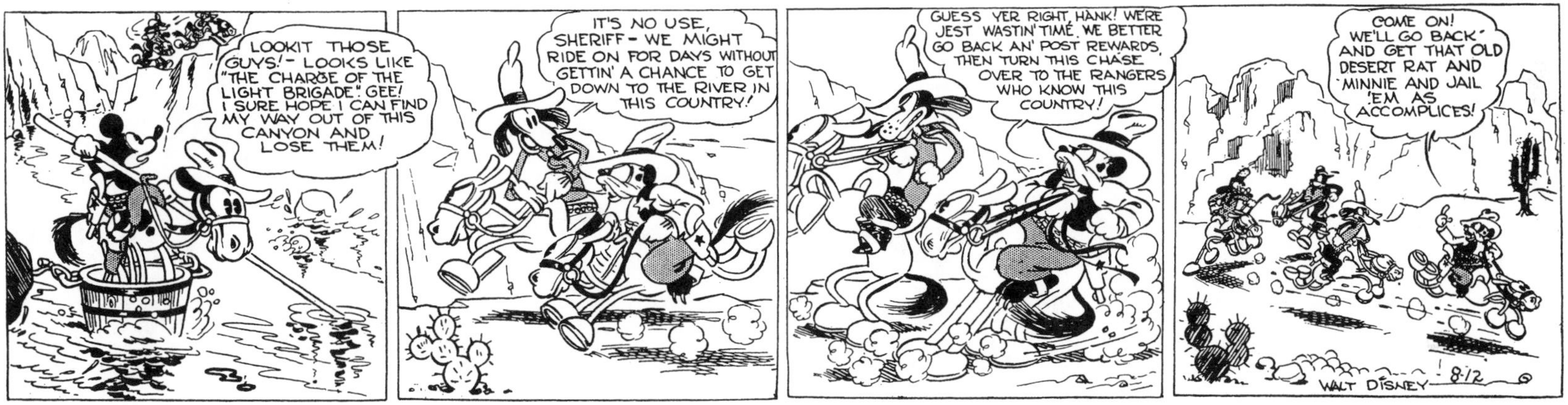
LOOKIT THOSE GUYS! - LOOKS LIKE "THE CHARGE OF THE LIGHT BRIGADE". GEE! I SURE HOPE I CAN FIND MY WAY OUT OF THIS CANYON AND LOSE THEM!
IT'S NO USE, SHERIFF - WE MIGHT RIDE ON FOR DAYS WITHOUT GETTIN' A CHANCE TO GET DOWN TO THE RIVER IN THIS COUNTRY!
GUESS YER RIGHT, HANK! WE'RE JEST WASTIN' TIME. WE BETTER GO BACK AN' POST REWARDS, THEN TURN THIS CHASE OVER TO THE RANGERS WHO KNOW THIS COUNTRY!
COME ON! WE'LL GO BACK AND GET THAT OLD DESERT RAT AND MINNIE AND JAIL 'EM AS ACCOMPLICES!
WALT DISNEY 8-12

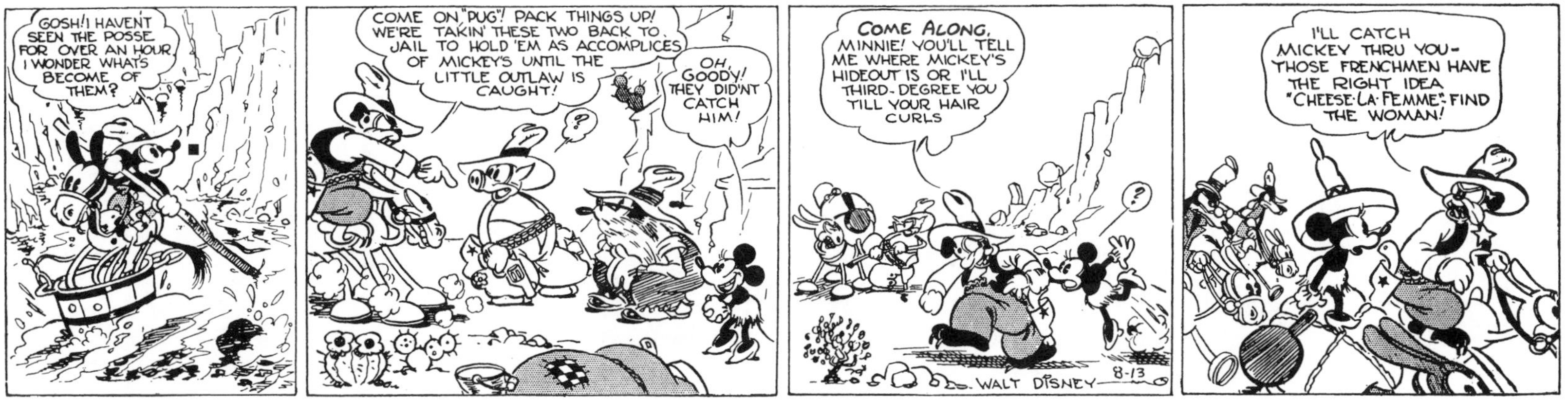
GOSH! I HAVEN'T SEEN THE POSSE FOR OVER AN HOUR. I WONDER WHAT'S BECOME OF THEM?
COME ON "PUG"! PACK THINGS UP! WE'RE TAKIN' THESE TWO BACK TO JAIL TO HOLD 'EM AS ACCOMPLICES OF MICKEY'S UNTIL THE LITTLE OUTLAW IS CAUGHT!
?
OH, GOODY! THEY DIDN'T CATCH HIM!
COME ALONG, MINNIE! YOU'LL TELL ME WHERE MICKEY'S HIDEOUT IS OR I'LL THIRD-DEGREE YOU TILL YOUR HAIR CURLS
?
WALT DISNEY 8-13
I'LL CATCH MICKEY THRU YOU - THOSE FRENCHMEN HAVE THE RIGHT IDEA "CHEESE-LA-FEMME" - FIND THE WOMAN!

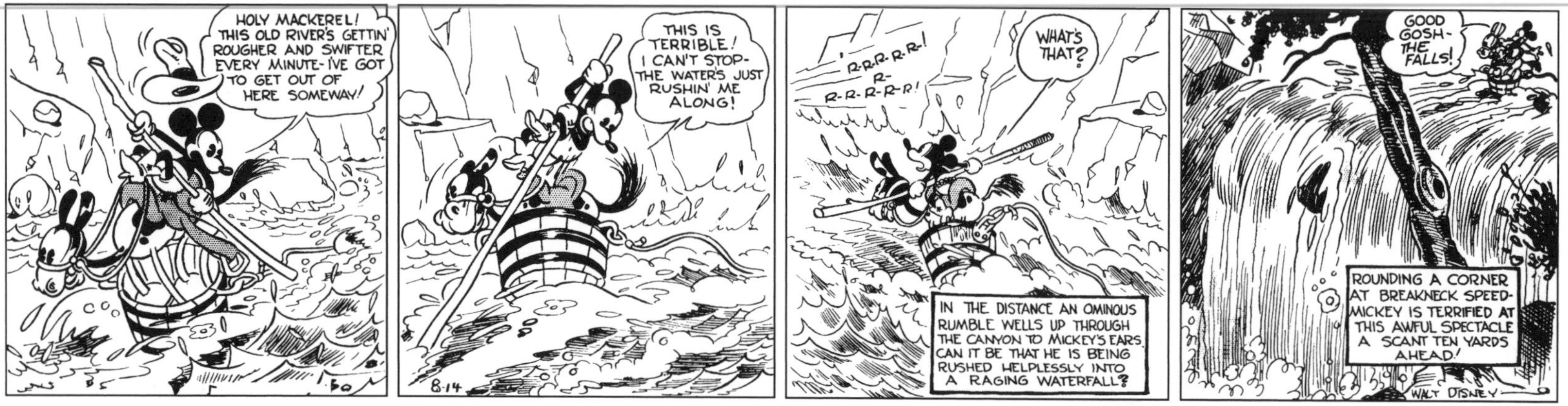

HOLY MACKEREL! THIS OLD RIVER'S GETTIN' ROUGHER AND SWIFTER EVERY MINUTE- I'VE GOT TO GET OUT OF HERE SOMEWAY!
THIS IS TERRIBLE! I CAN'T STOP- THE WATER'S JUST RUSHIN' ME ALONG!
8-14
R-R-R-R-R-! R- R-R-R-R-R!
WHAT'S THAT?
IN THE DISTANCE AN OMINOUS RUMBLE WELLS UP THROUGH THE CANYON TO MICKEY'S EARS. CAN IT BE THAT HE IS BEING RUSHED HELPLESSLY INTO A RAGING WATERFALL?
GOOD GOSH- THE FALLS!
ROUNDING A CORNER AT BREAKNECK SPEED- MICKEY IS TERRIFIED AT THIS AWFUL SPECTACLE A SCANT TEN YARDS AHEAD!
WALT DISNEY

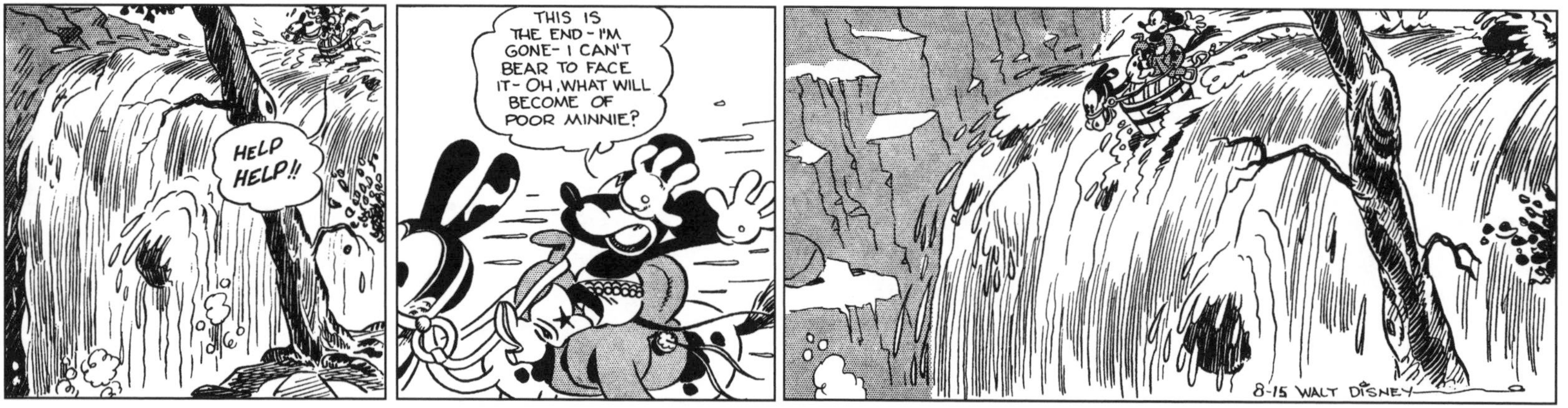

HELP HELP!!
THIS IS THE END- I'M GONE- I CAN'T BEAR TO FACE IT- OH, WHAT WILL BECOME OF POOR MINNIE?
8-15 WALT DISNEY

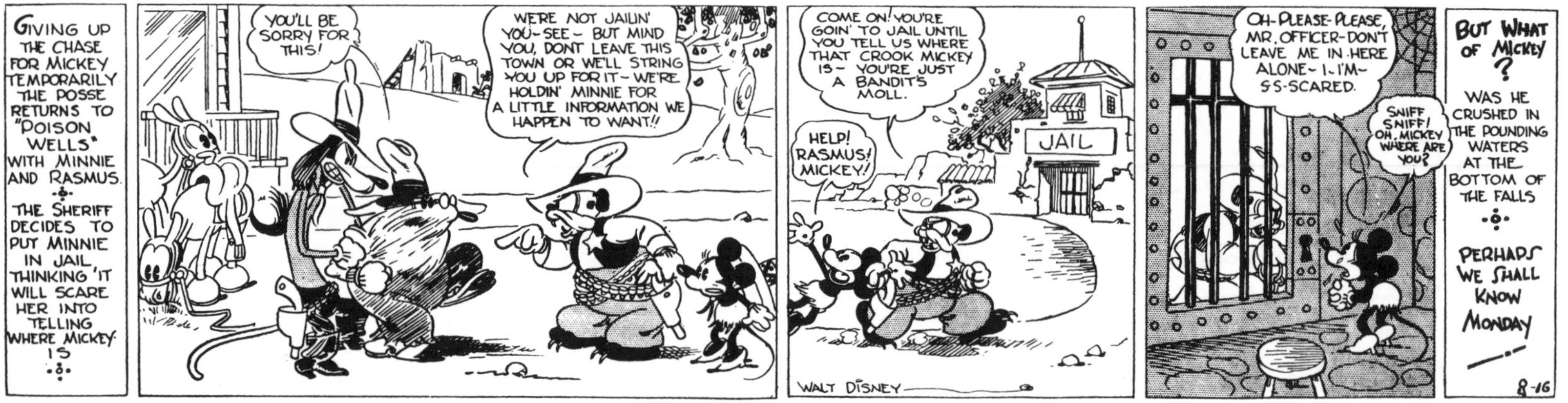

GIVING UP THE CHASE FOR MICKEY TEMPORARILY THE POSSE RETURNS TO "POISON WELLS" WITH MINNIE AND RASMUS.
THE SHERIFF DECIDES TO PUT MINNIE IN JAIL, THINKING 'IT WILL SCARE HER INTO TELLING WHERE MICKEY IS
YOU'LL BE SORRY FOR THIS!
WE'RE NOT JAILIN' YOU- SEE- BUT MIND YOU, DONT LEAVE THIS TOWN OR WE'LL STRING YOU UP FOR IT- WE'RE HOLDIN' MINNIE FOR A LITTLE INFORMATION WE HAPPEN TO WANT!!
COME ON! YOU'RE GOIN' TO JAIL UNTIL YOU TELL US WHERE THAT CROOK MICKEY IS- YOU'RE JUST A BANDIT'S MOLL.
HELP! RASMUS! MICKEY!
JAIL
WALT DISNEY
OH- PLEASE- PLEASE, MR. OFFICER- DON'T LEAVE ME IN HERE ALONE- I- I'M- S-S-SCARED.
SNIFF SNIFF! OH, MICKEY WHERE ARE YOU?
BUT WHAT OF MICKEY?
WAS HE CRUSHED IN THE POUNDING WATERS AT THE BOTTOM OF THE FALLS
PERHAPS WE SHALL KNOW MONDAY
8-16

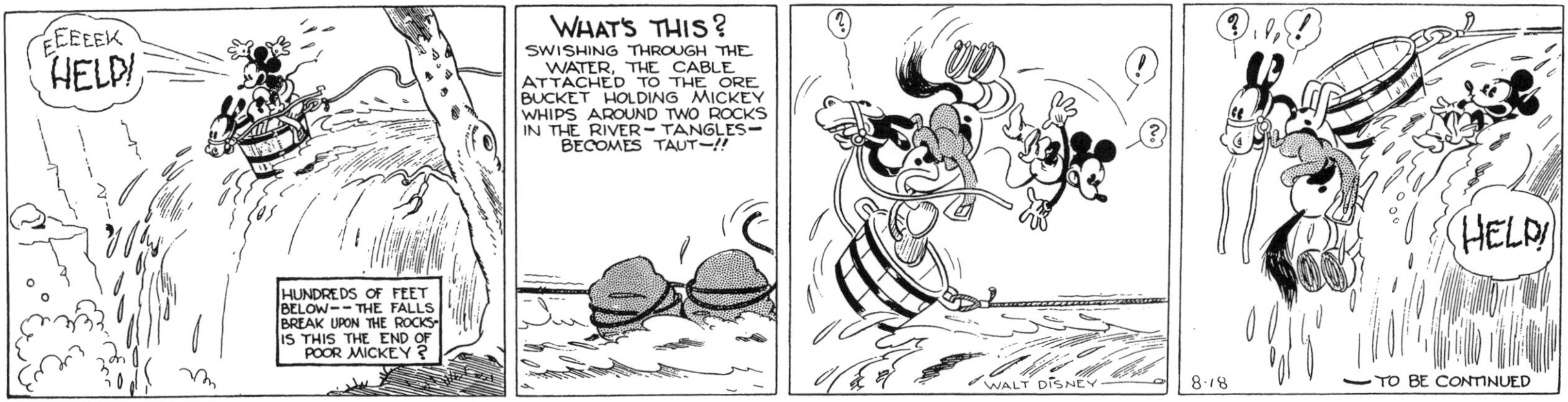
EEEEEK HELP!
HUNDREDS OF FEET BELOW-- THE FALLS BREAK UPON THE ROCKS- IS THIS THE END OF POOR MICKEY?
WHAT'S THIS? SWISHING THROUGH THE WATER, THE CABLE ATTACHED TO THE ORE BUCKET HOLDING MICKEY WHIPS AROUND TWO ROCKS IN THE RIVER- TANGLES- BECOMES TAUT-!!
WALT DISNEY
HELP!
8-18
—TO BE CONTINUED

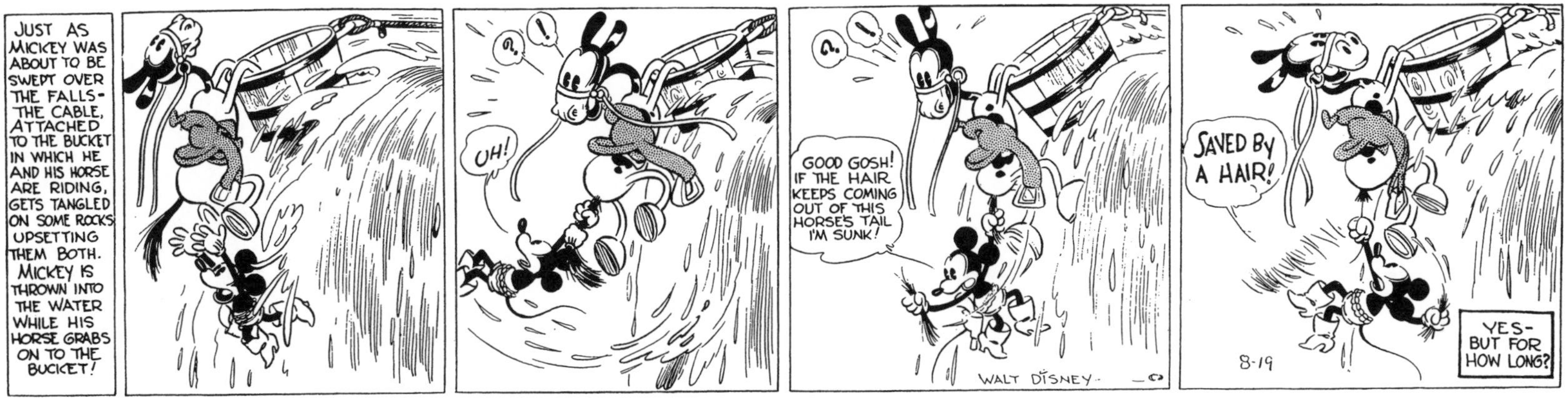
JUST AS MICKEY WAS ABOUT TO BE SWEPT OVER THE FALLS- THE CABLE, ATTACHED TO THE BUCKET IN WHICH HE AND HIS HORSE ARE RIDING, GETS TANGLED ON SOME ROCKS UPSETTING THEM BOTH. MICKEY IS THROWN INTO THE WATER WHILE HIS HORSE GRABS ON TO THE BUCKET!
UH!
GOOD GOSH! IF THE HAIR KEEPS COMING OUT OF THIS HORSE'S TAIL I'M SUNK!
WALT DISNEY
SAVED BY A HAIR!
8-19
YES- BUT FOR HOW LONG?

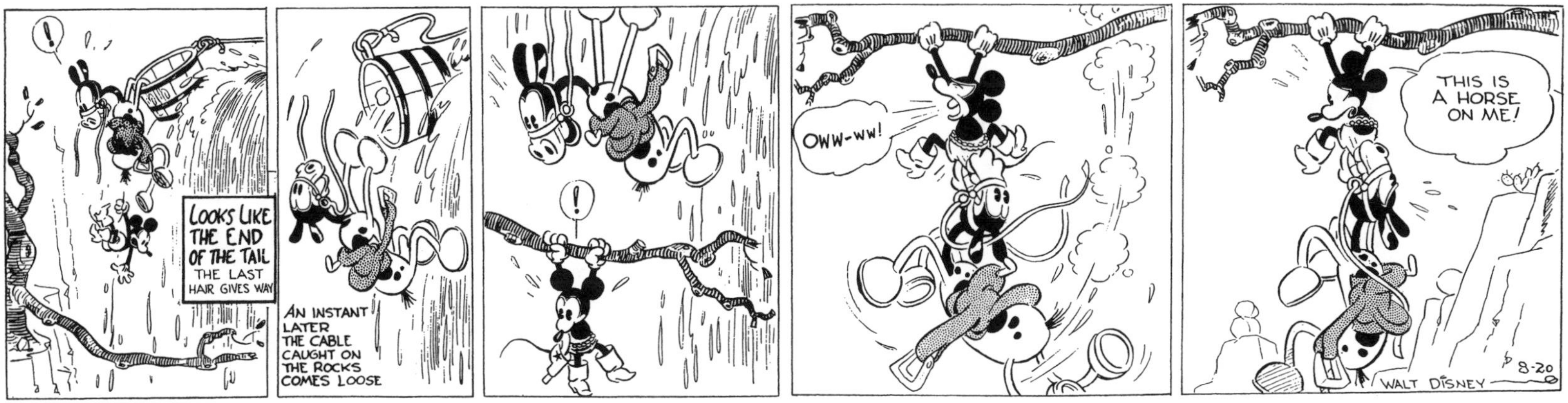
LOOKS LIKE THE END OF THE TAIL THE LAST HAIR GIVES WAY
AN INSTANT LATER THE CABLE CAUGHT ON THE ROCKS COMES LOOSE
OWW-WW!
THIS IS A HORSE ON ME!
8-20
WALT DISNEY

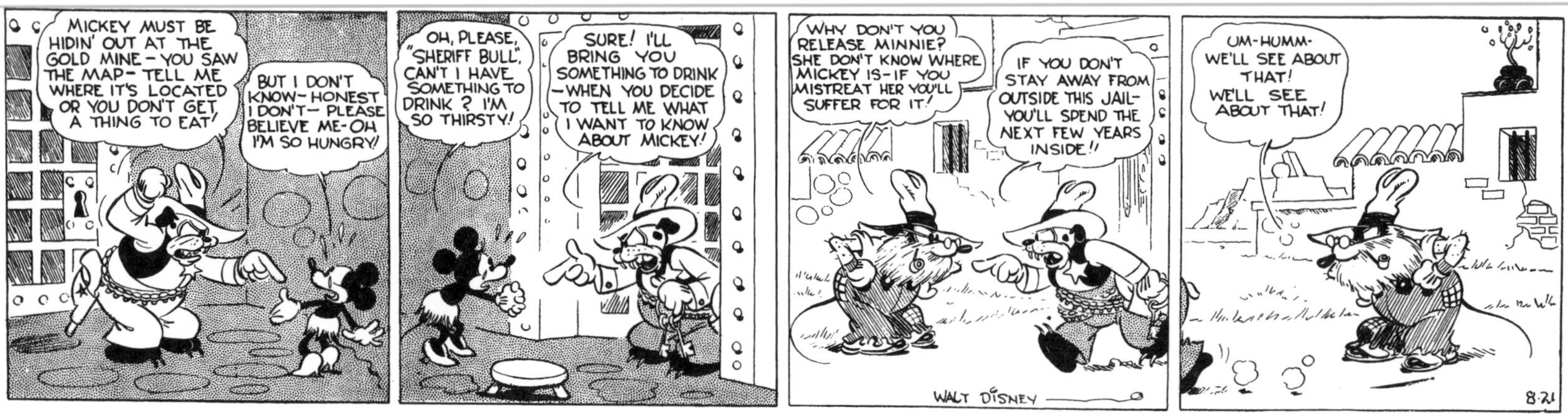
MICKEY MUST BE HIDIN' OUT AT THE GOLD MINE – YOU SAW THE MAP – TELL ME WHERE IT'S LOCATED OR YOU DON'T GET A THING TO EAT!
BUT I DON'T KNOW – HONEST I DON'T – PLEASE BELIEVE ME – OH I'M SO HUNGRY!
OH, PLEASE, "SHERIFF BULL", CAN'T I HAVE SOMETHING TO DRINK? I'M SO THIRSTY!
SURE! I'LL BRING YOU SOMETHING TO DRINK – WHEN YOU DECIDE TO TELL ME WHAT I WANT TO KNOW ABOUT MICKEY!
WHY DON'T YOU RELEASE MINNIE? SHE DON'T KNOW WHERE MICKEY IS – IF YOU MISTREAT HER YOU'LL SUFFER FOR IT!
IF YOU DON'T STAY AWAY FROM OUTSIDE THIS JAIL – YOU'LL SPEND THE NEXT FEW YEARS INSIDE!!
WALT DISNEY
UM-HUMM – WE'LL SEE ABOUT THAT! WE'LL SEE ABOUT THAT!
8-21

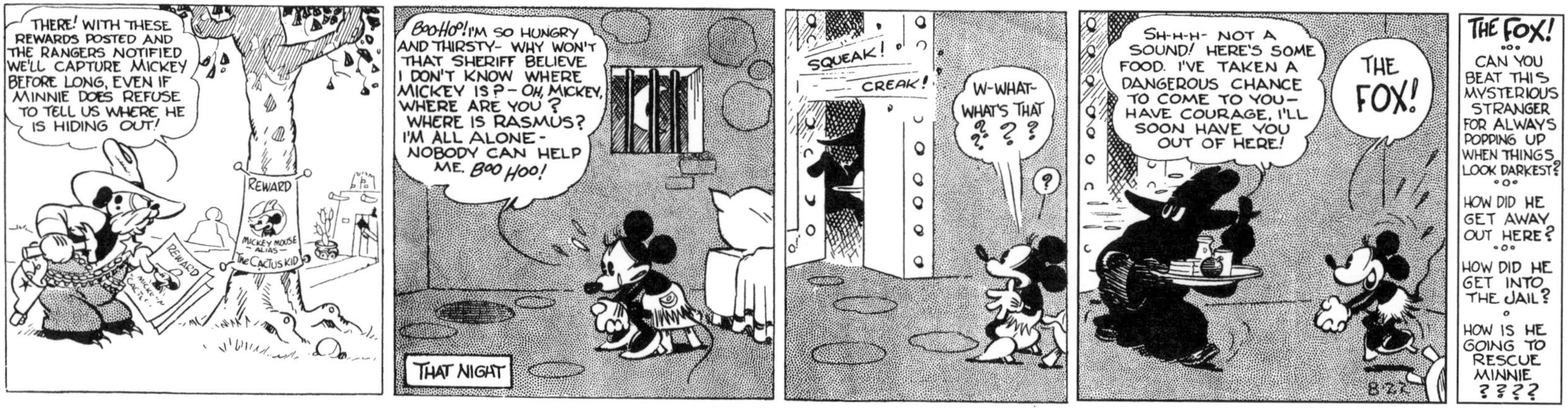
THERE! WITH THESE REWARDS POSTED AND THE RANGERS NOTIFIED WE'LL CAPTURE MICKEY BEFORE LONG, EVEN IF MINNIE DOES REFUSE TO TELL US WHERE HE IS HIDING OUT!
REWARD
MICKEY MOUSE ALIAS The CACTUS KID
REWARD
BOO-HOO! I'M SO HUNGRY AND THIRSTY – WHY WON'T THAT SHERIFF BELIEVE I DON'T KNOW WHERE MICKEY IS? – OH, MICKEY, WHERE ARE YOU? WHERE IS RASMUS? I'M ALL ALONE – NOBODY CAN HELP ME. BOO HOO!
THAT NIGHT
SQUEAK!
CREAK!
W-WHAT – WHAT'S THAT ???
?
SH-H-H- NOT A SOUND! HERE'S SOME FOOD. I'VE TAKEN A DANGEROUS CHANCE TO COME TO YOU – HAVE COURAGE, I'LL SOON HAVE YOU OUT OF HERE!
THE FOX!
8-22
THE FOX!
CAN YOU BEAT THIS MYSTERIOUS STRANGER FOR ALWAYS POPPING UP WHEN THINGS LOOK DARKEST?
HOW DID HE GET AWAY OUT HERE?
HOW DID HE GET INTO THE JAIL?
HOW IS HE GOING TO RESCUE MINNIE ????

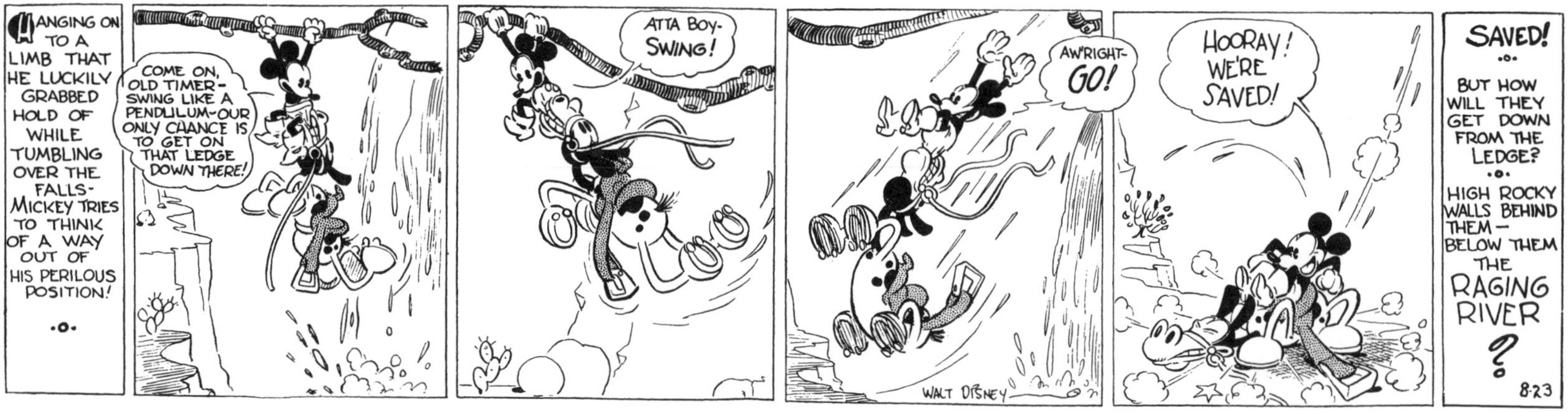
HANGING ON TO A LIMB THAT HE LUCKILY GRABBED HOLD OF WHILE TUMBLING OVER THE FALLS – MICKEY TRIES TO THINK OF A WAY OUT OF HIS PERILOUS POSITION!
COME ON, OLD TIMER – SWING LIKE A PENDULUM – OUR ONLY CHANCE IS TO GET ON THAT LEDGE DOWN THERE!
ATTA BOY – SWING!
AW'RIGHT – GO!
WALT DISNEY
HOORAY! WE'RE SAVED!
SAVED!
BUT HOW WILL THEY GET DOWN FROM THE LEDGE?
HIGH ROCKY WALLS BEHIND THEM – BELOW THEM THE RAGING RIVER
?
8-23

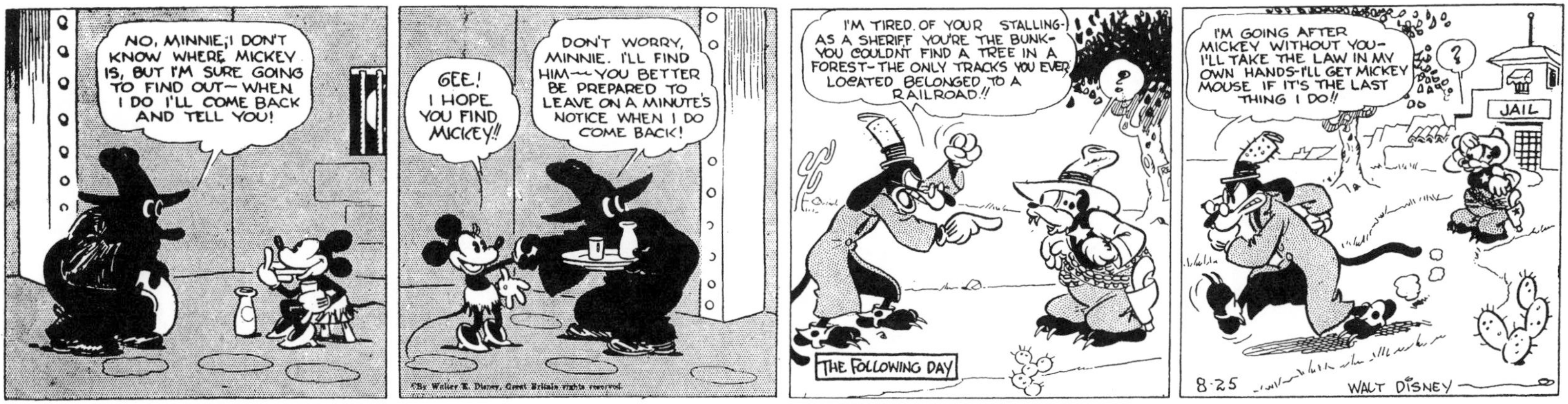
NO, MINNIE, I DON'T KNOW WHERE MICKEY IS, BUT I'M SURE GOING TO FIND OUT— WHEN I DO I'LL COME BACK AND TELL YOU!
GEE! I HOPE YOU FIND MICKEY!!
DON'T WORRY, MINNIE. I'LL FIND HIM—YOU BETTER BE PREPARED TO LEAVE ON A MINUTE'S NOTICE WHEN I DO COME BACK!
©By Walter E. Disney, Great Britain rights reserved.
I'M TIRED OF YOUR STALLING-AS A SHERIFF YOU'RE THE BUNK-YOU COULDN'T FIND A TREE IN A FOREST-THE ONLY TRACKS YOU EVER LOCATED BELONGED TO A RAILROAD!!
THE FOLLOWING DAY
I'M GOING AFTER MICKEY WITHOUT YOU-I'LL TAKE THE LAW IN MY OWN HANDS-I'LL GET MICKEY MOUSE IF IT'S THE LAST THING I DO!!
?
JAIL
8-25
WALT DISNEY

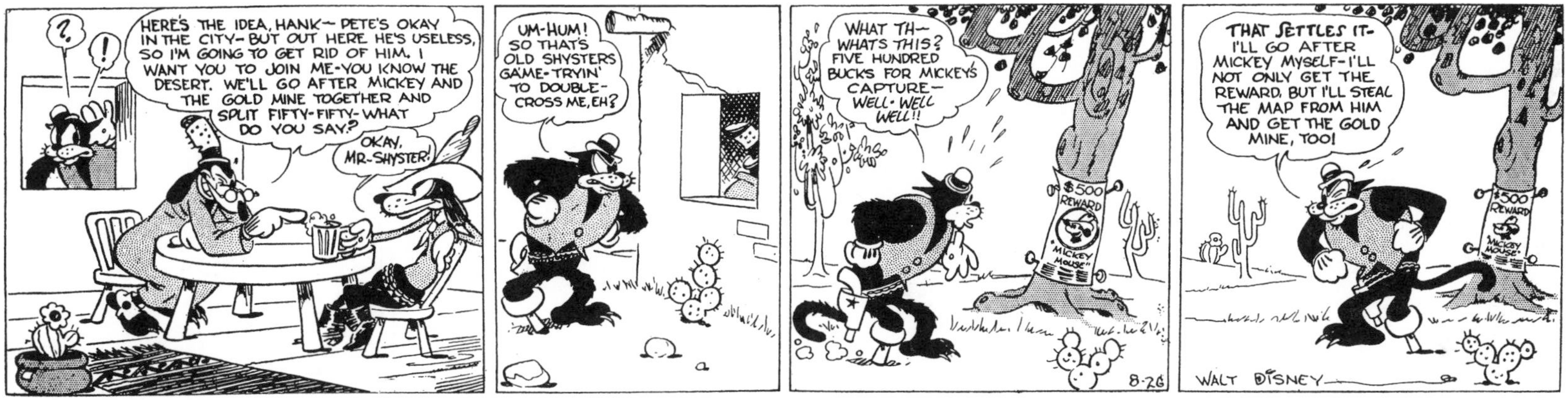
?
!
HERE'S THE IDEA, HANK— PETE'S OKAY IN THE CITY- BUT OUT HERE HE'S USELESS, SO I'M GOING TO GET RID OF HIM. I WANT YOU TO JOIN ME-YOU KNOW THE DESERT. WE'LL GO AFTER MICKEY AND THE GOLD MINE TOGETHER AND SPLIT FIFTY-FIFTY- WHAT DO YOU SAY?
OKAY, MR-SHYSTER!
UM-HUM! SO THAT'S OLD SHYSTERS GAME-TRYIN' TO DOUBLE-CROSS ME, EH?
WHAT TH— WHAT'S THIS? FIVE HUNDRED BUCKS FOR MICKEY'S CAPTURE— WELL-WELL WELL!!
$500 REWARD
"MICKEY MOUSE"
8-26
THAT SETTLES IT- I'LL GO AFTER MICKEY MYSELF-I'LL NOT ONLY GET THE REWARD, BUT I'LL STEAL THE MAP FROM HIM AND GET THE GOLD MINE, TOO!
$500 REWARD
MICKEY MOUSE
WALT DISNEY

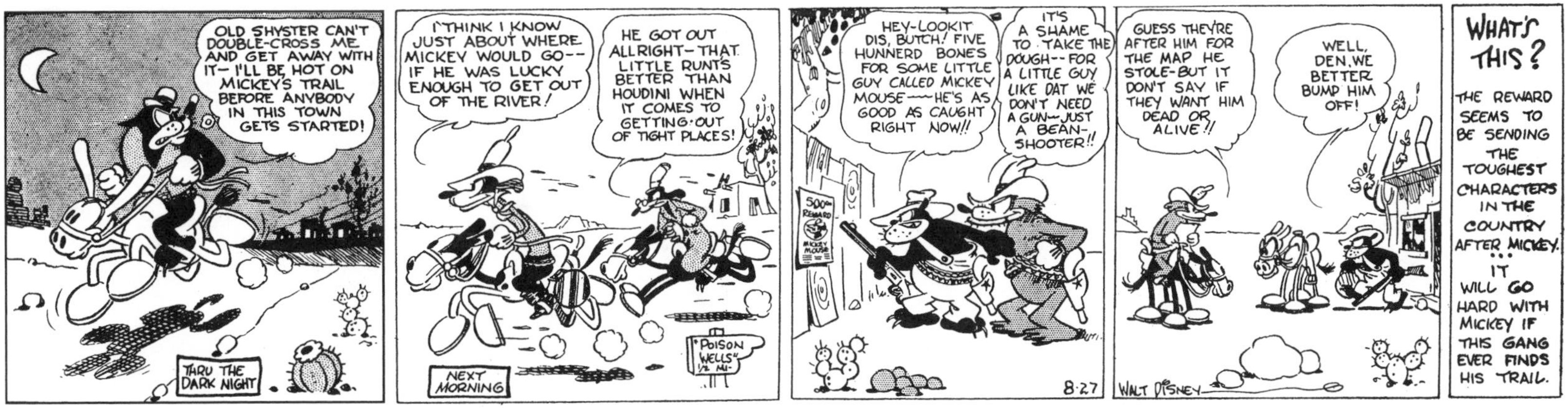
OLD SHYSTER CAN'T DOUBLE-CROSS ME AND GET AWAY WITH IT— I'LL BE HOT ON MICKEY'S TRAIL BEFORE ANYBODY IN THIS TOWN GETS STARTED!
THRU THE DARK NIGHT
I THINK I KNOW JUST ABOUT WHERE MICKEY WOULD GO— IF HE WAS LUCKY ENOUGH TO GET OUT OF THE RIVER!
HE GOT OUT ALLRIGHT- THAT LITTLE RUNT'S BETTER THAN HOUDINI WHEN IT COMES TO GETTING OUT OF TIGHT PLACES!
NEXT MORNING
"POISON WELLS" 1/2 MI.
HEY-LOOKIT DIS, BUTCH! FIVE HUNNERD BONES FOR SOME LITTLE GUY CALLED MICKEY MOUSE——HE'S AS GOOD AS CAUGHT RIGHT NOW!!
IT'S A SHAME TO TAKE THE DOUGH—FOR A LITTLE GUY LIKE DAT WE DON'T NEED A GUN—JUST A BEAN-SHOOTER!!
500 REWARD MICKEY MOUSE
8-27
GUESS THEY'RE AFTER HIM FOR THE MAP HE STOLE-BUT IT DON'T SAY IF THEY WANT HIM DEAD OR ALIVE!!
WELL, DEN, WE BETTER BUMP HIM OFF!
WALT DISNEY
WHAT'S THIS?
THE REWARD SEEMS TO BE SENDING THE TOUGHEST CHARACTERS IN THE COUNTRY AFTER MICKEY. . . . IT WILL GO HARD WITH MICKEY IF THIS GANG EVER FINDS HIS TRAIL.

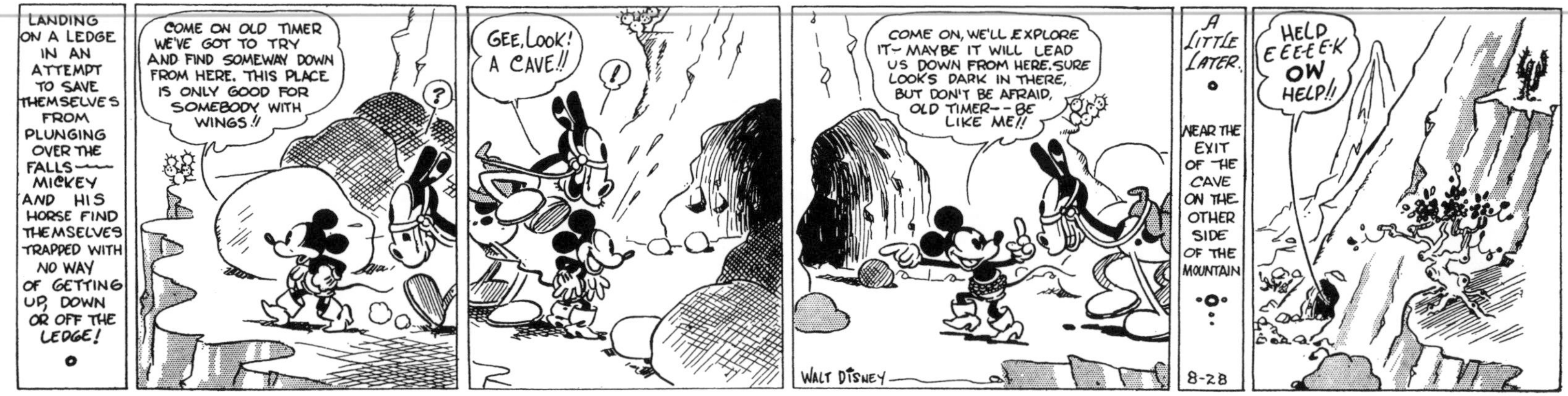
LANDING ON A LEDGE IN AN ATTEMPT TO SAVE THEMSELVES FROM PLUNGING OVER THE FALLS— MICKEY AND HIS HORSE FIND THEMSELVES TRAPPED WITH NO WAY OF GETTING UP, DOWN OR OFF THE LEDGE!
COME ON OLD TIMER WE'VE GOT TO TRY AND FIND SOMEWAY DOWN FROM HERE. THIS PLACE IS ONLY GOOD FOR SOMEBODY WITH WINGS!!
?
GEE, LOOK! A CAVE!!
!
COME ON, WE'LL EXPLORE IT— MAYBE IT WILL LEAD US DOWN FROM HERE. SURE LOOK'S DARK IN THERE, BUT DON'T BE AFRAID, OLD TIMER—BE LIKE ME!!
WALT DISNEY
A LITTLE LATER.
NEAR THE EXIT OF THE CAVE ON THE OTHER SIDE OF THE MOUNTAIN
8-28
HELP EEEE-E-K OW HELP!!

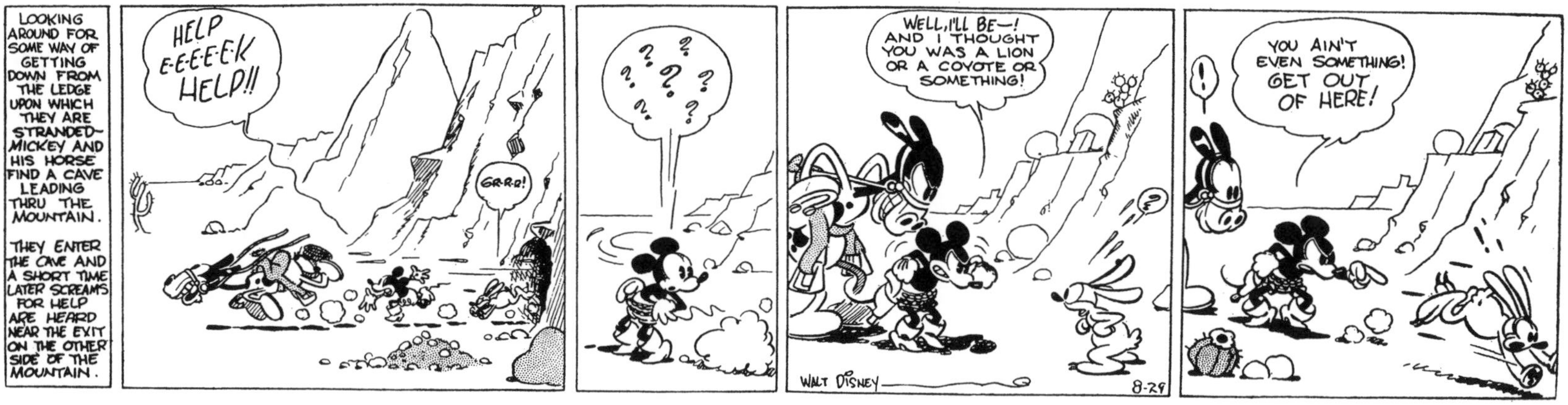
LOOKING AROUND FOR SOME WAY OF GETTING DOWN FROM THE LEDGE UPON WHICH THEY ARE STRANDED— MICKEY AND HIS HORSE FIND A CAVE LEADING THRU THE MOUNTAIN.
THEY ENTER THE CAVE AND A SHORT TIME LATER SCREAMS FOR HELP ARE HEARD NEAR THE EXIT ON THE OTHER SIDE OF THE MOUNTAIN.
HELP E-E-E-E-E-K HELP!!
GR-R-R!
? ? ? ? ? ? ?
WELL, I'LL BE—! AND I THOUGHT YOU WAS A LION OR A COYOTE OR SOMETHING!
WALT DISNEY
8-29
!
YOU AIN'T EVEN SOMETHING! GET OUT OF HERE!

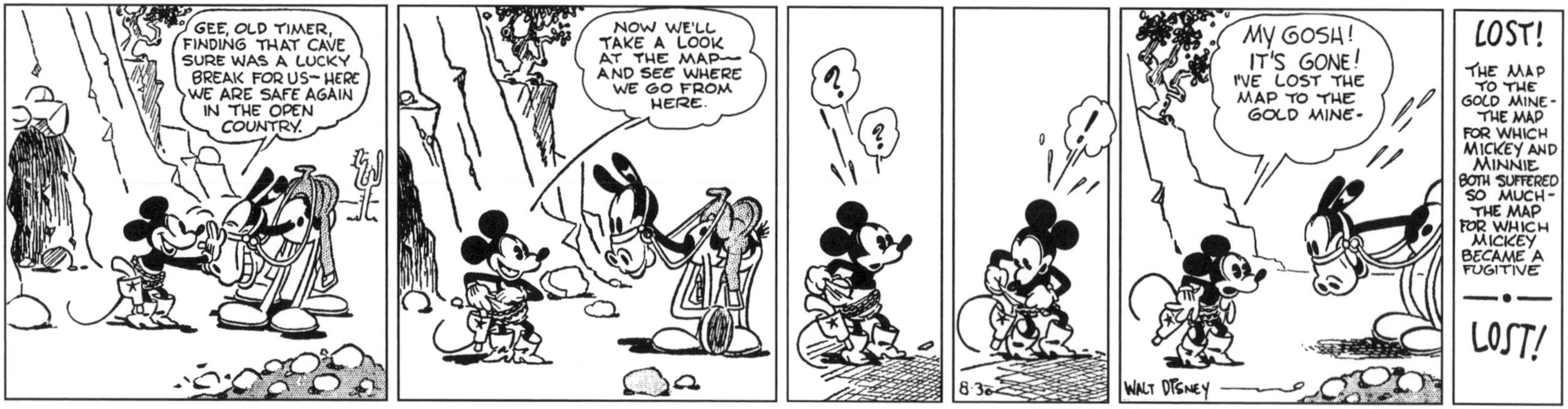
GEE, OLD TIMER, FINDING THAT CAVE SURE WAS A LUCKY BREAK FOR US— HERE WE ARE SAFE AGAIN IN THE OPEN COUNTRY.
NOW WE'LL TAKE A LOOK AT THE MAP— AND SEE WHERE WE GO FROM HERE.
?
?
!
8-30
MY GOSH! IT'S GONE! I'VE LOST THE MAP TO THE GOLD MINE-
WALT DISNEY
LOST!
THE MAP TO THE GOLD MINE- THE MAP FOR WHICH MICKEY AND MINNIE BOTH SUFFERED SO MUCH- THE MAP FOR WHICH MICKEY BECAME A FUGITIVE
LOST!

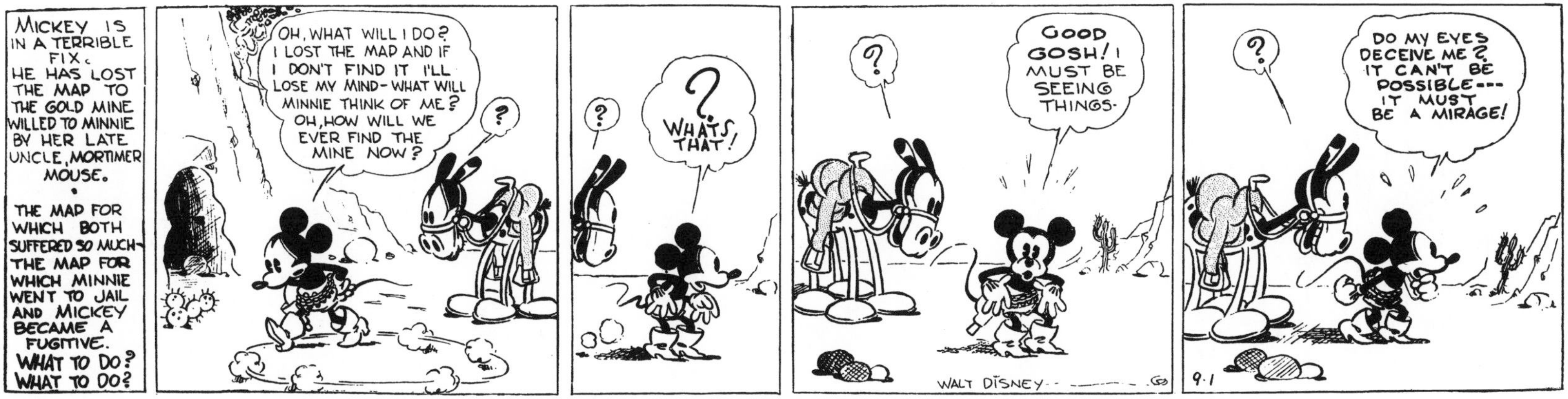
MICKEY IS IN A TERRIBLE FIX. HE HAS LOST THE MAP TO THE GOLD MINE WILLED TO MINNIE BY HER LATE UNCLE, MORTIMER MOUSE.
THE MAP FOR WHICH BOTH SUFFERED SO MUCH— THE MAP FOR WHICH MINNIE WENT TO JAIL AND MICKEY BECAME A FUGITIVE. WHAT TO DO? WHAT TO DO?
OH, WHAT WILL I DO? I LOST THE MAP AND IF I DON'T FIND IT I'LL LOSE MY MIND- WHAT WILL MINNIE THINK OF ME? OH, HOW WILL WE EVER FIND THE MINE NOW?
?
?
?
WHATS THAT!
?
GOOD GOSH! I MUST BE SEEING THINGS.
WALT DISNEY
?
DO MY EYES DECEIVE ME? IT CAN'T BE POSSIBLE--- IT MUST BE A MIRAGE!
9.1

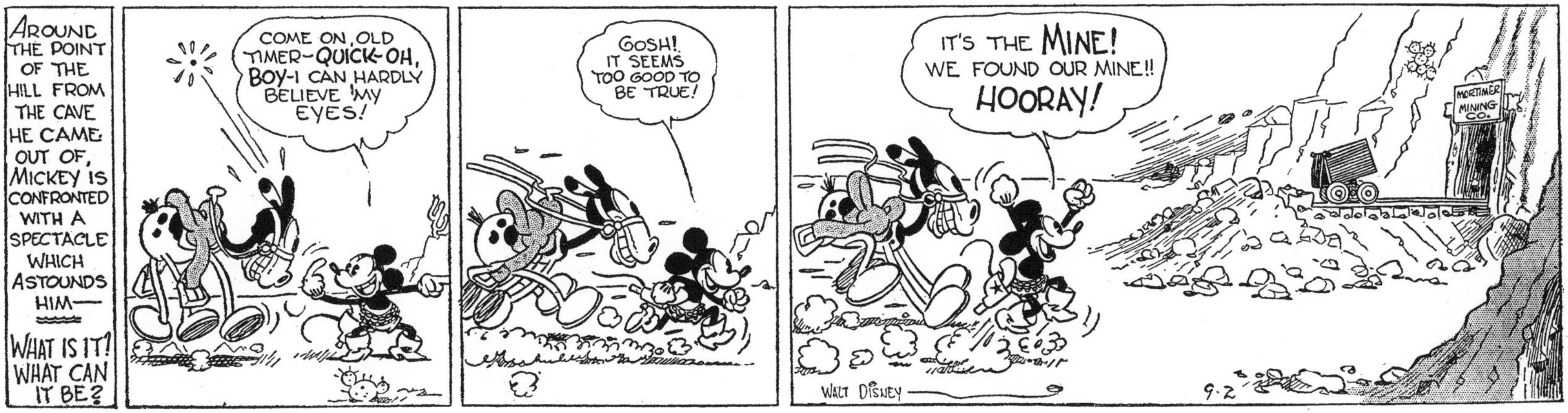
AROUND THE POINT OF THE HILL FROM THE CAVE HE CAME OUT OF, MICKEY IS CONFRONTED WITH A SPECTACLE WHICH ASTOUNDS HIM—
WHAT IS IT? WHAT CAN IT BE?
COME ON, OLD TIMER- QUICK-OH, BOY-I CAN HARDLY BELIEVE MY EYES!
GOSH! IT SEEMS TOO GOOD TO BE TRUE!
IT'S THE MINE! WE FOUND OUR MINE!! HOORAY!
MORTIMER MINING CO.
WALT DISNEY
9.2

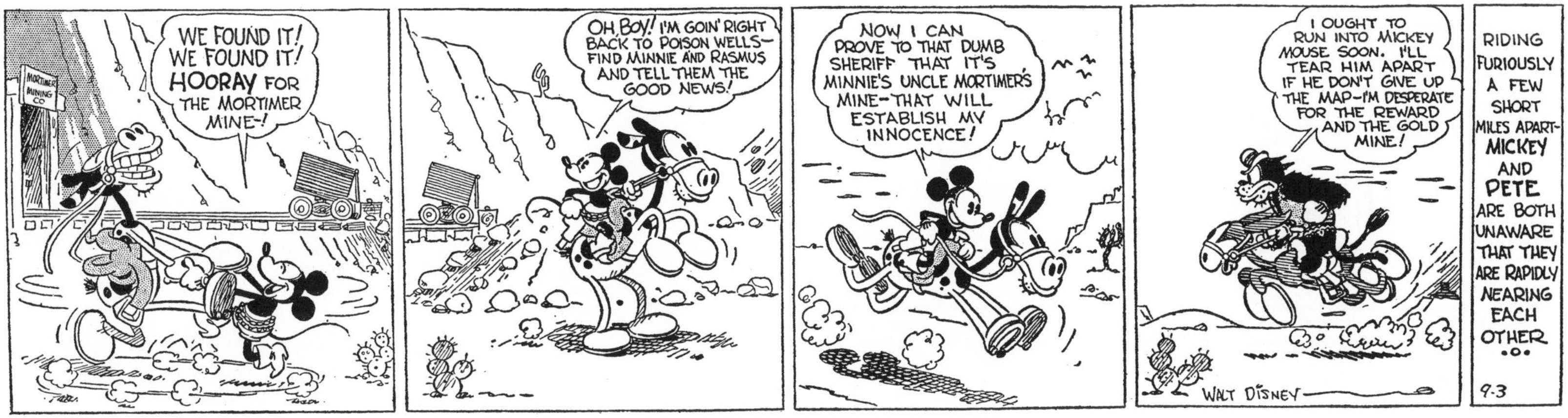
MORTIMER MINING CO
WE FOUND IT! WE FOUND IT! HOORAY FOR THE MORTIMER MINE!
OH, BOY! I'M GOIN' RIGHT BACK TO POISON WELLS— FIND MINNIE AND RASMUS AND TELL THEM THE GOOD NEWS!
NOW I CAN PROVE TO THAT DUMB SHERIFF THAT IT'S MINNIE'S UNCLE MORTIMER'S MINE—THAT WILL ESTABLISH MY INNOCENCE!
I OUGHT TO RUN INTO MICKEY MOUSE SOON. I'LL TEAR HIM APART IF HE DON'T GIVE UP THE MAP-I'M DESPERATE FOR THE REWARD AND THE GOLD MINE!
WALT DISNEY
RIDING FURIOUSLY A FEW SHORT MILES APART- MICKEY AND PETE ARE BOTH UNAWARE THAT THEY ARE RAPIDLY NEARING EACH OTHER
9.3

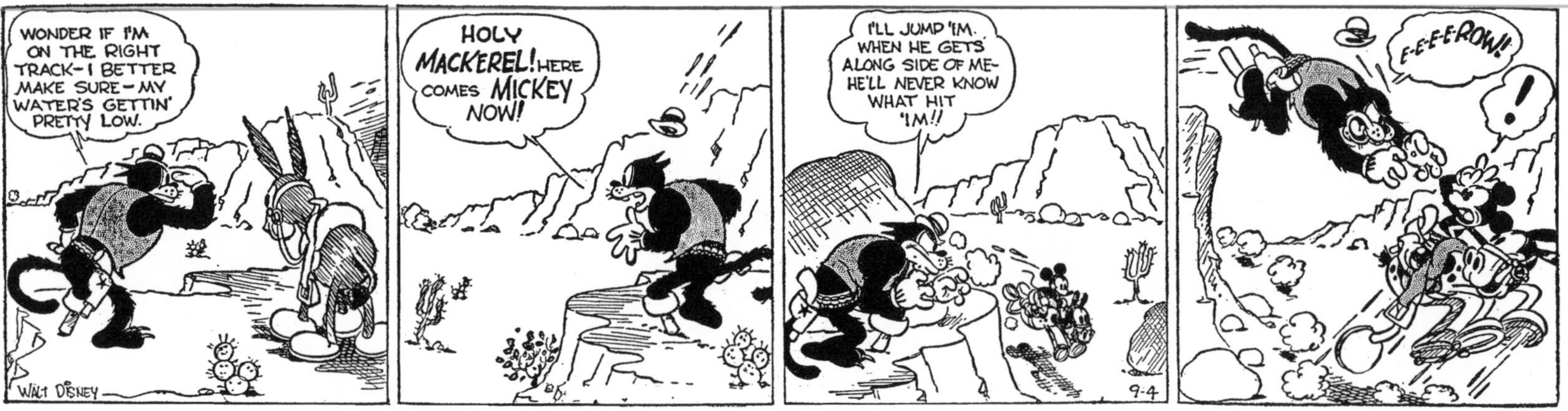
WONDER IF I'M ON THE RIGHT TRACK—I BETTER MAKE SURE—MY WATER'S GETTIN' PRETTY LOW.
WALT DISNEY
HOLY MACKEREL! HERE COMES MICKEY NOW!
I'LL JUMP 'IM. WHEN HE GETS ALONG SIDE OF ME—HE'LL NEVER KNOW WHAT HIT 'IM!!
9-4
E-E-E-E-ROW!
!

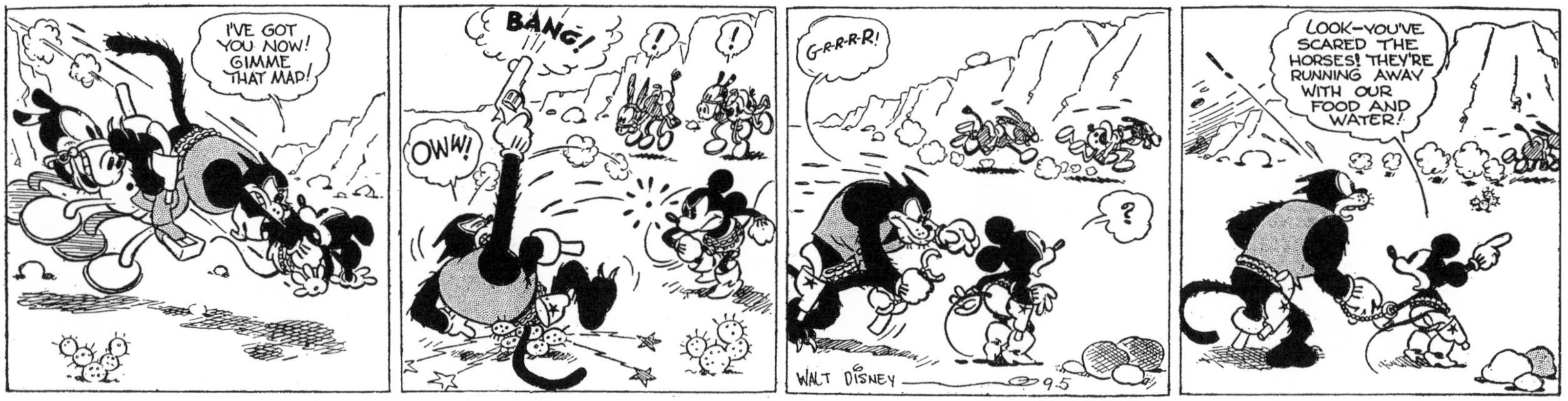
I'VE GOT YOU NOW! GIMME THAT MAP!
BANG!
OWW!
!
!
G-R-R-R-R!
?
WALT DISNEY
9-5
LOOK—YOU'VE SCARED THE HORSES! THEY'RE RUNNING AWAY WITH OUR FOOD AND WATER!

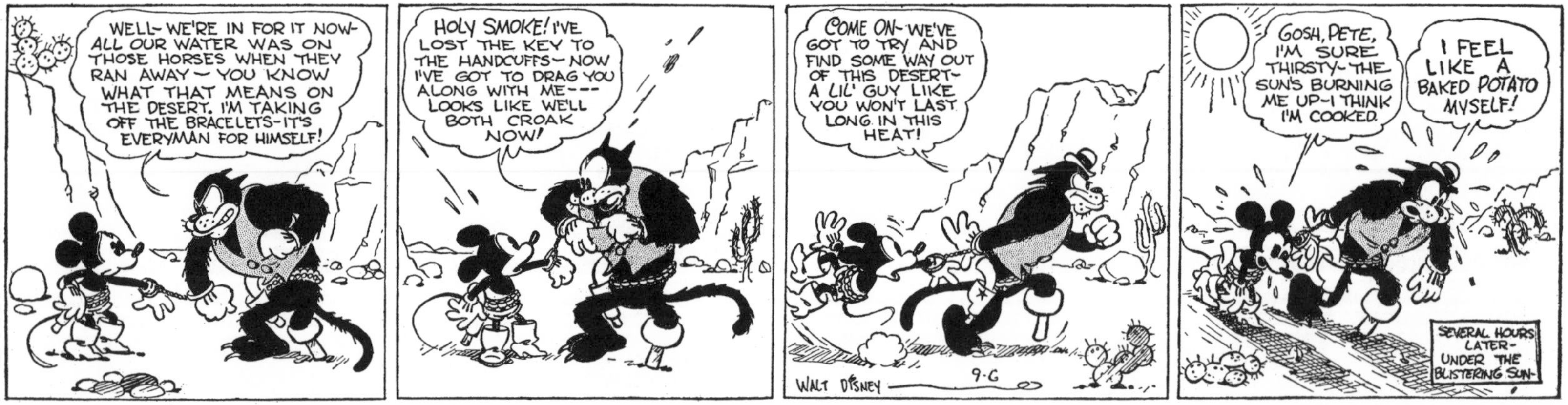
WELL—WE'RE IN FOR IT NOW—ALL OUR WATER WAS ON THOSE HORSES WHEN THEY RAN AWAY—YOU KNOW WHAT THAT MEANS ON THE DESERT. I'M TAKING OFF THE BRACELETS—IT'S EVERYMAN FOR HIMSELF!
HOLY SMOKE! I'VE LOST THE KEY TO THE HANDCUFFS—NOW I'VE GOT TO DRAG YOU ALONG WITH ME---LOOKS LIKE WE'LL BOTH CROAK NOW!
COME ON—WE'VE GOT TO TRY AND FIND SOME WAY OUT OF THIS DESERT—A LIL' GUY LIKE YOU WON'T LAST LONG IN THIS HEAT!
WALT DISNEY
9-6
GOSH, PETE, I'M SURE THIRSTY—THE SUN'S BURNING ME UP—I THINK I'M COOKED.
I FEEL LIKE A BAKED POTATO MYSELF!
SEVERAL HOURS LATER—UNDER THE BLISTERING SUN—

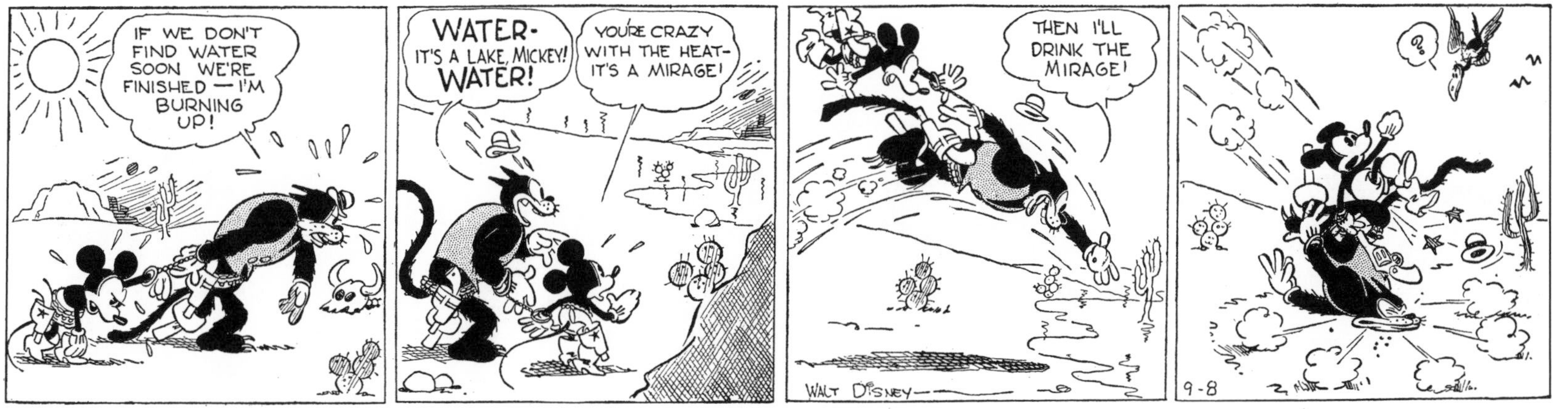
IF WE DON'T FIND WATER SOON WE'RE FINISHED — I'M BURNING UP!
WATER- IT'S A LAKE, MICKEY! WATER!
YOU'RE CRAZY WITH THE HEAT- IT'S A MIRAGE!
THEN I'LL DRINK THE MIRAGE!
WALT DISNEY
?
9-8

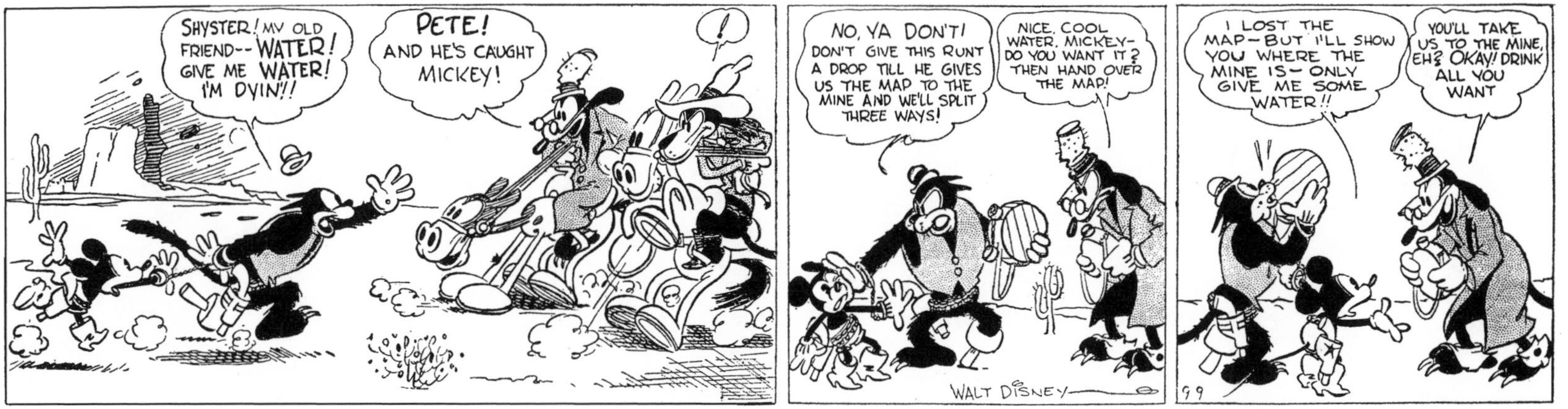
SHYSTER! MY OLD FRIEND-- WATER! GIVE ME WATER! I'M DYIN'!!
PETE! AND HE'S CAUGHT MICKEY!
!
NO, YA DON'T! DON'T GIVE THIS RUNT A DROP TILL HE GIVES US THE MAP TO THE MINE AND WE'LL SPLIT THREE WAYS!
NICE, COOL WATER, MICKEY- DO YOU WANT IT? THEN HAND OVER THE MAP!
WALT DISNEY
I LOST THE MAP—BUT I'LL SHOW YOU WHERE THE MINE IS—ONLY GIVE ME SOME WATER!!
YOU'LL TAKE US TO THE MINE, EH? OKAY! DRINK ALL YOU WANT
9-9

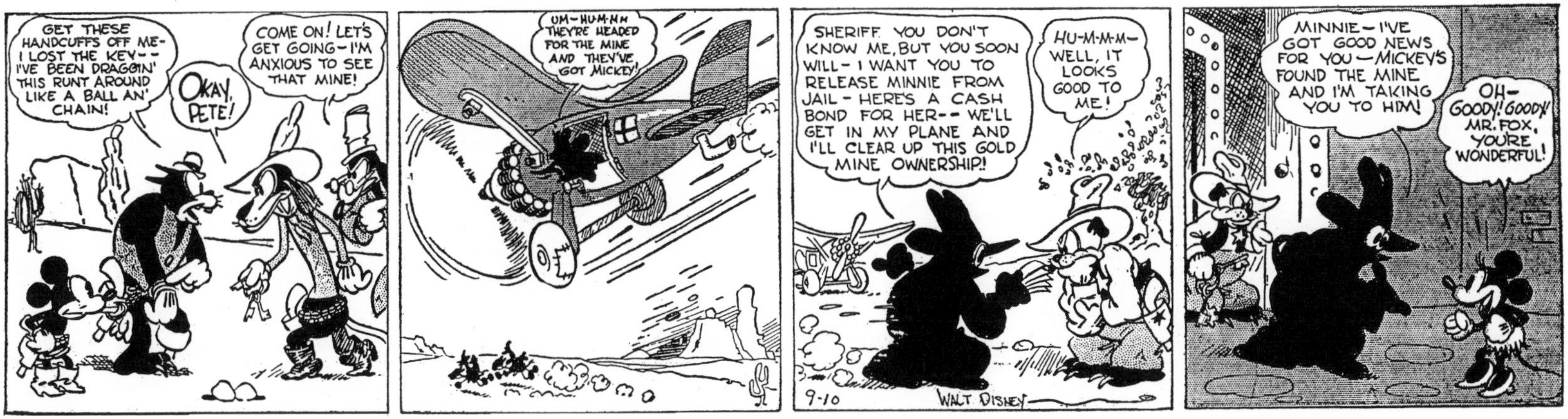
GET THESE HANDCUFFS OFF ME- I LOST THE KEY-- I'VE BEEN DRAGGIN' THIS RUNT AROUND LIKE A BALL AN' CHAIN!
OKAY, PETE!
COME ON! LET'S GET GOING-I'M ANXIOUS TO SEE THAT MINE!
UM-HUM-MM THEY'RE HEADED FOR THE MINE AND THEY'VE GOT MICKEY!
SHERIFF, YOU DON'T KNOW ME, BUT YOU SOON WILL- I WANT YOU TO RELEASE MINNIE FROM JAIL- HERE'S A CASH BOND FOR HER-- WE'LL GET IN MY PLANE AND I'LL CLEAR UP THIS GOLD MINE OWNERSHIP!
HU-M-M-M- WELL, IT LOOKS GOOD TO ME!
9-10
WALT DISNEY
MINNIE- I'VE GOT GOOD NEWS FOR YOU—MICKEY'S FOUND THE MINE AND I'M TAKING YOU TO HIM!
OH- GOODY! GOODY! MR. FOX, YOU'RE WONDERFUL!

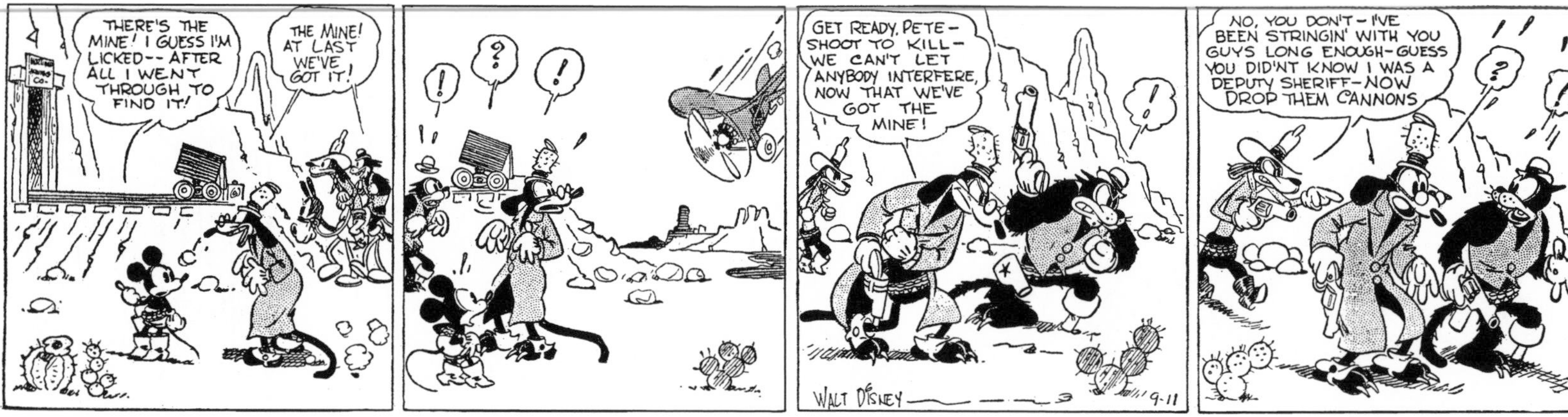
THERE'S THE MINE! I GUESS I'M LICKED-- AFTER ALL I WENT THROUGH TO FIND IT!
THE MINE! AT LAST WE'VE GOT IT!
!
?
!
GET READY, PETE - SHOOT TO KILL- WE CAN'T LET ANYBODY INTERFERE, NOW THAT WE'VE GOT THE MINE!
!
WALT DISNEY
9-11
NO, YOU DON'T - I'VE BEEN STRINGIN' WITH YOU GUYS LONG ENOUGH- GUESS YOU DIDN'T KNOW I WAS A DEPUTY SHERIFF- NOW DROP THEM CANNONS
?
!

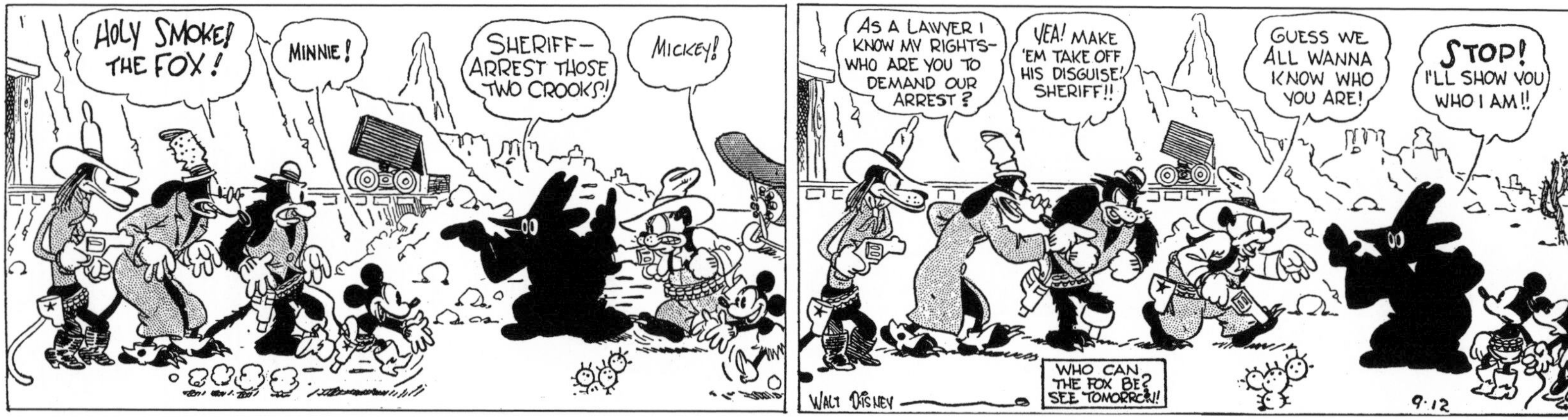
HOLY SMOKE! THE FOX!
MINNIE!
SHERIFF- ARREST THOSE TWO CROOKS!
MICKEY!
AS A LAWYER I KNOW MY RIGHTS- WHO ARE YOU TO DEMAND OUR ARREST?
YEA! MAKE 'EM TAKE OFF HIS DISGUISE! SHERIFF!!
GUESS WE ALL WANNA KNOW WHO YOU ARE!
STOP! I'LL SHOW YOU WHO I AM!!
WHO CAN THE FOX BE? SEE TOMORROW!!
WALT DISNEY
9-12

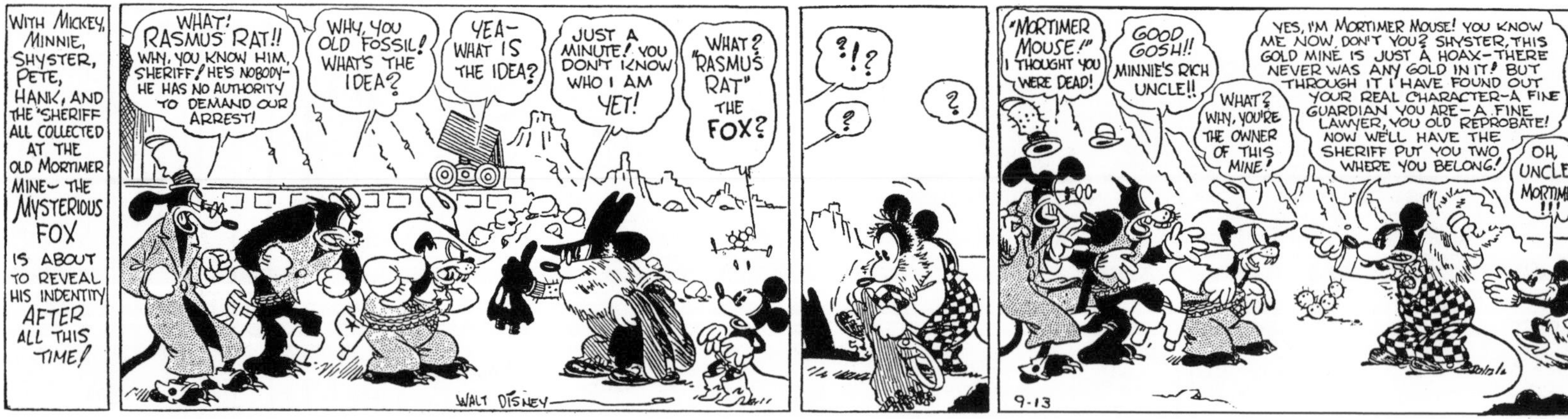
WITH MICKEY, MINNIE, SHYSTER, PETE, HANK, AND THE "SHERIFF" ALL COLLECTED AT THE OLD MORTIMER MINE- THE MYSTERIOUS FOX IS ABOUT TO REVEAL HIS INDENTITY AFTER ALL THIS TIME!
WHAT! RASMUS RAT!! WHY, YOU KNOW HIM, SHERIFF! HE'S NOBODY- HE HAS NO AUTHORITY TO DEMAND OUR ARREST!
WHY, YOU OLD FOSSIL! WHAT'S THE IDEA?
YEA- WHAT IS THE IDEA?
JUST A MINUTE! YOU DON'T KNOW WHO I AM YET!
WHAT? "RASMUS RAT" THE FOX?
WALT DISNEY
?!?
?
?
"MORTIMER MOUSE!" I THOUGHT YOU WERE DEAD!
GOOD GOSH!! MINNIE'S RICH UNCLE!!
WHAT? WHY, YOU'RE THE OWNER OF THIS MINE!
YES, I'M MORTIMER MOUSE! YOU KNOW ME NOW, DON'T YOU? SHYSTER, THIS GOLD MINE IS JUST A HOAX- THERE NEVER WAS ANY GOLD IN IT! BUT THROUGH IT I HAVE FOUND OUT YOUR REAL CHARACTER- A FINE GUARDIAN YOU ARE- A FINE LAWYER, YOU OLD REPROBATE! NOW WE'LL HAVE THE SHERIFF PUT YOU TWO WHERE YOU BELONG!
OH, UNCLE MORTIMER!!!
9-13

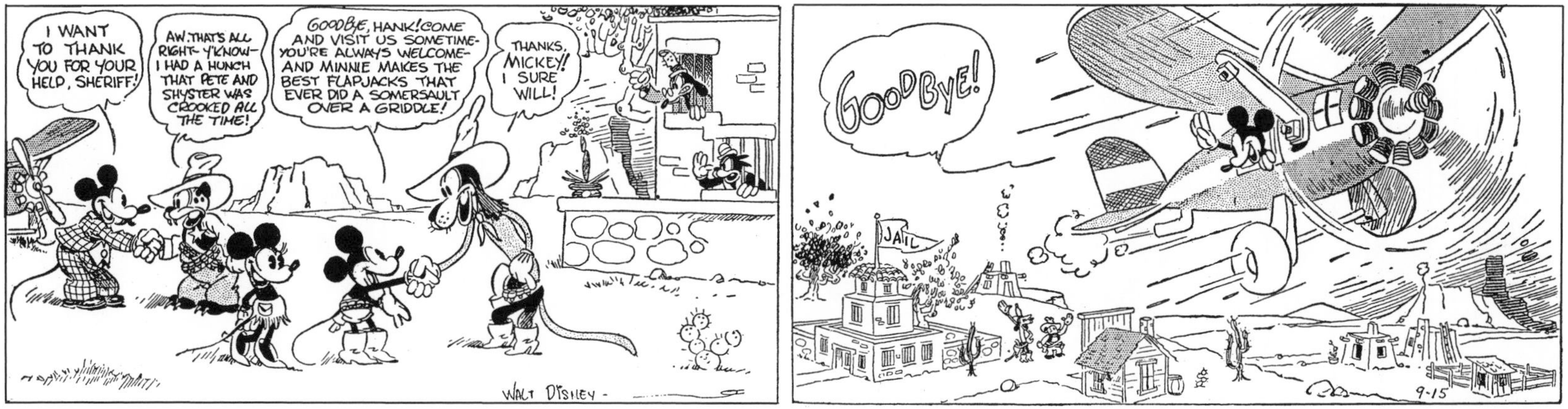
I WANT TO THANK YOU FOR YOUR HELP, SHERIFF!
AW. THAT'S ALL RIGHT— Y'KNOW— I HAD A HUNCH THAT PETE AND SHYSTER WAS CROOKED ALL THE TIME!
GOODBYE, HANK! COME AND VISIT US SOMETIME- YOU'RE ALWAYS WELCOME- AND MINNIE MAKES THE BEST FLAPJACKS THAT EVER DID A SOMERSAULT OVER A GRIDDLE!
THANKS, MICKEY! I SURE WILL!
WALT DISNEY
GOODBYE!
JAIL
9-15

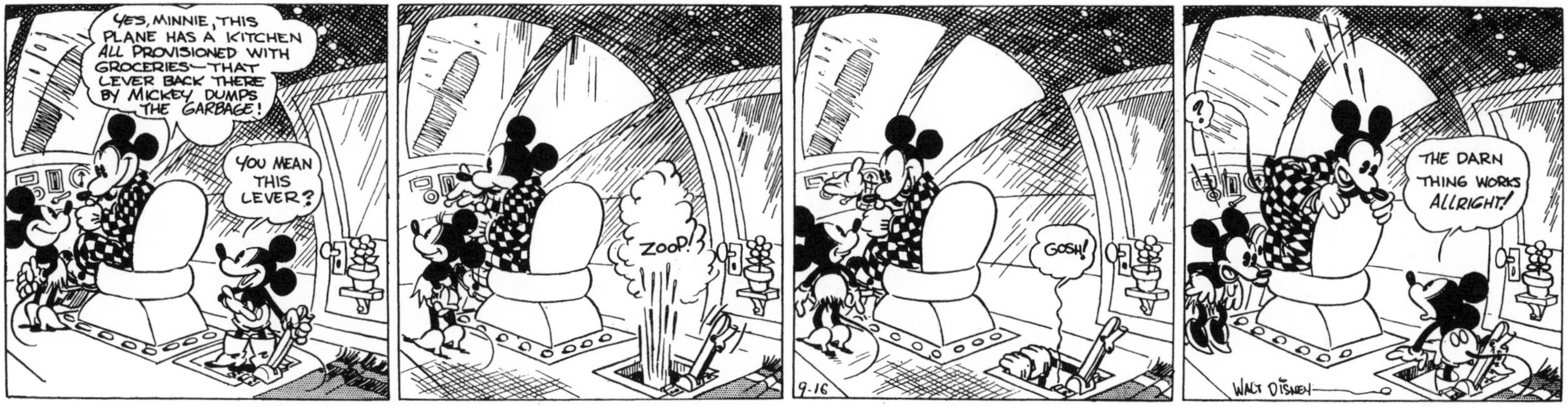
YES, MINNIE, THIS PLANE HAS A KITCHEN ALL PROVISIONED WITH GROCERIES— THAT LEVER BACK THERE BY MICKEY DUMPS THE GARBAGE!
YOU MEAN THIS LEVER?
ZOOP!
9-16
GOSH!
THE DARN THING WORKS ALLRIGHT!
WALT DISNEY

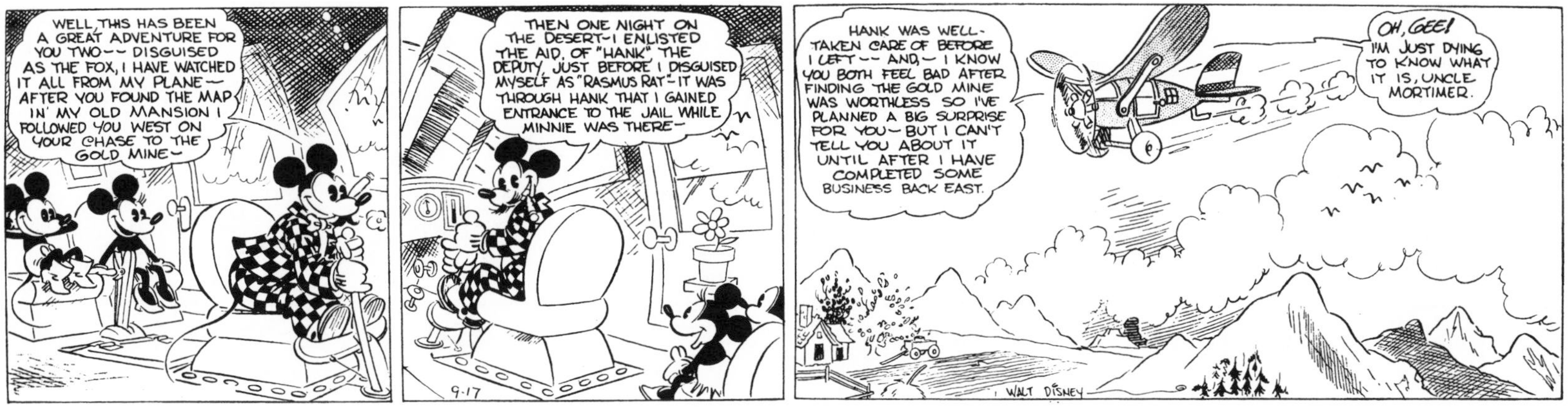
WELL, THIS HAS BEEN A GREAT ADVENTURE FOR YOU TWO— DISGUISED AS THE FOX, I HAVE WATCHED IT ALL FROM MY PLANE— AFTER YOU FOUND THE MAP IN MY OLD MANSION I FOLLOWED YOU WEST ON YOUR CHASE TO THE GOLD MINE—
THEN ONE NIGHT ON THE DESERT- I ENLISTED THE AID OF "HANK" THE DEPUTY, JUST BEFORE I DISGUISED MYSELF AS "RASMUS RAT"- IT WAS THROUGH HANK THAT I GAINED ENTRANCE TO THE JAIL WHILE MINNIE WAS THERE—
9-17
HANK WAS WELL-TAKEN CARE OF BEFORE I LEFT— AND,— I KNOW YOU BOTH FEEL BAD AFTER FINDING THE GOLD MINE WAS WORTHLESS SO I'VE PLANNED A BIG SURPRISE FOR YOU— BUT I CAN'T TELL YOU ABOUT IT UNTIL AFTER I HAVE COMPLETED SOME BUSINESS BACK EAST.
OH, GEE! I'M JUST DYING TO KNOW WHAT IT IS, UNCLE MORTIMER.
WALT DISNEY

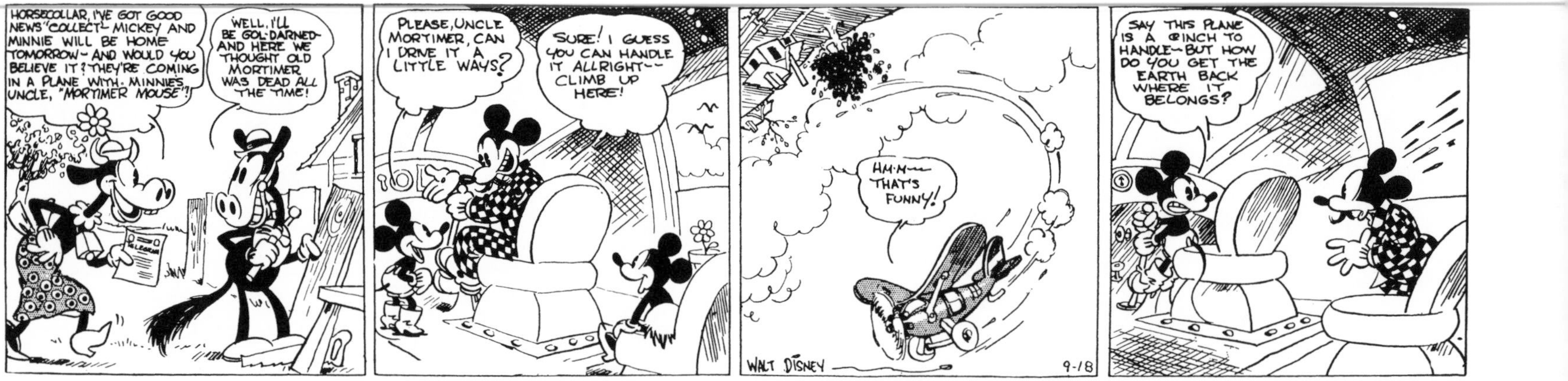
HORSECOLLAR, I'VE GOT GOOD NEWS "COLLECT"- MICKEY AND MINNIE WILL BE HOME TOMORROW- AND WOULD YOU BELIEVE IT? THEY'RE COMING IN A PLANE WITH MINNIE'S UNCLE, "MORTIMER MOUSE"!
WELL, I'LL BE GOL-DARNED- AND HERE WE THOUGHT OLD MORTIMER WAS DEAD ALL THE TIME!
PLEASE, UNCLE MORTIMER, CAN I DRIVE IT A LITTLE WAYS?
SURE! I GUESS YOU CAN HANDLE IT ALLRIGHT-- CLIMB UP HERE!
HM-M— THAT'S FUNNY!
WALT DISNEY
9-18
SAY THIS PLANE IS A CINCH TO HANDLE- BUT HOW DO YOU GET THE EARTH BACK WHERE IT BELONGS?

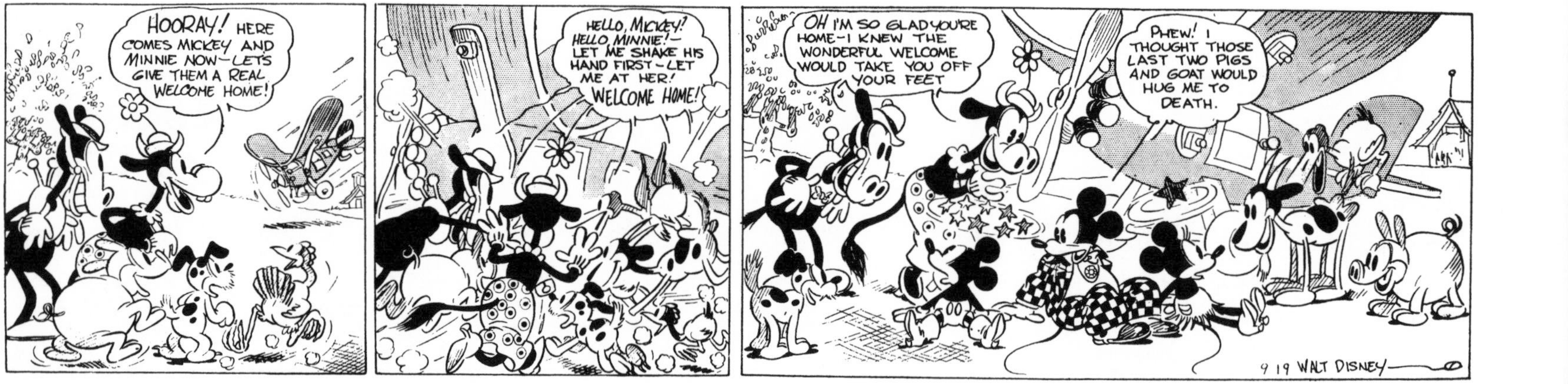
HOORAY! HERE COMES MICKEY AND MINNIE NOW- LET'S GIVE THEM A REAL WELCOME HOME!
HELLO, MICKEY! HELLO, MINNIE!- LET ME SHAKE HIS HAND FIRST- LET ME AT HER! WELCOME HOME!
OH I'M SO GLAD YOU'RE HOME- I KNEW THE WONDERFUL WELCOME WOULD TAKE YOU OFF YOUR FEET
PHEW! I THOUGHT THOSE LAST TWO PIGS AND GOAT WOULD HUG ME TO DEATH.
9 19 WALT DISNEY

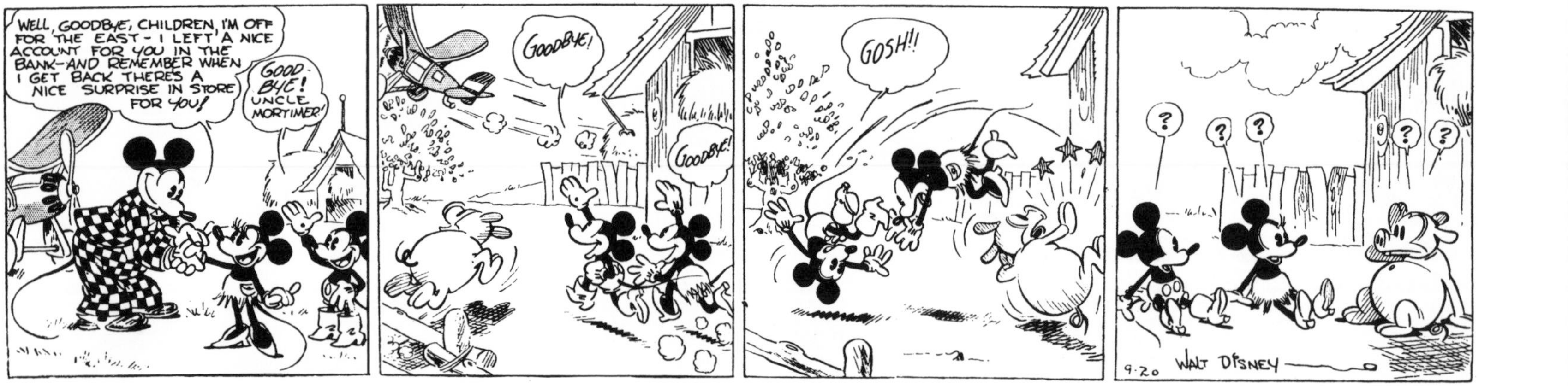
WELL, GOODBYE, CHILDREN, I'M OFF FOR THE EAST - I LEFT A NICE ACCOUNT FOR YOU IN THE BANK- AND REMEMBER WHEN I GET BACK THERE'S A NICE SURPRISE IN STORE FOR YOU!
GOOD-BYE! UNCLE MORTIMER!
GOODBYE!
GOODBYE!
GOSH!!
?
?
?
?
?
9-20
WALT DISNEY

MR. SLICKER AND THE EGG ROBBERS

PLUS! SHORT STORIES "MICKEY MOUSE MUSIC," "THE PICNIC," AND "TRAFFIC TROUBLES"

SEPTEMBER 22, 1930
–
JANUARY 17, 1931

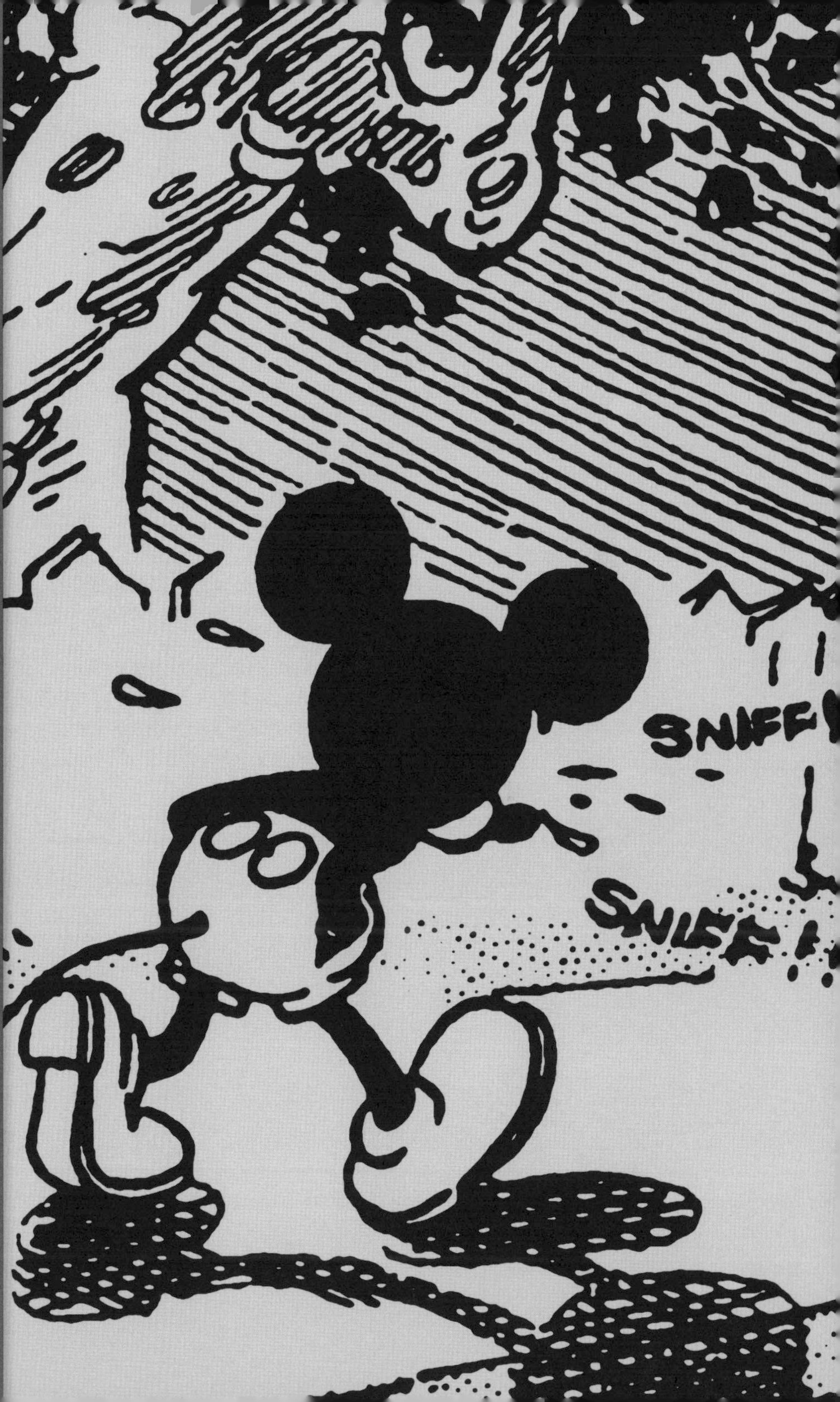

SNIFF!
SNIFF!

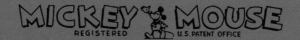

MICKEY MOUSE
REGISTERED U.S. PATENT OFFICE

SHEIKS AND LOVERS

Sometimes comic strips that seem innocent in one era become controversial in another. That's arguably the case with a one-week segment of "Mr. Slicker and the Egg Robbers," in which a lovelorn Mickey decides to end it once and for all. In 1930 as today, suicide was a grim fact of life; in 1930, however, it was far less common among youth. To tackle the concept with a young lead character like Mickey, then, was hardly to make undue light of a social ill. If anything, the story's treatment of suicide is proactive on those terms: its climax, in which Mickey firmly decides to stay alive, can easily be read as an authorial attempt to smarten up younger readers.

It was also an opportunity for humor, however unlikely. As later recollected by Floyd Gottfredson, Walt Disney pitched the idea to him as a comedy. "I said 'Walt, you're kidding!' He replied 'No, I'm not kidding. I think you could get a lot of funny stuff out of that.'"[1] Evidently, there were gags as well as pathos to be mined from the subject; but how would Floyd pull it off?

The answer appears to have come from filmic inspiration; suicide-as-comedy had been fodder for silent screen stars. Buster Keaton and Harold Lloyd ineptly tried rubbing themselves out in early 1920s shorts; Lloyd's *Haunted Spooks* (1920) even included the gag—reused by Mickey—of the hero jumping off a bridge only to land on a ship. But another inspiration for "Mr. Slicker" may well have been *The Suicide Sheik* (1929), an Oswald the Lucky Rabbit cartoon that Gottfredson likely saw while working as a projectionist.[2] Oswald's mishap with a falling safe added an extra twist to the backfiring-suicide concept: that of the backfires comically impacting passersby. While *Suicide Sheik* was actually a second-season Oswald short—made by former Disney crewmen without Walt's involvement—it's a safe bet to assume that its concepts hatched during Oswald's Disney tenure. Passing them on to Mickey wasn't much of a stretch.

In parting, we'd like to draw your attention to Minnie's mother and father, making their first of two appearances in this story. A close reading of "Mr. Slicker" reveals not just that Minnie lives at her parents' home, but that she still anticipates her college years. Such straightforward references to the Disney characters' actual ages would only very rarely be made in the years to come. [DG]

1 Floyd Gottfredson to Bill Blackbeard et al., *Mickey Mouse in Color* popular edition (New York: Pantheon, 1988), p. 107.

2 "As a projectionist in Utah, I had run all of Walt's 'Oswald the Lucky Rabbit' cartoons." Floyd Gottfredson to Jim Korkis, *Walt's People – Volume 8: Talking Disney with the Artists who Knew Him* (Bloomington: Xlibris, 2009), p. 278

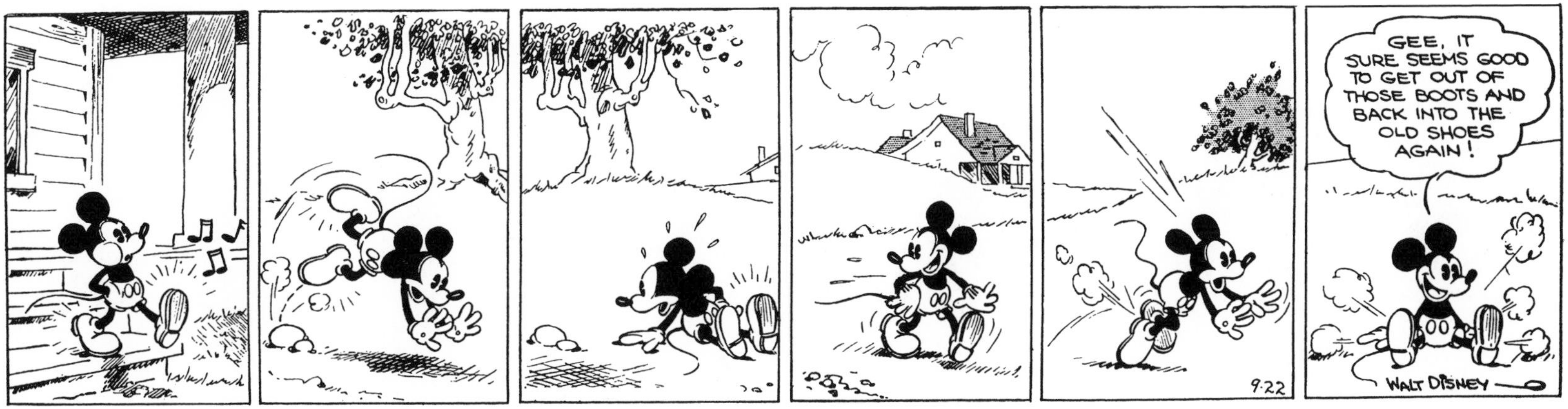
9-22
GEE, IT SURE SEEMS GOOD TO GET OUT OF THOSE BOOTS AND BACK INTO THE OLD SHOES AGAIN!
WALT DISNEY

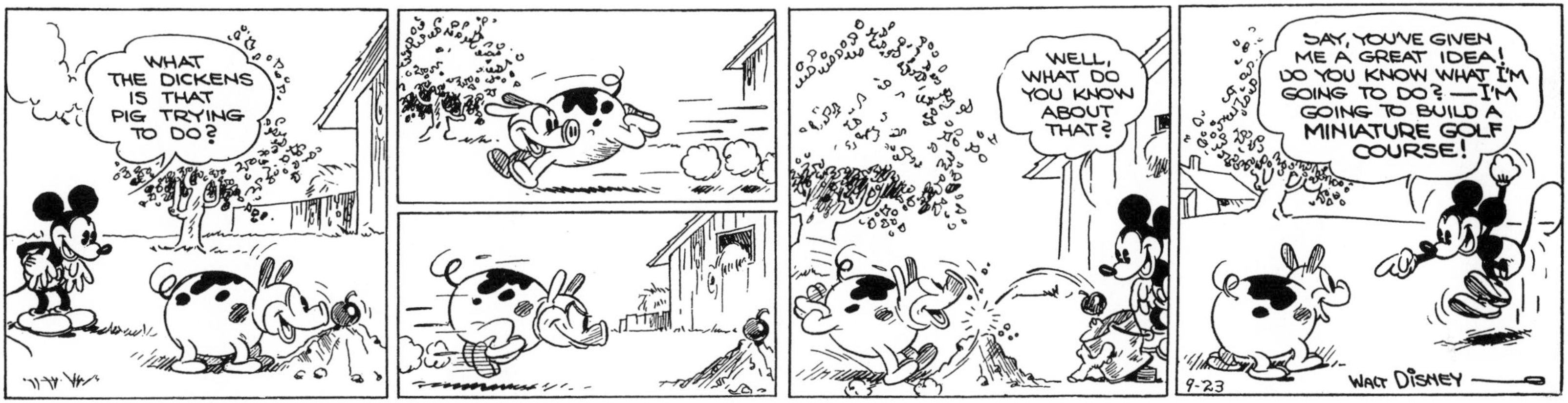
WHAT THE DICKENS IS THAT PIG TRYING TO DO?
WELL, WHAT DO YOU KNOW ABOUT THAT?
SAY, YOU'VE GIVEN ME A GREAT IDEA! DO YOU KNOW WHAT I'M GOING TO DO? —I'M GOING TO BUILD A MINIATURE GOLF COURSE!
9-23
WALT DISNEY

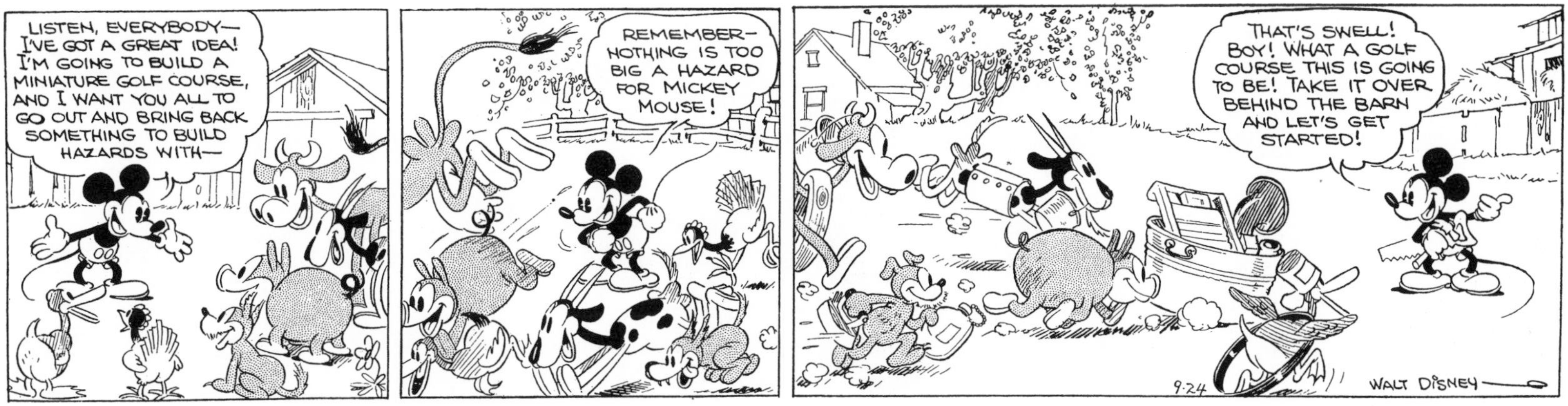
LISTEN, EVERYBODY— I'VE GOT A GREAT IDEA! I'M GOING TO BUILD A MINIATURE GOLF COURSE, AND I WANT YOU ALL TO GO OUT AND BRING BACK SOMETHING TO BUILD HAZARDS WITH—
REMEMBER— NOTHING IS TOO BIG A HAZARD FOR MICKEY MOUSE!
THAT'S SWELL! BOY! WHAT A GOLF COURSE THIS IS GOING TO BE! TAKE IT OVER BEHIND THE BARN AND LET'S GET STARTED!
9-24
WALT DISNEY

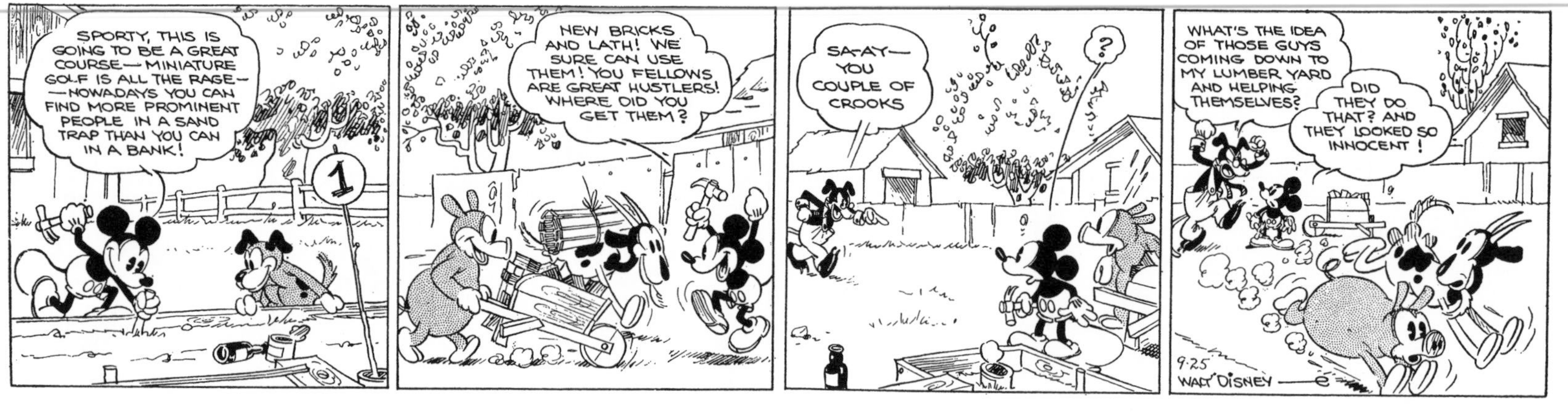
SPORTY, THIS IS GOING TO BE A GREAT COURSE— MINIATURE GOLF IS ALL THE RAGE— —NOWADAYS YOU CAN FIND MORE PROMINENT PEOPLE IN A SAND TRAP THAN YOU CAN IN A BANK!
1
NEW BRICKS AND LATH! WE SURE CAN USE THEM! YOU FELLOWS ARE GREAT HUSTLERS! WHERE DID YOU GET THEM?
SA-AY— YOU COUPLE OF CROOKS
?
WHAT'S THE IDEA OF THOSE GUYS COMING DOWN TO MY LUMBER YARD AND HELPING THEMSELVES?
DID THEY DO THAT? AND THEY LOOKED SO INNOCENT!
9-25
WALT DISNEY

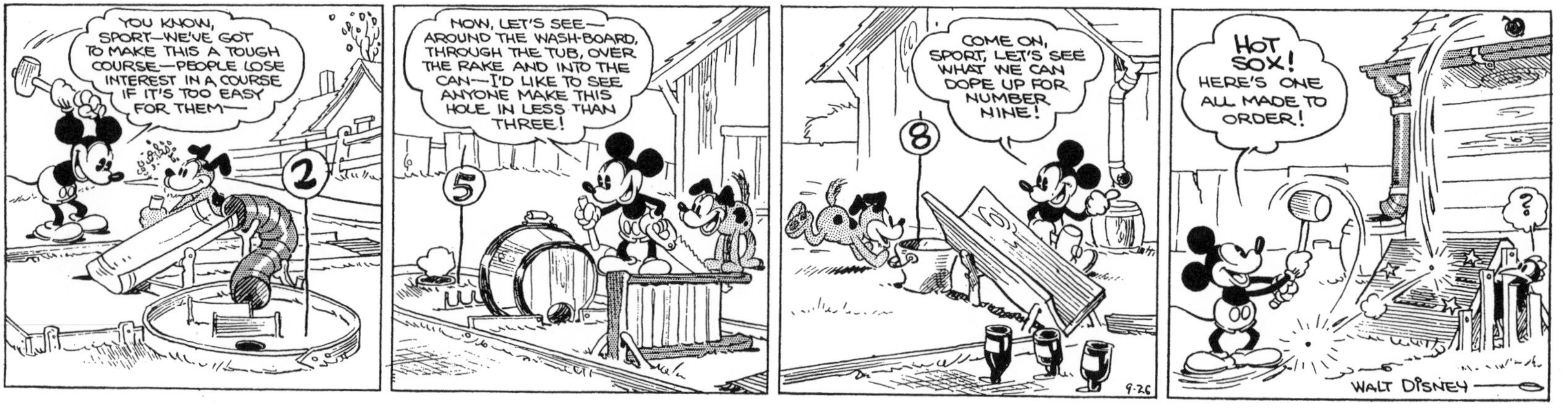
YOU KNOW, SPORT—WE'VE GOT TO MAKE THIS A TOUGH COURSE—PEOPLE LOSE INTEREST IN A COURSE IF IT'S TOO EASY FOR THEM—
2
NOW, LET'S SEE— AROUND THE WASH-BOARD, THROUGH THE TUB, OVER THE RAKE AND INTO THE CAN—I'D LIKE TO SEE ANYONE MAKE THIS HOLE IN LESS THAN THREE!
5
COME ON, SPORT, LET'S SEE WHAT WE CAN DOPE UP FOR NUMBER NINE!
8
9-26
HOT SOX! HERE'S ONE ALL MADE TO ORDER!
?
WALT DISNEY

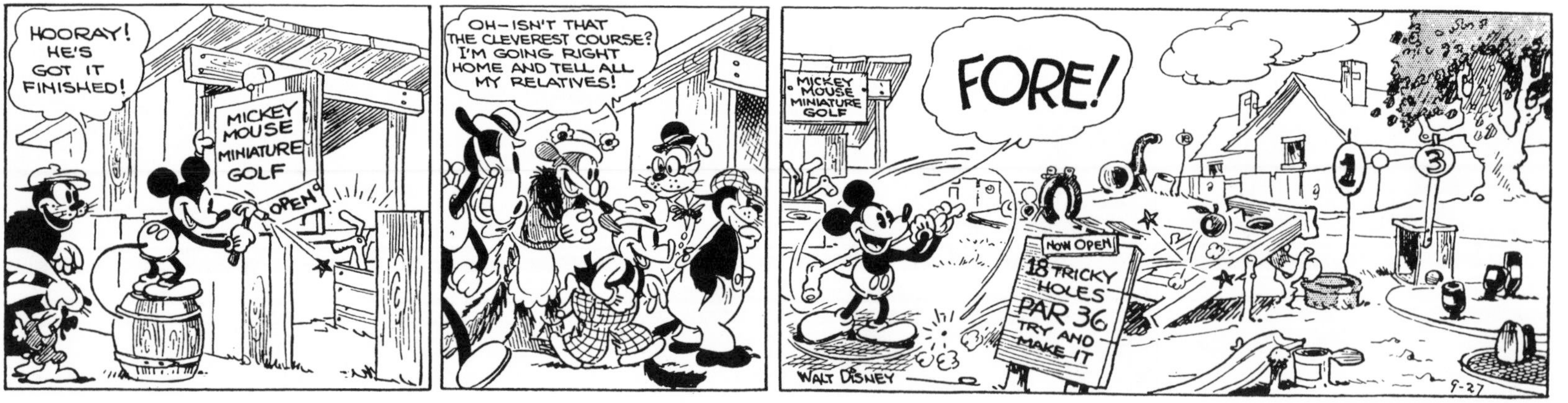
HOORAY! HE'S GOT IT FINISHED!
MICKEY MOUSE MINIATURE GOLF
OPEN
OH—ISN'T THAT THE CLEVEREST COURSE? I'M GOING RIGHT HOME AND TELL ALL MY RELATIVES!
MICKEY MOUSE MINIATURE GOLF
FORE!
NOW OPEN
18 TRICKY HOLES PAR 36 TRY AND MAKE IT
1
3
WALT DISNEY
9-27

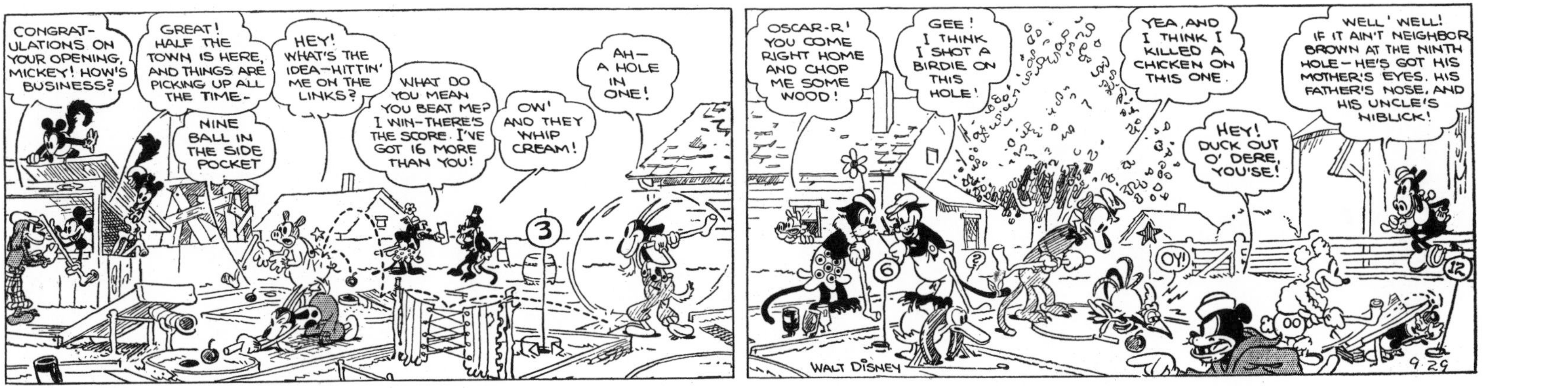
CONGRATULATIONS ON YOUR OPENING, MICKEY! HOW'S BUSINESS?
GREAT! HALF THE TOWN IS HERE, AND THINGS ARE PICKING UP ALL THE TIME-
NINE BALL IN THE SIDE POCKET
HEY! WHAT'S THE IDEA—HITTIN' ME ON THE LINKS?
WHAT DO YOU MEAN YOU BEAT ME? I WIN—THERE'S THE SCORE. I'VE GOT 16 MORE THAN YOU!
OW! AND THEY WHIP CREAM!
AH— A HOLE IN ONE!
3
OSCAR-R! YOU COME RIGHT HOME AND CHOP ME SOME WOOD!
GEE! I THINK I SHOT A BIRDIE ON THIS HOLE!
YEA, AND I THINK I KILLED A CHICKEN ON THIS ONE.
HEY! DUCK OUT O' DERE, YOU'SE!
OY!
6
WELL! WELL! IF IT AIN'T NEIGHBOR BROWN AT THE NINTH HOLE—HE'S GOT HIS MOTHER'S EYES, HIS FATHER'S NOSE, AND HIS UNCLE'S NIBLICK!
12
WALT DISNEY
9.29

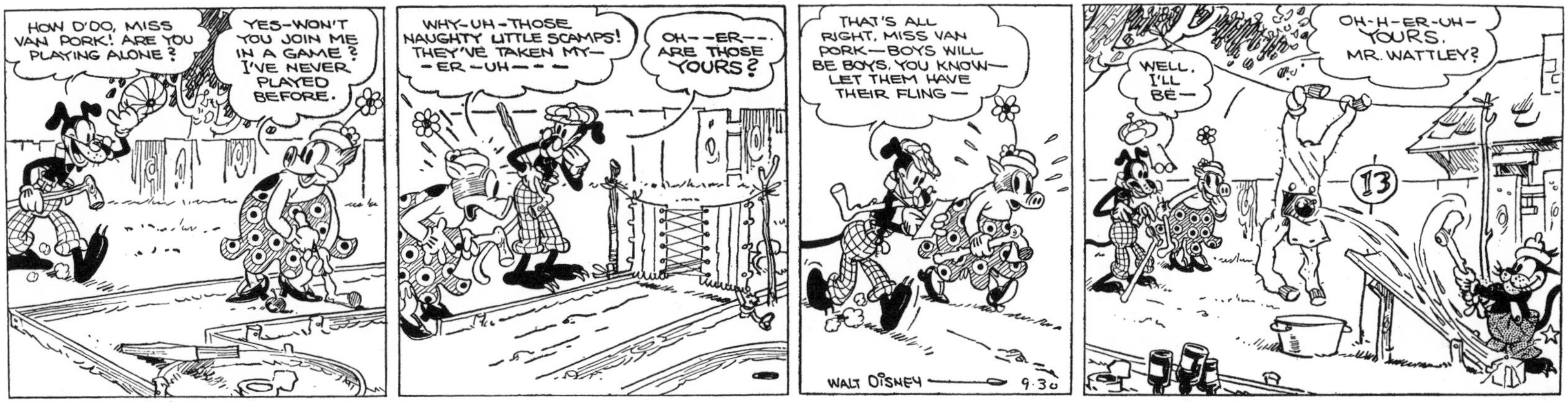
HOW D'DO, MISS VAN PORK! ARE YOU PLAYING ALONE?
YES—WON'T YOU JOIN ME IN A GAME? I'VE NEVER PLAYED BEFORE.
WHY-UH-THOSE NAUGHTY LITTLE SCAMPS! THEY'VE TAKEN MY— —ER—UH———
OH——ER—— ARE THOSE YOURS?
THAT'S ALL RIGHT, MISS VAN PORK—BOYS WILL BE BOYS, YOU KNOW—LET THEM HAVE THEIR FLING—
WALT DISNEY
9.30
WELL, I'LL BE—
OH-H-ER-UH— YOURS, MR. WATTLEY?
13

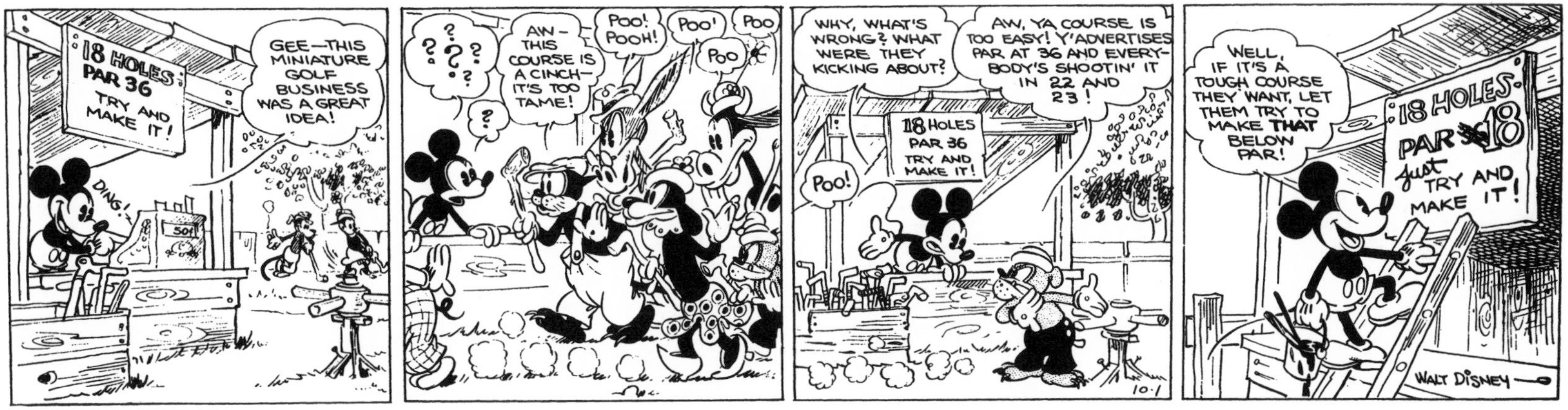
18 HOLES PAR 36 TRY AND MAKE IT!
GEE—THIS MINIATURE GOLF BUSINESS WAS A GREAT IDEA!
DING!
? ? ? ? ?
?
AW— THIS COURSE IS A CINCH— IT'S TOO TAME!
POO! POOH!
POO!
POO
POO
WHY, WHAT'S WRONG? WHAT WERE THEY KICKING ABOUT?
AW, YA COURSE IS TOO EASY! Y'ADVERTISES PAR AT 36 AND EVERYBODY'S SHOOTIN' IT IN 22 AND 23!
18 HOLES PAR 36 TRY AND MAKE IT!
POO!
10.1
WELL, IF IT'S A TOUGH COURSE THEY WANT, LET THEM TRY TO MAKE THAT BELOW PAR!
18 HOLES PAR 18 just TRY AND MAKE IT!
WALT DISNEY

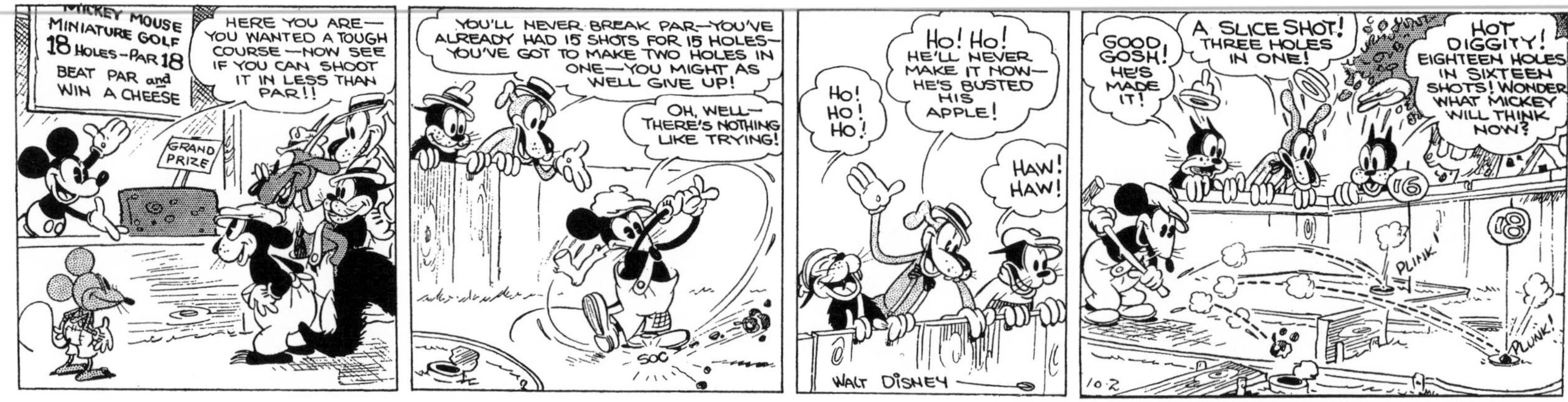
MICKEY MOUSE MINIATURE GOLF 18 HOLES—PAR 18 BEAT PAR and WIN A CHEESE
HERE YOU ARE—YOU WANTED A TOUGH COURSE—NOW SEE IF YOU CAN SHOOT IT IN LESS THAN PAR!!
GRAND PRIZE
YOU'LL NEVER BREAK PAR—YOU'VE ALREADY HAD 15 SHOTS FOR 15 HOLES—YOU'VE GOT TO MAKE TWO HOLES IN ONE—YOU MIGHT AS WELL GIVE UP!
OH, WELL—THERE'S NOTHING LIKE TRYING!
SOC
HO! HO! HO!
HO! HO! HE'LL NEVER MAKE IT NOW—HE'S BUSTED HIS APPLE!
HAW! HAW!
WALT DISNEY
GOOD GOSH! HE'S MADE IT!
A SLICE SHOT! THREE HOLES IN ONE!
HOT DIGGITY! EIGHTEEN HOLES IN SIXTEEN SHOTS! WONDER WHAT MICKEY WILL THINK NOW?
16
18
PLINK!
PLINK!
10-2

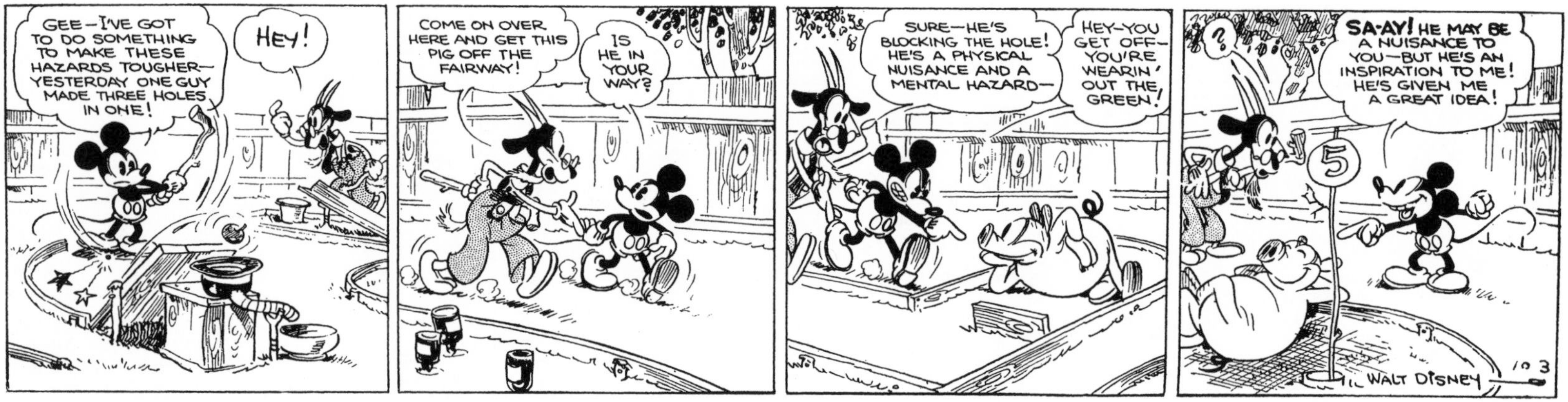
GEE—I'VE GOT TO DO SOMETHING TO MAKE THESE HAZARDS TOUGHER—YESTERDAY ONE GUY MADE THREE HOLES IN ONE!
HEY!
COME ON OVER HERE AND GET THIS PIG OFF THE FAIRWAY!
IS HE IN YOUR WAY?
SURE—HE'S BLOCKING THE HOLE! HE'S A PHYSICAL NUISANCE AND A MENTAL HAZARD—
HEY—YOU GET OFF—YOU'RE WEARIN' OUT THE GREEN!
?
SA-AY! HE MAY BE A NUISANCE TO YOU—BUT HE'S AN INSPIRATION TO ME! HE'S GIVEN ME A GREAT IDEA!
5
WALT DISNEY
10-3

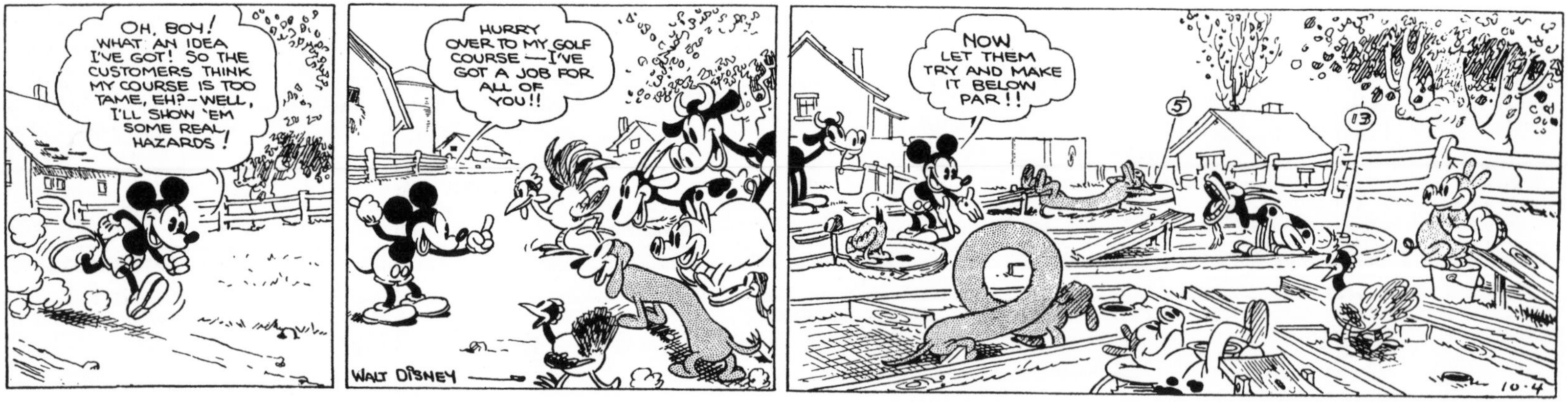
OH, BOY! WHAT AN IDEA I'VE GOT! SO THE CUSTOMERS THINK MY COURSE IS TOO TAME, EH?—WELL, I'LL SHOW 'EM SOME REAL HAZARDS!
HURRY OVER TO MY GOLF COURSE—I'VE GOT A JOB FOR ALL OF YOU!!
WALT DISNEY
NOW LET THEM TRY AND MAKE IT BELOW PAR!!
5
13
10-4

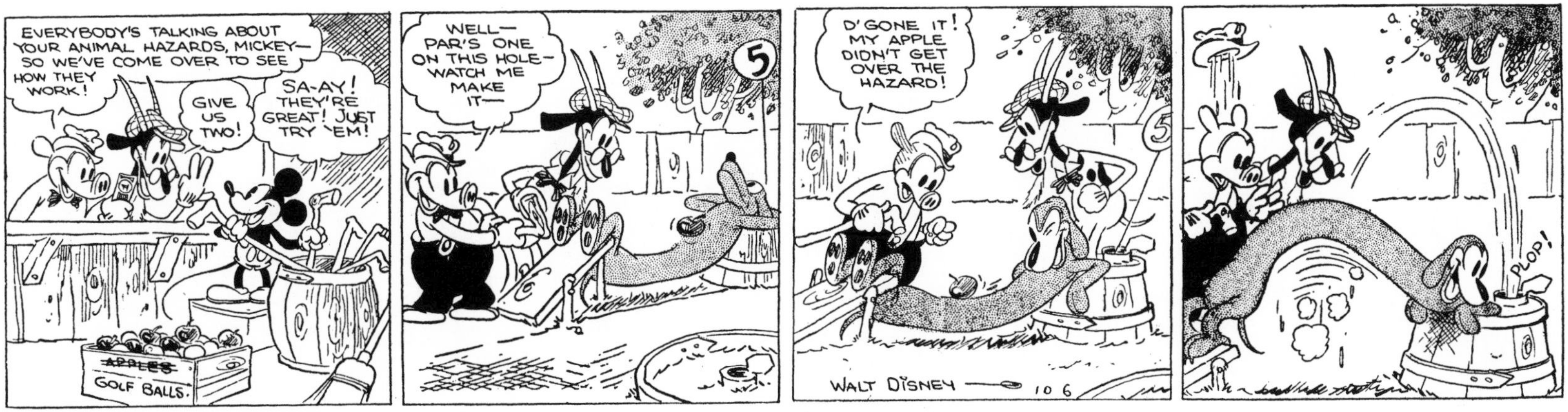
EVERYBODY'S TALKING ABOUT YOUR ANIMAL HAZARDS, MICKEY— SO WE'VE COME OVER TO SEE HOW THEY WORK!
GIVE US TWO!
SA-AY! THEY'RE GREAT! JUST TRY 'EM!
APPLES
GOLF BALLS.
WELL— PAR'S ONE ON THIS HOLE— WATCH ME MAKE IT—
5
D'GONE IT! MY APPLE DIDN'T GET OVER THE HAZARD!
5
WALT DISNEY
10 6
PLOP!

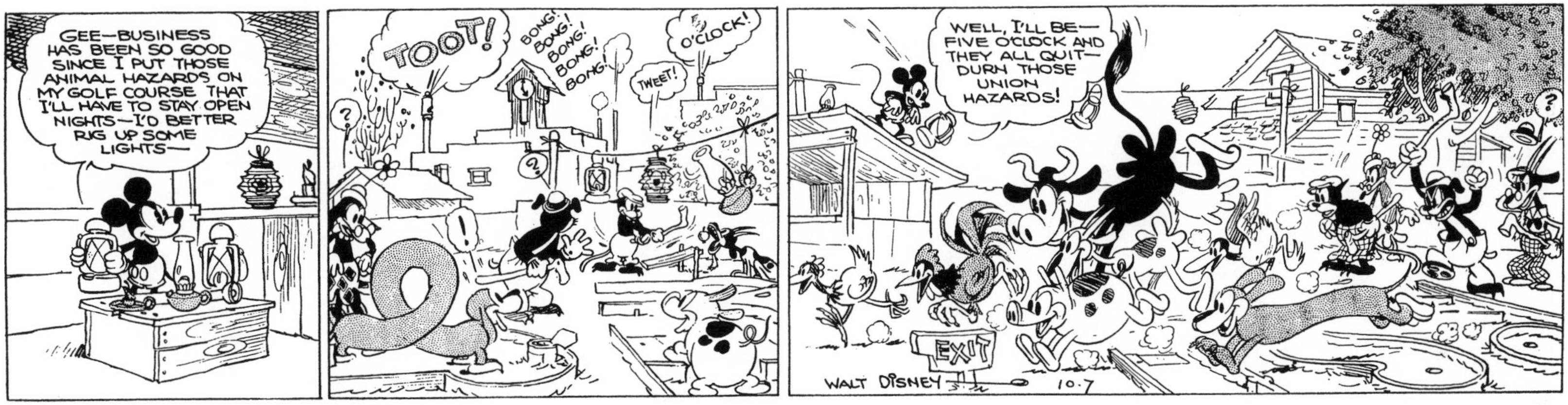
GEE—BUSINESS HAS BEEN SO GOOD SINCE I PUT THOSE ANIMAL HAZARDS ON MY GOLF COURSE THAT I'LL HAVE TO STAY OPEN NIGHTS—I'D BETTER RIG UP SOME LIGHTS—
TOOT!
BONG! BONG! BONG! BONG! BONG!
TWEET!
5 O'CLOCK!
WELL, I'LL BE— FIVE O'CLOCK AND THEY ALL QUIT— DURN THOSE UNION HAZARDS!
EXIT
WALT DISNEY
10-7

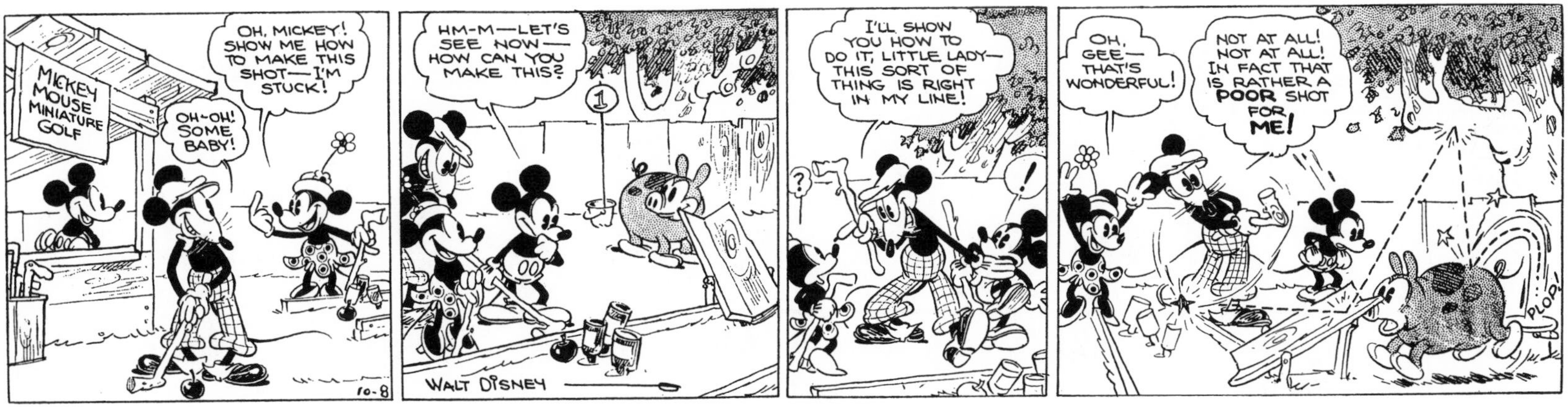
MICKEY MOUSE MINIATURE GOLF
OH, MICKEY! SHOW ME HOW TO MAKE THIS SHOT—I'M STUCK!
OH-OH! SOME BABY!
10-8
HM-M—LET'S SEE NOW— HOW CAN YOU MAKE THIS?
1
WALT DISNEY
I'LL SHOW YOU HOW TO DO IT, LITTLE LADY— THIS SORT OF THING IS RIGHT IN MY LINE!
OH, GEE— THAT'S WONDERFUL!
NOT AT ALL! NOT AT ALL! IN FACT THAT IS RATHER A **POOR** SHOT FOR **ME!**
PLOP!

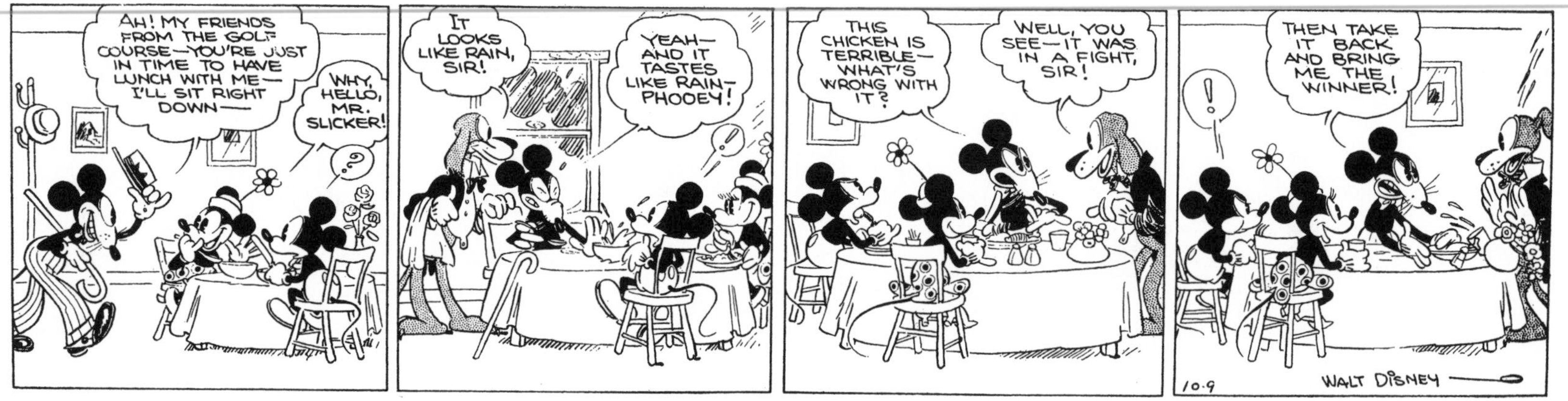
AH! MY FRIENDS FROM THE GOLF COURSE—YOU'RE JUST IN TIME TO HAVE LUNCH WITH ME—I'LL SIT RIGHT DOWN—
WHY, HELLO, MR. SLICKER!
?
IT LOOKS LIKE RAIN, SIR!
YEAH—AND IT TASTES LIKE RAIN-PHOOEY!
!
THIS CHICKEN IS TERRIBLE—WHAT'S WRONG WITH IT?
WELL, YOU SEE—IT WAS IN A FIGHT, SIR!
!
THEN TAKE IT BACK AND BRING ME THE WINNER!
10-9
WALT DISNEY

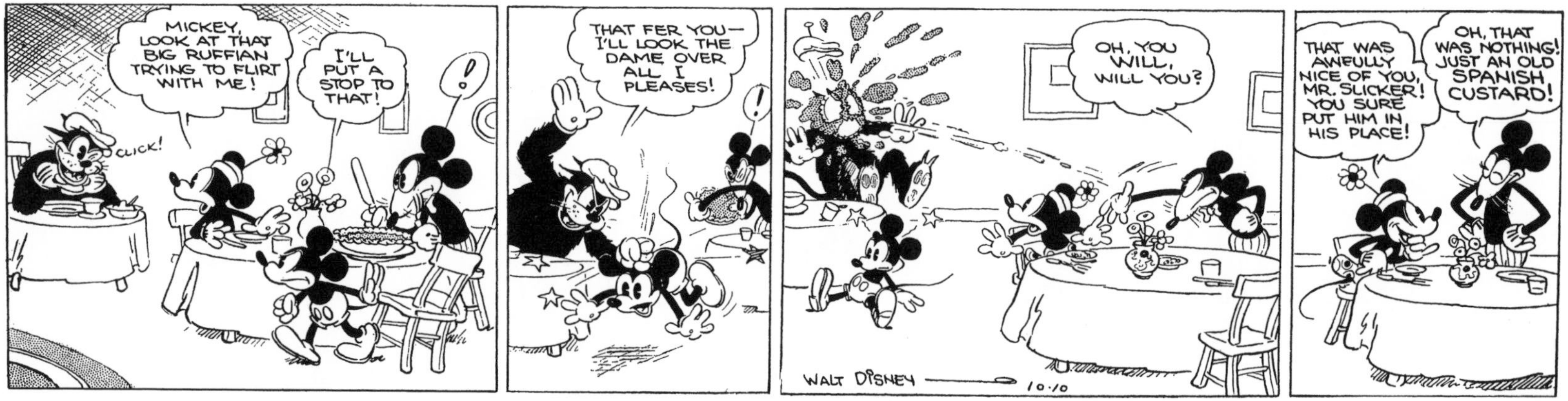
MICKEY, LOOK AT THAT BIG RUFFIAN TRYING TO FLIRT WITH ME!
CLICK!
I'LL PUT A STOP TO THAT!
!
THAT FER YOU—I'LL LOOK THE DAME OVER ALL I PLEASES!
!
OH, YOU WILL, WILL YOU?
WALT DISNEY
10-10
THAT WAS AWFULLY NICE OF YOU, MR. SLICKER! YOU SURE PUT HIM IN HIS PLACE!
OH, THAT WAS NOTHING! JUST AN OLD SPANISH CUSTARD!

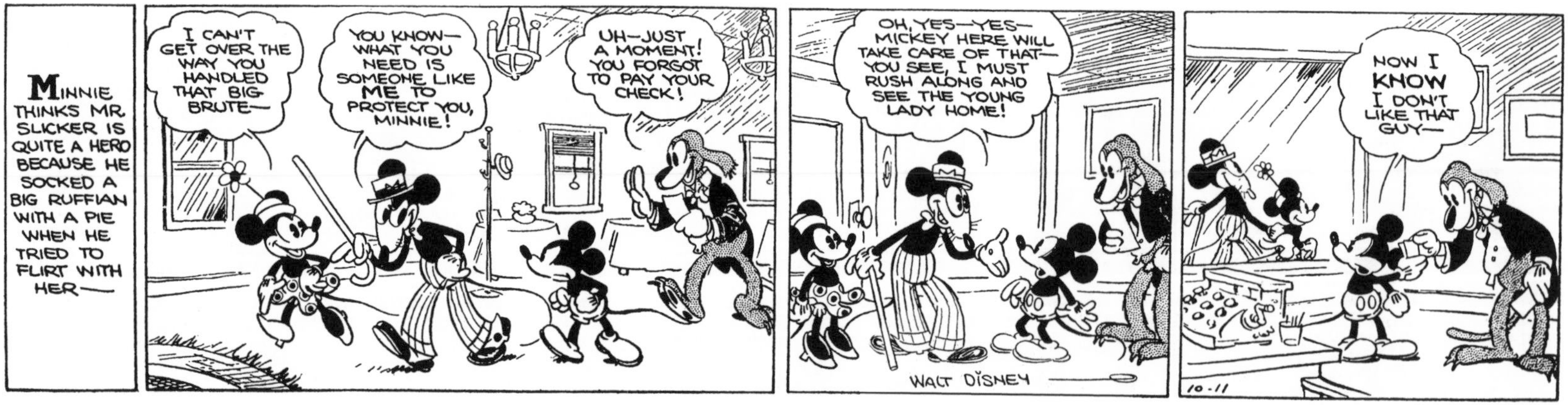
MINNIE THINKS MR. SLICKER IS QUITE A HERO BECAUSE HE SOCKED A BIG RUFFIAN WITH A PIE WHEN HE TRIED TO FLIRT WITH HER—
I CAN'T GET OVER THE WAY YOU HANDLED THAT BIG BRUTE—
YOU KNOW—WHAT YOU NEED IS SOMEONE LIKE ME TO PROTECT YOU, MINNIE!
UH—JUST A MOMENT! YOU FORGOT TO PAY YOUR CHECK!
OH, YES—YES—MICKEY HERE WILL TAKE CARE OF THAT—YOU SEE, I MUST RUSH ALONG AND SEE THE YOUNG LADY HOME!
WALT DISNEY
NOW I KNOW I DON'T LIKE THAT GUY—
10-11

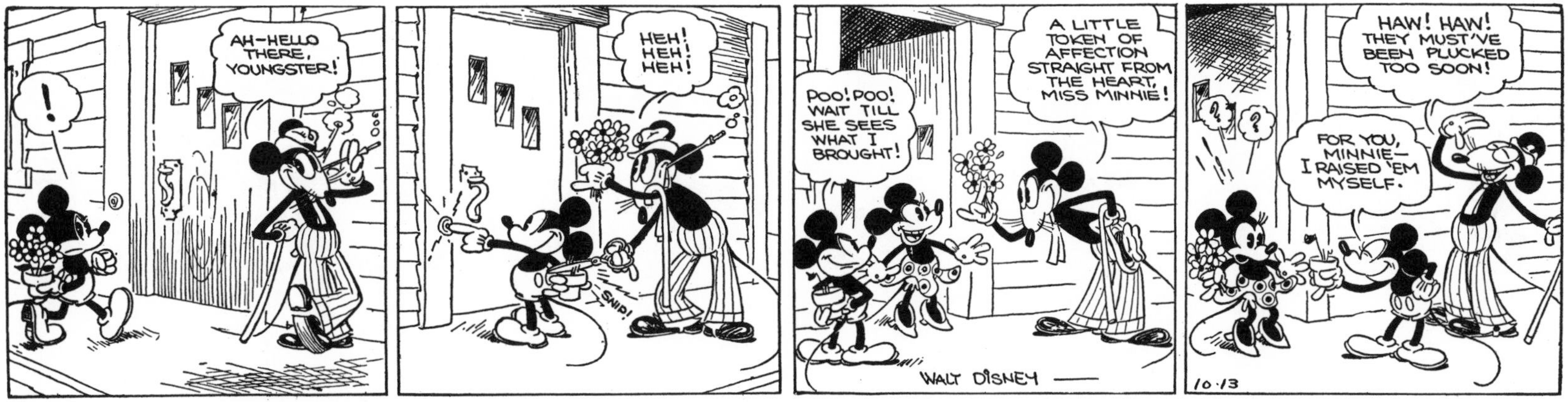
!
AH-HELLO THERE, YOUNGSTER!
HEH! HEH! HEH!
SNIP!
POO! POO! WAIT TILL SHE SEES WHAT I BROUGHT!
A LITTLE TOKEN OF AFFECTION STRAIGHT FROM THE HEART, MISS MINNIE!
WALT DISNEY
? ?
FOR YOU, MINNIE— I RAISED 'EM MYSELF.
HAW! HAW! THEY MUST'VE BEEN PLUCKED TOO SOON!
10·13

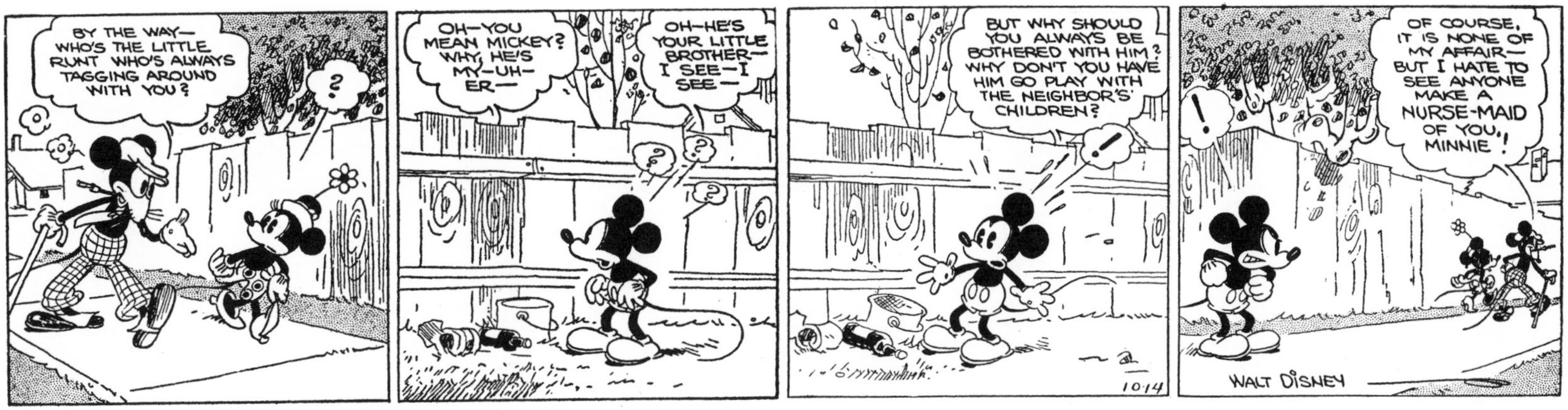
BY THE WAY— WHO'S THE LITTLE RUNT WHO'S ALWAYS TAGGING AROUND WITH YOU?
?
OH—YOU MEAN MICKEY? WHY, HE'S MY—UH— ER—
OH—HE'S YOUR LITTLE BROTHER— I SEE—I SEE—
? ? ?
BUT WHY SHOULD YOU ALWAYS BE BOTHERED WITH HIM? WHY DON'T YOU HAVE HIM GO PLAY WITH THE NEIGHBOR'S CHILDREN?
!
10·14
!
OF COURSE, IT IS NONE OF MY AFFAIR— BUT I HATE TO SEE ANYONE MAKE A NURSE-MAID OF YOU, MINNIE!
WALT DISNEY

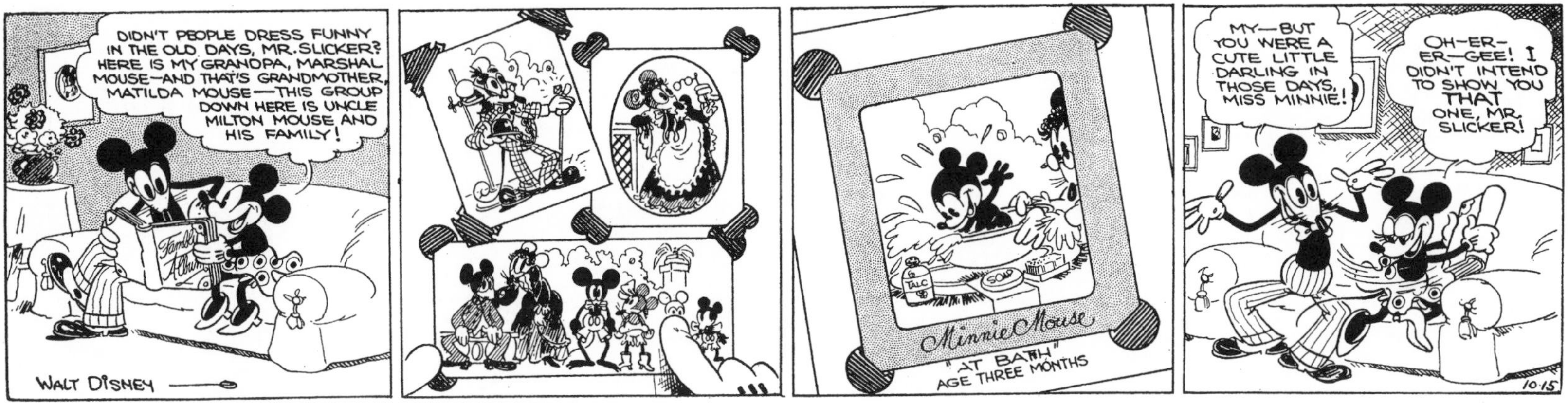
DIDN'T PEOPLE DRESS FUNNY IN THE OLD DAYS, MR. SLICKER? HERE IS MY GRANDPA, MARSHAL MOUSE—AND THAT'S GRANDMOTHER MATILDA MOUSE—THIS GROUP DOWN HERE IS UNCLE MILTON MOUSE AND HIS FAMILY!
Family Album
WALT DISNEY
TALC
SOAP
Minnie Mouse
"AT BATH"
AGE THREE MONTHS
MY—BUT YOU WERE A CUTE LITTLE DARLING IN THOSE DAYS, MISS MINNIE!
OH—ER— ER—GEE! I DIDN'T INTEND TO SHOW YOU THAT ONE, MR. SLICKER!
10·15

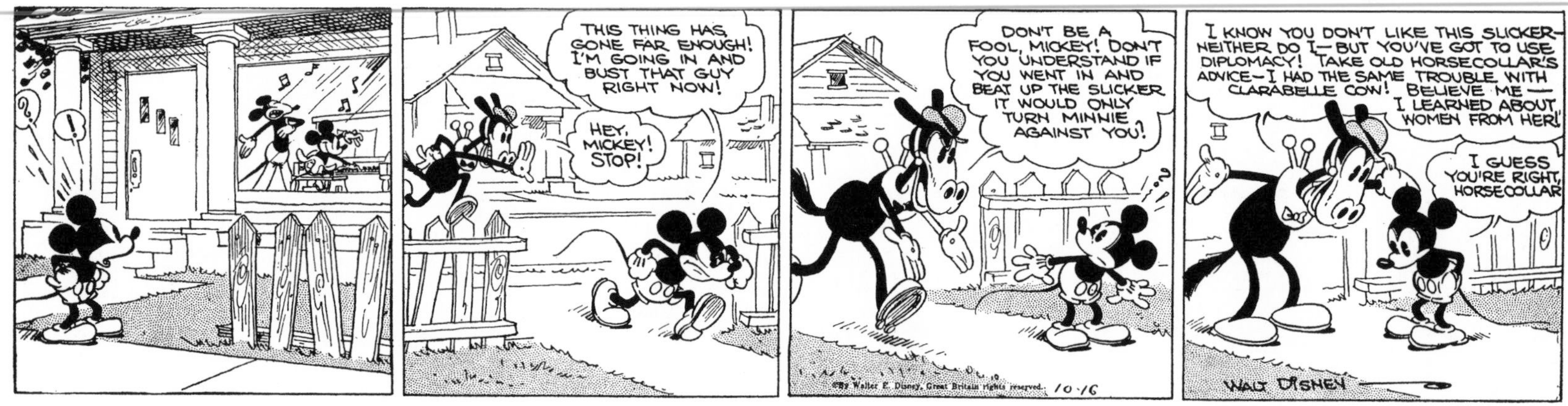
THIS THING HAS GONE FAR ENOUGH! I'M GOING IN AND BUST THAT GUY RIGHT NOW!
HEY, MICKEY! STOP!
DON'T BE A FOOL, MICKEY! DON'T YOU UNDERSTAND IF YOU WENT IN AND BEAT UP THE SLICKER IT WOULD ONLY TURN MINNIE AGAINST YOU!
©By Walter E. Disney, Great Britain rights reserved.
10-16
I KNOW YOU DON'T LIKE THIS SLICKER—NEITHER DO I—BUT YOU'VE GOT TO USE DIPLOMACY! TAKE OLD HORSECOLLAR'S ADVICE—I HAD THE SAME TROUBLE WITH CLARABELLE COW! BELIEVE ME—I LEARNED ABOUT WOMEN FROM HER!
I GUESS YOU'RE RIGHT, HORSECOLLAR
WALT DISNEY

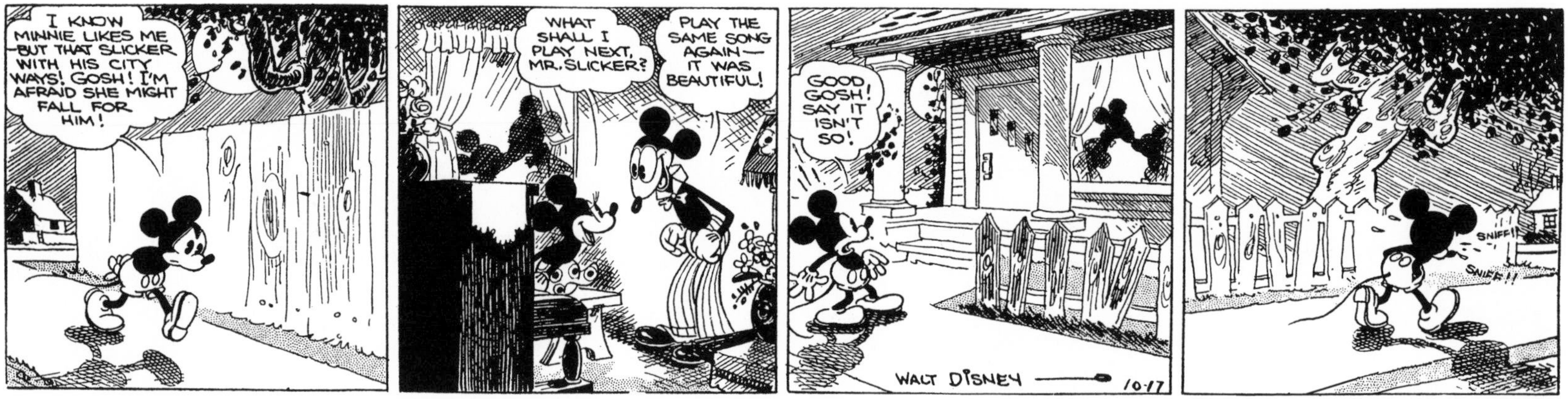
I KNOW MINNIE LIKES ME—BUT THAT SLICKER WITH HIS CITY WAYS! GOSH! I'M AFRAID SHE MIGHT FALL FOR HIM!
WHAT SHALL I PLAY NEXT, MR. SLICKER?
PLAY THE SAME SONG AGAIN—IT WAS BEAUTIFUL!
GOOD GOSH! SAY IT ISN'T SO!
WALT DISNEY
10-17
SNIFF!!
SNIFF!!

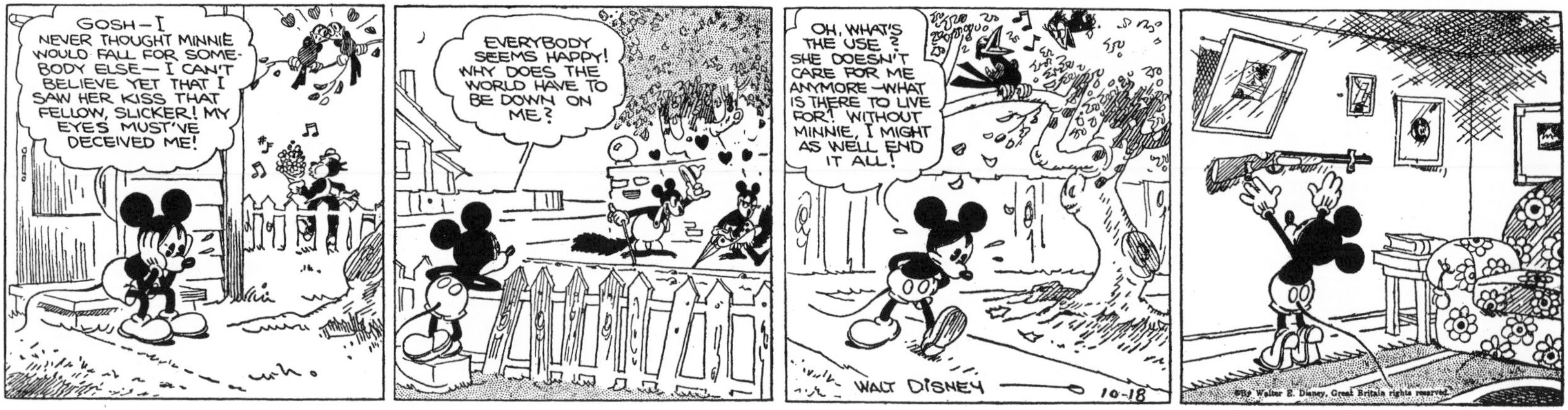
GOSH—I NEVER THOUGHT MINNIE WOULD FALL FOR SOMEBODY ELSE—I CAN'T BELIEVE YET THAT I SAW HER KISS THAT FELLOW, SLICKER! MY EYES MUST'VE DECEIVED ME!
EVERYBODY SEEMS HAPPY! WHY DOES THE WORLD HAVE TO BE DOWN ON ME?
OH, WHAT'S THE USE? SHE DOESN'T CARE FOR ME ANYMORE—WHAT IS THERE TO LIVE FOR? WITHOUT MINNIE, I MIGHT AS WELL END IT ALL!
WALT DISNEY
10-18
©By Walter E. Disney, Great Britain rights reserved.

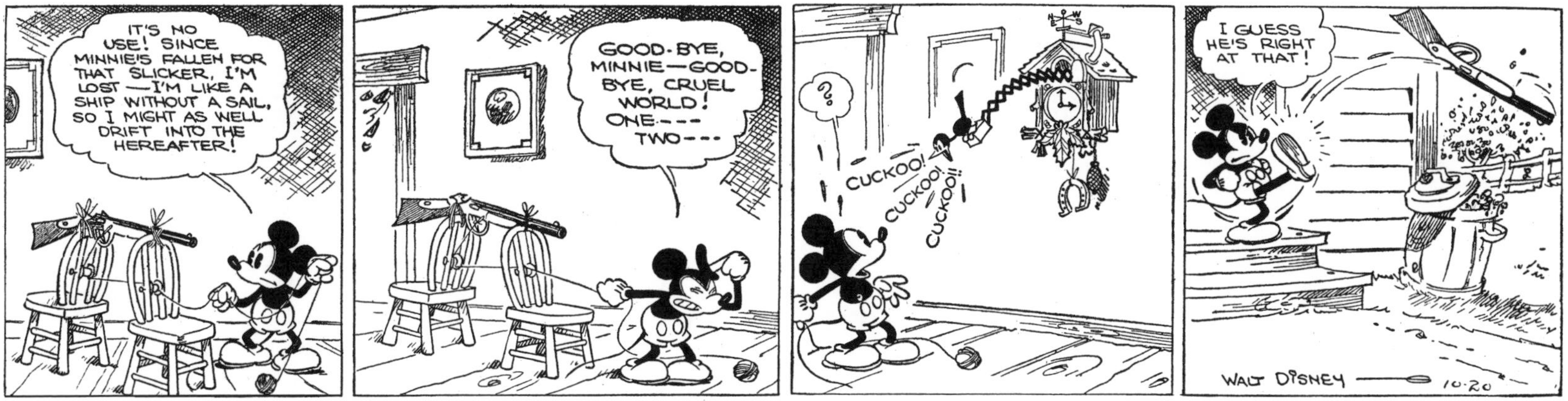
IT'S NO USE! SINCE MINNIE'S FALLEN FOR THAT SLICKER, I'M LOST—I'M LIKE A SHIP WITHOUT A SAIL, SO I MIGHT AS WELL DRIFT INTO THE HEREAFTER!
GOOD-BYE, MINNIE—GOOD-BYE, CRUEL WORLD! ONE--- TWO---
?
CUCKOO!
CUCKOO!
CUCKOO!!
I GUESS HE'S RIGHT AT THAT!
WALT DISNEY
10-20

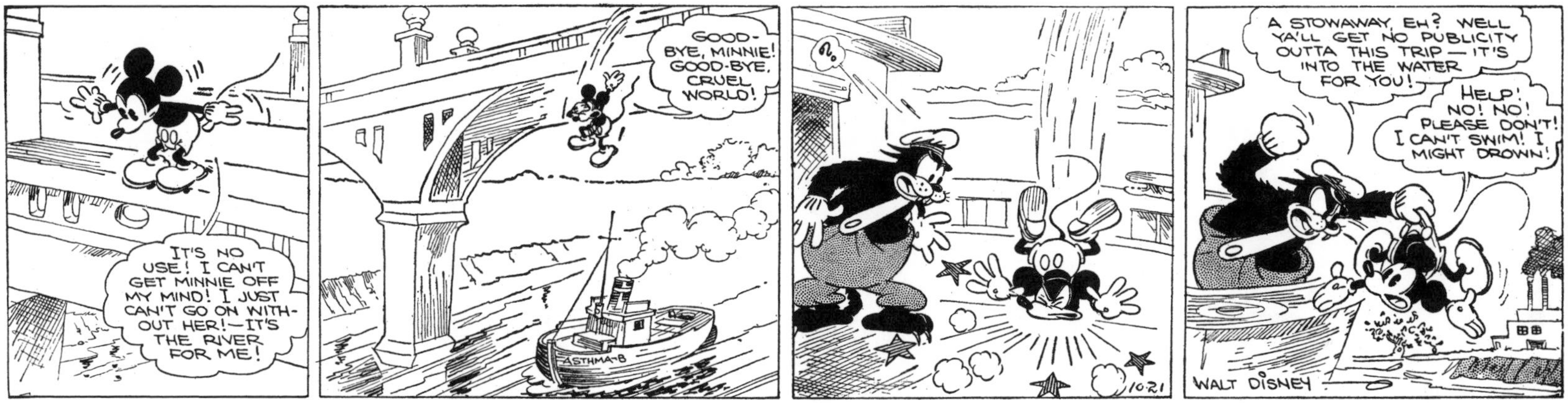
IT'S NO USE! I CAN'T GET MINNIE OFF MY MIND! I JUST CAN'T GO ON WITHOUT HER!—IT'S THE RIVER FOR ME!
GOOD-BYE, MINNIE! GOOD-BYE, CRUEL WORLD!
ASTHMA-B
?
10-21
A STOWAWAY, EH? WELL YA'LL GET NO PUBLICITY OUTTA THIS TRIP—IT'S INTO THE WATER FOR YOU!
HELP! NO! NO! PLEASE DON'T! I CAN'T SWIM! I MIGHT DROWN!
WALT DISNEY

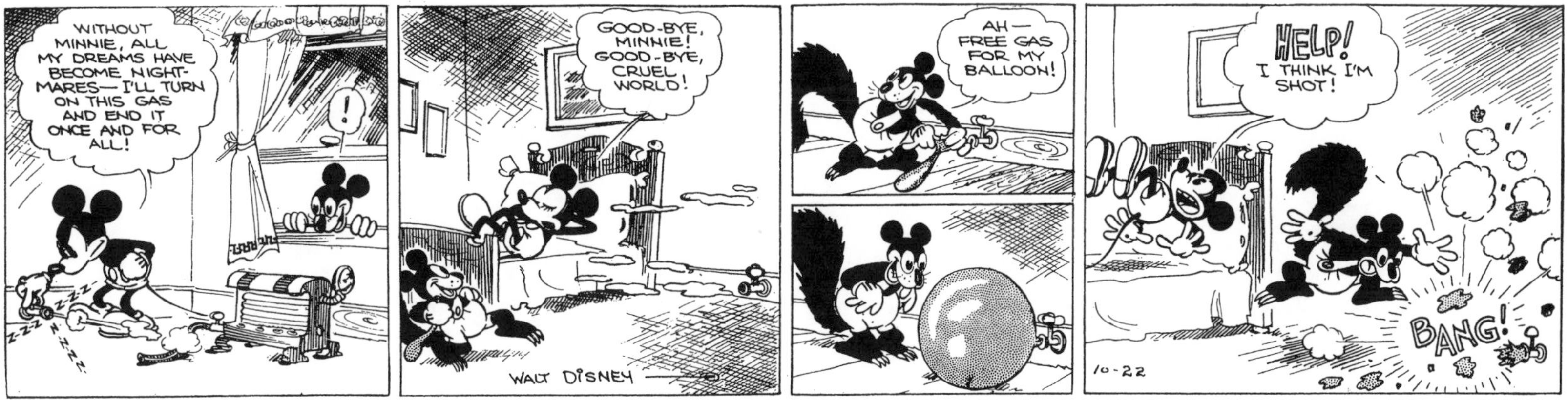
WITHOUT MINNIE, ALL MY DREAMS HAVE BECOME NIGHTMARES—I'LL TURN ON THIS GAS AND END IT ONCE AND FOR ALL!
!
GOOD-BYE, MINNIE! GOOD-BYE, CRUEL WORLD!
WALT DISNEY
AH—FREE GAS FOR MY BALLOON!
HELP! I THINK I'M SHOT!
BANG!
10-22

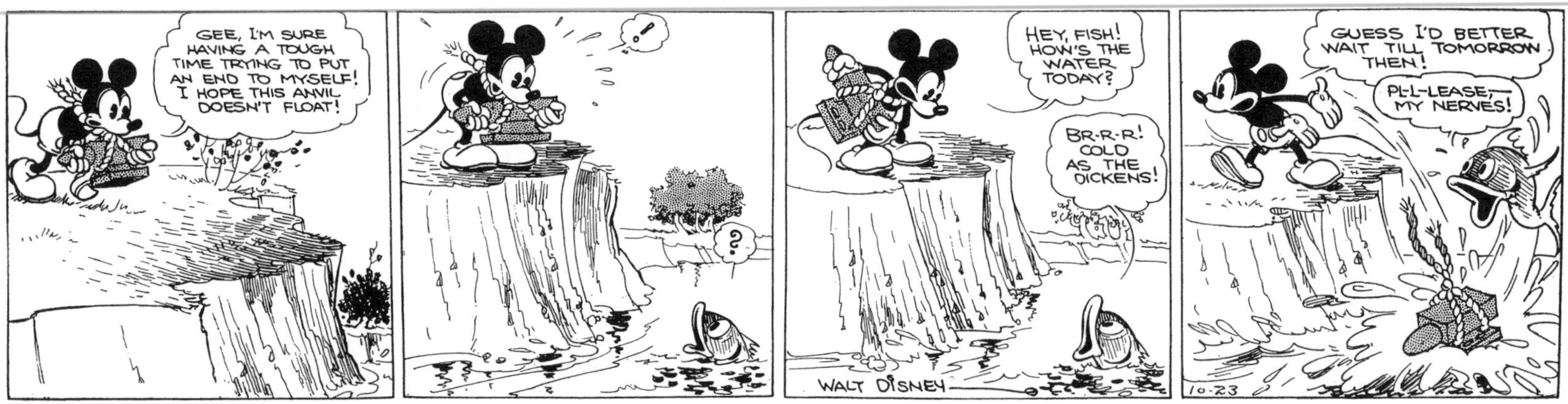
GEE, I'M SURE HAVING A TOUGH TIME TRYING TO PUT AN END TO MYSELF! I HOPE THIS ANVIL DOESN'T FLOAT!
!
?
HEY, FISH! HOW'S THE WATER TODAY?
BR-R-R! COLD AS THE DICKENS!
WALT DISNEY
GUESS I'D BETTER WAIT TILL TOMORROW THEN!
PL-L-LEASE,— MY NERVES!
10·23

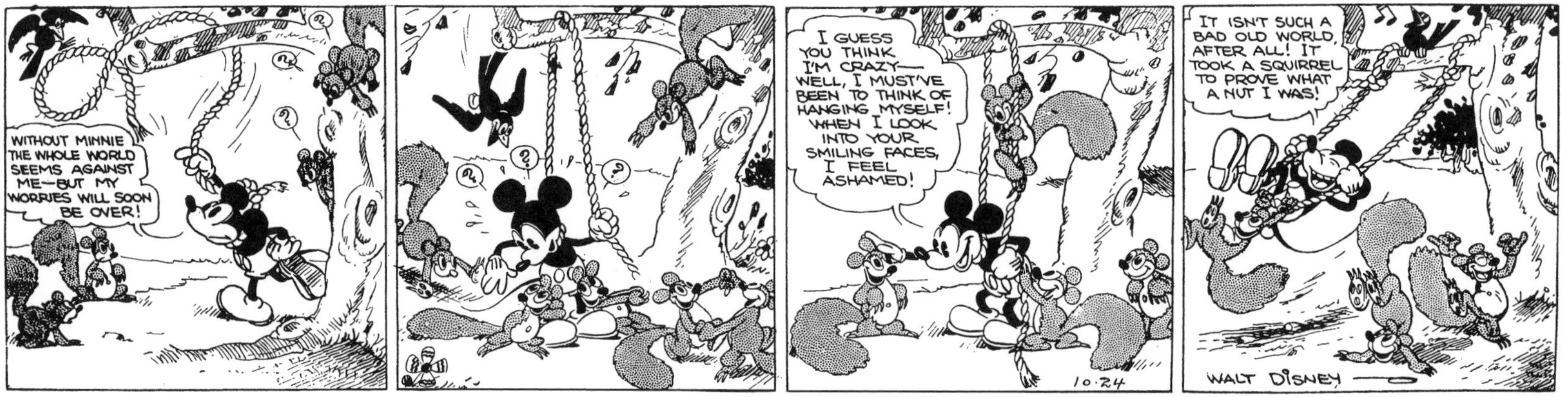
WITHOUT MINNIE THE WHOLE WORLD SEEMS AGAINST ME—BUT MY WORRIES WILL SOON BE OVER!
I GUESS YOU THINK I'M CRAZY— WELL, I MUST'VE BEEN TO THINK OF HANGING MYSELF! WHEN I LOOK INTO YOUR SMILING FACES, I FEEL ASHAMED!
10·24
IT ISN'T SUCH A BAD OLD WORLD, AFTER ALL! IT TOOK A SQUIRREL TO PROVE WHAT A NUT I WAS!
WALT DISNEY

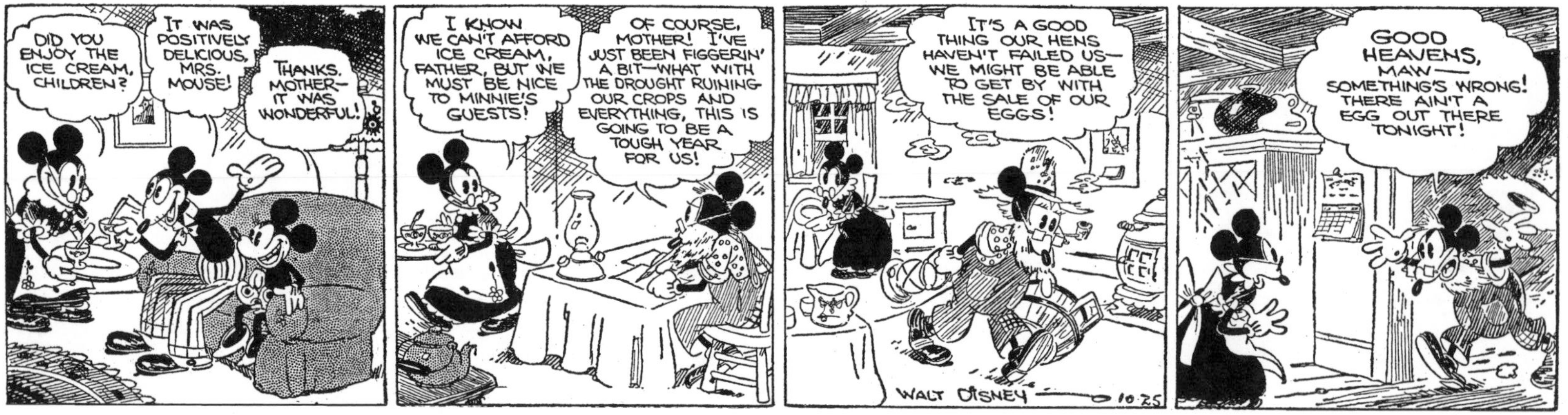
DID YOU ENJOY THE ICE CREAM, CHILDREN?
IT WAS POSITIVELY DELICIOUS, MRS. MOUSE!
THANKS, MOTHER— IT WAS WONDERFUL!
I KNOW WE CAN'T AFFORD ICE CREAM, FATHER, BUT WE MUST BE NICE TO MINNIE'S GUESTS!
OF COURSE, MOTHER! I'VE JUST BEEN FIGGERIN' A BIT—WHAT WITH THE DROUGHT RUINING OUR CROPS AND EVERYTHING, THIS IS GOING TO BE A TOUGH YEAR FOR US!
IT'S A GOOD THING OUR HENS HAVEN'T FAILED US— WE MIGHT BE ABLE TO GET BY WITH THE SALE OF OUR EGGS!
WALT DISNEY
10·25
GOOD HEAVENS, MAW— SOMETHING'S WRONG! THERE AIN'T A EGG OUT THERE TONIGHT!

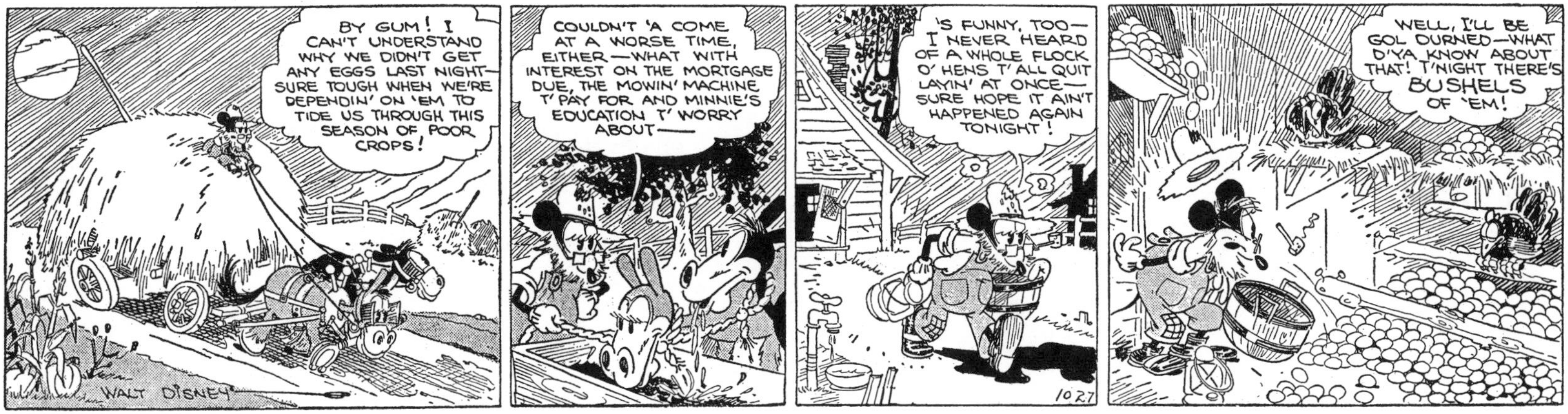
BY GUM! I CAN'T UNDERSTAND WHY WE DIDN'T GET ANY EGGS LAST NIGHT— SURE TOUGH WHEN WE'RE DEPENDIN' ON 'EM TO TIDE US THROUGH THIS SEASON OF POOR CROPS!
WALT DISNEY
COULDN'T 'A COME AT A WORSE TIME, EITHER—WHAT WITH INTEREST ON THE MORTGAGE DUE, THE MOWIN' MACHINE T' PAY FOR AND MINNIE'S EDUCATION T' WORRY ABOUT——
'S FUNNY, TOO— I NEVER HEARD OF A WHOLE FLOCK O' HENS T' ALL QUIT LAYIN' AT ONCE— SURE HOPE IT AIN'T HAPPENED AGAIN TONIGHT!
10-27
WELL, I'LL BE GOL DURNED—WHAT D'YA KNOW ABOUT THAT! T'NIGHT THERE'S BUSHELS OF 'EM!

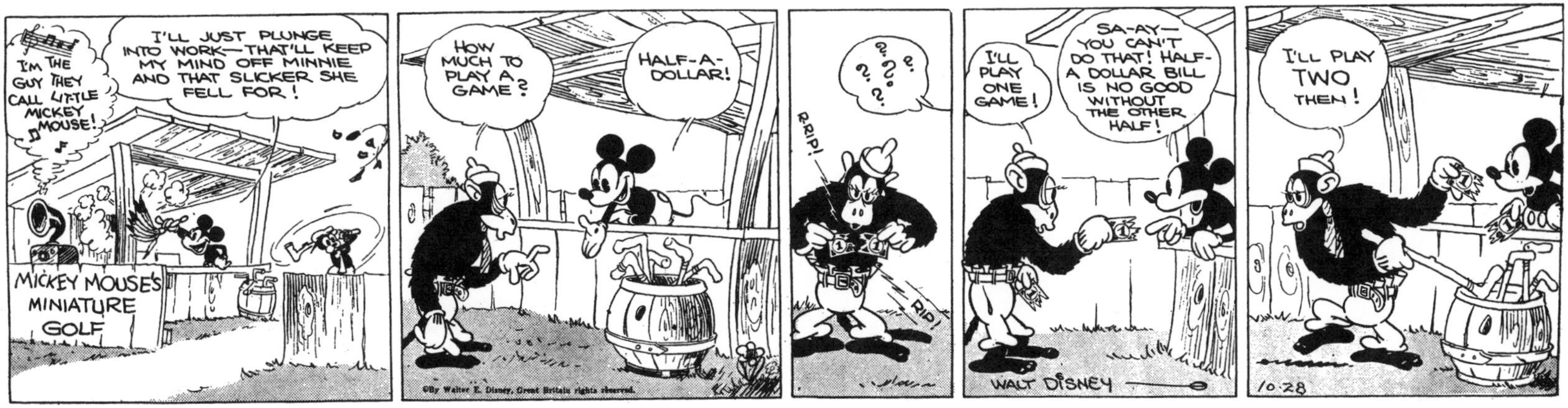
I'M THE GUY THEY CALL LITTLE MICKEY MOUSE!
I'LL JUST PLUNGE INTO WORK—THAT'LL KEEP MY MIND OFF MINNIE AND THAT SLICKER SHE FELL FOR!
MICKEY MOUSE'S MINIATURE GOLF
HOW MUCH TO PLAY A GAME?
HALF-A-DOLLAR!
©By Walter E. Disney, Great Britain rights reserved.
R-RIP!
? ? ? ? ?
RIP!
I'LL PLAY ONE GAME!
SA-AY— YOU CAN'T DO THAT! HALF-A DOLLAR BILL IS NO GOOD WITHOUT THE OTHER HALF!
WALT DISNEY
I'LL PLAY TWO THEN!
10-28

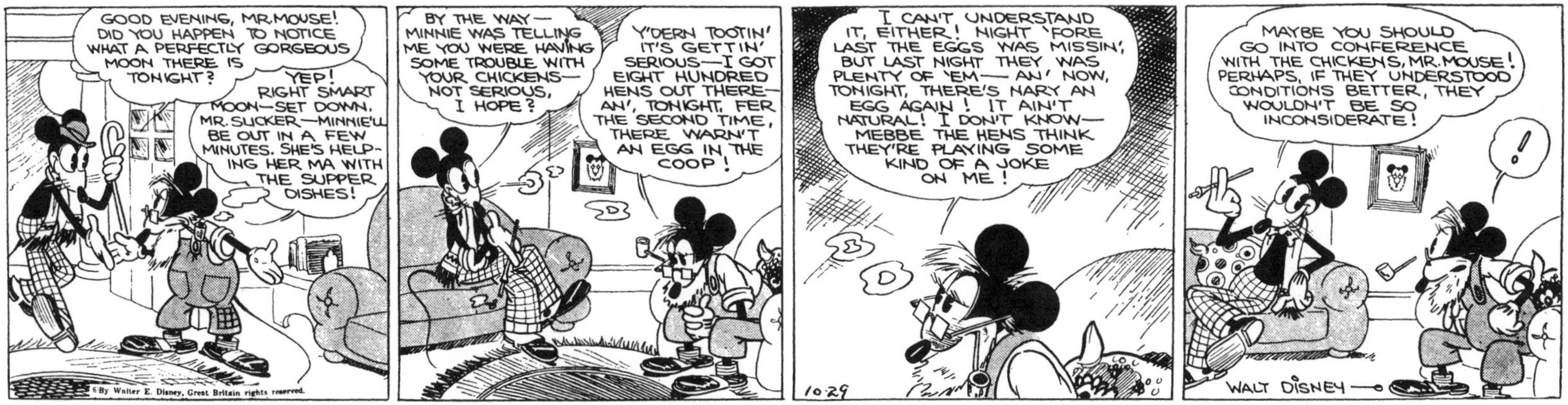
GOOD EVENING, MR. MOUSE! DID YOU HAPPEN TO NOTICE WHAT A PERFECTLY GORGEOUS MOON THERE IS TONIGHT?
YEP! RIGHT SMART MOON—SET DOWN, MR. SLICKER—MINNIE'LL BE OUT IN A FEW MINUTES. SHE'S HELPING HER MA WITH THE SUPPER DISHES!
©By Walter E. Disney, Great Britain rights reserved.
BY THE WAY— MINNIE WAS TELLING ME YOU WERE HAVING SOME TROUBLE WITH YOUR CHICKENS— NOT SERIOUS, I HOPE?
Y'DERN TOOTIN' IT'S GETTIN' SERIOUS—I GOT EIGHT HUNDRED HENS OUT THERE— AN', TONIGHT, FER THE SECOND TIME, THERE WARN'T AN EGG IN THE COOP!
I CAN'T UNDERSTAND IT, EITHER! NIGHT 'FORE LAST THE EGGS WAS MISSIN', BUT LAST NIGHT THEY WAS PLENTY OF 'EM— AN' NOW, TONIGHT, THERE'S NARY AN EGG AGAIN! IT AIN'T NATURAL! I DON'T KNOW— MEBBE THE HENS THINK THEY'RE PLAYING SOME KIND OF A JOKE ON ME!
10-29
MAYBE YOU SHOULD GO INTO CONFERENCE WITH THE CHICKENS, MR. MOUSE! PERHAPS, IF THEY UNDERSTOOD CONDITIONS BETTER, THEY WOULDN'T BE SO INCONSIDERATE!
!
WALT DISNEY

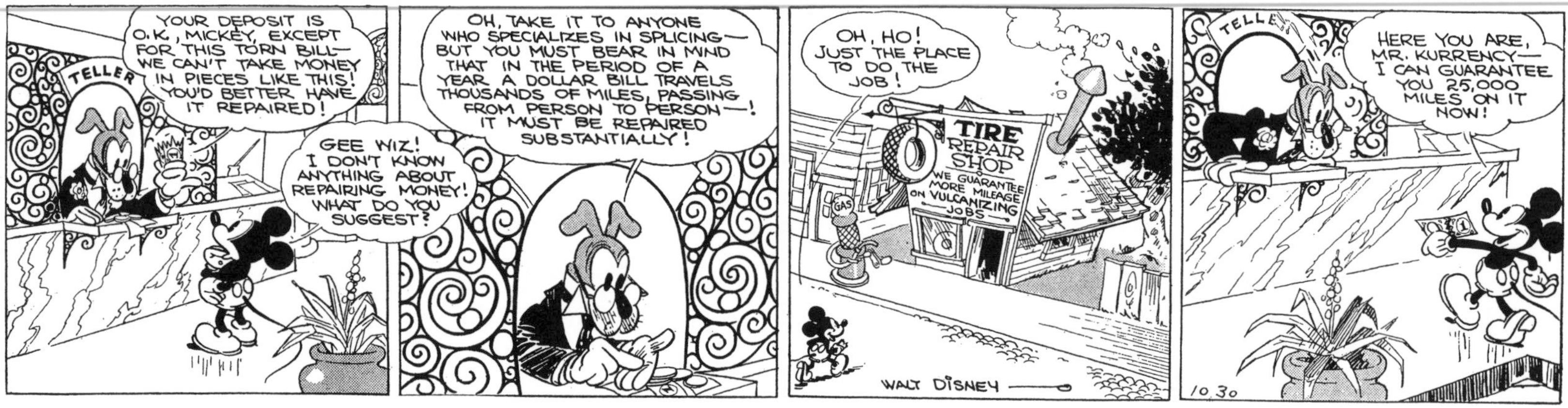
TELLER
YOUR DEPOSIT IS O.K., MICKEY, EXCEPT FOR THIS TORN BILL— WE CAN'T TAKE MONEY IN PIECES LIKE THIS! YOU'D BETTER HAVE IT REPAIRED!
GEE WIZ! I DON'T KNOW ANYTHING ABOUT REPAIRING MONEY! WHAT DO YOU SUGGEST?
OH, TAKE IT TO ANYONE WHO SPECIALIZES IN SPLICING— BUT YOU MUST BEAR IN MIND THAT IN THE PERIOD OF A YEAR A DOLLAR BILL TRAVELS THOUSANDS OF MILES, PASSING FROM PERSON TO PERSON—! IT MUST BE REPAIRED SUBSTANTIALLY!
OH, HO! JUST THE PLACE TO DO THE JOB!
TIRE REPAIR SHOP
WE GUARANTEE MORE MILEAGE ON VULCANIZING JOBS
GAS
WALT DISNEY
HERE YOU ARE, MR. KURRENCY— I CAN GUARANTEE YOU 25,000 MILES ON IT NOW!
10.30

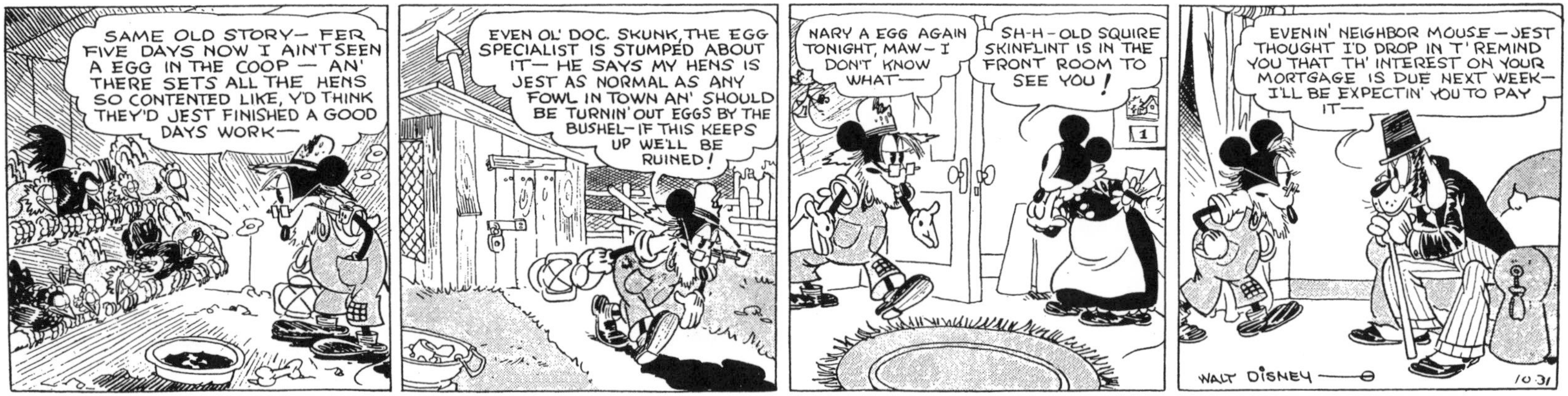
SAME OLD STORY— FER FIVE DAYS NOW I AIN'T SEEN A EGG IN THE COOP — AN' THERE SETS ALL THE HENS SO CONTENTED LIKE, Y'D THINK THEY'D JEST FINISHED A GOOD DAYS WORK—
EVEN OL' DOC. SKUNK, THE EGG SPECIALIST IS STUMPED ABOUT IT— HE SAYS MY HENS IS JEST AS NORMAL AS ANY FOWL IN TOWN AN' SHOULD BE TURNIN' OUT EGGS BY THE BUSHEL— IF THIS KEEPS UP WE'LL BE RUINED!
NARY A EGG AGAIN TONIGHT, MAW— I DON'T KNOW WHAT—
SH-H - OLD SQUIRE SKINFLINT IS IN THE FRONT ROOM TO SEE YOU!
EVENIN' NEIGHBOR MOUSE —JEST THOUGHT I'D DROP IN T' REMIND YOU THAT TH' INTEREST ON YOUR MORTGAGE IS DUE NEXT WEEK— I'LL BE EXPECTIN' YOU TO PAY IT—
WALT DISNEY
10.31

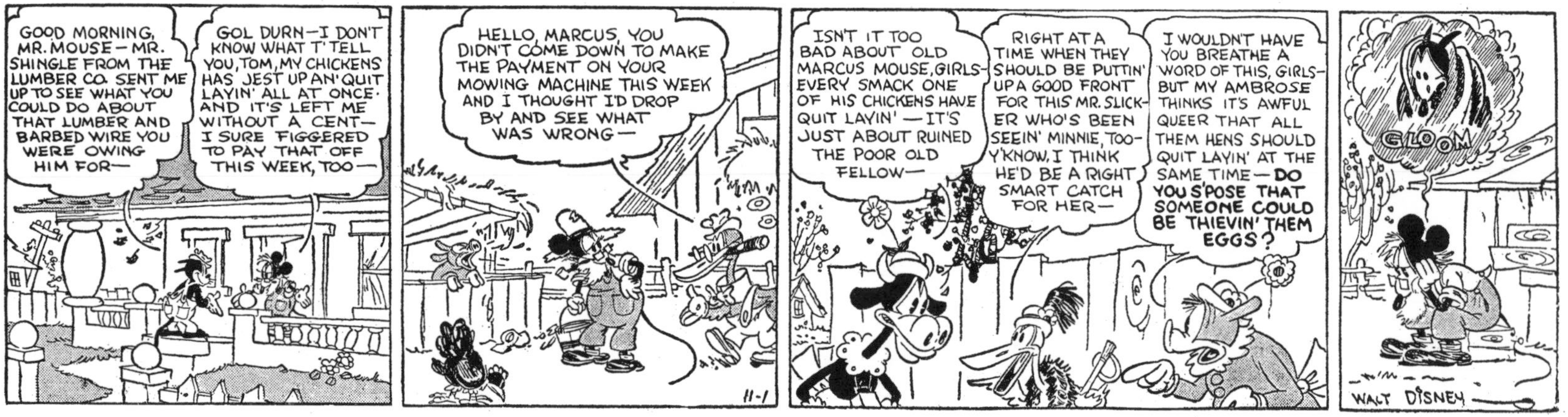
GOOD MORNING, MR. MOUSE— MR. SHINGLE FROM THE LUMBER CO. SENT ME UP TO SEE WHAT YOU COULD DO ABOUT THAT LUMBER AND BARBED WIRE YOU WERE OWING HIM FOR—
GOL DURN—I DON'T KNOW WHAT T' TELL YOU, TOM, MY CHICKENS HAS JEST UP AN' QUIT LAYIN' ALL AT ONCE. AND IT'S LEFT ME WITHOUT A CENT— I SURE FIGGERED TO PAY THAT OFF THIS WEEK, TOO—
HELLO, MARCUS, YOU DIDN'T COME DOWN TO MAKE THE PAYMENT ON YOUR MOWING MACHINE THIS WEEK AND I THOUGHT I'D DROP BY AND SEE WHAT WAS WRONG—
11-1
ISN'T IT TOO BAD ABOUT OLD MARCUS MOUSE, GIRLS— EVERY SMACK ONE OF HIS CHICKENS HAVE QUIT LAYIN' —IT'S JUST ABOUT RUINED THE POOR OLD FELLOW—
RIGHT AT A TIME WHEN THEY SHOULD BE PUTTIN' UP A GOOD FRONT FOR THIS MR. SLICKER WHO'S BEEN SEEIN' MINNIE, TOO— Y'KNOW, I THINK HE'D BE A RIGHT SMART CATCH FOR HER—
I WOULDN'T HAVE YOU BREATHE A WORD OF THIS, GIRLS— BUT MY AMBROSE THINKS IT'S AWFUL QUEER THAT ALL THEM HENS SHOULD QUIT LAYIN' AT THE SAME TIME— **DO YOU S'POSE THAT SOMEONE COULD BE THIEVIN' THEM EGGS?**
GLOOM
WALT DISNEY

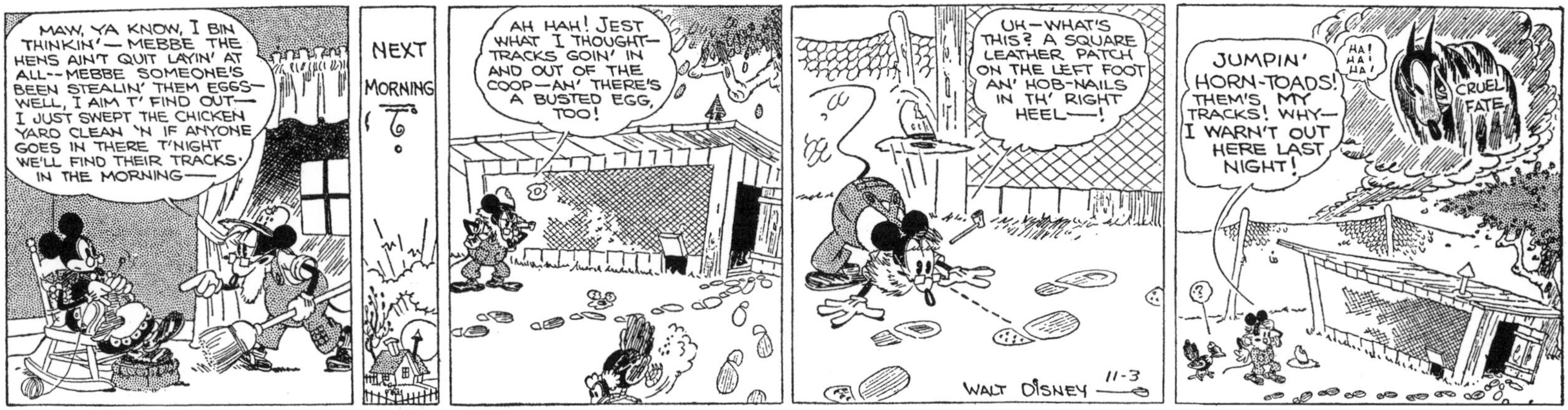
MAW, YA KNOW, I BIN THINKIN'—MEBBE THE HENS AIN'T QUIT LAYIN' AT ALL--MEBBE SOMEONE'S BEEN STEALIN' THEM EGGS—WELL, I AIM T' FIND OUT—I JUST SWEPT THE CHICKEN YARD CLEAN 'N IF ANYONE GOES IN THERE T'NIGHT WE'LL FIND THEIR TRACKS IN THE MORNING—
NEXT MORNING
AH HAH! JEST WHAT I THOUGHT—TRACKS GOIN' IN AND OUT OF THE COOP—AN' THERE'S A BUSTED EGG, TOO!
UH—WHAT'S THIS? A SQUARE LEATHER PATCH ON THE LEFT FOOT AN' HOB-NAILS IN TH' RIGHT HEEL—!
WALT DISNEY 11-3
JUMPIN' HORN-TOADS! THEM'S MY TRACKS! WHY—I WARN'T OUT HERE LAST NIGHT!
HA! HA! HA!
CRUEL FATE

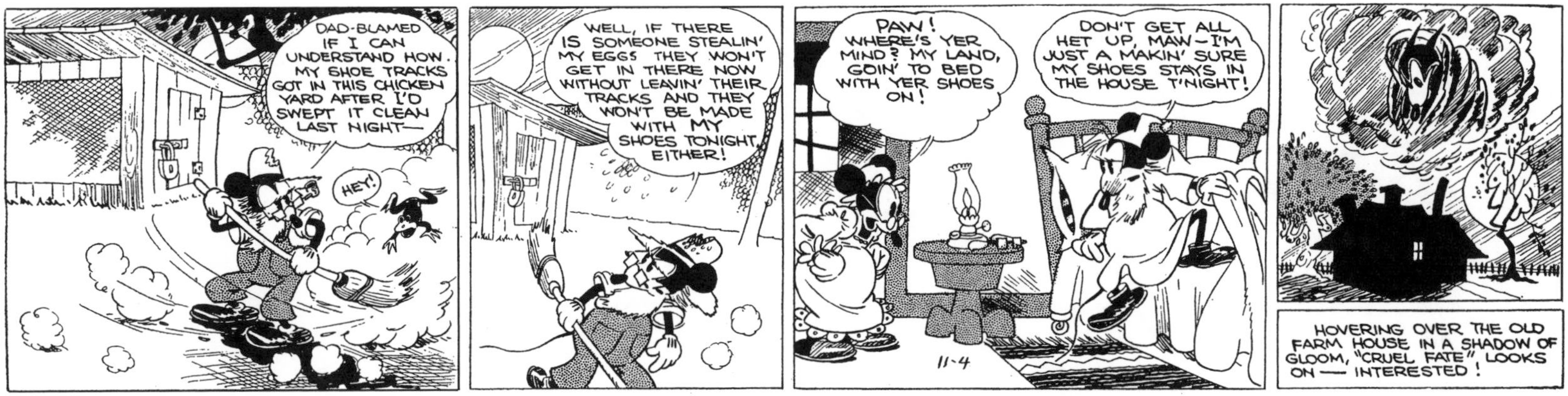
DAD-BLAMED IF I CAN UNDERSTAND HOW MY SHOE TRACKS GOT IN THIS CHICKEN YARD AFTER I'D SWEPT IT CLEAN LAST NIGHT—
HEY!
WELL, IF THERE IS SOMEONE STEALIN' MY EGGS THEY WON'T GET IN THERE NOW WITHOUT LEAVIN' THEIR TRACKS AND THEY WON'T BE MADE WITH MY SHOES TONIGHT, EITHER!
PAW! WHERE'S YER MIND? MY LAND, GOIN' TO BED WITH YER SHOES ON!
DON'T GET ALL HET UP, MAW—I'M JUST A MAKIN' SURE MY SHOES STAYS IN THE HOUSE T'NIGHT!
11-4
HOVERING OVER THE OLD FARM HOUSE IN A SHADOW OF GLOOM, "CRUEL FATE" LOOKS ON — INTERESTED!

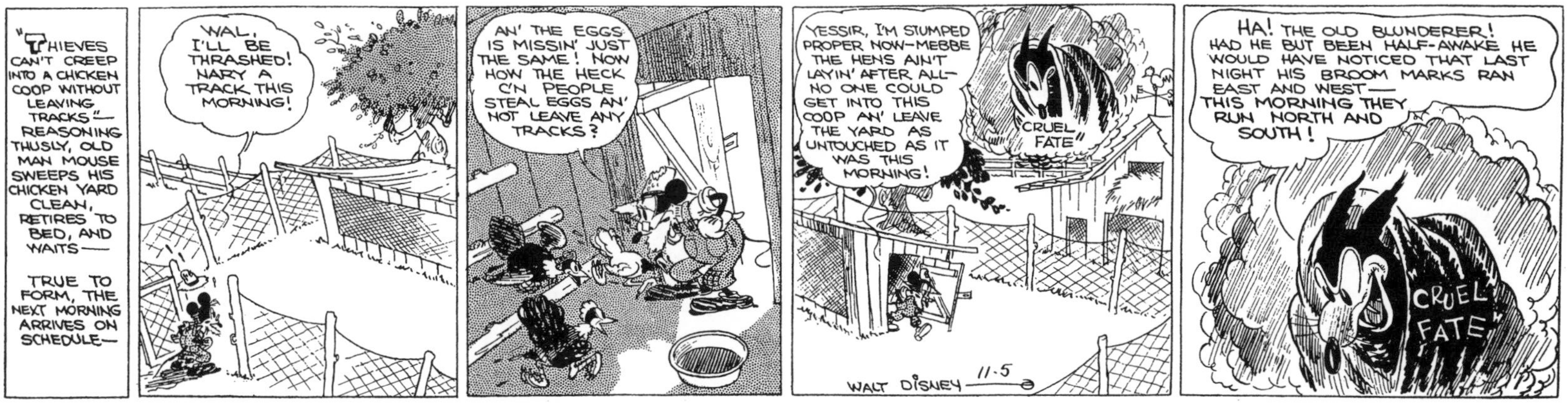
"THIEVES CAN'T CREEP INTO A CHICKEN COOP WITHOUT LEAVING TRACKS"—REASONING THUSLY, OLD MAN MOUSE SWEEPS HIS CHICKEN YARD CLEAN, RETIRES TO BED, AND WAITS—
TRUE TO FORM, THE NEXT MORNING ARRIVES ON SCHEDULE—
WAL, I'LL BE THRASHED! NARY A TRACK THIS MORNING!
AN' THE EGGS IS MISSIN' JUST THE SAME! NOW HOW THE HECK C'N PEOPLE STEAL EGGS AN' NOT LEAVE ANY TRACKS?
YESSIR, I'M STUMPED PROPER NOW—MEBBE THE HENS AIN'T LAYIN' AFTER ALL—NO ONE COULD GET INTO THIS COOP AN' LEAVE THE YARD AS UNTOUCHED AS IT WAS THIS MORNING!
"CRUEL FATE"
WALT DISNEY 11-5
HA! THE OLD BLUNDERER! HAD HE BUT BEEN HALF-AWAKE HE WOULD HAVE NOTICED THAT LAST NIGHT HIS BROOM MARKS RAN EAST AND WEST—THIS MORNING THEY RUN NORTH AND SOUTH!
"CRUEL FATE"

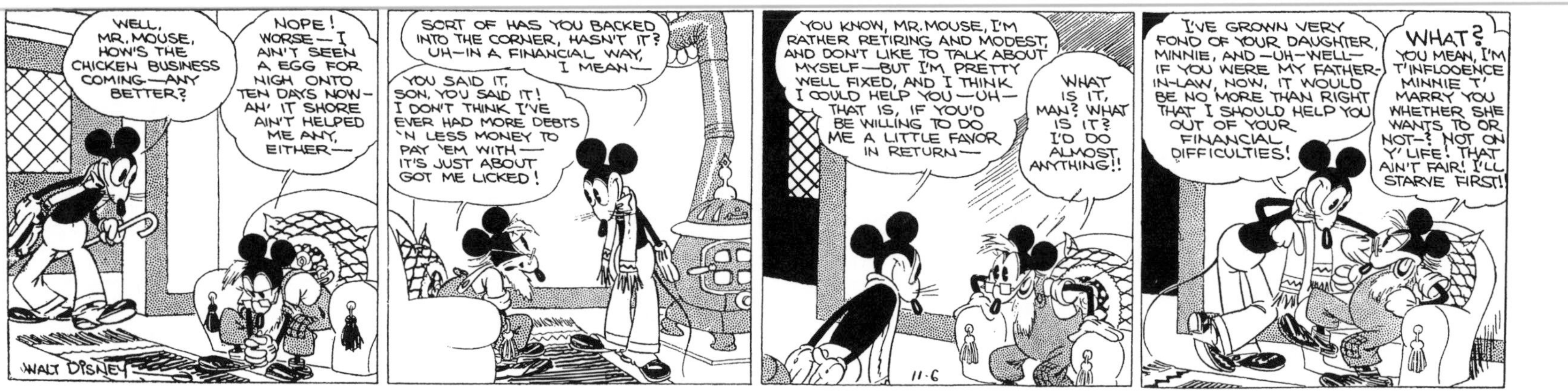
WELL, MR. MOUSE, HOW'S THE CHICKEN BUSINESS COMING—ANY BETTER?
NOPE! WORSE—I AIN'T SEEN A EGG FOR NIGH ONTO TEN DAYS NOW—AN' IT SHORE AIN'T HELPED ME ANY, EITHER—
WALT DISNEY
SORT OF HAS YOU BACKED INTO THE CORNER, HASN'T IT? UH—IN A FINANCIAL WAY, I MEAN—
YOU SAID IT, SON, YOU SAID IT! I DON'T THINK I'VE EVER HAD MORE DEBTS 'N LESS MONEY TO PAY 'EM WITH—IT'S JUST ABOUT GOT ME LICKED!
YOU KNOW, MR. MOUSE, I'M RATHER RETIRING AND MODEST, AND DON'T LIKE TO TALK ABOUT MYSELF—BUT I'M PRETTY WELL FIXED, AND I THINK I COULD HELP YOU—UH—THAT IS, IF YOU'D BE WILLING TO DO ME A LITTLE FAVOR IN RETURN—
WHAT IS IT, MAN? WHAT IS IT? I'D DO ALMOST ANYTHING!!
11·6
I'VE GROWN VERY FOND OF YOUR DAUGHTER, MINNIE, AND—UH—WELL—IF YOU WERE MY FATHER-IN-LAW, NOW, IT WOULD BE NO MORE THAN RIGHT THAT I SHOULD HELP YOU OUT OF YOUR FINANCIAL DIFFICULTIES!
WHAT? YOU MEAN, I'M T'INFLOOENCE MINNIE T' MARRY YOU WHETHER SHE WANTS TO OR NOT—? NOT ON Y' LIFE! THAT AIN'T FAIR! I'LL STARVE FIRST!

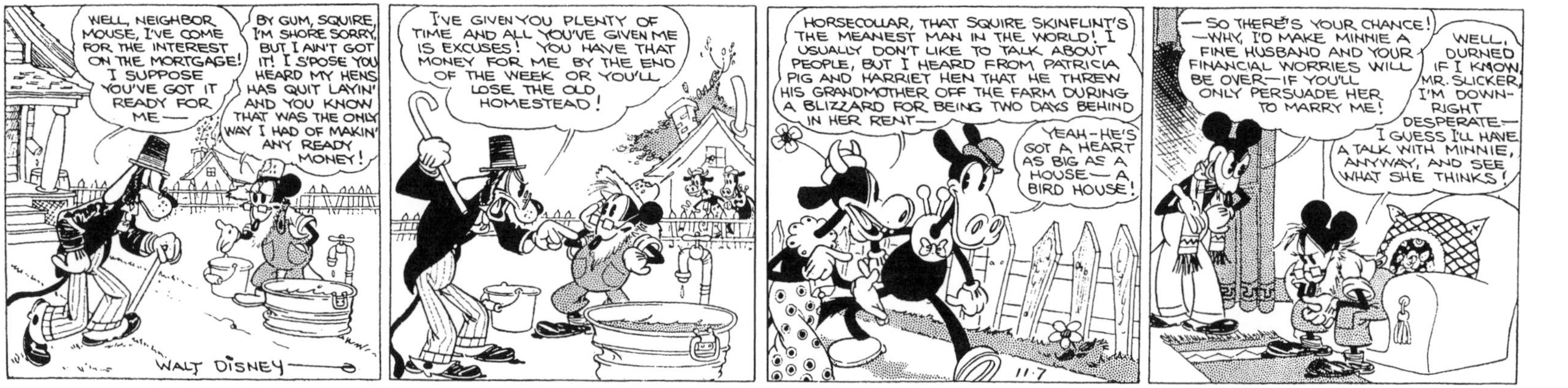
WELL, NEIGHBOR MOUSE, I'VE COME FOR THE INTEREST ON THE MORTGAGE! I SUPPOSE YOU'VE GOT IT READY FOR ME—
BY GUM, SQUIRE, I'M SHORE SORRY, BUT I AIN'T GOT IT! I S'POSE YOU HEARD MY HENS HAS QUIT LAYIN' AND YOU KNOW THAT WAS THE ONLY WAY I HAD OF MAKIN' ANY READY MONEY!
WALT DISNEY
I'VE GIVEN YOU PLENTY OF TIME AND ALL YOU'VE GIVEN ME IS EXCUSES! YOU HAVE THAT MONEY FOR ME BY THE END OF THE WEEK OR YOU'LL LOSE THE OLD HOMESTEAD!
HORSECOLLAR, THAT SQUIRE SKINFLINT'S THE MEANEST MAN IN THE WORLD! I USUALLY DON'T LIKE TO TALK ABOUT PEOPLE, BUT I HEARD FROM PATRICIA PIG AND HARRIET HEN THAT HE THREW HIS GRANDMOTHER OFF THE FARM DURING A BLIZZARD FOR BEING TWO DAYS BEHIND IN HER RENT—
YEAH—HE'S GOT A HEART AS BIG AS A HOUSE—A BIRD HOUSE!
11·7
—SO THERE'S YOUR CHANCE! —WHY, I'D MAKE MINNIE A FINE HUSBAND AND YOUR FINANCIAL WORRIES WILL BE OVER—IF YOU'LL ONLY PERSUADE HER TO MARRY ME!
WELL, DURNED IF I KNOW, MR. SLICKER, I'M DOWN-RIGHT DESPERATE—I GUESS I'LL HAVE A TALK WITH MINNIE, ANYWAY, AND SEE WHAT SHE THINKS!

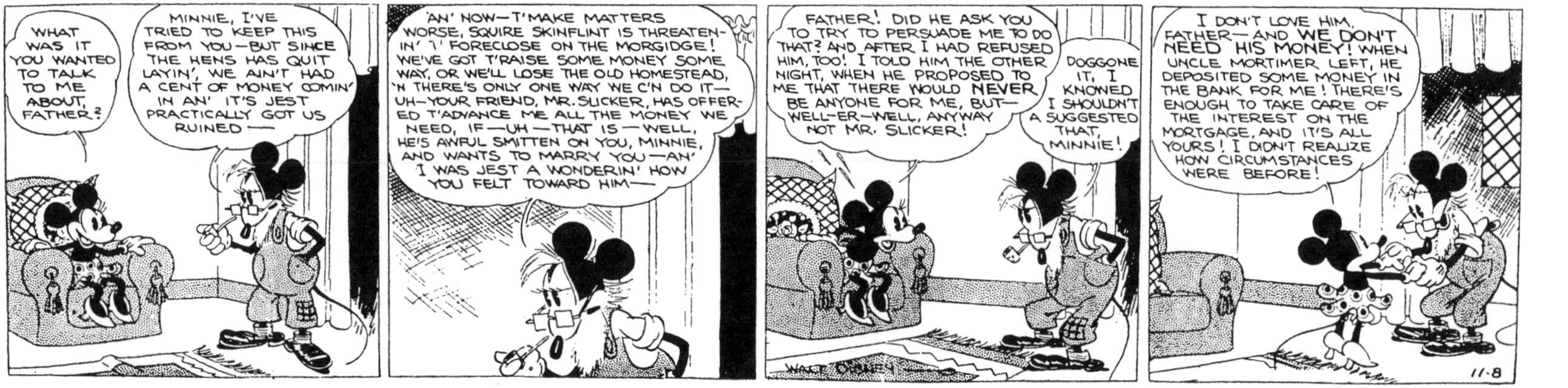
WHAT WAS IT YOU WANTED TO TALK TO ME ABOUT, FATHER?
MINNIE, I'VE TRIED TO KEEP THIS FROM YOU—BUT SINCE THE HENS HAS QUIT LAYIN', WE AIN'T HAD A CENT OF MONEY COMIN' IN AN' IT'S JEST PRACTICALLY GOT US RUINED—
AN' NOW—T'MAKE MATTERS WORSE, SQUIRE SKINFLINT IS THREATENIN' T' FORECLOSE ON THE MORGIDGE! WE'VE GOT T'RAISE SOME MONEY SOME WAY, OR WE'LL LOSE THE OLD HOMESTEAD, 'N THERE'S ONLY ONE WAY WE C'N DO IT—UH—YOUR FRIEND, MR. SLICKER, HAS OFFERED T'ADVANCE ME ALL THE MONEY WE NEED, IF—UH—THAT IS—WELL, HE'S AWFUL SMITTEN ON YOU, MINNIE, AND WANTS TO MARRY YOU—AN' I WAS JEST A WONDERIN' HOW YOU FELT TOWARD HIM—
FATHER! DID HE ASK YOU TO TRY TO PERSUADE ME TO DO THAT? AND AFTER I HAD REFUSED HIM, TOO! I TOLD HIM THE OTHER NIGHT, WHEN HE PROPOSED TO ME THAT THERE WOULD NEVER BE ANYONE FOR ME, BUT—WELL—ER—WELL, ANYWAY NOT MR. SLICKER!
DOGGONE IT, I KNOWED I SHOULDN'T A SUGGESTED THAT, MINNIE!
WALT DISNEY
I DON'T LOVE HIM, FATHER—AND WE DON'T NEED HIS MONEY! WHEN UNCLE MORTIMER LEFT, HE DEPOSITED SOME MONEY IN THE BANK FOR ME! THERE'S ENOUGH TO TAKE CARE OF THE INTEREST ON THE MORTGAGE, AND IT'S ALL YOURS! I DIDN'T REALIZE HOW CIRCUMSTANCES WERE BEFORE!
11·8

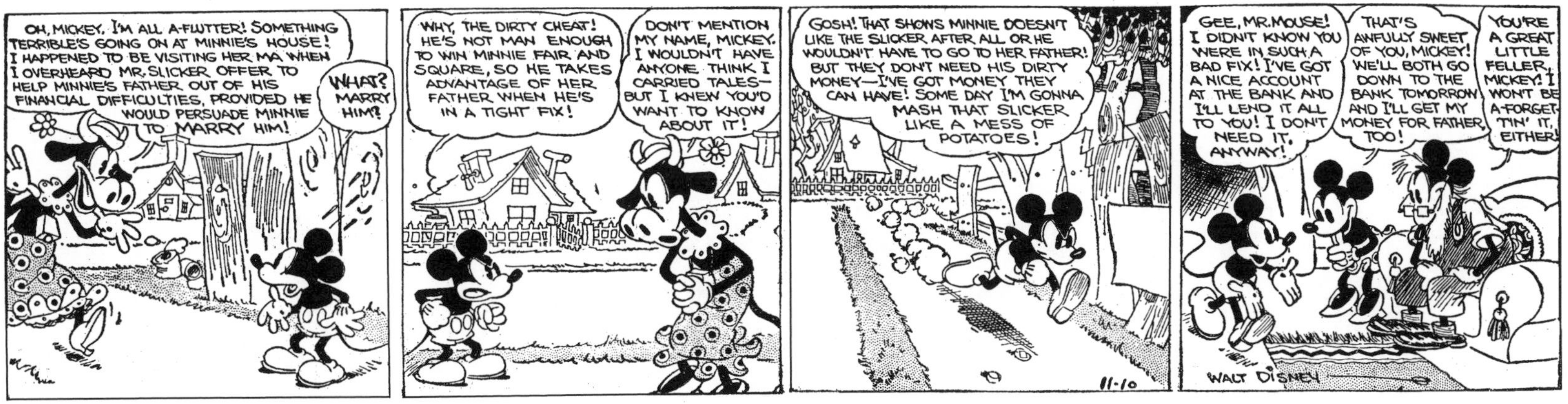
OH, MICKEY, I'M ALL A-FLUTTER! SOMETHING TERRIBLE'S GOING ON AT MINNIE'S HOUSE! I HAPPENED TO BE VISITING HER MA WHEN I OVERHEARD MR. SLICKER OFFER TO HELP MINNIE'S FATHER OUT OF HIS FINANCIAL DIFFICULTIES, PROVIDED HE WOULD PERSUADE MINNIE TO MARRY HIM!
WHAT? MARRY HIM?
WHY, THE DIRTY CHEAT! HE'S NOT MAN ENOUGH TO WIN MINNIE FAIR AND SQUARE, SO HE TAKES ADVANTAGE OF HER FATHER WHEN HE'S IN A TIGHT FIX!
DON'T MENTION MY NAME, MICKEY. I WOULDN'T HAVE ANYONE THINK I CARRIED TALES— BUT I KNEW YOU'D WANT TO KNOW ABOUT IT!
GOSH! THAT SHOWS MINNIE DOESN'T LIKE THE SLICKER AFTER ALL OR HE WOULDN'T HAVE TO GO TO HER FATHER! BUT THEY DON'T NEED HIS DIRTY MONEY—I'VE GOT MONEY THEY CAN HAVE! SOME DAY I'M GONNA MASH THAT SLICKER LIKE A MESS OF POTATOES!
11-10
GEE, MR. MOUSE! I DIDN'T KNOW YOU WERE IN SUCH A BAD FIX! I'VE GOT A NICE ACCOUNT AT THE BANK AND I'LL LEND IT ALL TO YOU! I DON'T NEED IT, ANYWAY!
THAT'S AWFULLY SWEET OF YOU, MICKEY! WE'LL BOTH GO DOWN TO THE BANK TOMORROW AND I'LL GET MY MONEY FOR FATHER, TOO!
YOU'RE A GREAT LITTLE FELLER, MICKEY! I WON'T BE A-FORGET-TIN' IT, EITHER!
WALT DISNEY

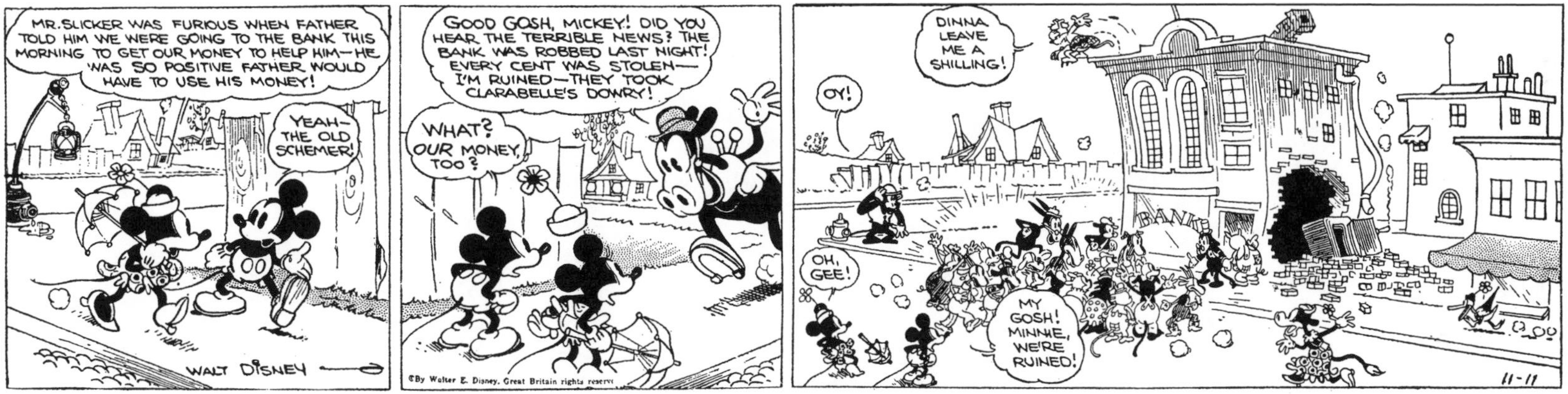
MR. SLICKER WAS FURIOUS WHEN FATHER TOLD HIM WE WERE GOING TO THE BANK THIS MORNING TO GET OUR MONEY TO HELP HIM—HE WAS SO POSITIVE FATHER WOULD HAVE TO USE HIS MONEY!
YEAH—THE OLD SCHEMER!
WALT DISNEY
GOOD GOSH, MICKEY! DID YOU HEAR THE TERRIBLE NEWS? THE BANK WAS ROBBED LAST NIGHT! EVERY CENT WAS STOLEN— I'M RUINED—THEY TOOK CLARABELLE'S DOWRY!
WHAT? OUR MONEY, TOO?
©By Walter E. Disney, Great Britain rights reserve
DINNA LEAVE ME A SHILLING!
OY!
OH, GEE!
MY GOSH! MINNIE, WE'RE RUINED!
BANK
11-11

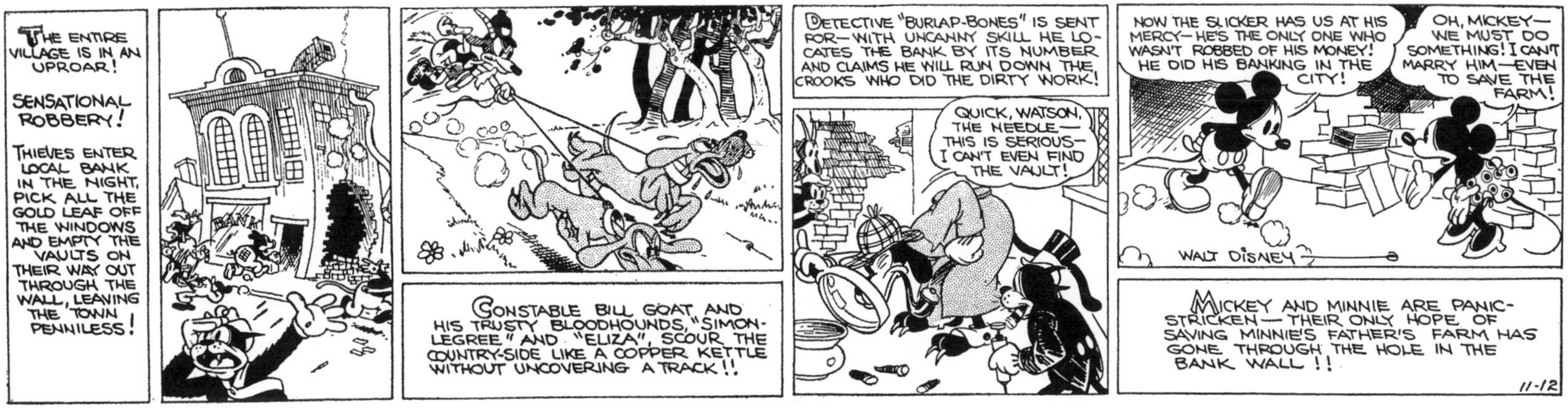
THE ENTIRE VILLAGE IS IN AN UPROAR!
SENSATIONAL ROBBERY!
THIEVES ENTER LOCAL BANK IN THE NIGHT, PICK ALL THE GOLD LEAF OFF THE WINDOWS AND EMPTY THE VAULTS ON THEIR WAY OUT THROUGH THE WALL, LEAVING THE TOWN PENNILESS!
BANK
CONSTABLE BILL GOAT AND HIS TRUSTY BLOODHOUNDS, "SIMON-LEGREE" AND "ELIZA", SCOUR THE COUNTRY-SIDE LIKE A COPPER KETTLE WITHOUT UNCOVERING A TRACK!!
DETECTIVE "BURLAP-BONES" IS SENT FOR—WITH UNCANNY SKILL HE LOCATES THE BANK BY ITS NUMBER AND CLAIMS HE WILL RUN DOWN THE CROOKS WHO DID THE DIRTY WORK!
QUICK, WATSON, THE NEEDLE—THIS IS SERIOUS—I CAN'T EVEN FIND THE VAULT!
NOW THE SLICKER HAS US AT HIS MERCY—HE'S THE ONLY ONE WHO WASN'T ROBBED OF HIS MONEY! HE DID HIS BANKING IN THE CITY!
OH, MICKEY—WE MUST DO SOMETHING! I CAN'T MARRY HIM—EVEN TO SAVE THE FARM!
WALT DISNEY
MICKEY AND MINNIE ARE PANIC-STRICKEN—THEIR ONLY HOPE OF SAVING MINNIE'S FATHER'S FARM HAS GONE THROUGH THE HOLE IN THE BANK WALL!!
11-12

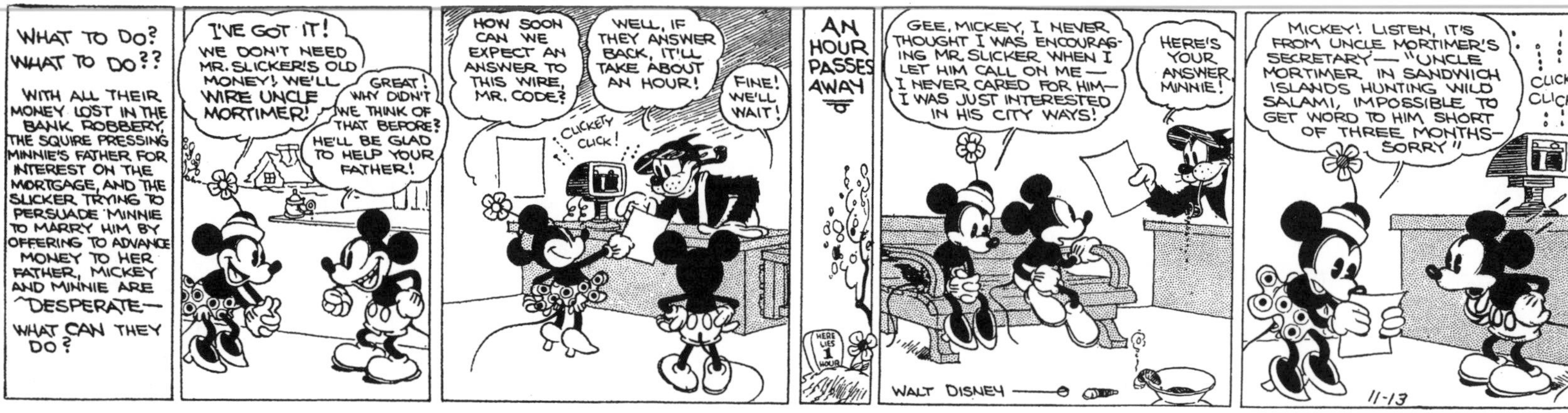
WHAT TO DO? WHAT TO DO??
WITH ALL THEIR MONEY LOST IN THE BANK ROBBERY, THE SQUIRE PRESSING MINNIE'S FATHER FOR INTEREST ON THE MORTGAGE, AND THE SLICKER TRYING TO PERSUADE MINNIE TO MARRY HIM BY OFFERING TO ADVANCE MONEY TO HER FATHER, MICKEY AND MINNIE ARE DESPERATE—
WHAT CAN THEY DO?
I'VE GOT IT! WE DON'T NEED MR. SLICKER'S OLD MONEY! WE'LL WIRE UNCLE MORTIMER!
GREAT! WHY DIDN'T WE THINK OF THAT BEFORE? HE'LL BE GLAD TO HELP YOUR FATHER!
HOW SOON CAN WE EXPECT AN ANSWER TO THIS WIRE, MR. CODE?
WELL, IF THEY ANSWER BACK, IT'LL TAKE ABOUT AN HOUR!
FINE! WE'LL WAIT!
CLICKETY CLICK!
AN HOUR PASSES AWAY
HERE LIES 1 HOUR
GEE, MICKEY, I NEVER THOUGHT I WAS ENCOURAGING MR. SLICKER WHEN I LET HIM CALL ON ME— I NEVER CARED FOR HIM— I WAS JUST INTERESTED IN HIS CITY WAYS!
HERE'S YOUR ANSWER, MINNIE!
WALT DISNEY
MICKEY! LISTEN, IT'S FROM UNCLE MORTIMER'S SECRETARY— "UNCLE MORTIMER IN SANDWICH ISLANDS HUNTING WILD SALAMI, IMPOSSIBLE TO GET WORD TO HIM SHORT OF THREE MONTHS— SORRY"
CLICK CLICK
11-13

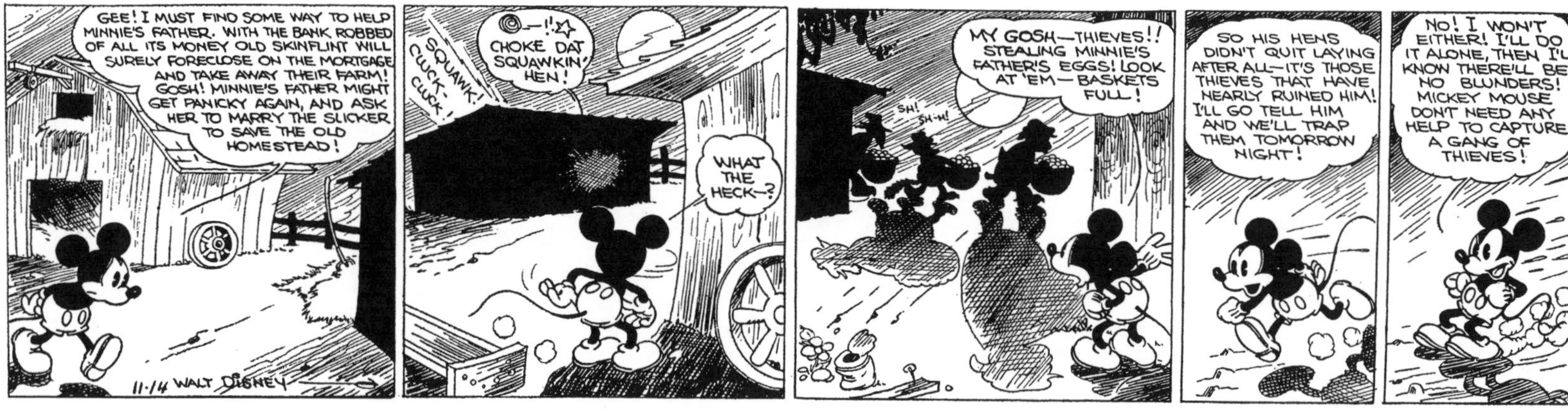
GEE! I MUST FIND SOME WAY TO HELP MINNIE'S FATHER. WITH THE BANK ROBBED OF ALL ITS MONEY OLD SKINFLINT WILL SURELY FORECLOSE ON THE MORTGAGE AND TAKE AWAY THEIR FARM! GOSH! MINNIE'S FATHER MIGHT GET PANICKY AGAIN, AND ASK HER TO MARRY THE SLICKER TO SAVE THE OLD HOMESTEAD!
11-14 WALT DISNEY
SQUAWK! CLUCK! CLUCK!
CHOKE DAT SQUAWKIN' HEN!
WHAT THE HECK—?
SH! SH-H!
MY GOSH—THIEVES!! STEALING MINNIE'S FATHER'S EGGS! LOOK AT 'EM— BASKETS FULL!
SO HIS HENS DIDN'T QUIT LAYING AFTER ALL—IT'S THOSE THIEVES THAT HAVE NEARLY RUINED HIM! I'LL GO TELL HIM AND WE'LL TRAP THEM TOMORROW NIGHT!
NO! I WON'T EITHER! I'LL DO IT ALONE, THEN I'LL KNOW THERE'LL BE NO BLUNDERS! MICKEY MOUSE DON'T NEED ANY HELP TO CAPTURE A GANG OF THIEVES!

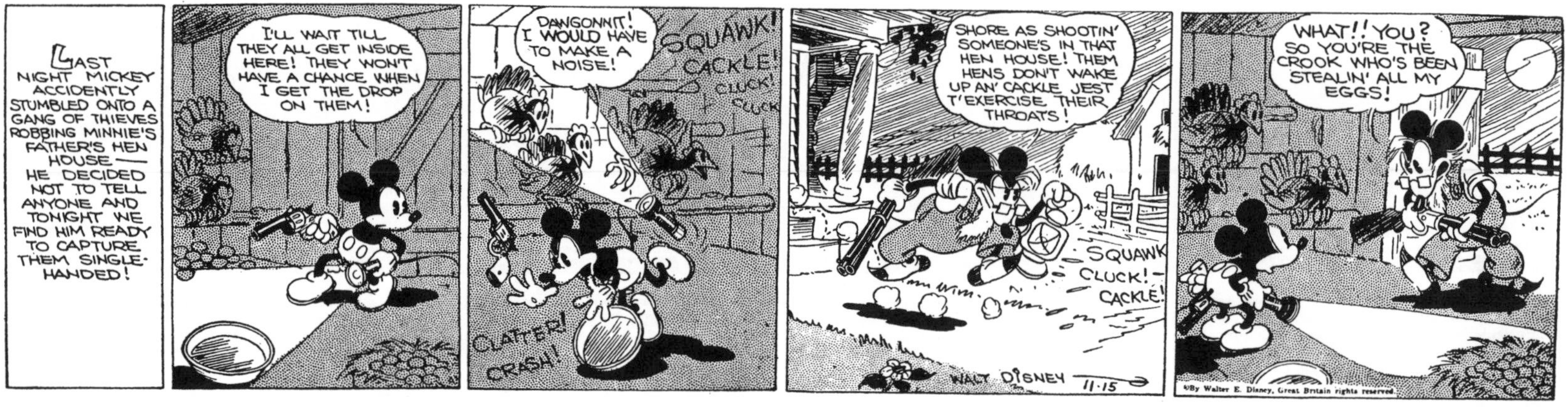
LAST NIGHT MICKEY ACCIDENTLY STUMBLED ONTO A GANG OF THIEVES ROBBING MINNIE'S FATHER'S HEN HOUSE— HE DECIDED NOT TO TELL ANYONE AND TONIGHT WE FIND HIM READY TO CAPTURE THEM SINGLE-HANDED!
I'LL WAIT TILL THEY ALL GET INSIDE HERE! THEY WON'T HAVE A CHANCE WHEN I GET THE DROP ON THEM!
DANGONNIT! I WOULD HAVE TO MAKE A NOISE!
SQUAWK! CACKLE! CLUCK! CLUCK
CLATTER! CRASH!
SHORE AS SHOOTIN' SOMEONE'S IN THAT HEN HOUSE! THEM HENS DON'T WAKE UP AN' CACKLE JEST T'EXERCISE THEIR THROATS!
SQUAWK CLUCK!- CACKLE!
WALT DISNEY 11-15
WHAT!! YOU? SO YOU'RE THE CROOK WHO'S BEEN STEALIN' ALL MY EGGS!
©By Walter E. Disney, Great Britain rights reserved.

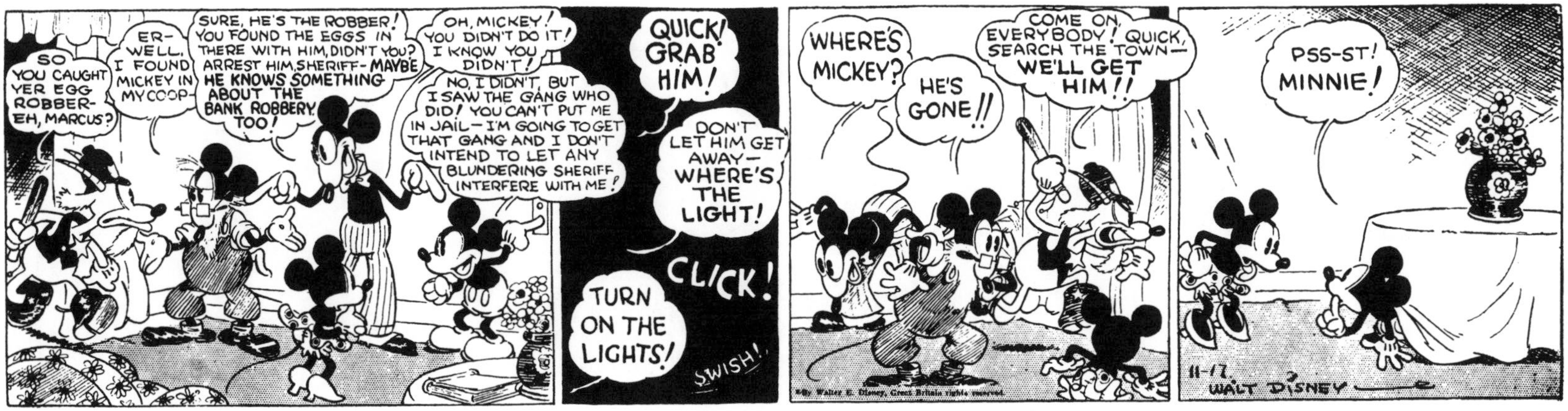
SO YOU CAUGHT YER EGG ROBBER— EH, MARCUS?
ER— WELL, I FOUND MICKEY IN MY COOP—
SURE, HE'S THE ROBBER! YOU FOUND THE EGGS IN THERE WITH HIM, DIDN'T YOU? ARREST HIM, SHERIFF— MAYBE HE KNOWS SOMETHING ABOUT THE BANK ROBBERY TOO!
OH, MICKEY! YOU DIDN'T DO IT! I KNOW YOU DIDN'T!
NO, I DIDN'T, BUT I SAW THE GANG WHO DID! YOU CAN'T PUT ME IN JAIL— I'M GOING TO GET THAT GANG AND I DON'T INTEND TO LET ANY BLUNDERING SHERIFF INTERFERE WITH ME!
QUICK! GRAB HIM!
DON'T LET HIM GET AWAY— WHERE'S THE LIGHT!
CLICK!
TURN ON THE LIGHTS!
SWISH!
WHERE'S MICKEY?
HE'S GONE!!
COME ON, EVERYBODY! QUICK, SEARCH THE TOWN— WE'LL GET HIM!!
PSS-ST! MINNIE!
11-17
WALT DISNEY

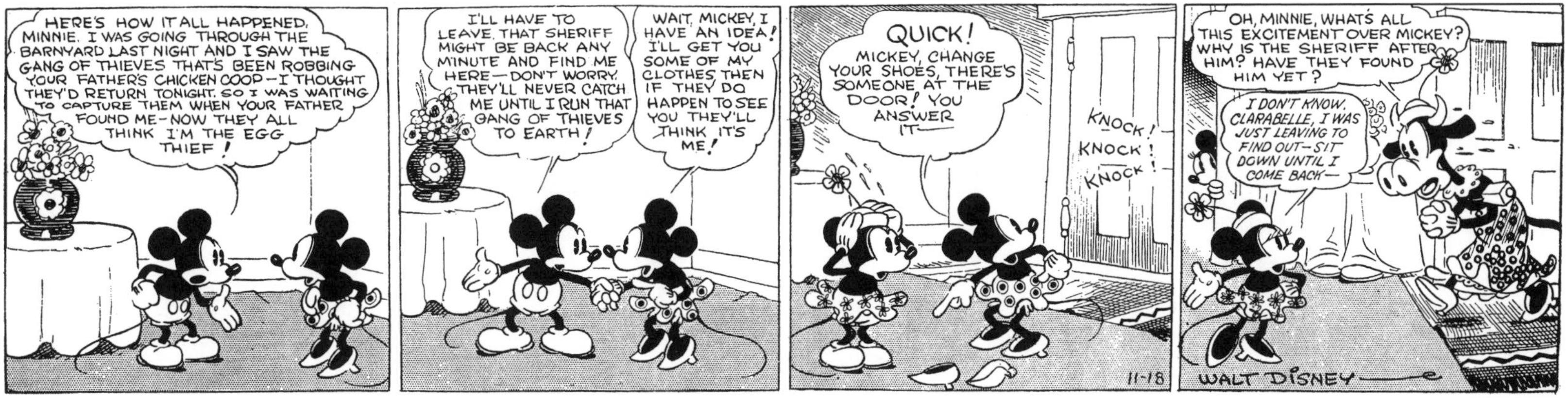
HERE'S HOW IT ALL HAPPENED, MINNIE. I WAS GOING THROUGH THE BARNYARD LAST NIGHT AND I SAW THE GANG OF THIEVES THAT'S BEEN ROBBING YOUR FATHER'S CHICKEN COOP— I THOUGHT THEY'D RETURN TONIGHT. SO I WAS WAITING TO CAPTURE THEM WHEN YOUR FATHER FOUND ME— NOW THEY ALL THINK I'M THE EGG THIEF!
I'LL HAVE TO LEAVE. THAT SHERIFF MIGHT BE BACK ANY MINUTE AND FIND ME HERE— DON'T WORRY. THEY'LL NEVER CATCH ME UNTIL I RUN THAT GANG OF THIEVES TO EARTH!
WAIT, MICKEY, I HAVE AN IDEA! I'LL GET YOU SOME OF MY CLOTHES, THEN IF THEY DO HAPPEN TO SEE YOU THEY'LL THINK IT'S ME!
QUICK! MICKEY, CHANGE YOUR SHOES, THERE'S SOMEONE AT THE DOOR! YOU ANSWER IT—
KNOCK! KNOCK! KNOCK!
11-18
OH, MINNIE, WHAT'S ALL THIS EXCITEMENT OVER MICKEY? WHY IS THE SHERIFF AFTER HIM? HAVE THEY FOUND HIM YET?
I DON'T KNOW, CLARABELLE, I WAS JUST LEAVING TO FIND OUT— SIT DOWN UNTIL I COME BACK—
WALT DISNEY

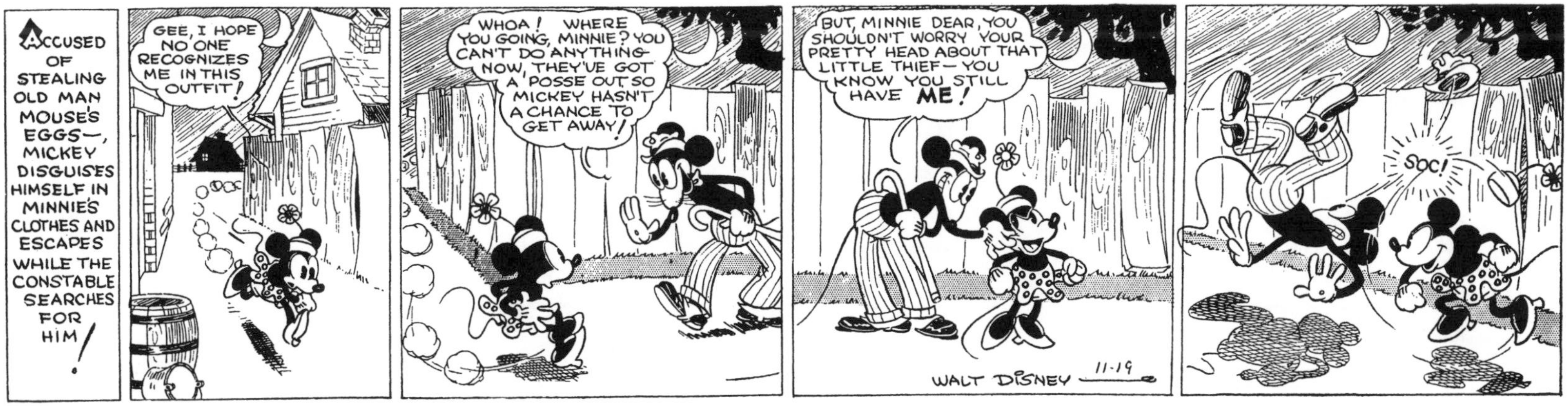
ACCUSED OF STEALING OLD MAN MOUSE'S EGGS—, MICKEY DISGUISES HIMSELF IN MINNIE'S CLOTHES AND ESCAPES WHILE THE CONSTABLE SEARCHES FOR HIM!
GEE, I HOPE NO ONE RECOGNIZES ME IN THIS OUTFIT!
WHOA! WHERE YOU GOING, MINNIE? YOU CAN'T DO ANYTHING NOW, THEY'VE GOT A POSSE OUT SO MICKEY HASN'T A CHANCE TO GET AWAY!
BUT, MINNIE DEAR, YOU SHOULDN'T WORRY YOUR PRETTY HEAD ABOUT THAT LITTLE THIEF— YOU KNOW YOU STILL HAVE ME!
WALT DISNEY 11-19
SOC!

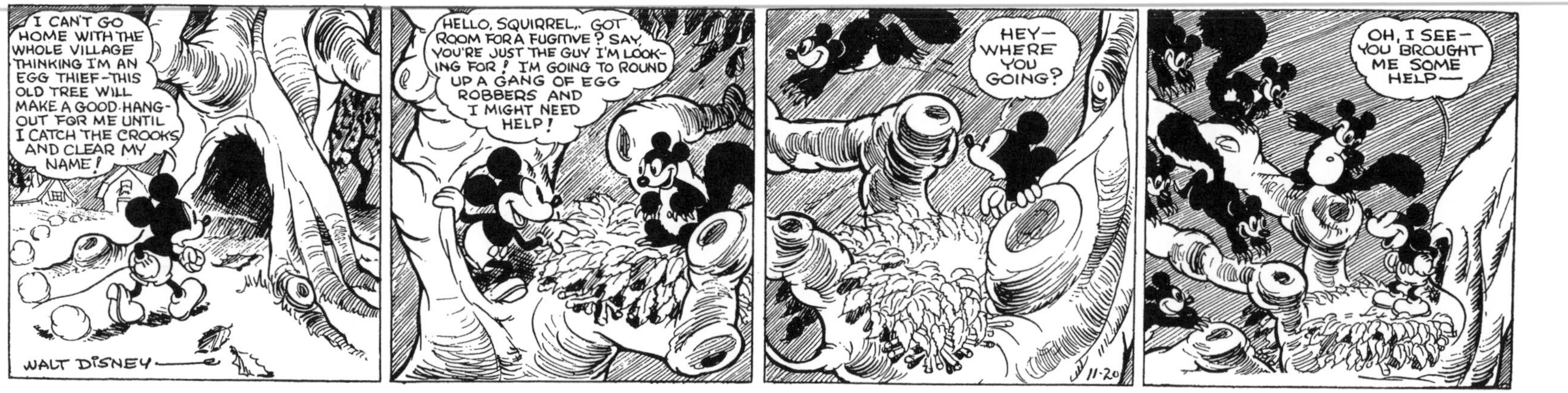
I CAN'T GO HOME WITH THE WHOLE VILLAGE THINKING I'M AN EGG THIEF—THIS OLD TREE WILL MAKE A GOOD HANG-OUT FOR ME UNTIL I CATCH THE CROOKS AND CLEAR MY NAME!
WALT DISNEY
HELLO, SQUIRREL,. GOT ROOM FOR A FUGITIVE? SAY, YOU'RE JUST THE GUY I'M LOOKING FOR! I'M GOING TO ROUND UP A GANG OF EGG ROBBERS AND I MIGHT NEED HELP!
HEY—WHERE YOU GOING?
11-20
OH, I SEE—YOU BROUGHT ME SOME HELP—

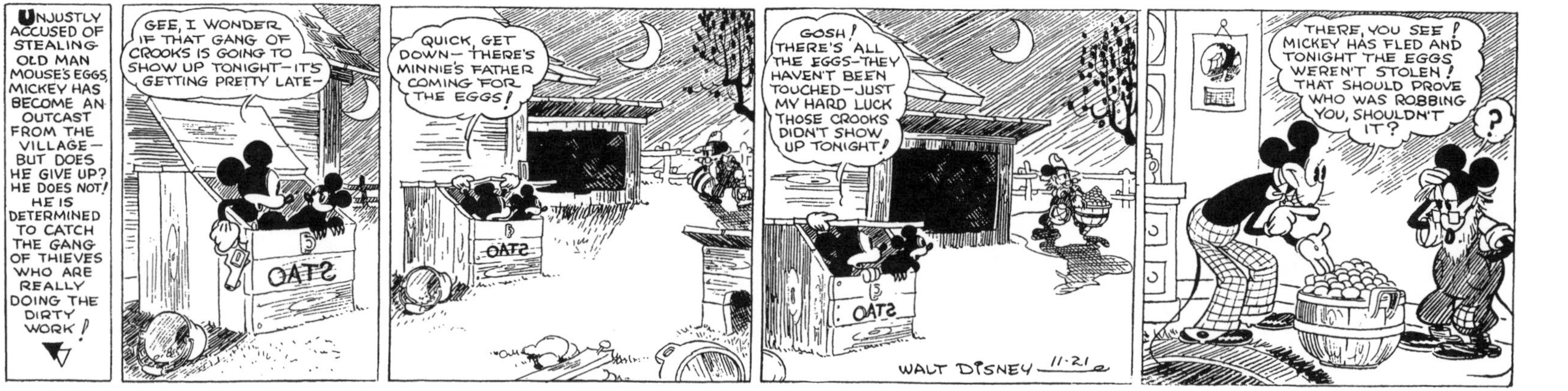
UNJUSTLY ACCUSED OF STEALING OLD MAN MOUSE'S EGGS, MICKEY HAS BECOME AN OUTCAST FROM THE VILLAGE—BUT DOES HE GIVE UP? HE DOES NOT! HE IS DETERMINED TO CATCH THE GANG OF THIEVES WHO ARE REALLY DOING THE DIRTY WORK!
GEE, I WONDER IF THAT GANG OF CROOKS IS GOING TO SHOW UP TONIGHT—IT'S GETTING PRETTY LATE—
OATS
QUICK, GET DOWN—THERE'S MINNIE'S FATHER COMING FOR THE EGGS!
OATS
GOSH! THERE'S ALL THE EGGS—THEY HAVEN'T BEEN TOUCHED—JUST MY HARD LUCK THOSE CROOKS DIDN'T SHOW UP TONIGHT!
OATS
WALT DISNEY 11-21
THERE, YOU SEE! MICKEY HAS FLED AND TONIGHT THE EGGS WEREN'T STOLEN! THAT SHOULD PROVE WHO WAS ROBBING YOU, SHOULDN'T IT?
?

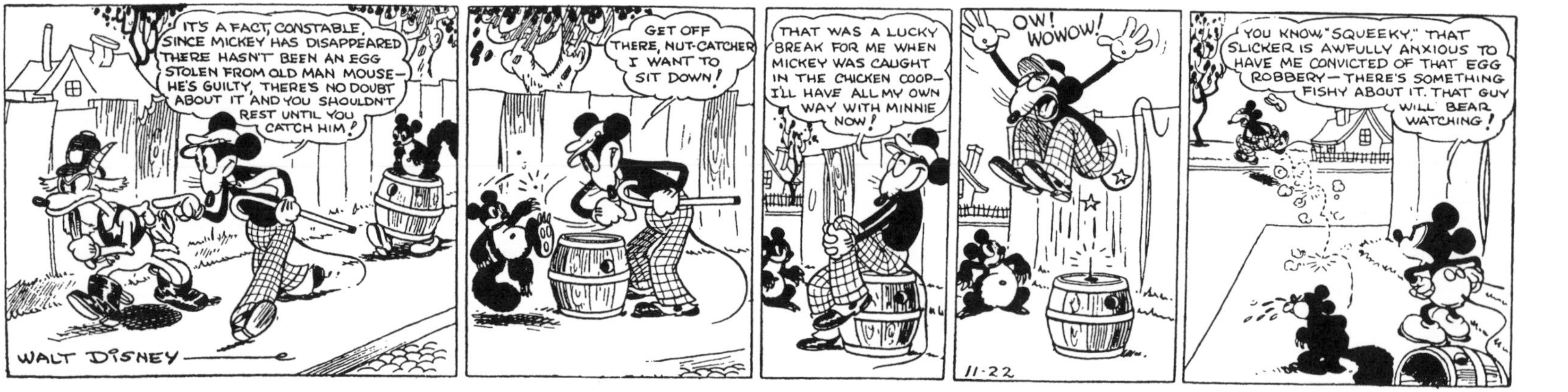
IT'S A FACT, CONSTABLE, SINCE MICKEY HAS DISAPPEARED THERE HASN'T BEEN AN EGG STOLEN FROM OLD MAN MOUSE—HE'S GUILTY, THERE'S NO DOUBT ABOUT IT AND YOU SHOULDN'T REST UNTIL YOU CATCH HIM!
WALT DISNEY
GET OFF THERE, NUT-CATCHER I WANT TO SIT DOWN!
THAT WAS A LUCKY BREAK FOR ME WHEN MICKEY WAS CAUGHT IN THE CHICKEN COOP—I'LL HAVE ALL MY OWN WAY WITH MINNIE NOW!
OW! WOWOW!
11-22
YOU KNOW, "SQUEEKY," THAT SLICKER IS AWFULLY ANXIOUS TO HAVE ME CONVICTED OF THAT EGG ROBBERY—THERE'S SOMETHING FISHY ABOUT IT. THAT GUY WILL BEAR WATCHING!

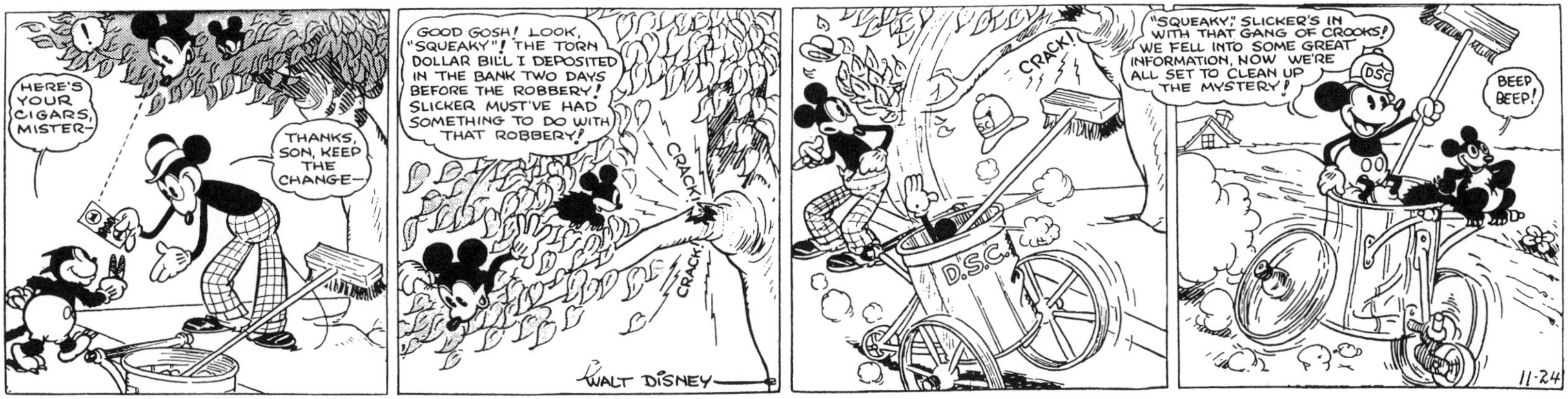
!
HERE'S YOUR CIGARS, MISTER—
THANKS, SON, KEEP THE CHANGE—
GOOD GOSH! LOOK, "SQUEAKY"! THE TORN DOLLAR BILL I DEPOSITED IN THE BANK TWO DAYS BEFORE THE ROBBERY! SLICKER MUST'VE HAD SOMETHING TO DO WITH THAT ROBBERY!
CRACK!
CRACK!
WALT DISNEY
CRACK!
D.S.C.
"SQUEAKY," SLICKER'S IN WITH THAT GANG OF CROOKS! WE FELL INTO SOME GREAT INFORMATION, NOW WE'RE ALL SET TO CLEAN UP THE MYSTERY!
BEEP BEEP!
DSC
11-24

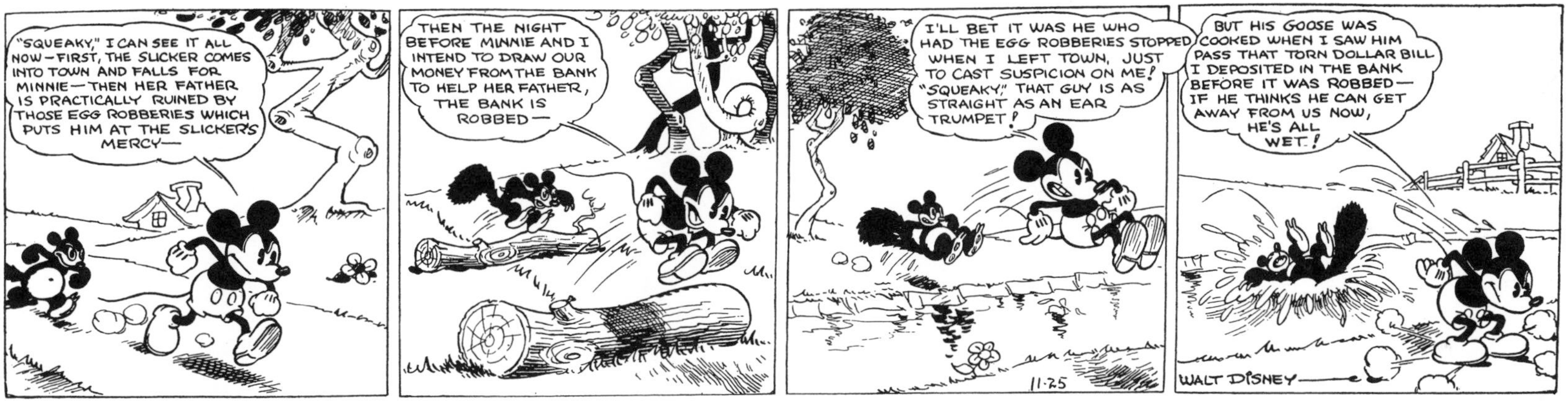
"SQUEAKY," I CAN SEE IT ALL NOW—FIRST, THE SLICKER COMES INTO TOWN AND FALLS FOR MINNIE—THEN HER FATHER IS PRACTICALLY RUINED BY THOSE EGG ROBBERIES WHICH PUTS HIM AT THE SLICKER'S MERCY—
THEN THE NIGHT BEFORE MINNIE AND I INTEND TO DRAW OUR MONEY FROM THE BANK TO HELP HER FATHER, THE BANK IS ROBBED—
I'LL BET IT WAS HE WHO HAD THE EGG ROBBERIES STOPPED WHEN I LEFT TOWN, JUST TO CAST SUSPICION ON ME! "SQUEAKY," THAT GUY IS AS STRAIGHT AS AN EAR TRUMPET!
11-25
BUT HIS GOOSE WAS COOKED WHEN I SAW HIM PASS THAT TORN DOLLAR BILL I DEPOSITED IN THE BANK BEFORE IT WAS ROBBED—IF HE THINKS HE CAN GET AWAY FROM US NOW, HE'S ALL WET!
WALT DISNEY

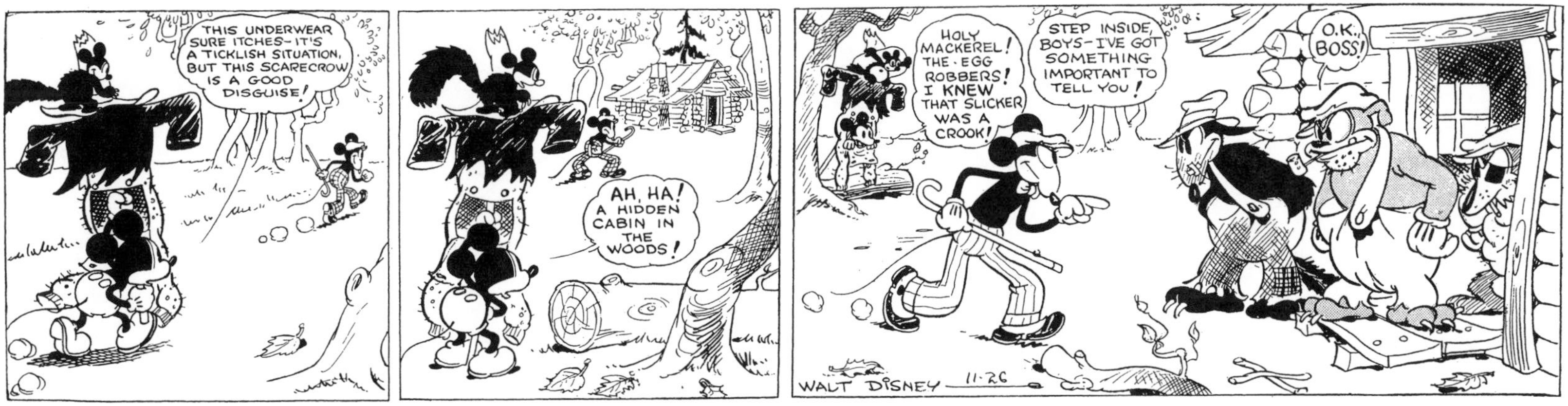
THIS UNDERWEAR SURE ITCHES—IT'S A TICKLISH SITUATION, BUT THIS SCARECROW IS A GOOD DISGUISE!
AH, HA! A HIDDEN CABIN IN THE WOODS!
HOLY MACKEREL! THE EGG ROBBERS! I KNEW THAT SLICKER WAS A CROOK!
STEP INSIDE, BOYS—I'VE GOT SOMETHING IMPORTANT TO TELL YOU!
O.K., BOSS!
WALT DISNEY 11-26

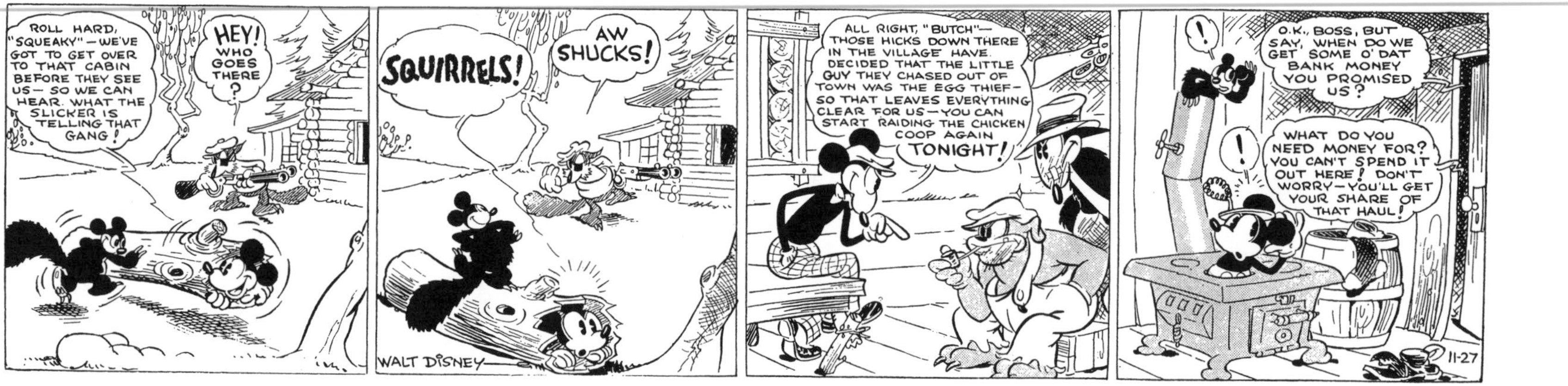
ROLL HARD, "SQUEAKY" — WE'VE GOT TO GET OVER TO THAT CABIN BEFORE THEY SEE US — SO WE CAN HEAR WHAT THE SLICKER IS TELLING THAT GANG!
HEY! WHO GOES THERE?
SQUIRRELS!
AW SHUCKS!
WALT DISNEY
ALL RIGHT, "BUTCH" — THOSE HICKS DOWN THERE IN THE VILLAGE HAVE DECIDED THAT THE LITTLE GUY THEY CHASED OUT OF TOWN WAS THE EGG THIEF — SO THAT LEAVES EVERYTHING CLEAR FOR US — YOU CAN START RAIDING THE CHICKEN COOP AGAIN TONIGHT!
!
O.K., BOSS, BUT SAY, WHEN DO WE GET SOME O' DAT BANK MONEY YOU PROMISED US?
!
WHAT DO YOU NEED MONEY FOR? YOU CAN'T SPEND IT OUT HERE! DON'T WORRY — YOU'LL GET YOUR SHARE OF THAT HAUL!
11-27

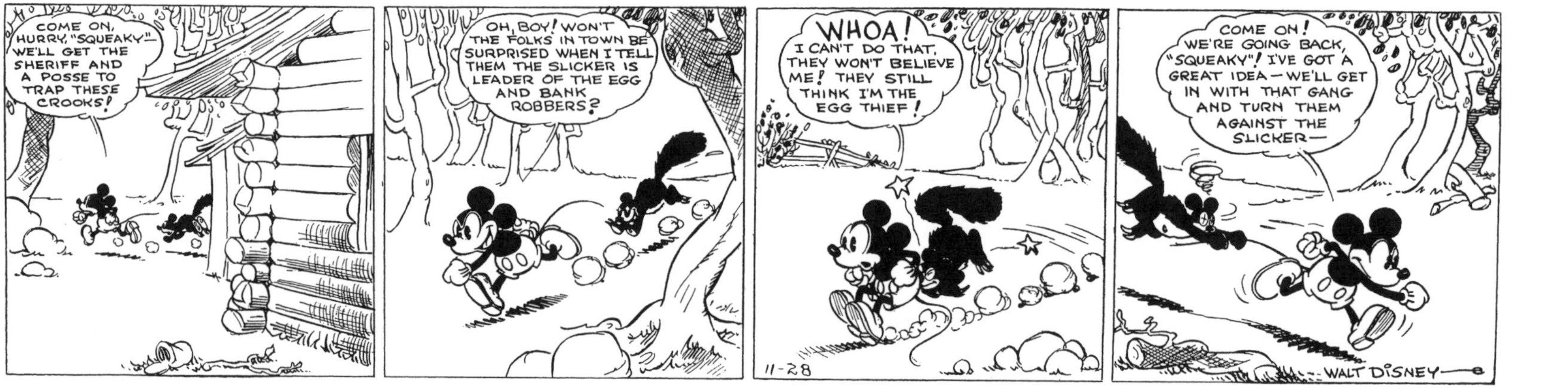
COME ON, HURRY, "SQUEAKY" — WE'LL GET THE SHERIFF AND A POSSE TO TRAP THESE CROOKS!
OH, BOY! WON'T THE FOLKS IN TOWN BE SURPRISED WHEN I TELL THEM THE SLICKER IS LEADER OF THE EGG AND BANK ROBBERS?
WHOA! I CAN'T DO THAT, THEY WON'T BELIEVE ME! THEY STILL THINK I'M THE EGG THIEF!
11-28
COME ON! WE'RE GOING BACK, "SQUEAKY"! I'VE GOT A GREAT IDEA — WE'LL GET IN WITH THAT GANG AND TURN THEM AGAINST THE SLICKER —
WALT DISNEY

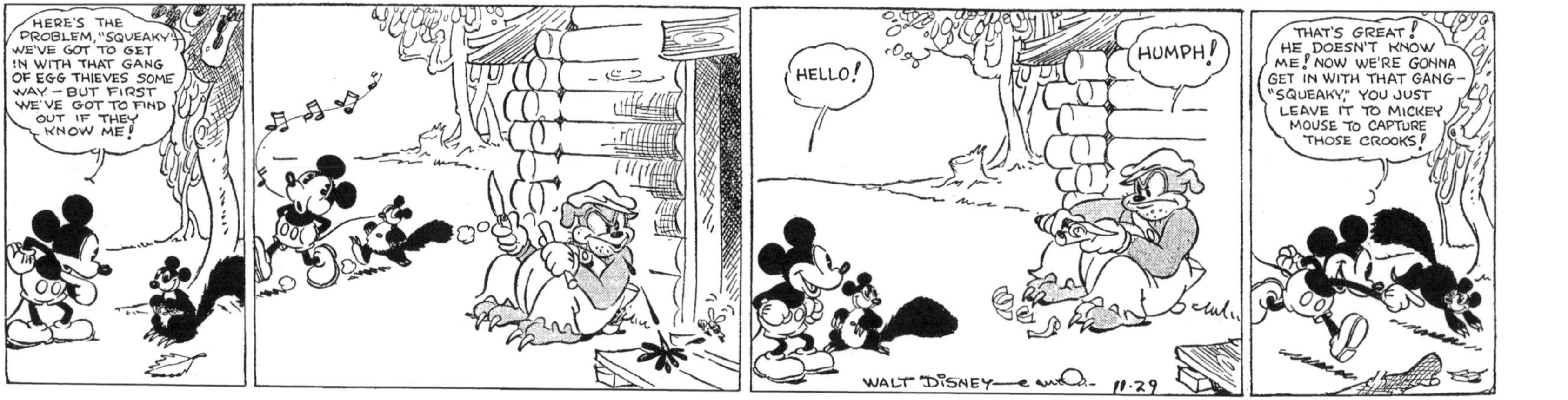
HERE'S THE PROBLEM, "SQUEAKY" — WE'VE GOT TO GET IN WITH THAT GANG OF EGG THIEVES SOME WAY — BUT FIRST WE'VE GOT TO FIND OUT IF THEY KNOW ME!
HELLO!
HUMPH!
WALT DISNEY
11-29
THAT'S GREAT! HE DOESN'T KNOW ME! NOW WE'RE GONNA GET IN WITH THAT GANG — "SQUEAKY," YOU JUST LEAVE IT TO MICKEY MOUSE TO CAPTURE THOSE CROOKS!

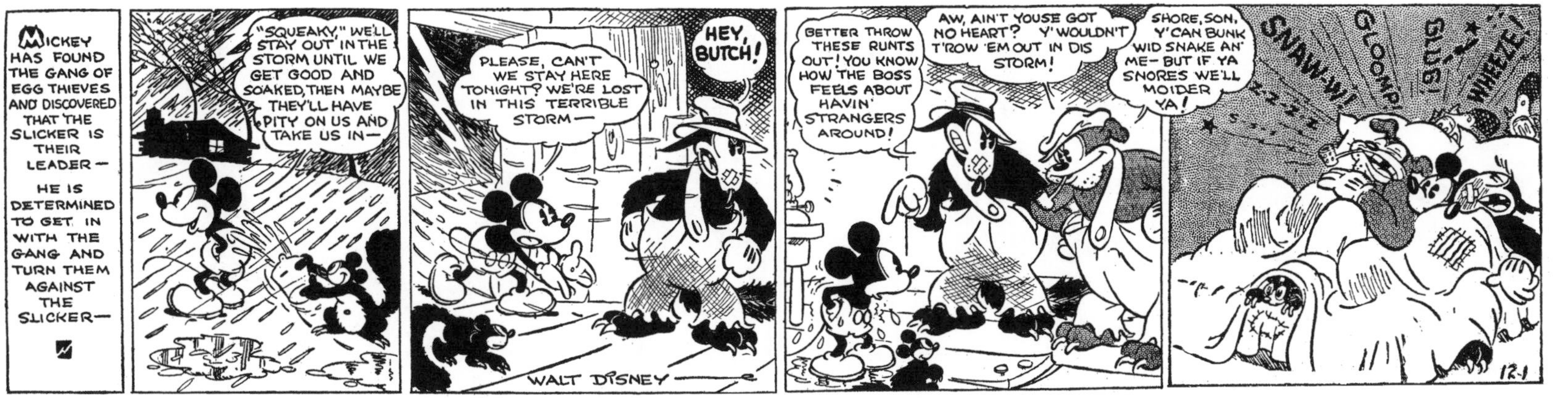
MICKEY HAS FOUND THE GANG OF EGG THIEVES AND DISCOVERED THAT THE SLICKER IS THEIR LEADER — HE IS DETERMINED TO GET IN WITH THE GANG AND TURN THEM AGAINST THE SLICKER —
"SQUEAKY," WE'LL STAY OUT IN THE STORM UNTIL WE GET GOOD AND SOAKED, THEN MAYBE THEY'LL HAVE PITY ON US AND TAKE US IN —
PLEASE, CAN'T WE STAY HERE TONIGHT? WE'RE LOST IN THIS TERRIBLE STORM —
HEY, BUTCH!
WALT DISNEY
BETTER THROW THESE RUNTS OUT! YOU KNOW HOW THE BOSS FEELS ABOUT HAVIN' STRANGERS AROUND!
AW, AIN'T YOUSE GOT NO HEART? Y' WOULDN'T T'ROW 'EM OUT IN DIS STORM!
SHORE, SON, Y' CAN BUNK WID SNAKE AN' ME — BUT IF YA SNORES WE'LL MOIDER YA!
SNAW-W!
GLOOMP!
GLUB!
WHEEZE!
12-1

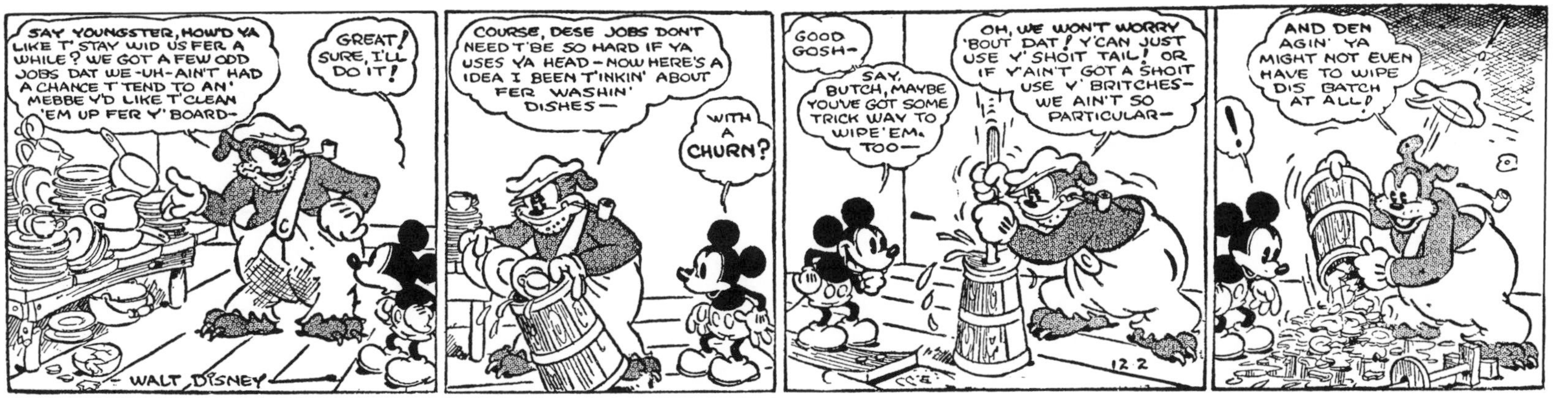
SAY YOUNGSTER, HOW'D YA LIKE T' STAY WID US FER A WHILE? WE GOT A FEW ODD JOBS DAT WE - UH - AIN'T HAD A CHANCE T' TEND TO AN' MEBBE Y'D LIKE T' CLEAN 'EM UP FER Y' BOARD —
GREAT! SURE, I'LL DO IT!
WALT DISNEY
COURSE, DESE JOBS DON'T NEED T' BE SO HARD IF YA USES YA HEAD — NOW HERE'S A IDEA I BEEN T'INKIN' ABOUT FER WASHIN' DISHES —
WITH A CHURN?
GOOD GOSH —
SAY, BUTCH, MAYBE YOU'VE GOT SOME TRICK WAY TO WIPE 'EM, TOO —
OH, WE WON'T WORRY 'BOUT DAT! Y' CAN JUST USE Y' SHOIT TAIL! OR IF Y' AIN'T GOT A SHOIT USE Y' BRITCHES — WE AIN'T SO PARTICULAR —
12-2
AND DEN AGIN' YA MIGHT NOT EVEN HAVE TO WIPE DIS BATCH AT ALL!

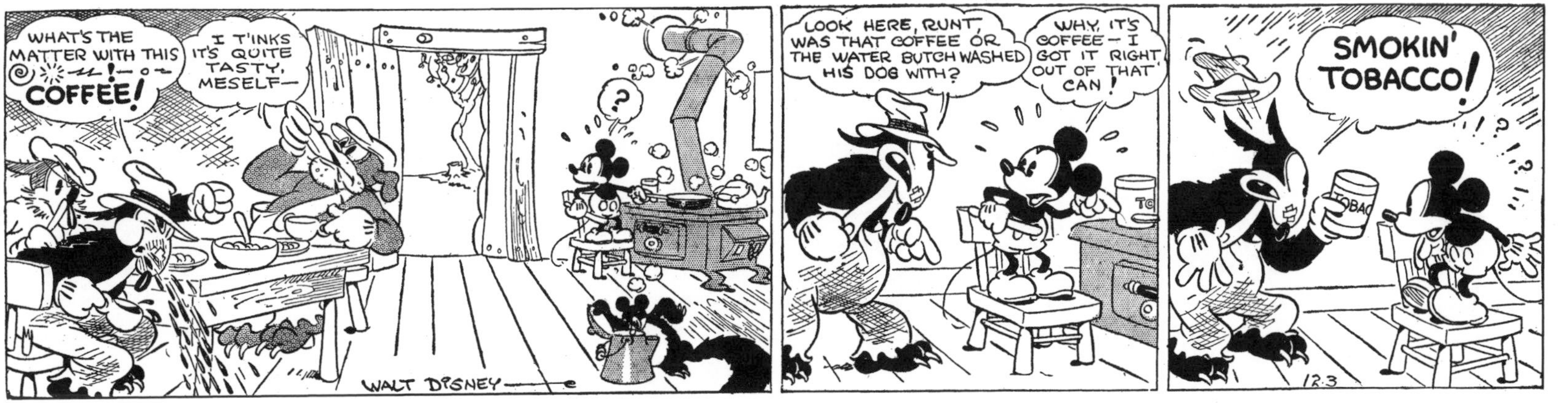
WHAT'S THE MATTER WITH THIS COFFEE!
I T'INKS IT'S QUITE TASTY, MESELF —
WALT DISNEY
LOOK HERE, RUNT, WAS THAT COFFEE OR THE WATER BUTCH WASHED HIS DOG WITH?
WHY, IT'S COFFEE — I GOT IT RIGHT OUT OF THAT CAN!
SMOKIN' TOBACCO!
12-3

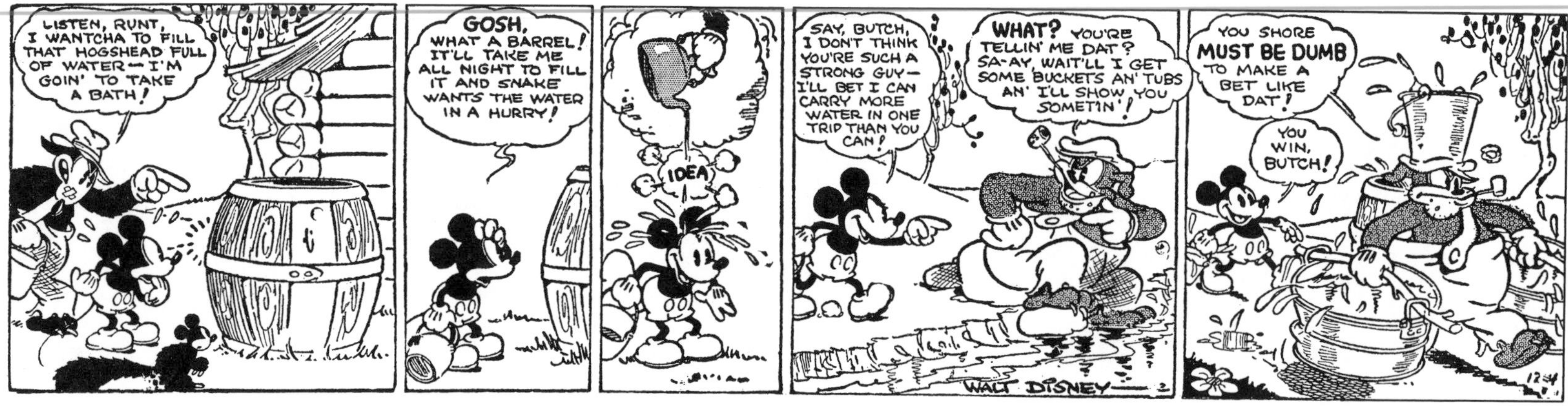
LISTEN, RUNT, I WANTCHA TO FILL THAT HOGSHEAD FULL OF WATER— I'M GOIN' TO TAKE A BATH!
GOSH, WHAT A BARREL! IT'LL TAKE ME ALL NIGHT TO FILL IT AND SNAKE WANTS THE WATER IN A HURRY!
IDEA
SAY, BUTCH, I DON'T THINK YOU'RE SUCH A STRONG GUY— I'LL BET I CAN CARRY MORE WATER IN ONE TRIP THAN YOU CAN!
WHAT? YOU'RE TELLIN' ME DAT? SA-AY, WAIT'LL I GET SOME BUCKETS AN' TUBS AN' I'LL SHOW YOU SOMETIN'!
WALT DISNEY
YOU SHORE MUST BE DUMB TO MAKE A BET LIKE DAT!
YOU WIN, BUTCH!
12-4

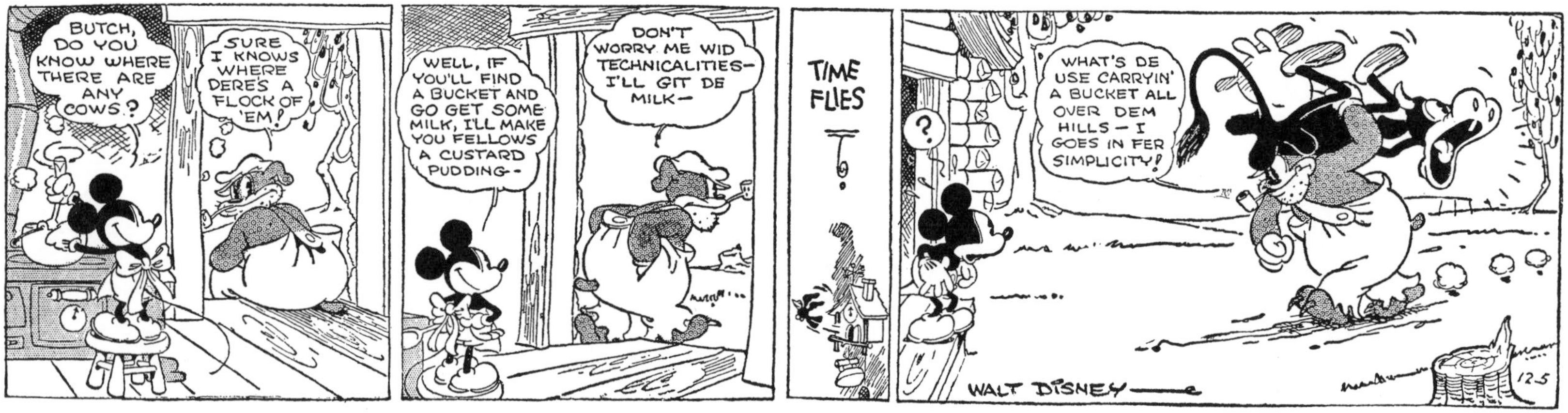
BUTCH, DO YOU KNOW WHERE THERE ARE ANY COWS?
SURE I KNOWS WHERE DERE'S A FLOCK OF 'EM!
WELL, IF YOU'LL FIND A BUCKET AND GO GET SOME MILK, I'LL MAKE YOU FELLOWS A CUSTARD PUDDING-
DON'T WORRY ME WID TECHNICALITIES- I'LL GIT DE MILK-
TIME FLIES
?
WHAT'S DE USE CARRYIN' A BUCKET ALL OVER DEM HILLS— I GOES IN FER SIMPLICITY!
WALT DISNEY
12-5

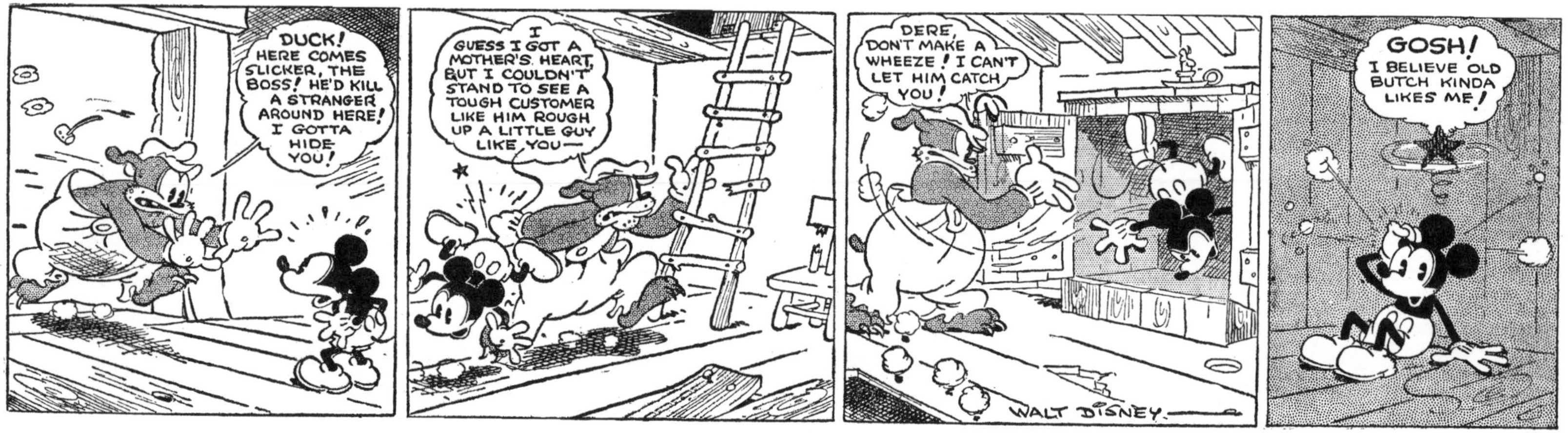
DUCK! HERE COMES SLICKER, THE BOSS! HE'D KILL A STRANGER AROUND HERE! I GOTTA HIDE YOU!
I GUESS I GOT A MOTHER'S HEART, BUT I COULDN'T STAND TO SEE A TOUGH CUSTOMER LIKE HIM ROUGH UP A LITTLE GUY LIKE YOU—
DERE, DON'T MAKE A WHEEZE! I CAN'T LET HIM CATCH YOU!
WALT DISNEY
GOSH! I BELIEVE OLD BUTCH KINDA LIKES ME!

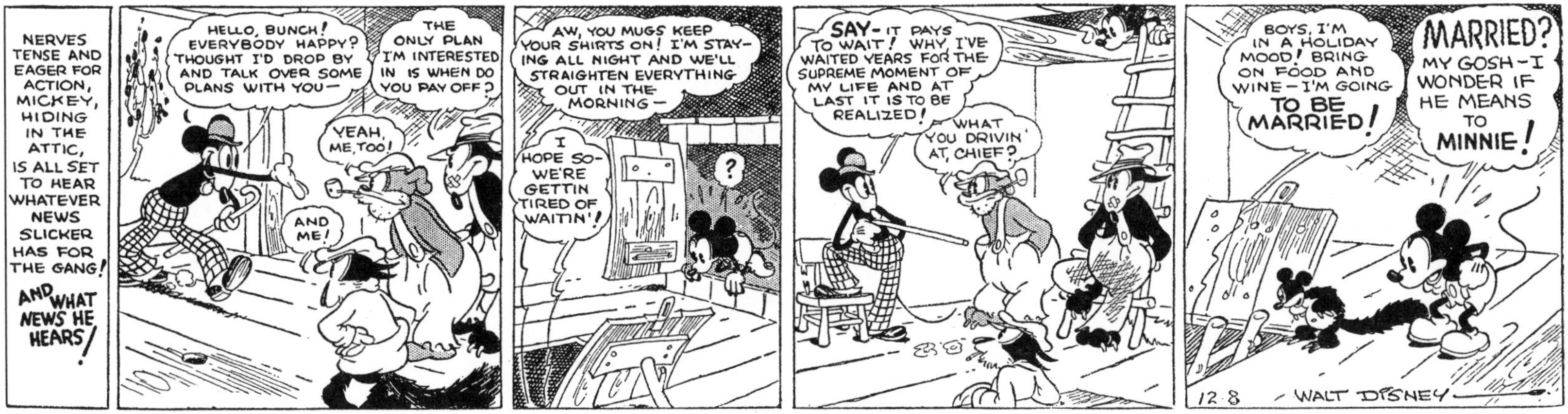
NERVES TENSE AND EAGER FOR ACTION, MICKEY, HIDING IN THE ATTIC, IS ALL SET TO HEAR WHATEVER NEWS SLICKER HAS FOR THE GANG!
AND WHAT NEWS HE HEARS!
HELLO, BUNCH! EVERYBODY HAPPY? THOUGHT I'D DROP BY AND TALK OVER SOME PLANS WITH YOU—
THE ONLY PLAN I'M INTERESTED IN IS WHEN DO YOU PAY OFF?
YEAH, ME, TOO!
AND ME!
AW, YOU MUGS KEEP YOUR SHIRTS ON! I'M STAYING ALL NIGHT AND WE'LL STRAIGHTEN EVERYTHING OUT IN THE MORNING—
I HOPE SO—WE'RE GETTIN TIRED OF WAITIN'!
?
SAY— IT PAYS TO WAIT! WHY, I'VE WAITED YEARS FOR THE SUPREME MOMENT OF MY LIFE AND AT LAST IT IS TO BE REALIZED!
WHAT YOU DRIVIN AT, CHIEF?
BOYS, I'M IN A HOLIDAY MOOD! BRING ON FOOD AND WINE—I'M GOING TO BE MARRIED!
MARRIED? MY GOSH—I WONDER IF HE MEANS TO MINNIE!
12·8
WALT DISNEY

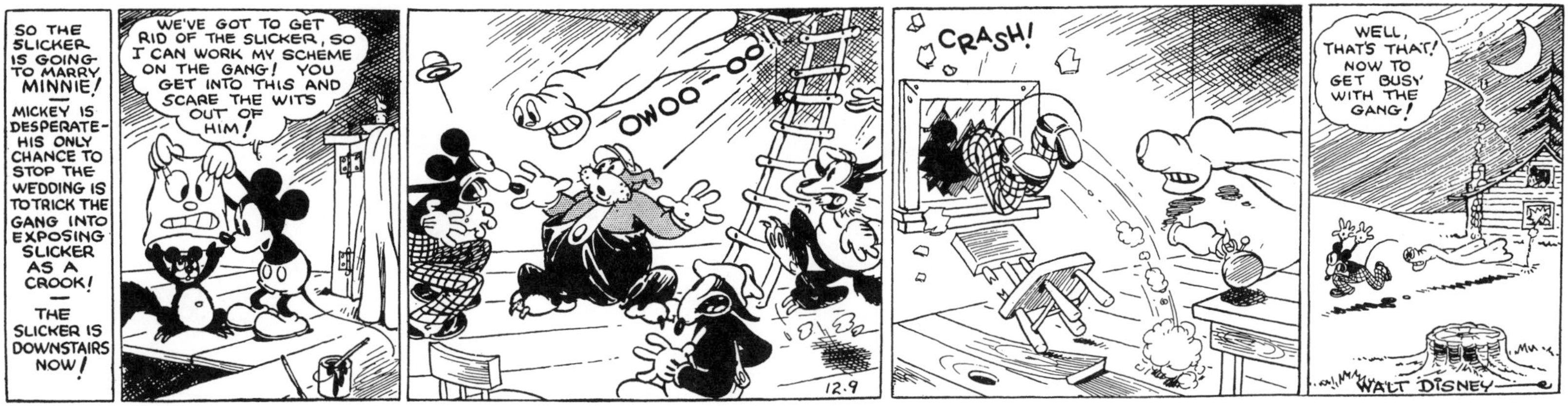
SO THE SLICKER IS GOING TO MARRY MINNIE! — MICKEY IS DESPERATE— HIS ONLY CHANCE TO STOP THE WEDDING IS TO TRICK THE GANG INTO EXPOSING SLICKER AS A CROOK! — THE SLICKER IS DOWNSTAIRS NOW!
WE'VE GOT TO GET RID OF THE SLICKER, SO I CAN WORK MY SCHEME ON THE GANG! YOU GET INTO THIS AND SCARE THE WITS OUT OF HIM!
OWOO-OO
12·9
CRASH!
WELL, THAT'S THAT! NOW TO GET BUSY WITH THE GANG!
WALT DISNEY

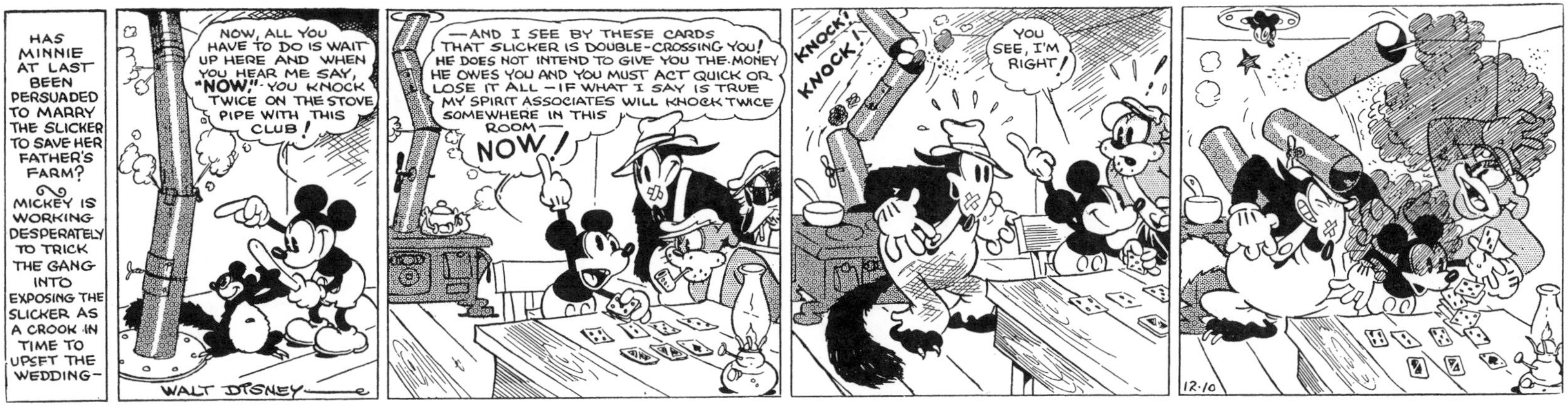
HAS MINNIE AT LAST BEEN PERSUADED TO MARRY THE SLICKER TO SAVE HER FATHER'S FARM?
MICKEY IS WORKING DESPERATELY TO TRICK THE GANG INTO EXPOSING THE SLICKER AS A CROOK IN TIME TO UPSET THE WEDDING—
NOW, ALL YOU HAVE TO DO IS WAIT UP HERE AND WHEN YOU HEAR ME SAY, "NOW!" YOU KNOCK TWICE ON THE STOVE PIPE WITH THIS CLUB!
WALT DISNEY
—AND I SEE BY THESE CARDS THAT SLICKER IS DOUBLE-CROSSING YOU! HE DOES NOT INTEND TO GIVE YOU THE MONEY HE OWES YOU AND YOU MUST ACT QUICK OR LOSE IT ALL—IF WHAT I SAY IS TRUE MY SPIRIT ASSOCIATES WILL KNOCK TWICE SOMEWHERE IN THIS ROOM—
NOW!
KNOCK! KNOCK!
YOU SEE, I'M RIGHT!
12·10

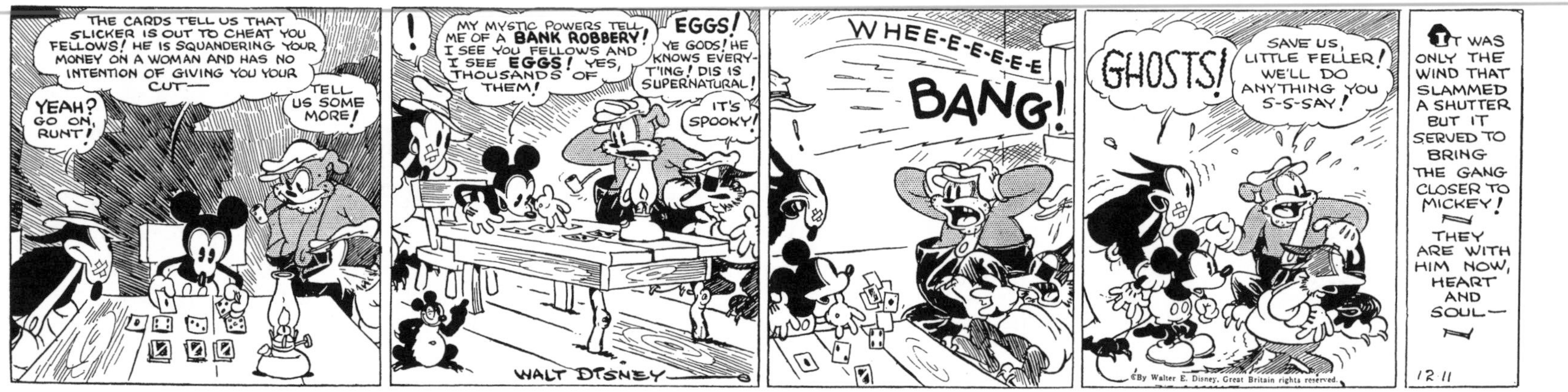
THE CARDS TELL US THAT SLICKER IS OUT TO CHEAT YOU FELLOWS! HE IS SQUANDERING YOUR MONEY ON A WOMAN AND HAS NO INTENTION OF GIVING YOU YOUR CUT—
YEAH? GO ON, RUNT!
TELL US SOME MORE!
!
MY MYSTIC POWERS TELL ME OF A BANK ROBBERY! I SEE YOU FELLOWS AND I SEE EGGS! YES, THOUSANDS OF THEM!
EGGS! YE GODS! HE KNOWS EVERY-T'ING! DIS IS SUPERNATURAL!
IT'S SPOOKY!
WALT DISNEY
WHEE-E-E-E-E-E
BANG!
!
GHOSTS!
SAVE US, LITTLE FELLER! WE'LL DO ANYTHING YOU S-S-SAY!
©By Walter E. Disney. Great Britain rights reserved.
IT WAS ONLY THE WIND THAT SLAMMED A SHUTTER BUT IT SERVED TO BRING THE GANG CLOSER TO MICKEY! THEY ARE WITH HIM NOW, HEART AND SOUL—
12.11

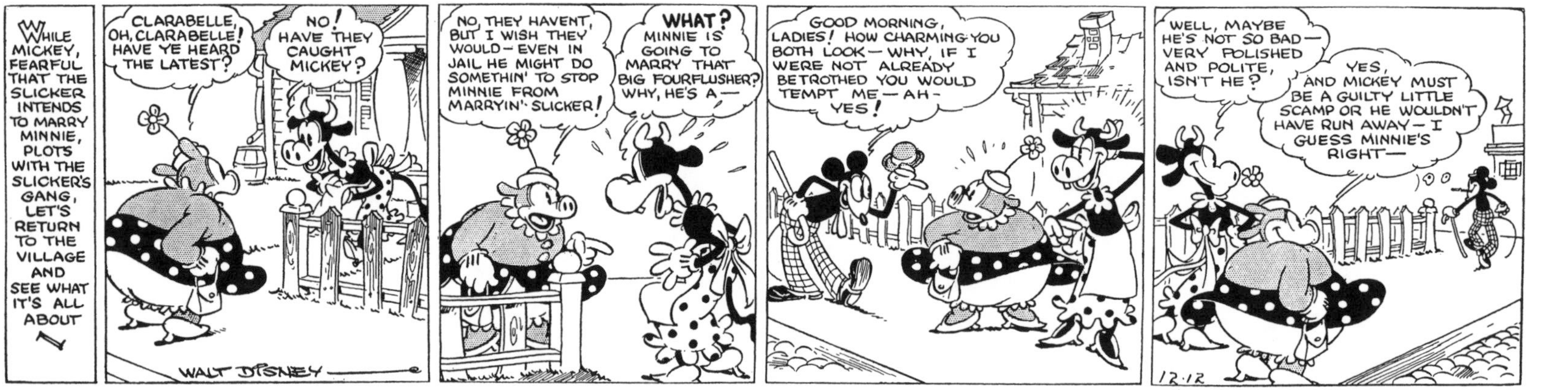
WHILE MICKEY, FEARFUL THAT THE SLICKER INTENDS TO MARRY MINNIE, PLOTS WITH THE SLICKER'S GANG, LET'S RETURN TO THE VILLAGE AND SEE WHAT IT'S ALL ABOUT
CLARABELLE, OH, CLARABELLE! HAVE YE HEARD THE LATEST?
NO! HAVE THEY CAUGHT MICKEY?
WALT DISNEY
NO, THEY HAVENT, BUT I WISH THEY WOULD—EVEN IN JAIL HE MIGHT DO SOMETHIN' TO STOP MINNIE FROM MARRYIN' SLICKER!
WHAT? MINNIE IS GOING TO MARRY THAT BIG FOURFLUSHER? WHY, HE'S A—
GOOD MORNING, LADIES! HOW CHARMING YOU BOTH LOOK—WHY, IF I WERE NOT ALREADY BETROTHED YOU WOULD TEMPT ME—AH—YES!
WELL, MAYBE HE'S NOT SO BAD—VERY POLISHED AND POLITE, ISN'T HE?
YES, AND MICKEY MUST BE A GUILTY LITTLE SCAMP OR HE WOULDN'T HAVE RUN AWAY—I GUESS MINNIE'S RIGHT—
12.12

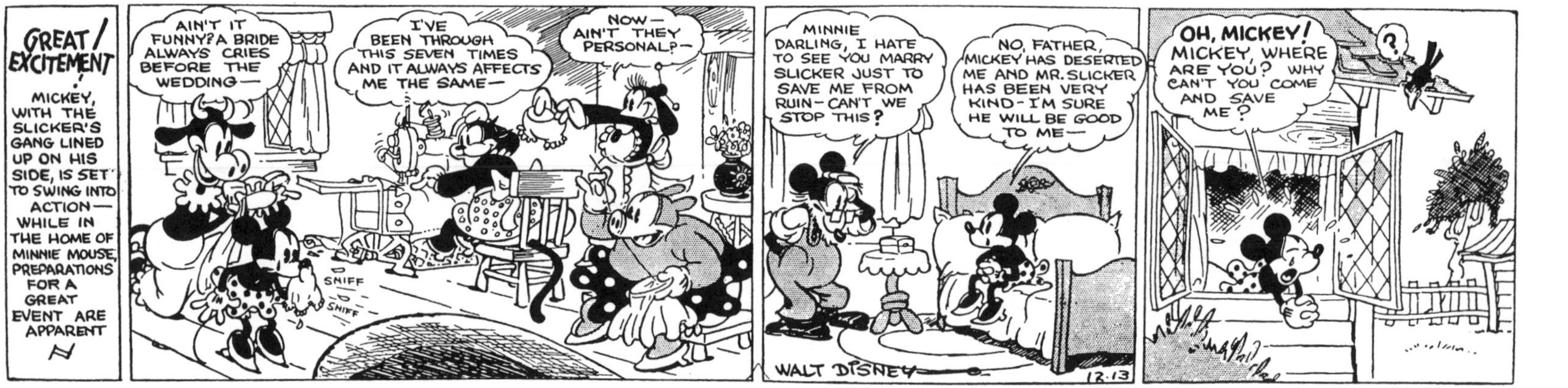
GREAT! EXCITEMENT!
MICKEY, WITH THE SLICKER'S GANG LINED UP ON HIS SIDE, IS SET TO SWING INTO ACTION—WHILE IN THE HOME OF MINNIE MOUSE, PREPARATIONS FOR A GREAT EVENT ARE APPARENT
AIN'T IT FUNNY? A BRIDE ALWAYS CRIES BEFORE THE WEDDING—
I'VE BEEN THROUGH THIS SEVEN TIMES AND IT ALWAYS AFFECTS ME THE SAME—
NOW—AIN'T THEY PERSONAL?—
SNIFF
SNIFF
MINNIE DARLING, I HATE TO SEE YOU MARRY SLICKER JUST TO SAVE ME FROM RUIN—CAN'T WE STOP THIS?
NO, FATHER, MICKEY HAS DESERTED ME AND MR. SLICKER HAS BEEN VERY KIND—I'M SURE HE WILL BE GOOD TO ME—
WALT DISNEY
12.13
OH, MICKEY! MICKEY, WHERE ARE YOU? WHY CAN'T YOU COME AND SAVE ME?
?

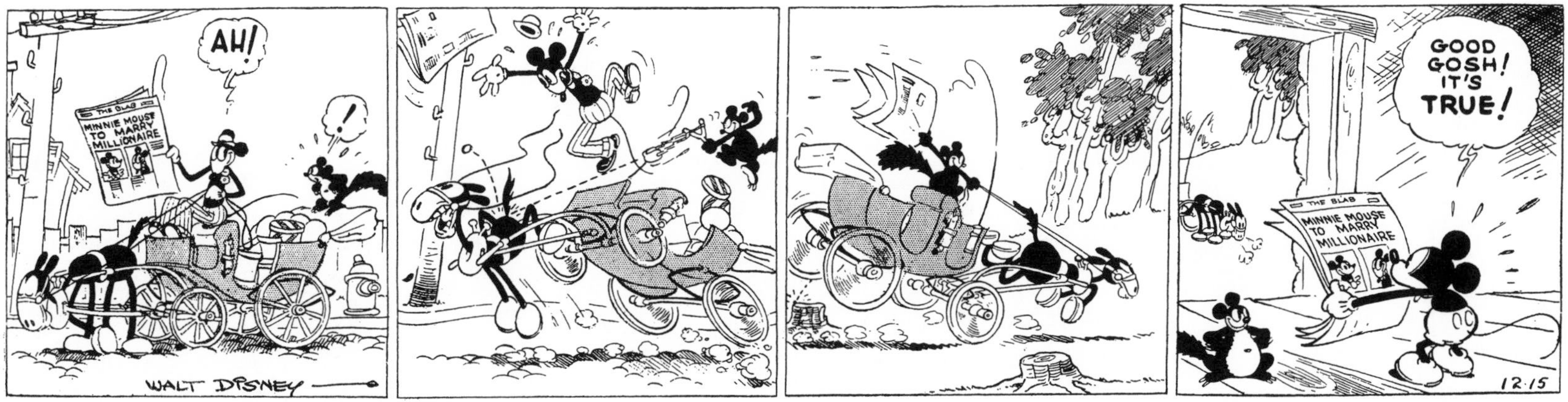

THE BLAB
MINNIE MOUSE TO MARRY MILLIONAIRE
AH!
!
WALT DISNEY
THE BLAB
MINNIE MOUSE TO MARRY MILLIONAIRE
GOOD GOSH! IT'S TRUE!
12·15

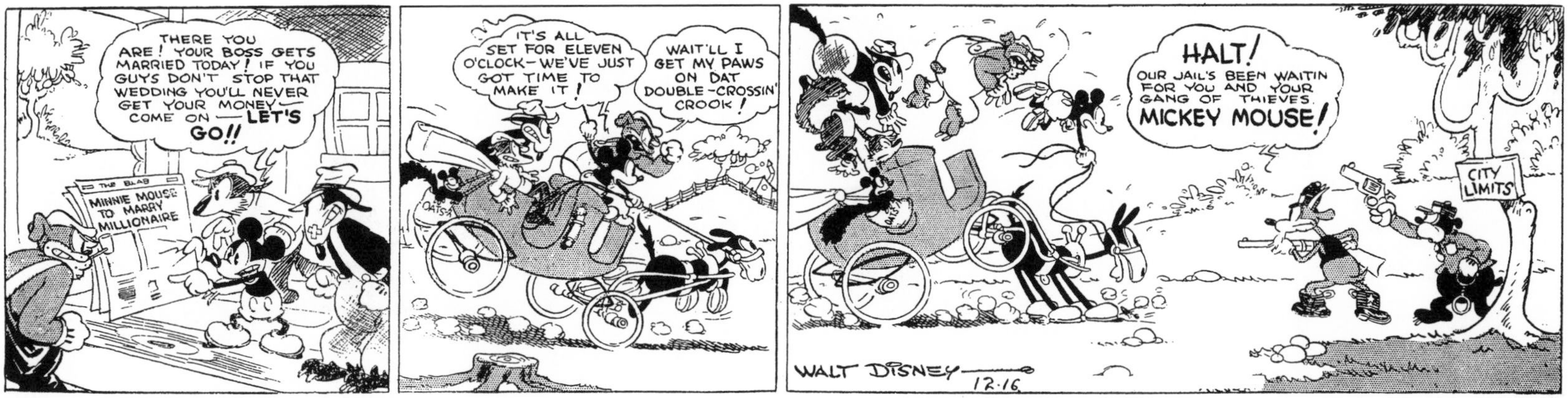

THERE YOU ARE! YOUR BOSS GETS MARRIED TODAY! IF YOU GUYS DON'T STOP THAT WEDDING YOU'LL NEVER GET YOUR MONEY— COME ON— LET'S GO!!
THE BLAB
MINNIE MOUSE TO MARRY MILLIONAIRE
IT'S ALL SET FOR ELEVEN O'CLOCK—WE'VE JUST GOT TIME TO MAKE IT!
WAIT'LL I GET MY PAWS ON DAT DOUBLE-CROSSIN' CROOK!
HALT!
OUR JAIL'S BEEN WAITIN FOR YOU AND YOUR GANG OF THIEVES. MICKEY MOUSE!
CITY LIMITS
WALT DISNEY
12·16

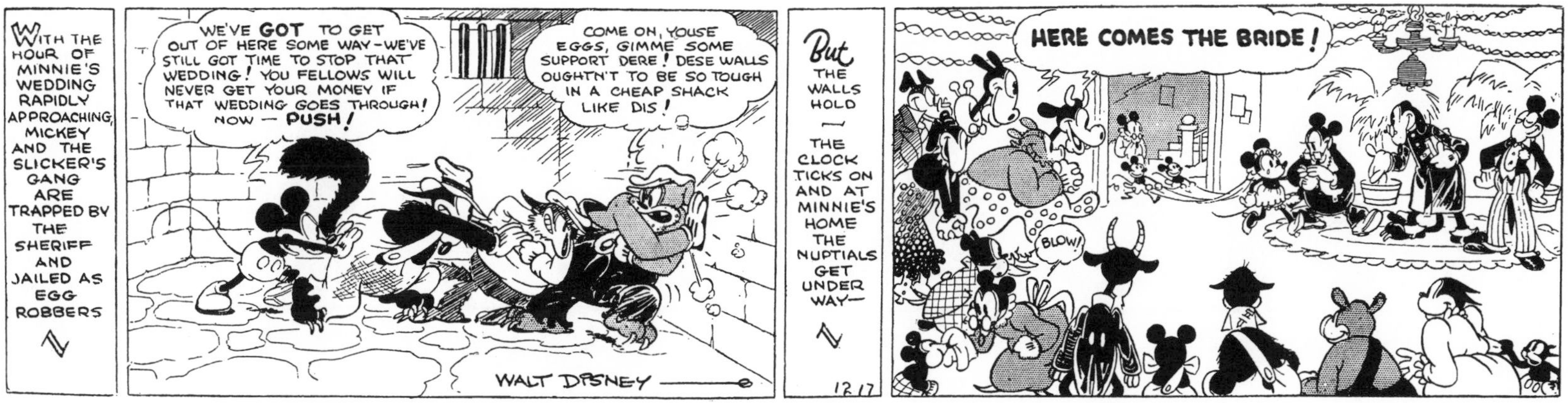

WITH THE HOUR OF MINNIE'S WEDDING RAPIDLY APPROACHING, MICKEY AND THE SLICKER'S GANG ARE TRAPPED BY THE SHERIFF AND JAILED AS EGG ROBBERS
WE'VE GOT TO GET OUT OF HERE SOME WAY—WE'VE STILL GOT TIME TO STOP THAT WEDDING! YOU FELLOWS WILL NEVER GET YOUR MONEY IF THAT WEDDING GOES THROUGH! NOW — PUSH!
COME ON, YOUSE EGGS, GIMME SOME SUPPORT DERE! DESE WALLS OUGHTN'T TO BE SO TOUGH IN A CHEAP SHACK LIKE DIS!
WALT DISNEY
But THE WALLS HOLD — THE CLOCK TICKS ON AND AT MINNIE'S HOME THE NUPTIALS GET UNDER WAY—
12·17
HERE COMES THE BRIDE!
BLOW!

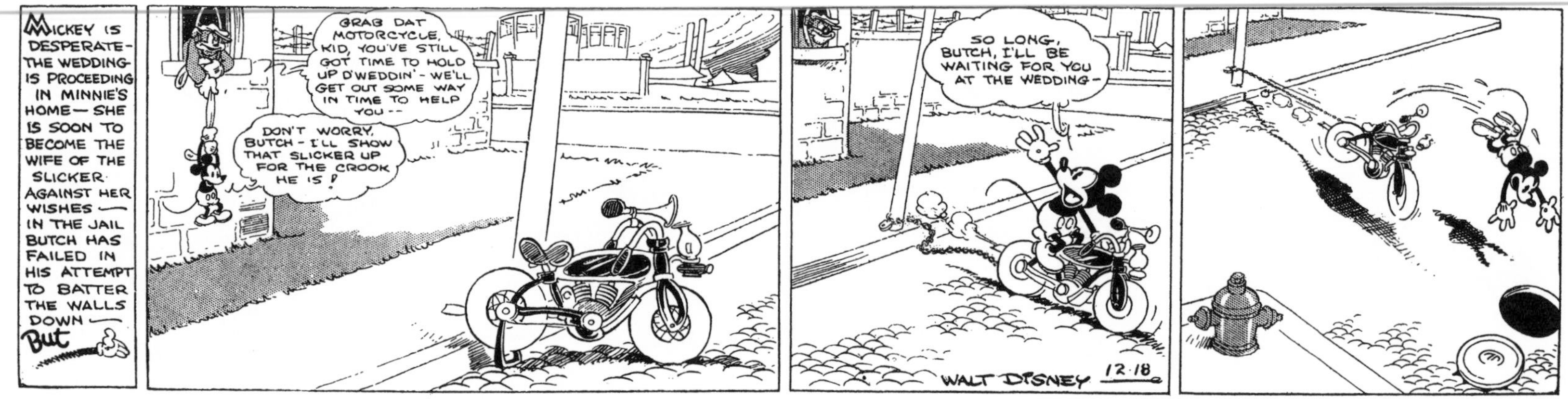
MICKEY IS DESPERATE- THE WEDDING IS PROCEEDING IN MINNIE'S HOME— SHE IS SOON TO BECOME THE WIFE OF THE SLICKER AGAINST HER WISHES — IN THE JAIL BUTCH HAS FAILED IN HIS ATTEMPT TO BATTER THE WALLS DOWN — But
GRAB DAT MOTORCYCLE, KID, YOU'VE STILL GOT TIME TO HOLD UP D'WEDDIN' - WE'LL GET OUT SOME WAY IN TIME TO HELP YOU --
DON'T WORRY, BUTCH - I'LL SHOW THAT SLICKER UP FOR THE CROOK HE IS!
SO LONG, BUTCH, I'LL BE WAITING FOR YOU AT THE WEDDING-
WALT DISNEY 12-18

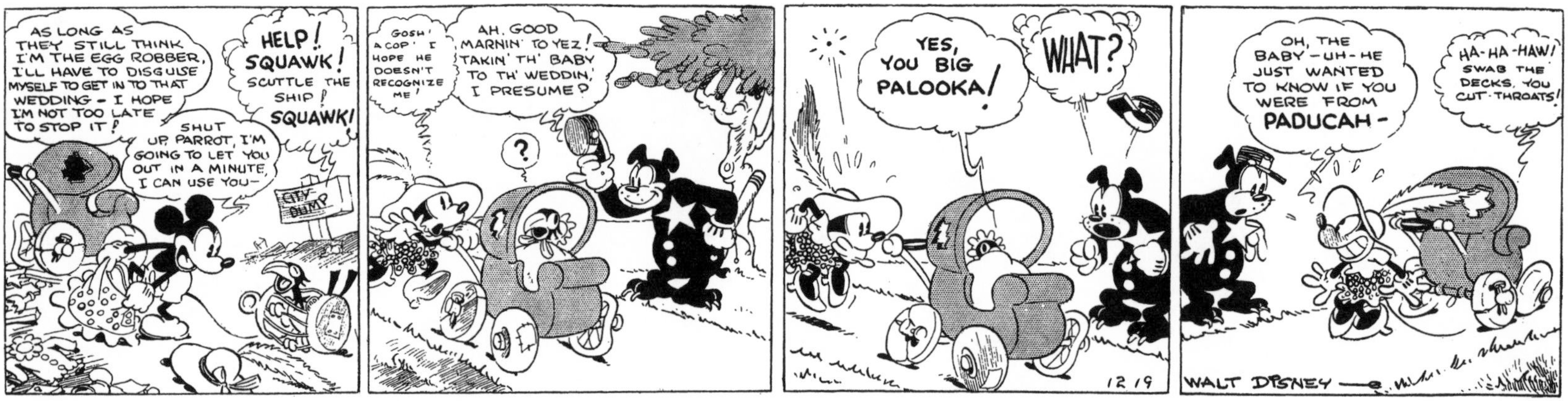
AS LONG AS THEY STILL THINK I'M THE EGG ROBBER, I'LL HAVE TO DISGUISE MYSELF TO GET IN TO THAT WEDDING - I HOPE I'M NOT TOO LATE TO STOP IT!
HELP! SQUAWK! SCUTTLE THE SHIP! SQUAWK!
SHUT UP, PARROT, I'M GOING TO LET YOU OUT IN A MINUTE, I CAN USE YOU-
CITY DUMP
GOSH! A COP! I HOPE HE DOESN'T RECOGNIZE ME!
AH, GOOD MARNIN' TO YEZ! TAKIN' TH' BABY TO TH' WEDDIN', I PRESUME?
?
YES, YOU BIG PALOOKA!
WHAT?
OH, THE BABY - UH - HE JUST WANTED TO KNOW IF YOU WERE FROM PADUCAH -
HA-HA-HAW! SWAB THE DECKS, YOU CUT-THROATS!
12 19
WALT DISNEY

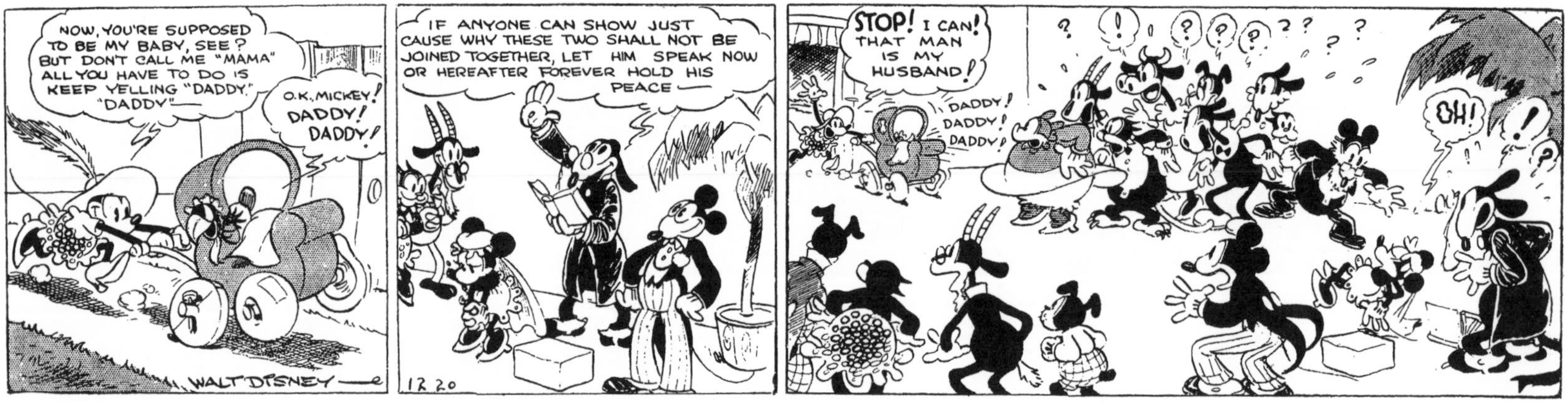
NOW, YOU'RE SUPPOSED TO BE MY BABY, SEE? BUT DON'T CALL ME "MAMA" ALL YOU HAVE TO DO IS KEEP YELLING "DADDY" "DADDY" —
O.K., MICKEY! DADDY! DADDY!
WALT DISNEY
IF ANYONE CAN SHOW JUST CAUSE WHY THESE TWO SHALL NOT BE JOINED TOGETHER, LET HIM SPEAK NOW OR HEREAFTER FOREVER HOLD HIS PEACE —
12 20
STOP! I CAN! THAT MAN IS MY HUSBAND!
DADDY! DADDY! DADDY!
OH!

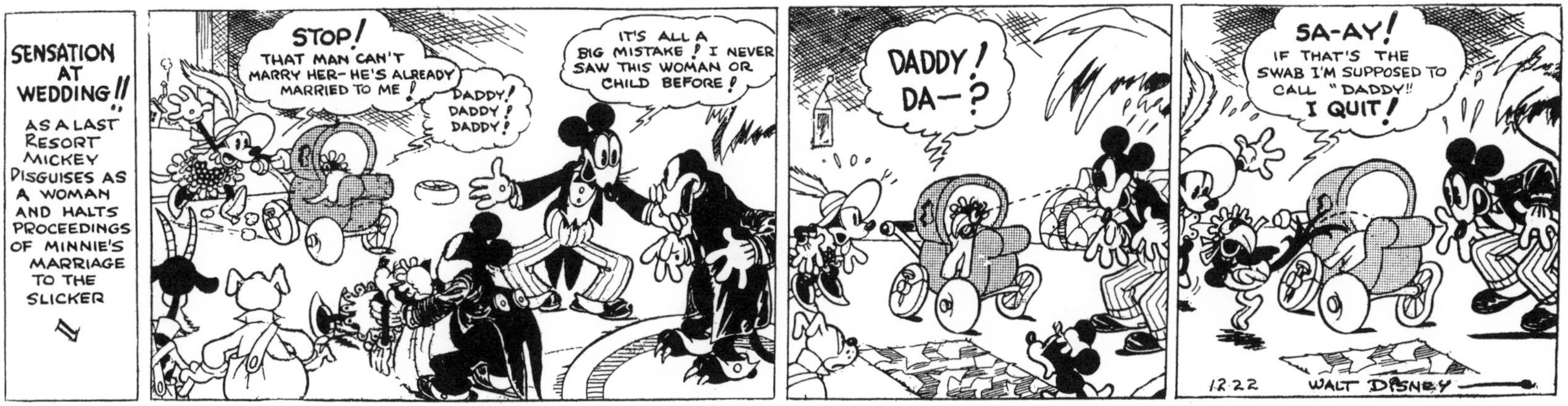
SENSATION AT WEDDING!!
AS A LAST RESORT MICKEY DISGUISES AS A WOMAN AND HALTS PROCEEDINGS OF MINNIE'S MARRIAGE TO THE SLICKER !!
STOP! THAT MAN CAN'T MARRY HER- HE'S ALREADY MARRIED TO ME!
DADDY! DADDY! DADDY!
IT'S ALL A BIG MISTAKE! I NEVER SAW THIS WOMAN OR CHILD BEFORE!
DADDY! DA-?
SA-AY! IF THAT'S THE SWAB I'M SUPPOSED TO CALL "DADDY!! I QUIT!
12.22
WALT DISNEY

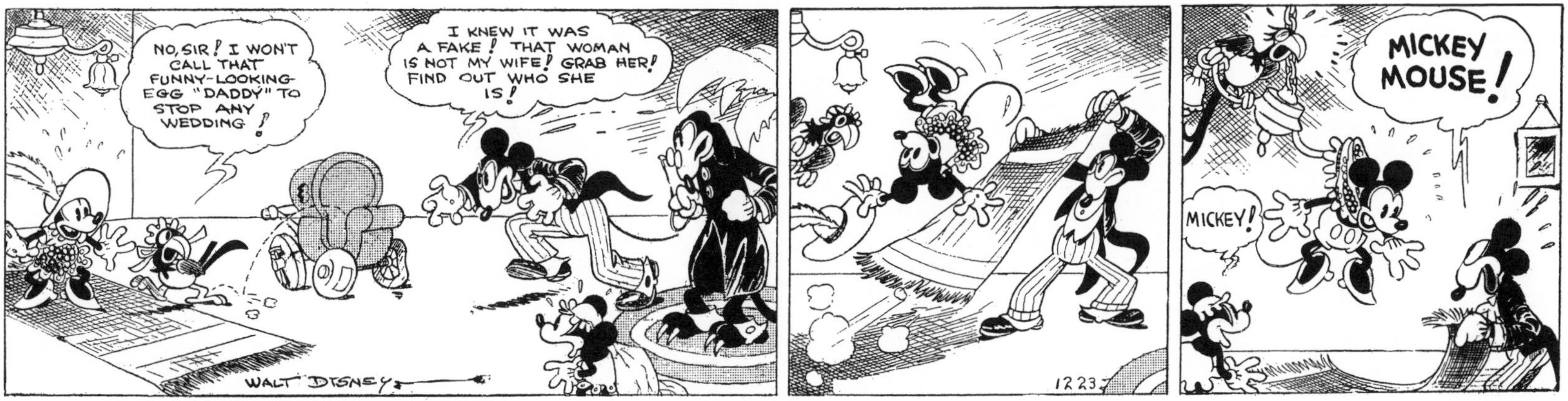
NO, SIR! I WON'T CALL THAT FUNNY-LOOKING EGG "DADDY" TO STOP ANY WEDDING!
I KNEW IT WAS A FAKE! THAT WOMAN IS NOT MY WIFE! GRAB HER! FIND OUT WHO SHE IS!
WALT DISNEY
12.23
MICKEY MOUSE!
MICKEY!

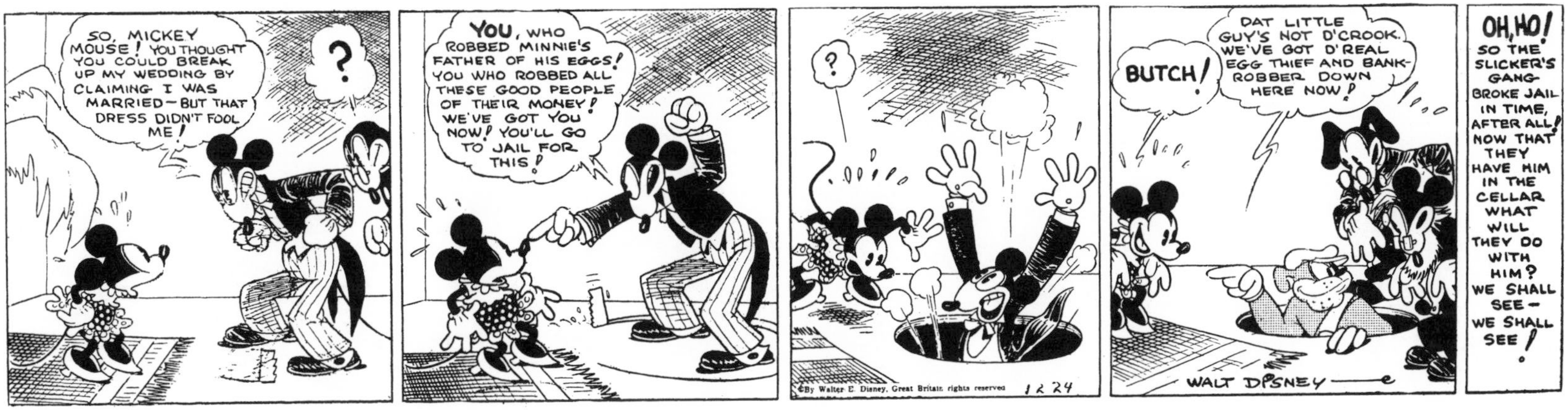
SO, MICKEY MOUSE! YOU THOUGHT YOU COULD BREAK UP MY WEDDING BY CLAIMING I WAS MARRIED—BUT THAT DRESS DIDN'T FOOL ME!
?
YOU, WHO ROBBED MINNIE'S FATHER OF HIS EGGS! YOU WHO ROBBED ALL THESE GOOD PEOPLE OF THEIR MONEY! WE'VE GOT YOU NOW! YOU'LL GO TO JAIL FOR THIS!
?
©By Walter E. Disney, Great Britain rights reserved
12.24
BUTCH!
DAT LITTLE GUY'S NOT D'CROOK. WE'VE GOT D'REAL EGG THIEF AND BANK-ROBBER DOWN HERE NOW!
WALT DISNEY
OH, HO! SO THE SLICKER'S GANG BROKE JAIL IN TIME, AFTER ALL! NOW THAT THEY HAVE HIM IN THE CELLAR WHAT WILL THEY DO WITH HIM? WE SHALL SEE— WE SHALL SEE!

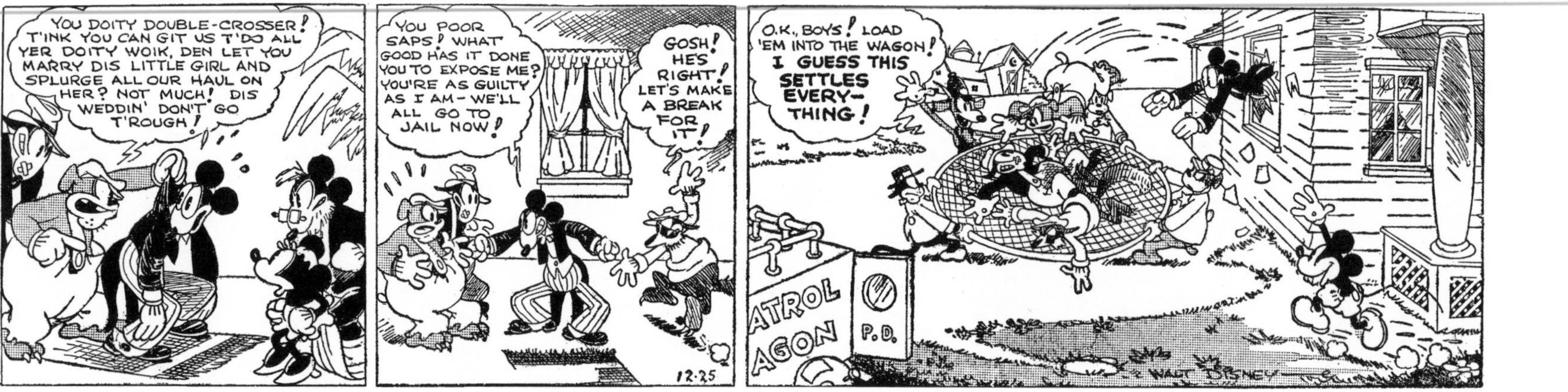
YOU DOITY DOUBLE-CROSSER! T'INK YOU CAN GIT US T'DO ALL YER DOITY WOIK, DEN LET YOU MARRY DIS LITTLE GIRL AND SPLURGE ALL OUR HAUL ON HER? NOT MUCH! DIS WEDDIN' DON'T GO T'ROUGH!
YOU POOR SAPS! WHAT GOOD HAS IT DONE YOU TO EXPOSE ME? YOU'RE AS GUILTY AS I AM - WE'LL ALL GO TO JAIL NOW!
GOSH! HE'S RIGHT! LET'S MAKE A BREAK FOR IT!
12-25
O.K., BOYS! LOAD 'EM INTO THE WAGON! I GUESS THIS SETTLES EVERY-THING!
ATROL AGON
P.D.
WALT DISNEY

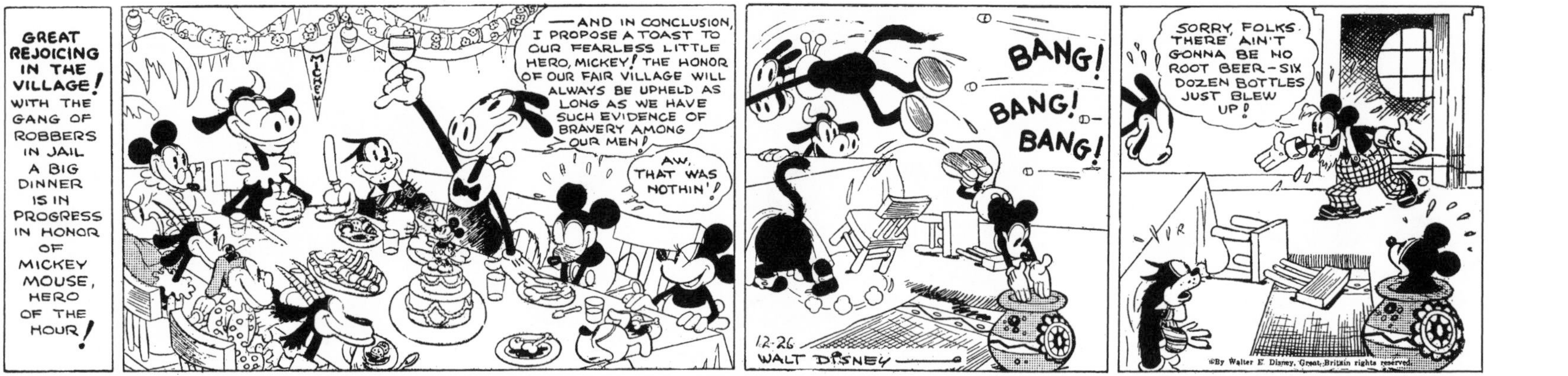
GREAT REJOICING IN THE VILLAGE! WITH THE GANG OF ROBBERS IN JAIL A BIG DINNER IS IN PROGRESS IN HONOR OF MICKEY MOUSE, HERO OF THE HOUR!
—AND IN CONCLUSION, I PROPOSE A TOAST TO OUR FEARLESS LITTLE HERO, MICKEY! THE HONOR OF OUR FAIR VILLAGE WILL ALWAYS BE UPHELD AS LONG AS WE HAVE SUCH EVIDENCE OF BRAVERY AMONG OUR MEN!
AW, THAT WAS NOTHIN'!
MICKEY
BANG!
BANG!
BANG!
12-26
WALT DISNEY
SORRY, FOLKS THERE AIN'T GONNA BE NO ROOT BEER-SIX DOZEN BOTTLES JUST BLEW UP!
©By Walter E Disney, Great Britain rights reserved.

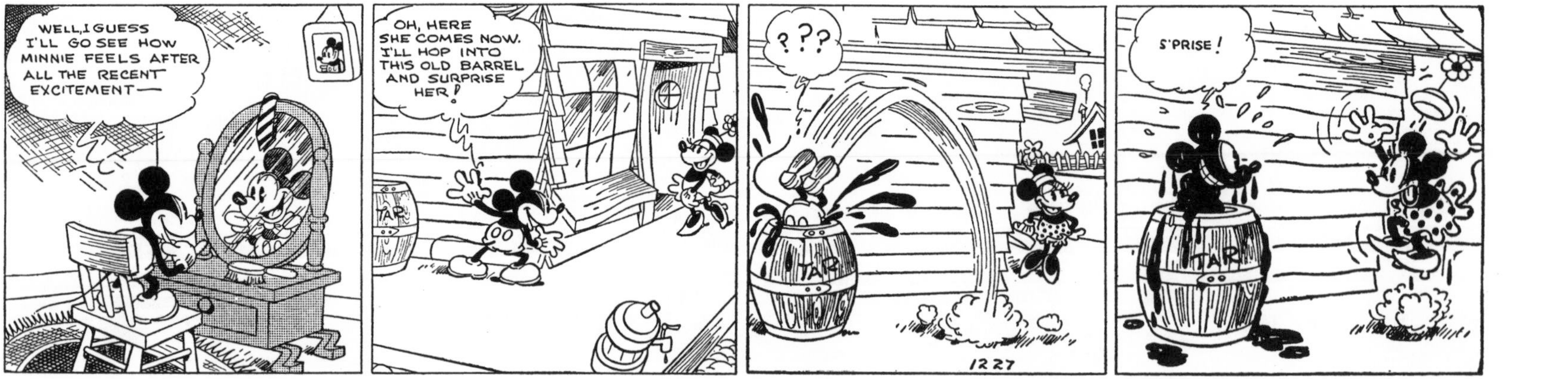
WELL, I GUESS I'LL GO SEE HOW MINNIE FEELS AFTER ALL THE RECENT EXCITEMENT—
OH, HERE SHE COMES NOW. I'LL HOP INTO THIS OLD BARREL AND SURPRISE HER!
TAR
???
TAR
12 27
S'PRISE!
TAR

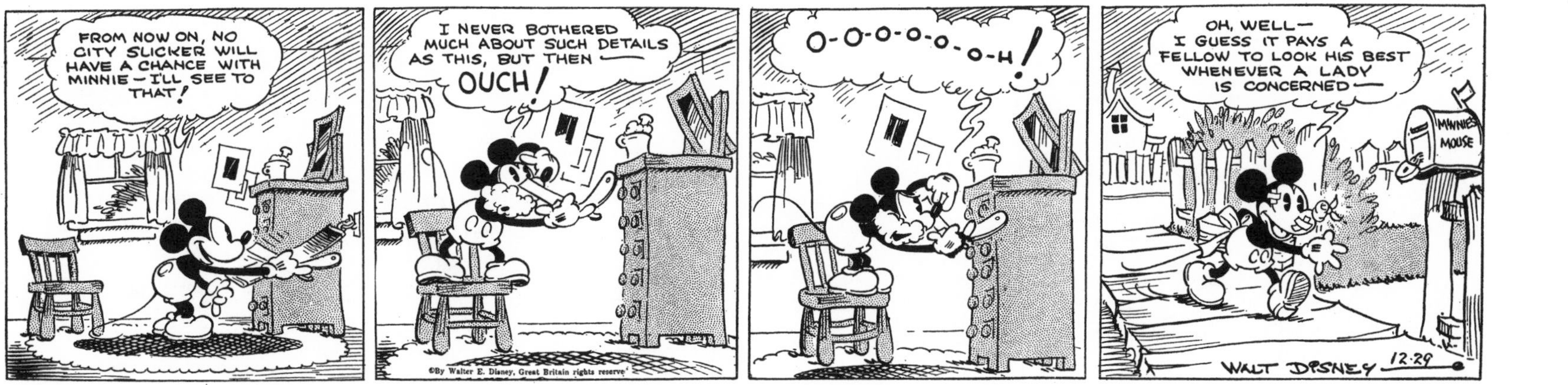
FROM NOW ON, NO CITY SLICKER WILL HAVE A CHANCE WITH MINNIE—I'LL SEE TO THAT!
I NEVER BOTHERED MUCH ABOUT SUCH DETAILS AS THIS, BUT THEN —
OUCH!
©By Walter E. Disney, Great Britain rights reserve
O-O-O-O-O-O-O-H!
OH, WELL— I GUESS IT PAYS A FELLOW TO LOOK HIS BEST WHENEVER A LADY IS CONCERNED—
MINNIE MOUSE
WALT DISNEY 12·29

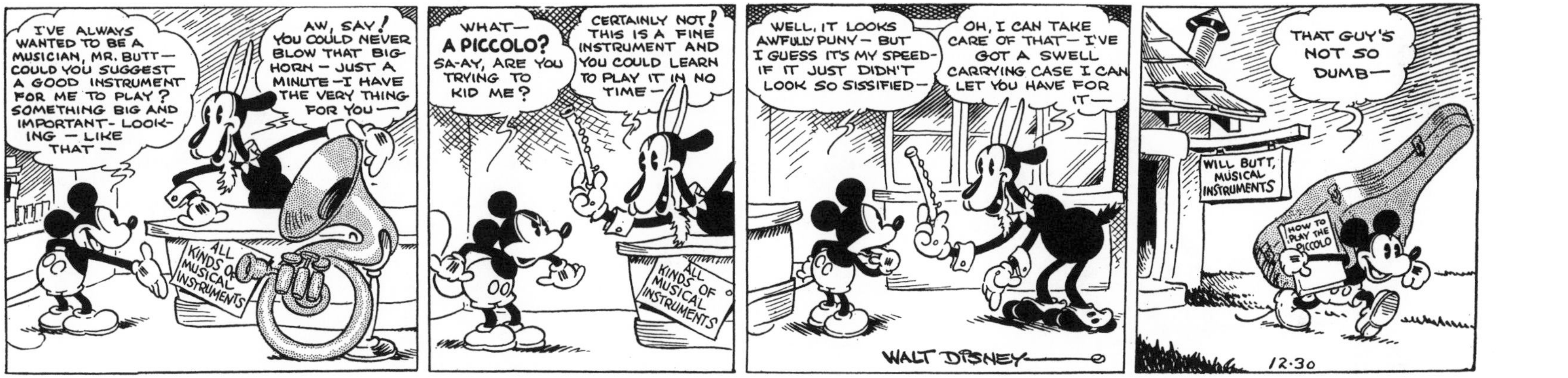
I'VE ALWAYS WANTED TO BE A MUSICIAN, MR. BUTT—COULD YOU SUGGEST A GOOD INSTRUMENT FOR ME TO PLAY? SOMETHING BIG AND IMPORTANT-LOOKING—LIKE THAT—
AW, SAY! YOU COULD NEVER BLOW THAT BIG-HORN—JUST A MINUTE—I HAVE THE VERY THING FOR YOU—
ALL KINDS OF MUSICAL INSTRUMENTS
WHAT— A PICCOLO? SA-AY, ARE YOU TRYING TO KID ME?
CERTAINLY NOT! THIS IS A FINE INSTRUMENT AND YOU COULD LEARN TO PLAY IT IN NO TIME—
ALL KINDS OF MUSICAL INSTRUMENTS
WELL, IT LOOKS AWFULLY PUNY—BUT I GUESS IT'S MY SPEED—IF IT JUST DIDN'T LOOK SO SISSIFIED—
OH, I CAN TAKE CARE OF THAT—I'VE GOT A SWELL CARRYING CASE I CAN LET YOU HAVE FOR IT—
WALT DISNEY
THAT GUY'S NOT SO DUMB—
WILL BUTT, MUSICAL INSTRUMENTS
HOW TO PLAY THE PICCOLO
12·30

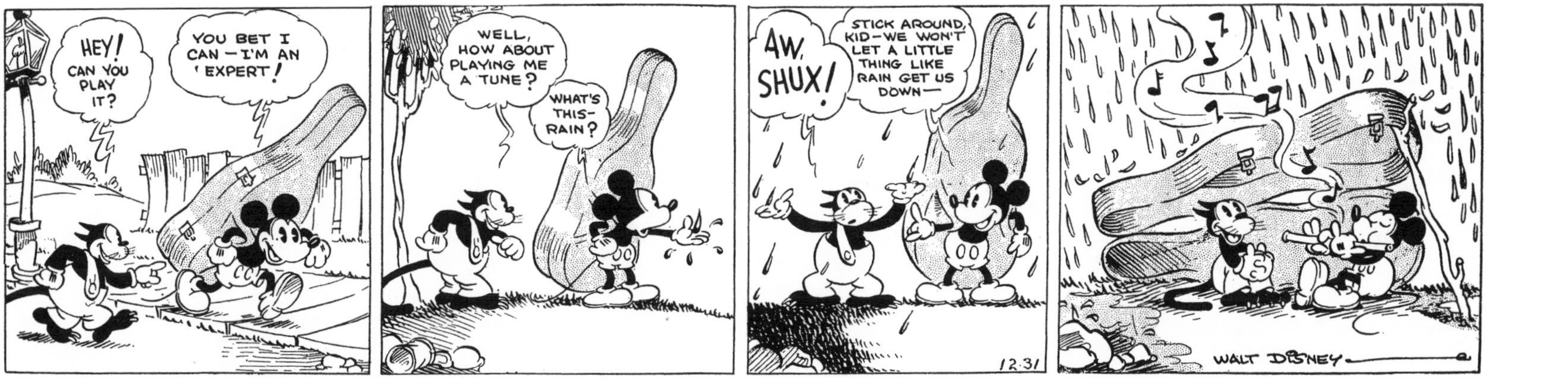
HEY! CAN YOU PLAY IT?
YOU BET I CAN—I'M AN 'EXPERT'!
WELL, HOW ABOUT PLAYING ME A TUNE?
WHAT'S THIS—RAIN?
12·31
AW, SHUX!
STICK AROUND, KID—WE WON'T LET A LITTLE THING LIKE RAIN GET US DOWN—
WALT DISNEY

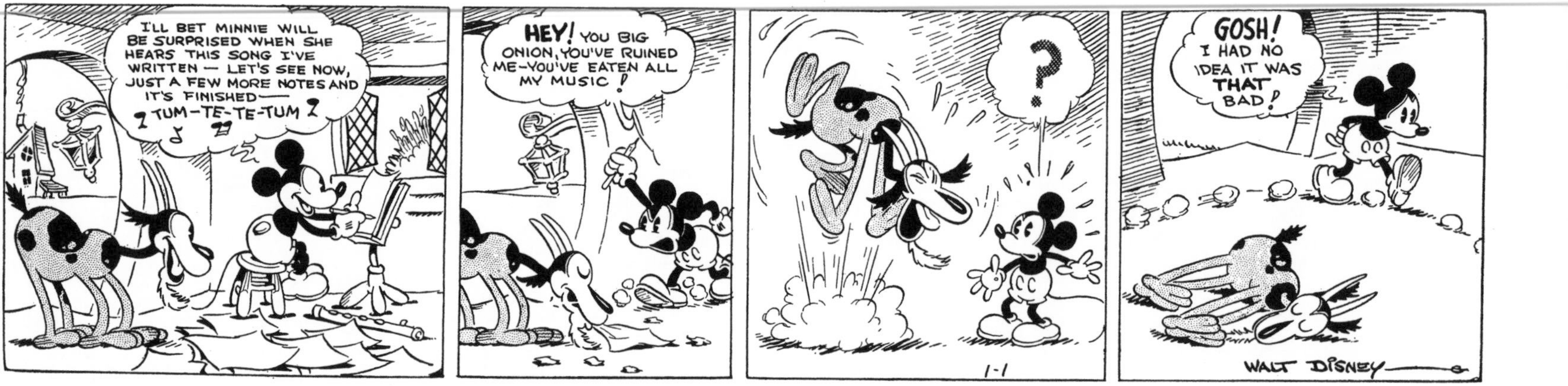
I'LL BET MINNIE WILL BE SURPRISED WHEN SHE HEARS THIS SONG I'VE WRITTEN — LET'S SEE NOW, JUST A FEW MORE NOTES AND IT'S FINISHED— TUM-TE-TE-TUM
HEY! YOU BIG ONION, YOU'VE RUINED ME-YOU'VE EATEN ALL MY MUSIC!
?
1-1
GOSH! I HAD NO IDEA IT WAS THAT BAD!
WALT DISNEY

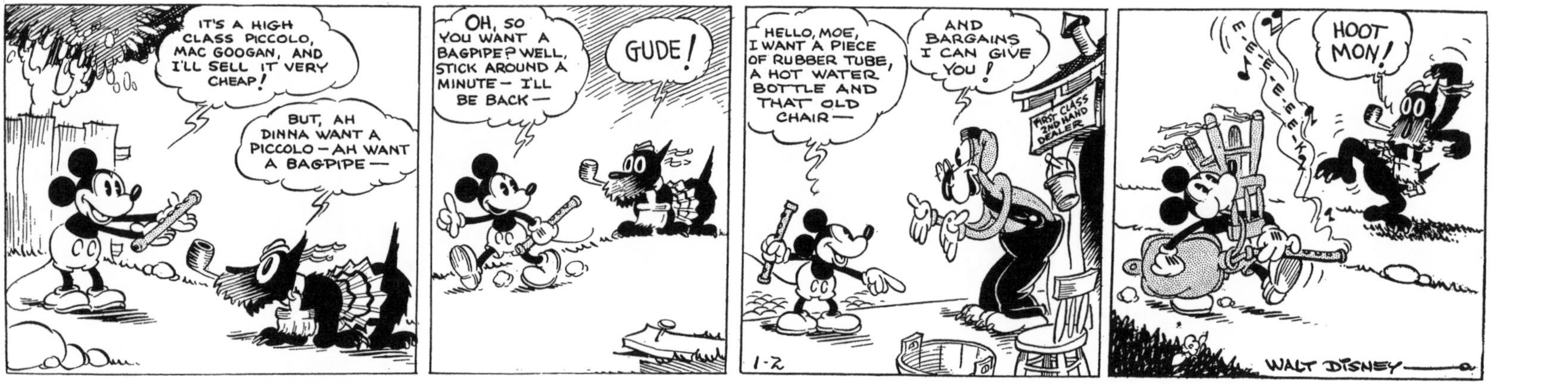
IT'S A HIGH CLASS PICCOLO, MAC GOOGAN, AND I'LL SELL IT VERY CHEAP!
BUT, AH DINNA WANT A PICCOLO—AH WANT A BAGPIPE—
OH, SO YOU WANT A BAGPIPE? WELL, STICK AROUND A MINUTE— I'LL BE BACK—
GUDE!
HELLO, MOE, I WANT A PIECE OF RUBBER TUBE, A HOT WATER BOTTLE AND THAT OLD CHAIR—
AND BARGAINS I CAN GIVE YOU!
FIRST CLASS 2ND HAND DEALER
1-2
E-E-E-E-E-E-K
HOOT MON!
WALT DISNEY

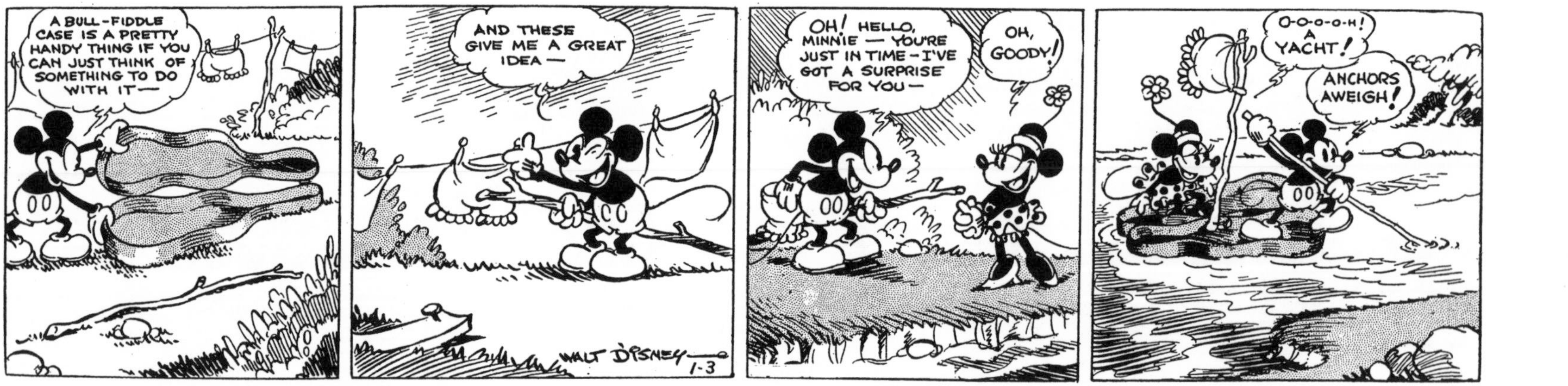
A BULL-FIDDLE CASE IS A PRETTY HANDY THING IF YOU CAN JUST THINK OF SOMETHING TO DO WITH IT—
AND THESE GIVE ME A GREAT IDEA—
WALT DISNEY
1-3
OH! HELLO, MINNIE — YOU'RE JUST IN TIME-I'VE GOT A SURPRISE FOR YOU—
OH, GOODY!
O-O-O-O-H! A YACHT!
ANCHORS AWEIGH!

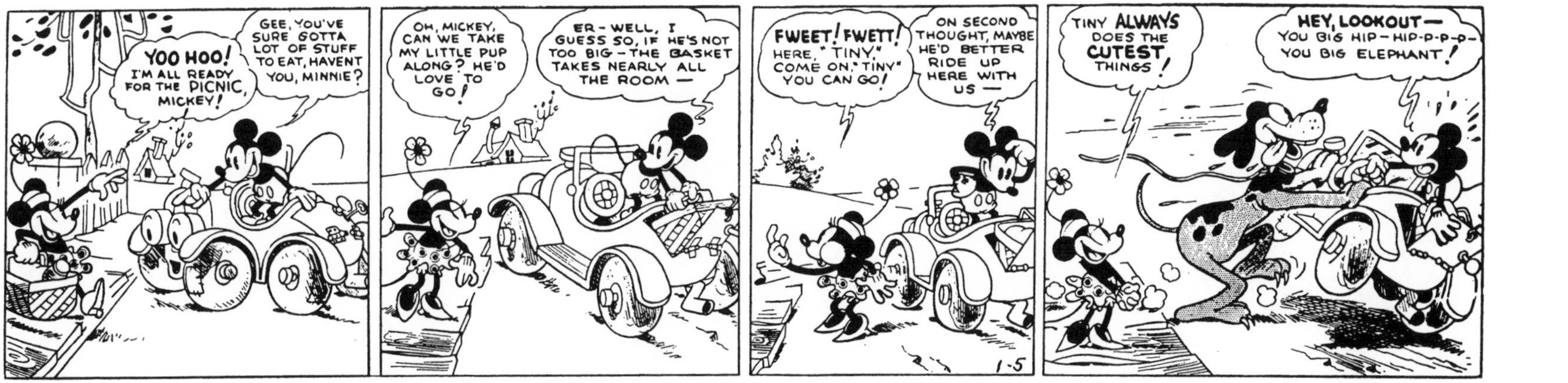
YOO HOO! I'M ALL READY FOR THE PICNIC, MICKEY!
GEE, YOU'VE SURE GOTTA LOT OF STUFF TO EAT, HAVENT YOU, MINNIE?
OH, MICKEY, CAN WE TAKE MY LITTLE PUP ALONG? HE'D LOVE TO GO!
ER-WELL, I GUESS SO, IF HE'S NOT TOO BIG - THE BASKET TAKES NEARLY ALL THE ROOM —
FWEET! FWETT! HERE, "TINY," COME ON, "TINY" YOU CAN GO!
ON SECOND THOUGHT, MAYBE HE'D BETTER RIDE UP HERE WITH US —
1-5
TINY ALWAYS DOES THE CUTEST THINGS!
HEY, LOOKOUT — YOU BIG HIP-HIP-P-P-P- YOU BIG ELEPHANT!

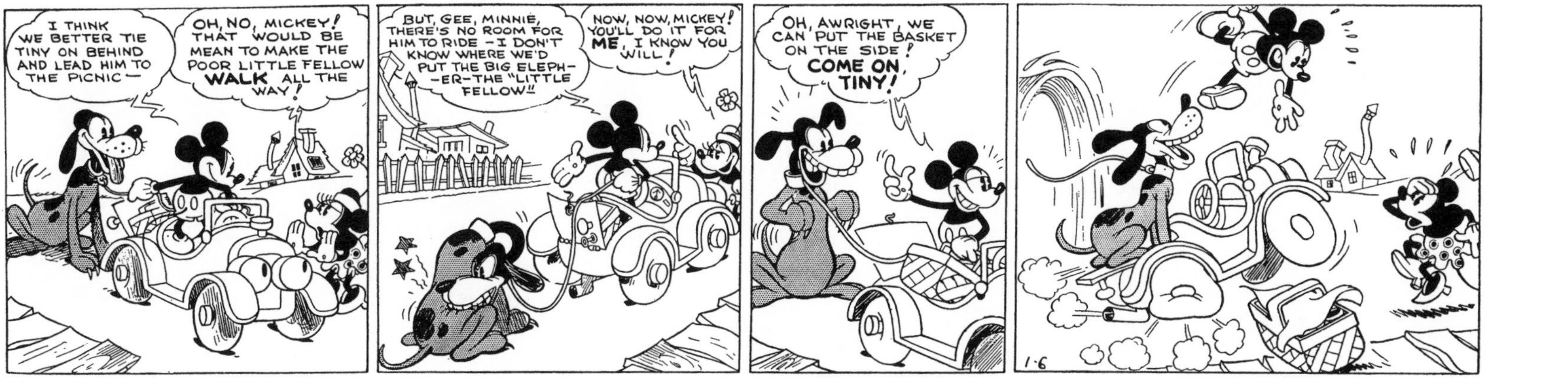
I THINK WE BETTER TIE TINY ON BEHIND AND LEAD HIM TO THE PICNIC —
OH, NO, MICKEY! THAT WOULD BE MEAN TO MAKE THE POOR LITTLE FELLOW WALK ALL THE WAY!
BUT, GEE, MINNIE, THERE'S NO ROOM FOR HIM TO RIDE - I DON'T KNOW WHERE WE'D PUT THE BIG ELEPH- -ER- THE "LITTLE FELLOW"!
NOW, NOW, MICKEY! YOU'LL DO IT FOR ME, I KNOW YOU WILL!
OH, AWRIGHT, WE CAN PUT THE BASKET ON THE SIDE! COME ON, TINY!
1-6

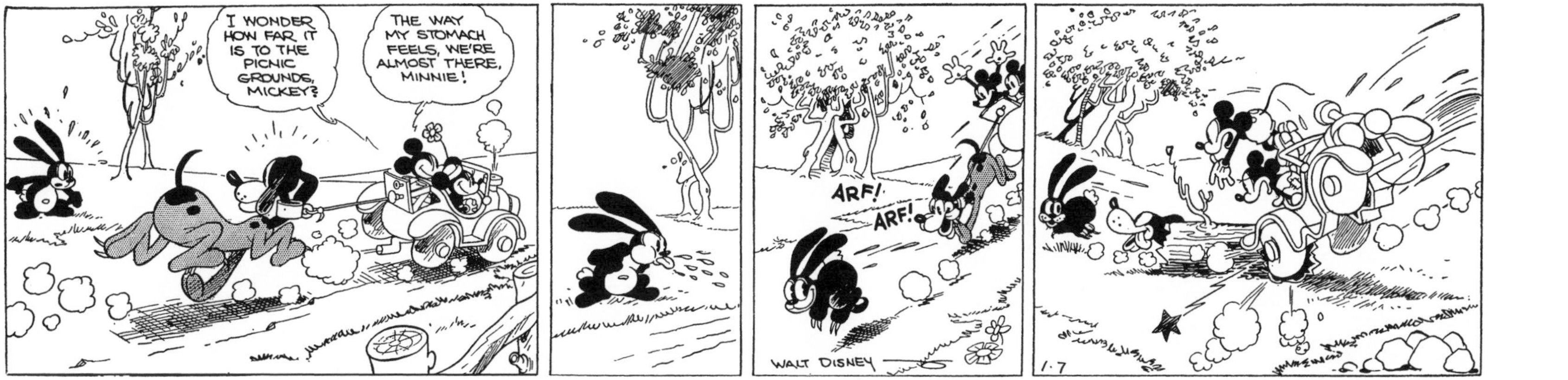
I WONDER HOW FAR IT IS TO THE PICNIC GROUNDS, MICKEY?
THE WAY MY STOMACH FEELS, WE'RE ALMOST THERE, MINNIE!
ARF!
ARF!
WALT DISNEY
1-7

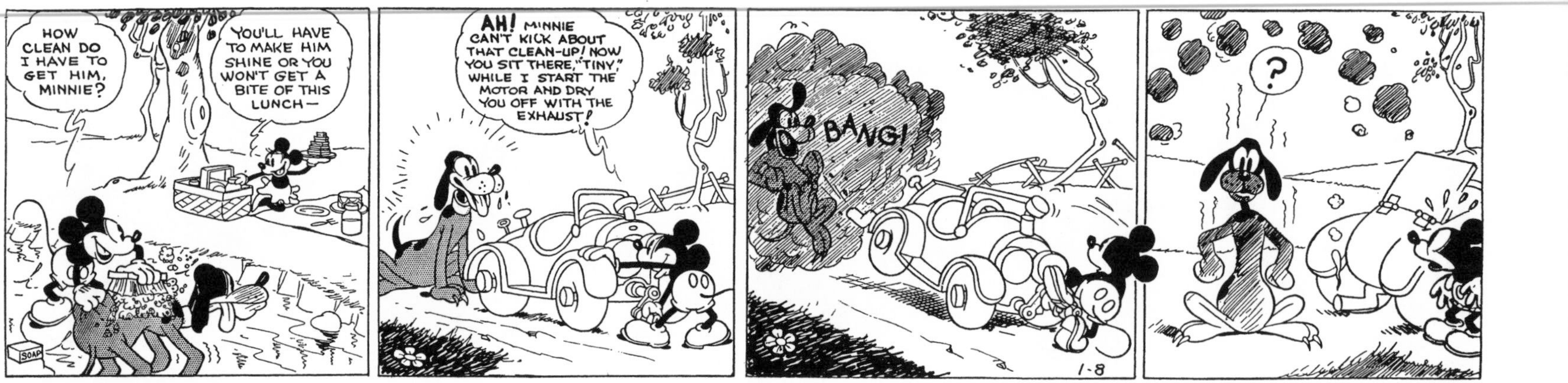
HOW CLEAN DO I HAVE TO GET HIM, MINNIE?
YOU'LL HAVE TO MAKE HIM SHINE OR YOU WON'T GET A BITE OF THIS LUNCH—
SOAP
AH! MINNIE CAN'T KICK ABOUT THAT CLEAN-UP! NOW YOU SIT THERE, "TINY," WHILE I START THE MOTOR AND DRY YOU OFF WITH THE EXHAUST!
BANG!
1-8
?

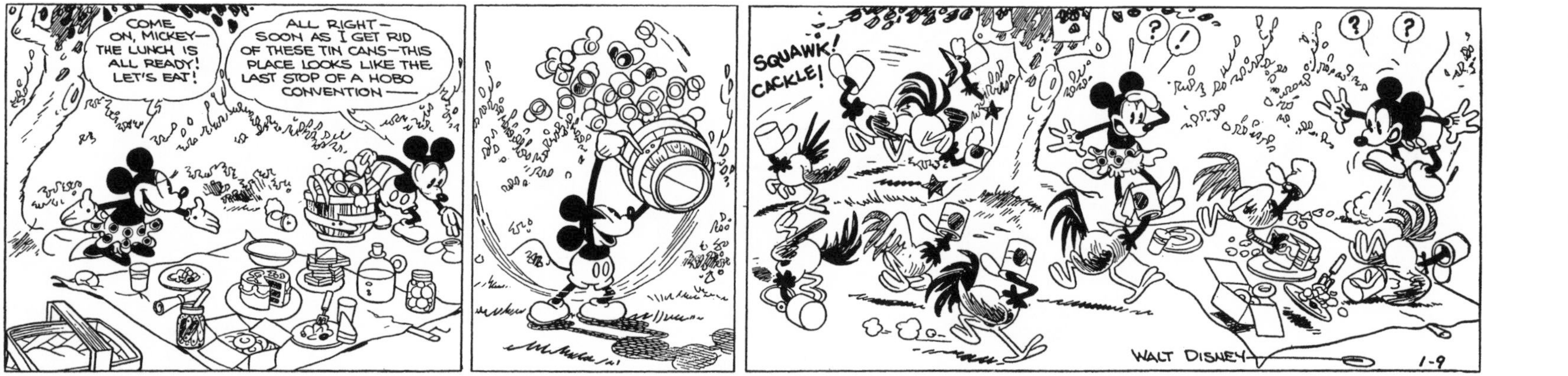
COME ON, MICKEY— THE LUNCH IS ALL READY! LET'S EAT!
ALL RIGHT— SOON AS I GET RID OF THESE TIN CANS—THIS PLACE LOOKS LIKE THE LAST STOP OF A HOBO CONVENTION——
SQUAWK! CACKLE!
? !
? ?
WALT DISNEY
1-9

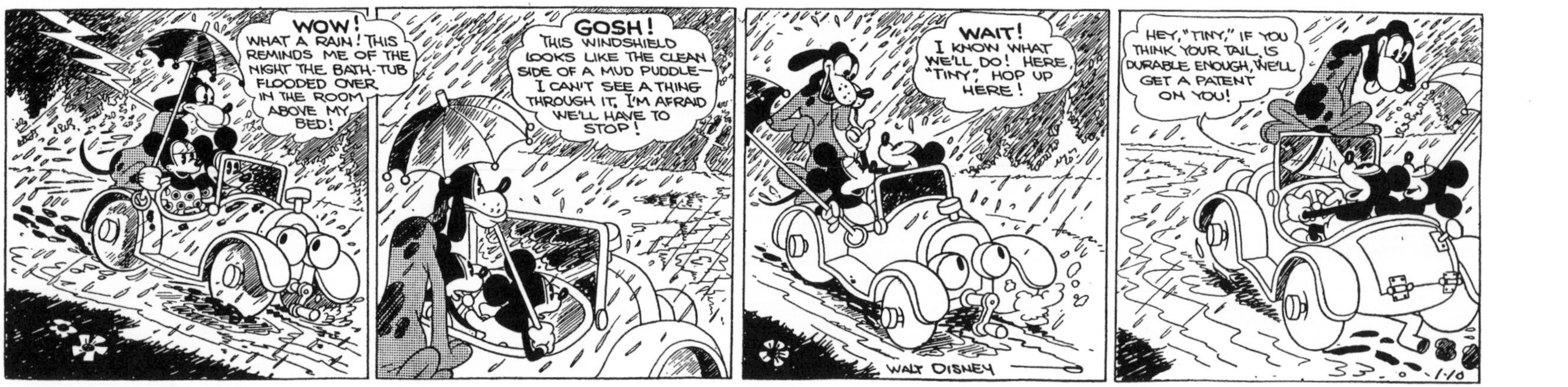
WOW! WHAT A RAIN! THIS REMINDS ME OF THE NIGHT THE BATH-TUB FLOODED OVER IN THE ROOM ABOVE MY BED!
GOSH! THIS WINDSHIELD LOOKS LIKE THE CLEAN SIDE OF A MUD PUDDLE— I CAN'T SEE A THING THROUGH IT. I'M AFRAID WE'LL HAVE TO STOP!
WAIT! I KNOW WHAT WE'LL DO! HERE, "TINY," HOP UP HERE!
WALT DISNEY
HEY, "TINY," IF YOU THINK YOUR TAIL IS DURABLE ENOUGH, WE'LL GET A PATENT ON YOU!
1-10

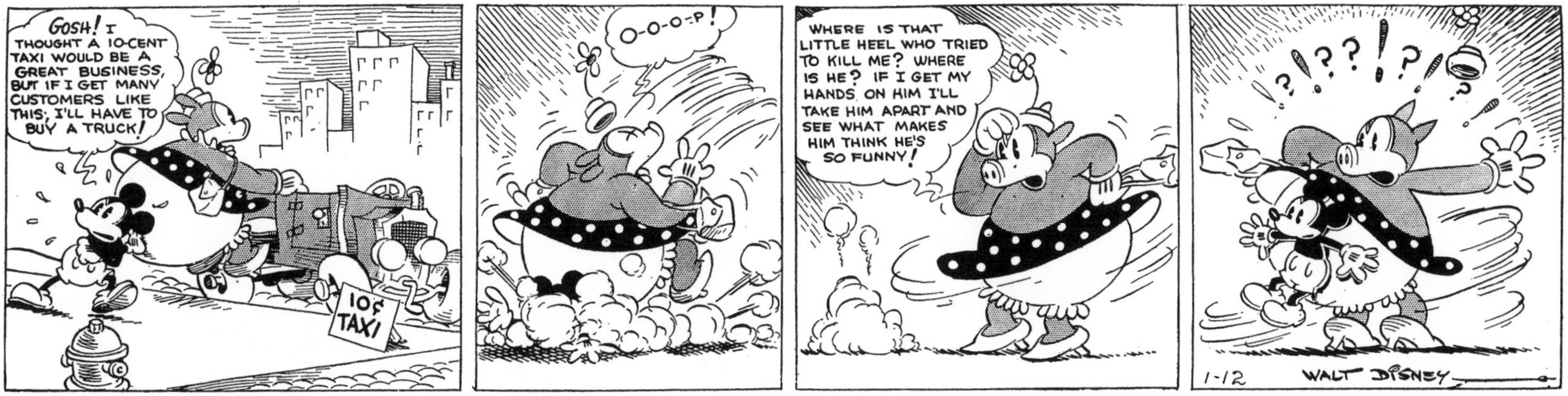
GOSH! I THOUGHT A 10-CENT TAXI WOULD BE A GREAT BUSINESS, BUT IF I GET MANY CUSTOMERS LIKE THIS, I'LL HAVE TO BUY A TRUCK!
10¢ TAXI
O-O-O-P!
WHERE IS THAT LITTLE HEEL WHO TRIED TO KILL ME? WHERE IS HE? IF I GET MY HANDS ON HIM I'LL TAKE HIM APART AND SEE WHAT MAKES HIM THINK HE'S SO FUNNY!
?!??!?!?
1-12
WALT DISNEY

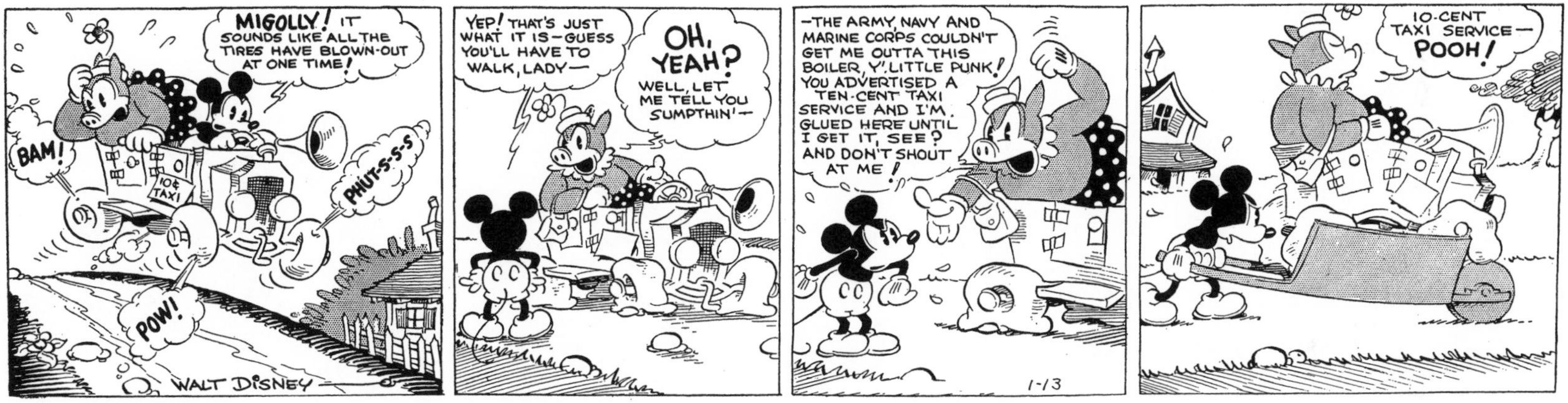
MIGOLLY! IT SOUNDS LIKE ALL THE TIRES HAVE BLOWN-OUT AT ONE TIME!
BAM!
10¢ TAXI
PHUT-S-S-S
POW!
WALT DISNEY
YEP! THAT'S JUST WHAT IT IS—GUESS YOU'LL HAVE TO WALK, LADY—
OH, YEAH? WELL, LET ME TELL YOU SUMPTHIN'—
—THE ARMY, NAVY AND MARINE CORPS COULDN'T GET ME OUTTA THIS BOILER, Y' LITTLE PUNK! YOU ADVERTISED A TEN-CENT TAXI SERVICE AND I'M GLUED HERE UNTIL I GET IT, SEE? AND DON'T SHOUT AT ME!
1-13
10-CENT TAXI SERVICE— POOH!

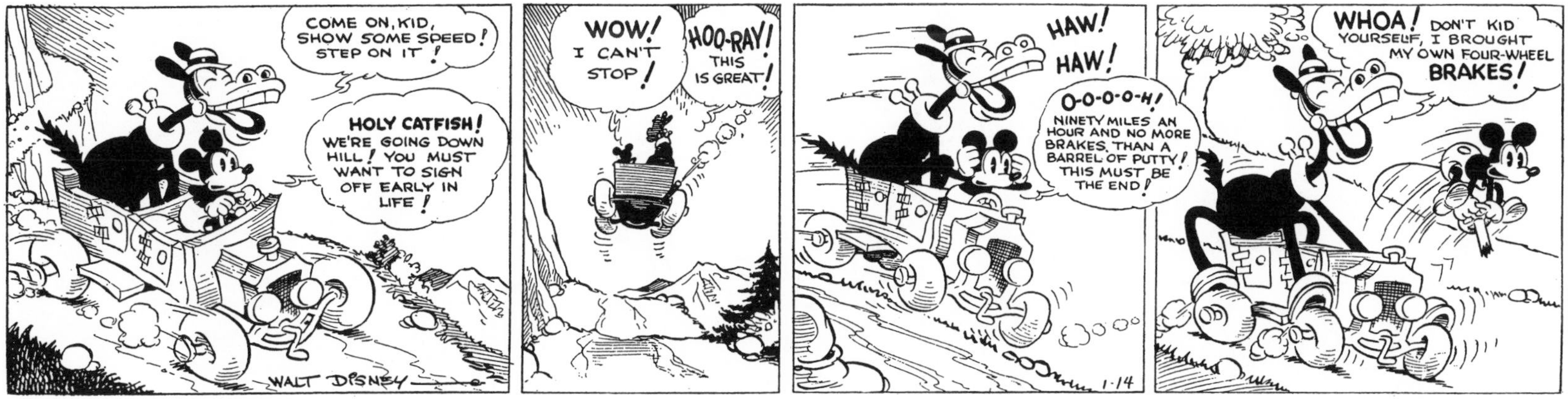
COME ON, KID, SHOW SOME SPEED! STEP ON IT!
HOLY CATFISH! WE'RE GOING DOWN HILL! YOU MUST WANT TO SIGN OFF EARLY IN LIFE!
WALT DISNEY
WOW! I CAN'T STOP!
HOO-RAY! THIS IS GREAT!
HAW! HAW!
O-O-O-O-H! NINETY MILES AN HOUR AND NO MORE BRAKES THAN A BARREL OF PUTTY! THIS MUST BE THE END!
1-14
WHOA! DON'T KID YOURSELF, I BROUGHT MY OWN FOUR-WHEEL BRAKES!

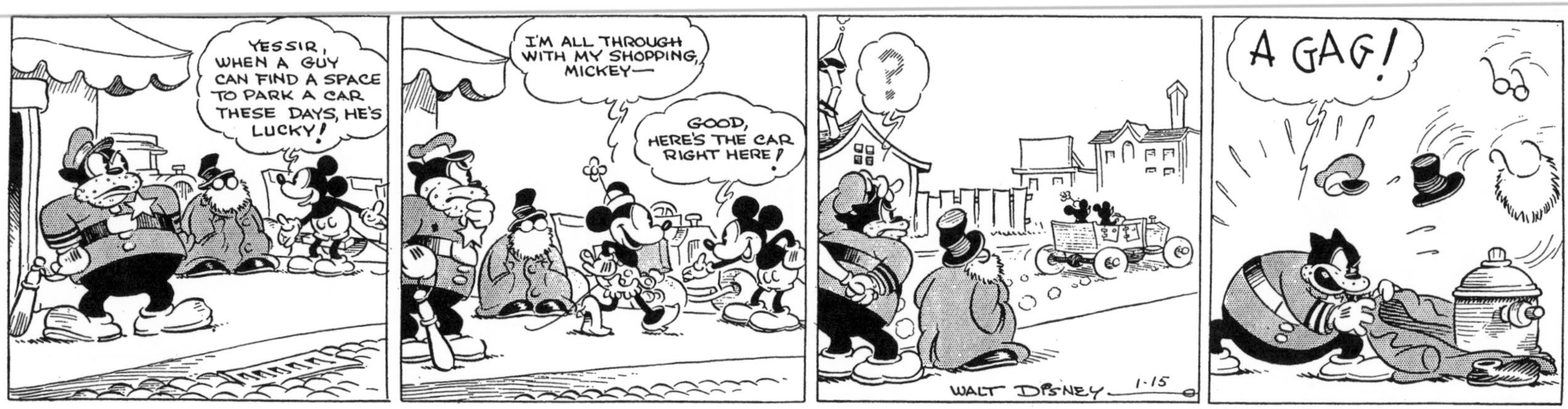
YESSIR, WHEN A GUY CAN FIND A SPACE TO PARK A CAR THESE DAYS, HE'S LUCKY!
I'M ALL THROUGH WITH MY SHOPPING, MICKEY—
GOOD, HERE'S THE CAR RIGHT HERE!
?
WALT DISNEY 1-15
A GAG!

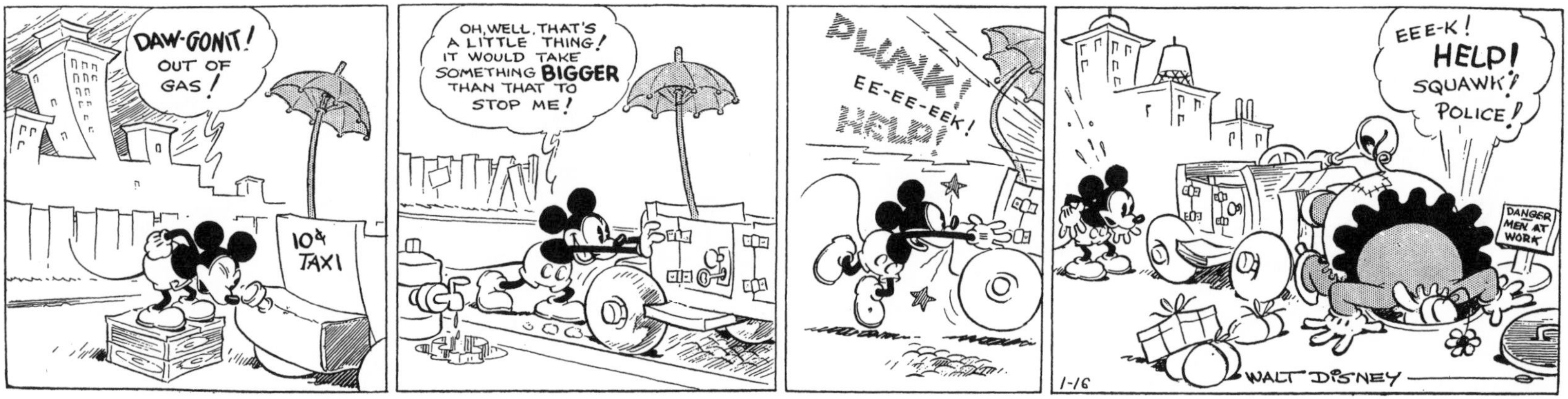
DAW-GONIT! OUT OF GAS!
10¢ TAXI
OH, WELL, THAT'S A LITTLE THING! IT WOULD TAKE SOMETHING BIGGER THAN THAT TO STOP ME!
PLUNK!
EE-EE-EEK!
HELP!
EEE-K! HELP! SQUAWK! POLICE!
DANGER MEN AT WORK
1-16
WALT DISNEY

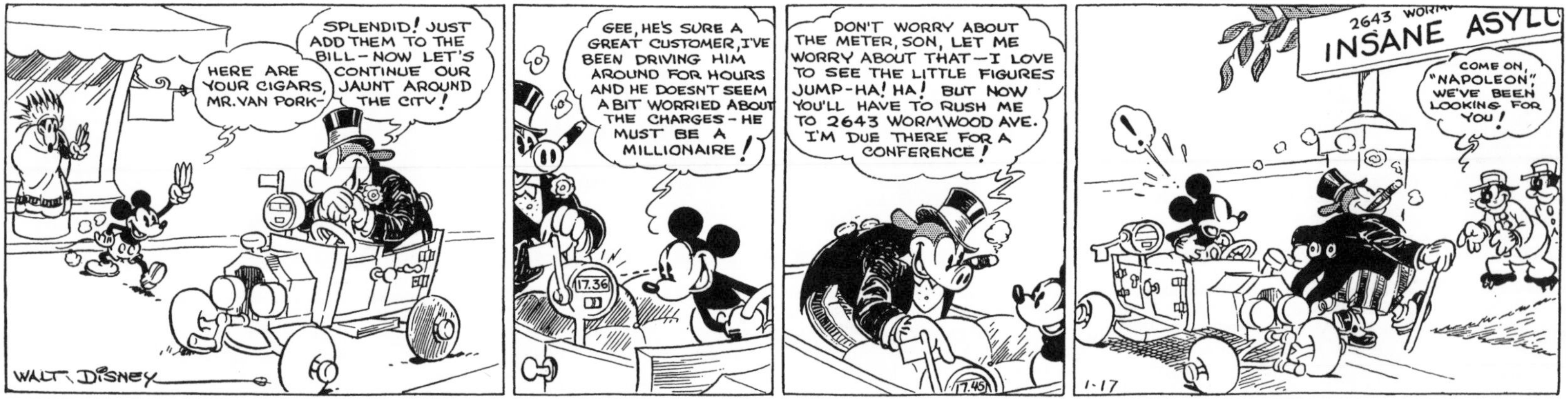
HERE ARE YOUR CIGARS, MR. VAN PORK—
SPLENDID! JUST ADD THEM TO THE BILL—NOW LET'S CONTINUE OUR JAUNT AROUND THE CITY!
WALT DISNEY
GEE, HE'S SURE A GREAT CUSTOMER, I'VE BEEN DRIVING HIM AROUND FOR HOURS AND HE DOESN'T SEEM A BIT WORRIED ABOUT THE CHARGES—HE MUST BE A MILLIONAIRE!
17.36
DON'T WORRY ABOUT THE METER, SON, LET ME WORRY ABOUT THAT—I LOVE TO SEE THE LITTLE FIGURES JUMP—HA! HA! BUT NOW YOU'LL HAVE TO RUSH ME TO 2643 WORMWOOD AVE. I'M DUE THERE FOR A CONFERENCE!
17.45
INSANE ASYLU
!
COME ON, "NAPOLEON", WE'VE BEEN LOOKING FOR YOU!
1-17

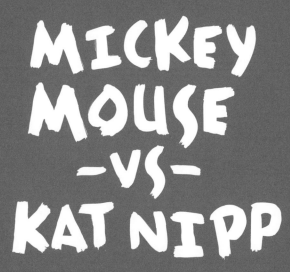

MICKEY MOUSE
-VS-
KAT NIPP

JANUARY 19, 1931
-
FEBRUARY 25, 1931

MICKEY MOUSE

REGISTERED U.S. PATENT OFFICE

KATNIPPERY

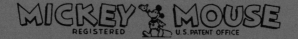

The greatest Disney comics have always appealed to adults as well as children. On a child's level, "Mickey Mouse Vs. Kat Nipp" is a simple cat and mouse game: cat holds territory; mouse uses tricks to put cat out of the way. Yet on another level, the story is slyly sophisticated. The grown-up significance of fights for "territory" could be found in any Depression-wracked big city; and let's not even start on the importance that Mickey and Nipp attach to their tails, which reflect prewar notions of masculinity via a crude kind of fashion consciousness.

Then, of course, there is the matter of Prohibition. While the story's home-brewed catnip drink—called by its Latin name, *nepeta cataria*—is obviously only a stand-in for liquor, Kat Nipp nevertheless refers to it as his "secret weakness," and it is mixed by a "moonshiner" who is suspicious of outside interference. The intent becomes most clear when Mickey uses the catnip to deprive Kat Nipp of his helpmate, Barnacle Bill. Gottfredson seems to have been saying that as tough as society's raffish elements might be, one could outwit and defeat them using their own weapons. 1930s bad guys might have been masters of the forbidden fruit, but they could just as easily become its victims; an empowering message for young Jazz Age readers.

The original "Kat Nipp" story also reflects the Jazz Age in its use of a crude, then-current social stereotype: a tough butcher's boy opines that Kat Nipp is still tougher by performing a crude "sissy" impersonation. While we can't entirely excuse clichés from a less enlightened time, we can ask that you read them as indicative of their era.

Kat Nipp himself survived his era, if only barely. Having first made a precomics debut in the 1929 cartoons *The Opry House, When the Cat's Away* (as "Tom Cat"), and *The Karnival Kid*, the bad guy would strike again in a 1938 Floyd Gottfredson Sunday strip (see page 120)—and in additional comics by the likes of Italy's Guglielmo Guastaveglia, Britain's Wilfred Haughton, and Denmark's Lars Jensen. [DG]

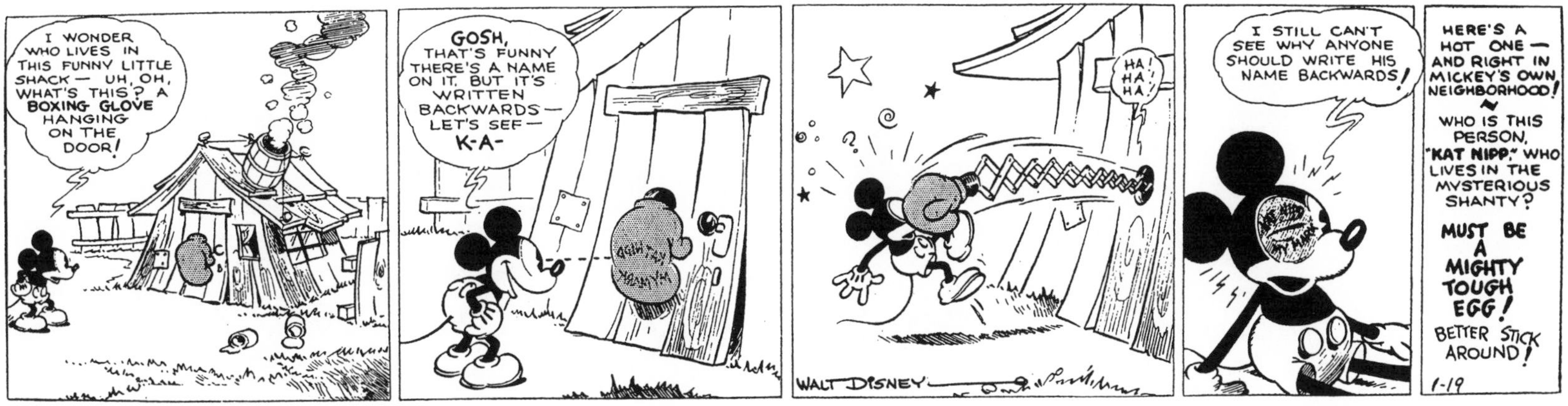
I WONDER WHO LIVES IN THIS FUNNY LITTLE SHACK— UH, OH, WHAT'S THIS? A BOXING GLOVE HANGING ON THE DOOR!
GOSH, THAT'S FUNNY THERE'S A NAME ON IT, BUT IT'S WRITTEN BACKWARDS— LET'S SEE— K-A-
HA! HA! HA!
WALT DISNEY
I STILL CAN'T SEE WHY ANYONE SHOULD WRITE HIS NAME BACKWARDS!
HERE'S A HOT ONE— AND RIGHT IN MICKEY'S OWN NEIGHBORHOOD!
WHO IS THIS PERSON, "KAT NIPP," WHO LIVES IN THE MYSTERIOUS SHANTY?
MUST BE A MIGHTY TOUGH EGG!
BETTER STICK AROUND!
1-19

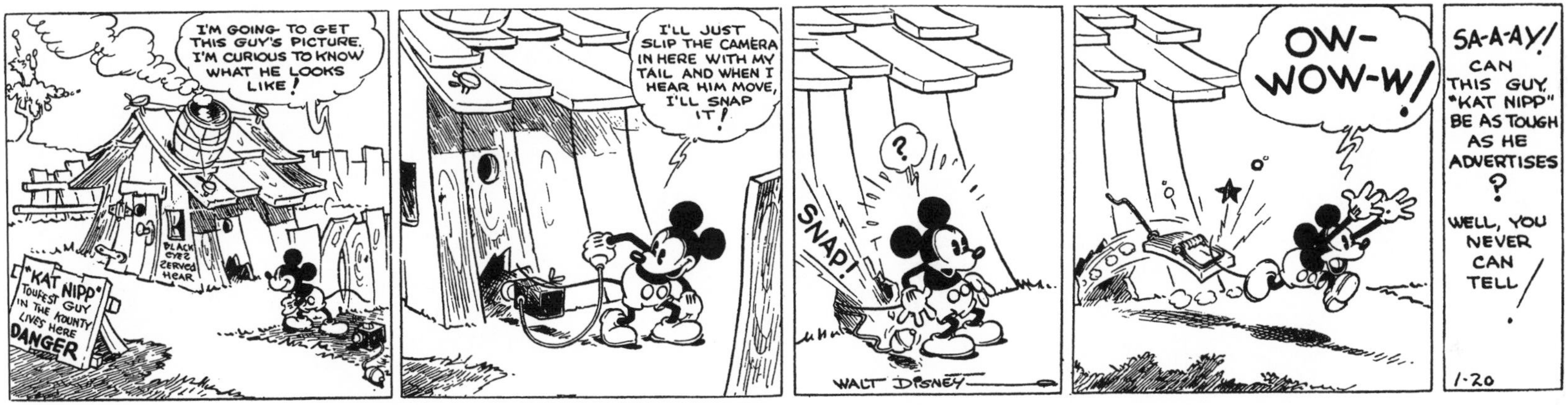
I'M GOING TO GET THIS GUY'S PICTURE. I'M CURIOUS TO KNOW WHAT HE LOOKS LIKE!
BLACK EYES ZERVED HEAR
"KAT NIPP" TOUFEST GUY IN THE KOUNTY LIVES HERE DANGER
I'LL JUST SLIP THE CAMERA IN HERE WITH MY TAIL AND WHEN I HEAR HIM MOVE, I'LL SNAP IT!
?
SNAP!
WALT DISNEY
OW-WOW-W!
SA-A-AY! CAN THIS GUY, "KAT NIPP" BE AS TOUGH AS HE ADVERTISES?
WELL, YOU NEVER CAN TELL!
1-20

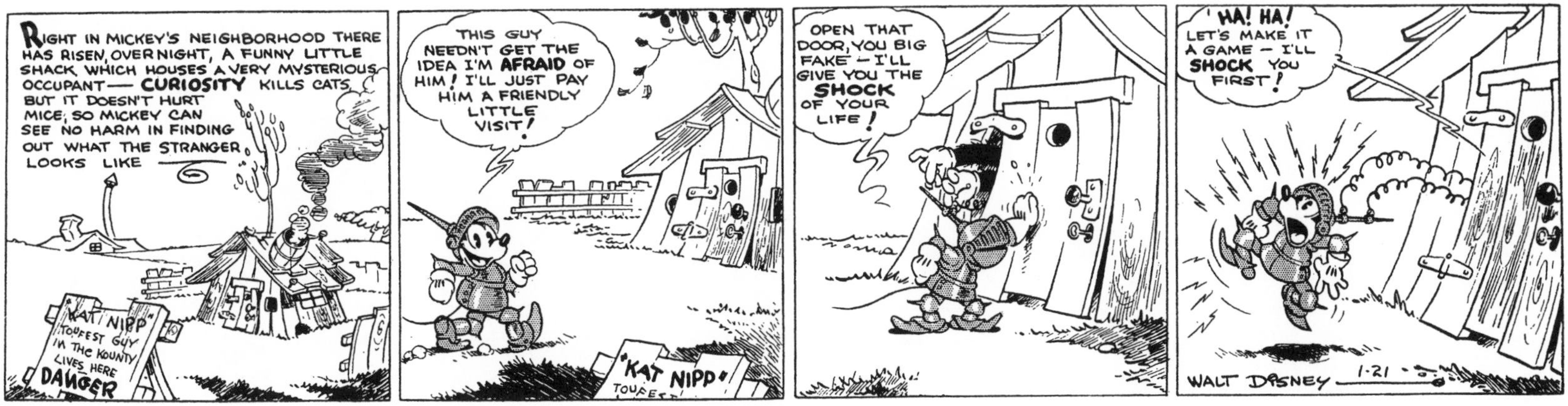
RIGHT IN MICKEY'S NEIGHBORHOOD THERE HAS RISEN, OVERNIGHT, A FUNNY LITTLE SHACK, WHICH HOUSES A VERY MYSTERIOUS OCCUPANT— CURIOSITY KILLS CATS, BUT IT DOESN'T HURT MICE, SO MICKEY CAN SEE NO HARM IN FINDING OUT WHAT THE STRANGER LOOKS LIKE—
"KAT NIPP" TOUFEST GUY IN THE KOUNTY LIVES HERE DANGER
THIS GUY NEEDN'T GET THE IDEA I'M AFRAID OF HIM! I'LL JUST PAY HIM A FRIENDLY LITTLE VISIT!
"KAT NIPP"
OPEN THAT DOOR, YOU BIG FAKE— I'LL GIVE YOU THE SHOCK OF YOUR LIFE!
HA! HA! LET'S MAKE IT A GAME— I'LL SHOCK YOU FIRST!
WALT DISNEY
1-21

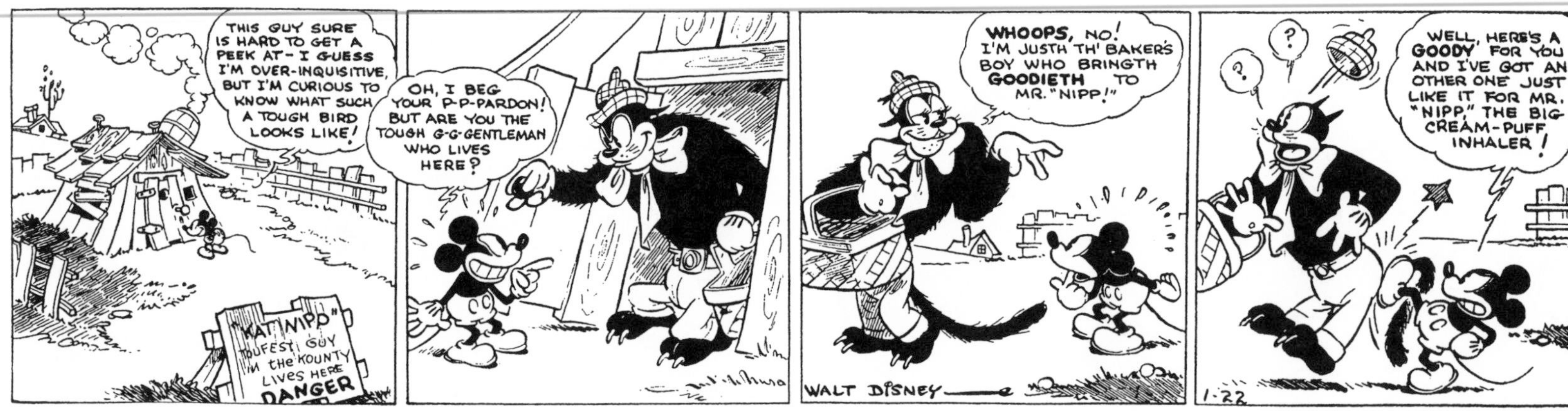
THIS GUY SURE IS HARD TO GET A PEEK AT– I GUESS I'M OVER-INQUISITIVE, BUT I'M CURIOUS TO KNOW WHAT SUCH A TOUGH BIRD LOOKS LIKE!
"KAT NIPP" TOUFEST GUY IN the KOUNTY LIVES HERE DANGER
OH, I BEG YOUR P-P-PARDON! BUT ARE YOU THE TOUGH G-G-GENTLEMAN WHO LIVES HERE?
WHOOPS, NO! I'M JUSTH TH' BAKER'S BOY WHO BRINGTH GOODIETH TO MR. "NIPP!"
WALT DISNEY
?
?
WELL, HERE'S A GOODY FOR YOU AND I'VE GOT ANOTHER ONE JUST LIKE IT FOR MR. "NIPP," THE BIG CREAM-PUFF INHALER!
1-22

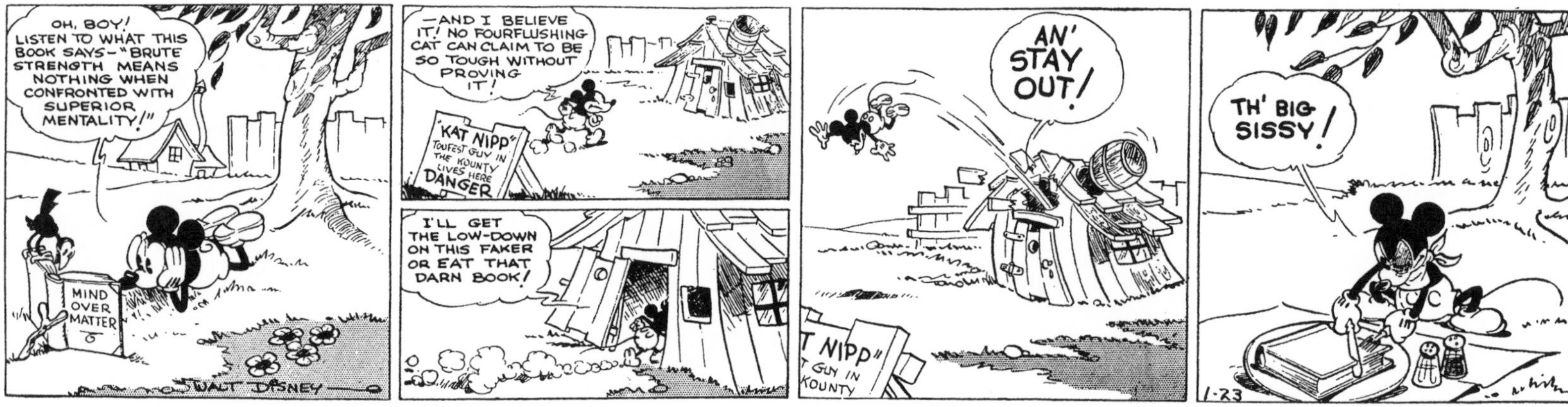
OH, BOY! LISTEN TO WHAT THIS BOOK SAYS–"BRUTE STRENGTH MEANS NOTHING WHEN CONFRONTED WITH SUPERIOR MENTALITY!"
MIND OVER MATTER
WALT DISNEY
—AND I BELIEVE IT! NO FOURFLUSHING CAT CAN CLAIM TO BE SO TOUGH WITHOUT PROVING IT!
"KAT NIPP" TOUFEST GUY IN THE KOUNTY LIVES HERE DANGER
I'LL GET THE LOW-DOWN ON THIS FAKER OR EAT THAT DARN BOOK!
AN' STAY OUT!
T NIPP" T GUY IN KOUNTY
TH' BIG SISSY!
1-23

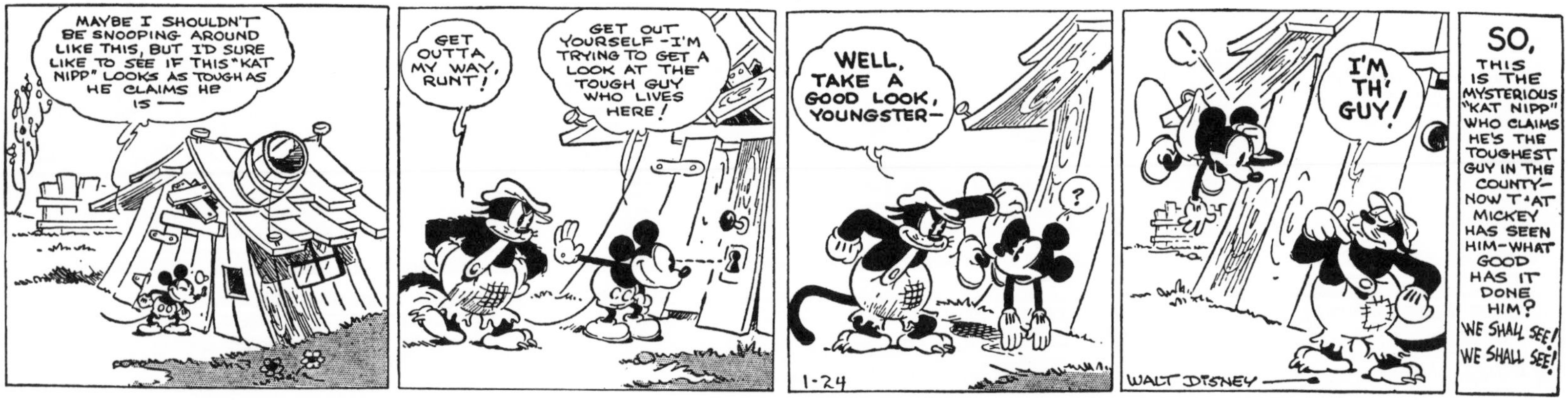
MAYBE I SHOULDN'T BE SNOOPING AROUND LIKE THIS, BUT I'D SURE LIKE TO SEE IF THIS "KAT NIPP" LOOKS AS TOUGH AS HE CLAIMS HE IS—
GET OUTTA MY WAY, RUNT!
GET OUT YOURSELF–I'M TRYING TO GET A LOOK AT THE TOUGH GUY WHO LIVES HERE!
WELL, TAKE A GOOD LOOK, YOUNGSTER–
?
1-24
!
I'M TH' GUY!
WALT DISNEY
SO, THIS IS THE MYSTERIOUS "KAT NIPP" WHO CLAIMS HE'S THE TOUGHEST GUY IN THE COUNTY– NOW THAT MICKEY HAS SEEN HIM–WHAT GOOD HAS IT DONE HIM?
WE SHALL SEE! WE SHALL SEE!

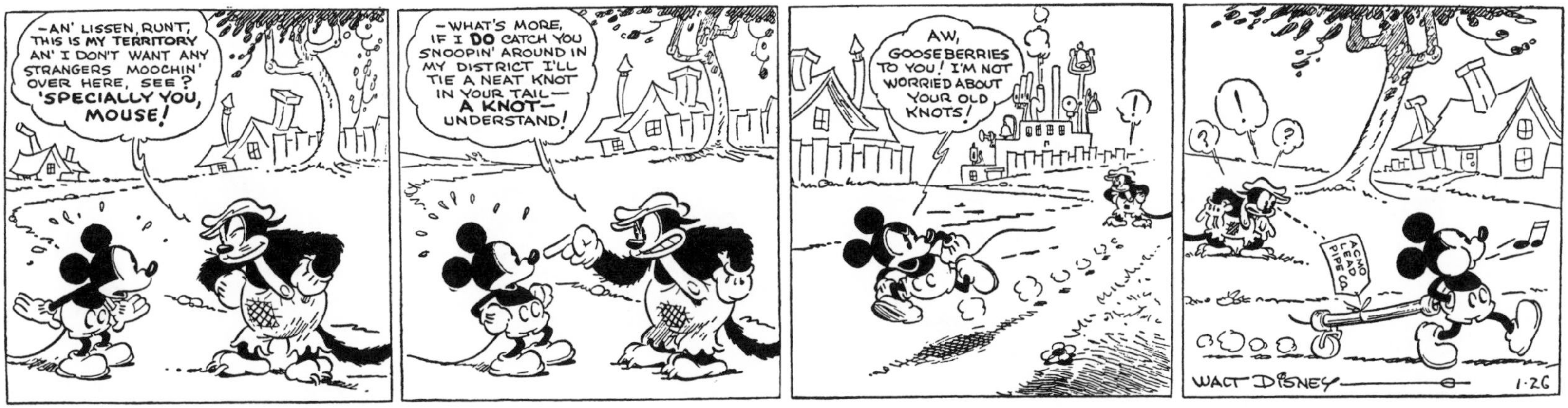
-AN' LISSEN, RUNT, THIS IS MY TERRITORY AN' I DON'T WANT ANY STRANGERS MOOCHIN' OVER HERE, SEE? 'SPECIALLY YOU, MOUSE!
-WHAT'S MORE, IF I DO CATCH YOU SNOOPIN' AROUND IN MY DISTRICT I'LL TIE A NEAT KNOT IN YOUR TAIL— A KNOT— UNDERSTAND!
AW, GOOSEBERRIES TO YOU! I'M NOT WORRIED ABOUT YOUR OLD KNOTS!
ACME LEAD PIPE CO.
WALT DISNEY
1·26

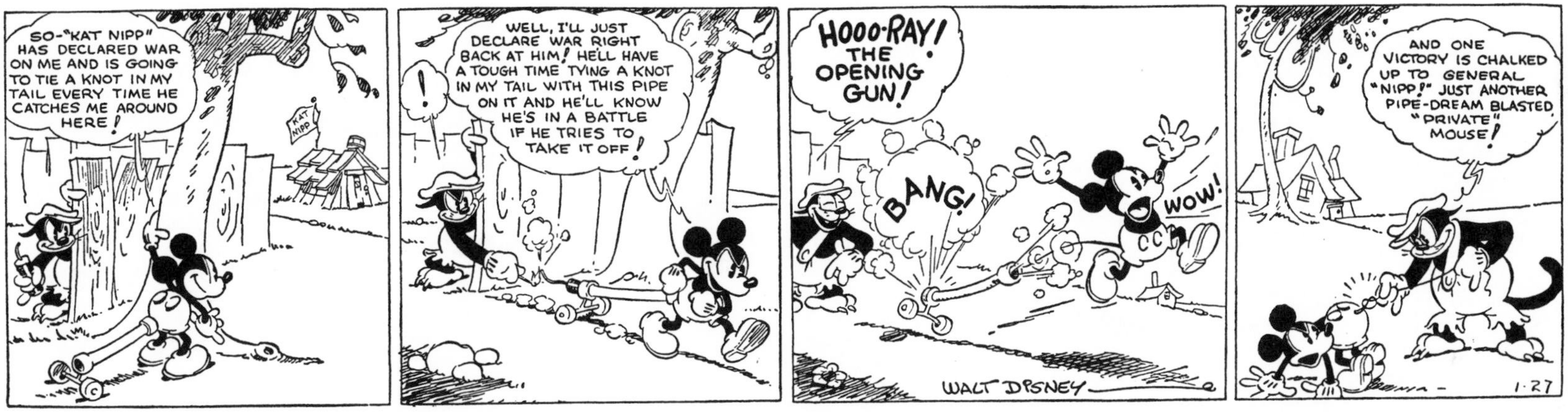
SO-"KAT NIPP" HAS DECLARED WAR ON ME AND IS GOING TO TIE A KNOT IN MY TAIL EVERY TIME HE CATCHES ME AROUND HERE!
KAT NIPP
WELL, I'LL JUST DECLARE WAR RIGHT BACK AT HIM! HE'LL HAVE A TOUGH TIME TYING A KNOT IN MY TAIL WITH THIS PIPE ON IT AND HE'LL KNOW HE'S IN A BATTLE IF HE TRIES TO TAKE IT OFF!
HOOO-RAY! THE OPENING GUN!
BANG!
WOW!
WALT DISNEY
AND ONE VICTORY IS CHALKED UP TO GENERAL "NIPP!" JUST ANOTHER PIPE-DREAM BLASTED "PRIVATE" MOUSE!
1·27

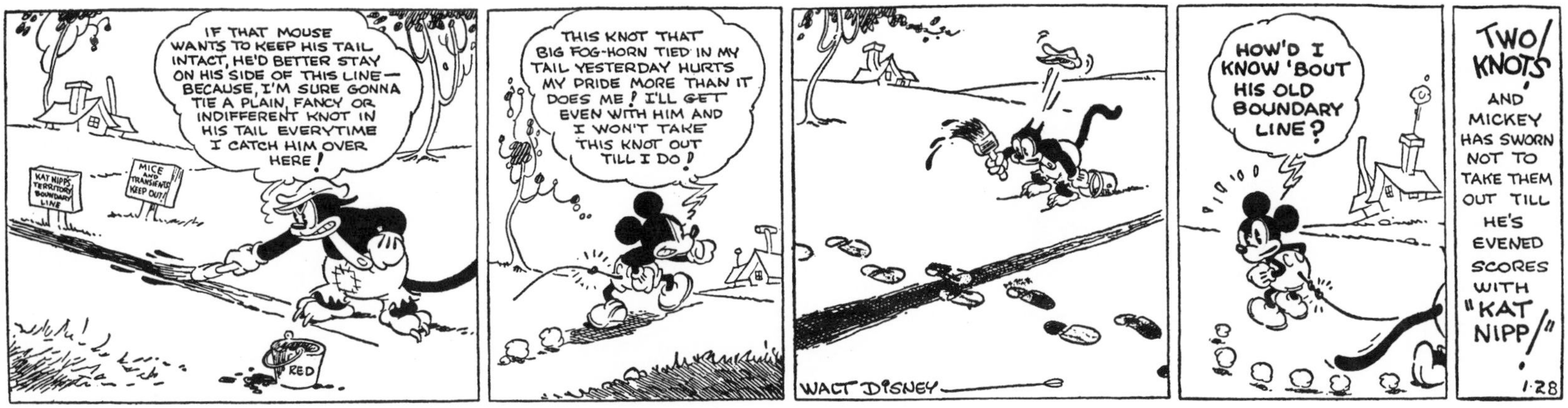
IF THAT MOUSE WANTS TO KEEP HIS TAIL INTACT, HE'D BETTER STAY ON HIS SIDE OF THIS LINE— BECAUSE, I'M SURE GONNA TIE A PLAIN, FANCY OR INDIFFERENT KNOT IN HIS TAIL EVERYTIME I CATCH HIM OVER HERE!
KAT NIPP'S TERRITORY BOUNDARY LINE
MICE AND TRANSIENTS KEEP OUT!
RED
THIS KNOT THAT BIG FOG-HORN TIED IN MY TAIL YESTERDAY HURTS MY PRIDE MORE THAN IT DOES ME! I'LL GET EVEN WITH HIM AND I WON'T TAKE THIS KNOT OUT TILL I DO!
WALT DISNEY
HOW'D I KNOW 'BOUT HIS OLD BOUNDARY LINE?
TWO KNOTS! AND MICKEY HAS SWORN NOT TO TAKE THEM OUT TILL HE'S EVENED SCORES WITH "KAT NIPP!"
1·28

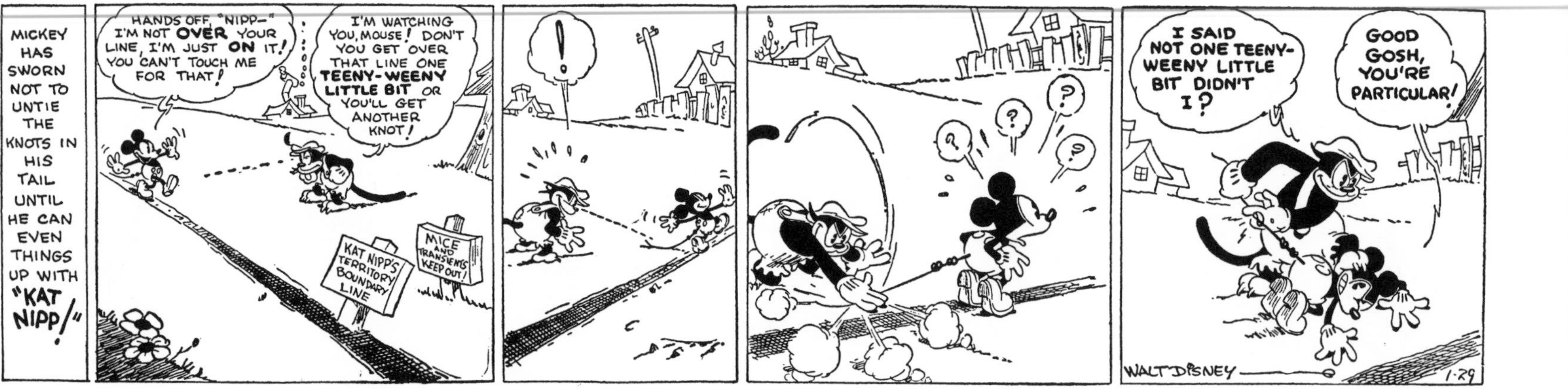
MICKEY HAS SWORN NOT TO UNTIE THE KNOTS IN HIS TAIL UNTIL HE CAN EVEN THINGS UP WITH "KAT NIPP!"
HANDS OFF, "NIPP—" I'M NOT OVER YOUR LINE, I'M JUST ON IT! YOU CAN'T TOUCH ME FOR THAT!
I'M WATCHING YOU, MOUSE! DON'T YOU GET OVER THAT LINE ONE TEENY-WEENY LITTLE BIT OR YOU'LL GET ANOTHER KNOT!
KAT NIPP'S TERRITORY BOUNDARY LINE
MICE AND TRANSIENTS KEEP OUT!
!
?
I SAID NOT ONE TEENY-WEENY LITTLE BIT DIDN'T I?
GOOD GOSH, YOU'RE PARTICULAR!
WALT DISNEY
1·29

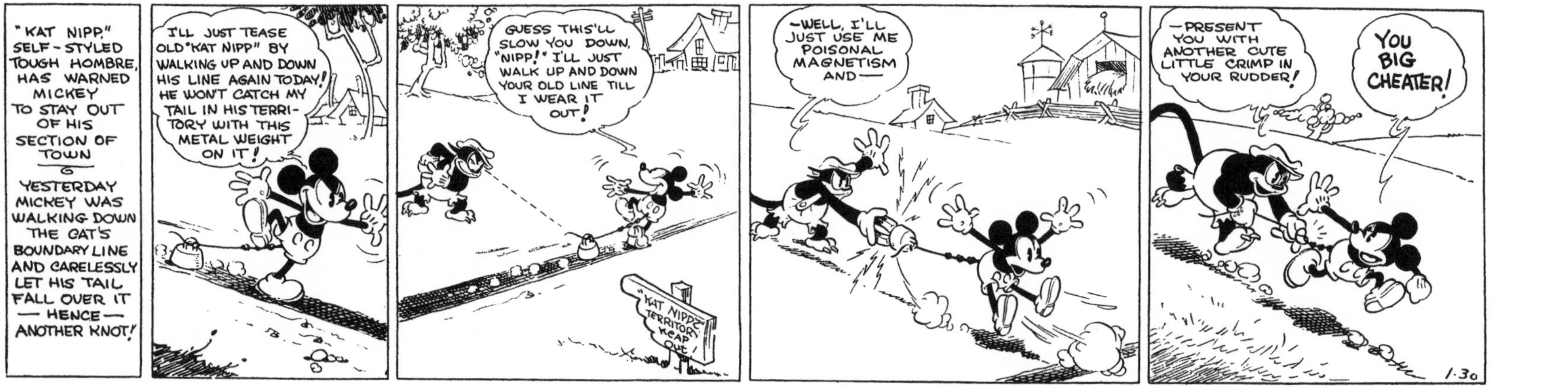
"KAT NIPP," SELF-STYLED TOUGH HOMBRE, HAS WARNED MICKEY TO STAY OUT OF HIS SECTION OF TOWN — YESTERDAY MICKEY WAS WALKING DOWN THE CAT'S BOUNDARY LINE AND CARELESSLY LET HIS TAIL FALL OVER IT — HENCE — ANOTHER KNOT!
I'LL JUST TEASE OLD "KAT NIPP" BY WALKING UP AND DOWN HIS LINE AGAIN TODAY! HE WON'T CATCH MY TAIL IN HIS TERRITORY WITH THIS METAL WEIGHT ON IT!
GUESS THIS'LL SLOW YOU DOWN, "NIPP!" I'LL JUST WALK UP AND DOWN YOUR OLD LINE TILL I WEAR IT OUT!
"KAT NIPP'S" TERRITORY KEAP OUT!
—WELL, I'LL JUST USE ME POISONAL MAGNETISM AND—
—PRESENT YOU WITH ANOTHER CUTE LITTLE CRIMP IN YOUR RUDDER!
YOU BIG CHEATER!
1·30

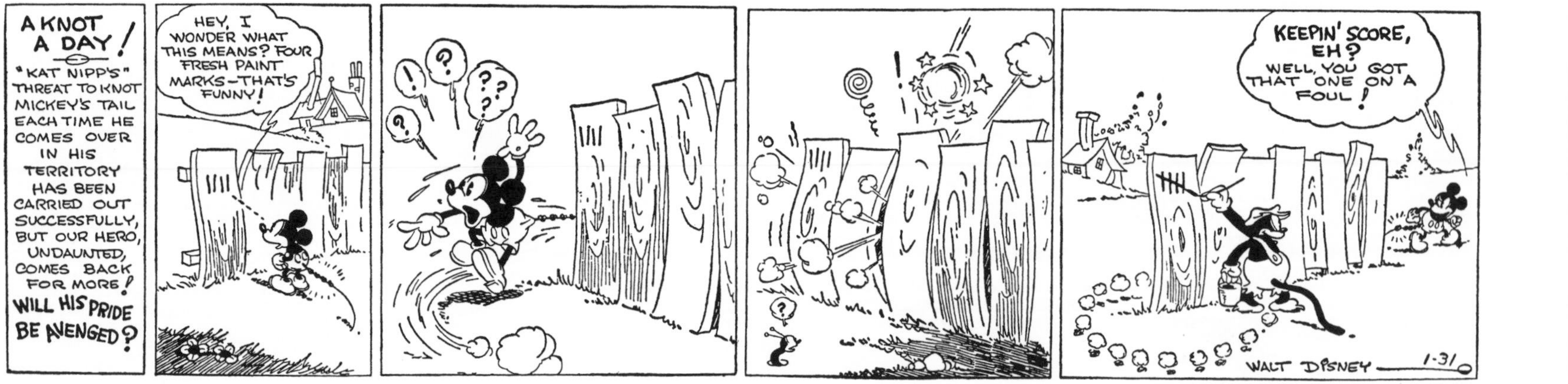
A KNOT A DAY! "KAT NIPP'S" THREAT TO KNOT MICKEY'S TAIL EACH TIME HE COMES OVER IN HIS TERRITORY HAS BEEN CARRIED OUT SUCCESSFULLY, BUT OUR HERO, UNDAUNTED, COMES BACK FOR MORE! WILL HIS PRIDE BE AVENGED?
HEY, I WONDER WHAT THIS MEANS? FOUR FRESH PAINT MARKS—THAT'S FUNNY!
KEEPIN' SCORE, EH? WELL, YOU GOT THAT ONE ON A FOUL!
WALT DISNEY
1·31

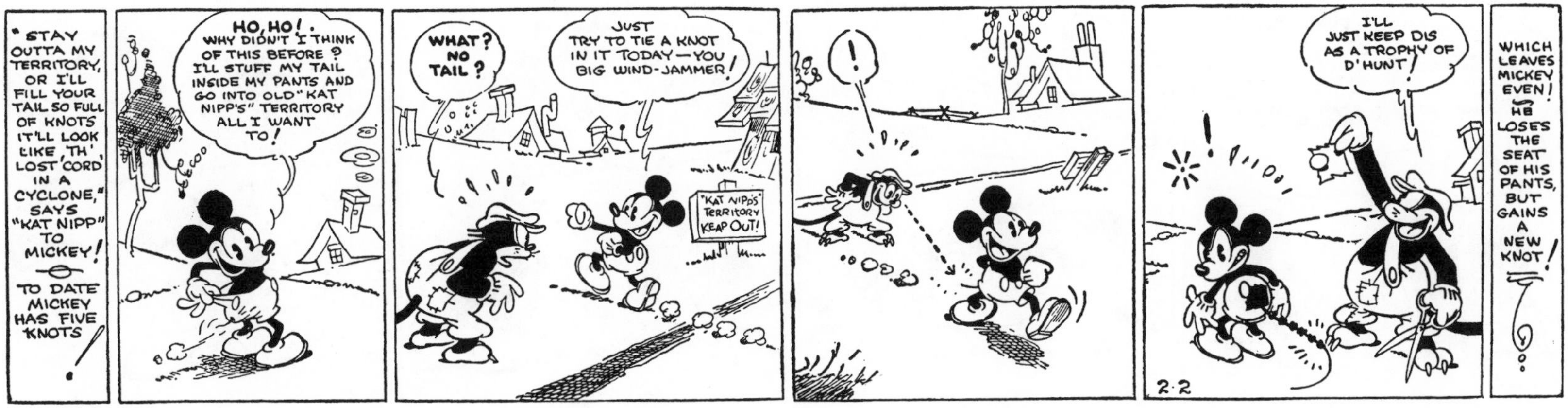
"STAY OUTTA MY TERRITORY, OR I'LL FILL YOUR TAIL SO FULL OF KNOTS IT'LL LOOK LIKE 'TH' LOST CORD' IN A CYCLONE," SAYS "KAT NIPP" TO MICKEY!
TO DATE MICKEY HAS FIVE KNOTS!
HO, HO! WHY DIDN'T I THINK OF THIS BEFORE? I'LL STUFF MY TAIL INSIDE MY PANTS AND GO INTO OLD "KAT NIPP'S" TERRITORY ALL I WANT TO!
WHAT? NO TAIL?
JUST TRY TO TIE A KNOT IN IT TODAY—YOU BIG WIND-JAMMER!
"KAT NIPP'S" TERRITORY KEAP OUT!
!
I'LL JUST KEEP DIS AS A TROPHY OF D' HUNT!
!
2-2
WHICH LEAVES MICKEY EVEN! HE LOSES THE SEAT OF HIS PANTS, BUT GAINS A NEW KNOT!

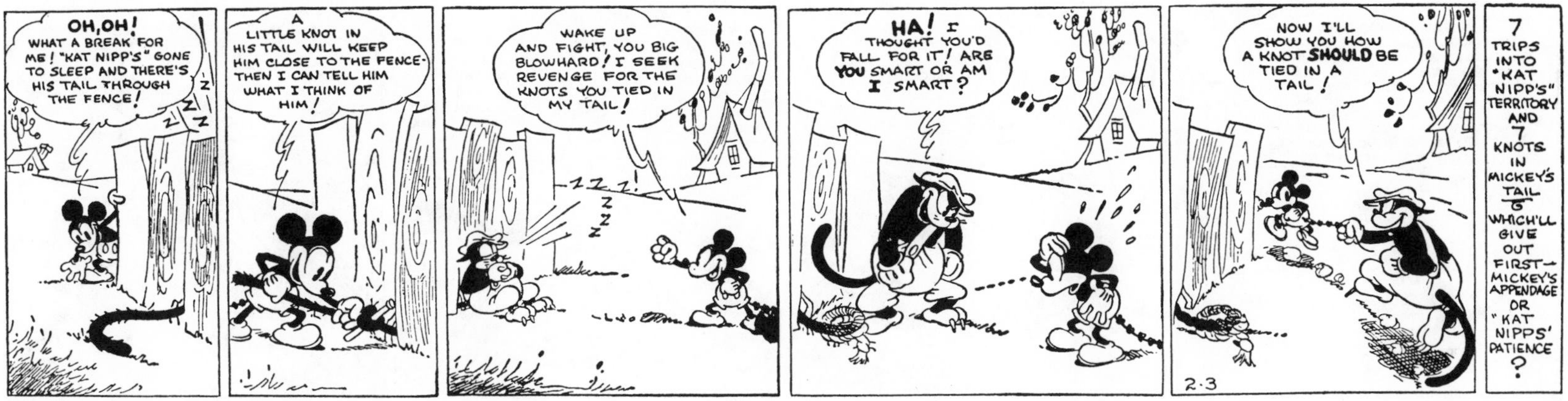
OH, OH! WHAT A BREAK FOR ME! "KAT NIPP'S" GONE TO SLEEP AND THERE'S HIS TAIL THROUGH THE FENCE!
Z Z Z
A LITTLE KNOT IN HIS TAIL WILL KEEP HIM CLOSE TO THE FENCE—THEN I CAN TELL HIM WHAT I THINK OF HIM!
WAKE UP AND FIGHT, YOU BIG BLOWHARD! I SEEK REVENGE FOR THE KNOTS YOU TIED IN MY TAIL!
Z Z Z Z Z
HA! I THOUGHT YOU'D FALL FOR IT! ARE YOU SMART OR AM I SMART?
NOW I'LL SHOW YOU HOW A KNOT SHOULD BE TIED IN A TAIL!
2-3
7 TRIPS INTO "KAT NIPP'S" TERRITORY AND 7 KNOTS IN MICKEY'S TAIL WHICH'LL GIVE OUT FIRST—MICKEY'S APPENDAGE OR "KAT NIPPS'" PATIENCE?

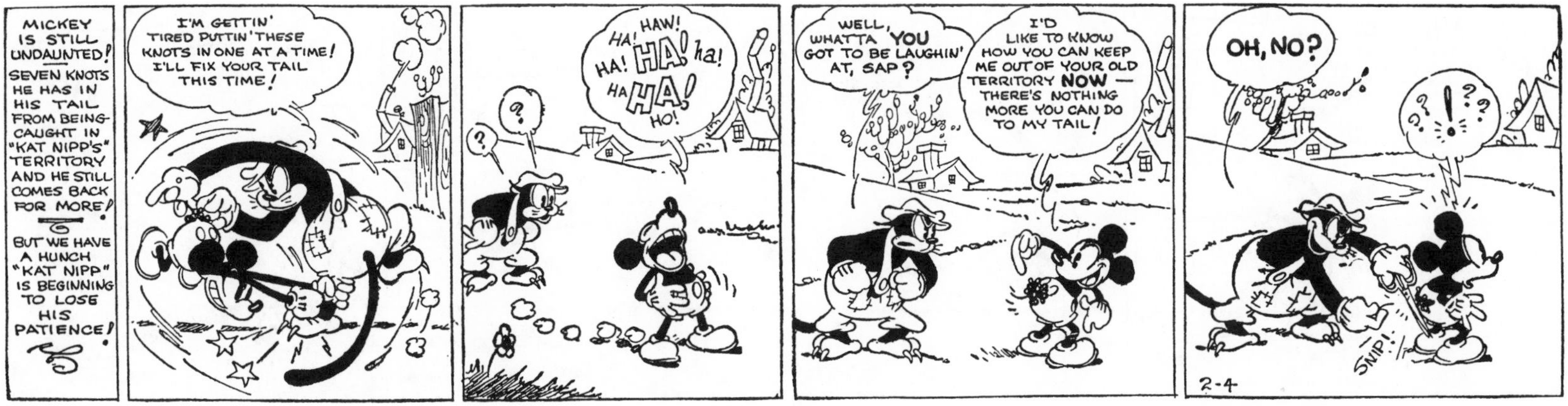
MICKEY IS STILL UNDAUNTED! SEVEN KNOTS HE HAS IN HIS TAIL FROM BEING-CAUGHT IN "KAT NIPP'S" TERRITORY AND HE STILL COMES BACK FOR MORE!
BUT WE HAVE A HUNCH "KAT NIPP" IS BEGINNING TO LOSE HIS PATIENCE!
I'M GETTIN' TIRED PUTTIN' THESE KNOTS IN ONE AT A TIME! I'LL FIX YOUR TAIL THIS TIME!
?
?
HA! HAW! HA! HA! ha! HA HA! HO!
WELL, WHATTA YOU GOT TO BE LAUGHIN' AT, SAP?
I'D LIKE TO KNOW HOW YOU CAN KEEP ME OUT OF YOUR OLD TERRITORY NOW—THERE'S NOTHING MORE YOU CAN DO TO MY TAIL!
OH, NO?
?? ! ??
SNIP!
2-4

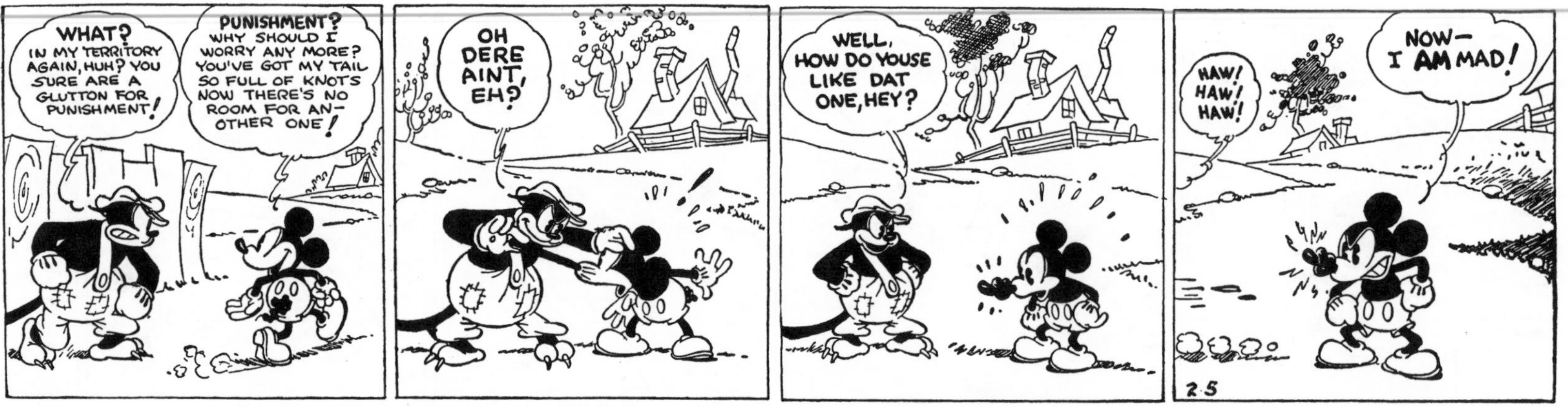
WHAT? IN MY TERRITORY AGAIN, HUH? YOU SURE ARE A GLUTTON FOR PUNISHMENT!
PUNISHMENT? WHY SHOULD I WORRY ANY MORE? YOU'VE GOT MY TAIL SO FULL OF KNOTS NOW THERE'S NO ROOM FOR ANOTHER ONE!
OH DERE AINT, EH?
WELL, HOW DO YOUSE LIKE DAT ONE, HEY?
HAW! HAW! HAW!
NOW— I AM MAD!
2·5

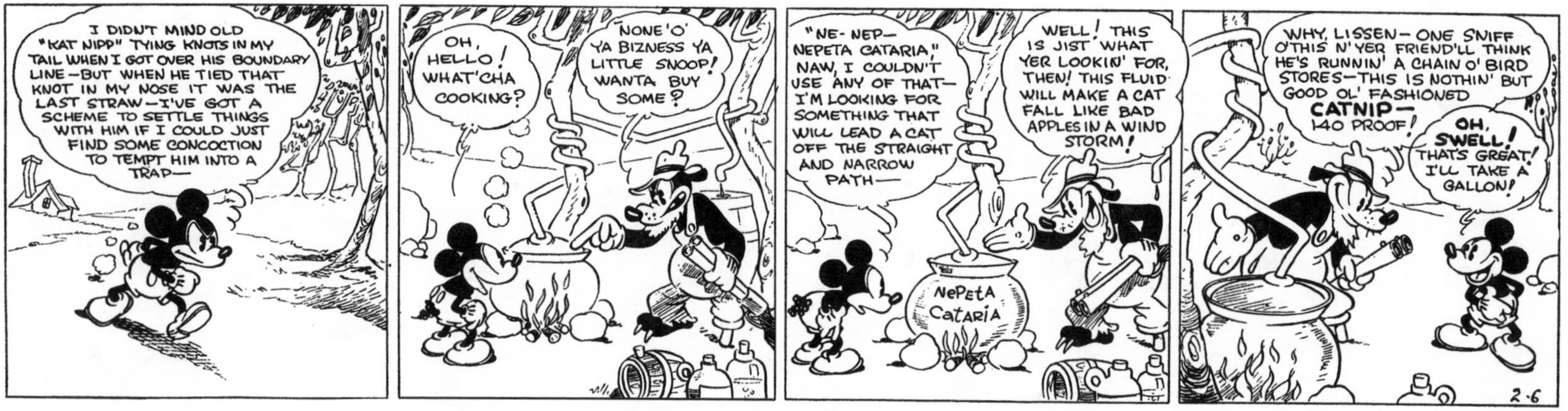
I DIDN'T MIND OLD "KAT NIPP" TYING KNOTS IN MY TAIL WHEN I GOT OVER HIS BOUNDARY LINE—BUT WHEN HE TIED THAT KNOT IN MY NOSE IT WAS THE LAST STRAW—I'VE GOT A SCHEME TO SETTLE THINGS WITH HIM IF I COULD JUST FIND SOME CONCOCTION TO TEMPT HIM INTO A TRAP—
OH, HELLO! WHAT'CHA COOKING?
NONE 'O' YA BIZNESS YA LITTLE SNOOP! WANTA BUY SOME?
"NE-NEP— NEPETA CATARIA," NAW, I COULDN'T USE ANY OF THAT— I'M LOOKING FOR SOMETHING THAT WILL LEAD A CAT OFF THE STRAIGHT AND NARROW PATH—
WELL! THIS IS JIST WHAT YER LOOKIN' FOR, THEN! THIS FLUID WILL MAKE A CAT FALL LIKE BAD APPLES IN A WIND STORM!
NePeta Cataria
WHY, LISSEN— ONE SNIFF O'THIS N' YER FRIEND'LL THINK HE'S RUNNIN' A CHAIN O' BIRD STORES—THIS IS NOTHIN' BUT GOOD OL' FASHIONED CATNIP— 140 PROOF!
OH, SWELL! THAT'S GREAT! I'LL TAKE A GALLON!
2·6

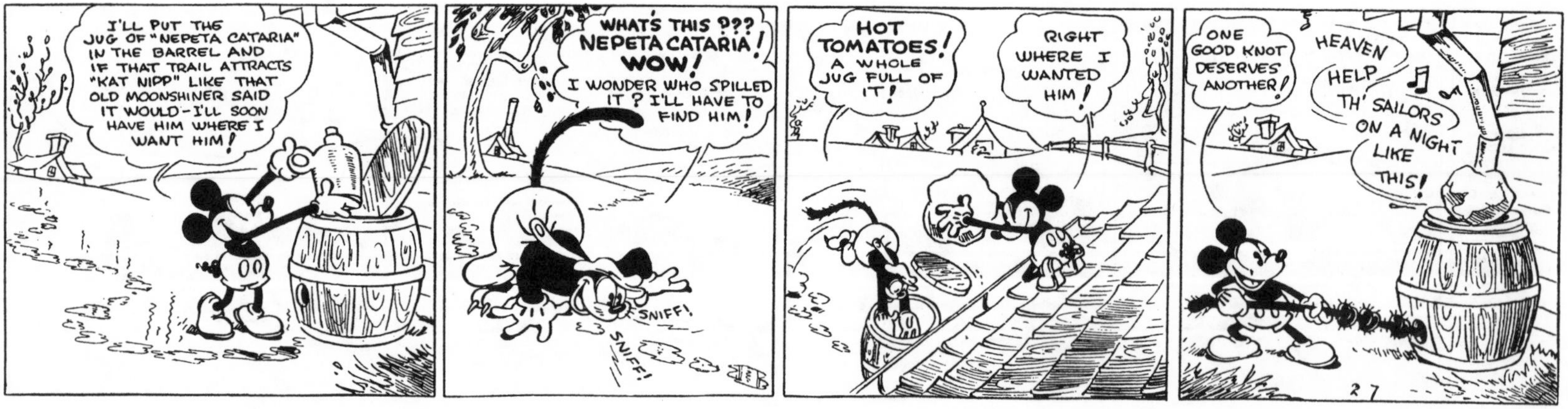
I'LL PUT THE JUG OF "NEPETA CATARIA" IN THE BARREL AND IF THAT TRAIL ATTRACTS "KAT NIPP" LIKE THAT OLD MOONSHINER SAID IT WOULD—I'LL SOON HAVE HIM WHERE I WANT HIM!
WHAT'S THIS ??? NEPETA CATARIA! WOW! I WONDER WHO SPILLED IT? I'LL HAVE TO FIND HIM!
SNIFF!
SNIFF!
HOT TOMATOES! A WHOLE JUG FULL OF IT!
RIGHT WHERE I WANTED HIM!
ONE GOOD KNOT DESERVES ANOTHER!
HEAVEN HELP TH' SAILORS ON A NIGHT LIKE THIS!
2·7

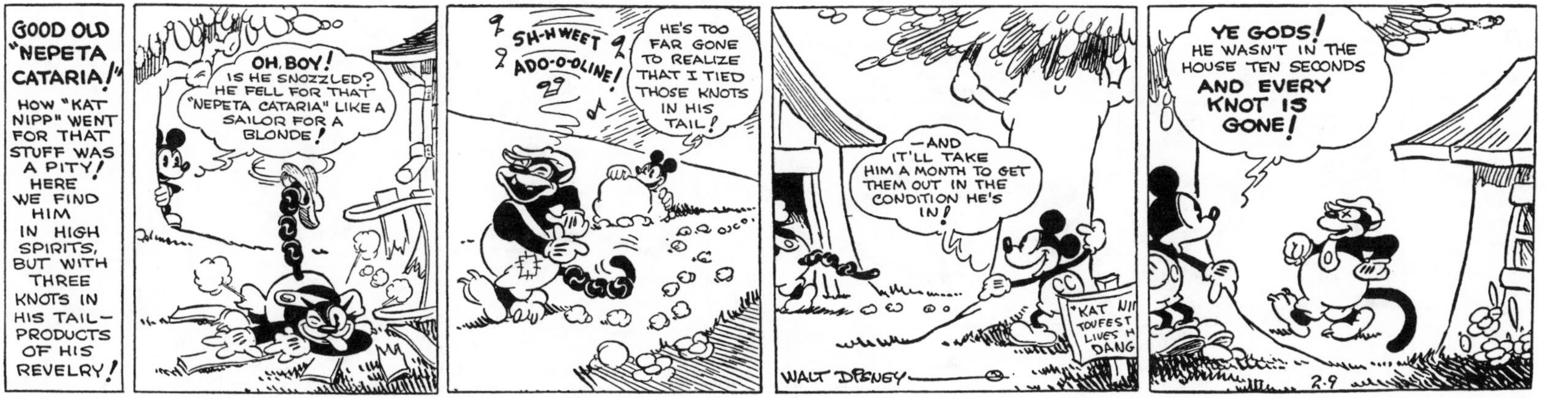
GOOD OLD "NEPETA CATARIA!" HOW "KAT NIPP" WENT FOR THAT STUFF WAS A PITY! HERE WE FIND HIM IN HIGH SPIRITS, BUT WITH THREE KNOTS IN HIS TAIL— PRODUCTS OF HIS REVELRY!
OH, BOY! IS HE SNOZZLED? HE FELL FOR THAT "NEPETA CATARIA" LIKE A SAILOR FOR A BLONDE!
SH-HWEET ADO-O-OLINE!
HE'S TOO FAR GONE TO REALIZE THAT I TIED THOSE KNOTS IN HIS TAIL!
—AND IT'LL TAKE HIM A MONTH TO GET THEM OUT IN THE CONDITION HE'S IN!
WALT DISNEY
YE GODS! HE WASN'T IN THE HOUSE TEN SECONDS AND EVERY KNOT IS GONE!
2-9

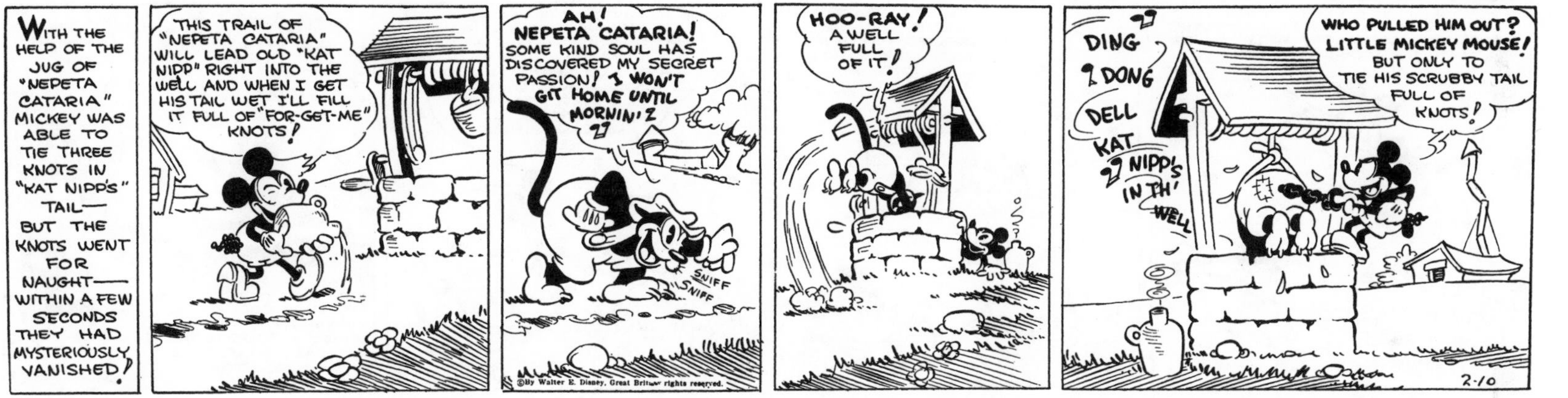
WITH THE HELP OF THE JUG OF "NEPETA CATARIA" MICKEY WAS ABLE TO TIE THREE KNOTS IN "KAT NIPP'S" TAIL— BUT THE KNOTS WENT FOR NAUGHT— WITHIN A FEW SECONDS THEY HAD MYSTERIOUSLY VANISHED!
THIS TRAIL OF "NEPETA CATARIA" WILL LEAD OLD "KAT NIPP" RIGHT INTO THE WELL AND WHEN I GET HIS TAIL WET I'LL FILL IT FULL OF "FOR-GET-ME" KNOTS!
AH! NEPETA CATARIA! SOME KIND SOUL HAS DISCOVERED MY SECRET PASSION! I WON'T GIT HOME UNTIL MORNIN'!
SNIFF SNIFF
©By Walter E. Disney, Great Britain rights reserved.
HOO-RAY! A WELL FULL OF IT!
DING DONG DELL KAT NIPP'S IN TH' WELL
WHO PULLED HIM OUT? LITTLE MICKEY MOUSE! BUT ONLY TO TIE HIS SCRUBBY TAIL FULL OF KNOTS!
2-10

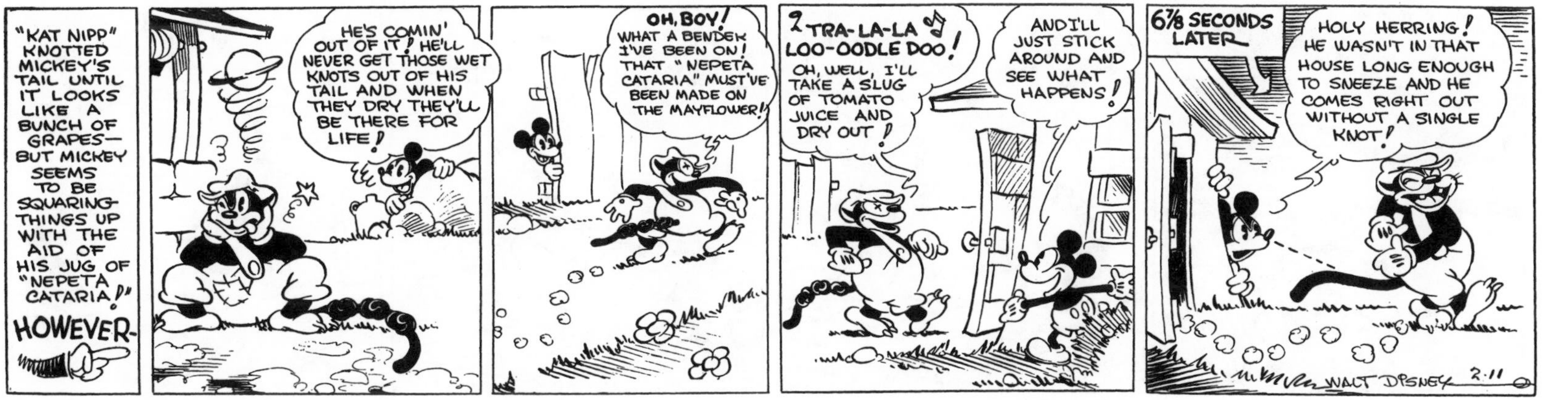
"KAT NIPP" KNOTTED MICKEY'S TAIL UNTIL IT LOOKS LIKE A BUNCH OF GRAPES— BUT MICKEY SEEMS TO BE SQUARING-THINGS UP WITH THE AID OF HIS JUG OF "NEPETA CATARIA!" HOWEVER-
HE'S COMIN' OUT OF IT! HE'LL NEVER GET THOSE WET KNOTS OUT OF HIS TAIL AND WHEN THEY DRY THEY'LL BE THERE FOR LIFE!
OH, BOY! WHAT A BENDER I'VE BEEN ON! THAT "NEPETA CATARIA" MUST'VE BEEN MADE ON THE MAYFLOWER!
TRA-LA-LA LOO-OODLE DOO! OH, WELL, I'LL TAKE A SLUG OF TOMATO JUICE AND DRY OUT!
AND I'LL JUST STICK AROUND AND SEE WHAT HAPPENS!
6⅞ SECONDS LATER
HOLY HERRING! HE WASN'T IN THAT HOUSE LONG ENOUGH TO SNEEZE AND HE COMES RIGHT OUT WITHOUT A SINGLE KNOT!
WALT DISNEY
2-11

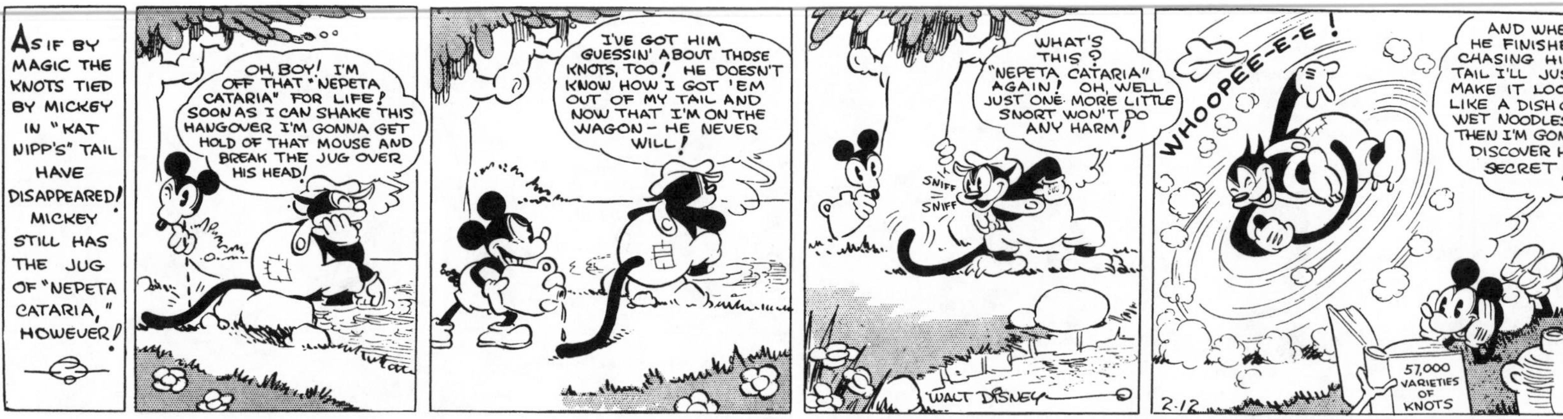
AS IF BY MAGIC THE KNOTS TIED BY MICKEY IN "KAT NIPP'S" TAIL HAVE DISAPPEARED! MICKEY STILL HAS THE JUG OF "NEPETA CATARIA," HOWEVER!
OH, BOY! I'M OFF THAT "NEPETA CATARIA" FOR LIFE! SOON AS I CAN SHAKE THIS HANGOVER I'M GONNA GET HOLD OF THAT MOUSE AND BREAK THE JUG OVER HIS HEAD!
I'VE GOT HIM GUESSIN' ABOUT THOSE KNOTS, TOO! HE DOESN'T KNOW HOW I GOT 'EM OUT OF MY TAIL AND NOW THAT I'M ON THE WAGON - HE NEVER WILL!
WHAT'S THIS? "NEPETA CATARIA" AGAIN! OH, WELL JUST ONE MORE LITTLE SNORT WON'T DO ANY HARM!
SNIFF
SNIFF
WALT DISNEY
WHOOPEE-E-E!
AND WHEN HE FINISHES CHASING HIS TAIL I'LL JUST MAKE IT LOOK LIKE A DISH OF WET NOODLES! THEN I'M GONNA DISCOVER HIS SECRET!
57,000 VARIETIES OF KNOTS
2.12

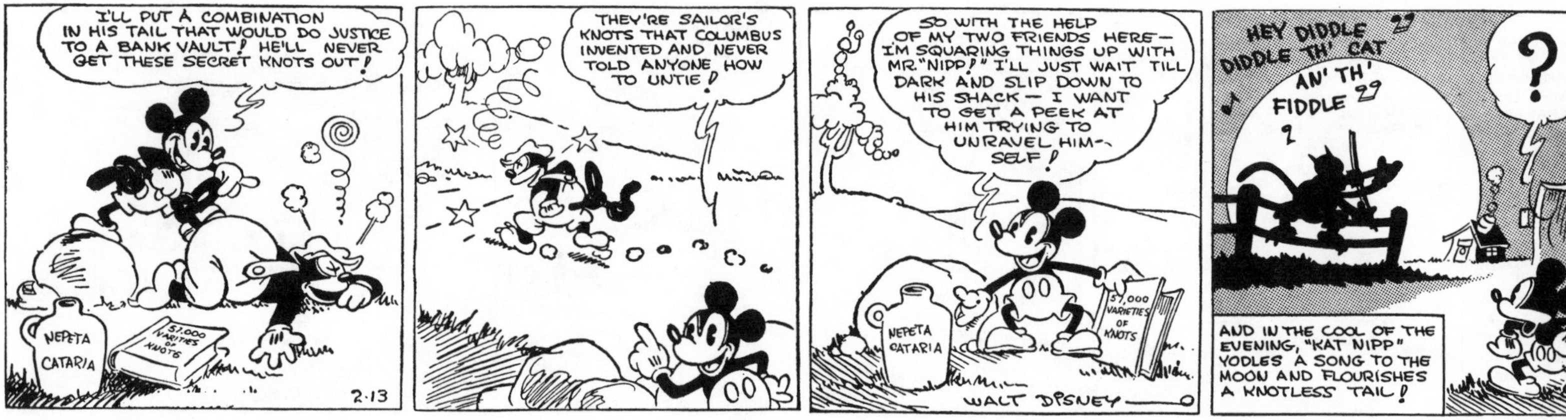
I'LL PUT A COMBINATION IN HIS TAIL THAT WOULD DO JUSTICE TO A BANK VAULT! HE'LL NEVER GET THESE SECRET KNOTS OUT!
NEPETA CATARIA
57,000 VARITIES OF KNOTS
2.13
THEY'RE SAILOR'S KNOTS THAT COLUMBUS INVENTED AND NEVER TOLD ANYONE HOW TO UNTIE!
SO WITH THE HELP OF MY TWO FRIENDS HERE— I'M SQUARING THINGS UP WITH MR. "NIPP!" I'LL JUST WAIT TILL DARK AND SLIP DOWN TO HIS SHACK — I WANT TO GET A PEEK AT HIM TRYING TO UNRAVEL HIM-SELF!
NEPETA CATARIA
57,000 VARIETIES OF KNOTS
WALT DISNEY
"HEY DIDDLE DIDDLE TH' CAT AN' TH' FIDDLE"
?
AND IN THE COOL OF THE EVENING, "KAT NIPP" YODLES A SONG TO THE MOON AND FLOURISHES A KNOTLESS TAIL!

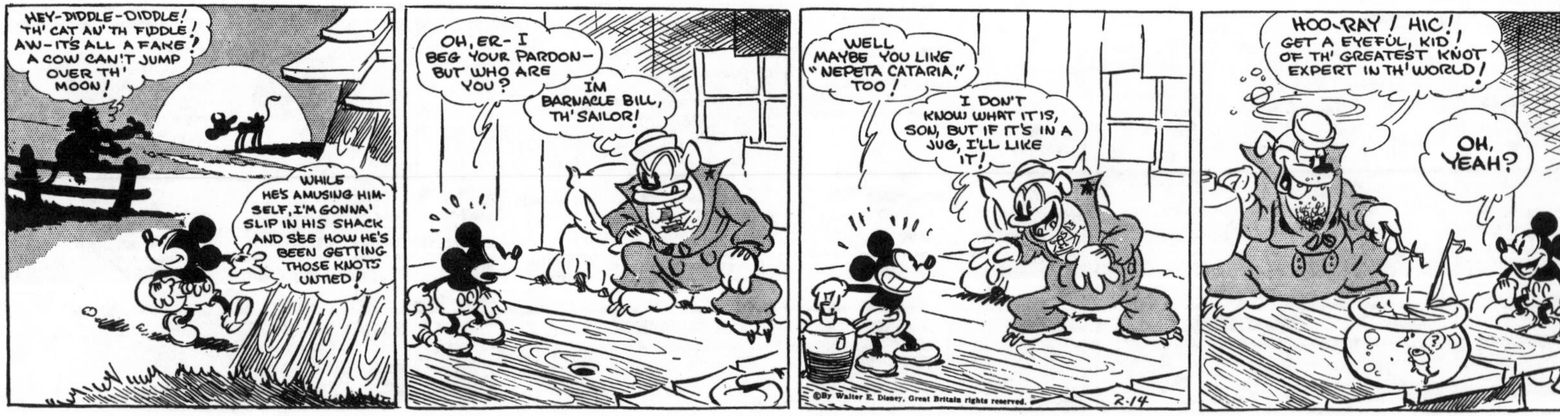
HEY-DIDDLE-DIDDLE! TH' CAT AN' TH FIDDLE! AW-IT'S ALL A FAKE! A COW CAN'T JUMP OVER TH' MOON!
WHILE HE'S AMUSING HIM-SELF, I'M GONNA' SLIP IN HIS SHACK AND SEE HOW HE'S BEEN GETTING THOSE KNOTS UNTIED!
OH, ER- I BEG YOUR PARDON- BUT WHO ARE YOU?
I'M BARNACLE BILL, TH' SAILOR!
WELL MAYBE YOU LIKE "NEPETA CATARIA," TOO!
I DON'T KNOW WHAT IT IS, SON, BUT IF IT'S IN A JUG, I'LL LIKE IT!
©By Walter E. Disney. Great Britain rights reserved.
2.14
HOO-RAY! HIC! GET A EYEFUL, KID! OF TH' GREATEST KNOT EXPERT IN TH' WORLD!
OH, YEAH?

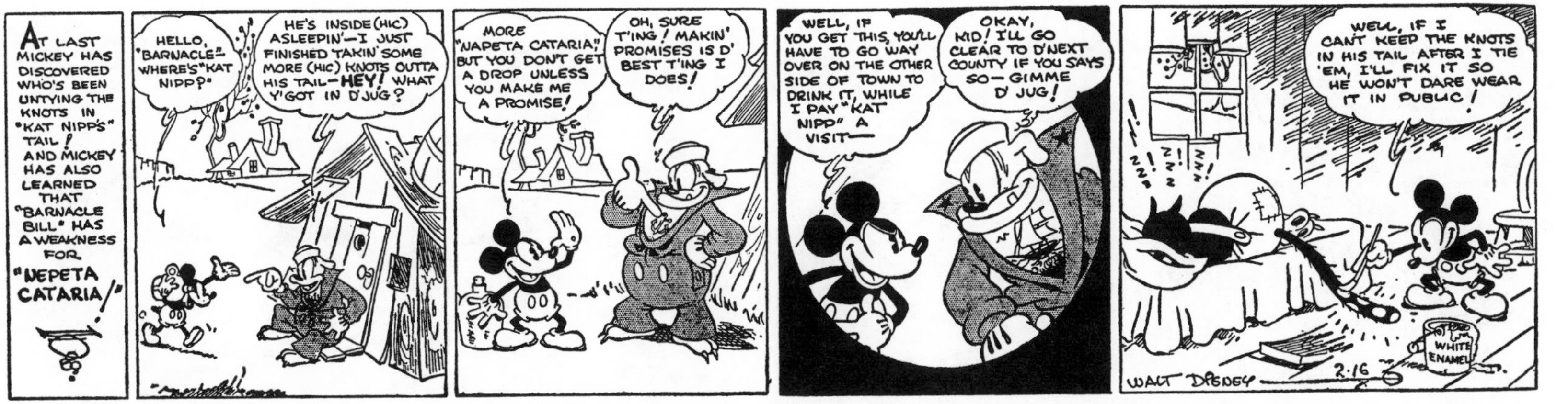
At last Mickey has discovered who's been untying the knots in "Kat Nipp's" tail! And Mickey has also learned that "Barnacle Bill" has a weakness for "Nepeta Cataria!"
HELLO, "BARNACLE"—WHERE'S "KAT NIPP?"
HE'S INSIDE (HIC) ASLEEPIN'—I JUST FINISHED TAKIN' SOME MORE (HIC) KNOTS OUTTA HIS TAIL—HEY! WHAT Y'GOT IN D' JUG?
MORE "NAPETA CATARIA," BUT YOU DON'T GET A DROP UNLESS YOU MAKE ME A PROMISE!
OH, SURE T'ING! MAKIN' PROMISES IS D' BEST T'ING I DOES!
WELL, IF YOU GET THIS, YOU'LL HAVE TO GO WAY OVER ON THE OTHER SIDE OF TOWN TO DRINK IT, WHILE I PAY "KAT NIPP" A VISIT—
OKAY, KID! I'LL GO CLEAR TO D'NEXT COUNTY IF YOU SAYS SO—GIMME D' JUG!
WELL, IF I CAN'T KEEP THE KNOTS IN HIS TAIL AFTER I TIE 'EM, I'LL FIX IT SO HE WON'T DARE WEAR IT IN PUBLIC!
WHITE ENAMEL
WALT DISNEY
2·16

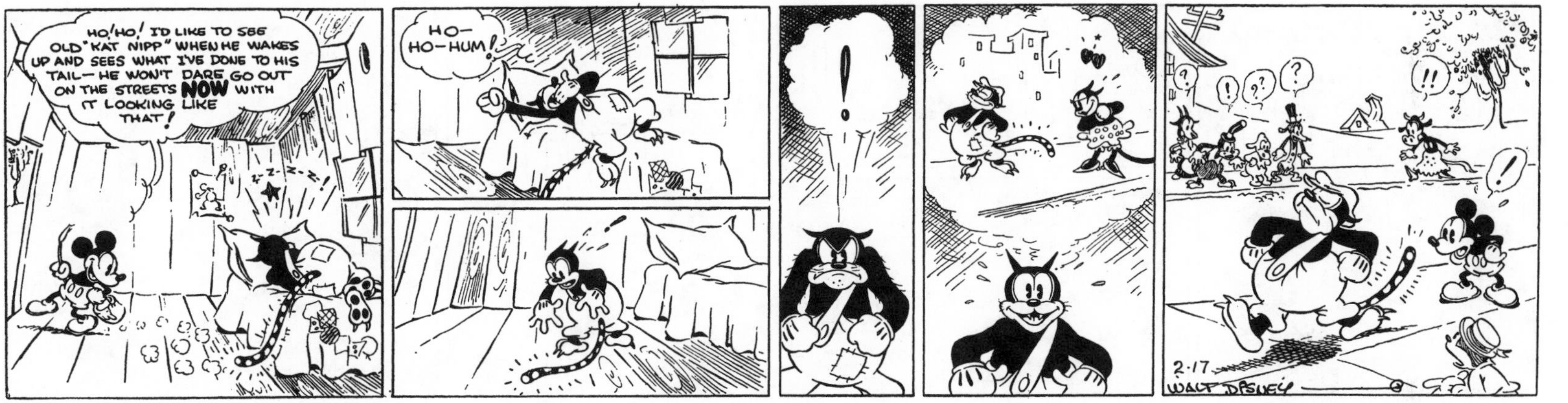
HO! HO! I'D LIKE TO SEE OLD "KAT NIPP" WHEN HE WAKES UP AND SEES WHAT I'VE DONE TO HIS TAIL—HE WON'T DARE GO OUT ON THE STREETS NOW WITH IT LOOKING LIKE THAT!
HO-HO-HUM!
!
2·17
WALT DISNEY

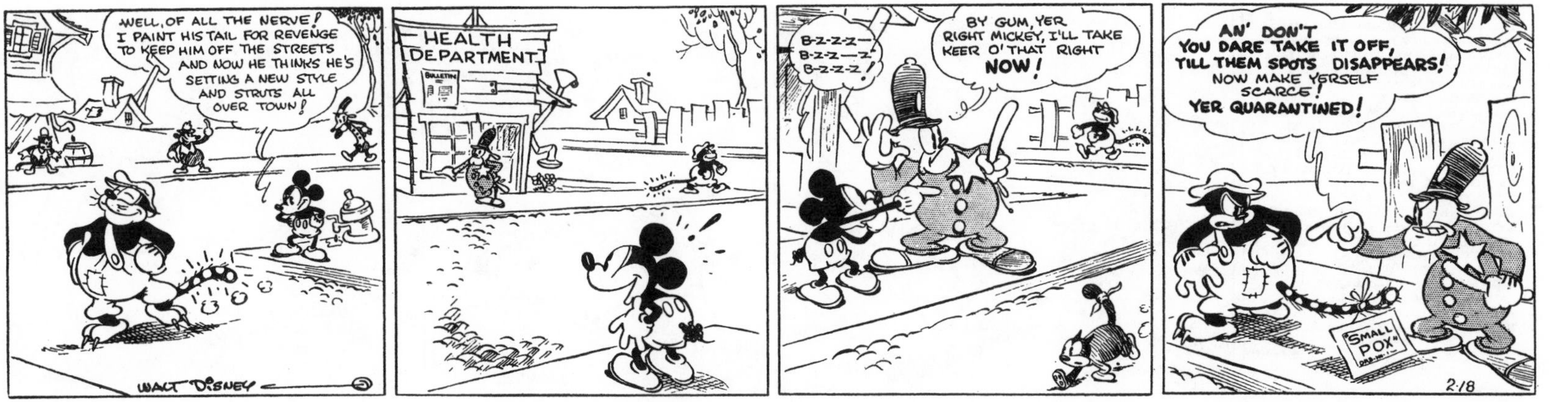
WELL, OF ALL THE NERVE! I PAINT HIS TAIL FOR REVENGE TO KEEP HIM OFF THE STREETS AND NOW HE THINKS HE'S SETTING A NEW STYLE AND STRUTS ALL OVER TOWN!
WALT DISNEY
HEALTH DEPARTMENT
B-Z-Z-Z— B-Z-Z—Z B-Z-Z-Z!
BY GUM, YER RIGHT MICKEY, I'LL TAKE KEER O' THAT RIGHT NOW!
AN' DON'T YOU DARE TAKE IT OFF, TILL THEM SPOTS DISAPPEARS! NOW MAKE YERSELF SCARCE! YER QUARANTINED!
SMALL POX
2·18

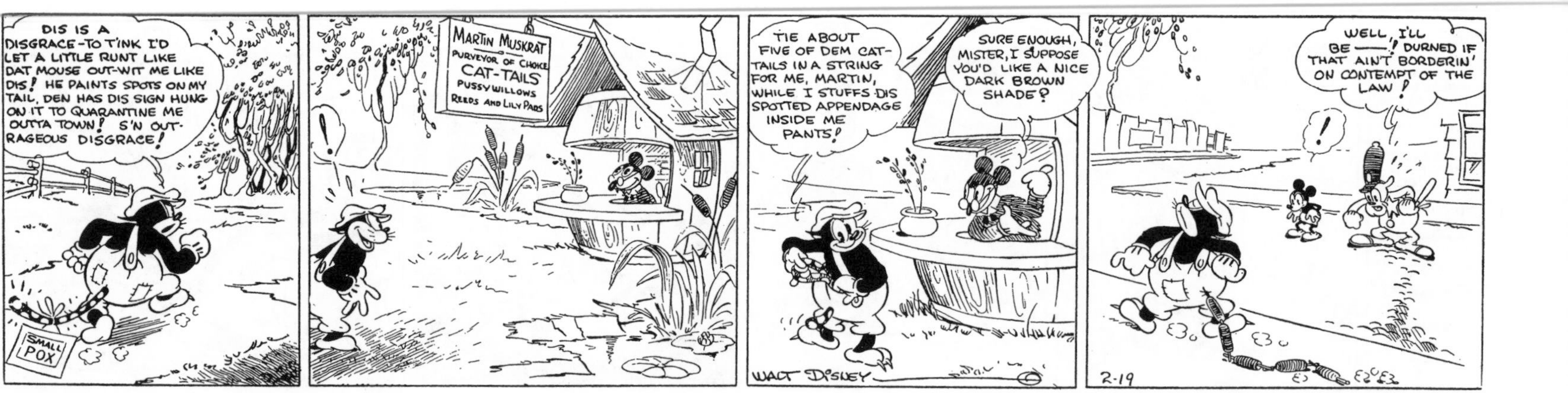
DIS IS A DISGRACE-TO T'INK I'D LET A LITTLE RUNT LIKE DAT MOUSE OUT-WIT ME LIKE DIS! HE PAINTS SPOTS ON MY TAIL, DEN HAS DIS SIGN HUNG ON IT TO QUARANTINE ME OUTTA TOWN! S'N OUT-RAGEOUS DISGRACE!
SMALL POX
MARTIN MUSKRAT
PURVEYOR OF CHOICE
CAT-TAILS
PUSSY WILLOWS
REEDS AND LILY PADS
!
TIE ABOUT FIVE OF DEM CAT-TAILS IN A STRING FOR ME, MARTIN, WHILE I STUFFS DIS SPOTTED APPENDAGE INSIDE ME PANTS!
SURE ENOUGH, MISTER, I SUPPOSE YOU'D LIKE A NICE DARK BROWN SHADE?
WALT DISNEY
WELL, I'LL BE——! DURNED IF THAT AIN'T BORDERIN' ON CONTEMPT OF THE LAW!
!
2-19

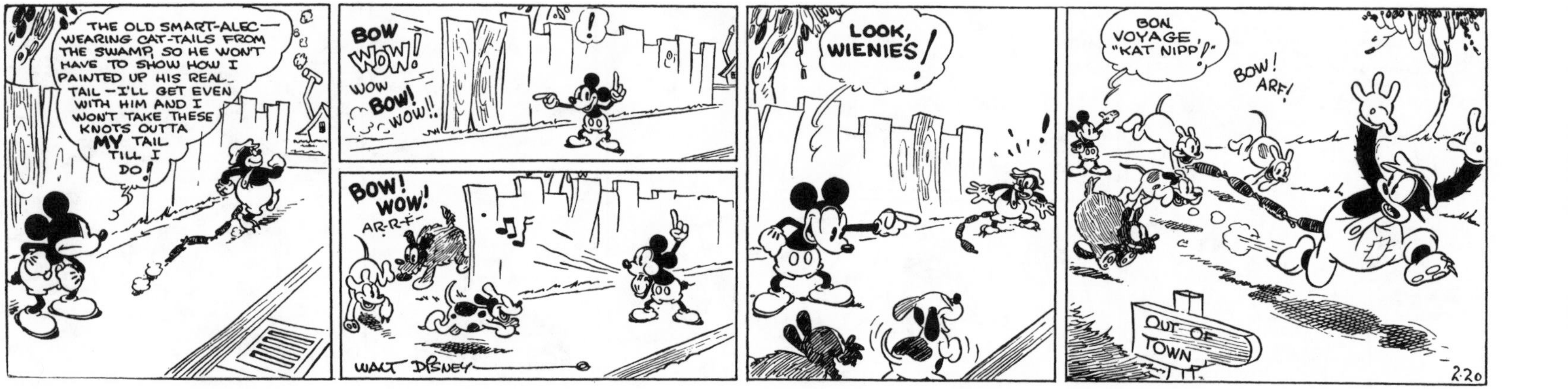
THE OLD SMART-ALEC— WEARING CAT-TAILS FROM THE SWAMP, SO HE WON'T HAVE TO SHOW HOW I PAINTED UP HIS REAL TAIL—I'LL GET EVEN WITH HIM AND I WON'T TAKE THESE KNOTS OUTTA MY TAIL TILL I DO!
BOW WOW! WOW BOW! WOW!!
!
BOW! WOW! AR-R-F
WALT DISNEY
LOOK, WIENIES!
BON VOYAGE, "KAT NIPP"!
BOW! ARF!
OUT OF TOWN
2-20

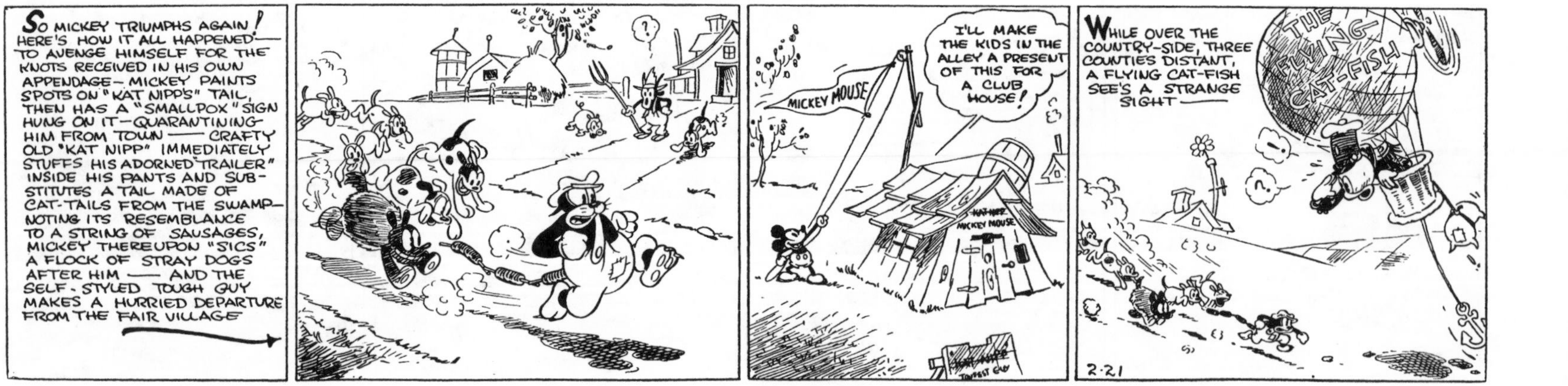
SO MICKEY TRIUMPHS AGAIN! HERE'S HOW IT ALL HAPPENED— TO AVENGE HIMSELF FOR THE KNOTS RECEIVED IN HIS OWN APPENDAGE—MICKEY PAINTS SPOTS ON "KAT NIPP'S" TAIL, THEN HAS A "SMALLPOX" SIGN HUNG ON IT—QUARANTINING HIM FROM TOWN —— CRAFTY OLD "KAT NIPP" IMMEDIATELY STUFFS HIS ADORNED "TRAILER" INSIDE HIS PANTS AND SUBSTITUTES A TAIL MADE OF CAT-TAILS FROM THE SWAMP- NOTING ITS RESEMBLANCE TO A STRING OF SAUSAGES, MICKEY THEREUPON "SICS" A FLOCK OF STRAY DOGS AFTER HIM —— AND THE SELF-STYLED TOUGH GUY MAKES A HURRIED DEPARTURE FROM THE FAIR VILLAGE
?
I'LL MAKE THE KIDS IN THE ALLEY A PRESENT OF THIS FOR A CLUB HOUSE!
MICKEY MOUSE
MICKEY MOUSE
WHILE OVER THE COUNTRY-SIDE, THREE COUNTIES DISTANT, A FLYING CAT-FISH SEE'S A STRANGE SIGHT ——
THE FLYING CAT-FISH
!
?
2-21

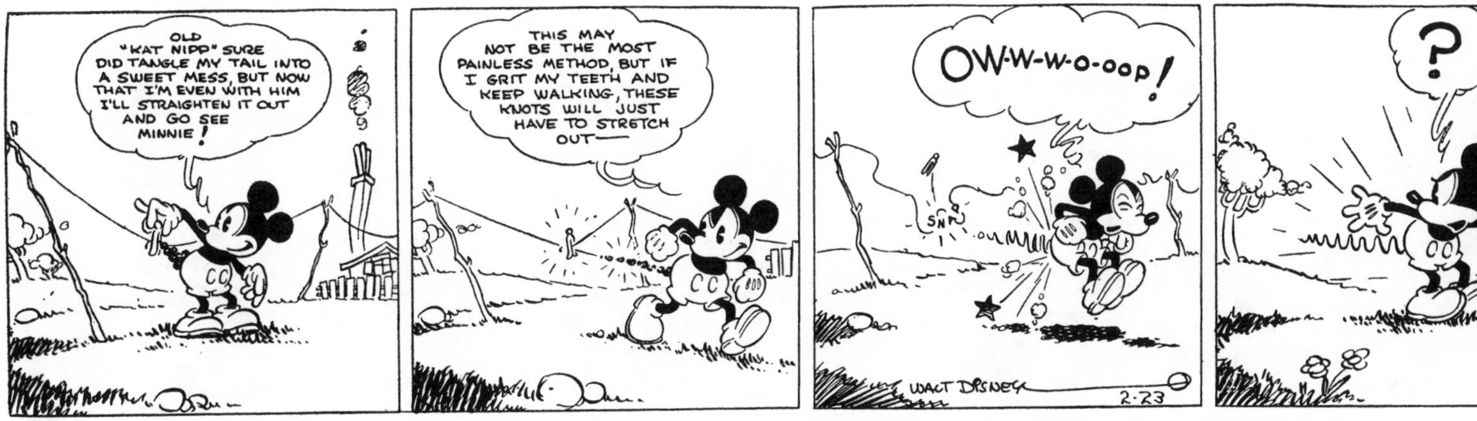
OLD "KAT NIPP" SURE DID TANGLE MY TAIL INTO A SWEET MESS, BUT NOW THAT I'M EVEN WITH HIM I'LL STRAIGHTEN IT OUT AND GO SEE MINNIE!
THIS MAY NOT BE THE MOST PAINLESS METHOD, BUT IF I GRIT MY TEETH AND KEEP WALKING, THESE KNOTS WILL JUST HAVE TO STRETCH OUT—
OW-W-W-O-O-OOP!
SNP
?
WALT DISNEY
2-23

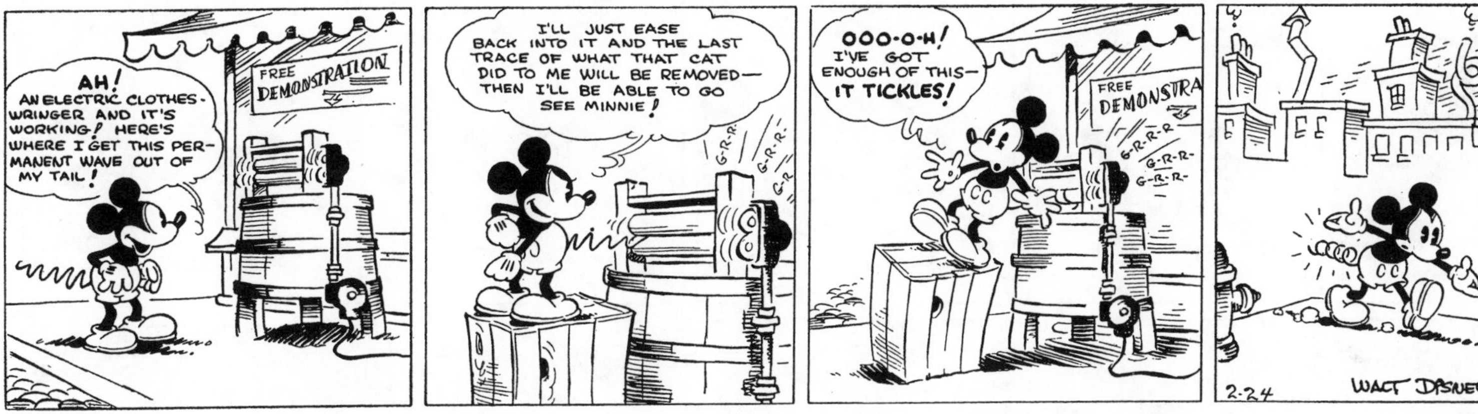
AH! AN ELECTRIC CLOTHES-WRINGER AND IT'S WORKING! HERE'S WHERE I GET THIS PERMANENT WAVE OUT OF MY TAIL!
FREE DEMONSTRATION
I'LL JUST EASE BACK INTO IT AND THE LAST TRACE OF WHAT THAT CAT DID TO ME WILL BE REMOVED— THEN I'LL BE ABLE TO GO SEE MINNIE!
G-R-R- G-R-R- G-R
OOO-O-H! I'VE GOT ENOUGH OF THIS— IT TICKLES!
FREE DEMONSTRA
G-R-R-R G-R-R- G-R-R-
2-24
WALT DISNEY

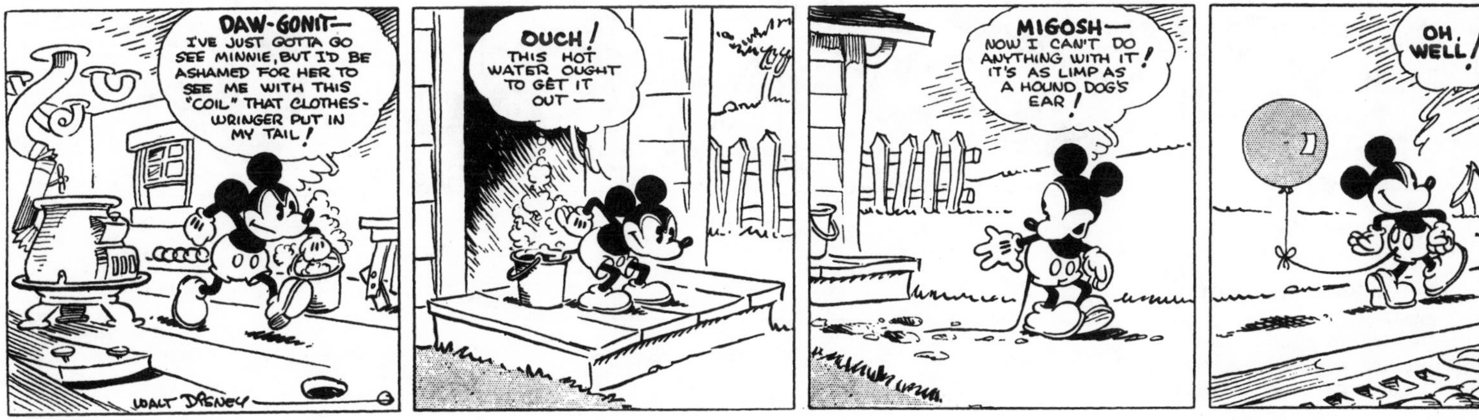
DAW-GONIT— I'VE JUST GOTTA GO SEE MINNIE, BUT I'D BE ASHAMED FOR HER TO SEE ME WITH THIS "COIL" THAT CLOTHES-WRINGER PUT IN MY TAIL!
WALT DISNEY
OUCH! THIS HOT WATER OUGHT TO GET IT OUT—
MIGOSH— NOW I CAN'T DO ANYTHING WITH IT! IT'S AS LIMP AS A HOUND DOG'S EAR!
OH, WELL!
2-25

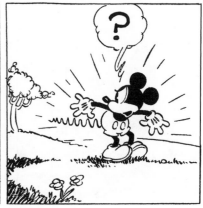

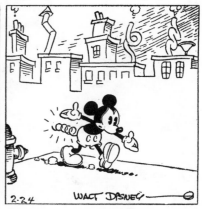

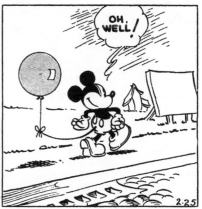

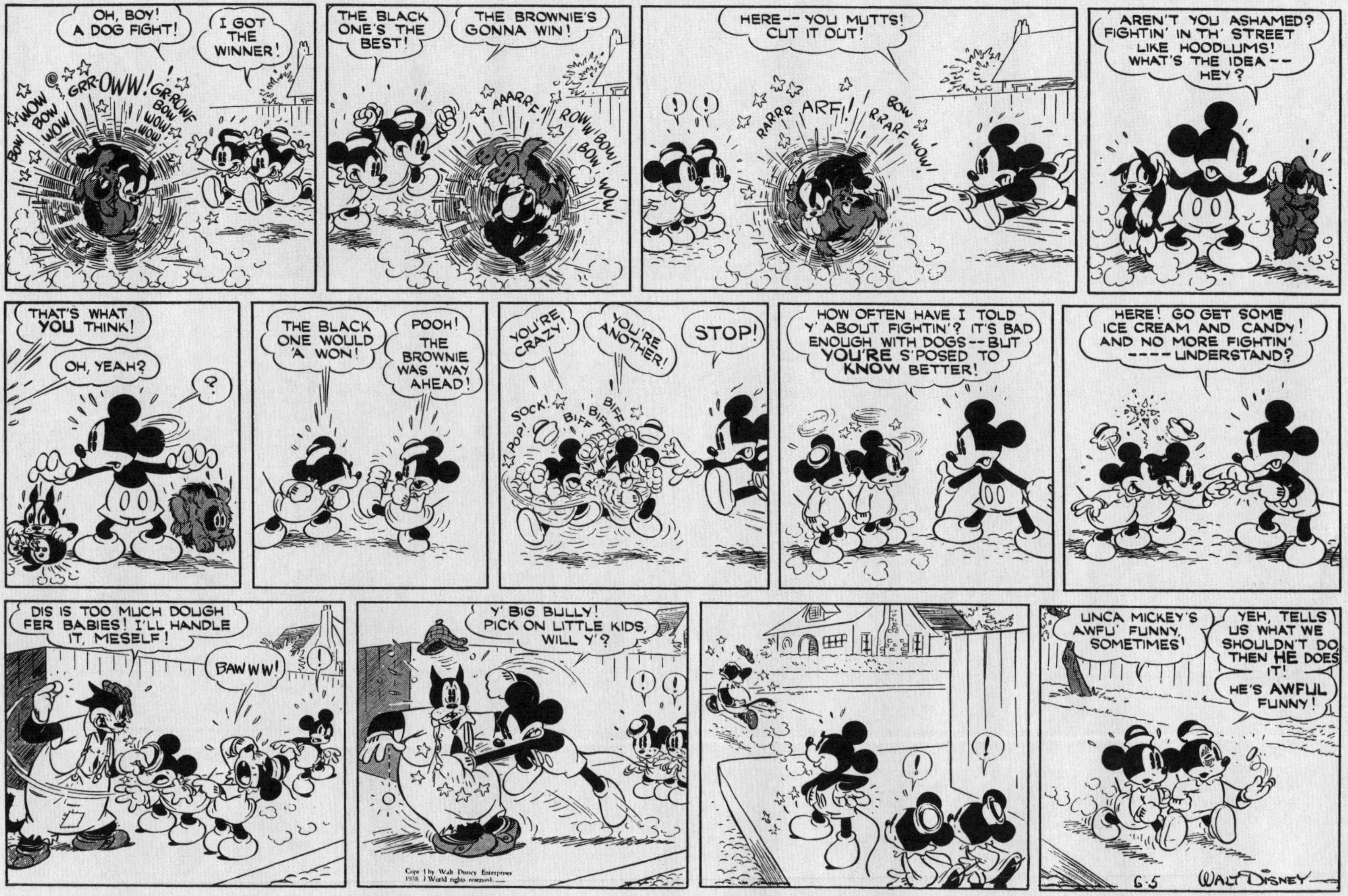
OH, BOY! A DOG FIGHT!
I GOT THE WINNER!
BOW WOW BOW WOW
GRR-OWW!
GR-ROWF BOW WOW! WOW
THE BLACK ONE'S THE BEST!
THE BROWNIE'S GONNA WIN!
AAARRF!
ROWW BOW! BOW WOW
HERE-- YOU MUTTS! CUT IT OUT!
RARRR ARF!
BOW RRARF WOW!
AREN'T YOU ASHAMED? FIGHTIN' IN TH' STREET LIKE HOODLUMS! WHAT'S THE IDEA -- HEY?
THAT'S WHAT YOU THINK!
OH, YEAH?
?
THE BLACK ONE WOULD 'A WON!
POOH! THE BROWNIE WAS 'WAY AHEAD!
YOU'RE CRAZY!
YOU'RE ANOTHER!
STOP!
SOCK! POP! BIFF BIFF BIFF
HOW OFTEN HAVE I TOLD Y' ABOUT FIGHTIN'? IT'S BAD ENOUGH WITH DOGS--BUT YOU'RE S'POSED TO KNOW BETTER!
HERE! GO GET SOME ICE CREAM AND CANDY! AND NO MORE FIGHTIN' ----UNDERSTAND?
DIS IS TOO MUCH DOUGH FER BABIES! I'LL HANDLE IT, MESELF!
BAWWW!
Y' BIG BULLY! PICK ON LITTLE KIDS, WILL Y'?
UNCA MICKEY'S AWFU' FUNNY, SOMETIMES!
YEH, TELLS US WHAT WE SHOULDN'T DO, THEN HE DOES IT!
HE'S AWFUL FUNNY!
6-5
WALT DISNEY

ABOVE: Rowr! Kat Nipp—or a reasonable facsimile thereof, complete with golf cap and Brooklyn twang—made a sudden reappearance in Floyd Gottfredson's Sunday strip for June 5, 1938. The strip got its later title, "He's Funny That Way," for a comic book reprint *Walt Disney's Comics and Stories* 11, 1941).

MICKEY MOUSE, BOXING CHAMPION

—AND—

HIGH SOCIETY

FEBRUARY 26, 1931
–
MAY 30, 1931

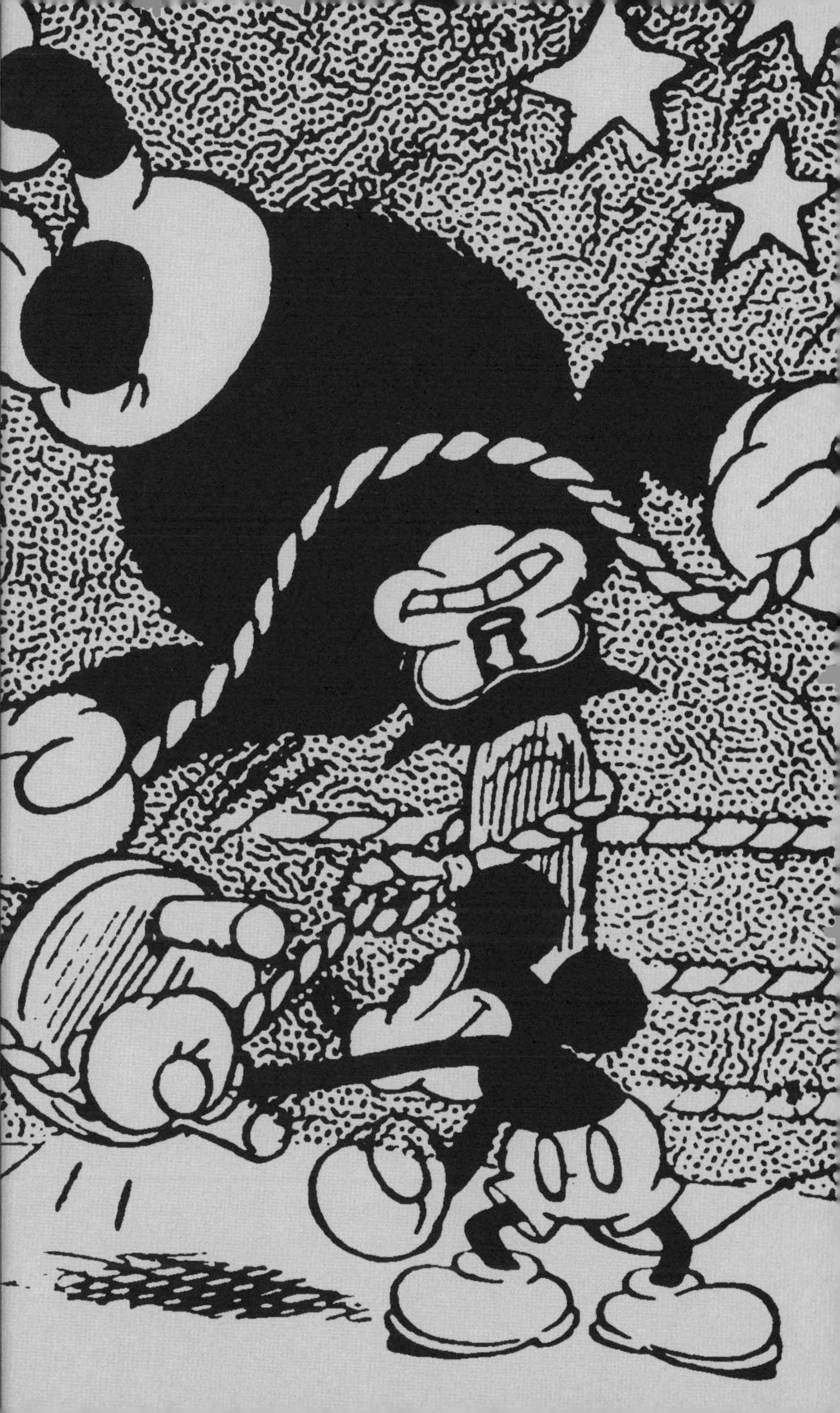

MICKEY MOUSE
REGISTERED U.S. PATENT OFFICE

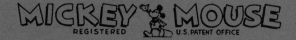

HIGH SOCIETY: REALITY SHOW EDITION

Life imitates art; and in "Mickey Mouse, Boxing Champion" and "High Society," Floyd Gottfredson set out to coordinate the two on purpose. When boxing champ Mickey took his photo for his fans, the captions requesting reader write-ins were actually the real deal. So were the photos, so to speak; Gottfredson and his team created an elaborate painted "photograph" (pictured on page 150) as one of Mickey's first-ever fan cards. How many fans would actually send in for one? Surely enough to boost the strip's success.

As things turned out, the strip didn't need much boosting. A monstrous 20,000 letters—at least according to a press release—made sending out the fan card replies into a Herculean task. "Let's get publicity," Floyd remembered Walt Disney as having told him later, "but for God's sake don't do that again!"[1]

In the end, however, the mountain of mail was good to have around: it made a handy prop for a real photo shoot. In early 1932, when Disney switched distributors from Columbia to United Artists, pictures of celebrity Mickey standing beside the huge pile of post became part of a promotional push.

We'd like to note that in the early 1930s, even a celebrity Mouse could set a bad example. Trick shooting, as briefly seen in "Boxing Champion," is dangerous in real life. Mickey certainly wouldn't endorse it today. [DG]

1 Walt Disney as quoted by Floyd Gottfredson to David R. Smith, *Mickey Mouse in Color* deluxe edition (Prescott: Another Rainbow, 1988), caption on p. 167.

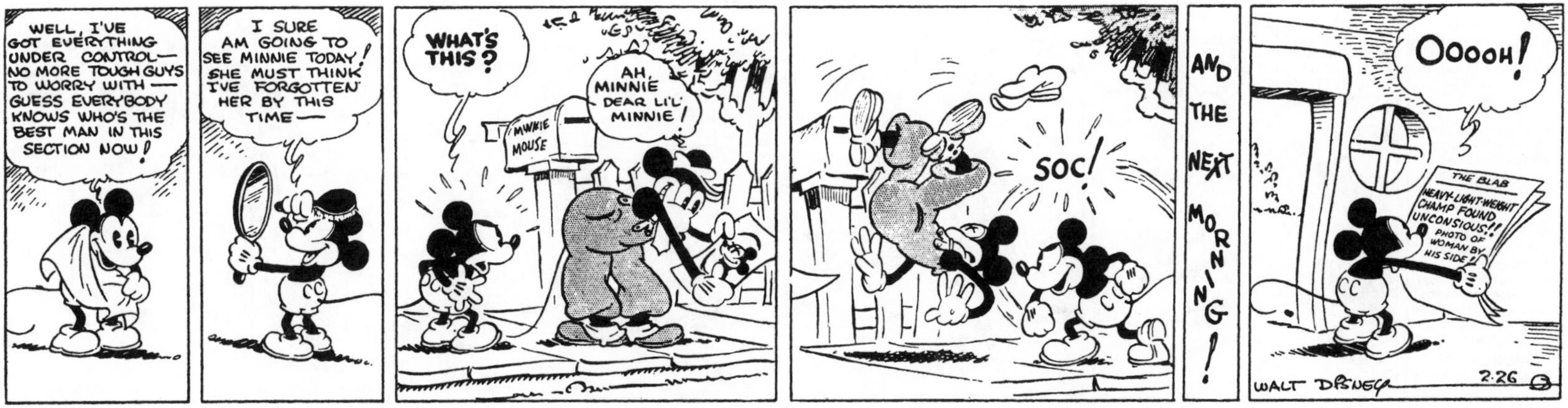
WELL, I'VE GOT EVERYTHING UNDER CONTROL— NO MORE TOUGH GUYS TO WORRY WITH— GUESS EVERYBODY KNOWS WHO'S THE BEST MAN IN THIS SECTION NOW!
I SURE AM GOING TO SEE MINNIE TODAY! SHE MUST THINK I'VE FORGOTTEN HER BY THIS TIME—
WHAT'S THIS?
AH, MINNIE DEAR LI'L' MINNIE!
MINNIE MOUSE
SOC!
AND THE NEXT MORNING!
OOOOH!
THE BLAB
HEAVY-LIGHT-WEIGHT CHAMP FOUND UNCONSIOUS!! PHOTO OF WOMAN BY HIS SIDE!
WALT DISNEY
2.26

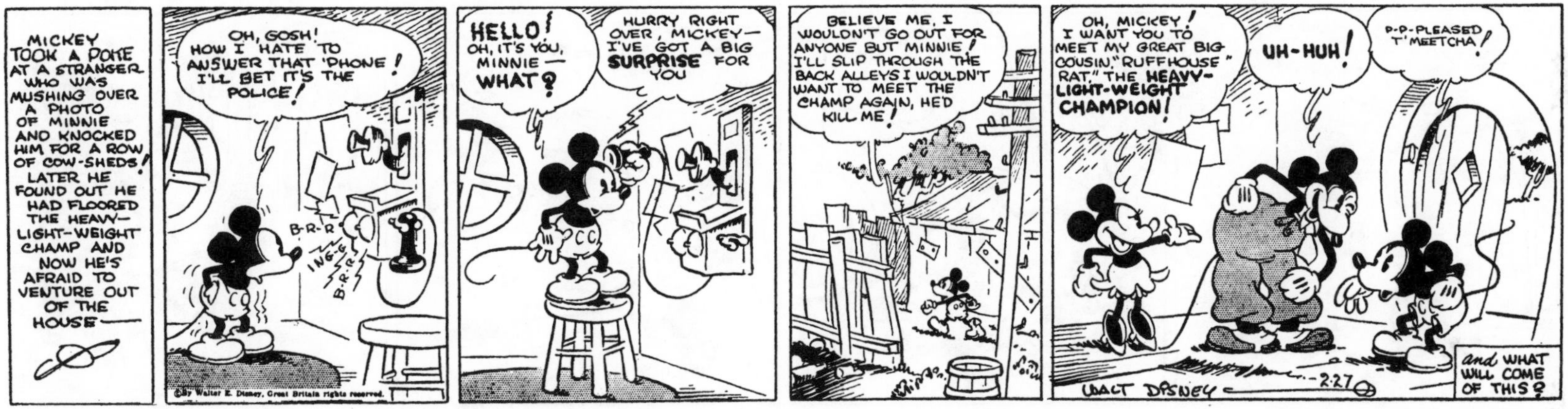
MICKEY TOOK A POKE AT A STRANGER WHO WAS MUSHING OVER A PHOTO OF MINNIE AND KNOCKED HIM FOR A ROW OF COW-SHEDS! LATER HE FOUND OUT HE HAD FLOORED THE HEAVY-LIGHT-WEIGHT CHAMP AND NOW HE'S AFRAID TO VENTURE OUT OF THE HOUSE—
OH, GOSH! HOW I HATE TO ANSWER THAT 'PHONE! I'LL BET IT'S THE POLICE!
B-R-R-ING-G B-R-R
©By Walter E. Disney, Great Britain rights reserved.
HELLO! OH, IT'S YOU, MINNIE— WHAT?
HURRY RIGHT OVER, MICKEY— I'VE GOT A BIG SURPRISE FOR YOU
BELIEVE ME, I WOULDN'T GO OUT FOR ANYONE BUT MINNIE! I'LL SLIP THROUGH THE BACK ALLEYS I WOULDN'T WANT TO MEET THE CHAMP AGAIN, HE'D KILL ME!
OH, MICKEY! I WANT YOU TO MEET MY GREAT BIG COUSIN, "RUFFHOUSE" RAT," THE HEAVY-LIGHT-WEIGHT CHAMPION!
UH-HUH!
P-P-PLEASED T'MEETCHA!
WALT DISNEY
2.27
and WHAT WILL COME OF THIS?

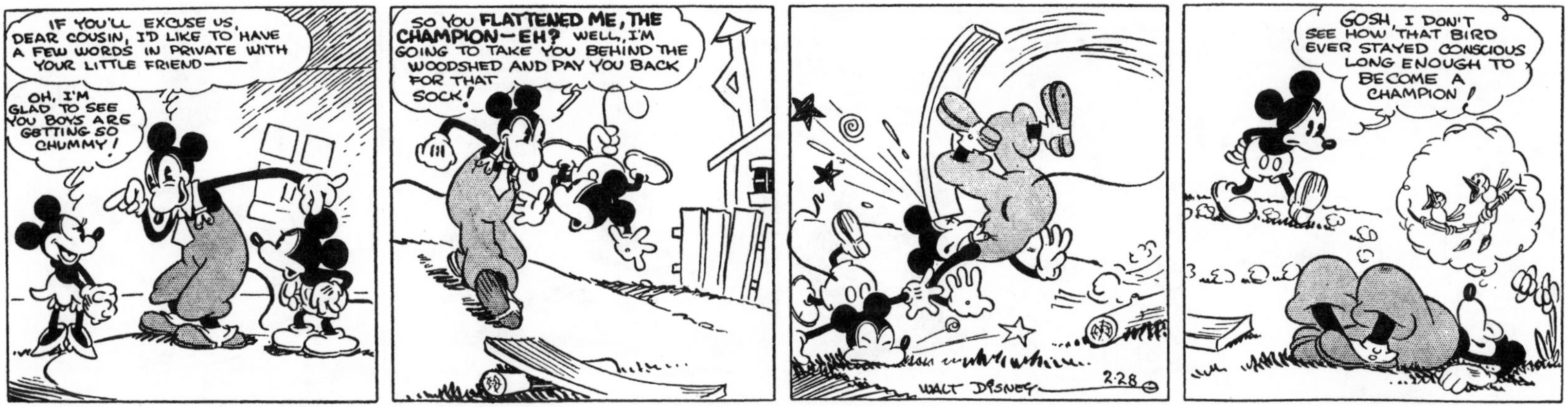
IF YOU'LL EXCUSE US, DEAR COUSIN, I'D LIKE TO HAVE A FEW WORDS IN PRIVATE WITH YOUR LITTLE FRIEND—
OH, I'M GLAD TO SEE YOU BOYS ARE GETTING SO CHUMMY!
SO YOU FLATTENED ME, THE CHAMPION—EH? WELL, I'M GOING TO TAKE YOU BEHIND THE WOODSHED AND PAY YOU BACK FOR THAT SOCK!
WALT DISNEY
2.28
GOSH, I DON'T SEE HOW THAT BIRD EVER STAYED CONSCIOUS LONG ENOUGH TO BECOME A CHAMPION!

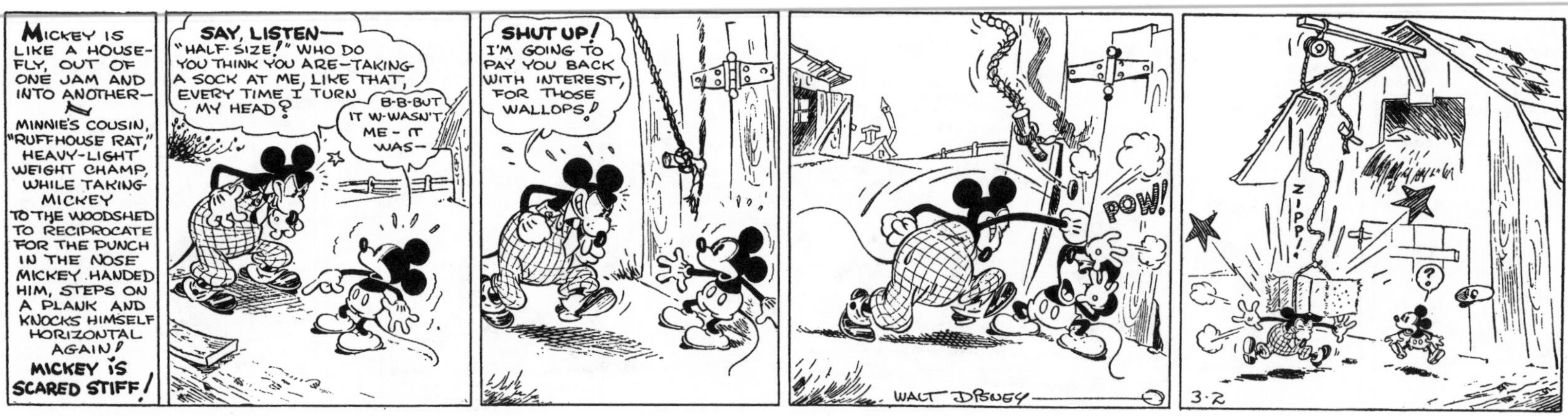
MICKEY IS LIKE A HOUSE-FLY, OUT OF ONE JAM AND INTO ANOTHER—
MINNIE'S COUSIN, "RUFFHOUSE RAT," HEAVY-LIGHT WEIGHT CHAMP, WHILE TAKING MICKEY TO THE WOODSHED TO RECIPROCATE FOR THE PUNCH IN THE NOSE MICKEY HANDED HIM, STEPS ON A PLANK AND KNOCKS HIMSELF HORIZONTAL AGAIN!
MICKEY IS SCARED STIFF!
SAY, LISTEN— "HALF-SIZE!" WHO DO YOU THINK YOU ARE—TAKING A SOCK AT ME, LIKE THAT, EVERY TIME I TURN MY HEAD?
B-B-BUT IT W-WASN'T ME - IT WAS—
SHUT UP! I'M GOING TO PAY YOU BACK WITH INTEREST, FOR THOSE WALLOPS!
POW!
ZIPP!
?
WALT DISNEY
3-2

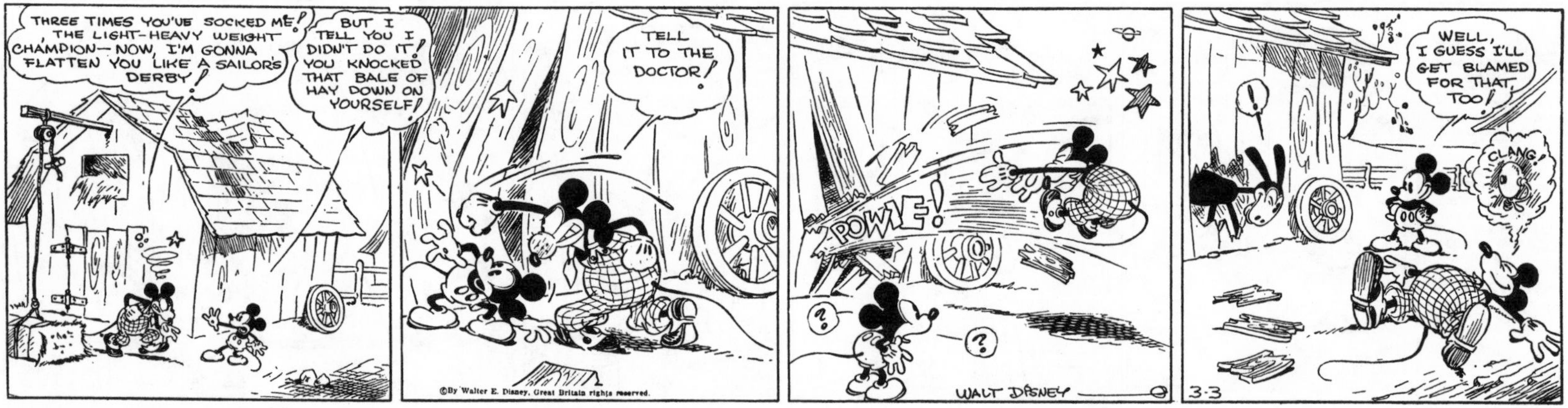
THREE TIMES YOU'VE SOCKED ME! , THE LIGHT-HEAVY WEIGHT CHAMPION— NOW, I'M GONNA FLATTEN YOU LIKE A SAILOR'S DERBY!
BUT I TELL YOU I DIDN'T DO IT! YOU KNOCKED THAT BALE OF HAY DOWN ON YOURSELF!
TELL IT TO THE DOCTOR!
©By Walter E. Disney, Great Britain rights reserved.
POWIE!
?
?
!
WELL, I GUESS I'LL GET BLAMED FOR THAT, TOO!
CLANG!
WALT DISNEY
3-3

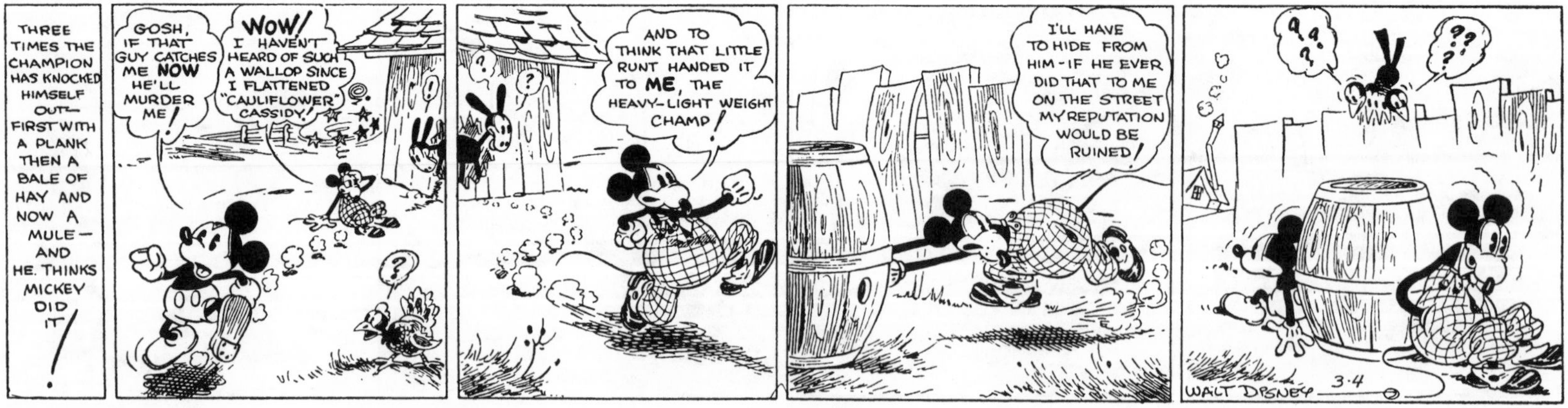
THREE TIMES THE CHAMPION HAS KNOCKED HIMSELF OUT— FIRST WITH A PLANK THEN A BALE OF HAY AND NOW A MULE— AND HE THINKS MICKEY DID IT!
GOSH, IF THAT GUY CATCHES ME NOW HE'LL MURDER ME!
WOW! I HAVEN'T HEARD OF SUCH A WALLOP SINCE I FLATTENED "CAULIFLOWER" CASSIDY!
?
AND TO THINK THAT LITTLE RUNT HANDED IT TO ME, THE HEAVY-LIGHT WEIGHT CHAMP!
I'LL HAVE TO HIDE FROM HIM - IF HE EVER DID THAT TO ME ON THE STREET MY REPUTATION WOULD BE RUINED!
WALT DISNEY
3-4

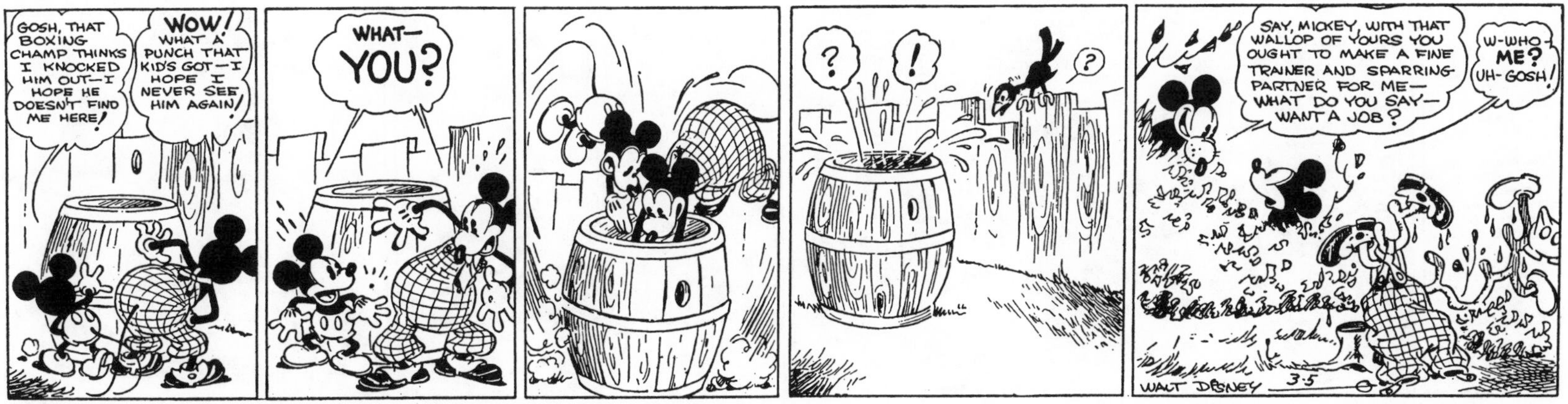
GOSH, THAT BOXING CHAMP THINKS I KNOCKED HIM OUT—I HOPE HE DOESN'T FIND ME HERE!
WOW! WHAT A PUNCH THAT KID'S GOT—I HOPE I NEVER SEE HIM AGAIN!
WHAT— YOU?
?
!
?
SAY, MICKEY, WITH THAT WALLOP OF YOURS YOU OUGHT TO MAKE A FINE TRAINER AND SPARRING-PARTNER FOR ME—WHAT DO YOU SAY—WANT A JOB?
W-WHO ME? UH-GOSH!
WALT DISNEY
3·5

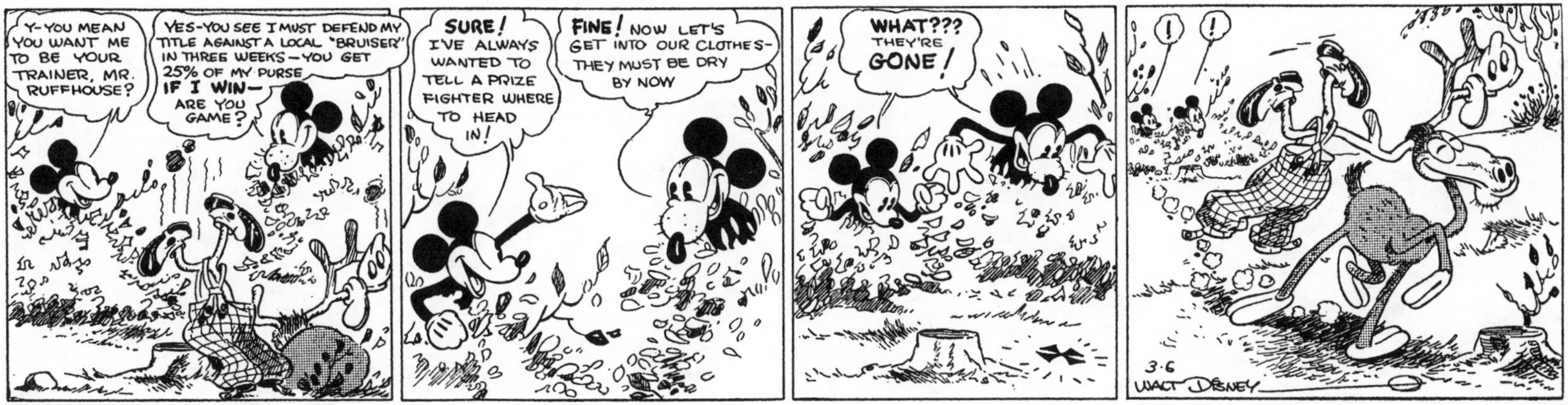
Y-YOU MEAN YOU WANT ME TO BE YOUR TRAINER, MR. RUFFHOUSE?
YES-YOU SEE I MUST DEFEND MY TITLE AGAINST A LOCAL "BRUISER" IN THREE WEEKS—YOU GET 25% OF MY PURSE IF I WIN—ARE YOU GAME?
SURE! I'VE ALWAYS WANTED TO TELL A PRIZE FIGHTER WHERE TO HEAD IN!
FINE! NOW LET'S GET INTO OUR CLOTHES-THEY MUST BE DRY BY NOW
WHAT??? THEY'RE GONE!
!
!
3·6
WALT DISNEY

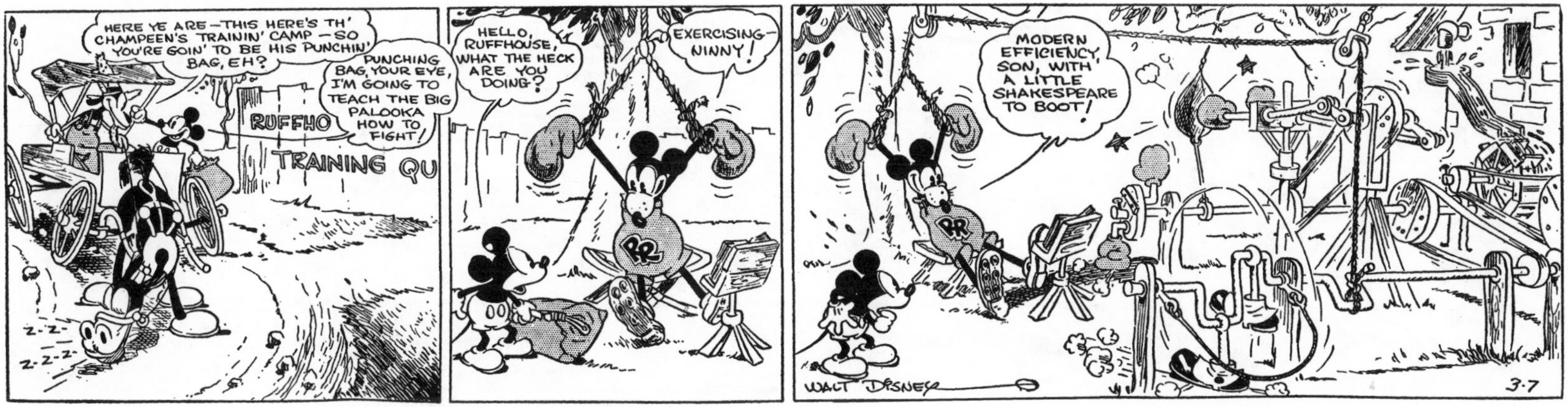
HERE YE ARE—THIS HERE'S TH' CHAMPEEN'S TRAININ' CAMP—SO YOU'RE GOIN' TO BE HIS PUNCHIN' BAG, EH?
PUNCHING BAG, YOUR EYE, I'M GOING TO TEACH THE BIG PALOOKA HOW TO FIGHT!
RUFFHO
TRAINING QU
Z-Z-
Z-Z-Z-
HELLO, RUFFHOUSE, WHAT THE HECK ARE YOU DOING?
EXERCISING-NINNY!
RR
MODERN EFFICIENCY, SON, WITH A LITTLE SHAKESPEARE TO BOOT!
RR
WALT DISNEY
3·7

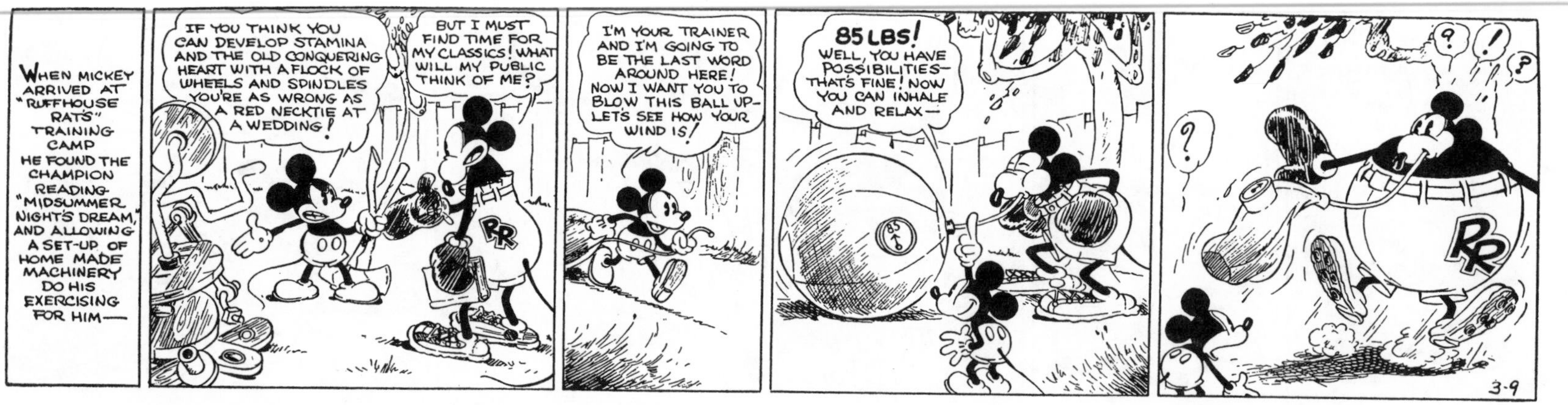
WHEN MICKEY ARRIVED AT "RUFFHOUSE RATS" TRAINING CAMP HE FOUND THE CHAMPION READING "MIDSUMMER NIGHT'S DREAM," AND ALLOWING A SET-UP OF HOME MADE MACHINERY DO HIS EXERCISING FOR HIM—
IF YOU THINK YOU CAN DEVELOP STAMINA AND THE OLD CONQUERING HEART WITH A FLOCK OF WHEELS AND SPINDLES YOU'RE AS WRONG AS A RED NECKTIE AT A WEDDING!
BUT I MUST FIND TIME FOR MY CLASSICS! WHAT WILL MY PUBLIC THINK OF ME?
I'M YOUR TRAINER AND I'M GOING TO BE THE LAST WORD AROUND HERE! NOW I WANT YOU TO BLOW THIS BALL UP- LET'S SEE HOW YOUR WIND IS!
85 LBS! WELL, YOU HAVE POSSIBILITIES— THAT'S FINE! NOW YOU CAN INHALE AND RELAX—
RR
?
?
!
?
3·9

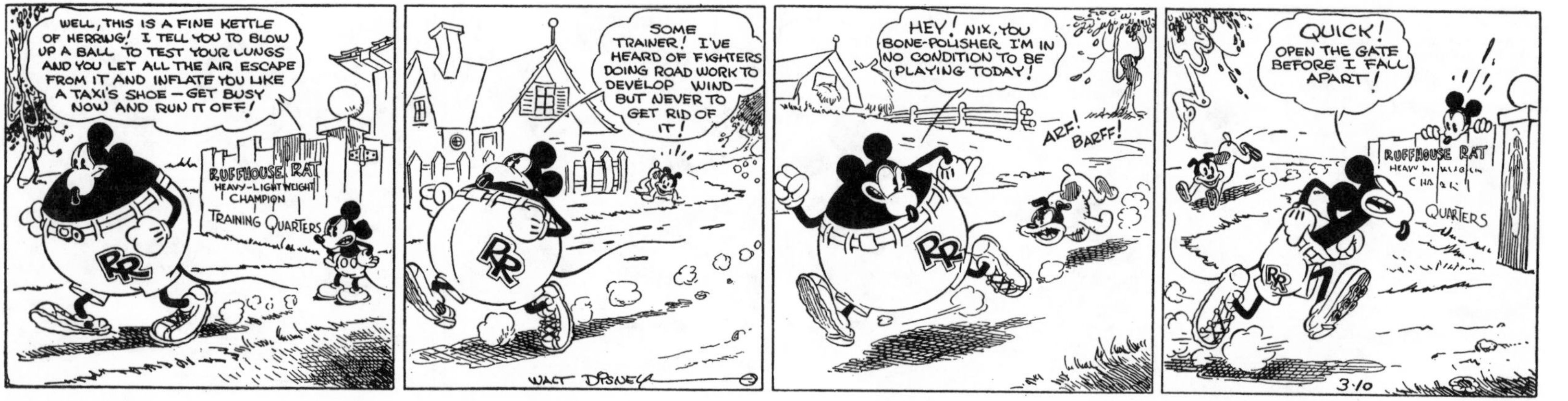
WELL, THIS IS A FINE KETTLE OF HERRING! I TELL YOU TO BLOW UP A BALL TO TEST YOUR LUNGS AND YOU LET ALL THE AIR ESCAPE FROM IT AND INFLATE YOU LIKE A TAXI'S SHOE — GET BUSY NOW AND RUN IT OFF!
RUFFHOUSE RAT
HEAVY-LIGHT WEIGHT CHAMPION
TRAINING QUARTERS
SOME TRAINER! I'VE HEARD OF FIGHTERS DOING ROAD WORK TO DEVELOP WIND— BUT NEVER TO GET RID OF IT!
WALT DISNEY
HEY! NIX, YOU BONE-POLISHER I'M IN NO CONDITION TO BE PLAYING TODAY!
ARF! BARFF!
QUICK! OPEN THE GATE BEFORE I FALL APART!
RUFFHOUSE RAT
QUARTERS
3·10

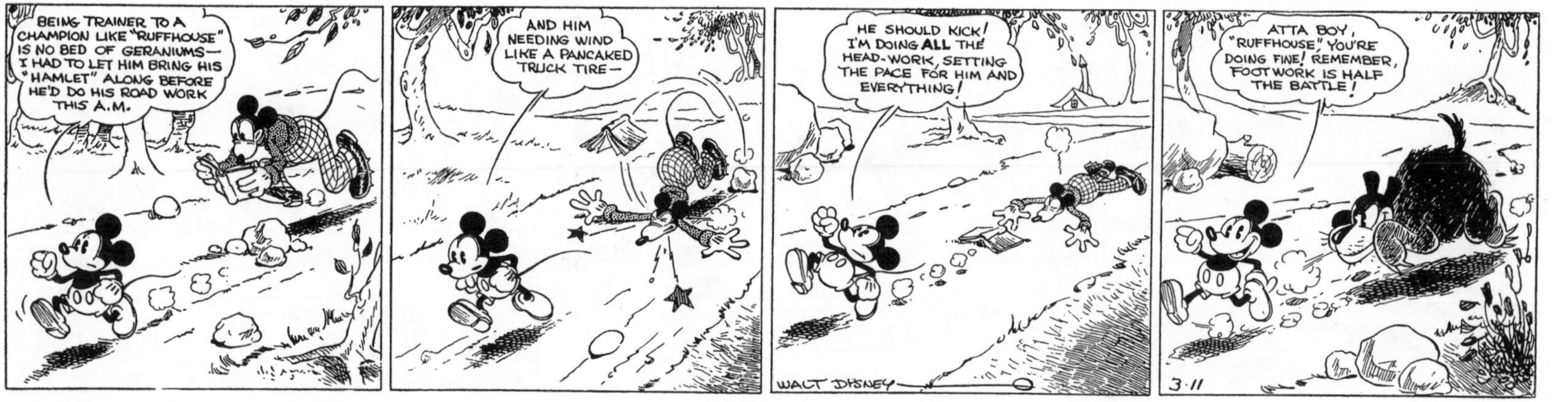
BEING TRAINER TO A CHAMPION LIKE "RUFFHOUSE" IS NO BED OF GERANIUMS— I HAD TO LET HIM BRING HIS "HAMLET" ALONG BEFORE HE'D DO HIS ROAD WORK THIS A.M.
AND HIM NEEDING WIND LIKE A PANCAKED TRUCK TIRE—
HE SHOULD KICK! I'M DOING ALL THE HEAD-WORK, SETTING THE PACE FOR HIM AND EVERYTHING!
WALT DISNEY
ATTA BOY, "RUFFHOUSE," YOU'RE DOING FINE! REMEMBER, FOOTWORK IS HALF THE BATTLE!
3·11

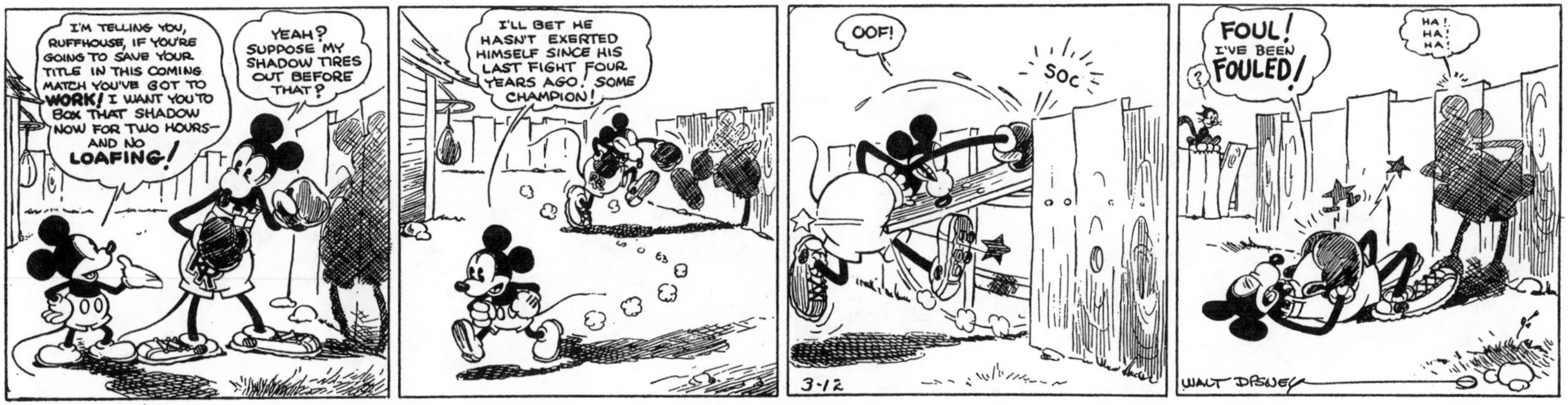
I'M TELLING YOU, RUFFHOUSE, IF YOU'RE GOING TO SAVE YOUR TITLE IN THIS COMING MATCH YOU'VE GOT TO WORK! I WANT YOU TO BOX THAT SHADOW NOW FOR TWO HOURS— AND NO LOAFING!
YEAH? SUPPOSE MY SHADOW TIRES OUT BEFORE THAT?
I'LL BET HE HASN'T EXERTED HIMSELF SINCE HIS LAST FIGHT FOUR YEARS AGO. SOME CHAMPION!
OOF!
SOC
3-12
FOUL! I'VE BEEN FOULED!
?
HA! HA! HA!
WALT DISNEY

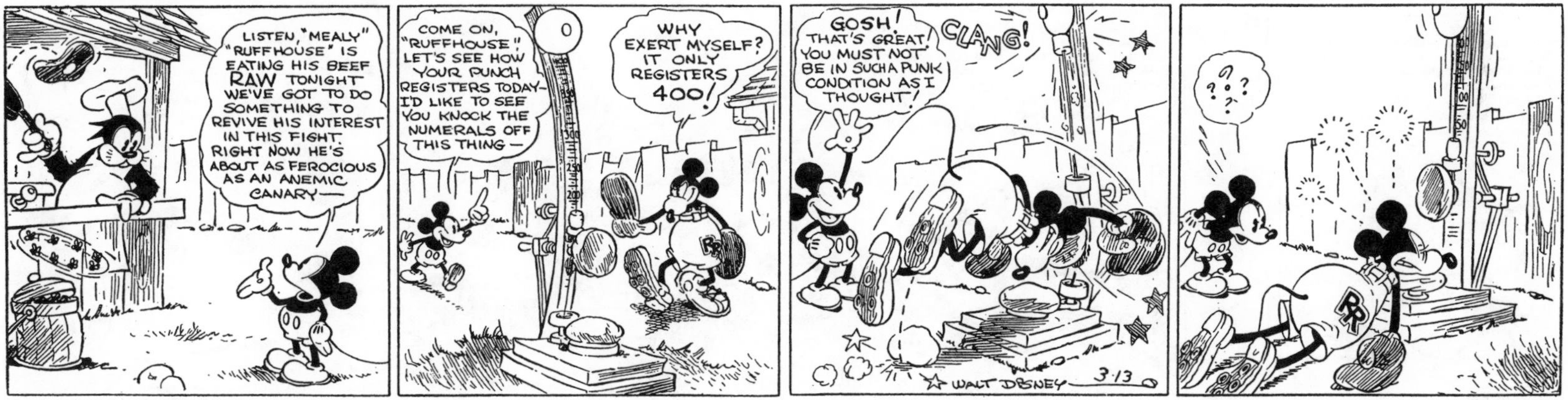
LISTEN, "MEALY" "RUFFHOUSE" IS EATING HIS BEEF RAW TONIGHT WE'VE GOT TO DO SOMETHING TO REVIVE HIS INTEREST IN THIS FIGHT. RIGHT NOW HE'S ABOUT AS FEROCIOUS AS AN ANEMIC CANARY—
COME ON, "RUFFHOUSE", LET'S SEE HOW YOUR PUNCH REGISTERS TODAY— I'D LIKE TO SEE YOU KNOCK THE NUMERALS OFF THIS THING—
WHY EXERT MYSELF? IT ONLY REGISTERS 400!
GOSH! THAT'S GREAT! YOU MUST NOT BE IN SUCH A PUNK CONDITION AS I THOUGHT!
CLANG!
WALT DISNEY 3-13
? ? ? ? ?

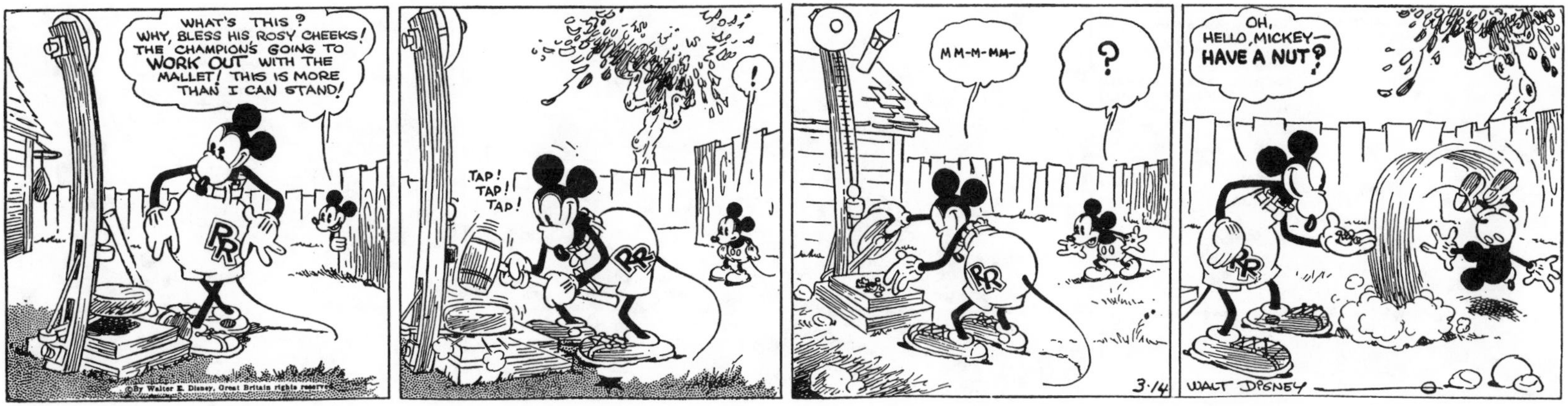
WHAT'S THIS? WHY, BLESS HIS ROSY CHEEKS! THE CHAMPION'S GOING TO WORK OUT WITH THE MALLET! THIS IS MORE THAN I CAN STAND!
© By Walter E. Disney, Great Britain rights reserved
TAP! TAP! TAP!
!
M-M-M-MM-
?
3-14
OH, HELLO, MICKEY— HAVE A NUT?
WALT DISNEY

FRANKLY, "RUFFHOUSE," AS YOUR TRAINER I'M DISGUSTED WITH YOU — HOW YOU EVER WON THE HEAVY LIGHT WEIGHT TITLE IS MORE THAN I CAN UNDERSTAND — YOU DON'T KNOW THE FIRST THING ABOUT TRAINING —
CALM YOURSELF, MICKEY, THAT'S MY SECRET — I WIN WITH A SUPER-SCIENTIFIC METHOD OF ULTRA-MODERN BOXING!
SUPER-WHICH? WHAT DO YOU MEAN?
PSYCHOLOGY AND A HYPNOTIC EYE — WATCH, I'LL DEMONSTRATE ON THIS ROOSTER —
WALT DISNEY 3-16

THAT ROOSTER SURE PUT THE SKIDS ON YOUR "HYPNOTIC EYE" RACKET — BETTER LAY OFF THAT "PSYCHOLOGY" STUFF — I DON'T THINK FIGHTERS AROUND HERE ARE INTELLIGENT ENOUGH TO BE LICKED BY IT —
While
BACK IN TOWN — IN THE OFFICES OF THE "DAILY EXPLOSION"
HEY — HOW COME YOU AIN'T HAD NO STORIES ABOUT THIS CHAMPEENSHIP FIGHT THAT'S COMIN' UP? THE CHAMPEEN'S BEEN IN TOWN FER TWO WEEKS NOW!
"CHAMPION?" FIGHT? WHAT FIGHT?
HEY! WHERE'S MY REPORTERS?
WHAT AM I PAYIN' THEM FOR?
DAILY EXPLOSION
!
PRESS ROOM — THE DAILY EXPLOSION
AND DON'T YOU SOMNAMBULISTS COME BACK 'TILL YOU GET A STORY THAT'LL TURN THE TOWN OVER!
3-17
WALT DISNEY

HEY, HYRUM, KNOW ANYTHING ABOUT "RUFFHOUSE RAT'S" CAULIFLOWER CAMP OUT IN THIS NEIGHBORHOOD?
RECKON YOU MEAN A PRIZEFIGHTIN' CAMP, EH? SURE — ONE MILE NORTH, TWO EAST, 'BOUT 40 RODS SOUTH TO TH' CRICK THEN FOLLER YER NOSE PAST HANK HOGG'S PLACE AN' THERE SHE BE!
BANG! BANG! BANG!
?
?
CRASH!
!
WALT DISNEY 3-18
DON'T BE ALARMED — WE'RE FROM THE "DAILY EXPLOSION" — WE'VE COME TO TAKE THE CHAMPION'S PICTURE — WHERE IS HE?

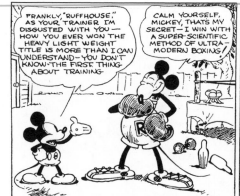

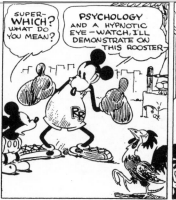

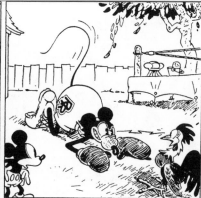

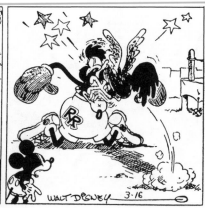

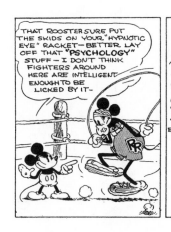

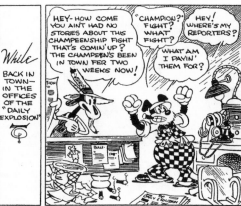

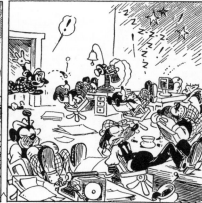

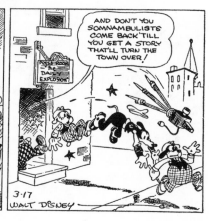

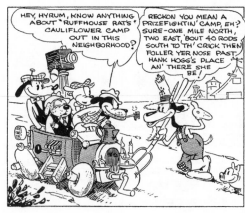

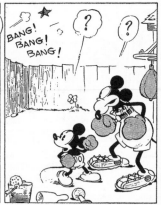

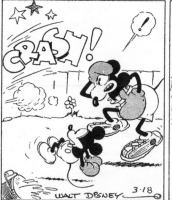

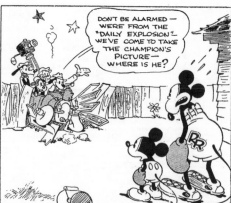

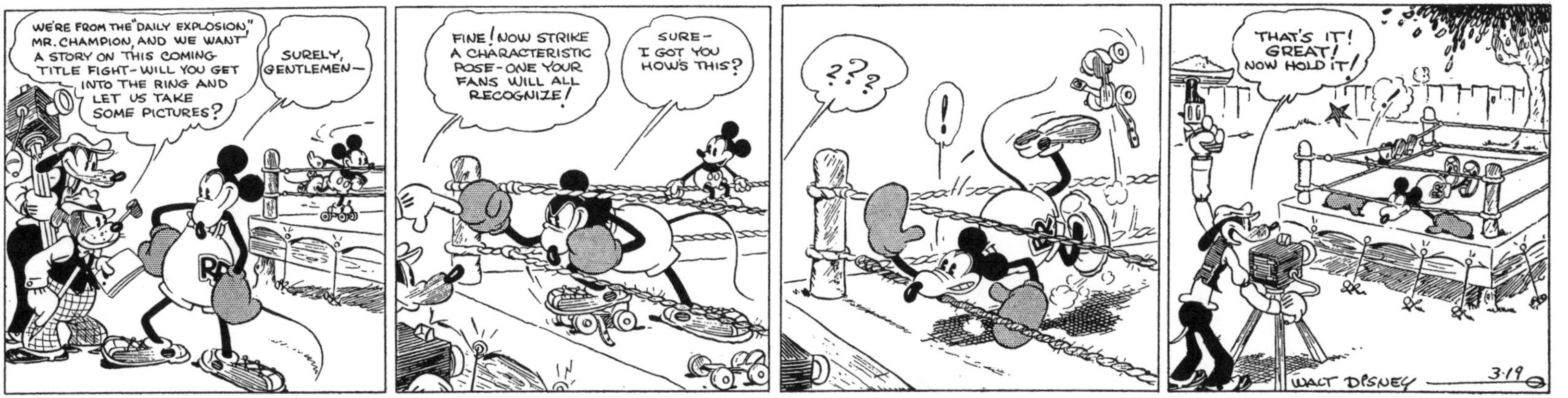
WE'RE FROM THE "DAILY EXPLOSION," MR. CHAMPION, AND WE WANT A STORY ON THIS COMING TITLE FIGHT – WILL YOU GET INTO THE RING AND LET US TAKE SOME PICTURES?
SURELY, GENTLEMEN –
FINE! NOW STRIKE A CHARACTERISTIC POSE – ONE YOUR FANS WILL ALL RECOGNIZE!
SURE – I GOT YOU HOW'S THIS?
???
!
THAT'S IT! GREAT! NOW HOLD IT!
WALT DISNEY 3·19

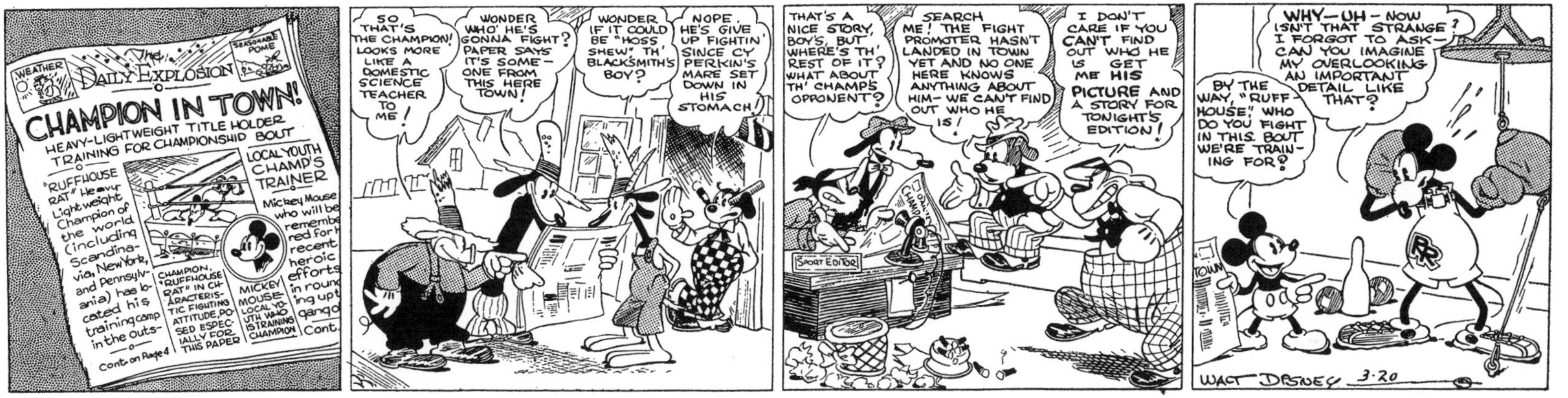
WEATHER
The DAILY EXPLOSION
SEASONABLE POME
CHAMPION IN TOWN!
HEAVY-LIGHTWEIGHT TITLE HOLDER TRAINING FOR CHAMPIONSHID BOUT
"RUFFHOUSE RAT" Heavy-Lightweight Champion of the world (including Scandinavia, New York, and Pennsylvania) has located his training camp in the outs-
Cont. on Page 4
CHAMPION, "RUFFHOUSE RAT" IN CHARACTERISTIC FIGHTING ATTITUDE, POSED ESPECIALLY FOR THIS PAPER
LOCAL YOUTH CHAMP'S TRAINER
Mickey Mouse who will be remembered for his recent heroic efforts in rounding up the gang o
Cont.
MICKEY MOUSE – LOCAL YOUTH WHO IS TRAINING CHAMPION
SO THAT'S THE CHAMPION! LOOKS MORE LIKE A DOMESTIC SCIENCE TEACHER TO ME!
WONDER WHO' HE'S GONNA FIGHT? PAPER SAYS IT'S SOME-ONE FROM THIS HERE TOWN!
WONDER IF IT COULD BE "HOSS SHEW," TH' BLACKSMITH'S BOY?
NOPE, HE'S GIVE UP FIGHTIN' SINCE CY PERKIN'S MARE SET DOWN IN HIS STOMACH!
THAT'S A NICE STORY, BOY'S, BUT WHERE'S TH' REST OF IT? WHAT ABOUT TH' CHAMP'S OPPONENT?
SEARCH ME! THE FIGHT PROMOTER HASN'T LANDED IN TOWN YET AND NO ONE HERE KNOWS ANYTHING ABOUT HIM – WE CAN'T FIND OUT WHO HE IS!
I DON'T CARE IF YOU CAN'T FIND OUT WHO HE IS GET ME HIS PICTURE AND A STORY FOR TONIGHT'S EDITION!
SPORT EDITOR
BY THE WAY, "RUFF-HOUSE," WHO DO YOU FIGHT IN THIS BOUT WE'RE TRAIN-ING FOR?
WHY – UH – NOW ISN'T THAT STRANGE? I FORGOT TO ASK – CAN YOU IMAGINE MY OVERLOOKING AN IMPORTANT DETAIL LIKE THAT?
TOWN
WALT DISNEY 3·20

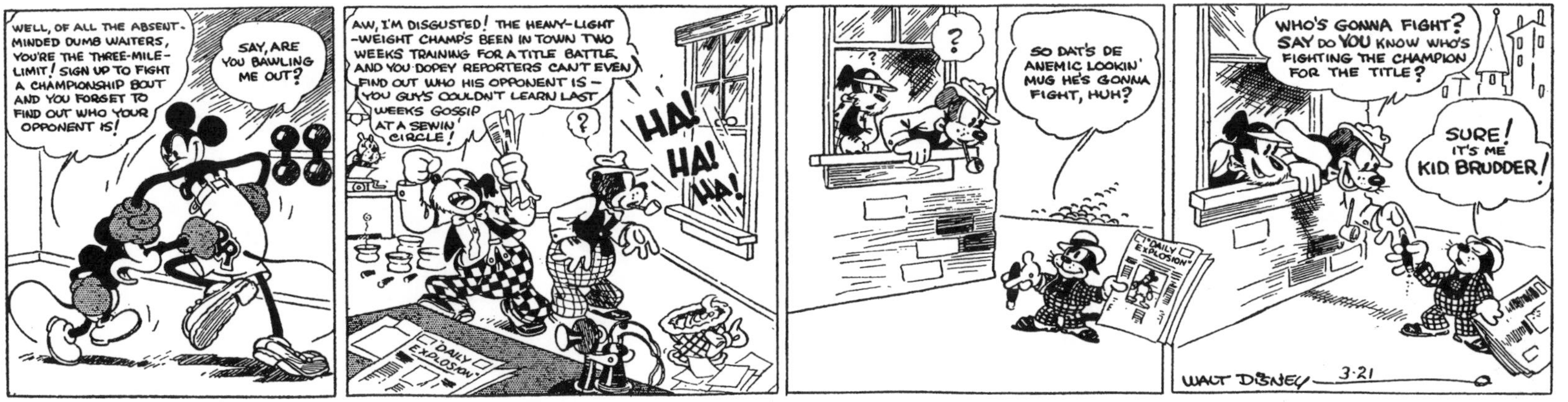
WELL, OF ALL THE ABSENT-MINDED DUMB WAITERS, YOU'RE THE THREE-MILE-LIMIT! SIGN UP TO FIGHT A CHAMPIONSHIP BOUT AND YOU FORGET TO FIND OUT WHO YOUR OPPONENT IS!
SAY, ARE YOU BAWLING ME OUT?
AW, I'M DISGUSTED! THE HEAVY-LIGHT-WEIGHT CHAMP'S BEEN IN TOWN TWO WEEKS TRAINING FOR A TITLE BATTLE, AND YOU DOPEY REPORTERS CAN'T EVEN FIND OUT WHO HIS OPPONENT IS – YOU GUYS COULDN'T LEARN LAST WEEKS GOSSIP AT A SEWIN' CIRCLE!
?
HA! HA! HA!
DAILY EXPLOSION
?
SO DAT'S DE ANEMIC LOOKIN' MUG HE'S GONNA FIGHT, HUH?
"DAILY EXPLOSION"
WHO'S GONNA FIGHT? SAY DO YOU KNOW WHO'S FIGHTING THE CHAMPION FOR THE TITLE?
SURE! IT'S ME KID BRUDDER!
WALT DISNEY 3·21

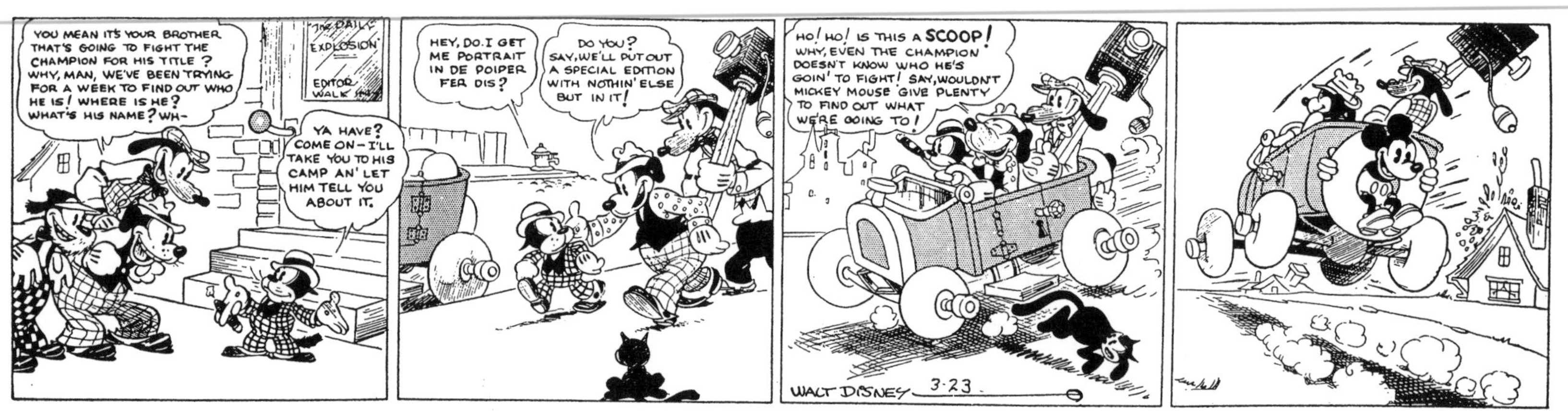

YOU MEAN IT'S YOUR BROTHER THAT'S GOING TO FIGHT THE CHAMPION FOR HIS TITLE? WHY, MAN, WE'VE BEEN TRYING FOR A WEEK TO FIND OUT WHO HE IS! WHERE IS HE? WHAT'S HIS NAME? WH-
YA HAVE? COME ON—I'LL TAKE YOU TO HIS CAMP AN' LET HIM TELL YOU ABOUT IT.
HEY, DO. I GET ME PORTRAIT IN DE POIPER FER DIS?
DO YOU? SAY, WE'LL PUT OUT A SPECIAL EDITION WITH NOTHIN' ELSE BUT IN IT!
HO! HO! IS THIS A SCOOP! WHY, EVEN THE CHAMPION DOESN'T KNOW WHO HE'S GOIN' TO FIGHT! SAY, WOULDN'T MICKEY MOUSE GIVE PLENTY TO FIND OUT WHAT WE'RE GOING TO!
WALT DISNEY 3·23

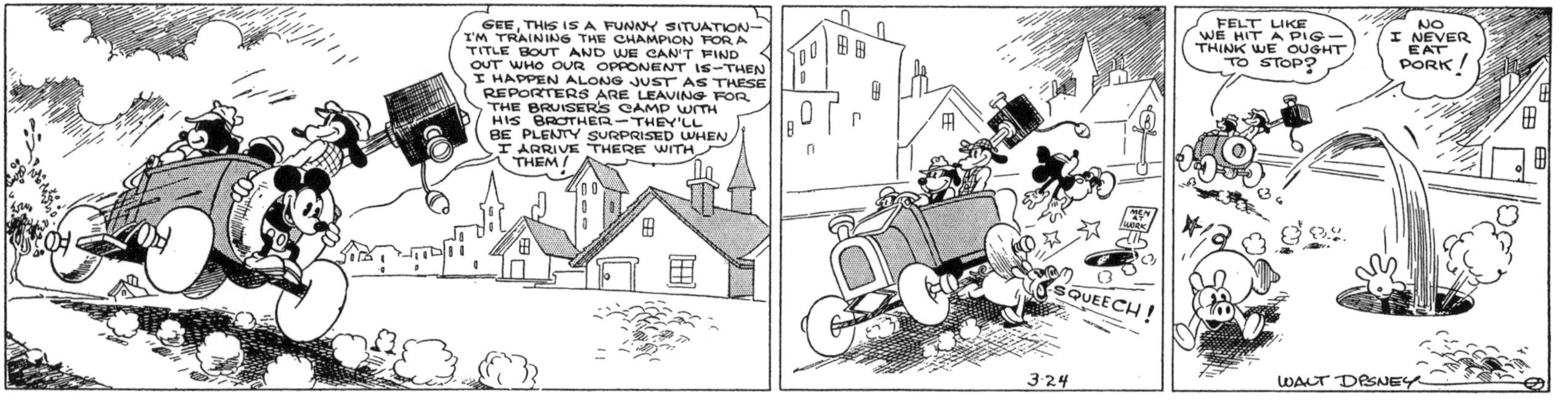

GEE, THIS IS A FUNNY SITUATION—I'M TRAINING THE CHAMPION FOR A TITLE BOUT AND WE CAN'T FIND OUT WHO OUR OPPONENT IS—THEN I HAPPEN ALONG JUST AS THESE REPORTERS ARE LEAVING FOR THE BRUISER'S CAMP WITH HIS BROTHER—THEY'LL BE PLENTY SURPRISED WHEN I ARRIVE THERE WITH THEM!
MEN AT WORK
SQUEECH!
3·24
FELT LIKE WE HIT A PIG—THINK WE OUGHT TO STOP?
NO I NEVER EAT PORK!
WALT DISNEY

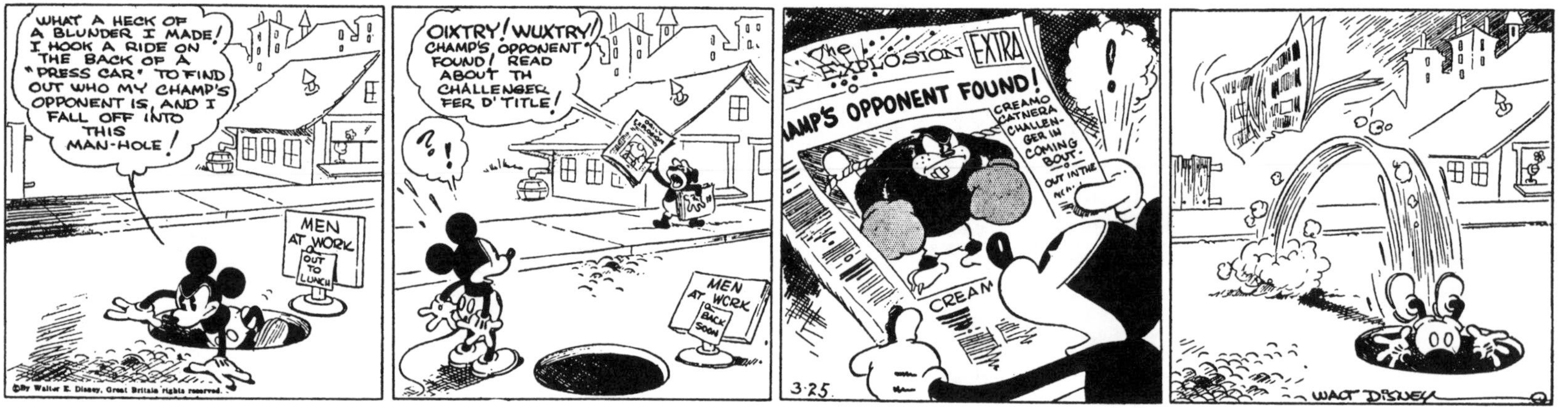

WHAT A HECK OF A BLUNDER I MADE! I HOOK A RIDE ON THE BACK OF A "PRESS CAR" TO FIND OUT WHO MY CHAMP'S OPPONENT IS, AND I FALL OFF INTO THIS MAN-HOLE!
MEN AT WORK
OUT TO LUNCH
©By Walter E. Disney. Great Britain rights reserved.
OIXTRY! WUXTRY! CHAMP'S OPPONENT FOUND! READ ABOUT TH CHALLENGER FER D' TITLE!
?!
MEN AT WORK
BACK SOON
The EXPLOSION EXTRA
CHAMP'S OPPONENT FOUND!
CREAMO CATNERA CHALLENGER IN COMING BOUT.
OUT IN THE
CREAM
!
3·25
WALT DISNEY

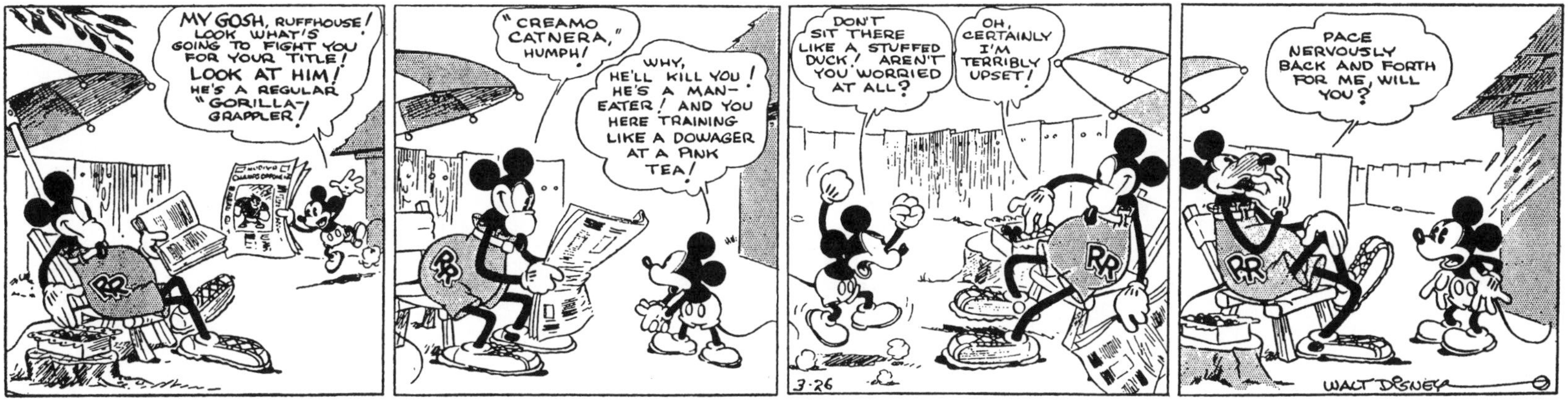
MY GOSH, RUFFHOUSE! LOOK WHAT'S GOING TO FIGHT YOU FOR YOUR TITLE! LOOK AT HIM! HE'S A REGULAR "GORILLA-GRAPPLER"!
"CREAMO CATNERA," HUMPH!
WHY, HE'LL KILL YOU! HE'S A MAN-EATER! AND YOU HERE TRAINING LIKE A DOWAGER AT A PINK TEA!
DON'T SIT THERE LIKE A STUFFED DUCK! AREN'T YOU WORRIED AT ALL?
OH, CERTAINLY I'M TERRIBLY UPSET!
3-26
PACE NERVOUSLY BACK AND FORTH FOR ME, WILL YOU?
WALT DISNEY

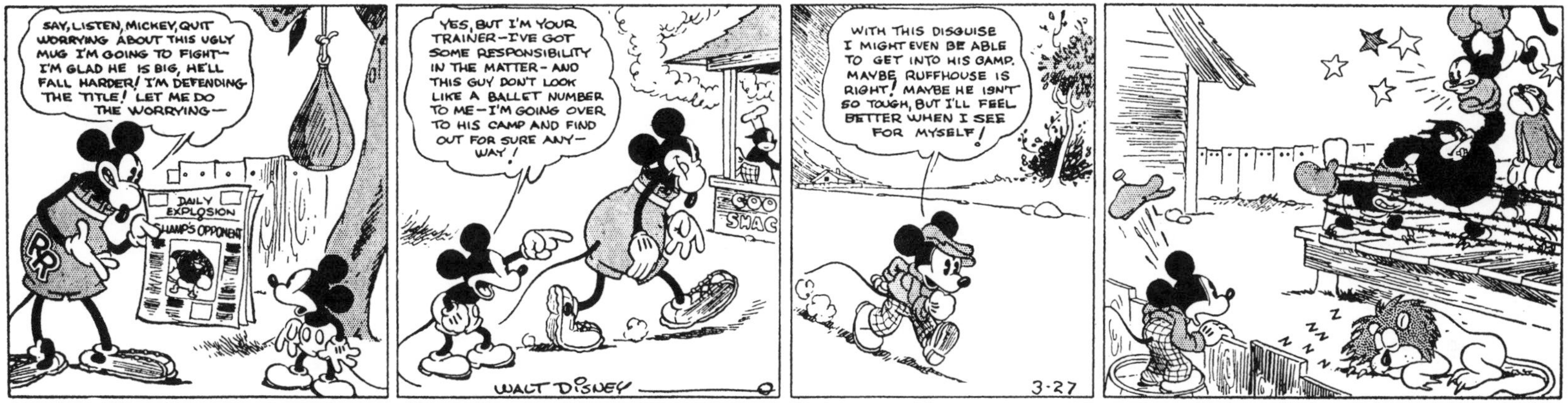
SAY, LISTEN, MICKEY, QUIT WORRYING ABOUT THIS UGLY MUG I'M GOING TO FIGHT— I'M GLAD HE IS BIG, HE'LL FALL HARDER! I'M DEFENDING THE TITLE! LET ME DO THE WORRYING—
DAILY EXPLOSION
CHAMP'S OPPONENT
YES, BUT I'M YOUR TRAINER—I'VE GOT SOME RESPONSIBILITY IN THE MATTER—AND THIS GUY DON'T LOOK LIKE A BALLET NUMBER TO ME—I'M GOING OVER TO HIS CAMP AND FIND OUT FOR SURE ANY-WAY!
WALT DISNEY
WITH THIS DISGUISE I MIGHT EVEN BE ABLE TO GET INTO HIS CAMP. MAYBE RUFFHOUSE IS RIGHT! MAYBE HE ISN'T SO TOUGH, BUT I'LL FEEL BETTER WHEN I SEE FOR MYSELF!
3-27
Z Z Z Z Z

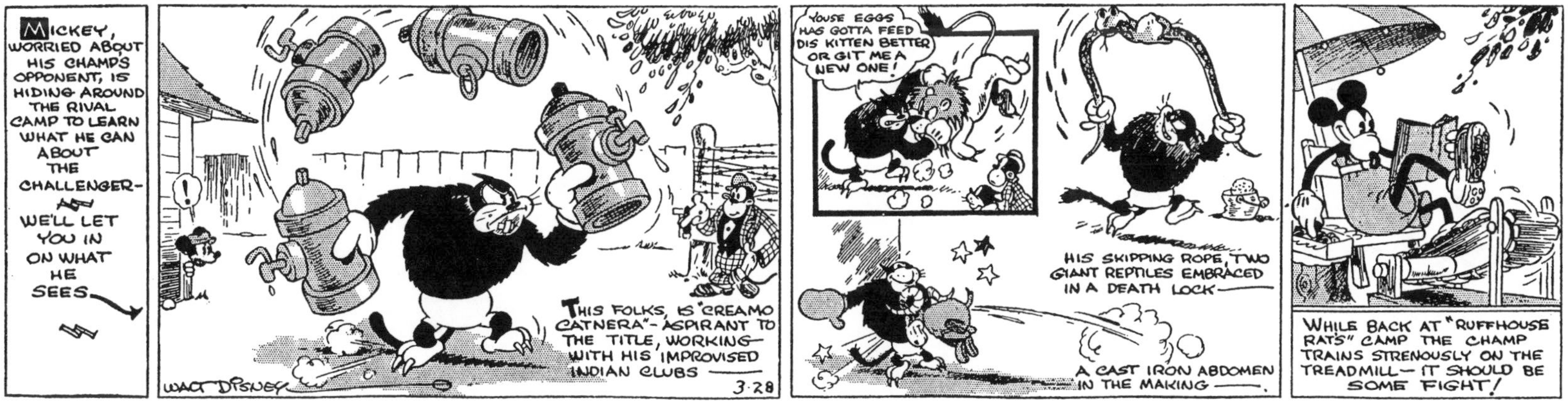
MICKEY, WORRIED ABOUT HIS CHAMP'S OPPONENT, IS HIDING AROUND THE RIVAL CAMP TO LEARN WHAT HE CAN ABOUT THE CHALLENGER— WE'LL LET YOU IN ON WHAT HE SEES
!
THIS FOLKS, IS "CREAMO CATNERA"—ASPIRANT TO THE TITLE, WORKING WITH HIS IMPROVISED INDIAN CLUBS
WALT DISNEY
3-28
YOUSE EGGS HAS GOTTA FEED DIS KITTEN BETTER OR GIT ME A NEW ONE!
HIS SKIPPING ROPE, TWO GIANT REPTILES EMBRACED IN A DEATH LOCK—
A CAST IRON ABDOMEN IN THE MAKING—
WHILE BACK AT "RUFFHOUSE RATS" CAMP THE CHAMP TRAINS STRENOUSLY ON THE TREADMILL—IT SHOULD BE SOME FIGHT!

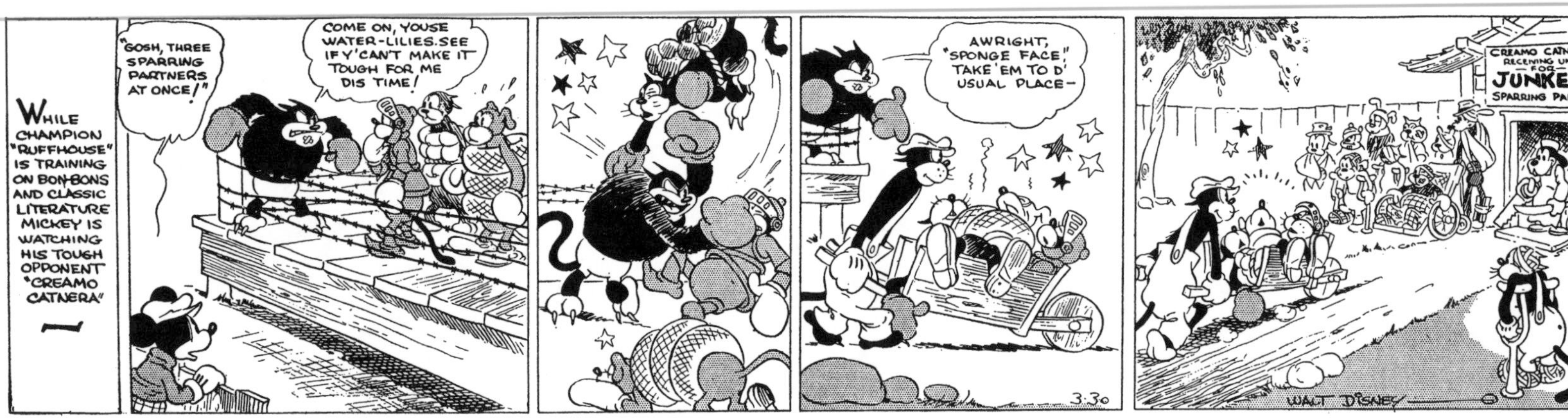
WHILE CHAMPION "RUFFHOUSE" IS TRAINING ON BON-BONS AND CLASSIC LITERATURE MICKEY IS WATCHING HIS TOUGH OPPONENT "CREAMO CATNERA"
"GOSH, THREE SPARRING PARTNERS AT ONCE!"
COME ON, YOUSE WATER-LILIES. SEE IF Y'CAN'T MAKE IT TOUGH FOR ME DIS TIME!
AWRIGHT, "SPONGE FACE" TAKE 'EM TO D' USUAL PLACE—
3·30
CREAMO CATNERA
RECEIVING UNIT
FOR
JUNKED
SPARRING PARTN
WALT DISNEY

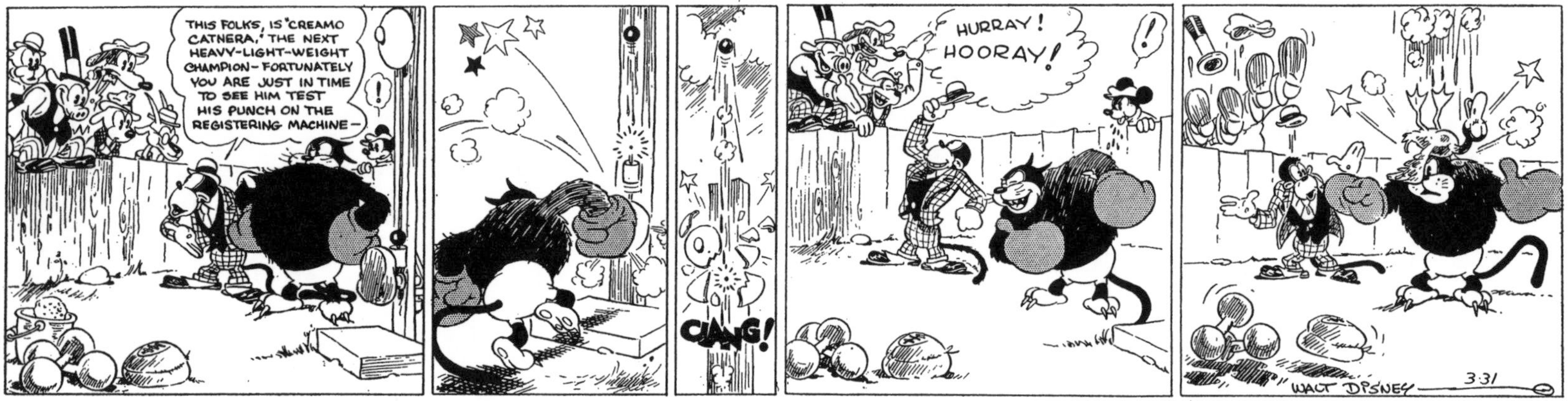
THIS FOLKS, IS "CREAMO CATNERA," THE NEXT HEAVY-LIGHT-WEIGHT CHAMPION—FORTUNATELY YOU ARE JUST IN TIME TO SEE HIM TEST HIS PUNCH ON THE REGISTERING MACHINE—
!
CLANG!
HURRAY! HOORAY!
!
WALT DISNEY
3·31

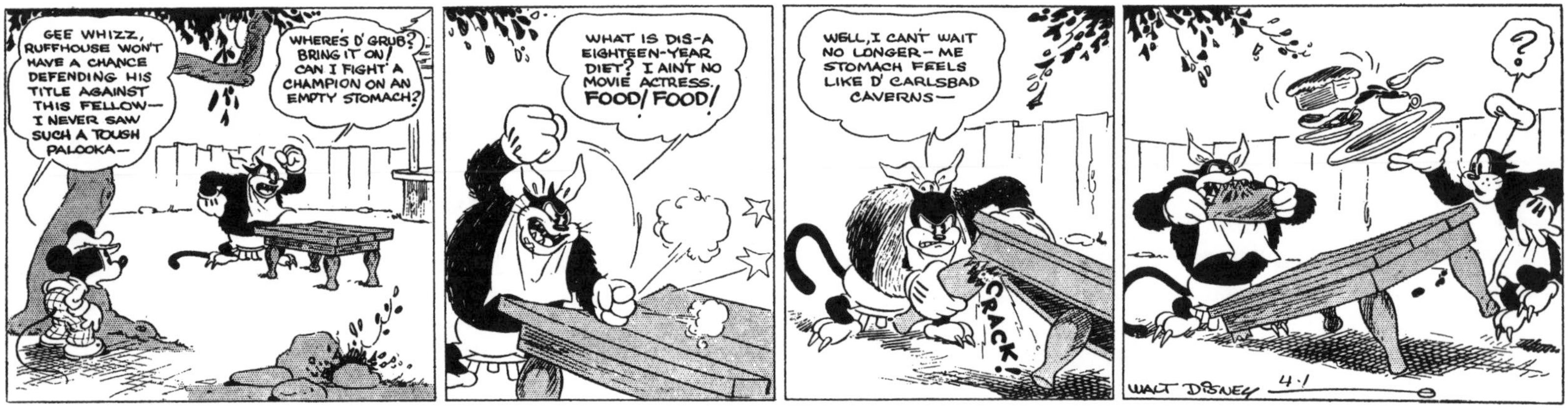
GEE WHIZZ, RUFFHOUSE WON'T HAVE A CHANCE DEFENDING HIS TITLE AGAINST THIS FELLOW— I NEVER SAW SUCH A TOUGH PALOOKA—
WHERE'S D' GRUB? BRING IT ON! CAN I FIGHT A CHAMPION ON AN EMPTY STOMACH?
WHAT IS DIS-A EIGHTEEN-YEAR DIET? I AIN'T NO MOVIE ACTRESS. FOOD! FOOD!
WELL, I CAN'T WAIT NO LONGER—ME STOMACH FEELS LIKE D' CARLSBAD CAVERNS—
CRACK!
?
WALT DISNEY
4·1

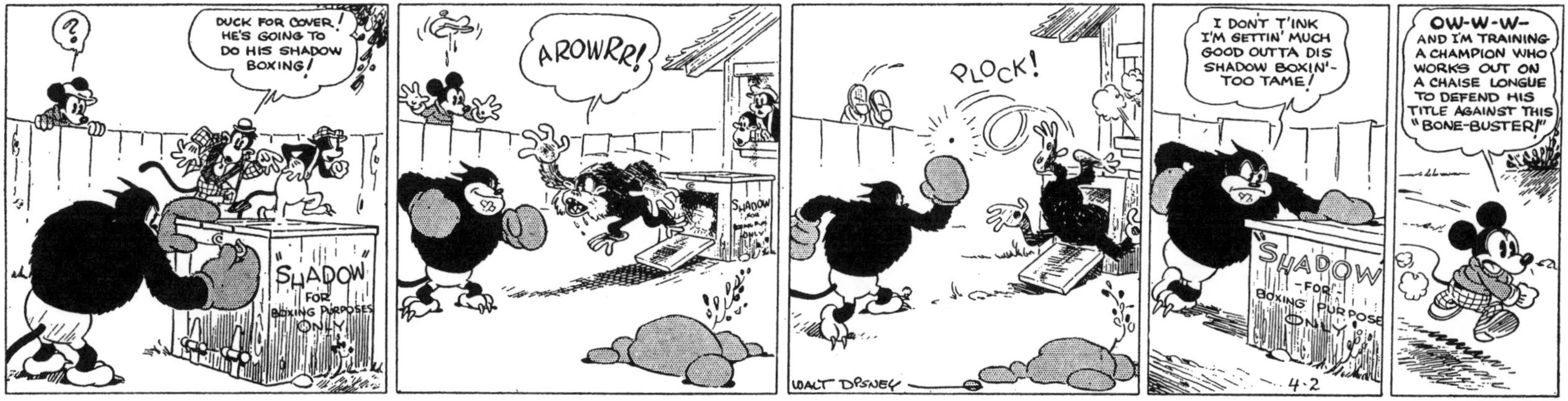
?
DUCK FOR COVER! HE'S GOING TO DO HIS SHADOW BOXING!
"SHADOW" FOR BOXING PURPOSES ONLY
AROWRR!
PLOCK!
WALT DISNEY
4·2
I DON'T T'INK I'M GETTIN' MUCH GOOD OUTTA DIS SHADOW BOXIN'- TOO TAME!
"SHADOW" -FOR- BOXING PURPOSES ONLY
OW-W-W- AND I'M TRAINING A CHAMPION WHO WORKS OUT ON A CHAISE LONGUE TO DEFEND HIS TITLE AGAINST THIS "BONE-BUSTER!"

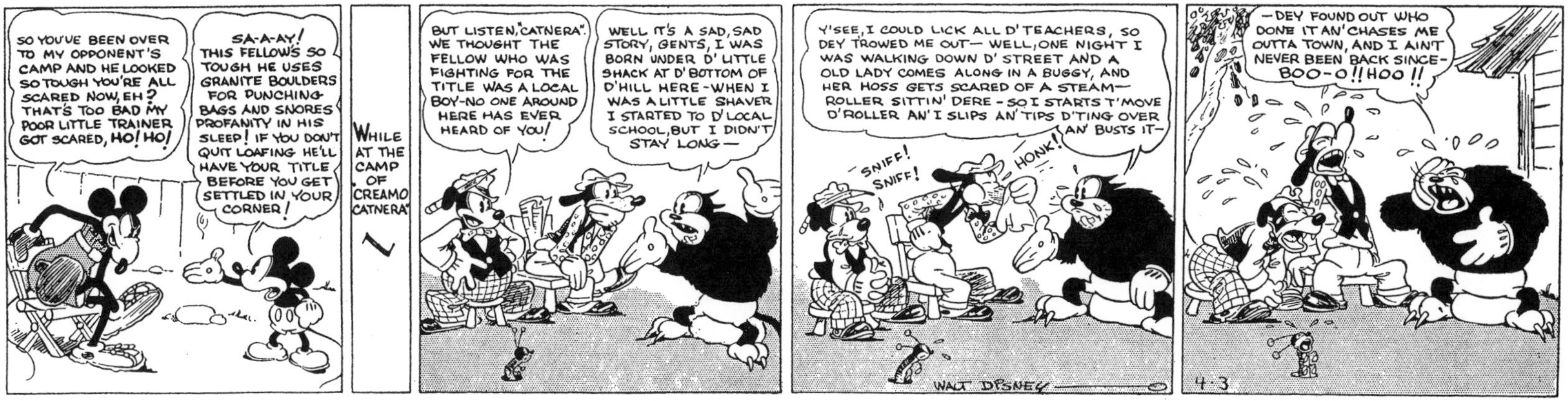
SO YOU'VE BEEN OVER TO MY OPPONENT'S CAMP AND HE LOOKED SO TOUGH YOU'RE ALL SCARED NOW, EH? THAT'S TOO BAD MY POOR LITTLE TRAINER GOT SCARED, HO! HO!
SA-A-AY! THIS FELLOW'S SO TOUGH HE USES GRANITE BOULDERS FOR PUNCHING BAGS AND SNORES PROFANITY IN HIS SLEEP! IF YOU DON'T QUIT LOAFING HE'LL HAVE YOUR TITLE BEFORE YOU GET SETTLED IN YOUR CORNER!
WHILE AT THE CAMP OF "CREAMO CATNERA"
BUT LISTEN, "CATNERA". WE THOUGHT THE FELLOW WHO WAS FIGHTING FOR THE TITLE WAS A LOCAL BOY-NO ONE AROUND HERE HAS EVER HEARD OF YOU!
WELL IT'S A SAD, SAD STORY, GENTS, I WAS BORN UNDER D' LITTLE SHACK AT D' BOTTOM OF D' HILL HERE-WHEN I WAS A LITTLE SHAVER I STARTED TO D' LOCAL SCHOOL, BUT I DIDN'T STAY LONG—
Y'SEE, I COULD LICK ALL D' TEACHERS, SO DEY TROWED ME OUT— WELL, ONE NIGHT I WAS WALKING DOWN D' STREET AND A OLD LADY COMES ALONG IN A BUGGY, AND HER HOSS GETS SCARED OF A STEAM-ROLLER SITTIN' DERE - SO I STARTS T' MOVE D' ROLLER AN' I SLIPS AN' TIPS D' TING OVER AN' BUSTS IT—
SNIFF! SNIFF!
HONK!
WALT DISNEY
—DEY FOUND OUT WHO DONE IT AN' CHASES ME OUTTA TOWN, AND I AIN'T NEVER BEEN BACK SINCE- BOO-O!! HOO!!
4·3

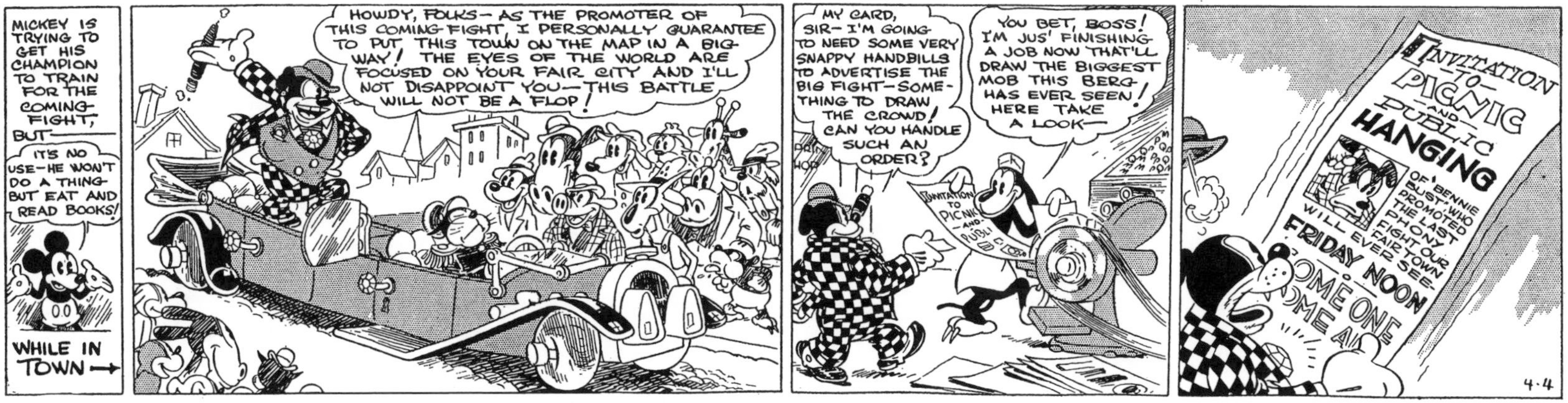
MICKEY IS TRYING TO GET HIS CHAMPION TO TRAIN FOR THE COMING FIGHT, BUT—
IT'S NO USE-HE WON'T DO A THING BUT EAT AND READ BOOKS!
WHILE IN TOWN →
HOWDY, FOLKS- AS THE PROMOTER OF THIS COMING FIGHT, I PERSONALLY GUARANTEE TO PUT THIS TOWN ON THE MAP IN A BIG WAY! THE EYES OF THE WORLD ARE FOCUSED ON YOUR FAIR CITY AND I'LL NOT DISAPPOINT YOU—THIS BATTLE WILL NOT BE A FLOP!
MY CARD, SIR- I'M GOING TO NEED SOME VERY SNAPPY HANDBILLS TO ADVERTISE THE BIG FIGHT-SOMETHING TO DRAW THE CROWD! CAN YOU HANDLE SUCH AN ORDER?
YOU BET, BOSS! I'M JUS' FINISHING A JOB NOW THAT'LL DRAW THE BIGGEST MOB THIS BERG HAS EVER SEEN! HERE TAKE A LOOK—
INVITATION -TO- PICNIC -AND- PUBLIC HANGING
OF BENNIE BUST WHO PROMOTED THE LAST PHONY FIGHT OUR FAIR TOWN WILL EVER SEE.
FRIDAY NOON
4·4

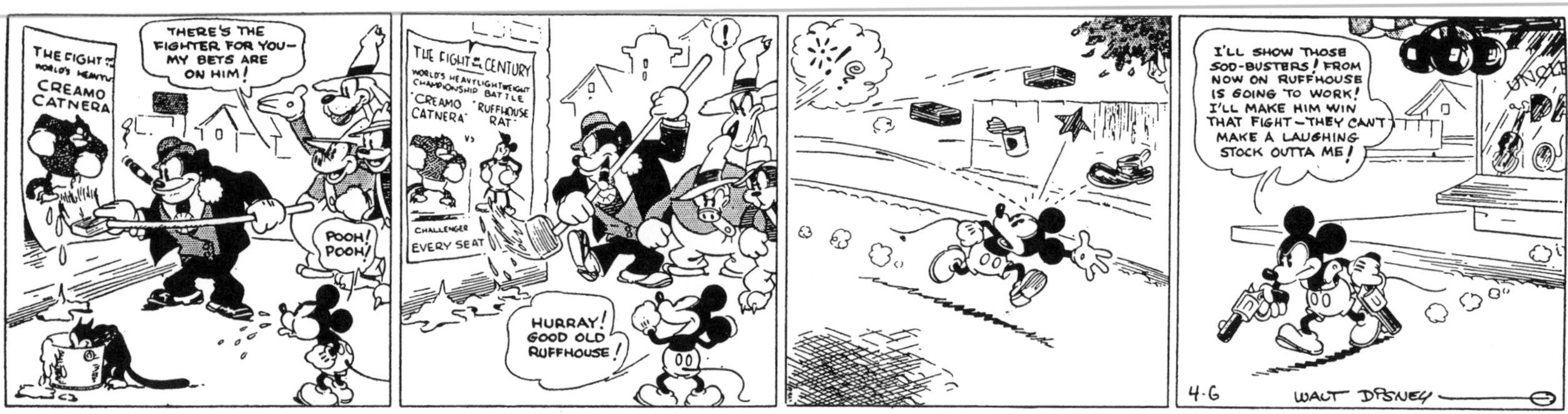
CREAMO CATNERA
THERE'S THE FIGHTER FOR YOU— MY BETS ARE ON HIM!
POOH! POOH!
THE FIGHT OF THE CENTURY
WORLD'S HEAVYLIGHTWEIGHT CHAMPIONSHIP BATTLE
"CREAMO CATNERA" VS "RUFFHOUSE RAT"
CHALLENGER
EVERY SEAT
HURRAY! GOOD OLD RUFFHOUSE!
I'LL SHOW THOSE SOD-BUSTERS! FROM NOW ON RUFFHOUSE IS GOING TO WORK! I'LL MAKE HIM WIN THAT FIGHT—THEY CAN'T MAKE A LAUGHING STOCK OUTTA ME!
4·6
WALT DISNEY

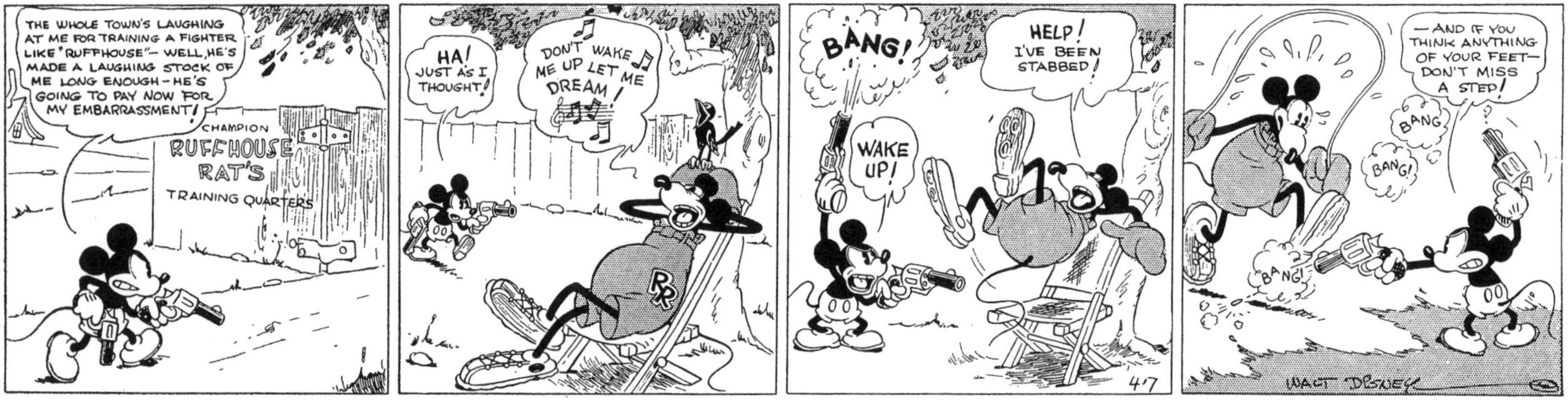
THE WHOLE TOWN'S LAUGHING AT ME FOR TRAINING A FIGHTER LIKE "RUFFHOUSE"— WELL, HE'S MADE A LAUGHING STOCK OF ME LONG ENOUGH—HE'S GOING TO PAY NOW FOR MY EMBARRASSMENT!
CHAMPION RUFFHOUSE RAT'S TRAINING QUARTERS
HA! JUST AS I THOUGHT!
DON'T WAKE ME UP LET ME DREAM!
RR
BANG!
WAKE UP!
HELP! I'VE BEEN STABBED!
4·7
—AND IF YOU THINK ANYTHING OF YOUR FEET— DON'T MISS A STEP!
BANG
BANG!
BANG!
WALT DISNEY

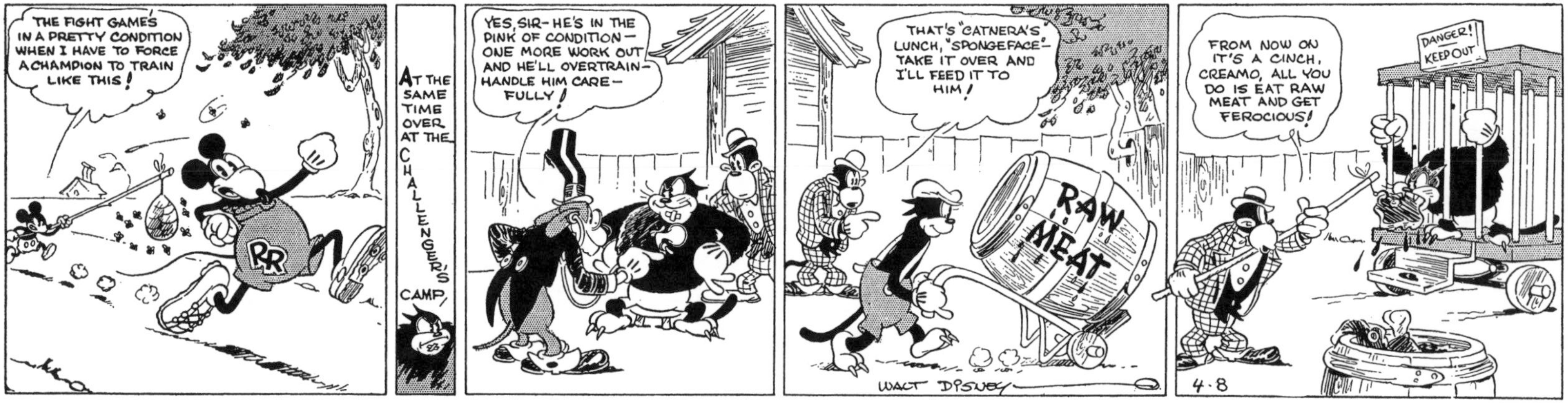
THE FIGHT GAME'S IN A PRETTY CONDITION WHEN I HAVE TO FORCE A CHAMPION TO TRAIN LIKE THIS!
RR
AT THE SAME TIME OVER AT THE CHALLENGER'S CAMP,
YES, SIR—HE'S IN THE PINK OF CONDITION— ONE MORE WORK OUT AND HE'LL OVERTRAIN— HANDLE HIM CARE-FULLY!
THAT'S "CATNERA'S" LUNCH, "SPONGEFACE"—TAKE IT OVER AND I'LL FEED IT TO HIM!
RAW MEAT
WALT DISNEY
FROM NOW ON IT'S A CINCH, CREAMO, ALL YOU DO IS EAT RAW MEAT AND GET FEROCIOUS!
DANGER! KEEP OUT
4·8

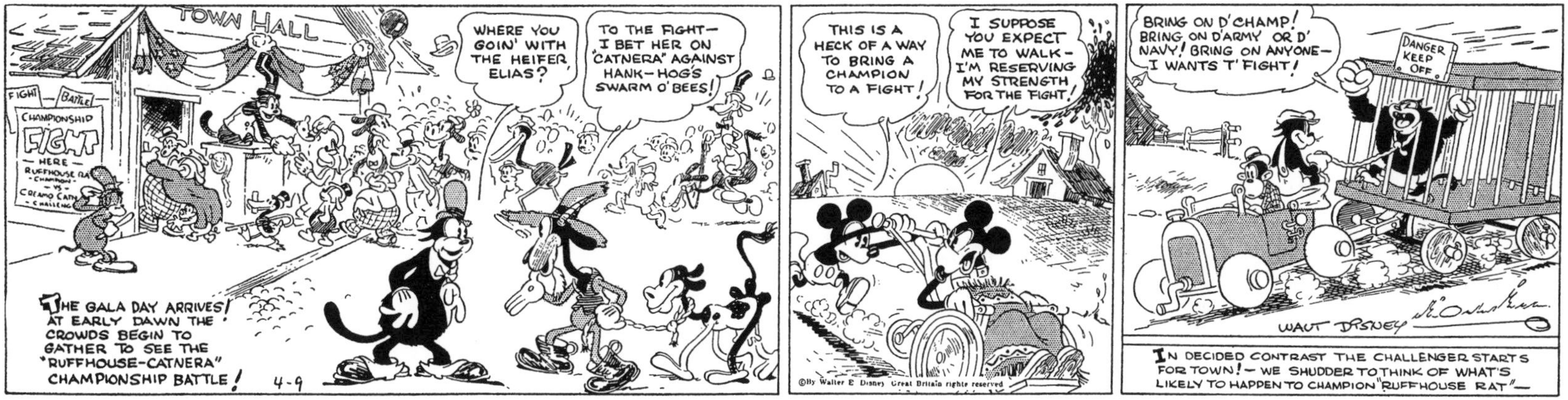
TOWN HALL
FIGHT
BATTLE
CHAMPIONSHIP FIGHT
HERE
THE GALA DAY ARRIVES! AT EARLY DAWN THE CROWDS BEGIN TO GATHER TO SEE THE "RUFFHOUSE-CATNERA" CHAMPIONSHIP BATTLE!
WHERE YOU GOIN' WITH THE HEIFER, ELIAS?
TO THE FIGHT— I BET HER ON "CATNERA" AGAINST HANK-HOG'S SWARM O' BEES!
4-9
THIS IS A HECK OF A WAY TO BRING A CHAMPION TO A FIGHT!
I SUPPOSE YOU EXPECT ME TO WALK— I'M RESERVING MY STRENGTH FOR THE FIGHT!
©By Walter E Disney Great Britain rights reserved
BRING ON D'CHAMP! BRING ON D'ARMY OR D' NAVY! BRING ON ANYONE— I WANTS T' FIGHT!
DANGER KEEP OFF
WALT DISNEY
IN DECIDED CONTRAST THE CHALLENGER STARTS FOR TOWN! — WE SHUDDER TO THINK OF WHAT'S LIKELY TO HAPPEN TO CHAMPION "RUFFHOUSE RAT"—

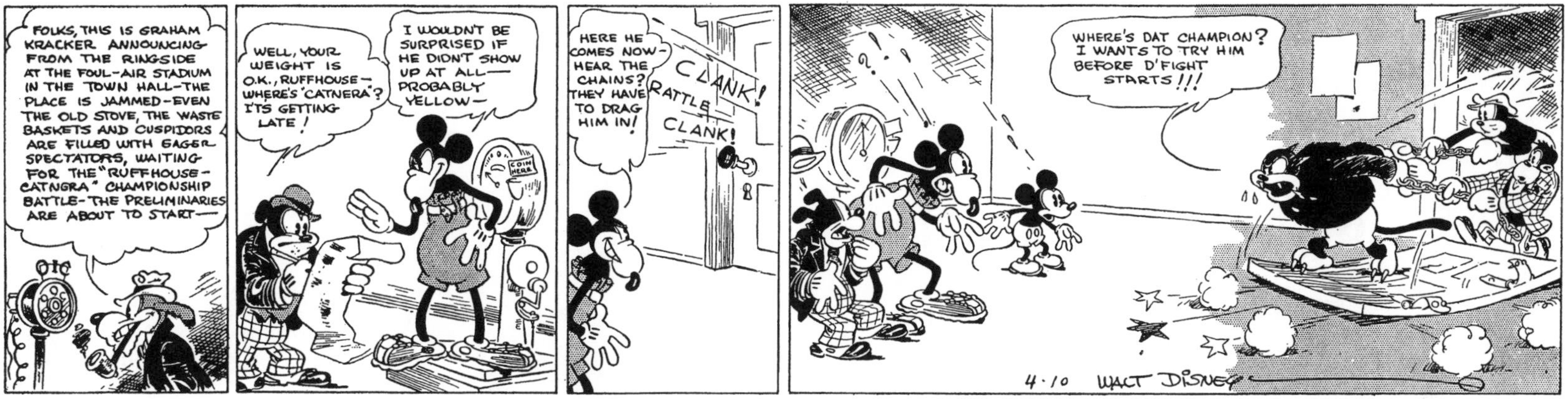
FOLKS, THIS IS GRAHAM KRACKER ANNOUNCING FROM THE RINGSIDE AT THE FOUL-AIR STADIUM IN THE TOWN HALL—THE PLACE IS JAMMED—EVEN THE OLD STOVE, THE WASTE BASKETS AND CUSPIDORS ARE FILLED WITH EAGER SPECTATORS, WAITING FOR THE "RUFFHOUSE-CATNGRA" CHAMPIONSHIP BATTLE—THE PRELIMINARIES ARE ABOUT TO START—
WELL, YOUR WEIGHT IS O.K., RUFFHOUSE— WHERE'S 'CATNERA'? IT'S GETTING LATE!
I WOULDN'T BE SURPRISED IF HE DIDN'T SHOW UP AT ALL— PROBABLY YELLOW—
COIN HERE
HERE HE COMES NOW— HEAR THE CHAINS? THEY HAVE TO DRAG HIM IN!
CLANK!
RATTLE
CLANK!
WHERE'S DAT CHAMPION? I WANTS TO TRY HIM BEFORE D'FIGHT STARTS!!!
4·10 WALT DISNEY

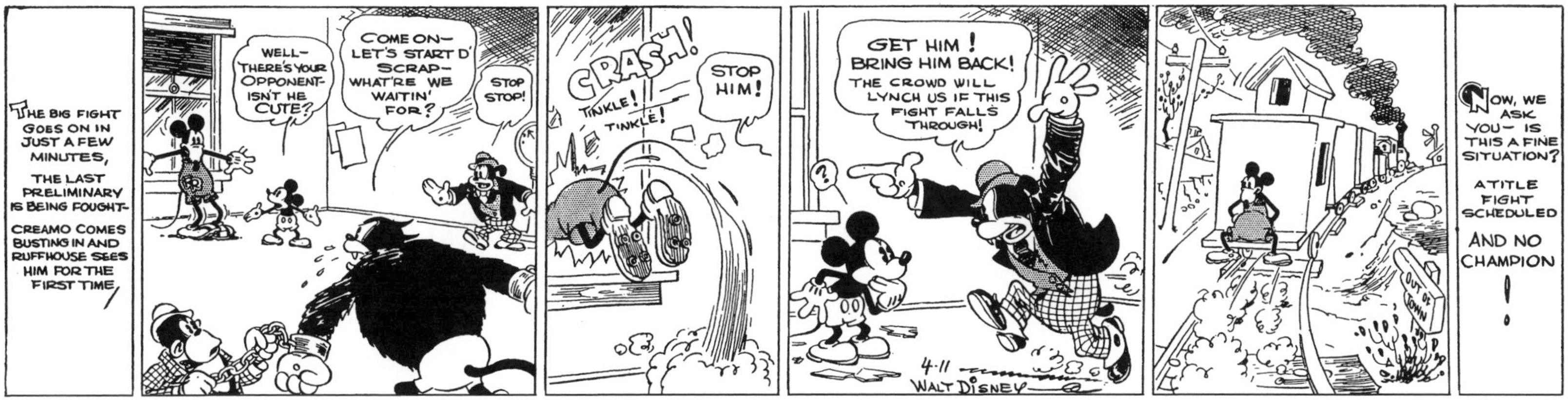
THE BIG FIGHT GOES ON IN JUST A FEW MINUTES, THE LAST PRELIMINARY IS BEING FOUGHT— CREAMO COMES BUSTING IN AND RUFFHOUSE SEES HIM FOR THE FIRST TIME!
WELL— THERE'S YOUR OPPONENT— ISN'T HE CUTE?
COME ON— LET'S START D' SCRAP— WHAT'RE WE WAITIN' FOR?
STOP STOP!
CRASH!
TINKLE! TINKLE!
STOP HIM!
GET HIM! BRING HIM BACK! THE CROWD WILL LYNCH US IF THIS FIGHT FALLS THROUGH!
4-11 WALT DISNEY
OUT OF TOWN
NOW, WE ASK YOU— IS THIS A FINE SITUATION? A TITLE FIGHT SCHEDULED AND NO CHAMPION!

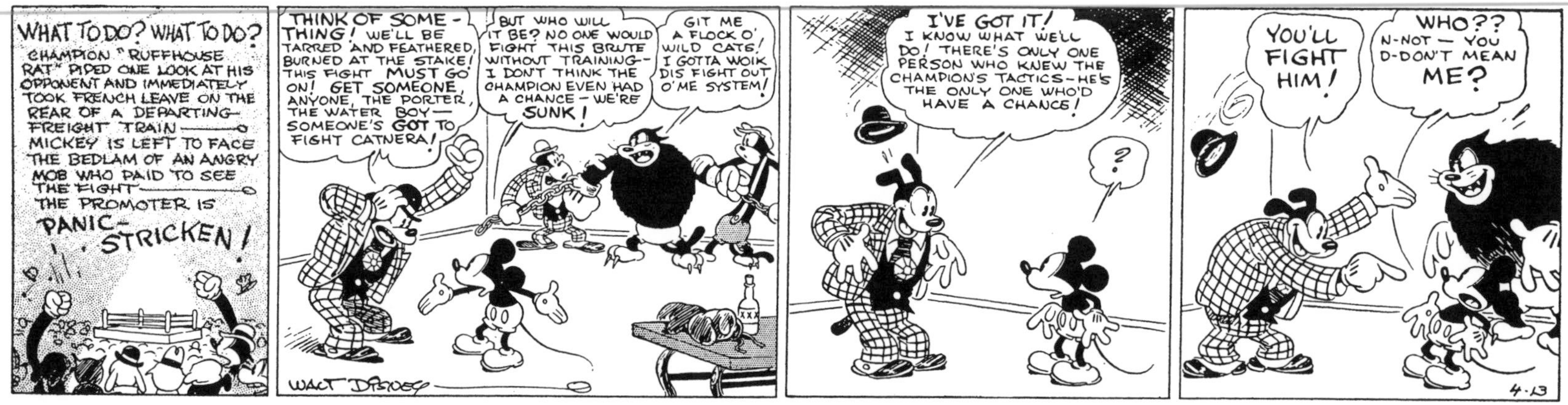
WHAT TO DO? WHAT TO DO?
CHAMPION "RUFFHOUSE RAT" PIPED ONE LOOK AT HIS OPPONENT AND IMMEDIATELY TOOK FRENCH LEAVE ON THE REAR OF A DEPARTING FREIGHT TRAIN — MICKEY IS LEFT TO FACE THE BEDLAM OF AN ANGRY MOB WHO PAID TO SEE THE FIGHT — THE PROMOTER IS PANIC-STRICKEN!
THINK OF SOMETHING! WE'LL BE TARRED AND FEATHERED, BURNED AT THE STAKE! THIS FIGHT MUST GO ON! GET SOMEONE, ANYONE, THE PORTER, THE WATER BOY — SOMEONE'S GOT TO FIGHT CATNERA!
BUT WHO WILL IT BE? NO ONE WOULD FIGHT THIS BRUTE WITHOUT TRAINING — I DON'T THINK THE CHAMPION EVEN HAD A CHANCE — WE'RE SUNK!
GIT ME A FLOCK O' WILD CATS! I GOTTA WOIK DIS FIGHT OUT O'ME SYSTEM!
XXX
WALT DISNEY
I'VE GOT IT! I KNOW WHAT WE'LL DO! THERE'S ONLY ONE PERSON WHO KNEW THE CHAMPION'S TACTICS — HE'S THE ONLY ONE WHO'D HAVE A CHANCE!
?
YOU'LL FIGHT HIM!
WHO?? N-NOT — YOU D-DON'T MEAN ME?
4-13

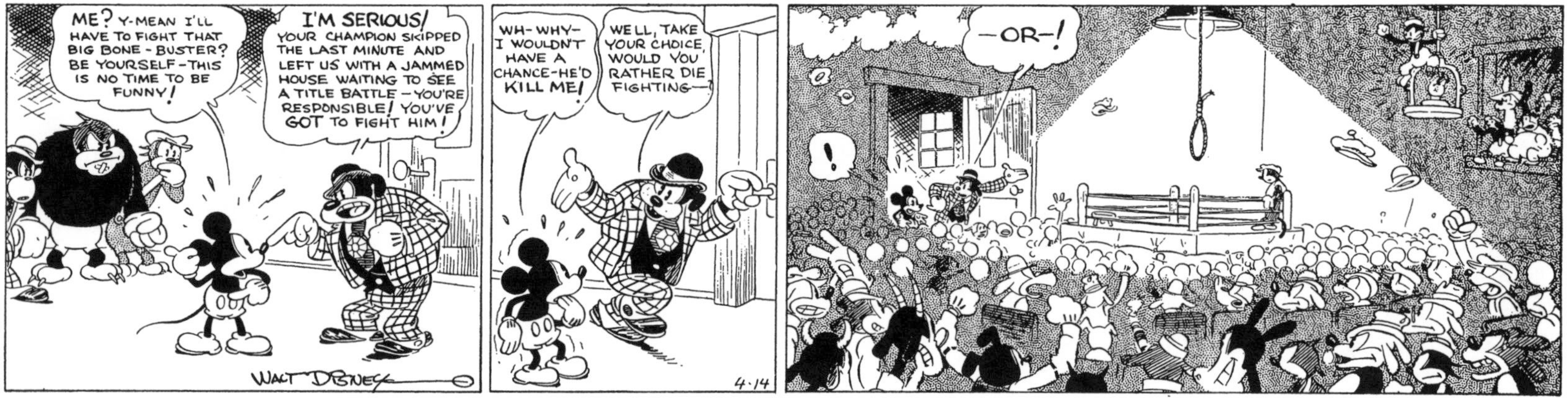
ME? Y-MEAN I'LL HAVE TO FIGHT THAT BIG BONE-BUSTER? BE YOURSELF — THIS IS NO TIME TO BE FUNNY!
I'M SERIOUS! YOUR CHAMPION SKIPPED THE LAST MINUTE AND LEFT US WITH A JAMMED HOUSE WAITING TO SEE A TITLE BATTLE — YOU'RE RESPONSIBLE! YOU'VE GOT TO FIGHT HIM!
WALT DISNEY
WH-WHY — I WOULDN'T HAVE A CHANCE — HE'D KILL ME!
WELL, TAKE YOUR CHOICE, WOULD YOU RATHER DIE FIGHTING —
4-14
— OR —!
!

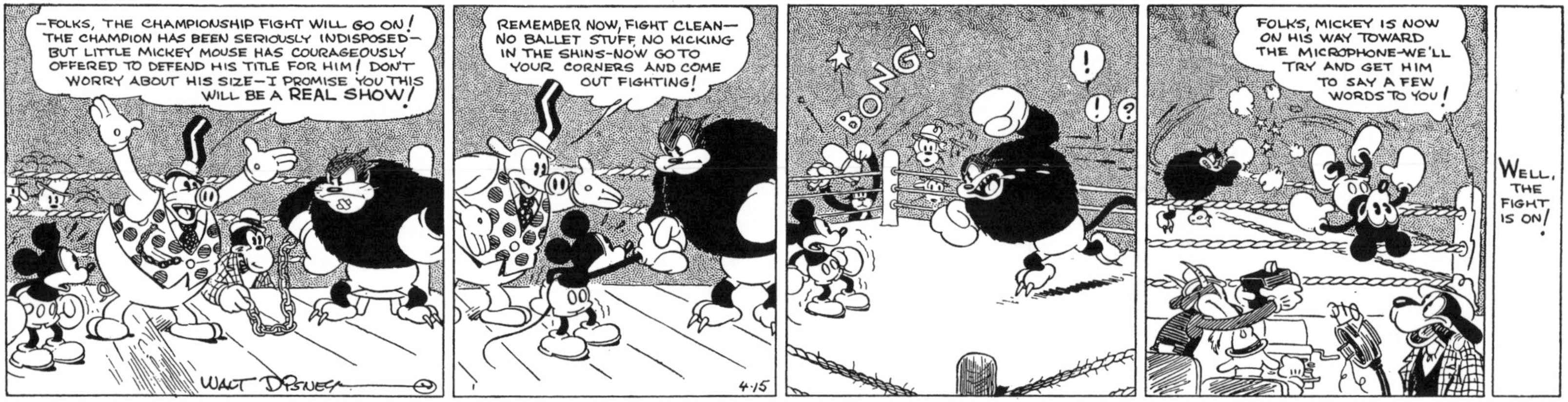
— FOLKS, THE CHAMPIONSHIP FIGHT WILL GO ON! THE CHAMPION HAS BEEN SERIOUSLY INDISPOSED — BUT LITTLE MICKEY MOUSE HAS COURAGEOUSLY OFFERED TO DEFEND HIS TITLE FOR HIM! DON'T WORRY ABOUT HIS SIZE — I PROMISE YOU THIS WILL BE A REAL SHOW!
WALT DISNEY
REMEMBER NOW, FIGHT CLEAN — NO BALLET STUFF, NO KICKING IN THE SHINS — NOW GO TO YOUR CORNERS AND COME OUT FIGHTING!
4-15
BONG!
!
!?
FOLKS, MICKEY IS NOW ON HIS WAY TOWARD THE MICROPHONE — WE'LL TRY AND GET HIM TO SAY A FEW WORDS TO YOU!
WELL, THE FIGHT IS ON!

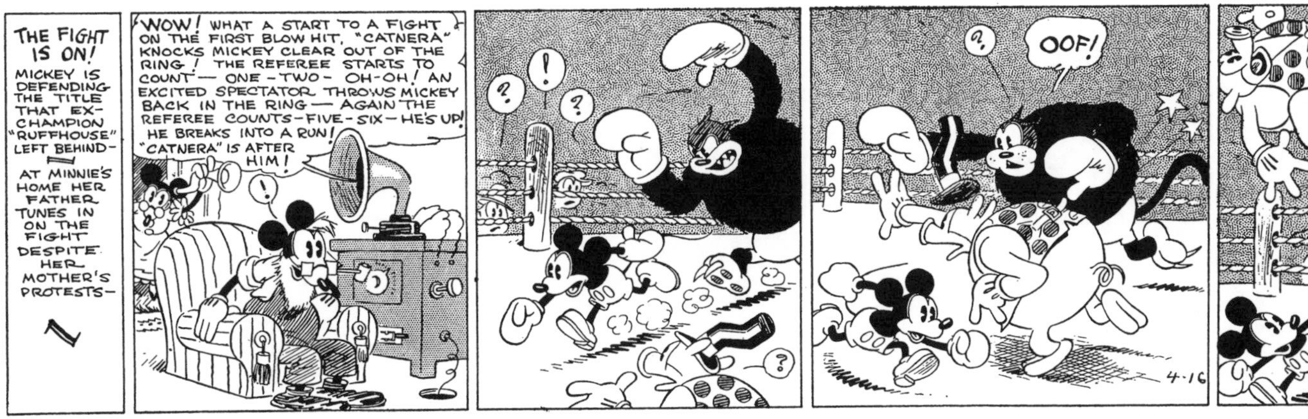
THE FIGHT IS ON!
MICKEY IS DEFENDING THE TITLE THAT EX-CHAMPION "RUFFHOUSE" LEFT BEHIND—
AT MINNIE'S HOME HER FATHER TUNES IN ON THE FIGHT DESPITE HER MOTHER'S PROTESTS—
WOW! WHAT A START TO A FIGHT ON THE FIRST BLOW HIT, "CATNERA" KNOCKS MICKEY CLEAR OUT OF THE RING! THE REFEREE STARTS TO COUNT — ONE - TWO - OH-OH! AN EXCITED SPECTATOR THROWS MICKEY BACK IN THE RING — AGAIN THE REFEREE COUNTS - FIVE - SIX - HE'S UP! HE BREAKS INTO A RUN! "CATNERA" IS AFTER HIM!
OOF!
GIT OUT O'HERE! YOU'RE JUST AN OBSTACLE IN ME PATH TO PROGRESS!
HO! HO!
HAW!
4·16
WALT DISNEY

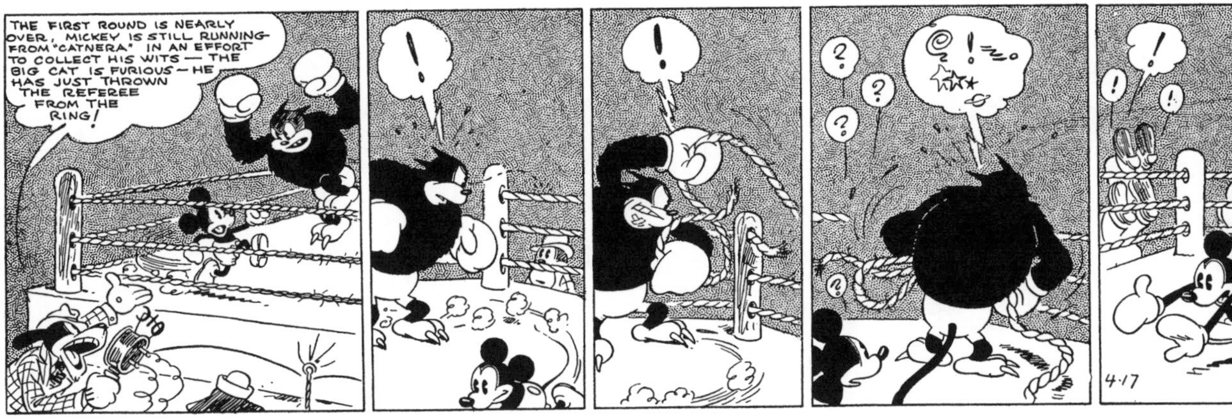
THE FIRST ROUND IS NEARLY OVER, MICKEY IS STILL RUNNING FROM "CATNERA" IN AN EFFORT TO COLLECT HIS WITS — THE BIG CAT IS FURIOUS — HE HAS JUST THROWN THE REFEREE FROM THE RING!
4·17
WALT DISNEY

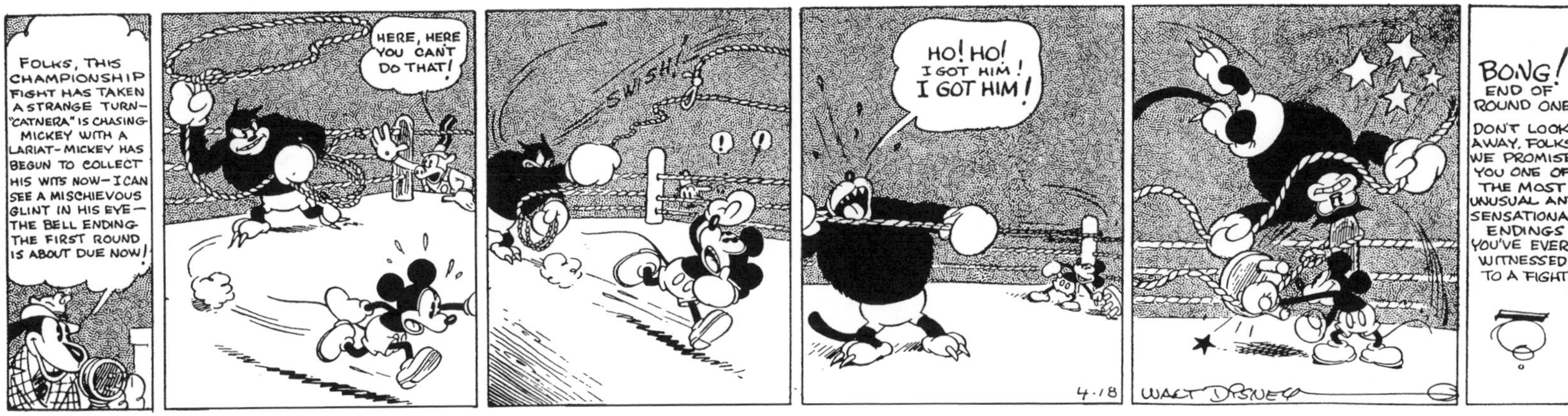
FOLKS, THIS CHAMPIONSHIP FIGHT HAS TAKEN A STRANGE TURN— "CATNERA" IS CHASING MICKEY WITH A LARIAT— MICKEY HAS BEGUN TO COLLECT HIS WITS NOW— I CAN SEE A MISCHIEVOUS GLINT IN HIS EYE— THE BELL ENDING THE FIRST ROUND IS ABOUT DUE NOW!
HERE, HERE YOU CAN'T DO THAT!
SWISH!
HO! HO! I GOT HIM! I GOT HIM!
4·18
WALT DISNEY
BONG! END OF ROUND ONE!
DON'T LOOK AWAY, FOLKS— WE PROMISE YOU ONE OF THE MOST UNUSUAL AND SENSATIONAL ENDINGS YOU'VE EVER WITNESSED TO A FIGHT!

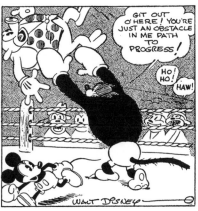

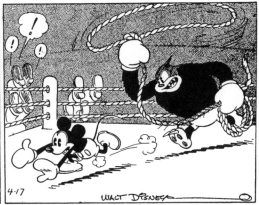

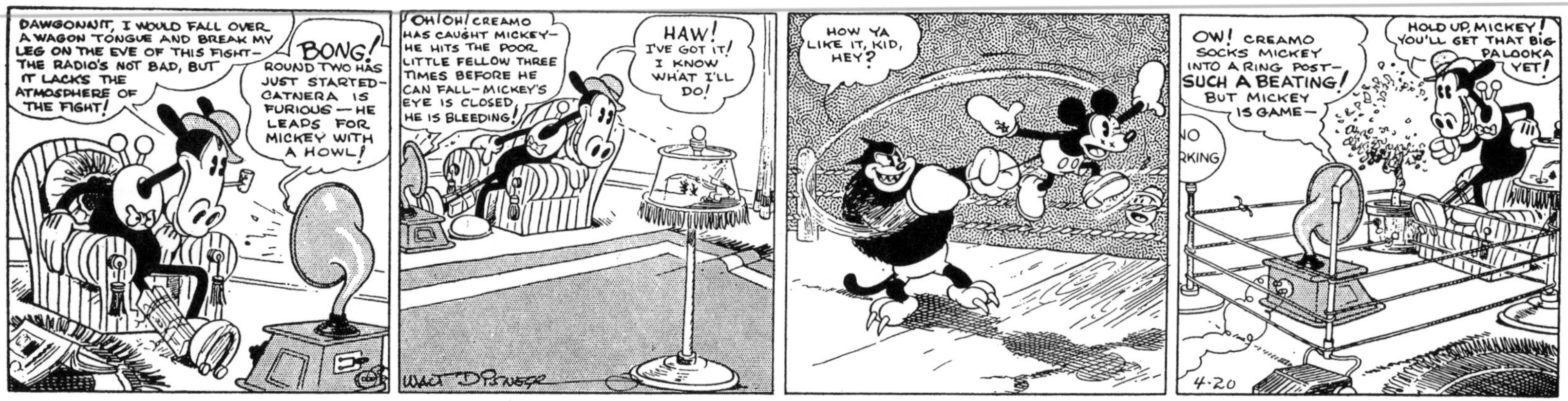
DAWGONNIT, I WOULD FALL OVER A WAGON TONGUE AND BREAK MY LEG ON THE EVE OF THIS FIGHT— THE RADIO'S NOT BAD, BUT IT LACKS THE ATMOSPHERE OF THE FIGHT!
BONG! ROUND TWO HAS JUST STARTED— CATNERA IS FURIOUS — HE LEADS FOR MICKEY WITH A HOWL!
OH! OH! CREAMO HAS CAUGHT MICKEY— HE HITS THE POOR LITTLE FELLOW THREE TIMES BEFORE HE CAN FALL—MICKEY'S EYE IS CLOSED HE IS BLEEDING!
HAW! I'VE GOT IT! I KNOW WHAT I'LL DO!
WALT DISNEY
HOW YA LIKE IT, KID, HEY?
OW! CREAMO SOCKS MICKEY INTO A RING POST— SUCH A BEATING! BUT MICKEY IS GAME—
HOLD UP, MICKEY! YOU'LL GET THAT BIG PALOOKA YET!
4·20

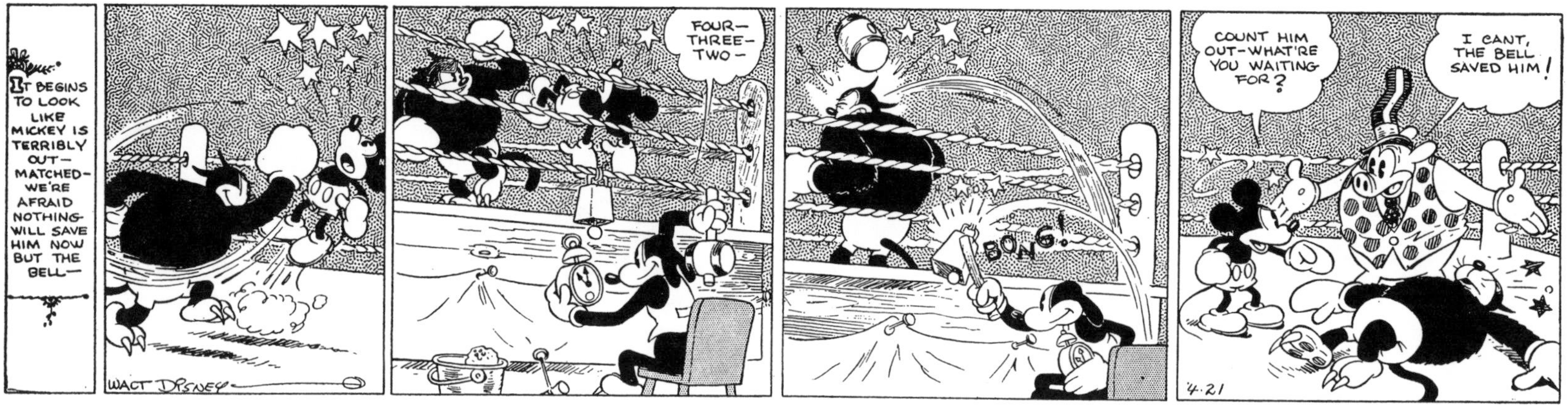
IT BEGINS TO LOOK LIKE MICKEY IS TERRIBLY OUT-MATCHED— WE'RE AFRAID NOTHING WILL SAVE HIM NOW BUT THE BELL—
WALT DISNEY
FOUR— THREE— TWO—
BONG!
COUNT HIM OUT—WHAT'RE YOU WAITING FOR?
I CANT, THE BELL SAVED HIM!
4·21

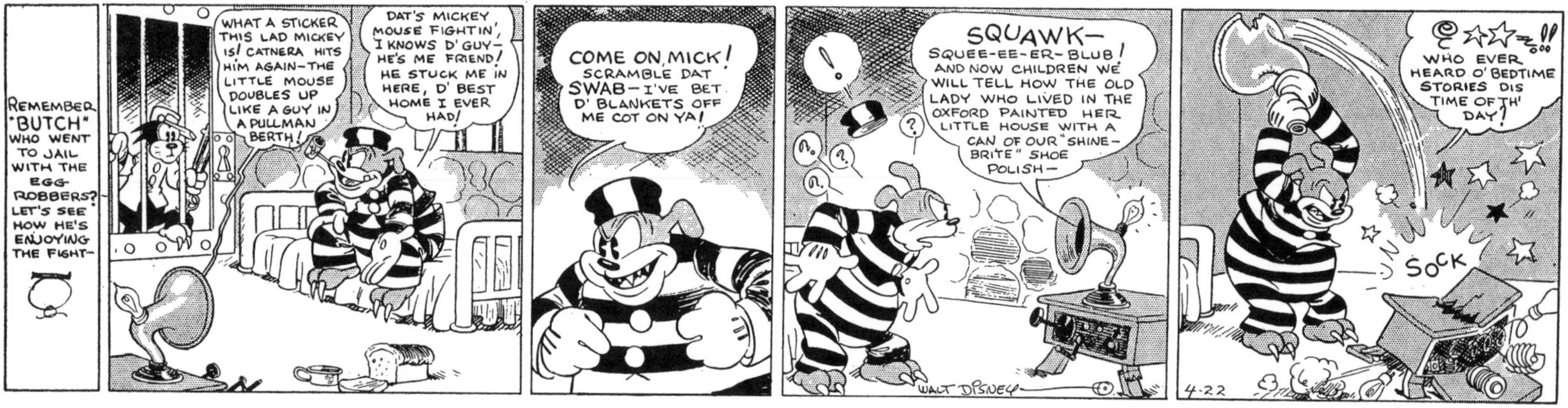
REMEMBER "BUTCH" WHO WENT TO JAIL WITH THE EGG-ROBBERS? LET'S SEE HOW HE'S ENJOYING THE FIGHT—
WHAT A STICKER THIS LAD MICKEY IS! CATNERA HITS HIM AGAIN—THE LITTLE MOUSE DOUBLES UP LIKE A GUY IN A PULLMAN BERTH!
DAT'S MICKEY MOUSE FIGHTIN', I KNOWS D' GUY— HE'S ME FRIEND! HE STUCK ME IN HERE, D' BEST HOME I EVER HAD!
COME ON, MICK! SCRAMBLE DAT SWAB—I'VE BET D' BLANKETS OFF ME COT ON YA!
SQUAWK— SQUEE-EE-ER-BLUB! AND NOW CHILDREN WE WILL TELL HOW THE OLD LADY WHO LIVED IN THE OXFORD PAINTED HER LITTLE HOUSE WITH A CAN OF OUR "SHINE-BRITE" SHOE POLISH—
WALT DISNEY
WHO EVER HEARD O' BEDTIME STORIES DIS TIME OF TH' DAY!
SOCK
4·22

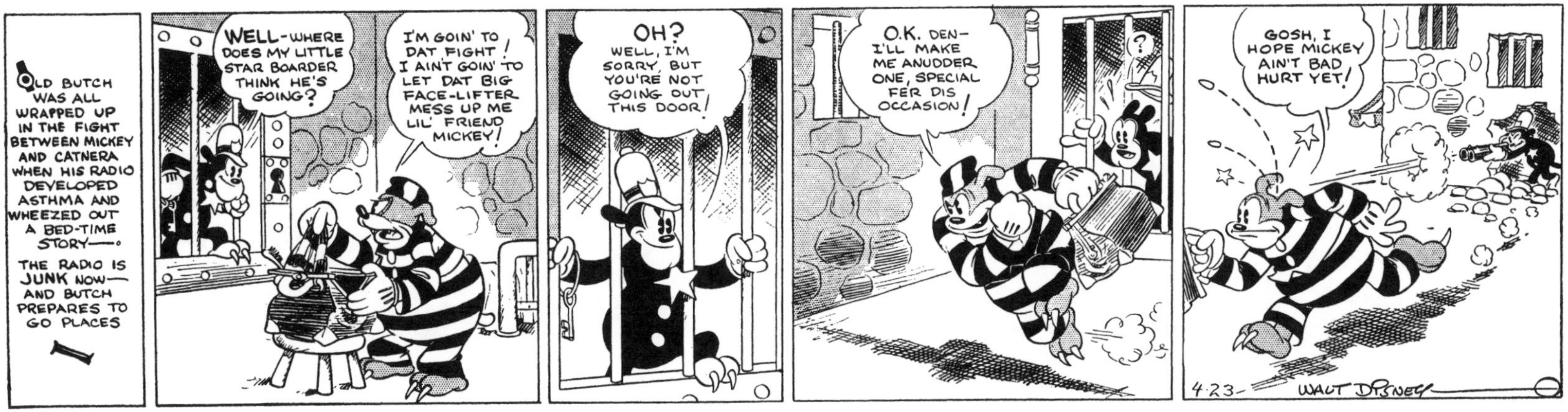
OLD BUTCH WAS ALL WRAPPED UP IN THE FIGHT BETWEEN MICKEY AND CATNERA WHEN HIS RADIO DEVELOPED ASTHMA AND WHEEZED OUT A BED-TIME STORY—.
THE RADIO IS JUNK NOW— AND BUTCH PREPARES TO GO PLACES
WELL-WHERE DOES MY LITTLE STAR BOARDER THINK HE'S GOING?
I'M GOIN' TO DAT FIGHT! I AIN'T GOIN' TO LET DAT BIG FACE-LIFTER MESS UP ME LIL' FRIEND MICKEY!
OH? WELL, I'M SORRY, BUT YOU'RE NOT GOING OUT THIS DOOR!
O.K. DEN- I'LL MAKE ME ANUDDER ONE, SPECIAL FER DIS OCCASION!
GOSH, I HOPE MICKEY AIN'T BAD HURT YET!
4-23-
WALT DISNEY

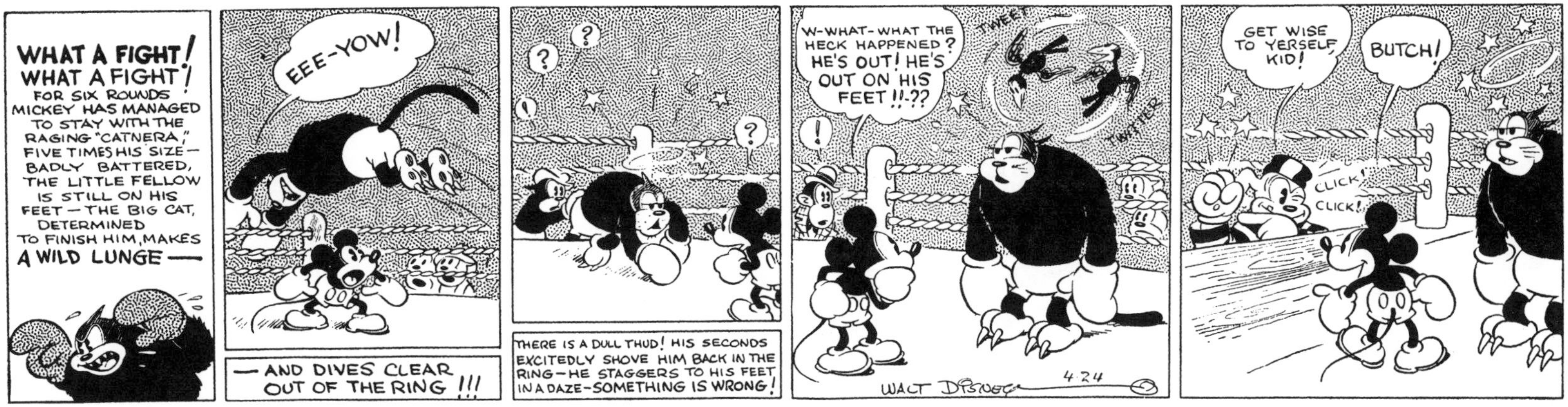
WHAT A FIGHT! WHAT A FIGHT! FOR SIX ROUNDS MICKEY HAS MANAGED TO STAY WITH THE RAGING "CATNERA," FIVE TIMES HIS SIZE- BADLY BATTERED, THE LITTLE FELLOW IS STILL ON HIS FEET—THE BIG CAT, DETERMINED TO FINISH HIM, MAKES A WILD LUNGE—
EEE-YOW!
—AND DIVES CLEAR OUT OF THE RING!!!
THERE IS A DULL THUD! HIS SECONDS EXCITEDLY SHOVE HIM BACK IN THE RING—HE STAGGERS TO HIS FEET IN A DAZE-SOMETHING IS WRONG!
W-WHAT-WHAT THE HECK HAPPENED? HE'S OUT! HE'S OUT ON HIS FEET!!-??
TWEET
TWITTER
WALT DISNEY
4-24
GET WISE TO YERSELF KID!
BUTCH!
CLICK!
CLICK!

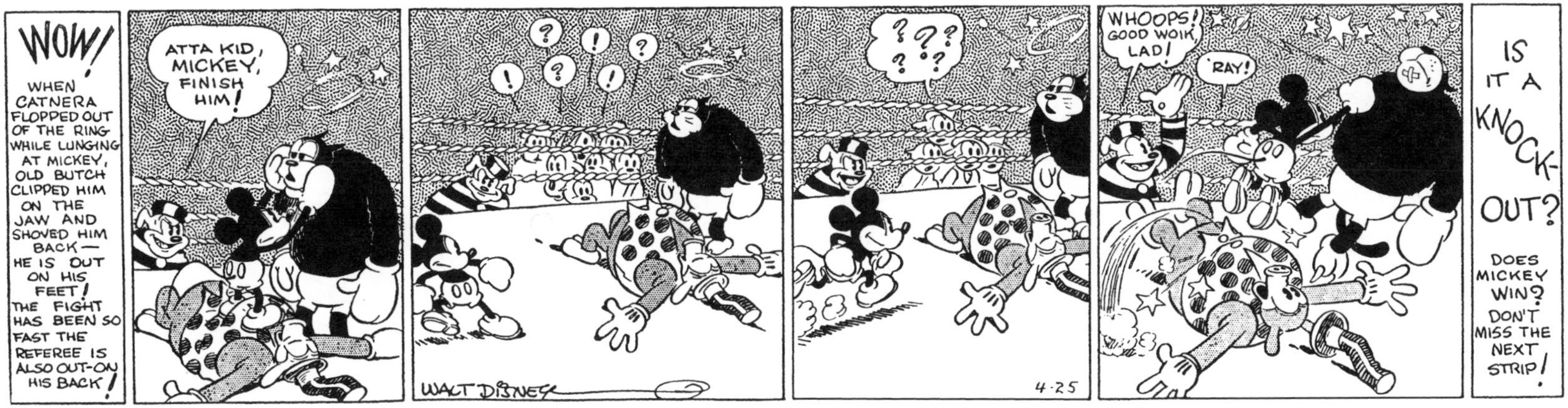
WOW! WHEN CATNERA FLOPPED OUT OF THE RING WHILE LUNGING AT MICKEY, OLD BUTCH CLIPPED HIM ON THE JAW AND SHOVED HIM BACK— HE IS OUT ON HIS FEET! THE FIGHT HAS BEEN SO FAST THE REFEREE IS ALSO OUT-ON HIS BACK!
ATTA KID, MICKEY, FINISH HIM!
WALT DISNEY
4-25
WHOOPS! GOOD WOIK LAD!
'RAY!
IS IT A KNOCK-OUT? DOES MICKEY WIN? DON'T MISS THE NEXT STRIP!

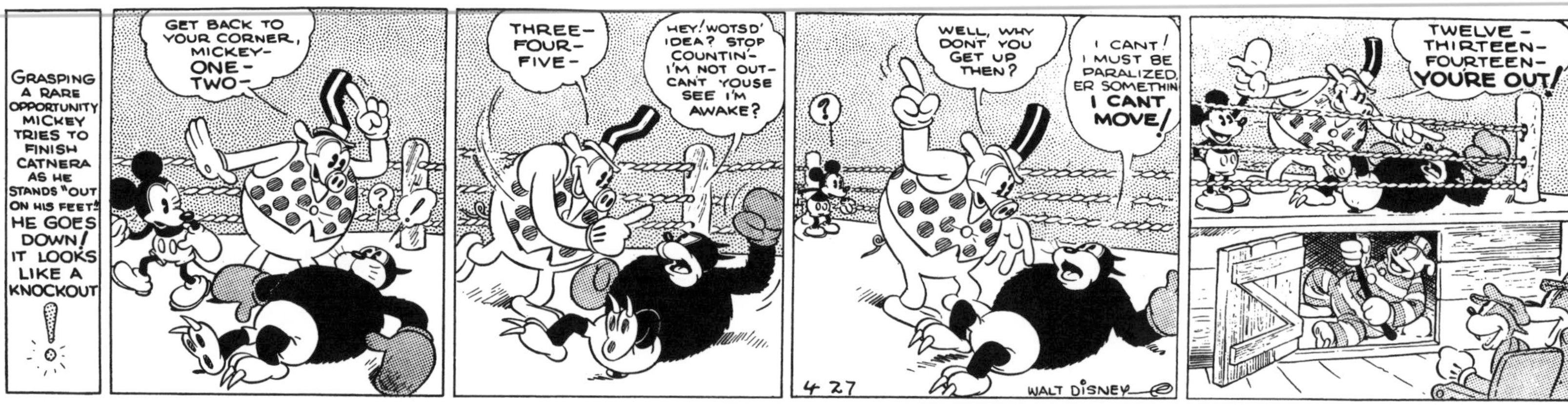
GRASPING A RARE OPPORTUNITY MICKEY TRIES TO FINISH CATNERA AS HE STANDS "OUT ON HIS FEET!" HE GOES DOWN! IT LOOKS LIKE A KNOCKOUT!
GET BACK TO YOUR CORNER, MICKEY- ONE- TWO-
?
!
THREE- FOUR- FIVE-
HEY! WOTSD' IDEA? STOP COUNTIN'- I'M NOT OUT- CAN'T YOUSE SEE I'M AWAKE?
?
WELL, WHY DONT YOU GET UP THEN?
I CANT! I MUST BE PARALIZED, ER SOMETHIN I CANT MOVE!
4 27
WALT DISNEY
TWELVE- THIRTEEN- FOURTEEN- YOU'RE OUT!

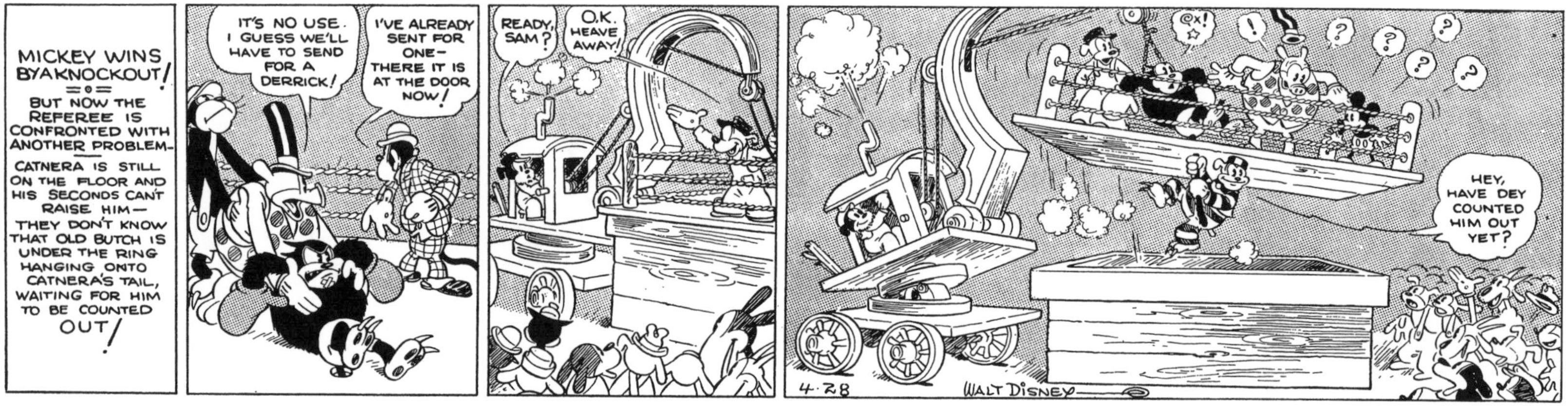
MICKEY WINS BY A KNOCKOUT! BUT NOW THE REFEREE IS CONFRONTED WITH ANOTHER PROBLEM- CATNERA IS STILL ON THE FLOOR AND HIS SECONDS CAN'T RAISE HIM— THEY DON'T KNOW THAT OLD BUTCH IS UNDER THE RING HANGING ONTO CATNERA'S TAIL, WAITING FOR HIM TO BE COUNTED OUT!
IT'S NO USE. I GUESS WE'LL HAVE TO SEND FOR A DERRICK!
I'VE ALREADY SENT FOR ONE- THERE IT IS AT THE DOOR NOW!
READY, SAM?
O.K. HEAVE AWAY!
HEY, HAVE DEY COUNTED HIM OUT YET?
4·28
WALT DISNEY

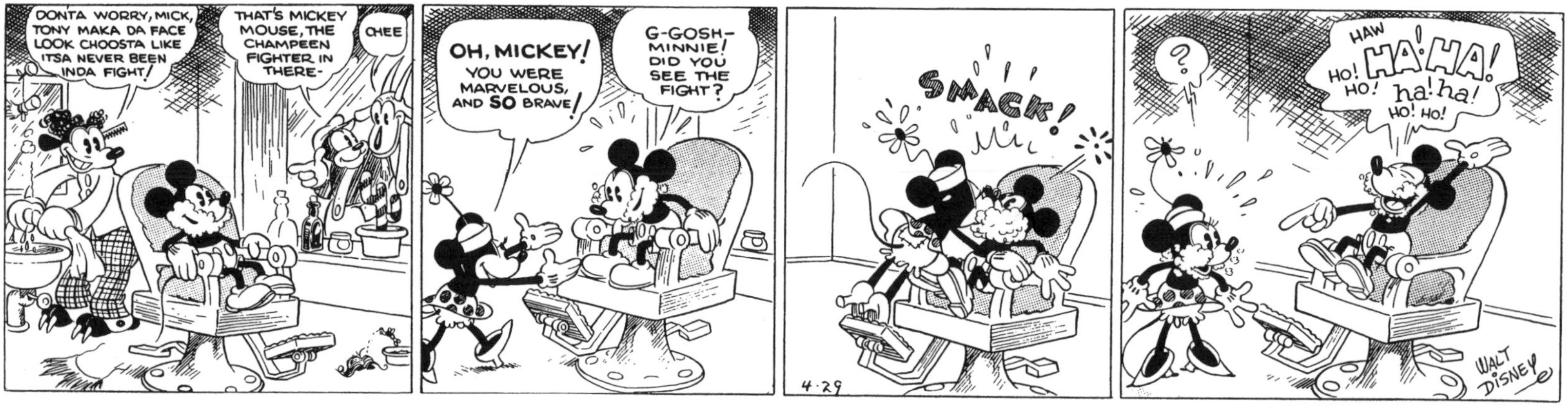
DONTA WORRY, MICK, TONY MAKA DA FACE LOOK CHOOSTA LIKE ITSA NEVER BEEN INDA FIGHT!
THAT'S MICKEY MOUSE, THE CHAMPEEN FIGHTER IN THERE-
CHEE
OH, MICKEY! YOU WERE MARVELOUS, AND SO BRAVE!
G-GOSH- MINNIE! DID YOU SEE THE FIGHT?
SMACK!
4·29
?
HAW HO! HO! HA! HA! ha! ha! HO! HO!
WALT DISNEY

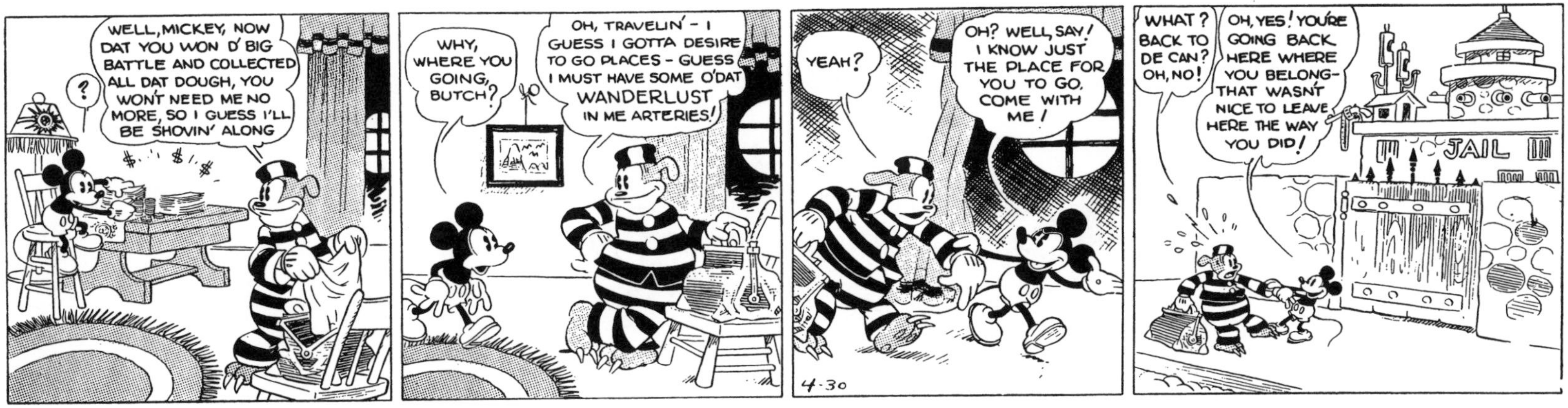
?
WELL, MICKEY, NOW DAT YOU WON D' BIG BATTLE AND COLLECTED ALL DAT DOUGH, YOU WON'T NEED ME NO MORE, SO I GUESS I'LL BE SHOVIN' ALONG
WHY, WHERE YOU GOING, BUTCH?
OH, TRAVELIN' - I GUESS I GOTTA DESIRE TO GO PLACES - GUESS I MUST HAVE SOME O'DAT WANDERLUST IN ME ARTERIES!
YEAH?
OH? WELL, SAY! I KNOW JUST THE PLACE FOR YOU TO GO. COME WITH ME!
4-30
WHAT? BACK TO DE CAN? OH, NO!
OH, YES! YOU'RE GOING BACK HERE WHERE YOU BELONG- THAT WASN'T NICE TO LEAVE HERE THE WAY YOU DID!
JAIL

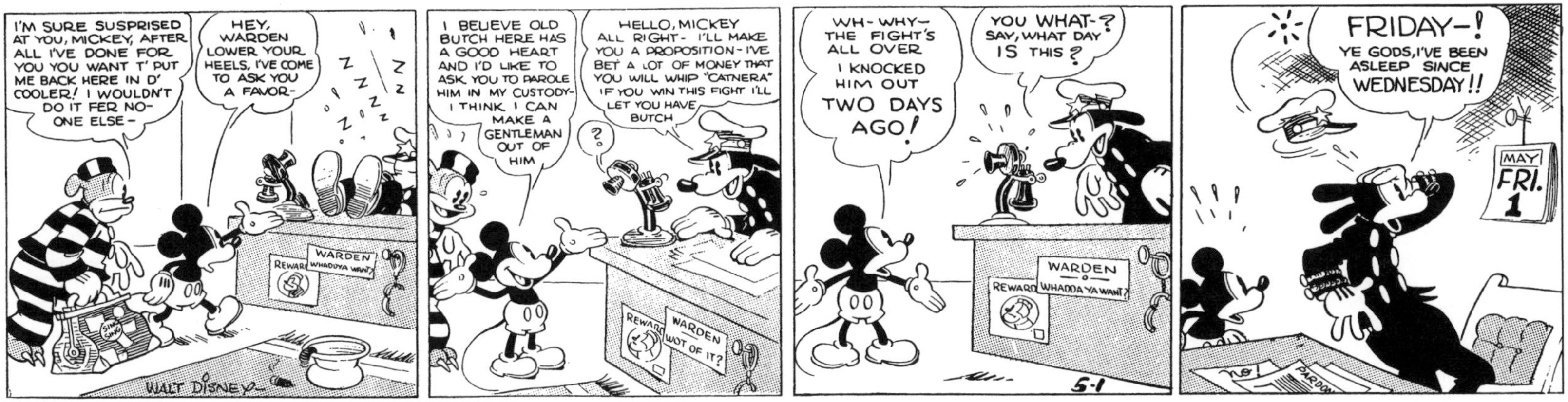
I'M SURE SUSPRISED AT YOU, MICKEY, AFTER ALL I'VE DONE FOR YOU YOU WANT T' PUT ME BACK HERE IN D' COOLER! I WOULDN'T DO IT FER NO-ONE ELSE-
HEY, WARDEN LOWER YOUR HEELS, I'VE COME TO ASK YOU A FAVOR-
WARDEN WHADDYA WANT?
WALT DISNEY
I BELIEVE OLD BUTCH HERE HAS A GOOD HEART AND I'D LIKE TO ASK YOU TO PAROLE HIM IN MY CUSTODY- I THINK I CAN MAKE A GENTLEMAN OUT OF HIM
HELLO, MICKEY ALL RIGHT- I'LL MAKE YOU A PROPOSITION- I'VE BET A LOT OF MONEY THAT YOU WILL WHIP "CATNERA" IF YOU WIN THIS FIGHT I'LL LET YOU HAVE BUTCH
?
WARDEN WOT OF IT?
WH-WHY- THE FIGHT'S ALL OVER I KNOCKED HIM OUT TWO DAYS AGO!
YOU WHAT-? SAY, WHAT DAY IS THIS?
WARDEN WHADDA YA WANT?
REWARD
5-1
FRIDAY-! YE GODS, I'VE BEEN ASLEEP SINCE WEDNESDAY!!
MAY FRI. 1

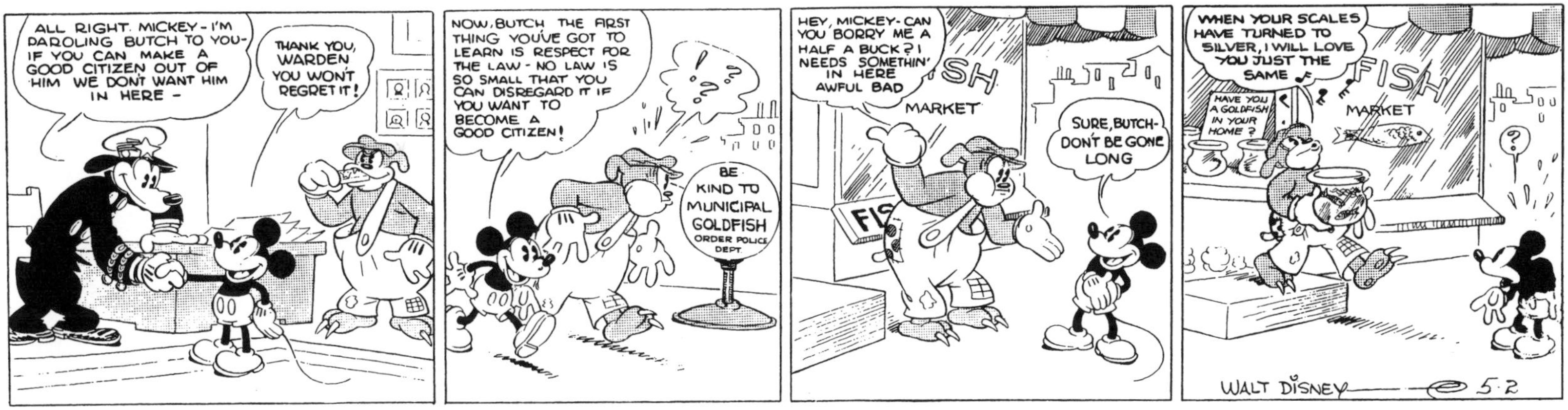
ALL RIGHT MICKEY- I'M PAROLING BUTCH TO YOU- IF YOU CAN MAKE A GOOD CITIZEN OUT OF HIM WE DON'T WANT HIM IN HERE-
THANK YOU, WARDEN YOU WON'T REGRET IT!
NOW, BUTCH THE FIRST THING YOU'VE GOT TO LEARN IS RESPECT FOR THE LAW - NO LAW IS SO SMALL THAT YOU CAN DISREGARD IT IF YOU WANT TO BECOME A GOOD CITIZEN!
BE KIND TO MUNICIPAL GOLDFISH ORDER POLICE DEPT
HEY, MICKEY- CAN YOU BORRY ME A HALF A BUCK? I NEEDS SOMETHIN' IN HERE AWFUL BAD
MARKET
SURE, BUTCH- DON'T BE GONE LONG
WHEN YOUR SCALES HAVE TURNED TO SILVER, I WILL LOVE YOU JUST THE SAME
HAVE YOU A GOLDFISH IN YOUR HOME?
FISH
MARKET
?
WALT DISNEY 5-2

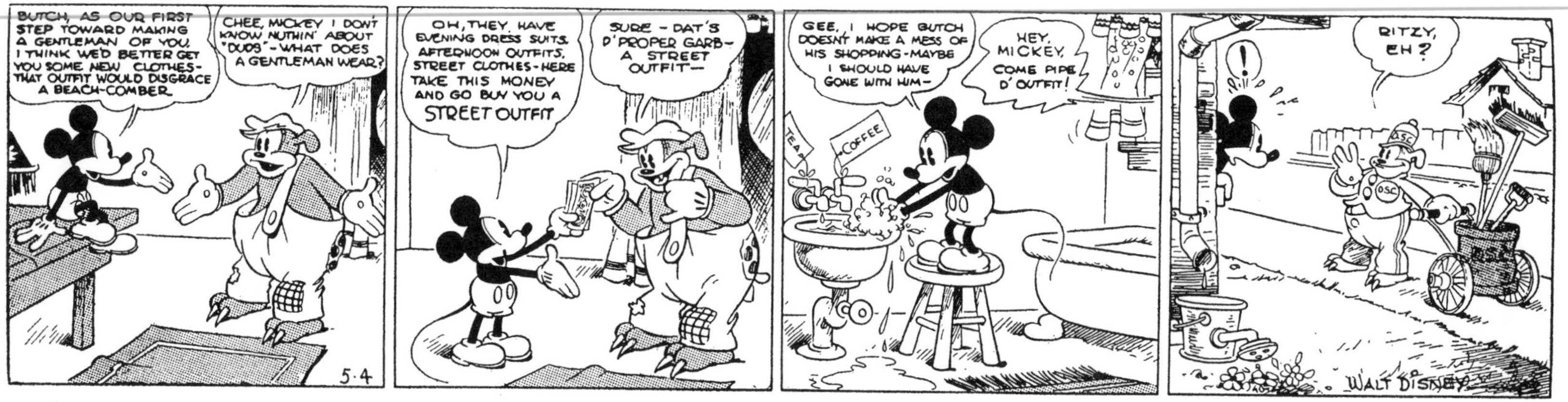
BUTCH, AS OUR FIRST STEP TOWARD MAKING A GENTLEMAN OF YOU, I THINK WE'D BETTER GET YOU SOME NEW CLOTHES- THAT OUTFIT WOULD DISGRACE A BEACH-COMBER
CHEE, MICKEY I DON'T KNOW NUTHIN' ABOUT "DUDS"-WHAT DOES A GENTLEMAN WEAR?
5·4
OH, THEY HAVE EVENING DRESS SUITS, AFTERNOON OUTFITS, STREET CLOTHES-HERE TAKE THIS MONEY AND GO BUY YOU A STREET OUTFIT
SURE - DAT'S D' PROPER GARB- A STREET OUTFIT—
GEE, I HOPE BUTCH DOESN'T MAKE A MESS OF HIS SHOPPING-MAYBE I SHOULD HAVE GONE WITH HIM-
HEY, MICKEY, COME PIPE D' OUTFIT!
TEA
COFFEE
!
RITZY, EH?
WALT DISNEY

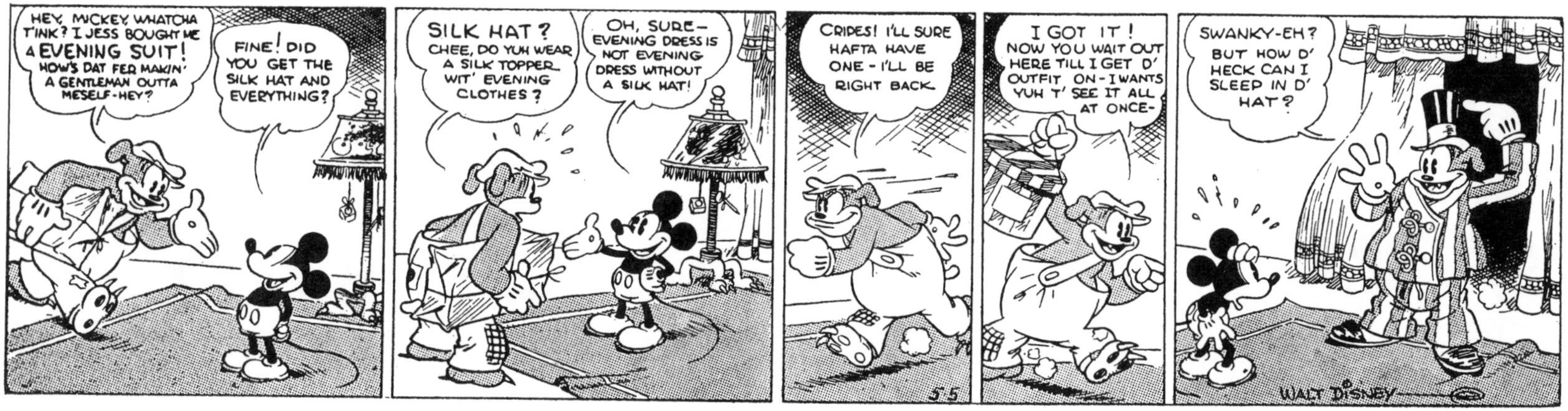
HEY, MICKEY, WHATCHA T'INK? I JESS BOUGHT ME A EVENING SUIT! HOW'S DAT FER MAKIN' A GENTLEMAN OUTTA MESELF-HEY?
FINE! DID YOU GET THE SILK HAT AND EVERYTHING?
SILK HAT? CHEE, DO YUH WEAR A SILK TOPPER WIT' EVENING CLOTHES?
OH, SURE- EVENING DRESS IS NOT EVENING DRESS WITHOUT A SILK HAT!
CRIPES! I'LL SURE HAFTA HAVE ONE - I'LL BE RIGHT BACK
5·5
I GOT IT! NOW YOU WAIT OUT HERE TILL I GET D' OUTFIT ON-I WANTS YUH T' SEE IT ALL AT ONCE-
SWANKY-EH? BUT HOW D' HECK CAN I SLEEP IN D' HAT?
WALT DISNEY

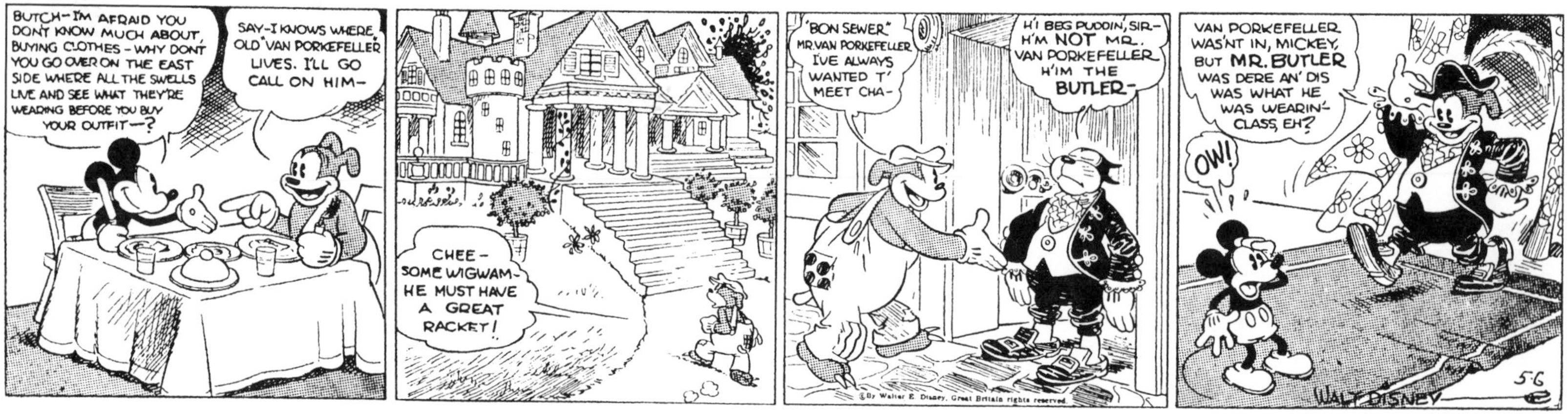
BUTCH-I'M AFRAID YOU DON'T KNOW MUCH ABOUT BUYING CLOTHES - WHY DON'T YOU GO OVER ON THE EAST SIDE WHERE ALL THE SWELLS LIVE AND SEE WHAT THEY'RE WEARING BEFORE YOU BUY YOUR OUTFIT—?
SAY-I KNOWS WHERE OLD VAN PORKEFELLER LIVES. I'LL GO CALL ON HIM-
CHEE- SOME WIGWAM- HE MUST HAVE A GREAT RACKET!
"BON SEWER" MR. VAN PORKEFELLER I'VE ALWAYS WANTED T' MEET CHA-
H'I BEG PUDDIN, SIR- H'M NOT MR. VAN PORKEFELLER H'IM THE BUTLER-
© By Walter E. Disney, Great Britain rights reserved
VAN PORKEFELLER WAS'NT IN, MICKEY, BUT MR. BUTLER WAS DERE AN' DIS WAS WHAT HE WAS WEARIN'- CLASS, EH?
OW!
5·6
WALT DISNEY

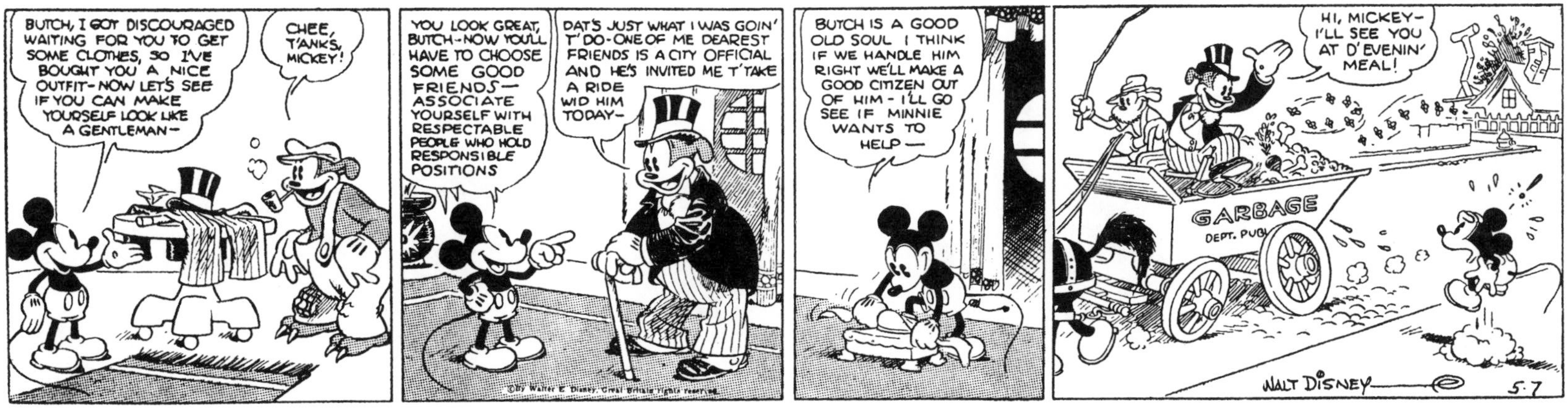
BUTCH, I GOT DISCOURAGED WAITING FOR YOU TO GET SOME CLOTHES, SO I'VE BOUGHT YOU A NICE OUTFIT - NOW LET'S SEE IF YOU CAN MAKE YOURSELF LOOK LIKE A GENTLEMAN -
CHEE, T'ANKS, MICKEY!
YOU LOOK GREAT, BUTCH - NOW YOU'LL HAVE TO CHOOSE SOME GOOD FRIENDS — ASSOCIATE YOURSELF WITH RESPECTABLE PEOPLE WHO HOLD RESPONSIBLE POSITIONS
DAT'S JUST WHAT I WAS GOIN' T' DO - ONE OF ME DEAREST FRIENDS IS A CITY OFFICIAL AND HE'S INVITED ME T' TAKE A RIDE WID HIM TODAY -
BUTCH IS A GOOD OLD SOUL I THINK IF WE HANDLE HIM RIGHT WE'LL MAKE A GOOD CITIZEN OUT OF HIM - I'LL GO SEE IF MINNIE WANTS TO HELP —
HI, MICKEY - I'LL SEE YOU AT D' EVENIN' MEAL!
GARBAGE
DEPT. PUBL
WALT DISNEY
5.7

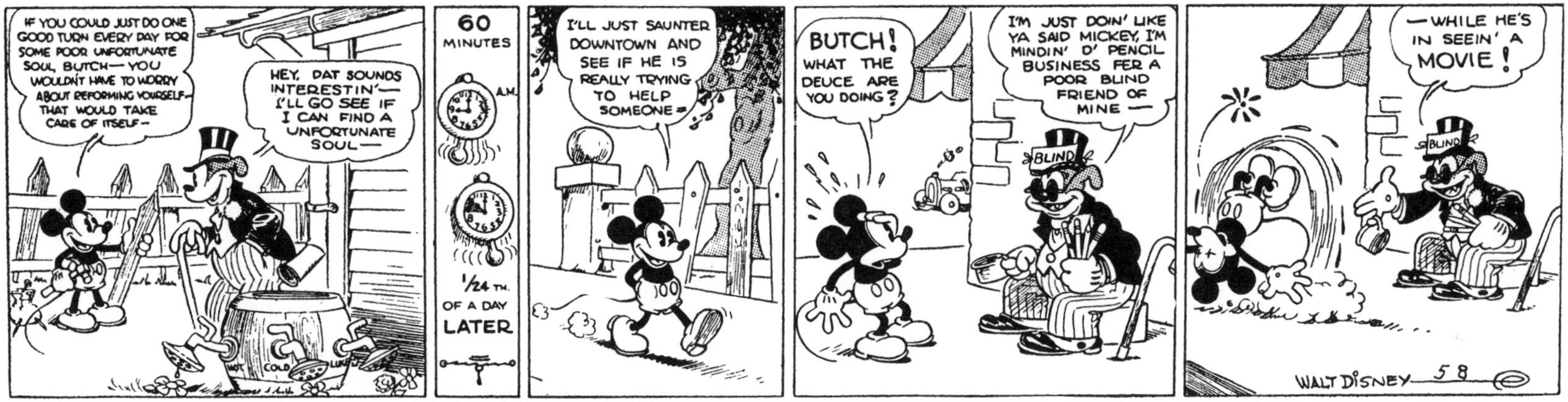
IF YOU COULD JUST DO ONE GOOD TURN EVERY DAY FOR SOME POOR UNFORTUNATE SOUL, BUTCH — YOU WOULDN'T HAVE TO WORRY ABOUT REFORMING YOURSELF - THAT WOULD TAKE CARE OF ITSELF -
HEY, DAT SOUNDS INTERESTIN' — I'LL GO SEE IF I CAN FIND A UNFORTUNATE SOUL —
HOT
COLD
60 MINUTES
A.M.
1/24 TH. OF A DAY LATER
I'LL JUST SAUNTER DOWNTOWN AND SEE IF HE IS REALLY TRYING TO HELP SOMEONE =
BUTCH! WHAT THE DEUCE ARE YOU DOING?
I'M JUST DOIN' LIKE YA SAID MICKEY, I'M MINDIN' D' PENCIL BUSINESS FER A POOR BLIND FRIEND OF MINE —
BLIND
— WHILE HE'S IN SEEIN' A MOVIE!
BLIND
WALT DISNEY 5 8

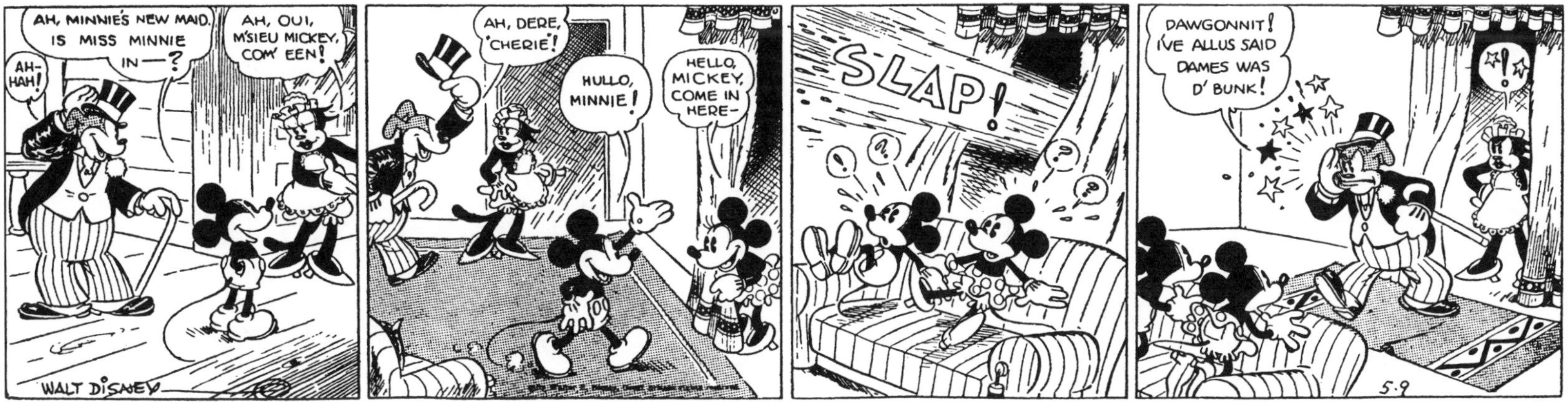
AH, MINNIE'S NEW MAID. IS MISS MINNIE IN —?
AH-HAH!
AH, OUI, M'SIEU MICKEY, COM' EEN!
WALT DISNEY
AH, DERE, 'CHERIE'!
HULLO, MINNIE!
HELLO, MICKEY, COME IN HERE -
SLAP!
DAWGONNIT! I'VE ALLUS SAID DAMES WAS D' BUNK!
5-9

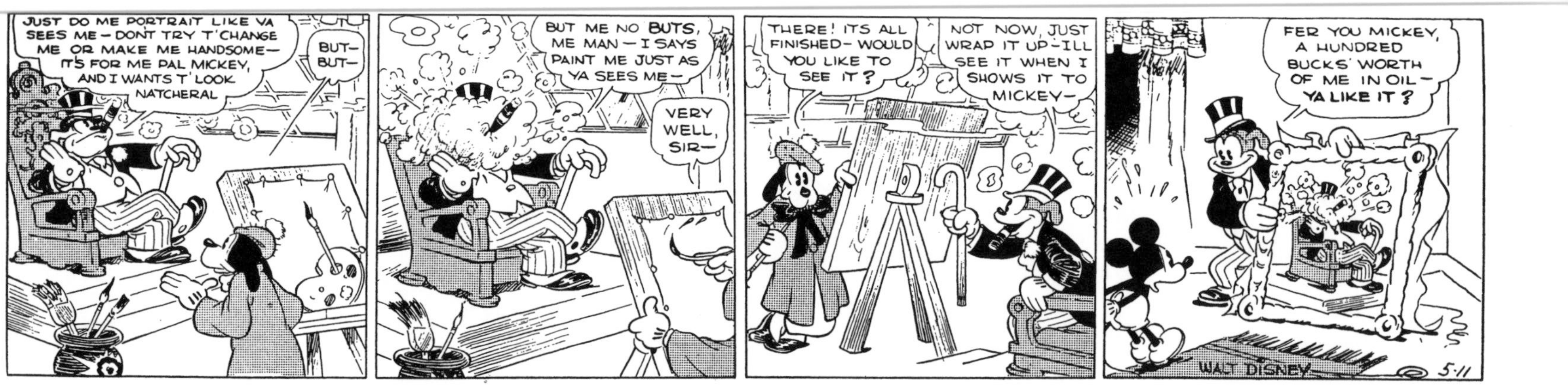
JUST DO ME PORTRAIT LIKE YA SEES ME — DON'T TRY T' CHANGE ME OR MAKE ME HANDSOME — IT'S FOR ME PAL MICKEY, AND I WANTS T' LOOK NATCHERAL
BUT- BUT-
BUT ME NO BUTS, ME MAN — I SAYS PAINT ME JUST AS YA SEES ME —
VERY WELL, SIR —
THERE! ITS ALL FINISHED- WOULD YOU LIKE TO SEE IT?
NOT NOW, JUST WRAP IT UP- I'LL SEE IT WHEN I SHOWS IT TO MICKEY —
FER YOU MICKEY, A HUNDRED BUCKS' WORTH OF ME IN OIL — YA LIKE IT?
WALT DISNEY
5-11

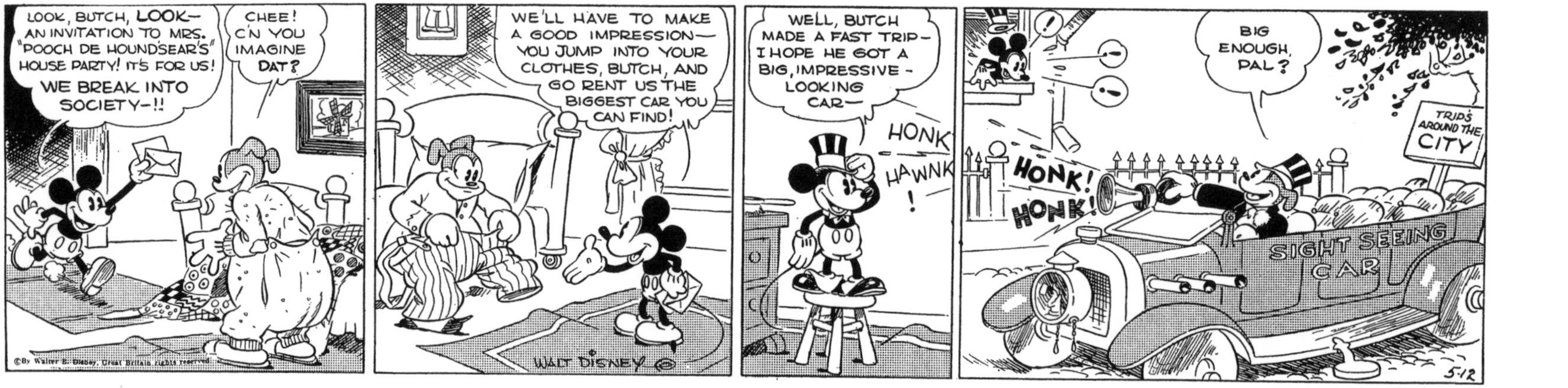
LOOK, BUTCH, LOOK — AN INVITATION TO MRS. "POOCH DE HOUNDSEAR'S" HOUSE PARTY! IT'S FOR US! WE BREAK INTO SOCIETY —!!
CHEE! C'N YOU IMAGINE DAT?
©By Walter E. Disney, Great Britain rights reserved
WE'LL HAVE TO MAKE A GOOD IMPRESSION — YOU JUMP INTO YOUR CLOTHES, BUTCH, AND GO RENT US THE BIGGEST CAR YOU CAN FIND!
WALT DISNEY
WELL, BUTCH MADE A FAST TRIP- I HOPE HE GOT A BIG, IMPRESSIVE - LOOKING CAR —
HONK
HAWNK!
BIG ENOUGH, PAL?
TRIPS AROUND THE CITY
HONK!
HONK!
SIGHT SEEING CAR
5-12

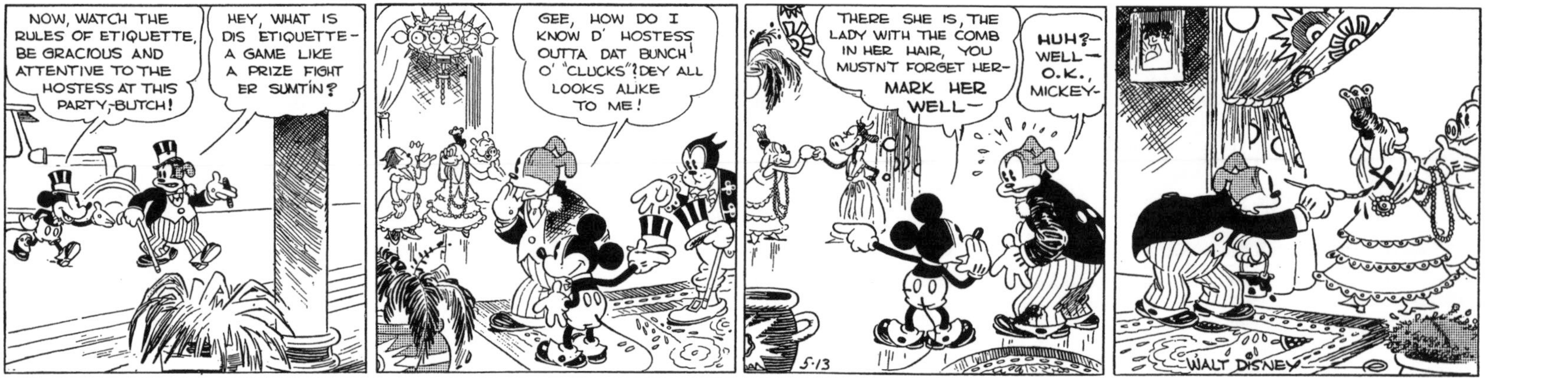
NOW, WATCH THE RULES OF ETIQUETTE, BE GRACIOUS AND ATTENTIVE TO THE HOSTESS AT THIS PARTY, BUTCH!
HEY, WHAT IS DIS ETIQUETTE - A GAME LIKE A PRIZE FIGHT ER SUMTIN?
GEE, HOW DO I KNOW D' HOSTESS OUTTA DAT BUNCH O' "CLUCKS"? DEY ALL LOOKS ALIKE TO ME!
THERE SHE IS, THE LADY WITH THE COMB IN HER HAIR, YOU MUSTN'T FORGET HER- MARK HER WELL —
HUH? — WELL — O.K., MICKEY-
5-13
WALT DISNEY

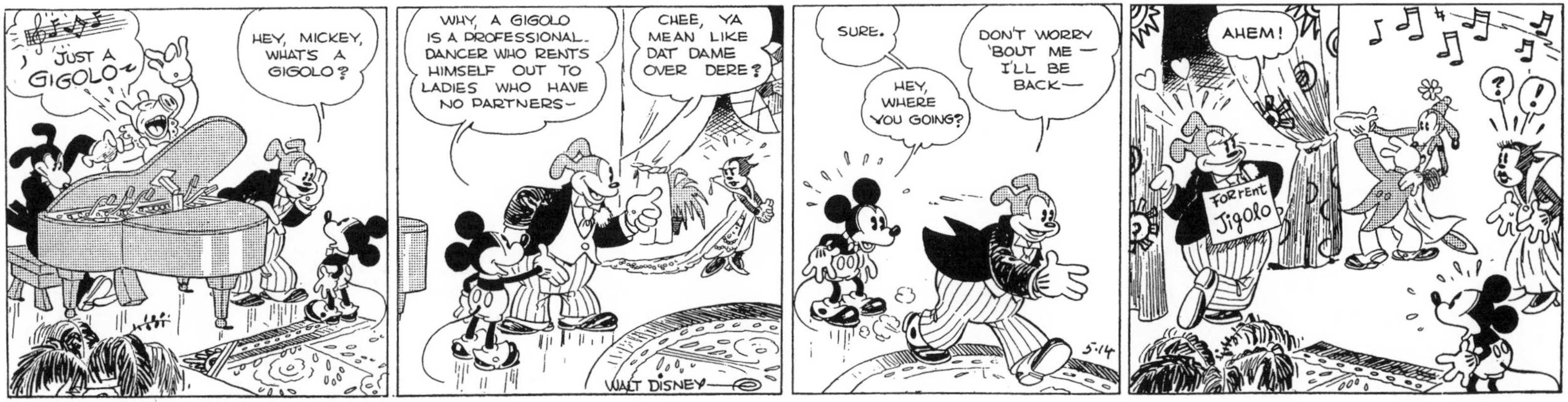
JUST A GIGOLO
HEY, MICKEY, WHAT'S A GIGOLO?
WHY, A GIGOLO IS A PROFESSIONAL DANCER WHO RENTS HIMSELF OUT TO LADIES WHO HAVE NO PARTNERS—
CHEE, YA MEAN LIKE DAT DAME OVER DERE?
WALT DISNEY
SURE.
HEY, WHERE YOU GOING?
DON'T WORRY 'BOUT ME— I'LL BE BACK—
5·14
AHEM!
FOR RENT Jigolo

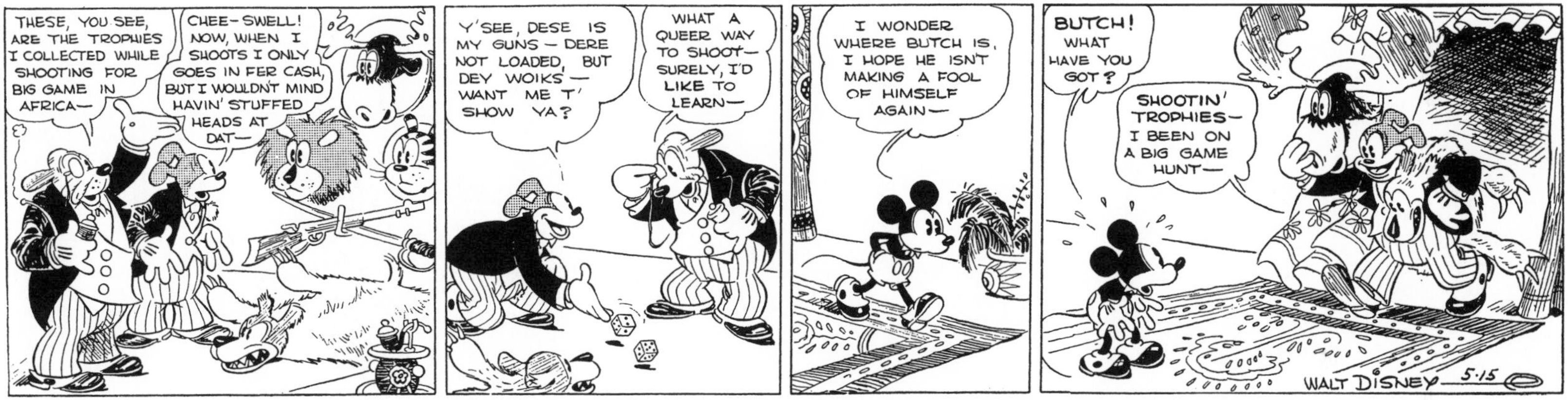
THESE, YOU SEE, ARE THE TROPHIES I COLLECTED WHILE SHOOTING FOR BIG GAME IN AFRICA—
CHEE-SWELL! NOW, WHEN I SHOOTS I ONLY GOES IN FER CASH, BUT I WOULDN'T MIND HAVIN' STUFFED HEADS AT DAT—
Y'SEE, DESE IS MY GUNS — DERE NOT LOADED, BUT DEY WOIKS'— WANT ME T' SHOW YA?
WHAT A QUEER WAY TO SHOOT— SURELY, I'D LIKE TO LEARN—
I WONDER WHERE BUTCH IS, I HOPE HE ISN'T MAKING A FOOL OF HIMSELF AGAIN—
BUTCH! WHAT HAVE YOU GOT?
SHOOTIN' TROPHIES— I BEEN ON A BIG GAME HUNT—
WALT DISNEY 5·15

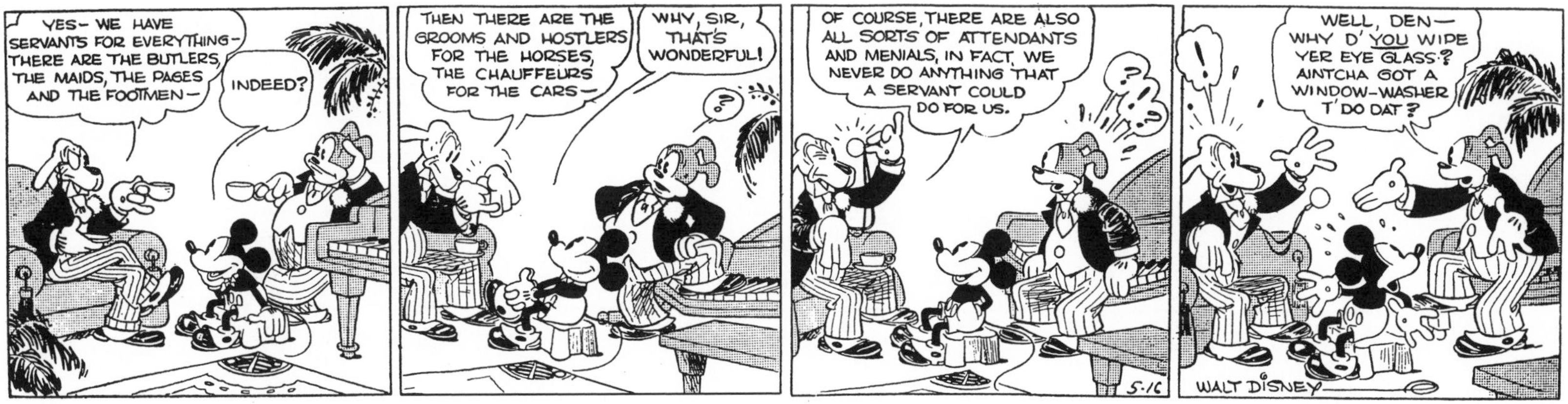
YES— WE HAVE SERVANTS FOR EVERYTHING— THERE ARE THE BUTLERS, THE MAIDS, THE PAGES AND THE FOOTMEN—
INDEED?
THEN THERE ARE THE GROOMS AND HOSTLERS FOR THE HORSES, THE CHAUFFEURS FOR THE CARS—
WHY, SIR, THAT'S WONDERFUL!
OF COURSE, THERE ARE ALSO ALL SORTS OF ATTENDANTS AND MENIALS, IN FACT, WE NEVER DO ANYTHING THAT A SERVANT COULD DO FOR US.
5·16
WELL, DEN— WHY D' YOU WIPE YER EYE GLASS? AINTCHA GOT A WINDOW-WASHER T' DO DAT?
WALT DISNEY

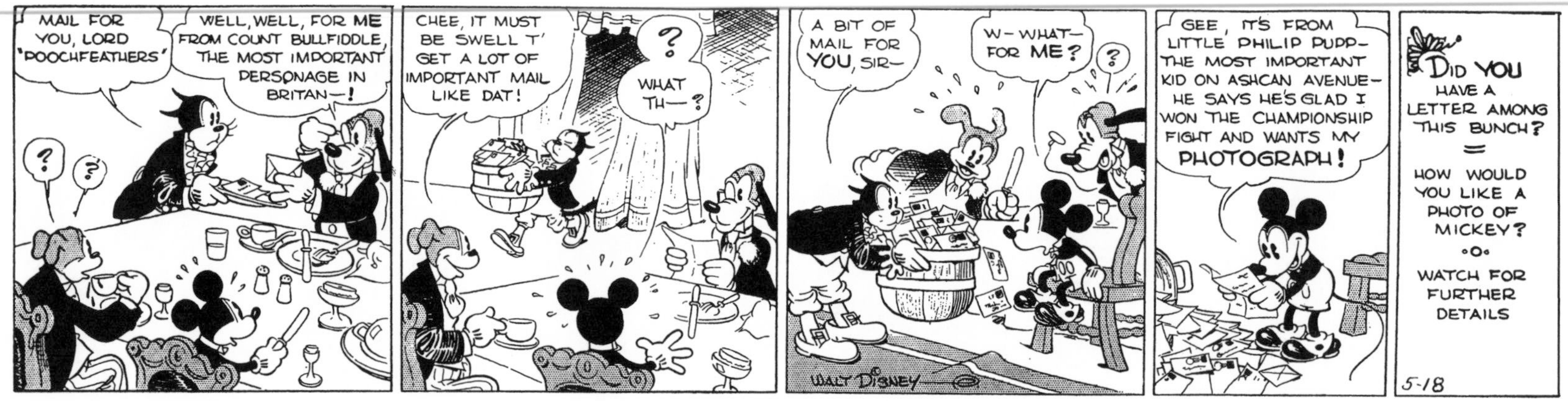
MAIL FOR YOU, LORD 'POOCHFEATHERS'
WELL, WELL, FOR ME FROM COUNT BULLFIDDLE, THE MOST IMPORTANT PERSONAGE IN BRITAN—!
?
?
CHEE, IT MUST BE SWELL T' GET A LOT OF IMPORTANT MAIL LIKE DAT!
?
WHAT TH—?
A BIT OF MAIL FOR YOU, SIR—
W—WHAT—FOR ME?
?
GEE, IT'S FROM LITTLE PHILIP PUPP—THE MOST IMPORTANT KID ON ASHCAN AVENUE—HE SAYS HE'S GLAD I WON THE CHAMPIONSHIP FIGHT AND WANTS MY PHOTOGRAPH!
WALT DISNEY
DID YOU HAVE A LETTER AMONG THIS BUNCH?
HOW WOULD YOU LIKE A PHOTO OF MICKEY?
WATCH FOR FURTHER DETAILS
5-18

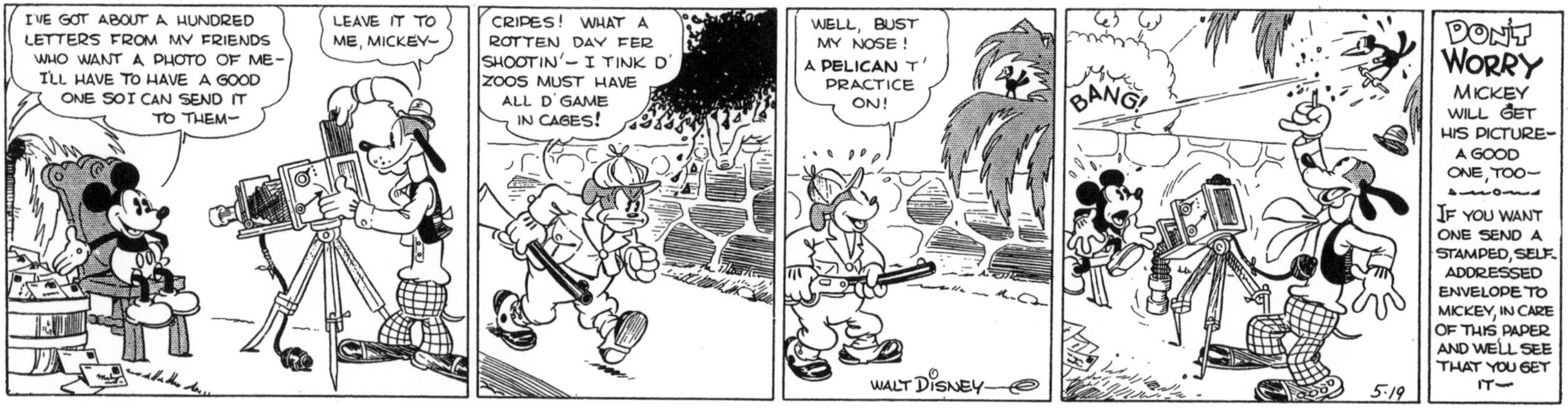
I'VE GOT ABOUT A HUNDRED LETTERS FROM MY FRIENDS WHO WANT A PHOTO OF ME—I'LL HAVE TO HAVE A GOOD ONE SO I CAN SEND IT TO THEM—
LEAVE IT TO ME, MICKEY—
CRIPES! WHAT A ROTTEN DAY FER SHOOTIN'—I TINK D' ZOOS MUST HAVE ALL D' GAME IN CAGES!
WELL, BUST MY NOSE! A PELICAN T' PRACTICE ON!
WALT DISNEY
BANG!
5·19
DON'T WORRY
MICKEY WILL GET HIS PICTURE—A GOOD ONE, TOO—
IF YOU WANT ONE SEND A STAMPED, SELF-ADDRESSED ENVELOPE TO MICKEY, IN CARE OF THIS PAPER AND WE'LL SEE THAT YOU GET IT—

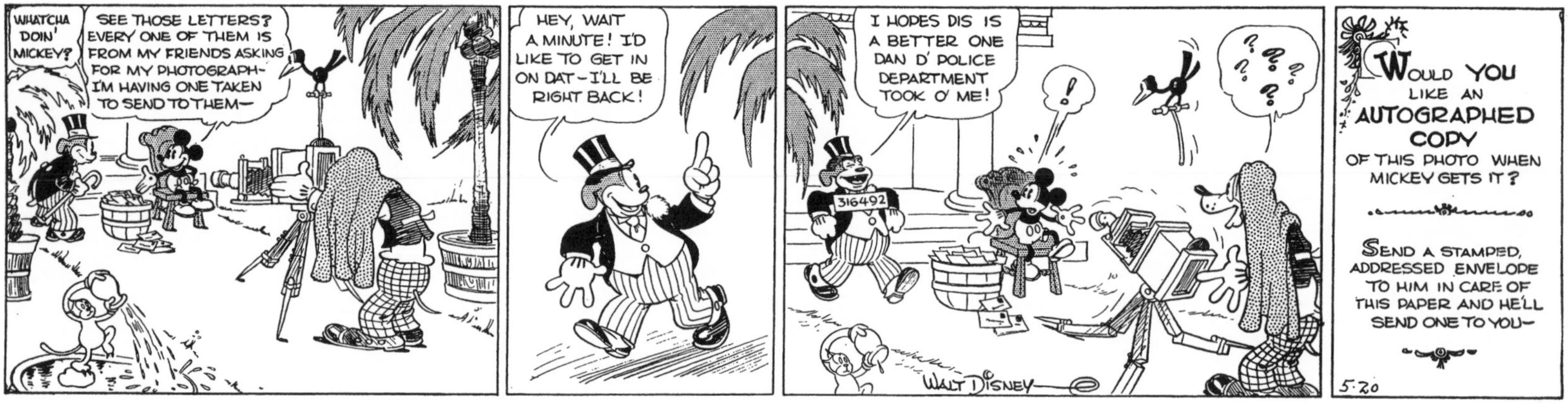
WHATCHA DOIN' MICKEY?
SEE THOSE LETTERS? EVERY ONE OF THEM IS FROM MY FRIENDS ASKING FOR MY PHOTOGRAPH—I'M HAVING ONE TAKEN TO SEND TO THEM—
HEY, WAIT A MINUTE! I'D LIKE TO GET IN ON DAT—I'LL BE RIGHT BACK!
I HOPES DIS IS A BETTER ONE DAN D' POLICE DEPARTMENT TOOK O' ME!
!
316492
WALT DISNEY
WOULD YOU LIKE AN AUTOGRAPHED COPY OF THIS PHOTO WHEN MICKEY GETS IT?
SEND A STAMPED, ADDRESSED ENVELOPE TO HIM IN CARE OF THIS PAPER AND HE'LL SEND ONE TO YOU—
5·20

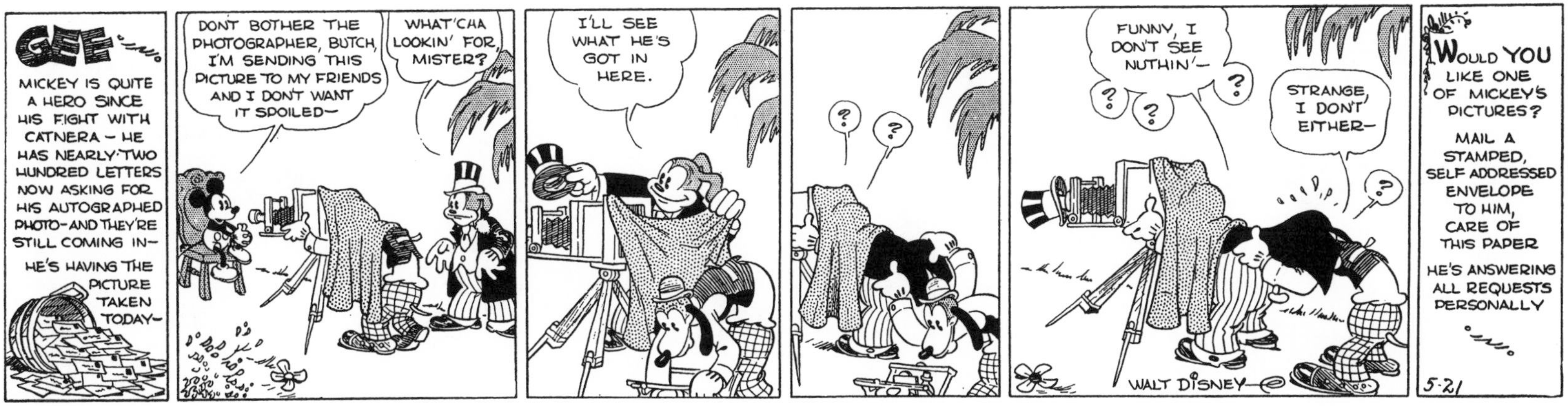
GEE
MICKEY IS QUITE A HERO SINCE HIS FIGHT WITH CATNERA – HE HAS NEARLY TWO HUNDRED LETTERS NOW ASKING FOR HIS AUTOGRAPHED PHOTO – AND THEY'RE STILL COMING IN–
HE'S HAVING THE PICTURE TAKEN TODAY–
DONT BOTHER THE PHOTOGRAPHER, BUTCH, I'M SENDING THIS PICTURE TO MY FRIENDS AND I DON'T WANT IT SPOILED–
WHAT'CHA LOOKIN' FOR, MISTER?
I'LL SEE WHAT HE'S GOT IN HERE.
?
?
FUNNY, I DON'T SEE NUTHIN'–
? ? ?
STRANGE, I DON'T EITHER–
?
WALT DISNEY
WOULD YOU LIKE ONE OF MICKEY'S PICTURES?
MAIL A STAMPED, SELF ADDRESSED ENVELOPE TO HIM, CARE OF THIS PAPER
HE'S ANSWERING ALL REQUESTS PERSONALLY
5·21

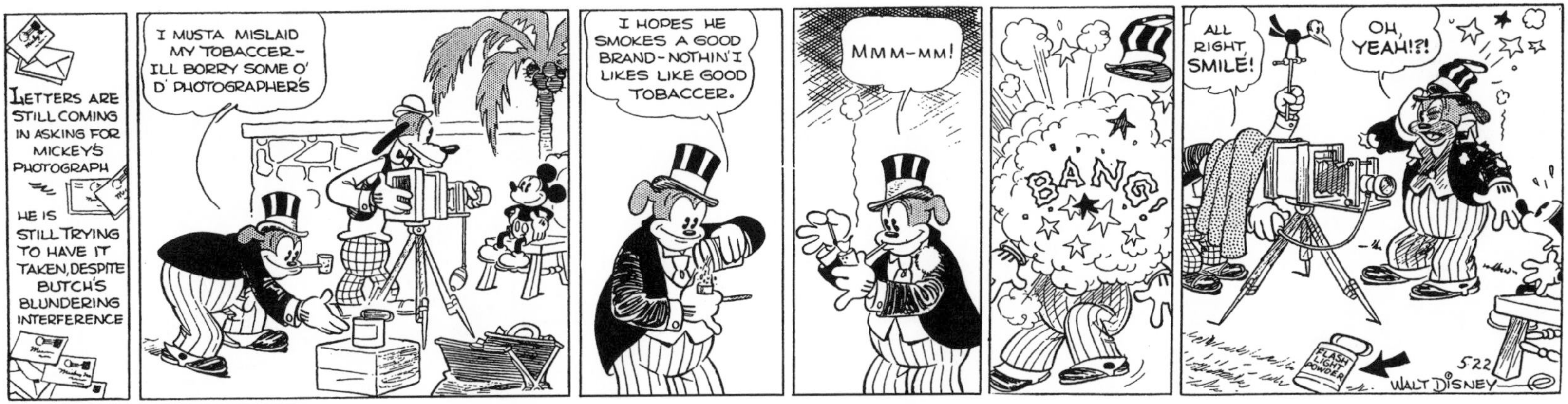
LETTERS ARE STILL COMING IN ASKING FOR MICKEY'S PHOTOGRAPH
HE IS STILL TRYING TO HAVE IT TAKEN, DESPITE BUTCH'S BLUNDERING INTERFERENCE
I MUSTA MISLAID MY TOBACCER– I'LL BORRY SOME O' D' PHOTOGRAPHER'S
I HOPES HE SMOKES A GOOD BRAND– NOTHIN' I LIKES LIKE GOOD TOBACCER.
MMM-MM!
BANG!
ALL RIGHT, SMILE!
OH, YEAH!?!
FLASH LIGHT POWDER
5·22
WALT DISNEY

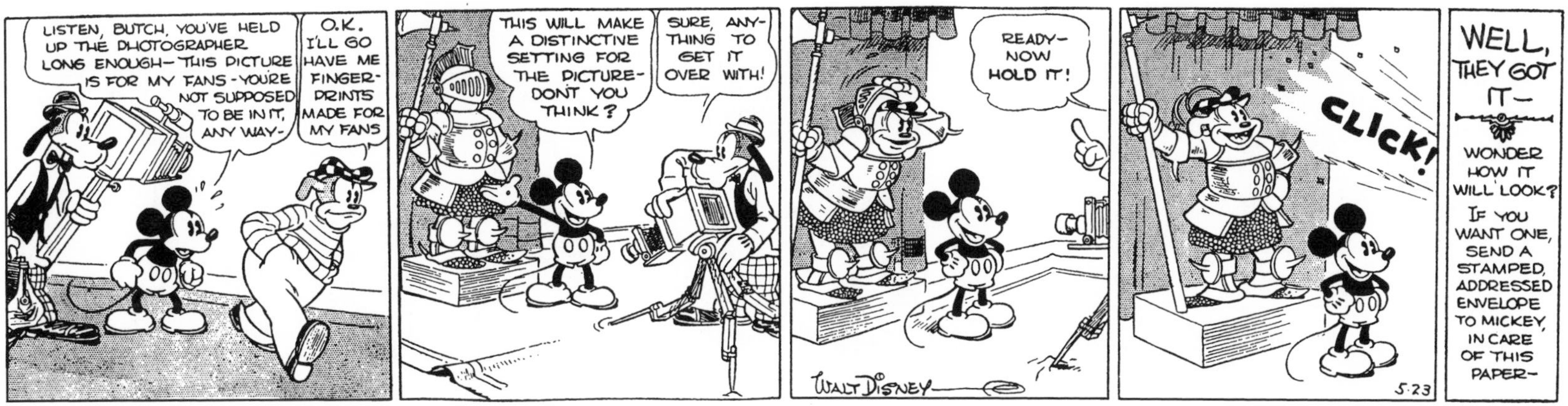
LISTEN, BUTCH, YOU'VE HELD UP THE PHOTOGRAPHER LONG ENOUGH– THIS PICTURE IS FOR MY FANS – YOU'RE NOT SUPPOSED TO BE IN IT, ANY WAY–
O.K. I'LL GO HAVE ME FINGER-PRINTS MADE FOR MY FANS
THIS WILL MAKE A DISTINCTIVE SETTING FOR THE PICTURE– DON'T YOU THINK?
SURE, ANY-THING TO GET IT OVER WITH!
READY– NOW HOLD IT!
WALT DISNEY
CLICK!
5·23
WELL, THEY GOT IT–
WONDER HOW IT WILL LOOK?
IF YOU WANT ONE, SEND A STAMPED, ADDRESSED ENVELOPE TO MICKEY, IN CARE OF THIS PAPER–

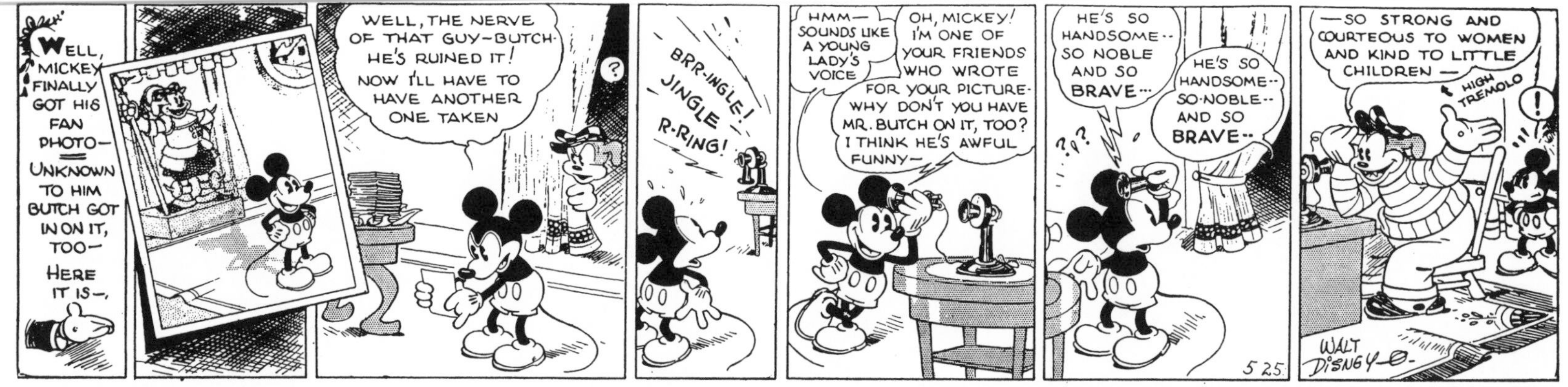
WELL, MICKEY FINALLY GOT HIS FAN PHOTO— UNKNOWN TO HIM BUTCH GOT IN ON IT, TOO— HERE IT IS—,
WELL, THE NERVE OF THAT GUY—BUTCH— HE'S RUINED IT! NOW I'LL HAVE TO HAVE ANOTHER ONE TAKEN
?
BRR-INGLE! JINGLE R-RING!
HMM— SOUNDS LIKE A YOUNG LADY'S VOICE
OH, MICKEY! I'M ONE OF YOUR FRIENDS WHO WROTE FOR YOUR PICTURE. WHY DON'T YOU HAVE MR. BUTCH ON IT, TOO? I THINK HE'S AWFUL FUNNY—
HE'S SO HANDSOME-- SO NOBLE AND SO BRAVE...
HE'S SO HANDSOME-- SO NOBLE-- AND SO BRAVE--
—SO STRONG AND COURTEOUS TO WOMEN AND KIND TO LITTLE CHILDREN —
HIGH TREMOLO
!
5 25
WALT DISNEY

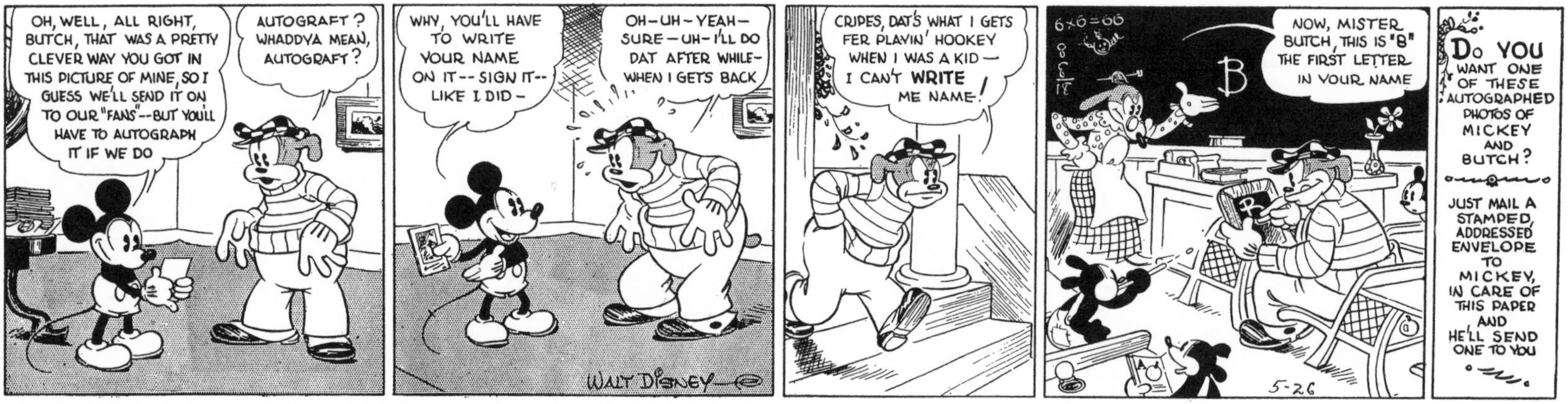
OH, WELL, ALL RIGHT, BUTCH, THAT WAS A PRETTY CLEVER WAY YOU GOT IN THIS PICTURE OF MINE, SO I GUESS WE'LL SEND IT ON TO OUR "FANS"--BUT YOU'LL HAVE TO AUTOGRAPH IT IF WE DO
AUTOGRAFT? WHADDYA MEAN, AUTOGRAFT?
WHY, YOU'LL HAVE TO WRITE YOUR NAME ON IT-- SIGN IT-- LIKE I DID—
OH—UH—YEAH— SURE—UH—I'LL DO DAT AFTER WHILE— WHEN I GETS BACK
WALT DISNEY
CRIPES, DAT'S WHAT I GETS FER PLAYIN' HOOKEY WHEN I WAS A KID— I CAN'T WRITE ME NAME!
6×6=66
NOW, MISTER BUTCH, THIS IS "B" THE FIRST LETTER IN YOUR NAME
B
5-26
DO YOU WANT ONE OF THESE AUTOGRAPHED PHOTOS OF MICKEY AND BUTCH?
JUST MAIL A STAMPED, ADDRESSED ENVELOPE TO MICKEY, IN CARE OF THIS PAPER AND HE'LL SEND ONE TO YOU

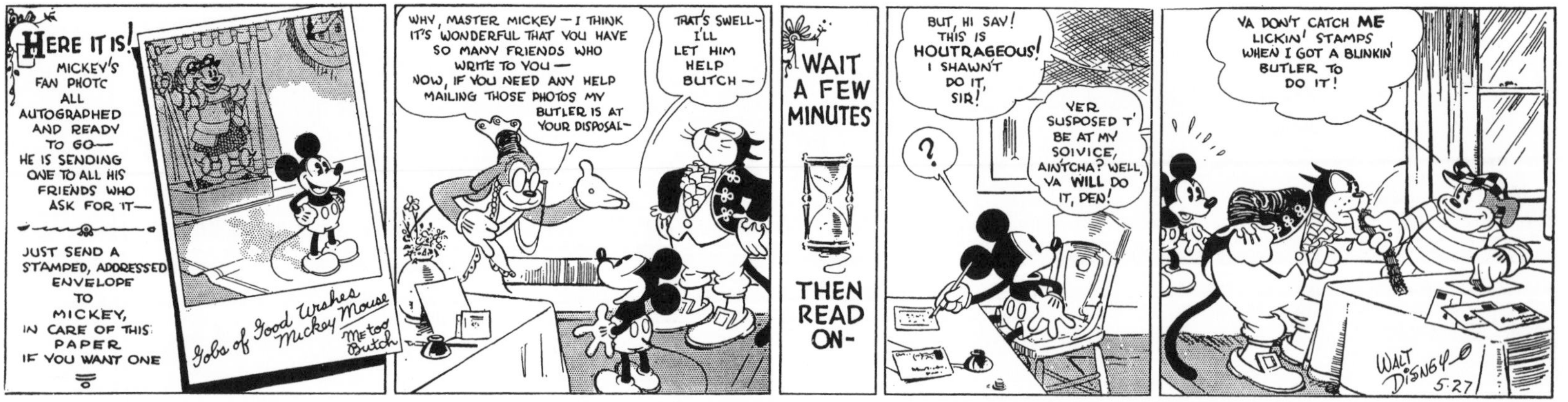
HERE IT IS! MICKEY'S FAN PHOTO ALL AUTOGRAPHED AND READY TO GO— HE IS SENDING ONE TO ALL HIS FRIENDS WHO ASK FOR IT—
JUST SEND A STAMPED, ADDRESSED ENVELOPE TO MICKEY, IN CARE OF THIS PAPER IF YOU WANT ONE
Gobs of Good Wishes Mickey Mouse
Me too Butch
WHY, MASTER MICKEY—I THINK IT'S WONDERFUL THAT YOU HAVE SO MANY FRIENDS WHO WRITE TO YOU— NOW, IF YOU NEED ANY HELP MAILING THOSE PHOTOS MY BUTLER IS AT YOUR DISPOSAL—
THAT'S SWELL— I'LL LET HIM HELP BUTCH—
WAIT A FEW MINUTES
THEN READ ON—
BUT, HI SAY! THIS IS HOUTRAGEOUS! I SHAWN'T DO IT, SIR!
?
YER SUPPOSED T' BE AT MY SOIVICE, AIN'TCHA? WELL, YA WILL DO IT, DEN!
YA DON'T CATCH ME LICKIN' STAMPS WHEN I GOT A BLINKIN' BUTLER TO DO IT!
WALT DISNEY
5-27

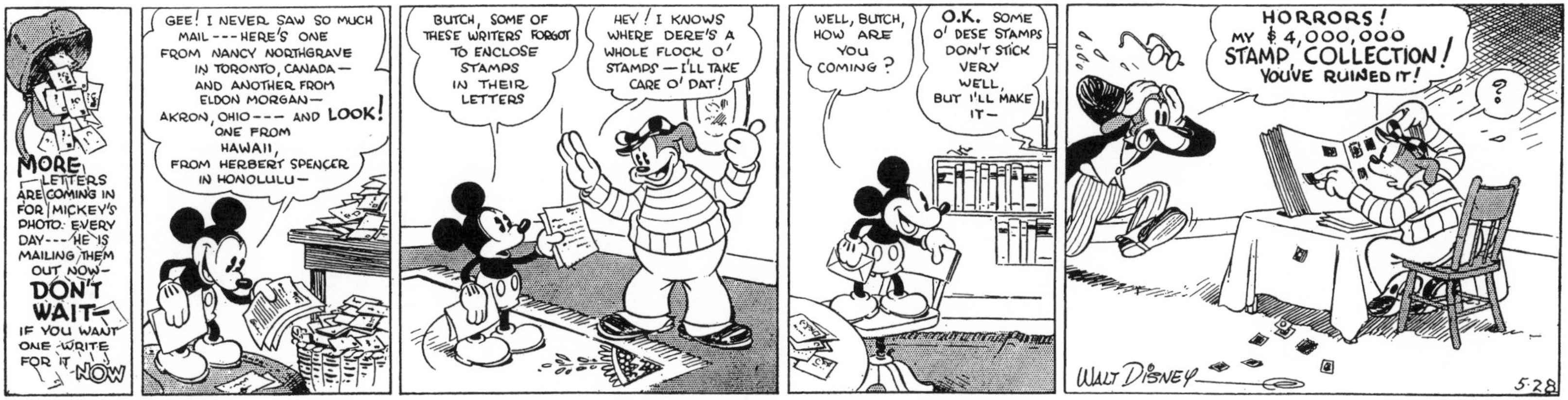
MORE LETTERS ARE COMING IN FOR MICKEY'S PHOTO. EVERY DAY--- HE IS MAILING THEM OUT NOW- DON'T WAIT- IF YOU WANT ONE WRITE FOR IT NOW
GEE! I NEVER SAW SO MUCH MAIL---HERE'S ONE FROM NANCY NORTHGRAVE IN TORONTO, CANADA— AND ANOTHER FROM ELDON MORGAN— AKRON, OHIO--- AND LOOK! ONE FROM HAWAII, FROM HERBERT SPENCER IN HONOLULU—
BUTCH, SOME OF THESE WRITERS FORGOT TO ENCLOSE STAMPS IN THEIR LETTERS
HEY! I KNOWS WHERE DERE'S A WHOLE FLOCK O' STAMPS—I'LL TAKE CARE O' DAT!
WELL, BUTCH, HOW ARE YOU COMING?
O.K. SOME O' DESE STAMPS DON'T STICK VERY WELL, BUT I'LL MAKE IT—
HORRORS! MY $ 4,000,000 STAMP COLLECTION! YOU'VE RUINED IT!
?
WALT DISNEY
5-28

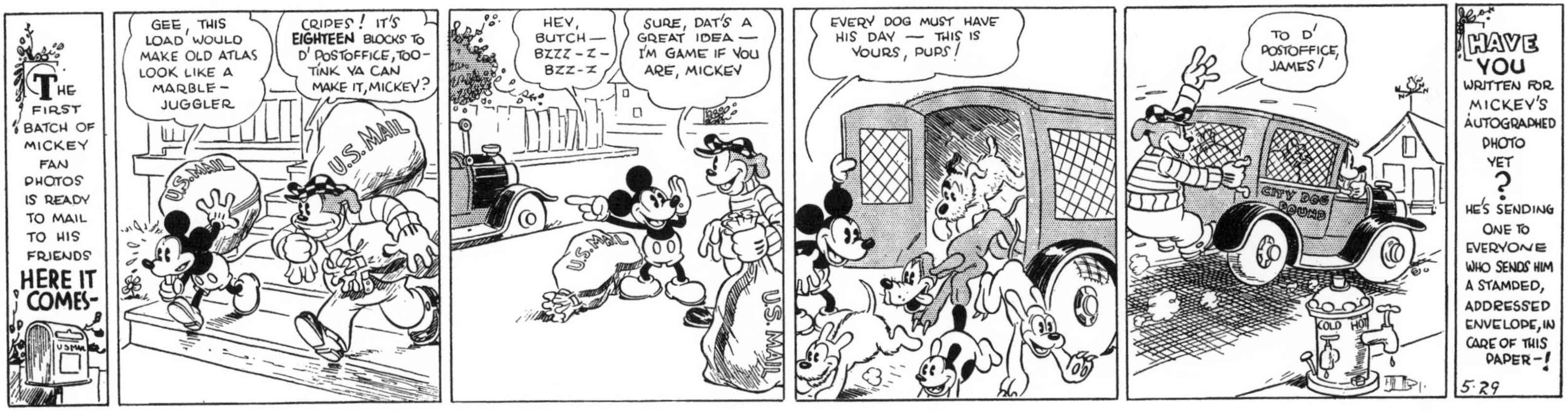
THE FIRST BATCH OF MICKEY FAN PHOTOS IS READY TO MAIL TO HIS FRIENDS' HERE IT COMES-
GEE, THIS LOAD WOULD MAKE OLD ATLAS LOOK LIKE A MARBLE-JUGGLER
CRIPES! IT'S EIGHTEEN BLOCKS TO D' POSTOFFICE, TOO-TINK YA CAN MAKE IT, MICKEY?
U.S. MAIL
HEY, BUTCH— BZZZ-Z— BZZ-Z
SURE, DAT'S A GREAT IDEA— I'M GAME IF YOU ARE, MICKEY
EVERY DOG MUST HAVE HIS DAY — THIS IS YOURS, PUPS!
TO D' POSTOFFICE, JAMES!
CITY DOG POUND
COLD HOT
HAVE YOU WRITTEN FOR MICKEY'S AUTOGRAPHED PHOTO YET? HE'S SENDING ONE TO EVERYONE WHO SENDS HIM A STAMPED, ADDRESSED ENVELOPE, IN CARE OF THIS PAPER-!
5-29

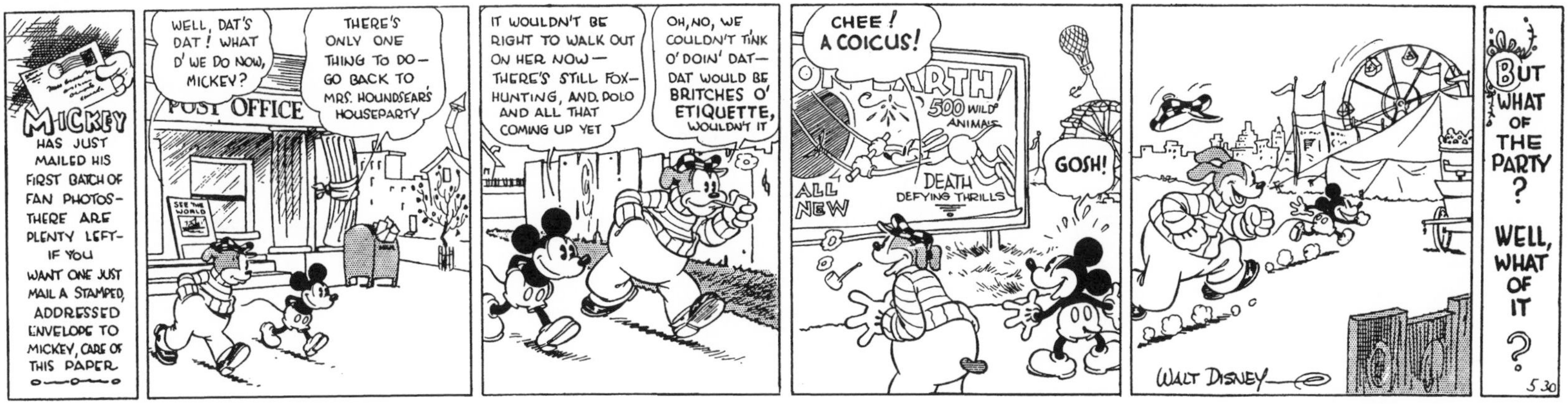
MICKEY HAS JUST MAILED HIS FIRST BATCH OF FAN PHOTOS- THERE ARE PLENTY LEFT- IF YOU WANT ONE JUST MAIL A STAMPED, ADDRESSED ENVELOPE TO MICKEY, CARE OF THIS PAPER
WELL, DAT'S DAT! WHAT D' WE DO NOW, MICKEY?
THERE'S ONLY ONE THING TO DO- GO BACK TO MRS. HOUNDSEAR'S HOUSEPARTY
POST OFFICE
SEE THE WORLD
IT WOULDN'T BE RIGHT TO WALK OUT ON HER NOW— THERE'S STILL FOX-HUNTING, AND POLO AND ALL THAT COMING UP YET
OH, NO, WE COULDN'T TINK O' DOIN' DAT- DAT WOULD BE BRITCHES O' ETIQUETTE, WOULDN'T IT
CHEE! A COICUS!
500 WILD ANIMALS
DEATH DEFYING THRILLS
ALL NEW
GOSH!
WALT DISNEY
BUT WHAT OF THE PARTY? WELL, WHAT OF IT?
5-30

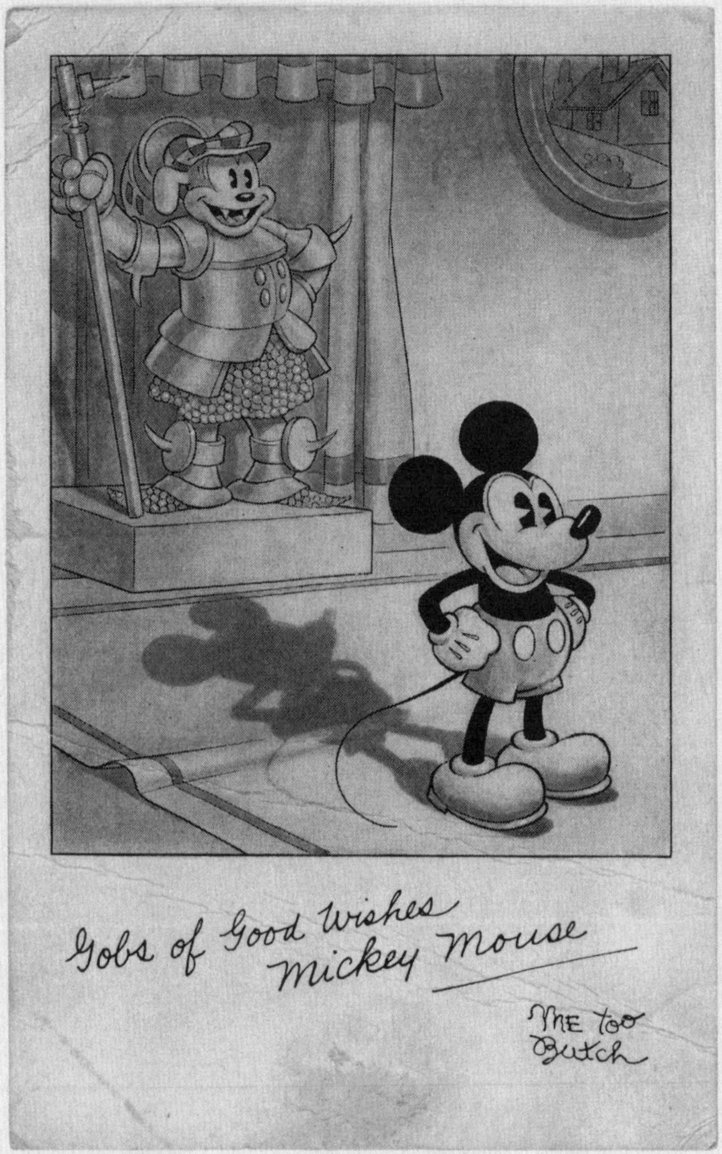
Gobs of Good Wishes
Mickey Mouse
Me too
Butch

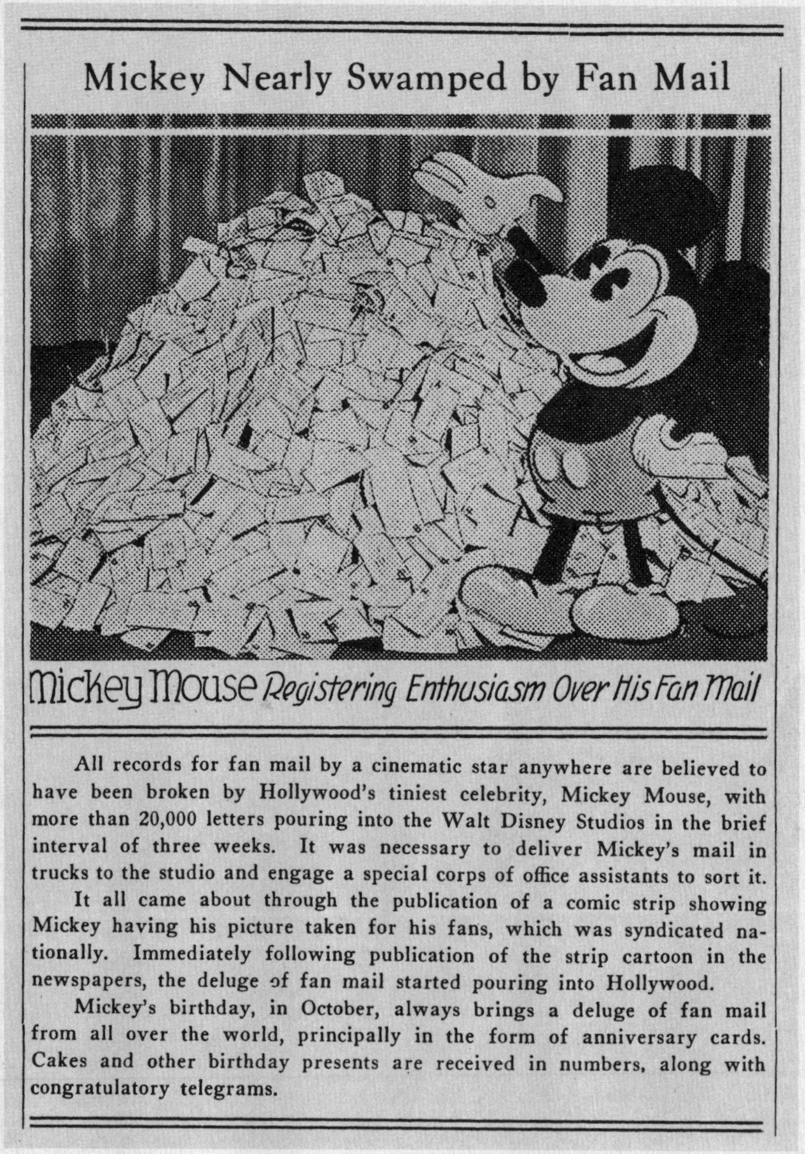

Mickey Nearly Swamped by Fan Mail

Mickey Mouse *Registering Enthusiasm Over His Fan Mail*

All records for fan mail by a cinematic star anywhere are believed to have been broken by Hollywood's tiniest celebrity, Mickey Mouse, with more than 20,000 letters pouring into the Walt Disney Studios in the brief interval of three weeks. It was necessary to deliver Mickey's mail in trucks to the studio and engage a special corps of office assistants to sort it.

It all came about through the publication of a comic strip showing Mickey having his picture taken for his fans, which was syndicated nationally. Immediately following publication of the strip cartoon in the newspapers, the deluge of fan mail started pouring into Hollywood.

Mickey's birthday, in October, always brings a deluge of fan mail from all over the world, principally in the form of anniversary cards. Cakes and other birthday presents are received in numbers, along with congratulatory telegrams.

LEFT: Gottfredson's giveaway "photo" of Mickey and Butch, 1931. Image courtesy Hake's Americana.

RIGHT: Disney/United Artists press release, 1932. Image courtesy Hake's Americana.

CIRCUS ROUSTABOUT
—AND—
PLUTO THE PUP

JUNE 1, 1931
–
JULY 18, 1931

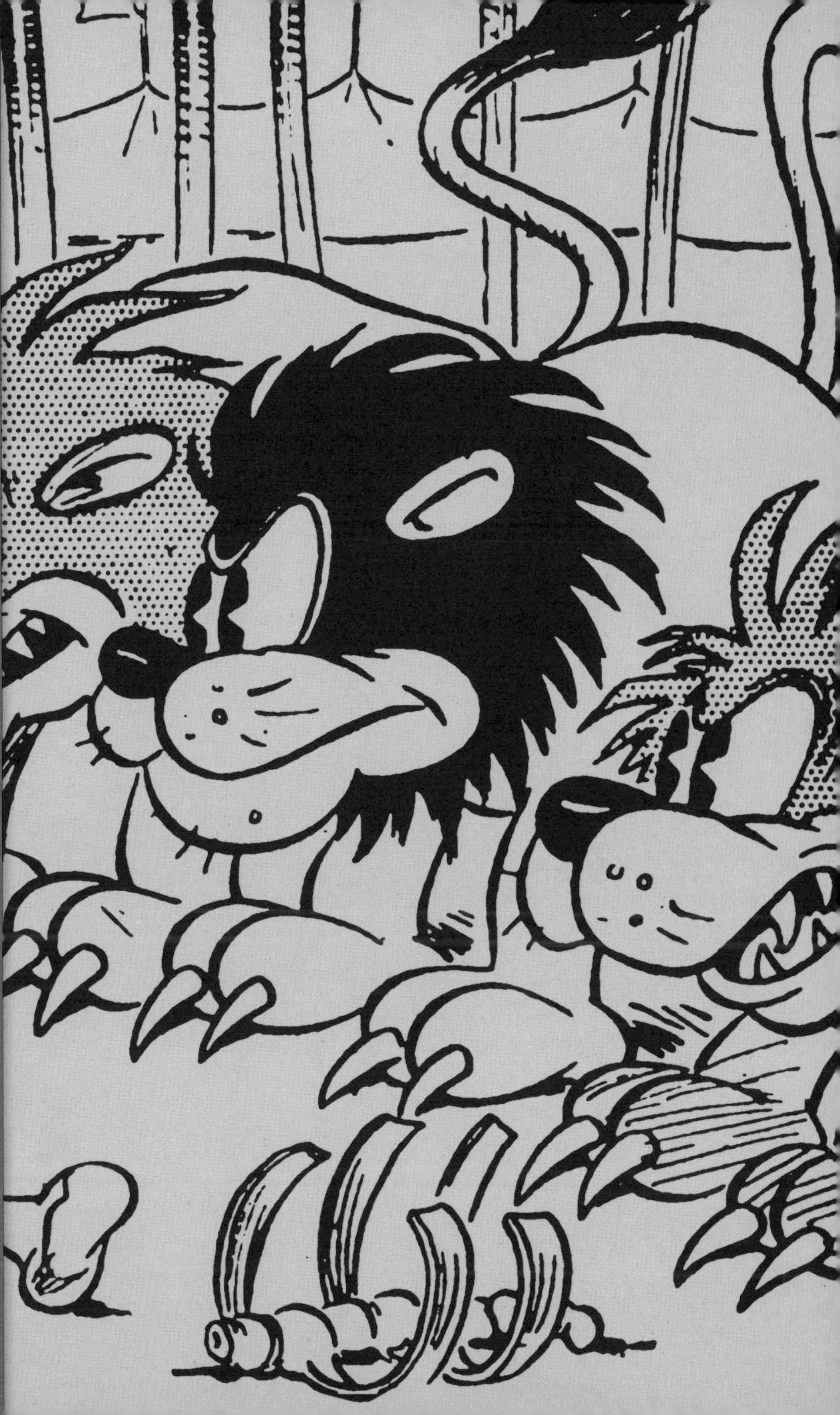

MICKEY MOUSE

REGISTERED U.S. PATENT OFFICE

MICK OF ALL TRADES

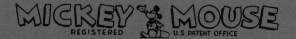

The "new job" plotline is a basic building block of comedy. Hero takes job. Hero has problems on job. Hero's problems build to comic crisis—or hero rises up from pratfalls to accomplish something more important. On the surface, "something more important" is often a crisis scenario that the hero must defuse. But "something" can also be a complex emotional arc for which the job provides the setting. This was the case in Charlie Chaplin's classic film *The Circus* (1928)—and so it seems to be, initially, in "Circus Roustabout," the first "job" story for Mickey Mouse.

On some level, the early Mickey himself was a kind of Chaplin figure. While not a societal outcast like Chaplin's Little Tramp, Gottfredson's Mouse shared the early Charlie's mischievous impulses and iconoclast stance. This made "job" stories especially fitting, not least because Mickey—like Charlie—could easily acquire a troublemaking reputation in a new-job environment. He might then need to prove his actual worth by impressing a skeptical workplace authority figure—or by defeating a bombastic, unlikeable one. In their circus job-stories, Mickey and Charlie do both.[1]

This is not to say that the two icons behaved identically. In a Chaplin film, the plot could be tragic as well as comic. In *The Circus*, we laugh as monkeys knock Charlie about; but we empathize when circumstances force the regretful Tramp to decline a female workmate's affection. In "Circus Roustabout," by contrast, the closest thing to an emotional investment is casually discarded; taken just as lightly as its surrounding work-gags. Gottfredson's job-story is just a job.

If anything, Mickey in 1931 bears more similarity to the Tramp of Charlie's 1910s films—a younger, naughtier figure—than to the contemporary, deeper Chaplin persona; this, perhaps, is the biggest difference between one workplace scenario and another. Of course, time would deepen Gottfredson's Mouse as well. Years later, in 1937's "Monarch of Medioka," a job-story could give Mickey the most difficult job of all—king!—and freely let it lead him into a multi-layered, exhausting personality crisis.

In 1931, our Mouse was still closer to an earlier school of comedy—and, apart from Chaplin, to his Disney predecessor Oswald the Lucky Rabbit, whose cat girlfriend anticipated Mlle. Maltese of "Circus Roustabout." [DG]

1 We won't give away the ending of Gottfredson's story here; suffice it to say that Mickey deals with both types of authority figures, while Charlie faces a single authority—Al the ringmaster—who incorporates both roles.

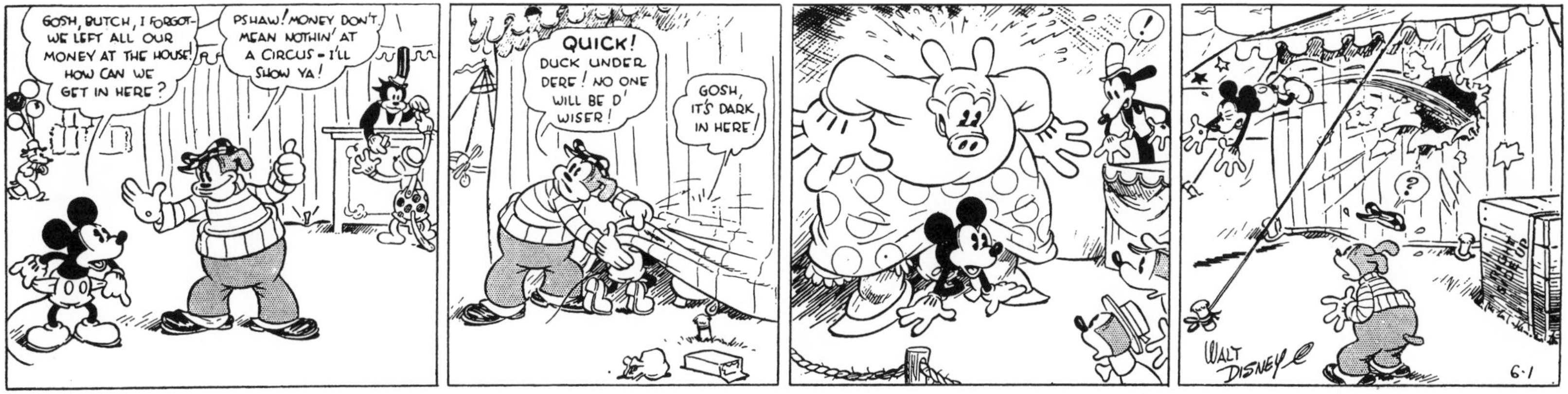

GOSH, BUTCH, I FORGOT- WE LEFT ALL OUR MONEY AT THE HOUSE! HOW CAN WE GET IN HERE?
PSHAW! MONEY DON'T MEAN NOTHIN' AT A CIRCUS — I'LL SHOW YA!
QUICK! DUCK UNDER DERE! NO ONE WILL BE D' WISER!
GOSH, IT'S DARK IN HERE!
!
?
WALT DISNEY
6·1

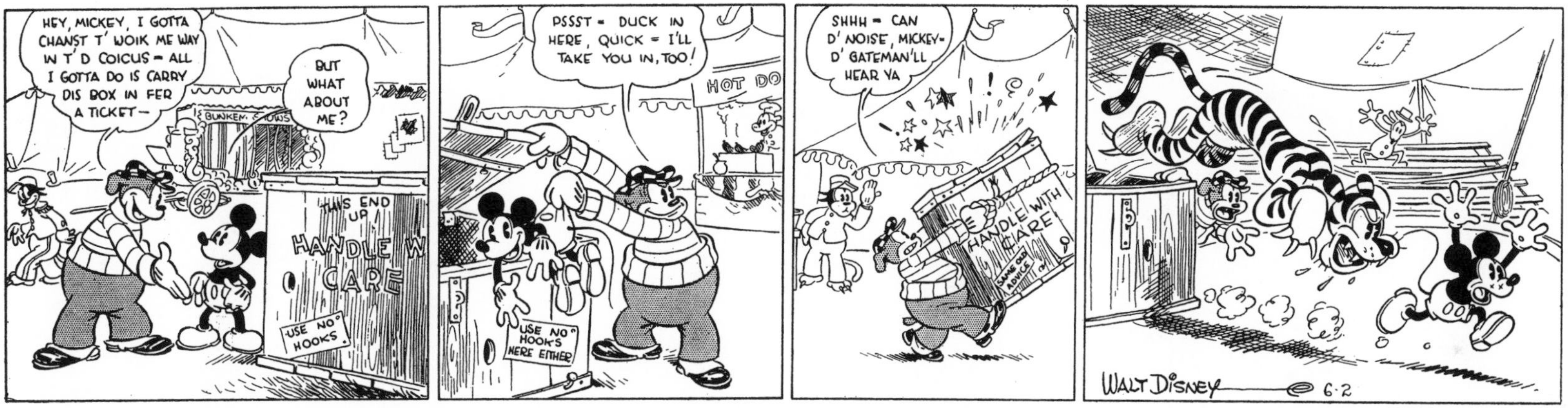

HEY, MICKEY, I GOTTA CHANST T' WOIK ME WAY IN T' D COICUS — ALL I GOTTA DO IS CARRY DIS BOX IN FER A TICKET—
BUT WHAT ABOUT ME?
BUNKEM SHOWS
THIS END UP
HANDLE W CARE
USE NO HOOKS
PSSST — DUCK IN HERE, QUICK — I'LL TAKE YOU IN, TOO!
HOT DO
USE NO HOOKS HERE EITHER
SHHH — CAN D' NOISE, MICKEY — D' GATEMAN'LL HEAR YA
HANDLE WITH CARE
WALT DISNEY
6·2

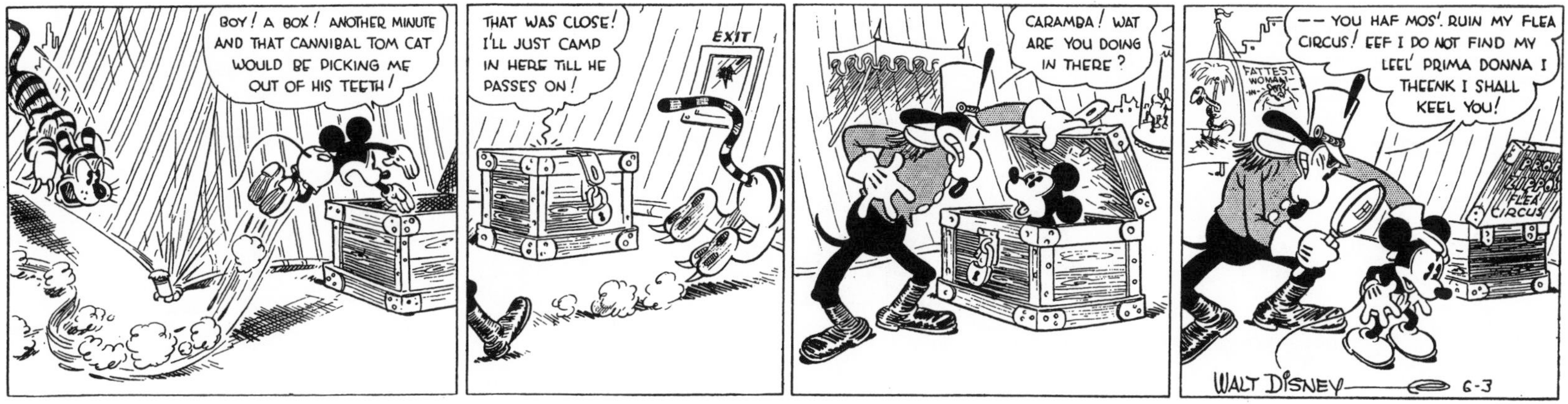

BOY! A BOX! ANOTHER MINUTE AND THAT CANNIBAL TOM CAT WOULD BE PICKING ME OUT OF HIS TEETH!
THAT WAS CLOSE! I'LL JUST CAMP IN HERE TILL HE PASSES ON!
EXIT
CARAMBA! WAT ARE YOU DOING IN THERE?
—— YOU HAF MOS'. RUIN MY FLEA CIRCUS! EEF I DO NOT FIND MY LEEL' PRIMA DONNA I THEENK I SHALL KEEL YOU!
FATTEST WOMAN
FLEA CIRCUS
WALT DISNEY
6-3

SAY! YOU'VE MADE A REGULAR NUISANCE OF YOURSELF AROUND HERE = I GUESS THE BEST WAY TO GET RID OF YOU IS TO GIVE YOU A JOB!
GOSH = SWELL! I'VE ALWAYS WANTED TO WORK FOR A CIRCUS!
I'VE GOT JUST THE JOB FOR A LITTLE RUNT LIKE YOU = COME ON OVER HERE!
RIGHT INSIDE = THEY'LL TAKE CARE OF YOU IN THERE!
GEE! THANKS A MILLION!
SLAM!
WALT DISNEY
6·4

WHAT A DIRTY TRICK THAT CIRCUS MANAGER PLAYED ON ME = LOCKING ME IN THIS LION CAGE!
© By Walter E. Disney, Great Britain rights reserved
HEY, BUTCH! GIVE ME THAT PAPER, QUICK!
?
MUSTARD
?
THERE = LOOK AT THAT!
!
MICKEY MOUSE SOCIAL LION!
MEETINGS EVERY SO OFTEN
CHEESE
6·5
WALT DISNEY

WE'RE IN A HECK OF A PICKLE! OUR ZEBRA HAS GONE A·W·O·L AND HE'S DUE FOR A PERFORMANCE IN AN HOUR = GRAB THIS PAINT AND GO STRIPE UP THAT MULE OVER THERE!
WORLD'S FINEST "MULE-STRIPERS!" THAT'S US, EH, BUTCH?
WELL, I'VE FINISHED, BUTCH = WHAT ABOUT YOU?
ME, TOO = COME AN' TAKE A SQUINT AT IT!
WALT DISNEY
6·6

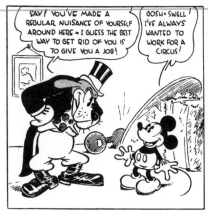

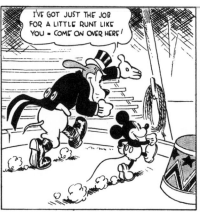

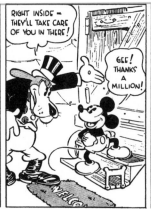

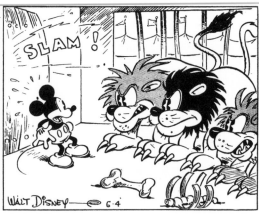

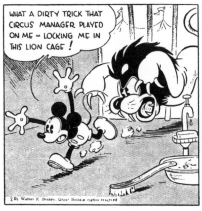

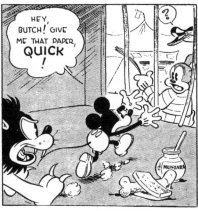

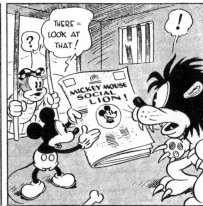

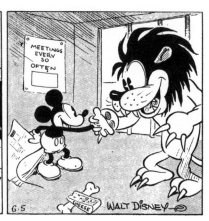

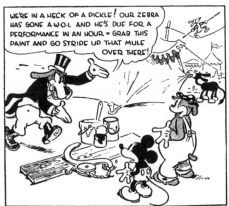

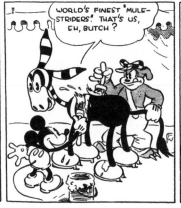

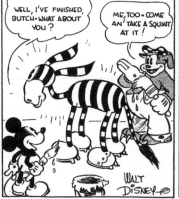

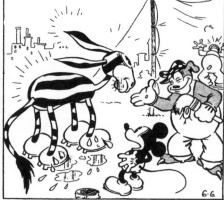

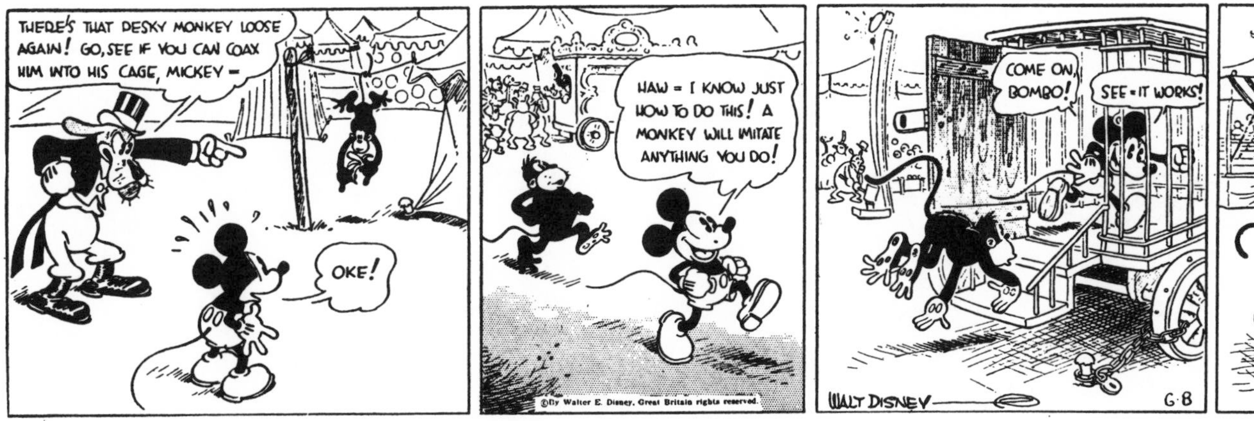
THERE'S THAT PESKY MONKEY LOOSE AGAIN! GO, SEE IF YOU CAN COAX HIM INTO HIS CAGE, MICKEY —
OKE!
HAW = I KNOW JUST HOW TO DO THIS! A MONKEY WILL IMITATE ANYTHING YOU DO!
©By Walter E. Disney. Great Britain rights reserved.
COME ON, BOMBO!
SEE = IT WORKS!
WALT DISNEY
6-8
SLAM!
BOM

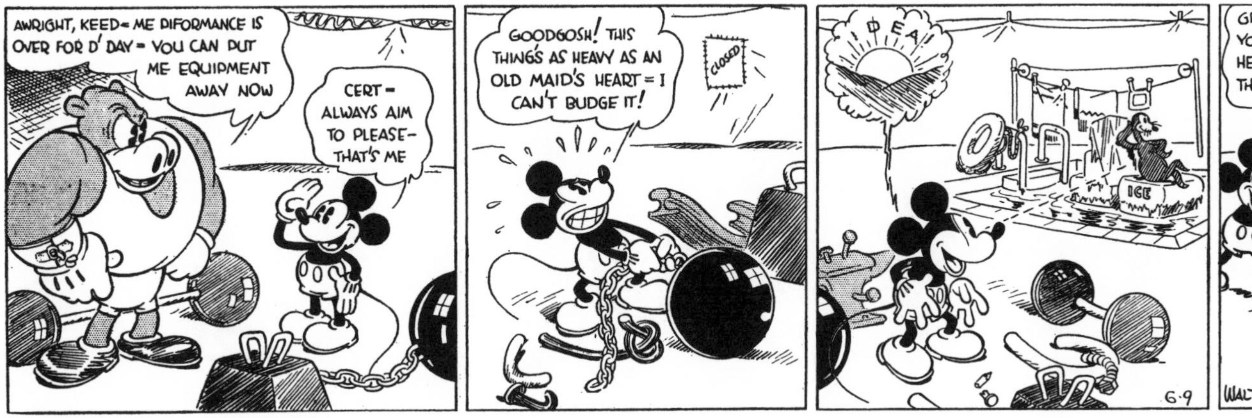
AWRIGHT, KEED = ME PERFORMANCE IS OVER FOR D' DAY = YOU CAN PUT ME EQUIPMENT AWAY NOW
CERT = ALWAYS AIM TO PLEASE — THAT'S ME
GOODGOSH! THIS THING'S AS HEAVY AS AN OLD MAID'S HEART = I CAN'T BUDGE IT!
CLOSED
IDEA!
ICE
6-9
GREAT WORK, ABIE — YOU'LL GET A NICE HERRING FOR THIS!
KEEP OUT
WALT DISNEY

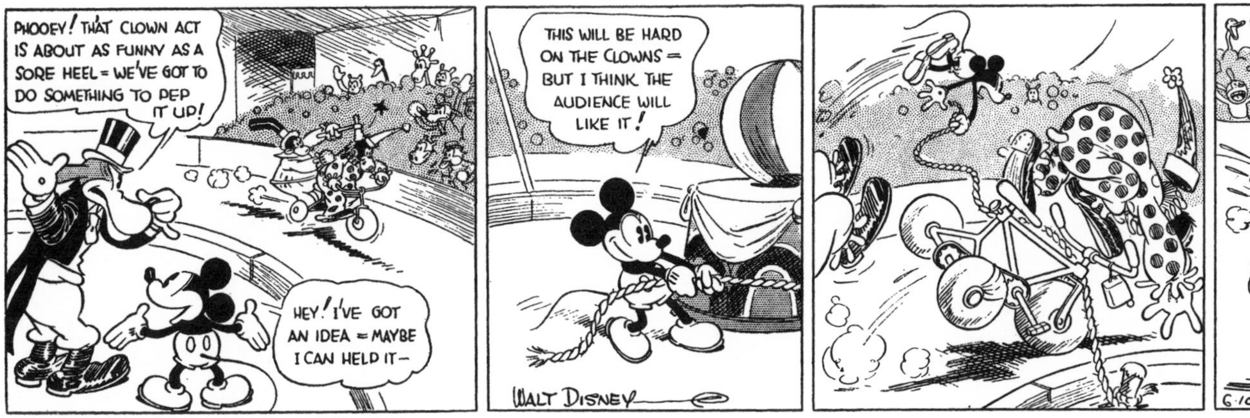
PHOOEY! THAT CLOWN ACT IS ABOUT AS FUNNY AS A SORE HEEL = WE'VE GOT TO DO SOMETHING TO PEP IT UP!
HEY! I'VE GOT AN IDEA = MAYBE I CAN HELP IT —
THIS WILL BE HARD ON THE CLOWNS = BUT I THINK THE AUDIENCE WILL LIKE IT!
WALT DISNEY
6-10

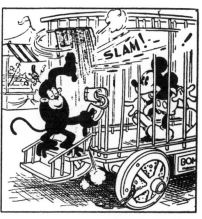

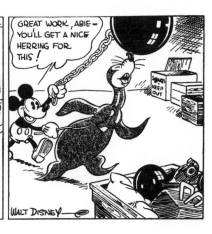

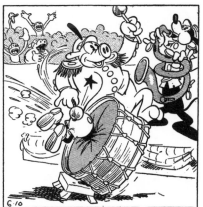

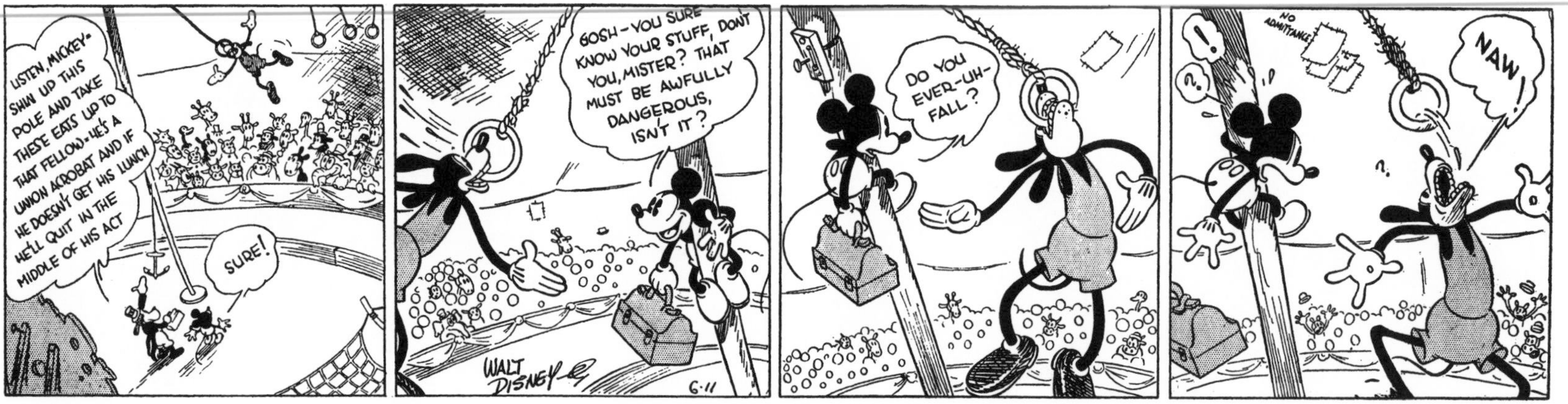
LISTEN, MICKEY- SHIN UP THIS POLE AND TAKE THESE EATS UP TO THAT FELLOW- HE'S A UNION ACROBAT AND IF HE DOESN'T GET HIS LUNCH HE'LL QUIT IN THE MIDDLE OF HIS ACT
SURE!
GOSH- YOU SURE KNOW YOUR STUFF, DON'T YOU, MISTER? THAT MUST BE AWFULLY DANGEROUS, ISN'T IT?
WALT DISNEY
6-11
DO YOU EVER-UH-FALL?
NO ADMITTANCE
!
?
NAW!

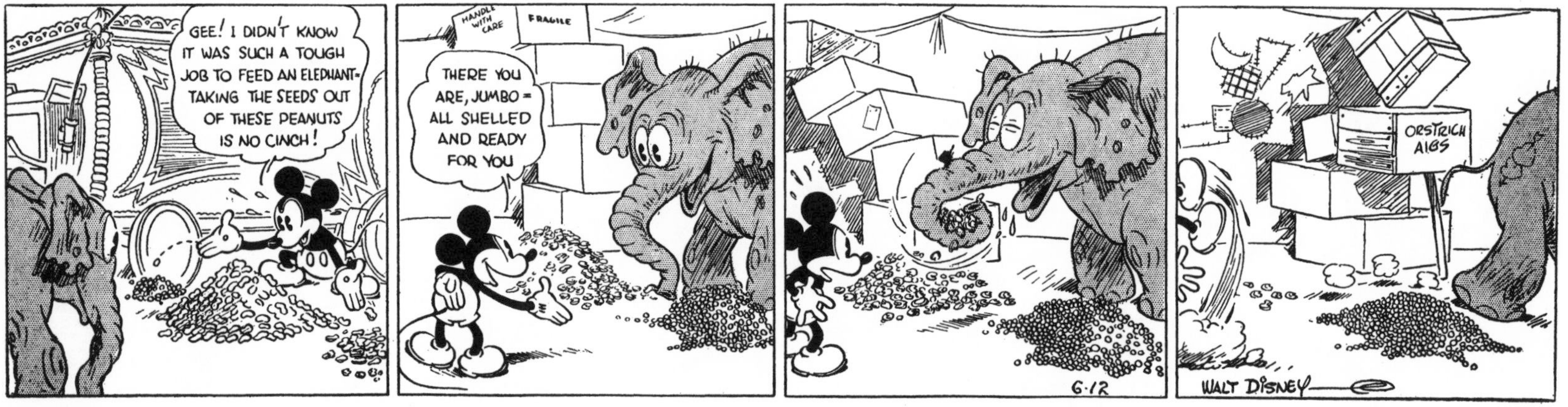
GEE! I DIDN'T KNOW IT WAS SUCH A TOUGH JOB TO FEED AN ELEPHANT- TAKING THE SEEDS OUT OF THESE PEANUTS IS NO CINCH!
HANDLE WITH CARE
FRAGILE
THERE YOU ARE, JUMBO= ALL SHELLED AND READY FOR YOU
6-12
ORSTRICH AIGS
WALT DISNEY

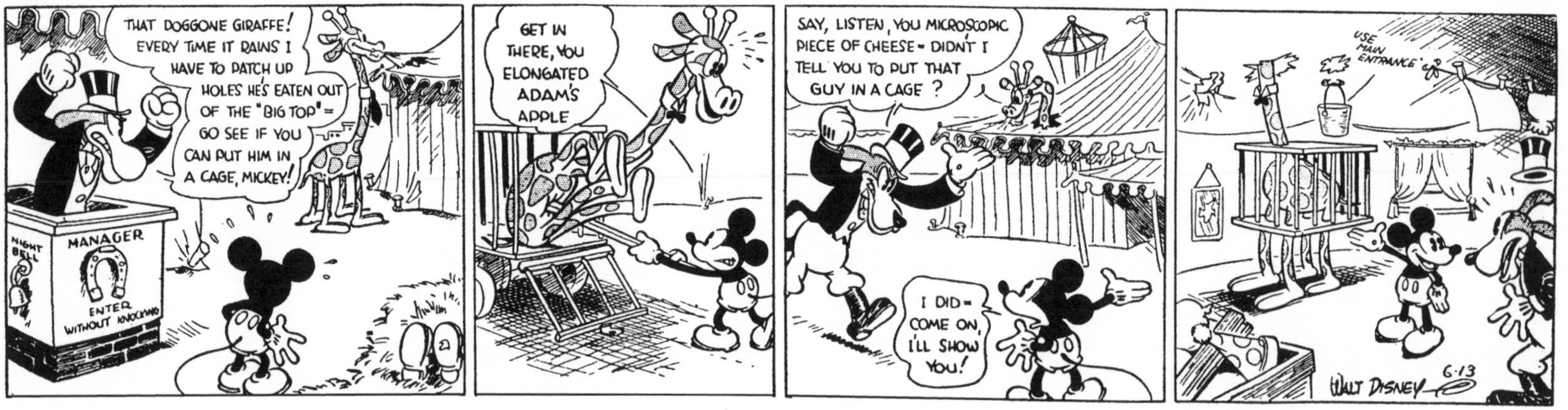
THAT DOGGONE GIRAFFE! EVERY TIME IT RAINS I HAVE TO PATCH UP HOLES HE'S EATEN OUT OF THE "BIG TOP"= GO SEE IF YOU CAN PUT HIM IN A CAGE, MICKEY!
NIGHT BELL
MANAGER
ENTER WITHOUT KNOCKING
GET IN THERE, YOU ELONGATED ADAM'S APPLE
SAY, LISTEN, YOU MICROSCOPIC PIECE OF CHEESE= DIDN'T I TELL YOU TO PUT THAT GUY IN A CAGE?
I DID= COME ON, I'LL SHOW YOU!
USE MAIN ENTRANCE
WALT DISNEY
6-13

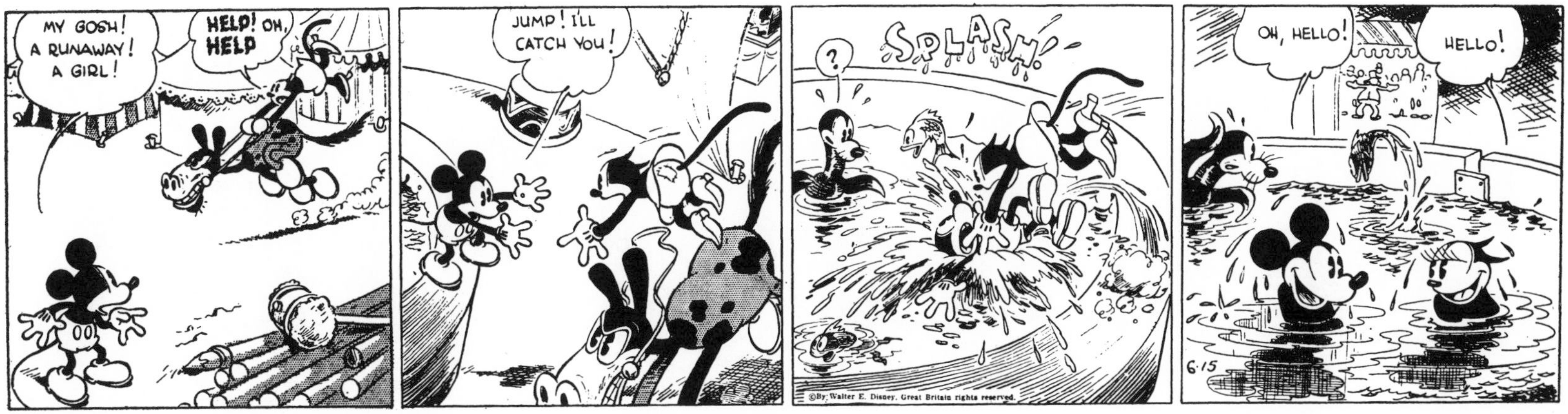
MY GOSH! A RUNAWAY! A GIRL!
HELP! OH, HELP
JUMP! I'LL CATCH YOU!
?
SPLASH!
©By Walter E. Disney, Great Britain rights reserved.
OH, HELLO!
HELLO!
6·15

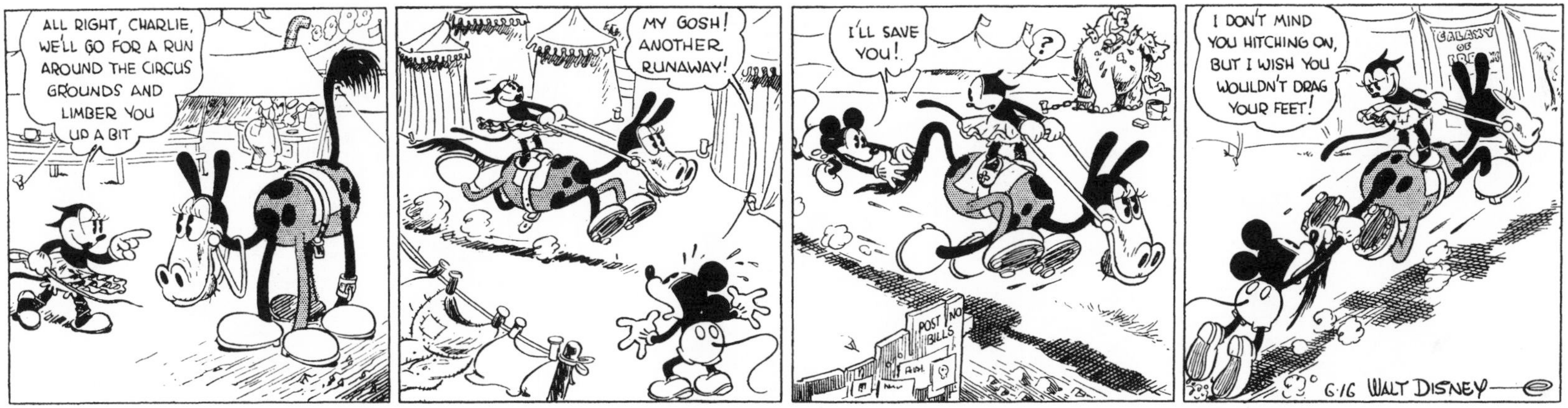
ALL RIGHT, CHARLIE, WE'LL GO FOR A RUN AROUND THE CIRCUS GROUNDS AND LIMBER YOU UP A BIT
MY GOSH! ANOTHER RUNAWAY!
I'LL SAVE YOU!
?
POST NO BILLS
I DON'T MIND YOU HITCHING ON, BUT I WISH YOU WOULDN'T DRAG YOUR FEET!
6·16 WALT DISNEY

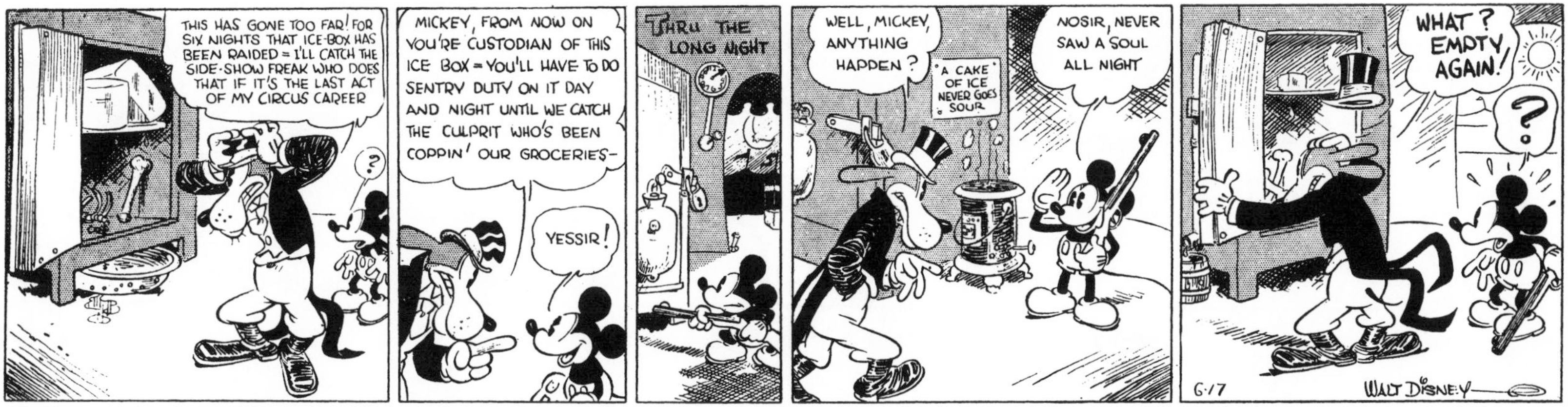
THIS HAS GONE TOO FAR! FOR SIX NIGHTS THAT ICE-BOX HAS BEEN RAIDED = I'LL CATCH THE SIDE-SHOW FREAK WHO DOES THAT IF IT'S THE LAST ACT OF MY CIRCUS CAREER
?
MICKEY, FROM NOW ON YOU'RE CUSTODIAN OF THIS ICE BOX = YOU'LL HAVE TO DO SENTRY DUTY ON IT DAY AND NIGHT UNTIL WE CATCH THE CULPRIT WHO'S BEEN COPPIN' OUR GROCERIES-
YESSIR!
THRU THE LONG NIGHT
WELL, MICKEY, ANYTHING HAPPEN?
A CAKE OF ICE NEVER GOES SOUR
NOSIR, NEVER SAW A SOUL ALL NIGHT
WHAT? EMPTY AGAIN!
?
6·17
WALT DISNEY

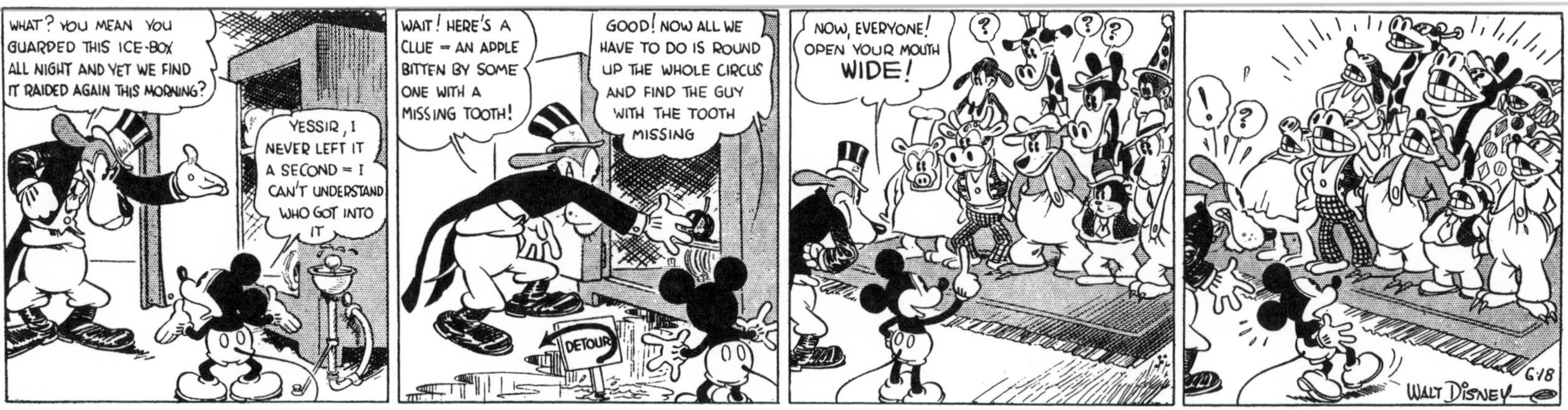
WHAT? YOU MEAN YOU GUARDED THIS ICE-BOX ALL NIGHT AND YET WE FIND IT RAIDED AGAIN THIS MORNING?
YESSIR, I NEVER LEFT IT A SECOND = I CAN'T UNDERSTAND WHO GOT INTO IT
WAIT! HERE'S A CLUE = AN APPLE BITTEN BY SOME ONE WITH A MISSING TOOTH!
GOOD! NOW ALL WE HAVE TO DO IS ROUND UP THE WHOLE CIRCUS AND FIND THE GUY WITH THE TOOTH MISSING
DETOUR
NOW, EVERYONE! OPEN YOUR MOUTH WIDE!
WALT DISNEY 6-18

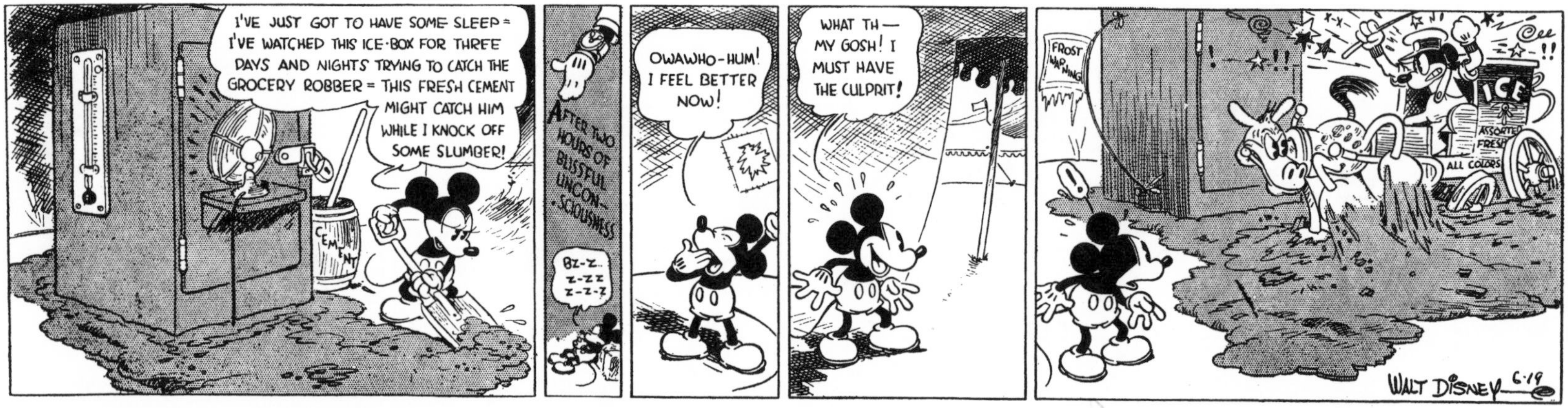
I'VE JUST GOT TO HAVE SOME SLEEP = I'VE WATCHED THIS ICE-BOX FOR THREE DAYS AND NIGHTS TRYING TO CATCH THE GROCERY ROBBER = THIS FRESH CEMENT MIGHT CATCH HIM WHILE I KNOCK OFF SOME SLUMBER!
CEMENT
AFTER TWO HOURS OF BLISSFUL UNCON-SCIOUSNESS
BZ-Z.. Z-Z Z Z-Z-Z
OWAWHO-HUM! I FEEL BETTER NOW!
WHAT TH— MY GOSH! I MUST HAVE THE CULPRIT!
FROST WARNING
ICE
ASSORTED FRESH
ALL COLORS
WALT DISNEY 6-19

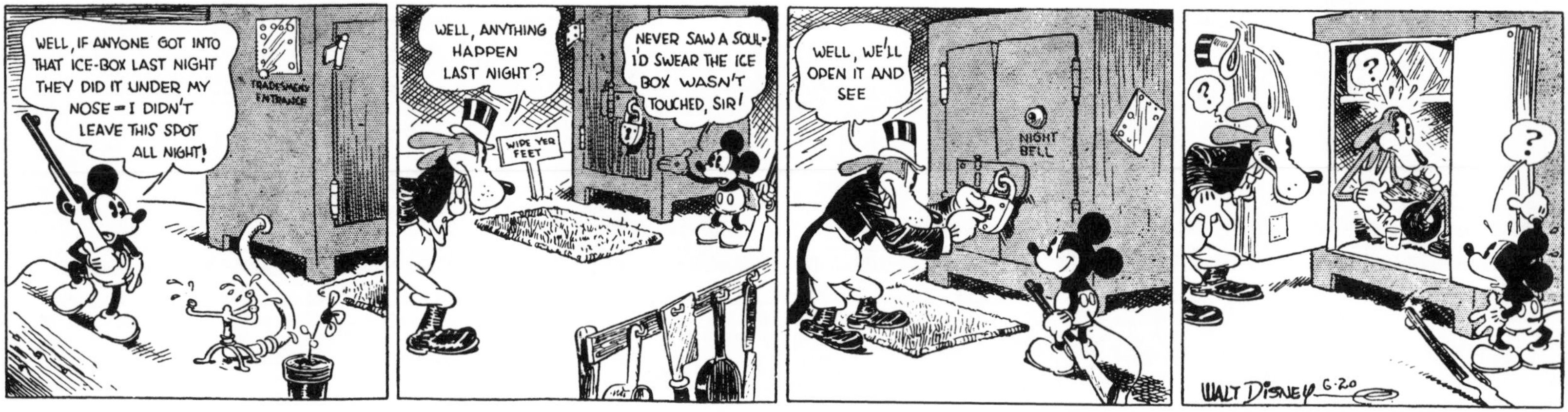
WELL, IF ANYONE GOT INTO THAT ICE-BOX LAST NIGHT THEY DID IT UNDER MY NOSE = I DIDN'T LEAVE THIS SPOT ALL NIGHT!
TRADESMEN'S ENTRANCE
WELL, ANYTHING HAPPEN LAST NIGHT?
NEVER SAW A SOUL. I'D SWEAR THE ICE BOX WASN'T TOUCHED, SIR!
WIPE YER FEET
WELL, WE'LL OPEN IT AND SEE
NIGHT BELL
WALT DISNEY 6-20

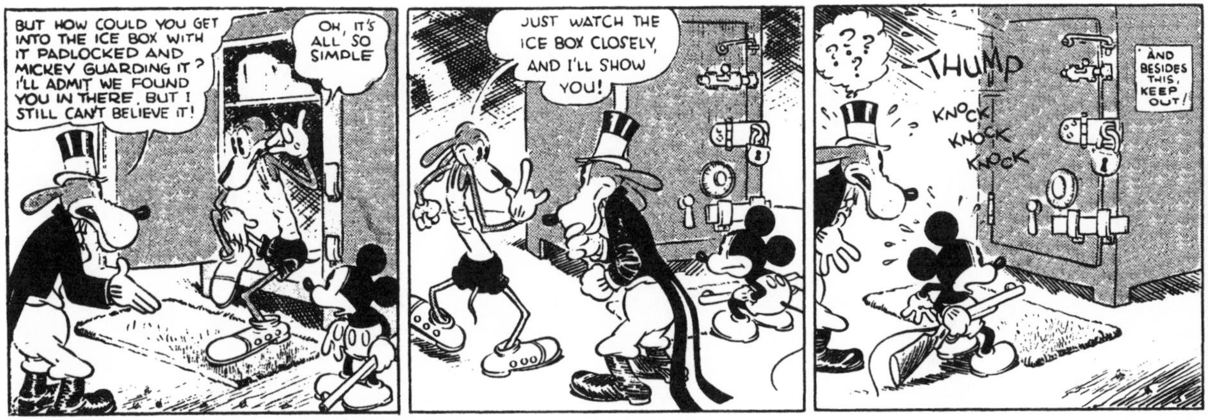
BUT HOW COULD YOU GET INTO THE ICE BOX WITH IT PADLOCKED AND MICKEY GUARDING IT? I'LL ADMIT WE FOUND YOU IN THERE, BUT I STILL CAN'T BELIEVE IT!
OH, IT'S ALL SO SIMPLE
JUST WATCH THE ICE BOX CLOSELY, AND I'LL SHOW YOU!
???
THUMP
KNOCK! KNOCK KNOCK
AND BESIDES THIS, KEEP OUT!
AND, WHAT'S MORE STAY OUT
WALT DISNEY
6.22

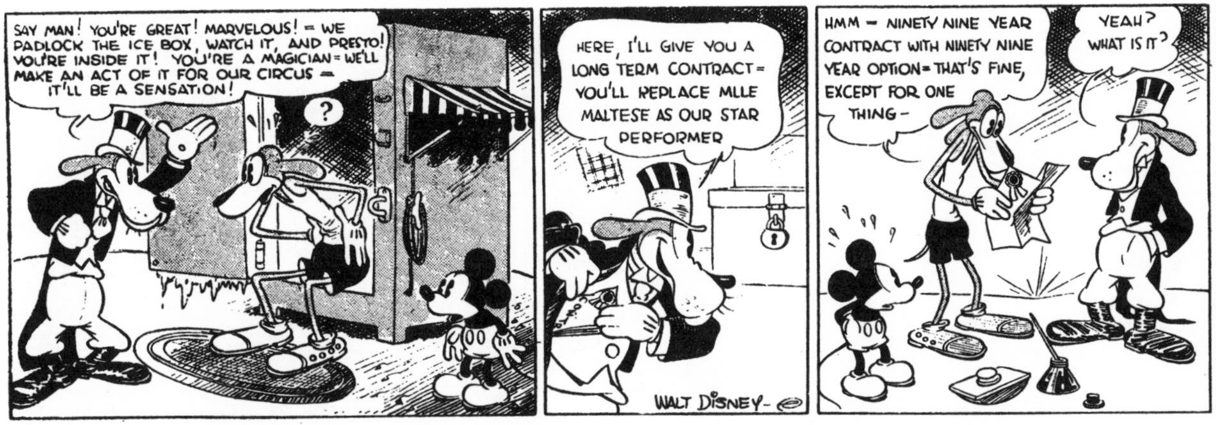
SAY MAN! YOU'RE GREAT! MARVELOUS! = WE PADLOCK THE ICE BOX, WATCH IT, AND PRESTO! YOU'RE INSIDE IT! YOU'RE A MAGICIAN = WE'LL MAKE AN ACT OF IT FOR OUR CIRCUS = IT'LL BE A SENSATION!
?
HERE, I'LL GIVE YOU A LONG TERM CONTRACT = YOU'LL REPLACE MLLE MALTESE AS OUR STAR PERFORMER
WALT DISNEY
HMM = NINETY NINE YEAR CONTRACT WITH NINETY NINE YEAR OPTION = THAT'S FINE, EXCEPT FOR ONE THING =
YEAH? WHAT IS IT?
IT DOESN'T SAY ANYTHING ABOUT A PENSION WHEN I RETIRE!
6.23

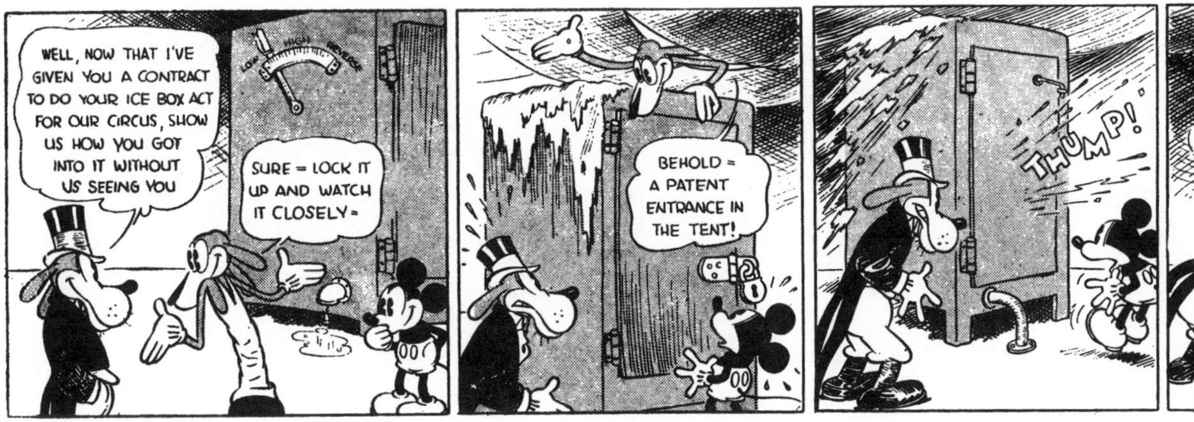
WELL, NOW THAT I'VE GIVEN YOU A CONTRACT TO DO YOUR ICE BOX ACT FOR OUR CIRCUS, SHOW US HOW YOU GOT INTO IT WITHOUT US SEEING YOU
SURE = LOCK IT UP AND WATCH IT CLOSELY =
BEHOLD = A PATENT ENTRANCE IN THE TENT!
THUMP!
YOU SEE, THERE IS NO **TOP** IN IT!
WALT DISNEY
6.24

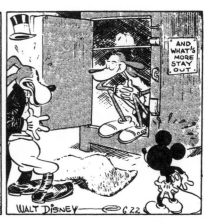

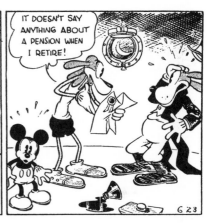

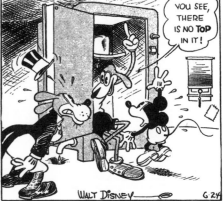

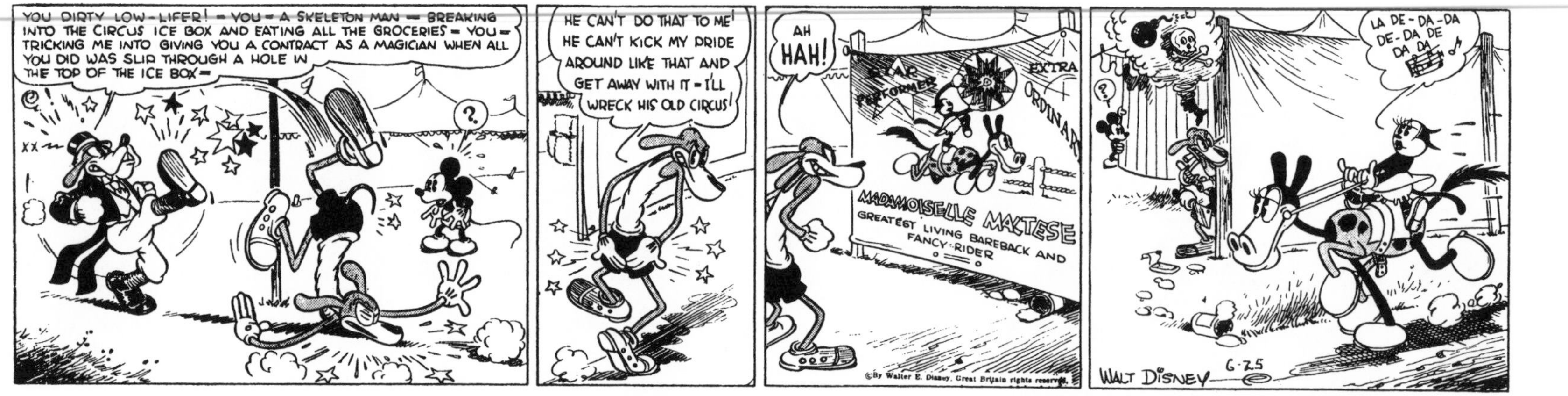
YOU DIRTY LOW-LIFER! = YOU = A SKELETON MAN = BREAKING INTO THE CIRCUS ICE BOX AND EATING ALL THE GROCERIES = YOU = TRICKING ME INTO GIVING YOU A CONTRACT AS A MAGICIAN WHEN ALL YOU DID WAS SLIP THROUGH A HOLE IN THE TOP OF THE ICE BOX =
?
HE CAN'T DO THAT TO ME! HE CAN'T KICK MY PRIDE AROUND LIKE THAT AND GET AWAY WITH IT = I'LL WRECK HIS OLD CIRCUS!
AH HAH!
STAR PERFORMER
EXTRA ORDINARY
MADAMOISELLE MALTESE
GREATEST LIVING BAREBACK AND FANCY RIDER
©By Walter E. Disney. Great Britain rights reserved.
?
LA DE-DA-DA DE-DA DE DA DA
WALT DISNEY
6-25

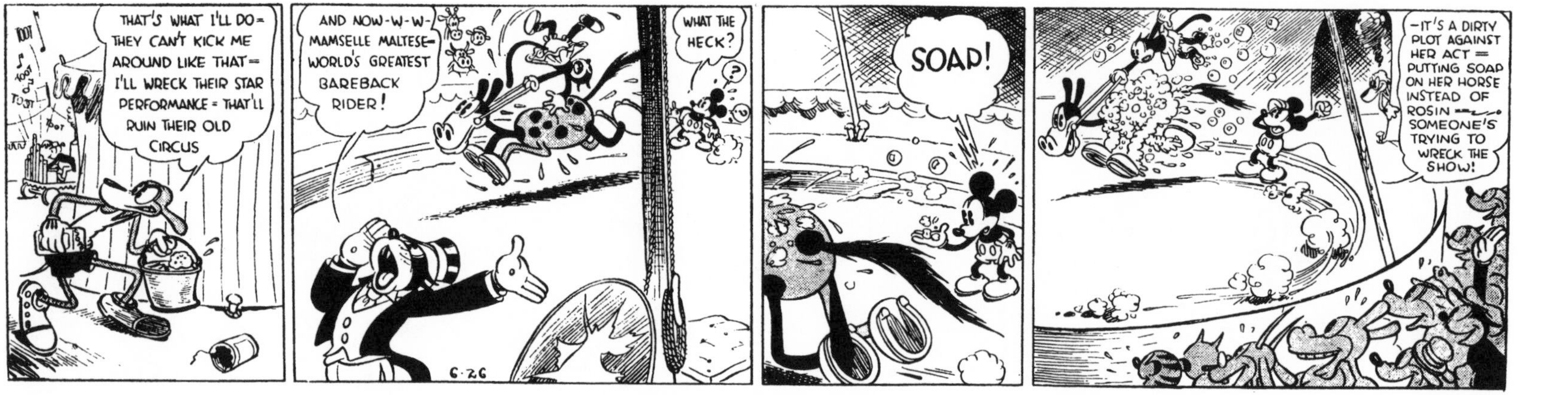
TOOT
THAT'S WHAT I'LL DO = THEY CAN'T KICK ME AROUND LIKE THAT = I'LL WRECK THEIR STAR PERFORMANCE = THAT'LL RUIN THEIR OLD CIRCUS
AND NOW-W-W MAMSELLE MALTESE = WORLD'S GREATEST BAREBACK RIDER!
WHAT THE HECK?
?
6-26
SOAP!
-IT'S A DIRTY PLOT AGAINST HER ACT = PUTTING SOAP ON HER HORSE INSTEAD OF ROSIN — SOMEONE'S TRYING TO WRECK THE SHOW!

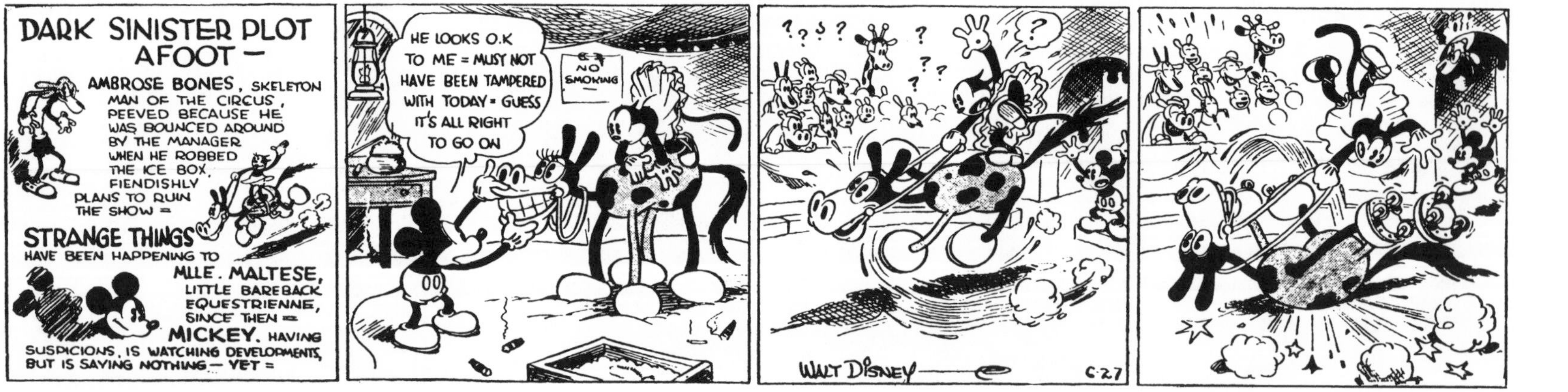
DARK SINISTER PLOT AFOOT —
AMBROSE BONES, SKELETON MAN OF THE CIRCUS, PEEVED BECAUSE HE WAS BOUNCED AROUND BY THE MANAGER WHEN HE ROBBED THE ICE BOX, FIENDISHLY PLANS TO RUIN THE SHOW =
STRANGE THINGS HAVE BEEN HAPPENING TO MLLE. MALTESE, LITTLE BAREBACK EQUESTRIENNE, SINCE THEN =
MICKEY, HAVING SUSPICIONS, IS WATCHING DEVELOPMENTS, BUT IS SAYING NOTHING — YET =
HE LOOKS O.K TO ME = MUST NOT HAVE BEEN TAMPERED WITH TODAY = GUESS IT'S ALL RIGHT TO GO ON
NO SMOKING
? ? ? ? ? ? ? ?
WALT DISNEY
6-27

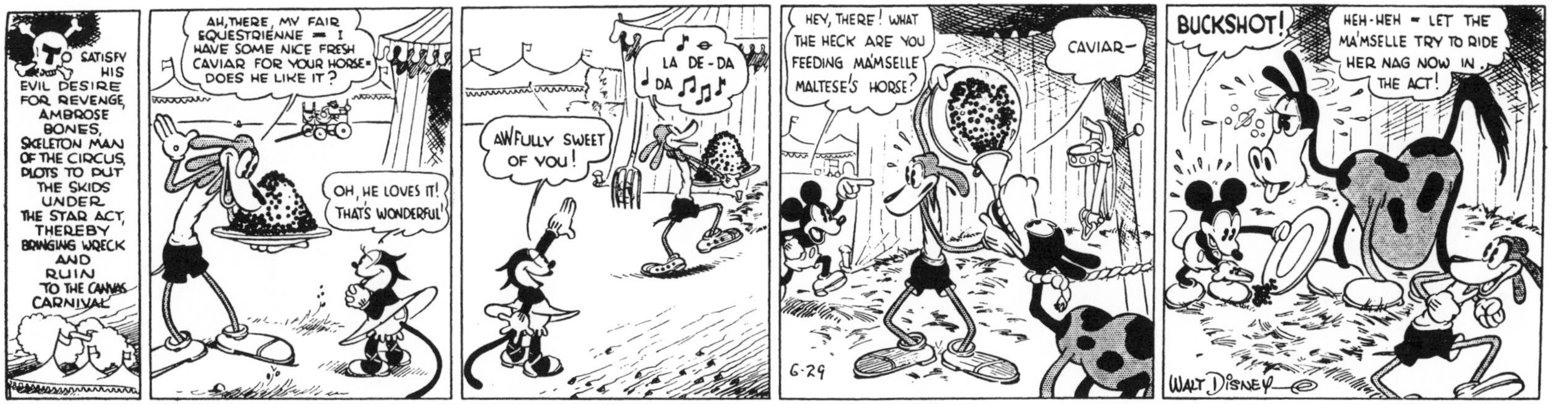
TO SATISFY HIS EVIL DESIRE FOR REVENGE, AMBROSE BONES, SKELETON MAN OF THE CIRCUS, PLOTS TO PUT THE SKIDS UNDER THE STAR ACT, THEREBY BRINGING WRECK AND RUIN TO THE CANVAS CARNIVAL
AH, THERE, MY FAIR EQUESTRIENNE = I HAVE SOME NICE FRESH CAVIAR FOR YOUR HORSE = DOES HE LIKE IT?
OH, HE LOVES IT! THAT'S WONDERFUL!
LA DE-DA DA
AWFULLY SWEET OF YOU!
HEY, THERE! WHAT THE HECK ARE YOU FEEDING MA'MSELLE MALTESE'S HORSE?
CAVIAR-
6-29
BUCKSHOT!
HEH-HEH = LET THE MA'MSELLE TRY TO RIDE HER NAG NOW IN THE ACT!
WALT DISNEY

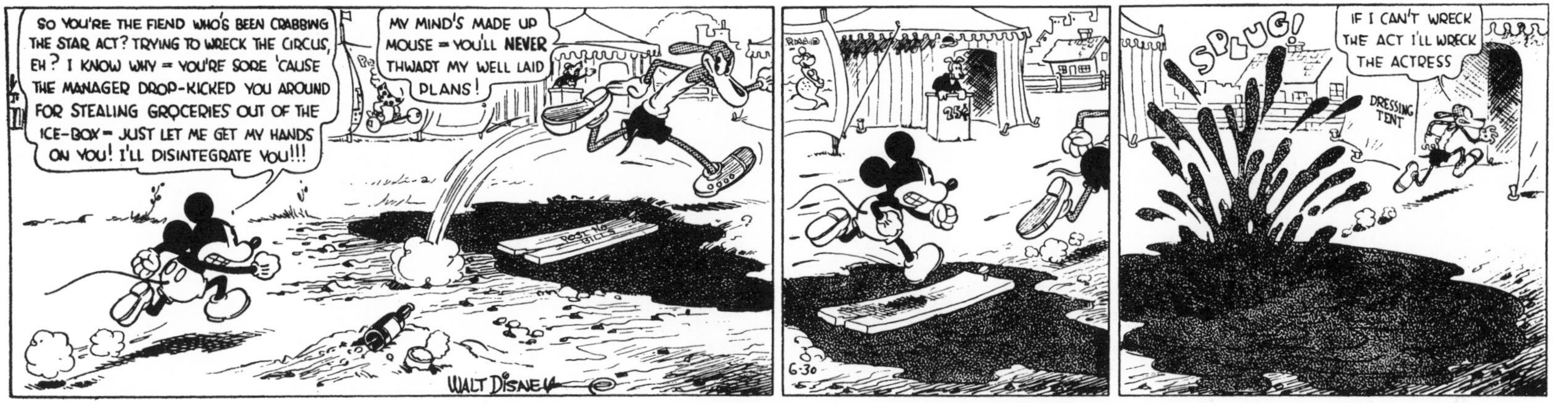
SO YOU'RE THE FIEND WHO'S BEEN CRABBING THE STAR ACT? TRYING TO WRECK THE CIRCUS, EH? I KNOW WHY = YOU'RE SORE 'CAUSE THE MANAGER DROP-KICKED YOU AROUND FOR STEALING GROCERIES OUT OF THE ICE-BOX = JUST LET ME GET MY HANDS ON YOU! I'LL DISINTEGRATE YOU!!!
MY MIND'S MADE UP MOUSE = YOU'LL NEVER THWART MY WELL LAID PLANS!
WALT DISNEY
6-30
SPLUG!
IF I CAN'T WRECK THE ACT I'LL WRECK THE ACTRESS
DRESSING TENT

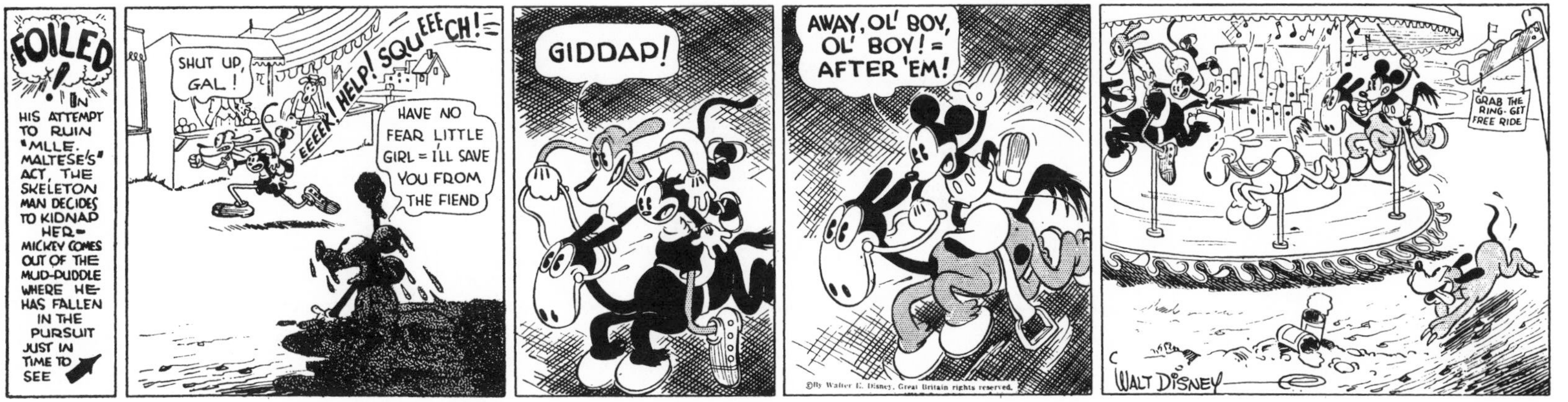
FOILED! IN HIS ATTEMPT TO RUIN "MLLE. MALTESE'S" ACT, THE SKELETON MAN DECIDES TO KIDNAP HER = MICKEY COMES OUT OF THE MUD-PUDDLE WHERE HE HAS FALLEN IN THE PURSUIT JUST IN TIME TO SEE
SHUT UP, GAL!
EEEEK! HELP! SQUEEECH!
HAVE NO FEAR LITTLE GIRL = I'LL SAVE YOU FROM THE FIEND
GIDDAP!
AWAY, OL' BOY, OL' BOY! = AFTER 'EM!
©By Walter E. Disney, Great Britain rights reserved.
GRAB THE RING - GET FREE RIDE
WALT DISNEY

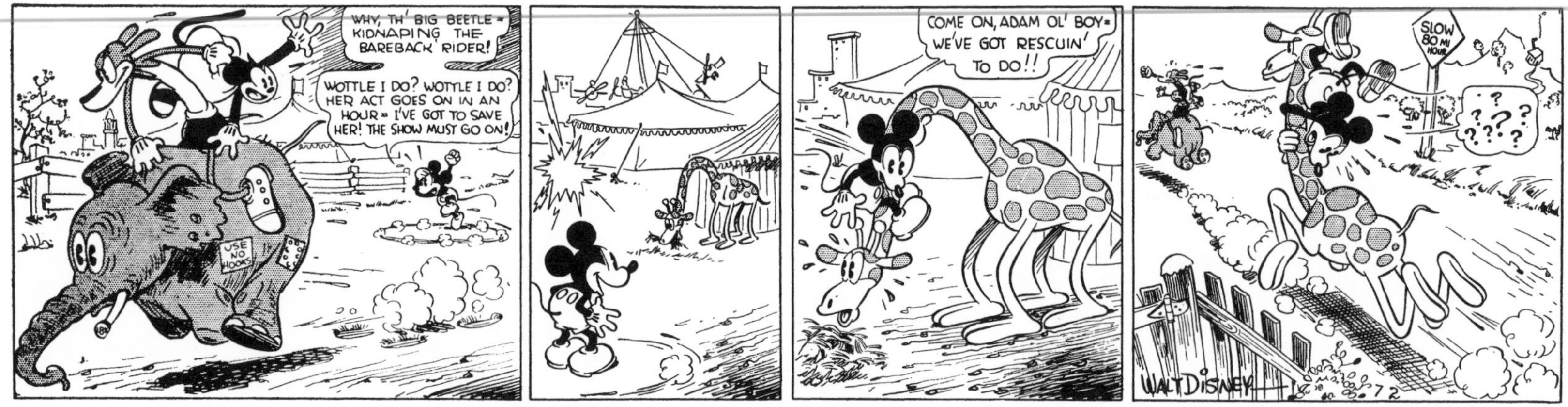
WHY, TH' BIG BEETLE= KIDNAPING THE BAREBACK RIDER!
WOTTLE I DO? WOTTLE I DO? HER ACT GOES ON IN AN HOUR= I'VE GOT TO SAVE HER! THE SHOW MUST GO ON!
USE NO HOOKS
COME ON, ADAM OL' BOY= WE'VE GOT RESCUIN' TO DO!!
SLOW 80 MI HOUR
? ? ? ? ?
WALT DISNEY
7-2

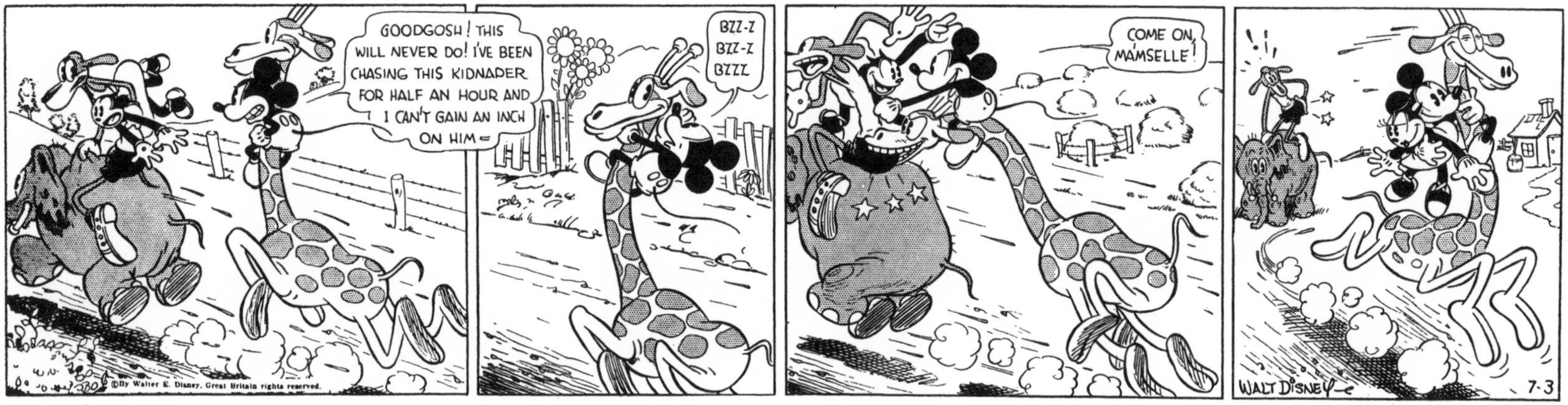
GOODGOSH! THIS WILL NEVER DO! I'VE BEEN CHASING THIS KIDNAPER FOR HALF AN HOUR AND I CAN'T GAIN AN INCH ON HIM=
©By Walter E. Disney. Great Britain rights reserved.
BZZ-Z BZZ-Z BZZZ
COME ON, MA'MSELLE!
WALT DISNEY
7-3

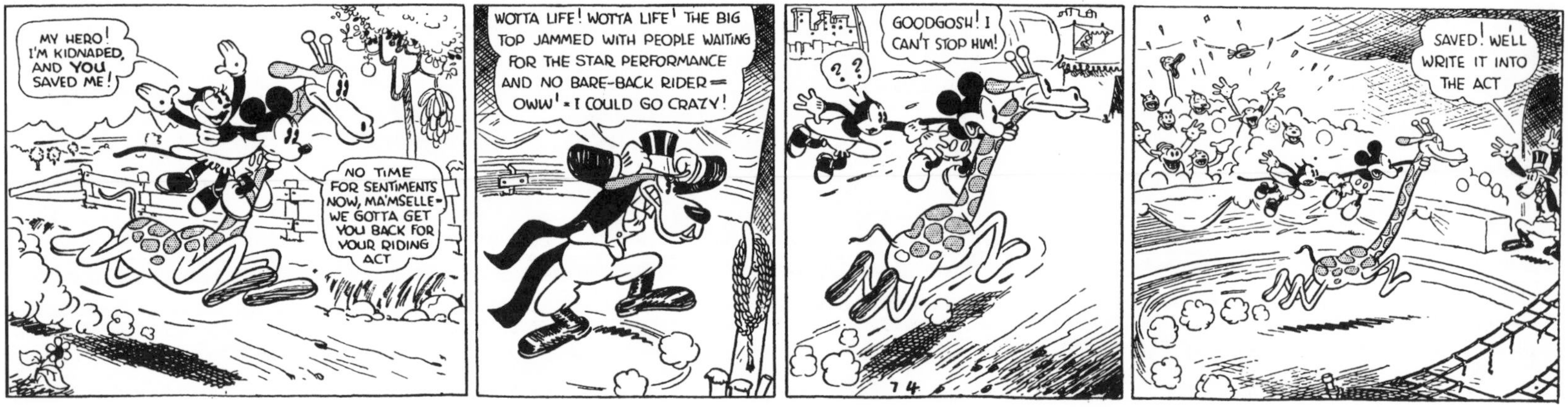
MY HERO! I'M KIDNAPED, AND YOU SAVED ME!
NO TIME FOR SENTIMENTS NOW, MA'MSELLE= WE GOTTA GET YOU BACK FOR YOUR RIDING ACT
WOTTA LIFE! WOTTA LIFE! THE BIG TOP JAMMED WITH PEOPLE WAITING FOR THE STAR PERFORMANCE AND NO BARE-BACK RIDER= OWW!= I COULD GO CRAZY!
? ?
GOODGOSH! I CAN'T STOP HIM!
7-4
SAVED! WE'LL WRITE IT INTO THE ACT

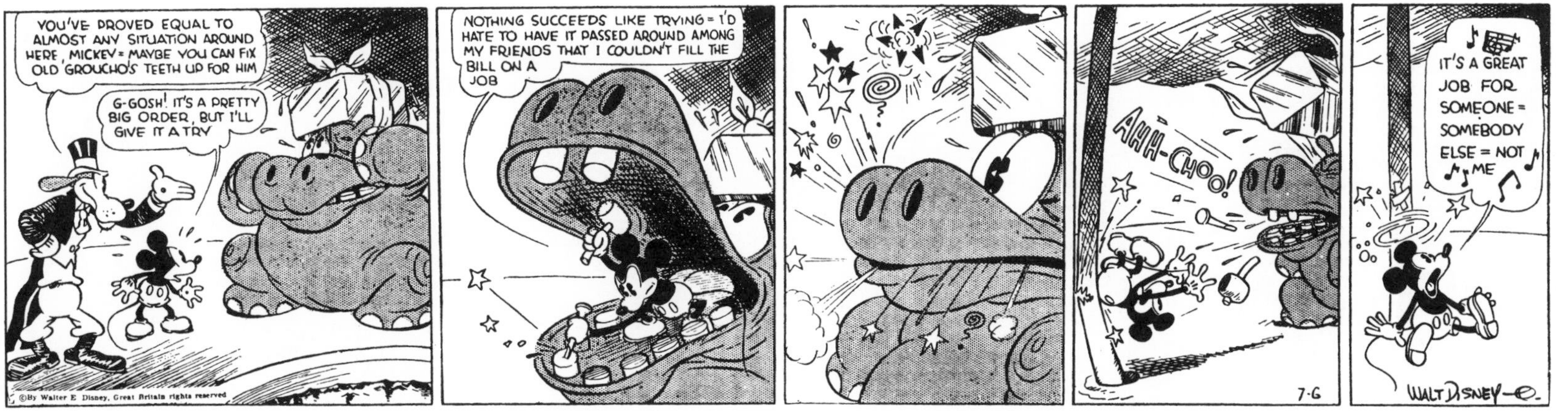
YOU'VE PROVED EQUAL TO ALMOST ANY SITUATION AROUND HERE, MICKEY = MAYBE YOU CAN FIX OLD 'GROUCHO'S TEETH UP FOR HIM
G-GOSH! IT'S A PRETTY BIG ORDER, BUT I'LL GIVE IT A TRY
©By Walter E. Disney, Great Britain rights reserved
NOTHING SUCCEEDS LIKE TRYING = I'D HATE TO HAVE IT PASSED AROUND AMONG MY FRIENDS THAT I COULDN'T FILL THE BILL ON A JOB
AHH-CHOO!
7·6
IT'S A GREAT JOB FOR SOMEONE = SOMEBODY ELSE = NOT ME
WALT DISNEY

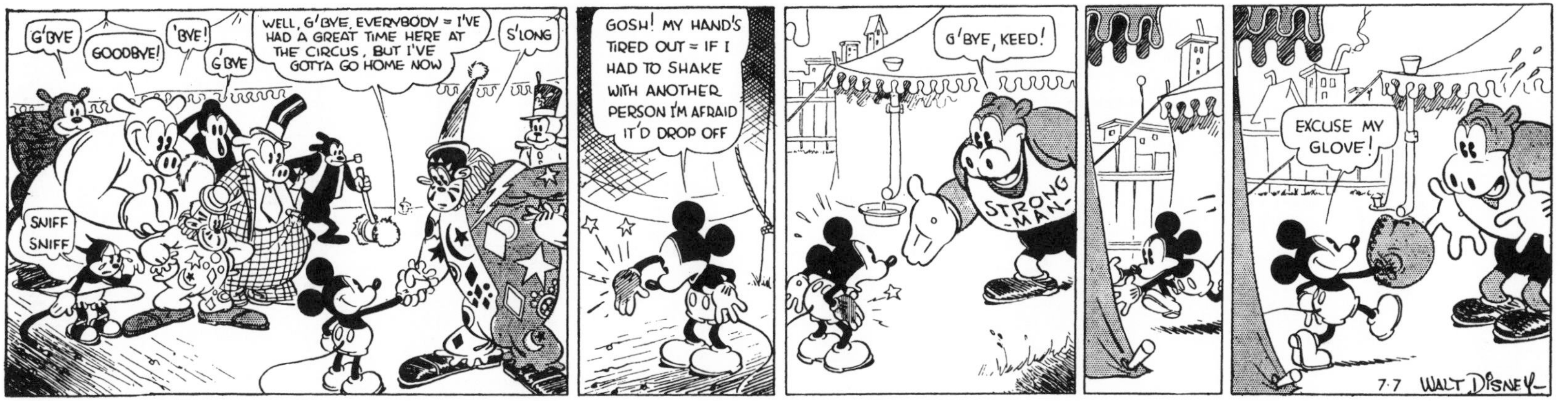
G'BYE
GOODBYE!
'BYE!
G'BYE
WELL, G'BYE, EVERYBODY = I'VE HAD A GREAT TIME HERE AT THE CIRCUS, BUT I'VE GOTTA GO HOME NOW
S'LONG
SNIFF SNIFF
GOSH! MY HAND'S TIRED OUT = IF I HAD TO SHAKE WITH ANOTHER PERSON I'M AFRAID IT'D DROP OFF
G'BYE, KEED!
STRONG -MAN-
EXCUSE MY GLOVE!
7·7
WALT DISNEY

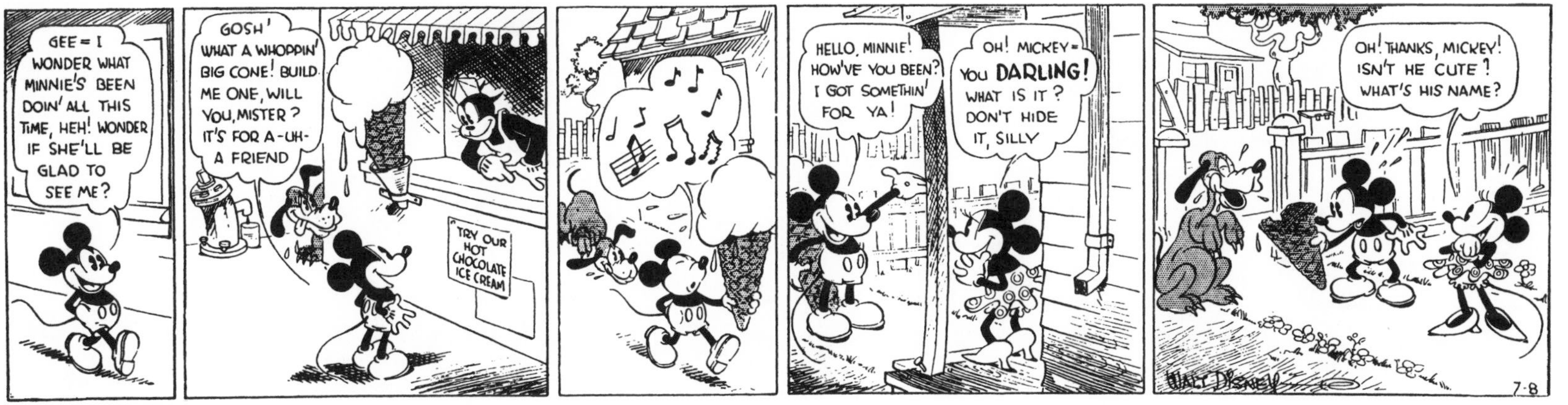
GEE = I WONDER WHAT MINNIE'S BEEN DOIN' ALL THIS TIME, HEH! WONDER IF SHE'LL BE GLAD TO SEE ME?
GOSH! WHAT A WHOPPIN' BIG CONE! BUILD ME ONE, WILL YOU, MISTER? IT'S FOR A-UH-A FRIEND
TRY OUR HOT CHOCOLATE ICE CREAM
HELLO, MINNIE! HOW'VE YOU BEEN? I GOT SOMETHIN' FOR YA!
OH! MICKEY = YOU DARLING! WHAT IS IT? DON'T HIDE IT, SILLY
OH! THANKS, MICKEY! ISN'T HE CUTE? WHAT'S HIS NAME?
WALT DISNEY
7·8

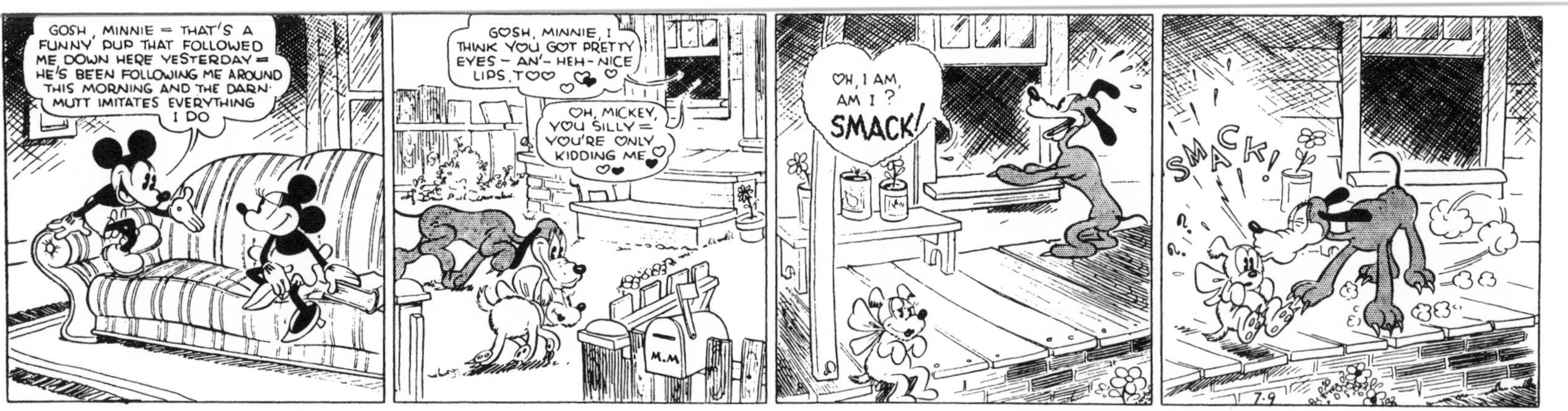
GOSH, MINNIE = THAT'S A FUNNY PUP THAT FOLLOWED ME DOWN HERE YESTERDAY = HE'S BEEN FOLLOWING ME AROUND THIS MORNING AND THE DARN MUTT IMITATES EVERYTHING I DO
GOSH, MINNIE, I THINK YOU GOT PRETTY EYES – AN'– HEH – NICE LIPS, TOO
OH, MICKEY, YOU SILLY = YOU'RE ONLY KIDDING ME
M.M
OH, I AM, AM I? SMACK!
SMACK!
7-9

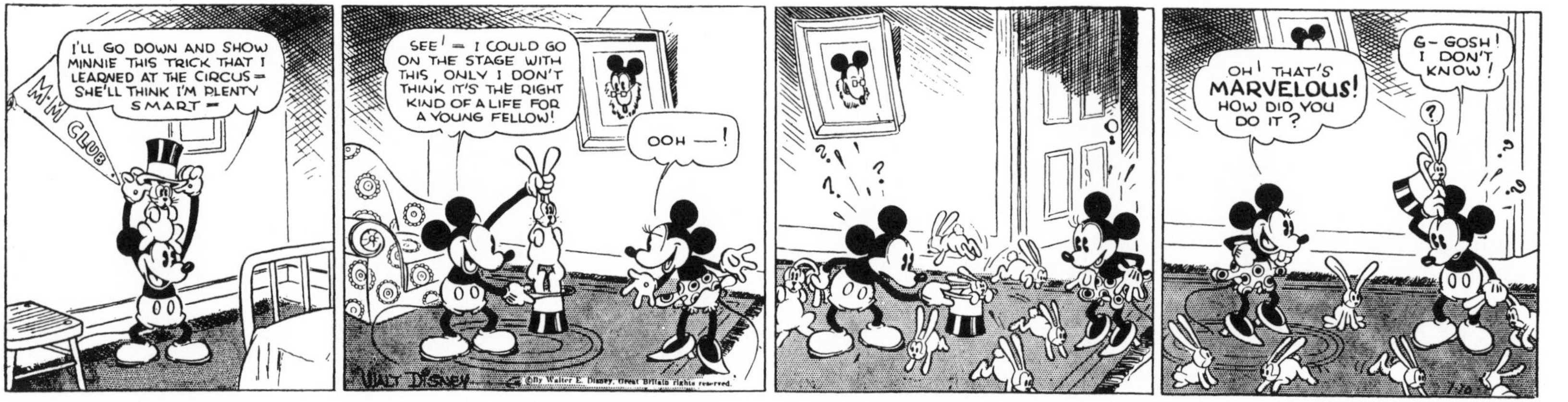
I'LL GO DOWN AND SHOW MINNIE THIS TRICK THAT I LEARNED AT THE CIRCUS = SHE'LL THINK I'M PLENTY SMART =
M-M CLUB
SEE! = I COULD GO ON THE STAGE WITH THIS, ONLY I DON'T THINK IT'S THE RIGHT KIND OF A LIFE FOR A YOUNG FELLOW!
OOH —!
WALT DISNEY
OH! THAT'S MARVELOUS! HOW DID YOU DO IT?
G-GOSH! I DON'T KNOW!
7-10

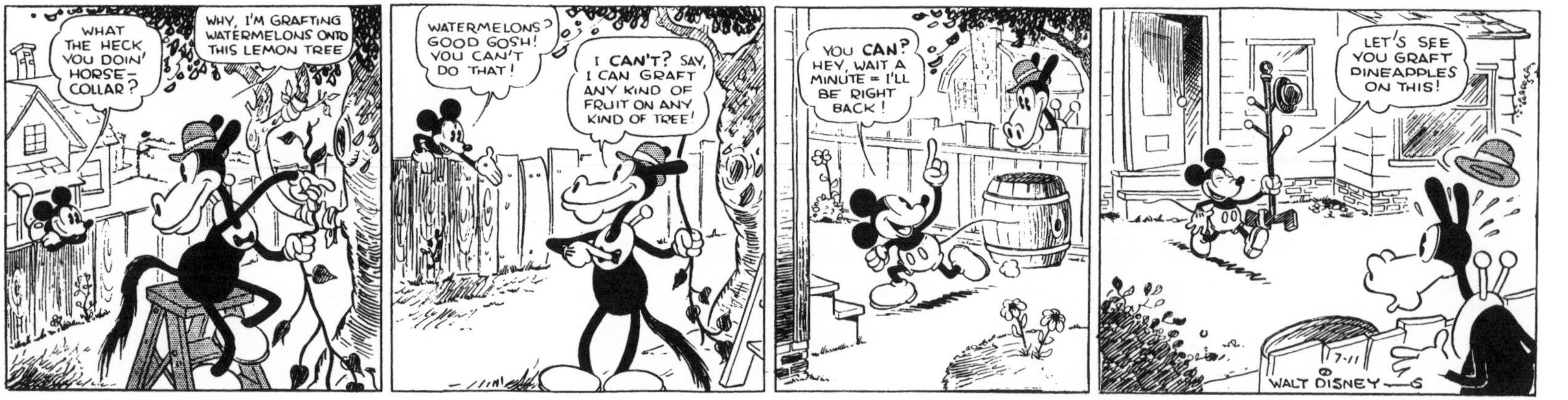
WHAT THE HECK YOU DOIN' HORSE-COLLAR?
WHY, I'M GRAFTING WATERMELONS ONTO THIS LEMON TREE
WATERMELONS? GOOD GOSH! YOU CAN'T DO THAT!
I CAN'T? SAY, I CAN GRAFT ANY KIND OF FRUIT ON ANY KIND OF TREE!
YOU CAN? HEY, WAIT A MINUTE = I'LL BE RIGHT BACK!
LET'S SEE YOU GRAFT PINEAPPLES ON THIS!
7-11
WALT DISNEY—S

HI, PLUTO GO GET IT, OL' BOY!
ARF! ARF!
WALT DISNEY
7-13

A NICE GOLDFISH POND WILL IMPROVE THE LOOKS OF MY YARD A LOT = GOSH! THIS GROUND'S HARD
WISH I COULD GET MR. WINKLE, THE BAKER, TO SHOW ME HOW TO MIX THE CEMENT
WALT DISNEY
7-14

GOSH, PLUTO = THERE'S SO MUCH DIRT ON YOU IT'S MAKING YOU THIN TO CARRY IT AROUND
THERE YOU ARE = CLEAN AS A PLATTER AT A FAMILY REUNION = WHEW! THANK GOSH I DON'T HAVE TO DO THAT AGAIN UNTIL NEXT SATURDAY
FLEA POWD
7-15

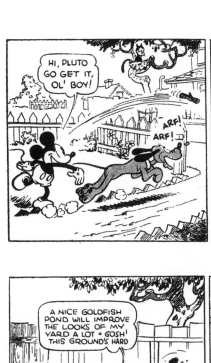

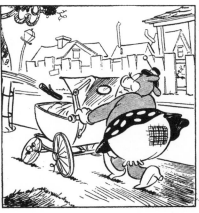

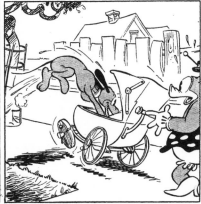

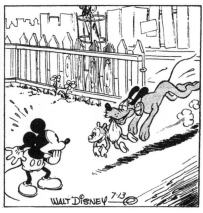

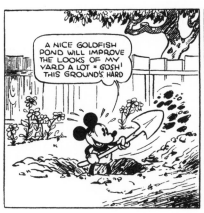

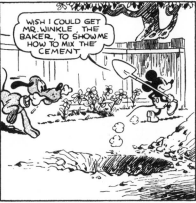

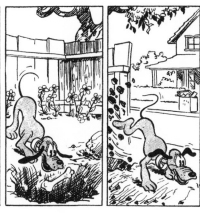

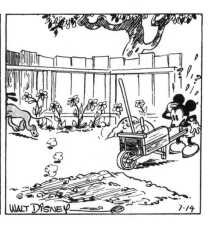

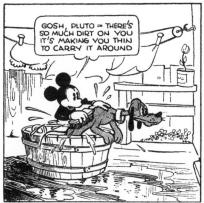

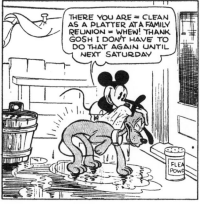

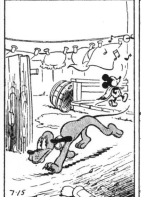

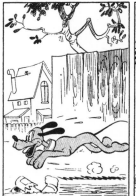

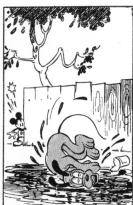

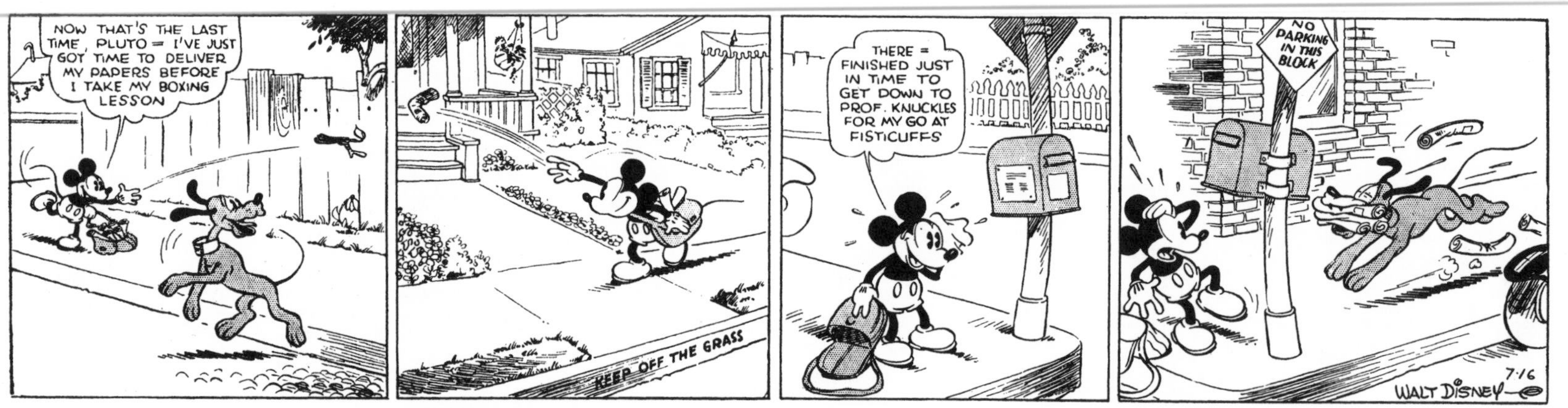
NOW THAT'S THE LAST TIME, PLUTO = I'VE JUST GOT TIME TO DELIVER MY PAPERS BEFORE I TAKE MY BOXING LESSON
KEEP OFF THE GRASS
THERE = FINISHED JUST IN TIME TO GET DOWN TO PROF. KNUCKLES FOR MY GO AT FISTICUFFS
NO PARKING IN THIS BLOCK
7-16
WALT DISNEY

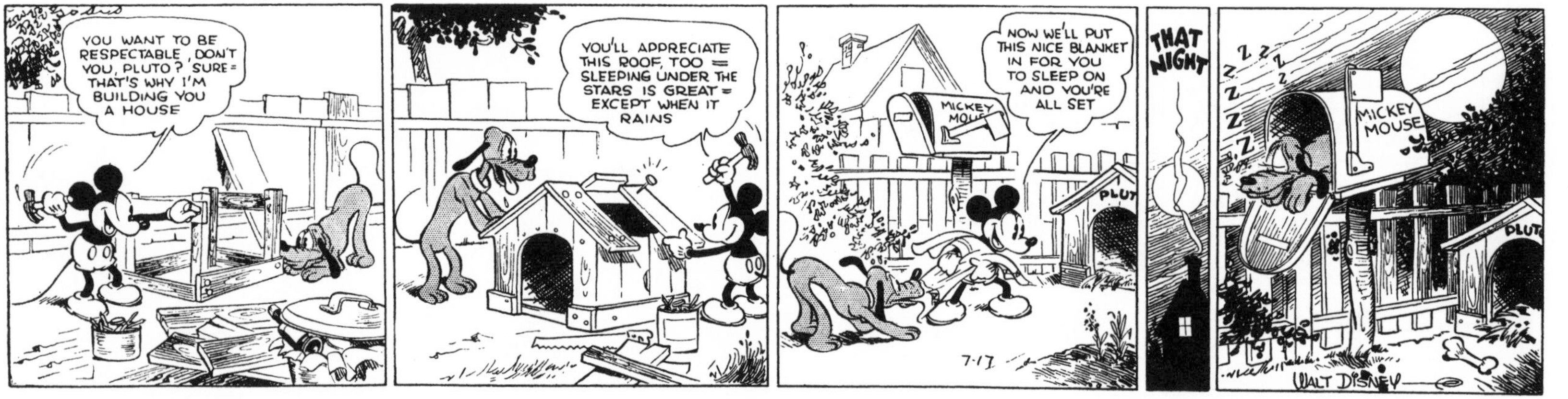
YOU WANT TO BE RESPECTABLE, DON'T YOU, PLUTO? SURE = THAT'S WHY I'M BUILDING YOU A HOUSE
YOU'LL APPRECIATE THIS ROOF, TOO = SLEEPING UNDER THE STARS IS GREAT = EXCEPT WHEN IT RAINS
NOW WE'LL PUT THIS NICE BLANKET IN FOR YOU TO SLEEP ON AND YOU'RE ALL SET
7-17
THAT NIGHT
Z Z Z
MICKEY MOUSE
WALT DISNEY

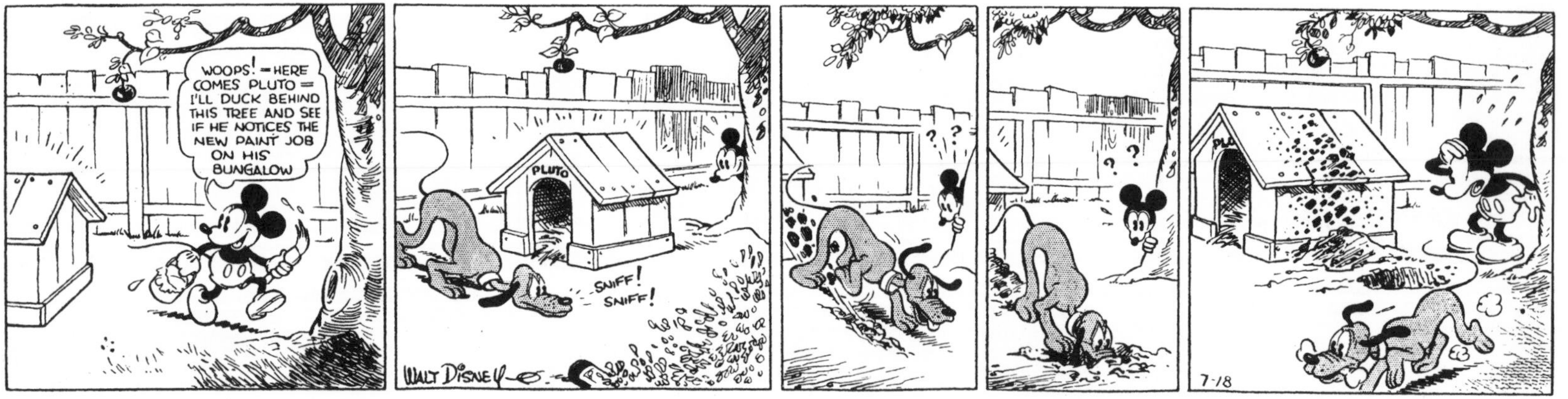
WOOPS! = HERE COMES PLUTO = I'LL DUCK BEHIND THIS TREE AND SEE IF HE NOTICES THE NEW PAINT JOB ON HIS BUNGALOW
PLUTO
SNIFF! SNIFF!
WALT DISNEY
? ?
? ?
7-18

MICKEY MOUSE AND THE RANSOM PLOT

JULY 20, 1931
–
NOVEMBER 7, 1931

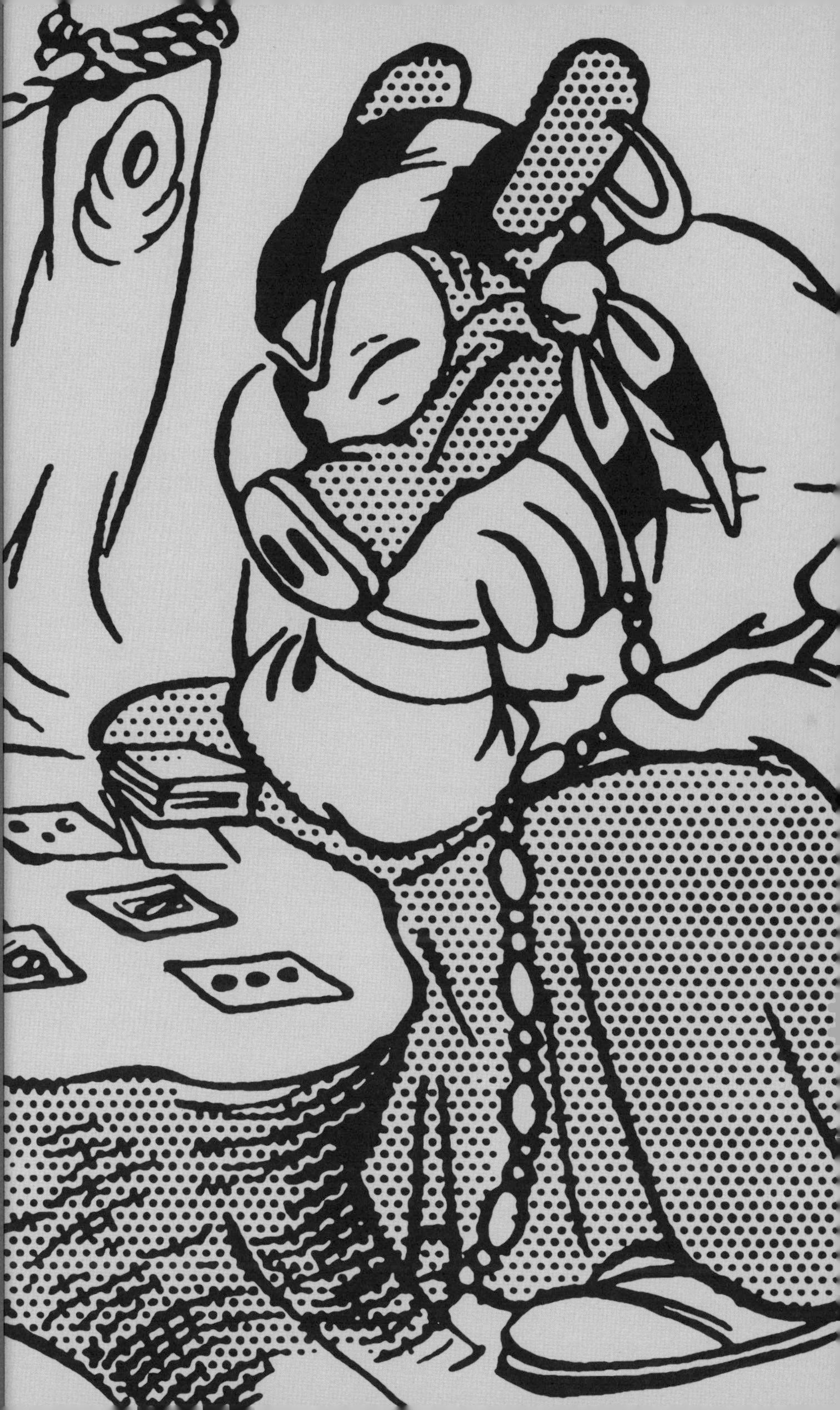

MICKEY MOUSE
REGISTERED U.S. PATENT OFFICE

MIDDLE-EURO MOUSE

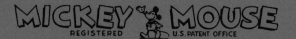

Romani, or gypsy culture is no longer a powerful force in the Western world. But prior to World War I, average citizens saw the situation differently. "Bohemia is of unlimited extent," explained J. G. Bertram, speaking more about popular myth than reality. "[The] arms of it stretch out to all quarters of the globe."[1] To some degree, this was true: Romani seemed to be everywhere because as migrants, populations got around. But the suggestion of power—implicit in the visual metaphor of stretching arms—was frankly erroneous.

From the British Romnichals to the middle European Kalderash, Romani peoples were hardly united enough to achieve across-the-board political representation. Instead, they were downtrodden and forced into positions of want, a situation that at once perpetuated—and was perpetuated by—the prejudices of citified Europeans and North Americans. An image of needy, romantic, slightly mysterious hillbillies grew up; and as befits anything mysterious, mainstream Westerners attributed more influence to it than the Romani people actually had.

From this misunderstanding emerged rather contradictory pop cultural artifacts. Gypsies were depicted as quaint, old-fashioned, and isolated—yet simultaneously unified and potent, with individual creators determining whether a given depiction bore more resemblance to actual Romani or to European Hatfields and McCoys. Sometimes gypsies were villains, entrapping hapless city folk in cunning ransom plots. Other times gypsies were heroes, whose supposedly down-home entertainments—"the life that all would like to lead," according to the classic operetta *The Bohemian Girl*—were idealized as a kind of good-natured 19th century counterculture.[2]

Floyd Gottfredson seems to have tried to have it both ways in "The Ransom Plot." The featured Romani characters are established as having shady, con artist leaders, but the rest are just carefree middle-European bumpkins—until the story suddenly calls for a crisis, whereupon much of the group rather unbelievably turn as piratical as their queen.

In retrospect, Gottfredson doesn't seem to have been truly comfortable with the melodrama tropes he was invoking. He is quick to show that some of the "tribe" are uncomfortable with their relatives' turn to the dark side; and when it comes time for Mickey to actually fight the clan, the entire family of dozens is beaten with surprising ease.

One gets the feeling that in a more progressive era—or in a more sophisticated story—this fundamentally whimsical Romani clan might have stayed on good terms with Mickey, perhaps to confront a more realistically menacing third party. In 1931, Gottfredson had yet to refine his approach; we urge that you judge the result as a relic of its time.

Another relic, we might point out, is the swastika depicted on tribal garments in the August 6 and 28 dailies. The symbol was seen as a harmless aboriginal icon before the Nazis came to power. [DG]

---

1 William Hazlitt, "The Characters of Shakespeare's Plays" (1817), in *Collected Works*, A. R. Wailer and A. Glover eds, 12 vols (London: J. M. Dent, 1902-1906), Vol. 1, p. 324.

2 Michael William Balfe and Alfred Bunn, *The Bohemian Girl: Opera in Three Acts* (Boston: Oliver Diston Company, 1882), p. 126.

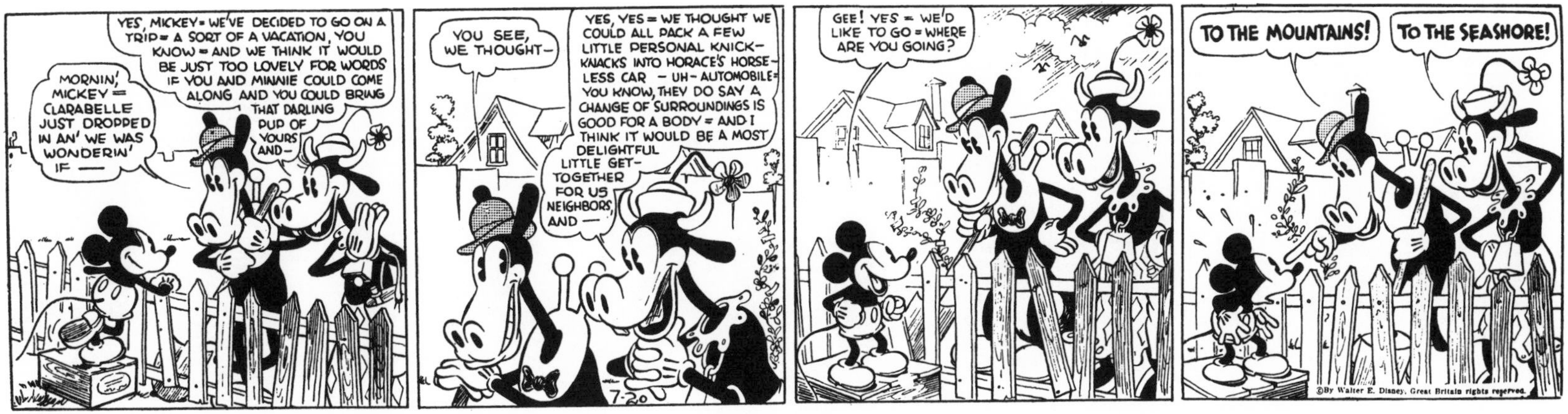
MORNIN', MICKEY = CLARABELLE JUST DROPPED IN AN' WE WAS WONDERIN' IF —
YES, MICKEY = WE'VE DECIDED TO GO ON A TRIP = A SORT OF A VACATION, YOU KNOW = AND WE THINK IT WOULD BE JUST TOO LOVELY FOR WORDS IF YOU AND MINNIE COULD COME ALONG AND YOU COULD BRING THAT DARLING PUP OF YOURS AND—
YOU SEE, WE THOUGHT—
YES, YES = WE THOUGHT WE COULD ALL PACK A FEW LITTLE PERSONAL KNICK-KNACKS INTO HORACE'S HORSE-LESS CAR — UH — AUTOMOBILE = YOU KNOW, THEY DO SAY A CHANGE OF SURROUNDINGS IS GOOD FOR A BODY = AND I THINK IT WOULD BE A MOST DELIGHTFUL LITTLE GET-TOGETHER FOR US NEIGHBORS, AND —
7-20
GEE! YES = WE'D LIKE TO GO = WHERE ARE YOU GOING?
TO THE MOUNTAINS!
TO THE SEASHORE!
©By Walter E. Disney, Great Britain rights reserved.

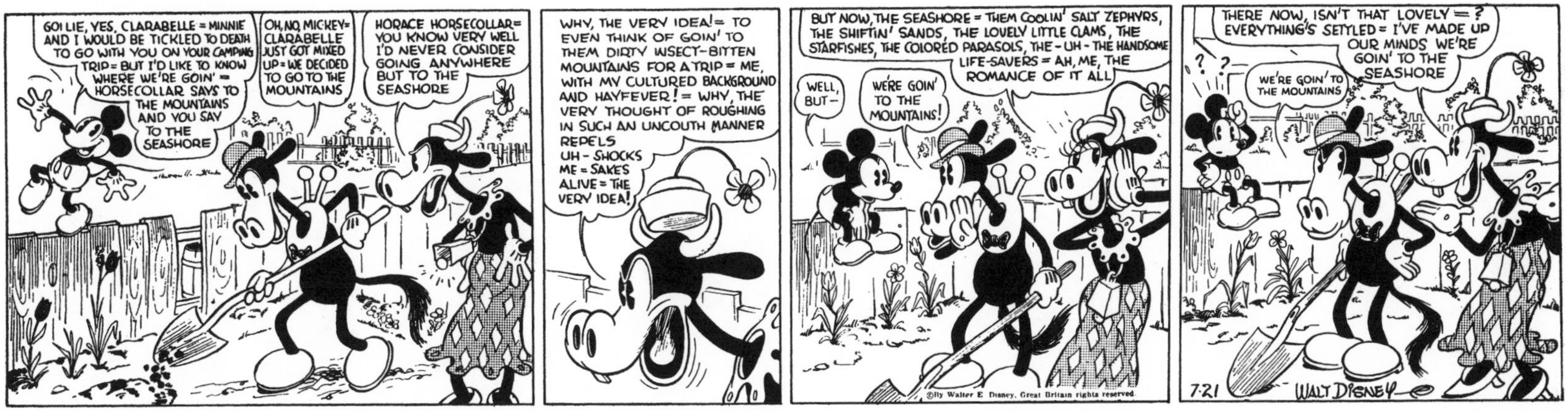
GOLLIE, YES, CLARABELLE = MINNIE AND I WOULD BE TICKLED TO DEATH TO GO WITH YOU ON YOUR CAMPING TRIP = BUT I'D LIKE TO KNOW WHERE WE'RE GOIN' = HORSECOLLAR SAYS TO THE MOUNTAINS AND YOU SAY TO THE SEASHORE
OH, NO, MICKEY = CLARABELLE JUST GOT MIXED UP = WE DECIDED TO GO TO THE MOUNTAINS
HORACE HORSECOLLAR = YOU KNOW VERY WELL I'D NEVER CONSIDER GOING ANYWHERE BUT TO THE SEASHORE
WHY, THE VERY IDEA! = TO EVEN THINK OF GOIN' TO THEM DIRTY INSECT-BITTEN MOUNTAINS FOR A TRIP = ME, WITH MY CULTURED BACKGROUND AND HAYFEVER! = WHY, THE VERY THOUGHT OF ROUGHING IN SUCH AN UNCOUTH MANNER REPELS UH - SHOCKS ME = SAKES ALIVE = THE VERY IDEA!
BUT NOW, THE SEASHORE = THEM COOLIN' SALT ZEPHYRS, THE SHIFTIN' SANDS, THE LOVELY LITTLE CLAMS, THE STARFISHES, THE COLORED PARASOLS, THE - UH - THE HANDSOME LIFE-SAVERS = AH, ME, THE ROMANCE OF IT ALL
WELL, BUT—
WE'RE GOIN' TO THE MOUNTAINS!
©By Walter E. Disney, Great Britain rights reserved.
THERE NOW, ISN'T THAT LOVELY = ? EVERYTHING'S SETTLED = I'VE MADE UP OUR MINDS WE'RE GOIN' TO THE SEASHORE
? ? —
WE'RE GOIN' TO THE MOUNTAINS
7-21
WALT DISNEY

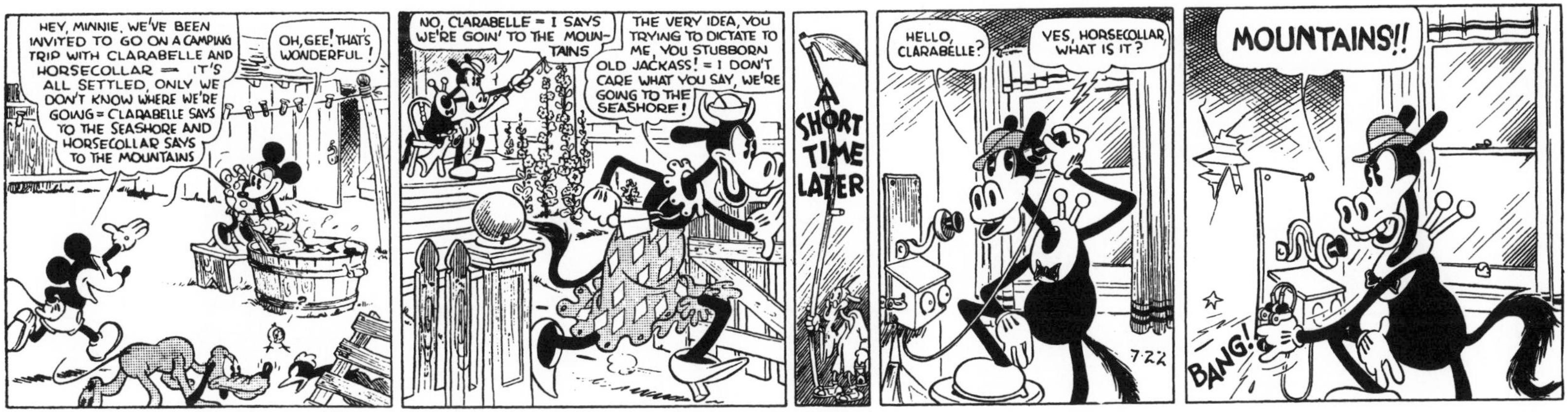
HEY, MINNIE, WE'VE BEEN INVITED TO GO ON A CAMPING TRIP WITH CLARABELLE AND HORSECOLLAR = IT'S ALL SETTLED, ONLY WE DON'T KNOW WHERE WE'RE GOING = CLARABELLE SAYS TO THE SEASHORE AND HORSECOLLAR SAYS TO THE MOUNTAINS
OH, GEE! THAT'S WONDERFUL!
NO, CLARABELLE = I SAYS WE'RE GOIN' TO THE MOUN-TAINS
THE VERY IDEA, YOU TRYING TO DICTATE TO ME, YOU STUBBORN OLD JACKASS! = I DON'T CARE WHAT YOU SAY, WE'RE GOING TO THE SEASHORE!
A SHORT TIME LATER
HELLO, CLARABELLE?
YES, HORSECOLLAR, WHAT IS IT?
7-22
MOUNTAINS!!
BANG!

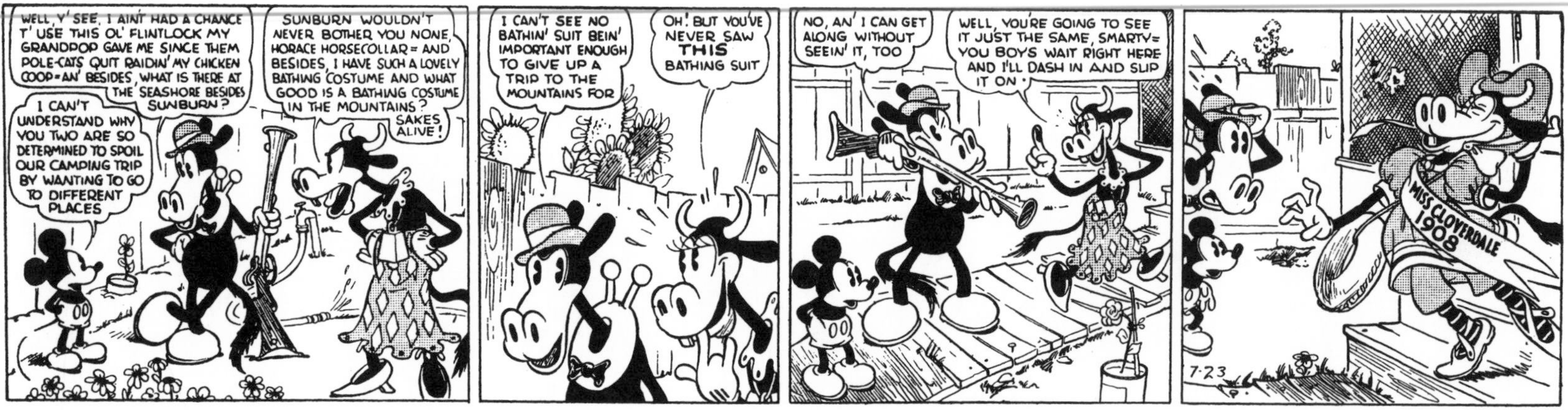

WELL, Y' SEE, I AIN'T HAD A CHANCE T' USE THIS OL' FLINTLOCK MY GRANDPOP GAVE ME SINCE THEM POLE-CATS QUIT RAIDIN' MY CHICKEN COOP=AN' BESIDES, WHAT IS THERE AT THE SEASHORE BESIDES SUNBURN?
I CAN'T UNDERSTAND WHY YOU TWO ARE SO DETERMINED TO SPOIL OUR CAMPING TRIP BY WANTING TO GO TO DIFFERENT PLACES
SUNBURN WOULDN'T NEVER BOTHER YOU NONE, HORACE HORSECOLLAR= AND BESIDES, I HAVE SUCH A LOVELY BATHING COSTUME AND WHAT GOOD IS A BATHING COSTUME IN THE MOUNTAINS?
SAKES ALIVE!
I CAN'T SEE NO BATHIN' SUIT BEIN' IMPORTANT ENOUGH TO GIVE UP A TRIP TO THE MOUNTAINS FOR
OH! BUT YOU'VE NEVER SAW THIS BATHING SUIT
NO, AN' I CAN GET ALONG WITHOUT SEEIN' IT, TOO
WELL, YOU'RE GOING TO SEE IT JUST THE SAME, SMARTY= YOU BOYS WAIT RIGHT HERE AND I'LL DASH IN AND SLIP IT ON.
MISS CLOVERDALE 1908
7-23

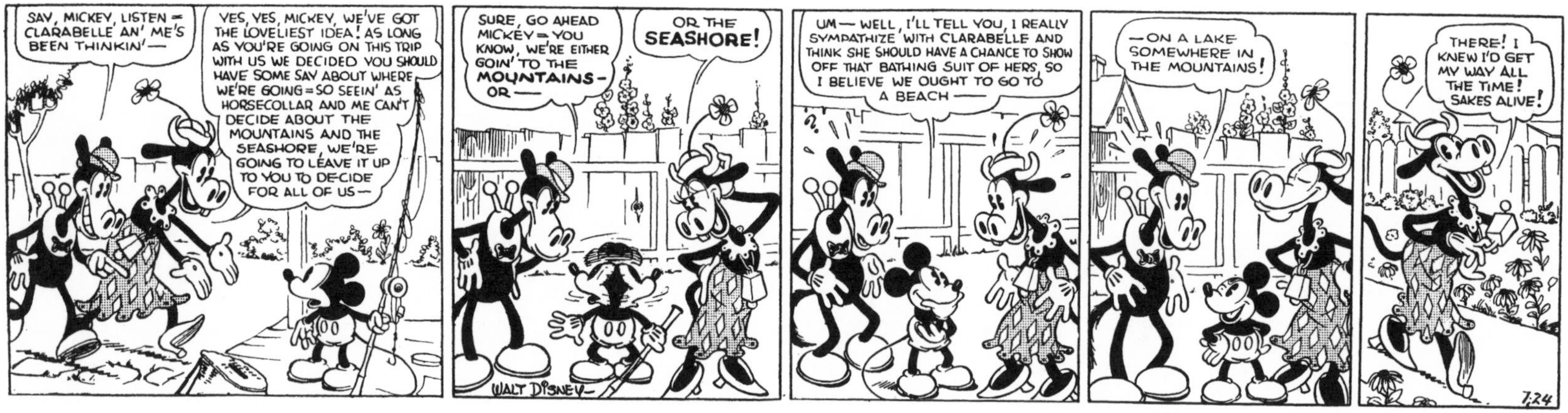

SAY, MICKEY, LISTEN= CLARABELLE AN' ME'S BEEN THINKIN'—
YES, YES, MICKEY, WE'VE GOT THE LOVELIEST IDEA! AS LONG AS YOU'RE GOING ON THIS TRIP WITH US WE DECIDED YOU SHOULD HAVE SOME SAY ABOUT WHERE WE'RE GOING=SO SEEIN' AS HORSECOLLAR AND ME CAN'T DECIDE ABOUT THE MOUNTAINS AND THE SEASHORE, WE'RE GOING TO LEAVE IT UP TO YOU TO DECIDE FOR ALL OF US—
SURE, GO AHEAD MICKEY= YOU KNOW, WE'RE EITHER GOIN' TO THE MOUNTAINS-OR—
OR THE SEASHORE!
WALT DISNEY
UM— WELL, I'LL TELL YOU, I REALLY SYMPATHIZE WITH CLARABELLE AND THINK SHE SHOULD HAVE A CHANCE TO SHOW OFF THAT BATHING SUIT OF HERS, SO I BELIEVE WE OUGHT TO GO TO A BEACH—
—ON A LAKE SOMEWHERE IN THE MOUNTAINS!
THERE! I KNEW I'D GET MY WAY ALL THE TIME! SAKES ALIVE!
7-24

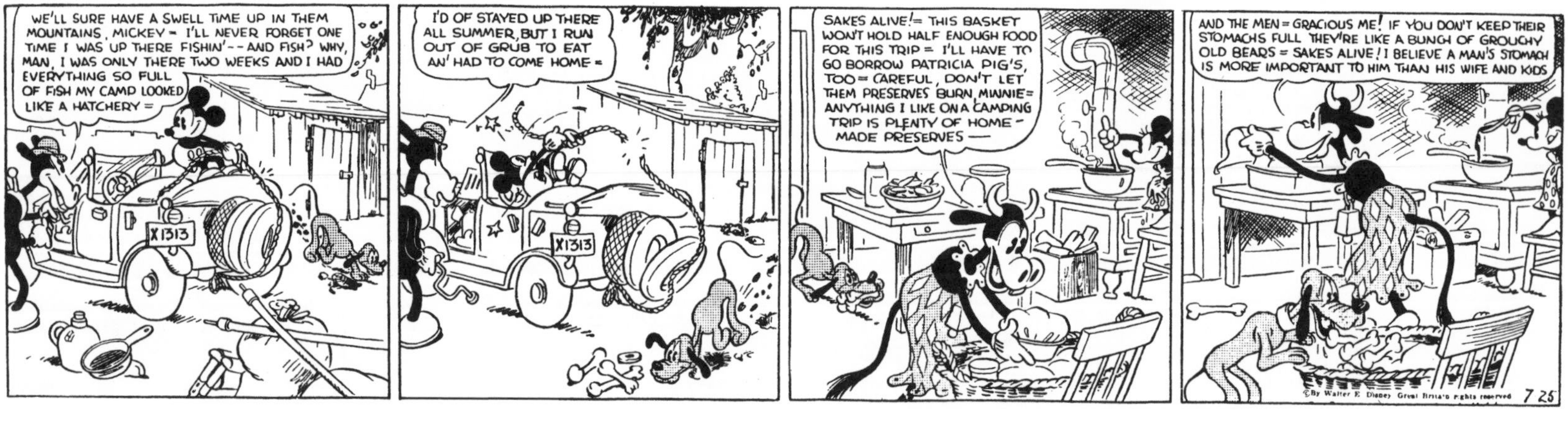

WE'LL SURE HAVE A SWELL TIME UP IN THEM MOUNTAINS, MICKEY= I'LL NEVER FORGET ONE TIME I WAS UP THERE FISHIN'--AND FISH? WHY, MAN, I WAS ONLY THERE TWO WEEKS AND I HAD EVERYTHING SO FULL OF FISH MY CAMP LOOKED LIKE A HATCHERY=
X1313
I'D OF STAYED UP THERE ALL SUMMER, BUT I RUN OUT OF GRUB TO EAT AN' HAD TO COME HOME=
X1313
SAKES ALIVE!= THIS BASKET WON'T HOLD HALF ENOUGH FOOD FOR THIS TRIP= I'LL HAVE TO GO BORROW PATRICIA PIG'S, TOO= CAREFUL, DON'T LET THEM PRESERVES BURN, MINNIE= ANYTHING I LIKE ON A CAMPING TRIP IS PLENTY OF HOME-MADE PRESERVES—
AND THE MEN= GRACIOUS ME! IF YOU DON'T KEEP THEIR STOMACHS FULL THEY'RE LIKE A BUNCH OF GROUCHY OLD BEARS= SAKES ALIVE! I BELIEVE A MAN'S STOMACH IS MORE IMPORTANT TO HIM THAN HIS WIFE AND KIDS
7-25

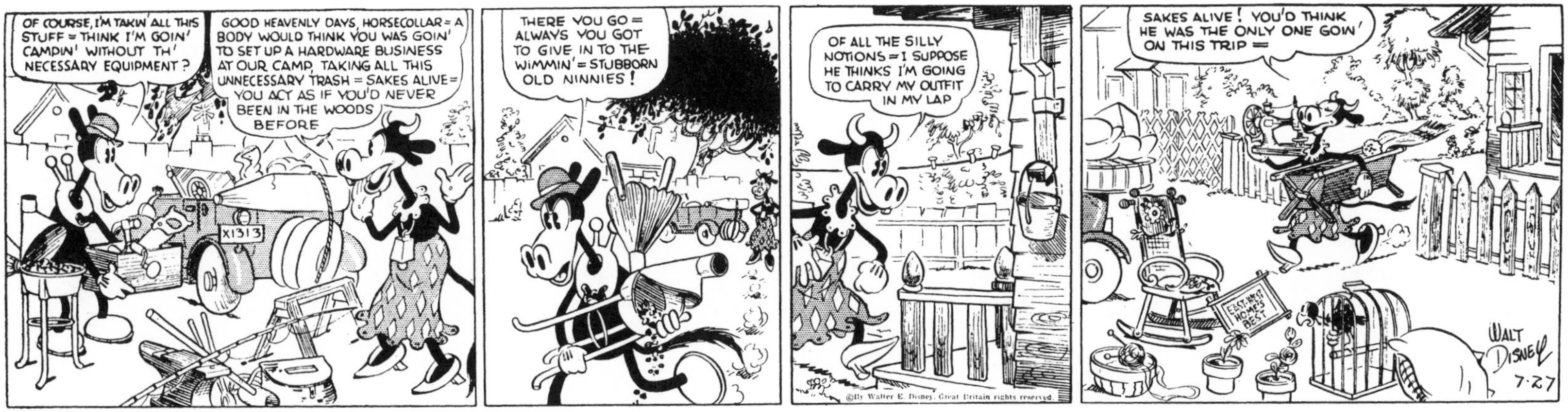
OF COURSE, I'M TAKIN' ALL THIS STUFF = THINK I'M GOIN' CAMPIN' WITHOUT TH' NECESSARY EQUIPMENT?
GOOD HEAVENLY DAYS, HORSECOLLAR = A BODY WOULD THINK YOU WAS GOIN' TO SET UP A HARDWARE BUSINESS AT OUR CAMP, TAKING ALL THIS UNNECESSARY TRASH = SAKES ALIVE = YOU ACT AS IF YOU'D NEVER BEEN IN THE WOODS BEFORE
X1313
THERE YOU GO = ALWAYS YOU GOT TO GIVE IN TO THE WIMMIN' = STUBBORN OLD NINNIES!
OF ALL THE SILLY NOTIONS = I SUPPOSE HE THINKS I'M GOING TO CARRY MY OUTFIT IN MY LAP
©By Walter E. Disney. Great Britain rights reserved.
SAKES ALIVE! YOU'D THINK HE WAS THE ONLY ONE GOIN' ON THIS TRIP =
WALT DISNEY
7-27

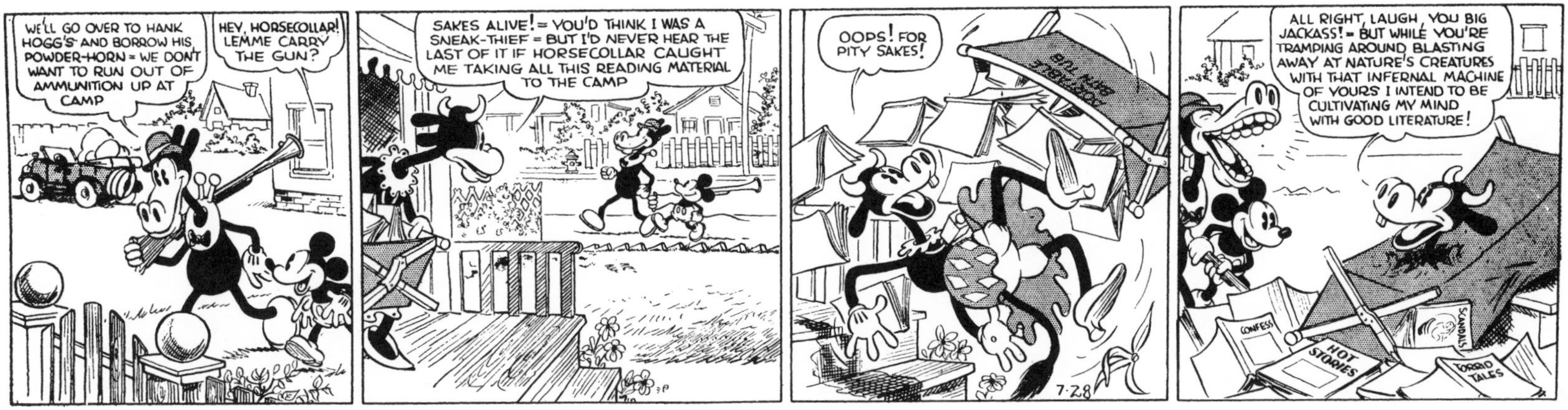
WE'LL GO OVER TO HANK HOGG'S AND BORROW HIS POWDER-HORN = WE DON'T WANT TO RUN OUT OF AMMUNITION UP AT CAMP
HEY, HORSECOLLAR! LEMME CARRY THE GUN?
SAKES ALIVE! = YOU'D THINK I WAS A SNEAK-THIEF = BUT I'D NEVER HEAR THE LAST OF IT IF HORSECOLLAR CAUGHT ME TAKING ALL THIS READING MATERIAL TO THE CAMP
OOPS! FOR PITY SAKES!
7-28
ALL RIGHT, LAUGH, YOU BIG JACKASS! = BUT WHILE YOU'RE TRAMPING AROUND BLASTING AWAY AT NATURE'S CREATURES WITH THAT INFERNAL MACHINE OF YOURS I INTEND TO BE CULTIVATING MY MIND WITH GOOD LITERATURE!
CONFESS
HOT STORIES
SCANDALS
TORRID TALES

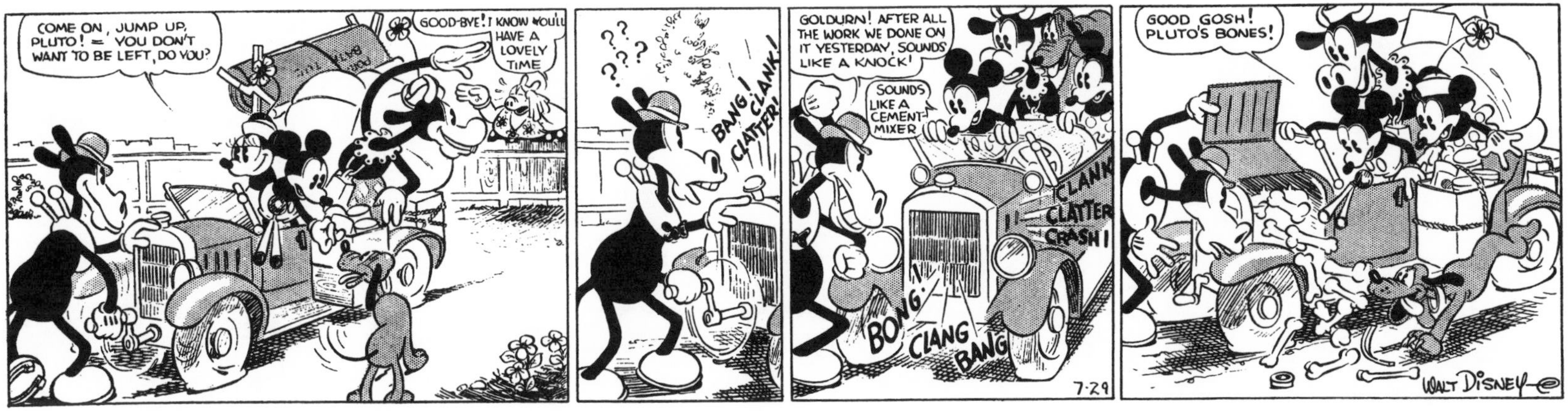
COME ON, JUMP UP, PLUTO! = YOU DON'T WANT TO BE LEFT, DO YOU?
GOOD-BYE!
I KNOW YOU'LL HAVE A LOVELY TIME
???
BANG! CLANK! CLATTER!
GOLDURN! AFTER ALL THE WORK WE DONE ON IT YESTERDAY, SOUNDS LIKE A KNOCK!
SOUNDS LIKE A CEMENT-MIXER
CLANK
CLATTER
CRASH!
BONG
CLANG
BANG
7-29
GOOD GOSH! PLUTO'S BONES!
WALT DISNEY

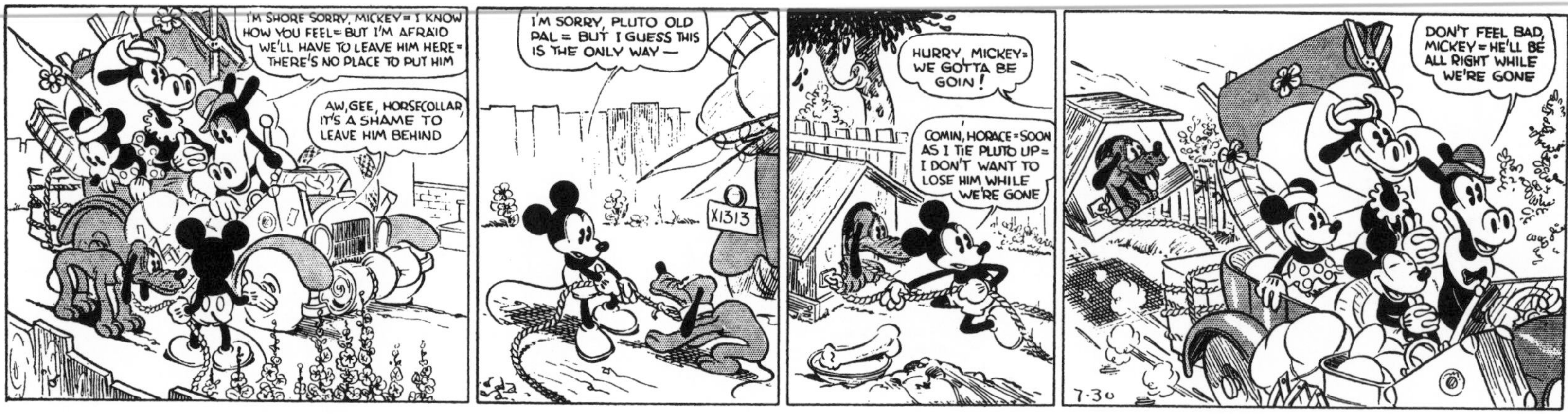
I'M SHORE SORRY, MICKEY = I KNOW HOW YOU FEEL = BUT I'M AFRAID WE'LL HAVE TO LEAVE HIM HERE = THERE'S NO PLACE TO PUT HIM
AW, GEE, HORSECOLLAR, IT'S A SHAME TO LEAVE HIM BEHIND
I'M SORRY, PLUTO OLD PAL = BUT I GUESS THIS IS THE ONLY WAY —
X1313
HURRY, MICKEY = WE GOTTA BE GOIN!
COMIN, HORACE = SOON AS I TIE PLUTO UP = I DON'T WANT TO LOSE HIM WHILE WE'RE GONE
DON'T FEEL BAD, MICKEY = HE'LL BE ALL RIGHT WHILE WE'RE GONE
7·30

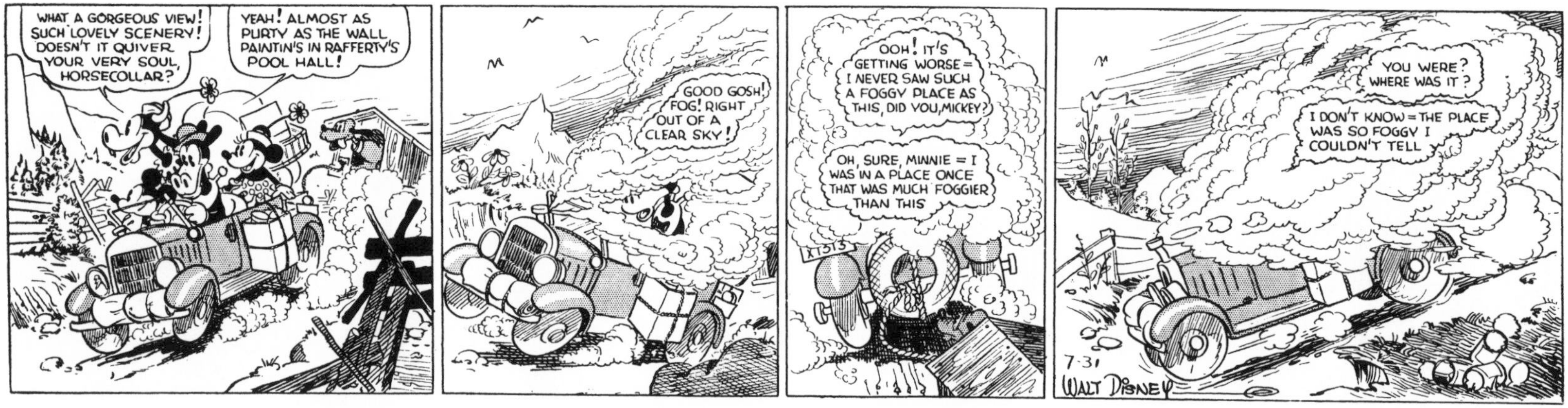
WHAT A GORGEOUS VIEW! SUCH LOVELY SCENERY! DOESN'T IT QUIVER YOUR VERY SOUL, HORSECOLLAR?
YEAH! ALMOST AS PURTY AS THE WALL PAINTIN'S IN RAFFERTY'S POOL HALL!
GOOD GOSH! FOG! RIGHT OUT OF A CLEAR SKY!
OOH! IT'S GETTING WORSE = I NEVER SAW SUCH A FOGGY PLACE AS THIS, DID YOU, MICKEY?
OH, SURE, MINNIE = I WAS IN A PLACE ONCE THAT WAS MUCH FOGGIER THAN THIS
X1313
YOU WERE? WHERE WAS IT?
I DON'T KNOW = THE PLACE WAS SO FOGGY I COULDN'T TELL
7·31
WALT DISNEY

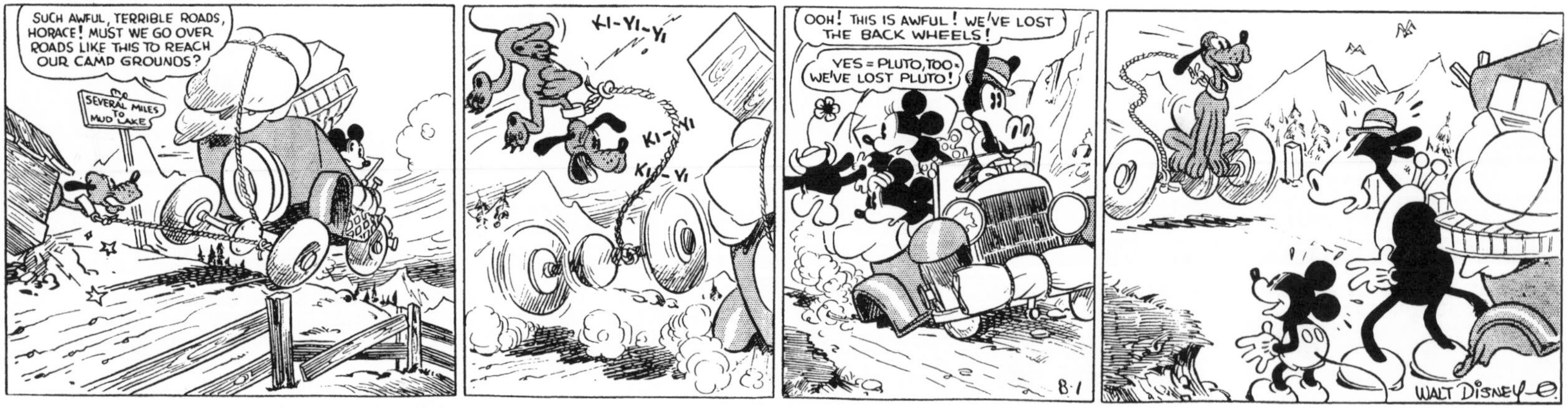
SUCH AWFUL, TERRIBLE ROADS, HORACE! MUST WE GO OVER ROADS LIKE THIS TO REACH OUR CAMP GROUNDS?
SEVERAL MILES TO MUD LAKE
KI-YI-YI
KI-YI
KI-YI
OOH! THIS IS AWFUL! WE'VE LOST THE BACK WHEELS!
YES = PLUTO, TOO = WE'VE LOST PLUTO!
8·1
WALT DISNEY

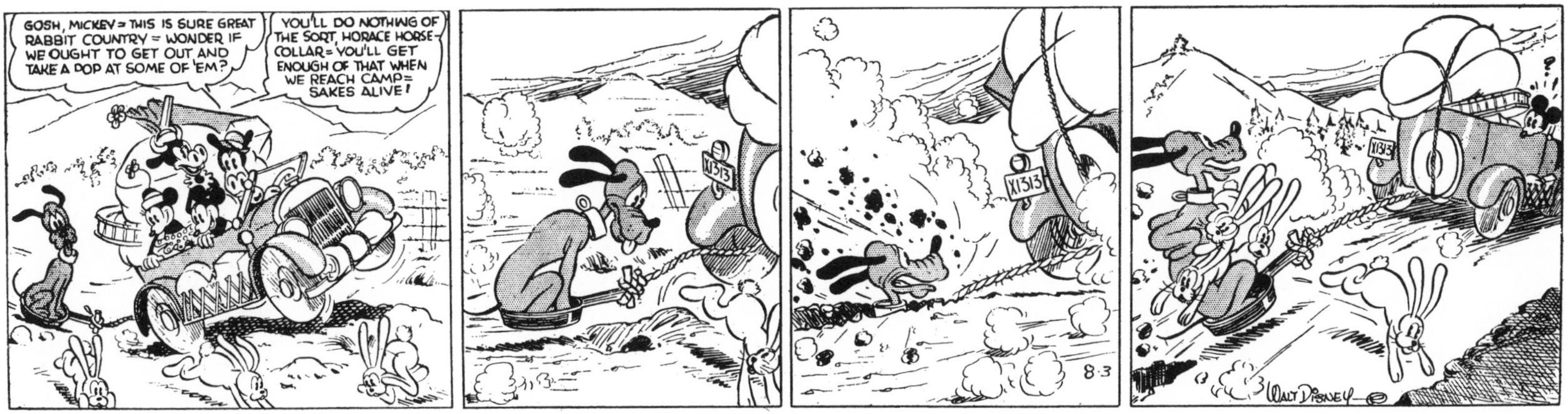
GOSH, MICKEY = THIS IS SURE GREAT RABBIT COUNTRY = WONDER IF WE OUGHT TO GET OUT AND TAKE A POP AT SOME OF 'EM?
YOU'LL DO NOTHING OF THE SORT, HORACE HORSE-COLLAR = YOU'LL GET ENOUGH OF THAT WHEN WE REACH CAMP = SAKES ALIVE!
X1313
X1313
X1313
8·3
WALT DISNEY

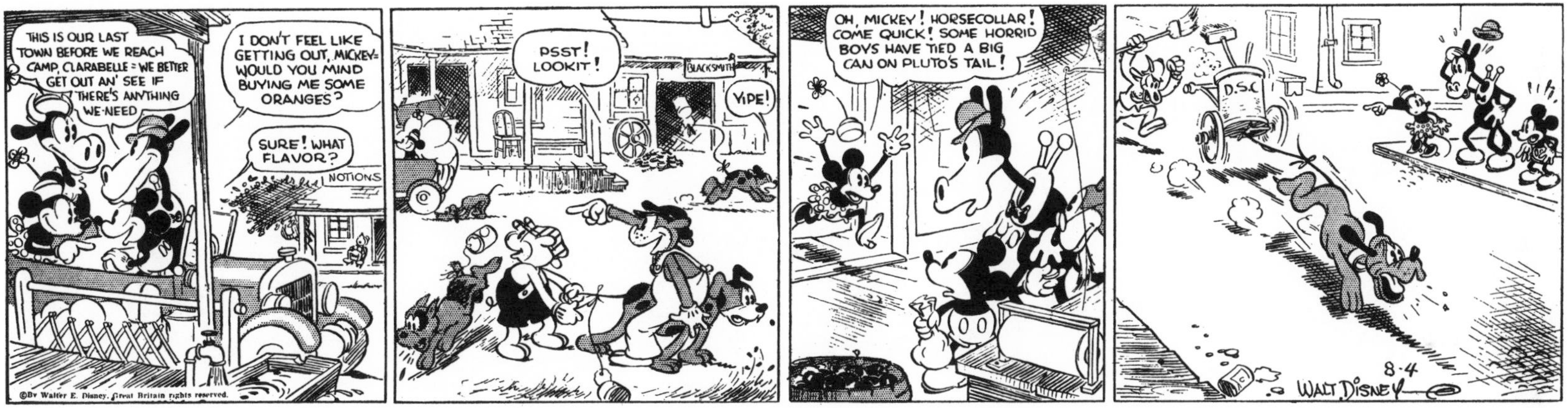
THIS IS OUR LAST TOWN BEFORE WE REACH CAMP, CLARABELLE = WE BETTER GET OUT AN' SEE IF THERE'S ANYTHING WE NEED
I DON'T FEEL LIKE GETTING OUT, MICKEY = WOULD YOU MIND BUYING ME SOME ORANGES?
SURE! WHAT FLAVOR?
NOTIONS
©By Walter E. Disney. Great Britain rights reserved.
PSST! LOOKIT!
BLACKSMITH
YIPE!
OH, MICKEY! HORSECOLLAR! COME QUICK! SOME HORRID BOYS HAVE TIED A BIG CAN ON PLUTO'S TAIL!
D.S.C.
8·4
WALT DISNEY

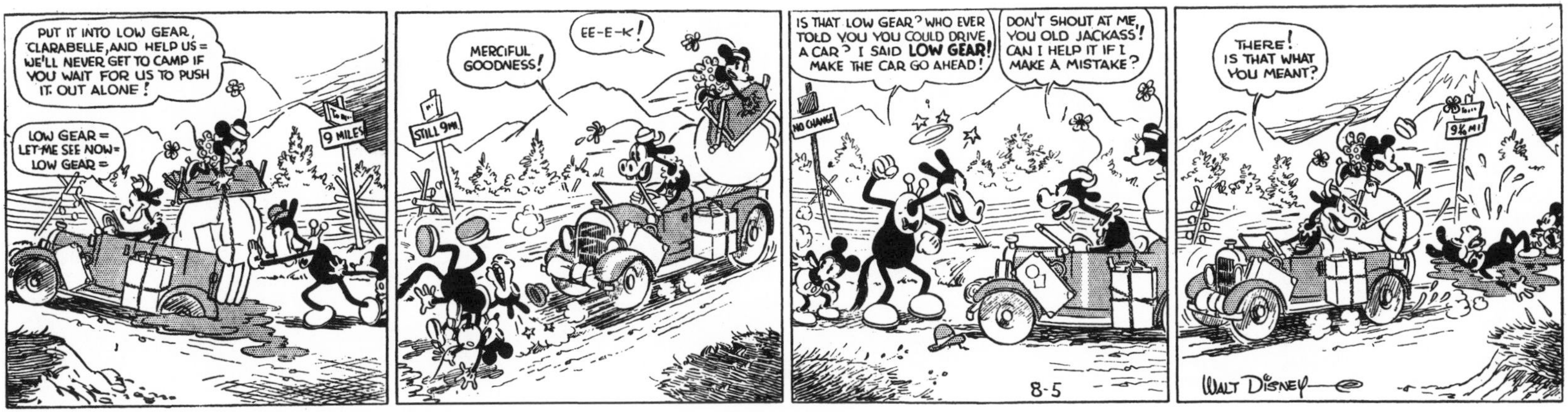
PUT IT INTO LOW GEAR, CLARABELLE, AND HELP US = WE'LL NEVER GET TO CAMP IF YOU WAIT FOR US TO PUSH IT OUT ALONE!
LOW GEAR = LET ME SEE NOW = LOW GEAR =
9 MILES
MERCIFUL GOODNESS!
EE-E-K!
STILL 9MI.
IS THAT LOW GEAR? WHO EVER TOLD YOU YOU COULD DRIVE A CAR? I SAID LOW GEAR! MAKE THE CAR GO AHEAD!
DON'T SHOUT AT ME, YOU OLD JACKASS! CAN I HELP IT IF I MAKE A MISTAKE?
NO CHANGE
8-5
THERE! IS THAT WHAT YOU MEANT?
9½ MI
WALT DISNEY

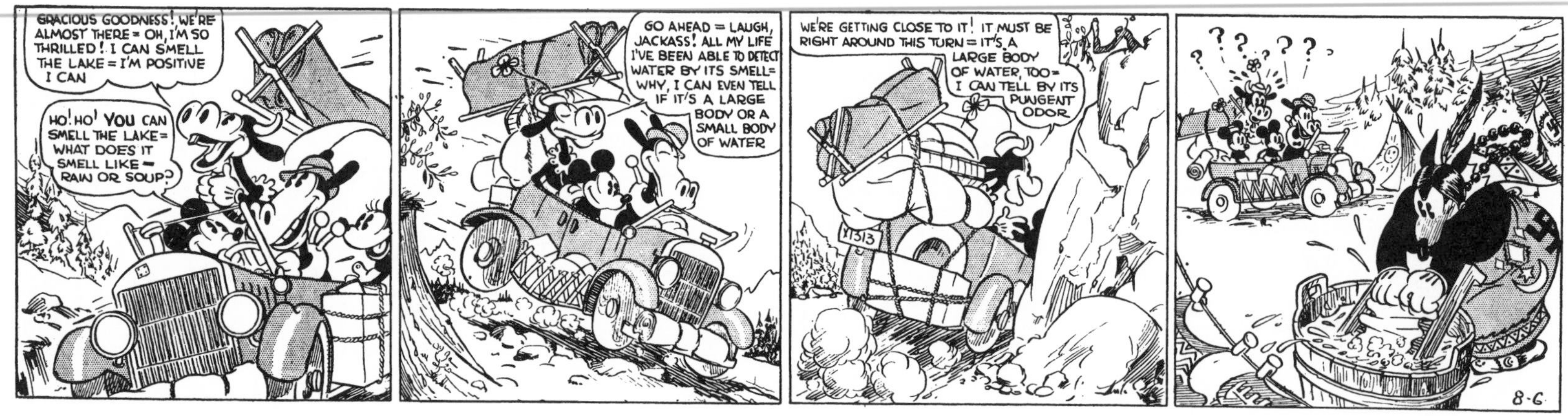
GRACIOUS GOODNESS! WE'RE ALMOST THERE = OH, I'M SO THRILLED! I CAN SMELL THE LAKE = I'M POSITIVE I CAN
HO! HO! YOU CAN SMELL THE LAKE = WHAT DOES IT SMELL LIKE — RAIN OR SOUP?
GO AHEAD = LAUGH, JACKASS! ALL MY LIFE I'VE BEEN ABLE TO DETECT WATER BY ITS SMELL = WHY, I CAN EVEN TELL IF IT'S A LARGE BODY OR A SMALL BODY OF WATER
WE'RE GETTING CLOSE TO IT! IT MUST BE RIGHT AROUND THIS TURN = IT'S A LARGE BODY OF WATER, TOO = I CAN TELL BY ITS PUNGENT ODOR
8-6

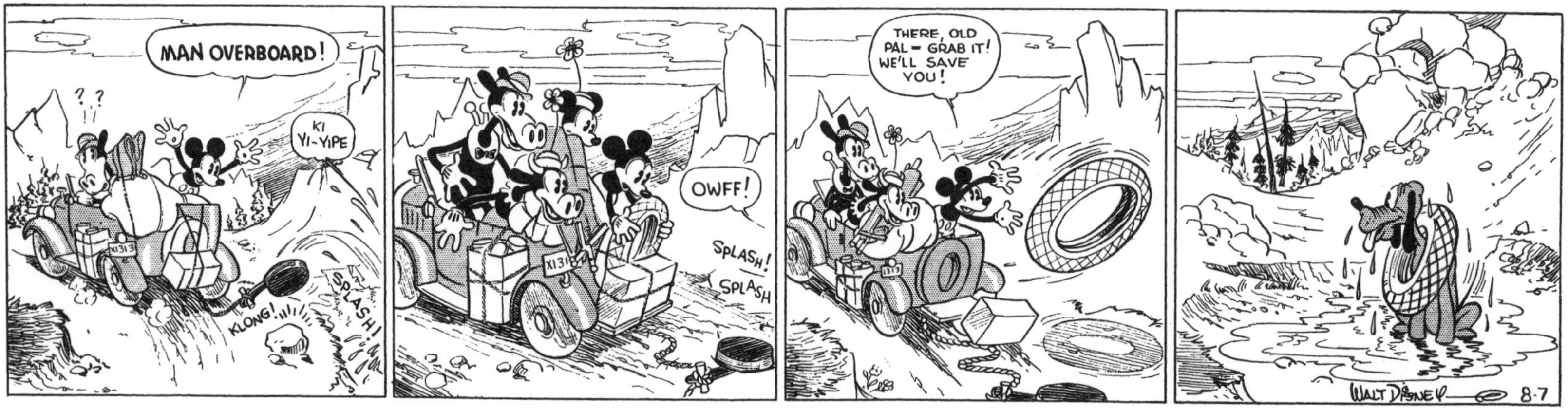
MAN OVERBOARD!
KI YI-YIPE
KLONG!
SPLASH!
OWFF!
SPLASH!
SPLASH
THERE, OLD PAL — GRAB IT! WE'LL SAVE YOU!
WALT DISNEY
8-7

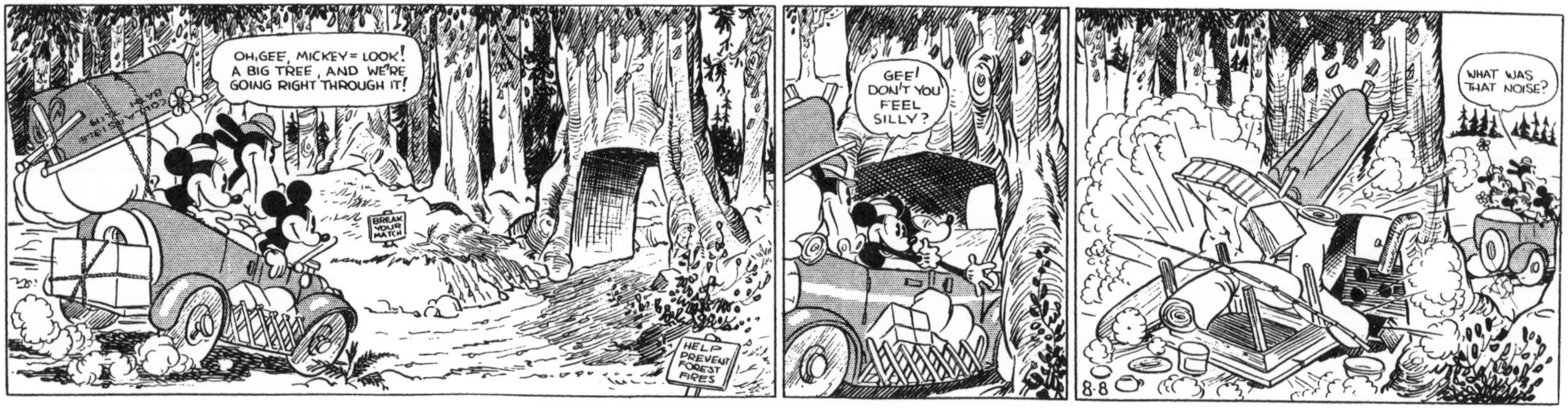
OH, GEE, MICKEY = LOOK! A BIG TREE, AND WE'RE GOING RIGHT THROUGH IT!
BREAK YOUR MATCH
HELP PREVENT FOREST FIRES
GEE! DON'T YOU FEEL SILLY?
WHAT WAS THAT NOISE?
8-8

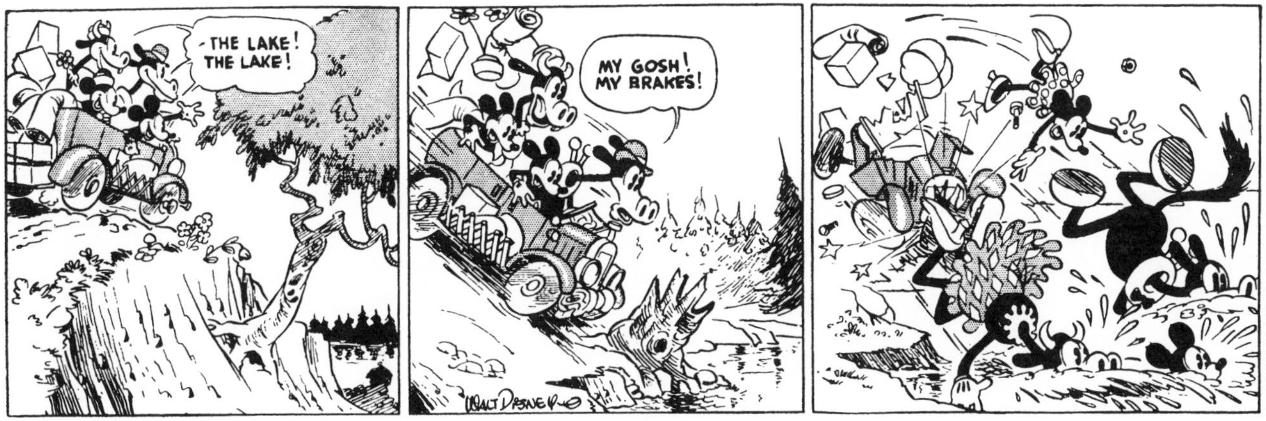
THE LAKE! THE LAKE!
MY GOSH! MY BRAKES!
WALT DISNEY
WELL, HERE'S THE CAMP = WHERE DO YOU WANT YOUR TENT PITCHED, CLARABELLE?
8·10

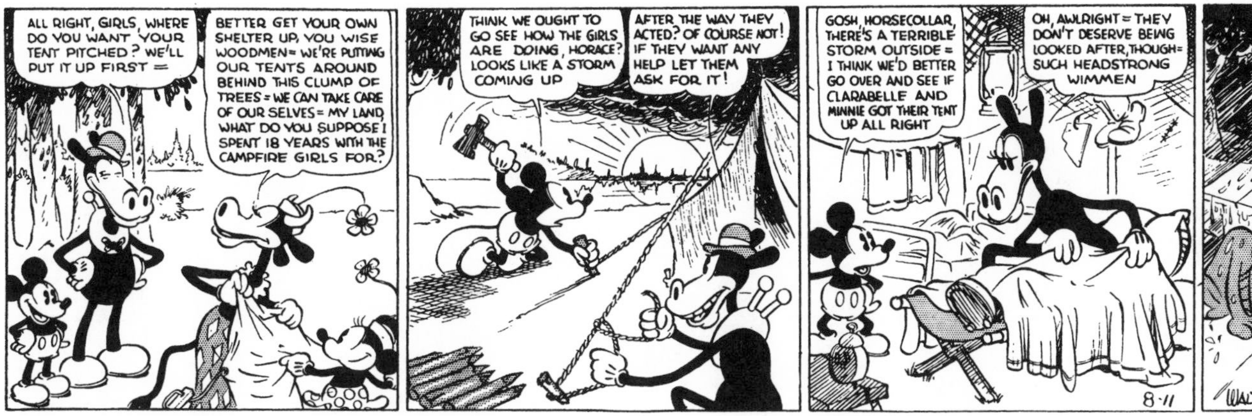
ALL RIGHT, GIRLS, WHERE DO YOU WANT YOUR TENT PITCHED? WE'LL PUT IT UP FIRST =
BETTER GET YOUR OWN SHELTER UP, YOU WISE WOODMEN = WE'RE PUTTING OUR TENTS AROUND BEHIND THIS CLUMP OF TREES = WE CAN TAKE CARE OF OUR SELVES = MY LAND, WHAT DO YOU SUPPOSE I SPENT 18 YEARS WITH THE CAMPFIRE GIRLS FOR?
THINK WE OUGHT TO GO SEE HOW THE GIRLS ARE DOING, HORACE? LOOKS LIKE A STORM COMING UP
AFTER THE WAY THEY ACTED? OF COURSE NOT! IF THEY WANT ANY HELP LET THEM ASK FOR IT!
GOSH, HORSECOLLAR, THERE'S A TERRIBLE STORM OUTSIDE = I THINK WE'D BETTER GO OVER AND SEE IF CLARABELLE AND MINNIE GOT THEIR TENT UP ALL RIGHT
OH, AWLRIGHT = THEY DON'T DESERVE BEING LOOKED AFTER, THOUGH = SUCH HEADSTRONG WIMMEN
8·11
Z-Z-Z-Z WE-E-E-E Z-Z-Z Z
WALT DISNEY

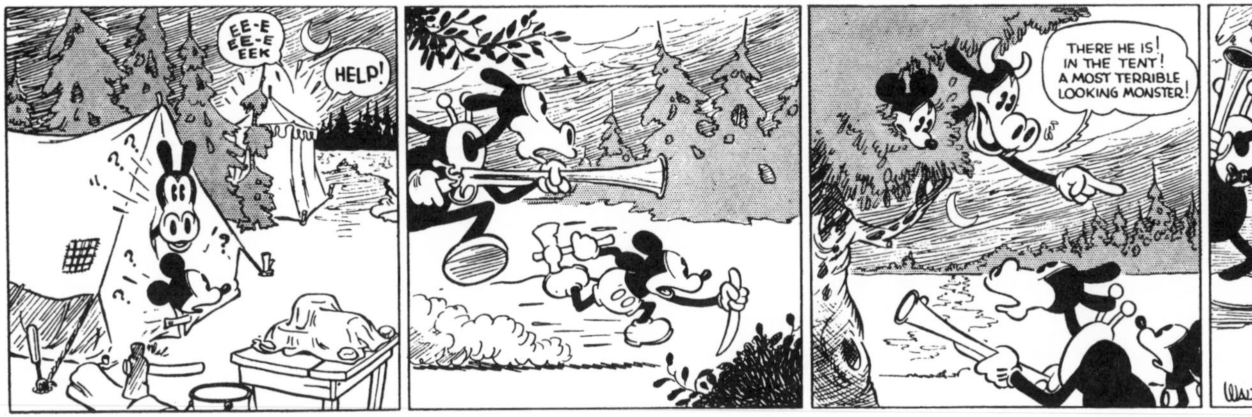
EE-E EE-E EEK
HELP!
THERE HE IS! IN THE TENT! A MOST TERRIBLE LOOKING MONSTER!
WALT DISNEY
8/12

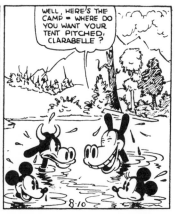

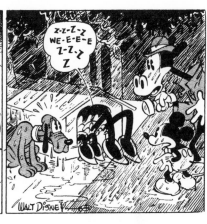

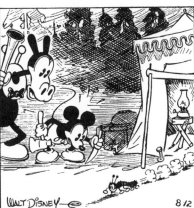

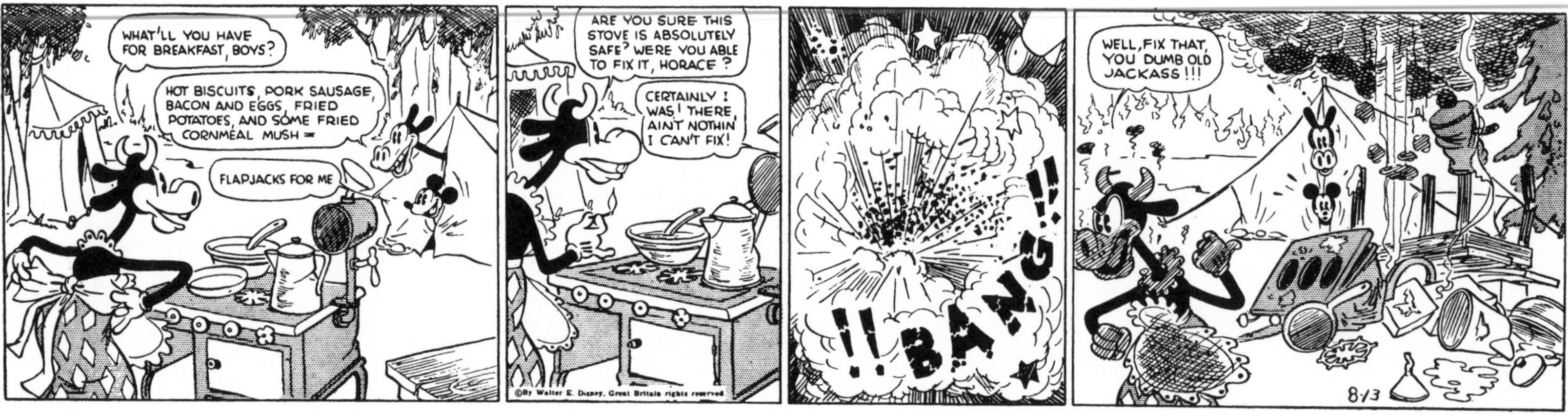
WHAT'LL YOU HAVE FOR BREAKFAST, BOYS?
HOT BISCUITS, PORK SAUSAGE, BACON AND EGGS, FRIED POTATOES, AND SOME FRIED CORNMEAL MUSH =
FLAPJACKS FOR ME
ARE YOU SURE THIS STOVE IS ABSOLUTELY SAFE? WERE YOU ABLE TO FIX IT, HORACE?
CERTAINLY! WAS! THERE AIN'T NOTHIN' I CAN'T FIX!
©By Walter E. Disney, Great Britain rights reserved
!! BANG !!
WELL, FIX THAT, YOU DUMB OLD JACKASS!!!
8-13

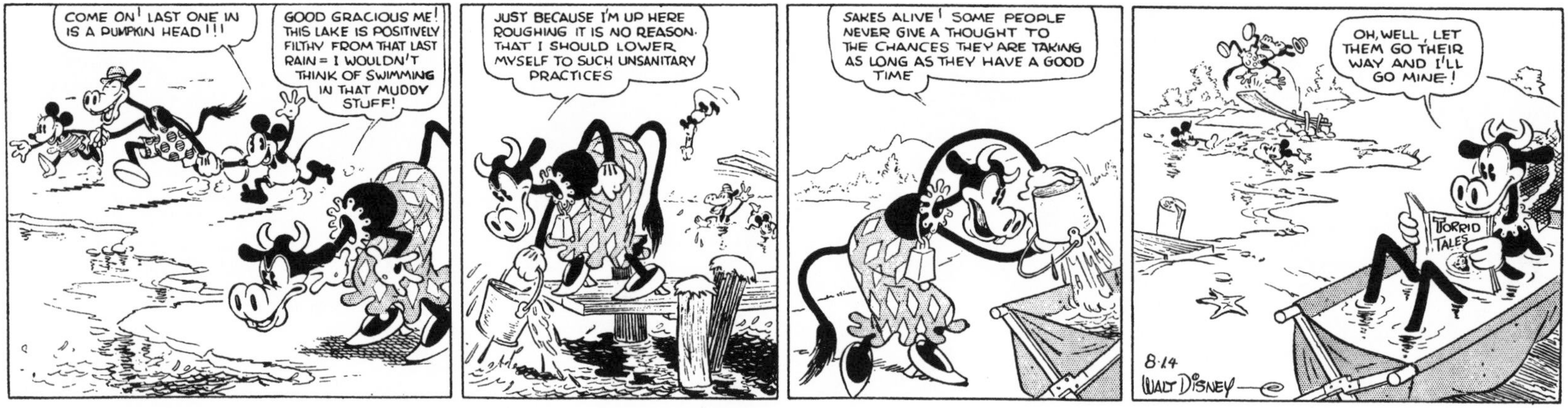
COME ON! LAST ONE IN IS A PUMPKIN HEAD!!!
GOOD GRACIOUS ME! THIS LAKE IS POSITIVELY FILTHY FROM THAT LAST RAIN = I WOULDN'T THINK OF SWIMMING IN THAT MUDDY STUFF!
JUST BECAUSE I'M UP HERE ROUGHING IT IS NO REASON THAT I SHOULD LOWER MYSELF TO SUCH UNSANITARY PRACTICES
SAKES ALIVE! SOME PEOPLE NEVER GIVE A THOUGHT TO THE CHANCES THEY ARE TAKING AS LONG AS THEY HAVE A GOOD TIME
OH, WELL, LET THEM GO THEIR WAY AND I'LL GO MINE!
TORRID TALES
8-14
WALT DISNEY

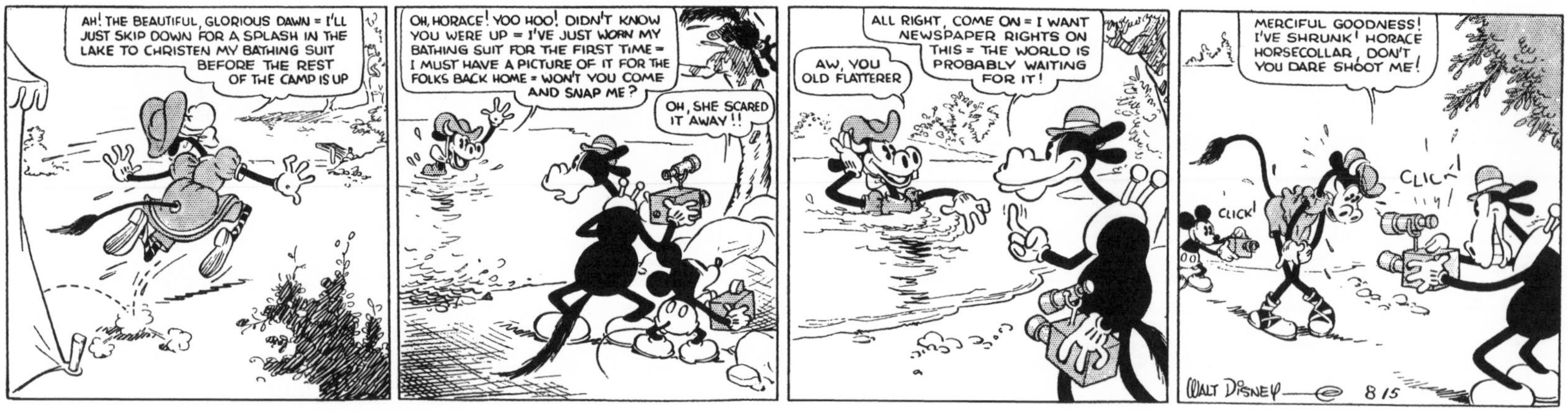
AH! THE BEAUTIFUL, GLORIOUS DAWN = I'LL JUST SKIP DOWN FOR A SPLASH IN THE LAKE TO CHRISTEN MY BATHING SUIT BEFORE THE REST OF THE CAMP IS UP
OH, HORACE! YOO HOO! DIDN'T KNOW YOU WERE UP = I'VE JUST WORN MY BATHING SUIT FOR THE FIRST TIME = I MUST HAVE A PICTURE OF IT FOR THE FOLKS BACK HOME = WON'T YOU COME AND SNAP ME?
OH, SHE SCARED IT AWAY!!
AW, YOU OLD FLATTERER
ALL RIGHT, COME ON = I WANT NEWSPAPER RIGHTS ON THIS = THE WORLD IS PROBABLY WAITING FOR IT!
MERCIFUL GOODNESS! I'VE SHRUNK! HORACE HORSECOLLAR, DON'T YOU DARE SHOOT ME!
CLICK!
CLICK!
WALT DISNEY
8-15

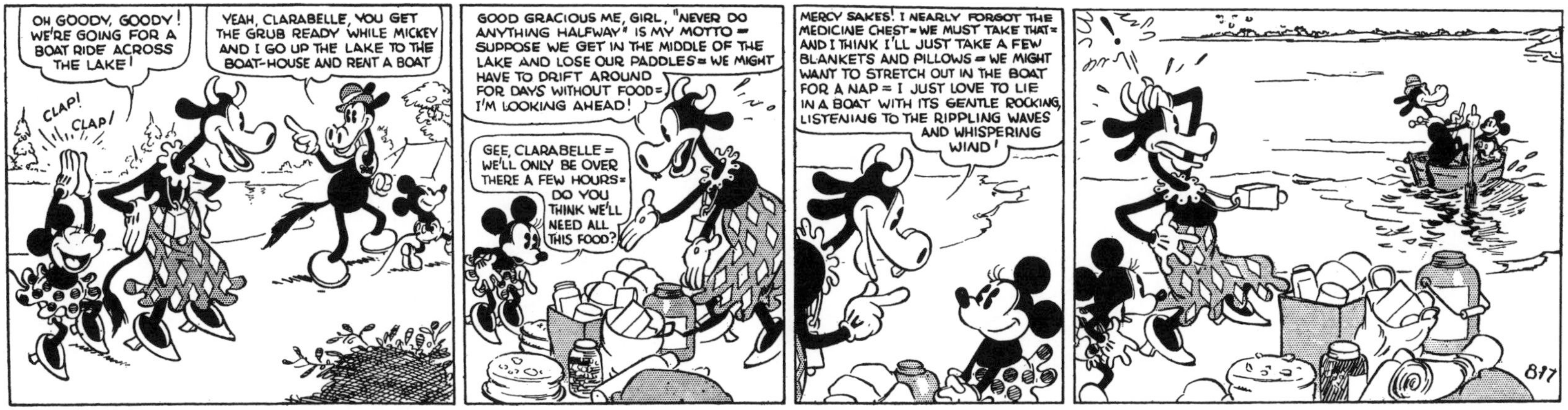
OH GOODY, GOODY! WE'RE GOING FOR A BOAT RIDE ACROSS THE LAKE!
CLAP! CLAP!
YEAH, CLARABELLE, YOU GET THE GRUB READY WHILE MICKEY AND I GO UP THE LAKE TO THE BOAT-HOUSE AND RENT A BOAT
GOOD GRACIOUS ME, GIRL, "NEVER DO ANYTHING HALFWAY" IS MY MOTTO = SUPPOSE WE GET IN THE MIDDLE OF THE LAKE AND LOSE OUR PADDLES = WE MIGHT HAVE TO DRIFT AROUND FOR DAYS WITHOUT FOOD = I'M LOOKING AHEAD!
GEE, CLARABELLE = WE'LL ONLY BE OVER THERE A FEW HOURS = DO YOU THINK WE'LL NEED ALL THIS FOOD?
MERCY SAKES! I NEARLY FORGOT THE MEDICINE CHEST = WE MUST TAKE THAT = AND I THINK I'LL JUST TAKE A FEW BLANKETS AND PILLOWS = WE MIGHT WANT TO STRETCH OUT IN THE BOAT FOR A NAP = I JUST LOVE TO LIE IN A BOAT WITH ITS GENTLE ROCKING, LISTENING TO THE RIPPLING WAVES AND WHISPERING WIND!
8-17

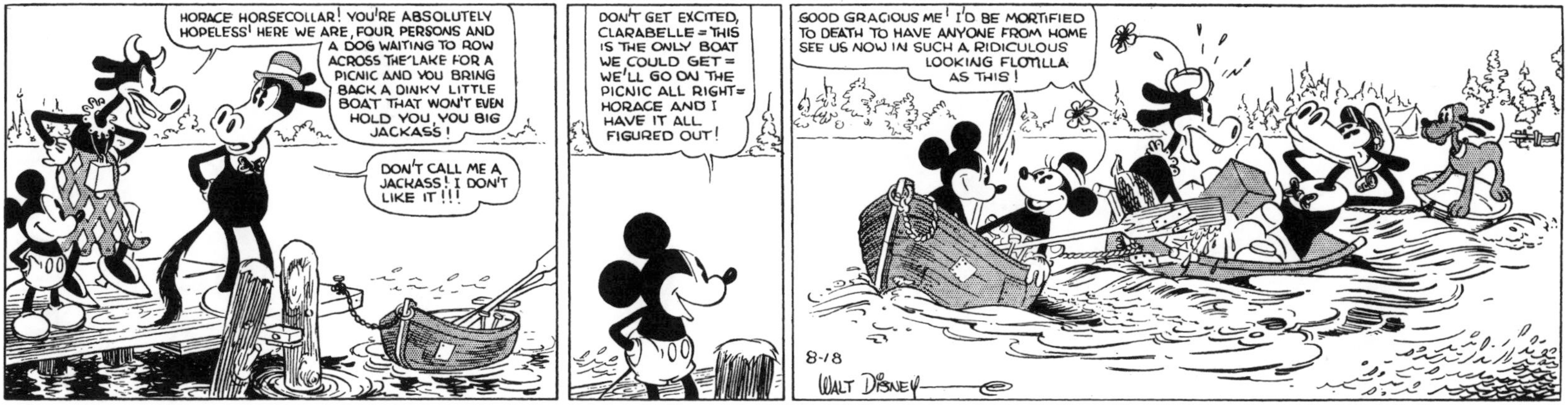
HORACE HORSECOLLAR! YOU'RE ABSOLUTELY HOPELESS! HERE WE ARE, FOUR PERSONS AND A DOG WAITING TO ROW ACROSS THE LAKE FOR A PICNIC AND YOU BRING BACK A DINKY LITTLE BOAT THAT WON'T EVEN HOLD YOU, YOU BIG JACKASS!
DON'T CALL ME A JACKASS! I DON'T LIKE IT!!!
DON'T GET EXCITED, CLARABELLE = THIS IS THE ONLY BOAT WE COULD GET = WE'LL GO ON THE PICNIC ALL RIGHT = HORACE AND I HAVE IT ALL FIGURED OUT!
GOOD GRACIOUS ME! I'D BE MORTIFIED TO DEATH TO HAVE ANYONE FROM HOME SEE US NOW IN SUCH A RIDICULOUS LOOKING FLOTILLA AS THIS!
8-18
WALT DISNEY

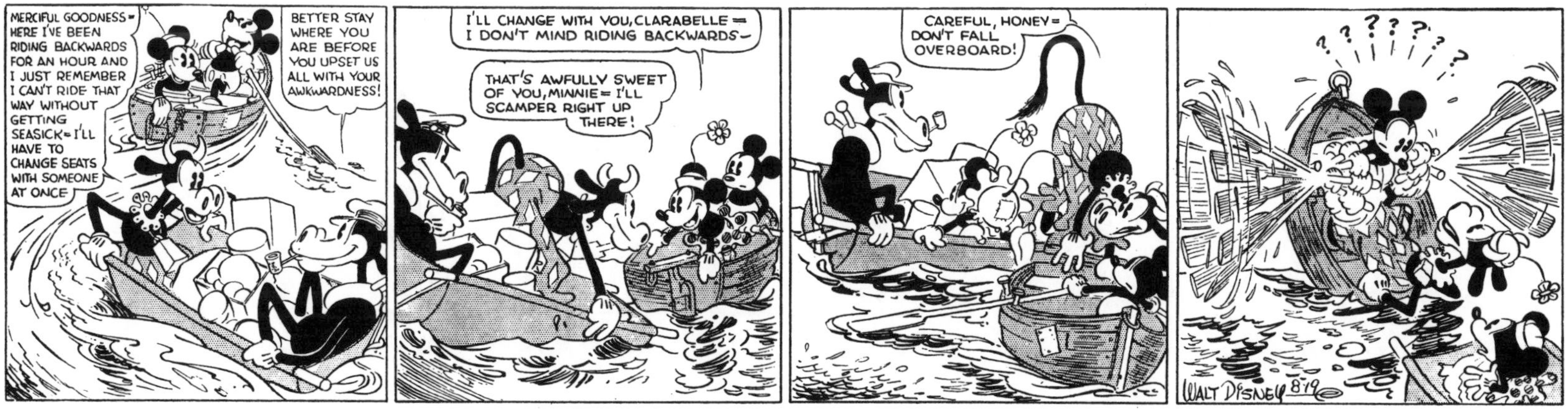
MERCIFUL GOODNESS = HERE I'VE BEEN RIDING BACKWARDS FOR AN HOUR AND I JUST REMEMBER I CAN'T RIDE THAT WAY WITHOUT GETTING SEASICK = I'LL HAVE TO CHANGE SEATS WITH SOMEONE AT ONCE
BETTER STAY WHERE YOU ARE BEFORE YOU UPSET US ALL WITH YOUR AWKWARDNESS!
I'LL CHANGE WITH YOU, CLARABELLE = I DON'T MIND RIDING BACKWARDS —
THAT'S AWFULLY SWEET OF YOU, MINNIE = I'LL SCAMPER RIGHT UP THERE!
CAREFUL, HONEY = DON'T FALL OVERBOARD!
? ? ? ? ? ? ?
WALT DISNEY 8-19

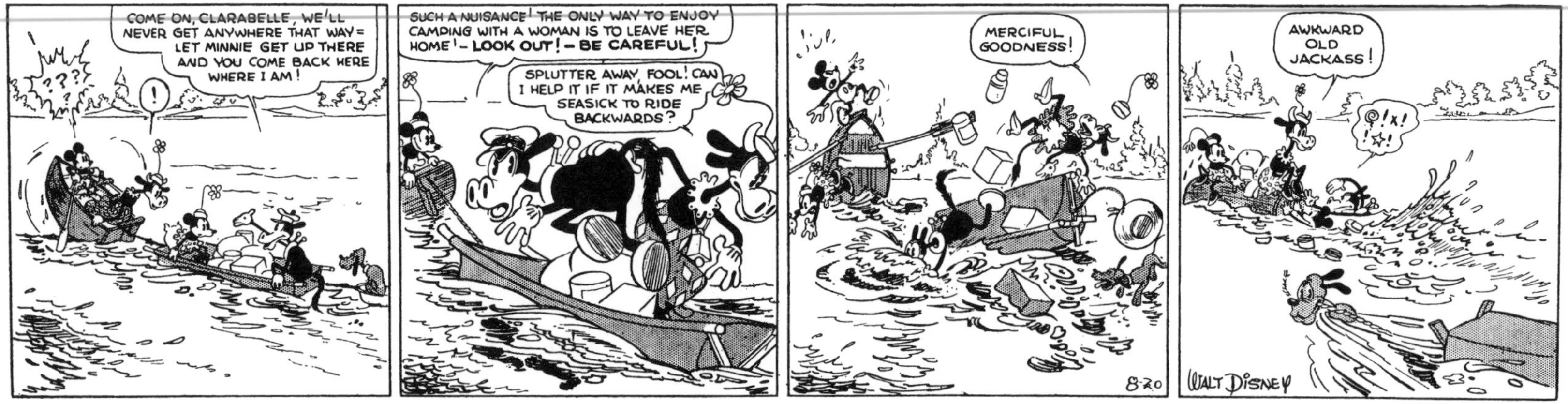
COME ON, CLARABELLE, WE'LL NEVER GET ANYWHERE THAT WAY= LET MINNIE GET UP THERE AND YOU COME BACK HERE WHERE I AM!
???
!
SUCH A NUISANCE! THE ONLY WAY TO ENJOY CAMPING WITH A WOMAN IS TO LEAVE HER HOME! – LOOK OUT! – BE CAREFUL!
SPLUTTER AWAY, FOOL! CAN I HELP IT IF IT MAKES ME SEASICK TO RIDE BACKWARDS?
MERCIFUL GOODNESS!
8·20
AWKWARD OLD JACKASS!
WALT DISNEY

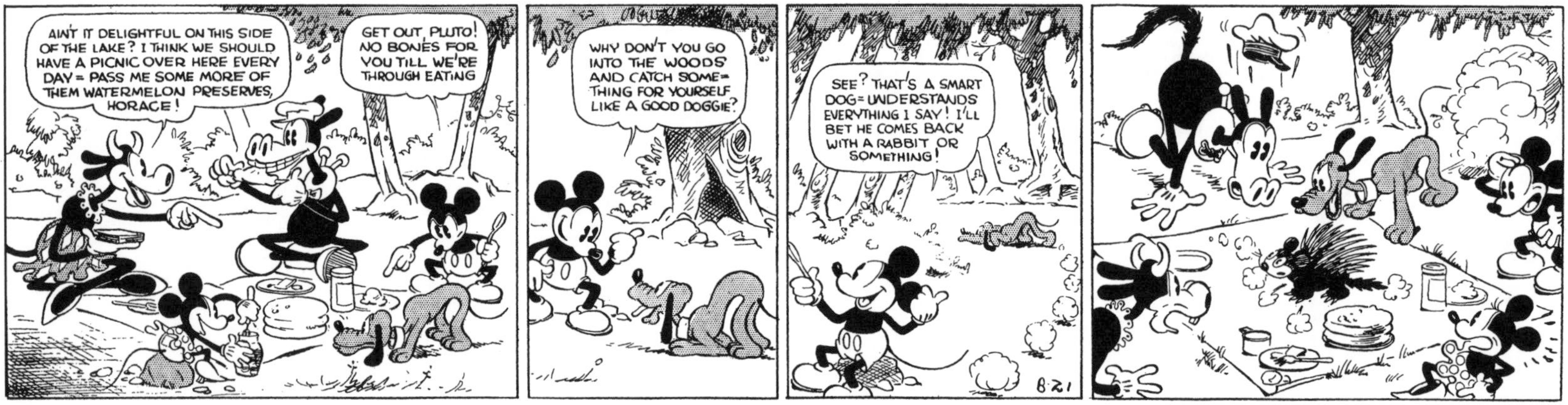
AIN'T IT DELIGHTFUL ON THIS SIDE OF THE LAKE? I THINK WE SHOULD HAVE A PICNIC OVER HERE EVERY DAY= PASS ME SOME MORE OF THEM WATERMELON PRESERVES, HORACE!
GET OUT, PLUTO! NO BONES FOR YOU TILL WE'RE THROUGH EATING
WHY DON'T YOU GO INTO THE WOODS AND CATCH SOME= THING FOR YOURSELF LIKE A GOOD DOGGIE?
SEE? THAT'S A SMART DOG= UNDERSTANDS EVERYTHING I SAY! I'LL BET HE COMES BACK WITH A RABBIT OR SOMETHING!
8·21

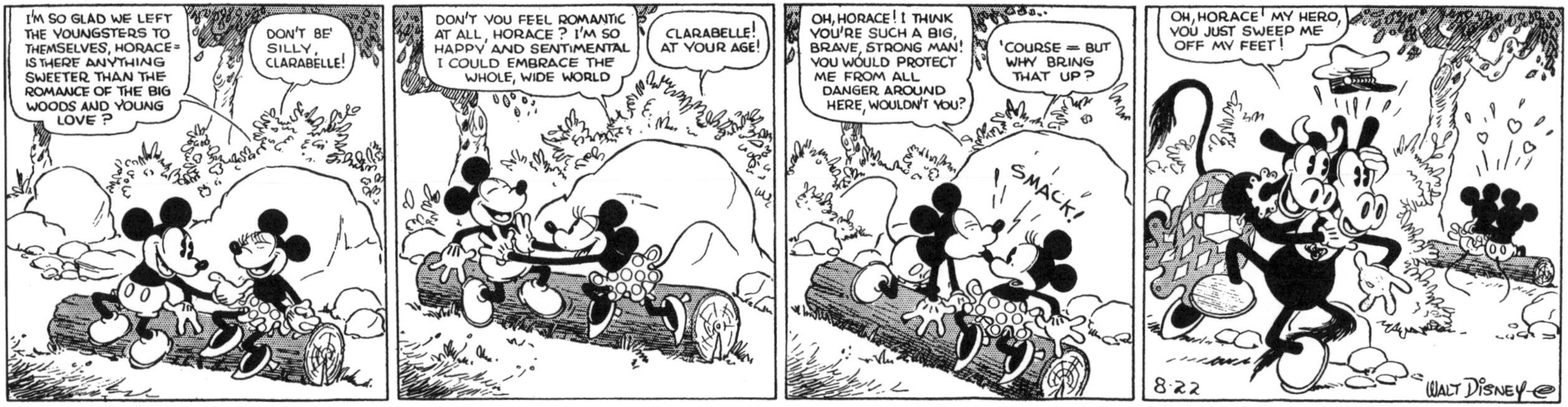
I'M SO GLAD WE LEFT THE YOUNGSTERS TO THEMSELVES, HORACE= IS THERE ANYTHING SWEETER THAN THE ROMANCE OF THE BIG WOODS AND YOUNG LOVE?
DON'T BE SILLY, CLARABELLE!
DON'T YOU FEEL ROMANTIC AT ALL, HORACE? I'M SO HAPPY AND SENTIMENTAL I COULD EMBRACE THE WHOLE, WIDE WORLD
CLARABELLE! AT YOUR AGE!
OH, HORACE! I THINK YOU'RE SUCH A BIG, BRAVE, STRONG MAN! YOU WOULD PROTECT ME FROM ALL DANGER AROUND HERE, WOULDN'T YOU?
'COURSE = BUT WHY BRING THAT UP?
SMACK!
OH, HORACE! MY HERO, YOU JUST SWEEP ME OFF MY FEET!
8·22
WALT DISNEY

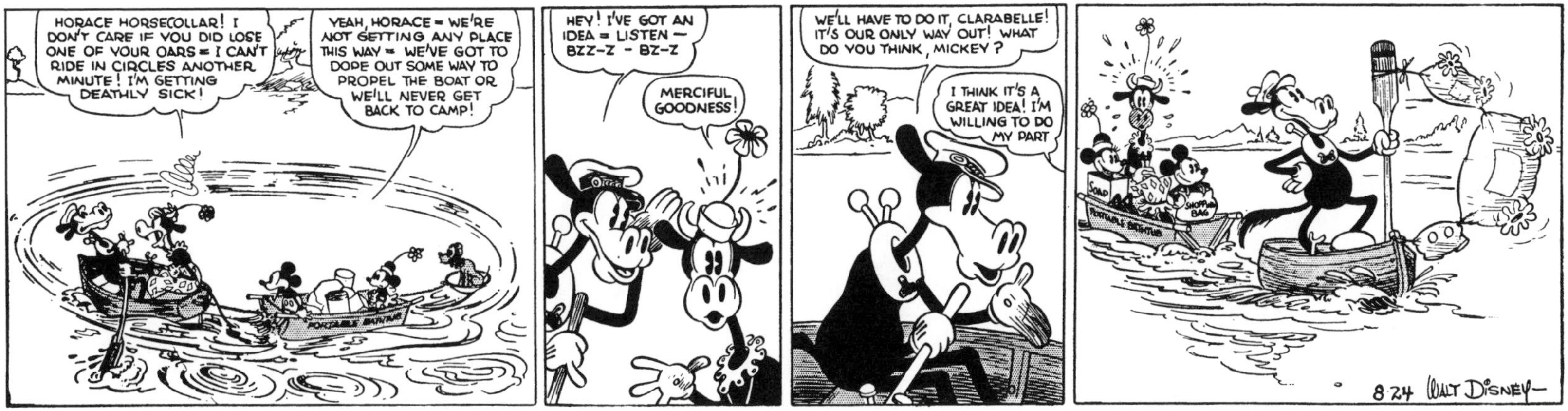
HORACE HORSECOLLAR! I DON'T CARE IF YOU DID LOSE ONE OF YOUR OARS = I CAN'T RIDE IN CIRCLES ANOTHER MINUTE! I'M GETTING DEATHLY SICK!
YEAH, HORACE = WE'RE NOT GETTING ANY PLACE THIS WAY = WE'VE GOT TO DOPE OUT SOME WAY TO PROPEL THE BOAT OR WE'LL NEVER GET BACK TO CAMP!
HEY! I'VE GOT AN IDEA = LISTEN — BZZ-Z – BZ-Z
MERCIFUL GOODNESS!
WE'LL HAVE TO DO IT, CLARABELLE! IT'S OUR ONLY WAY OUT! WHAT DO YOU THINK, MICKEY?
I THINK IT'S A GREAT IDEA! I'M WILLING TO DO MY PART
8·24 WALT DISNEY—

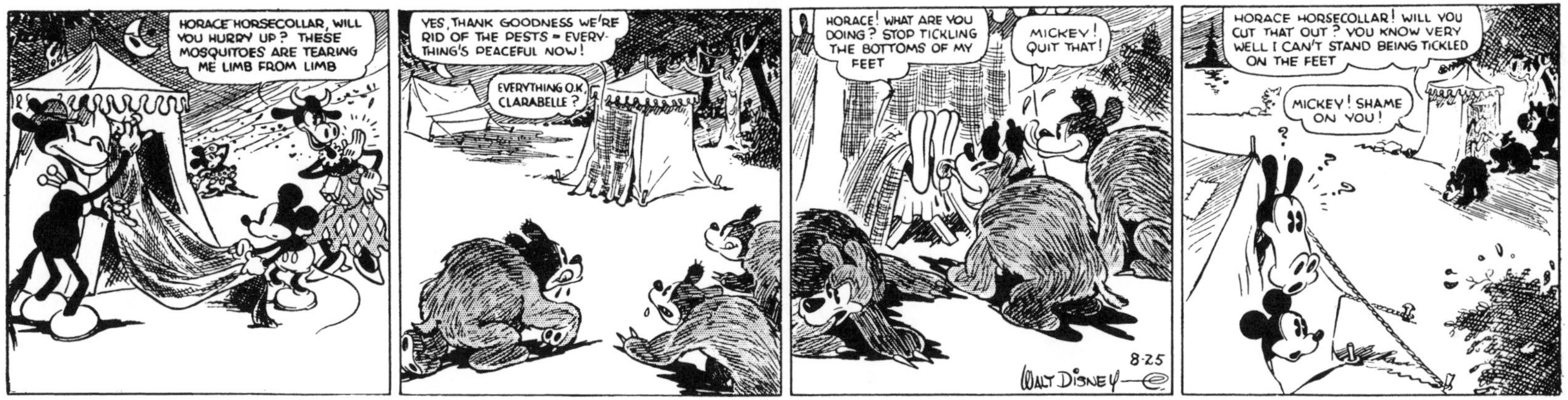
HORACE HORSECOLLAR, WILL YOU HURRY UP? THESE MOSQUITOES ARE TEARING ME LIMB FROM LIMB
YES, THANK GOODNESS WE'RE RID OF THE PESTS = EVERYTHING'S PEACEFUL NOW!
EVERYTHING O.K. CLARABELLE?
HORACE! WHAT ARE YOU DOING? STOP TICKLING THE BOTTOMS OF MY FEET
MICKEY! QUIT THAT!
8·25
WALT DISNEY
HORACE HORSECOLLAR! WILL YOU CUT THAT OUT? YOU KNOW VERY WELL I CAN'T STAND BEING TICKLED ON THE FEET
MICKEY! SHAME ON YOU!

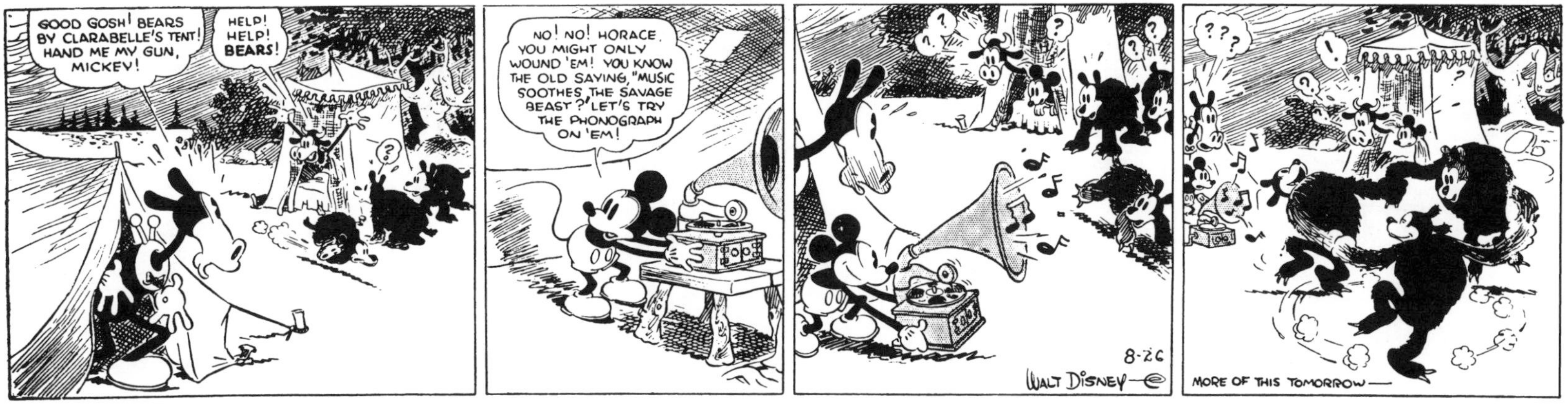
GOOD GOSH! BEARS BY CLARABELLE'S TENT! HAND ME MY GUN, MICKEY!
HELP! HELP! BEARS!
NO! NO! HORACE. YOU MIGHT ONLY WOUND 'EM! YOU KNOW THE OLD SAYING, "MUSIC SOOTHES THE SAVAGE BEAST"! LET'S TRY THE PHONOGRAPH ON 'EM!
8·26
WALT DISNEY
MORE OF THIS TOMORROW—

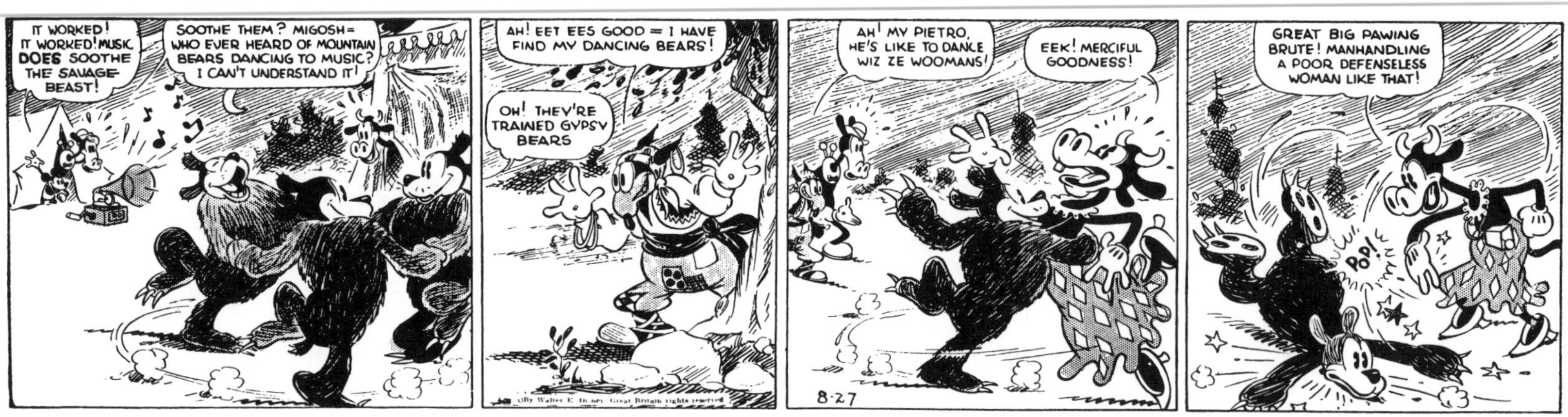
IT WORKED! IT WORKED! MUSIC DOES SOOTHE THE SAVAGE BEAST!
SOOTHE THEM? MIGOSH= WHO EVER HEARD OF MOUNTAIN BEARS DANCING TO MUSIC? I CAN'T UNDERSTAND IT!
AH! EET EES GOOD = I HAVE FIND MY DANCING BEARS!
OH! THEY'RE TRAINED GYPSY BEARS
AH! MY PIETRO, HE'S LIKE TO DANCE WIZ ZE WOOMANS!
EEK! MERCIFUL GOODNESS!
8-27
GREAT BIG PAWING BRUTE! MANHANDLING A POOR DEFENSELESS WOMAN LIKE THAT!
POP!

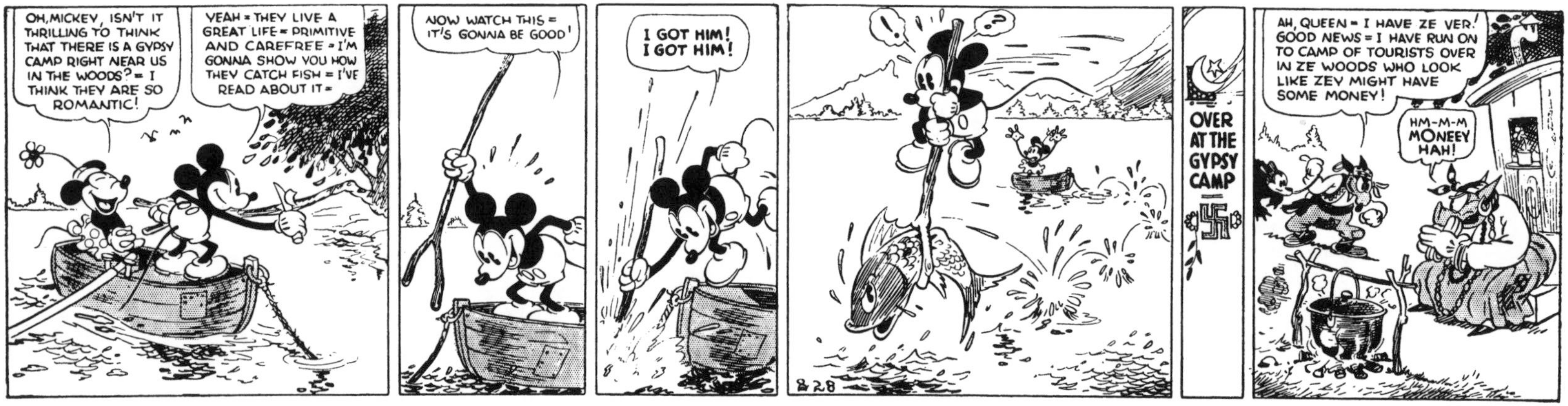
OH, MICKEY, ISN'T IT THRILLING TO THINK THAT THERE IS A GYPSY CAMP RIGHT NEAR US IN THE WOODS? = I THINK THEY ARE SO ROMANTIC!
YEAH = THEY LIVE A GREAT LIFE = PRIMITIVE AND CAREFREE = I'M GONNA SHOW YOU HOW THEY CATCH FISH = I'VE READ ABOUT IT =
NOW WATCH THIS = IT'S GONNA BE GOOD!
I GOT HIM! I GOT HIM!
8-28
OVER AT THE GYPSY CAMP
AH, QUEEN = I HAVE ZE VER' GOOD NEWS = I HAVE RUN ON TO CAMP OF TOURISTS OVER IN ZE WOODS WHO LOOK LIKE ZEY MIGHT HAVE SOME MONEY!
HM-M-M MONEEY HAH!

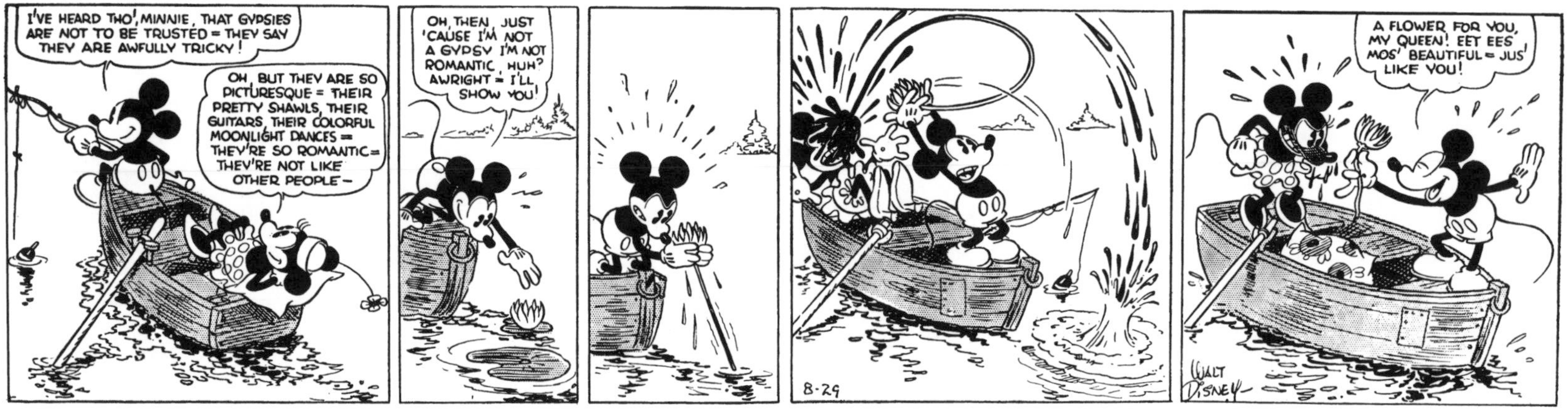
I'VE HEARD THO', MINNIE, THAT GYPSIES ARE NOT TO BE TRUSTED = THEY SAY THEY ARE AWFULLY TRICKY!
OH, BUT THEY ARE SO PICTURESQUE = THEIR PRETTY SHAWLS, THEIR GUITARS, THEIR COLORFUL MOONLIGHT DANCES = THEY'RE SO ROMANTIC = THEY'RE NOT LIKE OTHER PEOPLE -
OH, THEN JUST 'CAUSE I'M NOT A GYPSY I'M NOT ROMANTIC, HUH? AWRIGHT = I'LL SHOW YOU!
8-29
A FLOWER FOR YOU, MY QUEEN! EET EES MOS' BEAUTIFUL = JUS' LIKE YOU!
WALT DISNEY

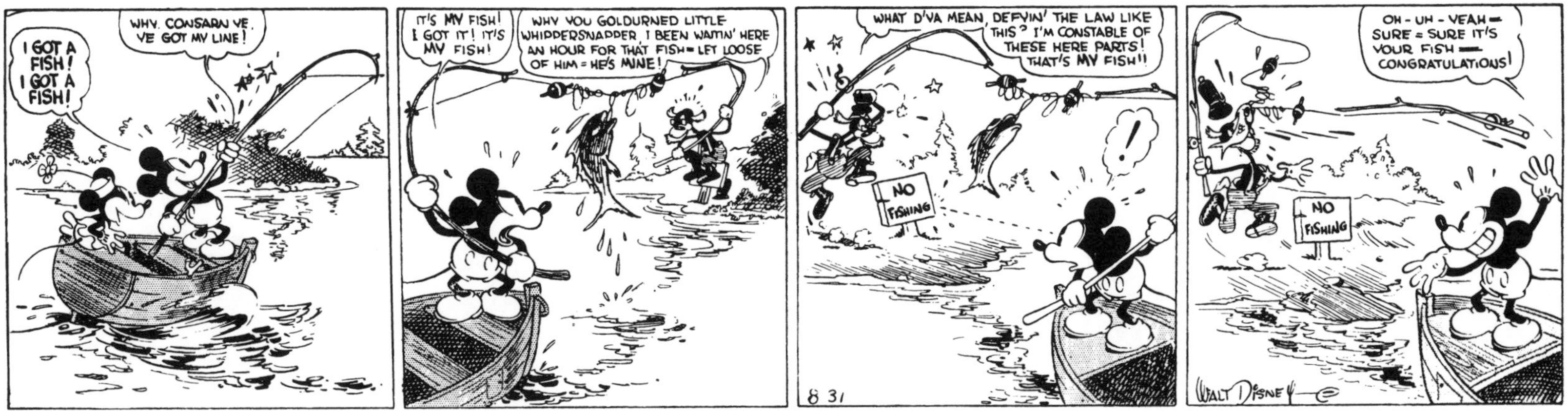
I GOT A FISH! I GOT A FISH!
WHY, CONSARN YE, YE GOT MY LINE!
IT'S MY FISH! I GOT IT! IT'S MY FISH!
WHY YOU GOLDURNED LITTLE WHIPPERSNAPPER, I BEEN WAITIN' HERE AN HOUR FOR THAT FISH = LET LOOSE OF HIM = HE'S MINE!
WHAT D'YA MEAN, DEFYIN' THE LAW LIKE THIS? I'M CONSTABLE OF THESE HERE PARTS! THAT'S MY FISH!!
NO FISHING
!
8 31
OH - UH - YEAH = SURE = SURE IT'S YOUR FISH — CONGRATULATIONS!
NO FISHING
WALT DISNEY

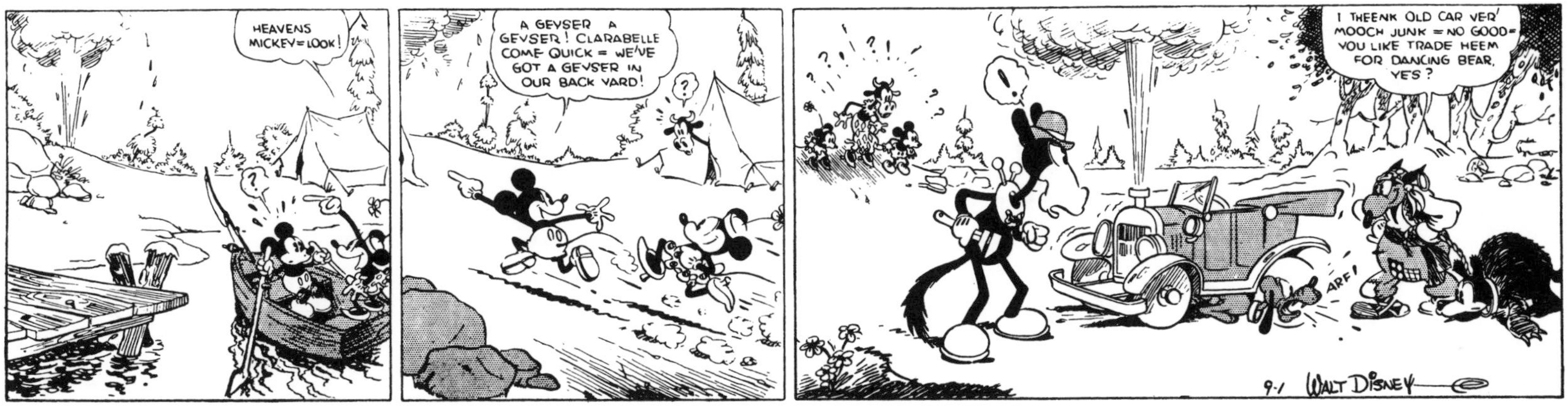
HEAVENS MICKEY = LOOK!
A GEYSER A GEYSER! CLARABELLE COME QUICK = WE'VE GOT A GEYSER IN OUR BACK YARD!
I THEENK OLD CAR VER' MOOCH JUNK = NO GOOD = YOU LIKE TRADE HEEM FOR DANCING BEAR, YES?
ARF!
9-1
WALT DISNEY

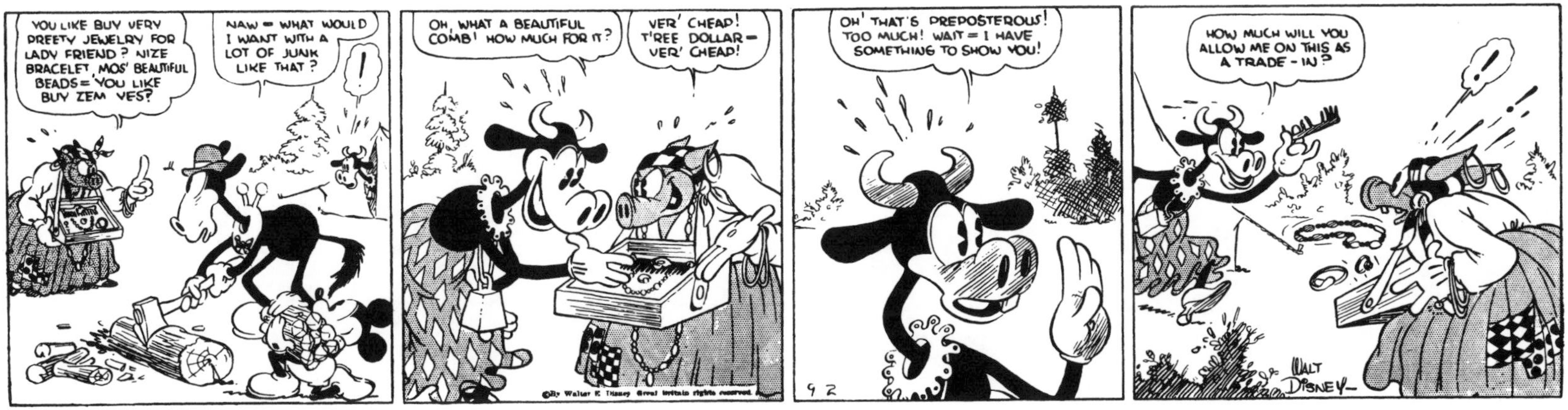
YOU LIKE BUY VERY PREETY JEWELRY FOR LADY FRIEND? NIZE BRACELET, MOS' BEAUTIFUL BEADS = YOU LIKE BUY ZEM YES?
NAW = WHAT WOULD I WANT WITH A LOT OF JUNK LIKE THAT?
!
OH, WHAT A BEAUTIFUL COMB! HOW MUCH FOR IT?
VER' CHEAP! T'REE DOLLAR — VER' CHEAP!
OH' THAT'S PREPOSTEROUS! TOO MUCH! WAIT = I HAVE SOMETHING TO SHOW YOU!
9 2
HOW MUCH WILL YOU ALLOW ME ON THIS AS A TRADE-IN?
!
WALT DISNEY

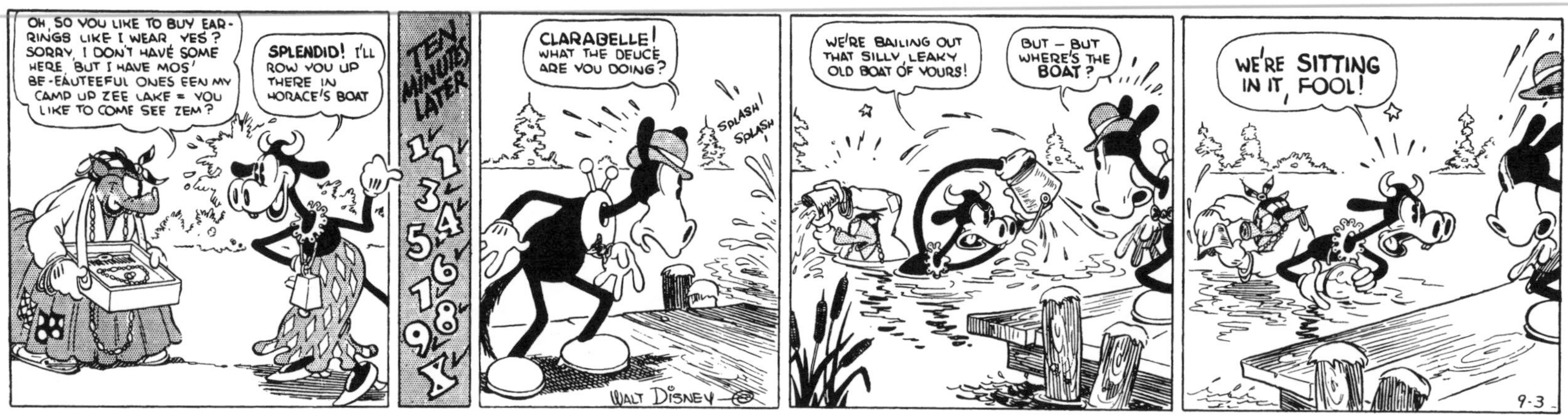
OH, SO YOU LIKE TO BUY EAR-RINGS LIKE I WEAR YES? SORRY, I DON'T HAVE SOME HERE, BUT I HAVE MOS' BE-EAUTEEFUL ONES EEN MY CAMP UP ZEE LAKE = YOU LIKE TO COME SEE ZEM?
SPLENDID! I'LL ROW YOU UP THERE IN HORACE'S BOAT
TEN MINUTES LATER
1 2 3 4 5 6 7 8 9 X
CLARABELLE! WHAT THE DEUCE ARE YOU DOING?
SPLASH! SPLASH!
WALT DISNEY
WE'RE BAILING OUT THAT SILLY, LEAKY OLD BOAT OF YOURS!
BUT — BUT WHERE'S THE BOAT?
WE'RE SITTING IN IT, FOOL!
9-3

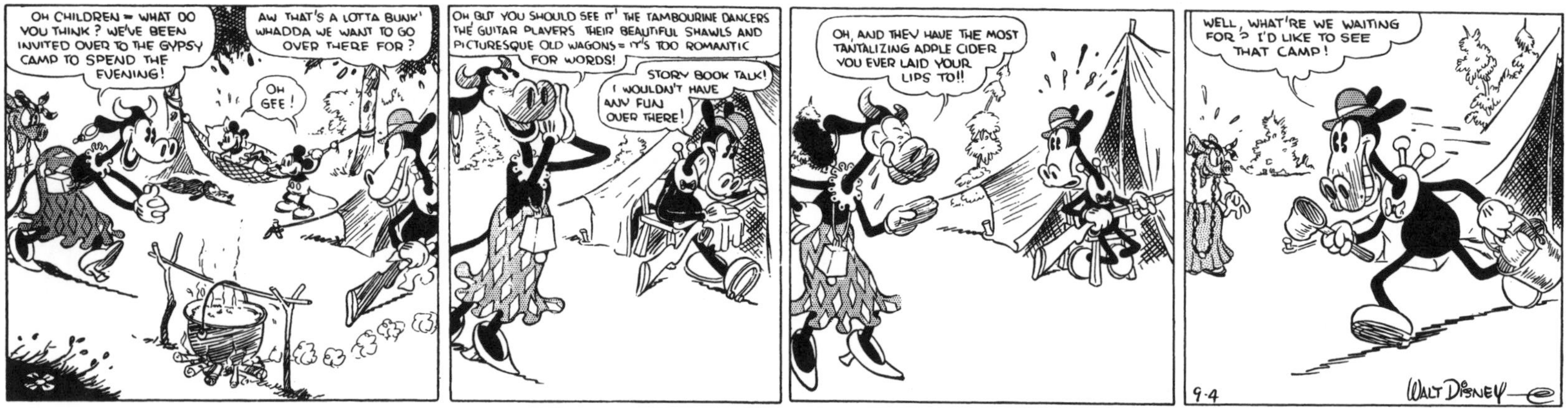
OH CHILDREN = WHAT DO YOU THINK? WE'VE BEEN INVITED OVER TO THE GYPSY CAMP TO SPEND THE EVENING!
AW THAT'S A LOTTA BUNK! WHADDA WE WANT TO GO OVER THERE FOR?
OH GEE!
OH BUT YOU SHOULD SEE IT! THE TAMBOURINE DANCERS THE GUITAR PLAYERS THEIR BEAUTIFUL SHAWLS AND PICTURESQUE OLD WAGONS = IT'S TOO ROMANTIC FOR WORDS!
STORY BOOK TALK! I WOULDN'T HAVE ANY FUN OVER THERE!
OH, AND THEY HAVE THE MOST TANTALIZING APPLE CIDER YOU EVER LAID YOUR LIPS TO!!
WELL, WHAT'RE WE WAITING FOR? I'D LIKE TO SEE THAT CAMP!
9-4
WALT DISNEY

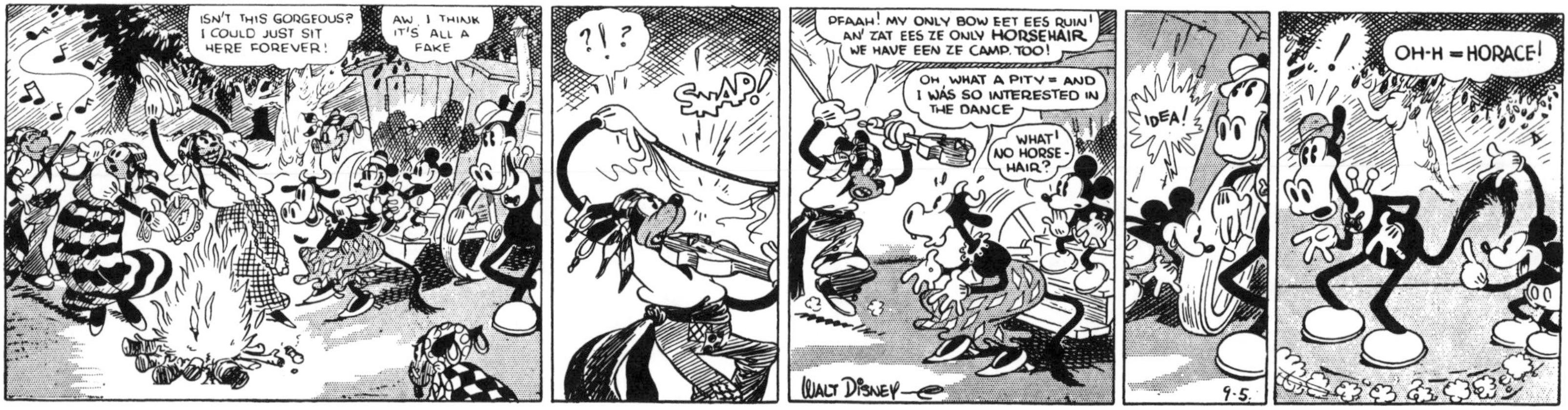
ISN'T THIS GORGEOUS? I COULD JUST SIT HERE FOREVER!
AW, I THINK IT'S ALL A FAKE
?!?
SNAP!
PFAAH! MY ONLY BOW EET EES RUIN! AN' ZAT EES ZE ONLY HORSEHAIR WE HAVE EEN ZE CAMP. TOO!
OH, WHAT A PITY = AND I WAS SO INTERESTED IN THE DANCE
WHAT! NO HORSE-HAIR?
WALT DISNEY
IDEA!
9-5
OH-H = HORACE!

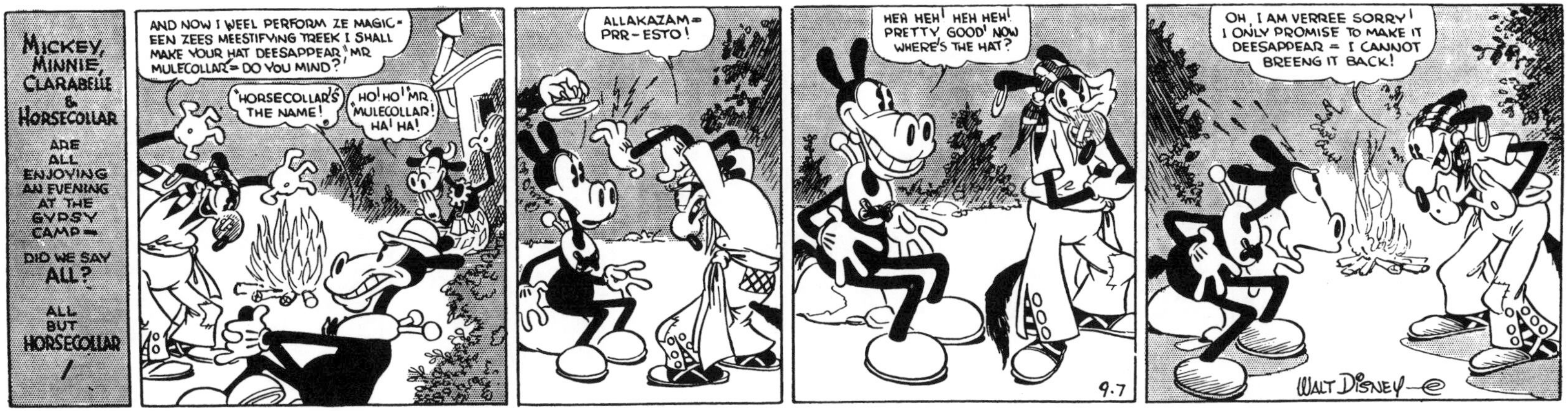
MICKEY, MINNIE, CLARABELLE & HORSECOLLAR ARE ALL ENJOYING AN EVENING AT THE GYPSY CAMP— DID WE SAY ALL? ALL BUT HORSECOLLAR!
AND NOW I WEEL PERFORM ZE MAGIC— EEN ZEES MEESTIFYING TREEK I SHALL MAKE YOUR HAT DEESAPPEAR! MR MULECOLLAR = DO YOU MIND?
"HORSECOLLAR'S THE NAME!
HO! HO! MR. MULECOLLAR! HA! HA!
ALLAKAZAM = PRR-ESTO!
HEH HEH! HEH HEH! PRETTY GOOD! NOW WHERE'S THE HAT?
9-7
OH, I AM VERREE SORRY! I ONLY PROMISE TO MAKE IT DEESAPPEAR = I CANNOT BREENG IT BACK!
WALT DISNEY

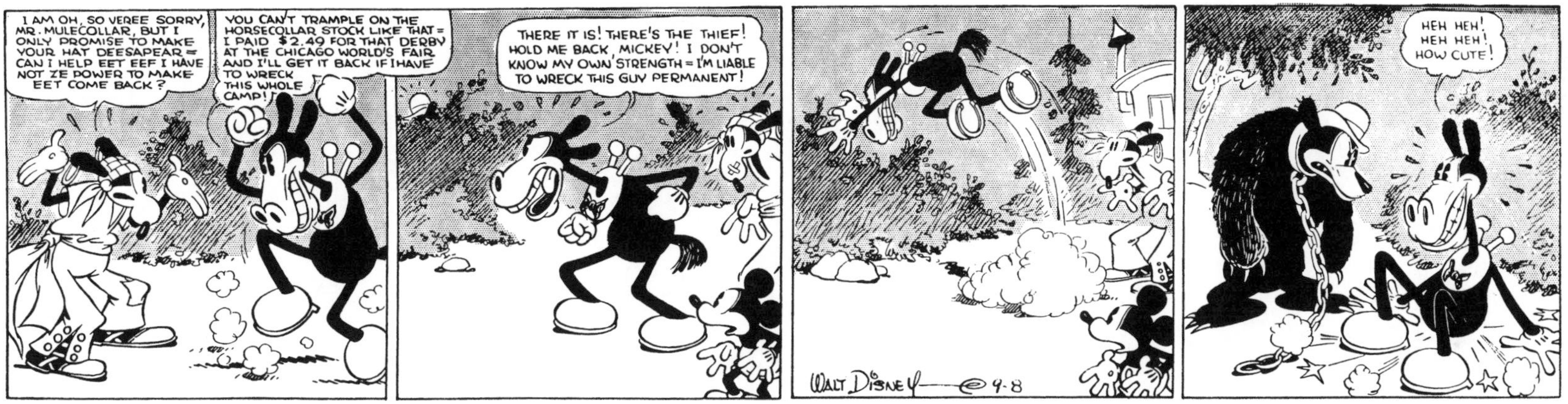
I AM OH, SO VEREE SORRY, MR. MULECOLLAR, BUT I ONLY PROMISE TO MAKE YOUR HAT DEESAPPEAR = CAN I HELP EET EEF I HAVE NOT ZE POWER TO MAKE EET COME BACK?
YOU CAN'T TRAMPLE ON THE HORSECOLLAR STOCK LIKE THAT = I PAID $2.49 FOR THAT DERBY AT THE CHICAGO WORLD'S FAIR AND I'LL GET IT BACK IF I HAVE TO WRECK THIS WHOLE CAMP!
THERE IT IS! THERE'S THE THIEF! HOLD ME BACK, MICKEY! I DON'T KNOW MY OWN STRENGTH = I'M LIABLE TO WRECK THIS GUY PERMANENT!
WALT DISNEY 9-8
HEH HEH! HEH HEH! HOW CUTE!

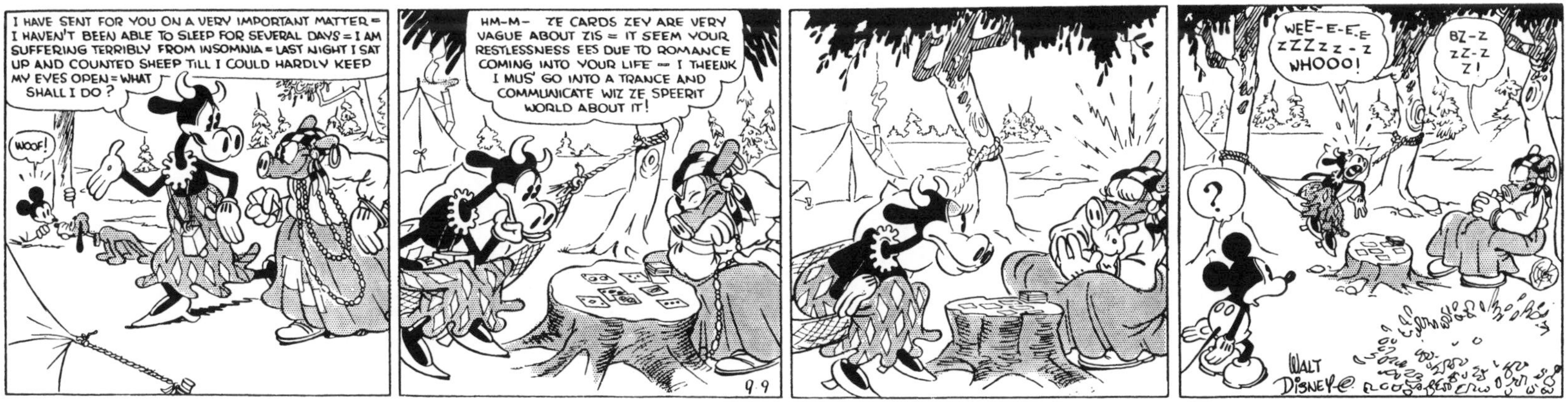
I HAVE SENT FOR YOU ON A VERY IMPORTANT MATTER = I HAVEN'T BEEN ABLE TO SLEEP FOR SEVERAL DAYS = I AM SUFFERING TERRIBLY FROM INSOMNIA = LAST NIGHT I SAT UP AND COUNTED SHEEP TILL I COULD HARDLY KEEP MY EYES OPEN = WHAT SHALL I DO?
WOOF!
HM-M— ZE CARDS ZEY ARE VERY VAGUE ABOUT ZIS = IT SEEM YOUR RESTLESSNESS EES DUE TO ROMANCE COMING INTO YOUR LIFE — I THEENK I MUS' GO INTO A TRANCE AND COMMUNICATE WIZ ZE SPEERIT WORLD ABOUT IT!
9-9
?
WEE-E-E-E ZZZZz z-z WHOOO!
BZ-Z ZZ-Z Z!
WALT DISNEY

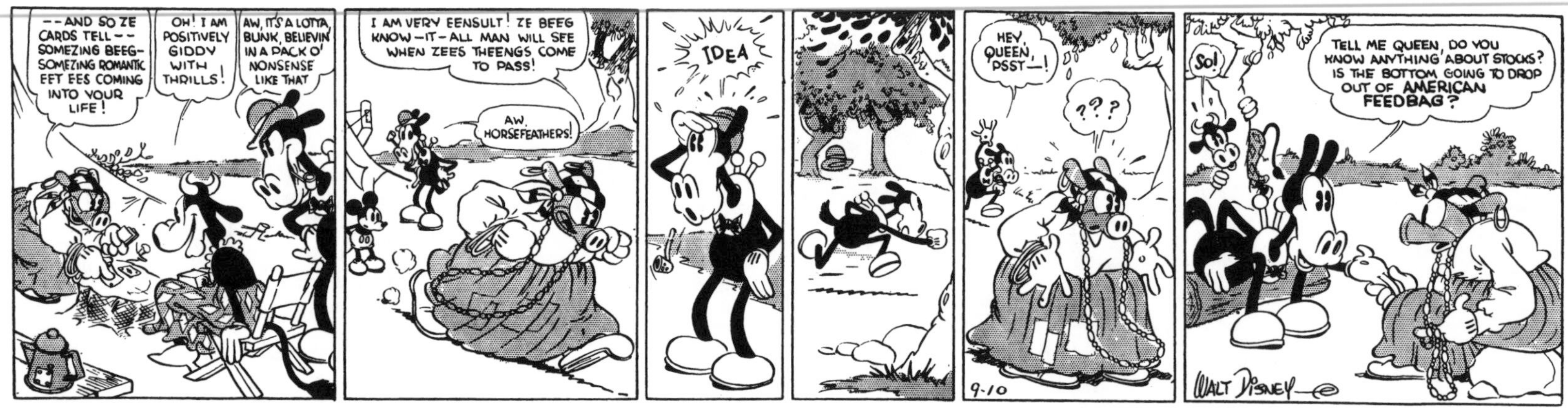
--AND SO ZE CARDS TELL-- SOMEZING BEEG-- SOMEZING ROMANTIC EET EES COMING INTO YOUR LIFE!
OH! I AM POSITIVELY GIDDY WITH THRILLS!
AW, IT'S A LOTTA BUNK, BELIEVIN' IN A PACK O' NONSENSE LIKE THAT
I AM VERY EENSULT! ZE BEEG KNOW-IT-ALL MAN WILL SEE WHEN ZEES THEENGS COME TO PASS!
AW, HORSEFEATHERS!
IDEA
HEY, QUEEN, PSST--!
???
9-10
SO!
TELL ME QUEEN, DO YOU KNOW ANYTHING ABOUT STOCKS? IS THE BOTTOM GOING TO DROP OUT OF AMERICAN FEEDBAG?
WALT DISNEY

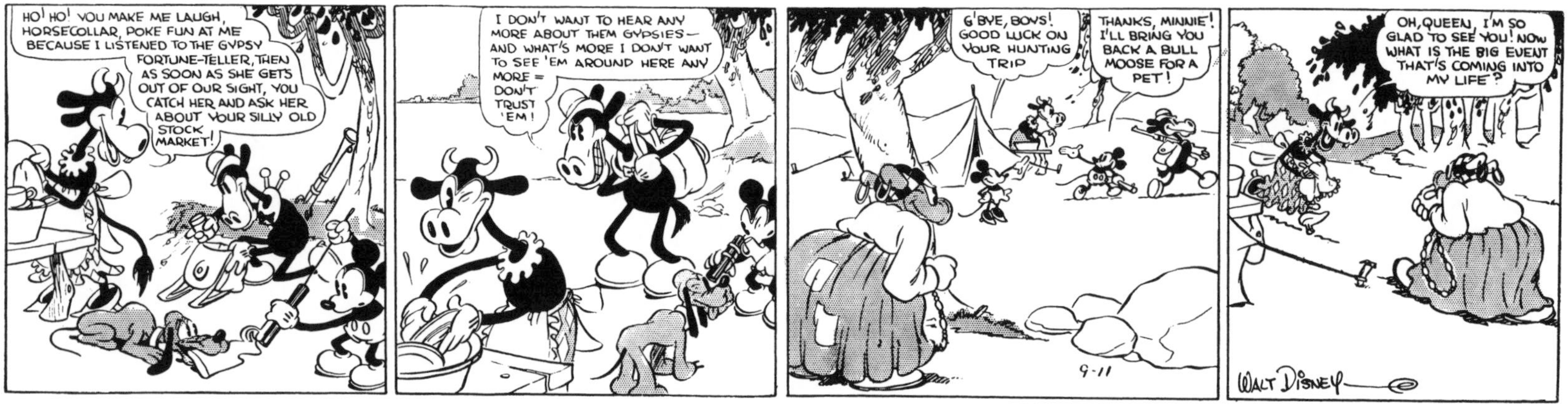
HO! HO! YOU MAKE ME LAUGH, HORSECOLLAR, POKE FUN AT ME BECAUSE I LISTENED TO THE GYPSY FORTUNE-TELLER, THEN AS SOON AS SHE GETS OUT OF OUR SIGHT, YOU CATCH HER AND ASK HER ABOUT YOUR SILLY OLD STOCK MARKET!
I DON'T WANT TO HEAR ANY MORE ABOUT THEM GYPSIES-- AND WHAT'S MORE I DON'T WANT TO SEE 'EM AROUND HERE ANY MORE = DON'T TRUST 'EM!
G'BYE, BOYS! GOOD LUCK ON YOUR HUNTING TRIP
THANKS, MINNIE! I'LL BRING YOU BACK A BULL MOOSE FOR A PET!
9-11
OH, QUEEN, I'M SO GLAD TO SEE YOU! NOW WHAT IS THE BIG EVENT THAT'S COMING INTO MY LIFE?
WALT DISNEY

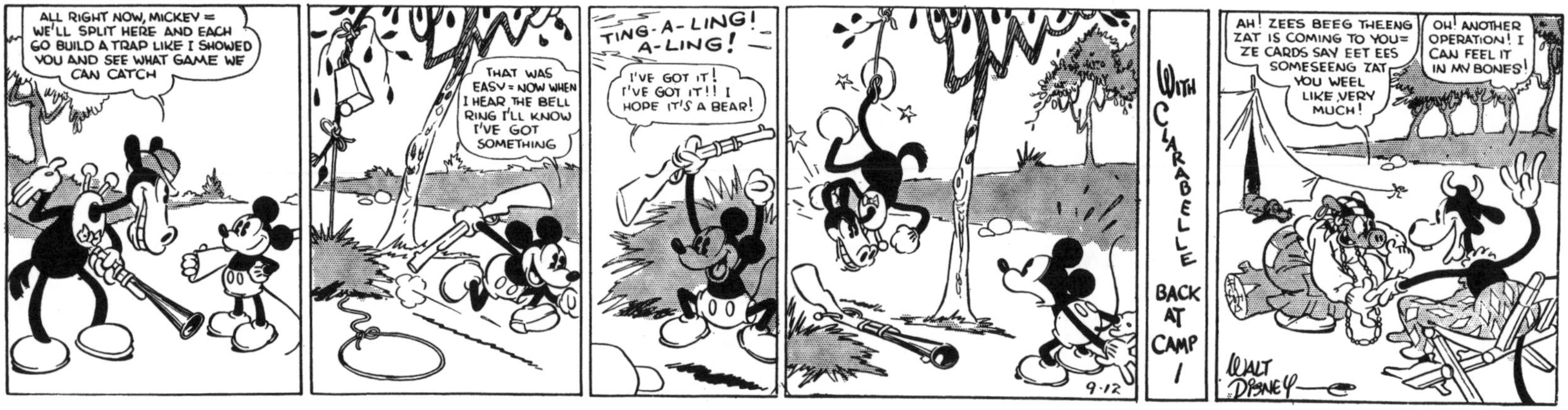
ALL RIGHT NOW, MICKEY = WE'LL SPLIT HERE AND EACH GO BUILD A TRAP LIKE I SHOWED YOU AND SEE WHAT GAME WE CAN CATCH
THAT WAS EASY = NOW WHEN I HEAR THE BELL RING I'LL KNOW I'VE GOT SOMETHING
TING-A-LING! A-LING!
I'VE GOT IT! I'VE GOT IT!! I HOPE IT'S A BEAR!
9-12
WITH CLARABELLE BACK AT CAMP!
AH! ZEES BEEG THEENG ZAT IS COMING TO YOU= ZE CARDS SAY EET EES SOMESEENG ZAT YOU WEEL LIKE VERY MUCH!
OH! ANOTHER OPERATION! I CAN FEEL IT IN MY BONES!
WALT DISNEY

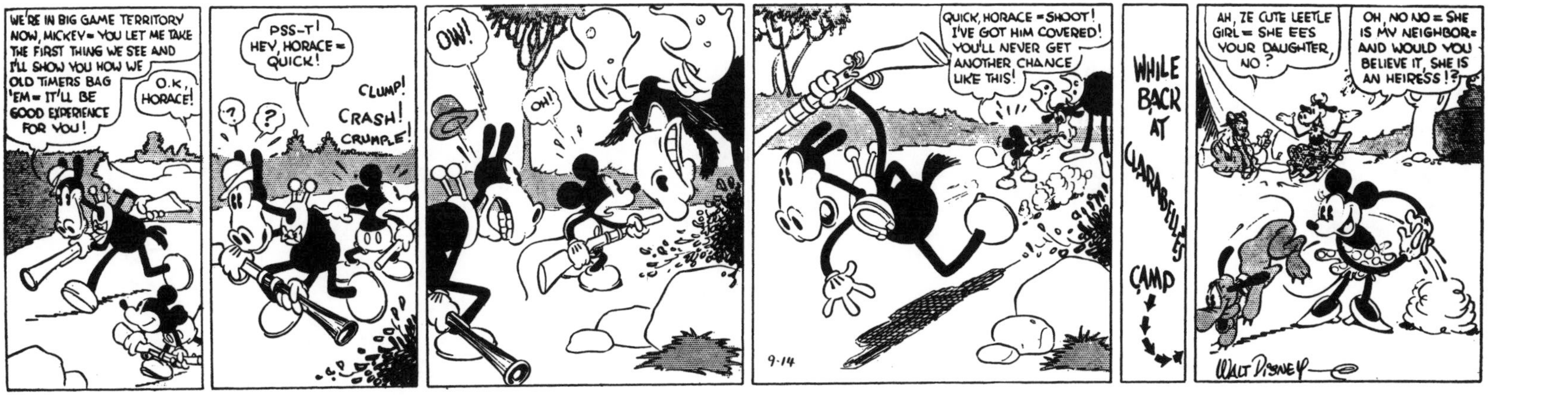
WE'RE IN BIG GAME TERRITORY NOW, MICKEY= YOU LET ME TAKE THE FIRST THING WE SEE AND I'LL SHOW YOU HOW WE OLD TIMERS BAG 'EM= IT'LL BE GOOD EXPERIENCE FOR YOU!
O.K., HORACE!
PSS-T! HEY, HORACE= QUICK!
?
?
CLUMP! CRASH! CRUMPLE!
OW!
OH!
QUICK, HORACE=SHOOT! I'VE GOT HIM COVERED! YOU'LL NEVER GET ANOTHER CHANCE LIKE THIS!
9-14
WHILE BACK AT CLARABELLE'S CAMP
AH, ZE CUTE LEETLE GIRL= SHE EES YOUR DAUGHTER, NO?
OH, NO NO= SHE IS MY NEIGHBOR= AND WOULD YOU BELIEVE IT, SHE IS AN HEIRESS!?
WALT DISNEY

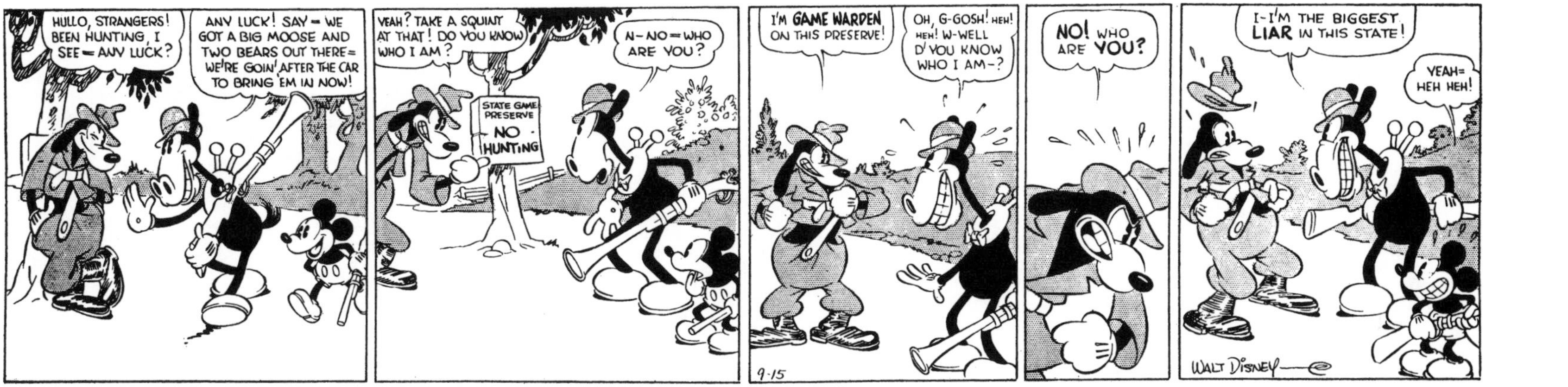
HULLO, STRANGERS! BEEN HUNTING, I SEE= ANY LUCK?
ANY LUCK! SAY= WE GOT A BIG MOOSE AND TWO BEARS OUT THERE= WE'RE GOIN' AFTER THE CAR TO BRING 'EM IN NOW!
YEAH? TAKE A SQUINT AT THAT! DO YOU KNOW WHO I AM?
STATE GAME PRESERVE
NO HUNTING
N-NO= WHO ARE YOU?
I'M GAME WARDEN ON THIS PRESERVE!
OH, G-GOSH! HEH! HEH! W-WELL D'YOU KNOW WHO I AM-?
NO! WHO ARE YOU?
9-15
I-I'M THE BIGGEST LIAR IN THIS STATE!
YEAH= HEH HEH!
WALT DISNEY

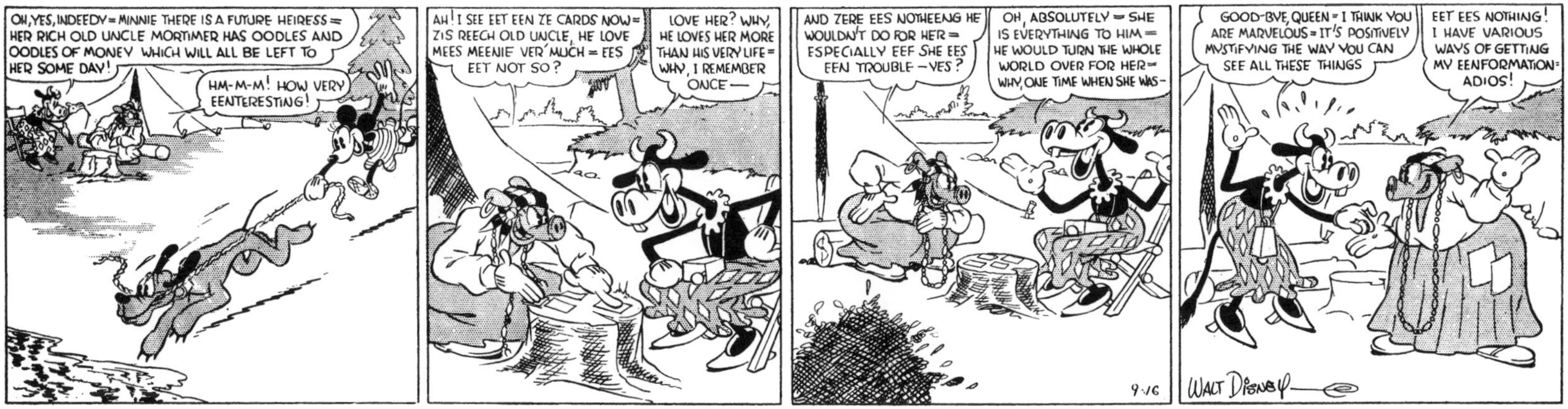
OH, YES, INDEEDY= MINNIE THERE IS A FUTURE HEIRESS= HER RICH OLD UNCLE MORTIMER HAS OODLES AND OODLES OF MONEY WHICH WILL ALL BE LEFT TO HER SOME DAY!
HM-M-M! HOW VERY EENTERESTING!
AH! I SEE EET EEN ZE CARDS NOW= ZIS REECH OLD UNCLE, HE LOVE MEES MEENIE VER' MUCH= EES EET NOT SO?
LOVE HER? WHY, HE LOVES HER MORE THAN HIS VERY LIFE= WHY, I REMEMBER ONCE—
AND ZERE EES NOTHEENG HE WOULDN'T DO FOR HER= ESPECIALLY EEF SHE EES EEN TROUBLE—YES?
OH, ABSOLUTELY= SHE IS EVERYTHING TO HIM= HE WOULD TURN THE WHOLE WORLD OVER FOR HER= WHY, ONE TIME WHEN SHE WAS-
9-16
GOOD-BYE, QUEEN= I THINK YOU ARE MARVELOUS= IT'S POSITIVELY MYSTIFYING THE WAY YOU CAN SEE ALL THESE THINGS
EET EES NOTHING! I HAVE VARIOUS WAYS OF GETTING MY EENFORMATION= ADIOS!
WALT DISNEY

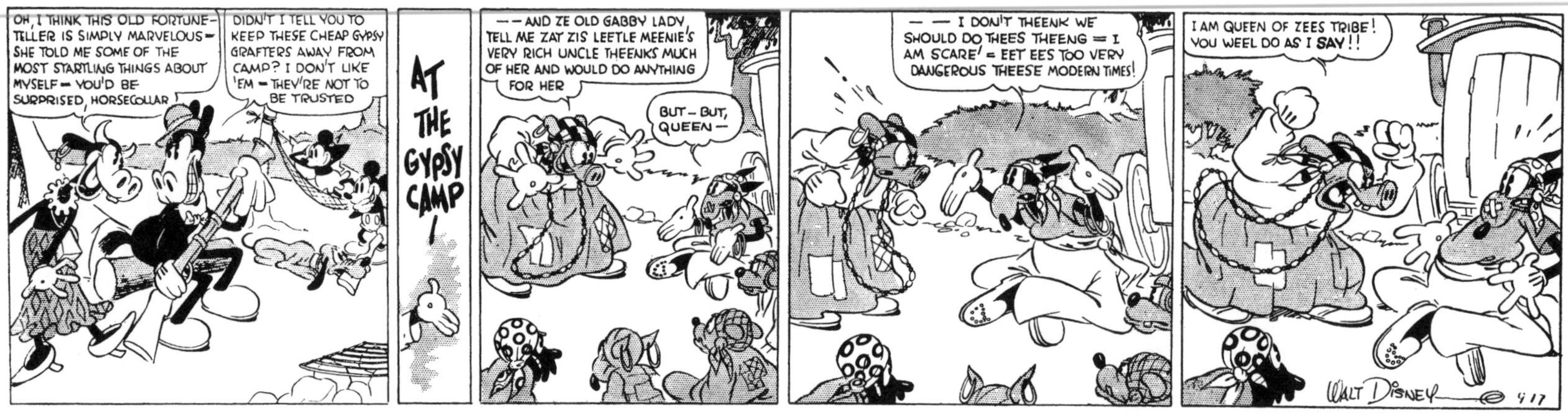

OH, I THINK THIS OLD FORTUNE-TELLER IS SIMPLY MARVELOUS— SHE TOLD ME SOME OF THE MOST STARTLING THINGS ABOUT MYSELF— YOU'D BE SURPRISED, HORSECOLLAR
DIDN'T I TELL YOU TO KEEP THESE CHEAP GYPSY GRAFTERS AWAY FROM CAMP? I DON'T LIKE 'EM — THEY'RE NOT TO BE TRUSTED
AT THE GYPSY CAMP!
— — AND ZE OLD GABBY LADY, TELL ME ZAT ZIS LEETLE MEENIE'S VERY RICH UNCLE THEENKS MUCH OF HER AND WOULD DO ANYTHING FOR HER
BUT— BUT, QUEEN —
— — I DON'T THEENK WE SHOULD DO THEES THEENG — I AM SCARE' — EET EES TOO VERY DANGEROUS THEESE MODERN TIMES!
I AM QUEEN OF ZEES TRIBE! YOU WEEL DO AS I SAY!!
WALT DISNEY 9-17

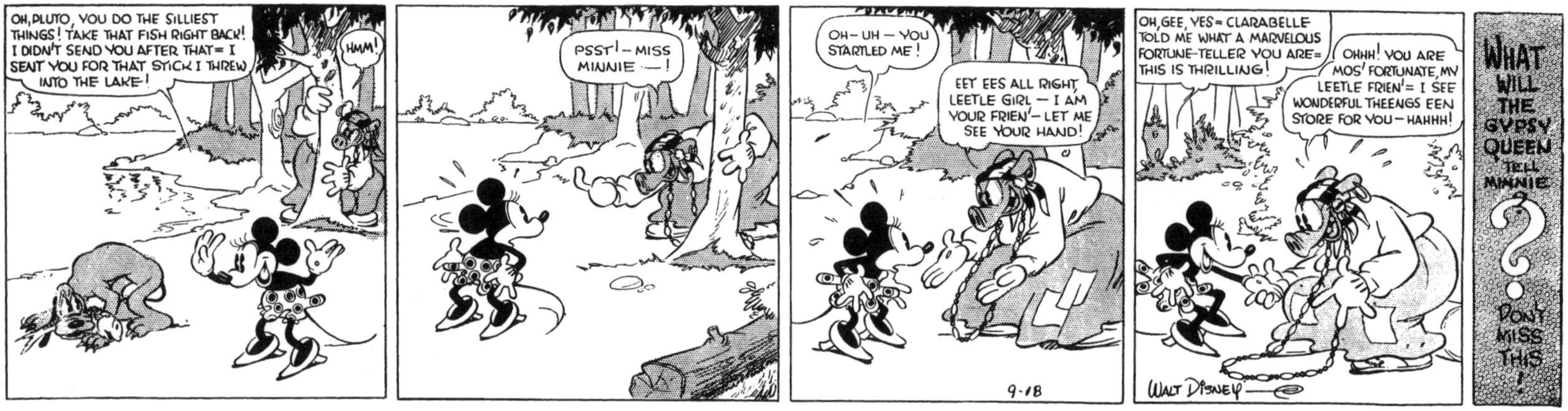

OH, PLUTO, YOU DO THE SILLIEST THINGS! TAKE THAT FISH RIGHT BACK! I DIDN'T SEND YOU AFTER THAT— I SENT YOU FOR THAT STICK I THREW INTO THE LAKE!
HMM!
PSST! — MISS MINNIE —!
OH— UH — YOU STARTLED ME!
EET EES ALL RIGHT, LEETLE GIRL — I AM YOUR FRIEN'— LET ME SEE YOUR HAND!
9-18
OH, GEE, YES— CLARABELLE TOLD ME WHAT A MARVELOUS FORTUNE-TELLER YOU ARE— THIS IS THRILLING!
OHHH! YOU ARE MOS' FORTUNATE, MY LEETLE FRIEN'— I SEE WONDERFUL THEENGS EEN STORE FOR YOU— HAHHH!
WALT DISNEY
WHAT WILL THE GYPSY QUEEN TELL MINNIE?
?
DON'T MISS THIS!

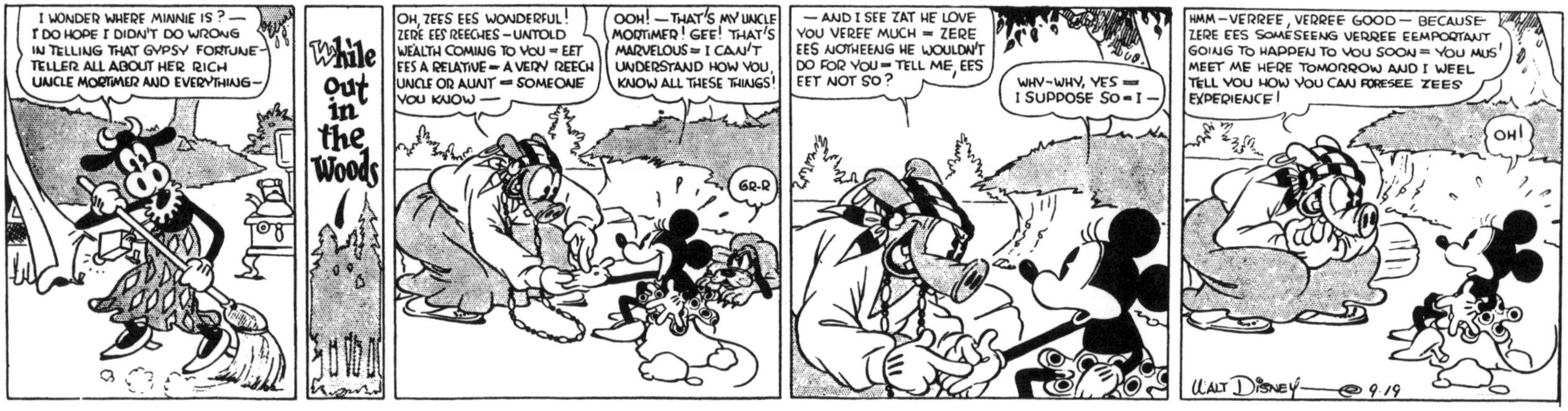

I WONDER WHERE MINNIE IS? — I DO HOPE I DIDN'T DO WRONG IN TELLING THAT GYPSY FORTUNE-TELLER ALL ABOUT HER RICH UNCLE MORTIMER AND EVERYTHING—
While out in the Woods!
OH, ZEES EES WONDERFUL! ZERE EES REECHES — UNTOLD WEALTH COMING TO YOU — EET EES A RELATIVE — A VERY REECH UNCLE OR AUNT — SOMEONE YOU KNOW —
OOH! — THAT'S MY UNCLE MORTIMER! GEE! THAT'S MARVELOUS— I CAN'T UNDERSTAND HOW YOU KNOW ALL THESE THINGS!
GR-R
— AND I SEE ZAT HE LOVE YOU VERREE MUCH — ZERE EES NOTHEENG HE WOULDN'T DO FOR YOU— TELL ME, EES EET NOT SO?
WHY— WHY, YES — I SUPPOSE SO— I —
HMM — VERREE, VERREE GOOD — BECAUSE ZERE EES SOMESEENG VERREE EEMPORTANT GOING TO HAPPEN TO YOU SOON — YOU MUS' MEET ME HERE TOMORROW AND I WEEL TELL YOU HOW YOU CAN FORESEE ZEES EXPERIENCE!
OH!
WALT DISNEY 9-19

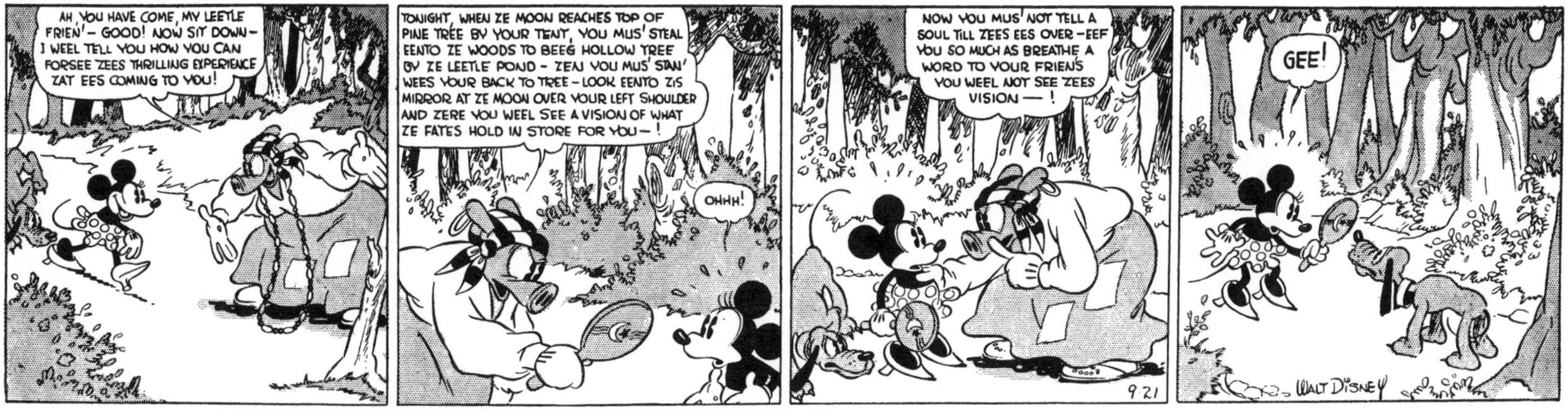
AH, YOU HAVE COME, MY LEETLE FRIEN' – GOOD! NOW SIT DOWN – I WEEL TELL YOU HOW YOU CAN FORSEE ZEES THRILLING EXPERIENCE ZAT EES COMING TO YOU!
TONIGHT, WHEN ZE MOON REACHES TOP OF PINE TREE BY YOUR TENT, YOU MUS' STEAL EENTO ZE WOODS TO BEEG HOLLOW TREE BY ZE LEETLE POND – ZEN YOU MUS' STAN' WEES YOUR BACK TO TREE – LOOK EENTO ZIS MIRROR AT ZE MOON OVER YOUR LEFT SHOULDER AND ZERE YOU WEEL SEE A VISION OF WHAT ZE FATES HOLD IN STORE FOR YOU – !
OHHH!
NOW YOU MUS' NOT TELL A SOUL TILL ZEES EES OVER – EEF YOU SO MUCH AS BREATHE A WORD TO YOUR FRIENS YOU WEEL NOT SEE ZEES VISION — !
9 21
GEE!
WALT DISNEY

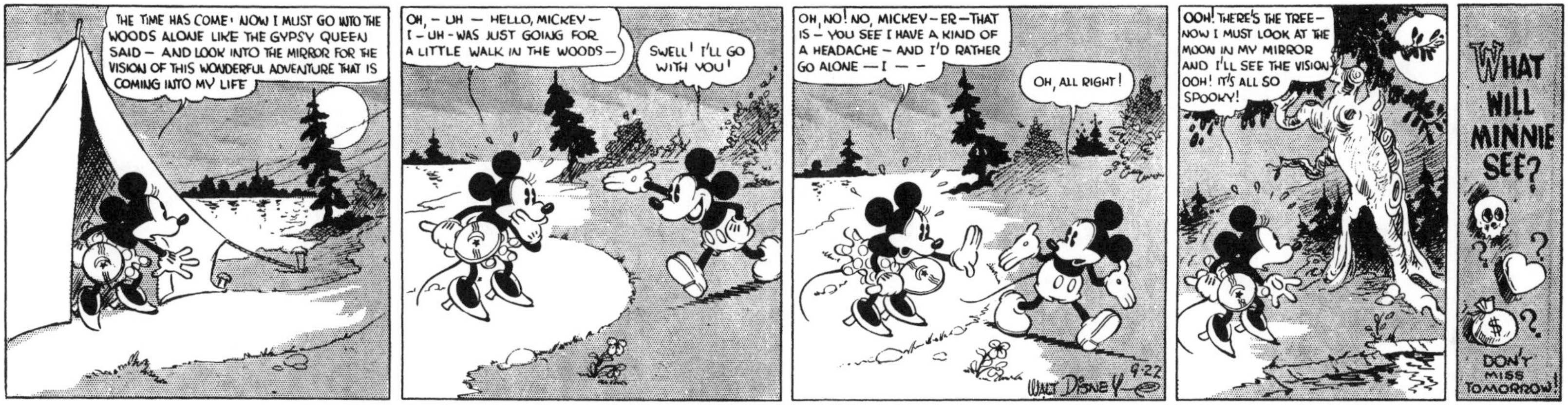
THE TIME HAS COME! NOW I MUST GO INTO THE WOODS ALONE LIKE THE GYPSY QUEEN SAID – AND LOOK INTO THE MIRROR FOR THE VISION OF THIS WONDERFUL ADVENTURE THAT IS COMING INTO MY LIFE
OH, – UH – HELLO, MICKEY – I – UH – WAS JUST GOING FOR A LITTLE WALK IN THE WOODS –
SWELL! I'LL GO WITH YOU!
OH, NO! NO, MICKEY – ER – THAT IS – YOU SEE I HAVE A KIND OF A HEADACHE – AND I'D RATHER GO ALONE – I – –
OH, ALL RIGHT!
9-22
WALT DISNEY
OOH! THERE'S THE TREE – NOW I MUST LOOK AT THE MOON IN MY MIRROR AND I'LL SEE THE VISION OOH! IT'S ALL SO SPOOKY!
WHAT WILL MINNIE SEE?
DON'T MISS TOMORROW!

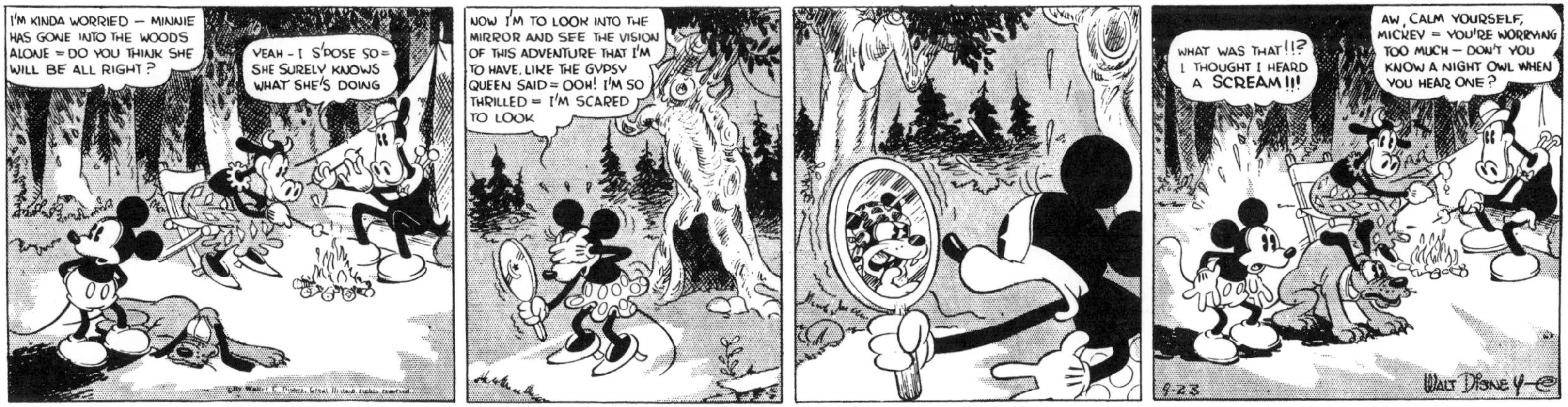
I'M KINDA WORRIED – MINNIE HAS GONE INTO THE WOODS ALONE = DO YOU THINK SHE WILL BE ALL RIGHT?
YEAH – I S'POSE SO = SHE SURELY KNOWS WHAT SHE'S DOING
NOW I'M TO LOOK INTO THE MIRROR AND SEE THE VISION OF THIS ADVENTURE THAT I'M TO HAVE, LIKE THE GYPSY QUEEN SAID = OOH! I'M SO THRILLED = I'M SCARED TO LOOK
9-23
WHAT WAS THAT!!? I THOUGHT I HEARD A SCREAM!!!
AW, CALM YOURSELF, MICKEY = YOU'RE WORRYING TOO MUCH – DON'T YOU KNOW A NIGHT OWL WHEN YOU HEAR ONE?
WALT DISNEY

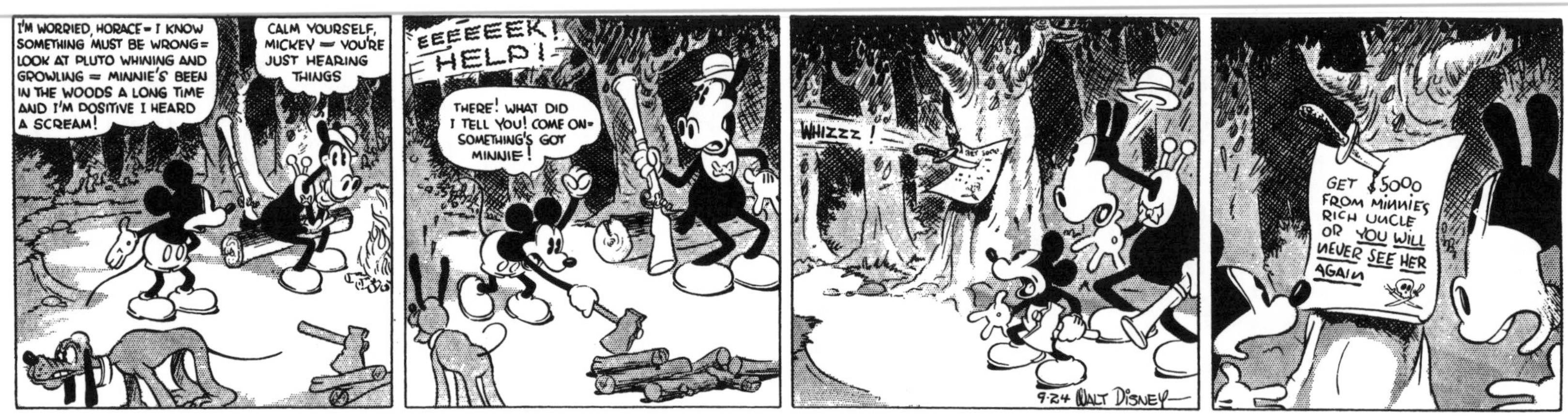
I'M WORRIED, HORACE = I KNOW SOMETHING MUST BE WRONG = LOOK AT PLUTO WHINING AND GROWLING = MINNIE'S BEEN IN THE WOODS A LONG TIME AND I'M POSITIVE I HEARD A SCREAM!
CALM YOURSELF, MICKEY = YOU'RE JUST HEARING THINGS
EEEEEEK! HELP!
THERE! WHAT DID I TELL YOU! COME ON = SOMETHING'S GOT MINNIE!
WHIZZZ!
9·24 WALT DISNEY
GET $5000 FROM MINNIE'S RICH UNCLE OR YOU WILL NEVER SEE HER AGAIN

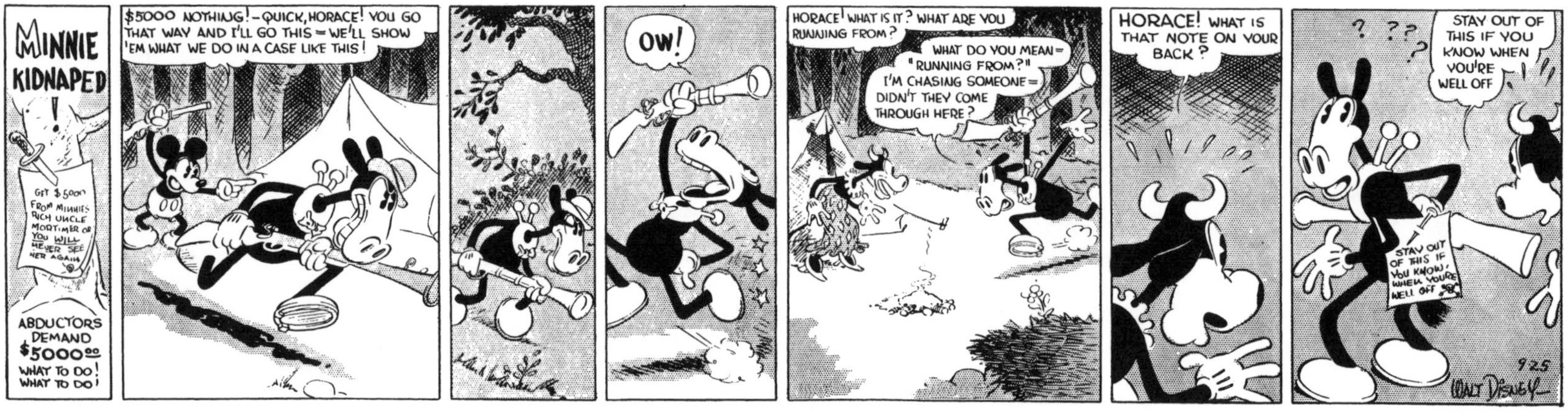
MINNIE KIDNAPED!
GET $5000 FROM MINNIES RICH UNCLE MORTIMER OR YOU WILL NEVER SEE HER AGAIN
ABDUCTORS DEMAND $5000.00
WHAT TO DO! WHAT TO DO!
$5000 NOTHING! – QUICK, HORACE! YOU GO THAT WAY AND I'LL GO THIS = WE'LL SHOW 'EM WHAT WE DO IN A CASE LIKE THIS!
OW!
HORACE! WHAT IS IT? WHAT ARE YOU RUNNING FROM?
WHAT DO YOU MEAN = "RUNNING FROM?" I'M CHASING SOMEONE = DIDN'T THEY COME THROUGH HERE?
HORACE! WHAT IS THAT NOTE ON YOUR BACK?
STAY OUT OF THIS IF YOU KNOW WHEN YOU'RE WELL OFF
STAY OUT OF THIS IF YOU KNOW, WHEN YOU'RE WELL OFF
9·25
WALT DISNEY

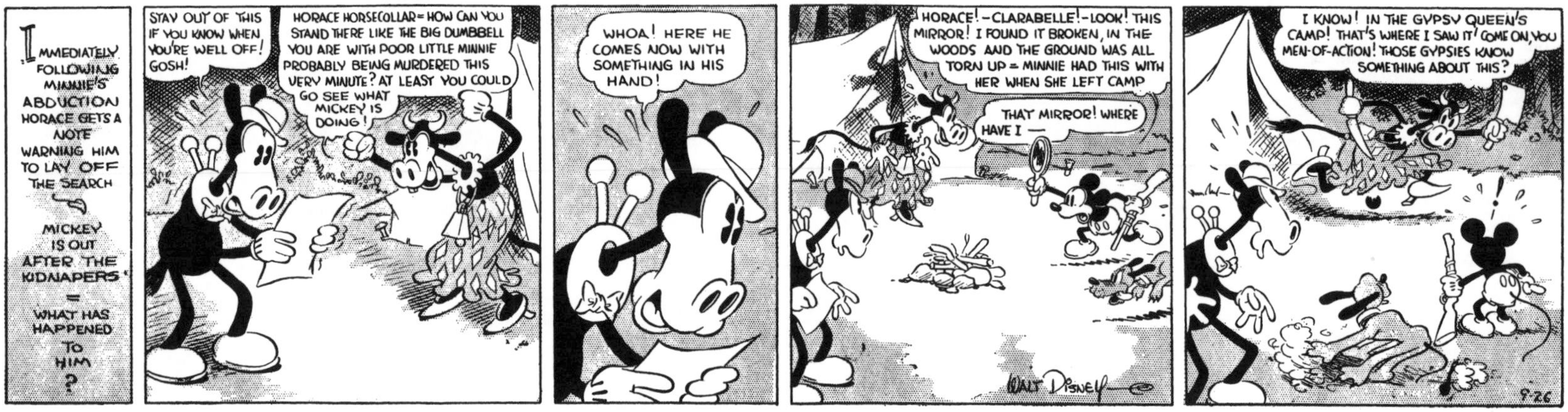
IMMEDIATELY FOLLOWING MINNIE'S ABDUCTION HORACE GETS A NOTE WARNING HIM TO LAY OFF THE SEARCH
MICKEY IS OUT AFTER THE KIDNAPERS = WHAT HAS HAPPENED TO HIM ?
STAY OUT OF THIS IF YOU KNOW WHEN YOU'RE WELL OFF! GOSH!
HORACE HORSECOLLAR = HOW CAN YOU STAND THERE LIKE THE BIG DUMBBELL YOU ARE WITH POOR LITTLE MINNIE PROBABLY BEING MURDERED THIS VERY MINUTE? AT LEAST YOU COULD GO SEE WHAT MICKEY IS DOING!
WHOA! HERE HE COMES NOW WITH SOMETHING IN HIS HAND!
HORACE! – CLARABELLE! – LOOK! THIS MIRROR! I FOUND IT BROKEN, IN THE WOODS AND THE GROUND WAS ALL TORN UP = MINNIE HAD THIS WITH HER WHEN SHE LEFT CAMP
THAT MIRROR! WHERE HAVE I —
WALT DISNEY
I KNOW! IN THE GYPSY QUEEN'S CAMP! THAT'S WHERE I SAW IT! COME ON, YOU MEN-OF-ACTION! THOSE GYPSIES KNOW SOMETHING ABOUT THIS?
9·26

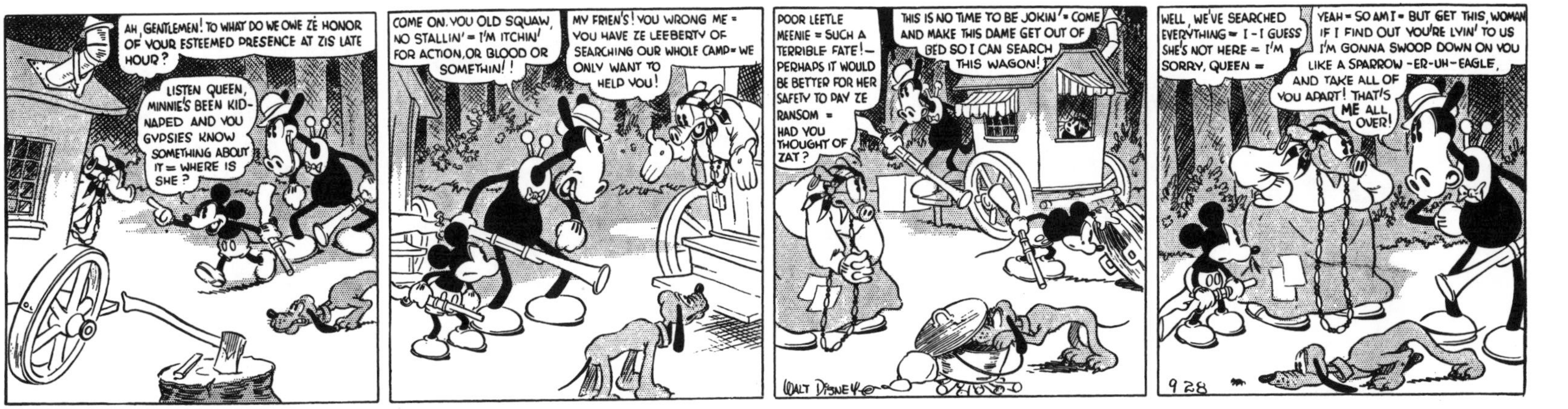
AH, GENTLEMEN! TO WHAT DO WE OWE ZE HONOR OF YOUR ESTEEMED PRESENCE AT ZIS LATE HOUR?
LISTEN QUEEN, MINNIE'S BEEN KIDNAPED AND YOU GYPSIES KNOW SOMETHING ABOUT IT = WHERE IS SHE?
COME ON. YOU OLD SQUAW, NO STALLIN' = I'M ITCHIN' FOR ACTION, OR BLOOD OR SOMETHIN'!!
MY FRIEN'S! YOU WRONG ME = YOU HAVE ZE LEEBERTY OF SEARCHING OUR WHOLE CAMP = WE ONLY WANT TO HELP YOU!
POOR LEETLE MEENIE = SUCH A TERRIBLE FATE! — PERHAPS IT WOULD BE BETTER FOR HER SAFETY TO PAY ZE RANSOM = HAD YOU THOUGHT OF ZAT?
THIS IS NO TIME TO BE JOKIN' = COME AND MAKE THIS DAME GET OUT OF BED SO I CAN SEARCH THIS WAGON!
WALT DISNEY
WELL, WE'VE SEARCHED EVERYTHING = I - I GUESS SHE'S NOT HERE = I'M SORRY, QUEEN =
YEAH = SO AM I = BUT GET THIS, WOMAN IF I FIND OUT YOU'RE LYIN' TO US I'M GONNA SWOOP DOWN ON YOU LIKE A SPARROW -ER-UH- EAGLE, AND TAKE ALL OF YOU APART! THAT'S ME ALL OVER!
9 28

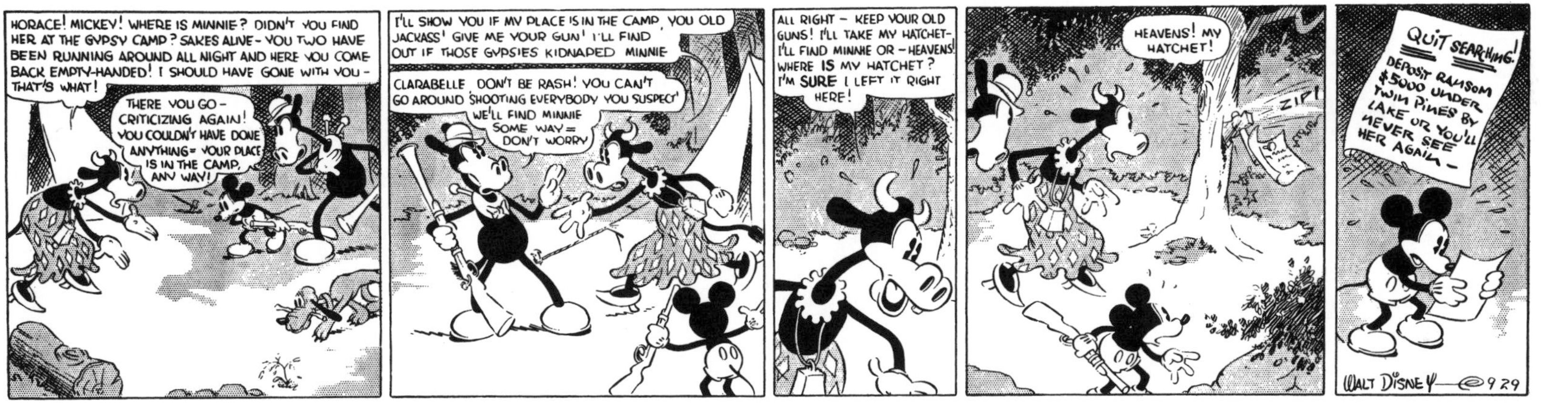
HORACE! MICKEY! WHERE IS MINNIE? DIDN'T YOU FIND HER AT THE GYPSY CAMP? SAKES ALIVE - YOU TWO HAVE BEEN RUNNING AROUND ALL NIGHT AND HERE YOU COME BACK EMPTY-HANDED! I SHOULD HAVE GONE WITH YOU - THAT'S WHAT!
THERE YOU GO - CRITICIZING AGAIN! YOU COULDN'T HAVE DONE ANYTHING = YOUR PLACE IS IN THE CAMP, ANY WAY!
I'LL SHOW YOU IF MY PLACE IS IN THE CAMP, YOU OLD JACKASS! GIVE ME YOUR GUN! I'LL FIND OUT IF THOSE GYPSIES KIDNAPED MINNIE
CLARABELLE, DON'T BE RASH! YOU CAN'T GO AROUND SHOOTING EVERYBODY YOU SUSPECT
WE'LL FIND MINNIE SOME WAY = DON'T WORRY
ALL RIGHT - KEEP YOUR OLD GUNS! I'LL TAKE MY HATCHET - I'LL FIND MINNIE OR - HEAVENS! WHERE IS MY HATCHET? I'M SURE I LEFT IT RIGHT HERE!
HEAVENS! MY HATCHET!
ZIP!
QUIT SEARCHING!
DEPOSIT RANSOM $5000 UNDER TWIN PINES BY LAKE OR YOU'LL NEVER SEE HER AGAIN —
WALT DISNEY ©9 29

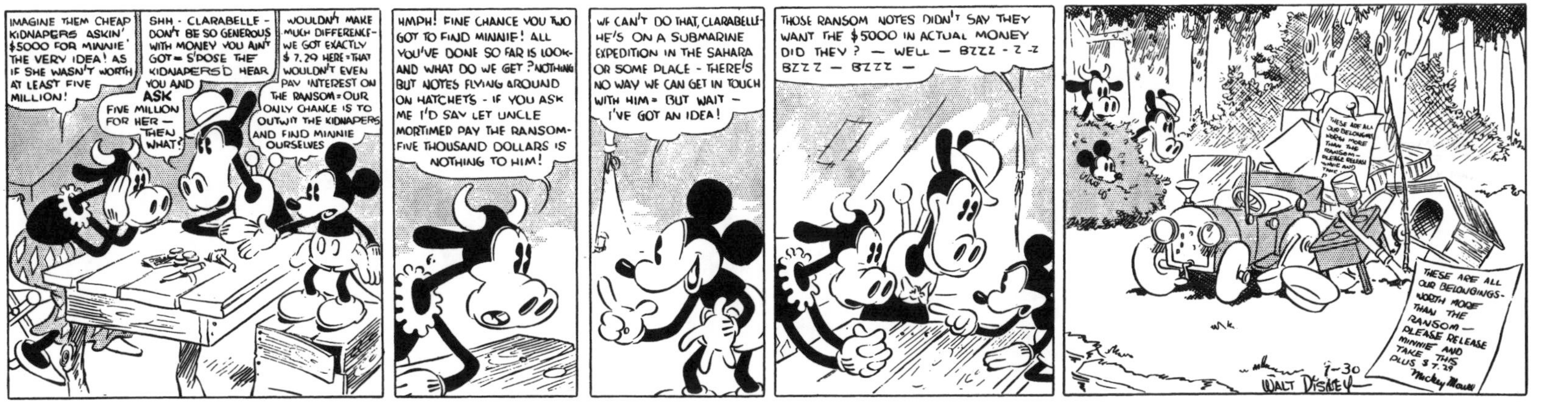
IMAGINE THEM CHEAP KIDNAPERS ASKIN' $5000 FOR MINNIE THE VERY IDEA! AS IF SHE WASN'T WORTH AT LEAST FIVE MILLION!
SHH - CLARABELLE - DON'T BE SO GENEROUS WITH MONEY YOU AIN'T GOT = S'POSE THE KIDNAPERS'D HEAR YOU AND ASK FIVE MILLION FOR HER — THEN WHAT?
WOULDN'T MAKE MUCH DIFFERENCE - WE GOT EXACTLY $7.29 HERE = THAT WOULDN'T EVEN PAY INTEREST ON THE RANSOM = OUR ONLY CHANCE IS TO OUTWIT THE KIDNAPERS AND FIND MINNIE OURSELVES
HMPH! FINE CHANCE YOU TWO GOT TO FIND MINNIE! ALL YOU'VE DONE SO FAR IS LOOK - AND WHAT DO WE GET? NOTHING BUT NOTES FLYING AROUND ON HATCHETS - IF YOU ASK ME I'D SAY LET UNCLE MORTIMER PAY THE RANSOM - FIVE THOUSAND DOLLARS IS NOTHING TO HIM!
WE CAN'T DO THAT, CLARABELLE - HE'S ON A SUBMARINE EXPEDITION IN THE SAHARA OR SOME PLACE - THERE'S NO WAY WE CAN GET IN TOUCH WITH HIM = BUT WAIT - I'VE GOT AN IDEA!
THOSE RANSOM NOTES DIDN'T SAY THEY WANT THE $5000 IN ACTUAL MONEY DID THEY? — WELL — BZZZ - Z - Z BZZZ — BZZZ —
THESE ARE ALL OUR BELONGINGS - WORTH MORE THAN THE RANSOM - PLEASE RELEASE MINNIE AND TAKE THIS PLUS $7.29 Mickey Mouse
9-30
WALT DISNEY

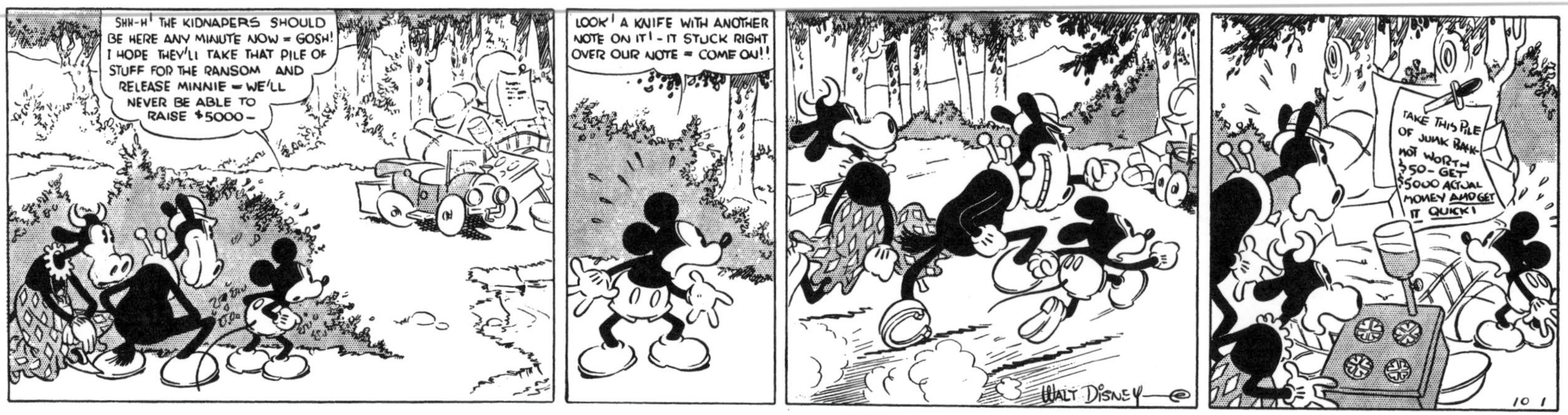
SHH-H! THE KIDNAPERS SHOULD BE HERE ANY MINUTE NOW = GOSH! I HOPE THEY'LL TAKE THAT PILE OF STUFF FOR THE RANSOM AND RELEASE MINNIE = WE'LL NEVER BE ABLE TO RAISE $5000 -
LOOK! A KNIFE WITH ANOTHER NOTE ON IT! - IT STUCK RIGHT OVER OUR NOTE = COME ON!!
WALT DISNEY
TAKE THIS PILE OF JUNK BACK NOT WORTH $50 - GET $5000 ACTUAL MONEY AND GET IT QUICK!
10 1

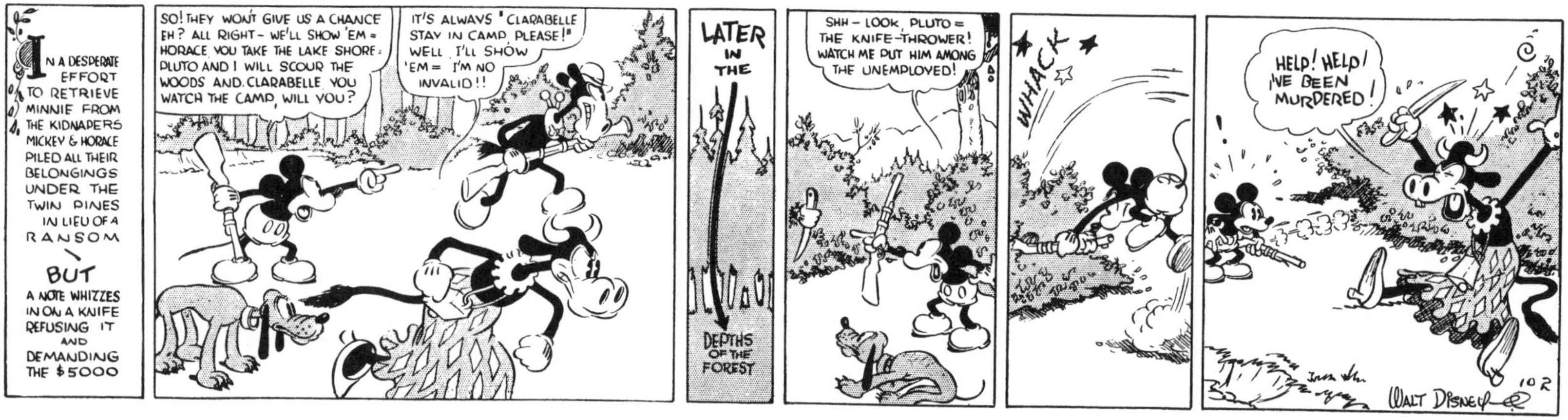
IN A DESPERATE EFFORT TO RETRIEVE MINNIE FROM THE KIDNAPERS MICKEY & HORACE PILED ALL THEIR BELONGINGS UNDER THE TWIN PINES IN LIEU OF A RANSOM
BUT
A NOTE WHIZZES IN ON A KNIFE REFUSING IT AND DEMANDING THE $5000
SO! THEY WON'T GIVE US A CHANCE EH? ALL RIGHT - WE'LL SHOW 'EM = HORACE, YOU TAKE THE LAKE SHORE: PLUTO AND I WILL SCOUR THE WOODS AND, CLARABELLE, YOU WATCH THE CAMP, WILL YOU?
IT'S ALWAYS "CLARABELLE STAY IN CAMP, PLEASE!" WELL, I'LL SHOW 'EM = I'M NO INVALID!!
LATER IN THE
DEPTHS OF THE FOREST
SHH - LOOK, PLUTO = THE KNIFE-THROWER! WATCH ME PUT HIM AMONG THE UNEMPLOYED!
WHACK
HELP! HELP! I'VE BEEN MURDERED!
WALT DISNEY
10 2

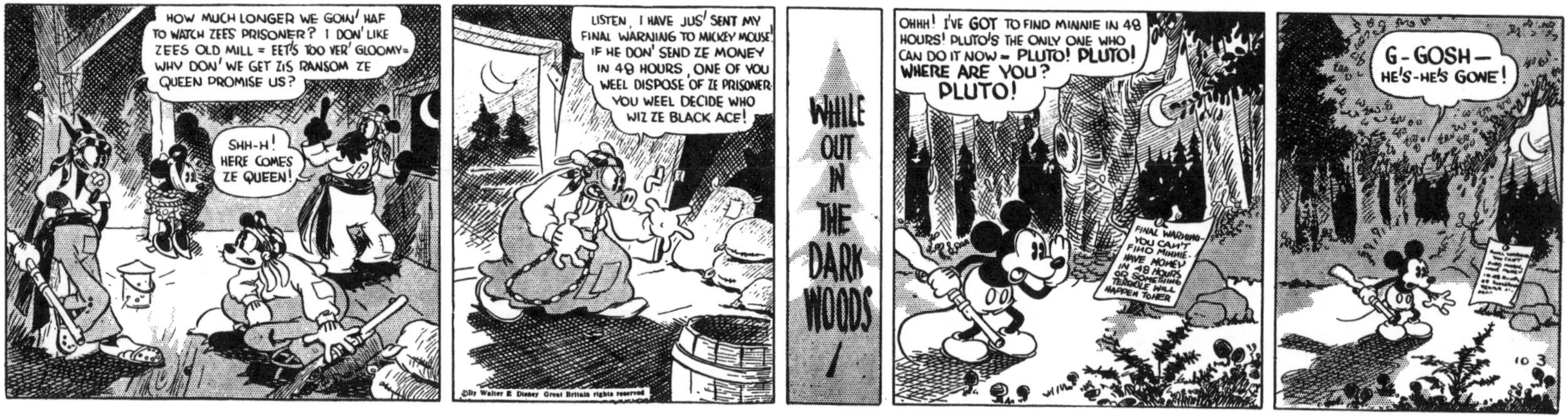
HOW MUCH LONGER WE GOIN' HAF TO WATCH ZEES PRISONER? I DON' LIKE ZEES OLD MILL = EET'S TOO VER' GLOOMY = WHY DON' WE GET ZIS RANSOM ZE QUEEN PROMISE US?
SHH-H! HERE COMES ZE QUEEN!
LISTEN, I HAVE JUS' SENT MY FINAL WARNING TO MICKEY MOUSE! IF HE DON' SEND ZE MONEY IN 48 HOURS, ONE OF YOU WEEL DISPOSE OF ZE PRISONER - YOU WEEL DECIDE WHO WIZ ZE BLACK ACE!
©by Walter E Disney Great Britain rights reserved
WHILE OUT IN THE DARK WOODS!
OHHH! I'VE GOT TO FIND MINNIE IN 48 HOURS! PLUTO'S THE ONLY ONE WHO CAN DO IT NOW = PLUTO! PLUTO! WHERE ARE YOU? PLUTO!
FINAL WARNING - YOU CAN'T FIND MINNIE HAVE MONEY IN 48 HOURS OR SOMETHING TERRIBLE WILL HAPPEN TO HER
G-GOSH - HE'S - HE'S GONE!
10 3

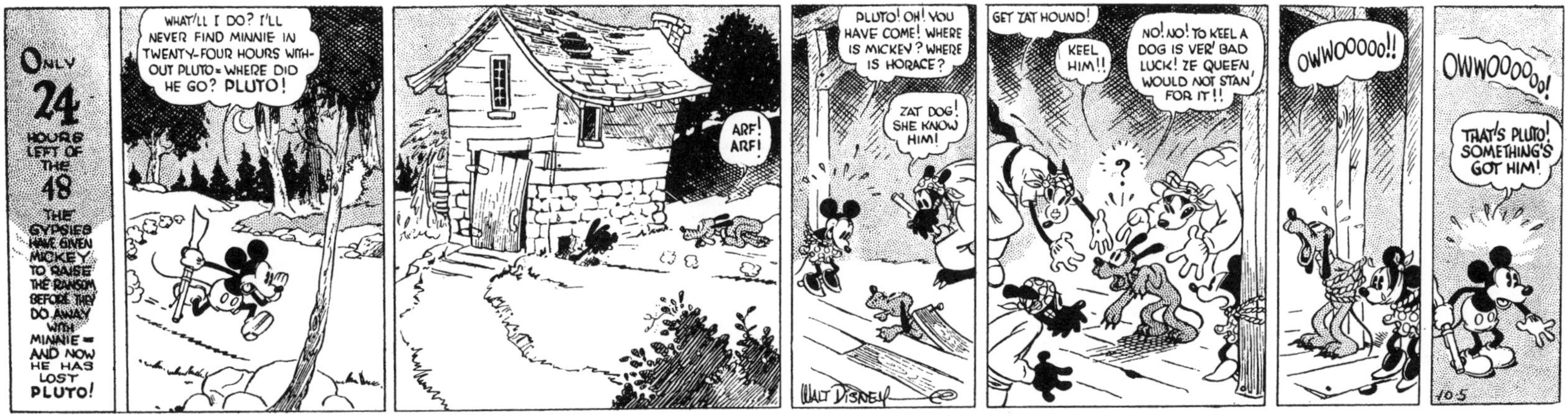
ONLY 24 HOURS LEFT OF THE 48 THE GYPSIES HAVE GIVEN MICKEY TO RAISE THE RANSOM BEFORE THEY DO AWAY WITH MINNIE = AND NOW HE HAS LOST PLUTO!
WHAT'LL I DO? I'LL NEVER FIND MINNIE IN TWENTY-FOUR HOURS WITH-OUT PLUTO = WHERE DID HE GO? PLUTO!
ARF! ARF!
PLUTO! OH! YOU HAVE COME! WHERE IS MICKEY? WHERE IS HORACE?
ZAT DOG! SHE KNOW HIM!
GET ZAT HOUND!
KEEL HIM!!
NO! NO! TO KEEL A DOG IS VER' BAD LUCK! ZE QUEEN WOULD NOT STAN' FOR IT!!
?
OWWOOOOO!!
OWWOOOOoo!
THAT'S PLUTO! SOMETHING'S GOT HIM!
WALT DISNEY
10-5

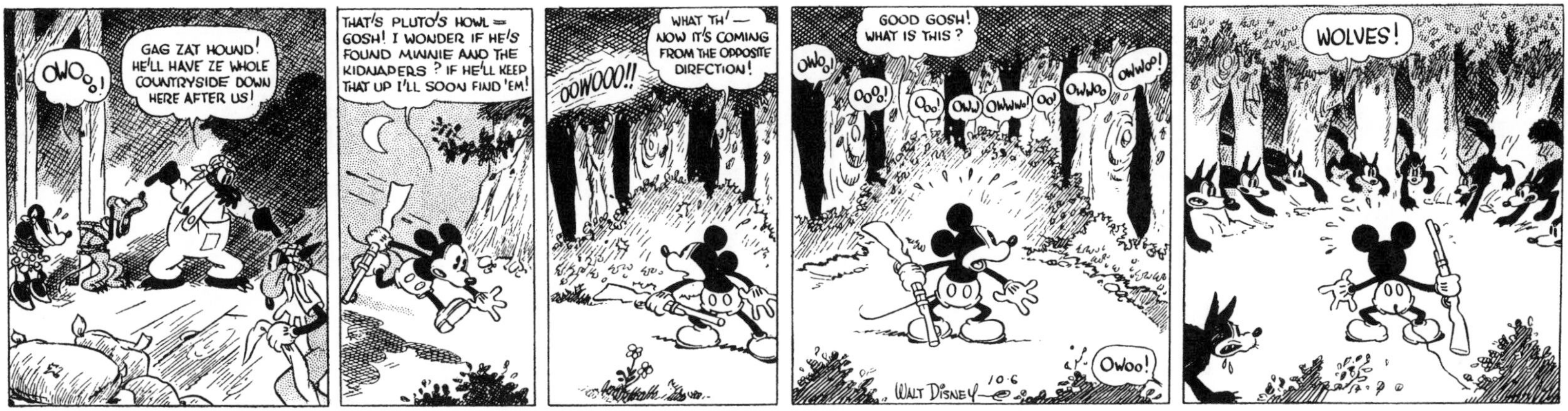
OWOoo!
GAG ZAT HOUND! HE'LL HAVE ZE WHOLE COUNTRYSIDE DOWN HERE AFTER US!
THAT'S PLUTO'S HOWL = GOSH! I WONDER IF HE'S FOUND MINNIE AND THE KIDNAPERS? IF HE'LL KEEP THAT UP I'LL SOON FIND 'EM!
OOWOOO!!
WHAT TH'! — NOW IT'S COMING FROM THE OPPOSITE DIRECTION!
GOOD GOSH! WHAT IS THIS?
Owoo!
WALT DISNEY
10-6
WOLVES!

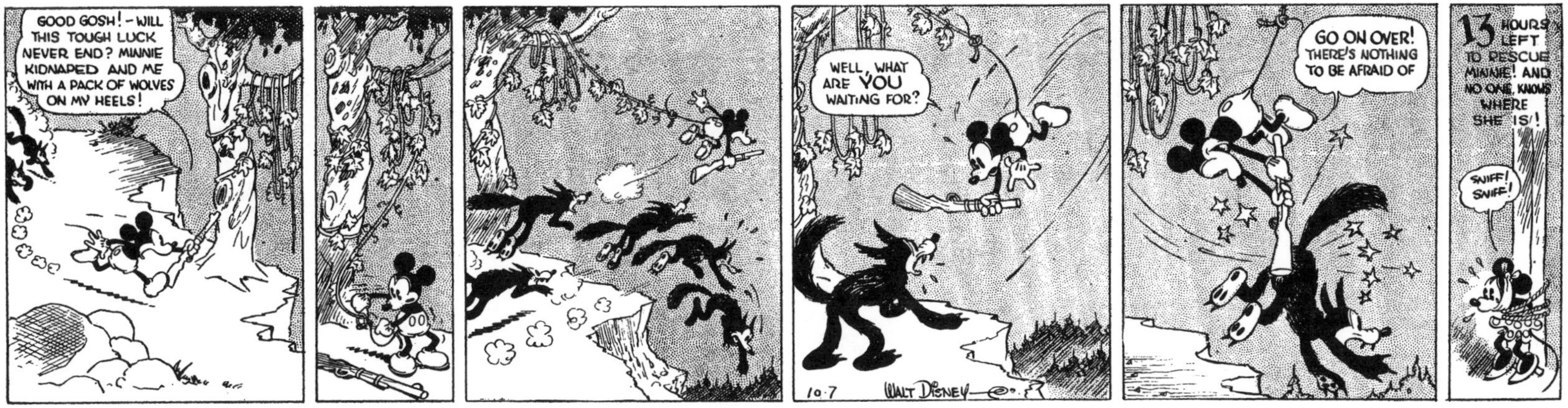
GOOD GOSH! - WILL THIS TOUGH LUCK NEVER END? MINNIE KIDNAPED AND ME WITH A PACK OF WOLVES ON MY HEELS!
WELL, WHAT ARE YOU WAITING FOR?
10-7
WALT DISNEY
GO ON OVER! THERE'S NOTHING TO BE AFRAID OF
13 HOURS LEFT TO RESCUE MINNIE! AND NO ONE KNOWS WHERE SHE IS!
SNIFF! SNIFF!

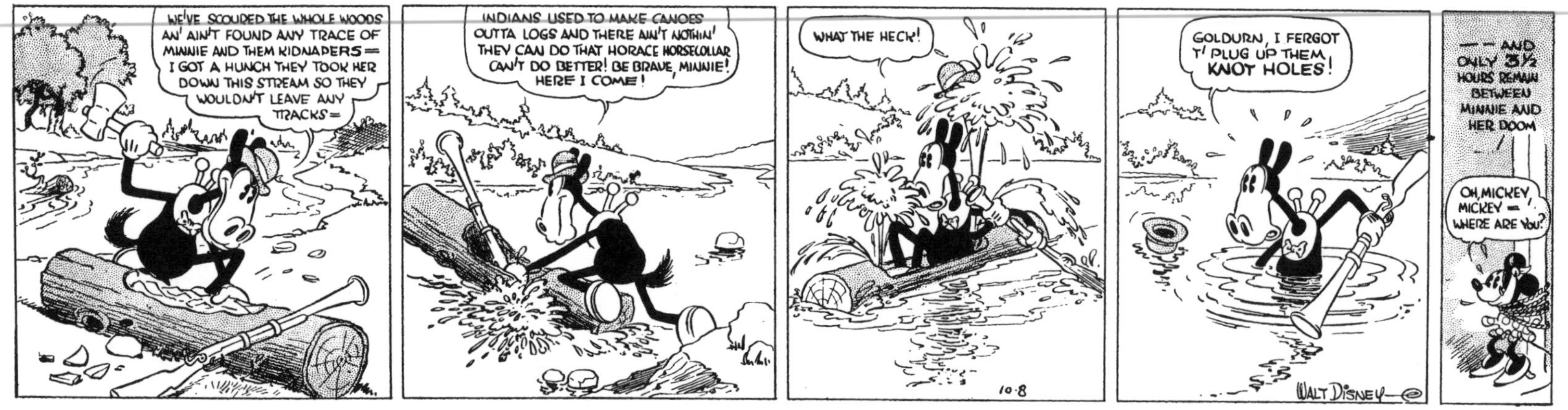
WE'VE SCOURED THE WHOLE WOODS AN' AIN'T FOUND ANY TRACE OF MINNIE AND THEM KIDNAPERS = I GOT A HUNCH THEY TOOK HER DOWN THIS STREAM SO THEY WOULDN'T LEAVE ANY TRACKS =
INDIANS USED TO MAKE CANOES OUTTA LOGS AND THERE AIN'T NOTHIN' THEY CAN DO THAT HORACE HORSECOLLAR CAN'T DO BETTER! BE BRAVE, MINNIE! HERE I COME!
WHAT THE HECK!
10-8
GOLDURN, I FERGOT T' PLUG UP THEM KNOT HOLES!
WALT DISNEY
— — AND ONLY 3½ HOURS REMAIN BETWEEN MINNIE AND HER DOOM
OH, MICKEY, MICKEY = WHERE ARE YOU?

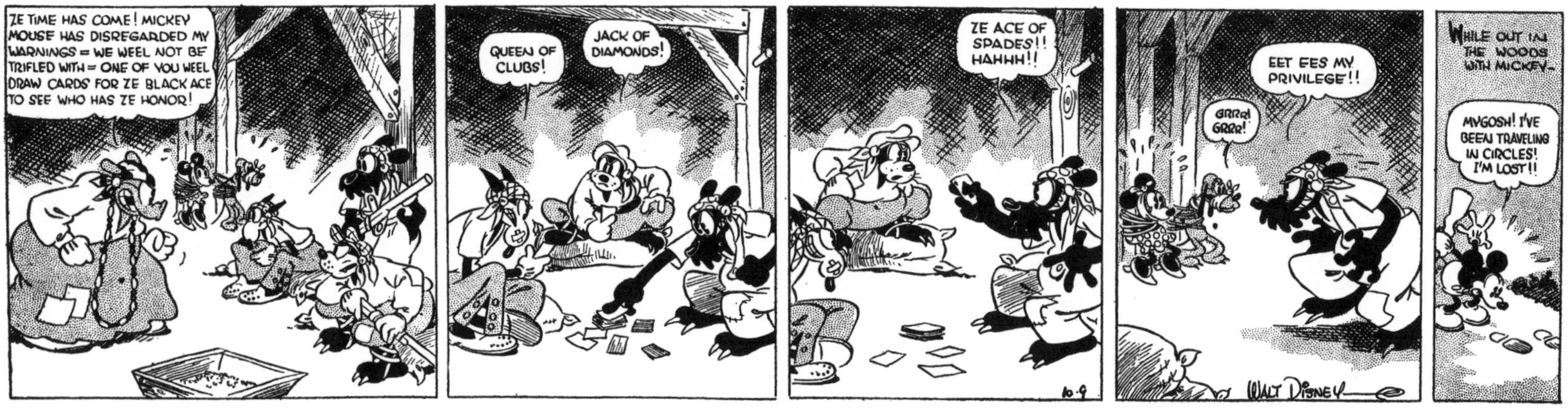
ZE TIME HAS COME! MICKEY MOUSE HAS DISREGARDED MY WARNINGS = WE WEEL NOT BE TRIFLED WITH = ONE OF YOU WEEL DRAW CARDS FOR ZE BLACK ACE TO SEE WHO HAS ZE HONOR!
QUEEN OF CLUBS!
JACK OF DIAMONDS!
ZE ACE OF SPADES!! HAHHH!!
10-9
EET EES MY PRIVILEGE!!
GRRR! GRRR!
WALT DISNEY
WHILE OUT IN THE WOODS WITH MICKEY—
MYGOSH! I'VE BEEN TRAVELING IN CIRCLES! I'M LOST!!

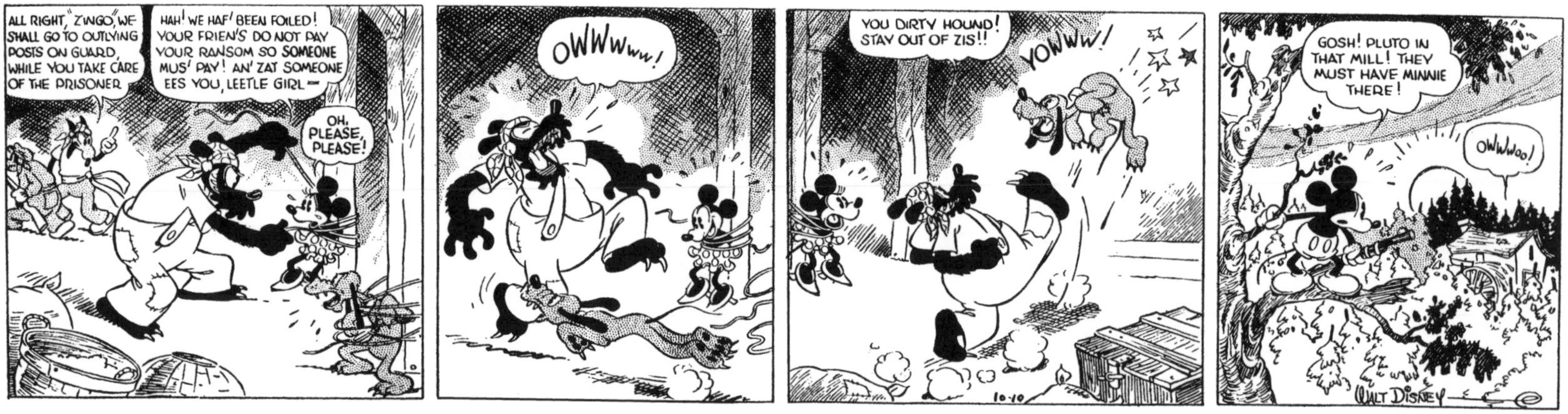
ALL RIGHT, "ZINGO," WE SHALL GO TO OUTLYING POSTS ON GUARD, WHILE YOU TAKE CARE OF THE PRISONER
HAH! WE HAF' BEEN FOILED! YOUR FRIEN'S DO NOT PAY YOUR RANSOM SO SOMEONE MUS' PAY! AN' ZAT SOMEONE EES YOU, LEETLE GIRL —
OH, PLEASE, PLEASE!
OWWWww!
YOU DIRTY HOUND! STAY OUT OF ZIS!!
YOWWW!
10-10
GOSH! PLUTO IN THAT MILL! THEY MUST HAVE MINNIE THERE!
OWWWoo!
WALT DISNEY

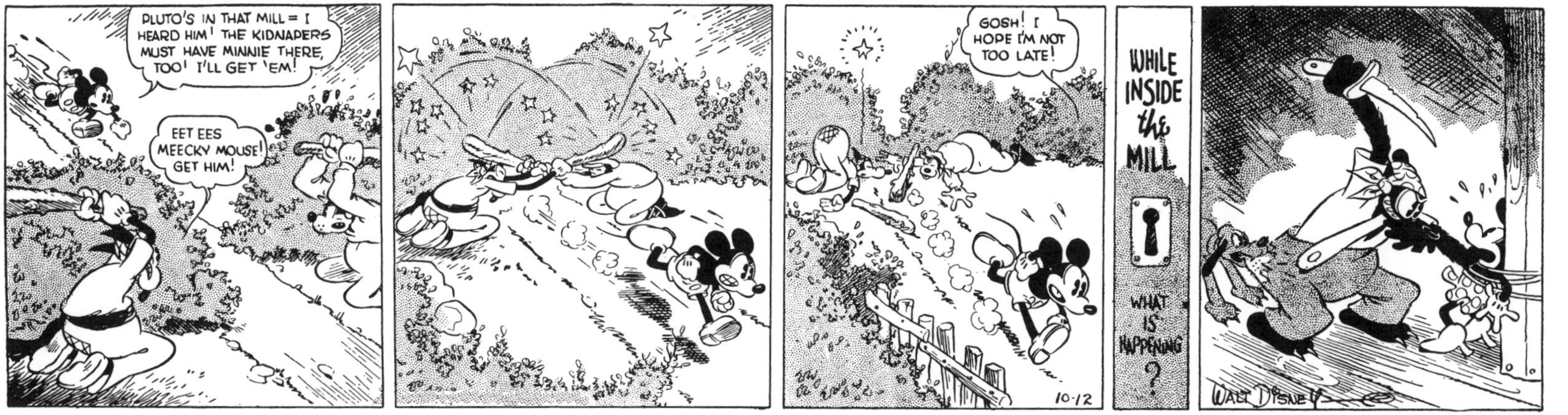
PLUTO'S IN THAT MILL = I HEARD HIM! THE KIDNAPERS MUST HAVE MINNIE THERE, TOO! I'LL GET 'EM!
EET EES MEECKY MOUSE! GET HIM!
GOSH! I HOPE I'M NOT TOO LATE!
10-12
WHILE INSIDE the MILL
WHAT IS HAPPENING ?
WALT DISNEY

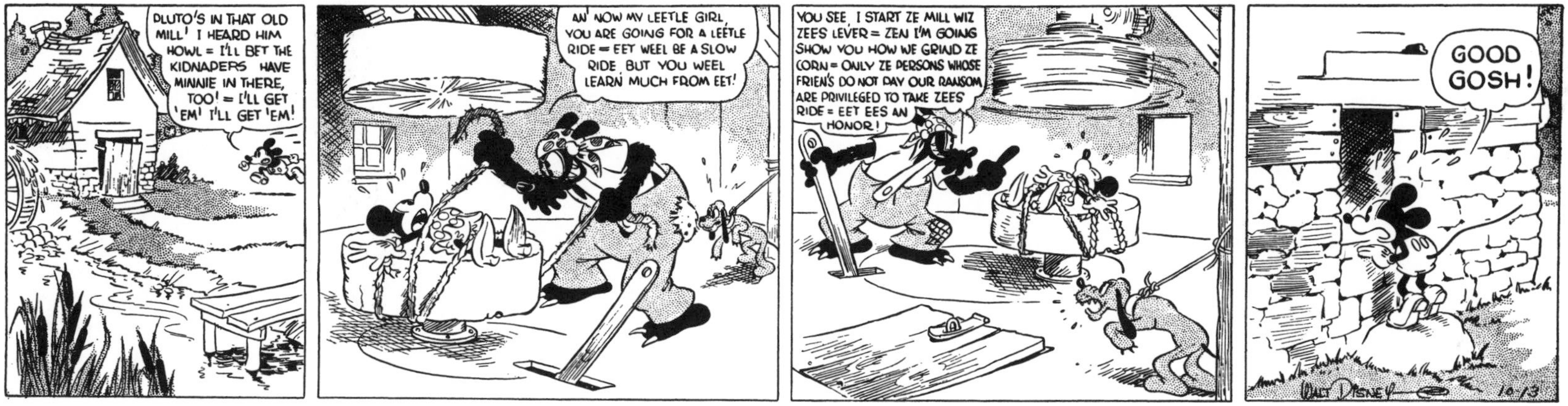
PLUTO'S IN THAT OLD MILL! I HEARD HIM HOWL = I'LL BET THE KIDNAPERS HAVE MINNIE IN THERE, TOO! = I'LL GET 'EM! I'LL GET 'EM!
AN' NOW MY LEETLE GIRL, YOU ARE GOING FOR A LEETLE RIDE = EET WEEL BE A SLOW RIDE BUT YOU WEEL LEARN MUCH FROM EET!
YOU SEE, I START ZE MILL WIZ ZEES LEVER = ZEN I'M GOING SHOW YOU HOW WE GRIND ZE CORN = ONLY ZE PERSONS WHOSE FRIEN'S DO NOT PAY OUR RANSOM ARE PRIVILEGED TO TAKE ZEES RIDE = EET EES AN HONOR!
GOOD GOSH!
WALT DISNEY
10-13

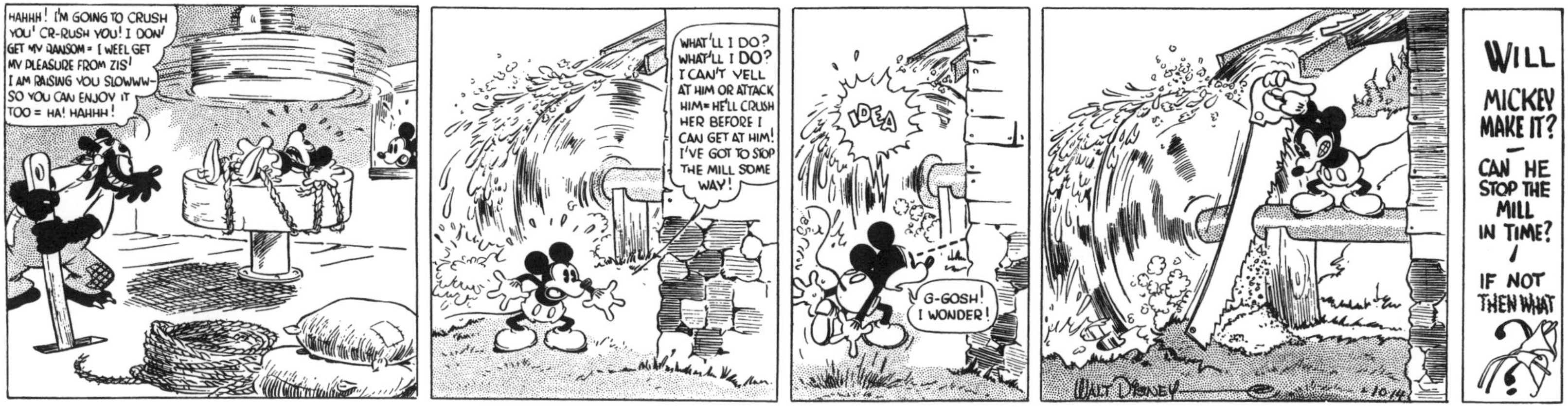
HAHHH! I'M GOING TO CRUSH YOU! CR-RUSH YOU! I DON' GET MY RANSOM = I WEEL GET MY PLEASURE FROM ZIS! I AM RAISING YOU SLOWWW- SO YOU CAN ENJOY IT TOO = HA! HAHHH!
WHAT'LL I DO? WHAT'LL I DO? I CAN'T YELL AT HIM OR ATTACK HIM = HE'LL CRUSH HER BEFORE I CAN GET AT HIM! I'VE GOT TO STOP THE MILL SOME WAY!
IDEA
G-GOSH! I WONDER!
WALT DISNEY
10-14
WILL MICKEY MAKE IT? - CAN HE STOP THE MILL IN TIME? / IF NOT THEN WHAT ?

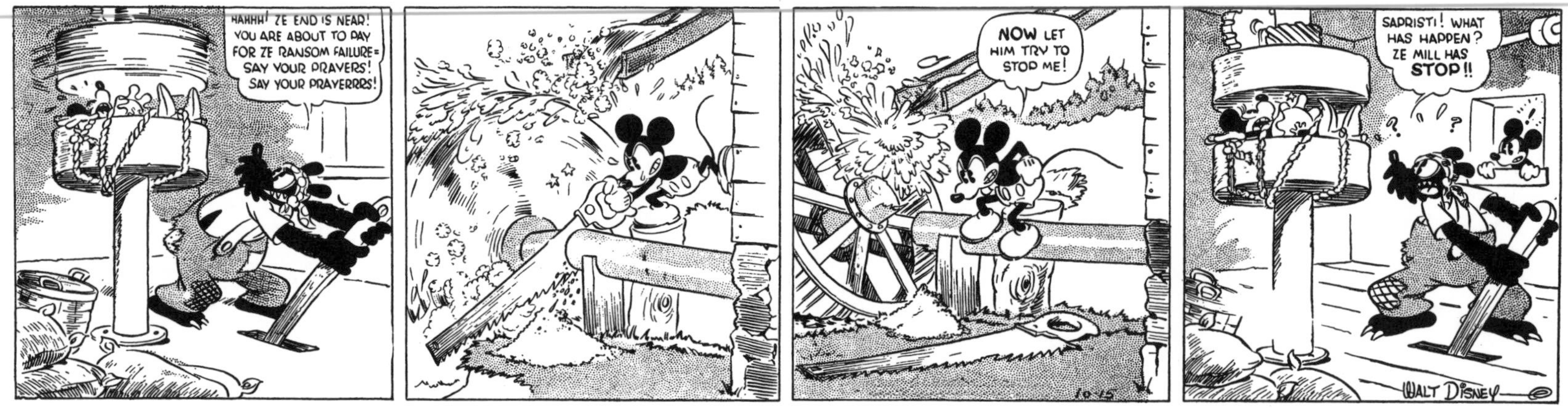
HAHHH! ZE END IS NEAR! YOU ARE ABOUT TO PAY FOR ZE RANSOM FAILURE= SAY YOUR PRAYERS! SAY YOUR PRAYERRRS!
NOW LET HIM TRY TO STOP ME!
10-15
SAPRISTI! WHAT HAS HAPPEN? ZE MILL HAS STOP!!
WALT DISNEY

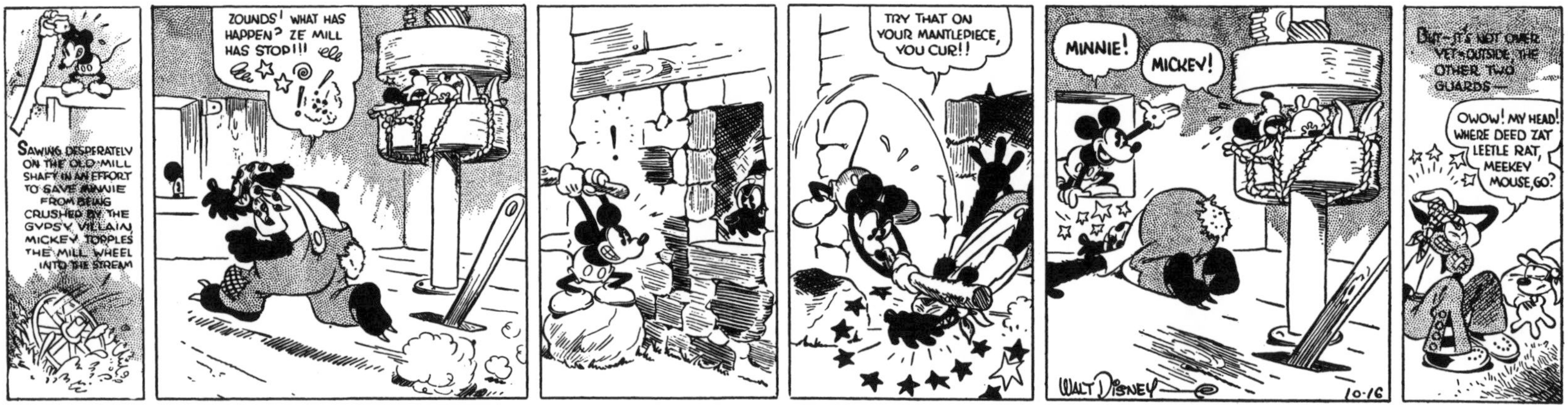
SAWING DESPERATELY ON THE OLD MILL SHAFT IN AN EFFORT TO SAVE MINNIE FROM BEING CRUSHED BY THE GYPSY VILLAIN, MICKEY TOPPLES THE MILL WHEEL INTO THE STREAM
ZOUNDS! WHAT HAS HAPPEN? ZE MILL HAS STOP!!!
TRY THAT ON YOUR MANTLEPIECE, YOU CUR!!
MINNIE!
MICKEY!
WALT DISNEY
10-16
BUT–IT'S NOT OVER YET–OUTSIDE, THE OTHER TWO GUARDS—
OWOW! MY HEAD! WHERE DEED ZAT LEETLE RAT, MEEKEY MOUSE, GO?

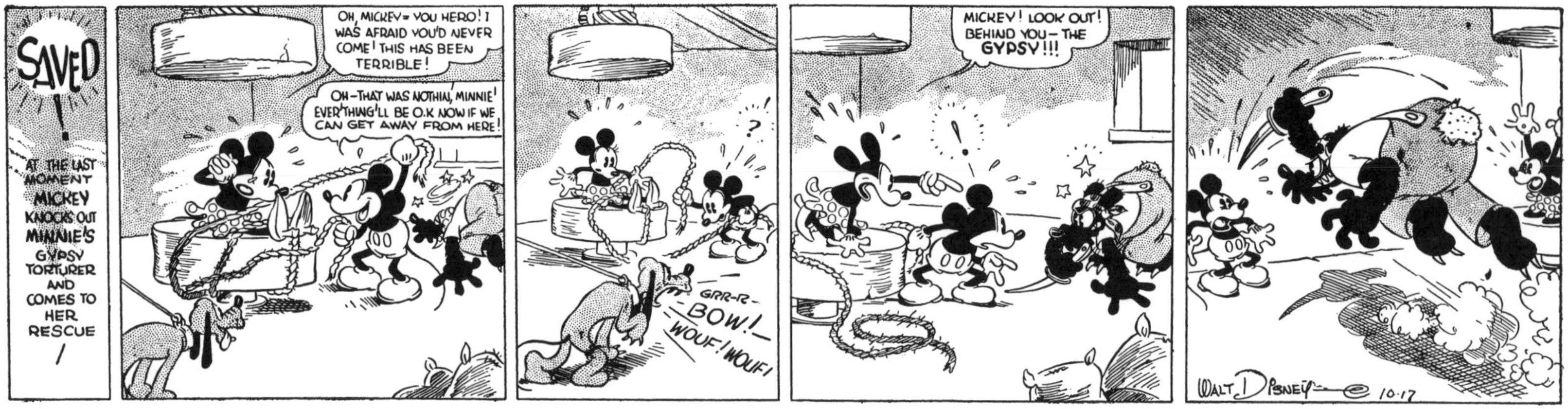
SAVED!
AT THE LAST MOMENT MICKEY KNOCKS OUT MINNIE'S GYPSY TORTURER AND COMES TO HER RESCUE!
OH, MICKEY= YOU HERO! I WAS AFRAID YOU'D NEVER COME! THIS HAS BEEN TERRIBLE!
OH–THAT WAS NOTHIN', MINNIE! EVERYTHING'LL BE O.K NOW IF WE CAN GET AWAY FROM HERE!
GRR-R-BOW!–WOUF! WOUF!
MICKEY! LOOK OUT! BEHIND YOU–THE GYPSY!!!
WALT DISNEY
10-17

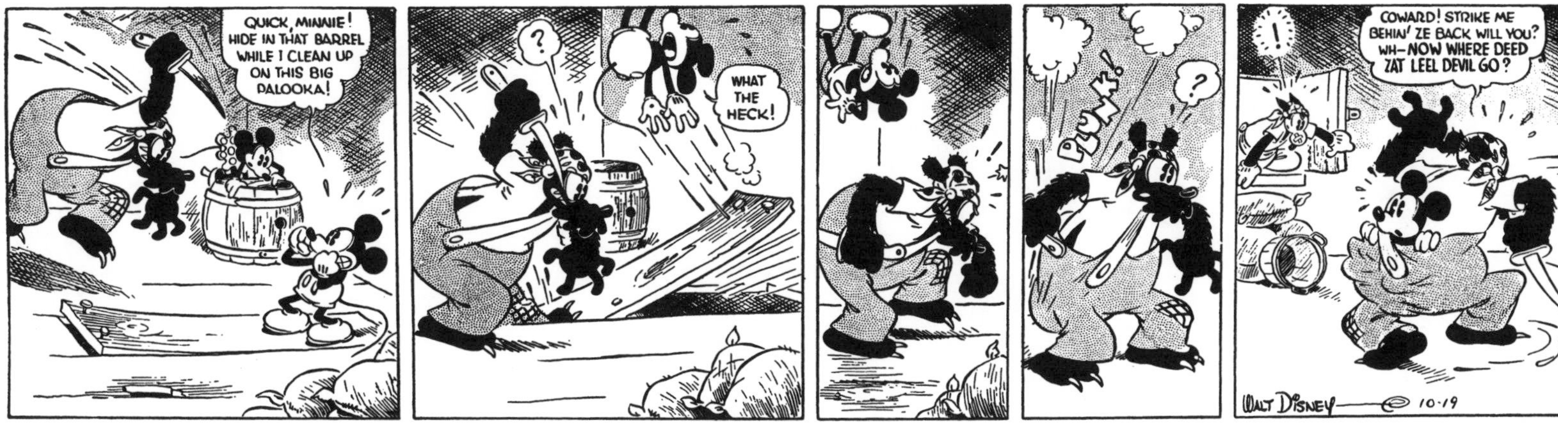
QUICK, MINNIE! HIDE IN THAT BARREL WHILE I CLEAN UP ON THIS BIG PALOOKA!
?
WHAT THE HECK!
PLUNK!
?
!
COWARD! STRIKE ME BEHIN' ZE BACK WILL YOU? WH—NOW WHERE DEED ZAT LEEL DEVIL GO?
WALT DISNEY
10-19

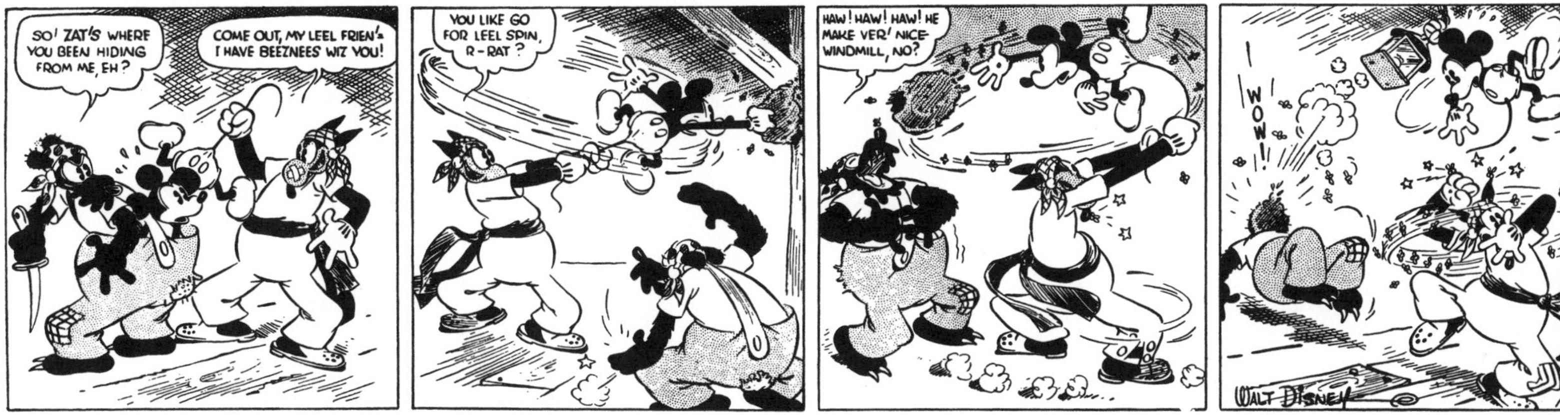
SO! ZAT'S WHERE YOU BEEN HIDING FROM ME, EH?
COME OUT, MY LEEL FRIEN'! I HAVE BEEZNEES WIZ YOU!
YOU LIKE GO FOR LEEL SPIN, R-RAT?
HAW! HAW! HAW! HE MAKE VER' NICE WINDMILL, NO?
WOW!
WALT DISNEY
10-20

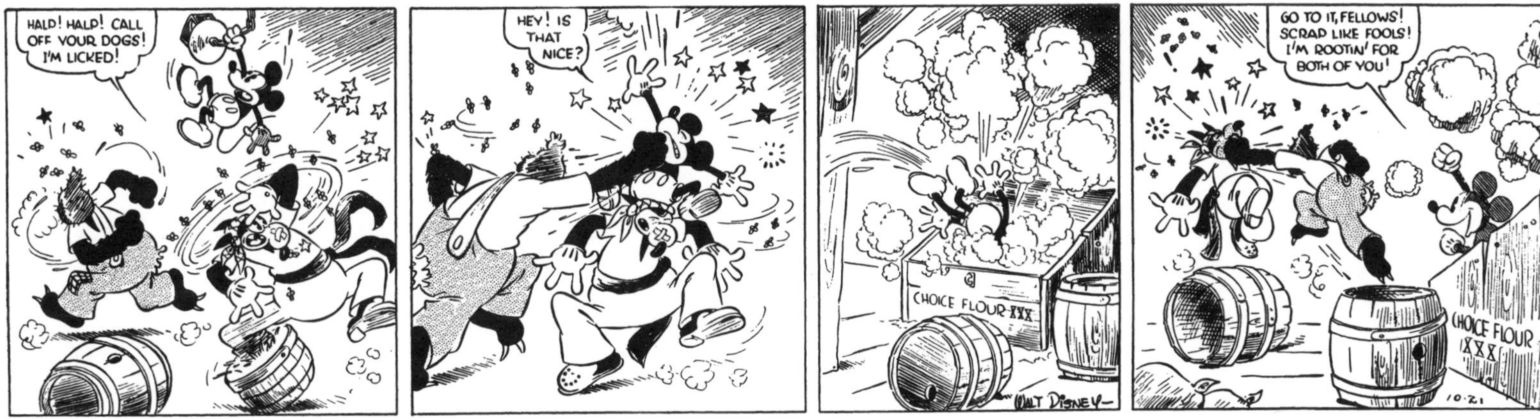
HALP! HALP! CALL OFF YOUR DOGS! I'M LICKED!
HEY! IS THAT NICE?
CHOICE FLOUR XXX
WALT DISNEY
GO TO IT, FELLOWS! SCRAP LIKE FOOLS! I'M ROOTIN' FOR BOTH OF YOU!
CHOICE FLOUR XXX
10-21

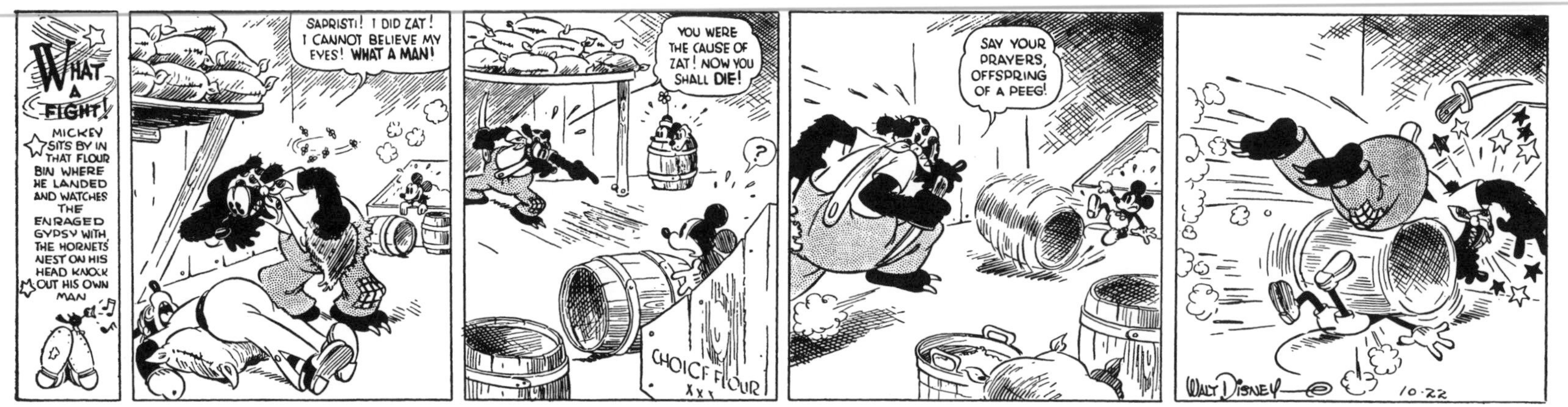
WHAT A FIGHT!
MICKEY SITS BY IN THAT FLOUR BIN WHERE HE LANDED AND WATCHES THE ENRAGED GYPSY WITH THE HORNETS' NEST ON HIS HEAD KNOCK OUT HIS OWN MAN
SAPRISTI! I DID ZAT! I CANNOT BELIEVE MY EYES! WHAT A MAN!
YOU WERE THE CAUSE OF ZAT! NOW YOU SHALL DIE!
?
CHOICE FLOUR XXX
SAY YOUR PRAYERS, OFFSPRING OF A PEEG!
WALT DISNEY
10·22

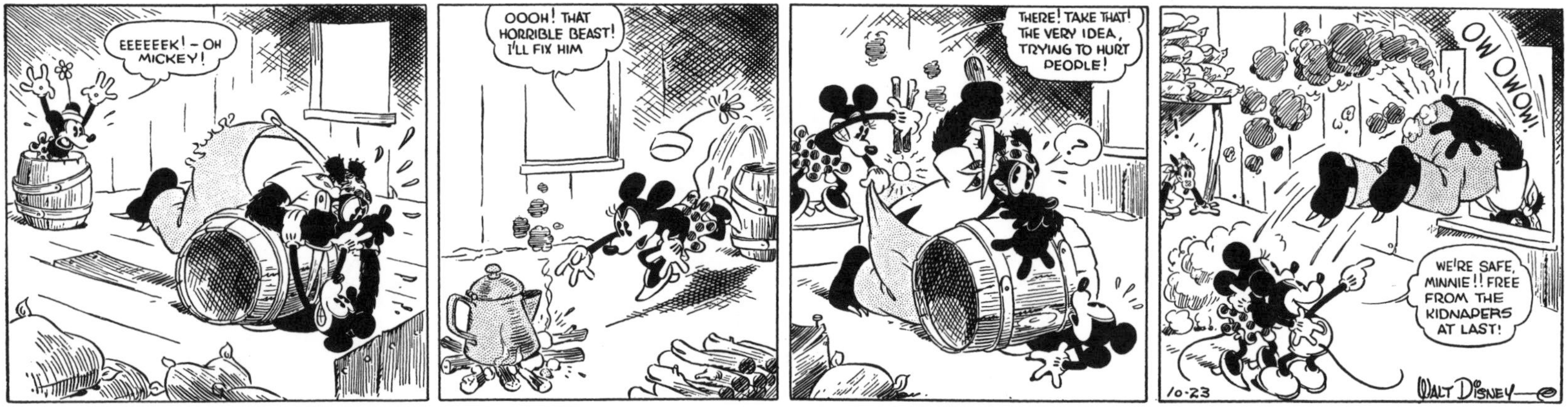
EEEEEEK! – OH MICKEY!
OOOH! THAT HORRIBLE BEAST! I'LL FIX HIM
THERE! TAKE THAT! THE VERY IDEA, TRYING TO HURT PEOPLE!
?
OW OW OW!
WE'RE SAFE, MINNIE!! FREE FROM THE KIDNAPERS AT LAST!
10-23
WALT DISNEY

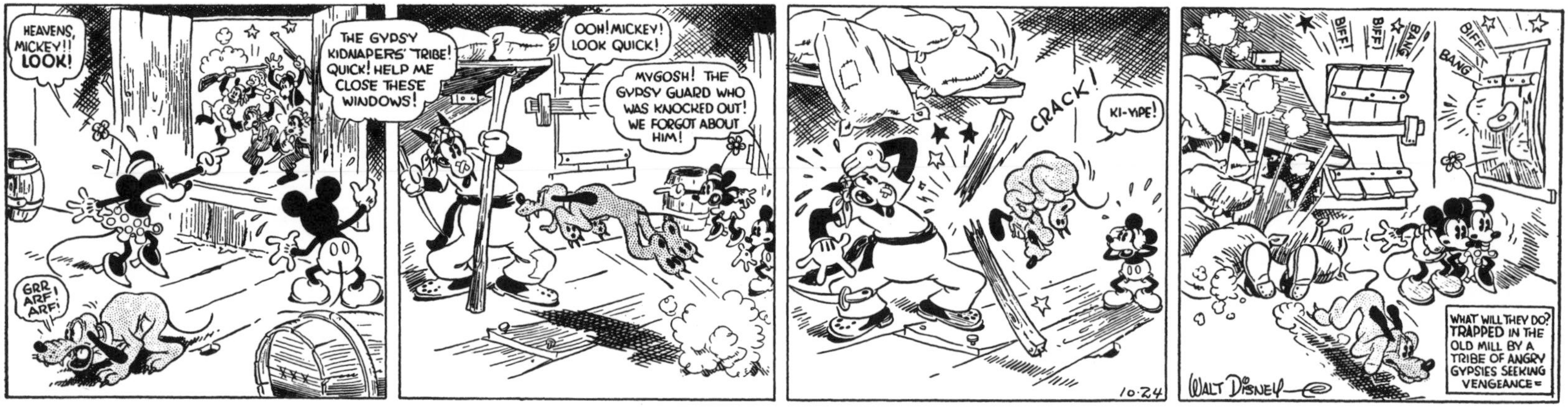
HEAVENS, MICKEY!! LOOK!
THE GYPSY KIDNAPERS' TRIBE! QUICK! HELP ME CLOSE THESE WINDOWS!
GRR ARF! ARF!
XXX
OOH! MICKEY! LOOK QUICK!
MYGOSH! THE GYPSY GUARD WHO WAS KNOCKED OUT! WE FORGOT ABOUT HIM!
CRACK!
KI-YIPE!
10·24
BIFF! BIFF! BANG BIFF! BANG
WHAT WILL THEY DO? TRAPPED IN THE OLD MILL BY A TRIBE OF ANGRY GYPSIES SEEKING VENGEANCE=
WALT DISNEY

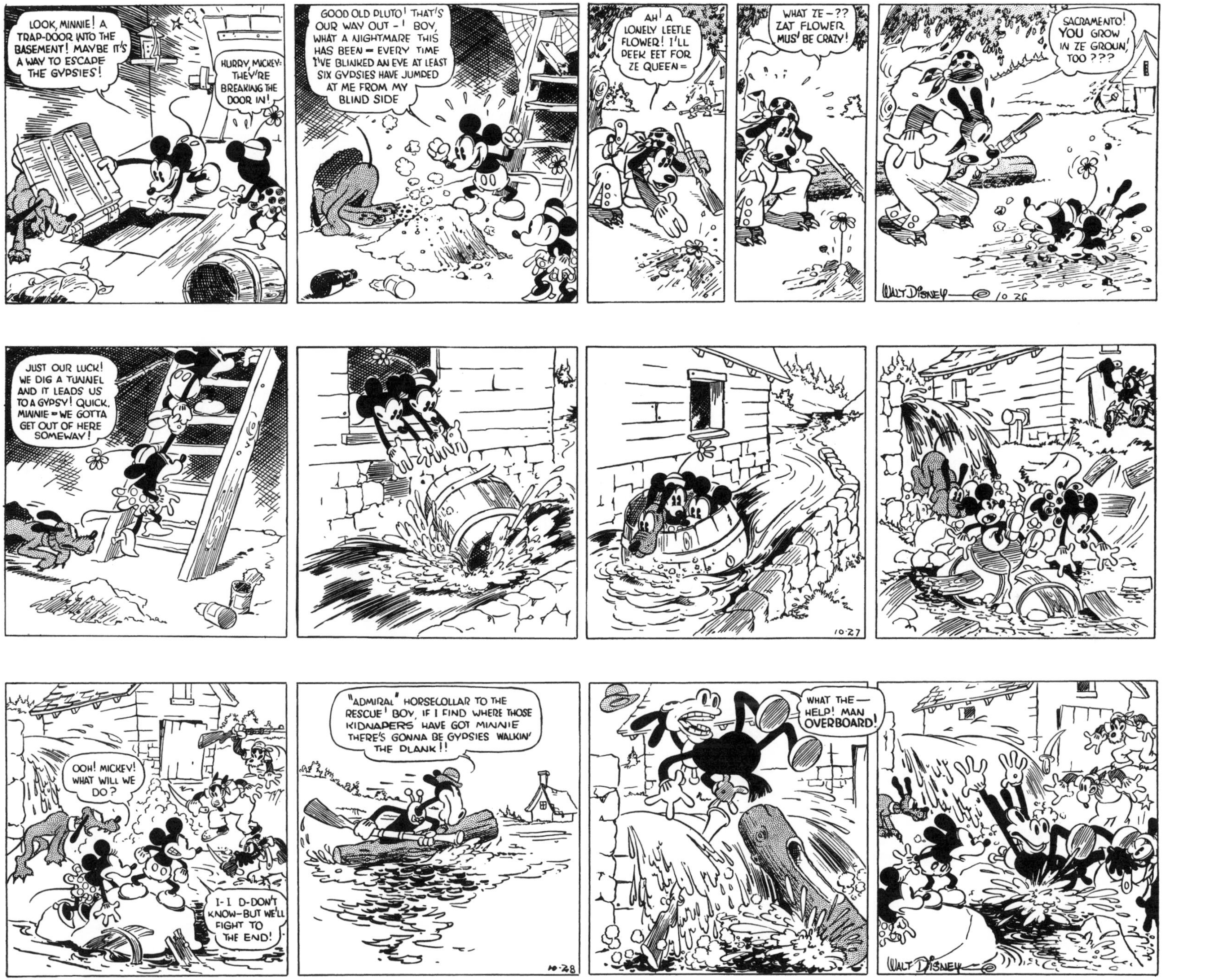
LOOK, MINNIE! A TRAP-DOOR INTO THE BASEMENT! MAYBE IT'S A WAY TO ESCAPE THE GYPSIES!
HURRY, MICKEY: THEY'RE BREAKING THE DOOR IN!
GOOD OLD PLUTO! THAT'S OUR WAY OUT—! BOY, WHAT A NIGHTMARE THIS HAS BEEN—EVERY TIME I'VE BLINKED AN EYE AT LEAST SIX GYPSIES HAVE JUMPED AT ME FROM MY BLIND SIDE
AH! A LONELY LEETLE FLOWER! I'LL PEEK EET FOR ZE QUEEN—
WHAT ZE—?? ZAT FLOWER MUS' BE CRAZY!
SACRAMENTO! YOU GROW IN ZE GROUN', TOO???
WALT DISNEY
10·26
JUST OUR LUCK! WE DIG A TUNNEL AND IT LEADS US TO A GYPSY! QUICK, MINNIE—WE GOTTA GET OUT OF HERE SOMEWAY!
10·27
OOH! MICKEY! WHAT WILL WE DO?
I-I D-DON'T KNOW—BUT WE'LL FIGHT TO THE END!
"ADMIRAL" HORSECOLLAR TO THE RESCUE! BOY, IF I FIND WHERE THOSE KIDNAPERS HAVE GOT MINNIE THERE'S GONNA BE GYPSIES WALKIN' THE PLANK!!
10·28
WHAT THE— HELP! MAN OVERBOARD!
WALT DISNEY

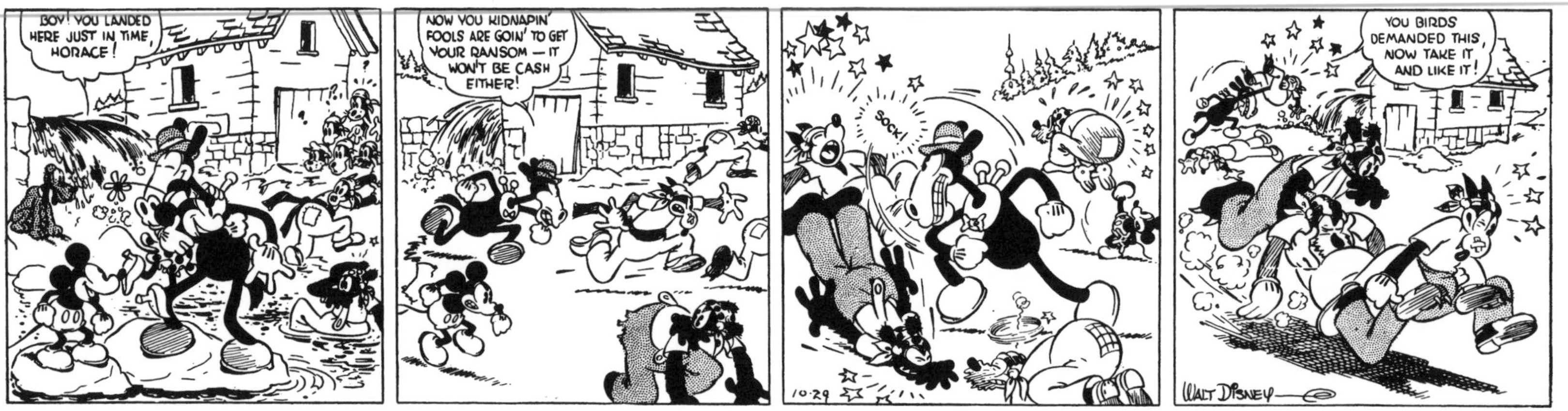
BOY! YOU LANDED HERE JUST IN TIME, HORACE!
NOW YOU KIDNAPIN' FOOLS ARE GOIN' TO GET YOUR RANSOM — IT WON'T BE CASH EITHER!
SOCK!
10·29
YOU BIRDS DEMANDED THIS, NOW TAKE IT AND LIKE IT!
WALT DISNEY

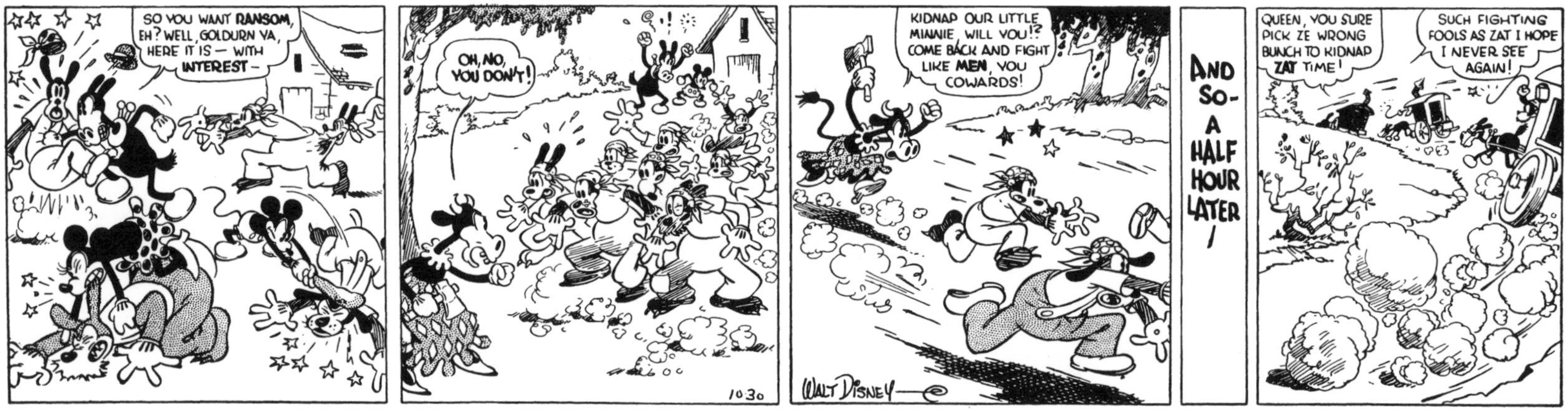
SO YOU WANT RANSOM, EH? WELL, GOLDURN YA, HERE IT IS — WITH INTEREST—
OH, NO, YOU DON'T!
10·30
KIDNAP OUR LITTLE MINNIE, WILL YOU!? COME BACK AND FIGHT LIKE MEN, YOU COWARDS!
WALT DISNEY
AND SO— A HALF HOUR LATER!
QUEEN, YOU SURE PICK ZE WRONG BUNCH TO KIDNAP ZAT TIME!
SUCH FIGHTING FOOLS AS ZAT I HOPE I NEVER SEE AGAIN!

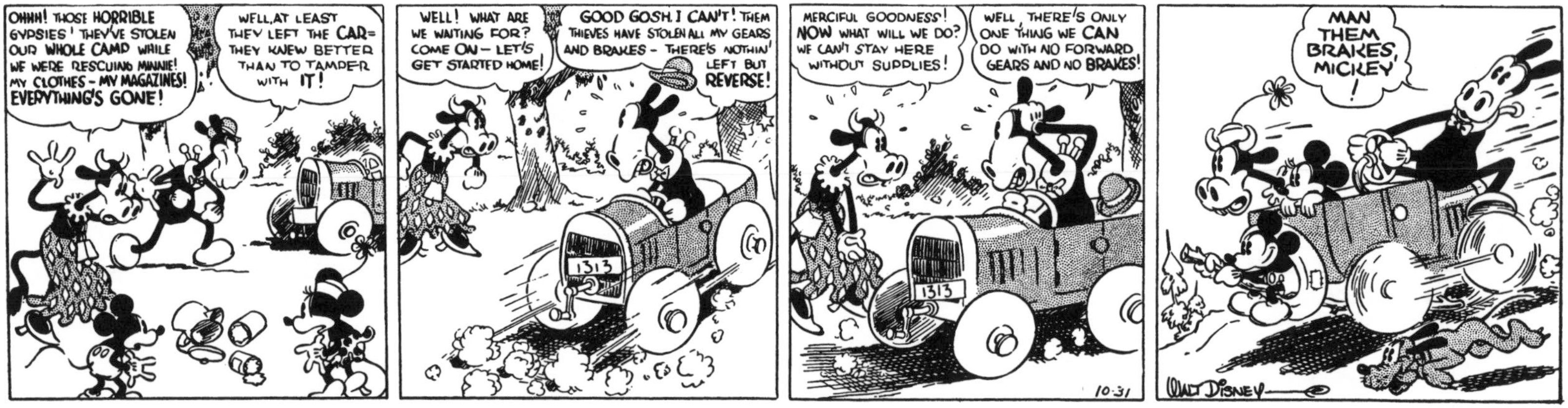
OHHH! THOSE HORRIBLE GYPSIES! THEY'VE STOLEN OUR WHOLE CAMP WHILE WE WERE RESCUING MINNIE! MY CLOTHES – MY MAGAZINES! EVERYTHING'S GONE!
WELL, AT LEAST THEY LEFT THE CAR= THEY KNEW BETTER THAN TO TAMPER WITH IT!
WELL! WHAT ARE WE WAITING FOR? COME ON – LET'S GET STARTED HOME!
GOOD GOSH, I CAN'T! THEM THIEVES HAVE STOLEN ALL MY GEARS AND BRAKES – THERE'S NOTHIN' LEFT BUT REVERSE!
1313
MERCIFUL GOODNESS! NOW WHAT WILL WE DO? WE CAN'T STAY HERE WITHOUT SUPPLIES!
WELL, THERE'S ONLY ONE THING WE CAN DO WITH NO FORWARD GEARS AND NO BRAKES!
1313
10·31
MAN THEM BRAKES, MICKEY!
WALT DISNEY

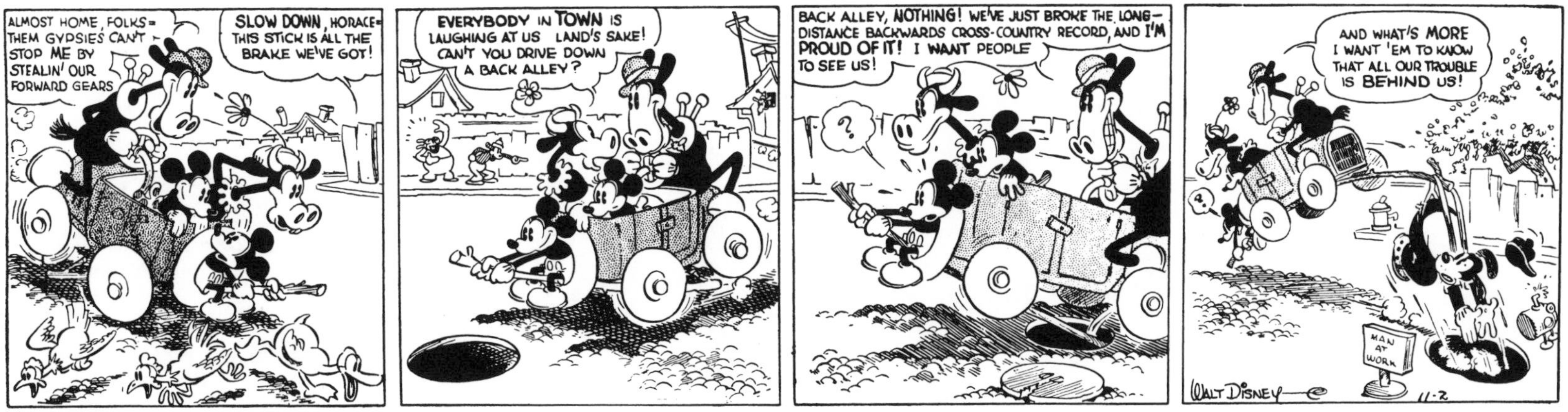
ALMOST HOME, FOLKS= THEM GYPSIES CAN'T STOP ME BY STEALIN' OUR FORWARD GEARS
SLOW DOWN, HORACE= THIS STICK IS ALL THE BRAKE WE'VE GOT!
EVERYBODY IN TOWN IS LAUGHING AT US LAND'S SAKE! CAN'T YOU DRIVE DOWN A BACK ALLEY?
BACK ALLEY, NOTHING! WE'VE JUST BROKE THE LONG-DISTANCE BACKWARDS CROSS-COUNTRY RECORD, AND I'M PROUD OF IT! I WANT PEOPLE TO SEE US!
?
AND WHAT'S MORE I WANT 'EM TO KNOW THAT ALL OUR TROUBLE IS BEHIND US!
MAN AT WORK
WALT DISNEY
11-2

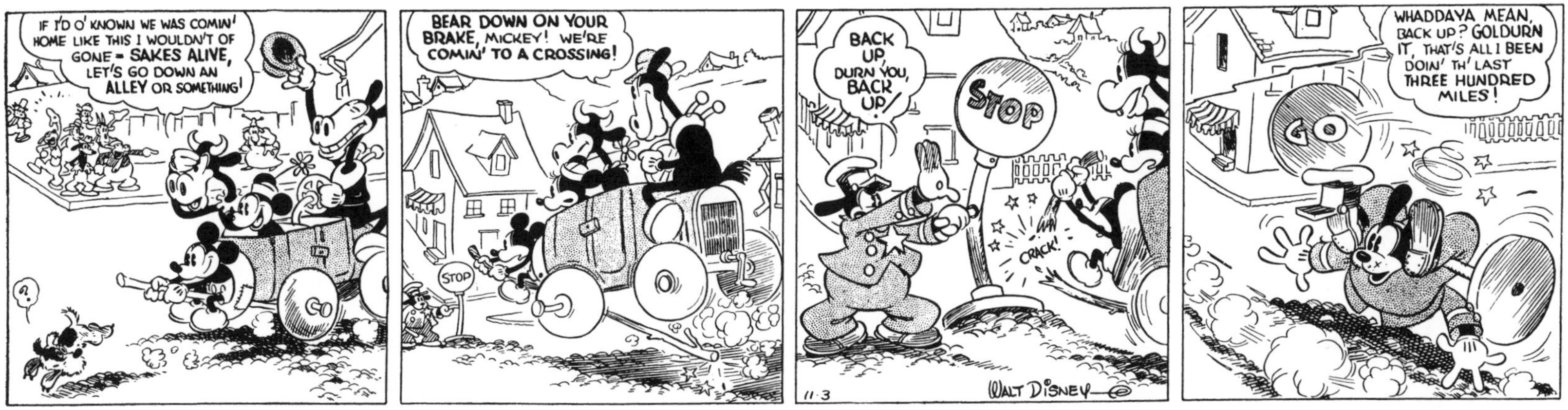
IF I'D O' KNOWN WE WAS COMIN' HOME LIKE THIS I WOULDN'T OF GONE= SAKES ALIVE, LET'S GO DOWN AN ALLEY OR SOMETHING!
?
BEAR DOWN ON YOUR BRAKE, MICKEY! WE'RE COMIN' TO A CROSSING!
STOP
BACK UP, DURN YOU, BACK UP!
STOP
CRACK!
11-3
WALT DISNEY
WHADDAYA MEAN, BACK UP? GOLDURN IT, THAT'S ALL I BEEN DOIN' TH' LAST THREE HUNDRED MILES!
GO

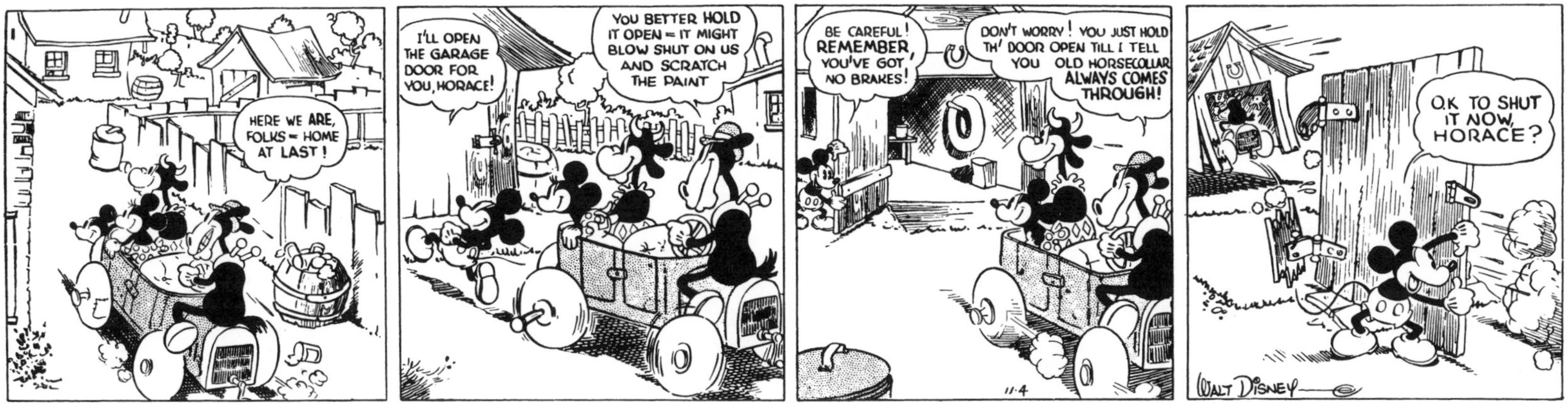
HERE WE ARE, FOLKS= HOME AT LAST!
I'LL OPEN THE GARAGE DOOR FOR YOU, HORACE!
YOU BETTER HOLD IT OPEN= IT MIGHT BLOW SHUT ON US AND SCRATCH THE PAINT
BE CAREFUL! REMEMBER, YOU'VE GOT NO BRAKES!
DON'T WORRY! YOU JUST HOLD TH' DOOR OPEN TILL I TELL YOU OLD HORSECOLLAR ALWAYS COMES THROUGH!
11-4
O.K. TO SHUT IT NOW, HORACE?
WALT DISNEY

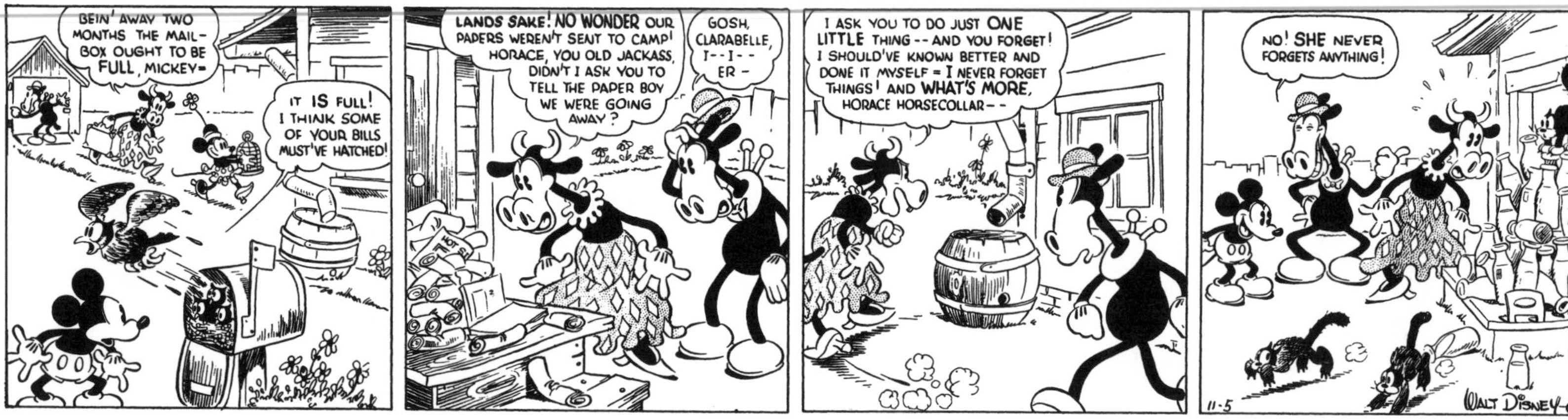
BEIN' AWAY TWO MONTHS THE MAIL-BOX OUGHT TO BE FULL, MICKEY=
IT IS FULL! I THINK SOME OF YOUR BILLS MUST'VE HATCHED!
LANDS SAKE! NO WONDER OUR PAPERS WEREN'T SENT TO CAMP! HORACE, YOU OLD JACKASS, DIDN'T I ASK YOU TO TELL THE PAPER BOY WE WERE GOING AWAY?
GOSH, CLARABELLE, I--I-- ER-
I ASK YOU TO DO JUST ONE LITTLE THING--AND YOU FORGET! I SHOULD'VE KNOWN BETTER AND DONE IT MYSELF = I NEVER FORGET THINGS! AND WHAT'S MORE, HORACE HORSECOLLAR--
NO! SHE NEVER FORGETS ANYTHING!
11-5
WALT DISNEY

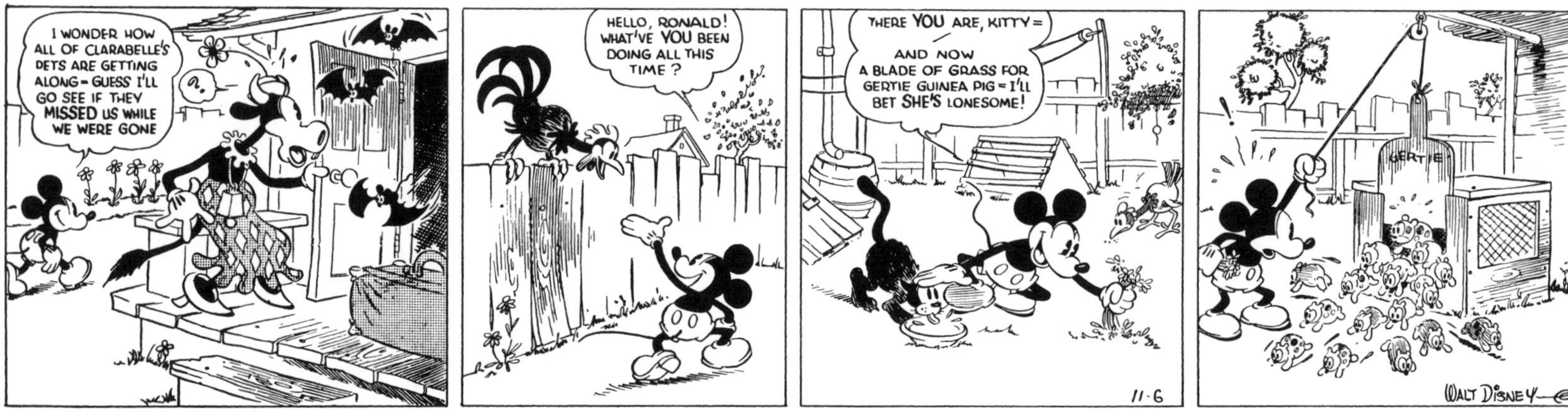
I WONDER HOW ALL OF CLARABELLE'S PETS ARE GETTING ALONG = GUESS I'LL GO SEE IF THEY MISSED US WHILE WE WERE GONE
HELLO, RONALD! WHAT'VE YOU BEEN DOING ALL THIS TIME?
THERE YOU ARE, KITTY =
AND NOW A BLADE OF GRASS FOR GERTIE GUINEA PIG = I'LL BET SHE'S LONESOME!
GERTIE
11-6
WALT DISNEY

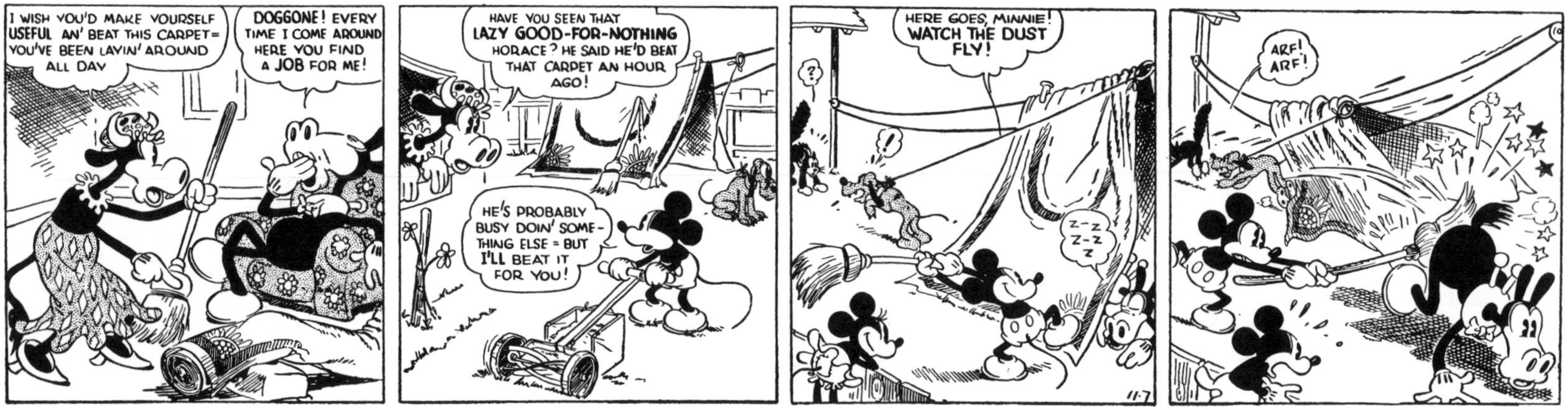
I WISH YOU'D MAKE YOURSELF USEFUL AN' BEAT THIS CARPET= YOU'VE BEEN LAYIN' AROUND ALL DAY
DOGGONE! EVERY TIME I COME AROUND HERE YOU FIND A JOB FOR ME!
HAVE YOU SEEN THAT LAZY GOOD-FOR-NOTHING HORACE? HE SAID HE'D BEAT THAT CARPET AN HOUR AGO!
HE'S PROBABLY BUSY DOIN' SOME-THING ELSE = BUT I'LL BEAT IT FOR YOU!
HERE GOES, MINNIE! WATCH THE DUST FLY!
Z-Z Z-Z Z
ARF! ARF!
11-7

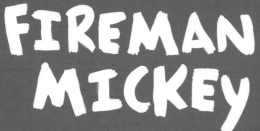

FIREMAN MICKEY
—AND—
CLARABELLE'S BOARDING HOUSE

NOVEMBER 9, 1931
–
JANUARY 9, 1932

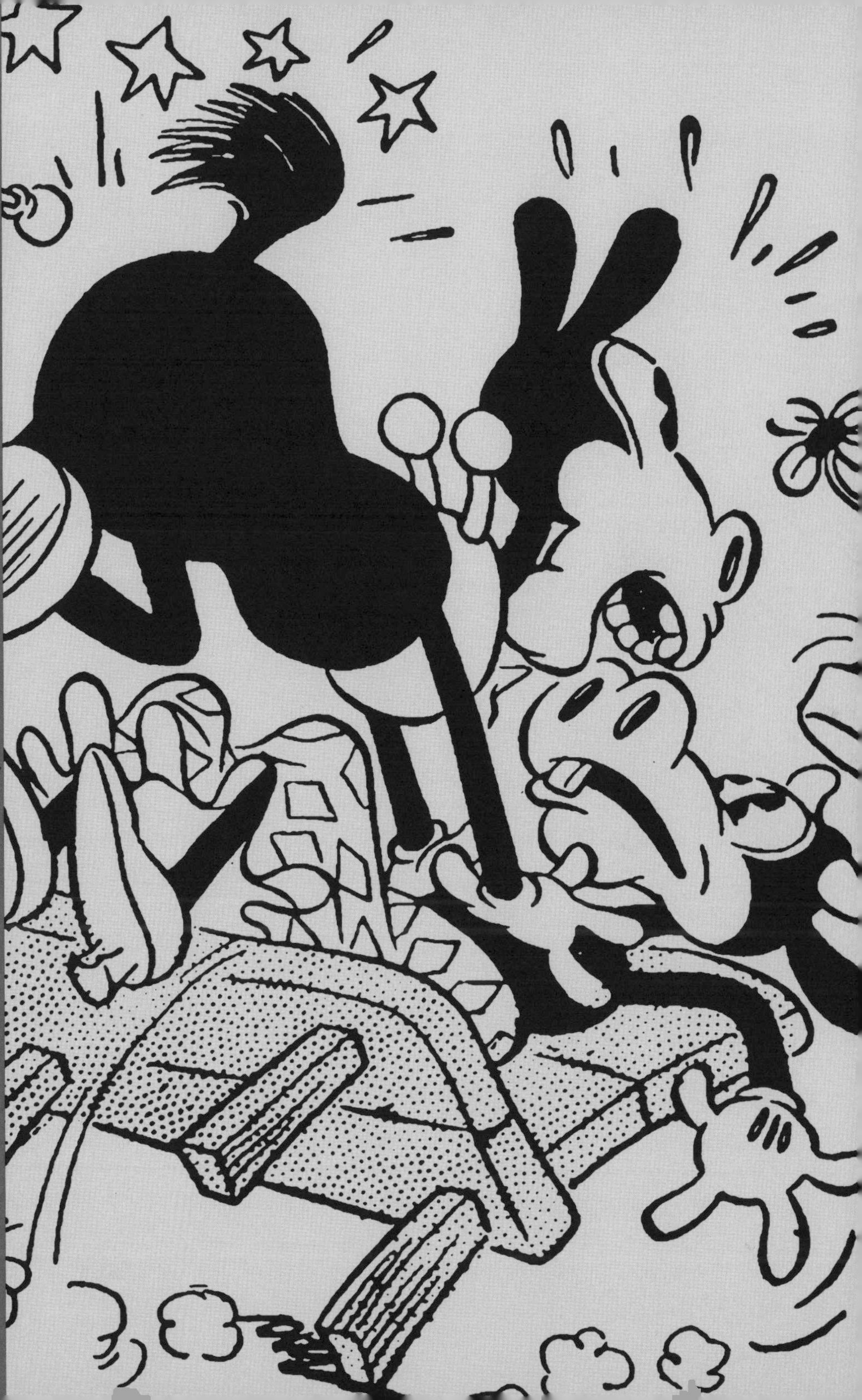

MICKEY MOUSE
REGISTERED U.S. PATENT OFFICE

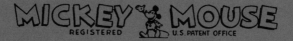

A MOUSE (AND A HORSE, AND A COW) AGAINST THE WORLD

Volume 1 of *Walt Disney's Mickey Mouse by Floyd Gottfredson* has spent a lot of time with Mickey and Minnie in their hometown.[1] We've seen Mickey's minigolf mishaps; his feud with Kat Nipp; and his unintended boxing match, all of which took place in the city known today as Mouseton. We've also witnessed many appearances by Mickey's and Minnie's close Mouseton friends: at this stage, we're primarily referring to Horace Horsecollar and Clarabelle Cow.[2]

Yet, oddly enough, we've seen little extended interaction between the Mice and these friends in their day-to-day hometown lives. "Mickey Mouse and the Ransom Plot," while bringing the gang together for a long, uninterrupted stretch, largely did so in an abstract, remote locale; and while Horace and Clarabelle did make appearances in the domestic-themed "Mr. Slicker" and "Boxing Champion," their roles were in no way lengthy or significant.

At last, however, in the gag stories "Fireman Mickey" and "Clarabelle's Boarding House," Gottfredson began to explore Mickey's relationship with these close friends in the domestic realm—and a milestone was reached. Themes of empathy, engagement, and bonding came to the fore as never before.

What did Mickey's extended cast mean to each other in the long term? As we shall see, Mickey cares about Horace and Clarabelle; enough to actively push them toward considering marriage. Clarabelle, uncommonly strategic, uses a checklist to plan her boarding house business. And while Mickey and Minnie themselves aren't ready to tie the knot, Mickey otherwise moves towards maturity: even if his help for city official Pop Weezil involves some childish behavior, it is a leap forward for Mickey to provide community service at all.

Gottfredson would later speak of Mickey, in his frequent underdog role, as a "mouse against the world," in conflict with a much larger society.[3] Such conflicts functioned best, of course, when Mickey's standing in society actively mattered to him. "Mr. Slicker" and "Boxing Champion" made it matter by forcing Mickey into dramatic roles: celebrity, fugitive, savior of the farm. In "Fireman Mickey" and "Clarabelle's Boarding House," by contrast, Mickey's standing finally matters for a reason we can identify with: because planning for the future is now realistically in Mickey's interest.

We'd like to ask, of course, that you excuse the odd unrealistic moment now and then. When "Cupid" Mickey fires arrows at unwitting victims, he's inarguably asking for trouble. [DG]

1 First named as "Silo Center" in 1932, Mickey's town was successively "Hometown" (1935) and "Mouseville" (1939). The modern name of Mouseton (1990-present) emerged to avoid conflict with Terrytoons, whose Mighty Mouse stories took place in Mouseville.

2 Called "Horse-Collar Horace" in 1930 press releases, Mickey's pal was just "Horsecollar" in the daily strip until "The Ransom Plot," where the modern version of his name first appeared. See the next volume of Fantagraphics' *Mickey Mouse* series for a lengthier profile of Horace and Clarabelle.

3 Floyd Gottfredson to David R. Smith, *Mickey Mouse in Color* deluxe edition (Prescott: Another Rainbow, 188), p. 164.

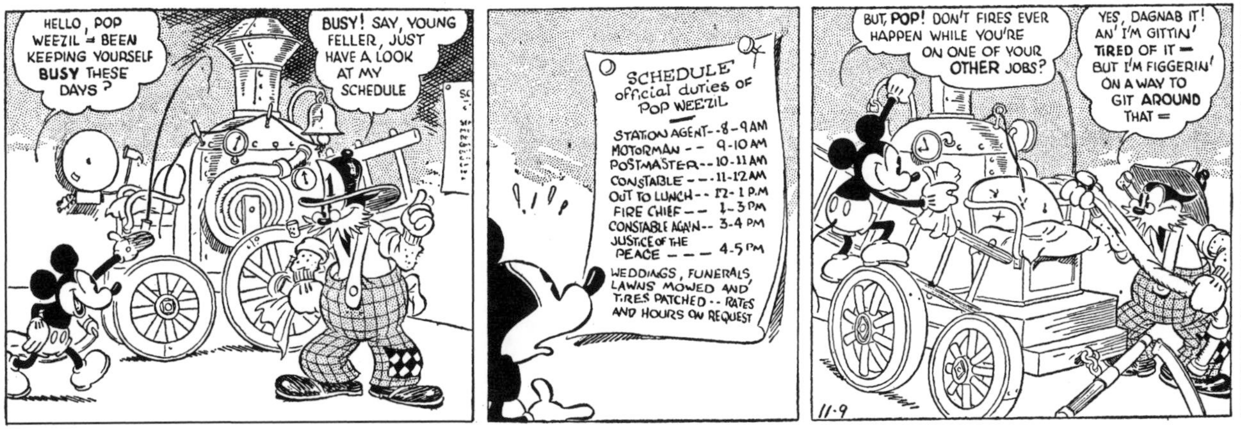
HELLO, POP WEEZIL = BEEN KEEPING YOURSELF BUSY THESE DAYS?
BUSY! SAY, YOUNG FELLER, JUST HAVE A LOOK AT MY SCHEDULE
SCHEDULE
official duties of Pop Weezil
STATION AGENT--8-9 AM
MOTORMAN -- 9-10 AM
POSTMASTER--10-11 AM
CONSTABLE --11-12 AM
OUT TO LUNCH--12-1 P.M.
FIRE CHIEF -- 1-3 PM
CONSTABLE AGAIN-- 3-4 PM
JUSTICE OF THE PEACE --- 4-5 PM
WEDDINGS, FUNERALS, LAWNS MOWED AND TIRES PATCHED -- RATES AND HOURS ON REQUEST
BUT, POP! DON'T FIRES EVER HAPPEN WHILE YOU'RE ON ONE OF YOUR OTHER JOBS?
YES, DAGNAB IT! AN' I'M GITTIN' TIRED OF IT — BUT I'M FIGGERIN' ON A WAY TO GIT AROUND THAT =
11-9
I'M GONNA TRY AN' GIT THE CITY COUNCIL T' PASS A LAW AG'IN' FIRES BREAKIN' OUT EXCEPT WHEN I'M ON FIRE DUTY
FIRE STATION # 1
MAIL
WALT DISNEY

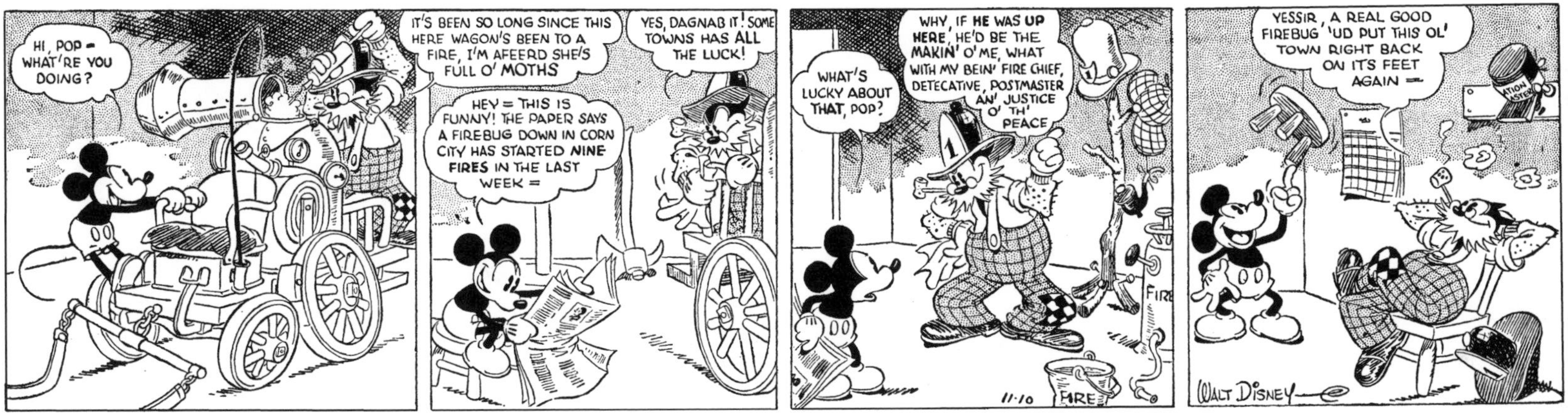
HI, POP — WHAT'RE YOU DOING?
IT'S BEEN SO LONG SINCE THIS HERE WAGON'S BEEN TO A FIRE, I'M AFEERD SHE'S FULL O' MOTHS
HEY = THIS IS FUNNY! THE PAPER SAYS A FIREBUG DOWN IN CORN CITY HAS STARTED NINE FIRES IN THE LAST WEEK =
YES, DAGNAB IT! SOME TOWNS HAS ALL THE LUCK!
WHAT'S LUCKY ABOUT THAT, POP?
WHY, IF HE WAS UP HERE, HE'D BE THE MAKIN' O' ME, WHAT WITH MY BEIN' FIRE CHIEF, DETECTIVE, POSTMASTER AN' JUSTICE O' TH' PEACE
FIRE
11-10
FIRE
YESSIR, A REAL GOOD FIREBUG 'UD PUT THIS OL' TOWN RIGHT BACK ON ITS FEET AGAIN =
WALT DISNEY

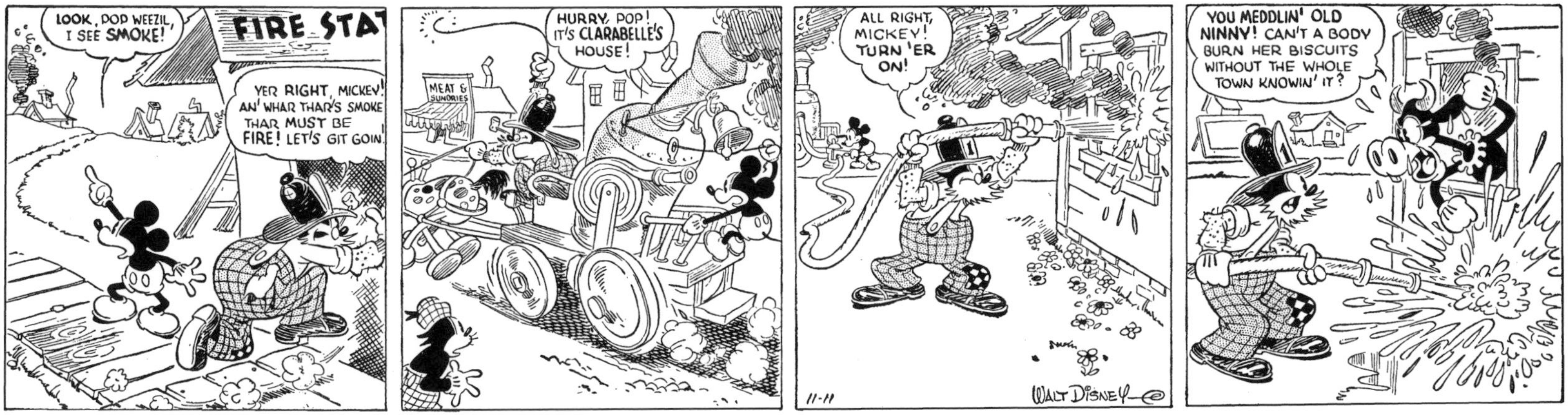
LOOK, POP WEEZIL, I SEE SMOKE!
FIRE STAT
YER RIGHT, MICKEY! AN' WHAR THAR'S SMOKE THAR MUST BE FIRE! LET'S GIT GOIN'!
MEAT & SUNDRIES
HURRY, POP! IT'S CLARABELLE'S HOUSE!
ALL RIGHT, MICKEY! TURN 'ER ON!
11-11
WALT DISNEY
YOU MEDDLIN' OLD NINNY! CAN'T A BODY BURN HER BISCUITS WITHOUT THE WHOLE TOWN KNOWIN' IT?

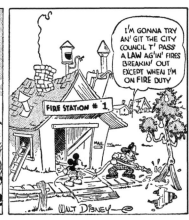

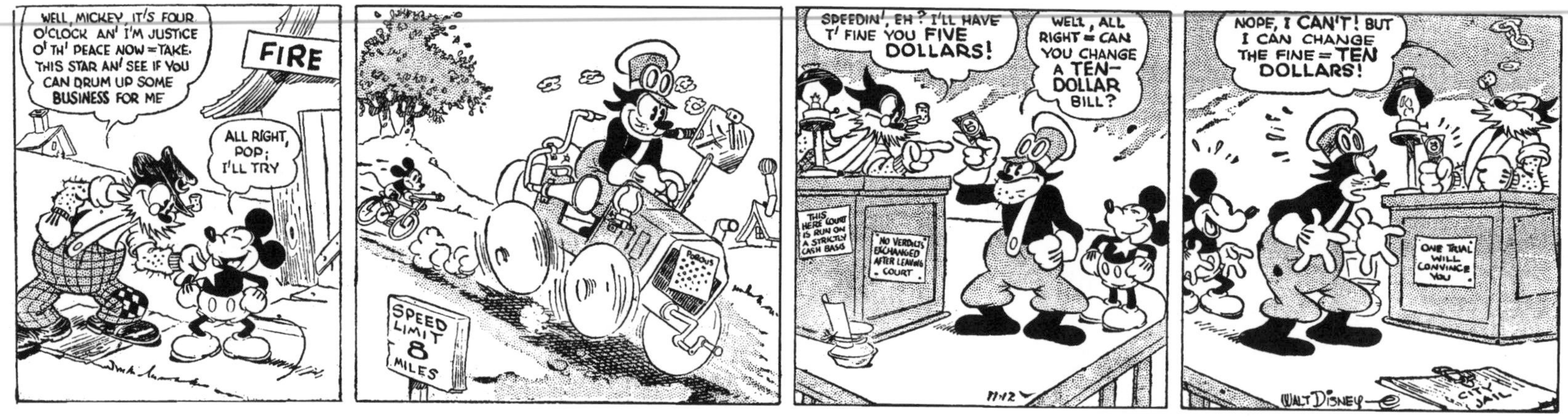
WELL, MICKEY, IT'S FOUR O'CLOCK AN' I'M JUSTICE O' TH' PEACE NOW = TAKE THIS STAR AN' SEE IF YOU CAN DRUM UP SOME BUSINESS FOR ME
FIRE
ALL RIGHT, POP; I'LL TRY
SPEED LIMIT 8 MILES
POROUS
SPEEDIN', EH? I'LL HAVE T' FINE YOU FIVE DOLLARS!
WELL, ALL RIGHT = CAN YOU CHANGE A TEN-DOLLAR BILL?
THIS HERE COURT IS RUN ON A STRICTLY CASH BASIS
NO VERDICTS EXCHANGED AFTER LEAVING COURT
11-12
NOPE, I CAN'T! BUT I CAN CHANGE THE FINE = TEN DOLLARS!
ONE TRIAL WILL CONVINCE YOU
WALT DISNEY
CITY JAIL

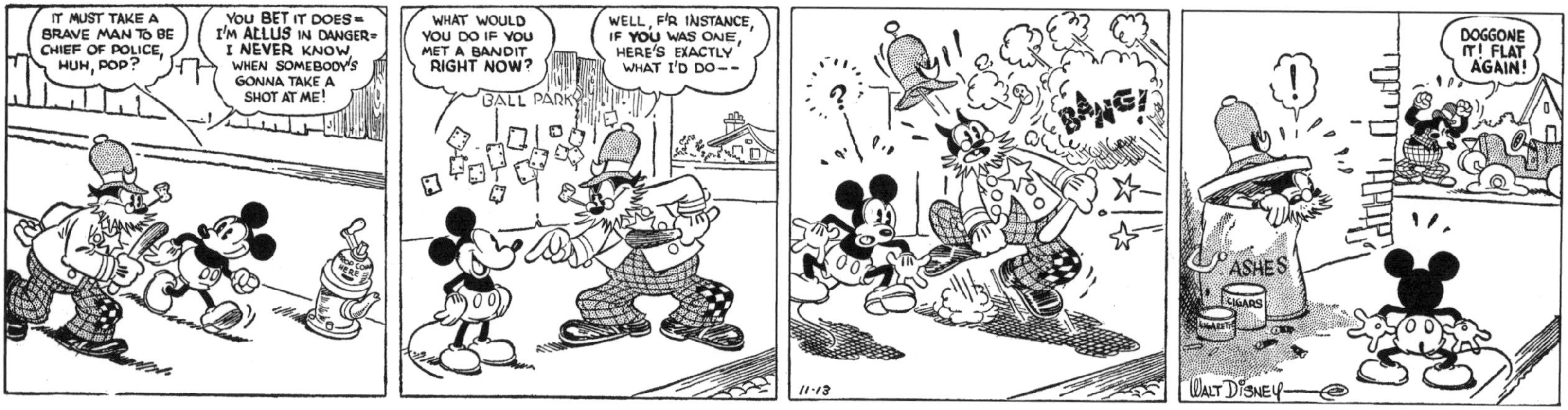
IT MUST TAKE A BRAVE MAN TO BE CHIEF OF POLICE, HUH, POP?
YOU BET IT DOES = I'M ALLUS IN DANGER = I NEVER KNOW WHEN SOMEBODY'S GONNA TAKE A SHOT AT ME!
WHAT WOULD YOU DO IF YOU MET A BANDIT RIGHT NOW?
WELL, F'R INSTANCE, IF YOU WAS ONE, HERE'S EXACTLY WHAT I'D DO--
BALL PARK
?
BANG!
11-13
DOGGONE IT! FLAT AGAIN!
!
ASHES
CIGARS
WALT DISNEY

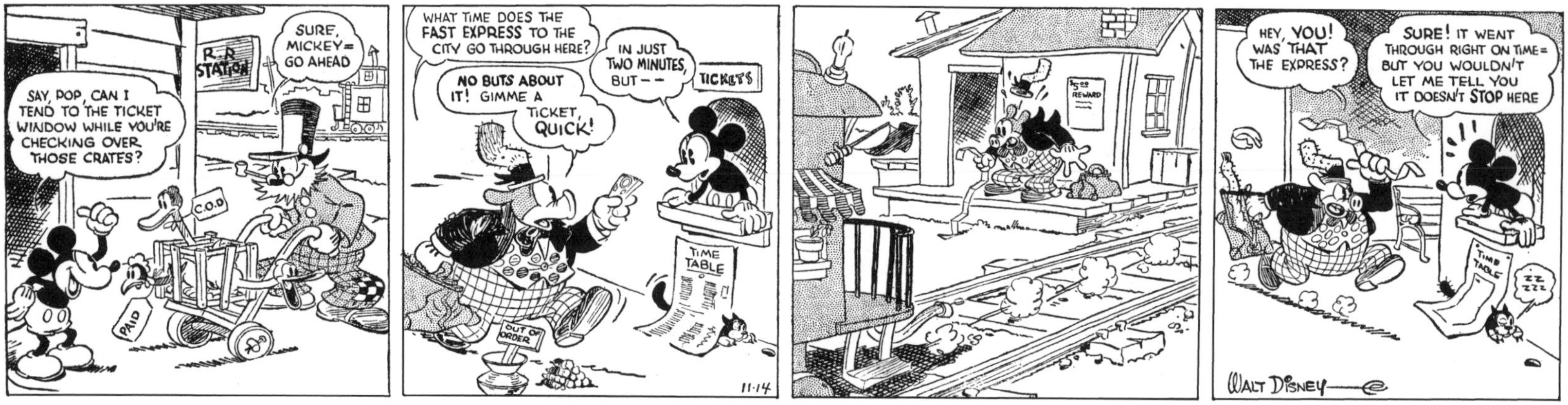
R.R. STATION
SURE, MICKEY = GO AHEAD
SAY, POP, CAN I TEND TO THE TICKET WINDOW WHILE YOU'RE CHECKING OVER THOSE CRATES?
C.O.D
PAID
WHAT TIME DOES THE FAST EXPRESS TO THE CITY GO THROUGH HERE?
IN JUST TWO MINUTES, BUT--
TICKETS
NO BUTS ABOUT IT! GIMME A TICKET, QUICK!
TIME TABLE
OUT OF ORDER
11-14
$5.00 REWARD
HEY, YOU! WAS THAT THE EXPRESS?
SURE! IT WENT THROUGH RIGHT ON TIME = BUT YOU WOULDN'T LET ME TELL YOU IT DOESN'T STOP HERE
TIME TABLE
ZZ ZZZ
WALT DISNEY

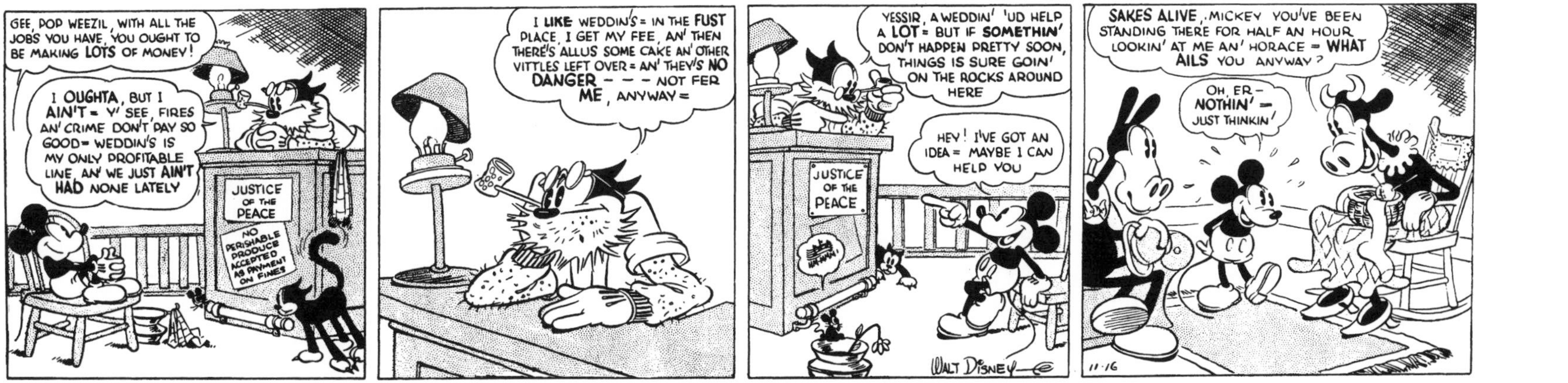

GEE, POP WEEZIL, WITH ALL THE JOBS YOU HAVE, YOU OUGHT TO BE MAKING LOTS OF MONEY!
I OUGHTA, BUT I AIN'T = Y' SEE, FIRES AN' CRIME DON'T PAY SO GOOD = WEDDIN'S IS MY ONLY PROFITABLE LINE, AN' WE JUST AIN'T HAD NONE LATELY
JUSTICE OF THE PEACE
NO PERISHABLE PRODUCE ACCEPTED AS PAYMENT ON FINES
I LIKE WEDDIN'S = IN THE FUST PLACE, I GET MY FEE, AN' THEN THERE'S ALLUS SOME CAKE AN' OTHER VITTLES LEFT OVER = AN' THEY'S NO DANGER - - - NOT FER ME, ANYWAY =
YESSIR, A WEDDIN' 'UD HELP A LOT = BUT IF SOMETHIN' DON'T HAPPEN PRETTY SOON, THINGS IS SURE GOIN' ON THE ROCKS AROUND HERE
HEY! I'VE GOT AN IDEA = MAYBE I CAN HELP YOU
JUSTICE OF THE PEACE
WALT DISNEY
SAKES ALIVE, MICKEY YOU'VE BEEN STANDING THERE FOR HALF AN HOUR LOOKIN' AT ME AN' HORACE = WHAT AILS YOU ANYWAY?
OH, ER- NOTHIN' - JUST THINKIN'
11-16

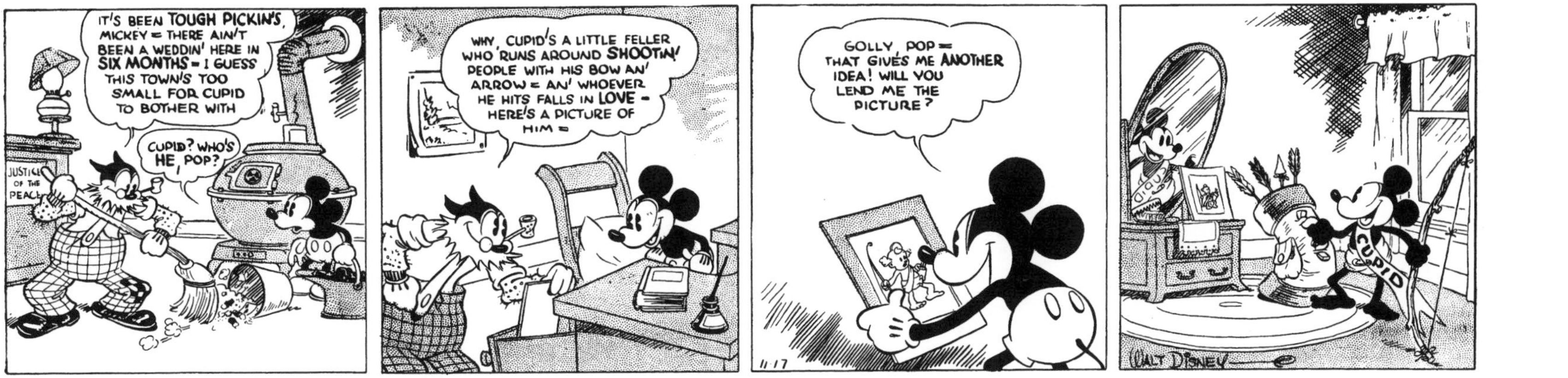

IT'S BEEN TOUGH PICKIN'S, MICKEY = THERE AIN'T BEEN A WEDDIN' HERE IN SIX MONTHS = I GUESS THIS TOWN'S TOO SMALL FOR CUPID TO BOTHER WITH
CUPID? WHO'S HE, POP?
WHY, CUPID'S A LITTLE FELLER WHO RUNS AROUND SHOOTIN' PEOPLE WITH HIS BOW AN' ARROW = AN' WHOEVER HE HITS FALLS IN LOVE - HERE'S A PICTURE OF HIM =
GOLLY, POP = THAT GIVES ME ANOTHER IDEA! WILL YOU LEND ME THE PICTURE?
11-17
CUPID
WALT DISNEY

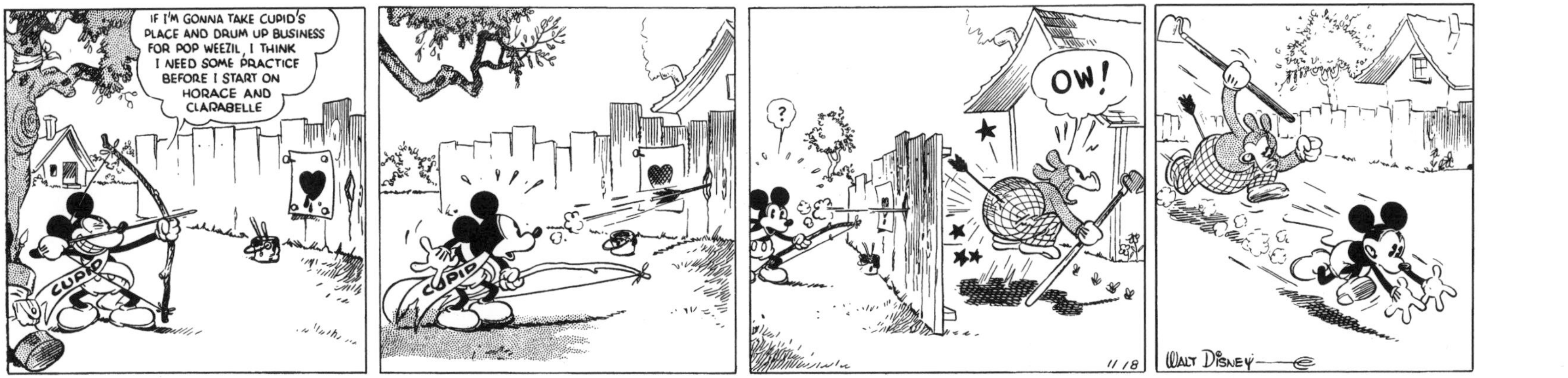

IF I'M GONNA TAKE CUPID'S PLACE AND DRUM UP BUSINESS FOR POP WEEZIL, I THINK I NEED SOME PRACTICE BEFORE I START ON HORACE AND CLARABELLE
CUPID
CUPID
?
OW!
11-18
WALT DISNEY

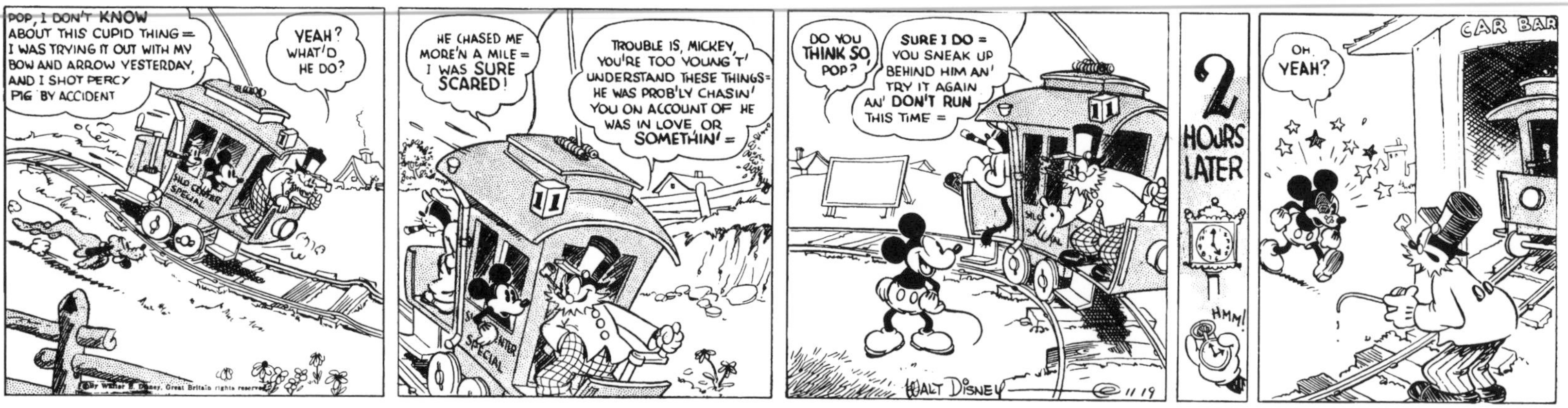
POP, I DON'T KNOW ABOUT THIS CUPID THING = I WAS TRYING IT OUT WITH MY BOW AND ARROW YESTERDAY, AND I SHOT PERCY PIG BY ACCIDENT
YEAH? WHAT'D HE DO?
HE CHASED ME MORE'N A MILE = I WAS SURE SCARED!
TROUBLE IS, MICKEY, YOU'RE TOO YOUNG T' UNDERSTAND THESE THINGS = HE WAS PROB'LY CHASIN' YOU ON ACCOUNT OF HE WAS IN LOVE, OR SOMETHIN' =
DO YOU THINK SO, POP?
SURE I DO = YOU SNEAK UP BEHIND HIM AN' TRY IT AGAIN AN' DON'T RUN THIS TIME =
WALT DISNEY
11-19
2 HOURS LATER
HMM!
CAR BAR
OH, YEAH?

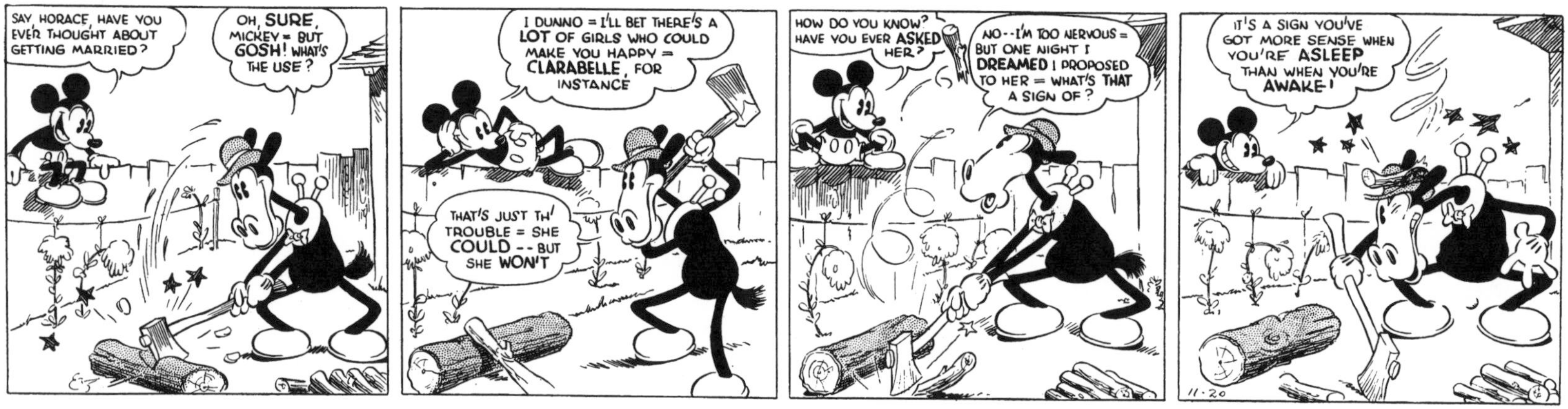
SAY, HORACE, HAVE YOU EVER THOUGHT ABOUT GETTING MARRIED?
OH, SURE, MICKEY = BUT GOSH! WHAT'S THE USE?
I DUNNO = I'LL BET THERE'S A LOT OF GIRLS WHO COULD MAKE YOU HAPPY = CLARABELLE, FOR INSTANCE
THAT'S JUST TH' TROUBLE = SHE COULD -- BUT SHE WON'T
HOW DO YOU KNOW? HAVE YOU EVER ASKED HER?
NO -- I'M TOO NERVOUS = BUT ONE NIGHT I DREAMED I PROPOSED TO HER = WHAT'S THAT A SIGN OF?
IT'S A SIGN YOU'VE GOT MORE SENSE WHEN YOU'RE ASLEEP THAN WHEN YOU'RE AWAKE!
11-20

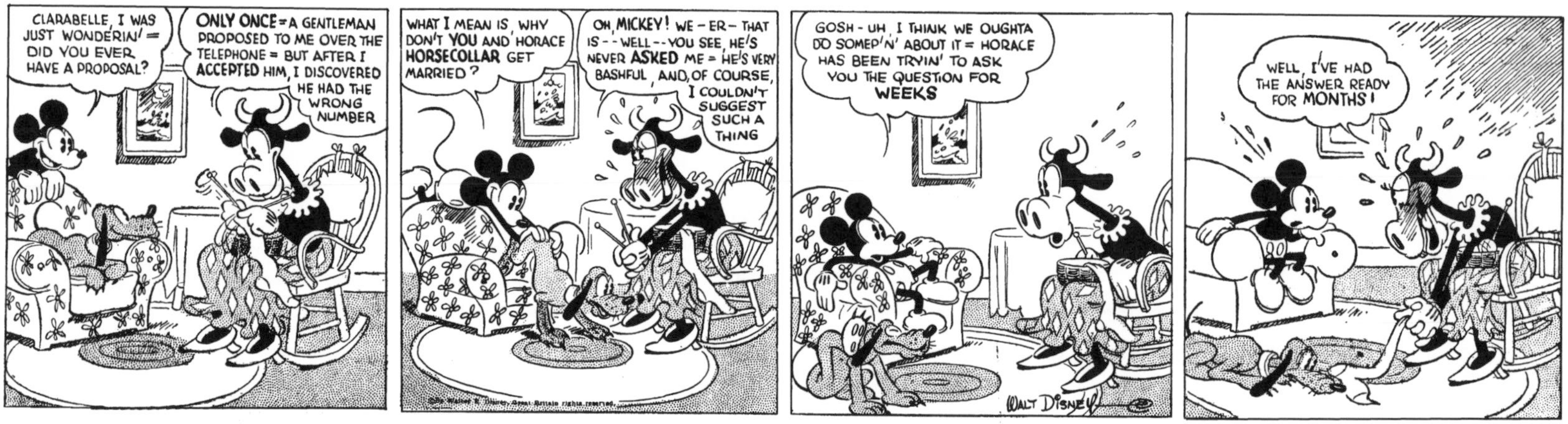
CLARABELLE, I WAS JUST WONDERIN' = DID YOU EVER HAVE A PROPOSAL?
ONLY ONCE = A GENTLEMAN PROPOSED TO ME OVER THE TELEPHONE = BUT AFTER I ACCEPTED HIM, I DISCOVERED HE HAD THE WRONG NUMBER
WHAT I MEAN IS, WHY DON'T YOU AND HORACE HORSECOLLAR GET MARRIED?
OH, MICKEY! WE - ER - THAT IS -- WELL -- YOU SEE, HE'S NEVER ASKED ME = HE'S VERY BASHFUL, AND, OF COURSE, I COULDN'T SUGGEST SUCH A THING
GOSH - UH, I THINK WE OUGHTA DO SOMEP'N' ABOUT IT = HORACE HAS BEEN TRYIN' TO ASK YOU THE QUESTION FOR WEEKS
WALT DISNEY
WELL, I'VE HAD THE ANSWER READY FOR MONTHS!

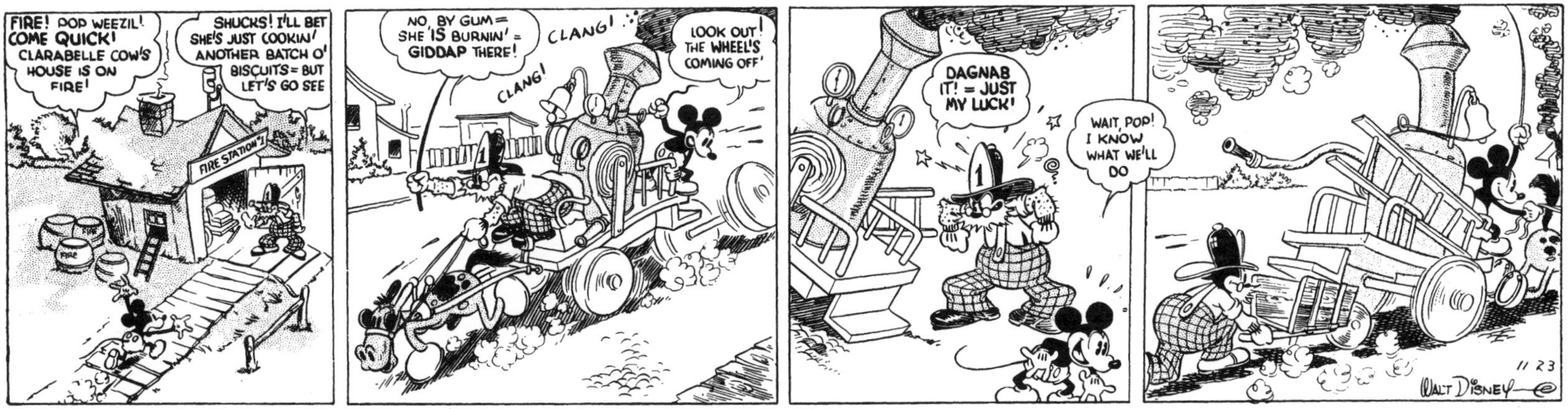
FIRE! POP WEEZIL! COME QUICK! CLARABELLE COW'S HOUSE IS ON FIRE!
SHUCKS! I'LL BET SHE'S JUST COOKIN' ANOTHER BATCH O' BISCUITS = BUT LET'S GO SEE
FIRE STATION
NO, BY GUM = SHE IS BURNIN' = GIDDAP THERE!
CLANG!
CLANG!
LOOK OUT! THE WHEEL'S COMING OFF!
DAGNAB IT! = JUST MY LUCK!
WAIT, POP! I KNOW WHAT WE'LL DO
11 23
WALT DISNEY

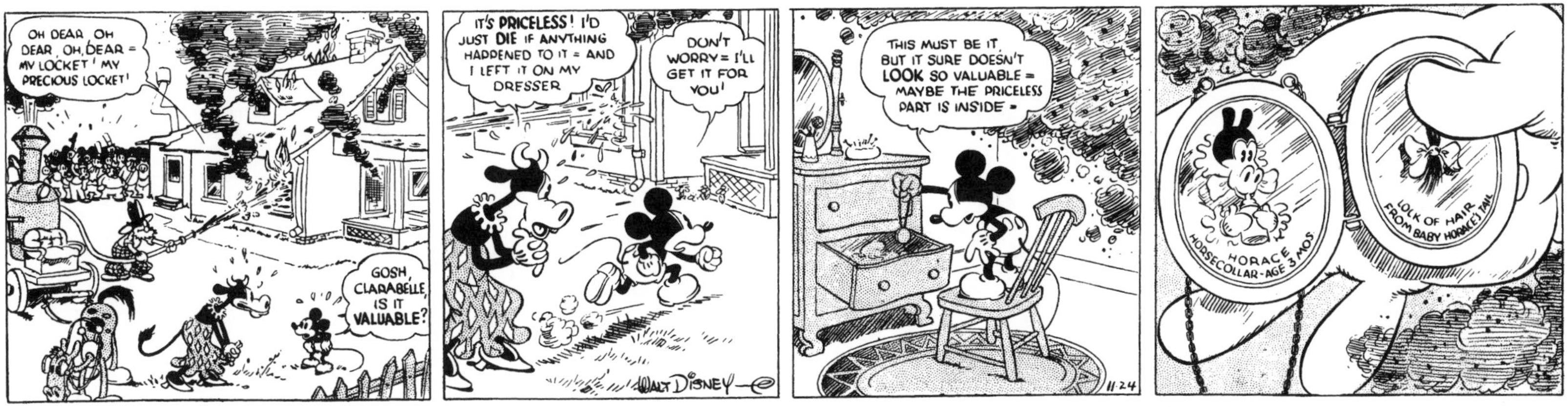
OH DEAR, OH DEAR, OH, DEAR = MY LOCKET! MY PRECIOUS LOCKET!
GOSH, CLARABELLE, IS IT VALUABLE?
IT'S PRICELESS! I'D JUST DIE IF ANYTHING HAPPENED TO IT = AND I LEFT IT ON MY DRESSER
DON'T WORRY = I'LL GET IT FOR YOU!
WALT DISNEY
THIS MUST BE IT, BUT IT SURE DOESN'T LOOK SO VALUABLE = MAYBE THE PRICELESS PART IS INSIDE =
11 24
HORACE HORSECOLLAR - AGE 3 MOS.
LOCK OF HAIR FROM BABY HORACE'S TAIL

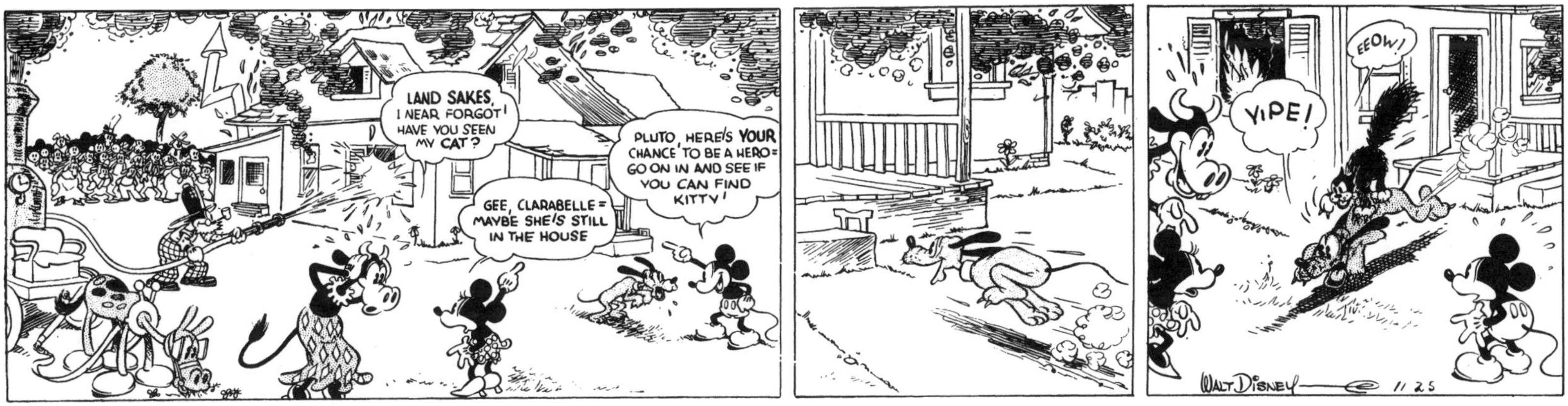
LAND SAKES, I NEAR FORGOT! HAVE YOU SEEN MY CAT?
GEE, CLARABELLE = MAYBE SHE'S STILL IN THE HOUSE
PLUTO, HERE'S YOUR CHANCE TO BE A HERO = GO ON IN AND SEE IF YOU CAN FIND KITTY!
EEOW!
YIPE!
WALT DISNEY
11 25

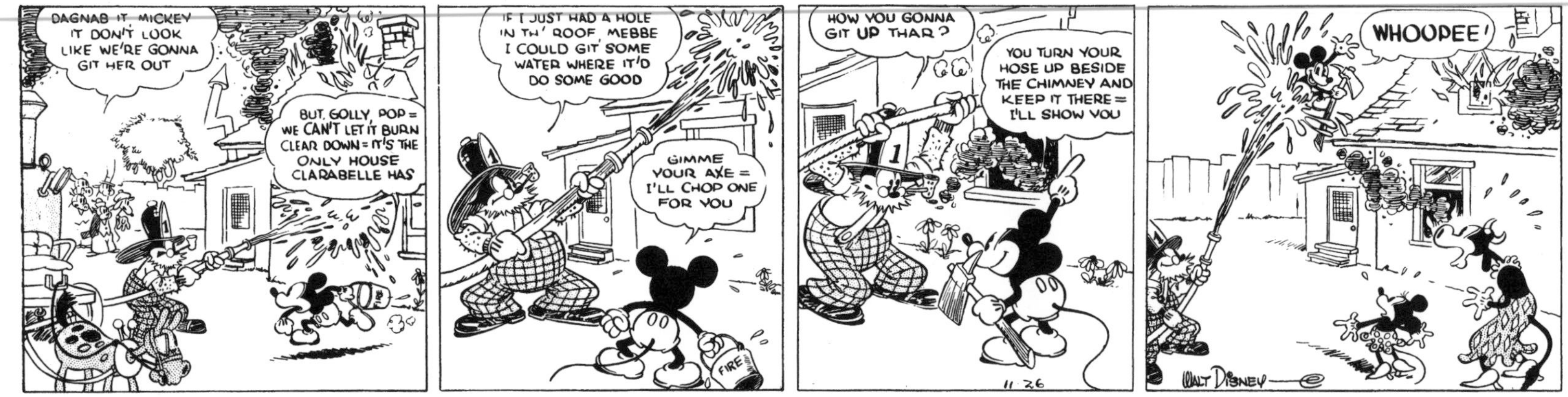
DAGNAB IT, MICKEY IT DON'T LOOK LIKE WE'RE GONNA GIT HER OUT
BUT, GOLLY, POP = WE CAN'T LET IT BURN CLEAR DOWN = IT'S THE ONLY HOUSE CLARABELLE HAS
IF I JUST HAD A HOLE IN TH' ROOF, MEBBE I COULD GIT SOME WATER WHERE IT'D DO SOME GOOD
GIMME YOUR AXE = I'LL CHOP ONE FOR YOU
FIRE
HOW YOU GONNA GIT UP THAR?
YOU TURN YOUR HOSE UP BESIDE THE CHIMNEY AND KEEP IT THERE = I'LL SHOW YOU
11 26
WHOOPEE!
WALT DISNEY

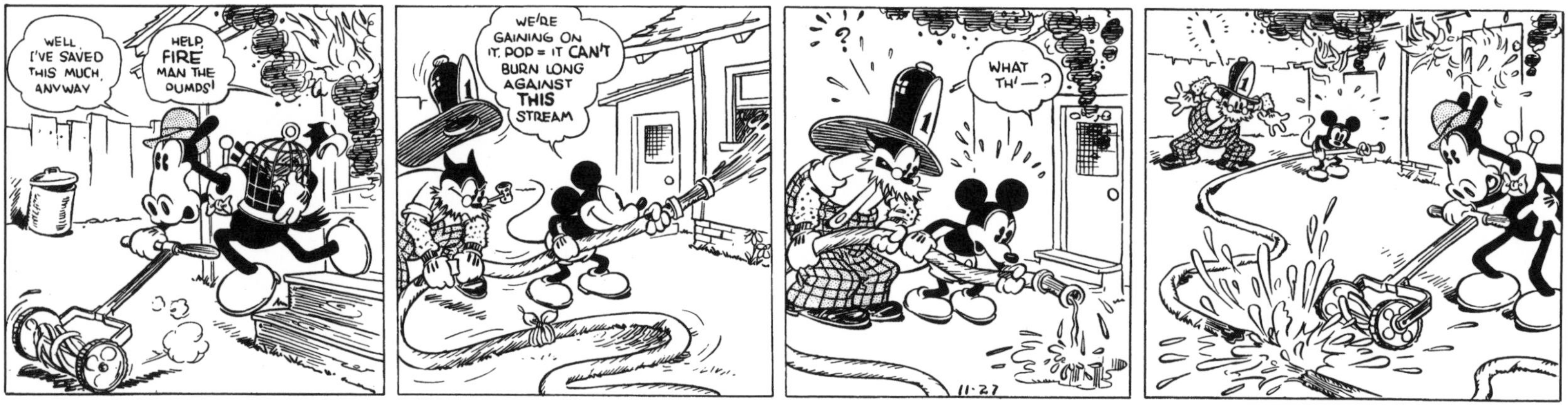
WELL, I'VE SAVED THIS MUCH, ANYWAY
HELP, FIRE, MAN THE PUMPS!
WE'RE GAINING ON IT, POP = IT CAN'T BURN LONG AGAINST THIS STREAM
WHAT TH'—?
11·27

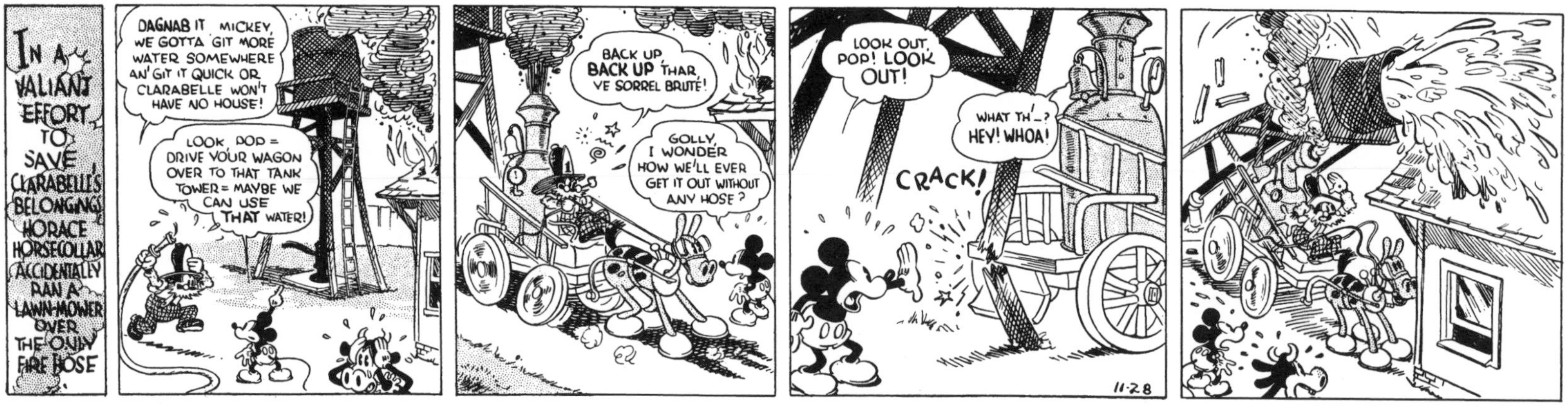
IN A VALIANT EFFORT TO SAVE CLARABELLE'S BELONGINGS HORACE HORSECOLLAR ACCIDENTALLY RAN A LAWN-MOWER OVER THE ONLY FIRE HOSE
DAGNAB IT, MICKEY, WE GOTTA GIT MORE WATER SOMEWHERE AN' GIT IT QUICK OR CLARABELLE WON'T HAVE NO HOUSE!
LOOK, POP = DRIVE YOUR WAGON OVER TO THAT TANK TOWER = MAYBE WE CAN USE THAT WATER!
BACK UP, BACK UP THAR, YE SORREL BRUTE!
GOLLY, I WONDER HOW WE'LL EVER GET IT OUT WITHOUT ANY HOSE?
LOOK OUT, POP! LOOK OUT!
WHAT TH'—? HEY! WHOA!
CRACK!
11·28

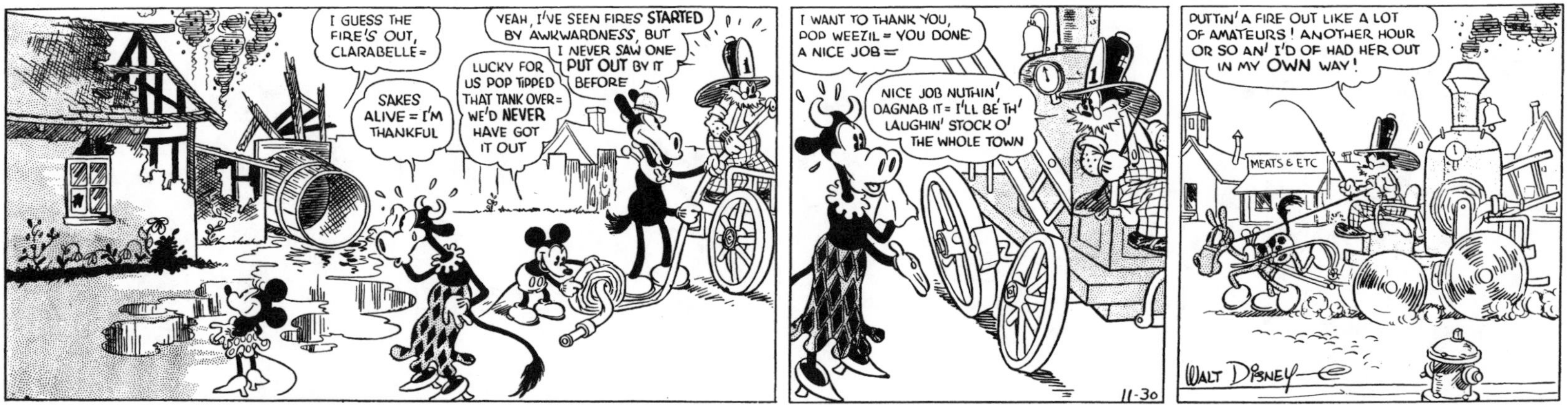
I GUESS THE FIRE'S OUT, CLARABELLE =
SAKES ALIVE = I'M THANKFUL
LUCKY FOR US POP TIPPED THAT TANK OVER = WE'D NEVER HAVE GOT IT OUT
YEAH, I'VE SEEN FIRES STARTED BY AWKWARDNESS, BUT I NEVER SAW ONE PUT OUT BY IT BEFORE
I WANT TO THANK YOU, POP WEEZIL = YOU DONE A NICE JOB =
NICE JOB NUTHIN', DAGNAB IT = I'LL BE TH' LAUGHIN' STOCK O' THE WHOLE TOWN
11-30
PUTTIN' A FIRE OUT LIKE A LOT OF AMATEURS! ANOTHER HOUR OR SO AN' I'D OF HAD HER OUT IN MY OWN WAY!
MEATS & ETC
WALT DISNEY

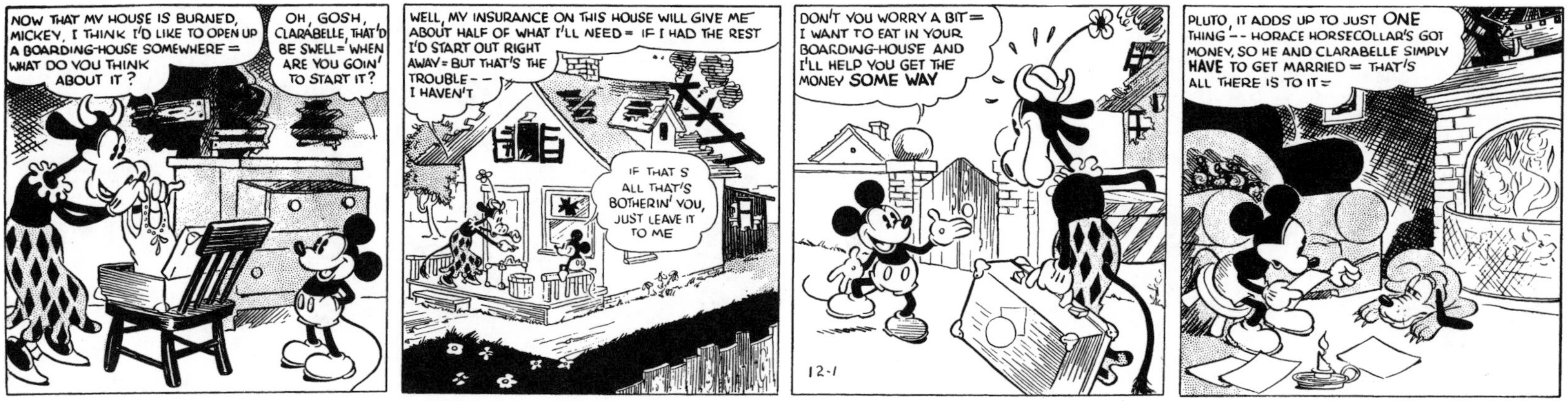
NOW THAT MY HOUSE IS BURNED, MICKEY, I THINK I'D LIKE TO OPEN UP A BOARDING-HOUSE SOMEWHERE = WHAT DO YOU THINK ABOUT IT?
OH, GOSH, CLARABELLE, THAT'D BE SWELL = WHEN ARE YOU GOIN' TO START IT?
WELL, MY INSURANCE ON THIS HOUSE WILL GIVE ME ABOUT HALF OF WHAT I'LL NEED = IF I HAD THE REST I'D START OUT RIGHT AWAY = BUT THAT'S THE TROUBLE -- I HAVEN'T
IF THAT'S ALL THAT'S BOTHERIN' YOU, JUST LEAVE IT TO ME
DON'T YOU WORRY A BIT = I WANT TO EAT IN YOUR BOARDING-HOUSE AND I'LL HELP YOU GET THE MONEY SOME WAY
12-1
PLUTO, IT ADDS UP TO JUST ONE THING -- HORACE HORSECOLLAR'S GOT MONEY, SO HE AND CLARABELLE SIMPLY HAVE TO GET MARRIED = THAT'S ALL THERE IS TO IT =

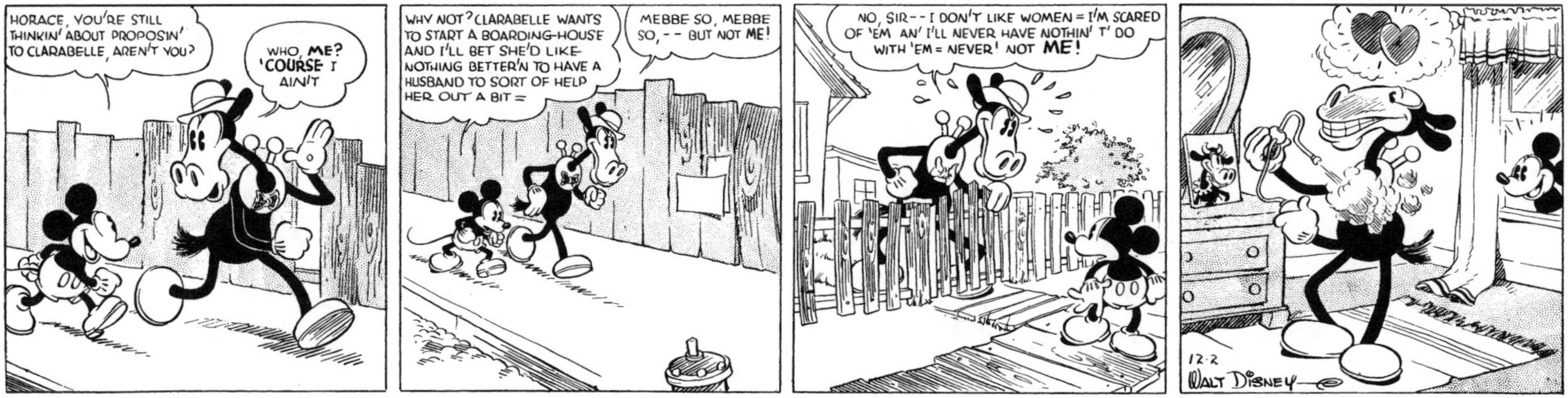
HORACE, YOU'RE STILL THINKIN' ABOUT PROPOSIN' TO CLARABELLE, AREN'T YOU?
WHO, ME? 'COURSE I AIN'T
WHY NOT? CLARABELLE WANTS TO START A BOARDING-HOUSE AND I'LL BET SHE'D LIKE NOTHING BETTER'N TO HAVE A HUSBAND TO SORT OF HELP HER OUT A BIT =
MEBBE SO, MEBBE SO, -- BUT NOT ME!
NO, SIR -- I DON'T LIKE WOMEN = I'M SCARED OF 'EM AN' I'LL NEVER HAVE NOTHIN' T' DO WITH 'EM = NEVER! NOT ME!
12-2
WALT DISNEY

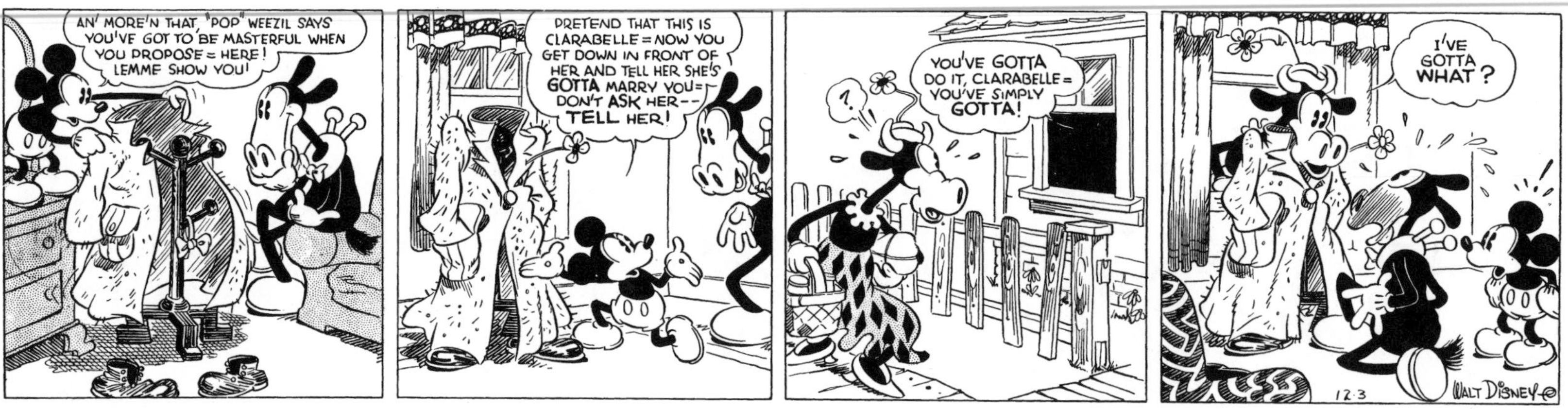
AN' MORE'N THAT, "POP" WEEZIL SAYS YOU'VE GOT TO BE MASTERFUL WHEN YOU PROPOSE = HERE! LEMME SHOW YOU!
PRETEND THAT THIS IS CLARABELLE = NOW YOU GET DOWN IN FRONT OF HER AND TELL HER SHE'S GOTTA MARRY YOU= DON'T ASK HER-- TELL HER!
YOU'VE GOTTA DO IT, CLARABELLE= YOU'VE SIMPLY GOTTA!
I'VE GOTTA WHAT?
12.3
WALT DISNEY

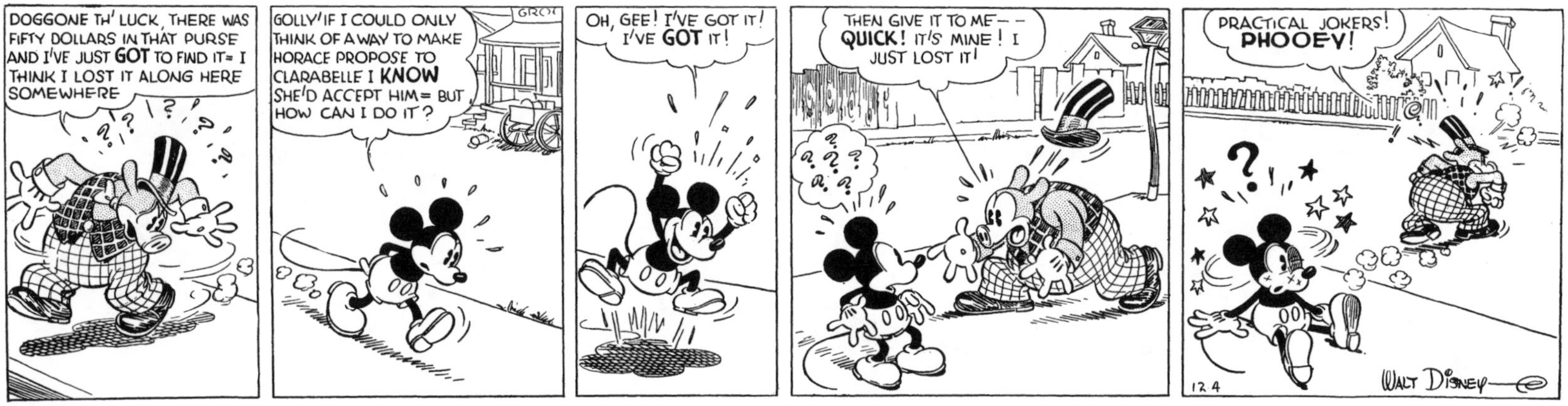
DOGGONE TH' LUCK, THERE WAS FIFTY DOLLARS IN THAT PURSE AND I'VE JUST GOT TO FIND IT= I THINK I LOST IT ALONG HERE SOMEWHERE
GOLLY! IF I COULD ONLY THINK OF A WAY TO MAKE HORACE PROPOSE TO CLARABELLE I KNOW SHE'D ACCEPT HIM= BUT HOW CAN I DO IT?
OH, GEE! I'VE GOT IT! I'VE GOT IT!
THEN GIVE IT TO ME-- QUICK! IT'S MINE! I JUST LOST IT!
PRACTICAL JOKERS! PHOOEY!
12.4
WALT DISNEY

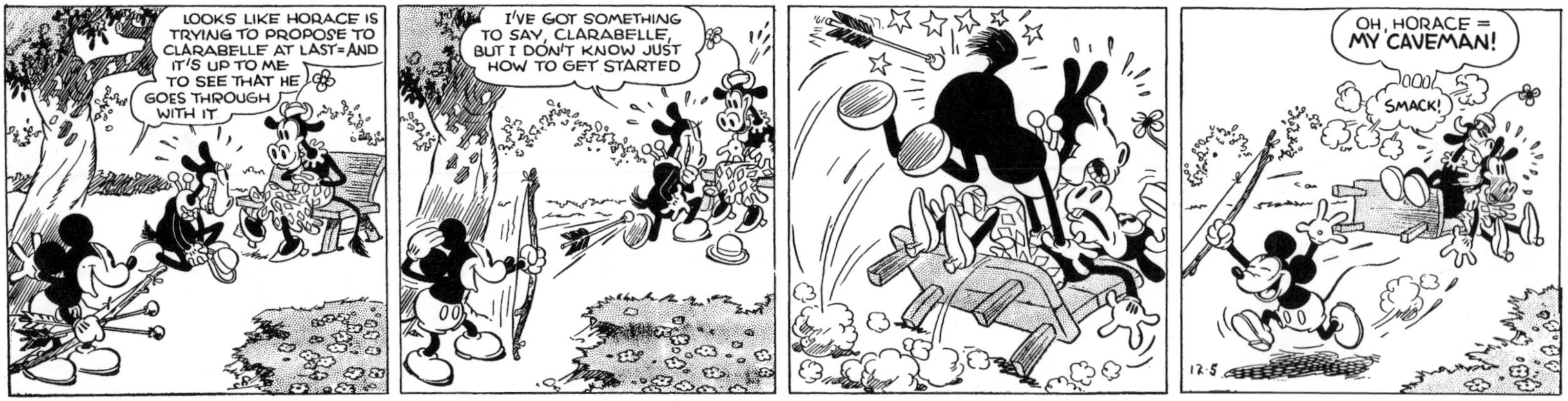
LOOKS LIKE HORACE IS TRYING TO PROPOSE TO CLARABELLE AT LAST= AND IT'S UP TO ME TO SEE THAT HE GOES THROUGH WITH IT
I'VE GOT SOMETHING TO SAY, CLARABELLE, BUT I DON'T KNOW JUST HOW TO GET STARTED
OH, HORACE = MY CAVEMAN!
SMACK!
12.5

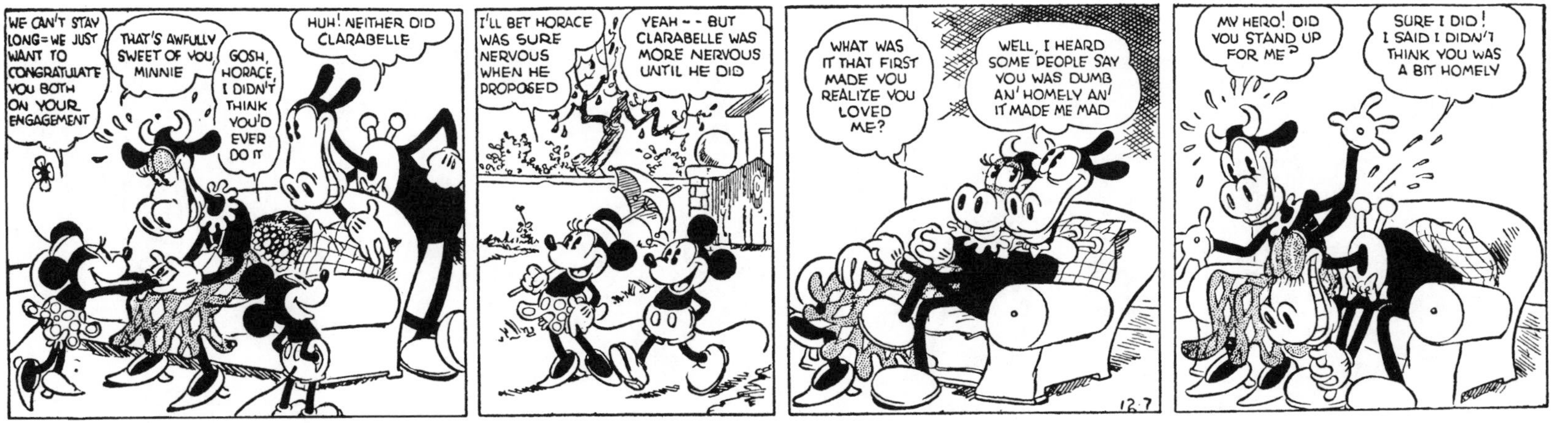
WE CAN'T STAY LONG=WE JUST WANT TO CONGRATULATE YOU BOTH ON YOUR ENGAGEMENT
THAT'S AWFULLY SWEET OF YOU, MINNIE
GOSH, HORACE, I DIDN'T THINK YOU'D EVER DO IT
HUH! NEITHER DID CLARABELLE
I'LL BET HORACE WAS SURE NERVOUS WHEN HE PROPOSED
YEAH -- BUT CLARABELLE WAS MORE NERVOUS UNTIL HE DID
WHAT WAS IT THAT FIRST MADE YOU REALIZE YOU LOVED ME?
WELL, I HEARD SOME PEOPLE SAY YOU WAS DUMB AN' HOMELY AN' IT MADE ME MAD
MY HERO! DID YOU STAND UP FOR ME?
SURE I DID! I SAID I DIDN'T THINK YOU WAS A BIT HOMELY
12-7

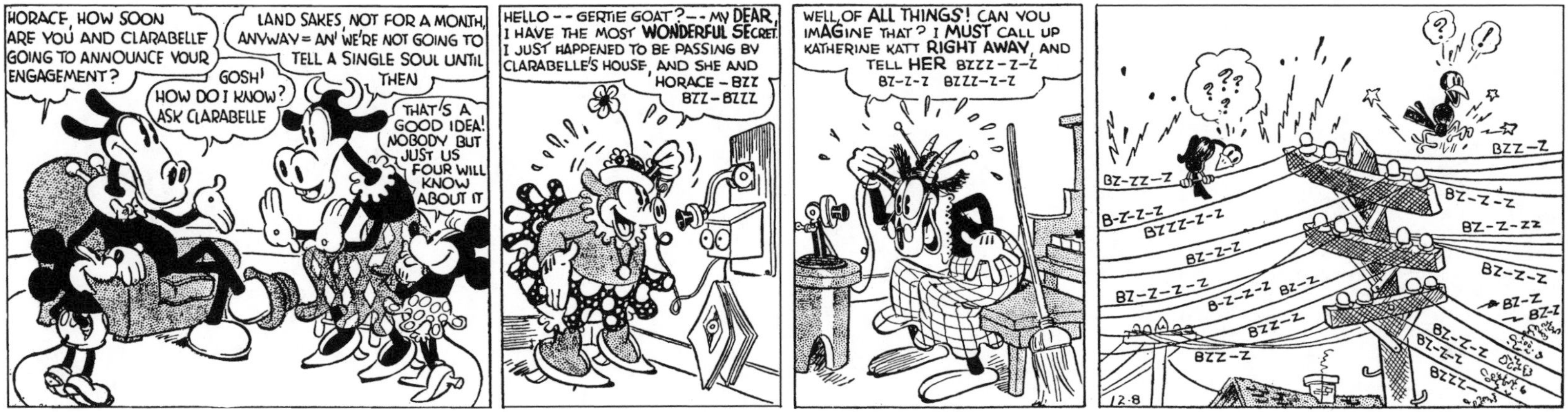
HORACE, HOW SOON ARE YOU AND CLARABELLE GOING TO ANNOUNCE YOUR ENGAGEMENT?
GOSH! HOW DO I KNOW? ASK CLARABELLE
LAND SAKES, NOT FOR A MONTH, ANYWAY=AN' WE'RE NOT GOING TO TELL A SINGLE SOUL UNTIL THEN
THAT'S A GOOD IDEA! NOBODY BUT JUST US FOUR WILL KNOW ABOUT IT
HELLO -- GERTIE GOAT? -- MY DEAR, I HAVE THE MOST WONDERFUL SECRET. I JUST HAPPENED TO BE PASSING BY CLARABELLE'S HOUSE, AND SHE AND HORACE - BZZ BZZ - BZZZ
WELL, OF ALL THINGS! CAN YOU IMAGINE THAT? I MUST CALL UP KATHERINE KATT RIGHT AWAY, AND TELL HER BZZZ - Z-Z BZ-Z-Z BZZZ-Z-Z
12-8
BZ-ZZ-Z
B-Z-Z-Z
BZZZ-Z-Z
BZ-Z-Z
BZ-Z-Z-Z
B-Z-Z-Z BZ-Z
BZZ-Z
BZZ-Z
BZZ-Z
BZ-Z-Z
BZ-Z-ZZ
BZ-Z-Z
BZ-Z
BZ-Z
BZ-Z-Z
BZ-Z-Z
BZZZ

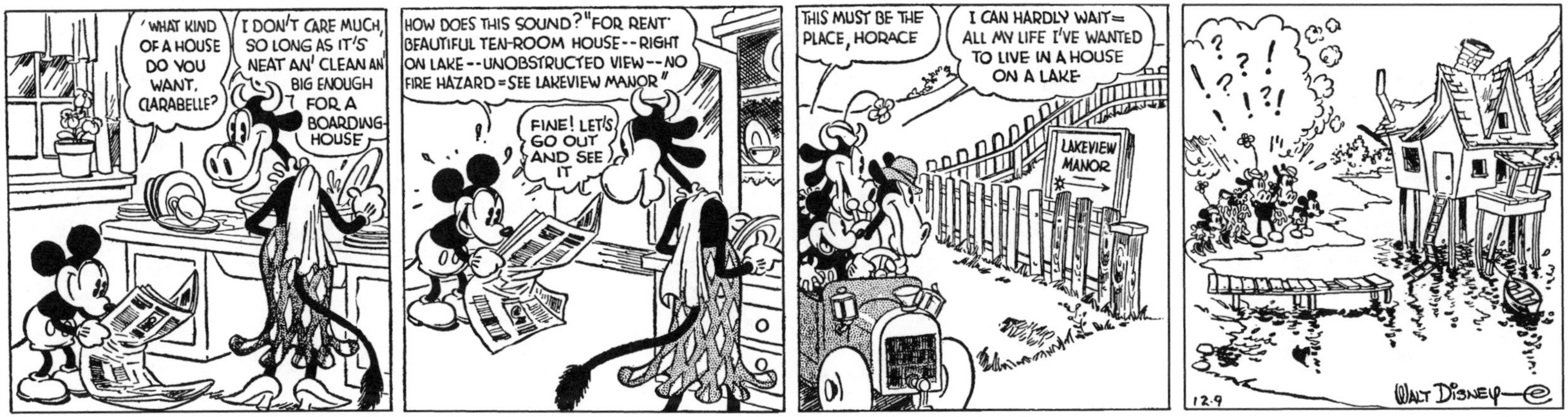
WHAT KIND OF A HOUSE DO YOU WANT, CLARABELLE?
I DON'T CARE MUCH, SO LONG AS IT'S NEAT AN' CLEAN AN' BIG ENOUGH FOR A BOARDING-HOUSE
HOW DOES THIS SOUND? "FOR RENT BEAUTIFUL TEN-ROOM HOUSE -- RIGHT ON LAKE -- UNOBSTRUCTED VIEW -- NO FIRE HAZARD=SEE LAKEVIEW MANOR"
FINE! LET'S GO OUT AND SEE IT
THIS MUST BE THE PLACE, HORACE
I CAN HARDLY WAIT= ALL MY LIFE I'VE WANTED TO LIVE IN A HOUSE ON A LAKE
LAKEVIEW MANOR
12-9
WALT DISNEY

YES, MISS COW, I HAVE THE VERY PLACE FOR YOU= IT'S LARGE ENOUGH FOR A BOARDING-HOUSE, AND IT'S IN A WONDERFUL NEIGHBORHOOD = I'LL MEET YOU THERE IN TWENTY MINUTES- - - CORNER OF 23RD AND - -
A.K. NUYEN
REAL ESTATE
HMMM! LOOKS VERY NICE, BUT HOW ABOUT THE NEIGHBORS? ARE THEY - - -
OH, YES - - THEY'RE NICE, QUIET, REFINED, HOME-LOVING PEOPLE = THE ONES NEXT DOOR, FOR INSTANCE - - -
- - - AND STAY OUT!
12-10
WALT DISNEY

WHO'D EVER OF THOUGHT IT'D BE SO HARD T' FIND A PLACE FOR MY BOARDING-HOUSE?
I TELL YOU WHAT= LET'S JUST GET IN THE CAR AND DRIVE AROUND = MAYBE WE'LL RUN ACROSS ONE
BEAUTIFUL HILLSIDE HOME
UNSURPASSED VIEW: OVERLOOKS ENTIRE COUNTRY: HANGING GARDENS: NO CLOSE NEIGHBORS: RENT REASONABLE: 1 BLOCK WEST
THAT SOUNDS PRETTY GOOD TO ME, MICKEY - LET'S HAVE A LOOK
12-11
WALT DISNEY

WELL, WE'RE PURTY NEAR THERE, FOLKS = WHEN HORACE HORSE-COLLAR STARTS OUT AFTER A HOUSE, HE FINDS ONE
THERE YOU ARE - - CLARABELLE'S AN' MY NEW BOARDIN' HOUSE = AN' WHAT'S MORE, THE RENT'S PAID FOR TH' FIRST MONTH = AIN'T SHE A DANDY?
WHY, YOU GREAT BIG - -
OH, FOR - -
OH, HORACE!
O' COURSE YOU UNDERSTAND, IT'LL HAVE T' BE FIXED UP A BIT
WALT DISNEY
12-12

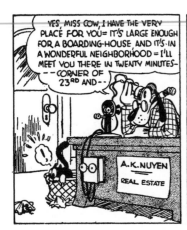

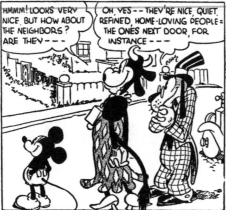

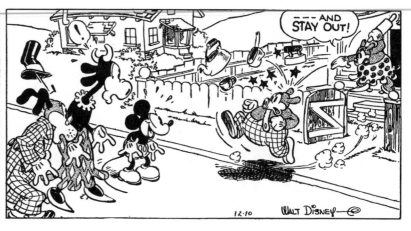

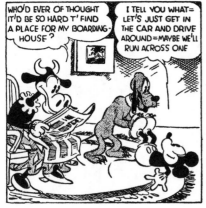

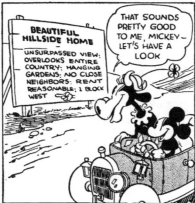

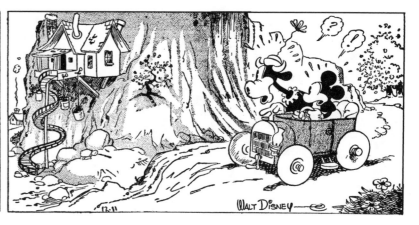

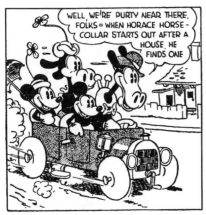

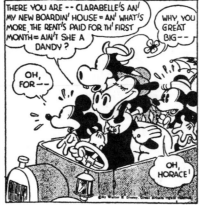

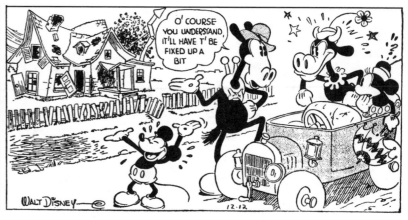

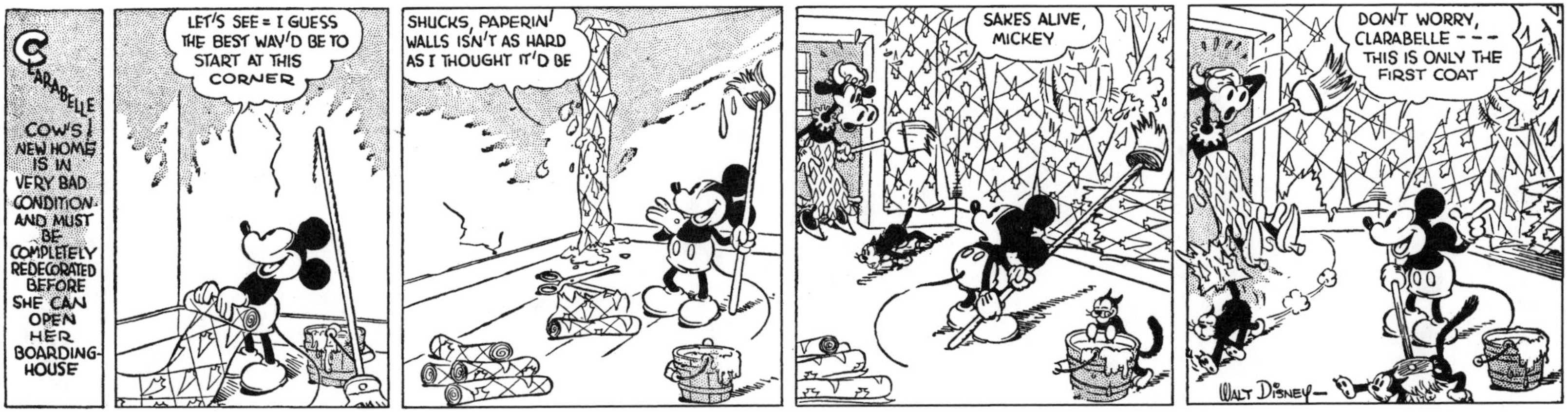
CLARABELLE COW'S NEW HOME IS IN VERY BAD CONDITION AND MUST BE COMPLETELY REDECORATED BEFORE SHE CAN OPEN HER BOARDING-HOUSE
LET'S SEE = I GUESS THE BEST WAY'D BE TO START AT THIS CORNER
SHUCKS, PAPERIN' WALLS ISN'T AS HARD AS I THOUGHT IT'D BE
SAKES ALIVE, MICKEY
DON'T WORRY, CLARABELLE - - - THIS IS ONLY THE FIRST COAT
WALT DISNEY

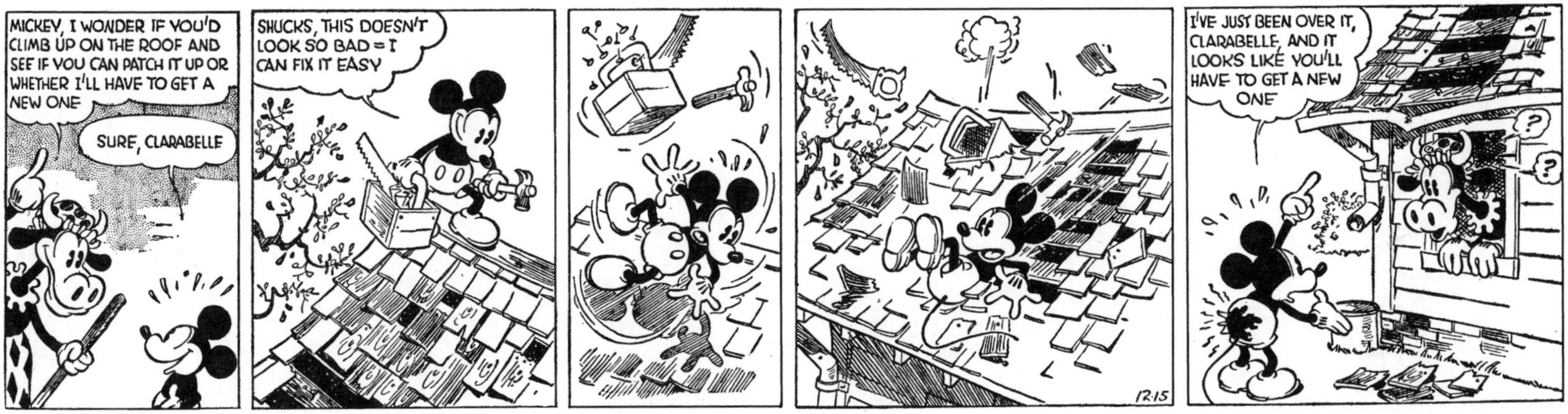
MICKEY, I WONDER IF YOU'D CLIMB UP ON THE ROOF AND SEE IF YOU CAN PATCH IT UP OR WHETHER I'LL HAVE TO GET A NEW ONE
SURE, CLARABELLE
SHUCKS, THIS DOESN'T LOOK SO BAD = I CAN FIX IT EASY
12-15
I'VE JUST BEEN OVER IT, CLARABELLE, AND IT LOOKS LIKE YOU'LL HAVE TO GET A NEW ONE
?
?

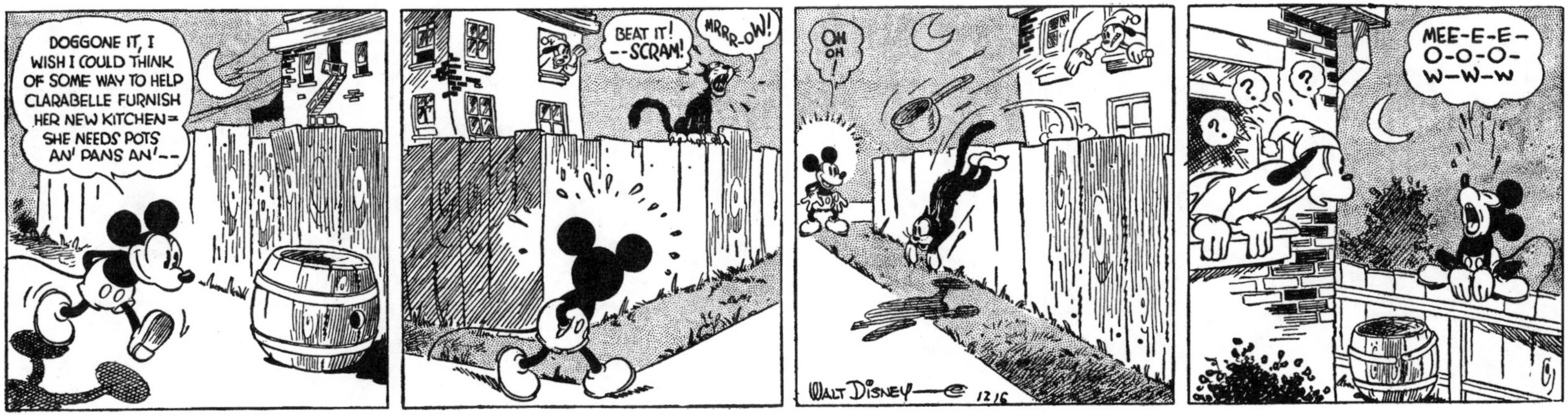
DOGGONE IT, I WISH I COULD THINK OF SOME WAY TO HELP CLARABELLE FURNISH HER NEW KITCHEN = SHE NEEDS POTS AN' PANS AN' - -
BEAT IT! - - SCRAM!
MRRR-OW!
OH OH
WALT DISNEY 12/16
?
?
?
MEE-E-E- O-O-O- W-W-W

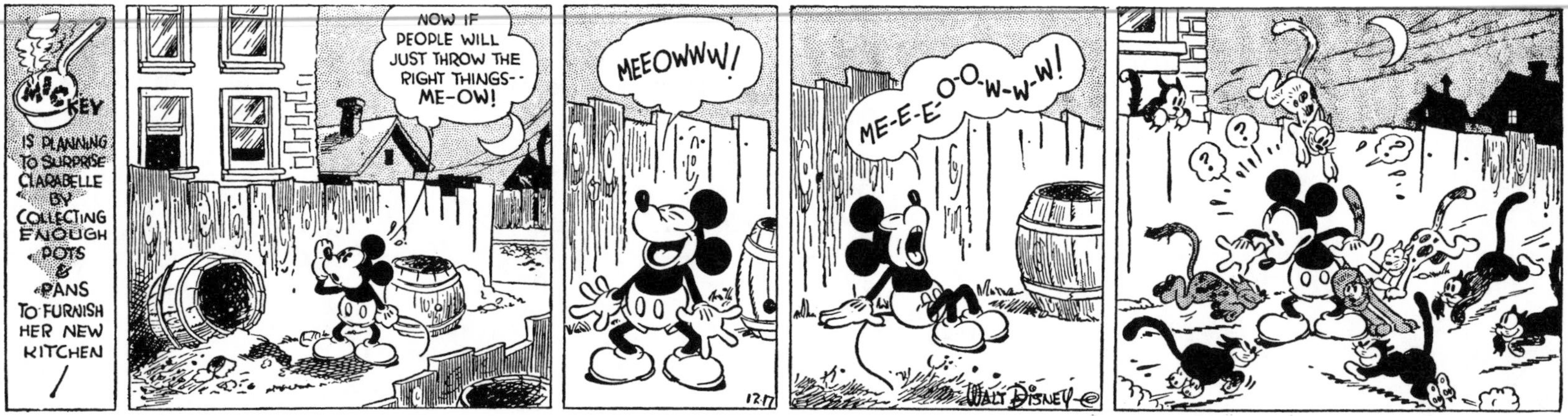
MICKEY IS PLANNING TO SURPRISE CLARABELLE BY COLLECTING ENOUGH POTS & PANS TO FURNISH HER NEW KITCHEN!
NOW IF PEOPLE WILL JUST THROW THE RIGHT THINGS-- ME-OW!
MEEOWWW!
ME-E-E-O-O-W-W-W!
WALT DISNEY
12-17

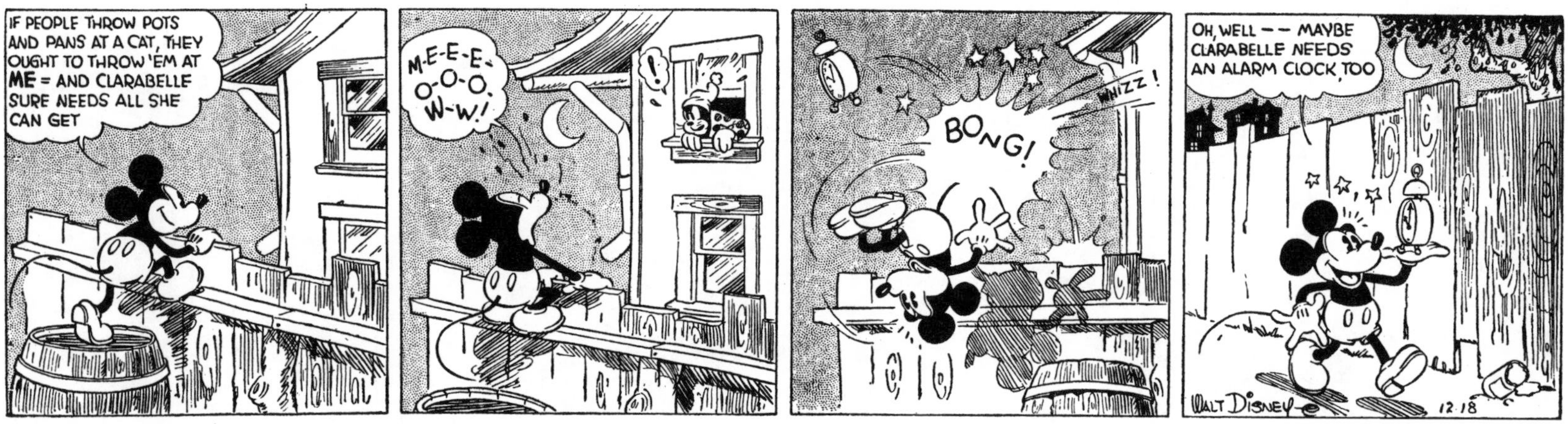
IF PEOPLE THROW POTS AND PANS AT A CAT, THEY OUGHT TO THROW 'EM AT ME = AND CLARABELLE SURE NEEDS ALL SHE CAN GET
M-E-E-E-O-O-O-W-W!
WHIZZ!
BONG!
OH, WELL -- MAYBE CLARABELLE NEEDS AN ALARM CLOCK, TOO
WALT DISNEY
12-18

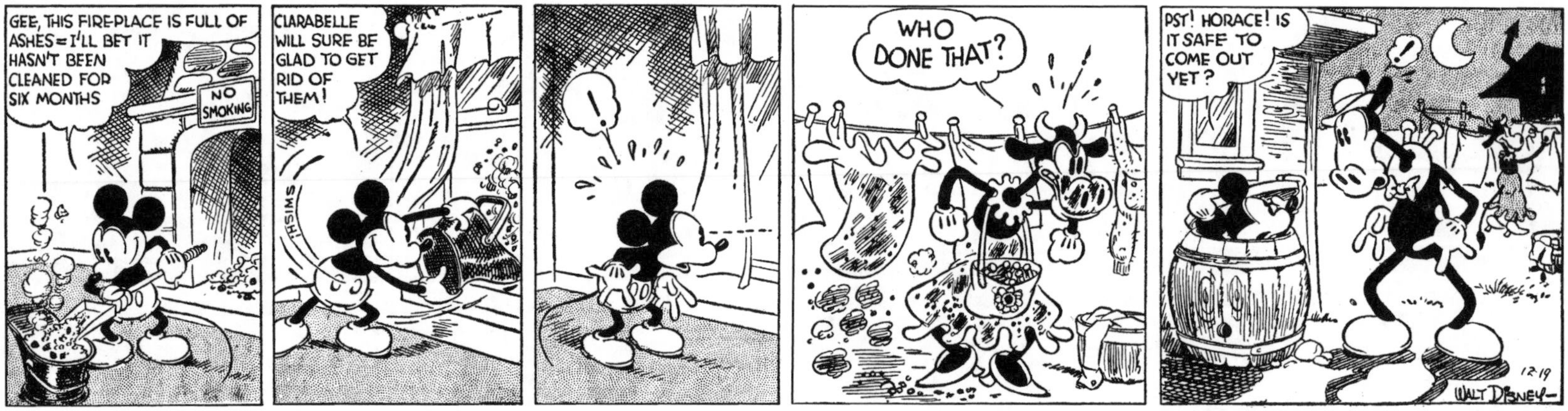
GEE, THIS FIRE-PLACE IS FULL OF ASHES = I'LL BET IT HASN'T BEEN CLEANED FOR SIX MONTHS
NO SMOKING
CLARABELLE WILL SURE BE GLAD TO GET RID OF THEM!
WHO DONE THAT?
PST! HORACE! IS IT SAFE TO COME OUT YET?
12-19
WALT DISNEY

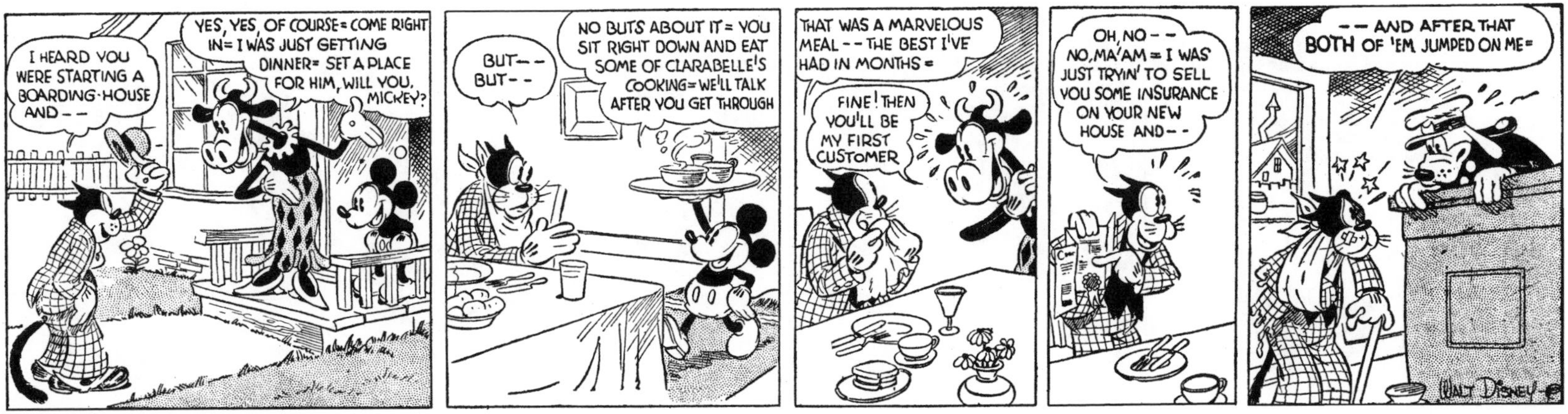
I HEARD YOU WERE STARTING A BOARDING-HOUSE AND --
YES, YES, OF COURSE= COME RIGHT IN= I WAS JUST GETTING DINNER= SET A PLACE FOR HIM, WILL YOU, MICKEY?
BUT-- BUT--
NO BUTS ABOUT IT= YOU SIT RIGHT DOWN AND EAT SOME OF CLARABELLE'S COOKING= WE'LL TALK AFTER YOU GET THROUGH
THAT WAS A MARVELOUS MEAL -- THE BEST I'VE HAD IN MONTHS=
FINE! THEN YOU'LL BE MY FIRST CUSTOMER
OH, NO -- NO, MA'AM= I WAS JUST TRYIN' TO SELL YOU SOME INSURANCE ON YOUR NEW HOUSE AND --
-- AND AFTER THAT BOTH OF 'EM JUMPED ON ME=
WALT DISNEY

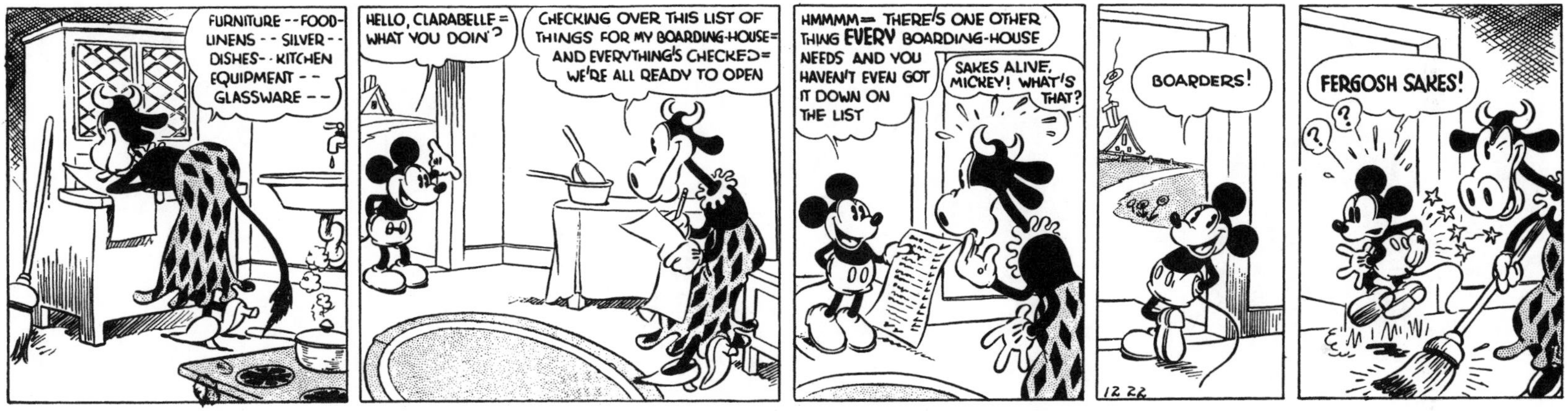
FURNITURE -- FOOD -- LINENS -- SILVER -- DISHES -- KITCHEN EQUIPMENT -- GLASSWARE --
HELLO, CLARABELLE= WHAT YOU DOIN'?
CHECKING OVER THIS LIST OF THINGS FOR MY BOARDING-HOUSE= AND EVERYTHING'S CHECKED= WE'RE ALL READY TO OPEN
HMMMM= THERE'S ONE OTHER THING EVERY BOARDING-HOUSE NEEDS AND YOU HAVEN'T EVEN GOT IT DOWN ON THE LIST
SAKES ALIVE, MICKEY! WHAT'S THAT?
BOARDERS!
12 22
FERGOSH SAKES!

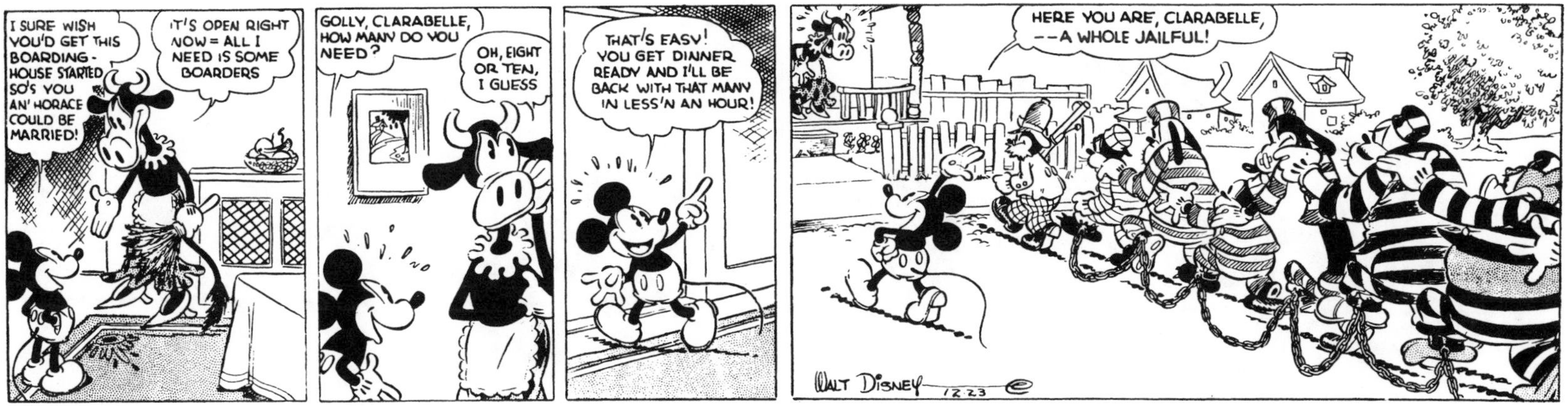
I SURE WISH YOU'D GET THIS BOARDING-HOUSE STARTED SO'S YOU AN' HORACE COULD BE MARRIED!
IT'S OPEN RIGHT NOW= ALL I NEED IS SOME BOARDERS
GOLLY, CLARABELLE, HOW MANY DO YOU NEED?
OH, EIGHT OR TEN, I GUESS
THAT'S EASY! YOU GET DINNER READY AND I'LL BE BACK WITH THAT MANY IN LESS'N AN HOUR!
HERE YOU ARE, CLARABELLE, -- A WHOLE JAILFUL!
WALT DISNEY 12 23

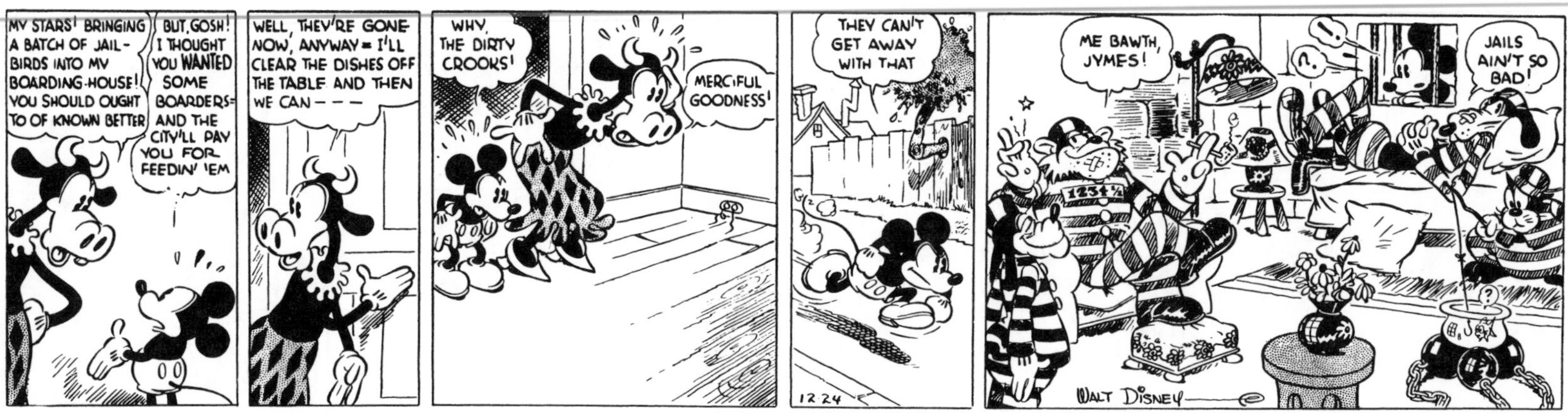
MY STARS! BRINGING A BATCH OF JAIL-BIRDS INTO MY BOARDING-HOUSE! YOU SHOULD OUGHT TO OF KNOWN BETTER
BUT, GOSH! I THOUGHT YOU WANTED SOME BOARDERS= AND THE CITY'LL PAY YOU FOR FEEDIN' 'EM
WELL, THEY'RE GONE NOW, ANYWAY= I'LL CLEAR THE DISHES OFF THE TABLE AND THEN WE CAN — — —
WHY, THE DIRTY CROOKS!
MERCIFUL GOODNESS!
THEY CAN'T GET AWAY WITH THAT
12 24
ME BAWTH, JYMES!
JAILS AIN'T SO BAD!
WALT DISNEY

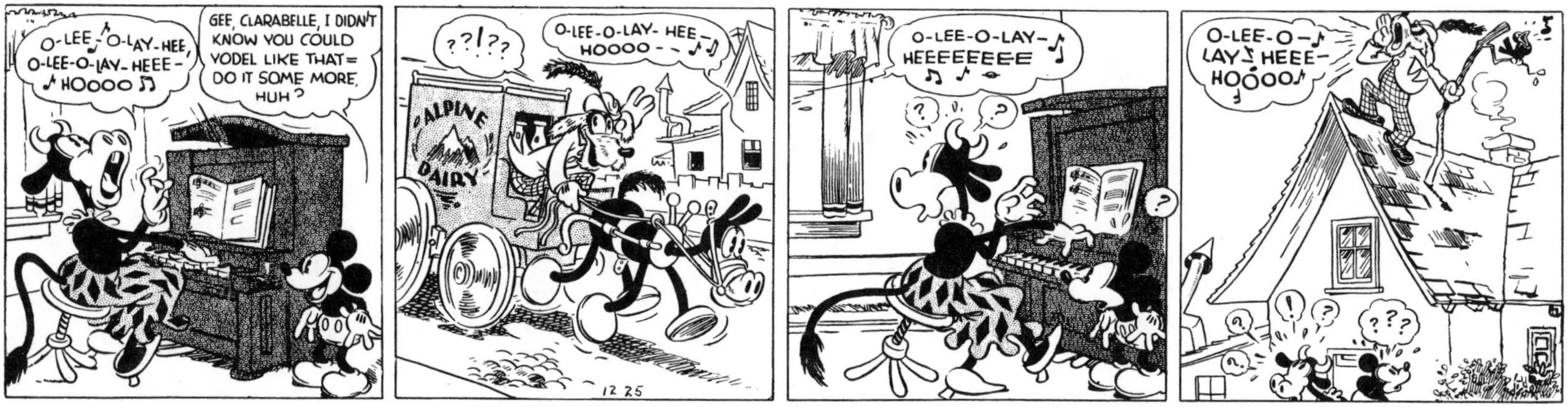
O-LEE-O-LAY-HEE, O-LEE-O-LAY-HEEE-HOOOO
GEE, CLARABELLE, I DIDN'T KNOW YOU COULD YODEL LIKE THAT= DO IT SOME MORE, HUH?
??!??
O-LEE-O-LAY-HEE-HOOOO — —
ALPINE DAIRY
12 25
O-LEE-O-LAY-HEEEEEEEE
O-LEE-O-LAY-HEEE-HOOOO

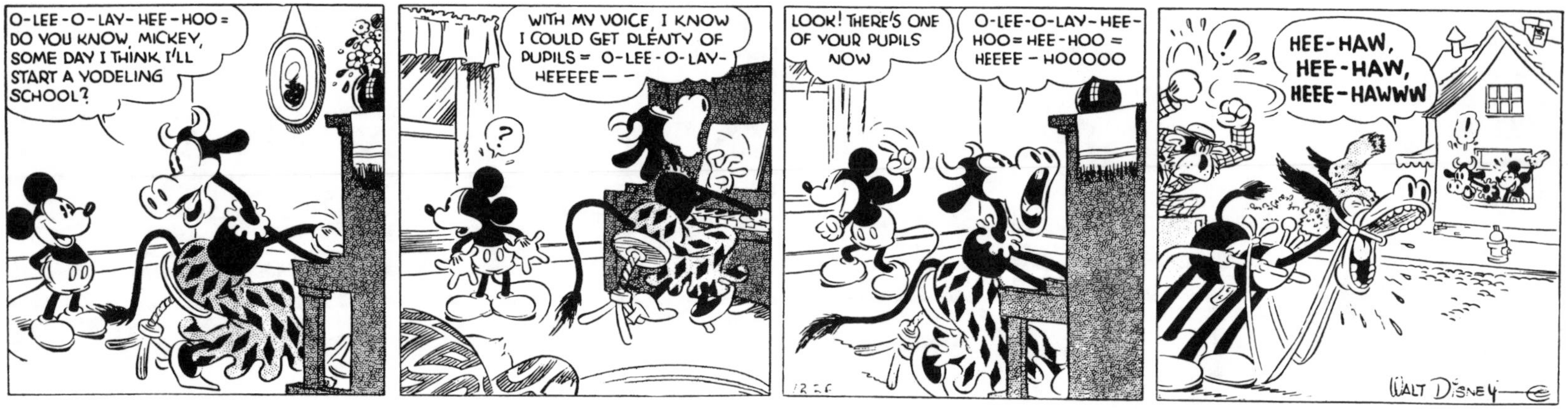
O-LEE-O-LAY-HEE-HOO= DO YOU KNOW, MICKEY, SOME DAY I THINK I'LL START A YODELING SCHOOL?
WITH MY VOICE, I KNOW I COULD GET PLENTY OF PUPILS= O-LEE-O-LAY-HEEEEE — —
LOOK! THERE'S ONE OF YOUR PUPILS NOW
O-LEE-O-LAY-HEE-HOO= HEE-HOO = HEEEE-HOOOOO
HEE-HAW, HEE-HAW, HEEE-HAWWW
WALT DISNEY

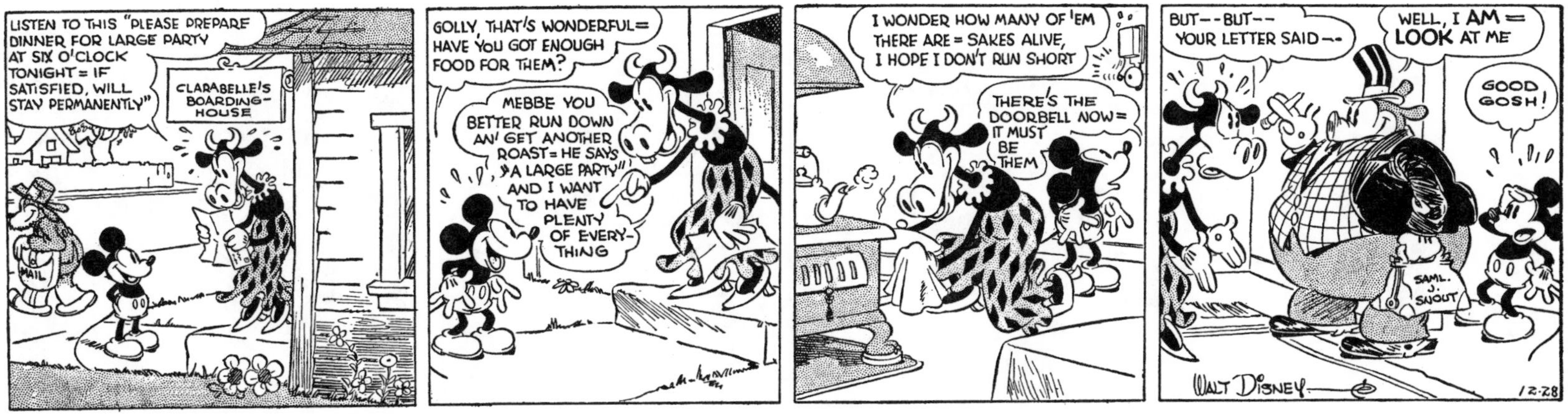
LISTEN TO THIS "PLEASE PREPARE DINNER FOR LARGE PARTY AT SIX O'CLOCK TONIGHT = IF SATISFIED, WILL STAY PERMANENTLY"
CLARABELLE'S BOARDING-HOUSE
MAIL
GOLLY, THAT'S WONDERFUL = HAVE YOU GOT ENOUGH FOOD FOR THEM?
MEBBE YOU BETTER RUN DOWN AN' GET ANOTHER ROAST = HE SAYS "A LARGE PARTY" AND I WANT TO HAVE PLENTY OF EVERY-THING
I WONDER HOW MANY OF 'EM THERE ARE = SAKES ALIVE, I HOPE I DON'T RUN SHORT
THERE'S THE DOORBELL NOW = IT MUST BE THEM
BUT--BUT-- YOUR LETTER SAID--
WELL, I **AM** = **LOOK** AT ME
GOOD GOSH!
SAML. J. SNOUT
WALT DISNEY
12-28

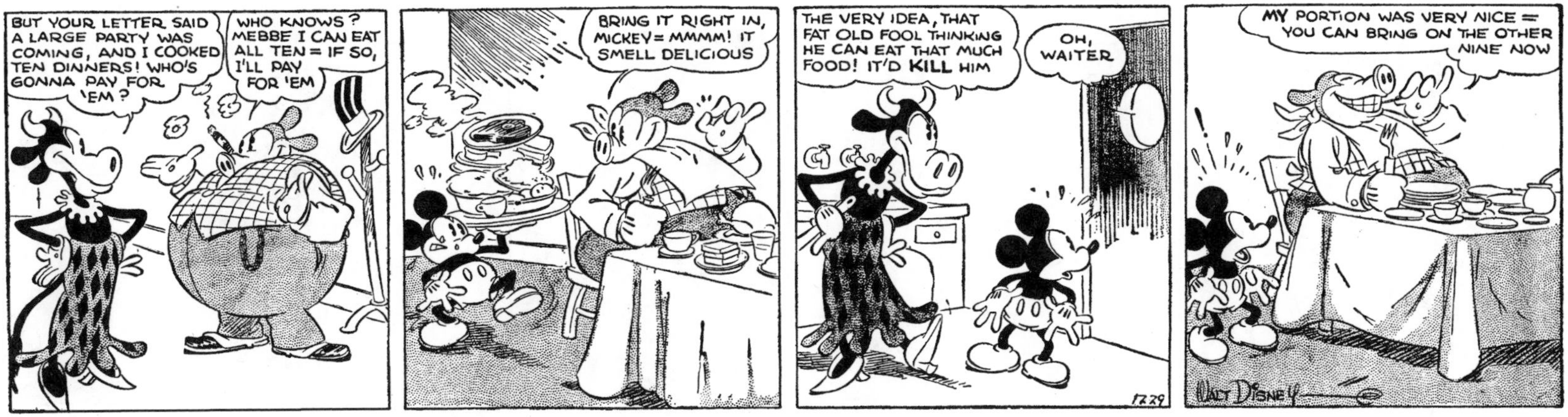
BUT YOUR LETTER SAID A LARGE PARTY WAS COMING, AND I COOKED TEN DINNERS! WHO'S GONNA PAY FOR 'EM?
WHO KNOWS? MEBBE I CAN EAT ALL TEN = IF SO, I'LL PAY FOR 'EM
BRING IT RIGHT IN, MICKEY = MMMM! IT SMELL DELICIOUS
THE VERY IDEA, THAT FAT OLD FOOL THINKING HE CAN EAT THAT MUCH FOOD! IT'D **KILL** HIM
OH, WAITER
12-29
MY PORTION WAS VERY NICE = YOU CAN BRING ON THE OTHER NINE NOW
WALT DISNEY

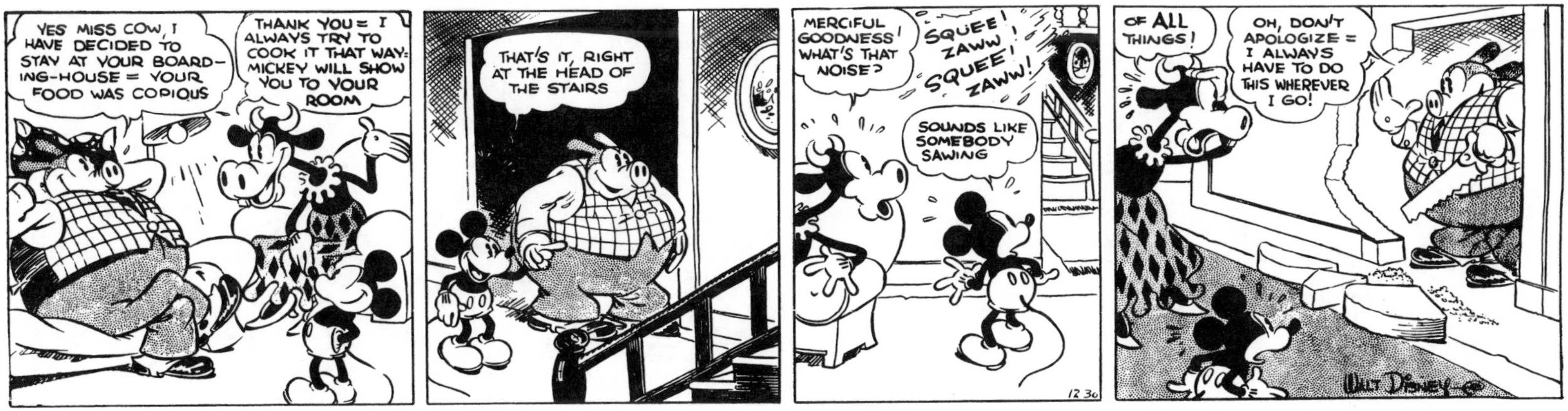
YES MISS COW, I HAVE DECIDED TO STAY AT YOUR BOARD-ING-HOUSE = YOUR FOOD WAS COPIOUS
THANK YOU = I ALWAYS TRY TO COOK IT THAT WAY = MICKEY WILL SHOW YOU TO YOUR ROOM
THAT'S IT, RIGHT AT THE HEAD OF THE STAIRS
MERCIFUL GOODNESS! WHAT'S THAT NOISE?
SQUEE ZAWW SQUEE ZAWW!
SOUNDS LIKE SOMEBODY SAWING
12-30
OF **ALL** THINGS!
OH, DON'T APOLOGIZE = I ALWAYS HAVE TO DO THIS WHEREVER I GO!
WALT DISNEY

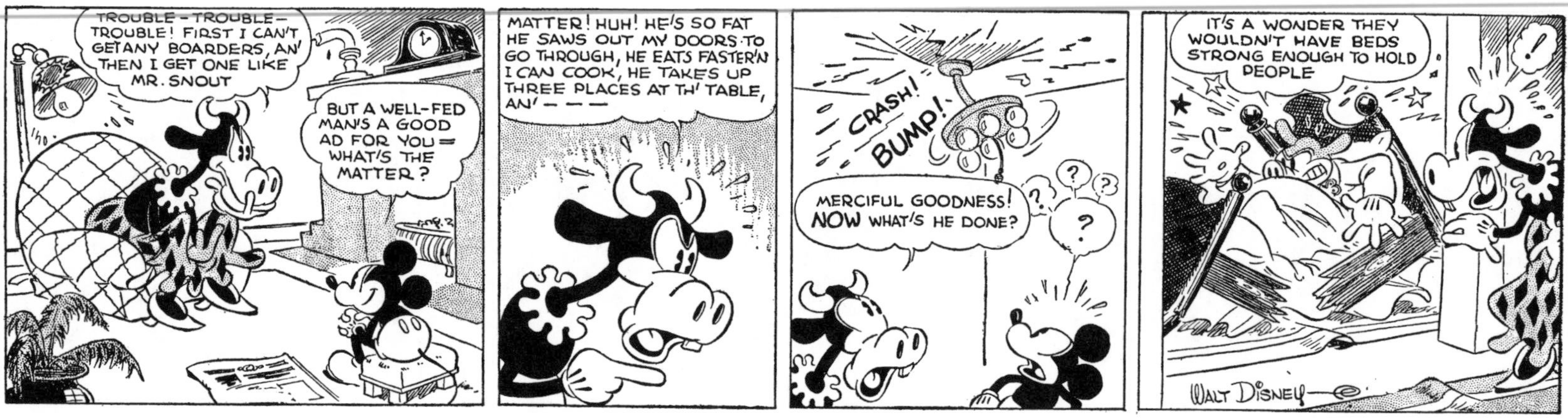
TROUBLE - TROUBLE - TROUBLE! FIRST I CAN'T GET ANY BOARDERS, AN' THEN I GET ONE LIKE MR. SNOUT
BUT A WELL-FED MAN'S A GOOD AD FOR YOU = WHAT'S THE MATTER?
MATTER! HUH! HE'S SO FAT HE SAWS OUT MY DOORS TO GO THROUGH, HE EATS FASTER'N I CAN COOK, HE TAKES UP THREE PLACES AT TH' TABLE, AN' — — —
CRASH!
BUMP!
MERCIFUL GOODNESS! NOW WHAT'S HE DONE?
IT'S A WONDER THEY WOULDN'T HAVE BEDS STRONG ENOUGH TO HOLD PEOPLE
WALT DISNEY

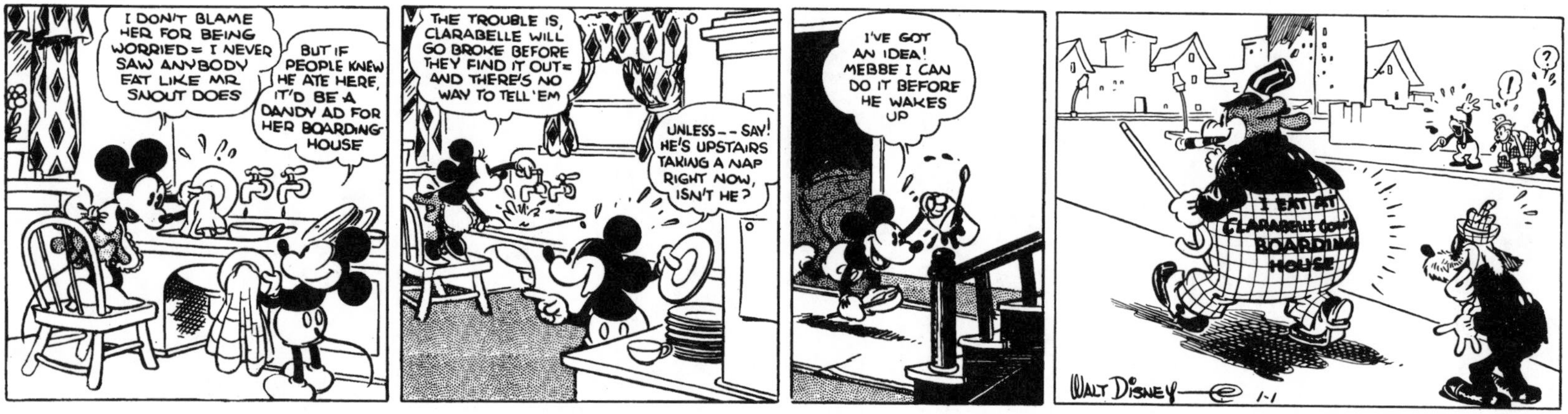
I DON'T BLAME HER FOR BEING WORRIED = I NEVER SAW ANYBODY EAT LIKE MR SNOUT DOES
BUT IF PEOPLE KNEW HE ATE HERE, IT'D BE A DANDY AD FOR HER BOARDING-HOUSE
THE TROUBLE IS, CLARABELLE WILL GO BROKE BEFORE THEY FIND IT OUT = AND THERE'S NO WAY TO TELL 'EM
UNLESS - - SAY! HE'S UPSTAIRS TAKING A NAP RIGHT NOW, ISN'T HE?
I'VE GOT AN IDEA! MEBBE I CAN DO IT BEFORE HE WAKES UP
I EAT AT CLARABELLE COW'S BOARDING HOUSE
WALT DISNEY
1-1

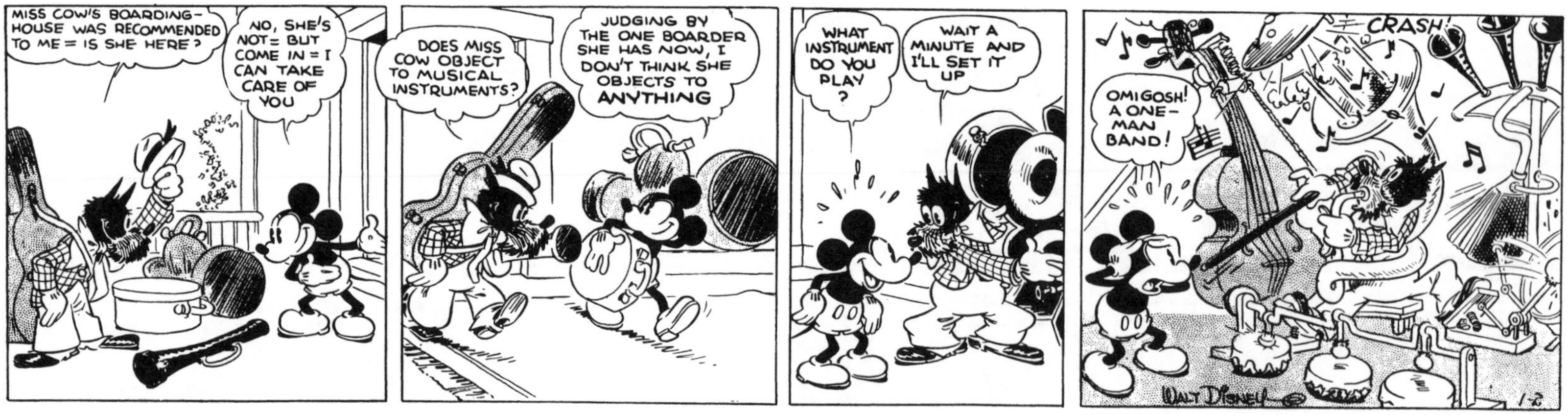
MISS COW'S BOARDING-HOUSE WAS RECOMMENDED TO ME = IS SHE HERE?
NO, SHE'S NOT = BUT COME IN = I CAN TAKE CARE OF YOU
DOES MISS COW OBJECT TO MUSICAL INSTRUMENTS?
JUDGING BY THE ONE BOARDER SHE HAS NOW, I DON'T THINK SHE OBJECTS TO ANYTHING
WHAT INSTRUMENT DO YOU PLAY?
WAIT A MINUTE AND I'LL SET IT UP
CRASH!
OMIGOSH! A ONE-MAN BAND!
WALT DISNEY
1-2

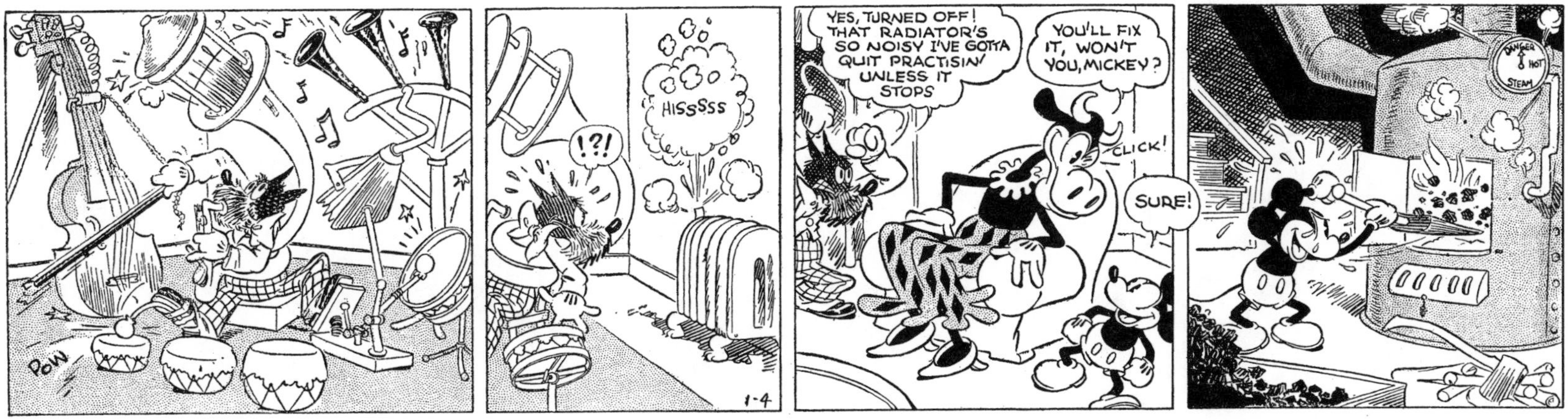
POW
!?!
HISSSSS
1-4
YES, TURNED OFF! THAT RADIATOR'S SO NOISY I'VE GOTTA QUIT PRACTISIN' UNLESS IT STOPS
YOU'LL FIX IT, WON'T YOU, MICKEY?
CLICK!
SURE!
DANGER HOT STEAM

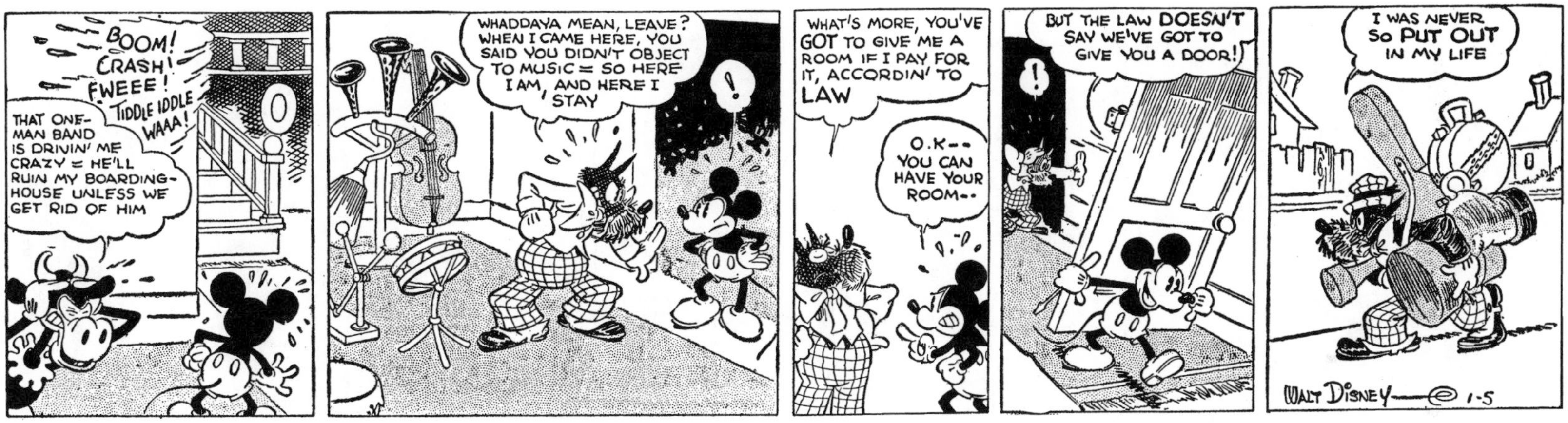
BOOM! CRASH! FWEEE! TIDDLE IDDLE WAAA!
THAT ONE-MAN BAND IS DRIVIN' ME CRAZY = HE'LL RUIN MY BOARDING-HOUSE UNLESS WE GET RID OF HIM
WHADDAYA MEAN, LEAVE? WHEN I CAME HERE, YOU SAID YOU DIDN'T OBJECT TO MUSIC = SO HERE I AM, AND HERE I STAY
!
WHAT'S MORE, YOU'VE GOT TO GIVE ME A ROOM IF I PAY FOR IT, ACCORDIN' TO LAW
O.K.-- YOU CAN HAVE YOUR ROOM--
!
BUT THE LAW DOESN'T SAY WE'VE GOT TO GIVE YOU A DOOR!
I WAS NEVER SO PUT OUT IN MY LIFE
WALT DISNEY 1-5

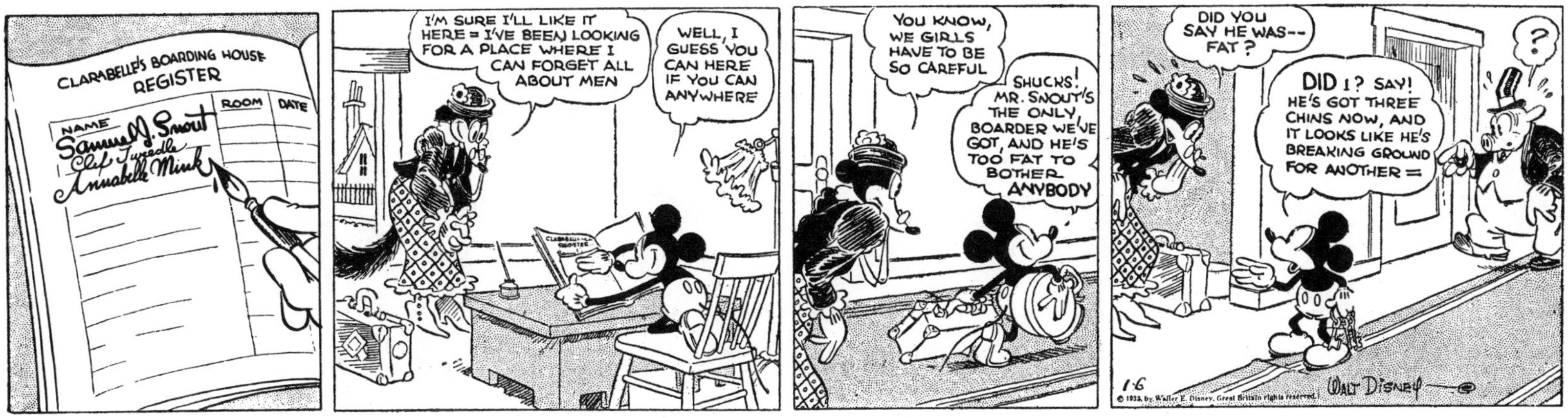
CLARABELLE'S BOARDING HOUSE REGISTER
NAME ROOM DATE
Samuel J. Snout
Clef Tweedle
Annabelle Mink
I'M SURE I'LL LIKE IT HERE = I'VE BEEN LOOKING FOR A PLACE WHERE I CAN FORGET ALL ABOUT MEN
WELL, I GUESS YOU CAN HERE IF YOU CAN ANYWHERE
YOU KNOW, WE GIRLS HAVE TO BE SO CAREFUL
SHUCKS! MR. SNOUT'S THE ONLY BOARDER WE'VE GOT, AND HE'S TOO FAT TO BOTHER ANYBODY
1-6
DID YOU SAY HE WAS--FAT?
?
DID I? SAY! HE'S GOT THREE CHINS NOW, AND IT LOOKS LIKE HE'S BREAKING GROUND FOR ANOTHER =
© 1933, by Walter E. Disney, Great Britain rights reserved.
WALT DISNEY

DON'T TELL A SOUL, BUT HORACE HORSE-COLLAR AND I ARE GOING TO BE MARRIED SOON
MY GOODNESS, YOU DON'T KNOW HOW LUCKY YOU ARE = I'VE NEVER FOUND A MAN
I SUPPOSE YOU LOOK UNDER YOUR BED EVERY NIGHT--LIKE THE REST OF US?
OH, YES, OF COURSE = BUT I'VE NEVER EVEN FOUND ONE THERE = TEE HEE
WELL, IT'S TIME FOR ME TO GO UP TO BED = GOOD-NIGHT
HO-HUM! PARDON ME!
1-7
EEEEEEK!
BOO!
THAT'S GRATITUDE FOR YOU!

?
WHIZZ!
BLOOMP!
GOLLY HORACE! WHAT HAPPENED?
I HAVEN'T GOT TH' SLIGHTEST IDEA
1-8
CLARABELLE AN' I WAS TALKIN' AN' SHE ASKED ME IF I'D STILL LOVE HER WHEN SHE'S OLD AN' HOMELY
AN' I--TRYIN' T' BE NICE--SAID SHE MIGHT GET OLDER, BUT SHE'D NEVER GET ANY HOMELIER
HAW HAW! HO! HO! HO! HO! HA! HA!
F'GOSH SAKES! NOW WHAT'RE YOU LAUGHIN' AT?
WALT DISNEY

YEAH--SHE'S WAITIN' FOR YOU INSIDE
FOR OUR ENGAGEMENT, CLARABELLE
OH, HORACE! YOU ANGEL, WHY, IT'S ADORABLE!
1-9
BUT WHAT DOES THIS MEAN? "TO PATRICIA--WITH LOVE!" HAVE YOU USED THIS BEFORE?
?
WELL--ER--YOU SEE--I--THAT IS--
PERCY PIG! WHERE'S THAT DIAMOND RING I TOLD YOU TO HAVE REPAIRED TODAY?
WELL, YOU SEE, PATRICIA, M'DEAR, --HORACE HORSE-COLLAR AND I--WELL, WE JUST SORTA GOT INTO A CARD GAME--AND--
WALT DISNEY

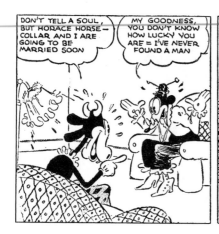

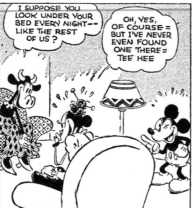

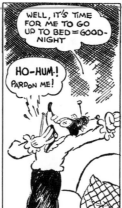

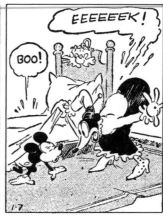

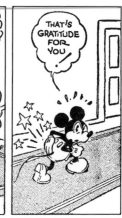

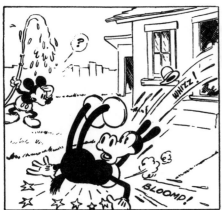

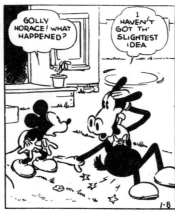

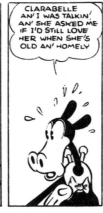

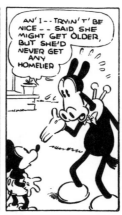

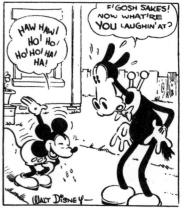

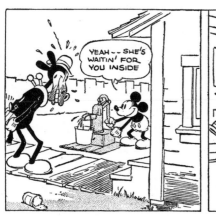

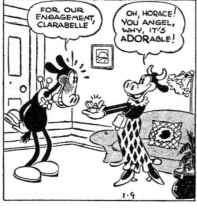

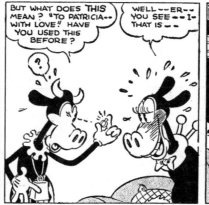

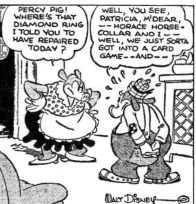

THE GOTTFREDSON ARCHIVES

Essays and Special Features

ABOVE: Ub Iwerks in 1929.

RIGHT: A later Mickey Mouse sizes up Iwerks' first 1928 mouse. This juxtaposition was created for Mickey's seventh birthday in 1935, with a caption calling the 1928 mouse "Mortimer Mouse, Walt Disney's original rendering of Mickey." An earlier, similar comparison—captioned identically—appeared in Feg Murray's syndicated newspaper feature, "Seein' Stars," on November 17, 1933.

OPPOSITE: Ub Iwerks' original 1928 sketch sheet, containing the first-ever drawings of Mickey and Minnie Mouse.

IN THE BEGINNING:
UB IWERKS
AND THE BIRTH OF MICKEY MOUSE

» BY THOMAS ANDRAE

THE *MICKEY MOUSE* COMIC STRIP reached its adventuresome peak—and the peak of its success—under Floyd Gottfredson. The strip was never Gottfredson's alone, though. Over the years he shared production duties with many other exceptional Disney studio writers and artists. But the most important "second man" on *Mickey Mouse* preceded Gottfredson's run entirely. This man was Ub Iwerks, the early partner of Walt's who animated the first Mickey cartoons, designed the character, and penciled the first 18 strips in the daily series. Iwerks' opening strips are must-reads for any Mickey strip fan. To view them in the proper context, however, we must take a closer look at Iwerks' Disney achievements—and at Mickey Mouse's origin.

The circumstances of Mickey Mouse's birth are shrouded in myth. Walt Disney always claimed that he created Mickey on the train to California from New York after having lost his first major cartoon star, Oswald the Lucky Rabbit. According to Disney, a mouse he had kept as a pet on a farm in Missouri inspired the creation of a mouse character he initially named Mortimer. The story goes that his wife Lillian thought the name made the mouse sound like a sissy, and renamed the character Mickey.

Although the official story has been repeated many times over the years, David R. Smith, Director emeritus of the Walt Disney Archives, has discounted it as "publicity fodder."[1] New evidence suggests that the legend of Mickey's birth must be drastically revised.

When Disney was asked in 1931 how Mickey was created, he admitted that he couldn't remember: "I can't say just how the idea came," said Disney. "We wanted another animal. We had a cat: a mouse naturally came to mind. We felt that the public—especially children—like animals that are 'cute' and little."[2] Lillian herself said that the Kansas City stories about Walt befriending mice were apocryphal: "We simply thought the mouse would make a cute character to animate."[3]

A more likely account of the mouse's origin involves the key role of Ub Iwerks. Iwerks, Walt's friend and colleague beginning in 1919, met Disney at Kansas City's Pesmen-Rubin Commercial Art Studio, then acted as lead animator on the vast majority of Disney's silent cartoon series. When Disney decided to make the first Mickey Mouse short, *Plane Crazy*, Iwerks was the only full-fledged animator he had. His other animators had been hired away by his distributor, Charles Mintz, along with Disney's cartoon star, Oswald. In a 1956 interview with a publicity agent at

ours—but they had cute ears."[5] "Walt designed a mouse, but it wasn't very good," claimed Otto Messmer, creator and designer of Felix the Cat. "He was long and skinny. Ub Iwerks redesigned the character."[6] It was Iwerks' drawing that became the model. As he described it: "pear-shaped body, ball on top, a couple of thin legs. You gave it long ears, it was a rabbit. Short ears, it was a cat. Ears hanging down, a dog. With an elongated nose it became a mouse. Mickey was the same basic figure initially"[7] Thus, Mickey is often described as being simply a reshaping of Oswald. But, as we shall see, the evolution of Mickey was much more complicated than that.

Mischievous rodents had been a stock-in-trade in the films and comic strips of the day. Ignatz Mouse was Krazy Kat's *bête noire* in George Herriman's famous comic strip, and Skiddoo the mouse bedeviled Felix the Cat in Messmer's cartoons and comic strip adventures. Mice were also featured players in Paul Terry's "Aesop's Film Fables," cartoons for which Walt professed great admiration. Disney had drawn a group of short-pantsed mice in this mold in a 1926 birthday card for his father, and made mice continuing bit players of his animation entourage in his silent films. The rodents figured so prominently that Hugh Harman featured them in a publicity poster he had drawn—with a photographed Walt surrounded by his characters—when the staff moved into Disney's new studio at Hyperion Avenue.

A sheet of Mickey sketches by Iwerks is a virtual Rosetta Stone concerning Mickey's birth, revealing for the first time the facts of Mickey's creation. Dating from 1928, it contains the earliest known drawings of the character.[8] Though these drawings were promoted as a piece of Studio history into the 1960s—one TV special even reenacted their creation[9]—they subsequently vanished for decades. Placed in a safe at Retlaw Enterprises, the Disney family company, by animator Bill Cottrell (Disney's

Disney's, Iwerks gave this account: "Walt came back to Hollywood discouraged, and Roy [Disney] and I joined him in a meeting to discuss the possibilities of a new character. I tried some sketches of dogs and cats. There were too many cats (Felix, Krazy, etc.), so I tried looking through a batch of magazines. In *Life* or *Judge* I ran into cartoons of animals by Meeker and I got the idea for a mouse. There hadn't been any good mouse characters. We weren't artists—there were almost none in the field—but we worked out a character and Lilly [Disney's wife] gave it a name and then we kicked ideas around and cooked up a story

about Lindbergh, who was a hero at the time."[4] *Plane Crazy* (1928) starred Mickey as a would-be-aviator trying to emulate his hero, Charles Lindbergh, who had recently flown solo from America to Paris.

Iwerks' mention of being inspired by an artist named Meeker in *Life* or *Judge* was likely a reference to cartoonist Clifton Meek, who drew the comic strip "The Adventures of Johnny Mouse" in the 1910s, and a series about unnamed mice for *Life* magazine in the early 1920s. "I grew up with those drawings," Walt told an interviewer, "They were different from

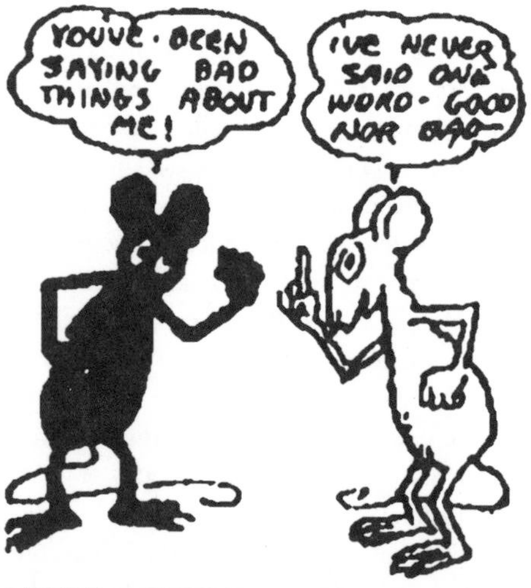
YOU'VE · BEEN SAYING BAD THINGS ABOUT ME!
I'VE NEVER SAID ONE WORD · GOOD NOR BAD—

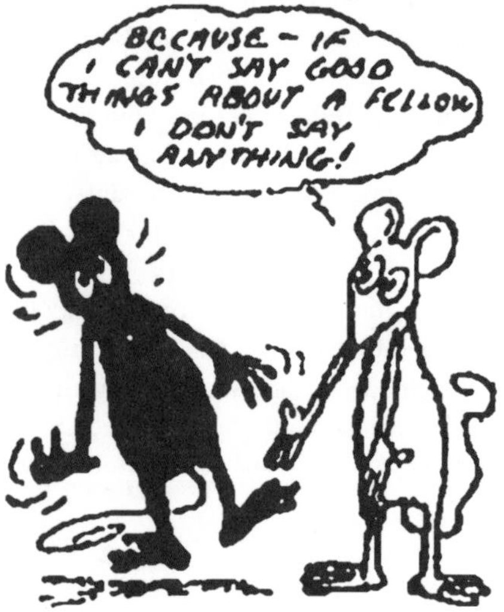
BECAUSE — IF I CAN'T SAY GOOD THINGS ABOUT A FELLOW I DON'T SAY ANYTHING!

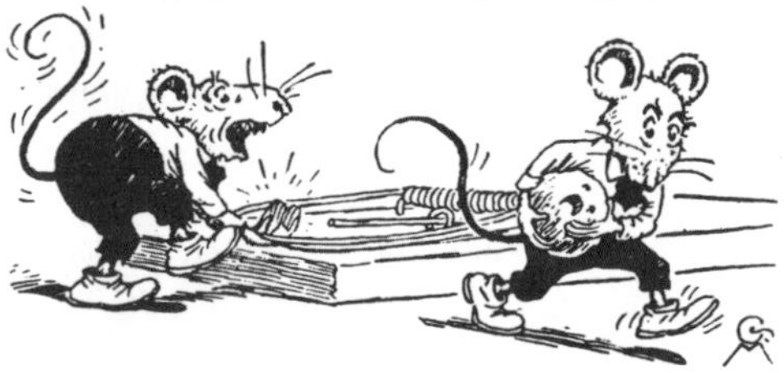

brother-in-law), they lay undiscovered by the family until years after his death.

The dating of the sketch sheet can be surmised from two non-Mickey images on the sheet. Iwerks drew a horseshoe at the top of the page and what appears to be a turkey's tail feathers on the far right margin. These images figure prominently in *Plane Crazy* (1928), the first-produced Mickey cartoon: in it, Minnie gives Mickey the horseshoe for luck. The mouse also uses turkey feathers as a tailfin for his second plane after the first plane crashes. These images suggest that the sketch sheet was done early in 1928, at the same time that Walt was writing the scenario for *Plane Crazy*. Thus the sketch sheet predates the *Plane Crazy* story sketches that were used in producing the film.

Looking at the sketch sheet today, one can deduce how Mickey's design came about. The drawing at the top left has Mickey in black knickers, a white blouse, bow tie, and flat shoes. This drawing is likely the first one done; indeed, it was singled out as the first drawing of Mickey in Studio publicity of the mid-1930s. The mouse's costume is remarkably similar to that of Meek's unnamed 1920s mice. Like Meek's 1920s mice, he has whiskers and side hair making him more mouse-like and less anthropomorphic than the final Mickey. On the lower right side of the sheet of drawings is the earliest known drawing of Minnie Mouse; from the start, her design shows that she was merely Mickey with eyelashes and a skirt.

Subsequent sketches on the page show how Disney and Iwerks gave Mickey a sleeker face more suitable for animation. They also experimented with Mickey's ears—initially giving him the rimmed, three-dimensional ears of Meek's 1920s mouse, then adapting the flat black circles of Meek's earlier Johnny Mouse, as well as earlier silent cartoon mice.[10] These ears became an important element of Mickey's iconography. They have an abstract design, so they remain round circles no matter how Mickey holds his head; thus, they do not belong to three-dimensional space. As John Updike points out, Mickey's ears belong "to an ideal realm of symbolization," Updike suggests, giving Mickey an aura of "cartoon resilience and indestructibility," a key aspect of his character.[11]

The 1928 Mickey sketch sheet also reflects experiments with Mickey's eyes, color and costume. Some images on the page show a white mouse; in time, Iwerks and Disney settled on black, perhaps to follow the designs of earlier silent cartoon mice. A circled Mickey design at the center of the page—undoubtedly okayed by Walt—is topless and wears short pants, and has large, goggle eyes without eyebrows: it is this design, or one close to it, that we see in Mickey's first-produced cartoon, *Plane Crazy* (1928). Notably, it includes some of the rat-like features of earlier cartoon mice in the *Alice* and *Oswald* shorts: a long snout and claw-like bare feet.[12] The more raffish appearance was emblematic of the mischievous and anarchic personality with which Disney imbued his star in his first cartoons.

Yet even after a circled model was okayed, Mickey continued to develop. Partway through *The Gallopin' Gaucho* (1928), Mickey traded his goggle eyes for oblong, floating eyes that recall the top left drawing on the sketch sheet. Significantly, another circled drawing on the sheet shows Mickey wearing the 1920s Meek character's costume; Disney was apparently ambivalent about making Mickey barefooted, and his flat shoes from this costume returned in *Gaucho* as well. With these changes came a rounder, less rodent-like appearance, revealing Disney's desire for a more anthropomorphic looking character.

Some aspects of Mickey took longer to nail down. While previous mouse characters on the screen had been small, rodent-sized figures, Disney and Iwerks generally gave Mickey a large stature suitable to a cartoon protagonist—but not all the time. Iwerks explained: "I don't recall any special meetings or discussions on how Mickey should look... We decided to make Mickey the size of a little boy. We couldn't have

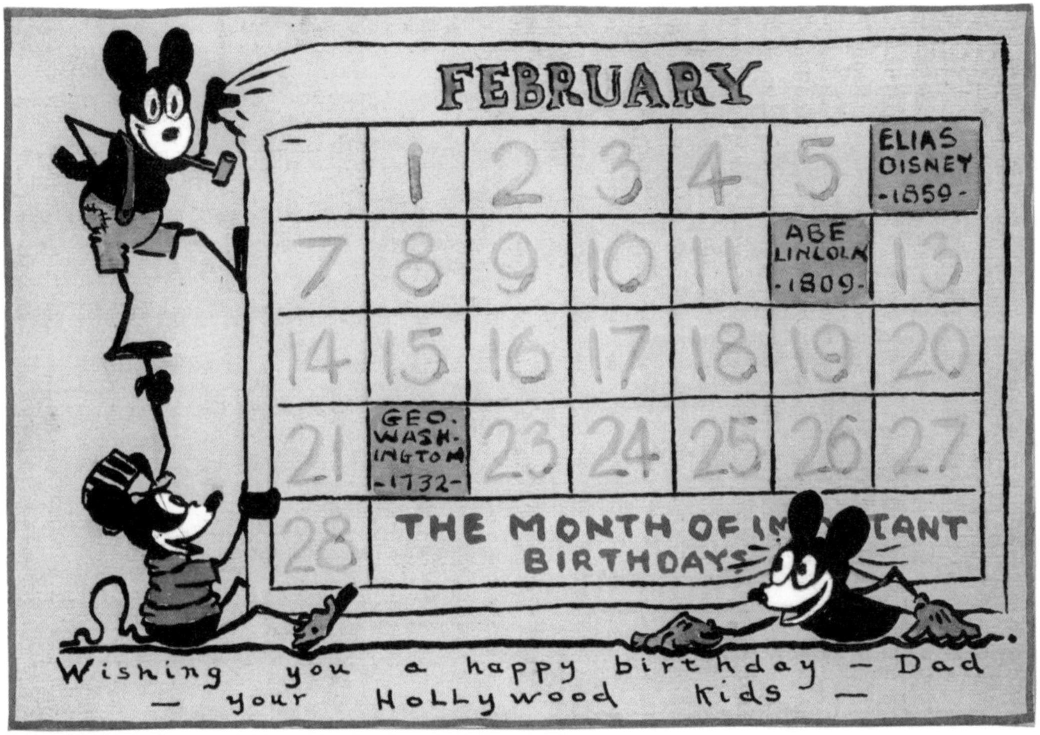
FEBRUARY
ELIAS DISNEY -1859-
ABE LINCOLN -1809-
GEO. WASHINGTON -1732-
THE MONTH OF IMPORTANT BIRTHDAYS
Wishing you a happy birthday — Dad
— your Hollywood Kids —

him mouse-size because of scale problems. We asked ourselves, 'What are people going to think?' The size we selected must have been right—people accepted him as a symbolic character, and though he looked like a mouse he was accepted as dashing and heroic."[13] However, in two early Mickey Mouse cartoons, *When the Cat's Away* and *The Barnyard Battle* (both 1929), Iwerks drew Mickey rodent-size, suggesting that Mickey's height had not yet been stabilized.

Mickey's personality was also in flux. According to Iwerks, the heroic image was central to Mickey: "Mickey was based on the character of Douglas Fairbanks Sr. He was the superhero of his day, always winning, gallant and swashbuckling. Mickey's action was in that vein. He was never intended to be a sissy; he was always an adventurous character. I thought of him in that respect, and I had him do naturally the sort of things Doug Fairbanks would do. Some people got the idea that in *Plane Crazy* Mickey was patterned after Lindbergh. Well, Lindy flew the Atlantic, but he was no Doug Fairbanks. He was a hero to boys because of airplanes and what he accomplished flying the Atlantic. But Mickey wasn't Lindy, even though we used Lindy's story as the theme of the picture—he was still Doug Fairbanks."[14]

The Fairbanks influence can be seen clearly in Mickey's *Gallopin' Gaucho*, which was loosely based on Fairbanks' film *The Gaucho* (1927). However, Mickey is too impudent and anarchic to be called a hero in most of the early cartoons—and, with the exception of *Gallopin' Gaucho*, they often end not with Mickey's triumph but his comic failure. In *The Barn Dance* (1928), for example, the brutish feline Pete is a better dancer than Mickey; Mickey's effort to rebuff him is foiled, and Minnie leaves a sobbing Mickey behind on the dance floor.

Mickey's inconsistency—between mouse and man, between success and failure—carried over to Disney's and Iwerks' first Mickey comics. When Iwerks first met Disney at Pesmen-Rubin Studio, Iwerks notably recollected that Walt's "goal then was to do a comic strip, sort of *Mutt and Jeff* imitation."[15] Indeed, the first Mickey Mouse cartoons bore the byline, "A Walt Disney comic," referencing Walt's early desire to become a cartoonist. Perhaps because Disney had initially hoped to become a comic strip artist, he decided to write the first four months of the *Mickey Mouse* strip himself. Yet Iwerks had been the first man actually approached about doing a Mickey daily: "Because I had been doing the animation at the Disney Studio, I got a letter one day from King Features Syndicate asking me to do a Mickey Mouse comic strip. I turned the letter over to Walt—that wasn't my business. Walt made the deal, and I did the drawings for a few strips. Actually with all the animation work I had no time for comics. I had too much else to do."[16]

But Iwerks produced some comics anyway. And there, in the strip's first weeks, we see Iwerks and Disney's mouse—complete with uncertainties lingering from that first 1928 sketch sheet. Mickey has free-floating black eyes, but Iwerks' heavy use of eyebrow lines suggests a will to draw the earlier goggle eyes, and the more mischievous look that they brought. Mickey is generally the size of a child, but when he pals around with two vulture chicks—in a post-Iwerks Walt-written sequence—he can be much smaller. He is also a combination hero/failure, but time would smooth this out: the way to go was shown by Mickey's first-strip introduction as a naïve farm boy, suggesting that youth, not

OPPOSITE: Meek, a mouse: Clifton Meek's black-furred, abstract Johnny Mouse in 1913, and his *Life* mice of the early 1920s. Images courtesy Gunnar Andreassen and Fredrik Strömberg.

LEFT: Walt Disney drew this 1926 birthday card for his father, populating it with mice that prefigure Mickey.

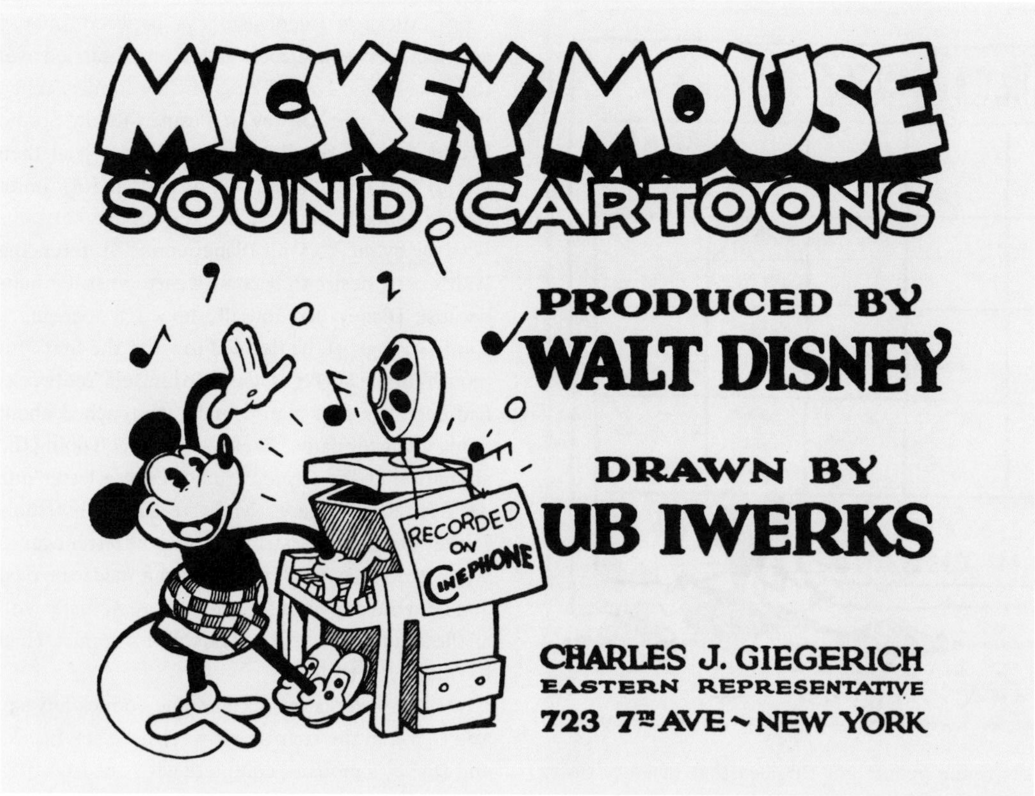

ABOVE: Iwerks advertising art from *The Film Daily Year Book*, 1929 edition. Image courtesy Mark Kausler.

ambiguity, was the cause of Mickey's imperfect success record.[17]

Walt's and Ub's partnership was ambiguous, too. Although Iwerks made an enormous contribution to the early Mickey cartoons, Disney remained responsible for much of the storyline and imbuing Mickey with a personality. Early Mickey cartoons thus bore the byline, "A Walt Disney Comic; Drawn by Ub Iwerks." Sometimes the matter of who had control over animating the cartoons led to conflicts. As early as *Steamboat Willie* (1928), the two men disagreed about the timing of sequences and the management of other animators. Then, one night at a Hollywood party, when a young boy asked Walt for an autographed drawing of Mickey, Walt turned to Ub and said, "Why don't you draw Mickey and I'll autograph it?" Frustrated by his lack of public credit and the ongoing arguments with Walt, Ub said, "Draw your own—Mickey!" and stormed out.[18]

For years, the two were at odds: Iwerks left Disney in January 1930, where he created Flip the Frog, Willie Whopper, and numerous color cartoons at his own animation studio. But Iwerks returned to Disney in 1940 to begin a new career as head of the studio's special effects lab. His breakthroughs, including the optical printer and traveling matte system, won him two Academy Awards before his death in 1971. His friendship with Walt resumed for as long as both lived—with squabbles over Mickey long past. •

1 "The Man and His Mouse," *West*, *San Jose Mercury News*, June 19, 1988, p. 7.

2 *American Magazine*, March, 1931, p. 15.

3 Neal Gabler, *Walt Disney: The Triumph of the American Imagination* (New York: Alfred A. Knopf, 2007), p. 113.

4 Ub Iwerks interview, 1956, Walt Disney Archives. Iwerks later recanted on crediting Lillian with naming Mickey; see Gabler, p. 114.

5 Gabler also argues for Disney's use of Meek's mouse as a model for Mickey, p. 113.

6 John Culhane, "A Mouse for All Seasons," *Saturday Revue*, Sept. 11, 1978, p. 50.

7 Ibid.

8 The Walt Disney Family Museum labels these drawings as "the earliest known drawings of Mickey Mouse... done around 1928," *San Francisco Chronicle*, April 1, 2009.

9 "The Mickey Mouse 40th Anniversary Show" (1968) marks an early use—perhaps the first—of the reenactment footage; it was later reused in the introduction to Disney's 1984 *Limited Gold Edition* VHS cassettes.

10 An earlier Johnny-inspired Disney mouse appears in *Goldie Locks and the Three Bears* (1922), one of Disney's Kansas City-produced Laugh-O-Grams fairy tale cartoons.

11 Craig Yoe and Janet Morra-Yoe, *The Art of Mickey Mouse* (New York: Disney Editions, 1993), p. 2.

12 However, Iwerks and Disney drew the bare feet as toeless blocks in *Plane Crazy*, perhaps because this was easier to animate.

13 Iwerks, 1956, WDA.

14 Interview with Iwerks by George Sherman, July 30, 1970, WDA.

15 David Smith, Iwerks interview, 1969-1971.

16 George Sherman, Iwerks interview, 1970.

17 See "The Cast: Mickey and Minnie" (page 255) for a closer look at these developments.

18 Leslie Iwerks and John Kenworthy, *The Hand Behind the Mouse: An Intimate Biography of Ub Iwerks* (New York: Disney Editions, 2001), p. 83.

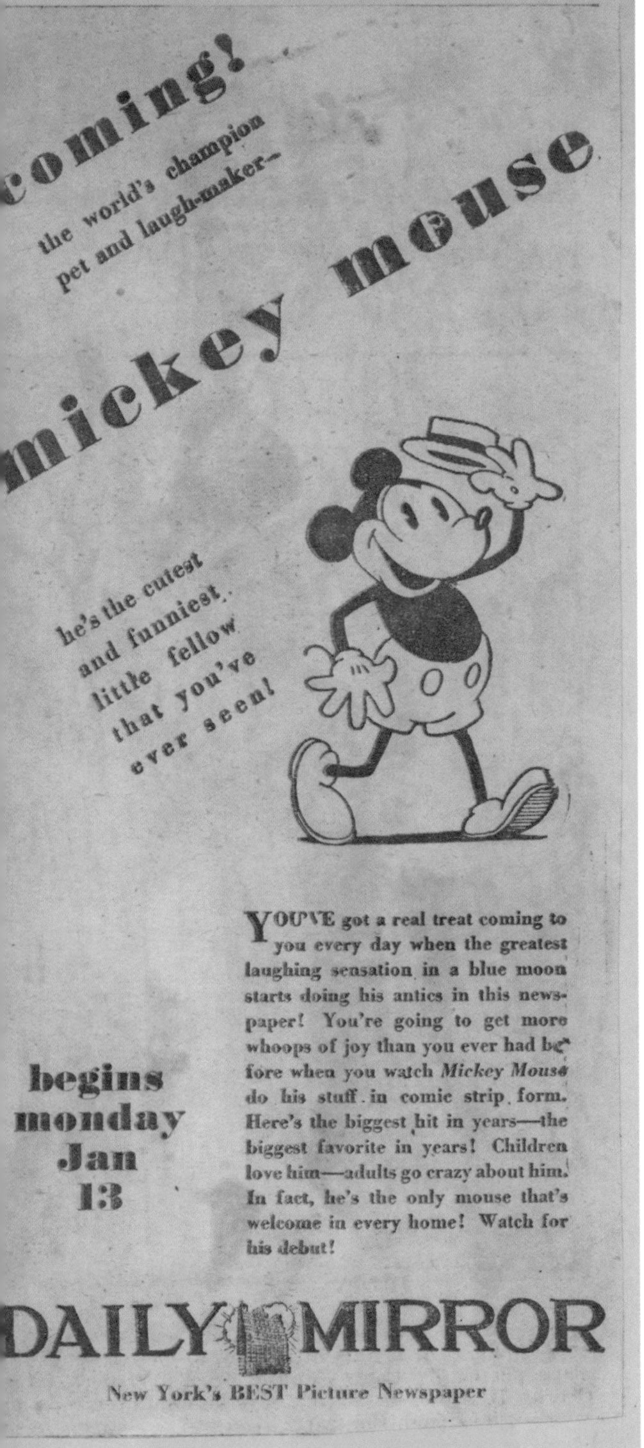
coming!
the world's champion
pet and laugh-maker—
mickey mouse
he's the cutest
and funniest
little fellow
that you've
ever seen!
YOU'VE got a real treat coming to you every day when the greatest laughing sensation in a blue moon starts doing his antics in this newspaper! You're going to get more whoops of joy than you ever had before when you watch *Mickey Mouse* do his stuff in comic strip form. Here's the biggest hit in years—the biggest favorite in years! Children love him—adults go crazy about him! In fact, he's the only mouse that's welcome in every home! Watch for his debut!
begins
monday
Jan
13
DAILY MIRROR
New York's BEST Picture Newspaper

Starting the Strip

» BY DAVID GERSTEIN

FOR GENERATIONS, comics have been among the Walt Disney Company's most important storytelling forms. In many countries, Disney comics remain a bestselling media venue for Mickey, Donald Duck, and other studio stars; in Finland, they are the bestselling weekly periodicals of any kind.[1] But every empire has to start somewhere. In 1956, Walt Disney recalled the funnies' launch in a fairly casual manner—with the studio having started to make comics just in time for others to demand them:

> "[*In 1929 we were looking for*] *ways to exploit characters like the Mouse. The most obvious was a comic strip. So I started work on a comic strip hoping I could sell it to one of the syndicates. As I was producing the first one, a letter came to me from King Features wanting to know if I would be interested in doing a comic strip featuring Mickey Mouse. Naturally I accepted their offer.*"[2]

But as we've just seen (page 226), Mickey co-creator Ub Iwerks remembered King having contacted *him*, not Walt; and *before* any strips were produced, not partway through their making.

Whose memory was right? Well—both and neither, as the saying goes. June 1929 indeed found Walt Disney thinking about comics. But actual work on them hadn't started. Charles Giegerich, Disney's account representative with distributor Pat Powers, suggested getting a move on:

> *I cannot say what success we would have in placing a comic page with the newspaper syndicates, but it certainly would be good publicity. If you will send me a couple of sample pages, I will take it up with the syndicates and find out what can be done in the matter.*[3]

Sample pages—hmm. Finding time to produce comics was harder than just talking about it. Evidence suggests that a month later, no samples had been made; had Disney proposed something the studio had no time for?

Enter another man with a proposition: Joseph Connolly, President of King Features Syndicate. His frankly fanboyish letter to "U. B. Iwerk, Esq." [sic] was written July 24:

> *I think your mouse animation is one of the funniest features I have ever seen in the movies. Please consider producing one in comic strip form for newspapers. If you can find time to do one, I shall be very interested in seeing some specimens.*[4]

As if following entertainment-mogul stereotypes to a tee, Connolly showed little knowledge

LEFT: A launch ad as published in the New York *Mirror*. Vignette by unknown artist; note Mickey's five-fingered right hand.

forget all your troubles!

I'll make you forget 'em!

BANISH dull care — forget your woes! For *Mickey Mouse* is coming to town. the wonderful animal cartoon that has swept the country like a prairie fire in the greatest wave of popular acclaim ever accorded a comic-art personality.

of actual entertainment production processes. He seemed to think Iwerks handled everything related to Mickey himself; if Ub didn't have time for a strip, there'd be no one else to produce one.

The supposed lone eagle replied to Connolly on July 30:

hello, everybody!

here I am!

MICKEY MOUSE is the greatest comic hit in years! He's known from one end of the globe to the other—for he appears on the screens of a thousand movie theatres nightly. And now, for the first time, this pet of the nation is going to perform for you, as a daily comic strip!

Mickey Mouse

will scamper right into your heart the first time you see him! And he'll tickle your funny-bone for a salvo of laughs! Kiddies yell *for* him—grown-ups yell *at* him and his inimitable antics. For *Mickey Mouse* is, without doubt, the funniest comic strip creation in a blue moon! Watch for his first appearance!

We would be glad to consider producing Mickey in comic strips for newspapers and we are today writing our Eastern representative, Mr. Charles Giegerich, at 723 Seventh Ave., informing him that you are interested and asking that he get in touch with you.

After we have received further information, we will proceed with the making up of several specimens for your approval.[5]

Iwerks' words clarified that no samples had yet been created. But Disney, writing to Giegerich, painted the picture of a careful comics task force at work:

It has been our belief for some time that Mickey would work up into a wonderful little comic strip and we have been laying plans to take care of the work involved...[6]

Yet it cannot have taken much plan-laying for Disney to decide—as he finally did—to write *Mickey* himself while Iwerks handled the art. Indeed, that would seem to have been the most obvious solution.

But it was a solution that made for delays, as heavy cartoon production really did block production of sample strips. Letters in August and September showed Walt caught unawares by lack of time, while Giegerich grumbled about the samples' absence.[7] On October 19 Disney admitted to Connolly:

The comic strip is an entirely new angle for us and we have been somewhat puzzled as to the best policy to carry out in this strip. The artist that we have had working on this angle has made up quite a few specimens but we have not as yet been able to satisfy ourselves with the results.[8]

This dreary statement almost seemed to signal a sputtering end to proceedings. But one month later—on November 18—those samples were finally sent to King Features, and the result was bliss.

What had finally brought the strip into focus? We're not fully certain; no rejected preliminary "specimens" seem to survive to tell us. But the early published *Mickey* dailies plumped for a "policy" of the most predictable kind: they were based directly on recent cartoons, an obvious story source.

let me chase
away the blues!

On December 30, a telegram from King Features outlined big plans:

NEW YORK MIRROR WISHES TO BEGIN PUBLICITY ON MICKEY MOUSE NEXT WEEK AND START STRIP WEEK THEREAFTER STOP IN ABSENCE OF FORMAL CONTRACT MAY WE HAVE YOUR PERMISSION TO TELL MIRROR TO GO AHEAD STOP WHEN WILL THIRD [WEEK OF STRIPS] REACH US STOP PLEASE WIRE COLLECT ANSWERS BOTH THESE QUESTIONS STOP PROSPECTS EXCELLENT THAT MICKEY WILL BE BIG COMIC HIT OF NINETEEN THIRTY.[9]

Mickey Mouse was promoted in the *Mirror* with a big King Features launch pack; slogans and callout images were everywhere. But it seems that only one other paper, the *Oakland Post-Enquirer*, ran the strip from its January 13 start. *Mickey* was slow to pick up steam; perhaps because its format was somewhat undecided. In principle, the strip told an ongoing story; in practice, the majority of strips were gag-a-day, linked only by characters and setting.

By March 1930 a new direction was needed. Floyd Gottfredson later recalled how King "asked Walt to change [the strip's] story line to a continuous adventure [serial]. This was the trend in comic strips at that time, following the huge success of *The Gumps* which had that kind of continuity."[10] From "big comic hit" to hasty fad-follower; how quickly glory fades.

Yet how fast *Mickey* was to recover; in what proved an enduring, exciting, decades-long series of adventures, a mouse was about to roar. If you have read this book from the start, you'll already know the heights that Walt Disney—and Floyd Gottfredson—would hit in just a few months.

But now let's jump back to January 13, 1930, and see where it all began: with "Lost on a Desert Island," the loosely-themed Mickey story that preceded King's request to go all-adventure. Every aspect of this tentative tale—from its visual milieu to its cultural references—bespeaks 1929 small-town America; or, more precisely, the way small-town America saw itself in 1929, however divorced from reality such perceptions may have been. Characters' language is antiquated: a flying vehicle is an "aeroplane" and a car a "flivver." Mickey shouts "by gollies" and sings "Boop-boop-a-doop," the catchphrase of then-famous film and Broadway performers (as well as cartoon icon Betty Boop, who at the time had yet to make her debut).

Slapstick, too, is of the period. Numerous jokes are based around simple embarrassment: a blow to the head, a loss of one's pants. Casual comedy is derived from firearms; we wouldn't see today's Mickey treat weapons this raucously.

And then there is the Other—the way that 1929 pop culture represented those who came from cultures outside America's white Anglo-Saxon majority. Films and fiction were filled with broadly exaggerated, often intentionally comical images of Africans, African-Americans, Italians, and others "not like us." In the case of "Lost on a Desert Island,"

MICKEY MOUSE

You've seen him in the

"TALKIES"—

Now you can see him EVERY DAY in the

WALT DISNEY'S
MICKEY MOUSE

OPPOSITE: Generic ad templates from King Features launch pack, January 1930. Vignette by Ub Iwerks and Win Smith, adapted from January 17, 1930 daily strip.

ABOVE: Generic ad template from King Features launch pack. Newspapers were meant to insert their name in the blurb and—presumably—put a slogan or logo onto the vignette's blank blackboard. Vignette by Win Smith, adapted from the 1930-32 Mickey Mouse cartoon main title card.

LEFT: Generic ad template from King Features launch pack. Minnie vignette by Les Clark and Win Smith, adapted from 1929 publications model sheet.

229.

PAQUITO
Semanario ilustrado para chicos y grandes
10¢
EN TODA LA REP.!

LES AVENTURES
DE MICKEY
HACHETTE

TOPOLINO
NELL'ISOLA MISTERIOSA
2 LIRE
CONTIENE UNA FIGURINA PREMIO TOPOLINO
GLI ALBI D'ORO
EDIZIONI WALT DISNEY · MONDADORI

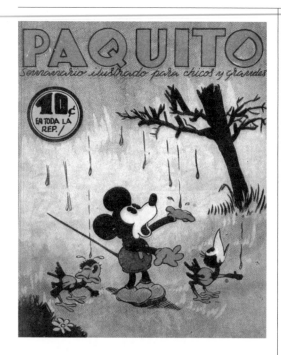

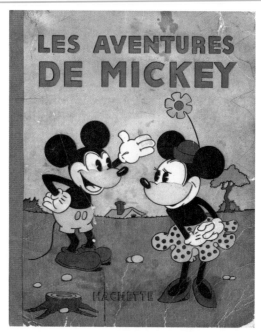

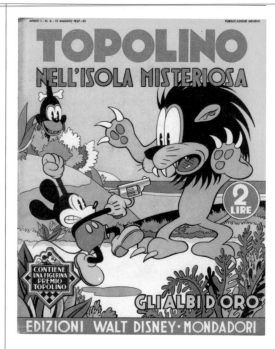

it's island natives who are caricatured, here as cannibals speaking a Pig Latin-like pidgin. The natives' Tarzan-style loincloths in one panel display a swavastika—or backwards swastika—icon, perceived as an aboriginal peace symbol in those pre-Third Reich days.

In general in the 1930s, stereotypes were seen by many as a natural element of humoristic shorthand—they were "what you used," as a creator of fiction, when you didn't want to go to the trouble of developing a nuanced incidental character from scratch. So second nature were these clichés, in fact, that the comics community's most outspoken supporters of civil rights—notably Walt Kelly and Theodor "Dr. Seuss" Geisel—could casually employ them at the time without pausing to think about their impact. Though the exact nature of this impact is hard to define, it cannot be disputed that close-minded individuals used negative stereotypes to bolster their racist views, and that the general absence of positive archetypes was demoralizing.

We hope you will read "Lost on a Desert Island" as a document of its less enlightened time—but also as a fascinating glimpse into the rigors of starting a comic strip, and as an essential dry run for classic stories that came later. We've been given the opportunity to enjoy this comic creation in full, so let's look for the spirit of wonder and exploration that remains a part of it. •

The author wishes to thank J. B. Kaufman for sharing invaluable research material.

ABOVE: Cover to Mexican *Paquito* comic (1935) illustrating "Lost on a Desert Island." Artist and issue number unknown; image courtesy Didier Ghez.

CENTER: Cover to French *Albums Mickey* 1 (1931), collecting "Lost on a Desert Island." Artist unknown.

FAR RIGHT: Cover to Italian *Albo D'Oro* 37005 (1937), illustrating "Lost on a Desert Island." Art by Michele Rubino; image courtesy Leonardo Gori.

1 Nationalencyklopedin, "Finland: Massmedier." Nationalencylopedin government website, http://www.ne.se/finland/massmedier (accessed August 30, 2010).

2 Walt Disney, 1956 quote reprinted in Cecil Munsey, *Disneyana* (New York: Hawthorn Books, Inc., 1974), p.16.

3 Charles J. Giegerich, letter to Walt Disney, June 8, 1929.

4 Joseph Connolly, letter to Ub Iwerks, July 24, 1929.

5 Ub Iwerks, letter to Joseph Connolly, July 30, 1929.

6 Walt Disney, letter to Charles J. Giegerich, July 30, 1929.

7 Munsey, ibid.

8 Walt Disney, letter to Joseph Connolly, October 19, 1929.

9 King Features Syndicate, telegram to Disney, December 30, 1929.

10 Floyd Gottfredson, introduction to *Walt Disney Best Comics—Mickey Mouse* (New York: Abbeville Press, Inc., 1978), p. 11.

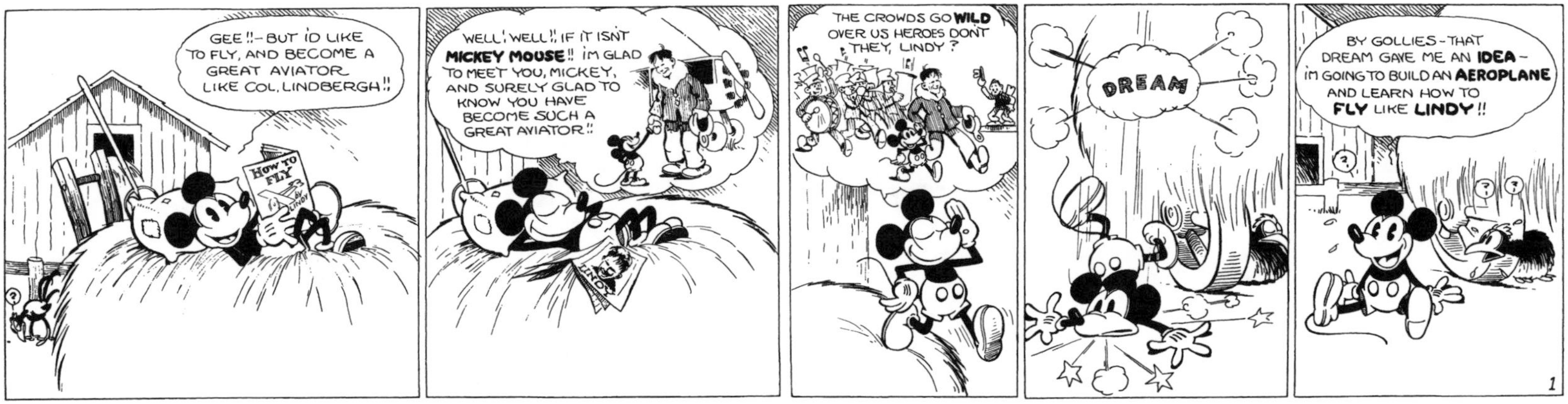
GEE!!-BUT I'D LIKE TO FLY, AND BECOME A GREAT AVIATOR LIKE COL. LINDBERGH!!
HOW TO FLY
WELL! WELL!! IF IT ISN'T **MICKEY MOUSE**!! I'M GLAD TO MEET YOU, MICKEY, AND SURELY GLAD TO KNOW YOU HAVE BECOME SUCH A GREAT AVIATOR!!
THE CROWDS GO **WILD** OVER US HEROES DON'T THEY, LINDY?
DREAM
BY GOLLIES-THAT DREAM GAVE ME AN **IDEA**-I'M GOING TO BUILD AN **AEROPLANE** AND LEARN HOW TO **FLY** LIKE **LINDY**!!
1

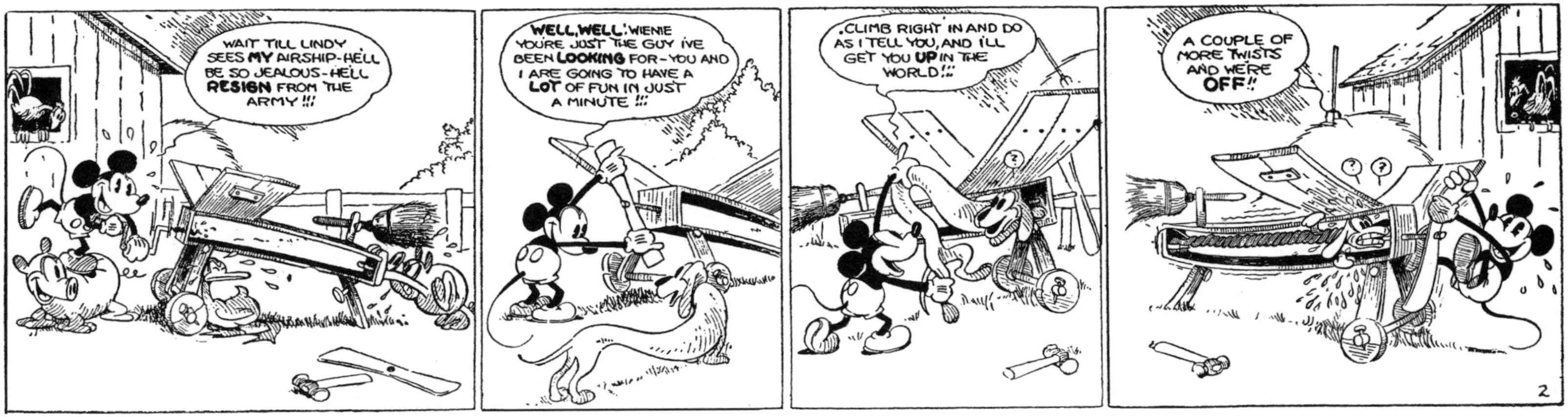
WAIT TILL LINDY SEES **MY** AIRSHIP-HE'LL BE SO JEALOUS-HE'LL **RESIGN** FROM THE ARMY!!!
WELL, WELL! WIENIE YOU'RE JUST THE GUY I'VE BEEN **LOOKING** FOR-YOU AND I ARE GOING TO HAVE A **LOT** OF FUN IN JUST A MINUTE!!!
CLIMB RIGHT IN AND DO AS I TELL YOU, AND I'LL GET YOU **UP** IN THE WORLD!!!
A COUPLE OF MORE TWISTS AND WE'RE **OFF**!!
2

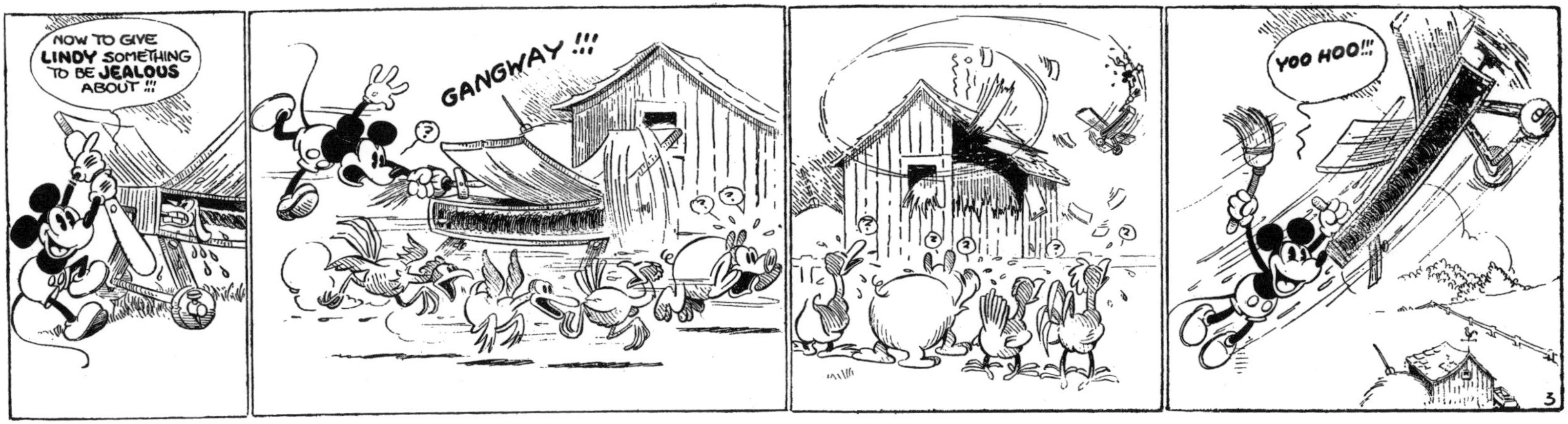
NOW TO GIVE **LINDY** SOMETHING TO BE **JEALOUS** ABOUT!!!
GANGWAY!!!
YOO HOO!!!
3

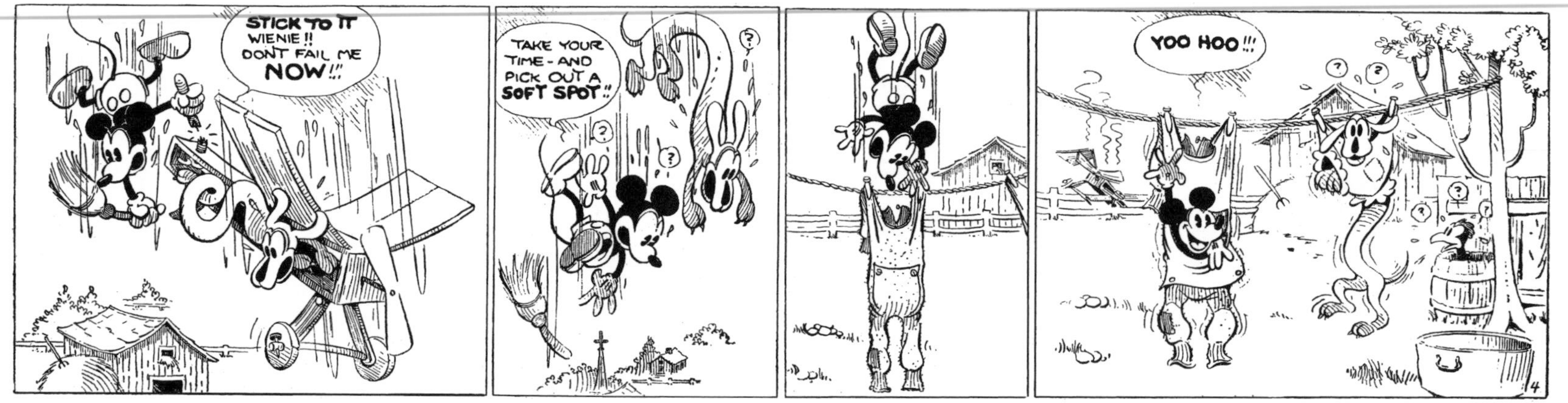
STICK TO IT WIENIE!! DONT FAIL ME NOW!!
TAKE YOUR TIME - AND PICK OUT A SOFT SPOT!!
YOO HOO!!!
4

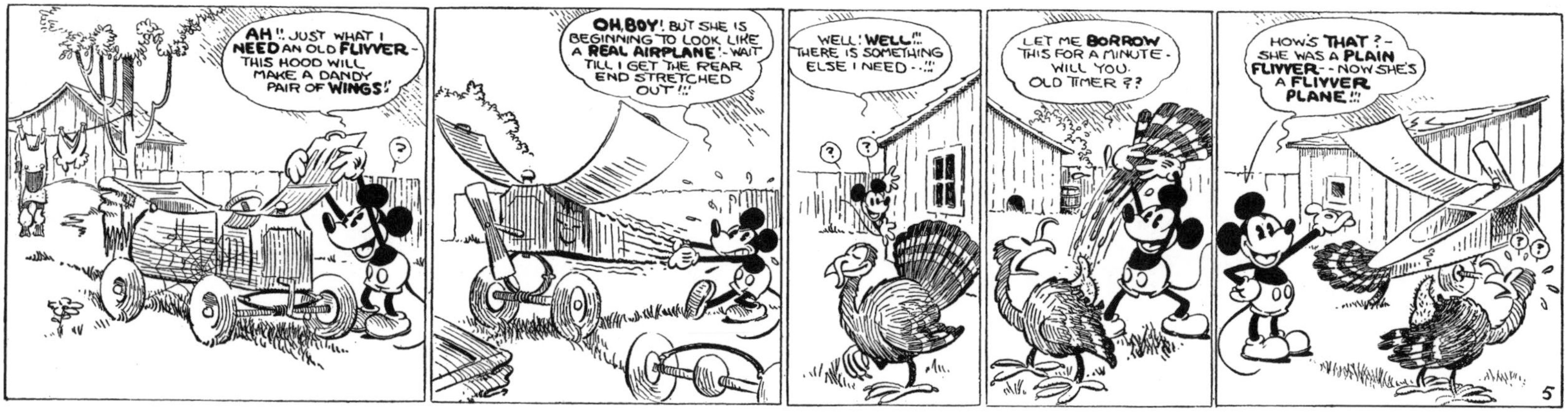
AH!! JUST WHAT I NEED AN OLD FLIVVER - THIS HOOD WILL MAKE A DANDY PAIR OF WINGS!!
OH, BOY! BUT SHE IS BEGINNING TO LOOK LIKE A REAL AIRPLANE!- WAIT TILL I GET THE REAR END STRETCHED OUT!!
WELL! WELL!! THERE IS SOMETHING ELSE I NEED - -!!
LET ME BORROW THIS FOR A MINUTE - WILL YOU, OLD TIMER ??
HOW'S THAT ? - SHE WAS A PLAIN FLIVVER - - NOW SHE'S A FLIVVER PLANE!!!
5

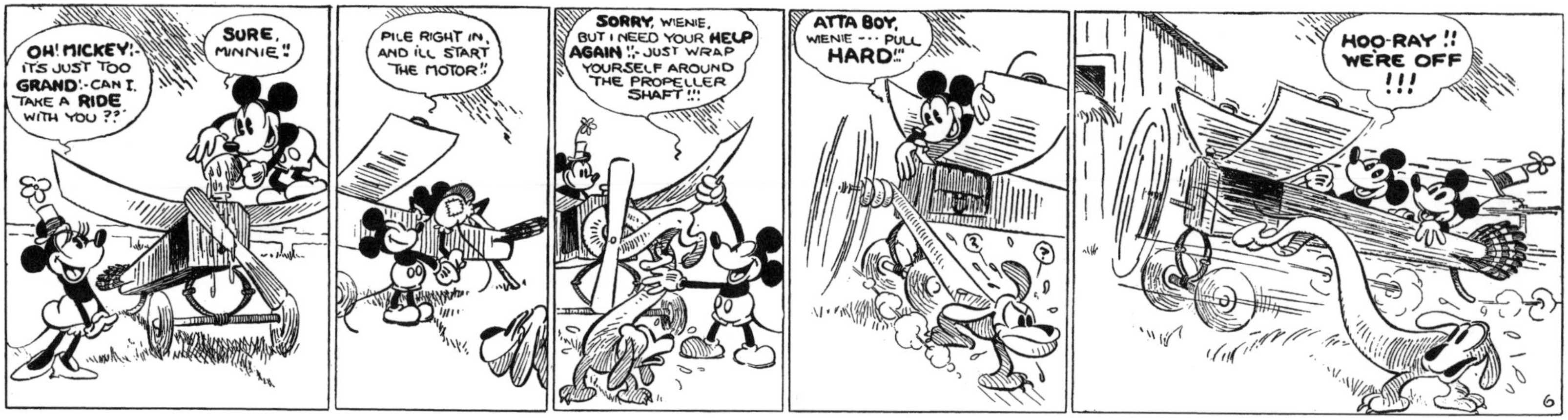
OH! MICKEY!- IT'S JUST TOO GRAND!- CAN I TAKE A RIDE WITH YOU ??
SURE, MINNIE!!
PILE RIGHT IN, AND I'LL START THE MOTOR!!
SORRY, WIENIE, BUT I NEED YOUR HELP AGAIN!!- JUST WRAP YOURSELF AROUND THE PROPELLER SHAFT!!!
ATTA BOY, WIENIE - - - PULL HARD!!
HOO-RAY!! WE'RE OFF!!!
6

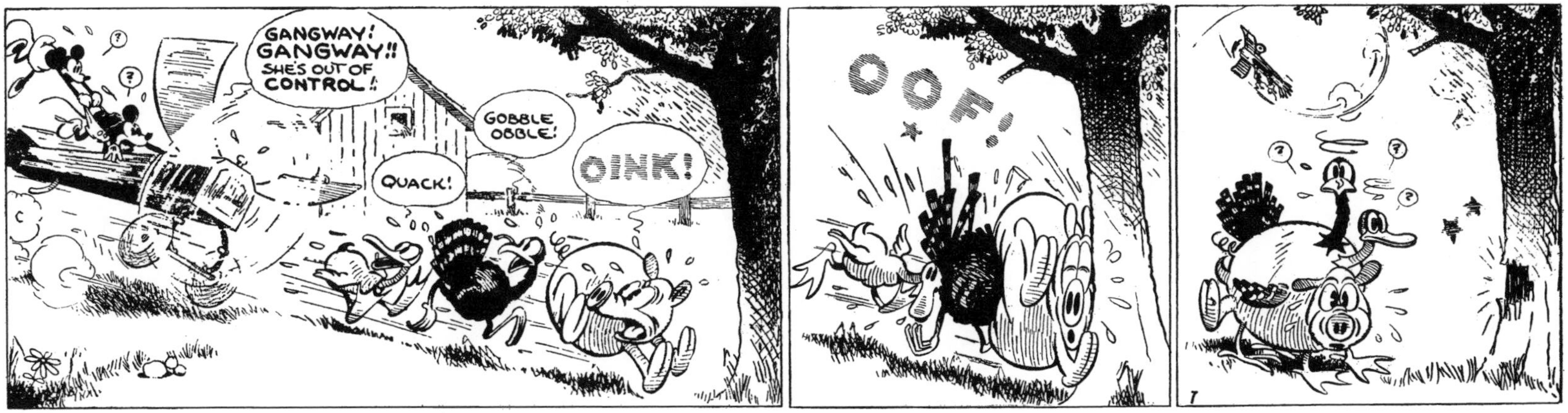
GANGWAY! GANGWAY!! SHE'S OUT OF CONTROL!!
GOBBLE OBBLE!
QUACK!
OINK!
OOF!
7

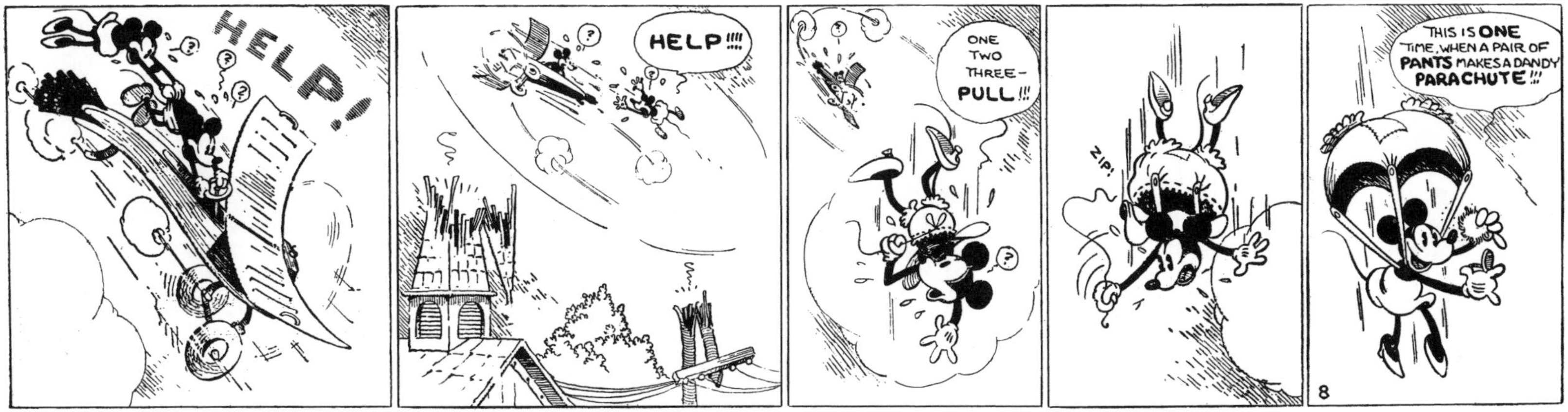
HELP!
HELP!!!!
ONE TWO THREE- PULL!!!
ZIP!
THIS IS ONE TIME, WHEN A PAIR OF PANTS MAKES A DANDY PARACHUTE!!!
8

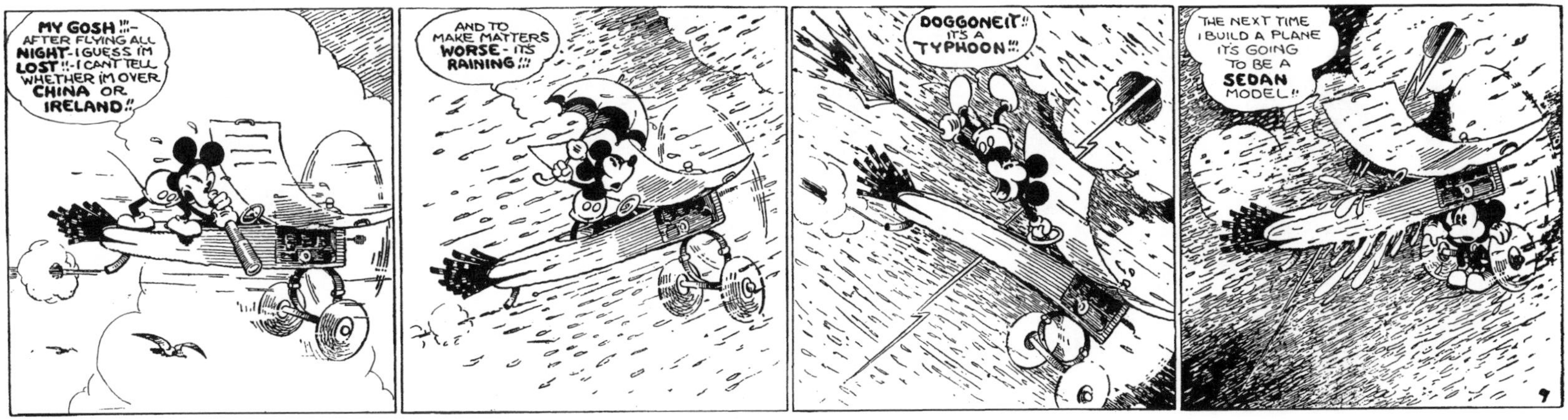
MY GOSH!!- AFTER FLYING ALL NIGHT- I GUESS I'M LOST!!- I CAN'T TELL WHETHER I'M OVER CHINA OR IRELAND!!
AND TO MAKE MATTERS WORSE- IT'S RAINING!!!
DOGGONE IT!! IT'S A TYPHOON!!!
THE NEXT TIME I BUILD A PLANE IT'S GOING TO BE A SEDAN MODEL!!
9

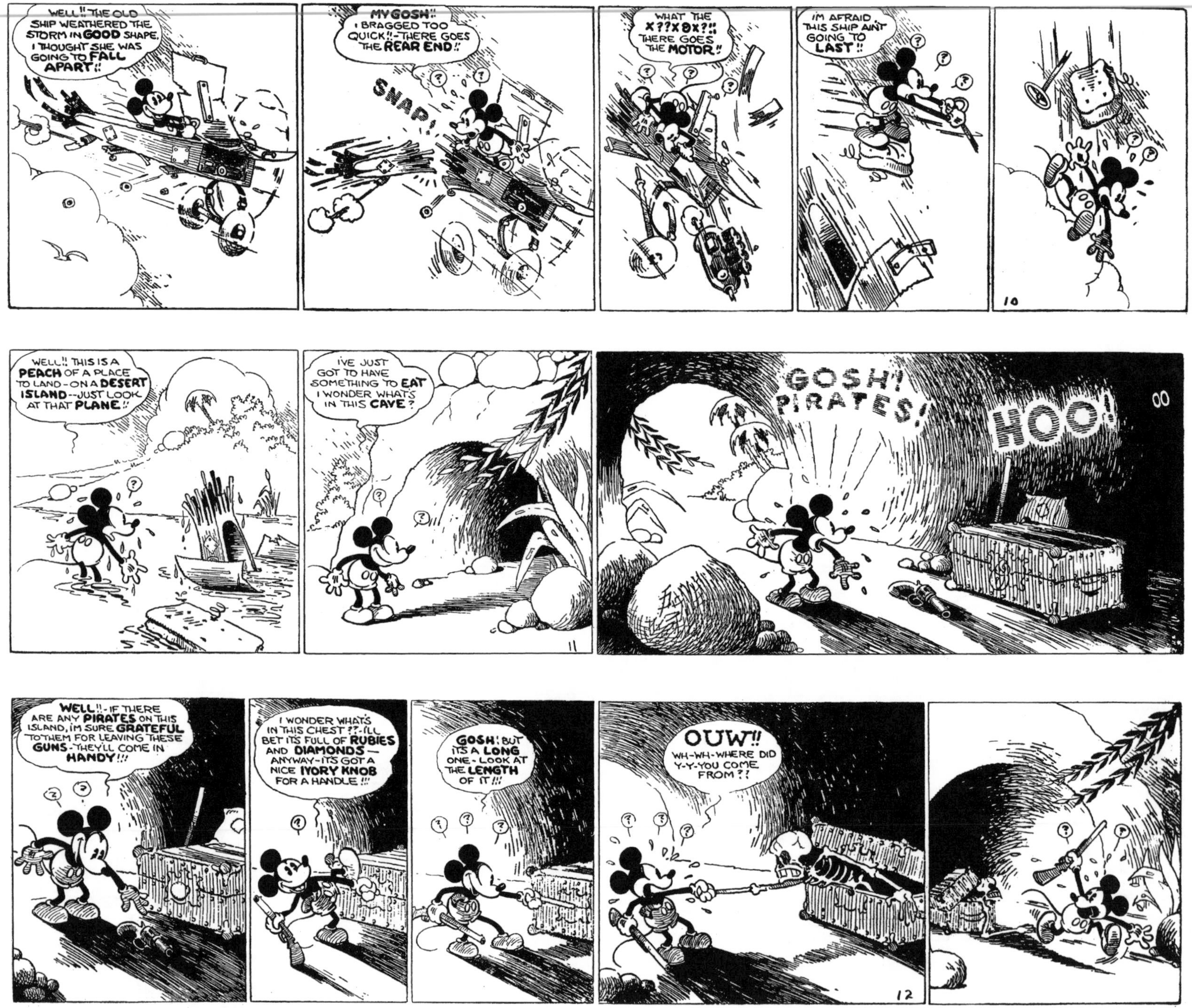
WELL!! THE OLD SHIP WEATHERED THE STORM IN GOOD SHAPE. I THOUGHT SHE WAS GOING TO FALL APART!!
MY GOSH!! I BRAGGED TOO QUICK!!--THERE GOES THE REAR END!!
SNAP!
WHAT THE X??X 9X?!! THERE GOES THE MOTOR!!
IM AFRAID, THIS SHIP AINT GOING TO LAST!!
10
WELL!! THIS IS A PEACH OF A PLACE TO LAND--ON A DESERT ISLAND--JUST LOOK AT THAT PLANE!!
I'VE JUST GOT TO HAVE SOMETHING TO EAT I WONDER WHAT'S IN THIS CAVE?
11
GOSH! PIRATES!
HOO!
OO
WELL!!--IF THERE ARE ANY PIRATES ON THIS ISLAND, IM SURE GRATEFUL TO THEM FOR LEAVING THESE GUNS--THEY'LL COME IN HANDY!!!
I WONDER WHAT'S IN THIS CHEST??--I'LL BET ITS FULL OF RUBIES AND DIAMONDS--ANYWAY--IT'S GOT A NICE IVORY KNOB FOR A HANDLE!!!
GOSH! BUT ITS A LONG ONE--LOOK AT THE LENGTH OF IT!!!
OUW!! WH-WH-WHERE DID Y-Y-YOU COME FROM??
12

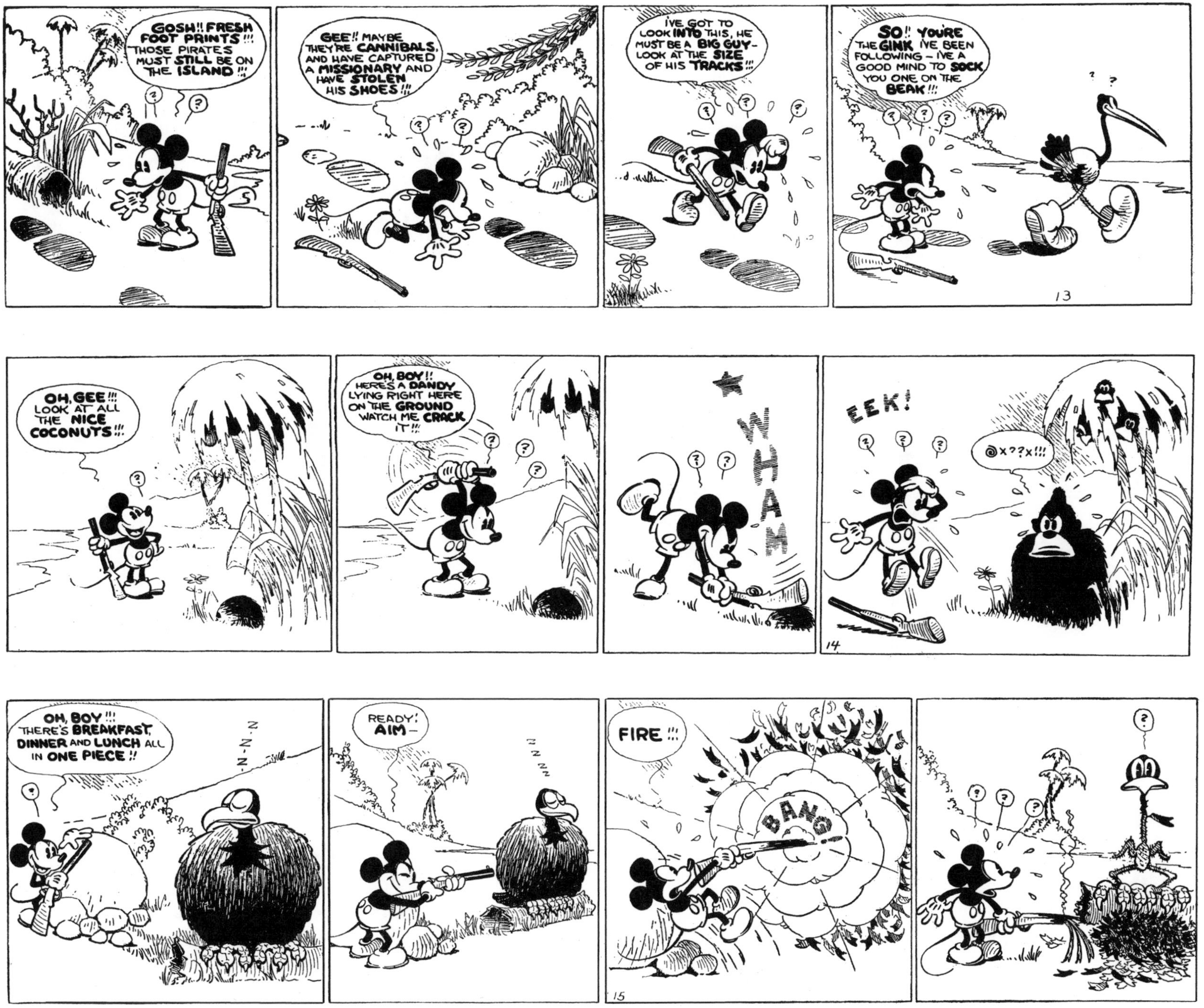
GOSH!! FRESH FOOT PRINTS!!! THOSE PIRATES MUST STILL BE ON THE ISLAND!!!
GEE!! MAYBE THEY'RE CANNIBALS, AND HAVE CAPTURED A MISSIONARY AND HAVE STOLEN HIS SHOES!!!
I'VE GOT TO LOOK INTO THIS, HE MUST BE A BIG GUY- LOOK AT THE SIZE OF HIS TRACKS!!!
SO!! YOU'RE THE GINK I'VE BEEN FOLLOWING - I'VE A GOOD MIND TO SOCK YOU ONE ON THE BEAK!!!
13
OH, GEE!!! LOOK AT ALL THE NICE COCONUTS!!!
OH, BOY!! HERE'S A DANDY LYING RIGHT HERE ON THE GROUND WATCH ME CRACK IT!!!
WHAM
EEK!
x??x!!!
14
OH, BOY!!! THERE'S BREAKFAST, DINNER AND LUNCH ALL IN ONE PIECE!!
Z-Z-Z
READY! AIM-
Z Z Z
FIRE!!!
BANG
15

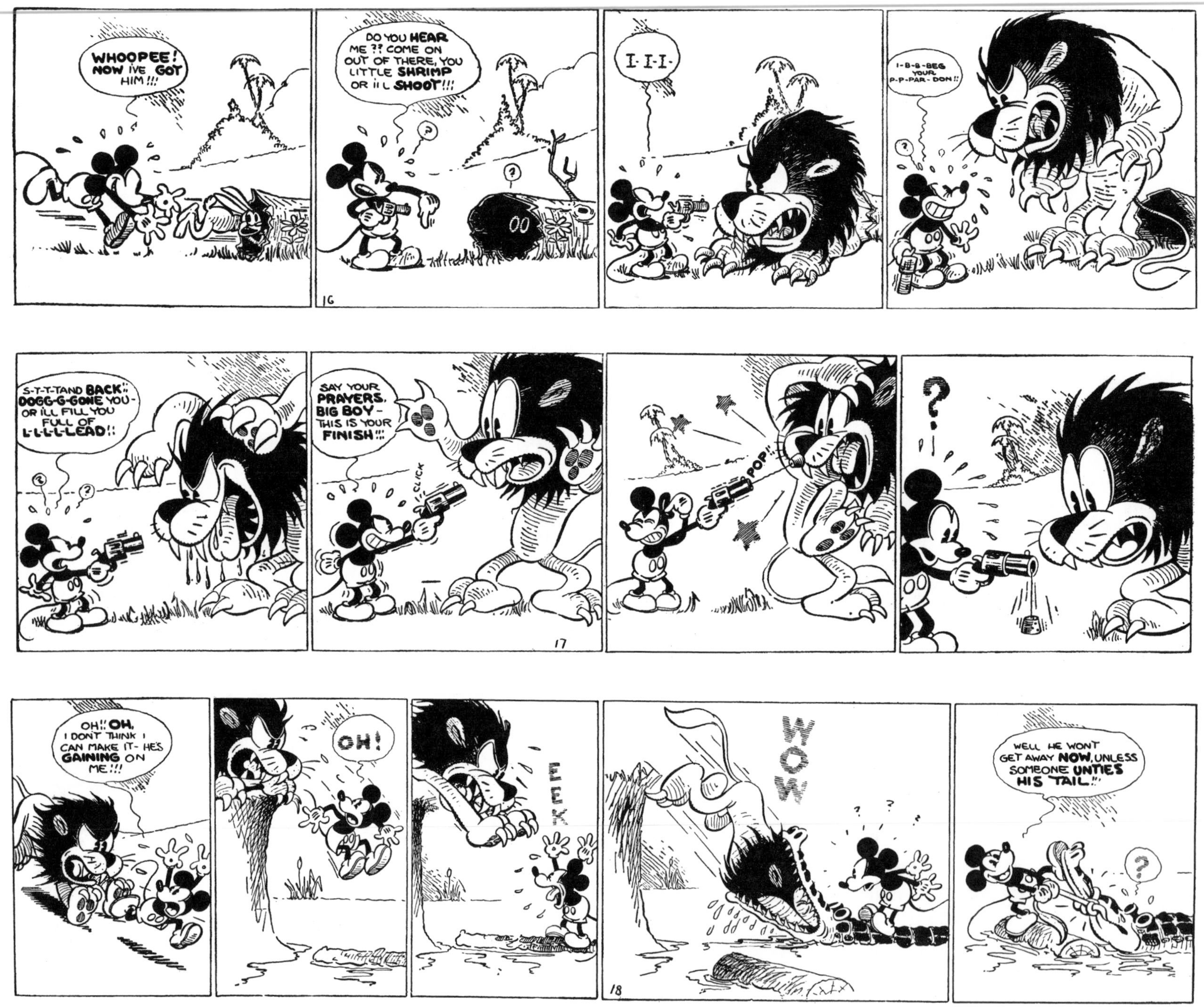
WHOOPEE! NOW I'VE GOT HIM!!!
DO YOU HEAR ME ?? COME ON OUT OF THERE, YOU LITTLE SHRIMP OR I'LL SHOOT!!!
16
I-I-I-
I-B-B-BEG YOUR P-P-PAR-DON!!
S-T-T-TAND BACK!! DOGG-G-GONE YOU - OR I'LL FILL YOU FULL OF L-L-L-L-LEAD!!
SAY YOUR PRAYERS, BIG BOY - THIS IS YOUR FINISH!!!
CLICK
17
POP!!
OH!! OH, I DON'T THINK I CAN MAKE IT - HE'S GAINING ON ME!!!
OH!
EEEK
WOW
18
WELL HE WON'T GET AWAY NOW, UNLESS SOMEONE UNTIES HIS TAIL!!

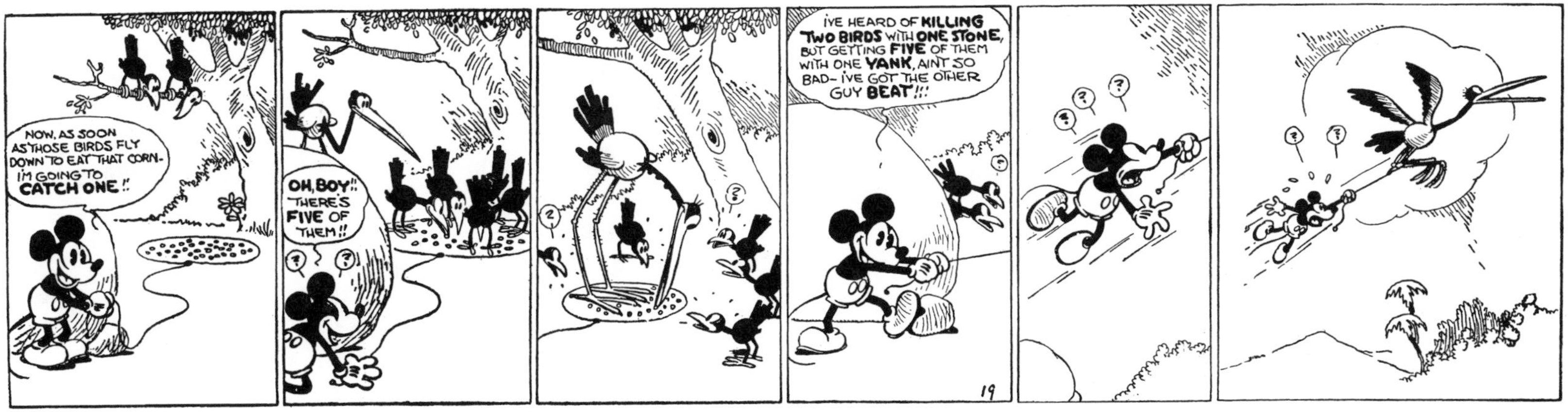
NOW, AS SOON AS THOSE BIRDS FLY DOWN TO EAT THAT CORN- I'M GOING TO CATCH ONE!!
OH, BOY!! THERE'S FIVE OF THEM!!
I'VE HEARD OF KILLING TWO BIRDS WITH ONE STONE, BUT GETTING FIVE OF THEM WITH ONE YANK, AINT SO BAD- I'VE GOT THE OTHER GUY BEAT!!!
19

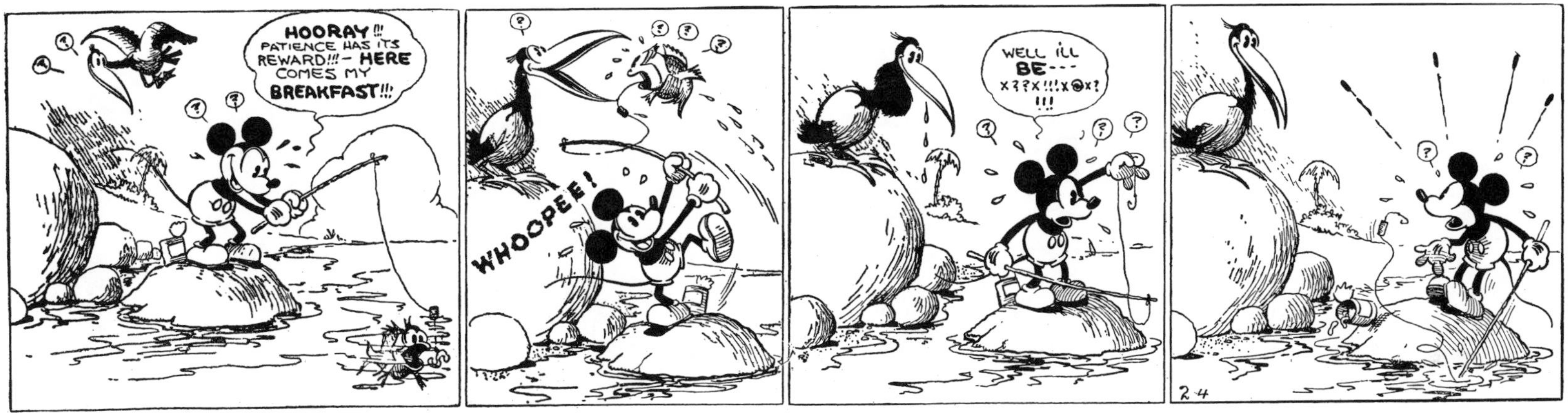
HOORAY!! PATIENCE HAS ITS REWARD!!!- HERE COMES MY BREAKFAST!!!
WHOOPEE!
WELL I'LL BE--- X??X!!!X@X? !!!
2-4

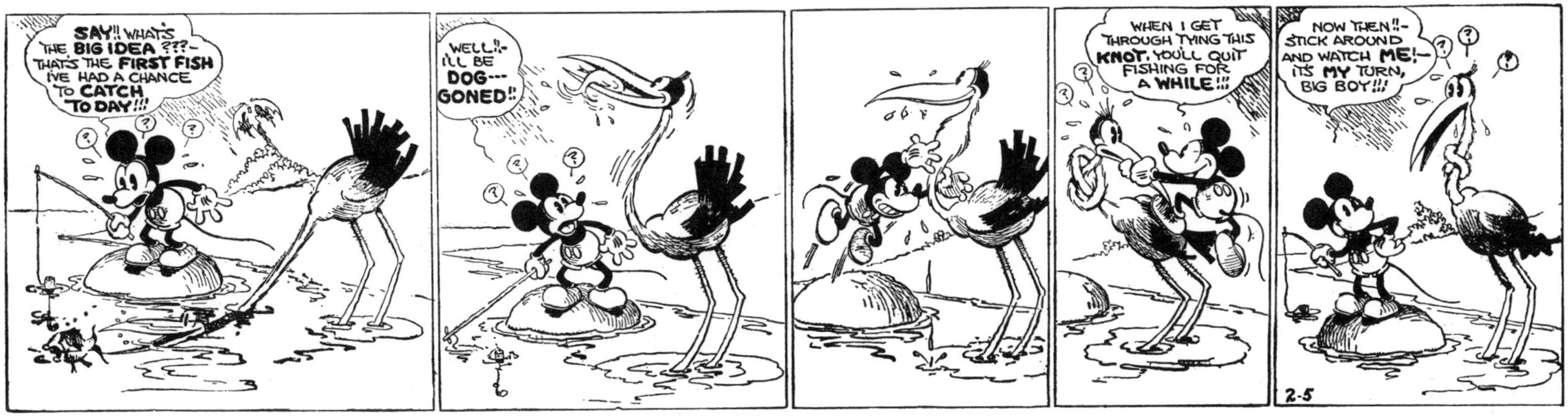
SAY!! WHAT'S THE BIG IDEA ???- THAT'S THE FIRST FISH I'VE HAD A CHANCE TO CATCH TO DAY!!!
WELL!!- I'LL BE DOG--- GONED!!
WHEN I GET THROUGH TYING THIS KNOT, YOU'LL QUIT FISHING FOR A WHILE!!!
NOW THEN!!- STICK AROUND AND WATCH ME!- IT'S MY TURN, BIG BOY!!!
2-5

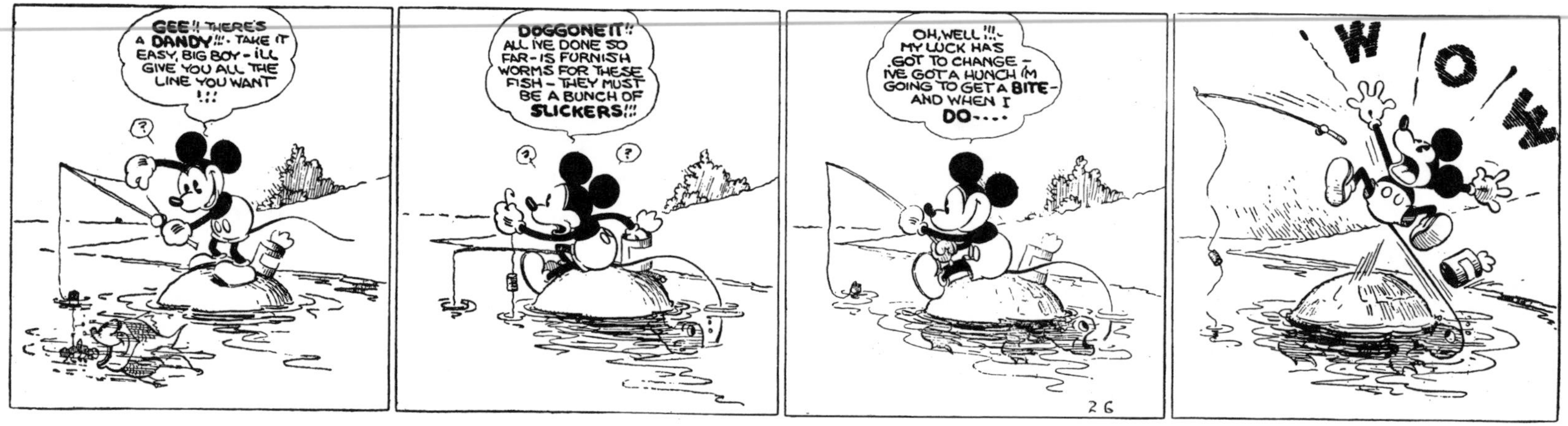
GEE!! THERE'S A DANDY!!!- TAKE IT EASY, BIG BOY - I'LL GIVE YOU ALL THE LINE YOU WANT !!!
DOGGONE IT!! ALL I'VE DONE SO FAR - IS FURNISH WORMS FOR THESE FISH - THEY MUST BE A BUNCH OF SLICKERS!!!
OH, WELL!!!- MY LUCK HAS GOT TO CHANGE - I'VE GOT A HUNCH I'M GOING TO GET A BITE - AND WHEN I DO....
2 6
WOW

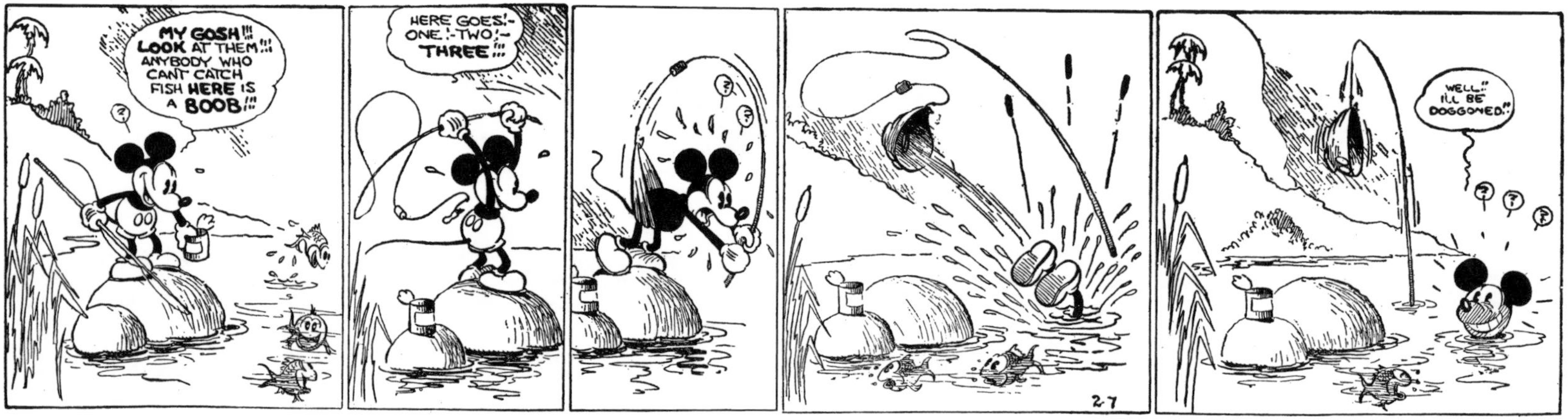
MY GOSH!!! LOOK AT THEM!!! ANYBODY WHO CAN'T CATCH FISH HERE IS A BOOB!!!
HERE GOES!- ONE!- TWO!- THREE!!!
2 7
WELL!! I'LL BE DOGGONED!!

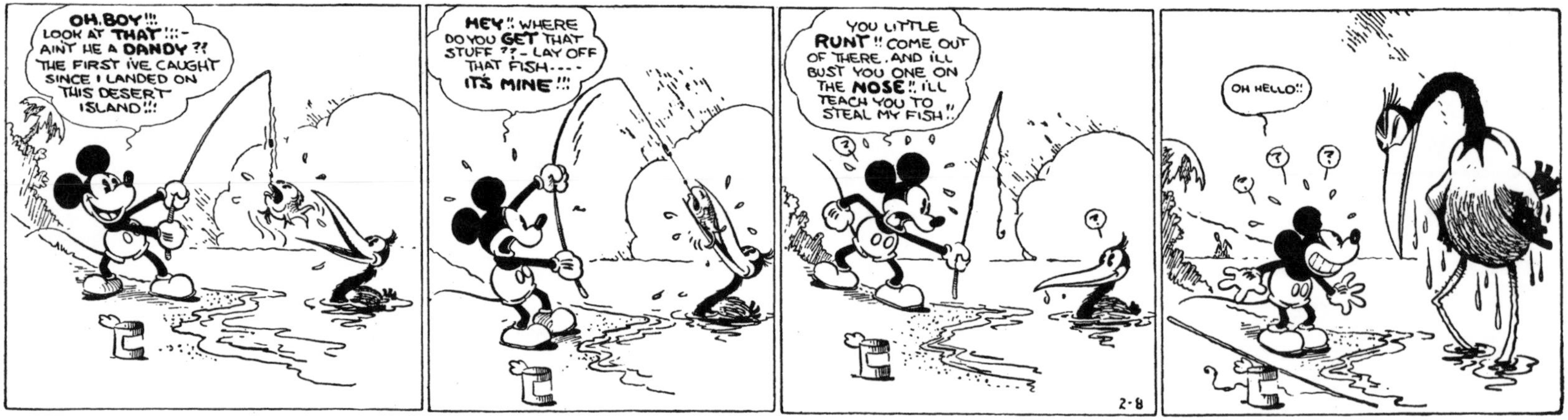
OH, BOY!!! LOOK AT THAT!!!- AIN'T HE A DANDY?? THE FIRST I'VE CAUGHT SINCE I LANDED ON THIS DESERT ISLAND!!!
HEY!! WHERE DO YOU GET THAT STUFF ??- LAY OFF THAT FISH--- IT'S MINE!!!
YOU LITTLE RUNT!! COME OUT OF THERE, AND I'LL BUST YOU ONE ON THE NOSE!! I'LL TEACH YOU TO STEAL MY FISH!!
2-8
OH HELLO!!

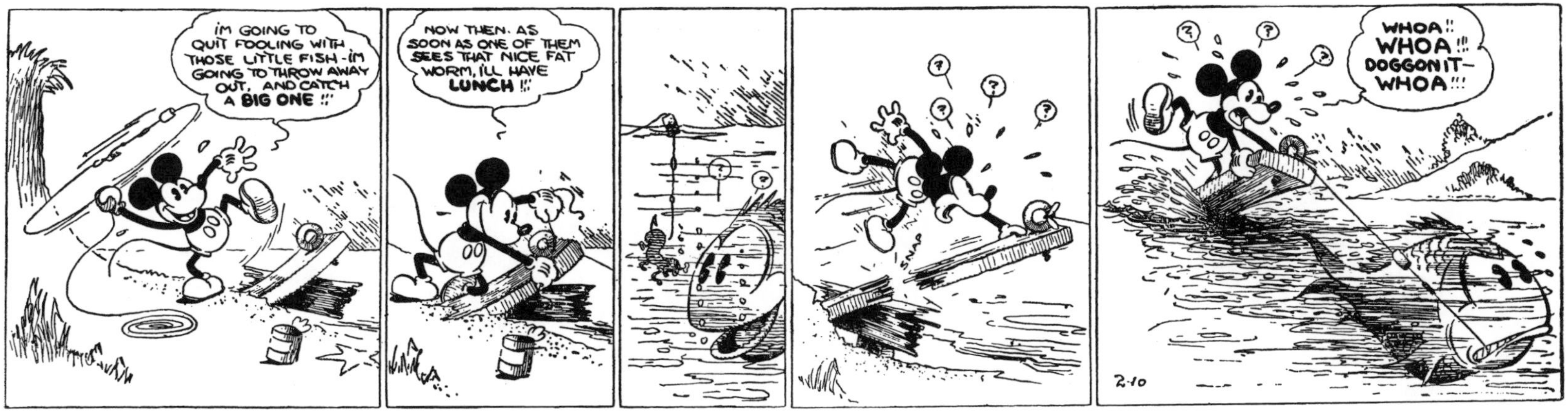
IM GOING TO QUIT FOOLING WITH THOSE LITTLE FISH - IM GOING TO THROW AWAY OUT, AND CATCH A BIG ONE !!
NOW THEN. AS SOON AS ONE OF THEM SEES THAT NICE FAT WORM, I'LL HAVE LUNCH !!
WHOA !! WHOA !!! DOGGONIT - WHOA !!!
2-10

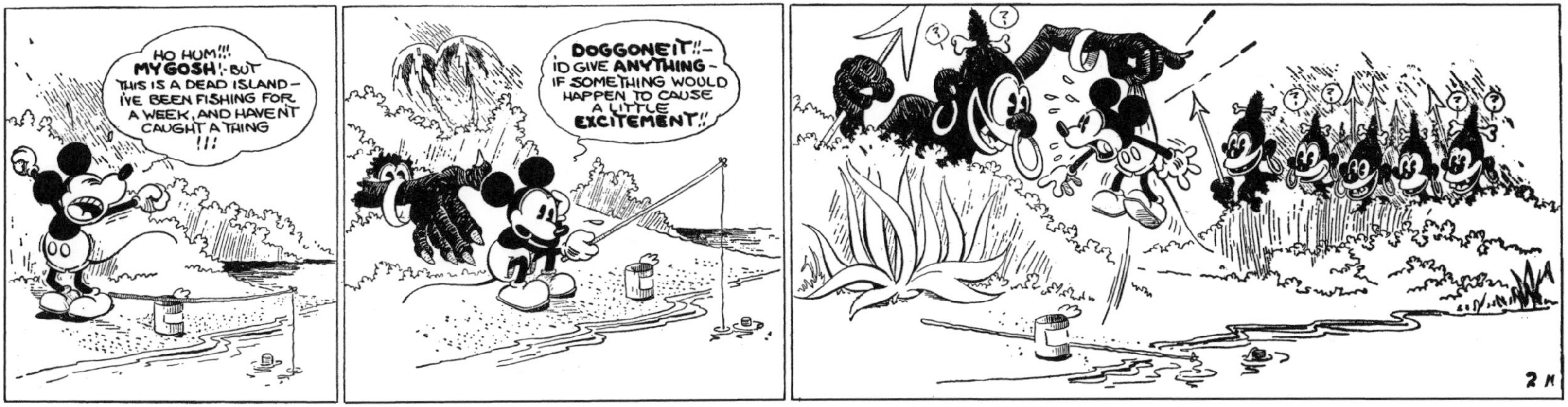
HO HUM !!! MY GOSH !- BUT THIS IS A DEAD ISLAND - I'VE BEEN FISHING FOR A WEEK, AND HAVENT CAUGHT A THING !!!
DOGGONEIT !!- I'D GIVE ANYTHING - IF SOMETHING WOULD HAPPEN TO CAUSE A LITTLE EXCITEMENT !!

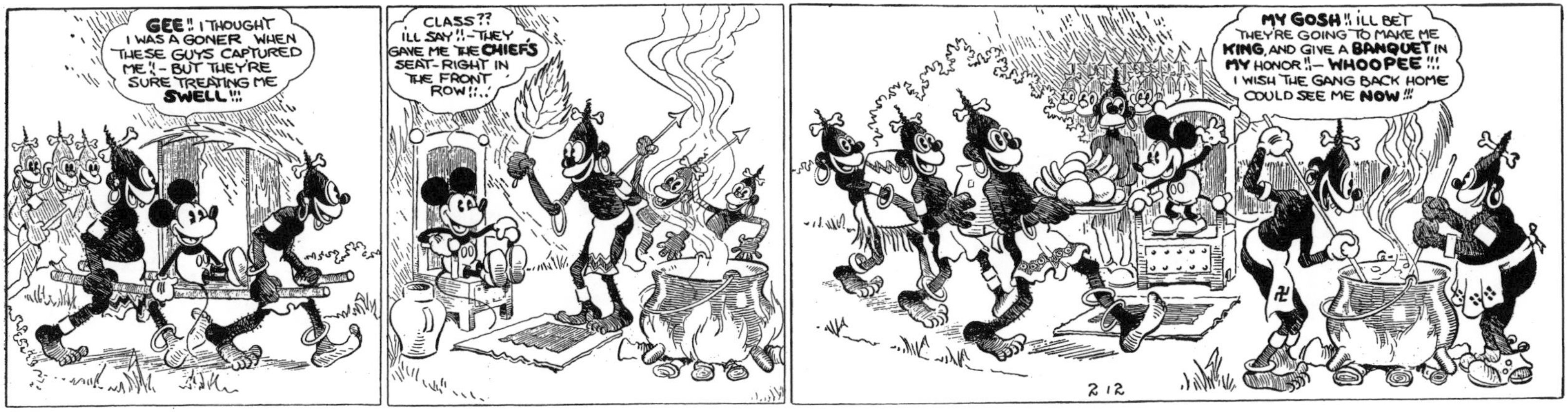
GEE !! I THOUGHT I WAS A GONER WHEN THESE GUYS CAPTURED ME !! - BUT THEY'RE SURE TREATING ME SWELL !!!
CLASS ?? I'LL SAY !! - THEY GAVE ME THE CHIEF'S SEAT - RIGHT IN THE FRONT ROW !!
MY GOSH !! I'LL BET THEY'RE GOING TO MAKE ME KING, AND GIVE A BANQUET IN MY HONOR !! - WHOOPEE !!! I WISH THE GANG BACK HOME COULD SEE ME NOW !!!
2 12

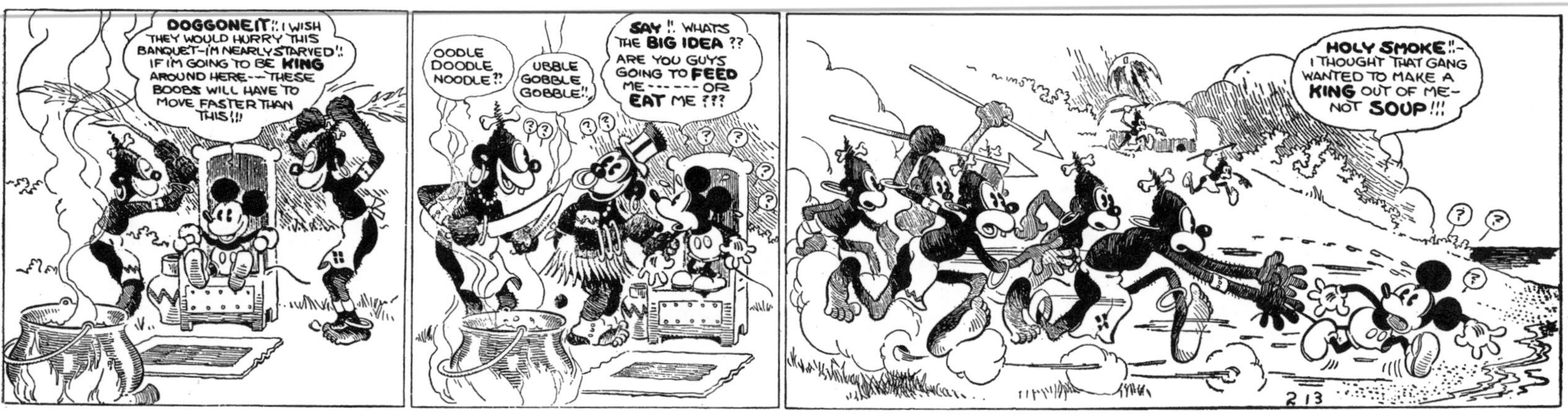
DOGGONE IT!! I WISH THEY WOULD HURRY THIS BANQUET—I'M NEARLY STARVED!! IF I'M GOING TO BE KING AROUND HERE— —THESE BOOBS WILL HAVE TO MOVE FASTER THAN THIS!!!
OODLE DOODLE NOODLE?!
UBBLE GOBBLE GOBBLE!!
SAY!! WHAT'S THE BIG IDEA?? ARE YOU GUYS GOING TO FEED ME------ OR EAT ME???
HOLY SMOKE!!— I THOUGHT THAT GANG WANTED TO MAKE A KING OUT OF ME— NOT SOUP!!!
2 13

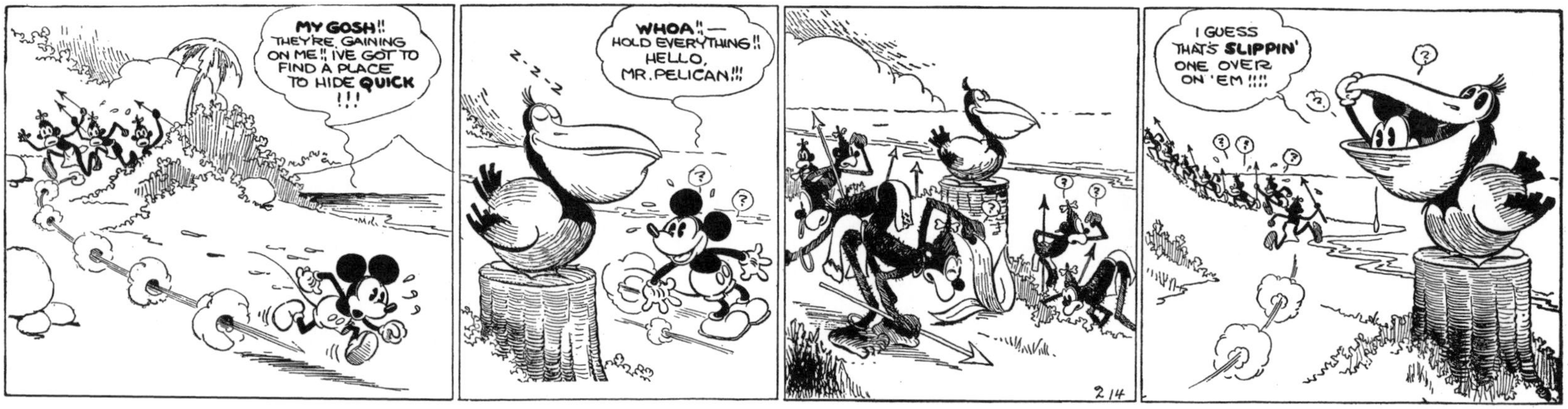
MY GOSH!! THEY'RE GAINING ON ME!! I'VE GOT TO FIND A PLACE TO HIDE QUICK!!!
Z-Z-Z
WHOA!!— HOLD EVERYTHING!! HELLO, MR. PELICAN!!!
2 14
I GUESS THAT'S SLIPPIN' ONE OVER ON 'EM!!!!

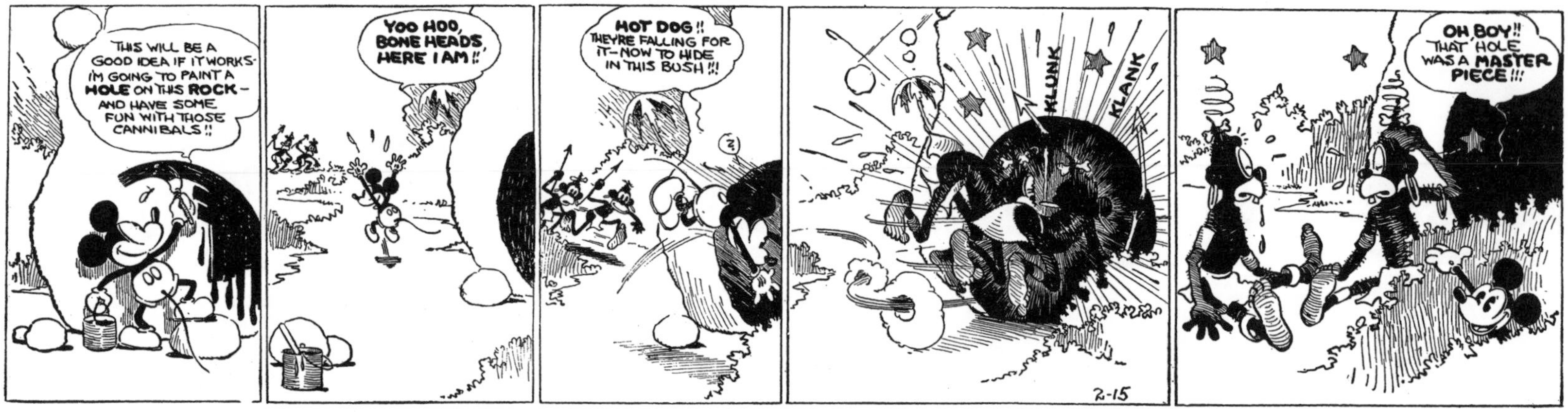
THIS WILL BE A GOOD IDEA IF IT WORKS—I'M GOING TO PAINT A HOLE ON THIS ROCK—AND HAVE SOME FUN WITH THOSE CANNIBALS!!
YOO HOO, BONE HEADS, HERE I AM!!
HOT DOG!! THEY'RE FALLING FOR IT—NOW TO HIDE IN THIS BUSH!!!
KLUNK
KLANK
2-15
OH BOY!! THAT HOLE WAS A MASTER PIECE!!!

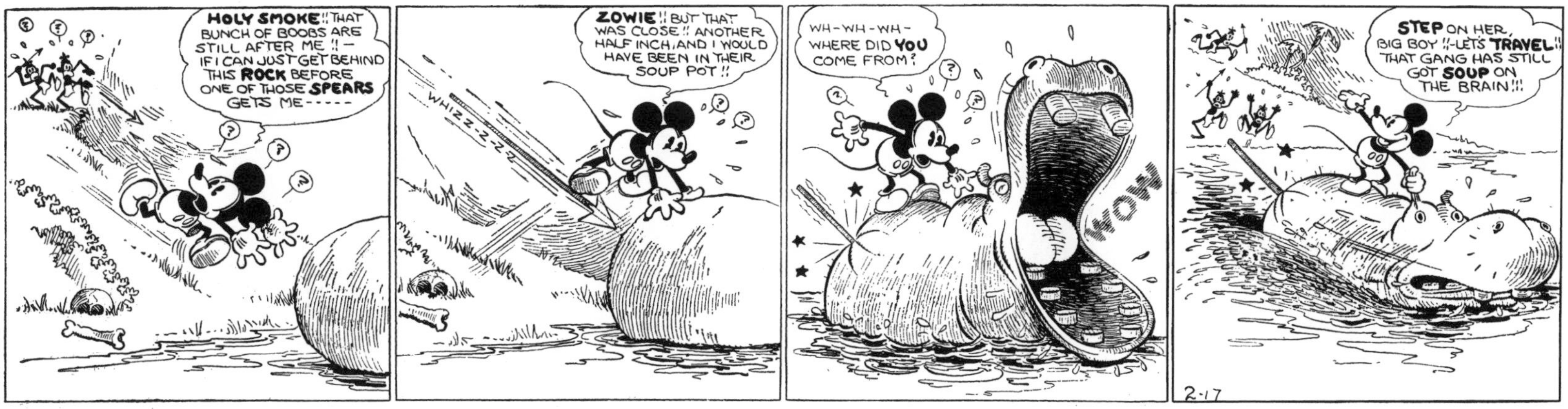
HOLY SMOKE!! THAT BUNCH OF BOOBS ARE STILL AFTER ME!!— IF I CAN JUST GET BEHIND THIS ROCK BEFORE ONE OF THOSE SPEARS GETS ME-----
WHIZZ-Z-Z
ZOWIE!! BUT THAT WAS CLOSE!! ANOTHER HALF INCH, AND I WOULD HAVE BEEN IN THEIR SOUP POT!!
WH-WH-WH- WHERE DID YOU COME FROM?
WOW
STEP ON HER, BIG BOY!!-LET'S TRAVEL!! THAT GANG HAS STILL GOT SOUP ON THE BRAIN!!!
2-17

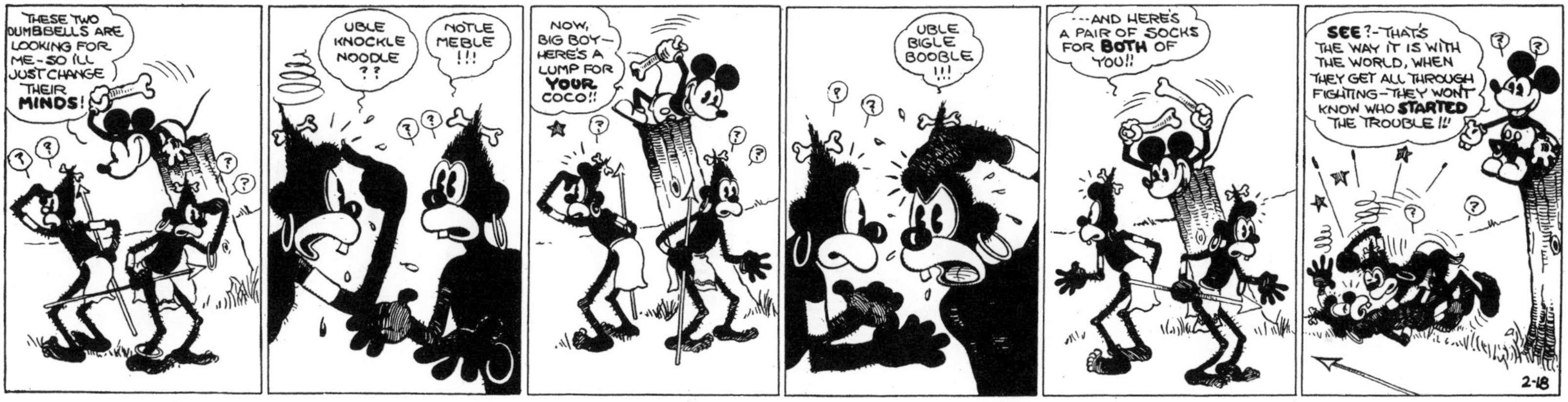
THESE TWO DUMBBELLS ARE LOOKING FOR ME-SO I'LL JUST CHANGE THEIR MINDS!
UBLE KNOCKLE NOODLE ??
NOTLE MEBLE !!!
NOW, BIG BOY— HERE'S A LUMP FOR YOUR COCO!!
UBLE BIGLE BOOBLE !!!
---AND HERE'S A PAIR OF SOCKS FOR BOTH OF YOU!!
SEE?-THAT'S THE WAY IT IS WITH THE WORLD, WHEN THEY GET ALL THROUGH FIGHTING-THEY WON'T KNOW WHO STARTED THE TROUBLE!!
2-18

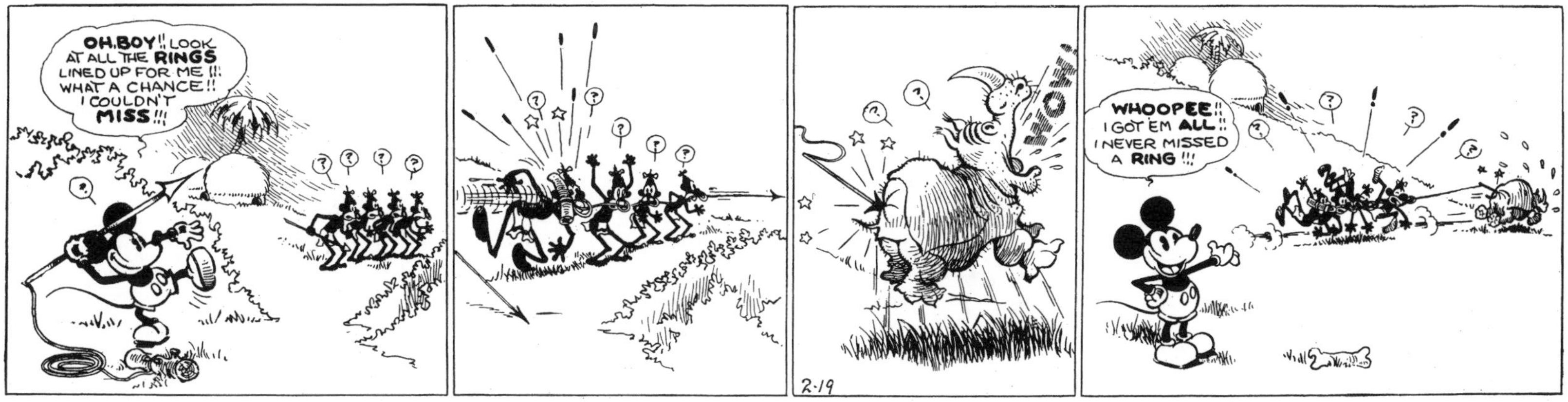
OH, BOY!! LOOK AT ALL THE RINGS LINED UP FOR ME!!! WHAT A CHANCE!! I COULDN'T MISS!!!
WOW!
2-19
WHOOPEE!! I GOT 'EM ALL!! I NEVER MISSED A RING!!!

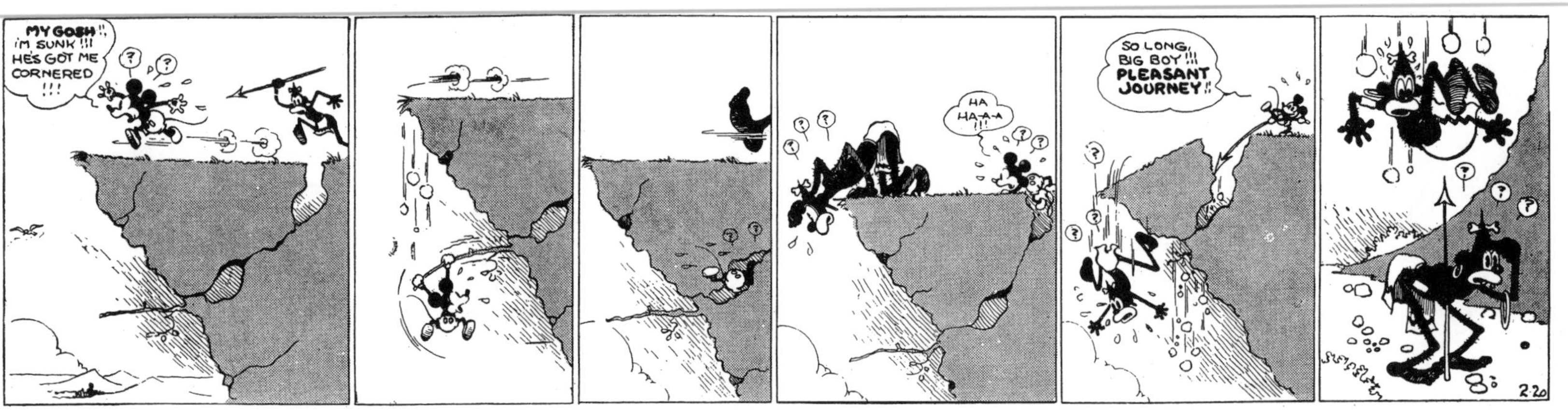
MY GOSH!! I'M SUNK!!! HE'S GOT ME CORNERED!!!
HA HA-A-A !!!
SO LONG, BIG BOY!!! PLEASANT JOURNEY!!
2-20

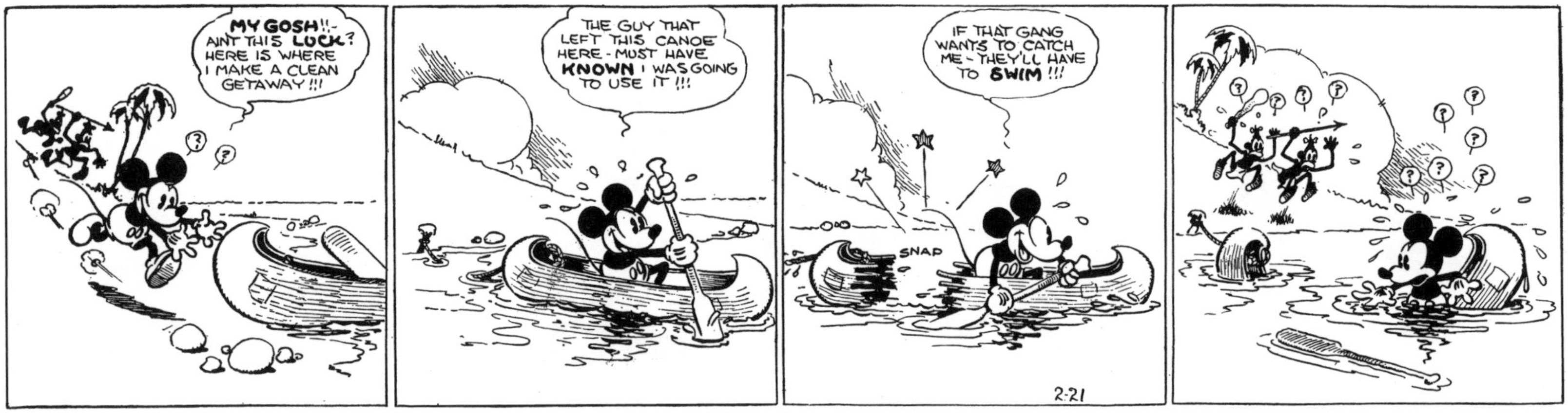
MY GOSH!!- AIN'T THIS LUCK? HERE IS WHERE I MAKE A CLEAN GETAWAY!!!
THE GUY THAT LEFT THIS CANOE HERE - MUST HAVE KNOWN I WAS GOING TO USE IT!!!
IF THAT GANG WANTS TO CATCH ME - THEY'LL HAVE TO SWIM!!!
SNAP
2-21

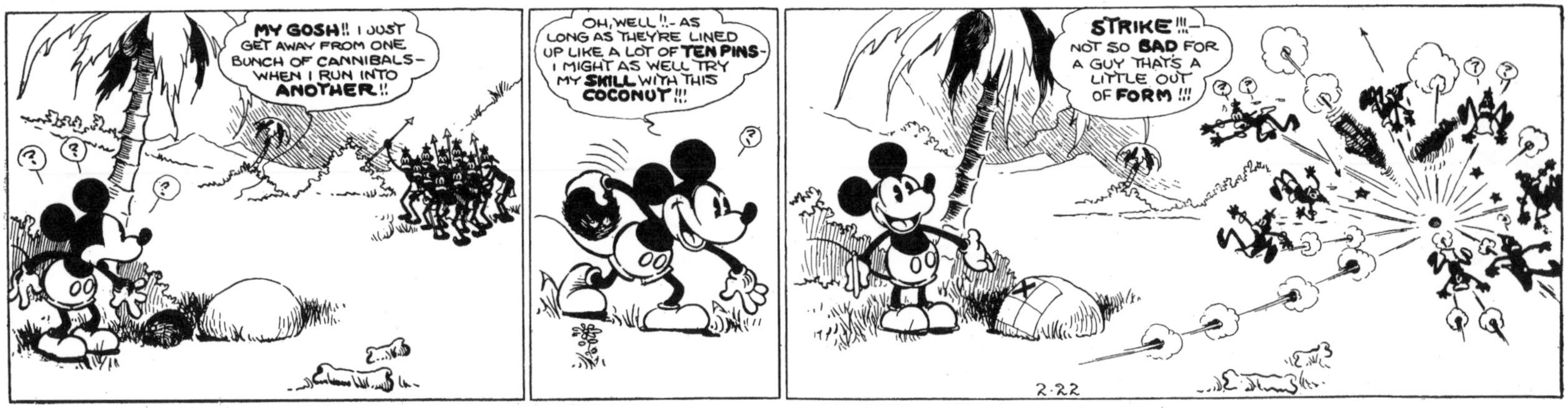
MY GOSH!! I JUST GET AWAY FROM ONE BUNCH OF CANNIBALS- WHEN I RUN INTO ANOTHER!!
OH, WELL!!- AS LONG AS THEY'RE LINED UP LIKE A LOT OF TEN PINS- I MIGHT AS WELL TRY MY SKILL WITH THIS COCONUT!!!
STRIKE!!!- NOT SO BAD FOR A GUY THAT'S A LITTLE OUT OF FORM!!!
2-22

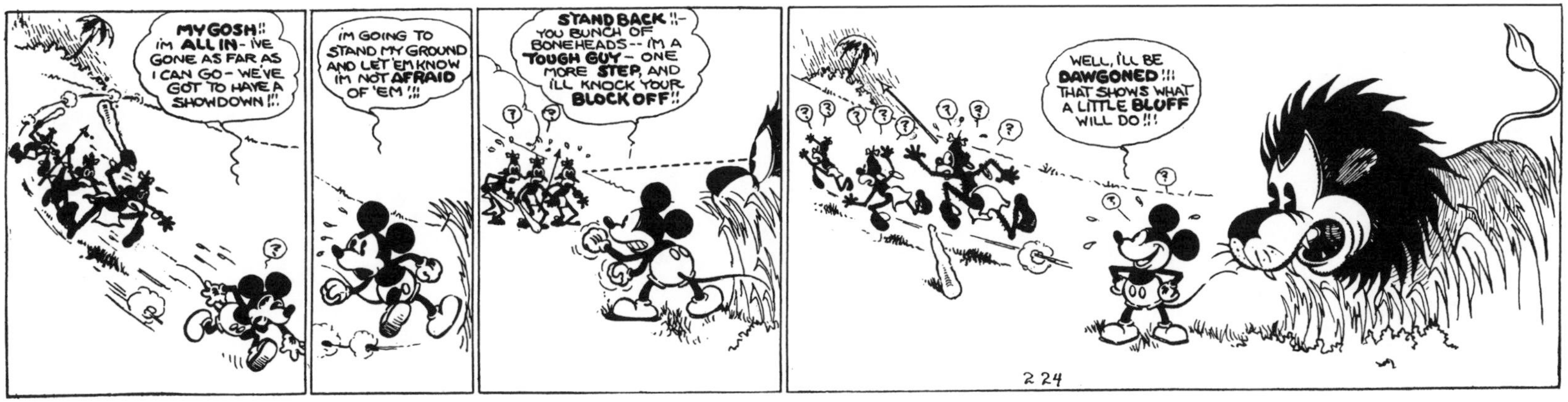
MY GOSH!! IM ALL IN – IVE GONE AS FAR AS I CAN GO – WE'VE GOT TO HAVE A SHOWDOWN!!!
IM GOING TO STAND MY GROUND AND LET 'EM KNOW IM NOT AFRAID OF 'EM!!!
STAND BACK!! – YOU BUNCH OF BONEHEADS -- IM A TOUGH GUY – ONE MORE STEP, AND ILL KNOCK YOUR BLOCK OFF!!
WELL, I'LL BE DAWGONED!!! THAT SHOWS WHAT A LITTLE BLUFF WILL DO!!!
2 24

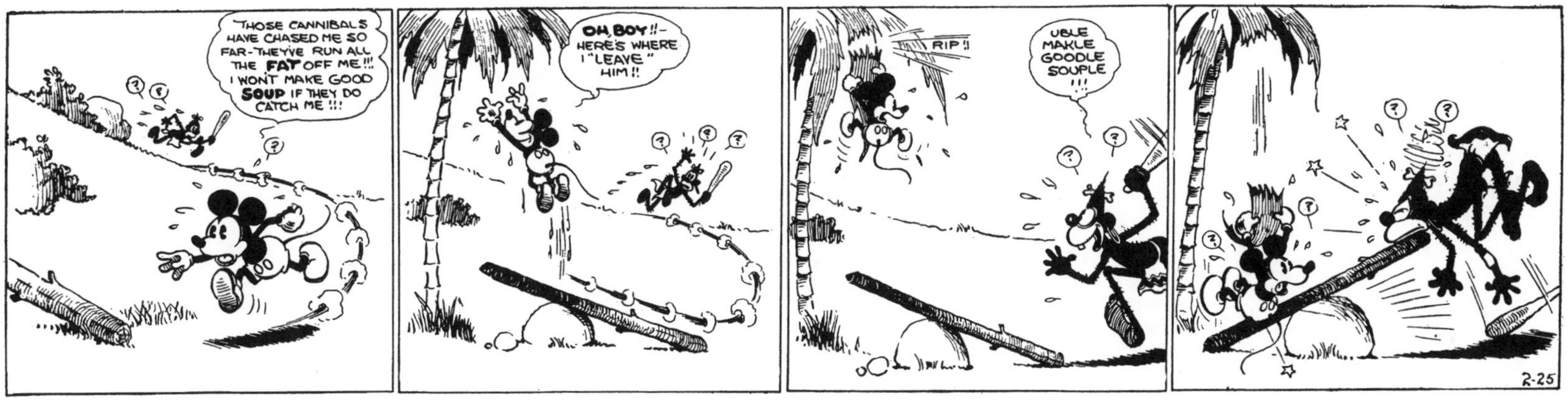
THOSE CANNIBALS HAVE CHASED ME SO FAR – THEY'VE RUN ALL THE FAT OFF ME!!! I WON'T MAKE GOOD SOUP IF THEY DO CATCH ME!!!
OH, BOY!! – HERE'S WHERE I "LEAVE" HIM!!
RIP!!
UBLE MAKLE GOODLE SOUPLE!!!
2-25

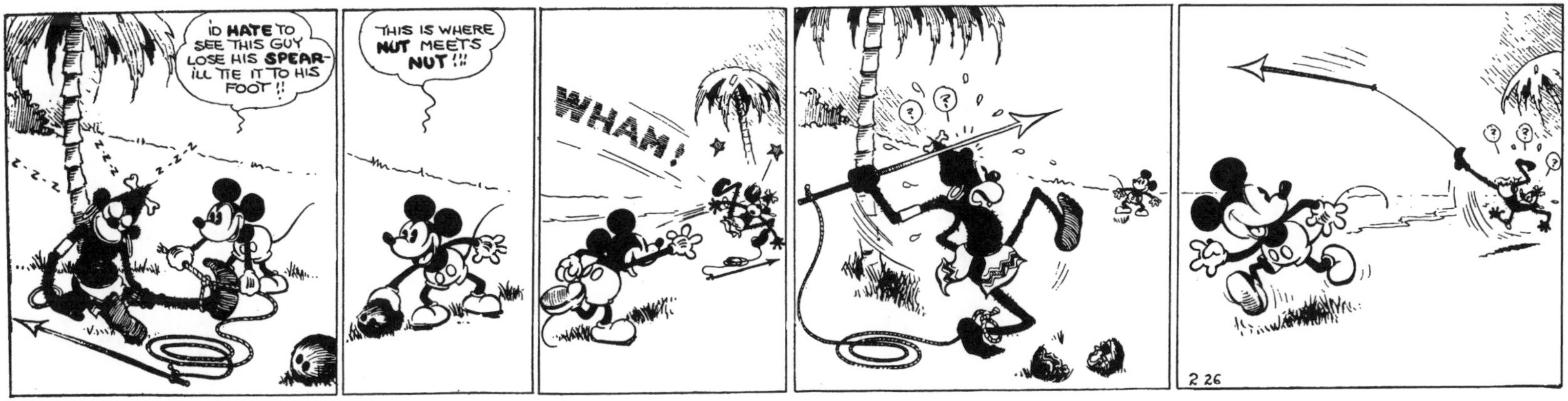
ID HATE TO SEE THIS GUY LOSE HIS SPEAR – ILL TIE IT TO HIS FOOT!!
THIS IS WHERE NUT MEETS NUT!!!
WHAM!
2 26

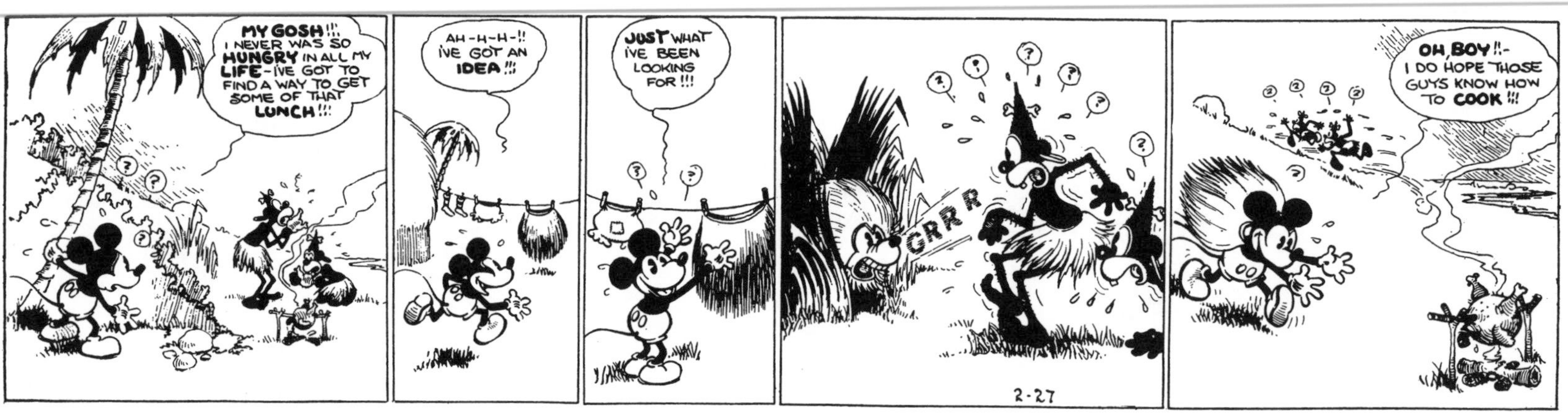
MY GOSH!!! I NEVER WAS SO HUNGRY IN ALL MY LIFE - I'VE GOT TO FIND A WAY TO GET SOME OF THAT LUNCH!!!
AH-H-H-!! I'VE GOT AN IDEA!!!
JUST WHAT I'VE BEEN LOOKING FOR!!!
GRRR
2-27
OH, BOY!!- I DO HOPE THOSE GUYS KNOW HOW TO COOK!!!

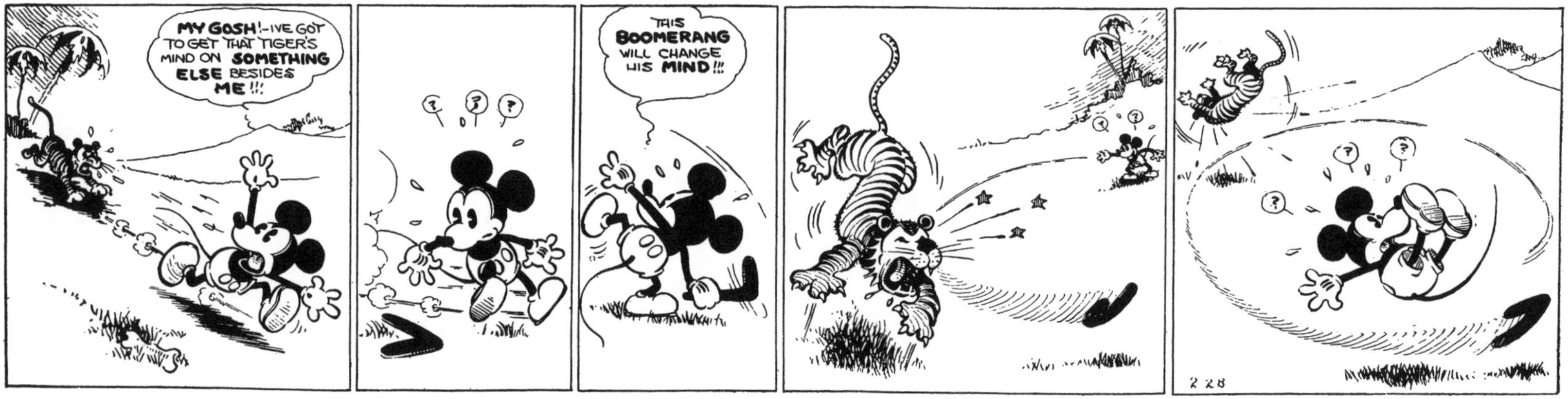
MY GOSH!- I'VE GOT TO GET THAT TIGER'S MIND ON SOMETHING ELSE BESIDES ME!!!
THIS BOOMERANG WILL CHANGE HIS MIND!!!
2 28

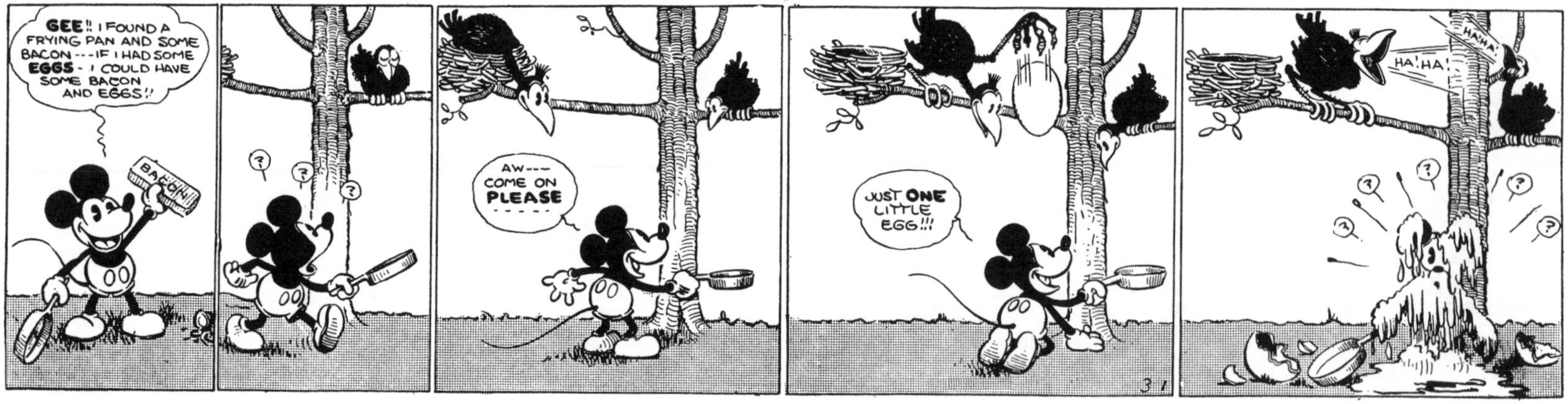
GEE!! I FOUND A FRYING PAN AND SOME BACON---IF I HAD SOME EGGS - I COULD HAVE SOME BACON AND EGGS!!
BACON
AW--- COME ON PLEASE -----
JUST ONE LITTLE EGG!!!
HA! HA!
HA HA!
3 1

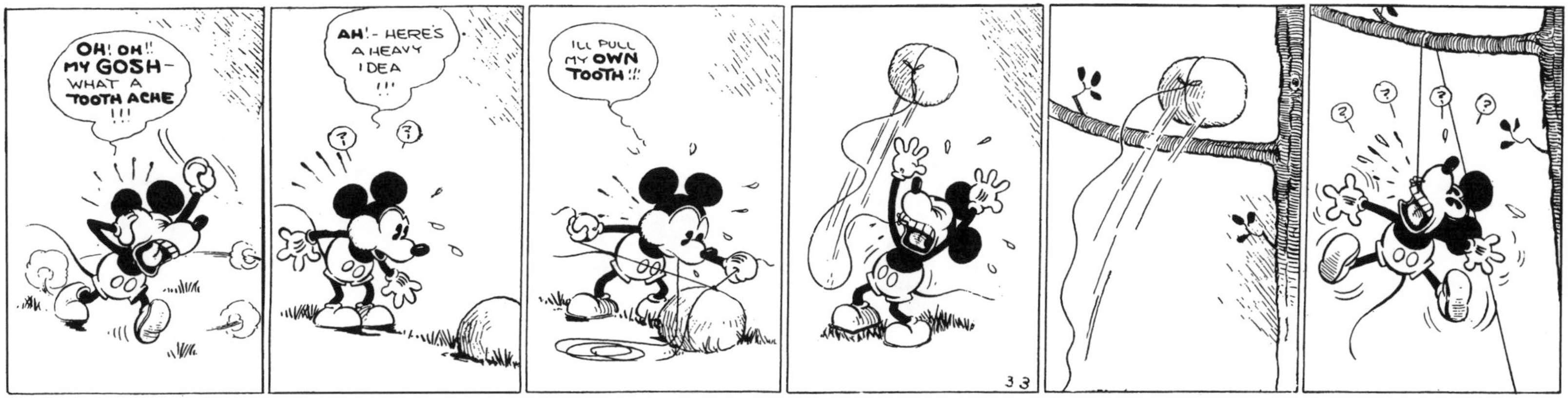
OH! OH!! MY GOSH— WHAT A TOOTH ACHE !!!
AH!- HERE'S A HEAVY IDEA !!!
I'LL PULL MY OWN TOOTH!!!
3-3

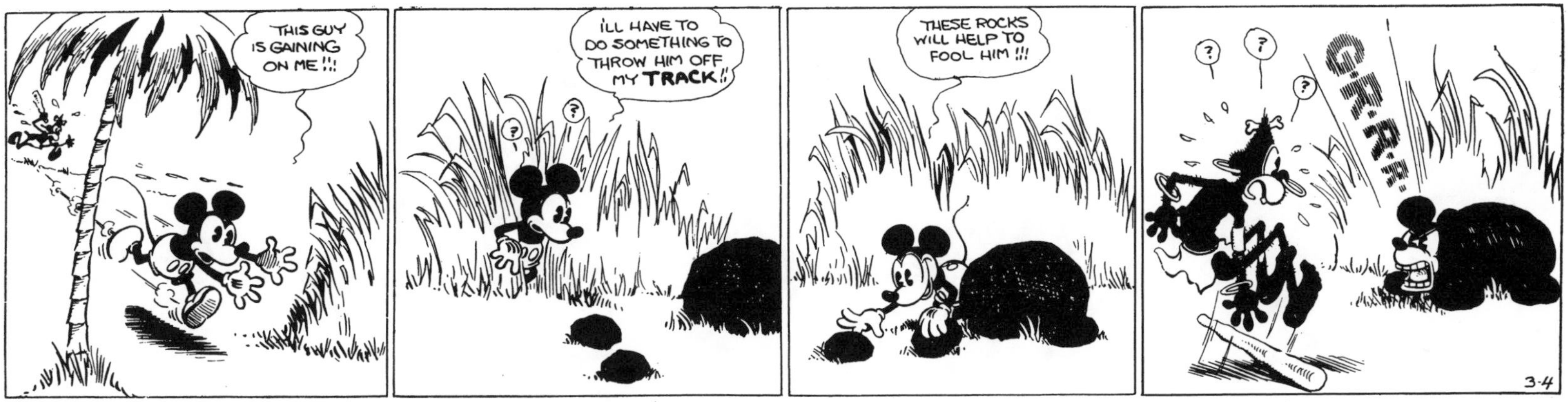
THIS GUY IS GAINING ON ME!!!
I'LL HAVE TO DO SOMETHING TO THROW HIM OFF MY TRACK!!
THESE ROCKS WILL HELP TO FOOL HIM!!!
G-R-R-R!
3-4

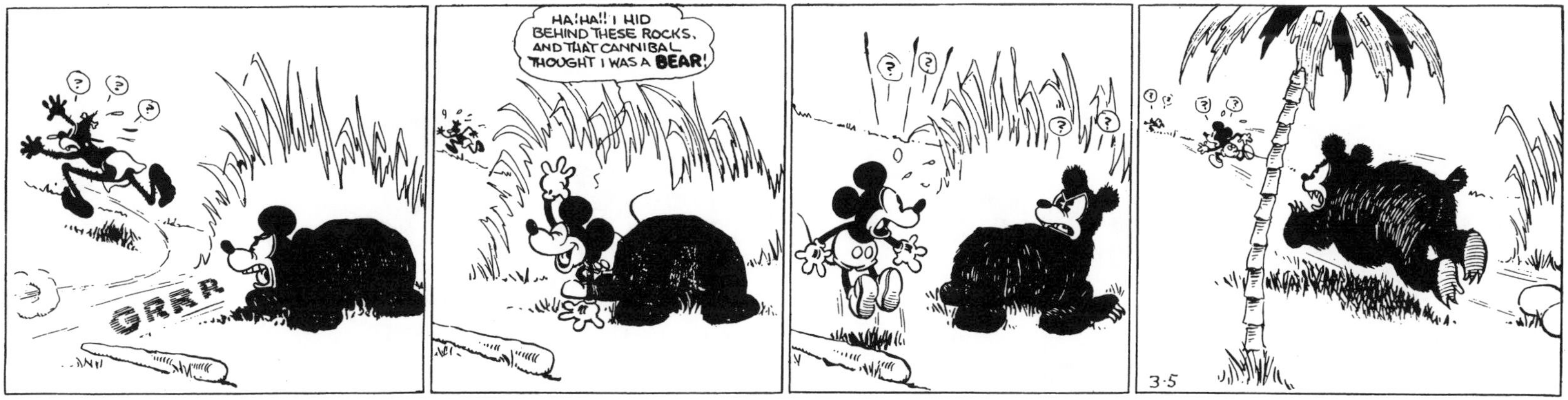
GRRR
HA!HA!! I HID BEHIND THESE ROCKS, AND THAT CANNIBAL THOUGHT I WAS A BEAR!
3-5

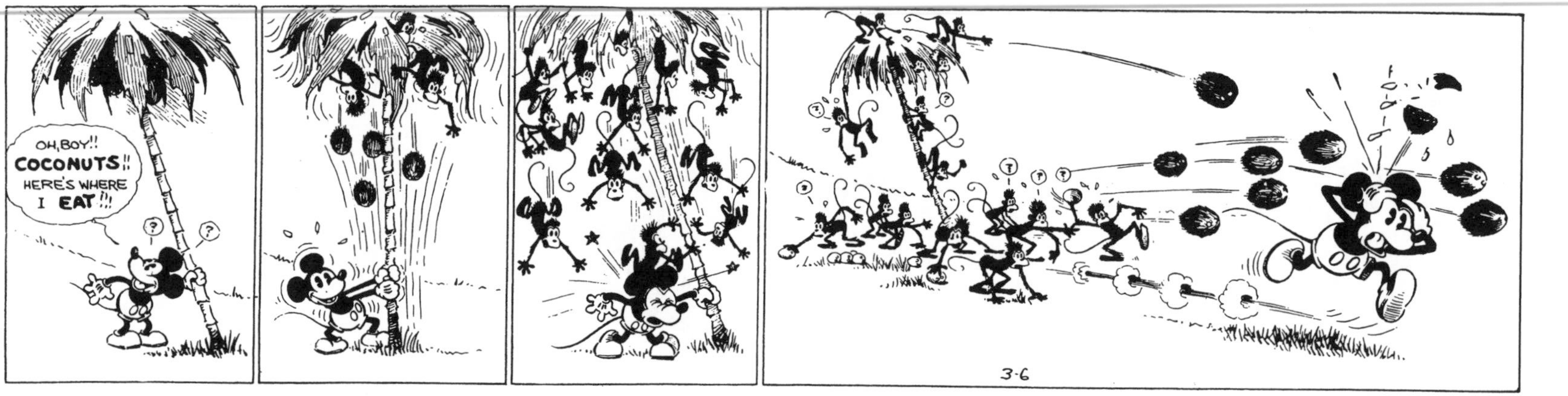
OH, BOY!! COCONUTS!! HERE'S WHERE I EAT!!!
3-6

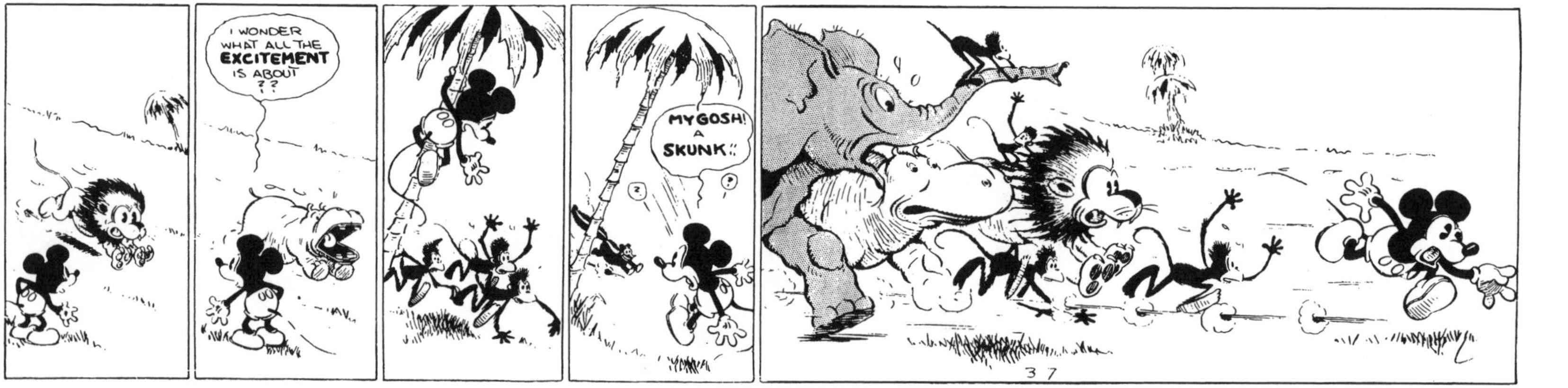
I WONDER WHAT ALL THE EXCITEMENT IS ABOUT ??
MY GOSH! A SKUNK!!
3 7

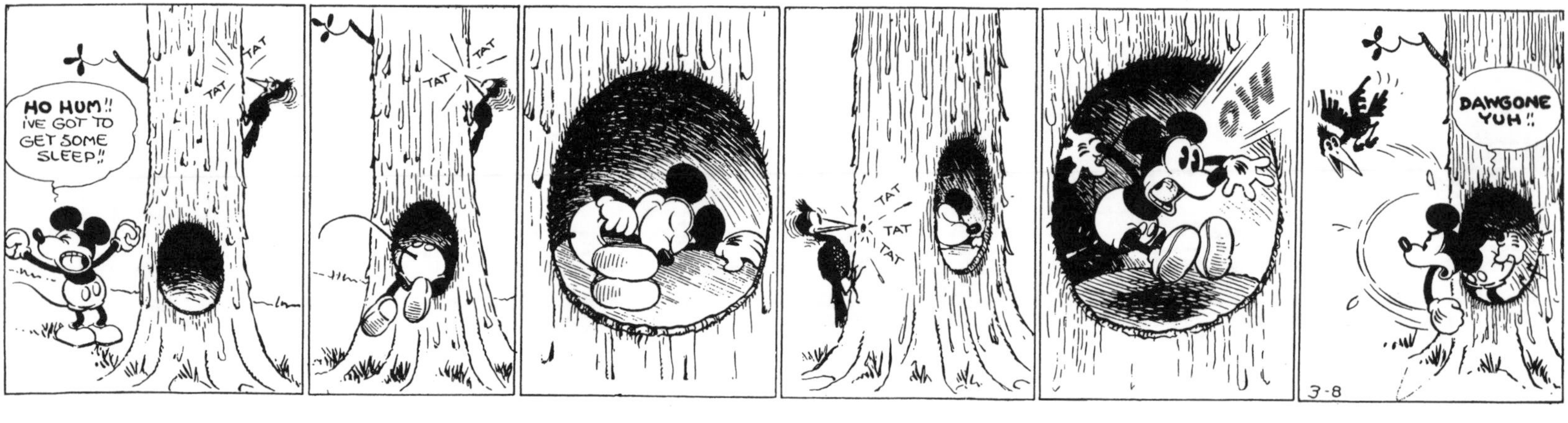
HO HUM!! I'VE GOT TO GET SOME SLEEP!!
TAT TAT
TAT TAT
TAT TAT TAT TAT
OW
DAWGONE YUH!!
3-8

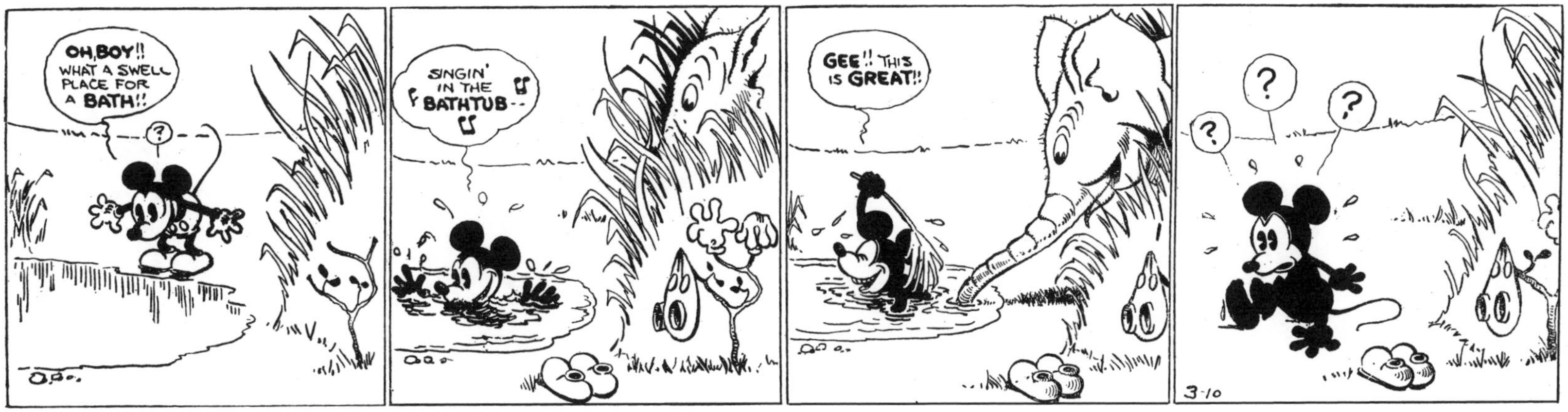
OH, BOY!! WHAT A SWELL PLACE FOR A BATH!!
SINGIN' IN THE BATHTUB
GEE!! THIS IS GREAT!!
3-10

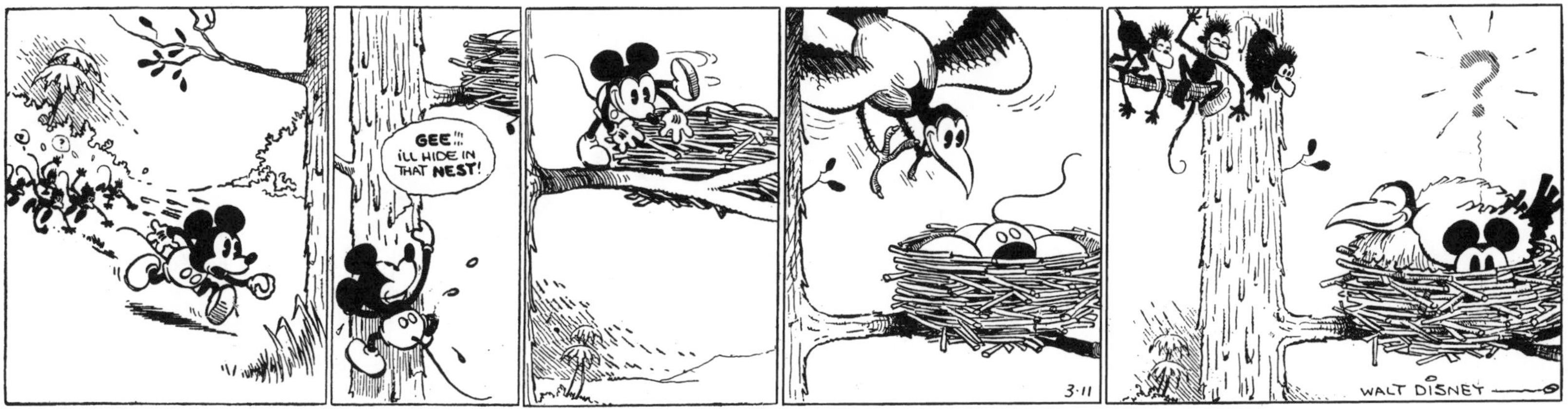
GEE!!! I'LL HIDE IN THAT NEST!
3-11
WALT DISNEY

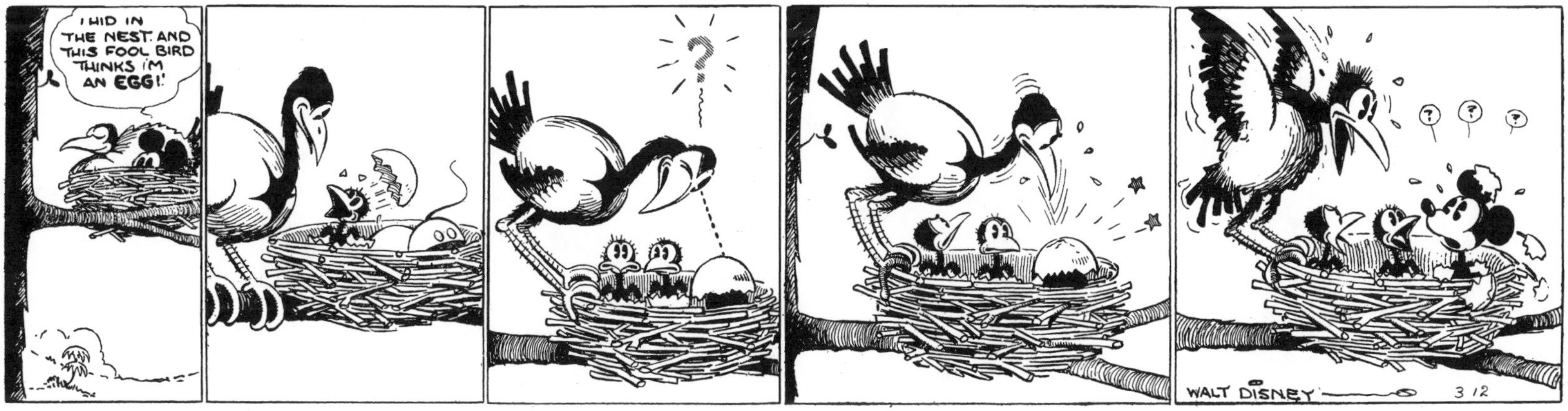
I HID IN THE NEST AND THIS FOOL BIRD THINKS I'M AN EGG!
WALT DISNEY
3 12

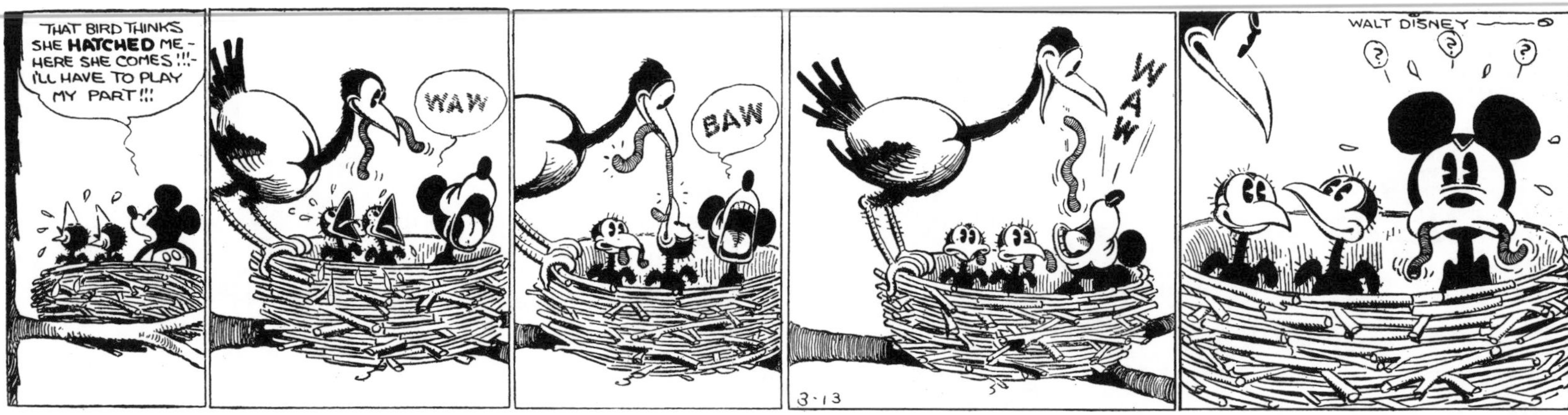
THAT BIRD THINKS SHE HATCHED ME — HERE SHE COMES !!! — I'LL HAVE TO PLAY MY PART !!!
WAW
BAW
WAW
WALT DISNEY
3·13

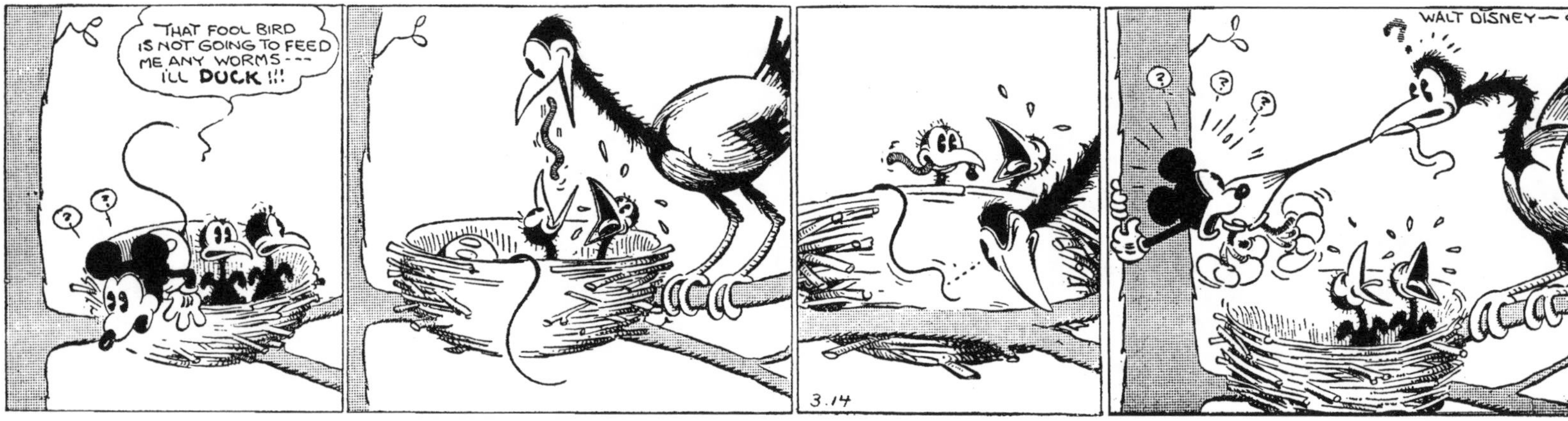
THAT FOOL BIRD IS NOT GOING TO FEED ME ANY WORMS --- I'LL DUCK !!!
3.14
WALT DISNEY

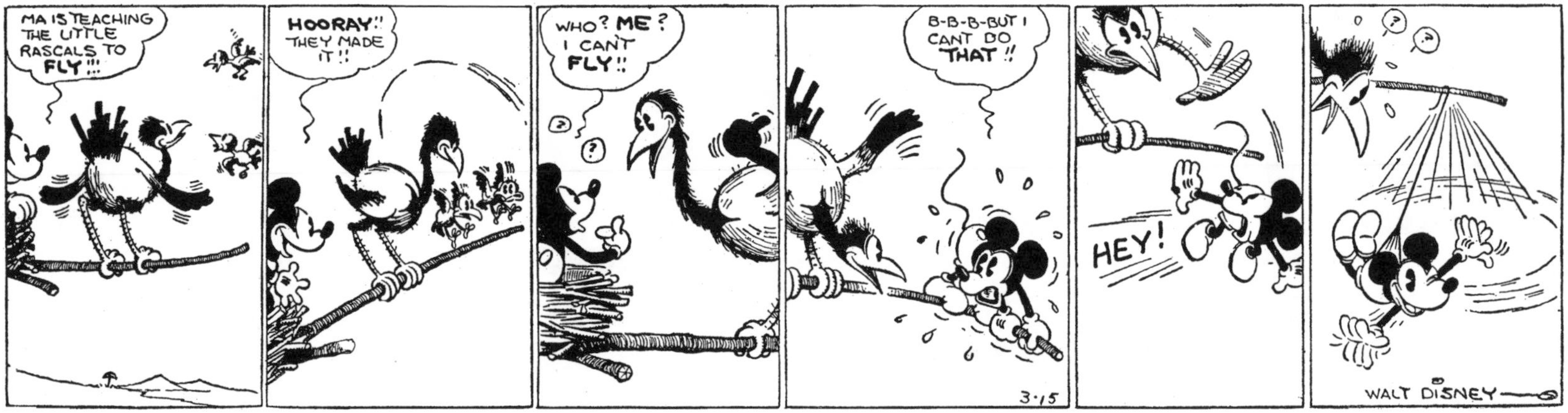
MA IS TEACHING THE LITTLE RASCALS TO FLY !!!
HOORAY !! THEY MADE IT !!
WHO ? ME ? I CAN'T FLY !!
B-B-B-BUT I CANT DO THAT !!
3·15
HEY!
WALT DISNEY

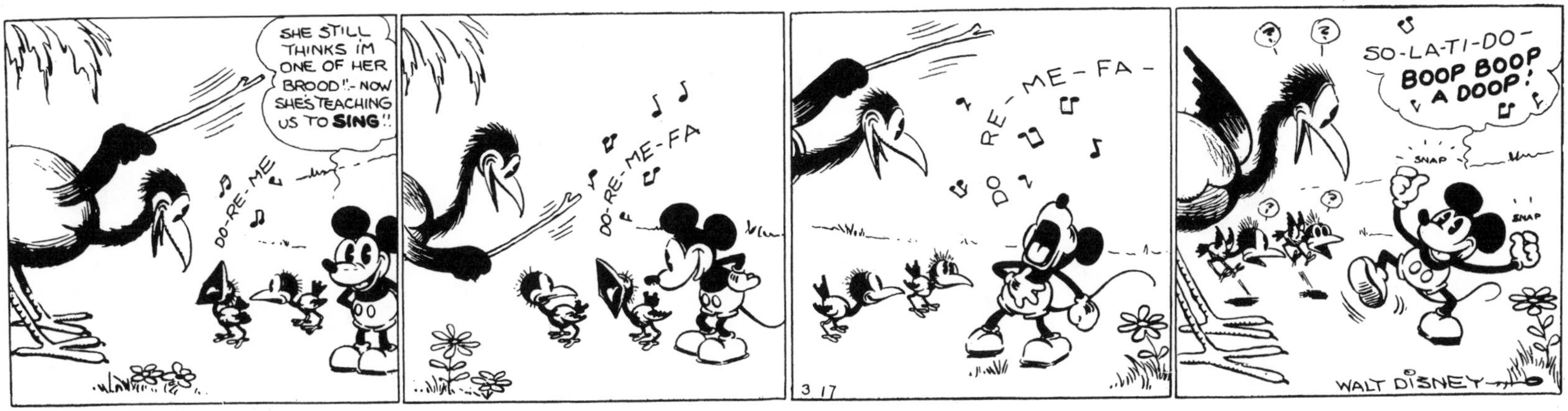
SHE STILL THINKS I'M ONE OF HER BROOD!!- NOW SHE'S TEACHING US TO SING!!
DO-RE-ME
DO-RE-ME-FA
DO RE-ME-FA-
SO-LA-TI-DO- BOOP BOOP A DOOP!
SNAP
SNAP
3 17
WALT DISNEY

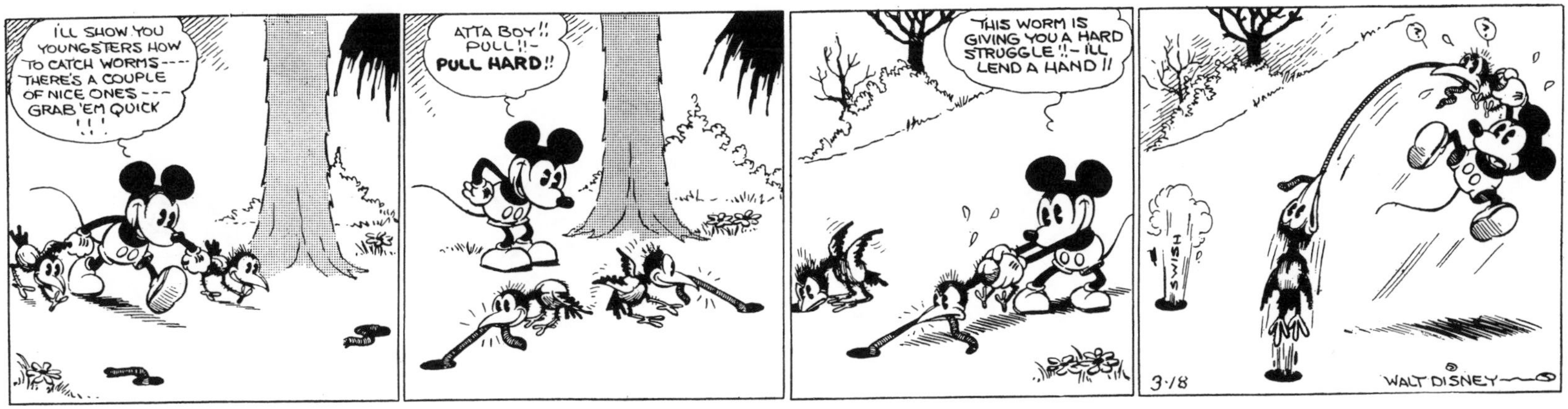
I'LL SHOW YOU YOUNGSTERS HOW TO CATCH WORMS---- THERE'S A COUPLE OF NICE ONES--- GRAB 'EM QUICK !!!
ATTA BOY!! PULL!!- PULL HARD!!
THIS WORM IS GIVING YOU A HARD STRUGGLE!!- I'LL LEND A HAND!!
SWISH
3·18
WALT DISNEY

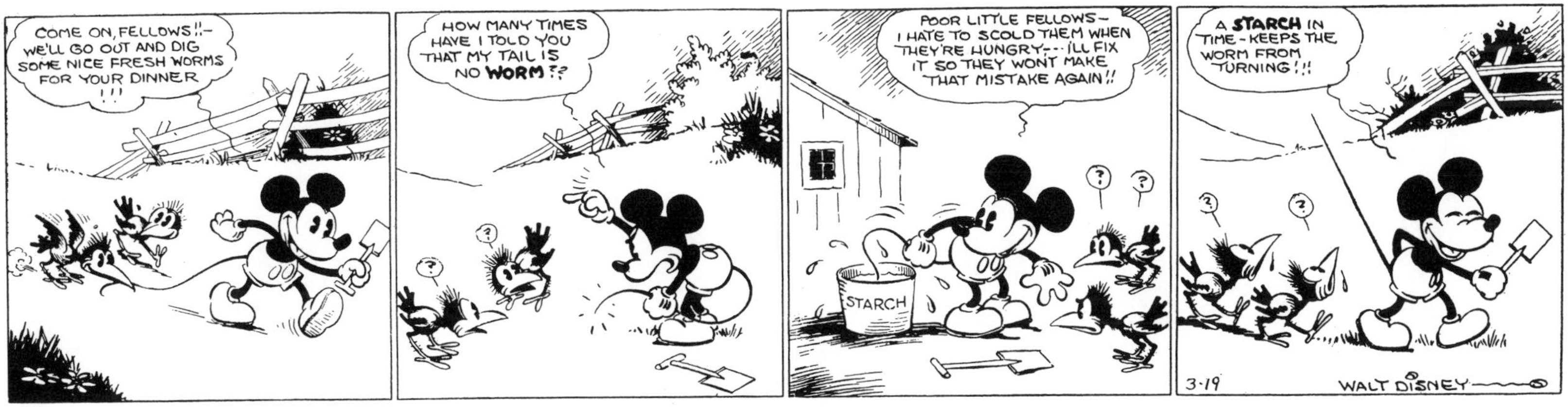
COME ON, FELLOWS!!- WE'LL GO OUT AND DIG SOME NICE FRESH WORMS FOR YOUR DINNER !!!
HOW MANY TIMES HAVE I TOLD YOU THAT MY TAIL IS NO WORM?!?
POOR LITTLE FELLOWS- I HATE TO SCOLD THEM WHEN THEY'RE HUNGRY--- I'LL FIX IT SO THEY WON'T MAKE THAT MISTAKE AGAIN!!
STARCH
A STARCH IN TIME- KEEPS THE WORM FROM TURNING!!!
3·19
WALT DISNEY

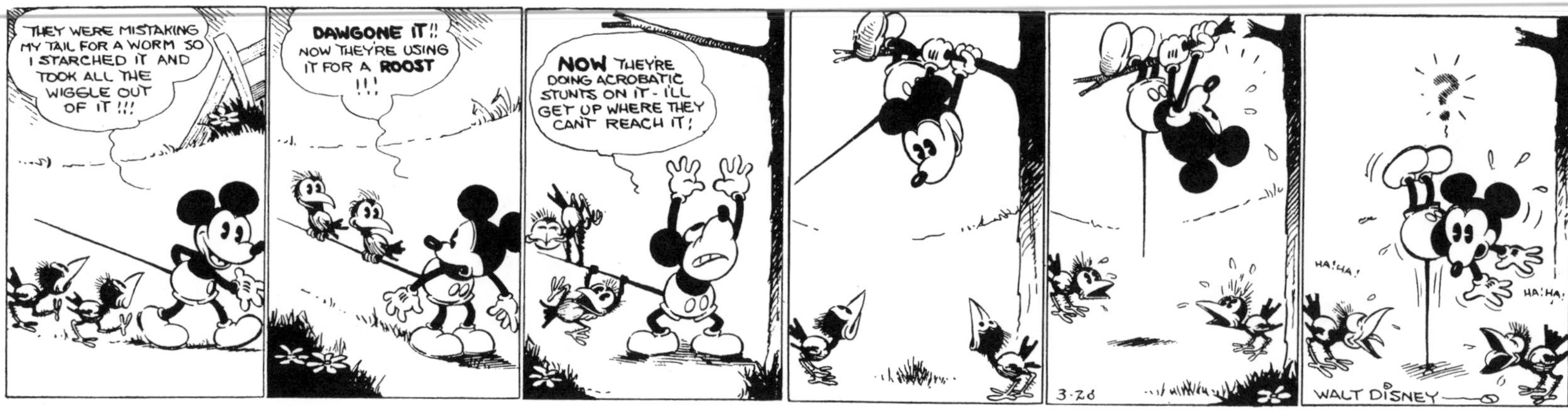
THEY WERE MISTAKING MY TAIL FOR A WORM SO I STARCHED IT AND TOOK ALL THE WIGGLE OUT OF IT !!!
DAWGONE IT!! NOW THEY'RE USING IT FOR A ROOST !!!
NOW THEY'RE DOING ACROBATIC STUNTS ON IT - I'LL GET UP WHERE THEY CAN'T REACH IT!
?
HA! HA!
HA! HA!
3-20
WALT DISNEY

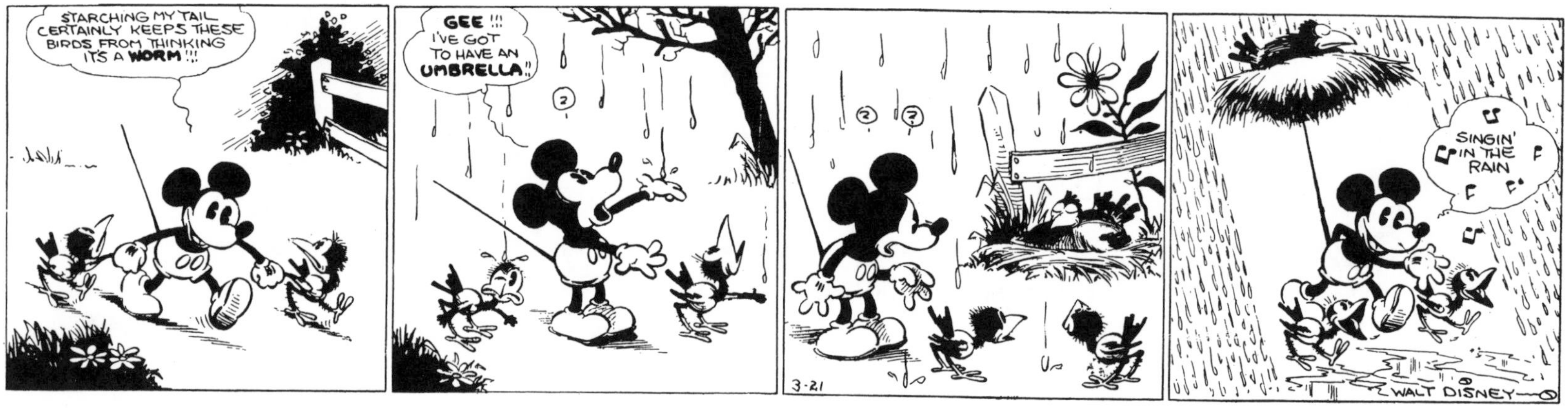
STARCHING MY TAIL CERTAINLY KEEPS THESE BIRDS FROM THINKING IT'S A WORM !!!
GEE !!! I'VE GOT TO HAVE AN UMBRELLA!!
SINGIN' IN THE RAIN
3-21
WALT DISNEY

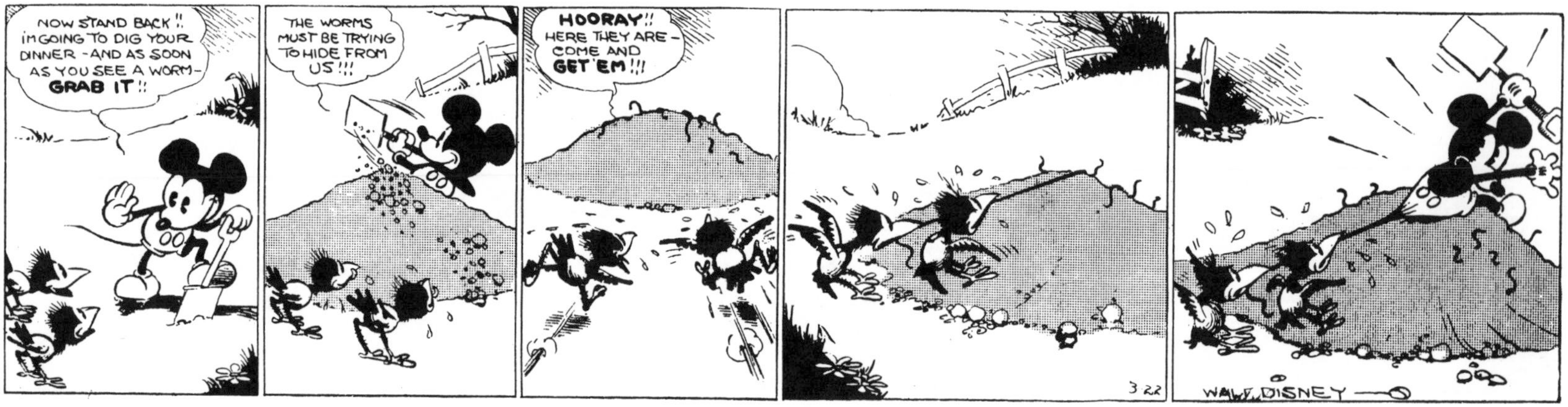
NOW STAND BACK!! I'M GOING TO DIG YOUR DINNER - AND AS SOON AS YOU SEE A WORM - GRAB IT!!
THE WORMS MUST BE TRYING TO HIDE FROM US!!!
HOORAY!! HERE THEY ARE - COME AND GET 'EM!!!
3-22
WALT DISNEY

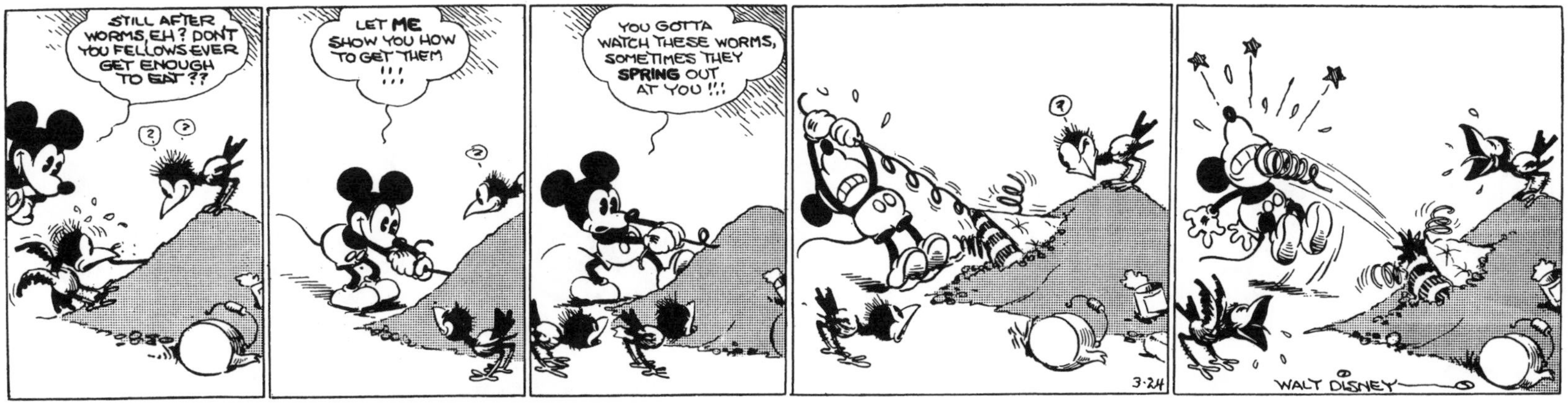
STILL AFTER WORMS, EH? DON'T YOU FELLOWS EVER GET ENOUGH TO EAT??
LET ME SHOW YOU HOW TO GET THEM !!!
YOU GOTTA WATCH THESE WORMS, SOMETIMES THEY SPRING OUT AT YOU!!!
3·24
WALT DISNEY

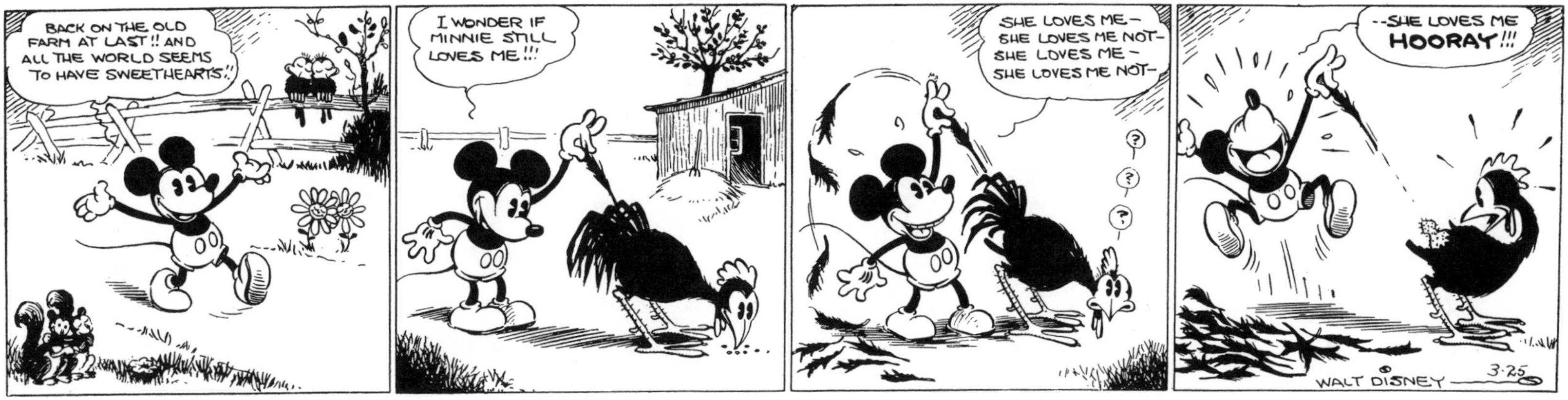
BACK ON THE OLD FARM AT LAST!! AND ALL THE WORLD SEEMS TO HAVE SWEETHEARTS!!
I WONDER IF MINNIE STILL LOVES ME!!!
SHE LOVES ME— SHE LOVES ME NOT— SHE LOVES ME— SHE LOVES ME NOT—
--SHE LOVES ME HOORAY!!!
WALT DISNEY 3·25

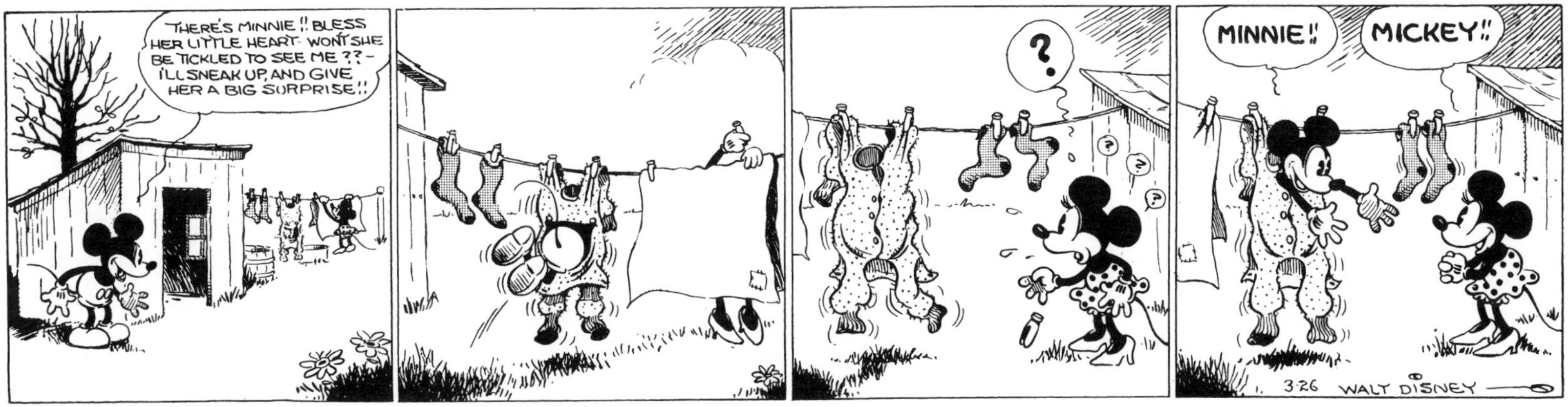
THERE'S MINNIE!! BLESS HER LITTLE HEART- WON'T SHE BE TICKLED TO SEE ME??- I'LL SNEAK UP, AND GIVE HER A BIG SURPRISE!!
?
MINNIE!!
MICKEY!!
3·26 WALT DISNEY

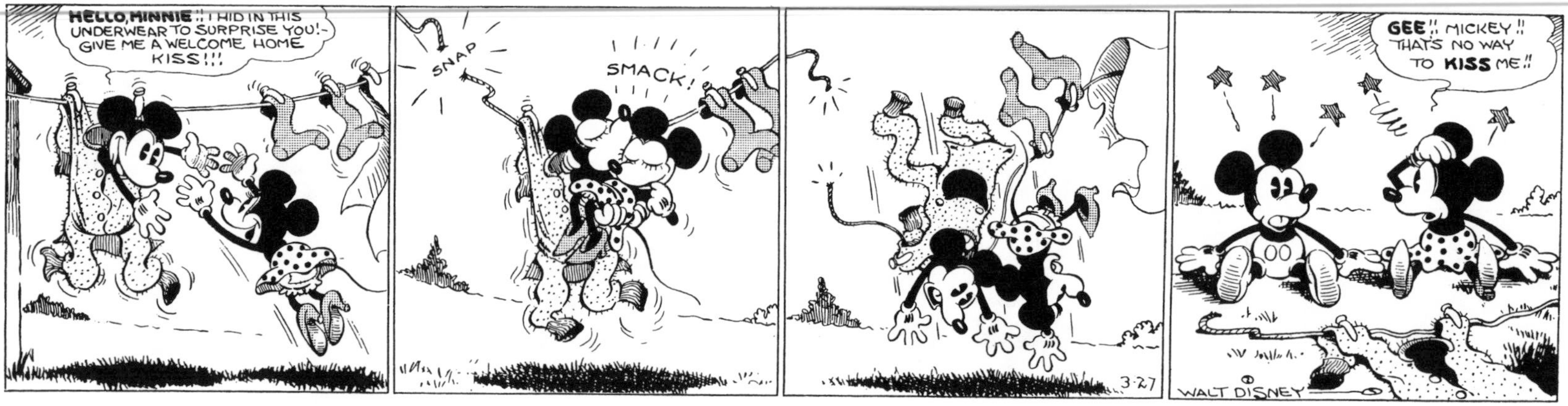
HELLO, MINNIE!! I HID IN THIS UNDERWEAR TO SURPRISE YOU!- GIVE ME A WELCOME HOME KISS!!!
SNAP
SMACK!
3-27
GEE!! MICKEY!! THAT'S NO WAY TO KISS ME!!
WALT DISNEY

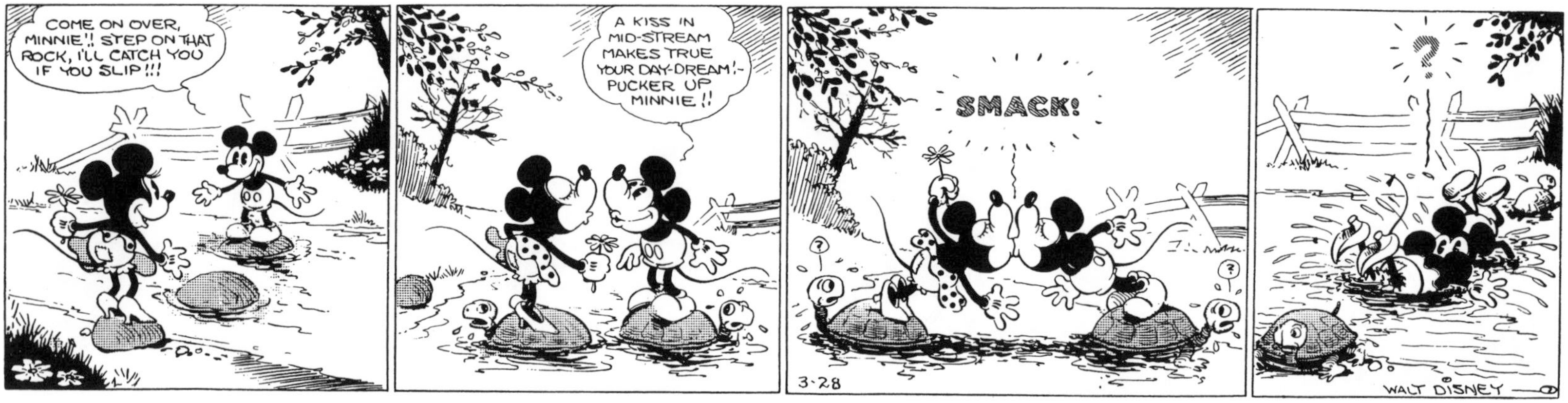
COME ON OVER, MINNIE!! STEP ON THAT ROCK, I'LL CATCH YOU IF YOU SLIP!!!
A KISS IN MID-STREAM MAKES TRUE YOUR DAY-DREAM!- PUCKER UP MINNIE!!
SMACK!
3-28
WALT DISNEY

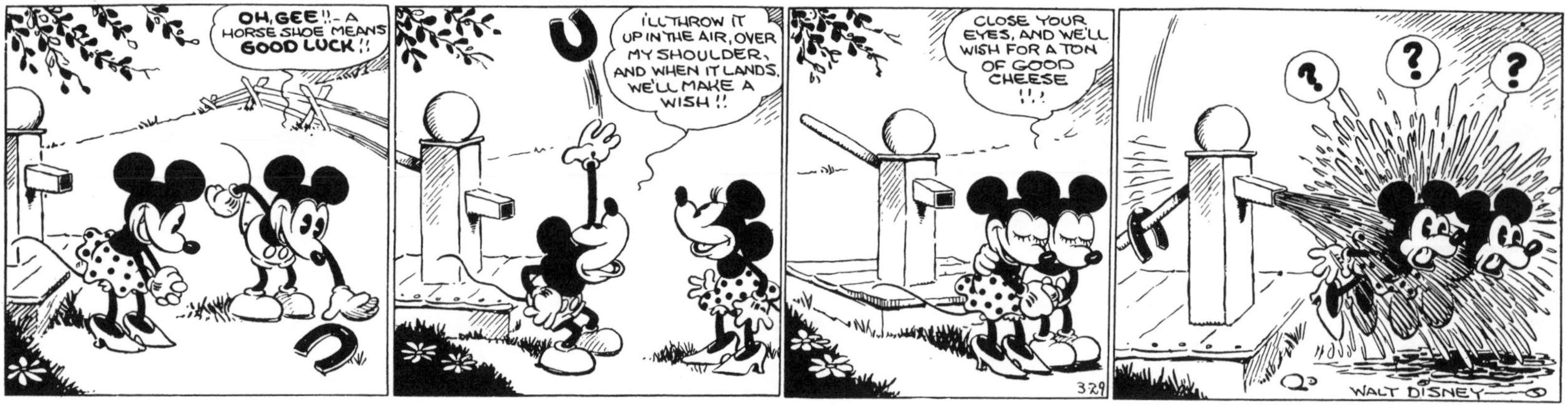
OH, GEE!!- A HORSE SHOE MEANS GOOD LUCK!!
I'LL THROW IT UP IN THE AIR, OVER MY SHOULDER, AND WHEN IT LANDS, WE'LL MAKE A WISH!!
CLOSE YOUR EYES, AND WE'LL WISH FOR A TON OF GOOD CHEESE!!!
3-29
WALT DISNEY

WHAT THE HECK'S
THE MATTER?? THIS
RADIO IS WORKING O.K.
BUT NOTHING COMES
OUT OF THE HORN!!

IT MUST BE
STOPPED UP!!
I'LL BLOW IT
OUT!!!

3·31 WALT DISNEY

ABOVE: Still from *Jungle Rhythm*.

ABOVE: Still from *Plane Crazy*.

ABOVE: Still from *Hell's Bells*.

WRITTEN AND DRAWN on what was at first an experimental basis, "Lost on a Desert Island" was hardly innovative in terms of plot or gag situations. In fact, quite a number of the story's gags were picked up from existing Disney cartoons.

The borrowing began with recent shorts. *Plane Crazy* (1928) was the source for the opening plane-building scenario, while *Jungle Rhythm* (1929) provided the jungle setting and lion model. *Hell's Bells* (1929), a Silly Symphony, showed a goblin using a cliff crevice to trick his pursuer—just as Mickey would do in the February 20 daily.

Walt also mined pre-Mickey silent cartoons for gags. Oswald the Lucky Rabbit's *Africa Before Dark* (1928) saw the bunny shoot the feathers off a bird and confront a big lion in a small log—anticipating Mickey's actions from January 29-31. *Alice Cans the Cannibals* (1925) birthed February 19's nose-ring gag. And the January 27 bird-in-boots scene dated back to *Cinderella* (1922), a Laugh-O-Gram fairy tale spoof that was among Walt's very first films.

Turnabout being fair play, the February 1 lion-and-crocodile gag was picked up for animation;

Mickey would perform it on-screen in *The Castaway* (1931), which went into production late in 1930. [DG]

OVERLEAF: Readers of "Lost on a Desert Island" might notice that Mickey flew over water to get to the island, then seemingly *walked* home. Italian Disney comics publisher Nerbini was apparently bothered by this narrative elision, and commissioned staff artist (and virtuoso Win Smith mimic) Giorgio Scudellari to create two strips to bridge it. A third Scudellari strip—an unrelated gag, albeit one that picks up from original strip #14 [page 235]—was also inserted earlier into the continuity. New English language dialogue and lettering by David Gerstein; art courtesy Leonardo Gori.

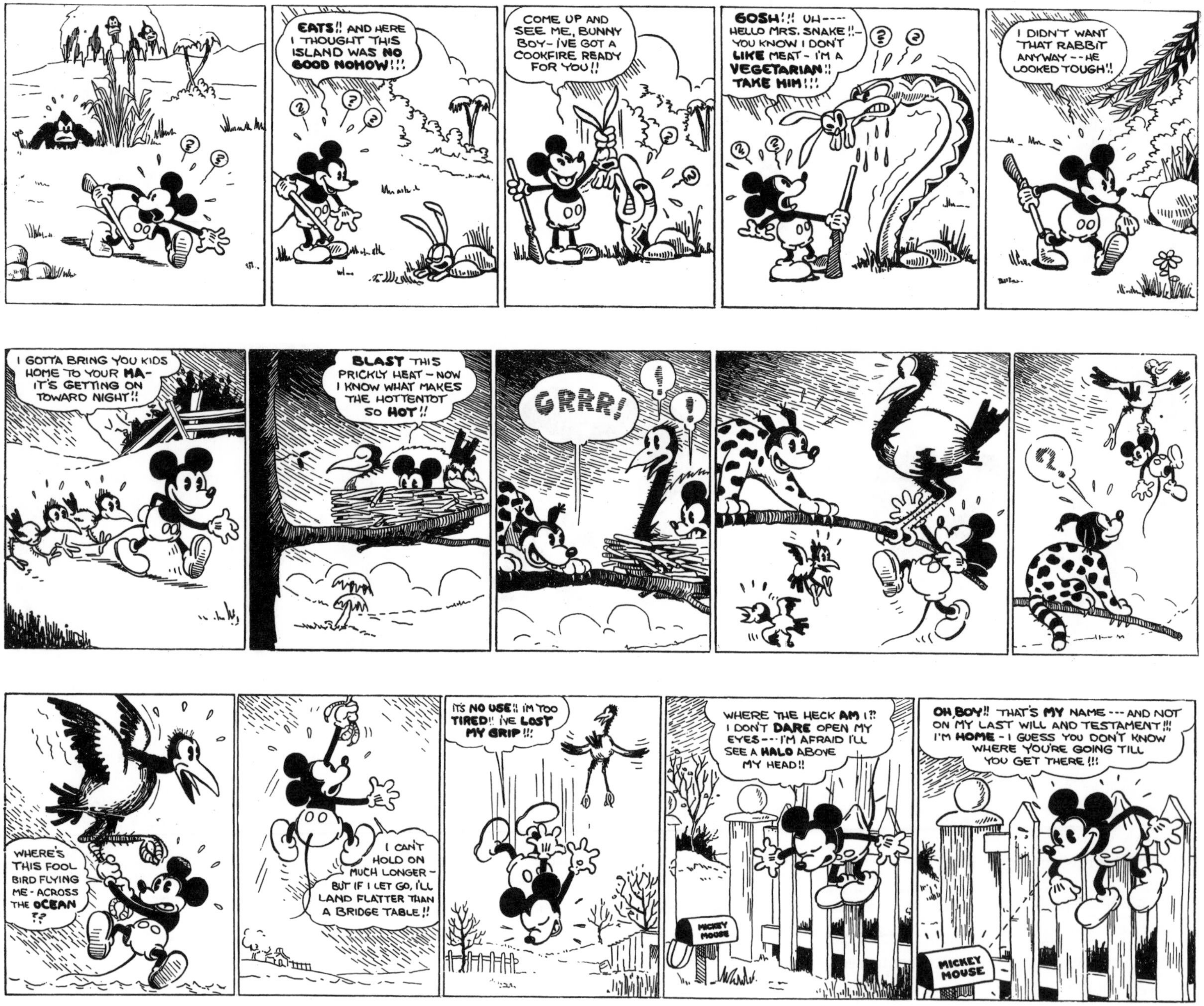
EATS!! AND HERE I THOUGHT THIS ISLAND WAS NO GOOD NOHOW!!!
COME UP AND SEE ME, BUNNY BOY– I'VE GOT A COOKFIRE READY FOR YOU!!
GOSH!!! UH---- HELLO MRS. SNAKE!!– YOU KNOW I DON'T LIKE MEAT– I'M A VEGETARIAN!! TAKE HIM!!!
I DIDN'T WANT THAT RABBIT ANYWAY -- HE LOOKED TOUGH!!
I GOTTA BRING YOU KIDS HOME TO YOUR MA– IT'S GETTING ON TOWARD NIGHT!!
BLAST THIS PRICKLY HEAT – NOW I KNOW WHAT MAKES THE HOTTENTOT SO HOT!!
GRRR!
WHERE'S THIS FOOL BIRD FLYING ME - ACROSS THE OCEAN ?!?
I CAN'T HOLD ON MUCH LONGER – BUT IF I LET GO, I'LL LAND FLATTER THAN A BRIDGE TABLE!!
IT'S NO USE!! I'M TOO TIRED!! I'VE LOST MY GRIP!!!
WHERE THE HECK AM I?? I DON'T DARE OPEN MY EYES --- I'M AFRAID I'LL SEE A HALO ABOVE MY HEAD!!
MICKEY MOUSE
OH BOY!! THAT'S MY NAME --- AND NOT ON MY LAST WILL AND TESTAMENT!!! I'M HOME – I GUESS YOU DON'T KNOW WHERE YOU'RE GOING TILL YOU GET THERE!!!
MICKEY MOUSE

"I only hope we never lose sight of one thing," Walt Disney often mused; his success "all started with a mouse." Of course, one could argue that Oswald the Lucky Rabbit had a year of success before Mickey. But Mickey, a character owned entirely by Walt, brought permanent success—as well as the concept of a fictional Disney world that could expand without interruption. Foremost beyond Mickey, in this world, came Minnie.

What kind of star characters did Walt Disney and Ub Iwerks create—what kind of heroes did Floyd Gottfredson inherit when he first became a comics person? As with any new creation, Mickey and Minnie were a bit inconsistent at the start. Mickey was definitely nailed down as both young and ambitious: his haystack dream in Walt's "Lost on a Desert Island" mirrored his bold goals in *Plane Crazy* (1928), the primal cartoon that inspired the comic. But how Mickey dealt with his ambitions varied wildly from one moment to the next.

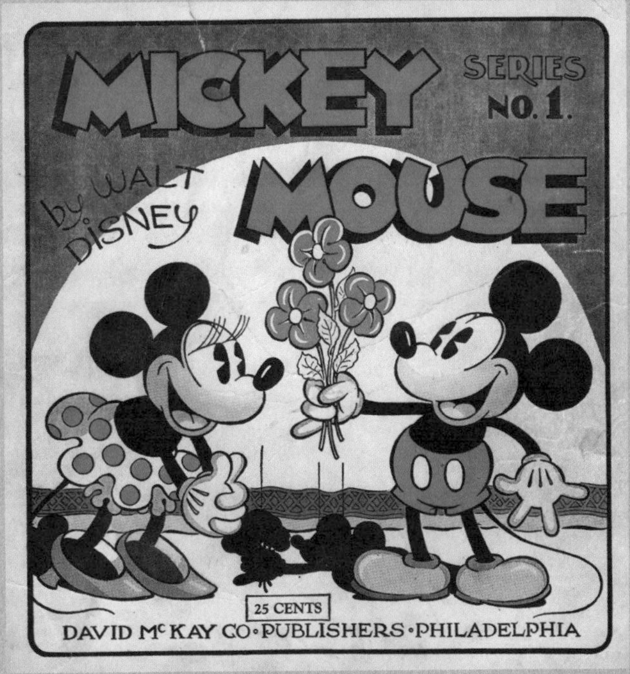
MICKEY MOUSE
SERIES NO. 1.
by WALT DISNEY
25 CENTS
DAVID McKAY CO·PUBLISHERS·PHILADELPHIA

Some strips showed a go-getter mouse full of genuine bravado; others showed a hero too timid to accomplish his goals. On February 29, 1930, Mickey bravely bluffs a whole gang of enemies; but on March 6, coconut-throwing monkeys are enough to scare him witless. On February 18, Mickey ponders human nature: "When they get all through fighting—they won't know who started the trouble!" But on April 24, Mickey's easy capture by Pegleg Pete recasts the philosopher as a foolhardy, impulsive klutz.

To some degree, the shifting personality of early Mickey matches that of many early comedy stars. In quest of laughs first and foremost, screen and fiction figures tossed consistency aside: nothing was out of character as long as it was funny at the moment. Cartoons like *The Jazz Fool* (1929) could even show Mickey permanently outsmarted by inanimate objects.

Floyd Gottfredson would help Mickey past this early, unsettled state. By summer 1930, Mickey was less likely to flee unless he had a plan in mind; less likely to be beaten without refocusing and rebounding—proving himself less a coward, a dufus, or a pushover than simply a youth caught, now and then, at an awkward moment. Animation picked up on the comics' changes: in *The Gorilla Mystery* (1930), Mickey initially runs from every threat, but repeatedly steels himself and returns to the fray.

Minnie gelled a little more quickly as a character. While referred to in an early ad as a "frivolous flapper," our leading lady was in fact thoughtful, careful, and reflective from the pre-Gottfredson start—perhaps less a function of Walt's careful planning than a faith in stereotypical "women's intuition." That said, the presence of this personality was ideal for the growth of both mice. By being careful and intuitive, Minnie could at once balance and provoke Mickey's impulsivity—challenging him to grow while, at the same time, disagreeing with him enough to keep him defiantly independent. Minnie was both Mickey's better half and his provocateur: ideal for the development of any adventure hero.

We'll be looking again at Mickey's and Minnie's ongoing development in Volume 4 of this series, six "comics years" from now. It will be fascinating to see what changes—and what stays the same. [DG]

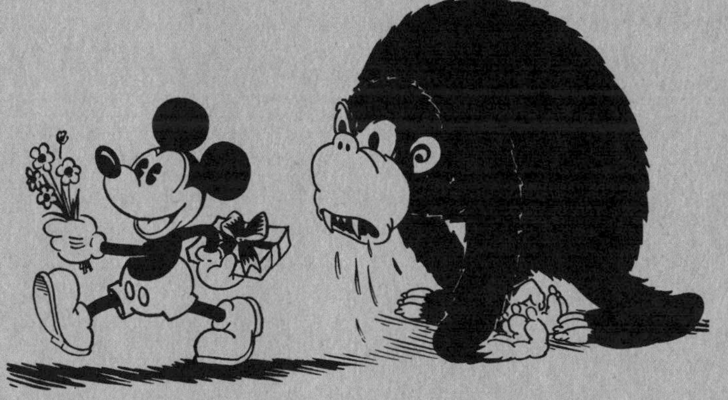

TOP: The happy couple shortly after their "adoption" by Gottfredson: Floyd's original cover drawing for *Mickey Mouse Series 1* (David McKay, 1931). Image courtesy Thomas Jensen.

BOTTOM: Publicity drawing for *The Gorilla Mystery* (1930), artist unknown. Courtesy Charles Shopsin.

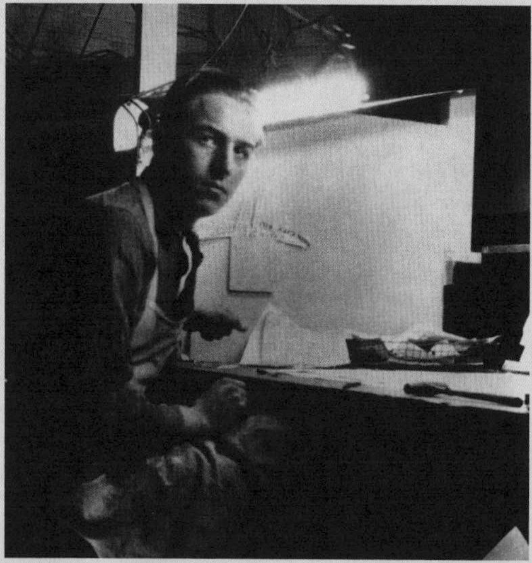

MICKEY MOUSE'S LIFE IN CARTOONS began with Walt Disney, so it was only fitting that his pre-Gottfredson comics career start with Disney, too. As recollected by daily strip co-creator Ub Iwerks (page 226), the youthful Walt longed to be a funny-page artist. Indeed, long before meeting Iwerks, he had moved toward that goal; Disney's years at Chicago's McKinley High School, for instance, found him writing and drawing for the school magazine *The Voice*.[1] Disney avidly created a mix of gag cartoons, serious illustrations, and political bromides at McKinley, but the gag cartoons outnumbered the others.

The gag cartoons also anticipated later developments. Historian Michael Barrier notes the similarity of Disney's *Voice* characters to those of George McManus' *Bringing Up Father*, the strip about domestic squabblers Maggie and Jiggs.[2] Chicago cartoonist Carey Orr, another influence, featured his *Kernel Cootie* in married feuds.[3] As late as 1920, when Disney created a putative daily strip called *Mr. George's Wife*, the inspiration was clear. George, like Jiggs or Cootie, just wanted to have fun. But when his spouse wasn't making life hard, he had trouble with bills, swindlers, and his noisy black cat. So beset by bad luck was George, in fact, that he seemed less a unique character than a one-note middle-aged grump. "I'm a happy married man," a bit player tells him in one strip. "You ought to be in a museum then," George replies. "You're a freak." The gag smacked less of personality than of joke books.

But Walt Disney was creative and anxious to grow—and he fast learned to move beyond stereotype. Disney's silent cartoons filled up with creative young heroes and their inventive solutions to problems: Julius the Cat in the *Alice Comedies* was one, and Oswald the Lucky Rabbit another. Notably, Oswald didn't start out that way: pilot film *Poor Papa* (1927) showed him as a George-like luckless, middle-aged family man. But Universal complained about that tired persona, and Disney rethought Oswald as a younger and snappier, if still hapless bunny.[4]

By the time Walt and Ub Iwerks created Mickey Mouse—and particularly, by the time they moved him into comic strips—Disney knew all about building colorful, rounded personalities. His Mickey is a naïve country boy at the bottom line, but dispenses wise-guy rural wisdom like a pro—or, better, like a kid trying to build self-confidence. "I've heard of killing two birds with one stone, but getting five of them with one yank ain't so bad," Walt's Mickey tells himself on February 3, 1930. "I've got the other guy beat!"

Mickey would move away from snappy one-liners as the strip became more adventurous, and as Walt's contribution receded. But Disney always kept thinking hard about Mickey, and about what methods of depicting Mickey felt most natural. "Cold animation comes from—a lack of real emotion about the characters," Disney told the *New York Herald-Tribune* in 1933. "Mickey's not a clown, he's just a human with a sense of humor."[5] The master's sensibility had left the days of *Mr. George's Wife*; Floyd Gottfredson, with his careful, emotional approach to Mickey, followed suit. [DG]

1 Michael Barrier, *The Animated Man: A Life of Walt Disney* (Berkeley: University of California Press, 2007), p. 21.

2 *Ibid.*

3 Mark Sonntag, "Carey Orr – Walt's Mentor." Tagtoonz, entry posted July 13, 2008, http://msonntag.blogspot.com/2008/07/carey-orr-walts-mentor.html (accessed December 17, 2010).

4 Russell Merritt and J. B. Kaufman, *Walt in Wonderland: The Silent Films of Walt Disney*, rev. ed. (Baltimore: Johns Hopkins Press, 2000), p. 87.

5 Walt Disney to Marguerite Tazelaar, "Mickey Mouse, Citizen of the World," *New York Herald-Tribune*, July 30, 1933.

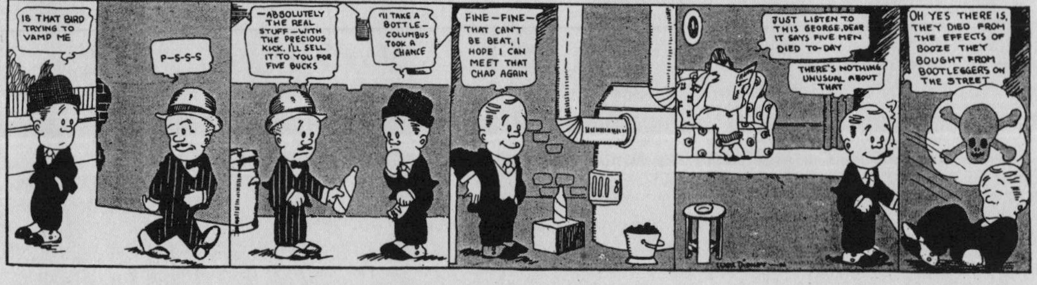
IS THAT BIRD TRYING TO VAMP ME
P-S-S-S
—ABSOLUTELY THE REAL STUFF—WITH THE PRECIOUS KICK. I'LL SELL IT TO YOU FOR FIVE BUCKS
I'LL TAKE A BOTTLE—COLUMBUS TOOK A CHANCE
FINE—FINE—THAT CAN'T BE BEAT, I HOPE I CAN MEET THAT CHAP AGAIN
JUST LISTEN TO THIS GEORGE, DEAR IT SAYS FIVE MEN DIED TO-DAY
THERE'S NOTHING UNUSUAL ABOUT THAT
OH YES THERE IS. THEY DIED FROM THE EFFECTS OF BOOZE THEY BOUGHT FROM BOOTLEGGERS ON THE STREET

ABOVE: Walt Disney in 1923, not long after his first comics attempts.

RIGHT: George gets into his usual bad luck. Story and art by Walt Disney, c. 1920. Image courtesy The Walt Disney Family Foundation.

...AND WIN SMITH

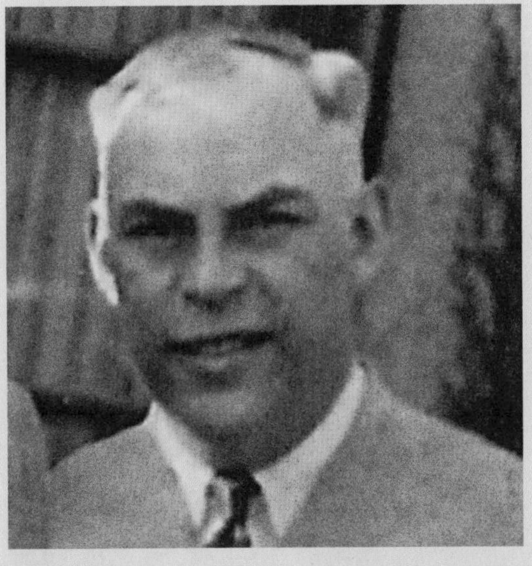

ABOVE: Win Smith, January 1930. Image courtesy Michael Barrier.

WHEN THE NEW GENERATION RISES, the old guard sometimes falls. In taking over art chores on the *Mickey Mouse* newspaper strip, Floyd Gottfredson replaced Win Smith (1887-c. 1941)—but the substitution was about more than one artist swapping for another. It was also about age and privilege. "At that time I was 24, and Walt was 27," Gottfredson would later recount.[1] "We considered Win an old man. He was 43."

If Gottfredson and Disney saw Smith as a geezer, however, Smith had his own age-based biases about his colleagues. At the time, Walt wanted Smith—then handling all of the art chores on *Mickey Mouse*—to write the strip as well. Smith refused, claiming seniority: "No goddamn young whippersnapper's going to tell me what to do." Walt might have been on good grounds to fire Smith for the insult; but Smith quit on his own, leaving the studio that day.[2]

Of course, Smith's career didn't end with his walkout. Gottfredson himself recollected that Smith—earlier a newspaper illustrator—traveled to San Francisco to resume his old line of work. But in the Depression, jobs were harder to find.[3] Soon Smith was back in comics, drawing short-lived strips starring Ub Iwerks' *Flip the Frog* (c. 1931) and Hugh Harman's and Rudolf Ising's *Bosko* (1934-1935). 1937 found Smith in animation, working as a story man for Universal's post-Disney *Oswald* shorts. And 1940 saw Smith writing and drawing "Penguin Pete" (later "Pat, Patsy and Pete"), a comic book filler for Western Publishing. In 1941, "Pete" found its final home in Western's new *Looney Tunes and Merrie Melodies Comics*, for which Smith also drew a single Bugs Bunny tale. Shortly after completing a "Pete" story for *Looney Tunes* 2 (1941), Smith passed away.[4]

Did Smith regret having left Disney? His later jobs seem to provide some clues. Bosko, though created before Mickey Mouse, bore a family resemblance to him—enough to suggest that Smith might have sought out the Harman-Ising job for its similarity to what he had left behind. *Flip the Frog*, meanwhile, gave Smith the chance to reconnect with a Disney colleague—Ub Iwerks, Smith's art partner on the *Mickey Mouse* daily strip.

If Smith didn't wish to take back his 1930 walkout, he did seem to become nostalgic for his Disney days. [DG]

1 Floyd Gottfredson to Arn Saba, "Mickey's Other Master." *The Comics Journal* 120 (March 1988), p. 53.

2 *Ibid.*

3 *Ibid.*, p. 54.

4 Roger Armstrong to Bill Blackbeard, *Walt's People – Volume 4: Talking Disney with the Artists who Knew Him* (Bloomington: Xlibris, 2007), p. 209.

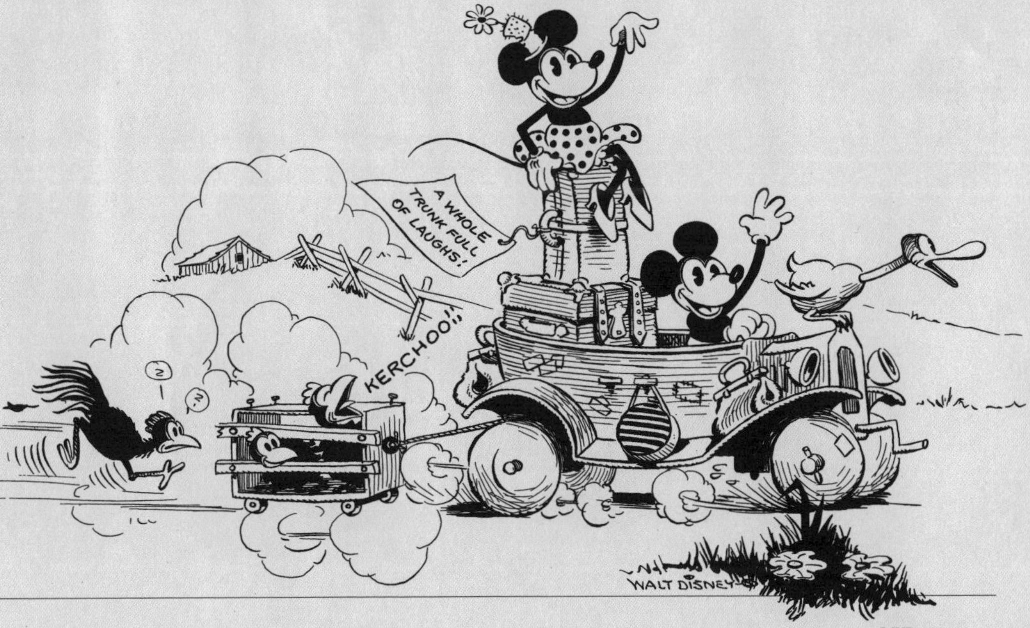
A WHOLE TRUNK FULL OF LAUGHS!
KERCHOO!!
WALT DISNEY

RIGHT: Publicity drawing for the *Mickey Mouse* daily strip, 1930. Art by Win Smith. Image courtesy Joakim Gunnarsson.

Gottfredson's World: MICKEY MOUSE IN DEATH VALLEY

Every country that loves Mickey Mouse has had its own edition—or editions—of Floyd Gottfredson's epics. And each country's Disney comics publisher has tried to make its own version unique, usually by asking homegrown talent to create their own covers or vignettes based on the stories.

In our *Mickey Mouse* series we're proud to anthologize these images, both foreign and domestic, old and new—and give you a sense of how far Floyd's classic adventures have traveled over the years. Look for more of these galleries over the coming pages. [DG]

MICKEY
CHERCHEUR D'OR
HACHETTE

TOPOLINO
NELLA VALLE INFERNALE
2 LIRE
CONTIENE UNA FIGURINA PREMIO TOPOLINO
GLI ALBI D'ORO
EDIZIONI WALT DISNEY · MONDADORI

LE JOURNAL DE MICKEY
B.D.
Suis MICKEY DANS LA VALLÉE INFERNALE
MINI-GUIDE
PLEIN DE JEUX POUR LES VOYAGES
Joue avec Disney PARADE
2 chances de gagner dans ton journal

OR

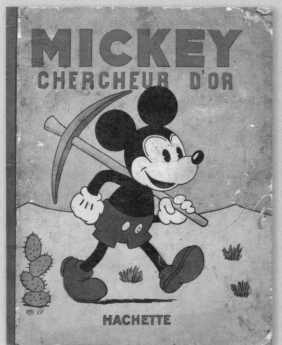

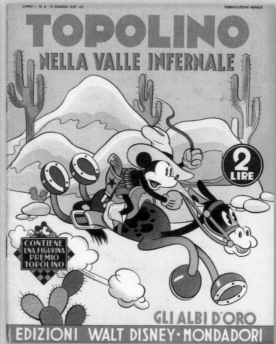

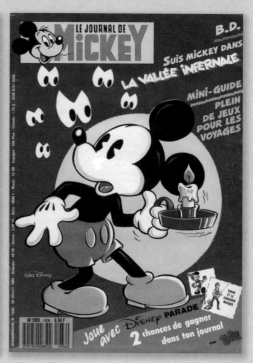

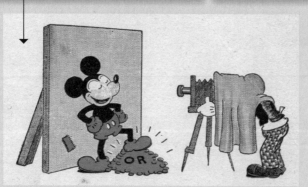

LEFT: Cover and title page vignette from French *Albums Mickey* 2 (1932). Artist unknown.

CENTER: Cover to Italian *Albo d'Oro* 6 (1937). Art by Michele Rubino; image courtesy Leonardo Gori.

RIGHT: Cover to French *Le Journal de Mickey* 1936 (1989). Art attributed to Patrice Croci.

UNCLOAKING THE FOX

» BY DAVID GERSTEIN

"Ther saugh I first the derke ymaginyng
Of felonye, and al the compassyng...
The smylere, with the knyfe under the cloke..."
— Geoffrey Chaucer, *The Canterbury Tales*

ONE OF FICTION'S classic archetypes, the shrouded man has forever been a mainstay of popular horror. What author, in search of a quick shiver, has not looked toward the thrill—and dread—of the unknown? If a character's motive or identity is effectively hidden from sight, it doesn't even matter whether the individual is good or evil; the uncertainty alone is enough to give us the chills. Chaucer's smiling rogue can hide his villainy, but so can a wholly innocent figure be mistaken for a terror. What intimidates readers as much as a possible whammy is the discomforting nature of concealment itself.

Two men obviously aware of this were Walt Disney and Win Smith, launching 1930's "Mickey Mouse in Death Valley" continuity. Pushed by King Features into making Mickey's world more adventuresome than before, Disney and Smith took the introduction of multilayered mystery characters as a necessary first step. Crooked lawyer Sylvester Shyster, a rogue who at various times feigned goodness, reflected the figurative interpretation of Chaucer's concept: in the story, a cynical Mickey even references the cloaked knife. But Minnie's Uncle Mortimer, in disguise as "The Fox," took the *Canterbury* image one step further by literalizing it. The Fox's cloak was the genuine article—physically concealing both Mortimer and his alternate alias "Rasmus Rat." And while Disney's—and later Gottfredson's—intent was eventually to show Mortimer/Rasmus as Sylvester's heroic opposite number, a certain amount of ambiguity crept into the portrayal, underlining the fundamentally dehumanizing nature of disguise. When first introduced, "Rasmus" evinces an obvious evil leer—never subsequently explained—at Mickey and Minnie's plight. And while the final revelation of Mortimer's identity wraps everything up to Mickey's satisfaction, the reader has to wonder why Mortimer waited so long to reveal his true identity; an earlier revelation might have kept Mickey and Minnie out of many life-threatening scrapes.

NOW THAT I'VE FREED YOU — HURRY TO MINNIE'S RESCUE — SHE IS IN DANGER!! — SHYSTER'S GANG ARE TRYING TO SCARE HER INTO SIGNING THE PAPERS!!

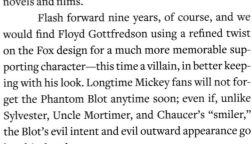

Perhaps, one might speculate, Disney, Smith, and Gottfredson themselves began "Death Valley" unsure of where the plot would lead, only pinning down the disguised Mortimer's true identity and motive some distance through the serial. If so, one could almost count the novice continuity-builders as players in their own adventure: foiled—or at least compromised—by the ongoing mystery of their cloaked co-star's split personality.

Speaking visually, the look of the Fox disguise came from a number of sources. As depicted in media at the time, cloaked mystery men tended to wear ghostly, one-color coverall sheets; evil characters, in the melodrama tradition, favored black sheets in particular. In keeping with the serial story's spirit of uncertainty, the good-guy Fox dressed in black despite being kindly—or perhaps, it must be allowed, because several likely visual models had been evil. The dastardly "Phantom" in *Slick Sleuths* (1926), a Mutt and Jeff film cartoon, looked remarkably like the Fox. So did some interpretations of Fantômas, the arch-criminal antihero of numerous French novels and films.

Flash forward nine years, of course, and we would find Floyd Gottfredson using a refined twist on the Fox design for a much more memorable supporting character—this time a villain, in better keeping with his look. Longtime Mickey fans will not forget the Phantom Blot anytime soon; even if, unlike Sylvester, Uncle Mortimer, and Chaucer's "smiler," the Blot's evil intent and evil outward appearance go hand-in-hand. •

LEFT: Mutt and Jeff meet a "Fox" prototype in *Slick Sleuths* (Dick Huemer/Associated Animators, 1926). Film courtesy Tom Stathes.

BOX
MONDAY
THE CHASE IS STILL ON PETE AND SHYSTER ARE AHEAD WITH THE MAP— STOLEN FROM MINNIE— BUT—MICKEY AND MINNIE ARE HOT ON THEIR HEELS SOMETHING'S DUE TO HAPPEN SOON!
COME ON PETE WE'LL GO IN AND HAVE A MEAL FOR A CHANGE - I'M FED UP ON YOUR COOKING!
SEZ YOU!
RESTAU
HA HA PETE I HAVE TO LAUGH WHEN I THINK HOW WE LET MICKEY AND MINNIE FIND THIS MAP AND THEN GRABBED IT FROM THEM - THEY'LL NEVER OVER TAKE US NOW-
PARDON ME FOR GRABBING THIS MAP - BUT ITS AN OLD SHYSTER CUSTOM I LEARNED FROM YOU

THE CHASE IS STILL ON— PETE AND SHYSTER AHEAD WITH THE MAP— STOLEN FROM MINNIE BUT—MICKEY AND MINNIE ARE HOT ON THEIR HEELS —SOMETHING IS DUE TO HAPPEN SOON!!
COME ON, PETE, WE'LL GO IN AND HAVE A MEAL FOR A CHANGE — I'M FED UP ON YOUR COOKING!! AS A COOK YOU'D MAKE A GOOD SWORD SWALLOWER!
SEZ YOU!!
RESTAURANT
HOORAY! WE'VE CAUGHT UP TO THEM AT LAST IT'S OLD SHYSTER'S CAR!!
DURN IT! THE MAP ISN'T HERE —THEY MUST HAVE IT WITH THEM IN THE RESTAURANT!
HA, HA, PETE — I HAVE TO LAUGH WHEN I THINK HOW WE LET MICKEY AND MINNIE FIND THIS MAP AND THEN GRABBED IT FROM THEM— THEY'LL NEVER OVERTAKE US NOW.
6-2
WALT DISNEY
PARDON ME FOR GRABBING THIS MAP— BUT IT'S AN OLD SHYSTER CUSTOM I LEARNED FROM YOU!!

TOODLE OO!

TOODLE-OO, MR. SHYSTER. WE'LL DROP YOU A POSTCARD FROM DEATH VALLEY!!
RESTAURANT
DURN YOU LITTLE RUNTS— COME BACK HERE.!!
BANG!!
COUGH!!
TOODLE OOH!
QUICK WHAT'LL WE DO? SUGGEST SOMETHING! DON'T STAND THERE LIKE THE DUMBBELL YOU ARE!!
I'VE GOT IT, BOSS— WE'LL HOP ON THAT HORSE AND OVERTAKE THEM!!
6-3
YOU FATHEAD! THAT HORSE COULDN'T OVERTAKE A SNAIL WITH LUMBAGO— COME ON, WE'LL TRY AND GET AN AIRPLANE OR TRAIN!!
WALT DISNEY

Behind the Scenes: PENCIL MANIA

VERY FEW PENCIL DRAWINGS survive today for Floyd Gottfredson's early *Mickey Mouse* comics. Records are scanty enough that we're not even sure when—or for how long—pencil art and ink art were done on different sheets of paper. By 1947, we know pencils were inked directly on the same sheet, with inks thus obliterating pencils from existence.[1]

At the start, however, Gottfredson's pencil art was preserved separately. As such, the week of June 2, 1930 partly survives today, and to inspect it is fascinating. What stands out first is its expressiveness: at the pencil stage, Mickey's and Minnie's faces are far more dynamic than they ended up in inks.

Notable, too, is that Gottfredson's distinctive shorthand was largely replaced by another writer's work. Whodunit? Walt Disney Archives director emeritus David R. Smith doesn't believe the writing to be Walt's,[2] and Floyd only remembered a little more. "Walt, attempting to gag the continuities up... hired a writer from Screen Gems at Columbia, whose name I cannot recall... He'd go over and write gags on [the pencils] and bring them back to me. I'd then go over his stuff and edit it, because it was too wordy. He was only there temporarily, only a couple of months."[3] Soon enough, Floyd Gottfredson could stand on his own. [DG]

HANG ON, MINNIE! HANG ON GOSH! THESE ROADS ARE TERRIBLE!!
OH, MICKEY, I'M GETTING DIZZY — THIS CAR SEEMS LIKE IT'S GONNA FALL APART — THESE ROADS ARE TOO ROUGH!!!
AH, I'VE GOT AN IDEA!!
POST NO BILLS
RAILROAD CROSSING LOOK OUT FOR TRAMPS
GEE, MICKEY, BUT YOU'RE CLEVER I'M PROUD OF YOU!!
WE'LL THROW THESE TIRES AWAY AND TAKE TO THE RAILS— LEAVE IT TO MICKEY MOUSE TO GET IDEAS!
CLANG! CLANG!! TOOT! TOOT! CHOO! CHOO!
NEXT STOP DEATH VALLEY!
CLANG! CLANG!
TOOT! TOOT!! HEY, GET OFF THE TRACK, YOU DUMMY! YOU'RE HOLDING UP THE DEATH VALLEY SPECIAL!
CLANG! CLANG!
GET OFF THE TRACK I TELL YOU— YOU BIG FATHEAD — IT'S COWS LIKE YOU THAT MAKE TRAINS LATE!!
MICKEY, PLEASE DON'T BE SO ROUGH WITH HER. REMEMBER SHE MAY BE SOMEBODY'S MOTHER— TRY AND BE NICE TO HER!
PLEASE, MRS. COW, WILL YOU BE KIND ENOUGH TO REMOVE YOURSELF FROM THE TRACKS?— I'VE ALWAYS GIVEN COWS A BREAK— IN FACT, MINNIE AND I DRINK NOTHING BUT MILK!
HUMPH!!
WALT DISNEY

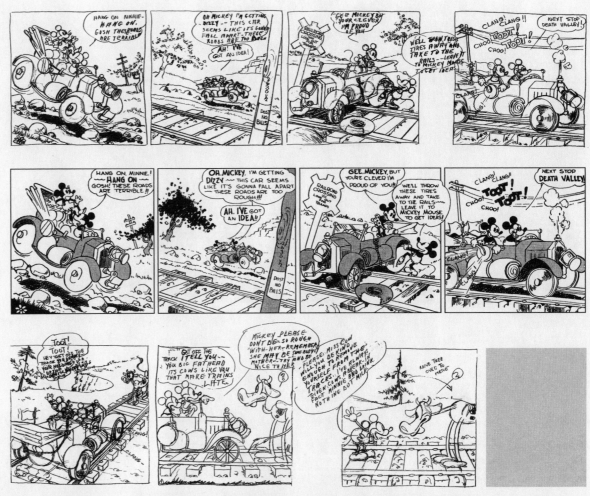

1 Photographs survive showing Gottfredson's "Shutterbug Mickey" (1947) as a work in progress, with some part-inked strips revealing pencil construction lines.

2 Bruce Hamilton: "The Year That Was 1930: A New Discovery!" in *Walt Disney's Comics and Stories* 632 (Prescott: Gladstone Publishing Ltd., 1999), p. 35.

3 Floyd Gottfredson to David R. Smith, *Mickey Mouse in Color* deluxe edition (Prescott: Another Rainbow, 1988), p. 159.

THAT'S IT MICKEY KEEP ON BEING NICE TO HER
DONT YOO SEE MRS. COW—THIS IS A MAP TO A GOLD MINE IN DEATH VALLEY AND WE'RE BEING CHASED BY A CROOKED LAWYER AND HIS HENCHMAN. IF THEY CATCH US THEY'LL TAKE THE MAP AND STEAL OUR GOLD MINE
DO YOU UNDERSTAND NOW DO YOU SEE WHAT IT MEANS TO US
FOR YOU TO GET OFF THE TRACK
SNIFF
SNIFF!!
BOO HOO
SNIFF—SNIFF

THATS NICE, MICKEY, KEEP ON BEING NICE TO HER. SHE'S STARTING TO WEAKEN!!
DON'T YOU SEE, MRS. COW— THIS IS A MAP TO A GOLD MINE IN DEATH VALLEY AND WE'RE BEING CHASED BY A CROOKED LAWYER AND HIS HENCHMAN— IF THEY CATCH US THEY'LL TAKE THE MAP AND STEAL OUR GOLD MINE!!
DO YOU UNDERSTAND NOW?— DO YOU SEE WHAT IT MEANS TO US FOR YOU TO GET OFF THE TRACK?
SNIFF— SNIFF— HOW CAN YOU BE SO CRUEL? IT DON'T MEAN MUCH TO YOU— JUST A LITTLE MOVE— BUT THINK WHAT IT MEANS TO US— ALL OUR EFFORTS AND HARD WORK WASTED AFTER GOING THRU ALL THOSE HARDSHIPS— AND THOSE BAD MEN MAY EVEN KILL US— DON'T YOU SEE NOW WHY YOU SHOULD MOVE?!
BOO HOO—!
6-6
WALT DISNEY

TOOT!! TOO-OO! TOOT!!
YOU WILL GET OFF THE TRACK AND LET US PASS
LOOK OUT MICKEY— THERE COMES A TRAIN!
TOOT! TOOT!
CLANG!

TOOT!! TOO—OO! TOOT!!
YOU WILL GET OFF THE TRACK AND LET US PASS
LOOK OUT, MICKEY— THERE COMES A TRAIN
TOOT!! TOOT!
TOOT!
CLANG!
MOO!
BAWW
CRASH!
BOOM!
BANG
POOR OLD COW— BUT IT WAS HER FAULT
THERE GOES OUR CAR, TOO
JN 2-30
6-7
WALT DISNEY

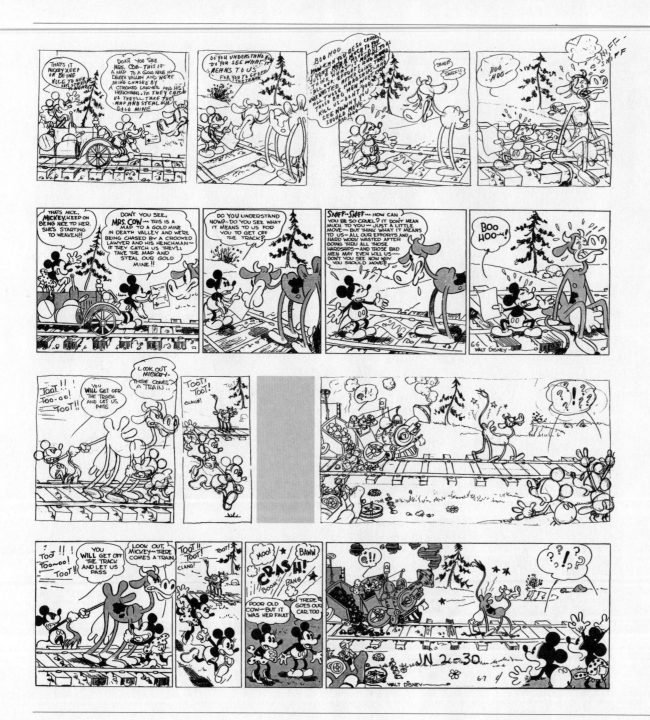

"Mr. Slicker and the Egg Robbers" has had several international covers over the years—including two rather infamous ones. Italy's *Le Nostre Leggendarie Imprese* 2 seems to illustrate both "Slicker" and "Mickey Mouse Vs. Kat Nipp," but neither story was really in the book. And France's *Albums Mickey* 3 portrayed an out-of-character vigilante Mickey not actually seen in Floyd's story. Yikes! [DG]

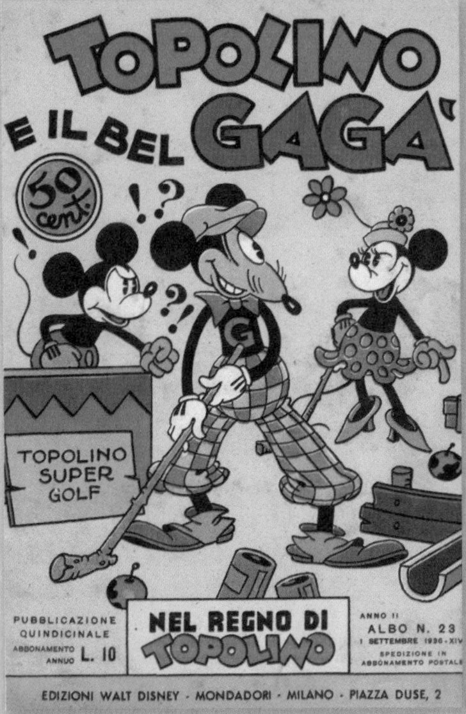
TOPOLINO
E IL BEL GAGA'
50 cent.
TOPOLINO SUPER GOLF
PUBBLICAZIONE QUINDICINALE
ABBONAMENTO ANNUO L. 10
NEL REGNO DI TOPOLINO
ANNO II
ALBO N. 23
EDIZIONI WALT DISNEY - MONDADORI - MILANO - PIAZZA DUSE, 2

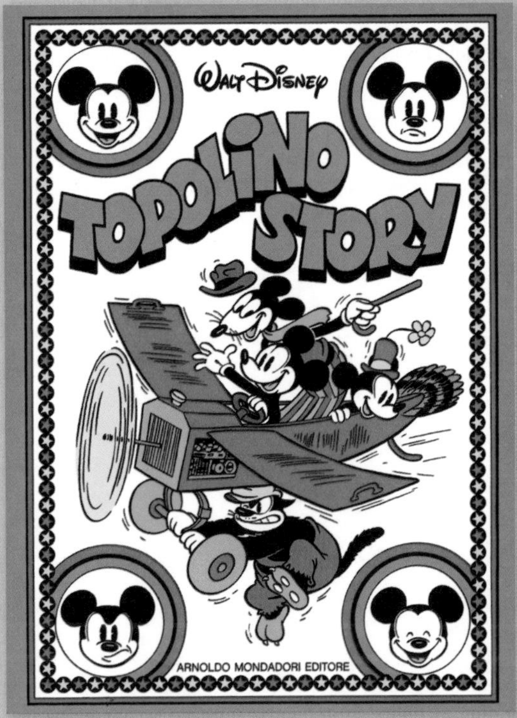
WALT DISNEY
TOPOLINO STORY
ARNOLDO MONDADORI EDITORE

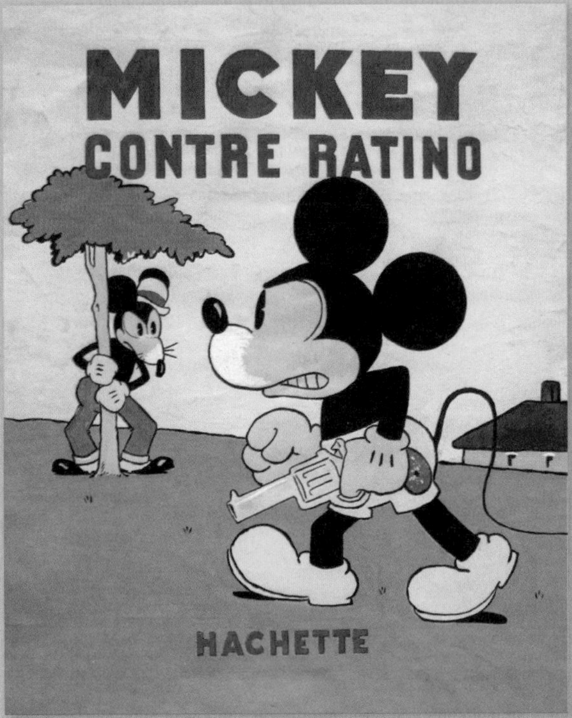
MICKEY
CONTRE RATINO
HACHETTE

LEFT: Cover to Italian *Nel Regno di Topolino* 23 (1936). Artist unknown.

CENTER: Cover to Italian *Le Nostre Leggendarie Imprese* 2 (1983), art by Marco Rota.

RIGHT: Original art for the cover to French *Albums Mickey* 3 (1932). Artist unknown (...and maybe it's better that way). Image courtesy Thibault de Trogoff.

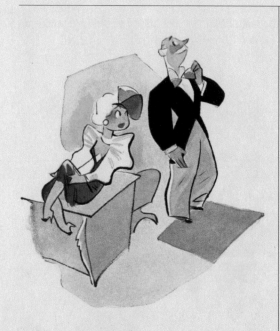

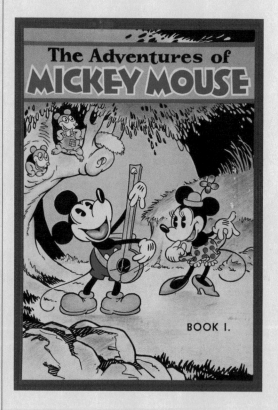

BORN IN VIRGINIA, Minnesota on May 17, 1905, Floyd Gottfredson's future inker/letterer showed an early talent for drawing—and an interest in going professional, which led him to Illinois' prestigious Art Institute of Chicago. After graduating, Nelson became a cartoonist, graphic designer and reporter for the *Chicago Daily News*. And it was the *News* that sent Nelson to California. Initially there to tour film studios on assignment, Roy ended up getting hired at Disney and spending two months as a *Mickey* daily strip inker.

Nelson had caricatured high-living 1920s partygoers for the *News*, and the bouncy style he used for such idle-class types seemed to lend itself to funny animal art. While the end date of Nelson's ink work on *Mickey* is not certain—he likely collaborated with his successor, Hardie Gramatky—Nelson's start date was definitely June 2, 1930, when his wild, distinctive lettering invaded voice balloons with a vengeance. Apart from inking and lettering Gottfredson's pencils, Nelson did the same for Jack King from June 9 to 21. Did Nelson ever try penciling himself? In part, perhaps; the week of June 30, while largely Gottfredson's work, includes sketchy scenery reminiscent of Nelson's solo art, as well as some oddly-proportioned characters.

Before leaving Disney, Nelson is believed to have worked on an early storybook, *The Adventures of Mickey Mouse, Book 1* (published 1931). Then it was back to Chicago, the *News*—and then a gig with *Esquire* magazine, for whom Nelson produced particularly memorable color illustrations.

From 1943-1946 Nelson served in the U.S. Army; after his discharge, he returned to Minnesota, where he drew for such clients as *The Sporting News*, the publisher Saalfield, and the Hearst media empire. Nelson married Marcella Colberg in 1950, but the couple didn't last long—poor Roy was diagnosed with lung cancer in 1953 and passed away in September 1956.

— Alberto Becattini and David Gerstein

WALT DISNEY'S
MICKEY MOUSE
WISHES YOU THE SEASON'S BEST.

The Adventures of
MICKEY MOUSE
BOOK I.

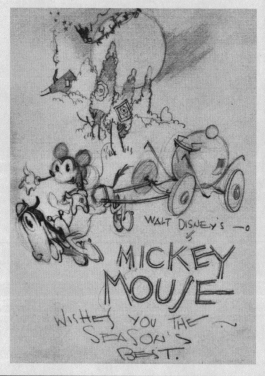

FAR LEFT: Roy Nelson watercolor illustration, 1930s. Image courtesy Shane Glines.

MIDDLE: Nelson's unused sketch for a Mickey Christmas card, 1930; see page 287 for Gottfredson's accepted design. Image courtesy Gunnar Andreassen.

ABOVE: *The Adventures of Mickey Mouse* (1931) is believed to contain some of Roy Nelson's art. Earl Duvall also contributed to this early children's book.

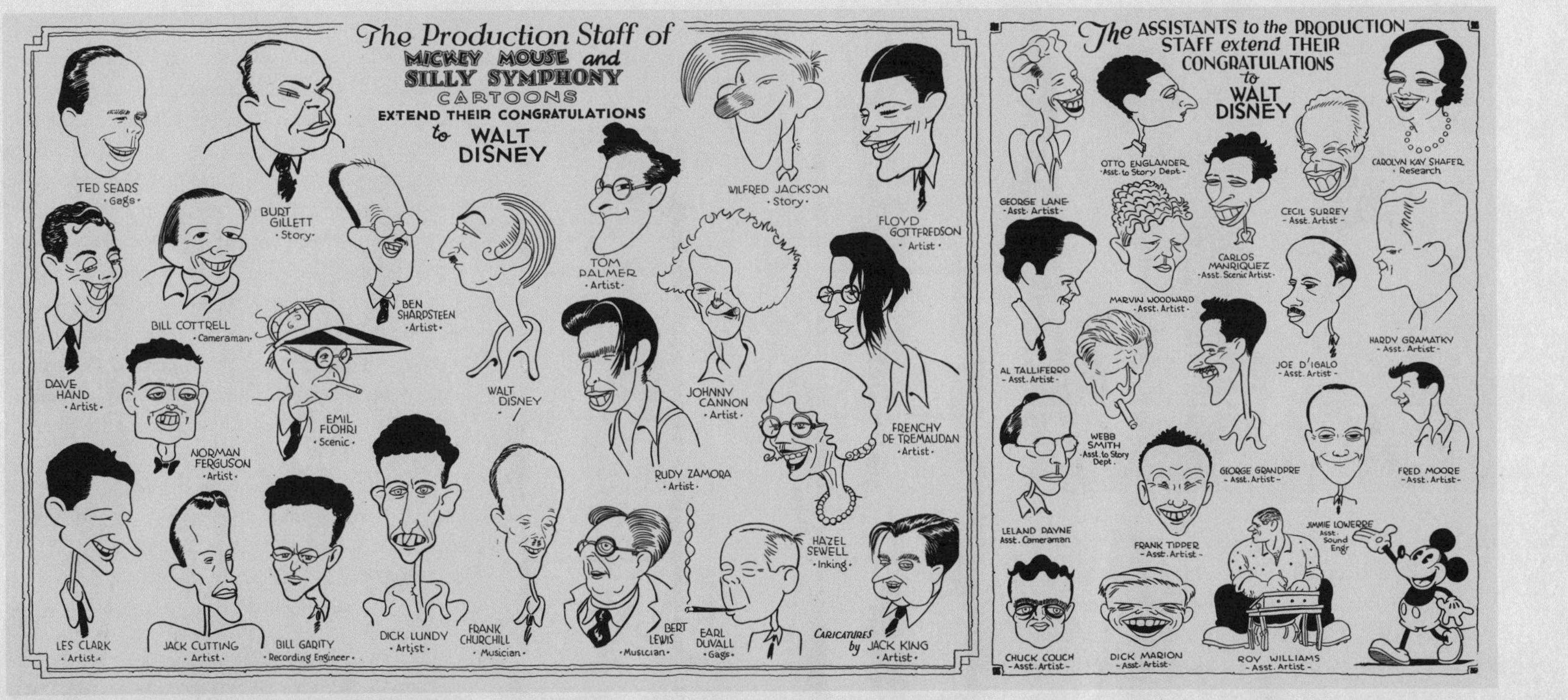
The Production Staff of
MICKEY MOUSE and
SILLY SYMPHONY
CARTOONS
EXTEND THEIR CONGRATULATIONS
to WALT DISNEY
TED SEARS · Gags ·
BURT GILLETT · Story ·
WILFRED JACKSON · Story ·
FLOYD GOTTFREDSON · Artist ·
TOM PALMER · Artist ·
BILL COTTRELL · Cameraman ·
BEN SHARPSTEEN · Artist ·
DAVE HAND · Artist ·
WALT DISNEY
JOHNNY CANNON · Artist ·
FRENCHY DE TREMAUDAN · Artist ·
EMIL FLOHRI · Scenic ·
NORMAN FERGUSON · Artist ·
RUDY ZAMORA · Artist ·
HAZEL SEWELL · Inking ·
LES CLARK · Artist ·
JACK CUTTING · Artist ·
BILL GARITY · Recording Engineer ·
DICK LUNDY · Artist ·
FRANK CHURCHILL · Musician ·
BERT LEWIS · Musician ·
EARL DUVALL · Gags ·
CARICATURES by JACK KING · Artist ·
The ASSISTANTS to the PRODUCTION STAFF extend THEIR CONGRATULATIONS to WALT DISNEY
OTTO ENGLANDER · Asst. to Story Dept. ·
CAROLYN KAY SHAFER · Research
GEORGE LANE · Asst. Artist ·
CECIL SURREY · Asst. Artist ·
CARLOS MANRIQUEZ · Asst. Scenic Artist ·
MARVIN WOODWARD · Asst. Artist ·
HARDY GRAMATKY · Asst. Artist ·
AL TALLIFERRO · Asst. Artist ·
JOE D'IGALO · Asst. Artist ·
WEBB SMITH · Asst. to Story Dept.
GEORGE GRANDPRE · Asst. Artist ·
FRED MOORE · Asst. Artist ·
LELAND PAYNE Asst. Cameraman
FRANK TIPPER · Asst. Artist ·
JIMMIE LOWERRE Asst. Sound Engr
CHUCK COUCH · Asst. Artist ·
DICK MARION · Asst. Artist ·
ROY WILLIAMS · Asst. Artist ·

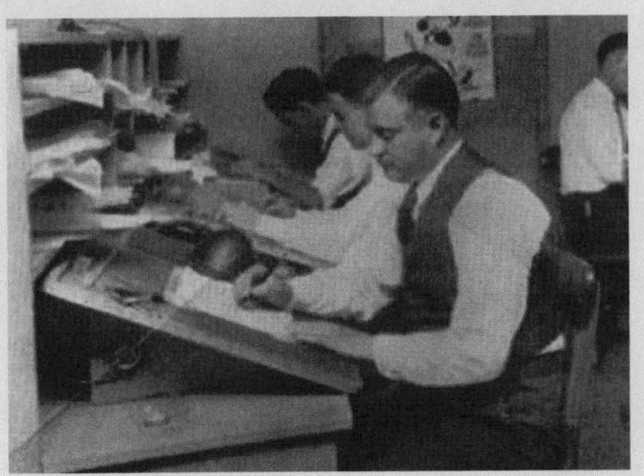

TOP: Jack King drew these studio staff caricatures for *Motion Picture Daily*, June 20, 1931. Image courtesy Cole Johnson.

BOTTOM: Jack King, c. late 1929. Image courtesy Alberto Becattini.

OF JAMES PATTON KING (1895-1958) we have less to say: if only because King's tenure on *Mickey Mouse* was shorter than almost anyone else's. King only drew the strip for two weeks: June 9-21, 1930. But two unusual weeks they were.

King's career began a decade earlier—and in animation, not comics. At Bray Studios in 1920, King directed shorts starring Judge Rummy and Silk Hat Harry, the dog-faced boozehounds created by cartoonist Tad Dorgan. Moving from Bray to Winkler Pictures in 1925, King became head *Krazy Kat* animator under director Bill Nolan. But when Nolan moved on—replaced by new directors Ben Harrison and Manny Gould—King seems to have followed Nolan to the exit. From June 1929, King was at Disney's, where he directed one Mickey cartoon, *Haunted House* (1929);[1] and, of course, drew his ill-fated run of daily strips.

For many years these strips' artist was unknown, but a cross-check with King's Disney animation work makes everything clear. Nobody else gave Mickey visible nails on the bottom of his shoes; nobody else drew *diagonal* pie-cuts in characters' eyes—or drew eyes pinched shut the same way. King even modeled the train's doggy fireman and mailman after Judge Rummy!

King stayed a Mickey animator for several years. Then he sojourned at Leon Schlesinger Productions, directing several early Porky Pig Looney Tunes; two featuring Lulu the Ostrich, his own creation. King then returned to Disney to direct several years of Donald Duck shorts—one of the first being *Donald's Ostrich* (1937). Old ostriches... uh, habits died hard.

—David Gerstein and Alberto Becattini

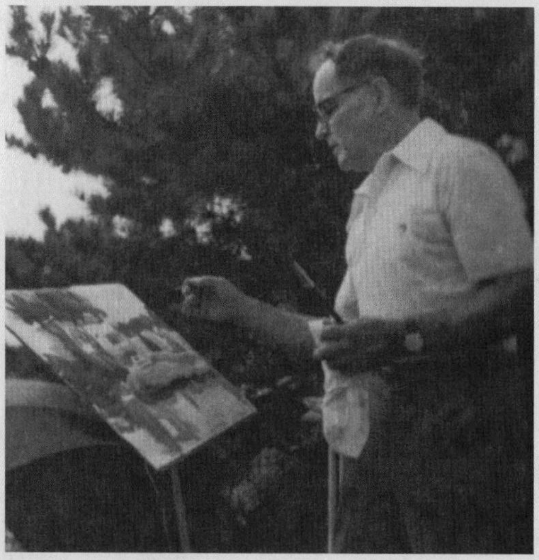

BORN APRIL 12, 1907 in Dallas, Hardie Gramatky had childhood dreams of becoming a cartoonist—always a positive sign! After attending Alhambra High School in San Gabriel, California (1923-27), Gramatky pursued his goal with the *Los Angeles Times*. While at first contributing to the *Times*' children's page, Gramatky expanded his duties by launching various weekly comic strips for the paper. The later 1920s saw Gramatky attending Stanford University, but he kept a hand in the funnies, assisting Charlie Plumb on his famous *Ella Cinders*.

1930 found Gramatky working with Disney, on a part-time basis at first.[2] He later recollected his first task as having been to illustrate a "comic book"[3] (most likely Saalfield's *Mickey Mouse Coloring Book*, published 1931; see page 268), though internal evidence suggests that some strip work came first.[4]

ABOVE: Hardie Gramatky, 1930s. Photo © Linda Gramatky Smith; used with permission.

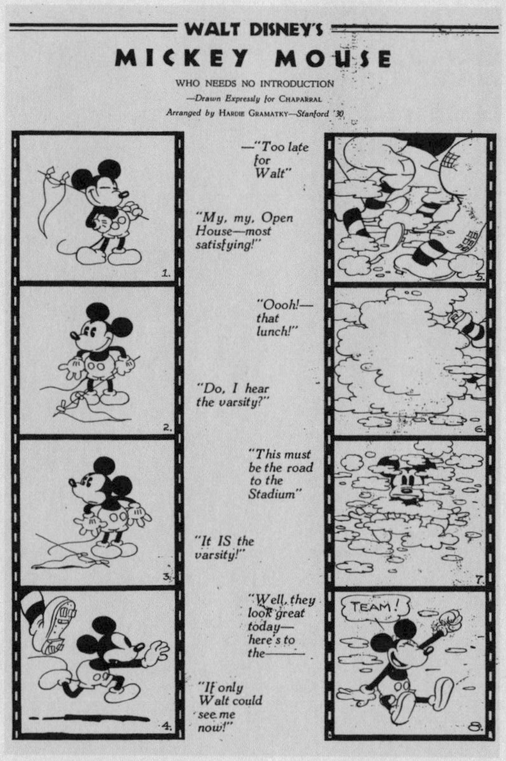
WALT DISNEY'S
MICKEY MOUSE
WHO NEEDS NO INTRODUCTION
—Drawn Expressly for CHAPARRAL
Arranged by HARDIE GRAMATKY—Stanford '30
—"Too late for Walt"
"My, my, Open House—most satisfying!"
"Oooh!—that lunch!"
"Do, I hear the varsity?"
"This must be the road to the Stadium"
"It IS the varsity!"
"Well, they look great today—here's to the———"
"If only Walt could see me now!"
TEAM!
1.
2.
3.
4.
5.
6.
7.
8.

RIGHT: Shortly after leaving his alma mater, Gramatky arranged for Mickey to make this appearance in the Stanford *Chaparral* magazine (c. 1931; Mickey poses largely copied from 1929 model sheet).

Gramatky became a full-time Disney staffer on November 3, 1930.[5] At this point it appears he forsook comics for the Animation Department, where he worked on various Mickey and Silly Symphony shorts up until 1936. Gramatky also helped to arrange Disney's famous evening art classes, taught by Don Graham at the Chouinard Art Institute.

Gramatky left Disney for New York in 1936, where he worked as a pictorial reporter with *Fortune* magazine—and honed his skill as a watercolor artist. One day, just for fun, Hardie was painting boats outside his waterfront studio—when the idea for a children's book came to him. "What would happen if a tug[boat] didn't want to tug?"[6] Gramatky soon wrote and painted the famous *Little Toot* (1939), starring a humanized tug, for publisher G. P. Putnam, and scored immediate success. In 1945, Disney bought the film rights to *Little Toot*, showcasing the tugboat's tale in a segment of *Melody Time* (1948).

As the years rolled by, Gramatky created new children's books—and went from strength to strength in watercolors, receiving honors from the likes of Chicago International (1942), the National Academy of Design, and the American Watercolor Society (both 1952). Gramatky was even included in Andrew Wyeth's list of America's twenty greatest watercolorists.[7]

While Gramatky passed away in 1979, his paintings are still sold as giclées today and exhibited in galleries around the world. His Mickey work, if a little more low-key, has also gotten around.

—Alberto Becattini and David Gerstein

The authors wish to thank historian Shane Glines (for Roy Nelson) and Linda Gramatky Smith (for Hardie Gramatky) for research assistance.

1 While most modern studio histories cite Walt Disney as having directed *Haunted House*, a surviving 1929 studio draft lists King as director.

2 Linda Gramatky Smith, conversations with the author, December 18 and 19, 2010.

3 Ibid.

4 The *Coloring Book* includes several illustrations adapted from Gramatky-inked September 1930 daily strip panels, suggesting that some comics had to have preceded the book.

5 "His first contract was dated November 3, 1930." David R. Smith, letter to Norma Yocum, March 8, 1979.

6 Linda Gramatky Smith, ibid.

7 M. Stephen Doherty, "Andrew Wyeth Picks 20 Great American Watercolorists." *Watercolor*, Fall 2006. The list's "greats" were specified as representing the greatest in both past and present.

THE ONE-OFF GOTTFREDSON SPIN-OFF

Kölnische Illustrierte Zeitung

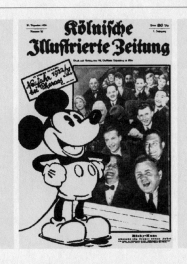

LATE 1930 AND EARLY 1931 found Gottfredson's *Mickey Mouse* becoming an international hit—and numerous local European cartoonists, some working for Disney licensees, wanted to take a crack at making Mickey comics of their own. Even if they only got one single, solitary chance.

The time: February 14, 1931. The place: Germany. The *Kölnische Illustrierte Zeitung* (Cologne Illustrated Times) had been printing Gottfredson's *Mickey* to great success. Then the German holiday of Fasching—a Mardi Gras-like carnival—came up on the calendar. The *Zeitung* wanted a Gottfredson strip to tie into this event, but none existed. So *Zeitung* cartoonist Frank Behmak took the opportunity to produce this original Disney strip, using recent dailies as a guide to drawing Mickey and Butch.[1]

Can you tell which strips the character poses come from? [DG]

Image courtesy Karsten Bracker.

1 J. P. Storm and M. Dreßler, *Im Reiche der Micky Maus: Walt Disney in Deutschland 1927-1945* (Berlin: Henschel Verlag GmbH, 1991), p. 196.

DANCE PALACE
I'LL GO COSTUMED AS MYSELF... NO ONE ELSE WOULD DARE!
COSTUME BALL TONIGHT!
WOW! EVERY-ONE DARED! GOSH, HOW'LL I PROVE I'M THE REAL MICKEY NOW?
!
BETCHA CAN'T DO THIS!
?
?
OH!
??
WHEE!
SHOW-OFF!
SCANDAL-MONGER!
NOT BAD, EH?
SCRAM
YOU TELL 'IM, DOORMAN!
TEE-HEE-HEE!
OUT !!
HMF! I ONLY WANTED TO SHOW 'EM THE LATEST STEP!
AFTER WALT DISNEY

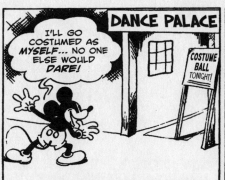

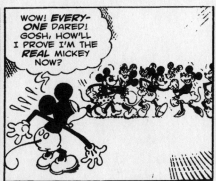

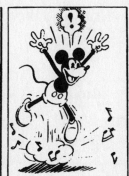

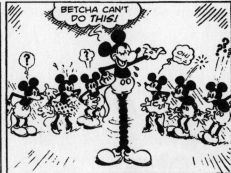

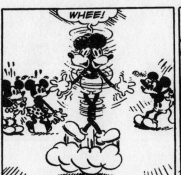

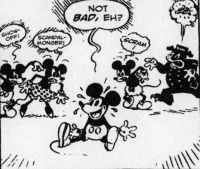

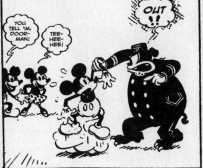

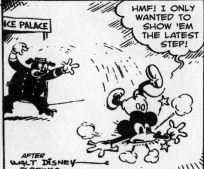

The Comics Dept. at Work: MICKEY MOUSE IN COLOR... AND BLACK & WHITE

Disney's Comic Strip Department also produced much non-strip art over the years. The first *Mickey Mouse Coloring Book*, published by Saalfield in 1931, was an early venue for this output, featuring numerous new Mickey vignettes—most drawn by Gottfredson inker Hardie Gramatky. Some of the images, however, strongly suggest Floyd's own layout and/or pencil work too.

Reprinted here and on the next few pages are those vignettes that, to our eyes, involve the greatest degree of Gottfredson involvement. The close resemblance of this giant-eared, beady-eyed Mickey to Floyd's "Death Valley" mouse suggests that the art was done in mid-1930. Comparing the vignettes to later strips in the "Death Valley" continuity—and earlier strips in "Mr. Slicker"—also reveals a number of borrowed character poses.

We believe all the finished ink work to be Gramatky's, with the single exception of the top right image on page 269, likely the work of Les Clark or Earl Duvall. Color, when included, is original; as a rule, Saalfield's coloring books featured some pre-colored images to help inspire young artists.

Special thanks to Mike Matei for help with restoration of images. [DG]

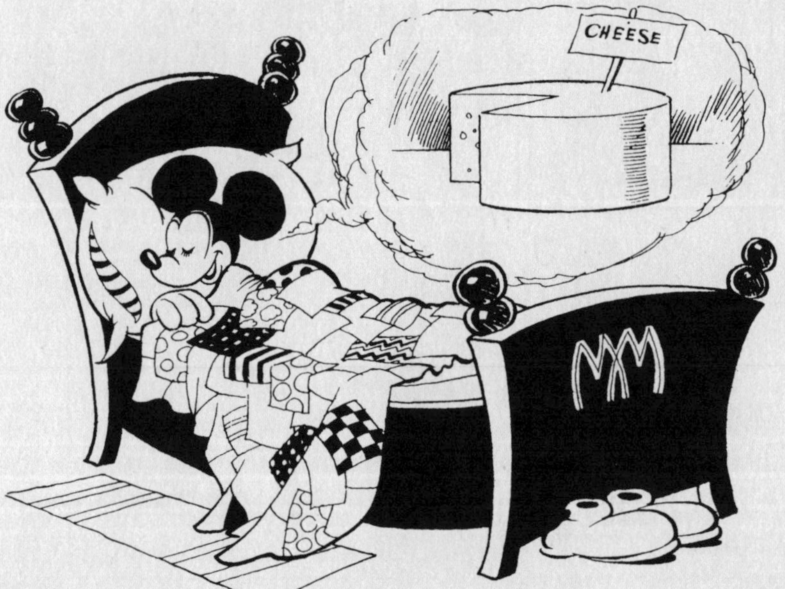
CHEESE
MM

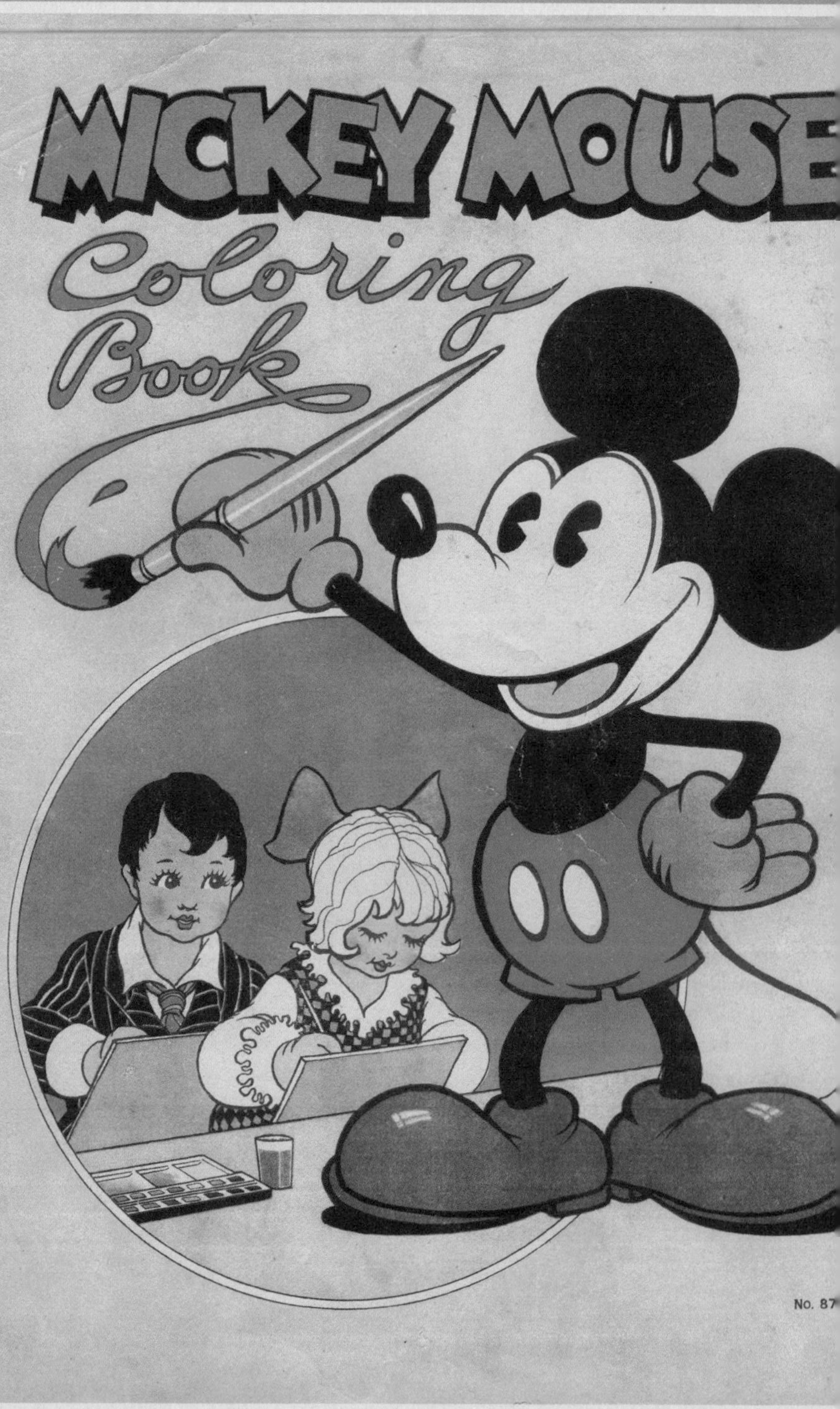
MICKEY MOUSE
Coloring Book
No. 87

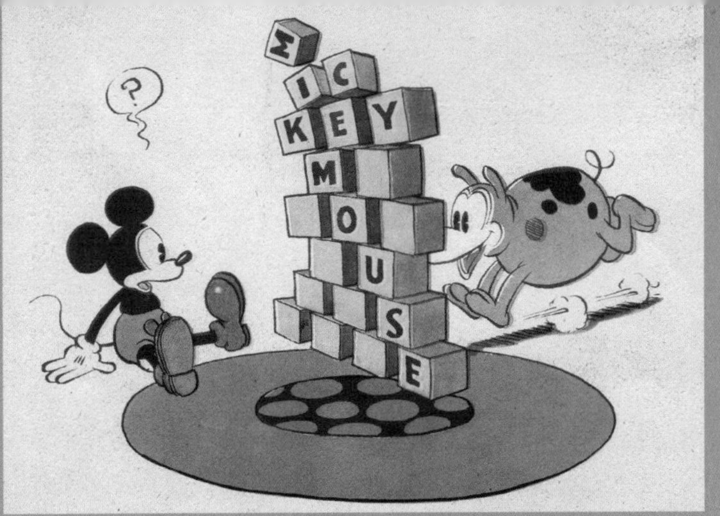
?
MICKEY MOUSE

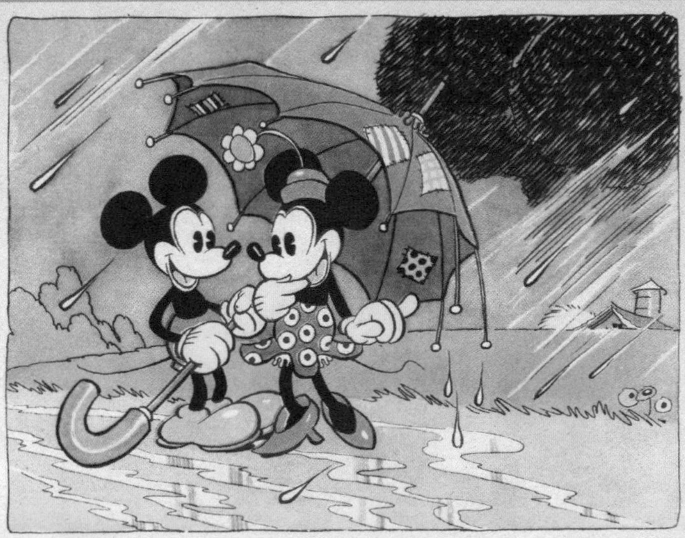

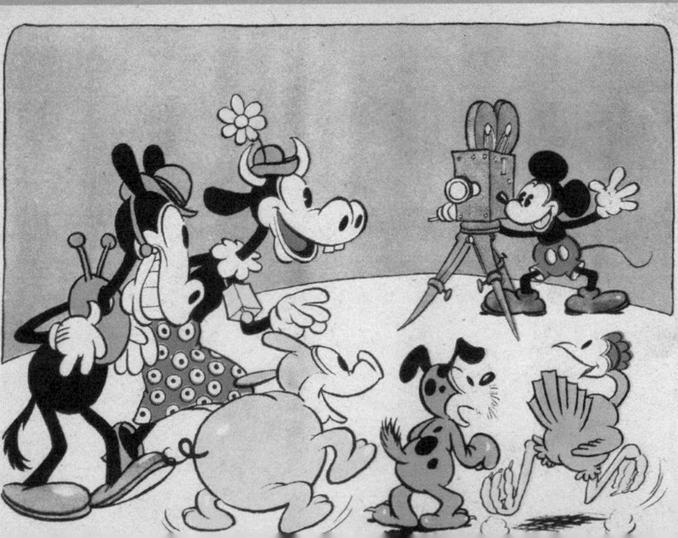

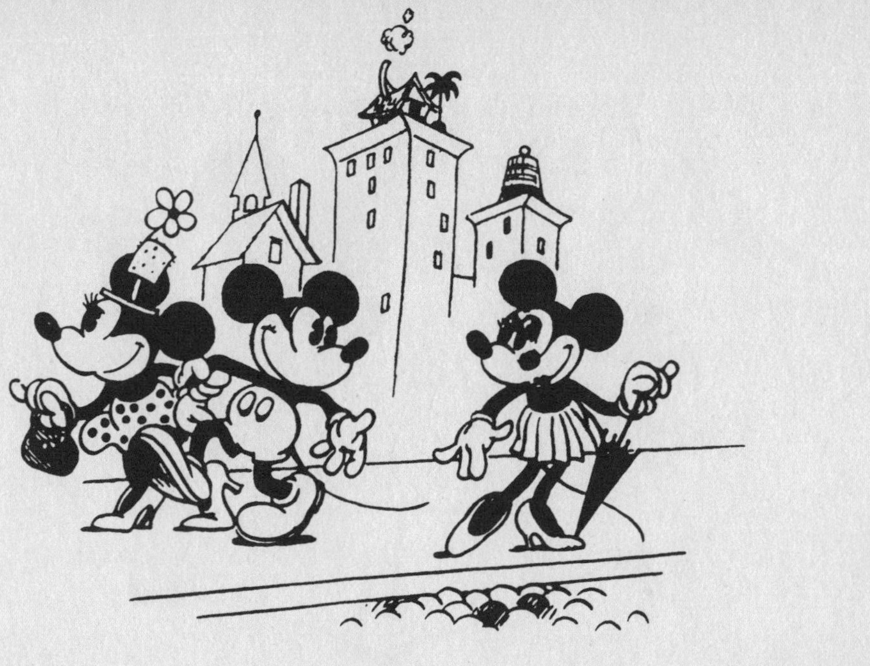

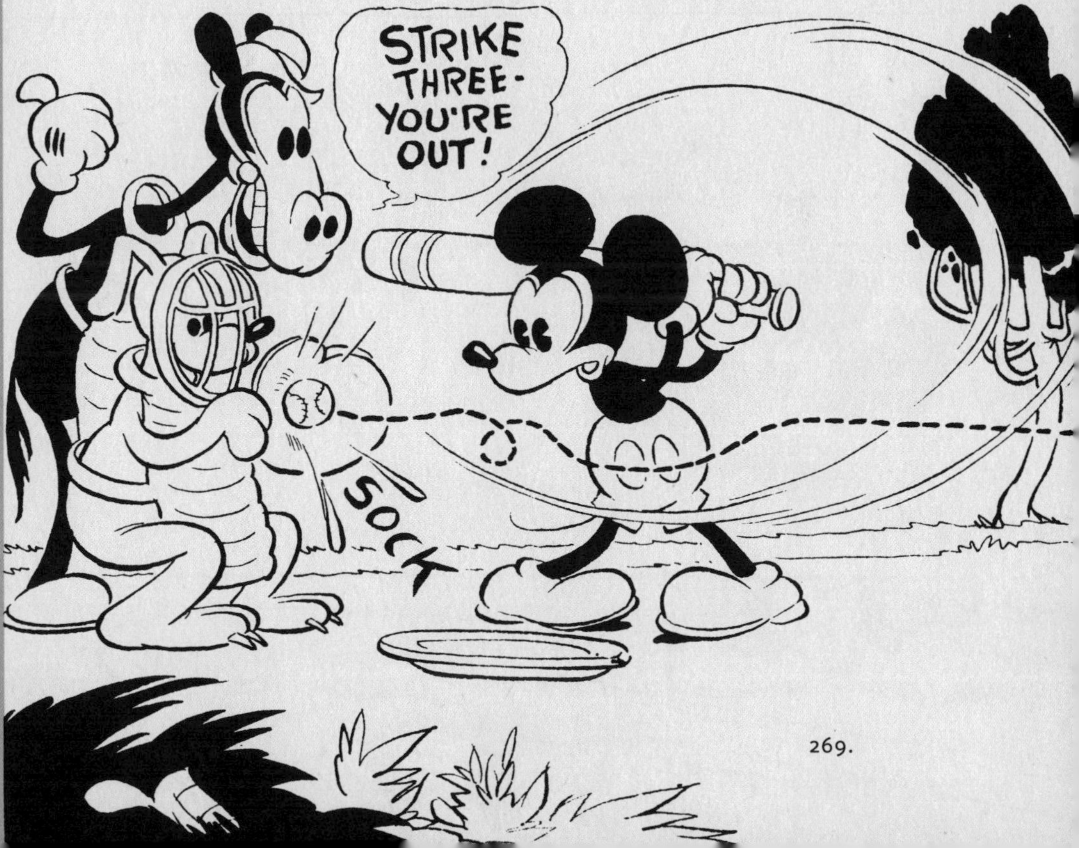
STRIKE THREE- YOU'RE OUT!
SOCK

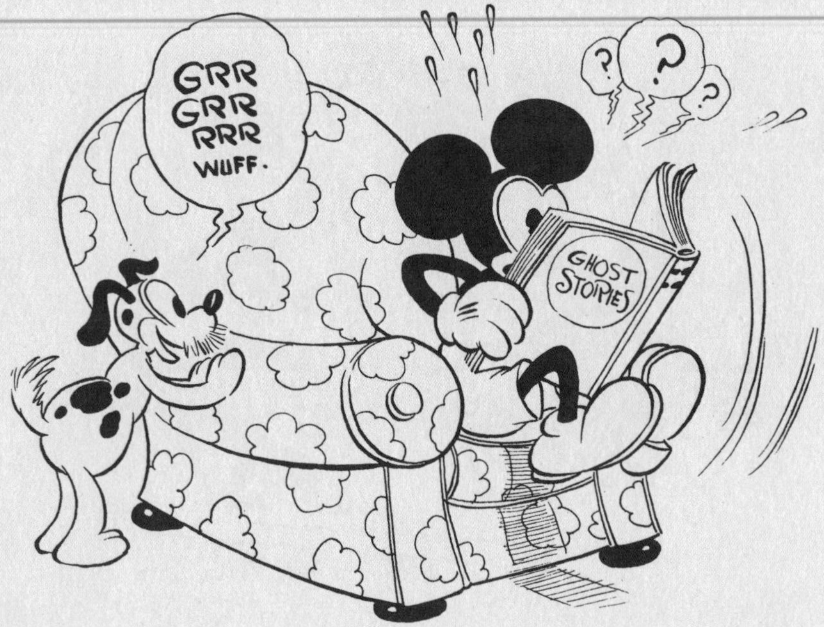
GRR
GRR
RRR
WUFF.
? ? ?
GHOST STORIES

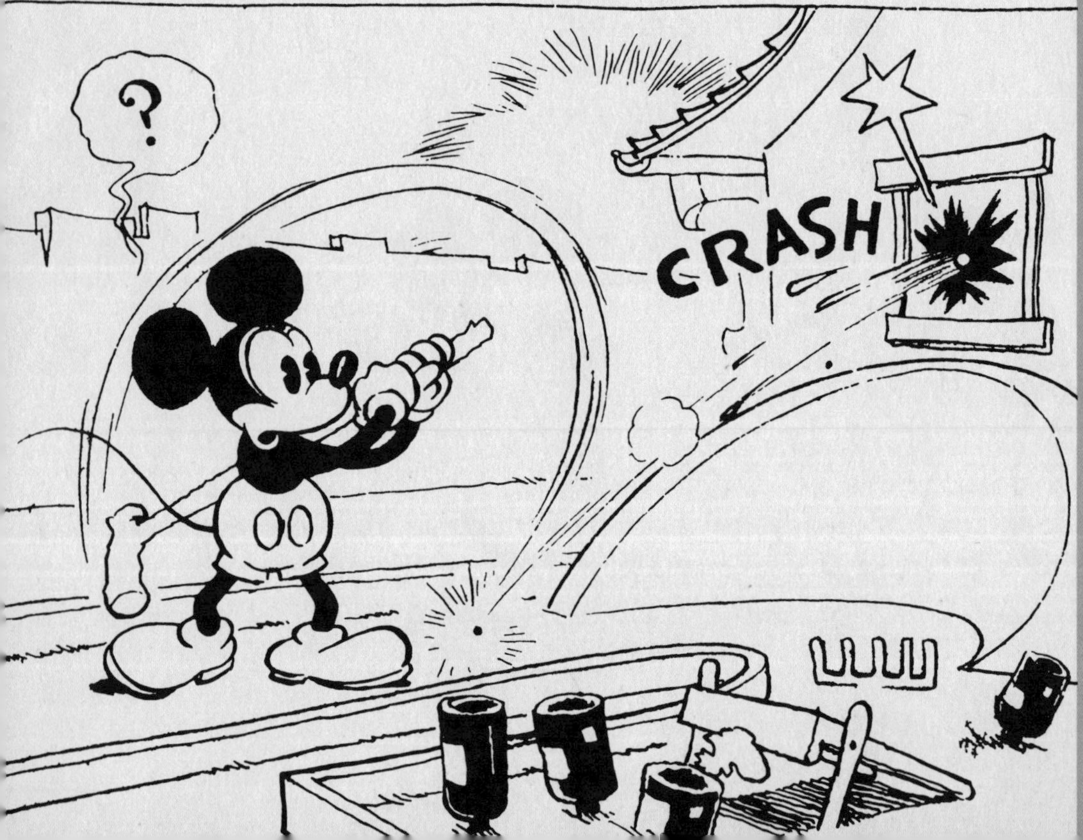
?
CRASH

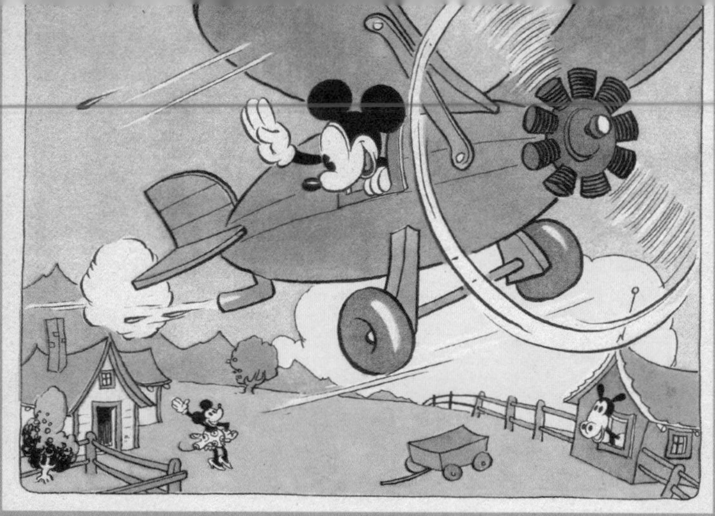

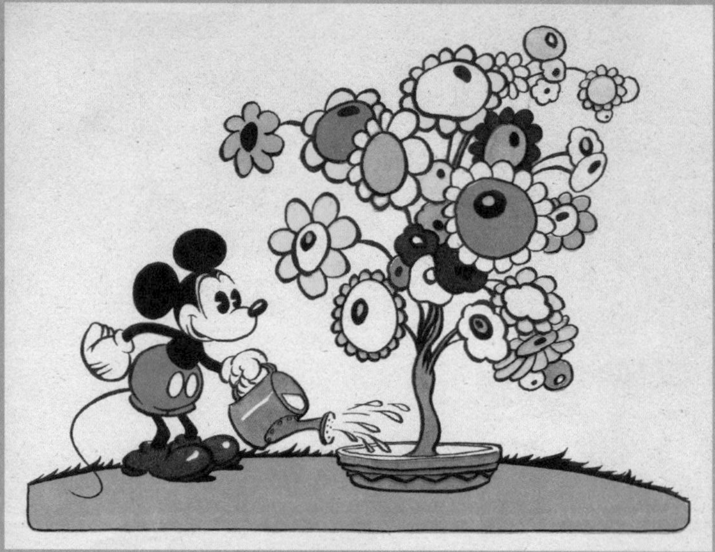

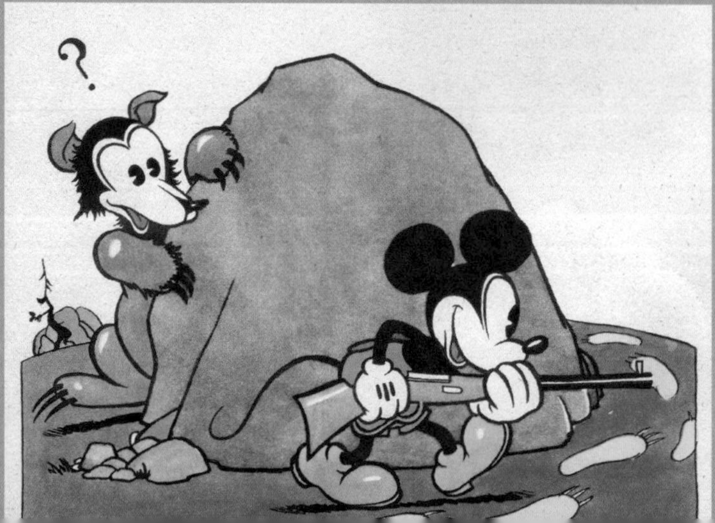
?

Gottfredson's World: MICKEY MOUSE vs. KAT NIPP

Somehow, the gods of comic book publishing frowned on Kat Nipp. While other Mickey stories had brand-new covers drawn for them in multiple countries, the tail-knotting bully got a 1930s cover in Italy alone—and instead of an original drawing, it consisted almost entirely of Gottfredson clip art.

But a cat always comes back. While perhaps not a *cover* star, Nipp has reappeared in various new comic book *stories* over the years. [DG]

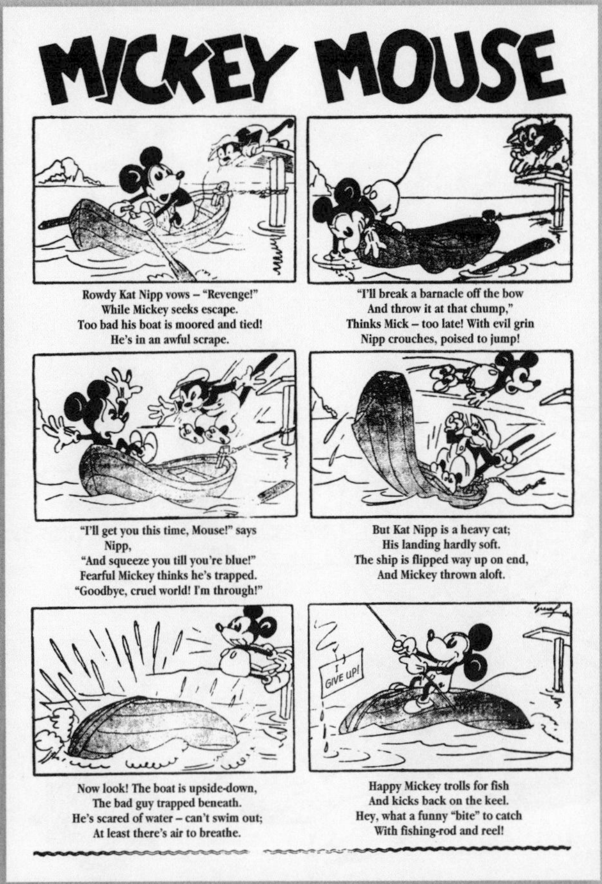
MICKEY MOUSE
Rowdy Kat Nipp vows – "Revenge!"
While Mickey seeks escape.
Too bad his boat is moored and tied!
He's in an awful scrape.
"I'll break a barnacle off the bow
And throw it at that chump,"
Thinks Mick – too late! With evil grin
Nipp crouches, poised to jump!
"I'll get you this time, Mouse!" says Nipp,
"And squeeze you till you're blue!"
Fearful Mickey thinks he's trapped.
"Goodbye, cruel world! I'm through!"
But Kat Nipp is a heavy cat;
His landing hardly soft.
The ship is flipped way up on end,
And Mickey thrown aloft.
I GIVE UP!
Now look! The boat is upside-down,
The bad guy trapped beneath.
He's scared of water – can't swim out;
At least there's air to breathe.
Happy Mickey trolls for fish
And kicks back on the keel.
Hey, what a funny "bite" to catch
With fishing-rod and reel!

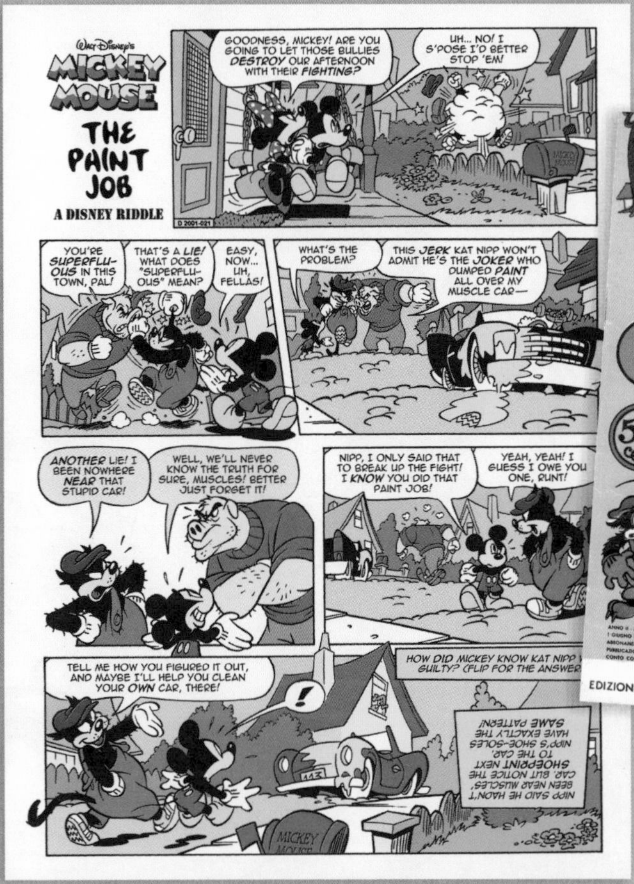
WALT DISNEY'S MICKEY MOUSE
THE PAINT JOB
A DISNEY RIDDLE
GOODNESS, MICKEY! ARE YOU GOING TO LET THOSE BULLIES DESTROY OUR AFTERNOON WITH THEIR FIGHTING?
UH... NO! I S'POSE I'D BETTER STOP 'EM!
YOU'RE SUPERFLUOUS IN THIS TOWN, PAL!
THAT'S A LIE! WHAT DOES "SUPERFLUOUS" MEAN?
EASY, NOW... UH, FELLAS!
WHAT'S THE PROBLEM?
THIS JERK KAT NIPP WON'T ADMIT HE'S THE JOKER WHO DUMPED PAINT ALL OVER MY MUSCLE CAR—
ANOTHER LIE! I BEEN NOWHERE NEAR THAT STUPID CAR!
WELL, WE'LL NEVER KNOW THE TRUTH FOR SURE, MUSCLES! BETTER JUST FORGET IT!
NIPP, I ONLY SAID THAT TO BREAK UP THE FIGHT! I KNOW YOU DID THAT PAINT JOB!
YEAH, YEAH! I GUESS I OWE YOU ONE, RUNT!
TELL ME HOW YOU FIGURED IT OUT, AND MAYBE I'LL HELP YOU CLEAN YOUR OWN CAR, THERE!
HOW DID MICKEY KNOW KAT NIPP WAS GUILTY? (FLIP FOR THE ANSWER.)
NIPP SAID HE HADN'T BEEN NEAR MUSCLES' CAR, BUT NOTICE THE SHOEPRINT NEXT TO THE CAR. NIPP'S SHOE-SOLES HAVE EXACTLY THE SAME PATTERN!
MICKEY MOUSE

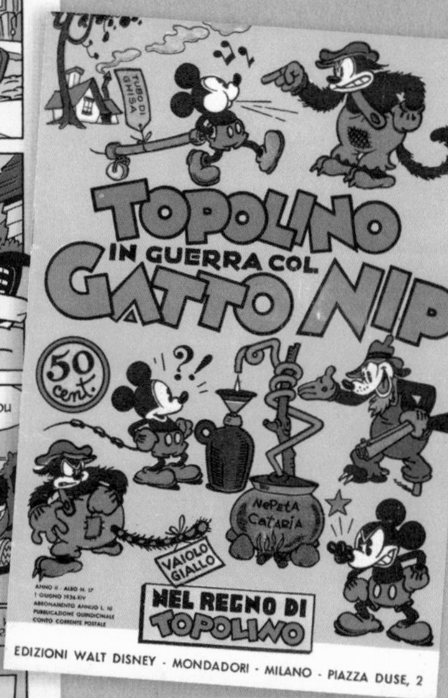
TUBO DI GHISA
TOPOLINO IN GUERRA COL GATTO NIP
50 cent.
NePeta CatARIA
VAIOLO GIALLO
ANNO II - ALBO N. 17
1 GIUGNO 1936-XIV
ABBONAMENTO ANNUO L. 10
PUBBLICAZIONE QUINDICINALE
CONTO CORRENTE POSTALE
NEL REGNO DI TOPOLINO
EDIZIONI WALT DISNEY - MONDADORI - MILANO - PIAZZA DUSE, 2

LEFT: Art by Guglielmo Guastaveglia (*Il Popolo di Roma* newspaper, August 6, 1931). Guastaveglia was the first Italian cartoonist to create original Disney comics. Image courtesy Leonardo Gori.

CENTER: Story by Lars Jensen, art by Xavier Vives Mateu (Danish *Anders And & Co.* 2002-33); English lettering by David Gerstein.

RIGHT: Collage "cover" to Italian *Nel Regno di Topolino* 17 (1936). Image courtesy Leonardo Gori.

Talk about spoilers. While "Mickey Mouse, Boxing Champion" got two beautiful covers to itself in the 1930s, Italian publisher Mondadori gave away a little too much about the story's ending—by showing an embarrassingly unscary Creamo Catnera flat on his back! [DG]

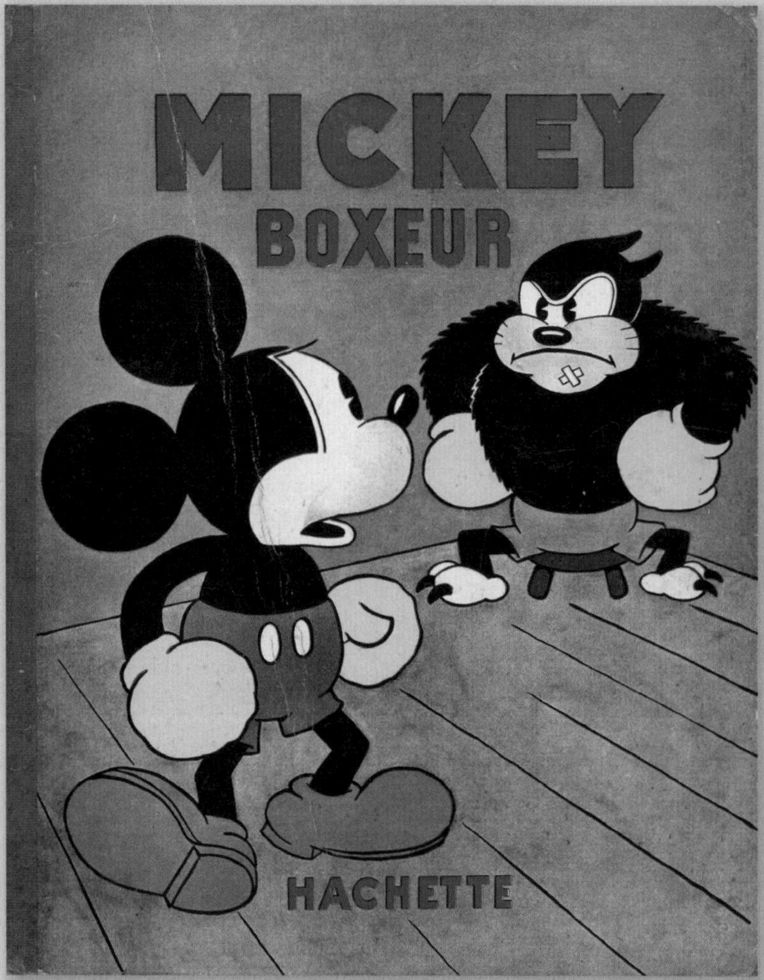
MICKEY
BOXEUR
HACHETTE

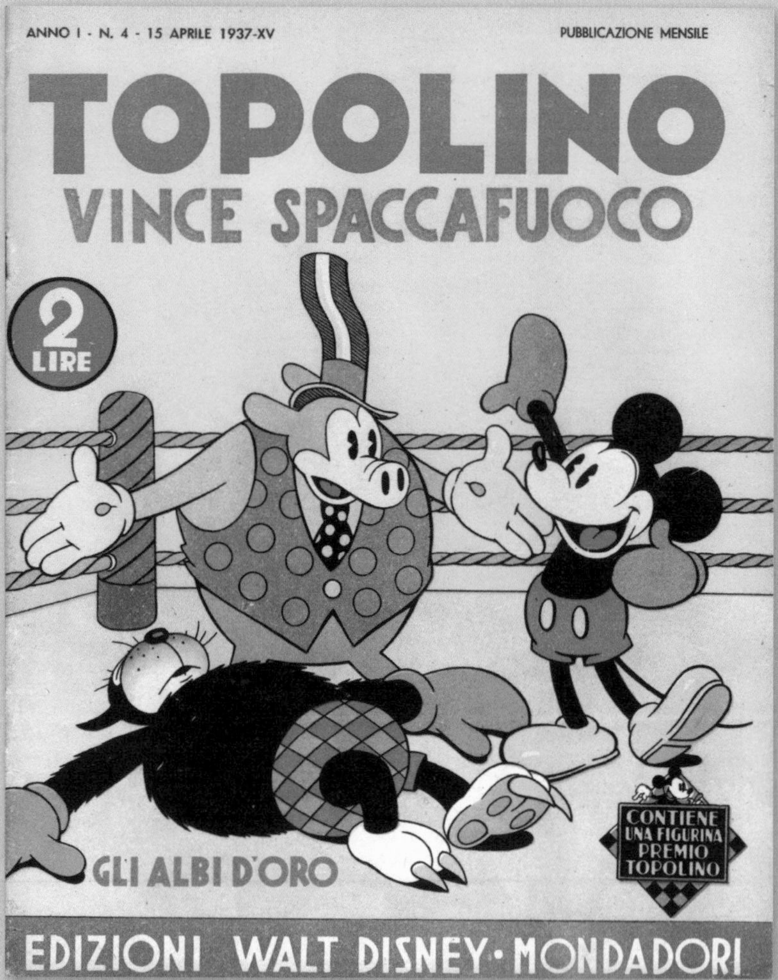
ANNO I - N. 4 - 15 APRILE 1937-XV
PUBBLICAZIONE MENSILE
TOPOLINO
VINCE SPACCAFUOCO
2 LIRE
GLI ALBI D'ORO
CONTIENE UNA FIGURINA PREMIO TOPOLINO
EDIZIONI WALT DISNEY·MONDADORI

LEFT: Cover to French *Album Mickey* 4 (1932). Artist unknown.

RIGHT: Cover to Italian *Albo d'Oro* 4 (1937). Art by Michele Rubino; image courtesy Leonardo Gori. Move along—no more boxing to see here.

Sharing the Spotlight: EARL DUVALL

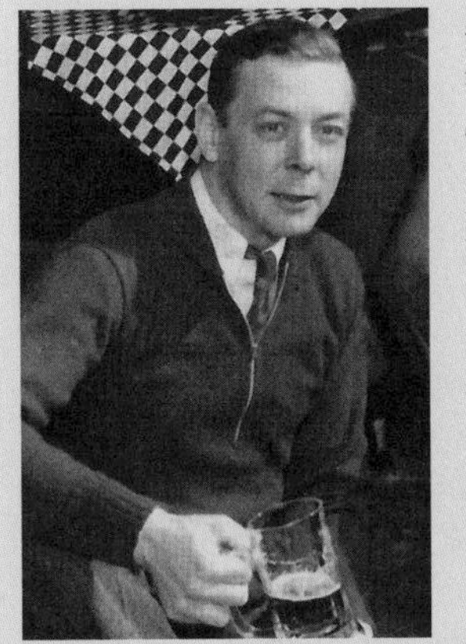

Born June 17, 1898, in a front room across from the Navy Yard, Washington, D. C. Public schools too difficult... entered business college. Big success at fourteen as page for U. S. Senator Joseph Weldon Bailey of Texas. Joe got in bad with Senate and Mrs. Duvall's son joined the regular army. Served during [World War I] at Hazelhurst Field, Mineola, New York. After the war hooked up with New York World *and then entered art department [at]* Washington Times. *Later with* Washington Post, *Bell Syndicate, New York. Came to California for no reason whatsoever and Walt gave me a job. Married, have one son and hay fever.*[1]

...THAT'S WHERE EARL DUVALL'S potted autobiography left off in 1931—when he and other Disney employees wrote quick bios *en masse* for a special *Motion Picture Daily* feature. Missing, however, were details of what Duvall *did* at Disney's. Though billed as a "gag man," Duvall in fact accomplished much more.

Like Hardie Gramatky before him, Duvall seems to have started out as a Disney part-timer or freelancer; like Gramatky, he spent much of his proving period inking *Mickey* dailies. *Mickey Mouse* was not Duvall's first comics job—in 1929, Earl jammed with Bob Pilgrim on Paramount Syndicate's *Christmas Adventure* strip—but *Mickey* is the earliest example we know of Duvall's talents being applied to *humor*. His bouncy ink line made a perfect match for Floyd Gottfredson's wild "Mickey Mouse Vs. Kat Nipp."

Notably, Duvall could also pencil Mickey, allowing him to draw specialty mouse designs for coloring books and games. He was also a layout artist and—yes—a gag man; as such, Duvall became a full-time Disney staffer in June 1931, the same month that he was profiled in *Motion Picture Daily.*[2]

When the *Mickey Mouse* Sunday page was launched in 1932, Duvall made his mark again. A *Silly Symphony* feature was the obvious top strip for *Mickey*, but the *Silly* shorts had few characters who could be adapted to such a strip. What to do? Then Duvall hit on fleshing out a bug mascot from *Silly* publicity: first for the *Silly* Sunday, then for a cartoon short, *Bugs in Love* (1932). Earl Duvall's Bucky Bug became a Disney comics mainstay. With his sweetheart June, his hobo pal Bo, and his unique rhyming dialogue, Bucky owned the *Silly* Sunday until 1934, got new comic book stories from 1943, and remains famous today in many European Disney venues.

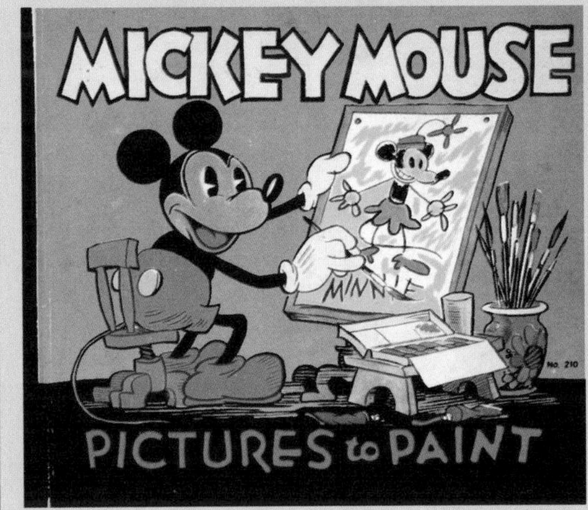
MICKEY MOUSE
MINNIE
PICTURES to PAINT

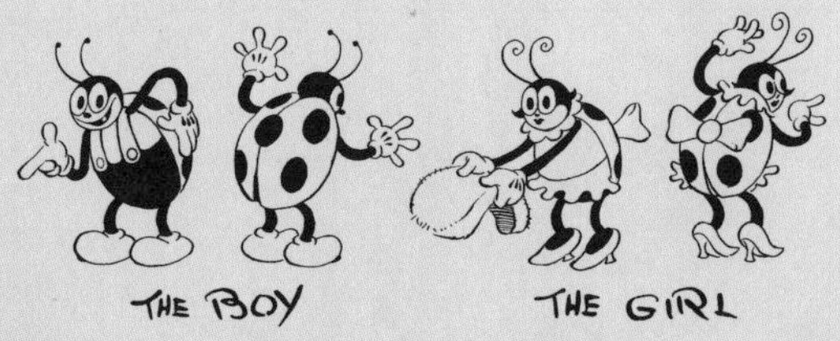
THE BOY
THE GIRL

As for Bucky's creator, Duvall penciled *Silly Symphonies* through mid-1932 and wrote it until 1933, when he left Disney—running out, it was claimed, on money owed to colleagues.[3] Later, on the Looney Tunes lot, Duvall tried to invent another star that clicked like Bucky—but Buddy, a dull human boy, wasn't it.[4] Visually, Buddy recalled silent-era cartoon kids; in action, he was a bore, without the verve, the rhyme scheme, or the fascinating bug world of Bucky Bug.

Desperate Duvall returned to insects in the Merrie Melody *Honeymoon Hotel* (1934), but he failed to make lightning bugs strike twice. Earl Duvall departed Schlesinger; first for Ub Iwerks' independent studio, then for a momentary return to Disney, then for obscurity. [DG]

ABOVE: Earl Duvall, future director of *Buddy's Beer Garden* (1933), in the early 1930s. Image courtesy Michael Barrier; photo © Hope Freleng Shaw, used with permission.

MIDDLE: Duvall cover drawing for an early children's book, 1931. For perhaps the only time, Mickey's tail is drawn and colored more like that of a real mouse.

FAR RIGHT: Duvall character models for *Bugs in Love* (1932), rendered before Bucky Bug or June had their later, svelter designs.

1 Earl Duvall et al., "The Personalities Behind the Laughs." *Motion Picture Daily*, June 20, 1931.

2 Michael Barrier, *Hollywood Cartoons* (New York: Oxford University Press, 1999), p. 105.

3 Jack Kinney, *Walt Disney and Assorted Other Characters* (New York: Harmony Books, 1988), p. 74.

4 Later Schlesinger/Warner director Bob Clampett identified Duvall as Buddy's creator. "Bob Clampett: An Interview With a Master Cartoon Maker and Puppeteer." *Funnyworld* 12, 1970.

The Cast: BUTCH

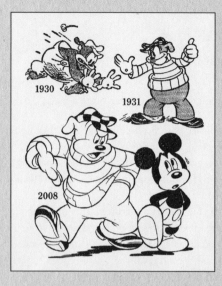

1930
1931
2008

A new writer brought onto an existing comics property never knows when he'll first "strike gold"—when he'll first introduce a new character memorable enough to join the recurring cast. Sometimes it never happens. Other times the new writer tries too hard, self-consciously building a stable of Mary Sues.

But sometimes the right chemistry is in play. A walk-on player is casually introduced as part of a single story—then seems to drift naturally into return appearances. Even then, though, stardom is not instant; it takes time to determine staying power, to work out bugs and tweak personality flaws. The more experience a writer has, the more easily character development comes.

Butch, Mickey's roughneck pal, was a test case for Floyd Gottfredson. Introduced as a villain's hired mook in "Mr. Slicker and the Egg Robbers," Butch began life as a generic grizzled, over-the-hill thug. But the more Floyd wrote of "old Butch," the more eccentric and memorable he became; protecting Mickey with a "mother's heart," lifting a live cow in his mighty grip. One can sense Gottfredson enjoying his new creation; so much so that Butch's later return, in "Mickey Mouse, Boxing Champion," came as no surprise.

But Floyd was not yet experienced in the ways of character building. Making Butch an ongoing player seems to have caused Gottfredson to rethink the tough guy's advanced age; perhaps the reasoning was that a good friend for Mickey ought to be his peer as well.

Thus, when featured in "Boxing Champion," convict Butch was still called "old"—but visually seemed to get younger, strip by strip. In the subsequent "High Society," a paroled Butch lost his modifier and behaved as if he were Mickey's own age. At times, the friendship between earnest Mickey and crude-but-amiable Butch mirrored that of Castor Oyl and Popeye in E. C. Segar's *Thimble Theatre*; tellingly, both Popeye and Butch broke out of prison single-handedly, and both Popeye and Butch seemed to grow younger over time. When Butch made a brief return to kindergarten in "High Society," his evolution into a well-meaning delinquent was complete.

Butch left Gottfredson's stories after 1931, but remained memorable for his unique personality—enough so that in the 1990s, Butch was revived as an ongoing member of the Mickey comics cast. His original geezer status, however, remains forgotten. In fact, today's Mickey would probably tell you that his roughneck chum still has a lot of growing up to do. [DG]

TOP: Butch then and now; modern image by César Ferioli (*Walt Disney's Comics and Stories* 689).

BOTTOM: Rejected first draft of the daily strip for May 2, 1931; compare with the published version on page 141. Image courtesy Alberto Becattini.

ALL RIGHT, MICKEY - I'M PAROLING BUTCH TO YOU - IF YOU CAN MAKE A GOOD CITIZEN OUT OF HIM WE DON'T WANT HIM IN HERE -
THANK YOU, WARDEN. YOU WON'T REGRET IT!
NOW, BUTCH - THE FIRST THING YOU'VE GOT TO LEARN IS RESPECT FOR THE LAW - NO LAW IS SO SMALL THAT YOU CAN DISREGARD IT IF YOU WANT TO BECOME A GOOD CITIZEN!
! ? ?
DO NOT SPIT ON SIDEWALK
ORDER POLICE DEPT.
©By Walter E. Disney. Great Britain rights reserved.
HEY, MICKEY - CAN YOU BORRY ME A HALF A BUCK? I NEEDS SOMETHIN' IN HERE AWFUL BAD
DWARE STORE
SURE, BUTCH - DON'T BE GONE LONG
YER RIGHT MICKEY IT AINT RIGHT - T' BUST EVEN THE LITTLE LAWS
SPECIAL SPITOONS 50¢
KDWARE STORE
SPUT!
?
WALT DISNEY 5-2

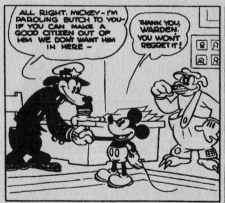

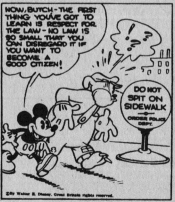

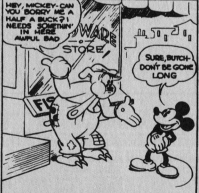

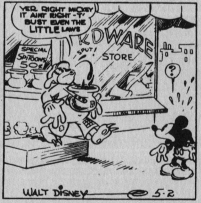

Sharing the Spotlight: AL TALIAFERRO

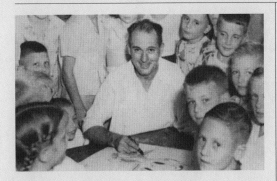

SOMETIMES A SORCERER'S APPRENTICE makes trouble for his master—with or without the help of a live broom. But other times, the apprentice is more than equal to his tasks, and ends up becoming a great conjuror himself. That's the story of Al Taliaferro (1905-1969), an assistant Mouse Man who turned master of the Duck.

Born on August 29, 1905 in Montrose, Colorado, Charles Alfred Taliaferro studied art history at California's Glendale High School, and learned to draw in part through a correspondence course.[1]

ABOVE: Al Taliaferro, mouse assistant—and duck pioneer, 1940s. Image courtesy The Walt Disney Company.

TOP RIGHT: Taliaferro's mature postwar designs for Donald and the gang. Promotional art, 1954.

BELOW: Mickey is surrounded by classic Taliaferro character types in the Sunday strip for January 30, 1938—inked but also partly penciled by Taliaferro.

PUBLISHERS'
GOLDEN
ANNIVERSARY
PASADENA
STAR-NEWS
COLORADO BLVD.
BEST WISHES!
WALT DISNEY
Copr. 1954, Walt Disney Productions
World Rights Reserved
Distributed by King Features Syndicate.

BANG
DON'T SHOOT! WE GIVE UP!
I DON'T KNOW HOW YOU DID IT, YOUNG FELLOW, BUT YOU'VE GOT A REWARD COMING TO YOU!
PD
!
SWELL! THEN I CAN GET A NEW TIRE IN PLACE OF THIS BLOW-OUT!
!
1·30

Al was working for a lighting firm in 1931 when he learned that Disney had jobs available. Easily passing muster with the boss, Taliaferro was given the task of inking Floyd Gottfredson's *Mickey Mouse* strips—and, soon, Earl Duvall's *Silly Symphonies* Sundays.

"I knew I was going to be a cartoonist," Taliaferro said in a 1968 interview. "I've always believed that if you want anything bad enough and you work hard enough for it, eventually you'll get it."[2] Taliaferro's smooth, rounded line style made him a natural complement for Gottfredson and Duvall. In late 1932, Duvall became "just" the writer on *Silly Symphonies*, leaving all the art to Taliaferro. Al's *Silly* solo work initially featured Bucky Bug, but his later tales of Big Bad Wolf, Max Hare, and Cookieland were no less inspired.

Taliaferro's ink work on *Mickey Mouse* continued on and off until 1938; though the studio record shows him "only" inking the strip, a lot of penciling in 1937-38 is visibly his as well—suggesting that often, Gottfredson all but yielded the field to him. By 1938, however, Taliaferro had little to gain by sticking with Mickey: he had found a new subject.

Taliaferro's first work with Donald Duck came in the *Silly* Sunday, where a 1934 "Wise Little Hen" serial constituted Donald's comics debut. Taliaferro, a personal fan of the maladjusted mallard, rooted to see more done with him. In 1936, his agitation led to a sixteen-month run of *Silly* Sundays starring the character. When those proved a success, Donald got his own daily strip in 1938, with Taliaferro as artist—a role he would keep until his death.

While Taliaferro rarely wrote the Donald strips he drew, he did suggest plot hooks and new characters to his scripters. In 1937, Taliaferro's creation of Donald's nephews Huey, Dewey, and Louie led to their debut on the screen; in 1940, Taliaferro's "small but mighty" mother-in-law Donnie Wheaton was the inspiration for stern farmer Grandma Duck.[3] Taliaferro also turned Bolivar, the St. Bernard from the cartoons *Alpine Climbers* and *More Kittens* (1936), into the Duck family dog—a role Bolivar retains in modern comics.

Al Taliaferro passed away just as Disney fans were first learning about his significance. Today, Taliaferro's classic strips are reprinted worldwide—and he is remembered not just for his own works, but for having created a Duck pantheon upon which the better-known Carl Barks later built. [DG]

1 Thomas Schrøder, "Al Taliaferro," *Anders And & Co. – Den komplette årgang 1960-2* (Copenhagen: Egmont Serieforlaget A/S, 2006), p. 7.

2 Al Taliaferro quoted in Jim Korkis, "Just Another Duck Man," *The Duckburg Times* 14 (April 28, 1982), p. 14.

3 Thomas Andrae, "The Legacy of Al Taliaferro," *Walt Disney's Comics and Stories* 522 (September 1987), p.15.

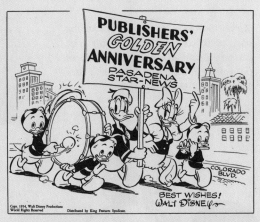

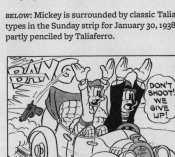

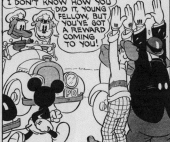

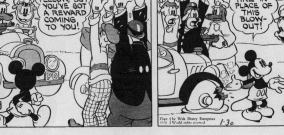

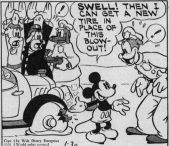

Mickey the last of the Great Troubadors, pays court to his Minnie with true classic passion. Minnie, in turn, adores the romantic rodent—"because I love Mice things," she explains shyly.

The Gottfredson Gang in "Their Own" Words

PART ONE

By David Gerstein

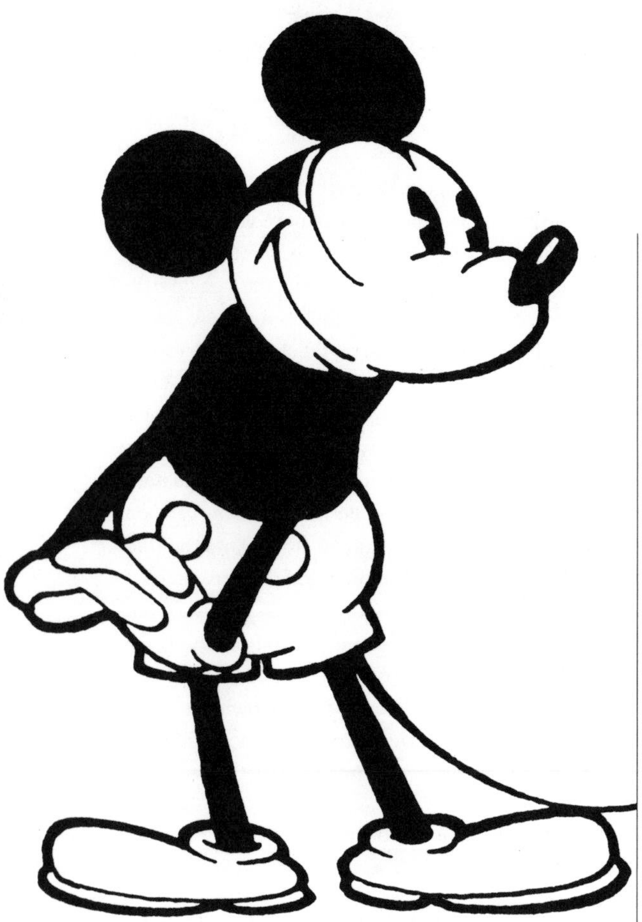

IN COMPARING DISNEY FILMS with Disney comics, modern fans can be forgiven for perceiving an amazing difference in tone. Characters at once brooding and philosophical in the daily strip became simple bounding, squealing animals on the silver screen. "I didn't realize how conditions were before," muses Gottfredson's Minnie in "Mr. Slicker and the Egg Robbers" (1930), after carefully analyzing an economic threat. In animation, the contemporary Minnie's most upstanding act was to dump hot coals down a bad guy's trousers (in *Pioneer Days*, also 1930).

What today's readers lack, in comparing cartoons to Gottfredson strips, is context. Rather than let films and comics languish in discontinuity, the 1930s Disney publicity machine forged a careful connection between its two main forms of output. The connection came in the form of carefully worded articles arranged with the press, fleshing out the cartoon characters as "actors" and celebrities. In a classic example of synergy, Gottfredson's strip began to reflect the same "reality": while Mickey was not presented as an actor, 1931's "High Society" gave him the status—and the pitfalls—of celebrity, too.

Like every celebrity, this famous Mickey was "interviewed" as part of the press onslaught. Authorized by Disney, but with an adult target group clearly in mind, the resulting pieces featured Tinseltown intrigue, embarrassing moments, and evidence of a Gottfredson-like youthful Mouse beneath a celebrity façade. But why not let these memorable relics do their own talking? In this volume of Fantagraphics' *Mickey Mouse* series we're excerpting rare tete-a-tetes with Mickey and Pluto, accompanied by their original Comic Strip Department illustrations. We'll bring you follow-up "chats" with Horace Horsecollar, Clarabelle Cow, and others in future volumes.

Be aware, by the way, that Disney's star characters no longer endorse or recommend certain unhealthy habits—like smoking!—that they occasionally display in these vintage pieces. [DG]

THIS SPREAD: Mickey vignette drawing by Les Clark. Minnie vignette by Earl Duvall, adapted from January 3, 1931 daily strip.

Confessions of MICKEY MOUSE

Mickey tells all! Read the thrilling story of the great mouse's life and loves!
By MORTIMER FRANKLIN

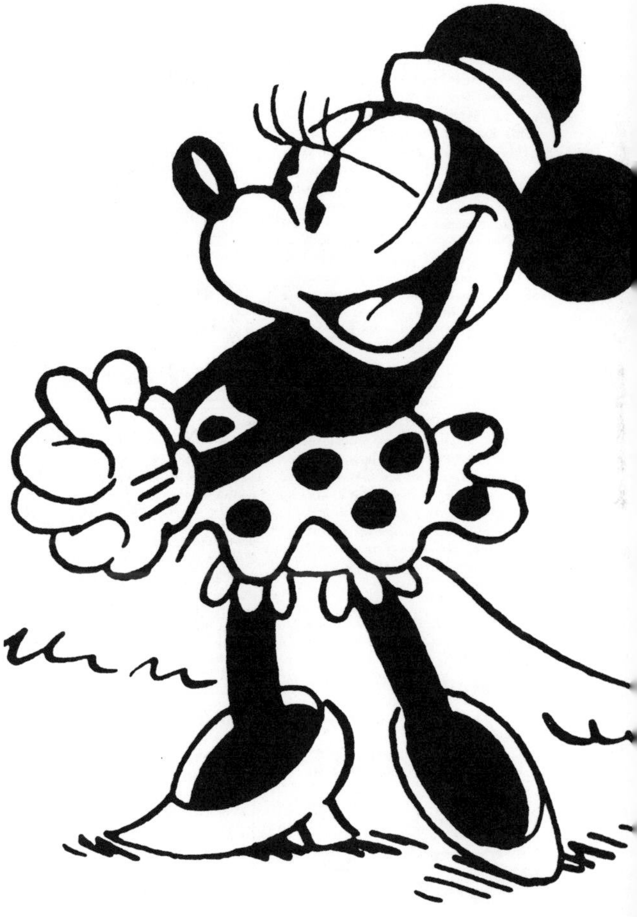

Excerpted from Screenland *Vol. XXIV No. 4, February 1932*

A "M. MOUSE—PRIVATE"

An august attendant ushered me in through the door on which the above legend was emblazoned in gold leaf.

Here, then, was that thrilling moment, the culmination of weeks of hoping and planning, when I was at last to interview the famous screen star, Mickey Mouse!

The opening door revealed him at the far end of a large room, reclining in a swivel chair behind an enormous glass-topped desk. The office exuded swank—deep, plushy rugs, heavy carved furniture, expensive-looking tapestries, exquisite floor-lamps. All was enveloped in a gentle half-light that seeped in through drawn curtains.

Miss Bloggs, the secretary who had granted me the appointment, met me at the door and presented me to my host. Some such greeting as a cheery slap on the back and a "Hi, Mickey!" had been in my mind. Instead, thoroughly awed, I took his paw almost reverently and mumbled, "Good morning, Mr. Mouse."

"Do sit down," he said indolently. "Do you prefer Russian cigarettes or Egyptian? Gold-tipped or straw?" He twirled a whisker elegantly, and I thought I detected more than a trace of the Oxford accent in his speech.

We lit our cigarettes, and then Mickey Mouse, without waiting for questions, began to talk rapidly and more than a bit pompously.

"I am deeply attached to my Art. To me it is the most important thing in life. I do not merely act my roles—I live them. My favorite poets are Shakespeare and Oscar Wilde. My favorite novel is 'A Tail of Two Cities.' My life's ambition is to play *Hamlet*. I am profoundly thrilled by the Essence of the Cosmic All, and yearn deeply to know the Inner Meaning of Life."

I sat there and gazed at him, forgetting to close my mouth, while he paused to take a breath. Then, as he observed my slightly deranged look, suddenly something happened to the young actor's face. Without otherwise changing his expression, he had given me a solemn wink!

"Oh, by the way, Miss Bloggs," he called, "would you mind running down to the bank and seeing if that statement is ready for me? And Wiggins"—

—CONTINUED ON PAGE 280

PRESS SHEET

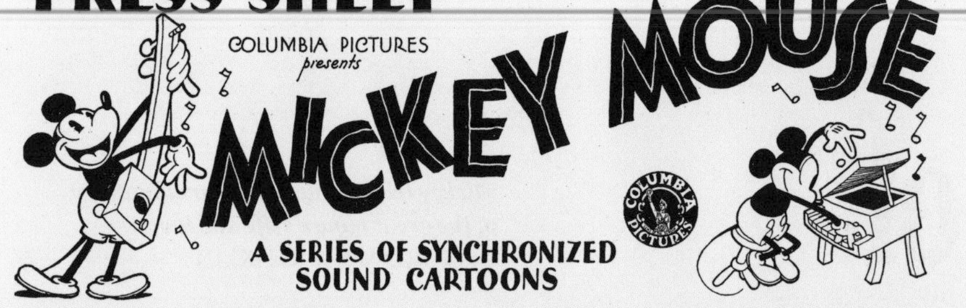

COLUMBIA PICTURES
presents
MICKEY MOUSE
A SERIES OF SYNCHRONIZED SOUND CARTOONS

DISTRIBUTED BY COLUMBIA PICTURES CORPORATION — 729 SEVENTH AVENUE, NEW YORK, N. Y.

WHIMSICAL 'MICKEY MOUSE' CARTOONS SUBJECT TO REGULAR FILM CENSORSHIP

The secret of the smooth, natural gestures characteristic of the Mickey Mouse cartoons is due to the fact that every care is taken to endow this popular screen favorite with almost human phrasing, action and tempo.

This beloved little ink spot can do anything a flesh and blood character can do. And in addition it performs fantastic whimsies which are possible only because Mickey can overcome natural obstacles and substance. But Walt Disney, Mickey's creator, tells us that his whimsical friend is subject to the same screen censorship that controls the destinies of the human heroes and heroines who do their stuff for the "talkies." In the latest Mickey Mouse release which comes to the .... Theatre on .... this ludicrous pen-and-ink child won't do anything that you and I couldn't do on the stage without blushing.

Mickey, a moral young mouse, never sings in his bath-tub unless the more delicate portions of his sinuous torso are concealed by a flock of rich, creamy suds. Mickey has a girl friend, Minnie, and while cartoon kisses aren't subject to clocking, yet Mickey makes certain that his camera conduct is always beyond reproach.

hello folks!
I'm here today!
MICKEY MOUSE
A WALT DISNEY COMIC
A Columbia Star
COLUMBIA PICTURES

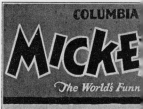

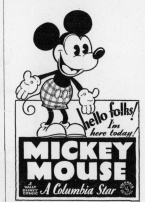

A CONSTANT REMINDER

that is sure to be a big attraction is the one sheet black-and-white poster illustrated above. It's worded so that it will be an eye-puller for any Mickey Mouse release. You should display it prominently in your lobby whenever Mickey Mouse comes to your theatre.

Mickey Mouse fans—and there are thousands and thousands of them—will eagerly look forward to seeing it. By using this poster in connection with the showing of the current release you will have an economical, striking one-sheet working for you all the time.

Hello Folks-
I'm here today!
MICKEY MOUSE
A WALT DISNEY COMIC
COLUMBIA PICTURES

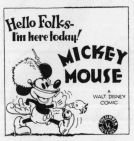

One Column Ad Cut or Mat No. 1

MICKEY MOUSE TITLES

THE FIRE FIGHTERS
THE CACTUS KID
PIONEER DAYS
GORILLA MYSTERY
THE PICNIC
FIDDLIN' AROUND
THE CHAIN GANG
THE BIRTHDAY PARTY

CAREFUL PLANNING EXACTING THOUGHT IN 'MICKEY MOUSE'

Takes Genius to Select Plots and Music

The next time you wipe the laugh drops off of your eyeglasses here at the .... Theatre, where Mickey Mouse cartoons are shown regularly as short features, remember, if you will, that the making of a six minute animated cartoon entails all of the careful thought, planning, writing and direction that goes into the making of many far more pretentious pictures that feature so-called 'live' actors and actresses.

Walt Disney, creator of Mickey Mouse, is an acknowledged production genius even out on the Hollywood coast, where the word genius is used grudgingly, at best.

According to the best authorities on the subject, Disney has the rare gift of rhythm and tempo that so many directors glibly discuss but seldom achieve.

How It Is Done

A successful cartoon doesn't "just happen." In the case of Mickey Mouse, a complete scenario containing plot, dialogue, gags and music is composed as carefully as though a million dollar production were to be translated to the screen. The action is generally adapted to the musical score, which is calculated not only for perfect synchronization, but in a manner designed to bring out the humorous accents and rhythms which are so characteristic of the Disney films.

After the musical score is completely transferred to the conductor's desk, the animation process progresses under the personal supervision of Mr. Disney, whose art staff includes some twenty draughtsmen who make the motion "frames" from Disney's key pictures, in addition to supplying the interesting backgrounds and cycloramic washes. It takes two weeks of hard, serious work to produce six minutes of laughs, and it costs between five and seven thousand dollars per reel.

"MICKEY MOUSE" NEWS SHORTS

Plant These Unique Items

STILLS

Get from your nearest Columbia Exchange the set of eight hilarious stills which show Mickey and Minnie Mouse in characteristic poses. Walt Disney has created masterpieces here. Display these stills effectively in your lobby. Put them in your local newspaper. Use them in your advertisements. They only cost ten cents apiece!

Mickey Mouse Leads Highly Moral Life

In the latest Mickey Mouse release, which comes to the .... Theatre on ...., you will see an animal who, although unhampered by a morality clause in his contract, is forced by the censors to lead a moral life.

Ohio recently banned a Mickey Mouse cartoon because a cartoon cow was portrayed reading a copy of Elinor Glyn's "Three Weeks." A German censorship board ruled: "The wearing of German military helmets by an army of cats which oppose the militia of mice is offensive to national dignity." And a Canadian board objected to the fact that a frollicking fish slapped a mermaid on the thigh with his fin.

Columbia Pictures
presents
MICKEY MOUSE
He Talks!
He Sings!
He Dances!

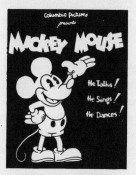

FLASH BANNER

Illustrated above is a gorgeous felt and metal banner the size of a one sheet (26 x 39). You can't beat it for splashing lobby and marquee display or for your theatre proper. You can get these banners for the astoundingly low price of $3.50 apiece. They'll quickly prove they're worth their weight in gold.

"Mickey Mouse" Makes Nation's Honor Roll

Mickey Mouse's sweetheart Minnie is all a-flutter. She says she always thought Mickey had it in him but now she knows. For in the latest Mickey Mouse release which comes to the .... Theatre on .... you will see a very famous character. Mickey has been awarded a place on the Honor Roll for 1930 along with other notables by the magazine, The Nation. Probably Mickey's grin couldn't be broader but in this latest release it almost seems so. He is obviously vastly amused by his mounting fame.

Mickey and Minnie Both Immortalized

Mickey Mouse and his sweetheart Minnie, who are to be seen in the latest Mickey Mouse release coming to the .... Theatre on ...., have come to new honors. For Mme. Taussaud in London has cabled Columbia Pictures asking Walt Disney, creator of the popular mouse, for permission to immortalize both Mickey and Minnie in wax figures to be placed permanently in her famous museum.

The notables of all ages and every country are represented in this collection, so the recognition of fictitious characters of the screen has caused much interest. It is said that Mickey is so popular in England that he is billed by British Theatre managers on the same scale as the greatest of Hollywood stars.

ONE SHEET POSTER

TO THE RIGHT, you will find A ONE SHEET POSTER ON Mickey Mouse, available in a complete series to illustrate each title. The poster is reproduced in brilliant colors from an original artistic drawing, and is a stock accessory. General illustration remains the same, but title imprint is changed for each release. Make generous use of this striking advertising unit.

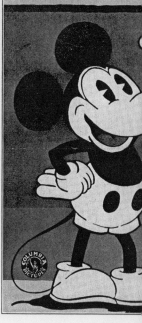

COLUMBIA
MICKE
The World's Funn
BARNYAR

ONE SH

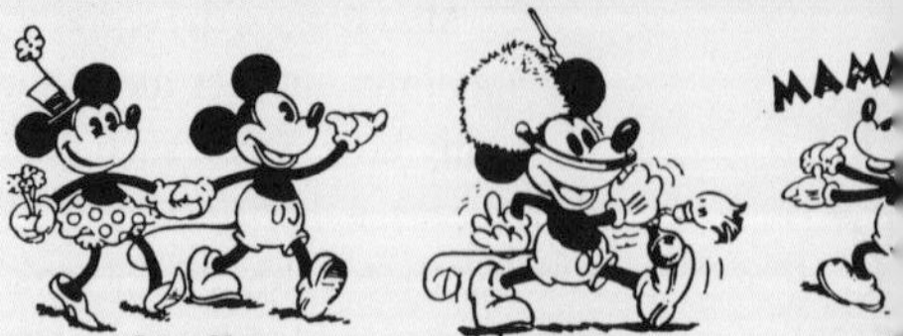

THESE WAGGISH, LAUGH-PROVOKING MICKEY MOUS
THEY MAKE SPLENDID ORIGINAL ADS AND THEY C
THE BIG ADS WHICH TELL

Mickey Mouse Poses

Available in Cuts or Mats

Cut or Mat— No. 2 — Cut or Mat— No. 3 — Cut or M No.

278. Print tie-ins were just one part of early Mickey publicity. This never-before-reprinted 1930 pressbook gives us a look at the bigger picture.

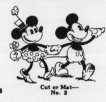

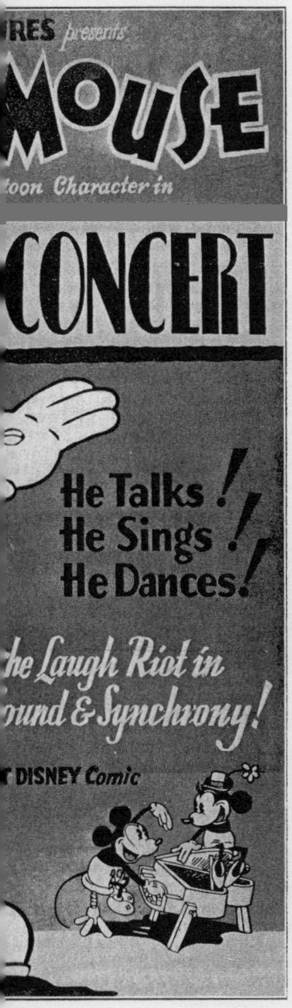
RES presents
MOUSE
toon Character in
CONCERT
He Talks!
He Sings!
He Dances!
he Laugh Riot in
ound & Synchrony!
T DISNEY Comic

OSTER

TEN CENT STORES SELL MICKEY BOOK

Columbia Pictures' Mickey Mouse animated cartoons will receive an additional boost via the 5-and-10-cent stores, all department stores having children's departments and toy departments, as well as all book and stationery shops, as a result of a recently effected tie-up.

The Walt Disney Studios, producers of the Mickey Mouse short subjects, have joined forces with Messrs. Bibo & Lang, Inc., music publishers, and are issuing a series of Mickey Mouse books as an exploitation boost in the popularity of this animated screen cartoon series. The first of these books, a 16 page, heavy-paper covered volume, size 9 x 12, and printed in a two-color job, has just been released during the past month.

The book, the circulation of which has reached tremendous proportions, deals with Mickey's adventures in Fairyland, and was written by Bobette Bibo. Her father, the publisher Irving Bibo, wrote an original ditty about Mickey's antics, the words and music of which are included in this first volume, and a most amusing game known as the Mickey Mouse journey, is another important feature of the new book. Studio cartoons by Walt Disney, creator of MICKEY MOUSE, profusely illustrate the work throughout.

11 x 14 LOBBY CARD

The attractive 11 x 14 black-and-white lobby card for Mickey Mouse is shown on the right hand corner of this page. The inimitable animal is announcing that he has arrived. That'll be good news for men, women, and children. Be sure and display this card prominently so they can't miss it. Incorporate it in your lobby set advertising your feature attraction.

SNAPPY REVIEWS OR RADIO SHORTS

The .... Theatre has a well-rounded program this week that is especially worth seeing because of ...., the latest Mickey Mouse cartoon. Here is clean, wholesome entertainment chock full of laughs and thrills. You can always feel sure that both you and the kiddies will have a "big time" when you see the hilarious antics of Mickey Mouse.

* * * * *

A sure cure for all this talk about depression and hard times is a trip to the .... Theatre this week. The famous Mickey Mouse cavorts all over the screen in a new and screamingly funny cartoon entitled .... Mickey can always be depended upon to dispel troubles but this latest laugh provoker .... is the best thing he has done yet.

* * * * *

The only trouble with the Mickey Mouse cartoons lies in the fact that they are much too short ...., Mickey's latest caper now on view at the .... Ther.tre, is so funny that you may have to borrow a handkerchief from your neighbor to wipe the tears of glee from your cheek—providing—your neighbor isn't rolling out in the aisles, convulsed with laughter himself. Long live Mickey.

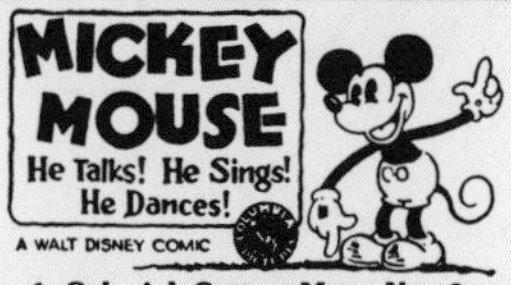
MICKEY MOUSE
He Talks! He Sings! He Dances!
A WALT DISNEY COMIC

1 Col. Ad Cut or Mat—No. 8

ACCESSORIES FOR MICKEY

POSTERS	
1 Sheet—Lithographed	$ .15 each
1 Sheet—Black & White	.15 each
LOBBY CARD	
11 x 14—Black & White	.10 each
BANNER	
Felt and Metal	3.50 each
ADS AND LINE CUTS	
Cuts	.25 per col.
Mats	.05 per col.
Two Teaser Ad Cuts	
Six Line Cuts	
STILLS	
8 to set (10c. apiece)	.80 per set

CAN BE PUT TO MANY HIGHLY PROFITABLE USES. EADILY AND ATTRACTIVELY INCORPORATED IN R FEATURE ATTRACTION.

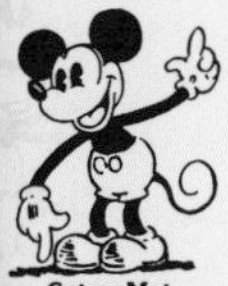

Cut or Mat—No. 5

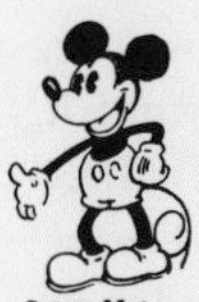

Cut or Mat—No. 6

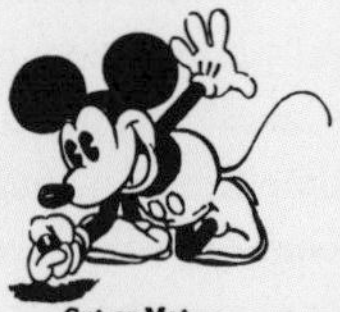

Cut or Mat—No. 7

Boost "Mickey" With These Drawings

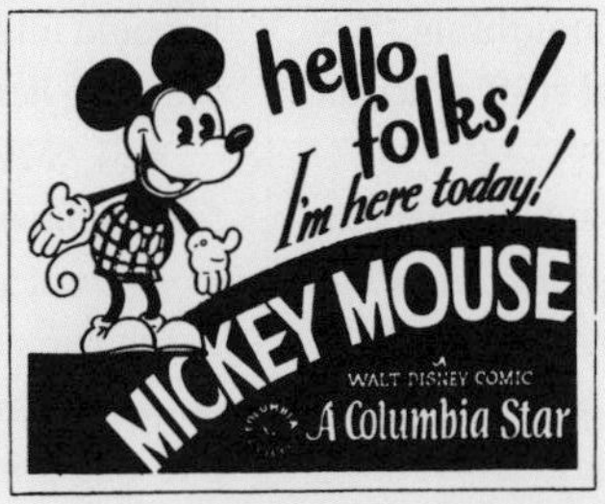
hello folks!
I'm here today!
MICKEY MOUSE
A WALT DISNEY COMIC
A Columbia Star

GET LONG PROFITS WITH THIS SHORT, SWEET SUBJECT

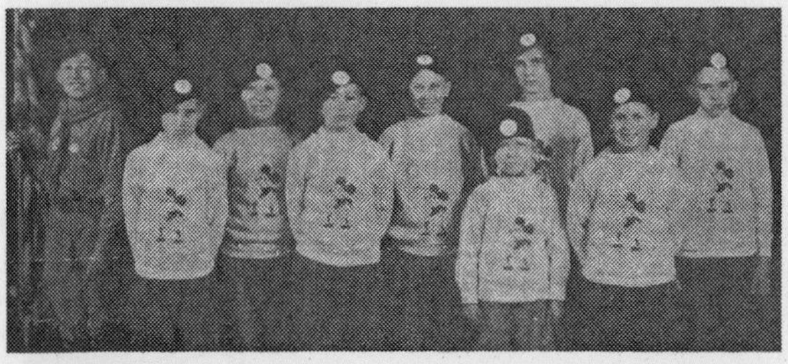

Just because Mickey Mouse sells itself as a universal favorite is no reason why the wise showman should neglect to keep on "plugging" this profitable, entertaining short.

Keep on reaching the kids, and you'll continue to fill those precious seats with kids and kids' parents.

Illustrated above, is a peach of a tie-up which has been tried and found to be a great piece of exploitation. Arrange with your local sporting goods shop to display a window of white athletic or sweat shirts imprinted with the picture of Mickey Mouse, as shown above. The attractiveness of the campaign can be increased if these sweaters are also shown in various color combinations.

If the boys and girls of your town are keen on ice skating, now is the time to promote an ice carnival, awarding tickets to your theatre for the contestant who most closely approximates the humorous antics of Mickey on the ice. Perhaps an outdoor Mickey Mouse costume party can be arranged on the ice, with prizes for the person whose costume and actions excel in imitation of the movie cartoon. Fancy skaters will vie eagerly in a test to see who can cut a Mickey figure on the ice.

Collegiate Tie-Ups

A similar plan which has proven itself at the high schools and even in some of the colleges is the Collegiate Slicker idea. In the picture shown at the bottom of this page, you will see a group of students attired in the conventional black rain coats imprinted with the Mickey Mouse title. One enterprising theatre man invited the youngsters to "go completely sophomore" by chalking up the quaint sayings collegiates delight in having scrawled across their slickers all over these exploitation slickers, limiting the wise cracks to subject matter referring to the Mouse. You might cash in on this idea further by having these slick slicker brigadeers parade up your main street, clad in these uniforms, announcing your Mickey Mouse showing, the date and the name of your theatre. Have them disperse AT your theatre, after you awarded free tickets to the winners of the wise crack authors. The newspapers should eat these stunts up because they make excellent copy with photographs.

Merchant Tie-Up

Here's another sure fire tie-up for you. Arrange a window display for Mickey Mouse with your butter and cheese merchant. An attractive window instantly calls to mind the association of mice and cheese. If he is a clever merchandiser, your cheese dealer will easily see the further advisability of making up small cube cheese samples, for distribution in your lobby. The tie-up, which will carry his name, address and a sample of his wares, is a great advertisement for him, and he, in turn can repay with a punchy bit of ballyhoo for you.

Interest Women

To the housewives in your town, I should appeal in the following manner: Have a cookie contest; offer prizes and publicity to the lady who makes a batch of cookies most resembling Mickey in some of his well-known poses. Impress upon the ladies that they must make their own moulds or forms for this purpose, and that here will be a genuine opportunity of publicly displaying their culinary art. Tie-up contest exhibits with grocery stores, etc., and carry this still farther by having the hardware firm in your town press a Mickey Mouse mould for cookie making, as a result of the publicity received during the home-made contest.

It would be a good idea to have these women contribute their cookies to the theatre management, who will announce that after the performance, the donations will be sold for the benefit of the unemployed or for any other popular local charity.

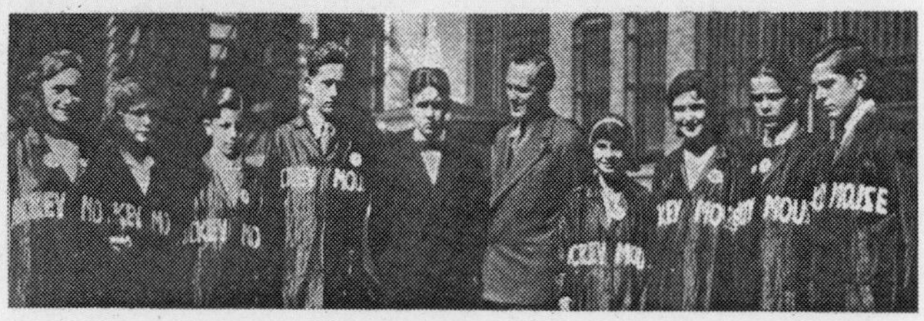

HOW TO USE THIS PRESS SHEET

In order to build up a regular patronage during the showing of the entire series of Mickey Mouse Cartoons, Columbia Pictures has designed this press sheet. The articles contained herein may be used with any release or as general stories for the entire series.

Animated sound cartoons are of such general interest that the longer articles presented herewith and describing the mechanics of making them are suitable for newspaper feature stories. Your editor would probably be glad to use them.

TEASERS AND CATCH LINES

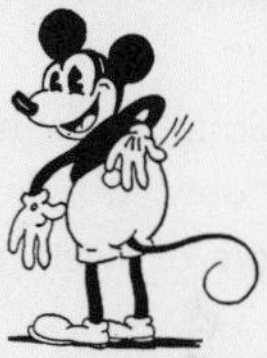

Mickey Mouse and Minnie Mouse — The Mice That Spice the Entertainment.

* * *

Outstanding Frollicking Fun Makers — Acclaimed by Press and Public.

* * *

Mickey Mouse on Your Marquee Means Money in Your Box Office.

* * *

Women Shriek (with laughter) When They See This Mouse —They Jump Up on Their Chairs and Cheer for Mickey.

* * *

No Room for Gloom When Mickey Mouse Appears.

* * *

A Sound of Revelry Tonight— Mickey Mouse is Here Again.

* * *

Hickory Dickory Dock — Mickey Mouse is on This Block.

* * *

A Movie Run That's Full of Fun.

Printed in U. S. A.

The cartoons cited on pressbook page two are *The Shindig* (1930) and *The Barnyard Battle* (1929). Pressbook image courtesy Walt Disney Archives.

this to the hovering attendant—"run over to the studio, won't you, and see if you can get a script of my next vehicle?"

After the door had closed behind his guardians, he listened for a moment. Then a broad grin overspread his face. Mr. Mouse, the tragicomic artist, disappeared; and Mickey, the gay, raffish, rowdy rodent, asserted himself.

"Whoops, it worked!" he cried, leaping out of his chair and executing a few rhumba steps on the top of his desk. "Now we can relax a bit. Here, have a *real* smoke!"

Kicking aside his beautiful jade cigarette holder, he opened a drawer in his desk and fished out a couple of swell nickel cigars. We lighted up forthwith.

"You know," said Mickey, gesticulating at me earnestly with the burnt match, "it's like that all the time. Since a couple of highbrow critics discovered that my stuff was Art, I've had to live up to it and be a doggoned artist instead of a plain, honest, fun-loving mouse. But you look like a regular guy—here, follow me."

In a jiffy he had climbed down from his chair and scuttled across the floor to the bookshelves that lined the opposite wall. There, behind a book on the bottom shelf, was a tiny hole in the wall through which Mickey dived before I realized what was up. As I stood nonplussed, wondering whether I was supposed to crawl in after him, a nearby tapestry lifted, and there stood Mickey in a little secret doorway, grinning broadly and beckoning me in.

"This is my den," he said rather proudly. "Come on in." It was a bare little cubby-hole whose only furniture was a small tin box, on which Mickey now squatted, and a three-legged stool, scarcely higher, to which he waved me. On the walls were a large-sized portrait of a young lady mouse, and a rough drawing of a cat's head to which clung some remnants of antique tomato.

"Target practice," explained Mickey, jerking a

Sweet domesticity. Mickey, once a rakish roué, claims that he's going to settle down now that he's found his real love. Well—maybe!

thumb toward it. "Ain't—isn't this a swell little dump? Nobody else knows about it—fixed it up all by myself. I often sneak in here for a quiet snooze, or to have a little snack. Look what I've got!"

Opening the lid of the tin box, he drew forth a small round whitish object.

"Cheese!" said Mickey joyfully, though quite superfluously. "Good old Limburger! Genuine pre-war, too!"

I declined a helping of the tidbit, and he fell to nibbling at it with great gusto. "I always keep a hunk of it in here," he explained between mouthfuls. "It's the only chance I get to enjoy the real stuff, since all this arty hoop-de-doo started.

"Walt wouldn't like it if he saw me ducking through holes—thinks it's too undignified. He's Mr. Disney, you know—the boss. I always call him Walt, except when speaking to him. He's a great little guy, all right—made me what I am today. Only thing is, he's been getting rather strict lately. And so has everybody else.

"I suppose you want to know all about my love life," continued the lad who made America mouse-conscious. "I'm engaged to Minnie Mouse right now, and it looks like the real thing this time. She's a field mouse, you know, and I always did like the out-door girl type." He leaned closer, and spoke in confidential tones. "It isn't generally known, but I've been married five times already. Four of 'em divorced me, and one was nabbed by a cat. So a mouse with my experience ought to know the right girl when he sees her. Minnie doesn't want to get married just yet—thinks it would interfere with her career. But just you watch me bring her around.

"My income?" Mickey seemed embarrassed for a moment. "Well, I really don't know how much I get, you see. Walt always takes most of it and puts it in the bank for me. But sometimes I manage to hold out a small roll, and then I have a swell time. I like the one-dollar bills best—they're nice and soft and juicy, and have a flavor all their own. Hundreds are good to chew on, they're so delightfully crisp. I don't care so much for the tens, but Minnie is saving them to make me a nice bath mat.

"I don't think very much of that endorsing idea, though of course I've been approached since I became famous. But I think maybe I'll let them use my signature on my favorite brand of hats—they're so nice to sleep in. I wouldn't take the money, of course; my idea is to use it to start a fund for the abolition of mousetraps. Talk about hobbies, that's mine. You know what they say about the man who makes a better mousetrap than his neighbor—that the world will beat a path to his door? Well, my idea is to change the slogan to: 'The world will beat him senseless.'

"How do I do all those acrobatic stunts like jumping rope with my tail and taking off my head and carrying it under my arm? Well, that would be giving away the secrets of the trade—but anyway, Walt taught me all of 'em, and believe me it was a grind. But it's a cinch when you've learned how. Look!"

With one step he had crossed the room and was running up the wall. He trotted carelessly up to the ceiling, where he did a brief tap dance, ending by stretching his tail down to touch the floor and sliding down it fireman fashion.

"Looks easy, doesn't it? Well, try it some time!

"Things aren't so bad with me at that," he added after a moment's reflection. "No use kicking, especially when I think of all the deserving mice who haven't even got a job. I'm well taken care of, and have my career, and all—except one thing." A shadow passed over his face.

"What's that?" I asked sympathetically.

"Why, it's those danged extras who support me in my pictures," he said slowly. "I mean especially the fellows who furnish the menace, whose job it is to almost get me on the screen. Well, how do I know but that some big bruiser of a hungry dog or cat won't get absent-minded and actually finish me some time while we're shooting? I interview every applicant for a part personally, give 'em intelligence tests and everything, but suppose sometime—just suppose—Oh, golly!"

"MICK-EY! MICK-EE!" came a voice through the thin wall of the den.

"Sh-h-h! They've missed us," said the boy star. "Come on—and you won't blab on me, will you?"

A quiet-looking, bespectacled gentleman strode over and grasped Mickey firmly by an ear.

"Where have you been, young fellow?" he chided, trying not quite successfully to suppress a smile. "Playing hookey again, eh?"

"Wh-why, no, Boss," said Mickey, "I was just showing this visitor my first editions."

"Has he been filling you up with all that bunk about his love life?" laughed Mr. Disney. "Mickey is an awful roué, isn't he? Come on now, old timer, you've got to rehearse that scene where you play a saxophone solo on an elephant's trunk."

"So long," waved Mickey. "And say," he added in a whisper, "drop in next week. I'm getting in a new stock of fromage—genuine stuff, right off the shelf!" •

LEFT: Kitchen vignette by Floyd Gottfredson (pencils) and Roy Nelson (inks), adapted from June 28, 1930 daily strip.

BELOW: Desert vignette by Floyd Gottfredson (pencils) and Roy Nelson (inks), adapted from July 17, 1930 daily strip.

On location! Mickey Mouse and his leading lady, Minnie, hike out into the desert on location for one of Mickey's thrillers.

The World's Dumbest Actor:
At the Park! His Woe! On Payroll!
By R.M. FINCH

World's Dumbest Actor

*** PLUTO, THE PUP ***

(He's From Eagle Rock)

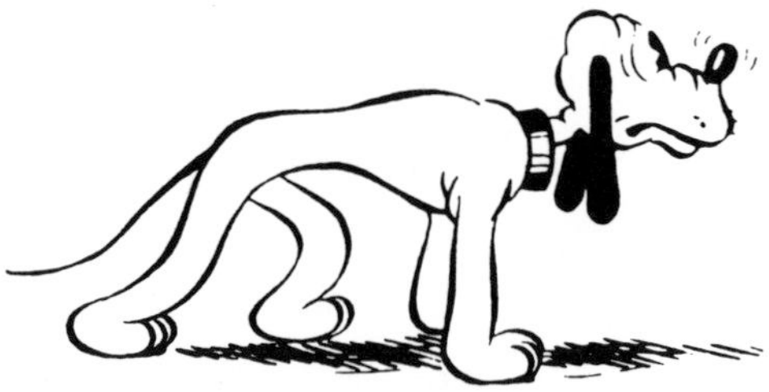

From the Los Angeles Illustrated Daily News, *October 20, 1931*

QUEST for Hollywood's dumbest motion picture actor took me to the Walt Disney studios during the noon hour, where I found Pluto the Pup sweltering in the sun, while the other members of the Mickey Mouse retinue reposed in the shade.

As I watched Pluto, dripping with perspiration, industriously fighting flies in the glaring sunshine, while Mickey Mouse, his sweetheart Minnie, Clarabelle Cow, Horse Collar Horace and other members of the company sat in the cool shadows, a battery of electric fans keeping the insect pests at a safe distance, I knew my long search was over.

Positively nothing could be dumber than that.

When I suggested to Pluto that we move into the shade while he told his life story, his sad eyes dropped in confusion.

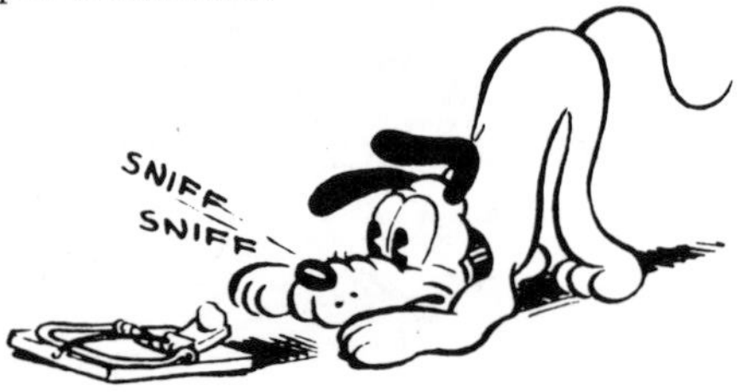
SNIFF
SNIFF

Sinking down upon his stomach, he rested his thin chin on his floppy paws and with his long, flea-bitten ears trailing in the dust, he told his sad story.

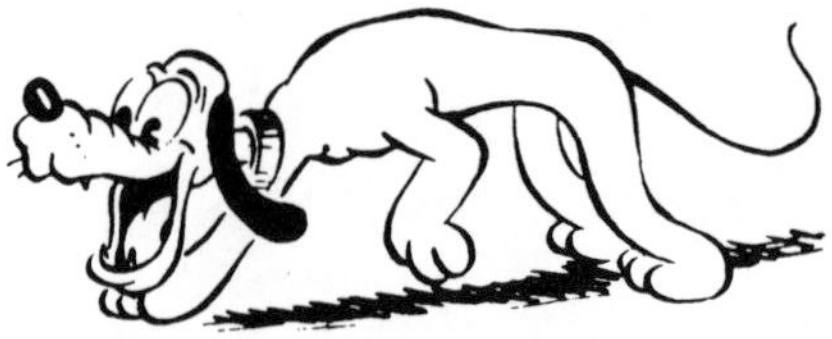

FROM EAGLE ROCK

"I was one of a litter of seven that saw the light of day in a kennel in Eagle Rock. From the very first I seemed to show a penchant for doing the right thing at the wrong time or the wrong thing at the right time, or just how would you say it?"

I waved him to go on.

"If there was a newly made flower bed, I chose it to dig me a cool nest to sleep in and got a larruping. If slippers were missing, it seemed that I always was caught playing with them, although my brothers and sisters, who filched them out of the closet, always managed to be elsewhere when they were recovered and I got the hiding.

"One day after I had mistaken an upstanding Brahma rooster for a potential playmate and nearly got my eyes scratched out with his spurs, the mistress of the house where I was born said to the master:

"'We've got to do something with Pluto. He's so simple nobody wants him and I think we'll have to put him on his own resources.'

"Now, wasn't that fine of them to single me out of the whole litter and give me the opportunity to be first to make my way in the world?

"The master mumbled something about the first time I crossed the street I would get ironed out by an automobile, but I paid no attention to it, so thrilled was I at the prospect of being my own boss.

"Little did I know then, in the exuberance of youth, the trials of being a vagabond.

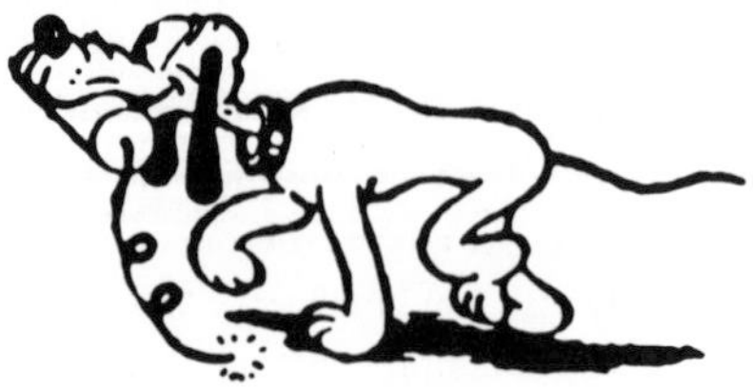

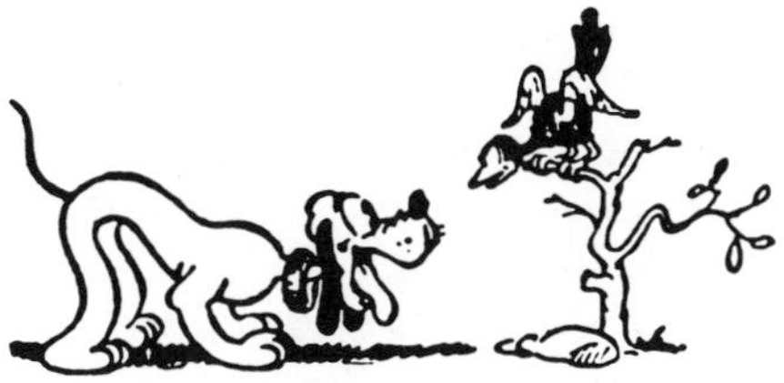

AT THE PARK

"I was taken out to Griffith park and dropped out of a car. After racing around in the company of a couple of strays, delighted by my new freedom and nearly getting shot for chasing chickens, I began to feel hungry.

"Faintly over the breeze came the whiff of a choice mutton bone. I followed my nose 'til it led me to a kennel not far away. The bone was resting before the door. Stupidly, I forgot to investigate whether there was anybody at home in the kennel and scarcely had got my teeth on the morsel when a white bull terrier came out and got me by the nape of the neck.

"I was bleeding in a hundred spots when I finally escaped. This split in my ear is a reminder of that terrible experience.

Pluto sighed sadly.

"But, how did you get into the films?" I asked.

"That's a funny one; I was coming to it.

"After ekeing out a miserable existence snatching morsels from garbage cans and gnawing bits from bones other dogs abandoned, one day a gang of street dogs stopped me. They told me that free bones were being put out by Mickey Mouse at the Disney studios and if I hurried I might get mine. They told me to walk right in without knocking.

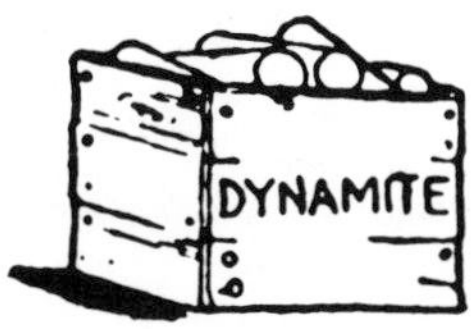
DYNAMITE

HIS WOE

"Imagine my embarrassment when I rushed into a big group of men surrounding Walt Disney—I found out later it was a scenario gag meeting—and the click-click was a drummer imitating a minstrel player with wooden 'bones.'

"In my confusion I knocked over a stand with a vase of flowers and, in attempting to recover my balance, stepped into an open bucket of paint. I was all ready to duck out when the swinging door slammed to on my tail.

"I let out a terrific ki-yi at the pain. One of the men grabbed me yelping by the scruff of the neck and was about to throw me out the window when Mr. Disney caught him by the arm.

"'Wait a minute,' he said.

"The man who held my struggling form interposed: 'Why, this pup is too dumb to live.'

" 'That's just the idea,' said Walt. 'He's exactly what we have been looking for. He hasn't a single human attribute in the way of intelligence. People will howl over his dumbness on the screen.

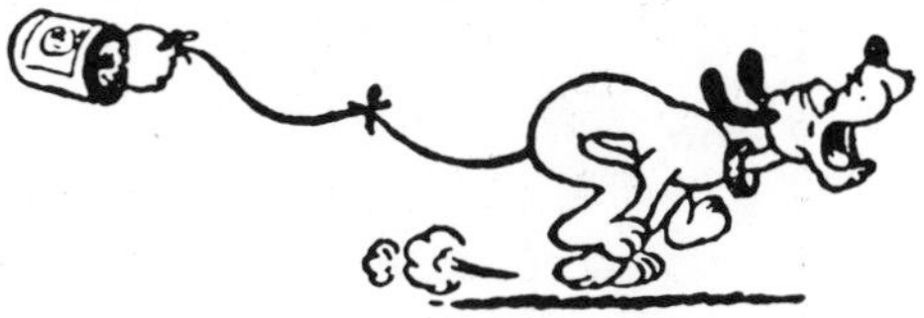

ON PAYROLL

"Well, to make a long story short, he ordered my wounded tail bandaged and put me on the payroll. For the first time in months I had milk and hamburger for supper.

"The next day he introduced me to the Mickey Mouse company and for the last two months I have been a regular actor in Mickey Mouse cartoons.

"Wasn't it sweet of him to say that?"

I left, my two months' quest ended. I had found the dumbest actor in the world! •

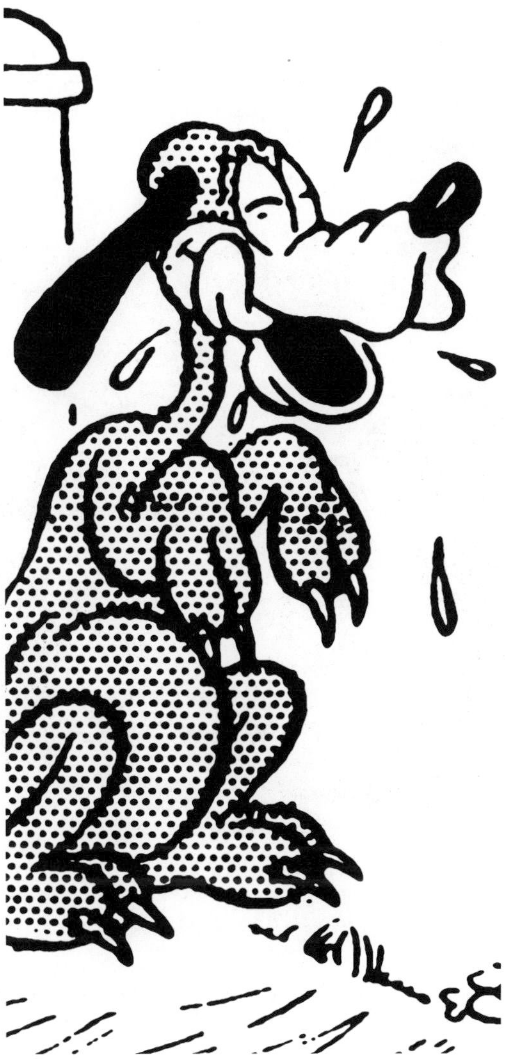

OPPOSITE: Vignette drawings attributed to Al Taliaferro.

THIS PAGE, LEFT AND MIDDLE: Vignette drawings attributed to Floyd Gottfredson.

ABOVE: Detail from July 8, 1931 daily strip; pencils by Floyd Gottfredson, inks by Al Taliaferro.

Gottfredson's World: STRANGE TALES OF LATE 1931

Who jinxed "Circus Roustabout," "Pluto the Pup," and "Fireman Mickey"? Each got but a single specialty drawing in the 1930s—one of which didn't even appear with its associated story! On the other hand, "Mickey Mouse and the Ransom Plot" received an embarrassment of riches. It got five covers to itself; three for variant editions of the same book!

For the first time, 1931 serials were feted with unique American cover art. In our coming volumes, we'll see more and more of this—following the action as Stateside Gottfredson reprints get fully underway.

The editors wish to thank Leonardo Gori and Thomas Jensen for contributing to our cover galleries. [DG]

ANNO I - N. 7 - 15 LUGLIO 1937 - XV
PUBBLICAZIONE MENSILE
TOPOLINO
E GLI ZINGARI
2 LIRE
CONTIENE UNA FIGURINA PREMIO TOPOLINO
GLI ALBI D'ORO
EDIZIONI WALT DISNEY · MONDADORI

TOPOLINO
DOMATORE E SALTIMBANCO
CENT. 50
SIGNORI LEONI, TRANQUILLIZZATEVI!... NON HO ALCUNA INTENZIONE DI FARVI DEL MALE!
ANNO PRIMO ALBO N. 9 30 SETTEMBRE 1935 - XIII
NEL REGNO DI TOPOLINO
PUBBLICAZIONE QUINDICINALE CONTO CORR. POSTALE
EDIZIONI WALT DISNEY - MONDADORI

TOPOLINO
ARCIERE
50 cent.
CUPIDO
ANNO II - ALBO N. 19
1 Luglio 1936 - XIV
NEL REGNO DI TOPOLINO
Pubblicaz. quindicinale
Conto Corrente Postale
EDIZIONI WALT DISNEY - MONDADORI

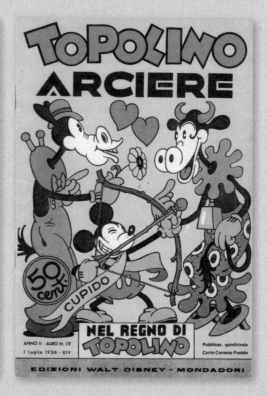

ABOVE LEFT: Cover to Italian *Albo D'Oro* 7 (1937), illustrating "Mickey Mouse and the Ransom Plot." Art by Michele Rubino; image courtesy Leonardo Gori.

ABOVE MIDDLE: Cover to Italian *Nel Regno di Topolino* 9 (1935), illustrating "Mickey Mouse, Circus Roustabout." Artist unknown; image courtesy Leonardo Gori. Mickey's voice balloon equates to "Settle down, Mr. Lion! I have no intention of harming you."

ABOVE RIGHT: Cover to Italian *Nel Regno di Topolino* 19 (1936), illustrating "Fireman Mickey." Art by Antonio Rubino; image courtesy Leonardo Gori.

OPPOSITE, TOP ROW: Covers to *Big Little Book* 717 in its two American editions and a British equivalent, *Great Big Midget Book* 1 (1933). All three books contained "Mickey Mouse and the Ransom Plot." British cover art reinked by Wilfred Haughton; images courtesy Hake's Americana.

OPPOSITE, BOTTOM LEFT: Cover to French *Albums Mickey* 5 (1932), illustrating "Mickey Mouse and the Ransom Plot." Artist unknown.

OPPOSITE, BOTTOM RIGHT: Title page from David McKay's *Mickey Mouse Series* 1 (1931), art attributed to Floyd Gottfredson. Oddly, while this image illustrates "Pluto the Pup," publisher David McKay put the actual "Pup" story into issue 2! Image courtesy Thomas Jensen.

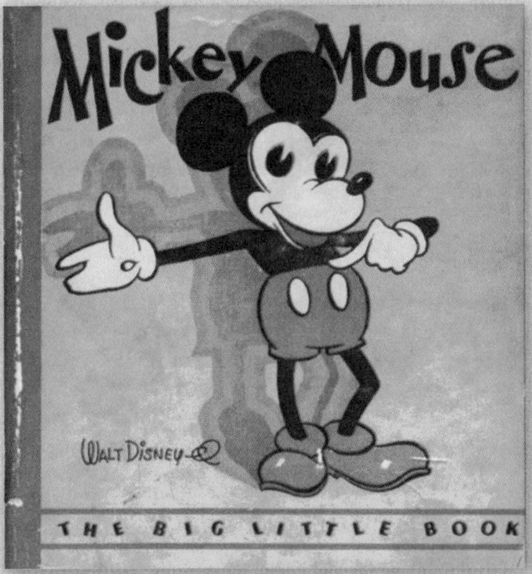
Mickey Mouse
WALT DISNEY
THE BIG LITTLE BOOK

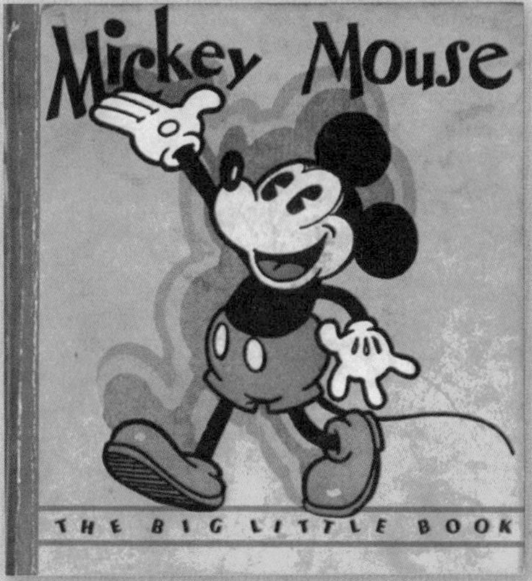
Mickey Mouse
THE BIG LITTLE BOOK

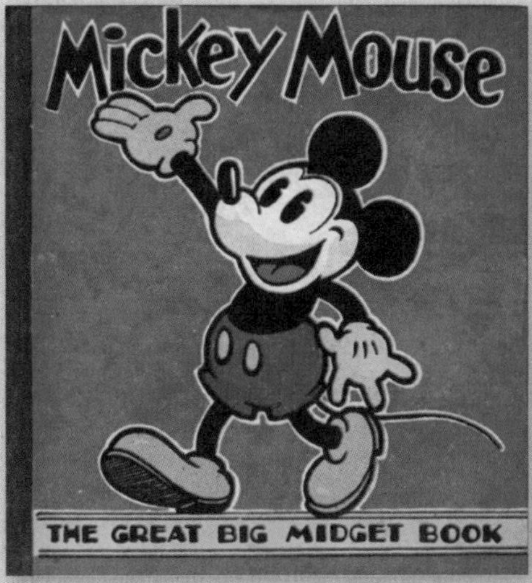
Mickey Mouse
THE GREAT BIG MIDGET BOOK

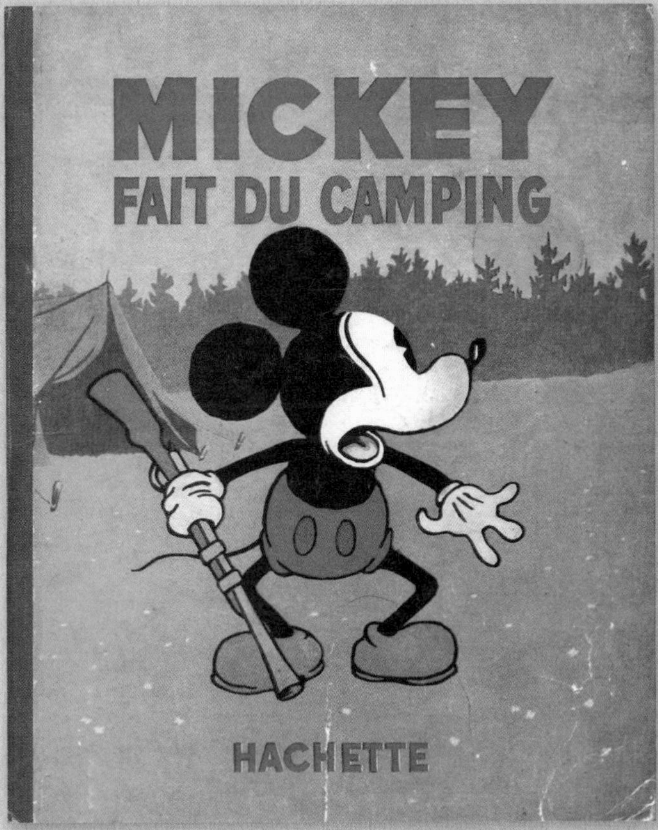
MICKEY
FAIT DU CAMPING
HACHETTE

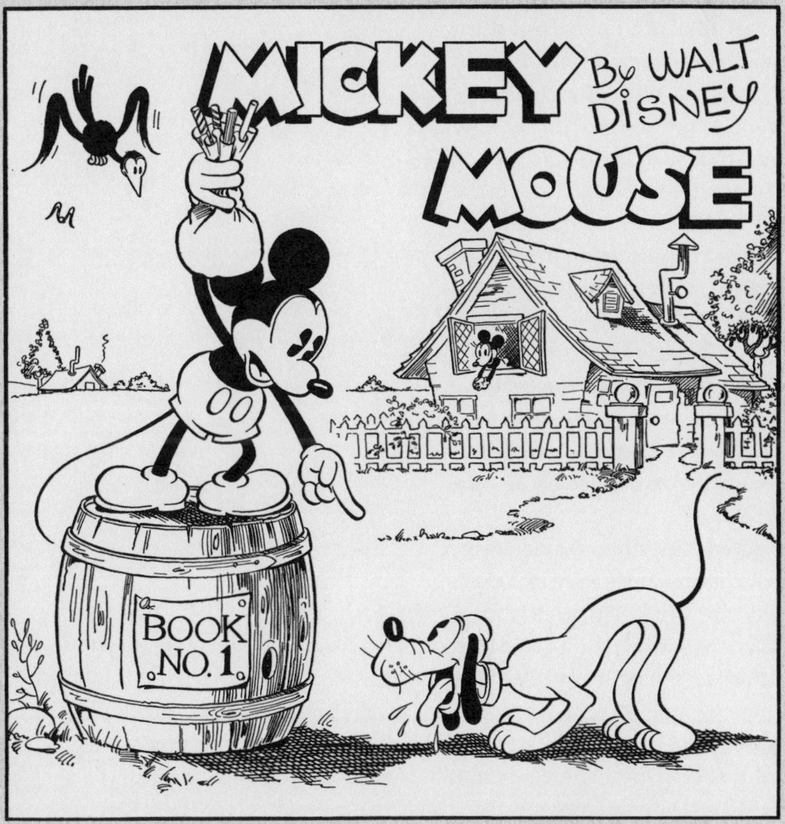
MICKEY
By WALT DISNEY
MOUSE
BOOK NO. 1

Run down the list of Disney heroes and you'll always find him: Mickey, Donald, Goofy... Pluto. Mickey's pet bloodhound spent years as a major focus character at Disney—and entered Mickey's comics life in late 1931, making a cameo appearance in Gottfredson's "Circus Roustabout" (July 1) and becoming the focus character in the subsequent "Pluto the Pup." But what did Pluto actually mean for Floyd Gottfredson, and for Floyd Gottfredson's Mickey Mouse?

It is helpful to look at what the dog first represented on film: an innovation and a foil. An innovation: when head animator Ub Iwerks left Disney in January 1930, the rest of the staff broke away from Iwerks' abstract, rubber-hose drawing style, and Pluto—created by Norm Ferguson—represented one of the first successfuls efforts to animate animals with more realistic features.[1] A foil: Pluto existed, at least initially, to create trouble for Mickey, with gags playing up the dog's stupidity. Confronting the Mouse with a realistic, but dumb animal was a new means of creating humor: not through a fantastic Iwerks beast, but through a proxy for audiences' own clumsy pets.

Several years into development, however, Pluto matured, and a 1936 character guide by writer Ted Sears tracked the changes. While Sears still called Pluto "not too smart," he found humor in the dog's "dumb reasoning"[2]—and the more Pluto reasoned on-screen, the less stupid and the more simply naïve and insecure he seemed. Pluto became not a fool, but a child; a viewpoint character for story men, in contrast with whom master Mickey now seemed like a strict, no-fun parent. How come? Perhaps staffers implicitly felt that there could be only one sympathetic figure per plot: story man Harry Reeves argued that "if you get Pluto [in a major role], you have to sacrifice Mickey."[3]

Luckily for us, Floyd Gottfredson sacrificed neither character. In his first stories with Pluto, Floyd's approach mirrored that of the first cartoons, with the dog as a friendly but unpredictable bag of trouble. Later, as Pluto grew smarter on-screen, Gottfredson finessed the changes as no animation team ever did. He allowed Pluto moments of independent (thought balloon) reasoning, letting us understand the dog's point of view; but he would then carefully switch viewpoints to Mickey, letting us feel for Mickey, not Pluto, when Pluto's mistakes caused problems. So there could be two sympathetic figures in a story; one just a little more sympathetic than the other.

It was a complicated balance, but it worked for Floyd. Pluto meant well; Mickey knew it but ended up embarrassed anyway; and the loyalty of two best friends generally stayed strong. [DG]

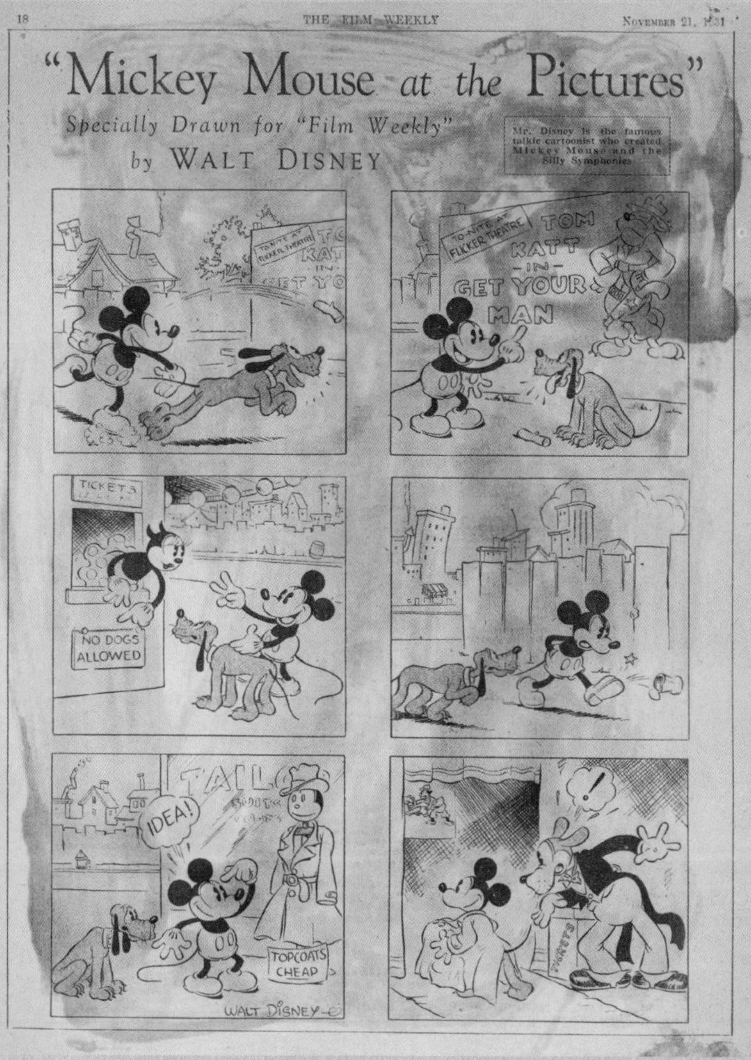
18
THE FILM WEEKLY
NOVEMBER 21, 1931
"Mickey Mouse at the Pictures"
Specially Drawn for "Film Weekly"
by WALT DISNEY
Mr. Disney is the famous talkie cartoonist who created Mickey Mouse and the Silly Symphonies
TO-NITE AT FLIKKER THEATRE
TOM KATT -IN- GET YOUR MAN
TICKETS
NO DOGS ALLOWED
IDEA!
TOPCOATS CHEAP
WALT DISNEY

ABOVE: This rare, early Pluto-centric strip was drawn by Gottfredson for the November 21, 1931 issue of *Film Weekly*—but its gag came from *Bobby Bumps and the Hypnotic Eye* (1919), a Bray Studios animated cartoon directed by Earl Hurd. Image courtesy Walt Disney Archives.

1 Michael Barrier, *Hollywood Cartoons* (New York: Oxford University Press, 1999), p. 75.

2 Ted Sears, "Pluto." Character analysis, c. 1936, p. 1.

3 Walt Disney, Harry Reeves, and George Stallings, story meeting on the unproduced cartoon *Spring Cleaning*, February 24, 1938, p. 1.

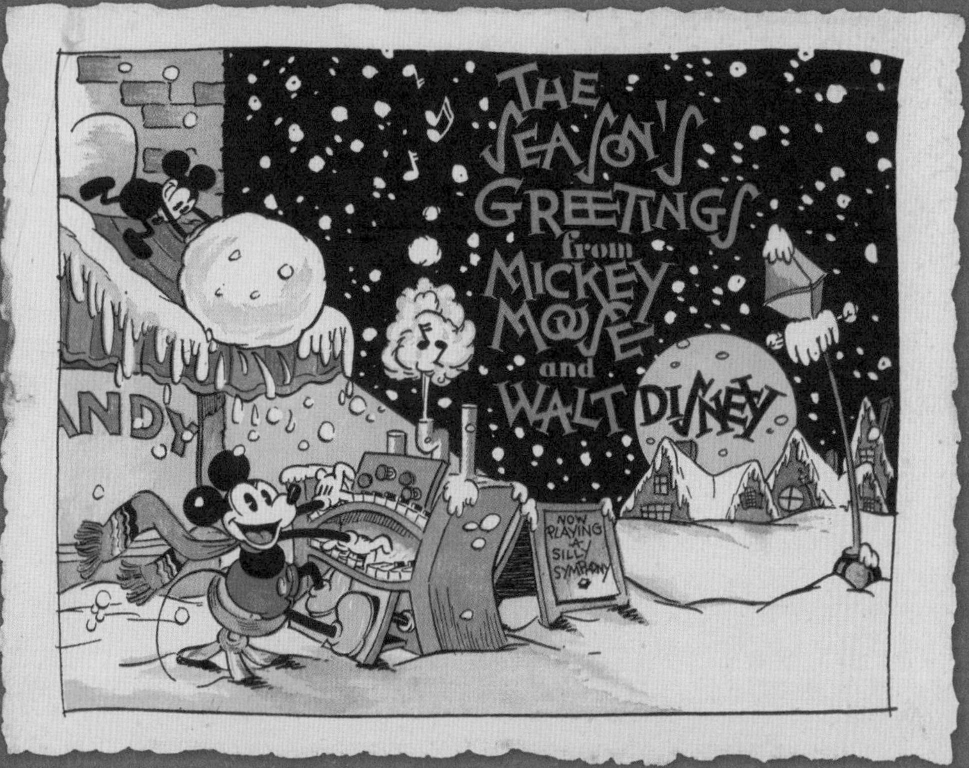
THE SEASON'S GREETINGS from MICKEY MOUSE and WALT DISNEY
NOW PLAYING A SILLY SYMPHONY
ANDY

"I have it on good authority that I was born in Utah. (No, Mormons don't wear horns.) Played hookey from art education by mailing empty envelopes to my correspondence school. My facial attributes are a composite of striking resemblances to Calvin Coolidge, Bull Montana and Richard Barthelmess. (Ed. Note—Please enclose 25¢ for all fan photos, to be mailed direct from Walt Disney Studio.) Awarded aluminum medal by four Marx Brothers for inventing collapsible jail with removable bars in 1928. Worked as projectionist until Will Hays organization discovered what was wrong with the industry, then suddenly decided to become a cartoonist. After 19 years at the drawing board have decided to take up art. Employed by Walt Disney for the past two years, and as long as Mickey pays the grocery bill, I can't kick."

— *Floyd Gottfredson*
Motion Picture Daily, *June 20, 1931*

LEFT: Disney studio Christmas card, 1930. Pencils by Floyd Gottfredson, inks attributed to Earl Duvall. Image from the Richard W. Hall collection, courtesy David Callahan.

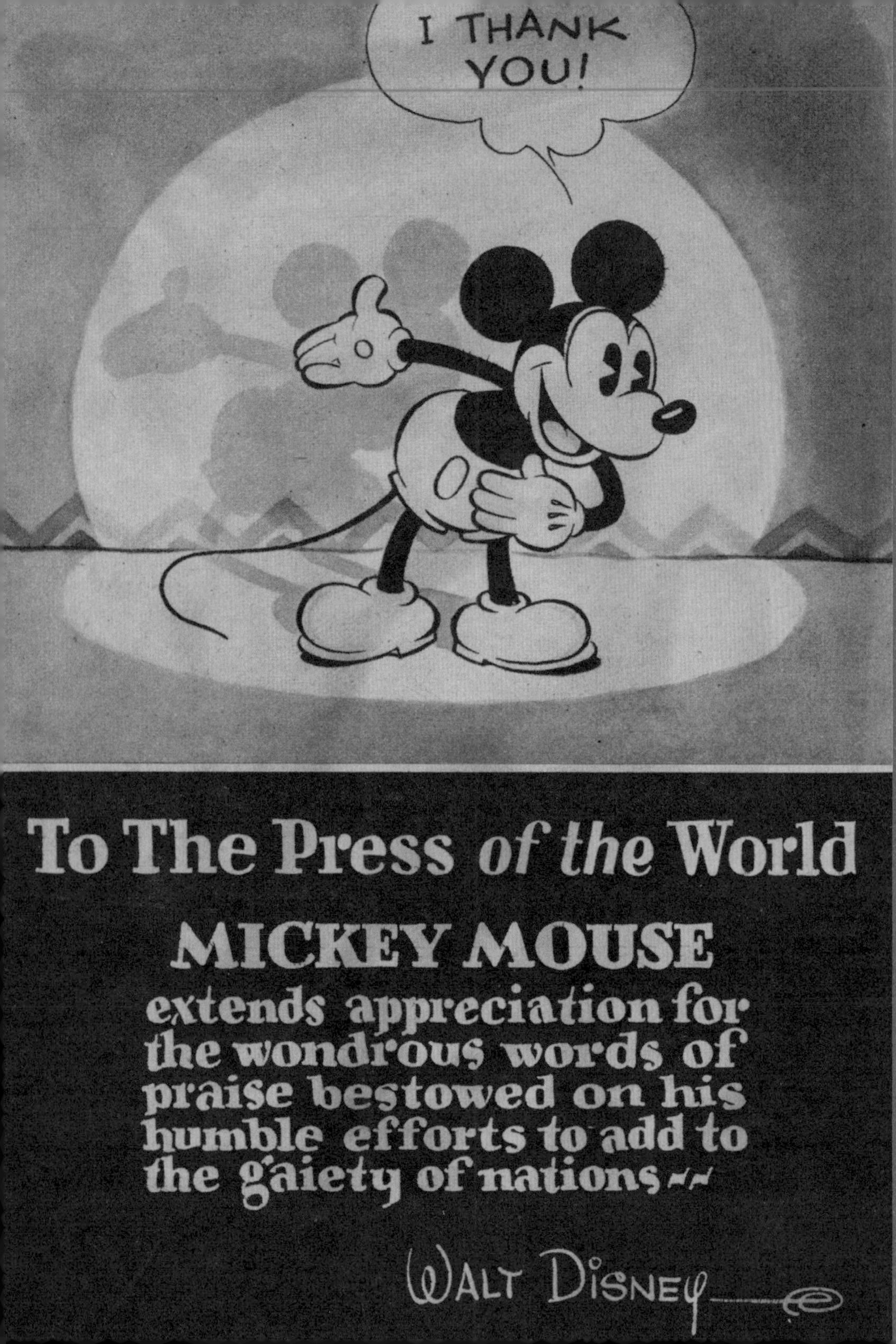

I THANK YOU!
To The Press of the World
MICKEY MOUSE
extends appreciation for the wondrous words of praise bestowed on his humble efforts to add to the gaiety of nations ~~
WALT DISNEY

ABOUT THE EDITORS

DAVID GERSTEIN's interest in the Disney Standard Characters began with his childhood viewing of *Plane Crazy* (1928) at a film retrospective. Today David is an animation and comics researcher, writer, and editor working extensively with the Walt Disney Company and its licensees.

David's published work includes *Mickey and the Gang: Classic Stories in Verse* (Gemstone 2005); *Walt Disney Treasures – Disney Comics: 75 Years of Innovation* (Gemstone 2006); *Walt Disney's Hall of Fame: Dick Kinney and Al Hubbard* (Egmont Serieforlaget 2009); and various issues of *Uncle Scrooge* (BOOM! Studios, ongoing). David has also worked with Disney in efforts to locate lost Oswald the Lucky Rabbit cartoons and to preserve the *Mickey Mouse* newspaper strips seen in this volume.

GARY GROTH co-founded Fantagraphics Books and *The Comics Journal* in 1976. And he is still at it.

LEFT: Specialty painting by Floyd Gottfredson (and—likely—unidentified others) for the *Los Angeles Times*' 50th anniversary edition, December 4, 1931. Image courtesy Walt Disney Archives.